EUDORA WELTY

EUDORA WELTY

COMPLETE NOVELS

The Robber Bridegroom
Delta Wedding
The Ponder Heart
Losing Battles
The Optimist's Daughter

THE LIBRARY OF AMERICA

The paper used in this publication meets the
minimum requirements of the American National Standard for
Information Sciences—Permanence of Paper for Printed
Library Materials, ANSI Z39.48—1984.

Distributed to the trade
in the United States by Penguin Putnam Inc.
and in Canada by Penguin Books Canada Ltd.

Library of Congress Catalog Number: 97–46702
For cataloging information, see end of Notes.
ISBN 1–883011–54–x

Third Printing
The Library of America—101

Manufactured in the United States of America

RICHARD FORD AND MICHAEL KREYLING
SELECTED THE CONTENTS AND WROTE THE NOTES
FOR THIS VOLUME

Contents

THE ROBBER BRIDEGROOM

To
Katherine Anne Porter

I

IT WAS the close of day when a boat touched Rodney's Landing on the Mississippi River and Clement Musgrove, an innocent planter, with a bag of gold and many presents, disembarked. He had made the voyage from New Orleans in safety, his tobacco had been sold for a fair price to the King's men. In Rodney he had a horse stabled against his return, and he meant to spend the night there at an inn, for the way home through the wilderness was beset with dangers.

As his foot touched shore, the sun sank into the river the color of blood, and at once a wind sprang up and covered the sky with black, yellow, and green clouds the size of whales, which moved across the face of the moon. The river was covered with foam, and against the landing the boats strained in the waves and strained again. River and bluff gave off alike a leaf-green light, and from the water's edge the red torches lining the Landing-under-the-Hill and climbing the bluff to the town stirred and blew to the left and right. There were sounds of rushing and flying, from the flourish of carriages hurrying through the streets after dark, from the bellowing throats of the flatboatmen, and from the wilderness itself, which lifted and drew itself in the wind, and pressed its savage breath even closer to the little galleries of Rodney, and caused a bell to turn over in one of the steeples, and shook the fort and dropped a tree over the racetrack.

Holding his bag of gold tight in his hand, Clement made for the first inn he saw under the hill. It was all lighted up and full of the sounds of singing.

Clement entered and went straight to the landlord and inquired, "Have you a bed for the night, where I will not be disturbed till morning?"

"Aye," replied the landlord, who brushed at a long mustache—an Englishman.

"But where have you left your right ear?" said Clement, pointing to the vacancy. Like all innocent men, he was proud of having one thing in the world he could be sharp about.

And the landlord was forced to admit that he had left the

3

ear pinned to a market cross in Kentucky, for the horse stealing he did.

Clement turned and went on up the road, and the storm
was worse. He asked at the next inn, which was equally glittering and bright, indeed he could not distinguish them in his
memory from one year's end to the next, if he might be ac-
commodated for the night.

"Aye," said the landlord, showing his front teeth all of
gold.

"But where have you left your left ear?" Clement asked,
and he had that man too. The fellow said it had been clipped
away in Nashville for the sad trouble he got into after the
cockfights.

On he went, the rain worse all the time, until it sounded
like the quarreling of wildcats in the cane, and at last, at the
very top of the hill, he found an inn where he was able to
pronounce the landlord honest.

"Since you appear to be a scrupulous man," he said, "I
would like to engage of you a bed for the night, with supper
and breakfast, if not too dear."

"To be sure," replied the landlord, the very image of a hare,
whose large ears were easily set a-trembling. "But, sir, this is
a popular house, if I may say so. You may have one bedfellow,
or even two, before the night is over."

At that very moment there came a loud gust of laughter
from the grogshop at the side—"Ho! Ho! Ho!"

"But it is early yet," the landlord said, his ears beginning
to quiver nonetheless. "If you go up at once, you will be able
to take first choice of place in the bed."

Clement stopped only to eat a supper of beefsteak, eggs,
bacon, turkey joints, johnnycake, pickled peaches, plum pie,
and a bowl of grog before saying good night to him.

"Pleasant dreams!" the landlord said, and the traveler went
up the winding stair.

Clement was the first man to the room. The storm was
unabated, the wind was shaking the house like a cat a mouse.
The rain had turned to hail. First he hid his moneybag under
that end of the pillow which was nearest the door, and then
he sat down to take off his boots before getting into bed,

such being the rule of the house. But before he got his first boot off, in walked a second traveler.

This was a brawny man six and a half feet high, with a blue coat, red shirt, and turkey feather stuck in his cap, and he held a raven on his finger which never blinked an eye, and could say,

> "Turn back, my bonny,
> Turn away home."

"Ah, stranger," said this fellow to Clement, striding up. "It's been a long time since we slept together."

"So it has," said Clement.

"Have you got the same old smell you had before?" asked the stranger, and Clement did not say no.

"Are you just as lousy as ever?" he roared, and Clement said he was.

"Then shake hands!"

Before Clement could get the second boot off, the third traveler walked in.

He was as brawny as the other, though but six feet tall, and dressed up like a New Orleans dandy, with his short coat knotted about him capewise. But for some reason he wore no hat, and his heavy yellow locks hung over his forehead and down to his shoulders.

"Ah, stranger," said he to the second traveler. "Crowded days! It's been a long time since our heads were side by side on the pillow."

"Long as forever!" sang out the other.

Then Clement knew they were all three strangers to one another, with the stormy night ahead.

When the third traveler removed his cloak, there was a little dirk hid in the knot, which he placed with his moneybag under the pillow. And there were the three bags of gold sitting there side by side, like hens on their nests. So Clement held up the snuffer over the light.

"Wait!" said the third traveler. "Are we dreaming already? We are going off without the last nightcap, gentlemen."

"Ho! Ho! Ho!" said the second traveler, punching himself in the forehead and kicking himself in the breeches. "That is a thing I seldom forget, for my mind is as bright as a gold piece."

All three of them sat and uncorked their jugs and at the same moment drank down. And when they looked up, the second traveler had drunk the whole jugful.

"Remarkable!" said the yellow-haired stranger, who had made way with half a jug. Poor Clement, who had swallowed only a fourth, could say nothing.

"That was only a finicky taste," replied the other, and throwing off his blue coat, he yelled, "Drink again!"

And he seized Clement's own jug out of his finger and emptied it.

"A master!" said Yellowhair. "But I dare say that is the end, the show is over. You can do no more."

"Ho! Ho!" said the other, and taking off his red shirt and filling his bristling chest with a breath of air, he seized the other's own jug and finished it off.

Then, sailing his cap in the air, he gave a whistle and a shake and declared that he was none other than Mike Fink, champion of all the flatboat bullies on the Mississippi River, and was ready for anything.

"Mike Fink! Well now," said the yellow-haired stranger, and putting his head to one side studied him with all the signs of admiration.

"Yes indeed I am," said the flatboatman crossly. "Am I not Mike Fink, as you live and breathe?" he roared at Clement.

It was a cautious night, but Clement believed him, until the yellow-haired stranger said, "Well, I doubt it."

"You doubt that I am Mike Fink? Nevertheless, it is true!" yelled the flatboatman. "Only look!" And he doubled up his fists and rippled the muscles on his arms up and down, as slow as molasses, and on his chest was the finest mermaid it was possible to have tattooed at any port. "I can pick up a grown man by the neck in each hand and hold him out at arm's length, and often do, too," yelled the flatboatman. "I eat a whole cow at one time, and follow her up with a live sheep if it's Sunday. Ho! ho! If I get hungry on a voyage, I jump off my raft and wade across, and take whatever lies in my path on shore. When I come near, the good folk take to their heels and run from their houses! I only laugh at the Indians, and I can carry a dozen oxen on my back at one time, and as for pigs, I tie them in a bunch and hang them to my belt!"

"Strike me dead!" said the yellow-haired stranger, and he yawned, got into bed, and shut his eyes.

"I'm an alligator!" yelled the flatboatman, and began to flail his mighty arms through the air. "I'm a he-bull and a he-rattlesnake and a he-alligator all in one! I've beat up so many flatboatmen and thrown them in the river I haven't kept a count since the flood, and I'm a lover of the women like you'll never see again." And he chanted Mike Fink's song: "I can outrun, outhop, outjump, throw down, drag out, and lick any man in the country!"

"Go down to the corner and buy yourself a new jug," said the yellow-haired stranger. His eyes were shut tight still, though Clement's, you may be sure, were open wide. "You're still nothing but an old buffalo."

"So I lie?" bellowed the flatboatman, and, leaping out of his breeches, he jumped across the room in three jumps and said, "Feast your eyes upon me and deny that I am Mike Fink."

Clement was ready to agree, but the yellow-haired stranger said, "Why, you're nothing but an old hoptoad, you will make me mad in a minute. Now what is it you want? If you want to fight, let us fight."

At that, the flatboatman gave one soul-reaching shout and jumped into the featherbed and burst it, and the yellow-haired stranger leaped up with a laugh, and the feathers blew all around the room like the chips in a waterspout. And out the window it was storming, and from the door the raven was saying,

> "Turn again, my bonny,
> Turn away home."

As for Clement, he removed himself, since he was a man of peace and would not be wanted on the scene, and held the candle where it would be safe and at the same time cast the best light, and all the while his bedfellows sliced right and left, picked each other up, and threw each other down for a good part of the night. And if he sneezed once, he sneezed a thousand times, for the feathers.

Finally the flatboatman said, "Let us stop and seize forty winks. We will take it up in the morning where we leave off tonight. Agreed?"

"Certainly," said the other, dropping him to the ground where he was about to throw him. "That is the rule Mike Fink would make, if he were here."

"Say once more that I am not Mike Fink and, peace or no peace, that will be your last breath!" cried the flatboatman. And then he said cunningly, "If by now you don't know who I am, *I* know who *you* are, that followed this rich planter to his bed."

"Take care," said the other.

"I will bet all the gold that lies under this pillow against the sickening buttons you wear sewed to your coat, that your name is Jamie Lockhart! Jamie Lockhart the——"

"Take care," said the other once more, and he half pulled out his little dirk.

"I say for the third time that your name is Jamie Lockhart, the I-forget-what," said the flatboatman. "And if that does not make it so, we will leave the decision to this gentleman, whose name has not yet been brought out in the open."

The poor planter could only say, "My name, about which there is no secret, is Clement Musgrove. But I do not know Jamie Lockhart, any more than I know Mike Fink, and will identify neither."

"I am Mike Fink!" yelled the flatboatman. "And that is Jamie Lockhart! And not the other way around, neither! You say you do not know who he is—do you not know *what* he is? He is a——" And he took hold of Clement like a mother bear and waltzed him around, whispering, "Say it! Say it! Say it!"

The poor man began to shake his head with wonder, and he did not like to dance.

But the yellow-haired stranger smiled at him and said coolly enough, "Say *who* I am forever, but dare to say *what* I am, and that will be the last breath of any man."

With that delivered, he lay down in the bed once more, and said to Mike Fink, "Blow out the candle."

The flatboatman immediately closed his mouth, put his breeches and shirt and his coat back on, blew out the candle, and fell into the bed on one side of Jamie Lockhart, if it was he, while the planter, deciding that affairs were at rest for the evening, lay down on the other.

But no sooner had Clement given a groan and got to the first delightful regions of sleep than he felt a hand seize his arm.

"Make no sound, as you value your life," whispered a voice. "But rise up out of the bed."

The storm was over, and the raven was still, but who knows whether he slept? It was the yellow-haired man who had whispered, and Clement had to wonder if now he should find out what Jamie Lockhart was. A murderer? A madman? A ghost? Some outlandish beast in New Orleans dress? He got to his feet and looked at his companion by the pure light of the moon, which by now was shining through the shutter. He was remarkably amiable to see. But by his look, nobody could tell what he would do.

So he led Clement to a corner, and then placed two bundles of sugar cane, that were standing by the wall, in their two places in the bed.

"Why is that?" said Clement.

"Watch and wait," said he, and gave him a flash in the dark from his white teeth.

And in the dead of the night up rose Mike Fink, stretching and giggling, and reaching with his hands he ripped up a long board from out of the floor.

As soon as it came under his touch, he exclaimed in a delighted whisper, "Particle of a flatboat you are! Oh, I would know you anywhere, I'd know you like a woman, I'd know you by your sweet perfume." He gave it a smack and said, "Little piece of flatboat, this is Mike Fink has got you by the tail. Now go to work and ruin these two poor sleeping fools!"

Then he proceeded to strike a number of blows with the plank, dividing them fairly and equally with no favorites between the two bundles of sugar cane lying between the feathers of the bed.

"There! And there! If we have left you one whole bone between you, I'm not the bravest creature in the world and this pretty thing never sprang from a flatboat," he said.

Next, reaching under the tatters of the pillow, he snatched all three bags of gold, like hot johnnycakes from a fire, and lying down and stretching his legs, he went to sleep at once, holding the gold in his two hands against his chest and dreaming about nothing else.

When all was still once more, Clement stretched forth his hand and said, "Are you Jamie Lockhart? I ask your name only in gratitude, and I do not ask you *what* you may be."

"I am Jamie Lockhart," said he.

"How can I thank you, sir, for saving my life?"

"Put it off until morning," said Jamie Lockhart. "For now, as long as we are supposed to be dead, we can sleep in peace."

He and the planter then fell down and slept until cockcrow.

Next morning Clement awoke to see Jamie Lockhart up and in his boots. Jamie gave him a signal, and he hid with him in the wardrobe and watched out through the crack.

So Mike Fink woke up with a belch like the roar of a lion.

"Next day!" announced Mike, and he jumped out of bed. With a rousing clatter the moneybags fell off his chest to the floor. "Gold!" he cried. Then he bent down and counted it, every piece, and then, as if with a sudden recollection, he stirred around in the bed with his finger, although he held his other hand over his eyes and would not look. "Nothing left of the two of them but the juice," said he.

Then Jamie Lockhart gave Clement a sign, and out they marched from the wardrobe, not saying a thing.

The flatboatman fell forward as if the grindstone were hung about his neck.

"Bogeys!" he cried.

"Good morning! Could this be Mike Fink?" inquired Jamie Lockhart politely.

"Holy Mother! Bogeys for sure!" he cried again.

"Don't you remember Jamie Lockhart, or has it been so long ago?"

"Oh, Jamie Lockhart, how do you feel?"

"Fine and fit."

"Did you sleep well?"

"Yes indeed," said Jamie, "except for some rats which slapped me with their tails once or twice in the night. Did you notice it, Mr. Musgrove?"

"Yes," said Clement, by the plan, "now that I think of it."

"I do believe they were dancing a Natchez Cotillion on my chest," said Jamie.

And at that the flatboatman cried "Bogeys!" for the last time, and jumped out the window. There he had left three sacks of gold behind him, Clement Musgrove's, Jamie Lockhart's and his own.

"Gone for good," said Jamie. "And so we will have to get rid of his gold somehow."

"Please be so kind as to dispose of that yourself," Clement said, "for my own is enough for me, and I have no interest in it."

"Very well," said he, "though it is the talking bird that takes my fancy more."

"You may have that and welcome. And now tell me what thing of mine you will accept, for you saved my life," said the planter in great earnestness.

Jamie Lockhart smiled and said, "I stand in need of one thing, it is true, and without it I may even be in danger of arrest."

"What is that?"

"A Spanish passport. It is only a formality, and a small matter, but I am a stranger in the Natchez country. It requires a recommendation to the Governor by a landowner like yourself."

"I will give it gladly," said Clement. "Before you go, I will write it out. But tell me—will you settle hereabouts?"

"Perhaps," said Jamie, making ready to go. "That is yet to be seen. Yet we shall surely meet again," he said, knotting the sleeves of his coat about his shoulders and taking up the bird on his left forefinger. It said at once, as though there it belonged,

> "Turn back, my bonny,
> Turn away home."

Clement decided then and there to invite this man to dine with him that very Sunday night. But first, being a gullible man, one given to trusting all listening people, Clement sat Jamie Lockhart down in the Rodney inn, looked him kindly in the face, and told him the story of his life.

"I was once married to a beautiful woman of Virginia," he said, "her name was Amalie. We lived in the peaceful hills. The first year, she bore me two blissful twins, a son and a daughter, the son named for me and the daughter named Rosamond. And it was not long before we set out with a few of the others, and were on our way down the river. That was the beginning of it all," said Clement, "the journey down. On the flatboat around our fire we crouched and looked at one another—I, my first wife Amalie, Kentucky Thomas and his wife Salome, and the little twins like cubs in their wrappings. The reason I ever came is forgotten now," he said. "I know I am not a seeker after anything, and ambition in this world never stirred my heart once. Yet it seemed as if I was caught up by what came over the others, and they were the same. There was a great tug at the whole world, to go down over the edge, and one and all we were changed into pioneers, and our hearts and our own lonely wills may have had nothing to do with it."

"Don't go fretting over the reason," said Jamie kindly, "for it may have been the stars."

"The stars shone down on all our possessions," said Clement, "as if they were being counted and found a small number. The stars shone brightly—too brightly. We could see too well then not to drift onward, too well to tie up and keep the proper vigil. At some point under the stars, the Indians lured us to shore."

"How did they do it?" asked Jamie. "What trick did they use? The savages are so clever they are liable to last out, no matter how we stamp upon them."

"The Indians know their time has come," said Clement. "They are sure of the future growing smaller always, and that lets them be infinitely gay and cruel. They showed their pleasure and their lack of surprise well enough, when we climbed and crept up to them as they waited on all fours, disguised in their bearskins and looking as fat as they could look, out from the head of the bluff."

"They took all your money, of course," said Jamie. "And I wonder how much it was you would have had to give. Only yesterday I heard of a case where travelers captured in the wilderness gave up three hundred doubloons, seventy-five bars of gold in six-by-eights, five hundred French guineas, and any number of odd pieces, the value of which you could not tell without weighing them—all together about fifteen thousand dollars."

But if he spoke a hint, Clement did not hear it. "The money was a little part," he said. "In their camp where we were taken—a clear-swept, devious, aromatic place under flowering trees—we were encircled and made to perform and go naked like slaves. We had to go whirling and dizzied in a dance we had never suspected lay in our limbs. We had to be humiliated and tortured and enjoyed, and finally, with the most precise formality, to be decreed upon. All of them put on their blazing feathers and stood looking us down as if we were little mice."

"This must have been long ago," said Jamie. "For they are not so fine now, and cannot do so much to prisoners as that."

"The son named after me was dropped into a pot of burning oil," said Clement, "and my wife Amalie fell dead out of the Indians' arms before the sight. This made the Indians shiver with scorn; they thought she should have lived on where she stood. In their contempt they turned me free, and put a sort of mark upon me. There is nothing that you can see, but something came out of their eyes. Kentucky Thomas was put to death. Then I, who had shed tears, and my child, that was a girl, and Salome, the ugly woman they were all afraid of, were turned into the wilderness, bound together. They beat us out with their drums."

"The Indians wanted you to be left with less than nothing," said Jamie.

"Like other devices tried upon a man's life, this could have compelled love," Clement said. "I walked tied beside this woman Salome, carrying my child, hungry and exhausted and in hiding for longer than I remember."

"And now she is your second wife," said Jamie, "and you have prospered, have you not?"

"From the first, Salome turned her eyes upon me with less question than demand, and that is the most impoverished gaze in the world. There was no longer anything but ambition left in her destroyed heart. We scarcely spoke to each other, but each of us spoke to the child. As I grew weaker, she grew stronger, and flourished by the struggle. She could have taken her two hands and broken our bonds apart, but she did not. I never knew her in any of her days of gentleness, which must have been left behind in Kentucky. The child cried, and she hushed it in her own way. One morning I said to myself, 'If we find a river, let that be a sign, and I will marry this woman,' but I did not think we would ever find a river. Then almost at once we came upon it—the whole Mississippi. A priest coming down from Tennessee on a flatboat to sell his whisky stopped when he saw us, cut us loose from each other, then married us. He fed us meat, blessed us, gave us a gallon of corn whisky, and left us where we were."

"And you turned into a planter on the spot," said Jamie, "and I wonder how much you are worth now!"

"There on the land which the King of Spain granted to me," said Clement, bent to tell his full story now or burst, "I built a little hut to begin with. But when my first tobacco was sold at the market, Salome, my new wife, entreated me in the night to build a better house, like the nearest settler's, and so I did. There was added the fine bedroom with a mirror to hang on the wall, and after the bedroom a separate larder, and behind the house a kitchen with a great oven. And behind the kitchen in a little pen was a brand-new pig, and tied beyond him to a tree was a fresh cow. A big black dog barked in the dooryard to keep anybody out, and a cock jumped on the roof of the house every morning and crowed loud enough to alarm the whole country.

" 'How is this, wife?' said I.

" 'We shall see,' Salome said. 'For it is impossible not to grow rich here.' "

"And she was right," said Jamie.

"Yes, she was right," Clement said. "She would stand inflexible and tireless, casting long black shadows from the candle she would be always carrying about the halls at night. She was never certain that we lived unmolested, and examined the rooms without satisfaction. Often she carried a rifle in the house, and she still does. You would see her eyes turn toward any open door, as true as a wheel. I brought her many gifts, more and more, that she would take out of their wrappings without a word and lay away in a chest."

"A woman to reckon with, your second wife," said Jamie with a musing smile.

Clement closed his lips then, but he remembered how in her times of love Salome was immeasurably calculating and just so, almost clock-like, in the way of the great Spanish automaton in the iron skirt in the New Orleans bazaar, which could play and beat a man at chess.

"As soon as possible," said Clement aloud, "I would bring her another present, to stop the guilt in my heart."

"Guilt is a burdensome thing to carry about in the heart," said Jamie. "I would never bother with it."

"Then you are a man of action," said Clement, "a man of the times, a pioneer and a free agent. There is no one to come to you saying 'I want' what you do not want. 'Clement,' Salome would say, 'I want a gig to drive in to Rodney.' 'Let us wait another year,' said I. 'Nonsense!' So there would be a gig. Next, 'Clement, I want a row of silver dishes to stand on the shelf.' 'But my dear wife, how can we be sure of the food to go in them?' And the merchants, you know, have us at their mercy. Nevertheless, my next purchase off the Liverpool ship was not a new wrought-iron plow, but the silver dishes. And it did seem that whatever I asked of the land I planted on, I would be given, when she told me to ask, and there was no limit to its favors."

"How is your fortune now?" asked Jamie, leaning forward on his two elbows.

"Well, before long a little gallery with four posts appeared across the front of my house, and we were sitting there in the evening; and new slaves sent out with axes were felling more trees, and indigo and tobacco were growing nearer and nearer to the river there under the black shadow of the forest. Then in one of the years she made me try cotton, and my fortune was made. I suppose that at the moment," said Clement in conclusion, but with no show of confidence (for to tell the truth, he was not sure exactly what he was worth), "I may be worth thousands upon thousands of gold pieces."

"You are a successful man," said Jamie, "willy-nilly."

"But on some of the mornings as I ride out," said Clement, "my daughter Rosamond runs and stops me on the path and says, 'Father, why was it you shouted out so loudly in the night?' And I tell her that I had a dream. 'What was your dream?' says she. 'In the dream, whenever I lie down, then it is the past. When I climb to my feet, then it is the present. And I keep up a struggle not to fall.' And Rosamond says, 'It is my own mother you love, swear it is so.' And Salome listens at the doors and I hear her say to herself, 'I had better wake him each morning just before his dream, which comes at dawn, and declare my rights.'" Clement sighed and said, "It is want that does the world's arousing, and if it were not for that, who knows what might not be interrupted?"

But Jamie said he must go, and reminded him of the passport that was needed.

"You have interested me very much," said Clement, when he had written it out; for the poor man was under the misapprehension that he now knew everything about Jamie, instead of seeing the true fact that Jamie now knew everything about him. "And in order to persuade you to settle near-by, and come and talk more to me in the evenings, I invite you to dine with me on next Sunday night. It is only three hours' ride away, and I will meet you here to show you the way."

"And I think I will come," said Jamie, his teeth flashing in a smile. But his look was strange indeed.

"I wish to introduce you," said Clement, nevertheless, "to Salome; and to my daughter Rosamond, who is so beautiful that she keeps the memory of my first wife alive and evergreen in my heart."

Then they both rode away—Clement through the wilderness to his plantation, and Jamie on an errand of his own, with the raven perched on his shoulder.

2

Away out in the woods from Rodney's Landing, in a clearing in the live-oaks and the cedars and the magnolia trees, with the Mississippi River a mile to the back and the Old Natchez Trace a mile to the front, was the house Clement Musgrove had built that had grown from a hut, and there was the smoke now coming out the chimney. So while he was riding home through the wilderness, there in the kitchen was his wife Salome, stirring a ladle in a pot of brew, and there at the window above was his daughter Rosamond, leaning out to sing a song which floated away on the air.

Rosamond was truly a beautiful golden-haired girl, locked in the room by her stepmother for singing, and still singing on, because it passed the time away better than anything else. This was the way the song began:

> "The moon shone bright, and it cast a fair light:
> 'Welcome,' says she, 'my honey, my sweet!
> For I have loved thee this seven long year,
> And our chance it was we could never meet.'
>
> Then he took her in his armes-two,
> And kissed her both cheek and chin,
> And twice or thrice he kissed this may
> Before they were parted in twin."

Before Rosamond came to the end of this love ballad, which was meant to be very long, Salome unlocked the door and there she stood like an old blackbird.

"Well, lazy thing," said she, "I need fresh herbs for the pot. There are some extra-large ones growing on the other side of the woods at the farthest edge of the indigo field. Go and pick them and don't come back till your apron is full."

And for a thing like this she would send Rosamond out alone every morning while her father was away, when he knew nothing of it. She would think that perhaps the Indians might kidnap the girl and adopt her into their tribe, and give her another name, or that a leopard might walk out between two trees and carry her off in his teeth before she could say a word.

For if Rosamond was as beautiful as the day, Salome was as ugly as the night, and all her gnashing of teeth made her none the better-looking.

So Rosamond said, "Yes, stepmother," and taking the time to dress herself in a light blue gown, bind her hair with a ribbon, and bake herself a little hoecake for a lunch, she made ready for her expedition.

"If you come back without the herbs, I'll break your neck," said the stepmother. "Now be gone!"

Rosamond on her way had to pass through a little locust grove, and as she walked underneath the boughs where the wild bees were humming, she always took hold of her mother's locket, which she wore on a silver chain, and the locket would seem to speak of its own accord. What it never failed to say was, "If your mother could see you now, her heart would break."

On she went then, and no sooner was she out of sight under the trees than up to the door rode Clement coming home on his horse. Salome had sent the girl away in the nick of time, and indeed she had had her eyes upon her husband since he was no more than a speck of dust, to see if she could tell from a distance what presents he was bringing; and she wanted to get her own name on the best ones.

Clement came in, and the first thing he said was, "Hello, wife, where is my little daughter gone?" for she had not run out to meet him, and that was as if the jessamines had not bloomed that year.

"Oh, she is safe enough, I have no doubt, and has forgotten us entirely," replied Salome, with a smile on her face all its own. "Her idleness has led her out of the house again, out dressed in her best, fit to meet the King there in the nettles, and not a word behind her of where she was going. Here I am keeping her dinner warm over the fire." For this was the way she would talk to her husband.

"My poor little daughter!" said Clement sadly. "It is a good thing that I married the woman who would look after my child," he said to himself, "or what would happen to her then?"

Then Salome gritted her teeth, but she saved up on her

anger to vent it in some grand way later, when the time was sure to come.

"How much did you get for your tobacco, and where are the presents you were to bring?" she said next.

"Here are the moneybags, count it for yourself when the table is cleared," said Clement, who would not cheat even a little midge of its pleasures. "And here is the packet of needles, the paper of pins, length of calico, pair of combs, orange, Madeira, and muscadine wine, the salt for the table, and all from the apothecary that he could provide."

"And is the silk gown for me too?" Salome asked, paying no heed to the rest but holding up to herself a beautiful dress the green of the sugar cane, and looking like an old witch dressed up for a christening.

"No, that is not for you, but for Rosamond," said Clement. "And so are the hairpins, and the petticoat stitched all around with golden thread, the like of which the young ladies are wearing in New Orleans."

"As if she were not vain enough as it is!" cried Salome. "And now these fancy things will be putting thoughts into her head, you mark my words, and away she will run, off with some river rat, like Livvie Lane and her sister Lambie on the next plantation, there within a week of each other."

Then Rosamond came back, with an apron full of herbs for the pot, and tried on the dress and the petticoat both before she would eat. What a sight she was! She pinned up her hair and she swept up and down the puncheon floor swaying like a swan, and flung her train about.

And the moment she saw Rosamond in the new clothes, Salome's heart felt like lead, and she had no more peace day or night.

"What have you been doing while I was gone?" said Clement when Rosamond had flung her arms around his neck to thank him, for she had never suspected that he would bring her anything except a childish and harmless toy.

"Oh, every day I go to the farthest edge of the indigo field, on the other side of the woods, and gather the herbs that grow there," said Rosamond, "for my stepmother will have no other kind. And today a little old panther came out from behind a holly tree and rubbed up against my side. I took him in my arms, to see what he would do, and he gave me a little purr. Just then the mother panther let go from the tree above my head, and down she lit on her feet, stirring up the leaves like a whirlwind and growling from end to end, like the gold organ in the Rodney church. She was ten feet long and she must have been nine feet high when her hair started rising, for she reached away over my head when I looked her up and down. The first thing I knew she took me up in her teeth, but very easy, by the sash, and carried me all the way home through the woods before she set me down at the gate. She swung me hard, and I knew she meant it for a lesson, and so I came away from her, and here I am, but the whole time I never dropped the leaf of one herb."

Now Rosamond was a great liar, and nobody could believe a word she said. But it took all the starch out of the stepmother, you can be sure, to send Rosamond out on a dangerous errand, hoping some ill might befall her, and then to have her come safely back with a tale of something even worse than she had wished upon her. As for Rosamond, she did not mean to tell anything but the truth, but when she opened her mouth in answer to a question, the lies would simply fall out like diamonds and pearls. Her father had tried scolding her, and threatening to send her away to the Female Academy, and then marching her off without her supper, but none of it had done any good, and so he let her alone. Now and then he remarked that if a man could be found anywhere in the world who could make her tell the truth, he would turn her over to him. Salome, on the other hand, said she should be given a dose of Dr. Peachtree.

"Next year, perhaps, she will submit to a tutor," said Clement to Salome, "and learn Greek and sewing and the guitar."

"Never! I will learn it all for myself," said poor Rosamond, and picking up the guitar, sure enough, she played "Fair as the Rose."

Near Clement's house, down in a gully, lived a poor widow and her six gawky daughters and her only son. The son, who was the youngest, was named Goat, because he could butt his way out the door when his mother left him locked in, and equally, because he could butt his way in when she left him locked out. Every time she would go off, and tell him to be sure not to stir from the house while she was gone, to any wrestling matches, horse races, gander pullings, shooting matches, turkey shoots, or cockfights whatever in Rodney, or she would knock his head off with the skillet, she would be sure to find him missing when she got back. And this in spite of all her promises to bring him presents, and so it was useless to bring him any. Goat was full of curiosity, and anything he found penned up he would let out, including himself. He had let loose all the little colts and pigs and calves and the flocks of geese, peahens, chickens, and turkeys in that part of the country, and he would let anything out of a trap, if he had to tear its leg off to do it.

Now by some manner and the way things come about, Salome had found a familiar in little Goat, and it was there in the back of her head to use him for her own ends. She could not buy him for a slave, because he was not in any degree a black African, but she took the old mother a quart jar of pickled peaches she had put up with her own hands, and looked so grand, that the mother freely gave her Goat for whatever occasion he was wanted, just so she got him back.

So the very next day after Clement brought Rosamond the silk dress like the dresses the Creole girls wore, and Salome's heart was getting no lighter but as heavy as iron, down crept the old stepmother behind the house into the gully and called away at Goat.

Goat, who had been left by the coals to watch a johnny-cake, came out through a hole in the door with his hair all matted up and the color of carrots, and his two eyes so crossed they looked like one. He smiled and he had every other tooth, but that was all. He stood there with his two big toes sticking up.

"I hope you are well, Goat," said Salome, giving her own brand of smile, and Goat said he had never felt better, as far as he could recollect.

"You remember that you are working for me, don't you, Goat?" said Salome.

"Yes indeed," said Goat, "until a better offer comes along."

"Then here is your work for today," said Salome, and she bent down as close to him as she dared, for he could have bitten her, and whispered a rigmarole into his ear.

"Leave it to me," said Goat afterwards. "You have not spoken to a deaf man."

So they sealed a bargain and Salome crept home to sit and wait.

In the meanwhile, Rosamond was fastening on her clothes, and she was putting on the new silk gown, for she was determined never again to wear any other. She pinned up her long hair with the pins. Then just as she was getting a look into the mirror, in walked Salome like a shadow across the sun.

"Well, my fine lady, I need herbs for the pot, for all that you got yesterday have lost their power today," she said. "Pick me nothing but the fine ones growing on the other side of the woods at the farthest edge of the indigo field. And don't dare to come home till you have filled your apron."

"Oh, but that will ruin my dress," cried poor Rosamond.

"That is because you are fool enough to wear it," said the stepmother, and so Rosamond had to go, and the stepmother called after her, "If you come back without the herbs, I'll wring your neck!"

Rosamond passed again through the little locust grove, and heard the golden hum of the bees, and took hold of the little locket. The locket spoke and said, "If your mother could see you now, her heart would break."

Then on she went, and this time, skulking along behind her, but well out of sight, was Goat, bent on his task and thinking as hard as he could so as not to forget it.

First Rosamond went through the woods and then she passed along the field of indigo, and finally she came to the very edge, which was by the side of a deep, dark ravine. And at the foot of this ravine ran the Old Natchez Trace, that old buffalo trail where travelers passed along and were set upon by the bandits and the Indians and torn apart by the wild animals.

There were the thorns and briars and among them the green herbs growing. No matter how many Rosamond picked, they always seemed to be just as thick the next day. So Rosamond held up her fine silk skirt and threw the herbs into it as she picked.

Now all this time, Goat had been keeping the little distance behind Rosamond, looking for his chance to finish her off. Those had been his directions in the long rigmarole Salome had whispered in his ear. If Rosamond were to take a look over the ravine's edge, he was to give her the right push, and if she were to fall into one of the bear traps he was to stop up his ears and not let her loose. And if anything whatever chanced to happen to her, he had only to remember to bring back a bit of her dress, all torn and rubbed in the dust, as a sign she was surely dead, and he would get his reward, a suckling pig.

Rosamond went about her business of gathering herbs, and if she saw or heard anything of Goat in the bush, she thought it was an Indian or a wildcat and paid no attention to it; for she was wearing her mother's locket, which kept her from the extravagant harms of the world and only let her in for the little ones.

It was not long before she opened her mouth and sang,

> "The moon shone bright, and it cast a fair light:
> 'Welcome,' says she, 'my honey, my sweet!
> For I have loved thee this seven long year,
> And our chance it was we could never meet.'"

And although she had never loved or known any man except her father, her voice was so sad and so sweet and full of love itself that Goat was on the very point of tears in the bushes.

No sooner had she finished the first verse of the song when there was a pounding of hoof-beats on the Trace below, and along under the crossed branches of the trees came riding none other than Jamie Lockhart, out for a devilment of some kind, with his face all stained in berry juice for a disguise.

When he heard Rosamond singing so sweetly, as if she had been practicing just for this, he had to look up, and as soon as he saw her he turned his horse straight up the bank and took it in three leaps.

"Good morning," said he, getting off his horse, a red

stallion named Orion, which at once began to graze upon the fine herbs growing under his nose.

"Good morning," said Rosamond, and she was so surprised that she let her skirt fall, and all the herbs she had gathered scattered to the wind.

"That is a grand dress you are wearing out for nothing," said Jamie, with a look coming into his eye.

"All my dresses are like this one," said Rosamond. "Only this is the worst of the lot, and that is why I don't care what happens to it."

"How lucky you are today, then, my girl," said Jamie, giving her a flash of his white teeth. "So put off the clothes you're wearing now, for I'm taking them with me."

"And who told you you might ask me for them?" cried Rosamond.

"No one tells me and no one needs to tell me," said Jamie, "for I am a bandit and I think of everything for myself."

And he led her by the hand into a clump of green willows, where they would not be seen by other travelers or bandits coming along the Trace.

"So pull your dress off over your head, my bonny, for you'll not go a step further with it on," he said.

"Well, then, I suppose I must give you the dress," said Rosamond, "but not a thing further."

"Oh!" spoke up Goat, where he was hiding behind the bush. "It's a shame now to take that off, for the petticoat is much too beautiful beneath."

But Rosamond was so busy with the little pins, which she took care to stick back in the dress, that she could not hear.

Then she stood before Jamie in the wonderful petticoat stitched all around with golden thread, and at once he must have that too.

"Put off your petticoat," he said, "for the dish requires the sauce."

The tears sprang for a moment to Rosamond's eyes, and she said to herself, "If my mother knew I had to give up the petticoat as well, her heart would break."

"Oh!" cried Goat from his hiding place, "never give up the spangled petticoat, for you are far too beautiful beneath!"

But at that moment Rosamond was so particular not to catch the tassels on the thorns that she never heard a thing.

Then she stood in front of Jamie in her cotton petticoats two deep, and he said, "Off with the smocks, girl, and be quick."

"Are you leaving me nothing?" cried Rosamond, darting glances all about her for help, but there wasn't any to be had, though Goat looked about too.

"I am taking some and all away with me," said Jamie. "Off with the rest."

"God help me," said Rosamond, who had sometimes imagined such a thing happening, and knew what to say. "Were you born of a woman? For the sake of your poor mother, who may be dead in her grave, like mine, I pray you to leave me with my underbody."

"Yes, I was born of a woman," said Jamie, "but for no birth that she bore or your mother bore either will I leave you with so much as a stitch, for I am determined to have all."

So Rosamond took off the first smock. "You may not know," said she, "that I have a father who has killed a hundred Indians and twenty bandits as well, and seven brothers that are all in hearty health. They will come after you for this, you may be sure, and hang you to a tree before you are an hour away."

"I will take all eight as they come, then," said Jamie, and he took out his airy little dirk. "Off with the last item," he said, "for I must hurry if a father and seven sons are waiting for the chase."

"Oh!" said Goat from the bush. "You are done for now, and my work is finished, and I might as well go home."

But Rosamond, who had imagined such things happening in the world, and what she would do if they did, reached up and pulled the pins out of her hair, and down fell the long golden locks, almost to the ground, but not quite, for she was very young yet. And as for hearing the sighs of little Goat, she was thinking of how ever she might look without a stitch on her, and would not have heard a thunderclap.

"Thank you, now," said Jamie, gathering up all the clothes from the grass and not forgetting the gold hairpins from

France that were scattered about. "But wait," he said, "which would you rather? Shall I kill you with my little dirk, to save your name, or will you go home naked?"

"Oh," cried Goat, "you are done for either way, but if you let him kill you now I will get a suckling pig."

"Why, sir, life is sweet," said Rosamond, looking up straight at him through the two curtains of her hair, "and before I would die on the point of your sword, I would go home naked any day."

"Then good-by," said Jamie, and leaping on his horse and crying "Success!", away he went, leaving her standing there.

When Rosamond reached home, the sun was straight up in the sky, and there were her father and stepmother sitting on either side of the front door in their chairs.

Salome said, "Rosamond, speak! Where are the pot-herbs I sent you for?"

But her father said, "In God's name, the child is as naked as a jay bird."

And he took hold of her and asked her what in the name of heaven had befallen her.

"Well, I will tell you," said Rosamond.

But first her father put over her his planter's coat, which doused her like a light, and said, "Before you begin, remember that truth is brief, for if you lie now, you will catch your death of a chill." And her stepmother's ears were opening like morning-glories to the sun.

Rosamond began and said, "Every day, I go to the farthest edge of the indigo field, on the other side of the woods, to gather the herbs that grow there, for my stepmother will have no other kind."

"Yes, yes," said poor Clement, "but make haste with the story."

"So on this day," said Rosamond, "I was gathering the herbs into my skirt and singing this song:

" 'Oh the moon shone bright, and it cast a fair light:
    "Welcome," says she, "my honey, my sweet——" ' "

"Never mind all the verses now," said Clement. "Skip over to the end."

"Well, in the end, there came the bandit," said Rosamond,

"riding his horse up the Old Natchez Trace. He was a very tall bandit with berry stains on his face so that nobody could tell what he looked like or who he was. His horse was as red as fire, and set to work right away biting off the tops of the herbs."

"Yes, no doubt," said Clement. "But hurry on with the news. The truth is longer than I thought."

"So he said 'Good morning,' and I said 'Good morning.' And I was so surprised to see him so polite that I dropped my skirt to the ground and all the herbs fell out, and that is why I did not bring them home."

"A likely excuse!" said Salome, and her eye traveled round to look for Goat, and her two hands went into fists to take him by the heels and shake his story out.

"What next, after the salutations?" poor Clement begged. "For something must go on from there, and this is the time I dread to hear what it was."

"Next, the bandit said, 'That's a grand dress you are wearing out for nothing,' for alas, I had on the New Orleans dress," said Rosamond, "and Father, for this, I never deserve to have another."

And her father said "Alas" too, for now he was going to hear what had happened to it.

"Well," said Rosamond, "the long and short of it is that the bandit took it, and took not only my dress but my petticoat with the golden tassels, my cotton petticoats, and, although I asked him in his mother's name to refrain, my underbody."

"And did he leave you then?" cried Clement.

"He left me then," said Rosamond, "though I had not been sure what he would do, my hair, brushed every night as it is, still being of uncertain length when I let it down."

And at first they did not believe her, but by dark she had told it the same way at least seven times, until there was nothing else to do but believe her, unless they jumped down the well.

"Where did the bastard go?" cried Clement, jumping to his feet the moment he was convinced, "for I will follow him and string him to a tree for this."

"I gave him my word that you would indeed, Father," said

Rosamond, "but he replied that there was no hope for you to saddle your horse for that, since he was aiming to cross the river into the wilds of Louisiana, where you could never get at him."

Nevertheless, Clement saddled his horse and rode all night, looking for the bandit, and finding nothing but the dark and cold.

But to Salome he said, "There is a thing the bandit did not count on, and it is this: I know the man to catch him where I cannot, the man who has the brains and the bravery and the very passport to do it. And that is Jamie Lockhart, the man who saved my life at the Rodney inn, and the very man to avenge my daughter's honor as well."

"But how do we know your daughter retains her honor?" asked Salome, gritting her teeth at the very thought of rescue. "Bandits, panthers, and the like indeed! The panther carries her gently in his teeth, and sets her down without harm, and the bandit robs her of every stitch she has on, and leaves her untouched. It is something to meditate about, my good husband!"

"Hold your tongue, woman!" cried Clement, full of anger, and for once he wondered if the stepmother really loved his little girl. Something seemed to fill the air like a black cloud, and the house shook as if from thunder.

When Rosamond appeared, dressed in her old blue gown, Clement asked her for the last time if she was quite sure she had not fallen into the bayou and gotten her dress wet, so that she had to leave it to dry there on the bank, with all her petticoats, and if they might not be there still.

But Rosamond said, "No, Father, it was a bandit that took them, and all just as I told you."

So Clement said, "Sunday night, which is tomorrow, I am bringing Jamie Lockhart to search out and kill this bandit of the woods. But in the meanwhile, stay away from the place where the pot-herbs grow, and never go there again. For next time, the bandit may do worse."

But Rosamond only opened the window and sang a song which floated away on the bright blue air.

Now back in the herb patch, Goat had seen everything and

lost track of nothing. But at the final point, seeing Rosamond separated from her clothes, he had had to make his mind up which to follow, and he had decided upon the clothes. It was evident that the clothes had cost money and Rosamond had not, and he was influenced by the bandit's choice in the matter as well. And besides, Goat knew better than not to place his hand before his eyes in the presence of naked ladies, or he would get the pillory, and that way he would have been sure to fall in the briars going home.

The bandit had galloped away like the wind and was a flicker on the hill, so Goat made haste to start off in that direction. He followed along up the Natchez Trace, keeping his eye out for the dress, and once he thought he saw it floating on the creek, but it was only the lily pads, and once he thought he saw it flying in the sky, but then he heard a distant moo, and it was only the old flying cow of Mobile going by. So eventually, after a day of starvation, he turned around and came back home.

The door was locked, but he butted his way into the kitchen and took up a loaf from the shovel and put it in his mouth.

"Hello, Mother," he said, "here I am back."

"Oh, cark and care," said his mother. "Did you bring any money?"

"No," he said, "but I have only to ask the rich lady for it, for I am doing a job of work for her and she is in debt to me."

"Are you sure she is rich," said the mother, "since she has paid you nothing?"

"All the surer," said Goat. "Rich she is, and a good thing for her, for she's as tall as a house, as dark as down a well, and as old as the hills, with such a face that's enough to make anybody die laughing or crying to see it, if they had nothing else to do."

"Then you'll do well to get your money from her," said the mother. "And get it in a hurry, or I'll brain you with the skillet for being so little comfort to me in my old age."

"I'm on my way now, as soon as I hear the news," said Goat. "What's the cry? Are my six sisters married off yet?"

"No more than they were before or ever will be," said the mother, "without a cent in the world to go with them."

"Well, you have only to wait till I bring the money home to see how the money works," said Goat. "Tell all six virgins to come in and brighten themselves up a little. Pack up their clothes, sit them on their chairs, and wait for my return."

So he was off up the hill and gave a whistle, and Salome came out in her hood and led him to the pear orchard, where the branches raining down to the ground hid them from sight.

"Well," said she, "did you follow her?"

"Like the lamb to school," said Goat.

"You saw it all?"

"I gave myself but one blink of the eye," said Goat.

"Then what of the moment when she stood there naked?" asked Salome, ready to burst for wanting to know.

"Oh, I shut my eyes for that," said Goat, whirling in a circle before her black frown. "For they'll never put me in the pillory for *you* to bail out."

"Why don't I kill you?" cried Salome furiously. "Ass! Fool! Then did you follow her still? What was the path she took home?"

"I followed the girl until she and the dress separated and took opposite ways," said Goat. "And since he chose the dress, I chose the dress, and went off hot after that, but it got away. Yet I recall one place now where I haven't looked, and that is in your bear trap."

"Fool!" cried Salome. "It is the girl I sent you to follow, and now the thing has happened which I looked for to happen, and you were blinking your eye! You have robbed me of my satisfaction, and robbed me of my proof. Idiot! Begone!" For she knew how to talk to Goat just like his own mother.

"First I would like my pay," said Goat.

"Here, take it then," said Salome, and she began boxing him well about the ears.

"That's enough," said Goat, "for I did not work quite that hard."

"One more chance will I give you," said Salome. "I think the girl will go out again in the morning. Follow her and never let her out of your sight. And whatever transpires, remember it as if it were written down and you could read, and come back and tell me."

"Consider it done," said Goat, and at once he jumped in a bush to hide.

Early the next morning, before the sun was up, the step-mother waked Rosamond and shook her till her bones rattled.

"Out of your bed, lazy girl," she said. "Your father has left already to ride to Rodney's Landing. He's buying the whisky, from Father O'Connell, for Jamie Lockhart to drink tonight when he brings him home for supper, and he's left you in my charge. So get up and milk the cows."

"Why should the slaves not milk the cows, for they do it every day and I have never done it before," said Rosamond, for it seemed to her that she had not got her dream dreamed out.

"Silence!" cried the stepmother. "I am punishing you, you stupid thing, for what happened yesterday. Have you forgotten already?"

So Rosamond got out of her bed, and while she was brushing her hair and tying it up, the stepmother made off with the little locket on the silver chain which had belonged to the girl's own mother, and Rosamond never missed it. Then Salome hurried away to her room hunched like an old rabbit over her prize.

Rosamond dressed and said her prayers and then she was out of the house and in the paddock milking the cows. But she found she did not mind it at all; for the creatures allowed her to lean her head against their soft foreheads, where their horns stood shining like the crescent moon, and they put out their warm tongues on her cheek, and not a one of them kicked her over for not knowing how a cow is milked, but let her go on with it in her own way.

When the rooster was crowing from the rooftop, Rosamond came round the house carrying the pail with the sound of the foam in it. The smell of night had not yet returned to the woods; and there was a star shining in the daylight. The gate was there at Rosamond's hand, and she touched it and it opened, and she went through; and up at the window was something dark looking down, her stepmother or the cat.

Rosamond found herself before she knew it at the edge of

the forest, and with the next step the house was out of sight. And she was still carrying the pail of milk in her hand.

It was so early that the green was first there, then not there in the treetops, but green seemed to beat on the air like a pulse. Once a redbird gave a call, for he too had been waked up in the dark, and had been purely compelled to sing this one note before the prism light of day would divert it into the old song. But Rosamond was not led by him to sing for herself, and only walked on and on into the woods.

The next sounds she heard were distant hoof-beats, lapping like the river waves against the sunrise. It was Jamie Lockhart coming on red Orion, the same as he had been before, in his robber's rags. He rode right up to her, and reached down his arms and lifted her up, pail of milk and all, into the saddle with scarcely a pause in his speed.

Up the ridge they went, and a stream of mist made a circle around them. Then it unwound and floated below in the hollows. The dark cedars sprang from the black ravine, the hanging fruit trees shone ahead on their crests and were hidden again by the cedars. The morning sky rolled slowly like a dark wave they were overtaking, but it had the sound of thunder. Over and over, the same hill seemed to rise beneath the galloping horse. Over and under was another sound, like horses following—was it her father, or an echo?—faster and faster, as they rode the faster.

Rosamond's hair lay out behind her, and Jamie's hair was flying too. The horse was the master of everything. He went like an arrow with the distance behind him and the dark wood closing together. On Rosamond's arm was the pail of milk, and yet so smoothly did they travel that not a single drop was spilled. Rosamond's cloak filled with wind, and then in the one still moment in the middle of a leap, it broke from her shoulder like a big bird, and dropped away below. Red as blood the horse rode the ridge, his mane and tail straight out in the wind, and it was the fastest kidnaping that had ever been in that part of the country.

Birds flew up like sparks from a flint. Nearer and nearer they came to the river, to the highest point on the bluff. A foam of gold leaves filled the willow trees. Taut as a string stretched over the ridge, the path ran higher and higher. Rosamond's head fell back, till only the treetops glittered in her eyes, which held them like two mirrors. So the sun mounted the morning cloud, and lighted the bluff and then the valley, which opened and showed the river, shining beneath another river of mist, winding and all the colors of flowers.

Then the red horse stood stock-still, and Jamie Lockhart lifted Rosamond down. The wild plum trees were like rolling smoke between him and the river, but he broke the branches and the plums rained down as he carried her under. He stopped and laid her on the ground, where, straight below, the river flowed as slow as sand, and robbed her of that which he had left her the day before.

Now when Rosamond got home from that expedition, the first thing Salome said to her was, "Well, where is the milk?"

Rosamond, whose head was spinning like a spindle, and who had not had her breakfast yet, said, "I dare say the red horse drank it up."

Then the stepmother knew everything. "You needn't tell me the story now," she said, "for I could tell it to you," and she licked her lip like a bear after a tasty dish of honey. Then she slapped the girl and dragged her into the house by her heels and propped her by the brooms and buckets and looked her up and down, and thought what she could do to her. And it was too bad the way she treated her the whole day.

"The house must be spotless for the arrival of the stranger," said Salome, "and it's tonight Jamie Lockhart is coming to deliver you from this fiend, though it's late in the day for that. And so it is up to you to wash the floor and polish the row of dishes and candlesticks and put fresh candles in, and sweep the hearth and lay the table and bring the water and clean the fowls and catch the pig and roast him, and get the loaves to baking in the ashes."

But if she thought Rosamond would open her mouth, she was sadly mistaken. The girl never complained a time, but took the beatings and the abusings with the tranquillity of an Indian savage, and cared nothing for how she might look.

"Yes, stepmother," she would say every time, and set to with no more care than if she were only threading a needle.

At dark, Clement rode home from Rodney, and Jamie Lockhart was riding beside him.

Salome was there at the door, in a great fancy gown and heels on her shoes to tilt her up, and with jewelry all over her so that she gave out spangles the way a porcupine gives out quills. So Jamie straightaway got out his presents, and for Salome he had brought a little gold snuffbox, which was just right.

Then at the top of her lungs Salome called Rosamond in from the kitchen, and if she had thought the girl had been making herself beautiful for Jamie Lockhart, she was badly mistaken. For Rosamond was in a sad state to be seen, with ashes all in her hair and soot on either cheek and her poor tongue all but hanging out, and her dress burned to a fringe all around from the coals, and altogether looking like a poor bewitched creature that could only go in circles.

So then Jamie saw Rosamond and they never recognized each other in the world, for the tables were turned; this time he was too clean and she was too dirty. You would think there had never been two lovers on earth with less memory of meeting in the past than Jamie and Rosamond. So he gave her a glance as if she were the peg on the wall where he would hang his hat if he had one, with never a moment's notice of that true worth which he had sampled, and handed her over his gift, which was nothing less than a paper of the pins taken from her own fine dress he had stolen.

Rosamond was so ragged and dirty that she could do no more than stand there in her tracks, and Clement had to speak up for her and say, "Thank you kindly, and the sweet little thing stands in need of pins to be sure, for she has lost them all as I will tell you with the whisky."

But Rosamond only batted her eyes and dropped her mouth open. As for Jamie, he shone like the sun from cleanliness, youth, wisdom, and satisfaction, and with the dirt and stain gone from his cheeks he was the perfect stranger to the bandit. So if Jamie did not see his kidnaped beauty standing before him, neither did Rosamond see the first sign of her dark lover, and that was that.

Jamie, whose motto was "Take first and ask afterward," had not learned Rosamond's name or where she lived, with her father and seven vengeful brothers, thinking to find out that information on his next ride through the vicinity of the indigo field, doing one thing at a time according to his practice. And besides, it was either love or business that traveled on his mind, never both at once, and this night it was business. For he had not let Clement go that first time without a memorandum of catching him again and finding more. He took a little walk around the room and began counting up to himself what the man's fortune might be, in case he could get hold of it all.

Then Salome told Rosamond to make haste in serving up the dinner, and she did, just as she was, in her rags. With her own hands she spread the abundance on the table and stood by and waited while the others ate and ate, and kept Jamie's glass filled to the top and even spilling over. And in between times she ran around the table and fanned with the peafowl feather fan to keep the flies away—but in a witless manner, so that once or twice she gave Jamie Lockhart a knock on the head. Clement was almost made to think at one time, when she turned a dipper of gravy into Jamie's lap, that this poor daughter of his did not wish to be rescued. And never once did she even say "I beg your pardon" to him.

Every time Clement said, "Why not take your proper seat, daughter, and let the servant wait upon us?" Rosamond would simply back out of sight, and finally the stepmother said, "She is doing this of her own choice, no doubt, to allow you a chance to talk, for it is a delicate matter with her to be rescued from a bandit, it never having happened to her before." And Jamie did not turn a hair, which made the old woman bite her lip.

"Leave us then, wife, since it is time for earnest conversation," said Clement.

Then Clement told Jamie Lockhart all—all, that is, that he knew himself, for the prize bird of the information was not yet in his net. And Jamie, gathering that some bandit had stolen some daughter's clothes on some spot in the forest wilds, thought that he must truly be a success in the world now, for the rest of them were copying him.

"Will you save the poor girl from this brigand, my friend?" asked Clement. "A reward of great price will be yours if you find the fellow and send such a menace to our womanhood out of the world."

"I cannot remain indifferent to such a request," said Jamie. "What is the reward you mention?"

"Deliver my daughter," said Clement, "and she is yours."

Then Jamie gave a start, you may be sure, to think of the poor disgraced creature that had let a peafowl feather fan knock his head off, as being his own wife. His eyes looked to the side, like a horse's near the quicksands, and the next moment he jumped up and said, "I must think first, for I am a busy man." And he began walking up and down.

Salome, whose ear had been at the crack, came to take his arm a while, and gave him a raring wink, and spoke a word to him of Rosamond's dreadful pride and conceit and how she needed her lesson, and he did not like the sound of that.

Then Clement took him by the other arm and said that a young thing so sweet and pure as his daughter, who sang the whole day long, and only looked this way for the one night because something had no doubt gone wrong in the kitchen, was more of a reward in herself than his house and lands put together, and Jamie could not say he liked the sound of that either.

Then Rosamond herself came forward, and putting her finger in her mouth like a little long-drawered creature from a covered wagon, said:

> "Here I stand all ragged and dirty!
> If you don't come kiss me I'll run like a turkey!"

And when he did, she had mustard on her mouth. And that was the last straw.

"Perhaps," said Jamie to himself as he walked up and down, "I should marry her, for she is rich and will be richer and then die, and all things come to him who waits, but that is not my motto. Why the devil could she not have been beautiful, like that little piece of sugar cane I found for myself in the woods? And it is not as if he had a choice of daughters, but the one only." He thought on, and said to himself, "The wife of a successful bandit should be a lady fit to wear fine dresses and jewels, and present an appearance to the world when we go to New Orleans, and make the rest rave with their jealousy. This young creature, however rich, is only a child with a dirty face, and I think the cat has her tongue as well, or the devil her brains."

And besides all that, it is a fact that in his heart Jamie carried nothing less than a dream of true love—something of gossamer and roses, though on this topic he never held conversation with himself, or let the information pass to a soul. And being a man of enterprise in everything, he had collected, whenever it happened to be convenient, numbers of clothes and jewels for this very unknown, that would deck a queen and be missed if a queen left them off. But as for finding this dream on earth, that Jamie was saving until the last, and he had done no work on it as yet except for that very morning; though he hated to waste that.

"What is your answer?" said Clement.

"Well, I will save her, then marry her," said Jamie, "but not now; for I must ride far tonight. I will do it tomorrow."

Clement took his hand and shook it, unable to thank him. Then the stepmother stuck out her wrist to him as if she wanted her hand kissed in the city manner, and when Jamie obliged her, he bowed, and she saw a little bit of berry juice sticking behind his ear. So she guessed everything.

"I wonder what presents he will be bringing next," said she in a loud whisper.

This angered Clement, who said to her, "You will find that men who are generous the way he is generous have needs to match."

Then Jamie waved his hand and rode away alone and still empty-handed, in the confusion of the moonlight, under the twining branches of the trees, bent on no one knew what.

Now as soon as Jamie had truly dishonored her, Rosamond began to feel a great growing pity for him. And the very next morning after he had come unrecognized to dinner, she set out of the house, carrying a lunch of a small cake she had baked especially, to find where he lived. Up in the window behind her something was looking down—it was either her stepmother or the cat. Rosamond forgot the locust grove, for her path lay another way.

How beautiful it was in the wild woods! Black willow, green willow, cypress, pecan, katalpa, magnolia, persimmon, peach, dogwood, wild plum, wild cherry, pomegranate, palmetto, mimosa, and tulip trees were growing on every side, golden-green in the deep last days of the Summer. Up overhead the cuckoo sang. A quail with her young walked fat as the queen across the tangled path. A flock of cardinals flew up like a fan opening out from the holly bush. The fox looked out from his hole.

On and on she went, deeper and deeper into the forest, and its sound was all around. She heard something behind her, but it was only a woodpecker pecking with his ivory bill. She thought there was a savage there, but it was only a deer which was looking so hard at her. Once she thought she heard a baby crying, but it was a wildcat down in the cane.

At last she crossed a dark ravine and came to a place where two long rows of black cedars were, and at the end sat a house with the door standing open. It was a little house not as pretty as her own, made of cedar logs all neatly put together, and looking and smelling like something good to eat.

So she began walking up the lane, holding the cake in her hands, and when she did she heard a voice saying,

> "Turn back, my bonny,
> Turn away home."

And there was a raven, sitting in a cage which hung at the window.

But she kept on until she got there, and then went up and

knocked modestly at the door. However, though her ears were filled with listening, there was no answer to be heard. So she looked through the window and then she looked through the door, but it was all dark and she could see nothing, and so she walked in.

"Is there anybody here?" she called.

But if there was an answer, she couldn't hear it, and so she walked through the house, from the one room to the other. She took a candle she carried in her apron and held it lighted before her. But nobody was there at all, except the raven in the cage, who said once more, when he saw her out of his bright eyes,

> "Turn again, my bonny,
> Turn away home."

"I'll do nothing of the kind," said Rosamond, who had had enough commands from her stepmother.

Everything was in the greatest disorder, bags and saddles lay in the middle of the floor, the remains of big fires lay as if suddenly quenched in the fireplaces. Jugs and long knives, coats and boots of all sizes, tallow candles, and a wonderful bridle of silver and gold were lying in a heap. A young rat sat up like a squirrel at the head of the table, in front of a row of dirty, empty plates. And there in the very middle of the table, close beside a platter with the head of a black bear on it, was Rosamond's own beautiful green silk dress, rolled up into a ball like a bundle of so many quilting pieces.

The first thing she did was to put on her own dress, and then, having nothing else to do, she rearranged all the furniture in the rooms and then washed all the plates and the big knives the robbers had been eating with. Then she hung everything on pegs that she could lift up, and shoveled away the ashes and got down on her knees and scrubbed the hearth until it shone brightly. She carried in the wood and laid a new fire, and was just putting the kettle on to boil when she heard a great clatter in the yard, and the robbers were coming home.

Rosamond hid behind a big barrel in the corner and in they came, with their spotted hounds panting around them. Jamie Lockhart rose up the tallest, his face all covered with the berry juice, just like the day before. He was the leader.

As soon as they saw what had happened to the house, they all stopped as dead as if they had been knocked on the head from behind.

"What grandeur is this?" shouted Jamie in anger.

"What bastard has been robbing the place?" cried the others. "For half the things are missing!"

Then they rushed about turning things over and pulling things down and looking under the tables and stools and between the featherbeds, undoing all of Rosamond's hard work, and at last they found Rosamond sitting behind the barrel, wearing her dress and eating her little cake.

"The first time we went away without a sentry to watch the door, a woman got in!" they said. "Kill her!" they cried.

And they were going to kill her, but she said, "Have some cake."

So each one of them took a piece of cake, and she said she had baked it herself.

The robbers began to argue about what to do with her then, but Jamie, who was their leader and was called nothing but "the Chief," said, "That business can wait till later. First we must count up our booty and divide it, for that is the order of affairs."

So they sat down to count up the worth of this and that, with one who could count keeping close track of it all, and Rosamond had to wait until they had finished.

"Now," said Jamie. "As to the girl, we must either keep her or kill her, for there is nothing midway about any of this."

"Kill her," said one, who was the smallest and who had gotten the smallest piece of cake.

"No, keep her," said the rest, "because she can cook for us and keep the fire up."

"That is settled then," said Jamie, "according to the vote of the band," and having sent them out to stable the horses, he grabbed Rosamond and kissed her as hard as he could, saying if the vote had gone otherwise he would have put the ones who voted wrong out of the way for keeps, since he was running things around there.

So Rosamond stayed and kept house for the robbers. And at first the life was like fairyland. Jamie was only with her in the hours of night, and rode away before the dawn, but he spoke as kind and sweet words as anyone ever could between the hours of sunset and sunrise.

In the daytime, in the silence of noon, while they were all away, she cooked and washed and baked and scrubbed, and sang every song she knew, backwards and forwards, until she was through with them. She washed the robbers' shirts till she wore them out with her washing, and then one evening they brought her home for a surprise a spinning-wheel that had come their way, at great inconvenience, and so she spun and manufactured all they would need for the cold Winter coming. She packed them lunches to take with them in the mornings, a bucket for each, in case they became separated before they would have their food at noon over the fire of an oak tree. And she wove a mat of canes and rushes and made them wipe their feet when they came in at the door.

So the day was hard but the night canceled out the day. When the moon went sailing like a boat through the heavens, between long radiant clouds, all lunar sand bars lying in the stream, and the stars like little fishes nibbled at the night, then it was time for the bandits to ride home. Rosamond waited alone but not afraid. At last they were there, and eating their hot supper, and Jamie came all weary from his riding and robbing, to fling off his sword and his boots and fall on the featherbed, where he would place his head on the softer pillow of her bosom and his face would settle down from all his adventures.

But when she tried to lead him to his bed with a candle, he would knock her down and out of her senses, and drag her there. However, if Jamie was a thief after Rosamond's love, she was his first assistant in the deed, and rejoiced equally in his good success.

She begged him every night to wash off the stains from his face so that she could see just once what he really looked like, and she swore that she believed he would be handsome, but he would never do it. He told her that this was for the best of reasons, and she had to be content with that. Sometimes she would wake up out of her first sleep and study his sleeping face, but she did not know the language it was written in. And she would look out the window and see a cloud put up a mask over the secret face of the moon, and she would hear the pitiful cries of the night creatures. Then it was enough to make her afraid, as if the whole world were circled by a band of Indian savages, and she would shake poor Jamie until he shouted up out of his sleep, and rouse him up to see his eyes come open. She would often wipe the rain away from his face when he came home, but nothing, it seemed, could penetrate those stains. No matter how she scrubbed, until he would let out a yell, the stains were just as dark as before. And sometimes, because he had told her that he had bound himself to an heiress, she was afraid he might get up and fly away through the window while she was fast asleep; so she would not let him go until up the gentle levee of the morning clouds the sun would climb to touch the brim, and the bandits flew over the ridge.

The only thing that divided his life from hers was the raiding and the robbing that he did, but that was like his other life, that she could not see, and so she contented herself with loving all that was visible and present of him as much as she was able.

The trees were golden under the sky. The grass was as soft as a dream and the wind blew like the long rising and falling breath of Summer when she has just fallen asleep. One day Jamie did not ride away with the others, and then the day was night and the woods were the roof over their heads. The tender flames of the myrtle trees and the green smoke of the cedars were the fires of their hearth. In the radiant noon they found the shade, and ate the grapes from the muscadine vines. The spice-dreams rising from the fallen brown pine needles floated through their heads when they stretched their limbs and slept in the woods. The stream lay still in the golden ravine, the water glowing darkly, the colors of fruits and nuts.

"Remember your own words," said the bandits to Jamie, as they were riding away without him to a rendezvous. " 'Who followeth not up his own work will fail.' "

"I cannot fail," said Jamie, and he half pulled out his little dirk.

For he thought he had it all divisioned off into time and place, and that many things were for later and for further away, and that now the world had just begun.

"All these treasures are for you," he said to Rosamond at night when the bounty was counted out.

"Thank you," she replied, and sorted and stored it all—even labeled it, with the date if she could keep account of it in the dream of time passing. And though she did not know when she would ever find use for a thousand pieces of English silver or the scalp of a Creek, she took tender care of each item.

And every night Jamie would come in with a mess of quail, bobolinks, purple finches, or bluebirds, which he would heap on the table and tell her to dress. Once he brought a heron, the color of Venetian glass, and it tasted as wild as a wild pear, but there was not enough of heron breast for any to eat except Jamie and Rosamond, and the rest ate buffalo meat in silence, under the smoke of the torches.

If her dead mother could have seen Rosamond then, she would never have troubled herself to come back one more time from the repose of Heaven to console and protect her, and could have fully given herself over to the joys of Paradise from then on; that is, if she could overlook from that place the fact that Jamie was a bandit; for Rosamond had quite forgotten the locket.

The only thing that could possibly keep her from being totally happy was that she had never seen her lover's face. But then the heart cannot live without something to sorrow and be curious over.

Now on the day that he had followed Rosamond to the robbers' house, all had gone well with Goat, and he was right at her heels, if she had turned around she would have been behind him, until she knocked at the robbers' door.

At first there had been no answer at all, and Goat decided they must have come on the wrong day. But then the raven had looked at them and said,

> "Turn back, my bonny,
> Turn away home."

So Goat, who never disobeyed any orders as plain as that, had turned at once and gone back to his mother.

"Hello, Mother, I'm home again," said he, butting his way

in to the kitchen. "A raven advised me to get back at once: what's the news?"

"Oh, cark and care," said his mother. "Did you bring back any money?"

"No," said he, "but I expect to receive some at any moment, for the lady I work for is very rich."

"Then it's a good thing," said his mother, "or I would be wishing I had strangled you at birth for all the comfort I get out of you."

"Are my six sisters married off yet?" asked Goat.

"They are just as they were yesterday, and that is unwed," said the mother.

"You have only to wait until I am paid for my work," said Goat, "and they will come rushing at all six of them as if they were in burning houses."

Then he told her good-by and set off up the hill to ask Salome for his pay.

"What, are you back so soon?" said Salome, when they had hidden in the orchard.

So he said he was back and that it was soon.

"Did you follow her this time?" Salome asked.

So he said yes, he followed her; that is, until a raven spoke up and told him it was time to go home.

"What raven?" cried Salome, for she did not know what raven he could mean.

Well, he said, it was simply the raven they kept to answer the door, he supposed, when they were not at home. And now might he have his pay?

"Go break your neck!" cried Salome. "Your mother should have strangled you in your cradle."

Goat said that made two that thought so, but that was not many. And he asked what if he came back to see her tomorrow, would she pay him then?

"Oh," said Salome, "when are you going to take your brains out and put them back in straight? Go to this house again, discount anything said to you by a raven, and when you find where Rosamond has gone, see what she does, and whether she cries or not, and come back and tell me."

"And when you have heard, will you pay me then?" asked Goat.

"Now you have it in your head," said Salome. "And get gone!"

Then she boxed both his ears and he set out, first passing through the chicken yard and letting a hen out of the coop, and then through the pigsty, where he let out a little pig with red spots. On second thought, he put both of these and a big red peach into his bag as advance payment to provide against starvation.

He was going along and going along through the deep woods, and went part of the way with a little wild boar that trotted as proudly as a horse, and had almost reached the robbers' house when he saw another place. There, up an avenue of cedar trees, at the entrance of a cave built of rock, sitting by a fire, was a bandit named the Little Harp, and he was just as ugly as it was possible to be. But Goat did not mind that, and sang out, "Good morning, mister! What are you up to? How are you feeling and how is everything with you? Is there anything that I could do for you? And how far is it from here to where the kidnaped young lady goes and raps on the door?"

Little Harp blinked his eyes and smiled, for nothing pleased him on a fine day like a lack of brains.

"Come here," said he, "and stay with me. I will give you work to do."

"Gladly," replied Goat, "but I am already working for another, a very rich lady, an old stepmother, who wants me to see that her stepdaughter is well kidnaped by a bandit. But I don't see why a young fellow like me could not take care of two commissions at one time."

"That is the way to talk," said the Little Harp. "You will come up in the world."

"How much are you going to pay me every month?" asked Goat, taking a seat on a rock and stretching his legs.

"Never mind," said the Little Harp. "Just do whatever I tell you, and you won't regret it."

"What will you want first," asked Goat, "if I do work for you?"

"Well," said Little Harp, "I might take a notion for a big fat hen."

"If that is all, I don't think that will be very hard," said

Goat, and reaching into his little bag he pulled out the hen, which indeed the Little Harp had been watching with watering mouth from the first moment, if he had not smelled it down the way. So the Little Harp took it. "I must consider," said he. He wrung the hen by the neck, plucked a feather off it, passed it through his little fire, and swallowed it down. "Yes, I believe you could do the work," he said. "You are hired. But now there is one thing that you must remember never to do, as long as you work for me. Never open the little trunk you will see standing by my featherbed inside the cave."

"If I do, you may cut off my ears," promised Goat.

"You may hear something say, 'Let me out,'" said Little Harp, "but you must answer, 'Not yet!' If you open the trunk even one inch, that will be the end of you."

"And will the money stop then too?" asked Goat.

"Completely," said Little Harp. "There is not a chance in the world of your ever getting another cent once you are dead."

"I agree to the terms," said Goat, and they shook hands.

"Now," said Goat, "what would you like me to do?"

"Well," said Little Harp, "I feel a fancy coming over me for a pig with red spots, but if that is impossible to find, don't look for it."

"Impossible my foot," said Goat. "I can get it for you as easy as breathing," and he pulled out his pig.

"Go pickle him," said Little Harp.

"Would you not rather have a peach?" asked Goat. "For that won't take as long."

"Yes," said the Little Harp, "I believe I would rather have a peach."

So he ate the peach on the spot, seed, fuzz, and all, and Goat asked him with the last swallow, "What next?"

"Next I would like a girl, kidnaped and brought to my door here," said Little Harp. "But I dare say you will not know where to find one."

"I have no kidnaped girl with me," said Goat, "but I have one in my mind. How soon do you want her?"

"By tomorrow," said Little Harp.

"It's as good as over with," said Goat. "You may imagine her now, skipping over the hill."

"Let me see her little finger first," said Little Harp. "Then, if I like that much, I will take her."

Goat was so overjoyed that he got up and did a little dance called "Rabbit Hash." Then away he went.

Little Harp went inside his cave and stretched his feet on the featherbed to wait.

Then there was a voice which had the sound of coming out of a little trunk, and it said, "Let me out!"

"Not yet!" cried Little Harp, and he began to cry, "Oh, you do plague me so, to be nothing more than a head wrapped up in blue mud, though I know your eyes and your tongue do stick out as red as fire, the way you came down off the pole in Rodney Square." And he said, "Oh, Big Harp, my brother, please stay in the trunk like a good head, and don't be after me eternally for raiding and murdering, for you give me no rest."

But the voice said, "Let me out!" all the while, even after the Little Harp fell asleep and went to snoring.

Back home in the gully, in came Goat, butting his way through the front door, which was locked, and they were all sitting around the table.

"Good news!" he cried, snatching up a johnnycake. "Sisters, the time for one of you has come. Arise and prepare yourself, for the time is set for tomorrow."

"The time for what?" they said.

"You must listen more closely, if you want to hear wonders," said Goat. "Sisters, all six of you point up your ears, and take this in with the full set of twelve. I am now working on the side for a gentleman up yonder in a cave, and when I said, 'What do you want?' he said first a hen, then a pig, then a peach, and before long he was dead for a wife. And although I do not speak all that runs to the end of my tongue, I conversed with myself behind my hand, and said, 'Here I am with six hopping virgin sisters in my own family, and my own house a nest of women—this job was designed for me in Heaven!' And I rushed here at once with the good news."

"Well," said the mother, "is he rich?" For she did all the talking for the six daughters.

"Oh, I am sure he must be rich," answered Goat, "for he

has, for one thing, a trunk so precious that he talks to it, and lets no one open it even to the extent of an inch."

So all the daughters there in a row began to sit up and toss their hair about.

"Is he handsome?" said the youngest.

"Well," said Goat, "I would not say outright that the gentleman is stamped with beauty, for when I saw him, his head was no larger than something off the orange tree, his forehead was full of bumps like an alligator's, and two teeth stuck out of his mouth like the broadhorns on a flatboat. He came out walking like a goose and dressed like a wild Indian. But beauty is no deeper than the outside, and besides, all six of you are as weighted down with freckles as a fig tree is with figs, which should render you modest."

"Which of us shall marry him?" they asked one another, and fell to giggling.

"Let us send him up the eldest," said the mother, "for she has waited the longest," and so that was decided.

"Be ready at sunup for the kidnaping," said Goat, "and be sure one of your little fingers is as sweet as a rose, or nothing will be doing."

At the same time, Clement and Salome were riding in the little cart over the plantation, which by now had all been harvested.

"Next year," said Salome, and she shaded her eagle eye with her eagle claw, and scanned the lands from east to west, "we must cut down more of the forest, and stretch away the fields until we grow twice as much of everything. Twice as much indigo, twice as much cotton, twice as much tobacco. For the land is there for the taking, and I say, if it can be taken, take it."

"To encompass so much as that is greedy," said Clement. "It would take too much of time and the heart's energy."

"All the same, you must add it on," said Salome. "If we have this much, we can have more." And she petted the little nut-shaped head of the peacock on her lap.

"Are you not satisfied already?" asked her husband.

"Satisfied!" cried Salome. "Never, until we have got rid of this house which is little better than a Kentuckian's cabin, with its puncheon floor, and can live in a mansion at least five stories high, with an observatory of the river on top of that, with twenty-two Corinthian columns to hold up the roof."

"My poor wife, you are ahead of yourself," said Clement, and he felt of her forehead to see if it were hot. And indeed it was burning like fire, for Salome worked her brain day and night to think up her wishes.

"I am doing well enough," said Salome. "It is you whose hand is cold."

"Then it is cold with grief," said Clement.

"Oh, now that that lazy, extravagant daughter of yours is no longer here," said Salome, "we shall be able to count much more on our plans, for now you have no one to will the money to, and so we may as well spend it at once."

"Hold your tongue, wife!" cried Clement, and he raised up and almost put his hands upon her, but he could not, for the poor contamination of her heart broke out through her words until it showed even on her skin, like the signs of the pox, and he could not punish her.

Then Salome, having Clement in her power, sent him out to make fresh application to the Governor for more acres, and resigned to that, he rode away to Rodney.

And there, staying once more at the inn where the landlord with the trembling ears kept hospitality for the travelers, Clement chanced to see Jamie Lockhart again, dressed as fine as anyone out of New Orleans in his button-sewn coat with the sleeves knotted around him capewise.

Now the truth is, Jamie had neglected poor Clement entirely, being so taken up with his daughter, and had never ridden back to do the thing he had promised, but only put it off. So he ran forward now to clasp his hand, and sat him down in the grogshop and bought him a glass of the best Kentucky whisky. Then he told him, as his excuse, that his business had carried him all of a sudden to New Orleans on the very night when he saw him last, where he had been from then till now, as busy as he had ever been in his life, and that he had therefore been unable to ride after the bandit who had frightened his daughter.

"However," said Jamie, "drink down bravely, for it is my

belief that the fellow will do her no more harm if he did not do it at first thoughts."

"Alas," said Clement, "while you were gone, he thought of it, for my child is stolen away."

Then the salt tears ran down his cheeks, and Jamie's heart was reached by the old man's sorrow, and after buying him another glass of whisky he spent the night in the same bed again without stealing a cent from him. Indeed, since he had not stolen it yet, he doubted if he ever would, for the old man had trusted the evil world and was the kind of man it would break your heart to rob.

"I have just succeeded in enlarging my plantation twice over," said Clement, when they met again in the morning, "though the size of anything whatever has nothing to do with the peace of mind. My wife will build a tower to overlook the boundaries of her land, while I ride its woods and know it to be a maze without end, for my love is lost in it."

So, in his soft feeling, Jamie declared before he knew it that he would track down this beast if it was the last thing he did, blow his brains out, and marry the poor daughter in the bargain.

For never once, due to the seven rampant brothers which his own kidnaped bride brought into the conversation now and again (whenever he recalled that he was promised to another), did the thought alight on Jamie's head that she might be for one moment the same as Clement's thumb-sucking child. It was the habit of the times for heiresses to disappear, as though swallowed up, and one more or less did not cause Jamie to stop and take notice.

"Tonight," said Jamie now, rising to his feet, "I will ride the woods to the north of here, and you must ride them to the south, and if the man has been running ahead of you, we will head him off."

Clement shook his hand, and when he could speak, it was to say once more, "Save her, and she is yours still."

On the plantation, Clement, inspired by Jamie to the hope of making a rescue that very night, ate a whole roast pig for supper and set out on horseback just as the stars began to come out.

He rode south on the Old Natchez Trace and then took another trail branching off to the deepest woods, a part he had never searched before. The wind shook the long beards of the moss. The lone owls hooted one by one and flew by his head as big as barrels. Near-by in the cane the wildcats frolicked and played, and on he rode, through the five-mile smell of a bear, and on till he came all at once to the bluff where deep down, under the stars, the dark brown wave of the Mississippi was rolling by. That was the place where he had found the river and married Salome. And if he had but known it, that was the place where Jamie Lockhart had carried his daughter, there under the meeting trees at the edge.

Clement's horse stopped, and all of a sudden there was a rustle of the leaves and a ghost or a shape went by behind him. In the next moment Clement was riding in pursuit, for he thought it was the bandit now for sure, and he rode and rode furiously, though it seemed to him that he had lost the way and that he was only charging in a circle; and this had happened to him before. But then he heard the same sound, and he brought his horse to a stop and jumped off his back. And although up until that moment he had thought all he defended too sacred for the privilege of violence, he now flung himself forward with such force that the wind left his body for a moment. He ran headlong through the dark, and then it seemed he clasped the very sound itself in his arms. He could feel the rude powerful grip of a giant or a spirit, and once he was brushed by a feather such as the savages wore, and they threshed about and beat down the earth for a long time. It was as dark as it could possibly be, for the stars seemed to have gone in and left the naked night overhead, and so Clement wrestled with his monster without any aid from the world at all. He tossed it to the ground and it flew up again, he bent it back with all his strength and it would not yield, it fought with the arms of a whirlwind and flung him on the ground, and he was about to give up, but then it clung to him like the Old Man of the Sea and he could not get out from under. At last with a great crash he threw himself upon it and it went down, and he sat there holding it down where it lay with his own body for the rest of the night, not daring to close his eyes for his concern, and for thinking he had won over wickedness. And it was not till the eye of the red sun looked over the ridge that Clement saw he had fought all night with a willow tree.

In the meanwhile, Jamie was riding the woods to the north and wishing he were home instead. He had just started to stain his face with the berry juice when he heard all of a sudden the sounds of screaming come out of a cave in the hillside.

"There, I have found the witless thing, without even trying," he said; "for it would be like her to scream at her bandit the whole night through and give him no peace, out of pure perversity." And he rode straight up to the door of the cave and threw a rock against it.

"One at a time!" came a voice from the inside. "If you're the next sister, you must wait till tomorrow!"

And "Oh! Oh! Oh!" came the screaming.

"Open up," cried Jamie. "If you're after doing a murder, I can give you aid."

"Can you now?" asked the Little Harp, for of course it was he inside with one of Goat's six sisters, and he came to the door and peeped through the chink.

"Here, you see, is the very rope to tie her up with," said Jamie, holding up nothing in the dark.

Then the Little Harp let him in, and Jamie followed him back in the cave to where he had one of Goat's sisters standing straight up in the middle of the floor with her apron tied over her head.

"Well, proud, dirty thing," said Jamie to her, for he had no doubt it was Clement's dim-witted daughter, and he gave her a mock kiss, "what are you doing inside there?"

"Oh! Oh! Oh!" she screamed back.

"She does nothing but scream," said the Little Harp. "That is her gift, and I would just as soon try to sleep in the room with a hyena."

"Why did you tie her up so snug?" asked Jamie. "You let the more dangerous hands and feet go free and only confine the harmless head."

"Oh, I have her blindfolded because she is so ugly," said the Little Harp. "I had her kidnaped sight unseen and test untested, you see, being given to understand she was in demand by another bandit, and never knowing that this was the masterpiece I would get. But as soon as I saw her little finger, I told her to go drown herself in the river."

"Oh!" screamed this sister of Goat's.

"But when I told her that," continued the Little Harp, "she told me that she was only one of six thriving sisters, all as strong as oxen, and that the whole company of them would come up here after me and beat my head to a pulp if I did not untie her."

"Ah yes, the brand of that speech is familiar to me," said Jamie, and he only laughed at the poor creature's fury, and gave her another peck that she did not know was coming.

"If you were to take your rope and tie the remainder of her up," said Little Harp, "do you suppose that would make her hush, or put her out of order for a little while?"

"That is a brilliant solution you have got there," said Jamie, thinking to have some fun with the two sillies, since the night was wasted anyway, and so he drew his hands around the girl's middle and gave her a little squeeze. But if she had screamed loudly enough before to be heard in church at Rodney, she screamed loudly enough next to be heard down at Fort Rosalie.

"That was wrong," said the Little Harp. "I would give anything for you not to have done that."

"There, we have got her started going louder instead of softer," said Jamie, "and I fear there will be no stopping her now. She will go on in this direction, getting louder and louder, until the rocks of this cave will come falling in, and bury us all alive. Why, my friend, don't you marry her instead?"

"Though it would keep me from deafness and a landslide, I would not do it," said the Little Harp, shaking his tiny head.

"Well, then," said Jamie, looking about, and thinking on the side that a bandit, however slow-witted, who could not do better than this cave must have something amiss somewhere. "How about putting the maiden in the trunk?"

"No! No! No! Never!" cried the Little Harp, and he ran and held the lid down. "For oh, the noise leaks out of the trunk too!" And he put his ear to the lock. "Listen!" he said.

But Jamie heard nothing at all, and at this show of silliness he thought it was time to change his tune. So he went to snatch up the girl without further dilly-dallying and take her home to Clement.

But the Little Harp came waddling forward like an old goose, and there held up in his right hand was the carving knife.

"I won't marry her," said he. "So come let's kill her! I'll hold her down, and you slice her down the center."

At this the poor girl nearly lost her voice, but she recovered it in time to scream a flock of bats down from the ceiling before she toppled over like the dead at their touch.

Jamie jumped with all his might on the Little Harp and dragged him in the corner.

"The game is over," said Jamie, "and the joke is told. You are not the fool I took you to be, but another fool entirely, and I ought to break all your bones where you need them most. Now tell me your name and I will tell you to get out of the country."

"My name is Little Harp, and my brother's name is Big Harp, but they cut off his head in Rodney and stuck it on a pole."

"Then get out of the country," said Jamie, "for I have heard of the Harps, that ran about leaving dead bodies over the countryside as thick as flies on the dumpling."

"Aha, but I know who you are too," said Little Harp, sticking out his tongue in a point, and his little eyes shining. "Your name is Jamie Lockhart and you are the bandit in the woods, for you have your two faces on together and I see you both."

At that, Jamie staggered back indeed, for he allowed no one who had seen him as a gentleman to see him as a robber, and no one who knew him as a robber to see him without the dark-stained face, even his bride.

He half pulled out his little dirk to kill the Little Harp then and there. But his little dirk, not unstained with blood, held back and would not touch the feeble creature. Something seemed to speak to Jamie that said, "This is to be your burden, and so you might as well take it." So he put the little dirk back and contented himself with one more blow with his arm, to knock the Little Harp's wind out for an hour or so.

Then he picked up the girl and set her up on his horse, still dead in her faint and sitting up as nice and stiff as a bird that is looked at by a snake, and so without bothering to unwrap her, Jamie took her off to Clement's house.

By now it was daylight, and he stopped and took the stain off the one side of his face and tied his coat about him, and then he knocked at the door.

"Here is your daughter," he said to Clement, and the old man nearly died with joy, but then he saw the foot sticking out and then the rough red hand. "My daughter has skin as white as a lily," he said, "and her foot is small.

"Oh, God in Heaven," he said, and then the apron fell off of its own accord and he saw the poor fish face looking at him. "Jamie Lockhart, you have rescued the wrong daughter. This is none of mine."

Then there was general misery, except for Goat's sister, who was rather pleased than sorry, now that the whole thing was over and she was not lying at the bottom of the river, and she went off home to tell the rest of her sisters the horrible things that had happened to her.

"But the worst of all," said Jamie to himself, as he stopped in the black ravine and stained his face again, "is that I have let the Little Harp go." He wondered now why he had done it, and he said, "This is going to be a burden to me," for he knew that by the time he got home, the Little Harp would have moved in.

4

THE NEXT MORNING, after the double failure to rescue his daughter from the bandit in the woods, Clement was sitting with his wife on his little veranda. All at once the front gate opened with a little sound, and there came Rosamond up the path.

They could hardly believe their eyes, until she had come and given them a kiss apiece.

"Well, where is your husband?" asked the stepmother.

"He sent his respects to my parents," said Rosamond, "but he is too busy to come himself."

Salome looked first at Rosamond's belt and then at her countenance, and was mortified to see no signs of humility in either place.

"Haughty and proud as ever, I see," she remarked, getting up to pace about her in a circle, "though the whole world knows you are no better than that gully girl who ran to the cave of the Little Harp and got blinders tied on her head for her trouble."

But Rosamond took out the presents she had brought back to them, very fine and expensive articles indeed, speaking well for her prosperity, and handed them out.

As for Clement, he embraced his daughter time after time, and was so filled with the joy of seeing her that he could not think up a single question to ask her.

So Salome said, "I dare say your robber-bridegroom has got enough of you and sent you packing."

"No, stepmother," said Rosamond, "for he will not let me leave his side."

"Then he keeps you a prisoner, does he?" cried Salome. "Just as I thought!"

"No, stepmother," said Rosamond, "for I stay of my own accord. But I thought of my father to whom I had not said good-by and it was more than I could bear, and I began to beg and to beg until at last this very morning I received permission to come here. But it is for a short time only."

"I dare say when you return you will find that your bird

has flown," said the stepmother next, for she pretended to know a great deal about the way of bandits.

"No, stepmother. We have a trust in one another that this separation cannot break," said Rosamond, but her stepmother only began to smile and ponder, and ponder and smile.

"Tell me, my ladybird," said Clement when he could speak through his delight and see through his tears, "are you happy?"

"Yes, Father," said Rosamond. "Although my husband is a bandit, he is a very good one."

"And does he bring you home fine clothes, dozens of beautiful dresses and petticoats too?" asked Salome, and Rosamond knew what she meant, but still she said, "Yes, indeed."

Then Clement thought, "She has met the man who can keep her from lying, and she is entirely out of the habit." And he was puzzled, and thought, "I should like to meet this strict bandit who has taught my daughter to be truthful."

"Where is your home, my child?" he asked.

"It is not far from here," said Rosamond, "but it might as well be a hundred miles, for it is so deep and dark in the woods, that no one knows the way out except my husband, who brought me."

Now the stepmother drew closer in upon Rosamond as she paced her circle, and said, "Does your husband kill the travelers where they stand, when he has finished with them, and leave them there in their blood, like all the rest?"

"I believe not," replied Rosamond, "but that I could not say, for he has never told me and I never asked him."

"What? You poor ignorant girl!" cried the stepmother. "I suppose you will say next that you do not even know his name for he has never told you!"

"That is correct," replied Rosamond.

"What!" cried the stepmother, and she was drawing in closer still. "You have been kept in darkness! Now do not tell me you have never seen the man by the light of day without his robber's disguise."

For although Goat had failed every time to make his report to Salome, she had divined these things for herself by means of the very wickedness in her heart.

"That is correct too," said Rosamond, and how her step-mother laughed to hear it, like a jay bird in the tree.

"Now tell us," said she finally, and she stood just above Rosamond's head looking down upon her, "whether or not you are truly married, in the eyes of heaven and the church."

So Rosamond looked back and forth between her father and her stepmother, and then, "Oh indeed," she said. "Father Danny O'Connell married us."

"God help him then," cried Clement, jumping to his feet, "for I see him on every journey I make to Rodney, and he has never told me."

"Ah, then, that is because the good father was drunk the day he married us," said Rosamond.

"Well, then, if he married you in the church, how is it you were not seen by the whole population of Rodney when you came down the steps?" said Salome.

"Oh, he did not marry us in the church," said Rosamond, "but at home in the woods."

"How did he know where to go, if I could not find it?" asked Clement, with his sorrow on his heart.

"That is because he did not go of his own knowledge or control," said Rosamond. "For my husband kidnaped him and brought him there. My husband rode down the streets of Rodney, and there was the priest, and he reached right down and got him like a hawk, and took him home. He was just a little drunk to begin with, so my husband set him up on his own horse, nicely sideways because of the cloth, and rode him home, and there on the hearth he married us, as drunk as a lord at the time, but very binding in the way he put it."

"How did poor Father O'Connell ever get so bad as that?" asked Clement. "For all that he is a good shot, a horse judge, and a sampler of Madeira, I have never seen Father O'Connell so beside himself he did not know which sinner he was giving an almo to on the streets."

"It was my husband that got him so drunk," said Rosamond. "First when they came, they had a little bragging contest, each surpassing the other until nobody won, and then my husband started a little contest to see who could empty the most from a jug for the count of ten, and all the rest stood around in a ring and they counted up to twenty-five. It was because of his sporting blood that Father O'Connell could not set down the jug, and he won."

"These competitions are dangerous things," said Clement. "I myself would have been the loser of more than my sense and my money once, if it had not been for Jamie Lockhart."

"And did the priest marry you then?" Salome asked, and she bent down over Rosamond and looked ready to gobble her up.

But Rosamond said, "Yes, then Father O'Connell said the marriage for my husband and me, and the whole house was decorated with flowers in gold vases," and her voice was as clear as a bell.

"It is strange that he remembers nothing of this," said Clement to himself. "He must have thought he had been only to fairyland, with all the glitter about, and never mentioned it."

There has to be a first time for everything, and at that moment the stepmother gave Rosamond a look of true friendship, as if Rosamond too had got her man by unholy means. But Rosamond began to wilt then, like a flower cut and left in the sun.

So the next day Salome got Rosamond away alone and they were sitting by the well, like a blood mother and daughter.

"My child," said the stepmother, "do I understand that you have never seen your husband's face?"

"Never," said Rosamond. "But I am sure he must be very handsome, for he is so strong."

"That signifies nothing," said the stepmother, "and works neither way. I fear, my dear, that you feel in your bosom a passion for a low and scandalous being, a beast who would like to let you wait on him and serve him, but will not do you the common courtesy of letting you see his face. It can only be for the reason that he is some kind of monster."

And she talked on until she saw the pride and triumph fading from Rosamond with every breath she took. For Rosamond did not think the trickery went so deep in her stepmother that it did not come to an end, but made her solid like an image of stone in the garden; and her time had come to believe her.

So Salome drew so close to Rosamond that they could look down the well and see one shadow, and she whispered in her ear, "There is one way to find out what your husband looks like, and if you want me to tell you: ask me."

"What way is that?" asked Rosamond, for at last she had to know.

"It is a little recipe, my dear, for removing berry stains," said Salome, "and there are no berry stains in the world so obstinate that this brew will not rub them out."

"What brew is that?" asked Rosamond, for she had to learn.

"Pay close attention, and stamp it on your brain," said the stepmother, "so you can remember it until you get home."

Then she repeated the recipe for removing berry stains from the face, as follows: Take three fresh eggs and break them into clear rain water. Stir until this is mixed, then boil it on the stove. Take the curd and set it off to cool. Add a little saffron, a little rue, and a little pepper. Throw into a quart of drinking-whisky and churn it up and down until it foams. Sponge it on, and the stains will go away.

"Remember that," said Salome. "It can't fail."

And then she reached down and pulled Rosamond's own mother's locket out of her little pouch and dangled it up before the girl.

"You forgot this, in your haste to leave," she said. "And you had better take it this time, for you might need it." Then she put it around Rosamond's neck and fastened it with her own hands.

She advised her to take one of the tomahawks with her also, to protect herself with, in case her husband should turn out to be too horrible to look at; but Rosamond was not that far gone that she would take it.

Then the girl thanked her for all her trouble and advice, and embraced her around the neck, and kissed her father, and said she intended to go back to her husband at once, sooner than she was expected, so as to surprise him.

"How happy he will be," said Clement. "And poor Jamie Lockhart!"

"Or how unhappy he will be, one or the other," said Salome, and then she ran in at the last moment to write the recipe for removing berry juice stains down on paper with her fine black quill, in case Rosamond might not remember everything that went into it.

While she was out of the way, it was Clement's time to speak to Rosamond alone, and he asked her about her husband for the last time.

"If being a bandit were his breadth and scope, I should find him and kill him for sure," said he. "But since in addition he loves my daughter, he must be not the one man, but two, and I should be afraid of killing the second. For all things are double, and this should keep us from taking liberties with the outside world, and acting too quickly to finish things off. All things are divided in half—night and day, the soul and body, and sorrow and joy and youth and age, and sometimes I wonder if even my own wife has not been the one person all the time, and I loved her beauty so well at the beginning that it is only now that the ugliness has struck through to beset me like a madness. And perhaps after the riding and robbing and burning and assault is over with this man you love, he will step out of it all like a beastly skin, and surprise you with his gentleness. For this reason, I will wait and see, but it breaks my heart not to have seen with my own eyes what door you are walking into and what your life has turned out to be."

Then Salome came running with the recipe written out and folded. "Hold this in your hand," she said.

So Rosamond took it and set out.

"Shall I walk part of the way with you?" her father called, but she went on alone, into the woods.

This time, Rosamond was afraid as she ran along, and she stumbled over the stones and was caught by the sharp thorns. She turned and looked behind her all the way, as if she were frightened of being followed by a beast which would tear her apart. A little whirlwind blew over the grass and pulled her hair down and tangled it with twigs. The little ravine was cold and gray, the mist lay on it, and the stream ran choked with yellow weeds, and the squirrels were shrieking through the woods.

At last she came to the lane between the two rows of cedars with the little house there at the end, and the door standing open and dark as before, but now scattered with fallen leaves. So she began walking up the lane, holding the little written recipe in her hand and wearing the locket around her neck, and she said, "If my mother could see me now, her heart would break."

But when she said that, a cloud rolled over the sky and a cold wind sprang up like Wintertime, and just as she came to the house the yellow lightning gave a flash like swords dueling over the rooftop. There at the window hung the raven in the cage, which had gone all rusty, and Rosamond had forgotten all about him. So he said,

> "Turn back, my bonny,
> Turn away home."

But in she went.

There in the dark hall she stood and looked through the door. All the bandits were there except her husband, and there was a strange bandit in his place, standing in the middle of the room while they lay on the floor and laughed at him. He was the ugliest man she had ever seen in her life, and she thought her heart would stop beating and her breath would stop in her throat before she could hide down behind the barrel, safe out of sight.

The whisky and the wine were going round, and the bandits were all as dirty and filthy as if she had left them for a year instead of a day. The whole house was tumbled and wrecked, with everything topsy-turvy and the rats back inside and running about unharmed. All her hard work had gone for nothing, and it was as if she had never done it.

The strange bandit was the Little Harp, who had moved in to live with Jamie Lockhart, not failing to bring his little trunk, which was there beside him. And all the men were lying about him and listening to him as if he were their chief, and nobody spoke of their real chief, or asked where he could be.

The jug went round from hand to hand, and soon all the robbers were drunk and the Little Harp was the drunkest of all.

"Where is the girl that you have here?" he cried. "Where do you keep her? Bring her in and give her to me!"

And then all the robbers laughed in great good spirits at the way the Little Harp asked for the girl that belonged to the king of the bandits, which was a thing they had often wished they could do themselves.

"She is away on a visit," they told the Little Harp, "and besides, she belongs to our chief."

"But your chief belongs to me!" cried the Little Harp. "He is bound over to me body and soul, because I saw what I saw and know what I know, and for that I may have his woman and all."

Then he set up such a din to have her that one of the robbers went out and brought in another young girl, but with long black hair, and pushed her through the circle into the Little Harp's arms.

"There she is!" they said to quiet him. And for a joke, it was an Indian girl.

He asked them first if they would swear she was not out of the gully but the true bride of the bandit king, and they all swore so long and so hard that Rosamond herself was almost ready to believe that she stood out in the room under the robbers' eyes and was not hiding down behind the barrel.

So the Little Harp said, "What will I do with her first? Bring her the Black Drink!"

The Black Drink was an Indian drink, and some people called it the Sleepy Drink, because whoever tasted it fell over like a dead man with his eyes rolled back, and could not be roused by anything in the world for three days.

So the girl fought and screamed, but they held the Black Drink to her lips and made her drink it and she fell over like the dead, with her hair and her arms swinging in front of her.

All the roomful laughed to see her, and the Little Harp took out his sharp knife and said, "Next I will cut off her little finger, for it offends me," and he cut off her wedding finger, and it jumped in the air and rolled across the floor into Rosamond's lap. But though she thought she would die of fright, Rosamond stayed where she was, as still as a mouse, and none of them saw where the finger went or hunted for it, for it had no ring on it.

"And now I will teach her the end of her life, for that is the thing she comes here lacking," said the Little Harp, and he threw the girl across the long table, among the plates and all, where the remains of all the meals lay where they were left, with the knives and forks sticking in them, and flung himself upon her before their eyes.

"You have killed her now," they said, and it was true: she was dead.

But just at that moment there was the sound of horse's hoofs, and next a terrible shout at the door, and Jamie Lockhart came in.

"What has he done?" he asked, and pointed to the Little Harp where he stood bragging among them all.

"I have killed your bride, and that is the first payment," said the Little Harp, holding up the sharp knife. "And the next thing, I will speak out your name and cast evil upon it."

"No, you will not!" shouted Jamie, and for the second time he leaped upon the Little Harp and with his two hands choked the wind out of him for a while.

"Take him away," he told the others, "for I will not have him sleeping with me. Roll him down the hill and let him lie, though if the wolves don't touch him, he'll be back with me tomorrow."

So the other bandits carried the Little Harp out and pitched him over the bushes, for Jamie still would not put an end to him: something would not let him have that satisfaction yet.

"Now what has he done?" Jamie cried, and he ran to the dead girl stretched on the table, but when he lifted up her hair it was black, and he saw it was the wrong girl. Then he could not speak at all, but fell upon his bed.

Then Rosamond came out from behind the barrel, and touched him where he lay, and told him she had returned, to lie by his side.

But when she woke up out of her first sleep, she looked at him dreaming there with his face stained dark with the berry juice, and she was torn as she had never been before with an anguish to know his name and his true appearance. For the coming of death and danger had only driven her into her own heart, and it was no matter what he had told her, she could wait no longer to learn the identity of her true love.

Up she got and away she crept, and made up the brew which would wipe away the stains. Then she crept back with some of it on a bit of rag. She took Jamie's head on her lap while he still slept and dreamed, and held up the lighted candle to see by, and set to her task. Lo and behold, the brew worked.

Jamie Lockhart opened his eyes and looked at her. The candle gave one long beam of light, which traveled between their two faces.

"You are Jamie Lockhart!" she said.

"And you are Clement Musgrove's silly daughter!" said he.

Then he rose out of his bed.

"Good-by," he said. "For you did not trust me, and did not love me, for you wanted only to know who I am. Now I cannot stay in the house with you."

And going straight to the window, he climbed out through it and in another moment was gone.

Then Rosamond tried to follow and climbed out after him, but she fell in the dust.

At the same moment, she felt the stirring within her that sent her a fresh piece of news.

And finally a cloud went over the moon, and all was dark night.

5

THE NEXT MORNING, when Rosamond came to her senses, she was still lying where she had fallen. This angered her enough, but then from her own bedroom window a head looked out. It was Goat.

"Who are you?" she said.

"Goat," he said.

"Why are you here?"

"I work here," said Goat, "and for the little locket you wear around your neck I will give you some news."

"This locket is all I have left in the world," said the poor girl. "And I already know everything and can learn nothing new."

"Do not be so sad as all that," said Goat, "and I will sing you a song."

Then he gave her a smile, where his teeth showed like a few stars on a cloudy evening, and he sang her the song he had heard her sing:

> "The moon shone bright, and it cast a fair light:
> 'Welcome,' says she, 'my honey, my sweet!
> For I have loved thee this seven long year,
> And our chance it was we could never meet.'
>
> Then he took her in his armes-two,
> And kissed her both cheek and chin,
> And twice or thrice he kissed this may
> Before they were parted in twin."

But then he had to stop, because her tears made his clothes liable to dampness.

"That is not the news," said Rosamond, "for that is an old story. I will certainly pay you nothing at all for singing it."

"Then I did it for nothing," said Goat, "and it is all the same to me. And now for the same price I will give you the real news, the latest news, the very truth! Only, it lacks rhyme."

"It will not be any better for me," said Rosamond.

"First: your husband is Jamie Lockhart, the bandit of the woods!" cried Goat. "Second: there was wicked murder done in Jamie Lockhart's house in the night! Third: the first man that brings in Jamie Lockhart's head will get a hundred pieces of gold, and the rest will go without! Fourth: the whole world around will be looking for Jamie Lockhart! Fifth: he jumped out the window and left you alone. And sixth: it all went just as she swore it would go, and I will get a suckling pig."

"Just as who swore it would go?" asked Rosamond, for she got a surprise at the end.

"Why, your stepmother, of course," said Goat, and he danced a jig called "Fiddle in the Ditch." "Everything has now worked out to the most perfect fraction of calculation."

"So you work for her!" said Rosamond. "Where have you been all night?"

"Ah! under your bed," said Goat. "And you never looked there. Then by the window, and I saw you wash his face, and I watched you tumble out after him when he told you good-by. And I have been on the lookout ever since, but I do not think he will come back, for what goes out the window seldom returns the same way."

"Leave me!" cried Rosamond. "And let me cry."

So Goat was leaving, but just then a voice said, "Let me out!" And there was the trunk that the Little Harp left, which they had forgotten to throw out after him.

"What did you say?" asked Goat, bending down to put his ear to the top. "Repeat it, please, for I am a little hard of hearing when there is conversation through a trunk."

"Let me out!" said the voice, a bit louder.

So Goat lifted up the lid. And there sat the head of Big Harp, Little Harp's brother, all wrapped up in the blue mud, and just as it came down off the pole in Rodney.

"Will you look what was doing the talking!" cried Goat, and pulled the head out by the hair, holding it up at arm's length so it turned round like a bird cage on a string, and admiring it from all directions.

Poor Rosamond, after one look, fainted again onto the grass, and Goat ran off and left her where she lay.

Setting the head atop his own head, he skipped off down

the hill, and he began to kick up his heels to the left and right and cry, "Jamie Lockhart is the bandit of the woods! And the bandit of the woods is Jamie Lockhart!"

But there was no time at all before the drums began to sound all around, north, south, east, and west, until the very leaves of the trees chattered with it. The branches slowly parted everywhere, and a multitude of faces looked out between.

Clement heard Goat's cry floating out of the forest, saying "Jamie Lockhart is the bandit of the woods! And the bandit of the woods is Jamie Lockhart!"

"Now there must be a choice made," he said. He walked away into the forest and placed the stones in a little circle around him and sat unheeded in the pine grove.

"What exactly is this now?" he said, for he too was concerned with the identity of a man, and had to speak, if only to the stones. "What is the place and time? Here are all possible trees in a forest, and they grow as tall and as great and as close to one another as they could ever grow in the world. Upon each limb is a singing bird, and across this floor, slowly and softly and forever moving into profile, is always a beast, one of a procession, weighted low with his burning coat, looking from the yellow eye set in his head." He stayed and looked at the place where he was until he knew it by heart, and could even see the changes of the seasons come over it like four clouds: Spring and the clear and separate leaves mounting to the top of the sky, the black flames of cedars, the young trees shining like the lanterns, the magnolias softly ignited; Summer and the vines falling down over the darkest caves, red and green, changing to the purple of grapes and the Autumn descending in a golden curtain; then in the nakedness of the Winter wood the buffalo on his sinking trail, pawing the ice till his forelock hangs in the spring, and the deer following behind to the salty places to transfix his tender head. And that was the way the years went by.

"But the time of cunning has come," said Clement, "and my time is over, for cunning is of a world I will have no part in. Two long ripples are following down the Mississippi behind the approaching somnolent eyes of the alligator. And like the tenderest deer, a band of copying Indians poses along the bluff to draw us near them. Men are following men down the Mississippi, hoarse and arrogant by day, wakeful and dreamless by night at the unknown landings. A trail leads like a tunnel under the roof of this wilderness. Everywhere the traps are set. Why? And what kind of time is this, when all is first given, then stolen away?

"Wrath and love burn only like the campfires. And even the appearance of a hero is no longer a single and majestic event like that of a star in the heavens, but a wandering fire soon lost. A journey is forever lonely and parallel to death, but the two watch each other, the traveler and the bandit, through the trees. Like will-o'-the-wisps the little blazes burn on the rafts all night, unsteady beside the shore. Where are they even so soon as tomorrow? Massacre is hard to tell from the performance of other rites, in the great silence where the wanderer is coming. Murder is as soundless as a spout of blood, as regular and rhythmic as sleep. Many find a skull and a little branching of bones between two floors of leaves. In the sky is the perpetual wheel of buzzards. A circle of bandits counts out the gold, with bending shoulders more slaves mount the block and go down, a planter makes a gesture of abundance with his riding whip, a flatboatman falls back from the tavern door to the river below with scarcely time for a splash, a rope descends from a tree and curls into a noose. And all around again are the Indians.

"Yet no one can laugh or cry so savagely in this wilderness as to be heard by the nearest traveler or remembered the next year. A fiddle played in a finished hut in a clearing is as vagrant as the swamp breeze. What will the seasons be, when we are lost and dead? The dreadful heat and cold—no more than the shooting star."

So while Clement was talking so long to himself on the lateness of the age, the Indians came closer and found him. A red hand dragged him to his feet. He looked into large, worldly eyes.

"The settlement has come, and the reckoning is here," said Salome. "Punishments and rewards are in order!" And she went out to the woods to look for Jamie Lockhart and have his head, for that was the kind of thing she had wanted to do all her life. So she had her claw shading her sharp eye, but her eye, from thinking of golden glitter, had possibly gotten too bright to see the dark that was close around her now, and while she scanned the sky the bush at her side came alive, and folded her to the ground.

"All I must do is cut off his head," said the Little Harp. "Then I can take his place. Advancement is only a matter of swapping heads about. I could be king of the bandits! Oh, the way to get ahead is to cut a head off!" said the Little Harp. And he looked about for some person to tell that to; but the face that looked back at him was redskinned and surrounded by feathers, and it wore a terrible frown. So the Little Harp was taken in the pose of a headhunter, with one knee raised and one arm high, with his hand around his sharp knife. Red arms twined around him like a soft net, and off he was borne, held fast in his gesture.

Rosamond, who had fallen on a thorn, eventually felt its prick. She came out of her faint and sat up on the ground.

"Where can I be?" she said, and when she looked behind her and saw the house of the robbers at the end of the lane of cedars, her memory could not collect it all at once, but went slowly up the path, gathering this and that little thing in its sight, until at last it went in at the front door, and she recollected all that had happened. So she began to cry.

"My husband was a robber and not a bridegroom," she said. "He brought me his love under a mask, and kept all the truth hidden from me, and never called anything by its true name, even his name or mine, and what I would have given him he liked better to steal. And if I had no faith, he had little honor, to deprive a woman of giving her love freely."

Weeping made her feel better, and so she went on with it. "Now I am deserted," she said. "I have been sent out of my happiness, even the house has thrown me out the window. Oh," she said, starting to her feet, "if I could only find my husband, I would tell him that he has broken my heart."

Holding out her arms she ran straight into the woods, but before she had gone far, an Indian savage appeared suddenly before her in the mask of a spotty leopard. So for the third time, Rosamond fell down in a faint, and the Indian carried her away.

As for Jamie, he had chosen this time of all the times to finish out his sleep, for he considered it had half been taken away from him the night before. There he lay on the ground under a plum tree, napping away with a smile on his face, while the paths of the innocent Clement and the greedy Salome and the mad Little Harp and the reproachful Rosamond all turned like the spokes of the wheel toward this dreaming hub. If the Indians had not stopped them off, he would have been dead three or four times and accused and forgiven once before he woke up. But while he still slept, the savages found him first, and lifted him, heavy with sleeping like a child, onto one of the little Asiatic horses they had, and tied him down with their sharp threads.

Then, to destroy the body of the maiden that had been contaminated, the Indians set fire to the robbers' house, and it went up in five points of red flame. The raven flew out over the treetops and was never seen again, and the forest was filled with the cry of the dogs.

So there they all ended in the Indian camp. One by one the savages had captured them all.

All, that is, except Goat, who, having turned the head of Big Harp loose on the world, could not get enough of running through the woods with it, crying, "Bring in his head! Bring in his head! A price is on his head!" In this manner he escaped, for the Indians searched in devious and secret ways only, in their revenge, and with his cry he shot straight through their fancy net.

Now this was a small camp, in a worn-away hollow stirred out by the river, the shell of a whirlpool, called the Devil's Punch Bowl. The rays of the sun had to beat down slantwise, and the Indians' dogs ran always in circles. So there all the young Indians danced at sunset, and the old Indians sat about folded up like women, with their withered knees by their ears. The small-boned ponies fed on the brown grass, and their teeth cut away with a scallopy sound. The yellow fires burned at regular places, and out of the cloud of smoke which hung in the shape of a flapping crow over the hut of the Chief, the odor of the dead blew round, for the venerated ancestors of the tribe were stretched inside upon their hammocks and gently swayed by the Autumn wind.

On this night, all the Indians, being very tired from their long day's work of revenge, fell back upon their mats and went to sleep with the sun. Having first made sure that all the prisoners were tied and left inside a hut, they put off punishing them until another day, for sleep had come to be sweeter than revenge.

So by the time the moon rose, Goat was running and scampering about the huts where the prisoners were tied, making no more noise than a swarm of gnats.

"Here are these great strong bullies tied up," he said, "and I am free."

So he looked in first one hut and then the other.

Poor Rosamond, on the point of fainting, and very hungry, was waiting for her death. Believing by now that she would never see her husband again, she thought dearly of that old life, and was fond of even the disguise he had worn.

"Now that I know his name is Jamie Lockhart, what has the news brought me?" she asked, and had only to look down at the ropes that bound her to see that names were nothing and untied no knots.

Goat, passing by and hearing her tears, recognized her at once by the sound, and popping his head through the chink in the door, he said, "Good evening, why are you crying?"

"Oh, I have lost my husband, and he has lost me, and we are both tied up to be killed in the morning," she cried.

"Then cry on," said Goat, "for I never expect to hear a better reason."

"Perhaps he is already dead," said Rosamond. "For I cannot believe, if he were alive, that he would not come and find me, whether he is tied up or not."

"If he is not dead now, he is as good as dead," said Goat. "Is there anything that I could do for you in his place?"

"Let me out!" begged Rosamond.

"Well, now," said Goat, "what will you give me?"

"Anything!" said Rosamond. "Do you want my locket?"

"No," said Goat. "I don't always want a locket."

"Then what do you want?"

"Will you let me come and live with you in the robbers' house when Jamie Lockhart and all the robbers are dead?"

"Yes," said Rosamond, "I will."

"And will you cook the meat and serve me at the same table where they sat?"

"Yes, yes," said Rosamond. "But let me out now."

"And will you let me come sleep in your little bed, and be my wife?" asked Goat.

"Yes!" cried Rosamond, and it was lucky for her she did not have to learn to tell a lie there on the spot, but already knew how.

"Then I ask no money," said Goat, and he stuck his little hand inside the door and lifted the latch. Then he came and bit the knots in two.

"Wait for me in the robbers' house," he whispered. "Have the kettle on the fire, and the bed turned down."

So Rosamond was free, and stole away to the woods.

Next Goat went by the hut where Salome was kept, and putting his head to the crack he said, "Good evening, why are you crying?"

"I am not crying!" said Salome, and indeed she was not, or anything like it. "Be gone! I need no one!"

So Goat let her stay.

Then, passing by the hut where Jamie and the Little Harp and the rest of the robbers were kept, Goat stopped and listened and heard a great quarreling. It was Jamie and the Little Harp, and the rest of the robbers were stretched out like the dead and snoring, and slept through the whole affair, for they were as tired as the Indians.

But at that moment the Little Harp said, "Quiet! I hear something just outside the door."

"What do you hear?" asked Jamie.

"I think it is a woodchuck," said the Little Harp, "from the scuffle in the leaves."

"Good evening," said Goat through the crack, in a voice like a woodchuck's. "The woodchucks have come, to see the big fight."

"What big fight?" said the Little Harp.

"Yours," said Goat. Then he did a little step, and Harp said, "Listen! I heard something running, and I think it is a squirrel."

"Good evening," said Goat through the crack, in the affected voice of a squirrel. "The squirrels have come, to see the big fight."

"What big fight?" said the Little Harp.

"Yours," said Goat.

Then he gave a grunt like a boar, and a hiss like a snake, and a sniff like a fox, and a scratch like a bear, and a howl like a wildcat, and a roar like a lion.

"Good evening," he said, roaring, "we have come to see the big fight."

"The Lord help us," said the Little Harp to Jamie, "but the fight must be going to be monstrous! I never knew there was even a lion about!"

"What fight?" asked Jamie, for he had heard none of this.

"Ours!" said the Little Harp. "Only we are tied up and can't get at it."

Just then Goat put his head in the crack.

"Good evening," he said, "could I do anything for you?"

"Here is our chance," said the Little Harp to Jamie. "This fellow works for me, and if I pay him enough, he will lift the latch and come in and untie us, and we can get at it."

"The sooner the better then," said Jamie, "for this might as well be gotten over with."

So the Little Harp promised Goat half of the reward money for Jamie's head and a brace of fighting turkeys, and Goat came in and untied him.

"So far, so good," said the Little Harp. "Now keep the enemy still tied for a bit, as I wish to do some work on him without the trouble I had before."

Then he pulled out a knife and walked up to Jamie and measured how far he was around the neck.

"The price is on this part of him," remarked the Little Harp to Goat, "so I think I will take the head and let the rest go, for this is all we need." And he was just about to cut off his head.

"Wait! Or we will have one head too many," said Goat. "At this very moment, the head that came out of your little trunk is resting on a new-cut pole in Rodney square under the name of Jamie Lockhart, the bandit of the woods."

"The Big Harp would kill me for that, if he were alive," said the Little Harp. "For he was very vain of his name, and after every robbery we ever did together, he would look back over his shoulder at what he had done, and call, 'We are the Harps!' as we ran to the woods."

"Don't cry for that," said Goat, "but look at the gold I have got. They said, 'Who killed Jamie Lockhart, and wrapped up his head so nice and brought it in?' and I said, 'I did.' And they trotted out the sack of gold before you could say 'Nebuchadnezzar.'" So he held up the gold.

"So far, so good," said the Little Harp. "Now turn the sum over to me." And he lifted the bag of gold out of Goat's hand.

"But it is my brain's money!" cried Goat.

"It is my brother's head!" cried the Little Harp.

"But I am Jamie Lockhart, the bandit of the woods!" cried Jamie. "This is all a madness!"

"Let it be untangled at once," said the Little Harp, sitting down between them and putting his great hand to his tiny head. "Now, first—I take back my words of yesterday—rash, headstrong words. And so you, sir, my good stranger, are *not* Jamie Lockhart, the bandit of the woods. And second, that is not your own head you are wearing, and third, I don't want it, and fourth, I won't have it."

"But I am Jamie Lockhart, the bandit of the woods!" cried Jamie. "Not a man in the world can say I am not who I am and what I am, and live!"

"Yes they can!" said the Little Harp. "I tell you you are not and never will be. I stand here and say Jamie Lockhart, the bandit of the woods, is dead, and his head rides a stick-horse in Rodney square, and here hot in my hand is the money that his life was worth."

"Now the time has come to fight!" cried Jamie.

There was a shy little smile on the Little Harp's face at that, and he said, "What's more, there is no more Big Harp any more, for his head is gone, and the Little Harp rules now. And for the proof of everything, I'm killing you now with my own two hands." With this, he rushed upon Jamie in full confidence. But Jamie leaped up and burst his ropes with one great strong breath, and caught him in the middle of the air.

And this time Jamie had no hesitations about what to do, but went for the Little Harp with all his might, and that was needed.

Goat, seeing that the fight had started at last, butted out through the door and sat on the roof of the hut like an owl. In the next moment out rolled the two men through the door after him, and they tore the turf and leveled whatever tree they fought under, until now and again an Indian woke up and quivered in his bed.

They fought the whole night through, till the sun came up. At last, just as the Little Harp had his knife point in Jamie's throat, and a drop of blood stood on it, Jamie pulled out his own little dirk and stopped the deed then and there.

The Little Harp, with a wound in his heart, heaved a deep sigh and a tear came out of his eye, for he hated to give up his life as badly as the deer in the woods.

So Jamie left him dead on the ground, tied in his own belt the reward that had been offered for his life, and started off a free man.

When the Indians gathered round and found themselves cheated of trying the two bandit leaders in court—one being already dead, and one being free—their fury was without bounds. So they rushed upon the rest of the robber band, the lazy ones who were still snoring in their places, and scalped them every one.

Then the drums began to beat, and to avenge the death of the Indian maiden, they sent for the beautiful girl they had captured to appear before their circle.

But Salome, in her hut, heard them coming for Rosamond, and she cried out and said, "What beautiful girl are you looking for? I am the most beautiful!" For she was jealous even of not being chosen the victim.

"What of the young girl with the golden hair?" said the Indians.

"She is dead!" cried Salome. Her voice rose to a great shout. "She is dead! I saw her die!"

Then a great groan went up from Clement, who heard her

from where he was bound in his hut. For like Rosamond, he believed her at last, when the day came.

"Alas!" said the Indians, sad and cheated once more. "How did the beautiful girl meet this early death?"

"She ran from the hut, escaping in the night," said Salome. "And a great spotted leopard came and carried her off between his teeth!"

So they went and looked, and sure enough, Rosamond was gone and there was no sign of her at all. "It must have been a leopard," they said.

"Now, will you choose me?" Salome asked.

So the Indians led her out into their circle and stood her up before them.

But before they could say anything at all to her, Salome opened her mouth and gave them a terrible, long harangue that made them put their fingers in their ears. She told them all she knew.

"It is the command of our Chief," they told her, "that you be still."

"I won't be still!" said she, and told them everything over.

"It is the command of the sun itself," they told her, "that you be still." But though they approached her, they did not lay their hands upon her, for she seemed dangerous to them.

"No one is to have power over me!" Salome cried, shaking both her fists in the smoky air. "No man, and none of the elements! I am by myself in the world."

Then they looked at one another. And Clement, from where he was bound, saw the sad faces of the Indians, like the faces of feverish children, and said to himself, "The savages have only come the sooner to their end; we will come to ours too. Why have I built my house, and added to it? The planter will go after the hunter, and the merchant after the planter, all having their day."

"The sun will lay his hand upon you," said the Indian Chief himself to Salome, speaking from the center of the circle. "The sun asks worship."

"The sun cannot punish me," cried Salome. "Punishment is always the proof. Why, I could punish the sun if I wished! For I have seen your sun with a shadow eating it, and I know it for a weak thing in the Winter, like all the rest of life!"

"She would throw mud on the face of the sun," said the Indians, drawing their circle in upon Salome and their hands lifting with their tomahawks, but not touching her.

Salome only laughed the more. "I can punish your sun if I wish!" she cried. "I will tell the sun now to stand still, and it will stand still!" And she threw back her head and called, "Sun! Stand where you are!"

Then anger came over all the faces of the Indians and dissolved the weariness that was there, and up sprang the young son of the Chief, bounding forward to the center of the circle. His hand went up for the first time above his father's, and he gave a command in a voice as strong as a buffalo's.

"You dared to command the sun!" he cried. "And you must dance for it."

Then his father raised his arms too, and all the other savages spread their arms high like the branches of trees, and moved inward.

"Dance!" they said. "If you dare to command the sun, dance!"

So Salome began to dance, whether she wanted to or whether she didn't, and the Indian Chief said, "If you stand still before the sun obeys you and stands still likewise, it is death for you."

So Salome danced and shouted, "Sun, retire! Go back, Sun! Sun, stand still!"

But it went on as it always had, and the Indian Chief said, "One like you cannot force him, for his home is above the clouds, in a tranquil place. He is the source of our tribe and of every thing, and therefore he does not and will not stand still, but continues forever."

So Salome danced. Out went her arms, hop went her bony feet, in and out went her head on her neck, like a hen that flies before the hawk. Around the fire they drummed her, and she danced till her limbs seemed all red-hot. One by one she cast off her petticoats, until at the end she danced as naked as a plucked goose, and faster and faster, until the dance was raveled out and she could dance no more. And still the sun went on as well as ever.

There she stood, blue as a thistle, and over she fell, stone dead.

"What man," said the Indian Chief, "owns the body of this woman?"

"I do," said Clement. "I own her body."

"Then take it and go free," said the Chief. Pity ran through all the grooves of his brown face.

So for the second time in his life, Clement was not held for a prisoner by the Indian savages, or put to death. The body of Salome was tied to a bony pony, and Clement was given the rope to lead it away.

Now Jamie all this time had been hiding in a gully, biding his time, and, by felling Indians, making his way through the woods to the rear of the huts. Then there was Goat beside him.

"Where are you going?" said Goat. "For I thought you were free and away."

"I am going where my wife is a prisoner, and get her and take her home if I lose my life for doing it," said Jamie. "For when I went off and left her, I had no idea what a big thing would come of it."

"Ah, but you are too late now," said Goat. "She believes you are dead, and is untied already and gone, and now she has promised to marry another husband. For seeing that you would be a dead man and I a live one, she has chosen me."

At that, Jamie half pulled out his little dirk again, but then he showed his teeth in a laugh. "It is too bad," said he, "that she did not tell you that she burns every piece of meat she sticks over the fire, and cannot sew a straight seam, and that her feet are cold in the bed at night."

"She did not," cried Goat. "It is a pity the cheating that goes on in a bargain."

"She is a noted liar," said Jamie, "that is known as far as the Bayou Pierre. And I only keep her because I stole her in the first place and have a soft sentiment about it."

"Still," said Goat, "I have something to expect for the work I have done. My tongue is hanging out from all my efforts."

"So it is," said Jamie.

"And it is not as if both my employers were not freshly dead and I will not have any more work," said Goat, "unless I scratch up something for myself."

"That is true," said Jamie.

"If there were such a thing as any reward money to be had," said Goat, "I should almost rather have that than either work or a wife."

"Hold out your hand, then," said Jamie, and he put the bag of gold into it. "That is the reward for a bandit's life, for the bandit's life is done with, though I must say I think it was worth more."

"Well and good," said Goat. "And know that this will be used to allow me to rest for a while, and then to buy a black cook, give all my sisters in marriage, and to enrich my mother in every way."

Then Jamie went on alone, and on foot, for his horse had been taken away from him and he had not found him yet. He went on and on and at last he came to the lane of the cedars.

But when he reached the place where the robbers' house had been, there was only a heap of cinders, with the long smoke cloud hanging over it. Then he searched and found the small bones lying in the embers, that had been the Indian maiden's. So he thought a trick had been played upon him after all, and that Rosamond was dead. And he ran wild through the woods.

6

ROSAMOND, in the meanwhile, was as lost as she could be in the woods, and making her way along the Old Natchez Trace. And of everybody she met she would ask the same question: "Have you seen Jamie Lockhart?" And they all said, "No indeed."

She was sadly tattered and torn, and tired from sleeping in hollow trees and keeping awake in the woods, so that she would not have been recognized by her own father, who, indeed, thought she was dead, carried off by a panther and eaten up.

So on one of the days she saw a man sleeping in the woods, and heard the sound of his horse near-by. And when she got up to the man, he had such a stature, though lying on the ground, she thought it would certainly be Jamie Lockhart having a nap. So she went up and touched him. But when he turned over he was the wrong man.

"You may wonder why I am taking a nap here in the middle of the day," the man said at once, sitting up and pulling the straws out of his hair. "Well, I can soon satisfy you as to that."

"Then do," said Rosamond, sitting down beside him, for she had had curiosity before and would have it again, and she thought, "Who knows? He may have seen my husband, since something knocked his wind out."

"I am a mail rider, an anonymous mail rider," said the tall man, "and over yonder is the mail to prove it, tied to the saddle and as safe as a church, for everybody gets out of the way when I come past. But I have just come from an adventure with the grandfather of all alligators, which you may or may not have met as you came along."

"Never an alligator did I see," said Rosamond, "though I saw a monstrous big fish look out of the lake as I passed by, which bared his fangs and whistled at me."

"Oh, but the alligator was worse than the fish," said the mail rider. "I have seen the fish. There he came, the alligator, waltzing as pretty as you please down between the sides of the Old Natchez Trace, and as long as anything you have ever seen come out of the water, ships and all. The first thing he did when he saw me coming was open his mouth, and I was riding so fast, so very fast, bent on my duty, that there was nothing to do but ride on, straight in the front door. And he clicked the latch and shot the bolt behind me."

"That was bad luck for Sunday," said Rosamond.

"And there were two other travelers in there already," said the mail rider.

"Did one have yellow hair?" asked Rosamond, for she thought that this was where Jamie Lockhart might have been, the victim of this fate.

"No, they were both too old for that," said the mail rider. "They never said a word. Luckily, I had just the moment before felt a desire for some persimmons, and not wishing to stop long enough to pick them one by one, I stuck out my hand as I rode by and pulled up the next persimmon tree by the roots. So I took it with me and ate from that as I went along. So, I propped the old alligator's mouth open with the persimmon tree."

"Were the persimmons ripe yet?" asked Rosamond.

"Hold back, madame," said the mail rider. "For this is what happened to me and not to you, and it is my business whether the persimmons were ripe or not. So the old grandfather said, 'Aaaaarh!' and gave such a horrid switch to his tail that his back teeth were rolling like thunder, but I didn't change my tune just because he didn't like it. First I took a good look around by the light of day, it being my first sight of an alligator's mouth from that direction. But teeth, teeth, nothing but teeth! I have never ridden my horse by so many teeth before. But when I said 'Gidyap!' and started back to civilization, do you know what happened?"

"Did he swallow you?" asked Rosamond.

"No indeed. How would he dare?" asked the mail rider. "But the persimmons on the persimmon tree were green, it being not quite late enough in the year to prop up an alligator with that kind of tree. And there, the way they draw up a mouth, they had drawn up the creature's mouth like a money-bag before I could ride as far as from me to you. So I couldn't get out and there I was."

"Did you make a noise?" asked Rosamond. "I have often

thought that would discourage an alligator who was swallowing people down."

"Noise was not the practical thing in that predicament," said the mail rider. "There was still left the tiniest, smallest hole you can imagine where I could see out into the world, and so dark it was inside that I saw the stars in the daytime. So I steered him around by the Big Dipper, with the other two fellows helping, all the way from East to West, and made him face full on the hot sun. And down it shone and ripened the persimmons on one side of the tree, while I built a little fire and ripened them on the other, though I had to use the merest bit of mail for the kindling, the other two fellows having nothing of use on them. So as soon as the persimmons were ripe, the alligator's mouth undrew, and I whipped up my horse and took my departure. And I suppose the others followed, though I never looked back to see. But the adventure has tired me, and I was lying down for a moment when you discovered me here."

"I am sorry to have disturbed your rest," said Rosamond. "But I wanted only to ask you a question. Have you seen Jamie Lockhart?"

At this, the mail rider jumped white to his feet and sat down whiter still. "Jamie Lockhart the ghost?" he said.

"God in Heaven, is he a ghost now?" cried Rosamond.

"I should say he is," said the rider. "And has been."

"Ah, how do you know?" cried Rosamond. "Tell me quickly what has happened."

"First, take a bite to eat," said he, and brought out a little napkin of meat and biscuit. And Rosamond, who had never been hungrier, accepted with thanks.

"To begin at the beginning," said the rider, "I won't say who I am. For that is a secret."

"Too much of this secrecy goes on in the world for my happiness," said Rosamond. "But skip over the dark spot and get on to the light."

"Where was I?" said he.

"You were saying that Jamie Lockhart is a ghost!" cried Rosamond. "How do you know?"

"That is easy to answer," said the mail rider. "I know he is a ghost because I made him one myself, with these very hands you see here holding the biscuit." Then he sighed and said, "But that was in the old days, and I dare say you don't believe that I was ever that big a figure in the world."

"Tell me the story straight," said Rosamond, "and leave yourself out."

"Oh, we had a terrible battle, Jamie Lockhart and I," said he. "It lasted through three nights running, and when we were through they had to get the floor and the roof switched back to their places, for we had turned the house inside out. Dozens and dozens of seagulls were dead, that had flown in off the river and got caught in the whirlwind of the fight. Hundreds of people were watching, and got their noses sliced off too, for standing too close."

"It's a wonder Jamie Lockhart did not kill you," said Rosamond.

"Do you know the reason?" said the mail rider. "It's because I killed him first. I beat him to a pulp—there was nothing left but the juice."

"I can hardly believe he would have let you," said Rosamond.

"The very next morning I saw his ghost," said the mail rider, "for it came in and said good morning to me, and not a scratch on it."

"And have you seen it since?" she said.

"At this very spot and at this very time yesterday," said he. "Why didn't you tell me in the first place that you were looking for Jamie Lockhart's ghost? For I know it well."

"Which direction was it going in?" asked Rosamond anxiously.

"In this very direction," said he. "I was riding along, and there it was, sitting on a gate. I knew that shape of a fine tall man with that illusion of yellow hair and that pretence of a coat tied on it like a cape. And I smelled the sulphur when it said, 'A nice evening for August.'

"So I said, 'Good evening, Jamie Lockhart's ghost.'

"And it smiled, and there were its same teeth.

"I asked it what it had been doing since the last time I saw it.

" 'Sitting on a gate,' said it.

" 'And are you unhappy or looking for anything?' says I, for I knew how ghosts are.

" 'Yes,' says it, 'I'm looking for my red horse Orion, have you seen its ghost flying along without its rider?'

"So I made haste to tell it where I had seen the horse, which had indeed passed me like the devil himself, going south, and the ghost said it was likely to be waiting by the old tavern door in Rodney's Landing, the very spot where we had had the fight and I had killed it. So the ghost went along with me till we got to Rodney, talking very amiable, but of course nothing we said was true. Though sure enough, there was the horse waiting like a tame mouse beside the tavern door. So it jumped on its back and off it went simply rising into the air, and said it was going to the New Orleans port for the purpose of taking a boat."

"Oh, I must prevent that," said Rosamond. "And you must take me along with you today and give me a ride. For I have a message for Jamie Lockhart from another world."

"Is it a message from out of the past for the old ghost?" asked the mail rider.

"No, it is from out of the future," said Rosamond. And she put it to him, "Did you ever before hear of an old ghost that was going to be a father of twins next week?"

"Oh!" he said. "Ghosts are getting more powerful every day in these parts. But ghost or no ghost, I wish now I had punched him in the nose, even if there was nothing there, for his rascality."

And he set Rosamond up on his horse in front of him, and laid on the whip, and they rode away down the Trace.

So while they were going along, some bandits rushed down upon them from a clump of pine trees, and told them to stop in their tracks for they meant to rob the mail.

"Pass on!" cried the mail rider. "This lady is soon to become a mother."

So the bandits lifted up their black hats to Rosamond and passed on up the Trace.

At the end of his run, he put her down, and Rosamond thanked him for his favors.

"Now, tell me your real name," said she, "for I must know

who it is I had to thank, for the way you have aided a poor deserted wife that is looking for her ghost of a husband."

At this request, the mail rider turned all red like the sunset, but at last he said, "Tell no one, but I am none other than Mike Fink! It would be outrageous if this were known, that the greatest flatboatman of them all came down in the world to be a mail rider on dry land. It would sound like the end of the world! Don't breathe it to a soul that you saw me this way, and you yourself must forget the disgrace as early as you can."

"How on earth did it happen?" asked Rosamond.

"It was enemies," said Mike Fink. "Men jealous of me. They found out that one day, after many years of heroism, I allowed myself to be cheated out of three little sacks of gold and a trained bird, and so they threw me out. All of them jumped on me at one time and it lasted a week, but they sent me up out of the river. They left me for dead on a sand bar in the Bayou Pierre. And so I came to this."

"Out of my gratitude to you, I will tell no one of your true identity," Rosamond promised. "And good luck to you. May you be restored to your proper place."

As a matter of fact, Rosamond told everyone she met, since she was not able to keep silent about it, but no one believed her, and so no harm was done.

Mike Fink rode away saying, "I will have to ride all night to make up for the deed of kindness I have done, and will probably be set upon by the bandits, who are waiting for my return trip when I have no shield before me, and be murdered for it."

But he was not, and in the end he did get back on the river and his name was restored to its original glory. And it is a good thing he never knew that he helped to restore the bride to a live and flourishing Jamie Lockhart, or that would have broken his heart in two.

So Rosamond went on, and by dint of begging one mail rider after another, and trotting upon one white pony after another black horse, she made her way clear to New Orleans.

The moment she reached the great city she made straight for the harbor.

The smell of the flapping fish in the great loud marketplace almost sent her into a faint, but she pressed on bravely along the water front, looking twice at every man she met, even if he looked thrice back at her, and at last she came to where a crowd of gentlemen and sailors were embarking on a great black ship going to Zanzibar. And sure enough, there in the middle, and taller than all the rest like a cornstalk in the cottonfield, was Jamie Lockhart, waving good-by to the shore.

"Jamie Lockhart!" she cried.

So he turned to see who it was.

"I came and found you!" she cried over all their heads.

Then he took his foot off the gangplank and came down and brought her home, not failing to take her by the priest's and marrying her on the way. And indeed it was in time's nick.

So in the Spring, Clement went on a trip from Rodney's Landing to New Orleans, and was walking about.

New Orleans was the most marvelous city in the Spanish country or anywhere else on the river. Beauty and vice and every delight possible to the soul and body stood hospitably, and usually together, in every doorway and beneath every palmetto by day and lighted torch by night. A shutter opened, and a flower bloomed. The very atmosphere was nothing but aerial spice, the very walls were sugar cane, the very clouds hung as golden as bananas in the sky. But Clement Musgrove was a man who could have walked the streets of Bagdad without sending a second glance overhead at the Magic Carpet, or heard the tambourines of the angels in Paradise without dancing a step, or had his choice of the fruits of the Garden of Eden without making up his mind. For he was an innocent of the wilderness, and a planter of Rodney's Landing, and this was his good.

So, holding a bag of money in his hand, he went to the docks to depart, and there were all the ships with their sails and their flags flying, and the seagulls dipping their wings like so many bright angels.

And as he was putting his foot on the gangplank, he felt a touch at his sleeve, and there stood his daughter Rosamond, more beautiful than ever, and dressed in a beautiful, rich white gown.

Then how they embraced, for they had thought each other dead and gone.

"Father!" she said. "Look, this wonderful place is my home now, and I am happy again!"

And before the boat could leave, she told him that Jamie Lockhart was now no longer a bandit but a gentleman of the world in New Orleans, respected by all that knew him, a rich merchant in fact. All his wild ways had been shed like a skin, and he could not be kinder to her than he was. They were the parents of beautiful twins, one of whom was named Clementine, and they lived in a beautiful house of marble and cypress wood on the shores of Lake Pontchartrain, with a hundred slaves, and often went boating with other merchants and their wives, the ladies reclining under a blue silk canopy; and they sailed sometimes out on the ocean to look at the pirates' galleons. They had all they wanted in the world, and now that she had found her father still alive, everything was well. Of course, she said at the end, she did sometimes miss the house in the wood, and even the rough-and-tumble of their old life when he used to scorn her for her curiosity. But the city was splendid, she said; it was the place to live.

"Is all this true, Rosamond, or is it a lie?" said Clement.

"It is the truth," she said, and they held the boat while she took him to see for himself, and it was all true but the blue canopy.

Then the yellow-haired Jamie ran and took him by the hand, and for the first time thanked him for his daughter. And as for him, the outward transfer from bandit to merchant had been almost too easy to count it a change at all, and he was enjoying all the same success he had ever had. But now, in his heart Jamie knew that he was a hero and had always been one, only with the power to look both ways and to see a thing from all sides.

Then Rosamond prepared her father a little box lunch with her own hands. She asked him to come and stay with them, but he would not.

"Good-by," they told each other as the wind filled the sails for the voyage home. "God bless you."

DELTA WEDDING

To
JOHN ROBINSON

I

THE NICKNAME of the train was the Yellow Dog. Its real name was the Yazoo-Delta. It was a mixed train. The day was the 10th of September, 1923—afternoon. Laura McRaven, who was nine years old, was on her first journey alone. She was going up from Jackson to visit her mother's people, the Fairchilds, at their plantation named Shellmound, at Fairchilds, Mississippi. When she got there, "Poor Laura, little motherless girl," they would all run out and say, for her mother had died in the winter and they had not seen Laura since the funeral. Her father had come as far as Yazoo City with her and put her on the Dog. Her cousin Dabney Fairchild, who was seventeen, was going to be married, but Laura could not be in the wedding for the reason that her mother was dead. Of these facts the one most persistent in Laura's mind was the most intimate one: that her age was nine.

In the passenger car every window was propped open with a stick of kindling wood. A breeze blew through, hot and then cool, fragrant of the woods and yellow flowers and of the train. The yellow butterflies flew in at any window, out at any other, and outdoors one of them could keep up with the train, which then seemed to be racing with a butterfly. Overhead a black lamp in which a circle of flowers had been cut out swung round and round on a chain as the car rocked from side to side, sending down dainty drifts of kerosene smell. The Dog was almost sure to reach Fairchilds before the lamp would be lighted by Mr. Terry Black, the conductor, who had promised her father to watch out for her. Laura had the seat facing the stove, but of course no fire was burning in it now. She sat leaning at the window, the light and the sooty air trying to make her close her eyes. Her ticket to Fairchilds was stuck up in her Madge Evans straw hat, in imitation of the drummer across the aisle. Once the Dog stopped in the open fields and Laura saw the engineer, Mr. Doolittle, go out and pick some specially fine goldenrod there—for whom, she could not know. Then the long September cry rang from the thousand unseen locusts, urgent at the open windows of the train.

Then at one place a white foxy farm dog ran beside the
Yellow Dog for a distance just under Laura's window, barking
sharply, and then they left him behind, or he turned back.
And then, as if a hand reached along the green ridge and all
of a sudden pulled down with a sweep, like a scoop in the
bin, the hill and every tree in the world and left cotton fields,
the Delta began. The drummer with a groan sank into sleep.
Mr. Terry Black walked by and took the tickets out of their
hats. Laura brought up her saved banana, peeled it down, and
bit into it.

Thoughts went out of her head and the landscape filled it.
In the Delta, most of the world seemed sky. The clouds were
large—larger than horses or houses, larger than boats or
churches or gins, larger than anything except the fields the
Fairchilds planted. Her nose in the banana skin as in the cup
of a lily, she watched the Delta. The land was perfectly flat
and level but it shimmered like the wing of a lighted dragonfly.
It seemed strummed, as though it were an instrument and
something had touched it. Sometimes in the cotton were trees
with one, two, or three arms—she could draw better trees
than those were. Sometimes like a fuzzy caterpillar looking in
the cotton was a winding line of thick green willows and cypresses, and when the train crossed this green, running on a
loud iron bridge, down its center like a golden mark on the
caterpillar's back would be a bayou.

When the day lengthened, a rosy light lay over the cotton.
Laura stretched her arm out the window and let the soot
sprinkle it. There went a black mule—in the diamond light of
far distance, going into the light, a child drove a black mule
home, and all behind, the hidden track through the fields was
marked by the lifted fading train of dust. The Delta buzzards,
that seemed to wheel as wide and high as the sun, with evening were going down too, settling into far-away violet tree
stumps for the night.

In the Delta the sunsets were reddest light. The sun went
down lopsided and wide as a rose on a stem in the west, and
the west was a milk-white edge, like the foam of the sea. The
sky, the field, the little track, and the bayou, over and over—all
that had been bright or dark was now one color. From the
warm window sill the endless fields glowed like a hearth in

firelight, and Laura, looking out, leaning on her elbows with her head between her hands, felt what an arriver in a land feels—that slow hard pounding in the breast.

"Fairchilds, Fairchilds!"

Mr. Terry Black lifted down the suitcase Laura's father had put up in the rack. The Dog ran through an iron bridge over James's Bayou, and past a long twilighted gin, its tin side looking first like a blue lake, and a platform where cotton bales were so close they seemed to lean out to the train. Behind it, dark gold and shadowy, was the river, the Yazoo. They came to the station, the dark-yellow color of goldenrod, and stopped. Through the windows Laura could see five or six cousins at once, all jumping up and down at different moments. Each mane of light hair waved like a holiday banner, so that you could see the Fairchilds everywhere, even with everybody meeting the train and asking Mr. Terry how he had been since the day before. When Mr. Terry set her on the little iron steps, holding her square doll's suitcase (in which her doll Marmion was horizontally suspended), and gave her a spank, she staggered, and was lifted down among flying arms to the earth.

"Kiss Bluet!" The baby was put in her face.

She was kissed and laughed at and her hat would have been snatched away but for the new elastic that pulled it back, and then she was half-carried along like a drunken reveler at a festival, not quite recognizing who anyone was. India hadn't come—"We couldn't find her"—and Dabney hadn't come, she was going to be married. They piled her into the Studebaker, into the little folding seat, with Ranny reaching sections of an orange into her mouth from where he stood behind her. Where were her suitcases? They drove rattling across the Yazoo bridge and whirled through the shady, river-smelling street where the town, Fairchild's Store and all, looked like a row of dark barns, while the boys sang "Abdul the Bulbul Amir" or shouted "Let Bluet drive!" and the baby was handed over Laura's head and stood between Orrin's knees, proudly. Orrin was fourteen—a wonderful driver. They went up and down the street three times, backing into cotton fields to turn around, before they went across the bridge again, homeward.

"That's to Marmion," said Orrin to Laura kindly. He waved at an old track that did not cross the river but followed it, two purple ruts in the strip of wood shadow.

"Marmion's my dolly," she said.

"It's not, it's where I was born," said Orrin.

There was no use in Laura and Orrin talking any more about what anything was. On this side of the river were the gin and compress, the railroad track, the forest-filled cemetery where her mother was buried in the Fairchild lot, the Old Methodist Church with the steamboat bell glinting pink in the light, and Brunswick-town where the Negroes were, smoking now on every doorstep. Then the car traveled in its cloud of dust like a blind being through the fields one after the other, like all one field but Laura knew they had names—the Mound Field, and Moon Field after Moon Lake. When they were as far as the overseer's house, Laura saw all the cousins lean out and spit, and she did too.

"I thought you all liked Mr. Bascom," she said, after they got by.

"It's not Mr. Bascom now, crazy," they said. "Is it, Bluet? Not Mr. Bascom now."

Then the car crossed the little bayou bridge, whose rackety rhythm she remembered, and there was Shellmound.

Facing James's Bayou, back under the planted pecan grove, it was gently glowing in the late summer light, the brightest thing in the evening—the tall, white, wide frame house with a porch all around, its bayed tower on one side, its tinted windows open and its curtains stirring, and even from here plainly to be heard a song coming out of the music room, played on the piano by a stranger to Laura. They curved in at the gate. All the way up the drive the boy cousins with a shout would jump and spill out, and pick up a ball from the ground and throw it, rocketlike. By the carriage block in front of the house Laura was pulled out of the car and held by the hand. Shelley had hold of her—the oldest girl. Laura did not know if she had been in the car with her or not. Shelley had her hair still done up long, parted in the middle, and a ribbon around it low across her brow and knotted behind, like a chariot racer. She wore a fountain pen on a chain now, and had her initials done in runny ink on her tennis shoes, over the ankle bones. Inside the house, the "piece" all at once ended.

"Shelley!" somebody called, imploringly.

"Dabney is an example of madness on earth," said Shelley now, and then she ran off, trailed by Bluet beating plaintively on a drum found in the grass, with a little stick. The boys were scattered like magic. Laura was deserted.

Grass softly touched her legs and her garter rosettes, growing sweet and springy for this was the country. On the narrow little walk along the front of the house, hung over with closing lemon lilies, there was a quieting and vanishing of sound. It was not yet dark. The sky was the color of violets, and the snow-white moon in the sky had not yet begun to shine. Where it hung above the water tank, back of the house, the swallows were circling busy as the spinning of a top. By the flaky front steps a thrush was singing waterlike notes from the sweet-olive tree, which was in flower; it was not too dark to see the breast of the thrush or the little white blooms either. Laura remembered everything, with the fragrance and the song. She looked up the steps through the porch, where there was a wooden scroll on the screen door that her finger knew how to trace, and lifted her eyes to an old fanlight, now reflecting a skyey light as of a past summer, that she had been dared—oh, by Maureen!—to throw a stone through, and had not.

She dropped her suitcase in the grass and ran to the back yard and jumped up with two of the boys on the joggling board. In between Roy and Little Battle she jumped, and the delights of anticipation seemed to shake her up and down.

She remembered (as one remembers first the eyes of a loved person) the old blue water cooler on the back porch—how thirsty she always was here!—among the round and square wooden tables always piled with snap beans, turnip greens, and onions from the day's trip to Greenwood; and while you drank your eyes were on this green place here in the back yard, the joggling board, the neglected greenhouse, Aunt Ellen's guineas in the old buggy, the stable wall elbow-deep in a vine. And in the parlor she knew was a clover-shaped footstool covered with rose velvet where she would sit, and sliding doors to the music room that she could open and shut. In the halls would be the rising smell of girls' fudge cooking, the sound of the phone by the roll-top desk going unanswered. She could remember mostly the dining room, the paintings by Great-Aunt Mashula that was dead, of full-blown yellow roses and a watermelon split to the heart by a jackknife, and every ornamental plate around the rail different because painted by a different aunt at a different time; the big table never quite cleared; the innumerable packs of old, old playing cards. She could remember India's paper dolls coming out flatter from the law books than hers from a shoe box, and smelling as if they were scorched from it. She remembered the Negroes, Bitsy, Roxie, Little Uncle, and Vi'let. She put out her arms like wings and knew in her fingers the thready pattern of red roses in the carpet on the stairs, and she could hear the high-pitched calls and answers going up the stairs and down. She thought of the upstairs hall where it was twilight all the time from the green shadow of an awning, and where an old lopsided baseball lay all summer in a silver dish on the lid of the paper-crammed plantation desk, and how away at either end of the hall was a balcony and the little square butterflies that flew so high were going by, and the June bugs knocking. She remembered the sleeping porches full of late sleepers, some strangers to her always among them when India led her through and showed them to her. She remembered well the cotton lint on ceilings and lampshades, fresh every morning like a present from the fairies, that made Vi'let moan.

Little Battle crowded her a little as he jumped, and she had to move down the board a few inches. They could play an endless game of hide-and-seek in so many rooms and up and down the halls that intersected and turned into dead-end porches and rooms full of wax begonias and elephant's-ears, or rooms full of trunks. She remembered the nights—the moon vine, the ever-blooming Cape jessamines, the verbena smelling under running feet, the lateness of dancers. A dizziness rose in Laura's head, and Roy crowded her now, but she jumped on, keeping in with their rhythm. She remembered life in the undeterminate number of other rooms going

on around her and India, where they lay in bed—life not stopping for a moment in deference to children going to sleep,
but filling with later and later laughter, with Uncle Battle reciting "Break! Break! Break!," the phone ringing its two longs
and a short for the Fairchilds, Aunt Mac reading the Bible
aloud (was she dead yet?), the visiting planters arguing with
Uncle Battle and her other uncle, Uncle George, from dining
room to library to porch, Aunt Ellen slipping by in the hall
looking for something or someone, the distant silvery creak
of the porch swing by night, like a frog's voice. There would
be little Ranny crying out in his dream, and the winding of
the Victrola and then a song called "I Wish I Could Shimmy
like my Sister Kate" or Uncle Pinck's favorite (where was he?),
Sir Harry Lauder singing "Stop Yer Ticklin', Jock." The girls
that were old enough, dressed in colors called jade and fla-
mingo, danced with each other around the dining-room table
until the boys came to get them, and could be watched from
the upper landing cavorting below, like marvelous mermaids
down a transparent sea.

In bed Laura and India would slap mosquitoes and tell each
other things. Last summer India had told Laura the showboat
that came on the high water and the same old Rabbit's Foot
Minstrel as always, and Laura told India "Babes in the
Wood," Thurston the Magician, Annette Kellerman in
"Daughter of the Gods," and Clara Kimball Young in
"Drums of Jeopardy," and if Laura went off to sleep, India
would choke her. She remembered the baying of the dogs at
night; and how Roy believed when you heard dogs bay, a
convict had got out of Parchman and they were after him in
the swamp; every night of the world the dogs would bay, and
Roy would lie somewhere in the house shaking in his bed.

Just then, with a last move down the joggling board, Roy
edged Laura off. She ran back to the steps and picked up her
suitcase again. Then her heart pounded: India came abruptly
around the house, bathed and dressed, busily watering the
verbena in the flower bed out of a doll's cream pitcher, one
drop to each plant. India too was nine. Her hair was all spun
out down her back, and she had a blue ribbon in it; Laura
touched her own Buster Brown hair, tangled now beyond
anyone's help. Their white dresses (Laura's in the suitcase,

folded by her father, and for a man to fold anything suddenly nearly killed her) were still identical, India had blue insertion run in the waist now and Laura had white, but the same little interlocking three hoops were briarstitched in the yokes, and their identical gold lockets still banged there against their chests.

"My mother is dead!" said Laura.

India looked around at her, and said "Greenie!"

Laura took a step back.

"We never did unjoin," said India. "Greenie!"

"All right," Laura said. "Owe you something." She stooped and put a pinch of grass in her shoe.

"You have to wash now," said India. She added, looking in her pitcher, "Here's you a drop of water."

All of a sudden Maureen ran out from under the pecan trees—the cousin who was funny in her head, though it was not her fault. Besides her own fine clothes, she got India's dresses that she wanted and India's ribbons, and India said she would get them till she died. She had never talked plain; every word was two words to her and had an "l" in it. Now she ran in front of Laura and straddled the walk at the foot of the steps. She danced from side to side with her arms spread, chanting, "Cou-lin Lau-la can-na get-la by-y!" She was nine too.

Roy and Little Battle ran up blandly as if they had never let Laura joggle with them at all, giving no recognition. Orrin walked tall as a man up from the bayou with a live fish he must have just caught, jumping on a string. He waved it at little Ranny, who at that moment rode out the front door and down the steps standing on the back of his tricycle, like Ben Hur, a towel tied around his neck and flying behind him. The dinner bell was ringing inside, over and over, the way Roxie rang—like an insistence against disbelief. Laura, avoiding sight of the fish, avoiding India's little drop, and Ranny and Maureen, made her way up the steps. Just as she reached the top, she threw up. There she waited, like a little dog.

But Aunt Ellen, though she was late for everything, was now running out the screen door with open arms. She was the mother of them all. Something fell behind her, her apron, as she came, and she was as breathless as any of her children.

Now she knelt and held Laura very firmly. "Laura—poor little motherless girl," she said. When Laura lifted her head, she kissed her. She sent India for a wringing-wet cloth.

Laura put her head on Aunt Ellen's shoulder and sank her teeth in the thick Irish lace on the collar of her white voile dress which smelled like sweet peas. She hugged her, and touched her forehead, the steady head held so near to hers with its flying soft hair and its erect bearing of gentle, explicit, but unfathomed alarm. With the cool on her face, she could see clearer and clearer, though it was almost dark now, the pearl-edged side comb so hazardously bringing up the strands of Aunt Ellen's dark hair. She let her go, and if she could she would have smoothed and patted her aunt's hair and cleared the part with her own fingers, and said, "Aunt Ellen, *you* must never mind!" But of course she couldn't.

Then she jumped up and ran after Orrin into the house, beating India to the table.

"Where's Uncle George?" Laura asked, looking from Uncle Battle around to everybody at the long, broad table. At suppertime, since she had come, she was expecting to see everybody gathered; but Uncle George and his wife, Aunt Robbie, would not drive in from Memphis until tomorrow; Aunt Tempe and her husband Uncle Pinck Summers and their daughter Mary Denis's little girl, Lady Clare Buchanan, were not driving over from Inverness until Mary Denis had her baby; and the two aunts from the Grove, Aunt Primrose and Aunt Jim Allen, had not come up to supper tonight. There was just Uncle Battle's and Aunt Ellen's family of children at the table—besides of course the two great-aunts, Great-Aunt Shannon and Great-Aunt Mac, and Cousin Maureen who lived here with them, and only one visitor, Dabney's best friend, Mary Lamar Mackey of Lookback Plantation—it was she who played the piano.

"Skeeta! Next!" called Uncle Battle resoundingly, fixing his eye on Laura. She passed her plate up to him. Uncle Battle, her mother's brother, with his corrugated brow, his planter's boots creaking under the table when he stood to carve the turkeys, was so tremendous that he always called children "Skeeta." His thick fair hair over his bulging brow had been combed with water before he came to the table, exactly like Orrin's, Roy's, Little Battle's, and Ranny's. As his eye roved over them, Laura remembered that he had broken every child at the table now from being left-handed. Laura was ever hopeful that she would see Uncle Battle the Fire-eater take up some fire and eat it, and thought it would be some night at supper.

"How Annie Laurie would have loved this very plate!" Uncle Battle said softly just now, holding up Laura's serving. "Breast, gizzard, and wing! Pass it, boy."

Even cutting up the turkeys at the head of his table, he was a rushing, mysterious, very laughing man to have had so many children coming up busy too, and he could put on a tender, irresponsible air, as if he were asking ladies and little girls, "Look at me! What can I do? Such a thing it all is!", and he meant Life—although he could also mention death and people's absence in an ordinary way. It was his habit to drive quickly off from the house at any time of the day or night—in a buggy or a car now. Automobiles had come in just as Uncle Battle got too heavy to ride his horse. He rode out to see work done or "trouble" helped; sometimes "trouble" came at night. When Negroes clear to Greenwood cut each other up, it was well known that it took Uncle Battle to protect them from the sheriff or prevail on a bad one to come out and surrender.

"Now eat it all!" Uncle Battle called to her as the plate reached her. But it was a joke, his giving her the gizzard, she saw, for it was her mother that loved it and she could not stand that piece of turkey. She did not dare tell him what he knew.

"Where is Dabney?" she asked, for it was Dabney they had been talking about ever since they sat down to the table, and her place by her father was empty.

"She'll be down directly," said Aunt Ellen. "She's going to be married, you know, Laura."

"Tonight?" asked Laura.

"Oh!" groaned Uncle Battle. "Oh! Oh!" He always groaned three times.

"Where is her husband now?" Laura asked.

"Now don't, Battle," said Aunt Ellen anxiously. "Laura

naturally wants to know how soon Dabney will marry Troy. Not till Saturday, dear."

"This is only Monday," Laura told her uncle consolingly.

"Oh, Papa's really *proud* of Dabney, no matter how he groans, because she won't wait till cotton picking's over," said Shelley. She was sitting beside Laura, and looked so seriously even at her, that the black grosgrain ribbon crossing her forehead almost indented it.

"I am, am I?" said Battle. "Suppose you help your mother serve the pickled peaches at your end."

When Laura looked at her plate, the gizzard was gone. She almost jumped to her feet—she almost cried to think of all that had happened to her. Next she was afraid she had eaten that bite without thinking. But then she saw Great-Aunt Shannon calmly eating the gizzard, on the other side of her. She had stolen it—Great-Aunt Shannon, who would talk conversationally with Uncle Denis and Aunt Rowena and Great-Uncle George, who had all died no telling how long ago, that she thought were at the table with her. But just now, after eating a little bit of something, the gizzard and a biscuit or so—"No more than a bird!" they protested—she was escorted, by Orrin, up to bed without saying a word. Great-Aunt Mac glared after her; Great-Aunt Mac was not dead at all. "Now be ashamed of yourself!" she called after her. "For starving yourself!"

The boys all looked at each other, and even unwillingly, they let smiles break out on their faces. The four boys were all ages—Orrin older than Laura, Roy, Little Battle, and Ranny younger—and constantly seeking one another, even at the table with their eyes, seeking the girls only for their audience when they hadn't one another. They were always rushing, chasing, flying, getting hurt—only eating and the knot of their napkins could keep them in chairs. All their knickerbockers, and Ranny's rompers, had fresh holes for Aunt Ellen in both knees every evening. They ate turkey until they bit their fingers and cried "Ouch!" They were so filled with their energy that once when Laura saw some old map on the wall, with the blowing winds in the corners, mischievous-eyed and round-cheeked, blowing the ships and dolphins around Scotland, Laura had asked her mother if they were India's four brothers. She loved them dearly. It was strange that it was India who had to be Laura's favorite cousin, since she would have given anything if the boy cousins would let her love them most. Of course she expected them to fly from her side like birds, and light on the joggling board, as they had done when she arrived, and to edge her off when she climbed up with them. That changed nothing.

The boys were only like all the Fairchilds, but it was the boys and the men that defined that family always. All the girls knew it. When she looked at the boys and the men Laura was without words but she knew that company like a dream that comes back again and again, each aspect familiar and longing not to be forgotten. Great Great-Uncle George on his horse, in his portrait in the parlor—the one who had been murdered by the robbers on the Natchez Trace and buried, horse, bridle, himself, and all, on his way to the wilderness to be near Great Great-Grandfather—even he, she had learned by looking up at him, had the family trait of quick, upturning smiles, instant comprehension of the smallest eddy of life in the current of the day, which would surely be entered in a kind of reckless pleasure. This pleasure either the young men copied from the older ones or the older ones always kept. The grown people, like the children, looked with kindling eyes at all turmoil, expecting delight for themselves and for you. They were shocked only at disappointment.

But boys and men, girls and ladies all, the old and the young of the Delta kin—even the dead and the living, for Aunt Shannon—were alike—no gap opened between them. Laura sat among them with her eyes wide. At any moment she might expose her ignorance—at any moment she might learn everything.

All the Fairchilds in the Delta looked alike—Little Battle, now, pushing his bobbed hair behind his ears before he took up a fresh drumstick, looked exactly like Dabney the way she would think at the window. They all had a fleetness about them, though they were tall, solid people with "Scotch legs"—a neatness that was actually a readiness for gaieties and departures, a distraction that was endearing as a lack of burdens. Laura felt their quality, their being, in the degree that they were portentous to her. For Laura found them all portentous—all except Aunt Ellen, who had only married into the family—Uncle George more than Uncle Battle for some reason, Dabney more than Shelley.

Without a primary beauty, with only a fairness of color (a thin-skinnedness, really) and an ease in the body, they had a demurring, gray-eyed way about them that turned out to be halfway mocking—for these cousins were the sensations of life and they knew it. (Why didn't Uncle George come on tonight—the best loved? Why wasn't Dabney on time to supper—the bride?) Things waited for them to appear, laughing to one another and amazed, in order to happen. They were forever, by luck or intuition, opening doors, discovering things, little or cherished things, running pell-mell down the stairs to meet people, ready to depart for vague and spontaneous occasions. Though everything came to Shellmound to them. All the girls got serenaded in the summertime—though Shelley last summer had said it pained her for Dabney to listen *that way*. They were never too busy for anything, they were generously and almost seriously of the moment: the past (even Laura's arrival today was past now) was a private, dull matter that would be forgotten except by aunts.

Laura from her earliest memory had heard how they "never seemed to change at all." That was the way her mother, who had been away from them down in Jackson where they would be hard to believe, could brag on them without seeming to. And yet Laura could see that they changed every moment. The outside did not change but the inside did; an iridescent life was busy within and under each alikeness. Laughter at something went over the table; Laura found herself with a picture in her mind of a great bowerlike cage full of tropical birds her father had shown her in a zoo in a city—the sparkle of motion was like a rainbow, while it was the very thing that broke your heart, for the birds that flew were caged all the time and could not fly out. The Fairchilds' movements were quick and on the instant, and that made you wonder, are they free? Laura was certain that they were *compelled*—their favorite word. Flying against the bad things happening, they kissed you in rushes of tenderness. Maybe their delight was part of their beauty, its flicker as it went by, and their kissing of not only you but everybody in a room was a kind of spectacle, an outward thing. But when they looked at you with their lighted eyes, picked you out in a room for a glance, waiting for you to say something in admiration or "conceit," to ask the smallest favor, of any of them you chose, and so to commit yourself forever—you could never question them again, you trusted them, that nothing more inward preoccupied them, for you adored them, and only wanted to be here with them, to be let run toward them. They are all as sweet as Ranny, she thought—all sweet right down to Ranny—Ranny being four and the youngest she could see at her end of the table, now angelically asleep in his chair with a little wishbone in his fist.

Just as Roxie was about to clear the table, Dabney gently but distractedly came in—dressed in blue, drying tears from her eyes, and murmuring to her mother as she passed her chair, "Oh, Mama, *that* was just because my brain isn't working; why did you bring up your children with faulty brains?"

"She ought to have drowned you when you were little," said Uncle Battle, and this was their extravagant way of talk. "Sit down, I saved you a wishbone and a heart besides what poor pickings is left."

"Run some more biscuit in the oven, Roxie," Ellen said. "I think too you'd better bring Miss Dabney a little ham, there's such a dearth of turkey to tempt her."

"Say it again, Mama," said Ranny, opening his eyes. Then he smiled at Dabney.

"What were you crying about—the worry you're bringing down on your father?" Battle said.

Holding out her plate for her father to serve (she sat close by him, at his right), Dabney smiled too, and waited. How beautiful she was—all flushed and knowing. Now they would tease her. An only child, Laura found teasing the thing she kept forgetting about the Delta cousins from one summer to the next. Uncle Battle might put the heart on Dabney's plate yet, knowing she could not bear to look at the heart; though Dabney would know what to do. Was it possible that it was because they loved one another so, that it made them set little traps to catch one another? They looked with shining eyes upon their kin, and all their abundance of love, as if it were a devilment, was made reckless and inspired or was belittled in fun, though never, so far, was it said out. They had never told Laura they loved her.

She sighed. "Where's Aunt Primrose and Aunt Jim Allen?"

"Why don't you ask any questions about who's here?" said India.

"They said I had to come see them and *tell* them first," said Dabney, beginning to eat hungrily. "Touchy, touchy."

"I'm touchy too," said Uncle Battle.

"Oh, *Laura!*" cried Dabney delightedly. "I didn't know you'd got here! Why, honey!" She flew around the table and kissed her.

"I came to your wedding," said Laura, casting pleased, shy glances all around.

"Oh, Laura, *you* want me to marry Troy, don't you? *You* approve, don't you?"

"Yes," said Laura. "I approve, Dabney!"

"You be in my wedding! You be a flower girl!"

"I can't," said Laura helplessly. "My mother died."

"Oh," cried Dabney, as if Laura had slapped her, running away from her and back to her place at the table, hiding her face. "It's just so *hard*, everything's just so *hard*. . . ."

"Here's your little ham, Miss Dab," said Roxie, coming in. "Do you good."

"Oh, Roxie, even you. No one will ever believe me, that I just can't swallow until Saturday. There's no use trying any more."

"You can bring the ice cream and cake then, Roxie," Aunt Ellen said. "It's Georgie's favorite cake, I do wish they could be here a day sooner!"

They sat sighing, eating cake, drinking coffee. The throb of the compress had never stopped. Laura could feel it now in the handle of her cup, the noiseless vibration that trembled in the best china, was within it.

It was hard to ever quite leave the dining room afte
It would be still faintly day, and not much coo
still sat, until the baby, who had hung teasi
coffee out of them from her high-chair ("

at the table!") wilted over like a little flower in her kimono with the butterfly sleeves and was kissed all around and carried up in flushed sleep in Dabney's overeager arms.

The table was in the middle of the large room, and there was little tendency to leave even that. But besides the old walnut-and-cane chairs (Great-Grandfather made them) there were easy chairs covered with cotton in a faded peony pattern, and rockers for the two great-aunts, sewing stands and fire shields beside them, all near the watery-green tile hearth. A spready fern stood in front of the grate in summertime, with a cricket in it now, that nobody could do anything about. Along the wall the china closets reflected the windows, except for one visible shelf where some shell-pattern candlesticks shone, and the Port Gibson epergne, a fan of Apostle spoons, and the silver sugar basket with the pierce-work in it and its old cracked purplish glass lining. At the other end of the room the Victrola stood like a big morning-glory and there, laid with somebody's game, was the card table Great-Grandfather also made out of his walnut trees when he cut his way in to the Yazoo wilderness. A long ornate rattan settee, upslanting at the ends, with a steep scrolled back, was in the bay alcove. In the half-moon of space behind it were marble pedestals and wicker stands each holding a fern of advanced size or a little rooted cutting, sometimes in bloom. Overhead, over the loaded plate rails, were square oil paintings of split melons and cut flowers by Aunt Mashula as a young girl.

This evening there was nobody but Uncle Battle to take cherry bounce, an anything alone he would not have it but with and took Bluet's doll out of his wandered in, Aunt Ellen wan-y wandered across the hall into play softly to herself, but no-anybody, could be persuaded on a stool and listened, lis-hile Dabney and Shelley and ss for a dance in Glen Alan, n the settee, each with her kinged feet in her sister's a waterfall the fronds of ub over them.

"Fan us, fan us, India," said Dabney, though the big overhead fan turned too.

"Ranny will fan you, before he goes to bed," India said, and Ranny came radiantly forward with Great-Aunt Shannon's palmetto.

"Ho hum," said Dabney. "You'd think I had nothing to do. I wonder if Troy is in from the fields."

"There's one speck of light left," said Shelley.

"Cousin Laura," said Orrin kindly, looking up from his book at her. He leaned on the table. "You weren't here, but Uncle George and Maureen nearly got killed."

"Uncle George?" Laura alone had not reclined; she stood looking into the big mirror over the sideboard which reflected the whole roomful of cousins.

"Ranny, you fan too hard. They nearly let the Yellow Dog run over them on the Dry Creek trestle." Dabney softly laughed from her prone position.

India moaned from the chair she was leaning over to read a book on the floor.

"It was almost a tragedy," said Shelley. She lifted up her head, then let it fall back.

"Why did they let the Yellow Dog almost run over them?" Laura made her way to the table and leaned on it to ask Orrin, who answered her gravely, with his finger in his place in the book. "Here's the way it was—" For all of them told happenings like narrations, chronological and careful, as if the ear of the world listened and wished to know surely.

"The whole family but Papa and Mama, and ten or twenty Negroes with us, went fishing in Drowning Lake. It will be two weeks ago Sunday. And so coming home we walked the track. We were tired—we were singing. On the trestle Maureen danced and caught her foot. I've done that, but I know how to get loose. Uncle George kneeled down and went to work on Maureen's foot, and the train came. He hadn't got Maureen's foot loose, so he didn't jump either. The rest of us did jump, and the Dog stopped just before it hit them and ground them all to pieces."

Uncle Battle looked at Dabney with a kind of outraged puffing of his sunburned cheeks, a glare in her direction like some fatherly malediction; whether it was meant for Dabney herself in front of his eyes, or for what he had heard, Laura could not tell. And as if glaring itself made him nervous he dandled the ragged doll heavily on his knee.

Dabney gave a half-smile. "The engineer looked out the window—he said he was sorry."

Laura looked at her gravely. "I'm glad I wasn't there," she told her.

Then Aunt Ellen came in, meditatively, as the hall clock finished striking two which meant it was eight. She had a feather on her skirt—had she been out for her precious guinea eggs? She was a slight, almost delicate lady, seeming exactly strong enough for what was needed of her life. She was scarcely taller than Orrin, and Dabney and Shelley had been both taller and bigger than their mother for two years. She walked into the roomful of family without immediately telling them anything. She was more restful than the Fairchilds. Her brown hair and her dark-blue eyes seemed part of her quietness—like the colors of water, reflective. Her Virginia voice, while no softer or lighter than theirs, was a less questioning, a never teasing one. It was a voice to speak to the one child or the one man her eyes would go to. They all watched her with soft eyes, but distractedly.

She was one of those little mothers that the wind seems almost to hurt, and they knew they needed to look after her. She held very straight in her back, like a little boy who can do right in dancing class. And while she meditated, she hurried—how she hurried! She was never slow—she was either still or darting. They said she had no need for hurry with a houseful of Negroes to do the first thing she told them. But she did not wait for them or anybody to wait on her. "Your mother is killing herself," Battle's sisters told the children. "But you can't do a thing in the world with her," they answered. "We're going to have to whip her or kill her before she'll lie down in the afternoons, even." They spoke of killing and whipping in the exasperation and helplessness of much love. Laura could see as far as that she was the opposite of a Fairchild, and that was a stopping point. Aunt Ellen would be seen busy in a room, where Aunt Tempe for instance was never seen except proceeding down halls, or seated. She never cared how she dressed any more than a child. Aunt Tempe said to India last summer, in the voice in which she always spoke to little girls, as if everything were a severe revelation, "When your mother goes to Greenwood she simply goes to the closet and says, 'Clothes, I'm going to Greenwood, anything that wants to go along, get on my back.' She has never learned what is reprehensible and what is not, in the Delta." She was often a little confused about her keys, and sometimes would ask Dabney, "What was I going for?" "Why am I here?" When she threw her head back dramatically, it meant she was listening for a baby. Her small sweetly shaped nose was sparingly freckled like a little girl's, like India's in summer. Sometimes, as when now she stood still for a moment in the room full of talking people, an unaccountable rosiness would jump into her cheeks and a look of merriment would make her eyes grow wide. Down low over the dinner table hung a lamp with a rectangular shade of tinted glass, like a lighted shoe-box toy, a "choo-choo boat" with its colored paper windows. In its light she would look over the room, at the youngest ones intertwining on the rug and hating so the approach of night, the older ones leaning across the cleared table, chasing each other in a circle, or reading, or lost to themselves on the flimsy settee; Battle pondering in his way or fuming, while from time to time the voices of the girls called out to the telephone would sound somewhere in the air like the twittering of birds—and it would be as if she had never before seen anything at all of this room with the big breasting china closets and the fruit and cake plates around the rail, had never watered the plants in the window, or encountered till now these absorbed, intent people—ever before in her life, Laura thought. At that moment a whisper might have said Look! to her, and the dining-room curtains might have traveled back on their rings, and there *they* were. Even some unused love seemed to Laura to be in Aunt Ellen's eyes when she gazed, after supper, at her own family. Could she get it? Laura's heart pounded. But the baby had dreams and soon she would cry out on the upper floor, and Aunt Ellen listening would run straight to her, calling to her on the way, and forgetting everything in this room.

2

How Ellen loved their wide and towering foreheads, their hairlines on the fresh skin silver as the edge of a peach, clean as a pencil line, dipping to a perfect widow's peak in every child she had. Their cheeks were wide and their chins narrow but pressed a little forward—lips caught, then parted, as if in constant expectation—so that their faces looked sturdy and resolute, unrevealing, from the side, but tender and heart-shaped from the front. Their coloring—their fair hair and their soot-dark, high eyebrows and shadowy lashes, the long eyes, of gray that seemed more luminous, more observant and more passionate than blue—moved her deeply and freshly in each child. Dear Orrin, talking so seriously now, the dignity in his look! And little Ranny with his burning cheeks and the silver bleach of summer on his hair, so deliberately wielding the fan over his sisters! She had never had a child to take after herself and would be as astonished as Battle now to see her own ways or looks dominant, a blue-eyed, dark-haired, small-boned baby lying in her arms. All the mystery of looks moved her, for she was with child once more.

In the men grown, in Battle and George, it was a paradoxical thing, the fineness and tenderness with the bulk and weight of their big bodies. All the Fairchild men (the old-maid sister, Jim Allen, would recite that like a bit of catechism) were six feet tall by the time they were sixteen and weighed two hundred pounds by the time they were forty. But Battle weighed two hundred and fifty, and groaned to be gentle as he was; and George, though he was not himself fat, was markedly bigger and fairer than any of them in the early portraits, as if he were not a throwback to the type (which had faltered but little, after all, through marriages with little women like her, like Laura Allen and Mary Shannon before her) but a new original—a sport of the tree itself. She guessed she apprehended everything through the way they looked and felt—George sometimes more than Battle. Battle wore the glower of fatherhood or its little undermask of helplessness, that George had not put on. And George had remained left-handed, the thing they all inherited, as was somehow visibly apparent not just momently but always—perhaps by such a

another Yellow Dog incident

thing as the part in his hair. Her secret tremor at Battle's determined breaking of her children's left-handedness made her cherish it like a failing in George.

The fineness in her men called to mind their unwieldiness, and the other way round, in a way infinitely endearing to her. The fineness could so soon look delicate—nobody could get tireder, fall sicker and more quickly so, than her men. She thought yet of the other brother Denis who was dead in France as holding this look; from the grave he gave her that look, partly of hurt: "How could I have been brought like this?" as Battle cried in the Far Field when his horse, unaccountably terrified at the old Yellow Dog one day, threw him and left him unable to raise himself from the ditch.

"Oh, it was cloudy, or we would have remembered it was time for the Dog," Orrin was saying, looking up from his book. "We wouldn't have made that mistake another day, when we could see the sun."

"The Dog was most likely running an hour late, and it wouldn't have done us any good." Dabney smiled. She twisted her foot in Shelley's hair, where they were lying together on the settee. "I'm making a hole in your net with my big toe."

"I won't lie here with you any longer," Shelley said languidly. But she did not move, or close her eyes fully. She looked rather dreamily down the slope of her own body, middy blouse, skirt, dark-blue stockings, and up Dabney's, light-blue stockings, light-blue swiss dress with one lace panel momently floating in Ranny's breeze, and Dabney's just-washed hair flying on her clasped hands behind her head. Dabney's face was suffused and soft now as Bluet's when she was waked from her nap. Her eyes seemed to swim in some essence not tears, but as bright—an essence that made the pupils large. The sisters looked now into each other's eyes, and as if there was no help for it, a flare leaped between them. . . .

There was a lusty cry from Maureen.

"She's caught the cricket. She's pulling his wings off—she'll kill the cricket." Roy was on his feet.

"Don't stop her, don't stop her. Let her have her way," Battle said, his voice rumbling in Ellen's ears.

"The cricket minded, I think," Ranny said, holding the fan still.

"Come help me make a cake before bedtime, Laura," said Ellen; now she saw Laura with forgetful eyes fastened on her. She's the poor little old thing, she thought. When a man alone has to look after a little girl, how in even eight months she will get long-legged and skinny. She will as like as not need to have glasses when school starts. He doesn't cut her hair, or he will cut it too short. How sharp her elbows are— Maureen looks like a cherub beside her—the difference just in their elbows!

"I'll be glad to, Aunt Ellen," Laura said, and put her hand in hers as if she were Ranny's age. She came along in a toiling little walk.

"Get out of the kitchen, Roxie. We want to make Mr. George and Miss Robbie a cake. They're coming tomorrow."

"You loves *them*," said Roxie. "You're fixin' to ask me to grate you a coconut, not get out."

"Yes, I am. Grate me the coconut." Ellen smiled. "I got fourteen guinea eggs this evening, and that's a sign I ought to make it, Roxie."

"Take 'em all: guineas," said Roxie belittlingly.

"Well, you get the oven hot." Ellen tied her apron back on. "You can grate me the coconut, and a lemon while you're at it, and blanch me the almonds. I'm going to let Laura pound me the almonds in the mortar and pestle."

"Is that very hard?" asked Laura, running out for a drink at the water cooler.

Ellen was breaking and separating the fourteen eggs. "Yes, I do want coconut," she murmured. For Ellen's hope for Dabney, that had to lie in something, some secret nest, lay in George's happiness. He had married "beneath" him too, in Tempe's unvarying word. When he got home from the war he married, in the middle of one spring night, little Robbie Reid, Old Man Swanson's granddaughter, who had grown up in the town of Fairchilds to work in Fairchild's Store.

She beat the egg whites and began creaming the sugar and butter, and saying a word from time to time to Laura who hung on the table and watched her, she felt busily consoled for the loss of Dabney to Troy Flavin by the happiness of George lost to Robbie. She remembered, as if she vigorously worked the memory up out of the mixture, a picnic at the Grove—the old place—an exuberant night in the spring before—it was not long after the death of Annie Laurie down in Jackson. Robbie had tantalizingly let herself be chased and had jumped in the river with George in after her, everybody screaming from where they lay. Dalliance, pure play, George was after that night—he was enchanted with his wife, he made it plain then. They were in moonlight. With great splashing he took her dress and petticoat off in the water, flung them out on the willow bushes, and carried her up screaming in her very teddies, her lost ribbon in his teeth, and the shining water running down her kicking legs and flying off her heels as she screamed and buried her face in his chest, laughing too, proud too.

The sisters'—Jim Allen's and Primrose's—garden ran right down to the water there—how could they have known their brother George would some day carry a dripping girl out of the river and fling her down thrashing and laughing on a bed of their darling sweet peas, pulling vines and all down on her? George flung himself down by her too and threw his wet arm out and drew her onto his fast-breathing chest. They lay there smiling and worn out, but twined together—appealing, shining in moonlight, and almost—somehow—threatening, Ellen felt. They were so boldly happy, with Dabney and Shelley there, with Primrose and Jim Allen trembling for their sweet peas if not daring to think of George's life risked, and India seizing the opportunity of running up and sprinkling them with pomegranate flowers and handfuls of grass to tickle them. Dabney had brought young Dickie Boy Featherstone along that night; they had sat timidly holding hands on the river bank, Dabney with a clover chain circling and festooning her like a net. They had chided Robbie, she had endangered George—he could not swim well for a wound of war. But no one can stare back more languorously and alluringly than a rescued woman, Ellen believed, from the memory of Robbie's slumbrous eyes and surfeited little smile as she lay on George's wet arm. George was delighted as by some passing transformation in her, speaking some word to her and making her

look away toward them overcome with merriment—as if she
had beguiled him in some obvious way he found absurd and
endearing—as if she had tried to arouse his jealousy, for instance, by flirting with another man.

As Ellen put in the nutmeg and the grated lemon rind she
diligently assumed George's happiness, seeing it in the Fairchild aspects of exuberance and satiety; if it was unabashed, it
was the best part true. But—adding the milk, the egg whites,
the flour, carefully and alternately as Mashula's recipe said—
she could be diligent and still not wholly sure—never wholly.
She loved George too dearly herself to seek her knowledge of
him through the family attitude, keen and subtle as that
was—just as she loved Dabney too much to see her propsect
without its risk, now family-deplored, around it, the happiness
covered with danger. "Look who Robbie Reid is!" they had
said once, and now, "Who is Troy Flavin?" Indeed, who was
Troy Flavin, beyond being the Fairchild overseer? Nobody
knew. Only that he had a little mother in the hills. It was
killing Battle; she heard him now, calling, "Dabney, Dabney!
Dickie Boy Featherstone's blowing his horn!" and at the telephone Dabney was talking softly to Troy, "I'm with Dickie
Boy Featherstone, gone to Glen Alan. . . . Good night. . . .
Good night. . . ." It seemed to Ellen that it was for every
one of them that added care pressed her heart on these late
summer nights ("Now you can taste, Laura," she said), care
that stirred in her and that she herself shielded, like the child
she carried.

"Now, Laura. Go get that little bottle of rose water off the
top shelf in the pantry. Climb where Roy climbs for the cooky
jar and you'll reach it. . . . Now be putting in a little rose
water as you go. Pound good."

She poured her cake out in four layer pans and set the first
two in the oven, gently shutting the door. "Be ready, Laura,
when I call you. Oh, save me twenty-four perfect halves—to
go on top. . . ."

She began with the rest of the eggs to make the filling; she
would just trust that Laura's paste would do, and make the
icing thick on top with the perfect almonds over it close
enough to touch.

"Smell my cake?" she challenged, as Dabney appeared radiant at the pantry door, then coming through, spreading her pink dress to let her mother see her. Ellen turned a little dizzily. Was the cake going to turn out all right? She was always nervous about her cakes. And for George she did want it to be nice—he was so appreciative. "*Don't* pound your poor finger, Laura."

"I wasn't going to, Aunt Ellen."

"Oh, Mother, am I beautiful—tonight?" Dabney asked urgently, almost painfully, as though she would run if she heard the answer.

Laura laid down the noisy pestle. Her lips parted. Dabney rushed across the kitchen and threw her arms tightly around her mother and clung to her.

Roxie, waiting on the porch, could be heard laughing, two high gentle notes out in the dark.

From an upper window India's voice came out on the soft air, chanting,

> Star light,
> Star bright,
> First star I've seen tonight,
> I wish I may, I wish I might
> Have the wish I wish tonight.

For a moment longer they all held still: India was wishing.

II

I⟨T WAS⟩ the next afternoon. Dabney came down the stairs
vaguely in time to the song Mary Lamar Mackey was rippling out in the music room—"Drink to Me Only with Thine
Eyes." "Oh, I'm a wreck," she sighed absently.

"Did you have your breakfast? Then run on to your aunts,"
said her mother, pausing in the hall below, pointing a silver
dinner knife at her. "You're a girl engaged to be married and
your aunts want to see you." "Your aunts" always referred to
the two old-maid sisters of her father's who lived at the Grove,
the old place on the river, Aunt Primrose and Aunt Jim Allen,
and not to Aunt Tempe who had married Uncle Pinck, or
Aunt Rowena or Aunt Annie Laurie who were dead. "I've got
all the Negroes your papa could spare me up here on the silver
and those miserable chandelier prisms—I don't want you underfoot, even."

"They saw me that Sunday they came up to dinner," said
Dabney, still on the stairs.

"But you weren't engaged that Sunday—or you hadn't told."

A veil came over Dabney's eyes—a sort of pleased mourn-
fulness.

"They'll ask me ten thousand questions."

"Let me go!" said India quickly. She was sitting on the
bottom step finishing a leaf hat. "I'm not really busy."

"Come on, then," said Dabney. She ran down and leaned
over her little sister and smiled at her for what seemed the
first time in years.

"I can come! I'll hop!" Bluet instantly came hopping up
with one shoe off, her sunny hair flying. In the corner Roxie's
little Sudie, who was "watching" her, stretched meek on the
floor with chin in hand. Little Battle tore through the house
but didn't stop a minute, except to spank Dabney hard. Mary
Lamar Mackey dreamily called, "Where are you all going?"

"Now get away from Dabney *everybody*, and let her go,"
said Ellen. "No, Dabney, not Ranny either, this time. You'll
dawdle and let him fall off the horse—and Primrose and Jim
Allen'll have to invite you to supper."

"Will they have spoon bread?" cried India.

"That's enough, India. You can carry that bucket of molasses if you're going, and I think I'll send a taste more of that blackberry wine—wait till I pour it off."

"You can wear this, Dabney." On her two forefingers India offered up the leaf hat to her sister, who had on a new dress.

"Oh, I couldn't! Never mind, you wear it," said Dabney. She herself fixed it on India's hair. Dabney had gotten awfully fixy, said the calm stare in India's eyes at that moment. The little girl set her jaw, Dabney frowned, and one of the rose thorns did scratch.

"Be sure that sack on the front porch gets to Jim Allen!" called their mother from the back porch. "Oh, where's my wine!"

"Vi'let! Vi'let!"

"Take Aunt Primrose my plaid wool and my cape pattern!" called Shelley from right under their feet. She was under the house looking for the key to the clock which she insisted had fallen through the floor. "In Mama's room! Vi'let!"

Dabney drew her brows together for a moment—Shelley was a year older than she was, and now that Dabney was the one getting married, she seemed to spend her time in the oddest places. She ought to be getting ready for Europe. She had to go in a month. She said she "simply couldn't" go to any of the bridge parties, that they were "just sixty girls from all over the Delta come to giggle in one house." She would hardly go to the dances, some nights. "Shelley, come out! . . . Mama, do you think they want *all* those hyacinth bulbs?" she called.

"They're onions! India, did you call Little Uncle to bring up Junie and Rob?"

"Little Uncle!"

"Wait a second, India," said Dabney. She caught at her sticking-out skirt. "You look plenty tacky, India—you're just the age where you look tacky and that's all there is to it." She sighed again, and ran lightly down the steps. "You ride with the onions, I'm going to see Troy tonight."

"Well, my golly," said India.

"We ought to send them back that candy dish—but can't send it back empty!" called Ellen in a falling voice.

Little Uncle and Vi'let got them loaded up on the horses and fixed all the buckets and sacks so they weren't very likely to fall open. "I don't know why we didn't take the car," Dabney said dreamily. They rode out the gate.

India said, "Haven't I got to see Troy, and the whole family got to see Troy, Troy, Troy, every single night the rest of our lives, besides the day? Does Troy hate onions? Does he declare he hates them? Does he hate peaches? Figs? Black-eyed peas?"

"We'll be further away than that," said Dabney, still dreamily.

It was a soft day, brimming with the light of afternoon. It was the fifth beautiful week, with only that one threatening day. The gold mass of the distant shade trees seemed to dance, to sway, under the plum-colored sky. On either side of their horses' feet the cotton twinkled like stars. Then a red-pop flew up from her nest in the cotton. Above in an unbroken circle, all around the wheel of the level world, lay silvery-blue clouds whose edges melted and changed into the pink and blue of sky. Girls and horses lifted their heads like swimmers. Here and there and far away the cotton wagons, of hand-painted green, stood up to their wheel tops in the white and were loaded with white, like cloud wagons. All along, the Negroes would lift up and smile glaringly and pump their arms—they knew Miss Dabney was going to step off Saturday with Mr. Troy.

A man on a black horse rode across their path at right angles, down Mound Field. He waved, his arm like a gun against the sky—it was Troy on Isabelle. A long stream of dust followed him, pink in the light. Dabney lifted her hand. "Wave, India," she said.

There was the distance where he still charmed her most— it was strange. Just here, coming now to the Indian mound, was where she really noticed him first—last summer, riding like this with India on Junie and Rob. (Though later, they would go clear to Marmion to sit in the moonlight by the old house and by the river, teasing and playing, when it was fall.) And she looked with joy, as if it marked the pre-eminent place, at the Indian mound topped with trees like a masted green boat on the cottony sea. That he was at this distance obviously not a Fairchild still filled her with an awe that had grown most easily from idle condescension—that made it hard to think of him as he would come closer. Troy, a slow talker, had been the object of little stories and ridicule at the table—then suddenly he was real. She shut her eyes. She saw a blinding light, or else was it a dark cloud—that intensity under her flickering lids? She rode with her eyes shut. Troy Flavin was the overseer. The Fairchilds would die, everybody said, if this happened. But now everybody seemed to be just too busy to die or not.

He was twice as old as she was now, but that was just a funny accident, thirty-four being twice seventeen, it wouldn't be so later on. When she was as much as twenty-five, he wouldn't be fifty! "Things will probably go on about as they do now," she would hear her mother say. "It isn't as if Dabney was going out of the Delta—like Mary Denis Summers." They would have Marmion, and Troy could manage the two places. "Marmion can't belong to Maureen!" she had cried, when she first asked. "Yes—not legally, but really," her father said; he thought it was complicated. So Dabney had said to Maureen, "Look, honey—will you give your house to me?" They had been lying half-asleep together in the hammock after dinner. And Maureen, hanging over her to look at her, her face close above hers, had chosen to smile radiantly. "Yes," she had said, "you can have my house-la, and a bite-la of my apple too." Oh, everything *could* be so easy! Virgie Lee, Maureen's mother, was not of sound mind and would have none of Marmion. It might have been more fun to ask George for the Grove, and see . . . but too late now, and the Grove was not the grandest place. Troy had simply slapped his hand on his saddle when she told him, at the way she could have Marmion with a little airy remark! She had blushed—surely that was flattery! Troy was slow on words.

"I don't hear anything but nice things about Troy," everybody was telling her. As though he were invisible, and only she had seen him! She thought of him proudly (he was right back of the mound now, she knew), a dark thundercloud, his slowness rumbling and his laugh flickering through in bright flashes; any "nice thing" would sound absurd—as if you were talking about a cousin, or a friend. Later they would laugh together about this. Uncle George would be on her side. He would treat it as if it wasn't any side, which would make it better—make it perfect . . . unless he got on Troy's side. He liked Troy. . . .

"There goes Pinchy, trying to come through," said India, to make Dabney open her eyes. Sure enough, there went Pinchy wandering in the cotton rows, Roxie's helper, not speaking to them at all but giving up every moment to seeking.

"I hope she comes through soon." Dabney frowned.

"I forgot the onions, too."

"Hyacinths, you mean."

"Onions. You're crazy as a June bug now, Dabney," said India thoughtfully. "Will I be like you?"

"You're crazy the way you forget things, onions or hyacinths either."

Troy was far to the right now—they had turned. They rode around the blue shadow of the Indian mound, and he was behind her. Faintly she could hear his busy shout, "Sylvanus! Sylvanus!"

"All the Fairchilds forget things," said India, beginning to gallop joyfully, making the wine splash.

They rode through the Far Field and into the pasture where three mules were looking out together from a green glade. The sedge was glowing, the round meadow had a bloom like fruit, and the sweet gums were like a soft curtain beyond, fading into the pink of the near sky. Here the season showed. Queen Anne's lace brushed their feet as they rode, and the tight green goldenrod knocked at them. She seemed to hear the rustle of the partridgy shadows.

Sometimes, Dabney was not so sure she was a Fairchild—sometimes she did not care, that was it. There were moments of life when it did not matter who she was—even where. Something, happiness—with Troy, but not necessarily, even the happiness of a fine day—seemed to leap away from identity as if it were an old skin, and that she was one of the Fairchilds was of no more need to her than the locust shells now hanging to the trees everywhere were to the singing locusts. What she felt, nobody knew! It would kill her father—of course for her to be a Fairchild was an inescapable thing, to him. And she would not take anything for the relentless way he was acting, not wanting to let her go. The caprices of his restraining power over his daughters filled her with delight now that she had declared what she could do. She felt a double pride between them now—it tied them closer than ever as they laughed, bragged, reproached each other and flaunted themselves. While her mother, who had never spoken the first word against her sudden decision to marry or questioned her wildness for Troy or her defiance of her father's wishes, in the whole two weeks, somehow defeated her. Dabney and her mother had gone into shells of mutual contemplation—like two shy young girls meeting in a country of a strange language. Perhaps it was only her mother's condition, thought Dabney, shaking her head a little. Only when she forgot herself, flashed out in the old way, shed tears, and begged her pardon, did Dabney feel again in her mother's quick kiss, like a peck, her watchfulness, the kind of pity for children that mothers might feel always until they were dead, reassuring to the mother and the little girl together.

Troy treated her like a Fairchild—he still did; he wouldn't stop work when she rode by even today. Sometimes he was so standoffish, gentle like, other times he laughed and mocked her, and shook her, and played like fighting—once he had really hurt her. How sorry it made him! She took a deep breath. Sometimes Troy was really ever so much like a Fairchild. Nobody guessed that, just seeing him go by on Isabelle! He had not revealed very much to her yet. He would—that dark shouting rider would throw back the skin of this very time, of this moment. . . . There would be a whole other world, with other cotton, even.

It was actually Uncle George who had shown her that there was another way to be—something else. . . . Uncle George, the youngest of the older ones, who stood in—who was—the very heart of the family, who was like them, looked like them (only by far, she thought, seeing at once his picnic smile, handsomer)—he was different, somehow. Perhaps the heart always was made of different stuff and had a different life from the rest of the body. She saw Uncle George lying on his arm on a picnic, smiling to hear what someone was telling, with a butterfly going across his gaze, a way to make her imagine all at once that in that moment he erected an entire, complicated house for the butterfly inside his sleepy body. It was very

strange, but she had felt it. She had then known something
he knew all along, it seemed then—that when you felt,
touched, heard, looked at things in the world, and found their
fragrances, they themselves made a sort of house within you,
which filled with life to hold them, filled with knowledge all
by itself, and all else, the other ways to know, seemed calculation and tyranny.

Blindly and proudly Dabney rode, her eyes shut against
what was too bright. Uncle George would be coming some
time today—she would be glad. He would be sweet to her,
sweet to Troy. In a way, their same old way, the family were
leaving any sweetness, any celebration and good wishing, to
Uncle George. They had said nothing very tender or final to
her yet; hardly anything at all excited, even, about the marriage—beyond her father's carrying on, that went without saying. They had put it off, she guessed, sighing. This was too
much in cotton-picking time, that was all—or else they still
had hope that she would not do this to them. Dabney smiled
again—she smiled as often as tears, once started, would
fall—her flickering eyes on India shaking her switch like a
wand at a scampering rabbit. Uncle George would come and
say something just right—or rather he would come and not
say any special thing at all, just show them the champagne he
brought for the wedding night, while Shelley, perhaps, was
coaxed to cry—and they would not fret or worry or hold back
any longer. Dabney herself would then be entirely happy.

"Has James's Bayou really got a whirlpool in the middle of
it?" cried India intensely.

"No, India, always no, but *you* stay out of it." They rode
into the tarnished light of a swampy place.

"But has it really got a ghost? Everybody knows it has."

"Then don't ask me every time. Just so she won't cry for
my wedding, that's all *I* ask!" Dabney sighed.

"I'd love her to cry for me," India said luringly. "Cry and
cry."

Just then, directly in front of them, Man-Son, one of the
Negroes, raised his hat. How strange—he should be picking
cotton, thought Dabney. But everything seemed to be happening strangely, some special way, now. Nodding sternly to
Man-Son, she remembered perfectly a certain morning away

back; of course, it was then she had discovered in Uncle George one first point where he differed from the other Fairchilds, and learned that one human being can differ, very excitingly, from another. As if everything had waited for her to be about to marry, for her to fall in love, it seemed to her that all, even memories and dreams, grew clear. . . .

It was a day in childhood, they were living at the Grove. She had wandered off—no older than India now—and had seen George come on a small scuffle, a scuffle with a knife, out in the woods—right here. George, thin, lanky, exultant, "wild," they said smilingly, had been down at the Grove from school that summer. Two of their little Negroes had flown at each other with extraordinary intensity here on the bank of the bayou. It was in the bright sun, in front of the cypress shadows. At the jerk-back of a little wrist, suddenly a knife let loose and seemed to fling itself in the air. Uncle George and Uncle Denis (who was killed the next year in the war) had just come out of the bayou, naked, so wet they shone in the sun, wet light hair hanging over their foreheads just alike, and they were stamping their feet, flinging out their arms, starting to wrestle and play, and Uncle George reached up and caught the knife. "I'll be damned," he said (at that she thought he was wounded) and turning, rushed in among the thrashing legs and arms. Uncle Denis walked off, slipping into his long-tailed shirt, just melted away into the light, laughing. Uncle George grabbed the little Negro that wanted to run, and pinned down the little Negro that was hollering. Somehow he held one, said "Hand me that," and tied up the other, tearing up his own shirt. He used his teeth and the Negroes' knife, and the young fighters were both as still as mice, though he said something to himself now and then.

It was a big knife—she was sure it was as big as the one Troy could pull out now. There was blood on the sunny ground. Uncle George cussed the little Negro for being cut like that. The other little Negro sat up all quiet and leaned over and looked at all Uncle George was doing, and in the middle of it his face crumpled—with a loud squall he went with arms straight out to Uncle George, who stopped and let him cry a minute. And then the other little Negro sat up off the ground, the small black pole of his chest striped with the shirt bandage, and climbed up to him too and began to holler, and he knelt low there holding to him the two little black boys who cried together melodiously like singers, and saying, still worriedly, "Damn you! Damn you both!" Then what did he do to them? He asked them their names and let them go. They had gone flying off together like conspirators. Dabney had never forgotten which two boys those were, and could tell them from the rest—Man-Son worked for them yet and was a good Negro, but his brother, the one with the scar on his neck, had given trouble, so Troy had got his way when he came, and her father had let him go.

When George turned around on the bayou, his face looked white and his sunburn a mask, and he stood there still and attentive. There was blood on his hands and both legs. He stood looking not like a boy close kin to them, but out by himself, like a man who had stepped outside—done something. But it had not been anything Dabney wanted to see him do. She almost ran away. He seemed to meditate—to refuse to smile. She gave a loud scream and he saw her there in the field, and caught her when she ran at him. He hugged her tight against his chest, where sweat and bayou water pressed her mouth, and tickled her a minute, and told her how sorry he was to have scared her like that. Everything was all right then. But all the Fairchild in her had screamed at his interfering—at his taking part—*caring* about anything in the world but them.

What things did he know of? There were surprising things in the world which did not surprise him. Wonderfully, he had reached up and caught the knife in the air. Disgracefully, he had taken two little black devils against his side. When he had not even laughed with them all about it afterwards, or told it like a story after supper, she was astonished, and sure then of a curious division between George and the rest. It was all something that the other Fairchilds would have passed by and scorned to notice—hadn't Denis, even?—that yet went to a law of his being, that came to it, like the butterfly to his sight. He could have lifted a finger and touched, held the butterfly, but he did not. The butterfly he loved, the knife not. The other Fairchilds never said but one thing about George and

Denis, who were always thought of together—that George and Denis were born sweet, and that they were not born sweet. Sweetness then could be the visible surface of profound depths—the surface of all the darkness that might frighten her. Now Denis was dead. And George loved the *world*, something told her suddenly. Not them! Not them in particular.

"Man-Son, what do you mean? You go get to picking!" she cried. She trembled all over, having to speak to him in such a way.

"Yes'm, Miss Dabney. Wishin' you'n Mr. Troy find you happiness."

They rode across the railroad track and on. The fields shone and seemed to tremble like a veil in the light. The song of distant pickers started up like the agitation of birds.

"Look pretty. Here we are," said India.

They were riding by the row of Negro houses and the manager's house. The horses lifted their noses, smelling the river. Little Matthew saw them and opened the back gate, swinging on it, and ran after them to help them off Junie and Rob. He put his little flat nose against the horses' long noses and spoke to them. Dabney and India loaded him up. Great-Grand-mother's magnolia, its lower branches taken root, spread over them. Only bits of sunlight, bright as butterflies, came through the dark tree.

The house at the Grove, a dove-gray box with its deep porch turned to the river breeze, stood under shade trees with its back to the Shellmound road. It was a cypress house on brick pillars now painted green and latticed over, and its double chimneys at either end were green too. There was an open deck, never walked any more, on its roof; it was Denis's place—he had loved to read poetry there. The garden, sun-faded, went down to the dusty moat in which the big cypresses stood like towers with doors at their roots. The bank of the river was willowy and bright, wild and unraked, and the shadowy Yazoo went softly colored and lying narrow and low in the time of year.

Aunt Primrose caught sight of them through the window of the kitchen ell, and agitatedly signaled to them that they

must go round to the front door and not on any account
come in at the back, and that she was caught in her boudoir
cap and was ashamed.

They waded through the side yard of mint and nodding
pink and white cosmos, the two pale bird dogs licking them.
Lethe flew out to help and fuss at Matthew, while Aunt
Primrose—they could hear her—spread the screen doors wide.
"Bless your hearts! Mercy! What all have you got there, always
come loaded!" she cried. A brown thrush, nesting once again
in September, flew out of the crape-myrtle tree at them and
made Dabney nearly drop the wine she was carrying herself,
to catch at her hair. Aunt Primrose, as if she should have
known that thrush would do that, ran out with little cries—
for she was the most tender-headed of the Fairchilds and
could not bear for anyone to have her hair caught or endangered.

India was allowed to go find Aunt Jim Allen, who was the
deaf aunt. She was in the first place India looked, the pantry,
tenderly writing out in her beautiful script the watermelon-
rind-preserve labels and singing in perfect tune, "Where Have
You Been, Billy Boy?" India tickled her neck with a piece of
verbena.

"Why, you monkey!" She was embraced.

Then, "Dabney!" and both aunts at last clutched the bride,
their voices stricken over her name.

"We'll sit in the parlor and Lethe will bring us some good
banana ice cream, that's what we'll do. (*Oh*, I was sorry when
the figs left!)" said Aunt Jim Allen.

"Then you'll have to turn straight around and start back,"
said Aunt Primrose.

They went on. "You're *looking* mighty pretty. I declare,
Dabney, if Sister Rowena had lived, I don't know what she
would have said. I don't believe she could have realized it.
Did you feel this way about Mary Denis Summers, Jim Allen?
I didn't." In their pinks and blues they looked like two plump
hydrangea bushes side by side. "She's having a baby right this
minute," India put in, while Dabney was saying, "It's some
of Mama's wine, and she apologizes if it's not as good as last
year, and Shelley's cape—she says please don't work too hard
on it and put out your eyes, but she could wear it on the

Berengaria and wrap up. And I'm afraid we forgot the hyacinths, but we can send them by Little Uncle in the morning."

Matthew, just now making his way in from the back, put
everything down on the carpet in one heap. Both aunts immediately ran and extracted all away, with soft cries.

"Neither Dabney nor me is scared to stay out after dark by
ourselves, Aunt Primrose," India said.

"Nonsense."

Dabney felt as if she had not been at the Grove with her
aunts since she was a little girl—all in two weeks they had
gone backward in time for her. She looked at them tenderly.

"I started you a cutting of the Seven-Sister rose the minute
I heard you were going to be married," said Aunt Primrose,
pointing her finger at her.

Aunt Primrose was the youngest aunt, she was next to
George, and Jim Allen had been next to Denis. They were
both pretty for old maids. Aunt Primrose had almost golden
hair, which she washed in camomile tea and waved on pale
steel curlers which after twenty years still snapped harshly and
fastened tightly, because her hair was so fine. Her skin was
fine and tender as Bluet's, and it had never had the midday
sun to touch it, or any sun without a hat or a parasol between
her and it. Her eyes were weak, but she could not be prevailed
on to wear ugly glasses. Her tiny ears, fine-lined and delicate,
had been pierced when she was seven years old (the last thing
her mother had done for her before the day she fell dead) and
she wore little straws through the holes until she was big
enough for diamonds. Her throat was full, with a mole like a
tiny cameo in its hollow, which sometimes struggled with the
beat of her heart, and her voice might have come out of such
a throat like a singer's, but it did not, being too soft and timid;
Aunt Jim Allen's came out strong. She was growing plumper
in the last few years, but she was always delicate and was
thought of as the little sister of the family. Her hands (with
her mother Laura Allen's rings) most naturally clasped, and
then suddenly flew apart—as if she were always eager to hear
your story, and then let it surprise her. She could not tolerate
a speck of dust in her house, and every room was ready for
the inspection of the Queen, Aunt Mac said belittlingly. Her
dresses, and Aunt Jim Allen's, were all dainty, with "touches,"

and they wore little sachets tied and tucked here and there underneath, smelling of clove pinks or violets, nothing "artificial." Aunt Primrose was sweet to Aunt Jim Allen and never said a cross word all day to her or to Lethe or any of the men or her manager. She loved everybody but there was one living man she adored and that was her brother George. "As well I might," she said. She was not scared to live in the house alone with Jim Allen, because she simply had faith nothing would happen to her.

Both of them would tell you that Jim Allen was the better cake maker, but Primrose was better with preserves and pickles and candy, and knew just the minute any named thing ought to be taken off the fire. They swore by Mashula Hines's cook book, and at other times read Mary Shannon's diary she kept when this was a wilderness, and it was full of things to make and the ways to set out cuttings and the proper times, along with all her troubles and provocations.

It was eternally cool in summer in this house; like the air of a dense little velvet-green wood it touched your forehead with stillness. Even the phone had a ring like a tiny silver bell. The Grove was really Uncle George's place now; but he had put his two unmarried sisters in the house and given them Little Joe to manage it, and gone to Memphis to practice law when he married that Robbie Reid. Matting lay along the halls, and the silver doorknobs were not quite round but the shape of little muffins, not perfect. Dabney went into the parlor. How softly all the doors shut, in this house by the river—a soft wind always pressed very gently against your closing. How quiet it was, without the loud driving noise of a big fan in every corner as there was at home, even when at moments *people* sighed and fell silent.

The parlor furniture was exactly like theirs, there were once double parlors here at the Grove, furnished identically in Mashula Hines's day, but how differently everything looked here. Grandmother's and Great-Grandmother's cherished things were so carefully kept here, and the Irish lace curtains were still good except for one little new place of Aunt Primrose's that shone out. Once a cyclone had come and drawn one pair of the curtains out the window and hung them in the top of a tall tree in the swamp, and Laura Allen had had

Negroes in the tree all one day instructed to get them down without tearing a thread, while her husband kept begging her to let them come help with the cows bellowing everywhere in the ditches, and then she had mended what could not help but be torn, so that no one could tell now which curtains they were.

There were two portraits of Mary Shannon in this room, on the dark wall the one Audubon painted down in Feliciana, where she visited home, which nobody liked, and over the mantelpiece the one Great-Grandfather did. It showed the Mary Shannon for whom he had cleared away and built the Grove—it had hung in the first little mud house; he had painted it one wintertime, showing her in a dark dress with arms folded and an expression of pure dream in the almost shyly drawn lips. There was a white Christmas rose from the new doorstep in her severely dressed hair. There were circles under her eyes—he had not been reticent there, for that was the year the yellow fever was worst and she had nursed so many of her people, besides her family and neighbors; and two hunters, strangers, had died in her arms. Shelley always thought, for some reason nobody understood, that this was why Great-Grandfather made her fold her arms and hide her hands, but India thought he could not draw hands, because she couldn't, and had not needed to try by giving her a good defiant pose. Dabney thought that Mary folded her arms because she would soon have her first child. Great-Grandfather only painted twice in his life, the romantic picture of his brother, in the library at home, and the realistic one of his wife—the two people he had in the world.

Mary seemed to look down at her and at the dear parlor, with the foolish, breakable little things in it. How sure and how alone she looked, the eyes so tired. What if you lived in a house all alone and away from everybody with no one but your husband?

"Dabney, where were you?" The aunts, with India holding their hands and swinging between them, came in. "Mary Denis Summers Buchanan has come through her ordeal—very well," said Aunt Jim Allen. "Tempe just telephoned from Inverness—didn't you hear us calling you? She wanted us to tell you it was a boy."

"I think Dabney's been eating green apples, but I feel all right," India said. Dabney stood watching them with her arms folded across herself, looking lost in wonder.

"Dabney! Do you feel a little . . . ? Run put back the spread and lie down on my bed." Aunt Primrose pulled her little bottle of smelling salts out of her pocket. "There's too much excitement in the world altogether," she said, with a kind of consoling, gentle fury that came on her sometimes.

"Why, India! I feel perfect!" laughed Dabney, feeling them all looking at her. And all the little parlor things she had a moment ago cherished she suddenly wanted to break. She had once seen Uncle George, without saying a word, clench his fist in the dining room at home—the sweetest man in the Delta. It is because people are mostly layers of violence and tenderness—wrapped like bulbs, she thought soberly; I don't know what makes them onions or hyacinths. She looked up and smiled back at the gay little knowing nods of her aunts. They all sat down on the two facing sofas and had a plate of banana ice cream and some hot fresh cake and felt better.

"Now hurry and start back," said Aunt Primrose. "Oh, you never do come, and when you do you never stay a minute! Oh—growing up, and marrying. India, you're still my little girl!" Aunt Primrose without warning kissed India rambunctiously and pulled her into her sacheted skirt.

Aunt Jim Allen took up her needle-point and the green-threaded needle. "I'm going to give you this stool cover with the calla lily, of *course*, Dabney. I'll have it ready by the time Battle can get Marmion ready, I dare say."

"Dabney will have to have some kind of little old wedding present from us to take home," said Aunt Primrose. "Jump up and pick you out something, honey. You take whatever you like. Don't want to see you hesitate."

"Oh—everything's so soon now," said Dabney, jumping up. "Papa said any kind of wedding I wanted I could have, if I had to get married at all, so I'm going to have shepherdess crooks and horsehair ruffled hats."

"Can anybody put their feet on the stool?" asked India. "Troy?"

"Hush, dear," said Aunt Primrose softly. "We *hope* not."

"I'm going to be coming down the stairs while Mary Lamar

Mackey plays—plays something—but you'll see it all," and Dabney was walking, rather gliding, around on the terribly slick parlor floor among all the little tables full of treasures. Some old friends of hers—two little china dogs—seemed to be going around with her.

"I'm a flower girl," said India, following her. "Cousin Laura McRaven's not one, because Aunt Annie Laurie is dead. Cousin Maureen and Cousin Lady Clare are flower girls. Bluet's wild to be the ring-bearer but she can't be—she's not a boy. That's Ranny."

"I'm going to have my bridesmaids start off in American Beauty and fade on out," said Dabney, turning about. "Two bridesmaids of each color, getting paler and paler, and then Shelley in flesh. She's my maid of honor."

"Of course," sighed Aunt Primrose.

"The Hipless Wonder," said India. "Her sweater belts go lower than anybody in *Virginia's*."

"Why, India."

"Then me in pure white," Dabney said. "Everything's from Memphis, but nothing's come."

"But if it does come, it will all be exquisite, honey," said Aunt Primrose a little dimly.

"Everything's from Memphis but me. I have Mama's veil and Mashula's train—I could hold a little flower from your yard, couldn't I?"

But both aunts looked a little gravely into her swaying glance.

"Who are the bridesmaids, Dabney, dear?" Aunt Jim Allen called out.

"Those fast girls I run with," said Dabney irresistibly. "The ones that dance all night barefooted . . ."

"Child!"

"She was just teasing," India said.

"Won't she take our present?" Aunt Primrose began to fan herself a little with the palmetto fan she had bound in black velvet so that when anyone wanted to pull it apart it couldn't be done.

"I hate to—I hate to take something you love!"

"Fiddlesticks!"

"We've never really *seen* Troy," Aunt Jim Allen said faintly.

She did sound actually frightened of Troy. "Not close *to*—
you know." She indicated the walls of the green-lit parlor with
her little ringed finger.

"You'll *have* to see him at the wedding," India told her
loudly. "He has red hair and cat eyes and a *mus*-tache."

"I'm going to have him trim that off, when we are married," said Dabney gravely.

"It's not as if you were going out of the Delta, of course,"
Aunt Jim Allen said, looking bemused from her little deaf
perch on the sofa. "Now it's time you chose something."

Dabney stopped, and her hand reached out and touched a
round flower bowl on the table in front of her. It was there
between the two china retrievers—was it the little bunny in
one mouth that looked like Aunt Jim Allen, and the little
partridge in the other that was Aunt Primrose? "I'd love a
flower bowl," she said.

"You didn't take the prettiest," warned India.

Both aunts rose to see.

"No, no! No, indeed, you'll not take that trifling little
thing! It's nothing but plain glass!"

"It came from Fairchild's Store!"

"Now you'll take something better than that, missy, something *we'd* want you to have," declared Aunt Primrose. She
marched almost stiffly around the room, frowning at all precious possessions. Then she gave a low croon.

"The night light! She must have the little night light!" She
stood still, pointing.

It was what they had all come to see when they were little
—the bribe.

"Oh, I couldn't." Dabney drew back, holding the flower
bowl in front of her.

"Put that down, child. She must have the night light, Jim
Allen," said Aunt Primrose, raising her small voice a clear octave. "Dabney shall have it. It's company. That's what it is.
That little light, it was company as early as I can remember
—when Papa and Mama died."

"As early as *I* can remember," said Aunt Jim Allen, making
her little joke about being the older sister.

"Dabney, Dabney, they're giving you the night light,"

whispered India, pulling at her sister's hand in a kind of anguish.

"I love it." Dabney ran up and kissed them both and gave them both a big hug to make up for waiting like that.

"And Aunt Mashula loved it—that waited for Uncle George, waited for him to come home from the Civil War till the lightning one early morning stamped her picture on the windowpane. *You*'ve seen it, India, it's *her* ghost you hear when you spend the night, breaking the window and crying up the bayou, and it's not an Indian maid, for what would she be doing, breaking our window to get out? The Indian maid would be crying nearer your place, where the mound is, if *she* cried."

"Jim Allen wants all the ghosts kept straight," said Aunt Primrose, flicking a bit of thread from her sister's dress.

"When did that Uncle George come back?" asked India.

"He never came back," said Aunt Primrose. "Nobody ever heard a single word. His brother Battle was killed and his brother Gordon was killed, and Aunt Shannon's husband Lucian Miles killed and Aunt Maureen's husband Duncan Laws, and yet she hoped. Our father and the children all gave up seeing him again in life. Aunt Mashula never did but she was never the same. She put her dulcimer away, you know. I remember her face. Only this little night light comforted her, she said. We little children would be envious to see her burn it every dark night."

"Who's Aunt Maureen?" asked India desultorily.

"Aunt Mac Lawes, sitting in your house right now," said Aunt Primrose rapidly. It made her nervous for people not to keep their kinfolks and their tragedies straight.

"Oh, it'll be company to you," Aunt Jim Allen said, while India, just to look at the little night light, began jumping up and down, rattling and jingling everything in the room. "There's nobody we'd rather have it, is there, Primrose, having no chick nor child at the Grove to leave it to?"

"I should say there isn't!" called Aunt Primrose to her. "Though George loved it, for a man. Where would that little Robbie put it, in Memphis? What would she *set* it on?" And taking a match from the mantelpiece she walked over to the little clay-colored object they all gazed at, sitting alone on its table, the pretty one with the sword scars on it. It was a tiny porcelain lamp with a cylinder chimney decorated with a fine brush, and an amazing little teapot, perfect spout and all, resting on its top.

"Shall we light it?"

India gave a single clap of the hands.

Aunt Primrose lighted the candle inside and stepped back, and first the clay-colored chimney grew a clear blush pink. The picture on it was a little town. Next, in the translucence, over the little town with trees, towers, people, windowed houses, and a bridge, over the clouds and stars and moon and sun, you saw a redness glow and the little town was all on fire, even to the motion of fire, which came from the candle flame drawing. In two high-pitched trebles the aunts laughed together to see, each accompanying and taunting the other a little with her delight, like the song and laughter of young children.

"Your tea would be nice and warm now if you had tea in the pot," said Aunt Primrose in an airy voice, and gave a dainty sound—almost a smack.

"Oh," said India gravely, "it's precious, isn't it?"

"You'll find it a friendly little thing," said Aunt Jim Allen, "if you're ever by yourself. Look! Only to light it, and you see the Great Fire of London, in the dark. Pretty—pretty—" She put it in Dabney's hand, still lighted, with its small teapot trembling. Aunt Primrose, with a respectful kind of look at Dabney, lifted the pot away and blew out the light.

Dabney held it, smiling. Then the aunts both drew back from the night light, as though Dabney had transformed it.

"Are you going to take it with you when you go on your honeymoon with Troy?" cried India.

"India Primrose Fairchild," said Aunt Primrose, looking at her own sister.

"Little girls don't talk about honeymoons," said Aunt Jim Allen. "They don't ask their sisters questions, it's not a bit nice."

"It's just that she loves the night light too," said Dabney. India took her around the waist and they went out together.

"Uncle George's coming from Memphis today. He's bring-ing champagne!" said Dabney over her shoulder.

"Mercy!" said both aunts. They smiled, looking faintly pink as they came to the door in the late sun. "I declare!" "George—wait till I get hold of him!" "He'll bring all the champagne in Memphis! We'll be tipsy, Primrose! He'll make this little family wedding into a Saturnalian feast! *That* will show people," Aunt Jim Allen said without hearing herself.

"Bless his heart," said Aunt Primrose. "When's he coming to see us? Tell him we expect him to noon dinner day *after* tomorrow. Ellen can have him first."

"You'll be coming up to dinner," said Dabney. "Aunt Tempe and Lady Clare and Uncle Pinck will be there and dying to see you."

"Mercy! Lady Clare!" said Aunt Primrose. "Don't let her do your mother the way she did at Annie Laurie's funeral, stamp her foot and get anything she wants."

"She's grown up more and been taking music," said Dabney, "and I've made her a flower girl."

She kissed them, with both hands around her present. Now that she was so soon to be married, she could see her whole family being impelled to speak to her, to say one last thing before she waved good-bye. She would long to stretch out her arms to them, every one. But they simply never looked deeper than the flat surface of any tremendous thing, that was all there was to it. They didn't try to understand *her* at all, her love, which they were free, welcome to challenge and question. In fact, here these two old aunts were actually *for-giving* it. All the Fairchilds were indulgent—indulgence was what she couldn't stand! The night light! Uncle George they indulged too, but they could never hurt him as they could hurt her—she *was* a little like him, only far beneath, powerless, a girl. He had an incorruptible, and hence unchallenging, sweetness of heart, and all their tender blaming could beat safely upon it, that solid wall of too much love.

"I declare I don't know how you're going to get a wedding present home on horseback—breakable," said Aunt Primrose rather perkily.

"Of course she can, and run out and cut those roses too, Dabney. You've got India to help carry things."

"Dabney can carry her night light home," said India. "I'll tote the little old bunch of flowers."

The others sat in the porch rockers and watched Dabney cut the red and white roses. "That's not enough—cut them all now, or we'll be mad."

"It's not like you were going away, or out of the Delta. Things aren't going to be any different, are they?" called Aunt Jim Allen. "Put those in something, child, and carry 'em to your mother. Tell her not to kill herself."

"Yes'm."

Aunt Primrose lifted one rose out of Dabney's bouquet as she went by. "What rose is that?" she asked her sister loudly.

"Why, I don't recognize it," said Aunt Jim Allen, taking it from her. "Don't recognize it at all."

They're never going to ask Dabney the questions, India meditated. She went up to Aunt Jim Allen and worried her, clasped and unclasped her harvest-moon breastpin, watching the way her sister went just a little prissily down the hall, being sent after a vase.

They don't make me say if I love Troy or if I don't, Dabney was thinking, clicking her heels in the pantry. But by the time she came back to the porch, the flowers in a Mason jar of water, she knew she would never say anything about love after all, if they didn't want her to. Suppose they were afraid to ask her, little old aunts. She thought of how they both drew back to see her holding their night light. They would give her anything, but they wouldn't touch it again now for the world. It was a wedding present.

But, "I hope I have a baby right away," she said loudly, just as she passed in front of them. India saw Dabney's jaw drop the moment it was out, just as her own did, though she herself felt a wonderful delight and terror that made her nearly smile.

"I bet you *do* have, Dabney," said India. She came up behind her and began to pull down on her and rub her and love her.

Aunt Primrose took a little sacheted handkerchief from her bosom and touched it to her lips, and a tear began to run down Aunt Jim Allen's dry, rice-powdered cheek. They looked at nothing, as ladies do in church.

"I've done enough," Dabney thought, frightened, not quite understanding things any longer. "I've done enough to them." They all kissed good-bye again, while the green and gold shadows burned from the river—the sun was going down.

Dabney's cheeks stung for a moment, while they were getting on their horses. The sisters rode away from the little house, and Dabney could not help it if she rode beautifully then and felt beautiful. Does happiness seek out, go to visit, the ones it can humble when it comes at last to show itself? The roses for their mother glimmered faintly on the steps of the aunts' house, left behind, and they couldn't go back.

They rode in silence. It was late, and the aunts might have been going to insist that they stay to supper, if Dabney hadn't said something a little ugly, a little unbecoming for Battle's daughter.

"The thorns of my hat hurt," said India.

She looked over at Dabney riding beside her, but would Dabney hear a word she said any more? Through parted lips her engaged sister breathed the soft blue air of seven o'clock in the evening on the Delta. In one easy hand she held the night light, the most enchanting thing in the world, and in the other hand she lightly held Junie's reins. The river wind stirred her hair. Her clear profile looked penitent and triumphant all in one, as if she were picked out and were riding alone into the world. India made a circle with her fingers, imagining she held the little lamp. She held it very carefully. It seemed filled with the mysterious and flowing air of night.

2

Just at sunset at Shellmound, meanwhile, Roxie and the others heard the sound of stranger-hoofs over the bayou bridge. Then coming over the grass in the yard rode Mr. George Fairchild—in his white clothes and all—on a horse they had never seen before. It was a sorrel filly with flax mane and tail and pretty stockings. "She's lady broke. She's wedding present for Miss Dab." But just then the little filly kicked her heels. "Bitsy always think he knows." "Wouldn't it be a sight did Mr. George pull out and take a little swallow out of his flask made all of gold, sitting where he is—like he do take?" "Miss Ellen! Here come Mr. George!"

"Where's Robbie?" Ellen called, running down the steps, light-footed as always at the sight of George coming. "Little Uncle!" she called to both sides, and Little Uncle came running.

Ranny, barefooted, came flying over the grass, and George put out an arm. Ranny leaped up and was pulled on beside him. He rode up with him sideways, both bare feet extended gracefully together like a captured maiden's. The little red filly almost danced—oh, she was so wet and tired. George was bareheaded now and his Panama hat was on the head of the little filly and she tossed at it.

"I came on Dabney's wedding present—where's Dabney?" he called.

"A horse! Ranny, look at Dabney's horse! Oh, George, you shouldn't.—Ranny, I thought you were in bed asleep."

"She was up at auction—I got on her and rode down." George dismounted and Little Uncle led the horse around the house with Ranny riding. "Little Uncle!" George ran after, and gave some kind of special directions, Ellen supposed, and accepted his hat from Little Uncle who bowed.

"All the way from Memphis? How long did it take you?" Ellen took hold of him and kissed him as if he had confessed a dark indulgence. "Just feel your forehead, you'll have the sunstroke if you don't get right in the house. Roxie!"

"Where's Dabney?" he asked again at the front door, and suddenly smiled at her, as if she might have been whimsical or foolish. She told him but he did not half listen. He was looking at her intently as they went through the hall and into the dining room. Nobody was there. He threw his coat and hat down and fell with a groan on the settee, which trembled under him the way it always did. "Warm day," he said at last, and shut his eyes. Roxie brought him the pitcher of lemonade, and he lifted up to drink a glass politely, but he would not have any cake just then. "I'll stretch a minute," he told Ellen, and at once his eyes shut again. She took his shoes off and he thanked her with a distant groan. She pulled the blinds a little, but he seemed far gone already with that intensity with which all the Fairchilds slept. In the darkened room his hair and all looked dark—turbulent and dark, almost Spanish. Spanish! She looked at him tenderly to have thought of such a far-fetched thing, and went out. The melting ice made a sound, and suddenly George did sigh heavily, as if protesting in his sleep.

"Poor man, he rode so *far*," she thought.

"I'm in trouble, Ellen!" he called after her, his voice wide awake and loud in the half-empty house. "Robbie's left me!"

She ran back to him. He still lay back with his eyes shut. The Spanish look was not exhaustion, it was misery.

"She left me four days and nights ago. I'm hoping she'll come on here—in time for the wedding." He opened his eyes, but looked at her unrevealingly. All the affront of Robbie Reid came in a downpour over Ellen, the affront she had all alone declared to be purely a little summer cloud.

"I never saw anybody get here as wrinkled up in my life." She kissed his cheek, and sat by him wordlessly for a little. "Why, Orrin's meeting the Southbound, just in case you all came that way," she said, still protesting.

"She took the car.—That's how I thought of a horse for Dabney." He grinned.

Bluet, barefooted, with a sore finger, and with her hair put up in rags, came into the dining room to be kissed. "Don't give me a lizard," she decided to beg him.

He asked for his coat and gave her some little thing wrapped up in paper which she took trustingly.

Shelley came in chasing Bluet, and listened stock-still. "She'd better not try to come here!" she cried, when she understood what Robbie had done. Her face was pale. "We wouldn't let her in. To do you like that—you, Uncle George!"

He groaned and sat up, rumpled and yawning.

Battle came in, groaning too, from the heat, and was told the news. He closed his eyes, and shouted for Roxie or anybody to bring him something cold to drink. Roxie came back with the lemonade. Then he fell into his chair, where he wagged the pitcher back and forth to cool it.

Ellen said, "Oh, don't tell Dabney—not yet—spoil her wedding—" She stopped in shame.

"Then don't tell India," said Shelley.

"And we can't let poor Tempe know—she just couldn't cope with this," said Battle in a soft voice. "Hard enough on Tempe to have Dabney marrying the way she is, and after Mary Denis married a Northern man and moved so far off. Can't tell Primrose and Jim Allen and hurt them."

"Of course don't tell any of the girls," George said, staring at Shelley unseeingly, his mouth an impatient line.

"Look, George," Battle said at length. "What's that sister of her's name? Rebel Reid! I bet you anything I've got Robbie's with Rebel."

"I've a very good notion she is," George said.

There were voices in the hall, Vi'let's and somebody's, a vaguely familiar voice.

"Troy's here. What's he doing here?" Ellen looked at Battle. "Oh—he's invited to supper."

"Man! Why don't you go get her, are you paralyzed? Then wring her neck. Did you go—are you going?" Battle turned his eyes from George to Ellen, Shelley, Bluet, and around to Troy—standing foxy-haired and high-shouldered in the door, his slow smile beginning—to invite indignation.

"What else is in your coat, Uncle George?" Ranny asked politely in the silence.

"No, I'm not going," George said. He watched Ranny and Bluet mildly as they went through his coat pulling everything out, and kept watching how Ranny squatted down opening a present with fingers careful enough to unlock some strange mystery in the world.

"Oh, George," Ellen was saying. "Oh, Battle." She looked from one to the other, then went to watch helplessly at the darkening window, where they could hear the horses coming. "Here's Dabney."

As Dabney and India rode in, Uncle George was coming down the front steps to meet them. He always met them like that, and they could tell him from anybody in the world. He called Dabney's name across the yard; his white shirt sleeve waved in the dark. He helped them down with the night light, and Dabney took it from him with a little predatory click of the tongue.

"Everything's fine with you, I hear," said George. "Troy's

in the house," and Dabney brushed against him and kissed him.

India saw Troy—he was a black wedge in the lighted window.

"It's all right," Dabney said, coolly enough, and ran up the steps.

But they heard it—running, she dropped the little night light, and it broke and its pieces scattered. They heard that but no cry at all—only the opening and closing of the screen door as she went inside.

India ran up to Uncle George and flung herself against his knees and beat on his legs. She could not stop crying, though Uncle George himself stayed out there holding her and in a little began teasing her about a little old piece of glass that Dabney would never miss.

III

I<small>T WAS</small> so hard to read at Shellmound. There was so much going on in real life. Laura had tried to read under the bed that morning, but Dabney had found her and pulled her out by the foot. Now with Volume I of *Saint Ronan's Well* inside her pinafore, next to her skin, she went tiptoeing in the direction of the library, where no one ever went at this hour. She could hear nothing, except the sounds of the Negroes, and the slow ceiling fan turning in the hall, and the submissive panting of the dogs just outside under the banana plants, lying up close to the house. Even Mary Lamar Mackey had gone to Greenwood.

Laura generally hesitated just a little in every doorway. Jackson was a big town, with twenty-five thousand people, and Fairchilds was just a store and a gin and a bridge and one big house, yet she was the one who felt like a little country cousin when she arrived, appreciating that she had come to where everything was dressy, splendid, and over her head. Demoniacally she tried to be part of it—she took a breath and whirled, went ahead of herself everywhere, then she would fall down a humiliated little girl whose grief people never seemed to remember. The very breath of preparation in the air, drawing in or letting out, hurried or deep and slow, made Dabney's wedding seem as fateful in the house as her mother's funeral had been, and she knew the serenity of this morning moment was only waiting for laughter or tears.

Even from the door, the library smelled of a tremendous dictionary that had come through high water and fire in Port Gibson and had now been left open on a stand, probably by Shelley. On the long wall, above the piles of bookcases and darker than the dark-stained books, was a painting of Great-Great-Uncle Battle, whose name was written on the flyleaf of the dictionary. It was done from memory by his brother, Great-Grandfather George Fairchild, a tall up-and-down picture on a slab of walnut, showing him on his horse with his saddlebags and pistols, pausing on a dark path between high banks, smiling not down at people but straight out into the room, his light hair gone dark as pressed wildflowers. His little black dogs, that he loved as a little boy, Great-Grandfather had put in too. Did he look as if he would be murdered? Certainly he did, and he was. Side by side with Old Battle's picture was one of the other brother, Denis, done by a real painter, changelessly sparkling and fair, though he had died in Mexico, "marching on a foreign land." Behind the glass in the bookcases hiding the books, and out on the tables, were the miniatures in velvet cases that opened like little square books themselves. Among them were Aunt Ellen's poor mother (who had married some Lord in England, or had died) and the three brothers and the husbands of Aunt Mac and Aunt Shannon, who could not be told apart from one another by the children; but no matter what hide-and-seek went on here, in this room where so many dead young Fair-childs, ruined people, were, there seemed to be always con-sciousness of their gazes, so courteous and meditative they were. Coming in, gratefully bringing out her book, Laura felt it wordlessly; the animation of the living generations in the house had not, even in forgetting identity, rebuked this gen-tleness, because the gentleness was still there in their own faces, part of the way they were made, the nervous, tender, pondering forehead, the offered cheek—the lonely body, broad shoulder, slender hand, the long pressing thigh of Old Battle Fairchild against his horse Florian.

She turned, and there by the mantel was Uncle George. Uncle George, every minute being welcomed and never alone, was alone now—except, that is, for Vi'let, leaning from a step-ladder with one knee on a bookcase, very slowly taking down the velvet curtains. He was rearing tall by the mantel, the gold clock and the children's switches at his head, wearing his white city clothes, but coatless, and his finger moved along the open edge of a blue envelope, which, in his hand then, appeared an object from a star. He gave Laura a serious look as she stood in the middle of the room, unconsciously offering him her open book with both hands. Over his shoulder stared the small oval portrait of Aunt Ellen in Virginia, stating flatly her early beauty, her oval face in the melancholy mood of a very young girl, the full lips almost argumentative.

There was nothing at all abstract in Uncle George's look,

like the abstraction of painted people, of most interrupted real people. There was only penetration in his look, and it reached to her. So serious was it that she backed away, out of the library, into the hall, and backwards out the screen door. Outside, she picked up a striped kitten that was stalking through the grass-blades, and held him to her, pressing against the tumult in her fingers and in his body. The willful little face was like a question close to hers, and the small stems of its breath came up and tickled her nose like flowers. In front of her eyes the cardinals were flying hard at their reflections in the car, drawn up in the yard now (they had got back from Greenwood). A lady cardinal was in the rosebush, singing so hard that she throbbed between her shoulder blades. Laura could see herself in the car door too, holding the kitten whose little foot stretched out. She stood looking at herself reflected there—as if she had gotten along so far like an adventurer in an invisible coat, as magical as it was unsuspected by her. Now she felt visible to everything.

The screen door opened behind her and Uncle George came out on the porch. They were calling him somewhere. She could see him in the red door, his hands were in his pockets and the letter was not showing on him.

"Skeeta! Like Shelley's kitten?" he remarked.

"No," she said, dropping it in the sheer perversity of excitement, because she thought that whatever had happened, he hoped Laura still liked Shelley's kitten. Now it chased the cardinals, which darted and scolded, though the lady cardinal sang on.

"What do you like best of anything in the world?" he asked, lighting his pipe now.

"Riddles," she answered.

"Uncle George!" they cried, but he began asking her, "As I was going to St. Ives." One thing the Fairchilds could all do was to take an old riddle and make it sound like a new one, their own. "One," she said, "you. You were going to St. Ives, all by yourself."

"Out of all those? Only me?" Then Dabney came out and grabbed him, and he looked over her head at Laura pretending he could not believe what he heard, as if he expected anything in the world to happen—a new answer to the riddle, which she, Laura, had not given him.

While they were all still seated around the table drinking their last coffee, Mr. Dunstan Rondo, the Methodist preacher at Fairchilds, paid a noon call. They were all tired, trying to make Aunt Shannon eat.

"Eat, Aunt Shannon, you've had no more than a bird."

"How can I eat, child," Aunt Shannon would say mysteriously, "when there's nothing to eat?"

They did not expect Mr. Rondo, they hardly knew him, but plainly, Ellen saw, he considered his dropping in a nice thing, since he was to marry Dabney and Troy so soon. Aunt Mac and Aunt Shannon vanished. The children started to run.

"Come back here!" Battle shouted. "You stay right here. Mr. Rondo, there's a baby too, somewhere."

"I'm afraid I'm not much of a Sunday School girl," Dabney told Mr. Rondo demurely as he took her hand. "But I'm the bride."

"By all means!" said Mr. Rondo, his voice hearty but uncertain. He sat in Battle's chair. Battle sat down on a little needle-point-covered stool and gave Mr. Rondo a rather argumentative look.

"I suppose you've met at some time or other my brother George, though he never put foot in a church that I know of. Fooling with practicing law in Memphis now—we're hoping he'll give it up and move back. He did plant the Grove over on the river, before he went to war."

Mr. Rondo and George shook hands.

"Why, I believe I married him," said Mr. Rondo.

"Of course! You did—you did. They got you out of bed in the middle of the night—you knew about it before we did!" Battle laughed at Mr. Rondo as at some failing in him.

"Is your wife the former Miss Roberta Reid from Fairchilds City?"

"Yes, sir."

"Yes, sir. That's who she is," Battle answered, also.

"And have they children?" asked Mr. Rondo, of Battle, as if that would be more polite.

Bluet, who never carried less than two things with her, hobbled in burdened under a suitcase and a croquet mallet. She was wearing a pair of Shelley's gun-metal stockings around her neck like a fur. "I'm their little girl," she said.

"They have not," said Battle. "And he loves them—eats mine up. He loves children and they love him. Look at Bluet kiss him." He scowled at Mr. Rondo.

"They get along beautifully, George and Robbie," said Ellen in open anxiety, making her way around the table toward Mr. Rondo. "It's in their faces—I don't know if you pay much attention to that kind of thing, Mr. Rondo?"

"In their faces?" Dabney asked, looking at her mother in astonishment.

"I was thinking of one picnic night, particularly, dear." Ellen's voice suddenly trembled.

"You mean when they put on the Rape of the Sabines down at the Grove?" asked Battle.

"A family picnic." Ellen smiled at the preacher firmly. "You should have come to dinner." She offered her hand, seeming to reproach him for not being invited. But Battle had said when she spoke of inviting him to one meal before the rehearsal supper, "Who wants a preacher to *eat* with them?" Mr. Rondo was so nice and plump, he looked as if he would have enjoyed the turkey too.

"A good deal, yes, a great deal in people's faces," he said.

"Well, entertain Mr. Rondo. Tell him about George on the trestle—I bet he'd like that," said Battle. "You tell it, Shelley."

"Oh, Papa, not me!" Shelley cried.

"Not *you?*"

"Let me," cried India. "I can tell it good—make everybody cry."

"All right, India."

"Very simply, now, India," said Ellen calmly. She sat up straight and held Ranny's hand.

"It was late in the afternoon!" cried India, joining her hands. She came close to Mr. Rondo and stood in front of him. "Just before the thunderstorm!"

Immediately in Shelley's delicate face Ellen could see reflected, as if she felt a physical blow now, the dark, rather brutal colors of the thunderclouded August landscape. "Simply, India."

"Let her alone, Ellen."

"What we'd been doing was fishing all Sunday morning in Drowning Lake. It was everybody but Papa and Mama—they missed it. It was me, Dabney, and Shelley, Orrin and Roy, Little Battle and Ranny and Bluet, Uncle George and Aunt Robbie—Mama, when's she coming? Soon? And Maureen. And Bitsy and Howard and Big Baby and Pinchy before she started seeking, and Sue Ellen's boys and everybody in creation."

"And Troy," said Dabney.

"Troy too. And then we didn't catch nothing. Came home on the railroad track, came through the swamp. Came to the trestle. Everybody wanted to walk it but Aunt Robbie said No. No indeed, she had city heels, and would never go on the trestle. So she sat down plump, but we weren't going to carry her! We started across. Then Shelley couldn't walk it either. She's supposed to be such a tomboy! And she couldn't look down. Everybody knows there isn't any water in Dry Creek in the summertime. Did you know that, Mr. Rondo?"

"I believe that is the case," said Mr. Rondo, when India waited.

"Well, Shelley went down the bank and walked through it. I was singing a song I know. 'I'll measure my love to show you, I'll measure my love to show you—'" *she has the microphone*

"That's enough of the song," said Dabney tensely.

" '—For we have gained the day!' Then Shelley said, 'Look! Look! The Dog!' and she yelled like a banshee and the Yellow Dog was coming creep-creep down the track with a flag on it." *personific*

"A flag!" cried Dabney.

"I looked, if you didn't," said India. "We said, 'Wait, wait! Go back! Stop! Don't run over us!' But *it* didn't care!"

"Mercy!" said Mr. Rondo. Bluet, who had never taken her eyes off him, laughed delightedly and circled round him. George watched her, a faint smile on his face.

"It couldn't stop, India, it wasn't that it didn't care."

Dabney frowned. "Mr. Doolittle was asleep. The engineer, you know." She smiled at Mr. Rondo.

"Who's telling this? Creep, creep. Then it was time for Aunt Robbie to jump up in her high heels and call 'George! Come back!' But he didn't. 'All right, sweethearts, jump,' Uncle George says, and the first one to jump was me. I landed on my feet and seat in an old snaky place. I made a horrible noise when I was going through the air—like this. . . . I looked up and saw Dabney get Ranny in her arms and jump holding him, the craziest thing she ever did, but Ranny said 'Do it again!' Creep, creep. Of course Roy hung by his hands instead of jumping, and Little Battle had to climb back and do it too. Look how ashamed they look! They got cinders in their eyes, both of them. Uncle George threw Bluet off, and Shelley picked her up. I forgot to say all the Negroes had run to the four corners of the earth and we could hear Pinchy yelling like a banshee from way up in a tree. That was before she started coming through."

"Go faster," said Dabney. "Mr. Rondo will get bored."

"Oh, well: Maureen caught her foot. She was dancing up there, and that's what she did—caught her foot good. Uncle George said to hold still a minute and he'd get it loose, but he couldn't get her foot loose at all. So creep, creep."

"It was coming fast!" cried Dabney. "Mr. Rondo, the whistle was blowing like everything, by that time!"

Mr. Rondo nodded, in a pleasant, searching manner.

"The whistle was blowing," said India, "but the Dog was not coming very fast. Aunt Robbie was crying behind us and saying, 'Come back, George!' and Shelley said, 'Jump, jump!' but he just stayed on the trestle with Maureen."

"Path of least resistance." Battle beamed at Mr. Rondo fiercely. "Path George's taken all his life."

"Hurry up, India," said Dabney. "Hurry up, India," said Ranny and Bluet, banging dessert spoons on the back of the preacher's chair.

"Now be still, or I won't let India go any further," Ellen said, her hand on her breast. Then Bluet beat her spoon very softly.

"Oh, well, Maureen said, 'Litt-la train-ain can-na get-la by-y,' and stuck her arms out."

Battle gave a short laugh. "India, you're a sight—you ought to go on the stage."

"Creep, creep." India smiled.

"Hurry up, India."

"Well, Maureen and Uncle George kind of wrestled with each other and both of them fell off, and anyway the Dog stopped in plenty time, and we all went home and Robbie was mad at Uncle George. I expect they had a fight all right. And that's all."

Bluet whimpered.

"Yes, that's all, Bluet," said Ellen. "India, you tell what you know about and then stop, that's the way."

"Now wait. Tell what Robbie said when it was all over, India," said Battle, turning the corners of his mouth down. "Listen, Mr. Rondo."

"Robbie said, 'George Fairchild, you didn't do this for *me*!' "

Battle roared with cross laughter from his stool.

Dabney cried, "You should have heard her!"

Shelley went white.

"Robbie said, 'George Fairchild, you didn't do this for *me*!' " India repeated. "Look, Shelley's upset."

"Shelley can't stand anything, it looks like, with all this Dabney excitement," said Battle. "Now don't let me see you cry."

"Leave me alone," Shelley said.

"She's crying," India said, with finality. "Look, Mr. Rondo: she's the oldest."

"Who is Maureen?" asked Mr. Rondo pleasantly. "Is she this little girl?" He pointed at Laura.

"Oh, no, I wasn't there," Laura said, a little fastidiously.

He was fully told, that Maureen had been dropped on her head as an infant, that her mother, Virgie Lee Fairchild, who had dropped her, ran away into Fairchilds and lived by herself, never came out, and that she wore her black hair hanging and matted to the waist, had not combed it since the day she let the child fall. "*You*'ve seen her!" Their two lives had stopped on that day, and so Maureen had been brought up at Shell-mound.

"Why, she's Denis's child!" they all said.

"She's just as much Fairchild as you are," said Battle. "So
don't ever let me catch you getting stuck up in your life." He
gave Laura a look.

"Is Maureen *my* first cousin?" Laura cried.

"We're kin to Maureen the same as we're kin to each
other," Shelley told her. "On the Fairchild side. Her papa was
Uncle Denis and he was killed in the war, don't you remember?"

"I forgot," said Laura. "When will she comb her hair?"

"We'll let you know when she does." Shelley and Dabney
giggled, looking at each other.

"I guess I'd better be going," said Mr. Rondo. "Midday's
a busy time to call."

"But I know she won't comb it for your wedding,
Dabney," said Battle. And he gave a hearty and rather pro-
longed laugh. "You might think your marrying Troy Flavin
would bring anything about, but it won't make your Aunt
Virgie Lee take the tangles out of her hair!" And he laughed
on, groaning, as if it hurt his side.

And Dabney suddenly left the table. She had to be called
three times, but when she came down she looked rather softened at being teased about her love before everybody. Mr.
Rondo had already taken his departure, promising to be back
to the rehearsal and supper on Friday night; they said they
would show him just what to do.

Ellen stood at the foot of the stairs holding a cup of broth.
George came out of the dining room lighting his pipe and
went to her.

"I know I should worry a little more about Aunt Shannon,"
she began, and he lifted the napkin and looked at the broth.
"Have a taste," she said, sighing.

"She's stubborn too," George said.

"I sent Laura up with this—but she wouldn't even drink it
for her. She sent the poor little thing back."

He nodded. Aunt Shannon never wept over Laura, as if she
could not do it over one motherless child, or give her any
immediate notice. In her the Fairchild oblivion to the member
of the family standing alone was most developed; just as in
years past its opposite, the Fairchild sense of emergency, a

dramatic instinct, was in its ascendancy, and she had torn herself to pieces over Denis's drinking and Denis's getting killed.
Insistently a little messenger or reminder of death, Laura
self-consciously struck her pose again and again, but she was
a child too familiar, too like all her cousins, too much one of
them (as they all were to one another a part of their very own
continuousness at times) ever to get the attention she begged
for. By Aunt Shannon in particular, the members of the family
were always looked on with that general tenderness and love
out of which the single personality does not come bolting and
clamorous, but just as easily emerges gently, like a star when
it is time, into the sky and by simply emerging drifts back into
the general view and belongs to the multitudinous heavens.
All were dear, all were unfathomable, all were constantly
speaking, as the stars would ever twinkle, imploringly or
not—so far, so far away.

"You take her the broth, George. I believe she would drink
it for you."

"Maybe so. Some days she thinks I'm Grandfather—or
Denis," he said without rancor.

She still held on to the bowl, not able to worry enough
about Aunt Shannon. How in his family's eyes George could
lie like a fallen tower as easily as he could be raised to extravagant heights! Now if he was fallen it was because of his ordinary wife, but once it had been because he gave away the
Grove, and before that something else. The slightest pressure
of his actions would modify the wonder, lower or raise it.
Whereas even the daily presence of Maureen and the shadowy
nearness of Virgie Lee had never taken anything away from
the pure, unvarying glory of Denis.

"Tell her to drink it for you," she said, and held out the
bowl to him very carefully. He took it with the touching help-
fulness of her son Ranny.

She watched him carrying it upstairs. Not for the first time,
she wondered whether, if it had never been for Denis, George
might not have been completely the hero to his family—instead of sometimes almost its hero and sometimes almost its
sacrificial beast. But she thought that she could tell (as George
turned on the landing and gave her a look as sweet as a child's
of not wanting her to be anxious) that he was more remark-

able than either, and not owing to Denis's spectacular life or death, but to his being in himself all that Denis no longer was, a human being and a complex man.

Battle came down the hall with a hangdog look, and she met him and comforted him for his impatience.

"If I weren't tied down," he said. "If I weren't tied down! I'd go find little Upstart Reid myself, and kill her. No, I'd set her and Flavin together and feed 'em to each other."

"Mr. Rondo came at the wrong time," Ellen said, kissing him. "It just wasn't a good day for Mr. Rondo."

"Go to sleep, Bluet, go to sleep," said Ellen monotonously to her baby. The house was nearly still; from below came faint noises from the kitchen, and from somewhere one little theme over and over on the piano. Mary Lamar Mackey played all day, the whole of her visit—as if the summer must speak a yearning each day through, yet never enough could she bring it to speak. Nocturnes were her joy.

"Go to sleep, Bluet, and I'll tell you my dream."

"Dream?"

Bluet was a gentle little thing, inquiring more gently than India, filled with attention, quick to show admiration and in-numerable kinds of small pleasures—she was younger. All day she worked, carrying on, like a busy housewife, her loves and hates without knowing her small life was an open window where they all looked in and smiled at her. Now she lay in one of the big white-painted iron sleeping-porch beds with the mosquito net folded back against its head; it was like a big baby buggy that, too, would carry her away somewhere against her will. "Do you hear the dove, Mama?" Outside the summer day shimmered and rustled, and the porch seemed to flow with light and shadow that traveled outwards.

In a low voice Ellen told her dream to put the child to sleep. With one hand she held down her little girl's leg, which wanted to kick like a dancer's. Gradually it gave up.

"Mama dreamed about a thing she lost long time ago be-fore you were born. It was a little red breastpin, and she wanted to find it. Mama put on her beautiful gown and she went to see. She went to the woods by James's Bayou, and on and on. She came to a great big tree."

"Great big tree," breathed the child.

"Hundreds of years old, never chopped down, that great big tree. And under the tree was sure enough that little breast-pin. It was shining in the leaves like fire. She went and knelt down and took her pin back, pinned it to her breast and wore it. Yes, she took her pin back—she pinned it to her breast—to her breast and wore it—away—away . . ."

Bluet's eyelids fell and her dancing leg was still. Her lips suddenly parted, but with a soft sigh and a rapid taking back of the lost breath she was past the moment when she could have protested. She was asleep for the afternoon.

The dream Ellen told Bluet was an actual one, for it would never have occurred to her to tell anything untrue to a child, even an untrue version of a dream. She often told dreams to Bluet at bedtime and nap time, for they were convenient—the only things she knew that were not real. Ellen herself had always rather trusted her dreams. It was her weakness, she knew, and it was right for the children as they grew up to deride her, and so she usually told them to the youngest. However, she dreamed the location of mistakes in the accounts and the payroll that her husband—not a born business man—had let pass, and discovered how Mr. Bascom had cheated them and stolen so much; and she dreamed whether any of the connection needed her in their various places, the Grove, Inverness, or the tenants down the river, and they always did when she got there. She dreamed of things the children and Negroes lost and of where they were, and often when she looked she did find them, or parts of them, in the dreamed-of places. She was too busy when she was awake to know if a thing was lost or not—she had to dream it.

It was the night before that she had the dream she lured Bluet to sleep with. Actually, it had been in the form of a warning; she had left that out, for Bluet's domestic but blood-thirsty little heart would have made her get up and dance on the bed to learn what a warning was. She was *warned* that her garnet brooch, a present in courting days from her husband, that had been lying around the house for years and then disappeared, lay in the leaves under a giant cypress tree on the other side of the bayou. She had certainly forgotten it during the confusion of the morning and of dinnertime, and since, when Dabney burst into tears and ran out crying, "Excuse me for *living*!" Now the feeling of being warned returned, rather pleasantly than not, to Ellen's bosom. She put a little sugared almond on Bluet's pillow, for her fairies' gift, and left the sleeping porch on tiptoe.

Then, while she was rubbing the silver and glass with a whole kitchen and back porch full of Negroes, Sylvanus, old Partheny's son, came to the door.

"Miss Ellen. Partheny send for you. Say please come."

"Has she had a spell?"

"She in one," said Sylvanus. "Say please Miss Ellen come. Not me stay with her, Mr. Troy git me."

"Run on back to the fields, Sylvanus, I'll go."

She took off her apron, after first filling a small pot with some of Aunt Shannon's broth, for she might as well stop at Little Uncle's, she thought, where his wife Sue Ellen was going to have another one and not doing well, and speak in person to Oneida too about helping to dress all the chickens.

She put her head in at the dining-room door. There were just the two old aunts awake and about; Aunt Shannon was downstairs now, calmly sewing a bit of stuff.

"I'm going out a little while," she said.

"The more fool you," said Aunt Mac.

Aunt Mac was three years younger than Aunt Shannon. She had dyed black hair that she pulled down, spreading its thin skein as far as it would go, about her tiny, rosy-lobed ears. Little black ringlets bounced across her forehead as if they alone were her hair and the rest were a cap, an old-fashioned winter toboggan with a small fuzzy ball at the peak, which was her impatient knot. She was little with age. Somewhere, in mastering her dignity over life, she had acquired the exaggerated walk of a small boy, under her long black skirt, and went around Shellmound with her old, wine-colored lip stuck out as if she invited a dare. Her cheekbones, like little gossamer-covered drums, stood out in her face, on which rice powder twinkled when she sat in her place under the brightest lamp. Her sharp, bright features looked out (though she was quite deaf now) as if she were indeed outdoors in her new cap, a bright boy or young soldier, stalking the territory of the wide world, looking for something to catch or maybe let get away, this time. She watched out; but very exactingly she dressed herself in mourning for her husband Duncan Laws, killed in the Battle of Corinth sixty years ago. A watch crusted with diamonds was always pinned to the little hollow of her breast, and she would make the children tell her the time by it, right or wrong. She whistled a tune sometimes, some vaguely militant or Presbyterian air that sounded archaic and perverse in a pantry, where she would sometimes fling open the cupboard doors to see how nearly starving they were. Her smile, when it came—often for India—was soft. She gave a trifling hobble sometimes now when she walked, but it seemed to be a flourish, just to look busy. Her eyes were re-markable, stone-blue now, and with all she had to do, she had read the Bible through nine times before she ever came to Shellmound and started it there. She and her sister Shannon had brought up all James's and Laura Allen's children, when they had been left, from Denis aged twelve to George aged three, after their dreadful trouble; were glad to do it—widows! And though Shannon drifted away sometimes in her mind and would forget where she was, and speak to Lucian as if he had not started out to war to be killed, or to her brother Battle the same way, or to her brother George as if he had been found and were home again, or to dead young Denis she had loved best—she, Mac, had never let go, never asked relenting from the present hour, and if anything should, God prevent it, happen to Ellen now, she was pre-pared to do it again, start in with young Battle's children, and bring them up. She would start by throwing Troy Flavin in the bayou in front of the house and letting the minnows chew him up.

But Aunt Shannon, when she would look around the room and know it, would catch her breath and ask for some-thing—for a palmetto fan, anything; as if life were so piteous that all people had better content themselves with was to be waited on hand and foot; tend or be tended, the wave would fall, and it was better to be tended.

Ellen took one of the big black cotton umbrellas out of the stand and went out. The sun did press down, like a hot white stone. The whole front yard was dazzling; it was covered with all the lace curtains of the house drying on stretchers. Just then here came Roy, riding on his billy goat, in and out, just not touching all the curtains.

"Oh, Roy! I did think you were asleep! Are you being careful?"

"I'll never touch a curtain or make the tiniest hole, Mama. Want to watch me?"

"No, I trust you."

"Can I ride along behind you, Mama, where you're going?"

"Not this time," she said.

She crossed the bayou bridge, almost treading on the butterflies lighting and clinging on the blazing, fetid boards, and walked leisurely down the other side on the old Marmion path (when there had been a river bridge up this far) through the trees. She had been weary today until now. It seemed to her that Dabney's wedding had made everybody feel a little headstrong this week, the children flying out of the house without even pretending to ask permission and herself not being able as well as usual to keep up with any of it.

It was a clamorous family, Ellen knew, and for her, her daughter Dabney and her brother-in-law George were the most clamorous. She knew George was importunate—how much that man hoped for! Much more than Battle. They should all fairly shield their eyes against that hope. Dabney did not really know yet for how much she asked. But where George was importunate, Dabney was almost greedy. Dabney was actually, at moments, almost selfish, and he was not. That is, she thought, frowning, George had not Dabney's kind of unselfishnss which is a dread of selfishness, but the thoughtless, hasty kind which is often cheated of even its flower, like a tender perennial that will disregard the winter earlier every year. . . . The umbrella was in her way now that she had come to the shade, and she could wish she had brought a little Negro along to carry it or the soup.

She noticed how many little paths crisscrossed and disappeared in here, the deeper she went. Who had made them? There had been more woods left standing here than she had remembered. The shade was nice. Moss from the cypresses hung deep overhead now, and by the water vines like pediments and arches reached from one tree to the next. She walked abstractedly, gently moving her extended hand with the closed umbrella in it from side to side, clearing the vines and mosquitoes from her path. There were trumpet vines and passion flowers. The cypress trunks four feet thick in the water's edge stood opened like doors of tents in Biblical engravings. How still the old woods were. Here the bayou banks were cinders; they said it was where the Indians burned their pottery, at the very last. The songs of the cotton pickers were far away, so were the hoofbeats of the horse the overseer rode (and once again, listening for them in spite of the quiet, she felt as if the cotton fields so solid to the sight had opened up and swallowed her daughter). Even inside this narrow but dense wood she found herself listening for sounds of the fields and house, walking along almost anxiously enough to look back over her shoulder—wondering if something needed her at home, if Bluet had waked up, if for some unaccountable reason Dabney had flown back from a party, calling her mother.

Then she heard a step, a starting up in the woods.

"Who's that?" she called sharply. "Come here to me."

There was no answer, but she saw, the way she moved in the woodsy light, it was a girl.

"Whose girl are you? Pinchy?" Pinchy, Roxie's helper, was coming through these days, and wandered around all day staring and moaning until she would see light. But Pinchy would answer Miss Ellen still.

"Are you one of our people? Girl, are you lost then?"

Still there was no answer, but no running away either. Ellen called, "Come here to me; I could tell, you are about the size of one of my daughters. And if you belong somewhere, I'm going to send you back unless they're mean to you, you can't hide with me, but if you don't belong anywhere, then I'll have to think. Now come out. My soup's getting cold here for an old woman."

Then since the girl remained motionless where she had been discovered, Ellen patiently made her way through the pulling vines and the old spider webs toward her. She was dimly aware of the chimney to the overseer's house stuck up through the trees, but in here it seemed an ancient place and for a moment the girl was not a trespasser but someone who lived in the woods, a dark creature not hiding, but waiting to be seen, careless on the pottery bank. Then she saw the corner of a little torn skirt poking out by the tree, almost of itself trembling.

"Come out, child. . . . It's luck I found you—I was just looking for a little pin I lost," she said.

"I haven't seen *no pin*," the girl said behind her tree.

When she heard the voice, Ellen stopped still. She peered. All at once she cried, "Aren't you a Negro?"

The girl still only waited behind a tree, but a quick, alert breath came from her that Ellen heard.

So she was white. A whole mystery of life opened up. Ellen waited by a tree herself, as if she could not go any farther through the woods. Almost bringing terror the thought of Robbie Reid crossed her mind. Then the girl seemed to become the more curious of the two; she looked around the tree. Ellen said calmly, "Come out here in the light."

She came out and showed herself, a beautiful girl, fair and nourished, round-armed. Not long ago she had been laughing or crying. She had been running. Her skin was white to transparency, her hazel eyes looking not downward at the state of her skirt but levelly into the woods around and the bayou.

"Stand still," said Ellen.

It was a thing she said habitually, often on her knees with pins in her mouth. She herself was sternly still, as if she expected presently to begin to speak—and speech at such a time would likely be stern questions that perhaps would find no answers. Yet at her side her arms slowly felt light and except for their burdens her hands would have gone out to the shadowy girl—she caught the motion back, feeling a cool breath as if a rabbit had run over her grave, or as if someone had seen her naked. She felt sometimes like a mother to the world, all that was on her! yet she had never felt a mother to a child this lovely.

The faint wind from the bayou blew in the girl's hair she had shaken out, marking somehow the time going by in the woods. None of her daughters stood this still in front of her, they tore from her side. Or even in the morning when she went to their beds to wake them, they never had a freshness like this, which the soiled cheek, the leafy hair, the wide-awake eyes made almost startling. None of her daughters, even Dabney, had a beauty which seemed to go out from them, as they stood still—every time she had ever said "Stand still," had she hoped for this beauty? In Ellen's mind dimly was that poetic expression *to shed* beauty. Now she comprehended it, as if a key to all the poetry Denis once read had been given to her here in the bayou woods when this girl without pouting or curiosity waited when told.

"Way out here in the woods!" said Ellen. "You'll bring mistakes on yourself that way." She waited a moment. "You're no Fairchilds girl or Inverness girl or Round Bayou or Greenwood girl. You're a stranger to me." The girl did not give her any answer and she said, "I don't believe *you* even know who I am."

"I haven't seen *no pin*," said the girl.

"You're at the end of the world out here! You're purely and simply wandering in the woods. I ought to take a stick to you."

"Nobody can say I stole *no pin*."

Ellen dropped the old black umbrella and took hold of the young girl's hand. It was small, calloused, and warm. "I wasn't speaking about any little possession to you. I suppose I was speaking about good and bad, maybe. I was speaking about men—men, our lives. But you don't know who I am."

The warm, quiet hand was not attempting to withdraw and not holding to hers either. How beautiful the lost girl was.

"I'm not stopping you," Ellen said. "I ought to turn you around and send you back—or make you tell me where you're going or think you're going—but I'm not. Look at me, I'm not stopping you," she said comfortably.

"You couldn't stop me," the girl said, comfortably also, and a half-smile, sweet and incredibly maternal, passed over her face. It made what she said seem teasing and sad, final and familiar, like the advice a mother is bound to give her girls. Ellen let the little hand go.

In the stillness a muscadine fell from a high place into the leaves under their feet, burying itself, and like the falling grape the moment of comfort seemed visible to them and dividing them, and to be then, itself, lost.

They took a step apart.

"I reckon I was the scared one, not you," Ellen said. She gathered herself together. "I reckon you scared me—first coming, now going. In the beginning I did think I was seeing something in the woods—a spirit (my husband declares one haunts his bayou here)—then I thought it was Pinchy, an ignorant little Negro girl on our place. It was when I saw you were—were a stranger—my heart nearly failed me, for some reason."

The girl looked down at the red glass buttons on her dress as if she began to feel a kind of pleasure in causing confusion.

"Which way is the big road, please ma'am?" she asked.

"That way." Ellen pointed explicitly with her umbrella, then drew it back slowly. "Memphis," she said. When her voice trembled, the name seemed to recede from something else into its legendary form, the old Delta synonym for pleasure, trouble, and shame.

The girl made her way off through the trees, and Ellen could hear the fallen branches break softly under her foot. A fleeting resentment that she did not understand flushed her cheeks; she thought, I didn't give her this little soup. But still listening after her, she knew that the girl did not care what she thought or would have given, what Ellen might have cast away with her; that she never looked back.

3

" 'Go in and out the window, go in and out the window . . .' "

They held hands, high and then low, and Shelley, who was It because she was the big girl, ran stooping under their arms, in and out. They were playing in the shade of the pecan trees, after naps and a ride to Greenwood after the groceries, Shelley, India, Bluet, Maureen, Ranny, and Laura. Cousin Lady Clare was just now sent by Aunt Mac out to play with them too. She had come ahead of Aunt Tempe, her grandmother, to Shellmound, come by herself on the Yellow Dog, and now went around with her lower teeth biting her upper lip like William S. Hart. Little Uncle's little boys were up in the yard, crisscrossing with two lawn mowers cutting the grass for the wedding. Far in the back, Howard was beating the rugs with a very slow beat. The sound of the lawn mowers was pleading; they seemed to be saying "Please . . . please." The children were keeping out of mischief so that other people could get something done; Shelley was obeying her mother too, and this lowered her some in the eyes of them all, white and colored.

" '. . . For we have gained the day.' "

Lady Clare said to Laura, "Ask Shelley can Troy French-kiss."

"I'm sure he can," Laura said loftily, for she had been here a day longer than Lady Clare, whatever French-kissing might be.

The song and the game were dreamlike to her. It was nice to have Shelley in the circle, but then it was lovely to have her out. It was funny how sometimes you wanted to be in a circle and then you wanted out of it in a rush. Sometimes the circle was for you, sometimes against you, if you were It. Sometimes in the circle you longed for the lone outsider to come in—sometimes you couldn't wait to close her out. It was never a good circle unless you were in it, catching hands, and knowing the song. A circle was ugly without you. She knew how ugly it was from the face Maureen would make to see it, and to change this she would let her in. Even if she did not, Maureen would get in. Maureen was a circle breaker. She was very strong. Once she had hold of you, she was so gentle and good at first, she would surprise you. She looked around with a soft, pink look on her face—in a minute it was a daring look, and the next minute she would try to break your finger bones. She liked to change a circle into "Crack the Whip," and with a jerk of her arm she could throw ten cousins to the ground and make them roll over.

They played "Running Water, Still Pond," "Fox in the Morning, Geese in the Evening," and then "Hide-and-Seek." Once Lady Clare was It, because she was carrying a little Chinese paper fan that folded back on tiny sticks, then Shelley was It again. Laura ran to her best hiding place, down on the ground behind the woodpile in the back yard. She waited a long time crouched over and nobody came to find her. From where she hid she could see the back of the house, hear the Negroes, and upstairs on the long sleeping porch she could see Uncle George walking up and down, up and down, smoking his pipe. She listened to the dark, dense rustling of the fig trees, and once she put a straw down a doodlebug hole and said the incantation in a very low voice.

Then she saw Maureen running by, and Maureen saw her. With a leap Maureen was up on her woodpile. She did not say a word. She looked over from the top, and then after a strange pause, as if she could think, she pushed the whole of the piled logs down on Laura, upsetting herself too. "Choo choo," said Maureen, and then she ran away.

Laura at first was surprised, and then with great effort she began to extricate herself. The surprise, the heavy weight, and the uncertainty of getting out kept her so busy that at first she did not miss them coming to look for her. She had on her next-best white dress, and long tears showed in it, and long scratches marked up her legs and arms. She had the taste of bark in her mouth and kept spitting on the ground, though the taste was still there. Inside the house the light, tinkling sounds went on; Roxie's high laugh, like a dove cry, rose softly and hung over the yard. And from farther away the sigh of the compress reminded her of Dabney, who had gone somewhere.

Harm—that was what Maureen intended, that was what she meant by her speechless gaze. That was what made her stay so close to them all, what drove her flying over the house, over the fields that way, after the others. That was what put extra sounds in her mouth. It was the harm inside her.

"She likes to spoil things," India had explained matter-of-factly, and matter-of-factly Laura had accepted it. But the cousins were a clan. They all said things, and they all kissed one another, and yet they all had secret, despiting ways to happiness. At hide-and-seek a trick could be played on Laura, for she was still outside. She herself would never mean from the start to push down and overwhelm, or withhold any secret intention or hope in relish and delight.

Pushing the heavy logs from her, she felt shorn of pleasure in her cousins and angry in not having known that this was how the Fairchilds wanted things to be, and how they would make things be, when it pleased them. Uncle George was nowhere to be seen, and she thought she heard Shelley laughing and calling his name down in the house. A feeling of their unawareness of her came over Laura and crushed her more heavily than the harm of Maureen and the logs of wood, and she thought surely her mother would cry in Heaven to see her now, if she had not cried so far.

She licked the blood away clean from her arms, and looked at her knees to see if some old scabs had come off—yes. She was as black and ugly as a little Negro. She tied her sash tight around her hips. Without looking up she crept around the yard, with her locket in her mouth, around the cistern on her hands and knees, keeping low not to be seen, her feet dragging numbly. Under the snowball bush she hit both feet with her fists until she could feel the sting, and then, picking all the cinders one by one out of her elbows and skirt and out of her Roman sandals, she walked around the house and darted in to Home, which was the trunk of a tree, without being caught.

At that moment, touching Home, her finger to the tree, she was not happy, not unhappy. "Free!" she called, looking around, not seeing the others anywhere, but she had them every one separate in her head.

Then she saw Uncle George walk out of the house and stare out into the late day. She wanted to call out to him, but something would not let her. Something told her, ever since the look he gave her, that it was right for him to stand apart, and that when he opened an envelope in a room no one should enter. Now she felt matter-of-factly intimate with it, with his stand and his predicament. She thought of herself as growing up beside Uncle George, the way some little flowers and vines have picked their tree, and so she felt herself sure of being near him. She knew quite objectively that *he* would not disown her and uproot her, that he loved any little green vine leaf, and now she felt inner warnings that this was a miracle of safety, strange in any house, and in her this miracle was guarded from the contamination even of thinking.

As if by smell, by the smell of his pipe, she knew that he out of all the Delta Fairchilds had kindness and that it was more than an acting in kindness, it was a waiting, a withholding, as if he could see a fire or a light, when he saw a human being—regardless of who it was, kin or not, even Aunt Ellen, to whom he called and waved now—and had never done the first thing in his life to dim it. This made him seem young—as young as she. On the other hand, when all night she could hear coming up the dark stair well his voice soft and loud with Uncle Battle's bark after it, chasing, she gathered that he was hard to please in some things and therefore old. Uncle George and Uncle Battle would argue or talk until Uncle Battle hollered out the window for Roxie or Ernest to come up to the house and fix them their nightcaps.

She stored love for Uncle George fiercely in her heart, she wished Shellmound would burn down and she could run in and rescue him, she prayed for God to bless him—for she felt they all crowded him so, the cousins, rushed in on him so, they smiled at him too much, inviting too much, daring him not to be faultless, and she would have liked to clear them away, give him room, and then—what? She would let him be mean and horrible—horrible to the horrible world.

Would she? She leaned her forehead against the tree, with some shimmering design about him in her head coming like a dream, in which she was clinging, protecting, fighting all in one, a Fairchild flourishing and flailing her arms about. Of course it was all one thing—it was one feeling. It was need. Need pulled you out of bed in the morning, showed you the day with everything crowded into it, then sang you to sleep at night as your mother did, need sent you dreams. Need did all this—when would it explain? Oh, some day. She waited now, and then each night fell asleep in the vise of India's arms. She imagined that one day—maybe the next, in the Fairchild house—she would know the answer to the heart's pull, just as it would come to her in school why the apple was pulled down on Newton's head, and that it was the way for girls in the world that they should be put off, put off, put off—and told a little later; but told, surely.

Uncle George came down the steps and walked slowly over the fresh-cut grass, not seeing her for she was behind the big pecan tree. All his secret or his problem, or what was in the blue letter, though she did not know what it was, was sharp to her to see him go by, weighty and real and as cutting (and perhaps as filled with dreaded life) as a seashell she had once come on, on the seashore, and unwittingly seized.

"Don't cry out here, Laura," said a soft voice.

It was Little Battle, in his overalls. He poked a cold biscuit with a little ham in it into her mouth, and because she was startled stood by while she swallowed it. Then they ran into the house. "Oh, Little Battle!"

4

Laura wanted so badly to be taken to their hearts (never wondering if she had not been, at any time before her own wish) that she almost knew what the Fairchilds were like, what to expect; but her wish was steadier than her vision and that itself kept her from knowing. Ellen saw it.

While she held supper for Dabney, late now at some brides-maid's party, Ellen had walked out in the yard to feel the cool. It was first-dark, and the thrushes were singing tirelessly from the trees. She had walked through the yard where the children were playing and Vi'let was gathering in the curtains, past the flower beds, down toward the bayou. The evening was hot; it was the fragrance of the lemon lilies that was cool, like the breath from a mountain well. From the house came a momentary discord on the piano keys. That was Shelley passing through the music room, putting her hands down over Mary Lamar Mackey's. Then the slow, dwelling melody went on.

Ellen looked down the road for Dabney. Stretching away, the cotton fields, slowly emptying, were becoming the color of the sky, a deepening blue so intense that it was like darkness itself. There was a feeling in the infinity of the Delta that even the bounded things, waiting, for instance, could go on for-ever. Over and over from the bayou woods came the one high note, then the three low notes of the dove.

At her feet the bayou ran, low, long since cleared of trees here, and all but motionless. She thought it was like a mirror that was time-darkened, no longer reflecting very much, but an entity in itself. She remembered old, disparaging Partheny when she got to her, going so ill-advised on foot. In Partheny's house in Brunswick-town she had bent over the cot where the old woman lay out straight with her long toes pointing up and her eyes looking at the ceiling. "Partheny, do you hear

me? Are you in a spell, Partheny?" Partheny was her nurse
when her oldest children were little.

"Oh, I done had it," Partheny had said. "It over by this
time. I were mindless, Miss Ellen. I were out of my house. I
were looking in de river. I were standing on Yazoo bridge wid
dis foot lifted. I were mindless, didn't know my name or name
of my sons. Hand stop me. Mr. Troy Flavin he were by my
side, gallopin' on de bridge. He laugh at me good—old
Partheny! Don't you jump in dat river, make good white folks
fish you out! No, sir, no, sir, I ain't goin' to do dat! Guides
me home. You can go on back now, go on back, Miss Ellen,
to your little girl puttin' on her weddin' veil. But don't set
your heels down! Go real still."

She heard someone coming from the house, and saw from
the glimmer of white clothes and the tall strolling walk of
"company" that it was George—he waved briefly. He looked
thin. Poor boy, he had not even eaten any to speak of, of the
good coconut cake she tried to tempt him with. The noise of
the children made him bite his lip, and he did not like Mary
Lamar Mackey, this time.

She had not even taken her apron off; she clasped her hands
before her. But he untied the apron when he came and threw
it over the branches of a little dogwood tree. "Forget everything out here," he said, and stood looking out.

"I saw a runaway girl in the bayou woods, George," she
said, "a white girl. Going just as fast to Memphis as she could
go. Purely loitering. I saw her peeping out from behind a tree,
the prettiest thing ever made. I very ill-advisedly went to
Brunswick-town on foot, by the short cut. There she was."
She had never thought of mentioning the girl or seeing her.
(Battle would say: "Ellen Fairchild, do you mean to tell me
you've been out alone, a lone woman on foot, in these fields
and woods? No gun either, I bet you all I've got.") But she
was tired, and sometimes now the whole world seemed rampant, running away from her, and she would always be carrying another child to bring into it.

Now she saw by the dense evening light—for she always
knew it when she saw it—a look on George's face that both
endeared him to her and reminded her of all her anxiety for
his comfort in life; the first source of the feeling, long ago,

might have been that look—she did not know. It was only a tender change of countenance, a smile—but it looked like the vanishing of suspense. There was gratification and regret in it, at something you said. It was as if he had known life could not go on without this thing—now, like a crash, a fall, it had come. So you, having begun, without knowing it, some unfinished story to him, would then tell everything, perhaps. She never altogether understood George's abrupt, tender smile —yet without thinking she would often find herself telling the very thing that brought it to his face. It could not be amusement—for she had nothing funny about her, not a bone in her body. For instance, now—surely he could not be simply enjoying the idea of herself brought up against a wild runaway girl? For her heart still felt the strain. And certainly she knew he would not laugh at a girl that wanted to run away.

"Not far from here at all," she said. "She was asking the way to the public road."

He said at once, "Yes, I met her, as I was coming in."

Then she was speechless. It was a thing she had never learned in her life, to expect that what has come to you, come in dignity to yourself in loneliness, will yet be shared, the secret never intact. She gazed into the evening star, her lips unreasonably pressed together.

"And did she ask the way to the Memphis road?" she asked then.

"Yes, and I took her over to the old Argyle gin and slept with her, Ellen," said George.

She seemed to let go in her whole body, and stood languidly still under her star a moment, then pulled her apron where it still shone white in the dogwood tree and tried to tie it back on.

George made an impatient sound. Sometimes he, the kindest of them all, would say a deliberate wounding thing—as if in assurance that nothing further might then hurt you. It was always some fact—all true—about himself, just a part of the fact, which was the same as a wild, free kind of self-assertion—it was his pride, too, speaking out. Then impatiently, as if you were too close to a fire, he pulled you away from your pain.

"She's older than you thought," he said. His voice distressed her by sounding grateful to her—was it simply because she had neither flinched nor disbelieved him or said, "It amounts to nothing," like a Fairchild quick to comfort?

She glanced toward George, though she could no longer see him. A feeling of uncontrollable melancholy came over her to see him in this half-light, which had so rested her before he came out. Dear George, whose every act could verge so closely on throwing himself away—what on earth would ever be worth that intensity with which he held it, the hurting intensity that was reflected back on him, from all passing things?

"Oh, George!" she cried, and then, "Sometimes I'm so afraid when Dabney marries she won't be happy in her life."

He patted her arm, yet not heavily or trying to turn her around. "Well, let's go in," she said. Yet she lingered, a little breeze seemed to stir over the bayou, and she was refreshed. George was the one person she knew in the world who did not have it in him to make of any act a facile thing or to make a travesty out of human beings—even, in spite of temptation at a time like this moment, of himself as one human being. (How the Fairchilds did talk on about their amazing short-comings, with an irony that she could not follow at all, and never rested in perfecting caricatures, little soulless images of themselves and each other that could not be surprised or hurt or changed! That way Battle, when they were first married, had told her something like this.) Only George left the world she knew as pure—in spite of his fierce energies, even here-sies—as he found it; still real, still bad, still fleeting and mysterious and hopelessly alluring to her.

She had feared for the whole family, somehow, at a time like this (being their mother, and the atmosphere heavy with the wedding and festivities hanging over their heads) when this girl, that was at first so ambiguous, and so lovely even to her all dull and tired—when she touched at their life, ran through their woods. She had not had a chance to face this fear before, for at the time she had had to cope with the runaway girl herself, who was only the age of her daughter Dabney, so she had believed. But at last she was standing quietly in the long twilight with George, bitterly glad (now it was certain: he was not happy) that he had been the one who had caught the girl, as if she had been thrown at them; for now was it not over?

Aware of his touch on her tired arm—for he was seldom, in the way the others were, demonstrative—she felt that he was, in reality, not intimate with this houseful at all, and that they did not know it—for a moment she thought she saw how it was.

All around them the lightning bugs had flashed to life. They flew slowly and near the earth—just beyond the reach now of India's hand.

"Ellen!" Battle called out, first from the window, then from the door. "Oh, Ellen, here's Troy! He's come up to supper! Ellen!"

"It's time to go in," Ellen said. "Dabney will be coming home and looking everywhere for her mother."

She knew she had provoked that smile again, in the blurred profile she looked into as they started up the garden. But she went in step with him through the dark wet grass, and breathed and sighed expectantly in the dark, as if before they reached the light and confusion of the house she could tell something promising and gentle to him.

"Look," George said.

Ranny was at their feet in the grass asleep—worn out—lying astride a stalk of sugar cane. George took him up without waking him, and carried him.

"He's gained!"

"He weighs thirty-six pounds."

Presently Ranny stirred, said something, and George set him down. Balancing and complaining like an old drunken man for a moment, he went forward on his own feet.

"What did he say?" Ellen asked.

"He said, 'Don't hold me.'"

Ranny, who always until now wanted dearly to be held, walked straight forward, and they sighed in amusement, drawing together, to see the little figure going in front of them, then beginning lightly, blindly, to trot, riding the horse of his mind in the big Delta night.

5

After Shelley had stayed her time in the room with Troy,
waiting for her sister, she excused herself to dress for the
Clarksdale dance. But up in her room, in her teddies, she sat
down on her cedar chest and unlocked her Trip Abroad diary,
lit a Fatima cigarette, and began to write. She had turned the
floor fan on her back and seat, and behind her as she wrote
the two ends of her little satin sash were dancing straight out.

Laura with her nightgown on stood in the door watching
her.

In Shelley's room, the best front one, there were medallions
on the wallpaper, each a gold frame with a face inside—which
Laura had thought were grandfathers and grandmothers,
probably from Port Gibson, until Shelley had told her they
weren't anybody—which was much more mysterious. The
wastebasket Shelley had woven in Crafts her summer at Camp.
Her bureau was decorated with a tray and powder-box and
jar set from her Dabney grandmother. The jars she had filled
with rose leaves and clove pinks the summer before, and now
and then, but not often, she still took the stoppers out and
smelled their last year's perfume. The mirror, on the side arm
of which her curling irons hung like a telephone, was stuck
all around with snapshots taken mostly on a trip with Mary
Denis Summers and some Yankees to the West, at which she
had had the worst time she ever had away from home; she
could not tell you why she kept their pictures, snooty faces
against dim yawning streaks of the Grand Canyon, daily in
view. Her silver comb and brush set had EVD on them—Aunt
Ellen's—the initials intertwined with raised lilies of the valley,
and the bristles worn curved as a thin shell now; luckily nobody brushed their hair any more. Her jewelry was inside a
little box Aunt Shannon, before she was so mixed up, had
given her; it was a present from her Great-Uncle Denis who
had sent it to her the year she was born, from off in the
Mexican War; it had a key with forked-tongued snakes on it.
Inside were a pair of her mother's gold bracelets with chains,
a silver butterfly ring from the Western trip, her Camp ring,
one of Uncle George's cuff links she had found when little
and had kept, her Great-Grandmother Mary Shannon's black

cameos, earrings, and pin, and her seed-pearl comb, and two or three diamond rings. Shelley would not be caught dead wearing any of them. She liked a garnet brooch of her mother's to pin her middy blouse together, but now she could not find it; Shelley said Dabney had probably borrowed it, it was Dabney who lost everything, or maybe India, who could dress herself up like a savage this summer, scavenging from room to room.

In the cedar chest underneath her now lay all the under-clothes she had received for graduation presents from high school and college in Virginia, some in little silk sacheted purses made to keep them in until she got married. There was one gown—Aunt Primrose had made it, of all people, Shelley said—of peach chiffon with a little peach chiffon coat that had a train, every edge picoted, and then embroidered all around with lover's knots: it was transparent. Shelley's mantel was wood and white marble, and the hearth was round and raised in a fat apron. The fireplace was now hidden by a per-fectly square silk screen painted by Aunt Tempe, with a bayou floating with wild ducks at sunset; a line of the ducks was rising at a right angle from the water and went straight to the upper corner like an arrow. On her mantel shelf was a gold china slipper, a souvenir of Mary Denis Summers's wedding, holding matches, and that was all, except for an incense burner and a photograph of Shelley in a Spanish comb and a great deal of piled hair, taken the year she graduated from Fairchilds High School. Shelley hated it. On the washstand was Shelley's glass with three stolen late-blooming Cape jes-samines from Miss Parnell Dortch's yard, now turned bright gold, still sweet. The bed was Aunt Ellen's from Virginia, a high square cool one with a mosquito net over it and a trundle bed underneath it. As a baby Shelley had slept on that, near her mother, and she despised having it still under her bed. There was no way on earth Shelley could get a lamp brought in to read by in bed. A long brass pole dangled from the center of the ceiling ending in two brass lilies from each of which a long, naked, but weak light bulb stuck out. "Plenty light to dress by, and you can read in the lower part of the house with your clothes on like other people," Uncle Battle said, favoring Dabney as he did and she never read, not having time. A paper kewpie doll batted about on a thread tied to the chandelier, that was all it was good for. Shelley wanted to read *The Beautiful and Damned* which was going around the Delta and to read it in bed, but she was about to give up hope. It was hard for her to even see how to write. In her closet were mostly evening dresses but enough middy blouses and pleated skirts hung at one end. All her shoes were flung in a heap on the floor, as if in despair. One green King Tut sandal was out in the middle of the room. Her peach ostrich mules were on her feet and as she wrote she from time to time lifted up her bare heels and waited a moment, tensely, before going on, like a mockingbird stretching in the grass. Momently, she put her Fatima cigarette ashes in her hair receiver.

"Go away, Laura!" said Shelley. "You aren't supposed to watch us every minute!"

Laura ran off, having the grace not to stick out her tongue as India would do.

Shelley was to go to Europe after the wedding, with Aunt Tempe—it was Aunt Tempe's graduation present; but she could not bring herself to wait that long before beginning to write in the book with the lock and key. The first entry was three weeks ago—"We all went fishing with Papa in Moon Lake, caught 103 fish, home in time, Indianola dance. Pee Wee Prentiss. Stomach ache. Dabney's favorite word is 'perfect.'" But already, so soon, she was writing long entries. Dressing a moment (they were calling her downstairs) and writing a moment, jumping up and down, she succeeded in getting the tulle dress, still hot from the iron, over her head and in filling in almost six pages of the diary. Her chest rose and fell in the little "starlight blue" dress, flat as a bathing suit against her heart.

Tonight again D. was cruel to T.F. and is keeping him waiting and then going out to one last dance. T. does not go home—waits for just a glimpse. He is interested because he thinks she must be smart. To provoke a man like him. Dabney does not even know it. Why doesn't it dawn on T.F. that none of the Fairchilds are smart, the way he means smart? Only now and then one of us is gifted, Aunt J.A. says—I am gifted at tennis—for no reason. We never wanted to be smart, one by one, but all together we have a wall, we are self-sufficient against people that come up knocking, we are solid to the outside. Does the world suspect? that we are all very private people? I think one by one we're all more lonely than private and more lonely than self-sufficient. I think Uncle G. takes us one by one. That is love—I think. He takes us one by one but Papa takes us all together and loves us by the bunch, which makes him a more cheerful man. Maybe we come too fast for Papa. One by one, we get it from Mashula and Laura Allen and Great-Grandfather all, we can be got at, hurt, killed—loved the same way—as things get to us. All the more us poor people to be cherished. I feel we should all be cherished but not all together in a bunch—separately, but not one to go unloved for the other loved. In the world, I mean. Shellmound and the world. Mamma says shame, that we forget about Laura, and we loved her mother so much we never mention her name or we would all cry. We are all unfair people. We are such sweet people to be so spoiled. George spoils us, does not reproach us, praises us, even, for what he feels is weak in us.

Maybe I can tell him yet, that I know where Robbie is, but so far I can't. The moment of telling, I cannot bring myself to that. I thought it would be easy at the supper table, but in the middle of supper now we all look at each other, all wondering—before a thing like Dabney's wedding, not knowing just what to do. Sometimes I believe we live most privately just when things are most crowded, like in the Delta, like for a wedding. I don't know what to do about anybody in the world, because it seems like you ought to do it soon, or it will be too late. I may not put any more in my diary at all till after the wedding. I wish now it would happen, and be past, I hate days, fateful days. I heard Papa talking about me to Uncle G. without knowing I was running by the library door not to meet T. when he came in (but waiting, I did) and Papa said I was the next one to worry about, I was prissy—priggish. Uncle G. said nobody could be born that way, they had to get humiliated. Can you be humiliated without knowing it? I would know it. He said I was not priggish, I only liked to resist. So does Dabney like it—I know. So does anybody but India, and young children.

When T. proposed to D. I think it was just because she was already so spoiled, he had to do something final to make her notice, and this did. That is not the way I want it done to me. Nobody tells T. a thing yet, and maybe we will never tell him anything. But I think he never minds at all. I think T. likes to size things up. I would never love him. I think he could tell tonight that Uncle G. has something on his mind, those sweet worry-lines across his brow and eyes—drinking all Papa's Bounce—because T. is the one who is always thinking of ways in or ways out, and I think he gets the smell of someone studying, as if it were one of the animals in trouble. Trouble acts up—he puts it down. But I know, trouble is not something fresh you never saw before that is coming just the one time, but is old, and your great-aunts not old enough to die yet can remember little hurts for sixty years just like the big hurts you know now, having your sister walk into something you dread and you cannot speak to her.

T. just sits and looks at a family that cherishes its weaknesses and belittles its strength. He is from the mountains—very slow. Where is his mother? Father? He is not a born gambler of any description. He considers D. not anything he is taking a chance on but a sure thing and wants her for sure. Robbie is another person like that and wants George for sure. I can't stand her! Maybe Europe will change everything. When I see the Leaning Tower of Pisa will I like Robbie any better? I doubt it. (Aunt T. will be with me all the time!) All of us wish G. did not want her and tell him and tell him, she is not worthy to wipe his feet. But he does want her, and suffers. He goes on. I do not know and cannot think how it was when Papa and Mama wanted each other. Of course they don't now, and don't suffer by now. I cannot think of any way of loving that would not fight the world, just speak to the world. Papa and Mama do not fight the world. They have let it in. Did they ever even lock a door. So much life and confusion has got in that there is nothing to stop it running over, like the magic pudding pot. The whole Delta is in and out of this house. Life may be stronger than Papa is. He let Troy in, and look, Troy took Dabney. Life is stronger than George, but George was not surprised, only he wants Robbie Reid. Life surprises Papa and it is Papa that surprise hurts. I think G. expects things to amount to more than you bargain for—and so do I. This scares me in the middle of a dance. Uncle G. scares me a little for knowing my fright. Papa is ashamed of it but G. does not reproach me—I think he upholds it. He expects things to be more than you think, and to mean something—something— He cherishes our weaknesses because they are just other ways that things are going to come to us. I think when you are strong you can squeeze them back and hold them from you a little while but where you are weak you run to meet them.

Shelley with a sigh leaned out of her window to rest. A whippoorwill was calling down in the bayou somewhere, and the hiss of the compress came softly and regularly as the sighing breath of night. She heard voices on the lawn. Dabney in a filmy dress was telling Troy good night. Shelley listened; how well she could hear and see from here she had not before realized or tried out.

Shelley's yellow Dog version

"Oh, I wish I didn't have to go to the old dance—or that you could dance, Troy!" cried Dabney. She clung to him, her voice troubled and tender. "Never mind, we'll soon be married."

"Sure," said Troy.

She clung to him more, as if she would be torn away, and looked over her shoulder at the night as if it almost startled her—indeed the soft air seemed to Shelley to be trembling with the fluctuation of starlight as with the pulsing of the compress on the river. Troy patted Dabney's shoulder.

"I hear your heart," she said right out, as if imploringly and yet to comfort him.

"I'll see you tomorrow," he said.

"Take care of yourself," she said.

"I will."

"It won't be long until I can take care of you."

There were tears in Shelley's eyes; their tenderness was almost pity as they clung together. She nearly cried with them.

"I have to go now, Troy, I have to."

She stood away. He stood with his arms hanging, and she went. Dickie Boy Featherstone put her in his open-top car.

Then Shelley heard Uncle George walk heavily over the porch and down the steps. She saw him strolling toward the gate, and smelled his pipe. "George!" He looked up and said how hot the night was. He went on. She could not say anything, she could not call it out a window. (It would seem so conceited of her, too.) She believed he went and stood on the bank of the bayou to smoke; she could see a patch of white through the Spanish daggers, though the mist drifted there now turning like foam in the luminous night. She leaned her forehead on the wall, the warm wallpaper pressed her head like a hand. . . .

The scene on the trestle was so familiar as to be almost indelible in Shelley's head, for her memory arrested the action and let her see it again and again, like a painting in a schoolroom, with colors vivid and thunderclouded, George and Maureen above locked together, and the others below with the shadow of the trestle on them. The engine with two wings of smoke above it, soft as a big bird, was upon them, coming as it would. George was no longer working at Maureen's caught foot. Their faces fixed, and in the instant alike, Maureen and Uncle George seemed to wait for the blow. Maureen's arms had spread across the path of the engine.

Shelley knew what had happened next, but the greatest pressure of uneasiness let her go after the one moment, as if the rest were a feat, a trick that would not work twice. The engine came to a stop. The tumbling denouement was what made them all laugh at the table. The apology of the engineer, old sleepy-head Mr. Doolittle that traded at the store! Shelley beat her head a time or two on the wall. And Maureen with no warning pushed with both her strong hands on George's chest, and he went over backwards to fall from the trestle, fall down in the vines to little Ranny's and old Sylvanus' wild cries. George did not even yet let her go, his hand reached for her pummeling hand and what he could not accomplish by loosening her foot or by pulling her up free, he accomplished by falling himself. Wrenched bodily, her heavy foot lifted and Maureen fell with him. And all the time the Dog had stopped, and Mr. Doolittle was looking from his little cab saying he was sorry, Mr. Fairchild! But George sat on the ground simply looking at Maureen. She had leaped up with alacrity, a taunting abandon, which seemed to hypnotize him. She leaped up and down on first one foot and then the other, strumming her lip.

There were things in that afternoon which gave Shelley an uneasiness she seemed to feel all alone, so that she hoarded the story even more closely to herself, would not tell it, and from night to night hesitated to put it down in her diary (though she looked forward to it all day). To begin with, there was the oblivious, tomboyish way she had led them all in walking too fast for Robbie in her high heels—a tomboy was only what she used to be, and wasn't now; all day Sunday, fishing and all, she had done it. Of course Robbie would wear the wrong heels, and it was right that she should be shown she dressed the wrong way, and should have to keep taking little runs to catch up, and finally be left as haughty as possible at the approach of a trestle. But then came Shelley's own shame in not being able to walk the trestle herself. No one would ever forget that about her, all their lives! She thought herself that it must have been premonition—with Uncle George along something was bound to happen, it was his recklessness that told her to hold back. Then there was the terror with which the engine filled her—that poky, familiar thing, it was sure to stop—of course she had no born terror of the Yellow Dog. Maureen's assumption that she could stop it by holding both her arms out across its path was more logical than you thought at first. But Shelley's deepest uneasiness came from Robbie's first words, "You didn't do this for *me*!" In her fury Robbie rose straight up as untouchable, foolish heels and all, away out of their hands all at once. . . . And how George had looked at her! ("Certainly he thinks nothing of danger, none of us ever has," her father had told Robbie later, when at the supper table she came to tears.) But Shelley felt that George and Robbie had hurt each other in a way so deep, so unyielding, that she was unequal to understanding it yet. She hoped to grasp it all, the worst, but fiercely feeling herself a young, unmarried, unengaged girl, she held the more triumphantly to her secret guess—that this confrontation on the trestle was itself the reason for Robbie's leaving George and for his not going after her. The guess made even his presence at Dabney's wedding take on the cast of assertion: here he was not looking for his wife. . . . But Dabney felt nothing of this, she felt no more about that black moment since she saw it was not fatal—when the engine stopped a hair's breadth from George and Maureen, she put up her elbows and did a little dance step with herself. After the train passed, Dabney and Troy had simply gone on up the railroad track and got engaged.

Was it possible that it was because of something strong *George* had felt, that the way a stroke of lightning can blaze a tree she could not forget that happening? Extravagantly responsible just as he was extravagantly reckless, what had he been prepared for—how many times before had something come very near to them and stopped?

Dabney if she knew would tell George in a minute, that Robbie was no farther away than Fairchild's Store this day, hiding from him and crying for him. But she could not enlighten him. She and Robbie had seen each other across the crowded room—a suspended cluster of long-handled popcorn poppers turned gently between them to block their vision—

and both their faces, her crying one too, went fixed, the way it was in High School: they did not speak.

She could hear under her window now the faint sound of the idling motor in some boy's automobile, and downstairs the Victrola ending "By the Light of the Stars" and then the dancers catching their breaths.

"Shelley, Shelley! Are you ever coming?" called Mary Lamar Mackey.

Then Shelley put a little coat of peach silk around her and went down, where at the foot of the stairs Piggy McReddy was waiting for her, shouting up, " 'I'm the Sheik of Araby!' "

6

Much later, in her room, Dabney opened her eyes. Perhaps she had only just gone to sleep, but the silver night woke her—the night so deep-advanced toward day that she seemed to breathe in a well, drenched with the whiteness of an hour that astonished her. It hurt her to lift her hand and touch at her forehead, for all seemed to be tenderness now, the night like herself, breathless and yet serene, unlooked-on. The daring of morning light impending would have to strike her when it reached her—not yet. The window invited her to see—her window. She got out of bed (her filmy dress like a sleeping moth clung to the chair) and the whole leafy structure of the outside seemed agitated and rustled, the shadows darted like birds. The gigantic sky radiant as water ran over the earth and around it. The old moon in the west and the planets of morning streamed their light. She wondered if she would ever know . . . the constellations. . . . The birds all slept. (The mourning dove that cried the latest must sleep the deepest of all.) What could she know now? But she could see a single leaf on a willow tree as far as the bayou's edge, such clarity as there was in everything. The cotton like the rolling breath of sleep overflowed the fields. Out into it, if she were married, she would walk now—her bare foot touch at the night's hour, firmly too, a woman's serious foot. She would walk on the clear night—angels, though, did that—tread it with love not this lonely, never this lonely, for under her foot would offer the roof, the chimney, the window of her husband, the solid house. Draw me in, she whispered, draw me in—open the window like my window, I am still only looking in where it is dark.

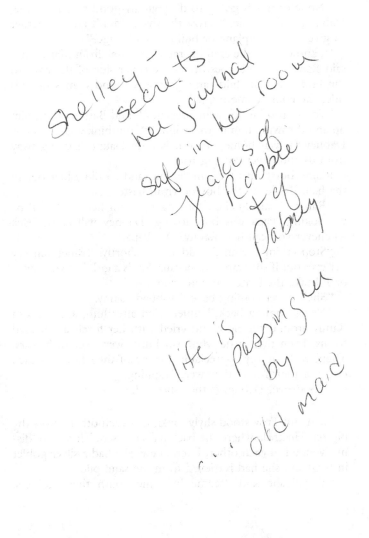

IV

"PAPA, Uncle George gave me a walking horse, red with four white socks and a star here!"

"Well, you didn't cry about that, did you?" said Battle.

"She's going to ride me!" said Ranny.

"None of this is going to do you any good that I can see, Dabney," said Battle, "across the river. I don't know whether to give you an airplane or build you a bridge."

"I know a way she could come back home from Marmion," said Ranny. "If she goes down the other side of the river to the bridge at Fairchilds and goes across and comes up this side, she could come home."

"You're too big for your breeches," said Battle, lifting him up and throwing him to the ceiling. "You think you can show Dabney the way home, do you? No, sir, Dabney's going away from us and never coming back."

Ranny burst into tears in the air, and so did Bluet out in the hall. Battle set the boy down in haste.

"Ranny!" said Shelley, looking up from her book. "Papa was joking. Papa was only joking. Dabney will come back whenever you call her, Ranny. Oh, Papa."

"Stop crying, Ranny," said Battle shortly. "Bluet can cry her eyes out if she wants to, because she's a girl, but you can't, or I'll take the switch to you promptly."

"She's never coming back," sobbed Ranny.

"Never coming back," Bluet cried after him, and hugged Ranny around the neck and cried with her forehead pressed to his. Even their little white sideburns were wet with tears. Then, without any appreciable change of their hold on each other or their noise, they were laughing.

"Good-bye, Dabney!" they shouted.

Ellen and Troy stood shyly looking at each other across the big red Heatrola where the back halls crossed. They were dismally afraid of each other, Ellen knew. She had a silver goblet in her hand she had retrieved from the sand pile.

"Troy," she said, "come help me polish these goblets.

Dabney's gone to Greenwood for the groceries. You don't mind finding me busy, do you?"

"I reckon all this is bound to make you busy," said Troy. He tiptoed around the Heatrola and followed her. She felt that he lightly peeped into the back door of the library as they went by. Primrose sat in there sewing some object—George had brought the aunts up this morning. As a matter of fact, Ellen noticed, it was a bridesmaid's lace mit, and even upon a blameless garment like a mit the sweet lady could not have satisfied herself her work would go perfectly with Troy peeping in. And indeed it was not perfect, but Primrose could never have had the thought occur to her that being a lady she could not sew a seam worthy of a lady, and would have undertaken anything in the trousseau.

"Where's Jim Allen?" she called. Primrose jumped, and drew the little mit to her. "Oh—it's Ellen! She's looking at your roses, though it's the heat of the day."

"She'll find them covered with blackspot," Ellen said regretfully. She led Troy back to the kitchen. Roy and a little stray Negro child were eating cold biscuits under Roxie's foot and feeding a small terrapin on the floor, and were sent out to the back yard. Aunt Mac, ignoring Roxie, Howard stringing beans, the children, and now Ellen and the young man, was ironing a stack of something on the trestle board in the back part of the kitchen.

They sat down at the scrubbed round table in the center. A June bug flying on a thread was tied to Troy's chair. "That's Little Battle's," Ellen said as if by divination. "You don't mind June bugs, do you?"

"Oh, no'm."

"Get you another chair if you do." She collected things from the dining room and pantry. "Here's the polish, here's you a rag, and you can take half these goblets. Roxie and Vi'let and Howard and all just have so much to do, and Pinchy at this time— Be particular you get in that little ridge."

"Yes'm."

"Wait. I'll get you a bite of cooky. That cup in your hand now will be Dabney's," she said, and Troy almost let it fall. "We have so many daughters—of course you have to divide things up. One daughter couldn't have more than her share."

She set a plate of cookies and a glass of buttermilk in front of him, went back and got him a cold drumstick. "Not that there's a contentious bone in any of my children's bodies.— That's Orrin's. Blessed Orrin likes silver too. He said, 'Mama, I want to have a silver cup of my own to shave out of when I'm grown,' and I told him it was surely his privilege."

"How old is Orrin now?" was all Troy could think of to reply, and Ellen could not think to save her life just then how old Orrin was.

"Here's one will be Dabney's, for you to shine. It was from the Dabneys—my family—brought over." She jumped up again and brought him a voluminous linen napkin to wipe his fingers on. "Don't leave that drumstick and let it waste. This is Dabney's cup."

Troy took it with his thumb and middle finger, sticking his forefinger well out.

"It won't say Sterling," called Aunt Mac from the ironing board. "That's because those things were made before there ever was an old Sterling, it's like B.C."

They polished in silence for a while. Troy added a little spit now and then, and held up each goblet critically but silently to see how Ellen thought it shone. His fingers were sprouted with his red hairs but they had a nice shape and they were kind, in Ellen's judgment.

"My little old mama made the prettiest quilts you ever laid your eyes on," he said, when he finally spoke. His foxy skin turned rosy with pleasure and his thick lashes growing in light-red bunches and points gave him a luxuriant, petlike look. He laid down his linen rag. "One called 'Trip around the World' and one called 'Four Doves at the Window.' 'Bouquet of Beauty,' that was one. . . ."

"And you asked your mother their names." Ellen looked at him as though he had done a commendable thing. "Where was your mother? Where was your home, Troy?" she asked softly. How she had wondered. Of course Battle would never have asked a man such a thing!

"My little mama ain't dead! No, ma'am, though she writes an infrequent letter and I take after her. Bear Creek, up Tishomingo Hills. She can crochet just as well as she can piece tops—hard to believe."

Why had Ellen wondered? She could have seen the little perched cabin in her mind any time, by just not trying. ("Howard," she said, "did you leave any strings on? Well, now, you take your hammer out under that cool fig tree and start making that altar Miss Dabney wants. Just do it your way—I can't even tell you how to start it.") She looked back at Troy. "Well, you're still Mississippi," she said, smiling.

"Though this don't seem like Mississippi to me," he said. "I mean at first. Two years back I would just as soon have been in Timbuktu as Fairchilds, not to see one hill."

"You were an only child? Like me?" she said, gently taking the goblet he had set down and putting her rag to it.

"Only boy."

Ellen could not imagine a boy not enumerating his sisters, but she nodded.

"I sure wish Dabney and myself could have one of Mammy's pretty quilts now, to lay on our bed."

"I guess your sisters ask her for them when they marry," she said rather breathlessly, and he nodded, as if to commend her. "Aunts," he said. "I had me three old-maid aunts that loved lots of cover." He cut his eye at Aunt Mac, who was by this time singing a Presbyterian hymn. "They were forever scared they'd get cold, and they had more quilts than you ever did see in your life. Lived on a mountain top. I'd go pay them a visit. They'd go to bed at sundown and I would sit up till about twelve o'clock before the fire, throwing on logs, getting the place hotter and hotter. Every time I'd throw on a log they'd throw off a quilt."

"Troy," she said, "I believe you're a tease too."

Troy straightened up, and taking a goblet as if it were unfinished business on the table between them, he attacked it with his rag, first spitting on it thinly between drawn lips. "Well, there's nothing easy about hills," he said. "And plenty like me have left them, four to my knowledge on one bend of the Tennessee River. They all come to the Delta. It sure gets you quick. By now, I can't tell a bit of difference between me and any Delta people you name. There's nothing easy about the Delta either, but it's just a matter of knowing how to handle your Negroes." He batted the June bug.

"Well, Troy, you know, if it was that at first, I believe there's more to it, and you'll be seeing there's a lot of life here yet that will take its time working out," said Ellen. She held up the goblet for him to see.

"What would it be?" Troy asked. He smiled down on her for the first time.

"The Delta's just like everywhere," she said mysteriously. "You keep taking things on, and you'll see. Things still take a little time. . . ."

Vi'let came in with a vase of wilted zinnias. "Miss Tempe's come in," she said. "Sent me out first thing to throw dead flowers out the parlor. Is it all right to throw 'em away?"

"It's all right, Vi'let, they're really dead. Go tell her Miss Ellen'll be there in a minute." She frowned over Troy's head. She was torn between her pride—presenting Troy naturally and now, to Tempe, and her conviction that she might wait just a little while about it.

"You can look for me back about sundown," Troy was saying. He stood up, put the chair up to the table again with the June bug, tired, hanging floodwards now, and took his hat off the top of the bread safe.

"Don't be late—it's supper and the rehearsal, remember. If those clothes and crooks haven't come, what'll we do?"

"Dey come," Roxie prophesied. "Ain't nothin' goin' to defeat Miss Dab, Miss Ellen."

Troy was bending in a polite bow to Aunt Mac. He started out and then stock-still asked Ellen, "Is she ironing *money*?"

"Why, that's the payroll," said Ellen. "Didn't you know Aunt Mac always washes it?"

"The payroll?" His hand started guiltily toward his money pocket.

"I get the money from the bank when I drive in, and she hates for them to give anything but new bills to a lady, the way they do nowadays. So she washes it."

"If that's what she wants to do, let her do it!" roared Battle. He was coming down the hall followed by four Negroes, all of them carrying big boxes. "Here's Dabney's doin's," he said. "All creation's coming out of Memphis. What must I do with it, throw it out the back door?"

"Take it quick, Roxie," said Ellen. "Vi'let! Howard! Aunt

Mac, you'll have to soon make way at the ironing board!" she cried to the old lady's ear.

"Tempe's here along with it," said Battle. "Come on, Troy, let's get out."

Troy walked a little gingerly out of the kitchen, as if he might be offered his salary before he got out, fresh and warm from the iron, but when Ellen pulled him from Battle and led him toward the cross hall by the side door and showed him the long present table set out there, he went easier.

"Now I'm really scared for you to touch Bohemian glass till after the wedding, Troy," she said earnestly. She took up a bit of it from the tray. "From Virginia," she said. "Dabney cousins that couldn't come. They sent an outrageous number of wine glasses."

"They sure are the prettiest things yet," he said, as she turned the flower-shaped glass in the light. He watched her worn, careful, ladylike hand with the bit of fragile glass sparkling around it.

"I love the hills," she said, glancing up. "I miss them even now."

He shook his head, smiling, at the distant past.

2

India, Laura, and Ranny were sitting on the parlor floor playing cassino when Aunt Tempe arrived, their six bare feet touching. A great lot of boxes came with her, Little Uncle went by two or three times with things, and Vi'let with the whitest dress box sailed to the back. Skipping in front, Lady Clare came in all over again under the aegis of Aunt Tempe and made a face at them. She looked around for the piano (as if it had ever been moved!) and sidling through the archway sat down and began to play "Country Gardens." Just at the door, India noticed, her father sent Aunt Tempe in with a nice, soft spank, and went off calling "Ellen! Ellen!"

Aunt Tempe, in a batik dress and a vibratingly large hat, entered (keeping time) and kissed all the jumping children. Then she straightened up from her kisses and admonitions and looked quickly around the parlor, as if to catch it before it

could compose itself. Howard, who kept coming in and standing motionless, studying the spot on the floor where he had
to put the altar, was caught in her gaze. " 'Scuse me," he said,
and vanished with his hammer. The big feet of Bitsy and
Bitsy's little boy, who was learning, hung inside the room; the
Negroes were washing the outside of the windows behind
thick white stuff, and talking to Maureen in the yard; if they
knew Aunt Tempe could see their feet, they would be moving
their rags.

India sat back on the floor and gazed at her aunt, admiring
the way she kept her hat on, and shuffling the cassino cards
gently. Aunt Tempe was about to call Vi'let—she did call
Vi'let and ask her what dead zinnias were doing in front of
the original Mr. George Fairchild? And where were Miss Ellen
and Miss Dabney—running around frantic upstairs? And
where was Mr. George? And where was just some *ice water*?
Out in the back they could hear Horace, Aunt Tempe's gog-
gly chauffeur, whistle at how hot it was at Shellmound, as
opposed to Inverness.

Aunt Tempe drew a breath and sighed. She made little turns
on her Baby Louis heels, and her soft plump shoulders came
in view like more bosoms in the back, over her corset. India
could read her mind. The table lamp provoked Aunt Tempe.
The three white marble Graces holding the shade in their six
arms, with dust unreachable in the folds of their draperies and
the dents of their eyes, were parading the whole lack of Shellmound to Aunt Tempe—it was *outdated*—it didn't do for
marrying girls off in. Of course Battle and Ellen would do the
place over, the day one of the children prevailed on them hard
enough—perhaps it would be quick little India—dress it up
and maybe brick it over, starting with the gates. One day they
would take up the floral rugs and the matting, and put in
something Oriental, and they would get rid, somehow, of that
Heatrola she hated to pass in the hall. They were only pro-
crastinating about it. But here Dabney was marrying, and still
the high, shabby old rooms went unchanged, for weddings or
funerals, with rocking chairs in them, little knickknacks and
playthings and treasures all shaken up in them together—and
those switches on the mantel would probably stay right there,
through the ceremony. On the table before her now a Tinker-

Toy windmill was sitting up and *running*—with the wedding two days off—right next to the exquisite tumbler with the Young Pretender engraved on it, that was her wedding present to Battle and Ellen—cracked now, and carelessly stuffed with a bouquet that could have been picked and put there by nobody but Bluet—black-eyed Susans, a little chewed rose, and a four-o'clock.

Aunt Tempe closed her eyes to see Mashula's dulcimer still hanging by that thin ribbon on the wall—did she know Shelley could take it down and play "Juanita" on it? India followed her gaze; it passed fleetingly over Uncle Pinck's coin collection from around the world, that Aunt Tempe had been tired of looking at in Inverness and taking out of little Shannon's mouth—and fell sadly on the guns that stood in the corner by the door and the pistols that rested on a little gilt and marble table in the bay window. "Those firearms!" she murmured, freshly distressed at their very thought, as if in her sensitive hearing she could hear them all go off at once. That was Somebody's gun—he had killed twelve bears every Saturday with it. And Somebody's pistol in the lady's workbox; he had killed a man with it in self-defense at Cotton Gin Port, and of the deed itself he had never brought himself to say a word; he had sent the pistol ahead of him by two Indian bearers to his wife, who had put it in this box and held her peace, a lesson to girls. There (India sighed with Aunt Tempe) was Somebody's Port Gibson flintlock, and Somebody's fowling piece he left behind him when he marched off to Mexico, never to be laid eyes on again. There were the Civil War muskets Aunt Mac watched over, an old Minie rifle coming to pieces before people's eyes. Grandfather's dueling pistols, that had not saved his life at all, were on the stand in a hard velvet case, and lying loose was Grandmother Laura Allen's little pistol that she carried in her riding skirt over Marmion, with a flower scratched with a penknife along the pearl handle, and Battle's, her father's, little toothmarks in it.

"Bang bang!" said Ranny.

"No longer a baby," Aunt Tempe sighed. She sat down in a rocker, and Vi'let brought a pitcher of her lemonade—so strong it would bring tears to the eyes. "And poor Laura," she said, reaching out at her and kissing her again. To her, girls were as obvious as peony plants, and you could tell from birth if they were going to bloom or not—she said so.

"I've brought Dabney a forty-piece luncheon set for the time being," she said, seeming to address Ranny. "I couldn't put my *mind* to anything more."

"How is Mary Denis's little new baby?" Ranny asked. "Is it still a boy?"

"Mm-hmm, and he's the image of me—except he has Titian hair," said Aunt Tempe. "That he got from Mr. Buchanan. It took wild horses to drag me away from Mary Denis at such a time, but I was prevailed on. I felt compelled to come to you."

"How is Mary Denis?" asked Ranny. "I love her!" He was sitting like a lamb at Aunt Tempe's feet, and letting her pet him.

"As well as I ever expected her to be, precious. She gets along very well considering she's married to a Yankee that wants his windows washed three times a week."

"They aren't though, are they?" cried India staunchly.

"Look, look! Aunt Tempe, look!" Dabney whirled in laughing, with flimsy boxes and tissue paper and chiffon ruffles flying.

"I should say they're not!" Aunt Tempe opened her arms and kissed Dabney three times under her big hat. (In the back, Vi'let was crying, "Miss Dab, ain't you 'shamed, you bring my dresses on back here!") "Mercy! You've always just washed your hair! Don't ever let this husband of yours, whoever he is, know you can cook, Dabney Fairchild, or you'll spend the rest of your life in the kitchen. That's the first thing I want to tell you."

"He doesn't know anything about me at all," Dabney laughed, dancing away in her mules around the wreath on the floral rug, whirling with her white wedding dress held to her. Her hair hung like a bright cloud down over her eyes and when she danced she scattered drops everywhere, except on her dress.

"Bring those affairs here to me, Ranny child," said Aunt Tempe.

"Oughtn't we to wait and let Dabney open everything that comes?"

Aunt Tempe shook out a dress and held it at an authoritative angle with her head tilted to match. "I must say I never heard of a *red wedding* before."

"American Beauty, Aunt Tempe!" cried India, teasingly whisking it from her and beginning to dance about after Dabney, holding it high.

"I stand corrected," said Aunt Tempe.

"They fade out before they get to Shelley and Dabney," Laura told her consolingly.

Maureen ran in, got Aunt Tempe's hug and kiss—and took, as if for her prize, the rosy dress slightly less bright and danced with it, nicely. The little girls went delicately though gleefully, and soundlessly on their bare feet. Laura too, with a sudden spring, had gently extracted the next dress from Aunt Tempe's fingers, and slid 1, 2, 3 into a ballroom waltz, hidden behind her pink cloud.

"Play, Lady Clare! Play till you drop," India's voice called.

Ranny leaped up and got under the wedding dress Dabney was holding, and then dancing frantically cried, "Let me out, let me out!"

"Slower, Lady Clare! Vi'let!" Aunt Tempe called, and Vi'let came and stood in the door with her hands on her hips. "If you don't press these dresses right away, you won't get a chance! They'll be worn out completely!"

"I *can't* go slower!" cried Lady Clare.

Outside, Bitsy and his little boy rubbed round peepholes in the window polish to see in, and laughed so appreciatively that they nearly fell out of the window, to India's ever-watchful delight as she pony-trotted.

"Well, of course I can't talk," said Aunt Tempe, looking fixedly at the bride dancing and the three dresses without any heads dancing around her, with Vi'let beginning to chase them. "My own daughter married a Yankee.—Naturally, I bring her to Memphis and Inverness to have her babies—*and* name them."

"It's not like Dabney was going out of the Delta," called the pale pink waltzing dress.

"Poor Mary Denis went clear to Illinois."

"Oh, Aunt Tempe, how's Mary Denis?" Dabney cried,

coming to a momentary stop. "I did so want her for a brides-maid!"

"She's thin as a rail and white as a ghost now!"

"I bet she's beautiful as ever! How much did her baby weigh?"

"Ten pounds, child: little George."

"Oh, how could you tear yourself away?" asked Dabney in a painful voice, holding a pose before the long mirror. She bent her arm and looked tenderly down over imaginary flowers. Vi'let smiled.

"I was prevailed on," said Aunt Tempe, but Dabney had run lightly out of the parlor again, snatching a flight of dresses and letting them fall over Vi'let, covering her as she giggled, with a bright cascade. Bluet, Maureen, Ranny, and Laura reeled after her, still under the spell, and Lady Clare was still playing "Country Gardens."

"The overseer," announced Aunt Tempe, nodding as if to imaginary people on both sides of the room, the tiniest smile on her face. India sat down and looked up at it.

They danced out, and Laura at the tail end would have danced her way upstairs too, dancing as if she were going to be in the wedding. The whole house was shaking like the joggling board or the compress, with dancing and "Country Gardens." Only in the hall Aunt Ellen stood leaning by the stairpost, leaning as if faint, her eyes and cheeks luminous. Just back of her, Roxie stood with a plate of coconut cake, erect and murmuring.

Uncle George, who had gone fishing before breakfast, had come in at that moment with a slam of the side door, stamping across the hall against the beat of bare feet. His face was burned and streaming, his white pants spotted with swamp mud. Behind him walked Howard's little boy, holding a string of fish—not very many and not very big.

Aunt Ellen and Uncle George, their gazes meeting, fell back while the laughing parade pushed and passed between them—Dabney gave George her passing kiss, and drops from her hair went in his eyes. Laura slowed down, and instead of going between them she waltzed from side to side; somehow she could not go between them, like the cousins. Her tingling feet were dancing but her body held her still in place, at a blind alley of desperation, as paralyzed from escape as a rabbit in sudden light.

It was the last thing she would have thought of—to pity Aunt Ellen or Uncle George at Shellmound, or to pity Maureen, just going around the turn of the stairs, dancing so sweetly today without fighting, or to pity Dabney who would always kiss just as quick as she saw. Where could she go just to hold out her arms and be taken, quickly—what other way, dark, out of sight of what was here and going by? She suddenly considered snatching Roxie's cake and running out the back. . . . She waltzed in a kind of crisis of agitation. People that she might even hate danced so sweetly just at the last minute, going around the turn, they made her despair. She felt she could never be able to hate anybody that hurt her in secret and in confidence, and that she was Maureen's secret the way Maureen was hers. Maureen! Dabney! Aunt Ellen! Uncle George! She almost called them, all—pleading. There was too much secrecy, too much pity at the stairs, she could not get by.

Uncle George suddenly shouted at the top of his voice, "That's enough!"

There was silence everywhere at Shellmound, prompt as India's gasps of half-distress, half-delight; then only Lady Clare's wistful complaint, "I don't know how to *ever* end it!" Wide-eyed, Roxie suddenly reached for Howard's little boy's hand, and he yielding George the fish they bolted. Where the clamor had been, Uncle George's two words shot out like one bird, then beat about the walls, struck in the rooms upstairs. Could Dabney bear it? Laura, who could not stop even then shuffling her foot, moved helplessly up and down in one place, wondering if Uncle George would kill her. Poor Aunt Primrose, who would not hurt anything on earth, appeared blinking at the library door, holding her little lace mit, nearly finished, before her breast.

Presently Dabney's light, excited laugh floated back at them from above, and then her face, bright and mischievous under the sparkling hair, looked smiling down over the rail, as if disembodied. Aunt Ellen looked up at her a minute and then said, "Dabney, you're supposed to be in Greenwood getting the groceries, dear," and walked serenely toward the parlor. Uncle George, his burned face still shining, came past Laura and she felt that she would turn to stone, but his fishy, tobacco-y hand came down ever so gently over her hair, and she stopped dancing.

Aunt Tempe's voice rose. "Why, bless your heart! George Fairchild! Come here and kiss your sister!"

Uncle George ran from her and from poor Aunt Primrose who looked after him without words. (The Fairchild men would just run from you sometimes.) He went to the back, holding out his fish. "Give them to the Negroes," Laura heard him tell somebody. Then Aunt Mac's voice: "Georgie, you look like Sin on Earth, wash your face at the kitchen sink!"

But I'm a poor little motherless girl, she thought, and sat down on the bottom step and cried a tear into the hem of her skirt, for herself. Before long she thought she'd go back to the kitchen and see what Aunt Mac would say to her.

"Ho hum," said India. She fell back on the floor and set a glass of lemonade on her diaphragm. "Aunt Tempe, I bet you don't know something you wish you did."

"What, child?" asked Aunt Tempe sharply.

"I bet you didn't know Aunt Robbie ran away from Uncle George and never is coming back."

"Hush your mouth, child."

"Yes, she did!"

"The nerve!" Aunt Tempe suddenly reached up and took off her hat. Her fine hair with the Memphis permanent wave sprang to life about her temples, like kitten ears.

India was not ever quite sure whose nerve Aunt Tempe spoke of—perhaps now her mother (she heard her coming) for not writing the news. Aunt Tempe carried the notion that her mother was snooty—the only one of her father's sisters who did; because her mother didn't write. "Rate," her mother said, in her Virginia accent, "I never rate." It was her Virginia snootiness that she would never "rate" anything, Aunt Tempe thought—people had to drop everything and come to Shellmound to find out.

"Ah! What has he done?" Aunt Tempe said, with her sisterly face alive to brotherly mischief. Then, "Oh, the mortification! Who told you, baby? And when?"

"I'm nine," said India. "No-*body* told me, but I *knew* way
back this morning."

"You knew what?" called Ellen warningly from the hall.
"You did get here!" she said to Aunt Tempe in that warm,
marveling voice with which she always welcomed people, no
matter how late she was doing it, as if some planet had mysteriously entered a fresh orbit and appeared at Shellmound.
She kissed Aunt Tempe's cheek—the softest cheek of the Fairchilds, which Aunt Tempe offered in a temporary manner like
a very expensive possession. After all (India could read her
mind as Aunt Tempe kissed back), she had been invited over
long-distance telephone, and she had been only barely able to
make out what *one* bolt from the blue was, that Dabney was
engaged—and then it was very unsatisfactory information;
they had let Bluet tell her the wedding day.

"Aunt Primrose and Aunt Jim Allen still don't know you
know what," India said, putting her arm soothingly around
Aunt Tempe's neck. "They don't even dream."

"Get away from me, India, you're always such a *hot*
child!—*Well-madam?*"

"How's Mary Denis?" asked Ellen as if the "Well-madam?"
were not Aunt Tempe's question first.

"Thin as a rail, white as a ghost. Only wild horses— The
baby's my image— Has Mr. Buchanan's Titian hair, Mr.
Buchanan's the same Yankee he ever was, demands the impossible. . . . Oh, the mortification of *life*, Ellen!"

"Now, Tempe, you're always further beside yourself than
you need to be," Ellen said. With the hand Aunt Tempe
couldn't see, she was very gently patting India's bare foot.

"Of course I am! And events come along and bear me out!
But nobody tells me!" Aunt Tempe poured out another glass
of lemonade and asked pitifully for a little tiny bit of sugar.
"Of course I know George and Battle both try to spare
me—Denis always spared me everything. It would kill me to
know all poor George must have gone through, what it's
driven him to!"

"India—you run out and tell Vi'let to stop whatever she's doing and come sweeten Aunt Tempe's lemonade to suit her—and take Lady Clare with you."

In the music room there was a stir as if Lady Clare roused out of some trance. "Did you hear me playing 'Country Gardens,' Aunt Ellen?" she cried, running in.

"Yes, dear, I was listening out in the hall," Ellen said. "You're a big strong girl, rounding out a little, I believe."

"I'm bigger than Laura," said Lady Clare. "I'm going out and turn around in the yard until it makes me drunk and I fall down and crack my head open."

"Now, Lady Clare—just because you're visiting!" said Aunt Tempe.

"I'm not going to tell Dabney you know what," said India as she walked out.

"That's a good girl, honey." Ellen looked at her proudly.

"She's got so many secrets from me, I'm not going to tell her mine! Maybe I'll tell her years later."

"Now! Straighten me out," Tempe said to Ellen, leaning not forward, but back.

"I can't imagine how India finds out things." Ellen was brooding. "It's just like magic."

"I don't worry about India!"

Ellen sighed. "I guess not yet.—Well, Dabney's going to marry Troy Flavin, just as we told you, and Robbie has run away from George and he won't say a word or go after her. Not connected, of course, but—"

"Two things always happen to the Fairchilds at once. Three! Have you forgotten Mary Denis having a baby at Inverness at the very moment all this was descending on you here?"

"No, I didn't forget," said Ellen. "I reckon there're enough Fairchilds for everything! But we're hoping this trouble of George's will blow over."

"Blow over! That's Battle's talk, I can hear him now. How, in the world?"

"Robbie might still come to the wedding."

"I'd like to see her! She'll get no welcome from me, flighty thing," said Tempe. "Bless George's heart! he lost his Fairchild temper." She smiled.

"Oh, Tempe. I think he's hurt," Ellen said. "You know George and Battle and all those men can't stand anybody to be ugly and cruel to them!"

"I know. And how can people hurt George?" Tempe asked. She turned up her soft face with a constricted look that was wonder, and searched Ellen's face.

"I don't know. . . . Remember Robbie's the one among us all we don't know very well," Ellen said, and then she faltered as if somehow she had conspired with Tempe's first thought, her surface of curiosity that had stopped her as she came into the room. "Vi'let, bring the sugar!" she called. "It's too late now for cake, isn't it, Tempe?"

"I don't think so. I know George's headstrong," said Tempe, piteously showing the palm of her little hand. "Nobody knows better than I do—the oldest sister! He's headstrong. Nobody has a bit of influence over him at all! But how can *she* think *she's* fit to take him down, Old Man Swanson's granddaughter? I could pull her eyes out this minute."

"I had led myself to believe they were happy," Ellen said. Vi'let was bringing the sugar on an unnecessarily big silver tray and Ellen watched her treat Tempe very specially and tell her how young and pretty she looked, not like no grandma, and she was going to bring her some of that cake. . . . "We're not telling Dabney about this until the wedding's over," she said, as Tempe sipped her lemonade.

"Pshaw! If Dabney's old enough to marry the overseer out of her father's fields, she's old enough to know what George and every other man does or is capable of doing. *I'll* tell her, the next time she dances in here."

"Tempe," said Ellen softly, "wait. Give Robbie just a little more time!"

"*Robbie?* Whose side are you on?"

"I'm on George's side! And Dabney's side . . . George is the sweetest boy in the world, but I think now it's up to Robbie—I think he's left it up to her. Tempe—we don't know—we don't know anything."

"All I know is Denis would have been in here begging my pardon half an hour ago—if *he* had yelled out 'That's enough!' like that with no warning, and my palpitations."

"Plate of cake, Miss Tempe," said Vi'let at her elbow.

"Here come me and Aunt Primrose!" India cried, singing her warning.

"Oh, Ellen—did you see how George tracked up your floor? It breaks my heart to see it. After Roxie spent the morning on her knees—now it all has to be done over.—Of course *he* don't know any better." She and Tempe kissed each other in a deprecatory, sisterly fashion. "He don't mean to. Tempe, we're getting fat. How is Mary Denis today?"

"Well, Mr. Buchanan thinks she looks 'just dandy!'" said Tempe.

"Tch!"

"He wants to raise up a lot of little Yankees in Illinois, regardless."

"Mary Denis is the prettiest thing that ever went out of the Delta."

"Have some cake, Primrose."

"It's a precious baby, too," Tempe sighed. "Looks so much like me, you'd catch your breath. (Oh, Mashula's coconut!) And you ought to see little Shannon—she's delighted. She can stamp her foot and say 'Scat!'"

"Oh, that little thing! I'd give anything if you could have brought her—the baby too!" cried Ellen.

"There is a limit on what I am able to do," Tempe said, and Ellen as if to make amends said, "Dabney will want to ask you all kinds of things, Tempe! I'm not much use to her, I'm afraid. She cried because the altar rocks—and I couldn't do a thing about it. Howard's banging on it, doing his best—I just wish somebody'd come by."

"And Battle is as helpless as a child with *machinery*. Well, everybody says Mary Denis's wedding was the most outstanding that has ever occurred in our part of the Delta. I won't say prettiest, because it was planned *al fresco* and it poured down—drenched the preacher—but it was the most outstanding once we'd moved inside."

"I remember it was," Ellen said. "Shelley and Dabney had such a good time being flower girls, scampering around. I couldn't come, being about to have—could it have been India?"

"Ha, ha," gloated India.

"Mr. Buchanan said he never saw so many cousins in his life, all scattering rose petals."

"Dabney's going to have shepherdess crooks, Aunt Tempe," said India.

"Good, *good*."

"Have you ever heard of such a thing?" Ellen said, marveling. "They haven't come, though. They're up there in Memphis still. Dabney makes Battle phone every day, the crook people and the cake people, and bless them out, but it doesn't do a bit of good."

"Let me at the phone," said Tempe, clutching the arms of her chair as though she were held back. "I'll call Pinck immediately and have him go to Memphis and bring the cake and the crooks in his own hands when he comes. Ah, and the flowers, are you sure of those?"

"We're not sure of anything," Ellen said. "Oh, Tempe, could you? The poor child will soon be beside herself."

"I couldn't do less."

"Pinck will wear himself out! But he's so wonderfully smart about everything in Memphis."

"He ought to be." Aunt Tempe went out to the telephone.

"I've nearly finished the mit." Aunt Primrose held it up, like a little empty net.

"Primrose!"

"I think they should have mits to carry those crooks," she said.

"I believe we're getting somewhere in spite of ourselves." Ellen took a breath. "Everything's done except get Howard's altar up and put the lace cloth over it to hide it good—and put your smilax and the candelabra around and wash all the punch cups from everywhere, got them in baskets—and get the flowers and the cake and the ice cream—Dabney wanted it in shapes, you know—and the crooks! George's champagne came, enough to kill us all. Now I'm thinking about the chicken salad—we've made two or three tubs and got it covered on ice—and do you think frozen tomato salad turned in the freezer would be a reproach on us for the rehearsal supper?"

"Mary Denis demanded a cold lobster aspic involving

moving the world," Tempe said, coming in. "Of course we moved it. Pinck said he would be delighted! I had to spell shepherdess—didn't you hear me calling you?"

"Dabney will be so thankful. Better wash a little faster on the windows, Bitsy and Floyd," Ellen called. "The rehearsal's tonight, there's not much time."

"Croesus, Mama!" cried Shelley, who was passing in the hall. "It's tomorrow night! Aunt Tempe, don't let her make it any sooner than it is."

"Have I got my times mixed up again!" Ellen put her hand to her forehead. "I told Troy it was tonight, and he didn't any more correct me than a spook. I was hoping we'd get somebody in the family could keep track of time."

"He just didn't want to be correcting you quite yet," said Tempe, with a brave smile. "I really think the house looks pretty well, Ellen!"

"Oh, do you think it looks all right?" Ellen looked around anxiously and yet in a kind of relief. "There was so little time to do much more than get the curtains washed and starched and the rugs beat."

"Child! They'll grind down so much chicken salad in everything it'll all have to be done over anyway," said Tempe in a dark voice.

"I thought in the long run, Primrose thought of it, we could just cover everything mostly with Southern smilax."

"Of course that will suffer with the dancing," said Primrose timidly.

"I consider our responsibility ceases with the cutting of the cake," Tempe declared. "Primrose, what are you putting your eyes out on now? Have you any idea how many bridesmaids there are in this wedding?"

"I set myself to finish this mit before I take a bite of dinner, and I will." Primrose accepted a little crumb of cake from Ellen. "It's my joy."

"I do hope," Tempe was saying, "you won't have the sliding doors open there in full view of Jim Allen's cornet. Jim Allen is forty-four years old in October and I can't think she would appreciate it."

"Oh, she wouldn't mind, Tempe," said Primrose. "Jim Allen's *beyond* all that."

"We have to have the doors open, so Mary Lamar can be heard perfectly playing for the wedding," Ellen said. "Or it would break Dabney's heart."

"It's a living shame these children don't take music," said Tempe. "India, now, *needs* to have music lessons: look at her." India was lying on the floor with her legs straight up in the air, listening.

"Well, there's nobody in Fairchilds giving lessons now," Ellen said, "since Miss Winona Deerfield married that traveling man that came through. If Sue Ellen would just get up from her bed and come back to these children, they'd be kept out of a lot." She suddenly smiled: Roy had come in, washed and combed, and silently opened *Quo Vadis?*

"You used to teach the early ones," said Tempe. "Don't deny it."

"Oh, I tried on Shelley. But I couldn't play pea-turkey now. Dabney's best friend Mary Lamar Mackey from over at Lookback plays if we want music—listen!" In the music room Mary Lamar, restored to the bench, softly began a Schubert song.

"Yes, but she takes it seriously," Aunt Tempe said, lifting a warning finger. "And Laura"—for Laura came in, trailing Roy—"it would be such a consolation to her when she's older."

"I'm not going to be in the wedding, Aunt Tempe," said Laura, veering to her.

"No, poor little girl, you."

"I went to tell Aunt Jim Allen but she was asleep in the dining room on the settee."

"Well, poor thing! She worked too hard counting cut-glass punch cups."

"She said 'Scat!' in her sleep when I looked at her."

"I'm glad it's cats and not rats she's dreaming about," Primrose said. "Oh, Ellen, she knows they're at the Grove—though I smile and don't let on I hear them." Primrose smiled now, a constricted little smile, as she talked. "You remember how rats madden poor Jim Allen, Tempe. If she thought we heard a rat she would be rushing screaming from the house now—maybe be killing us all, I don't know." She looked with her nervous smile toward Ellen. "That's one thing I want to talk over with George—rats. I want to ask him what to do about the rats in the Grove. It's George's house and he ought to know."

"Oh, but I'd wait till after the wedding, Primrose! Wait till—"

"I know," whispered Primrose, behind the little mit. "And Jim Allen—what she's been doing is hiding her tears—not wanting George and Battle to see her red eyes." When the music climbed again she whispered, "Spare Tempe!"

"Tempe knows—but Dabney doesn't. . . ." Ellen leaned over her, and walked to the window. Then she gave a cry. "Oh, who on earth can that be coming? Oh—it's Troy. Here comes Dabney's sweetheart, you all!" They peeped behind her. "Don't let him see us!"

"I believe to my soul *he's* got red hair!" cried Tempe.

"Let's us not move." India put her eye on Laura and Roy, but Roy was reading and heard nothing.

"I think he's a very steady, good boy," said Ellen. "And he's going to *learn*."

"That's a bad sign if I ever heard one," Tempe cried instantly. "My, he's in a hurry about it too. Flavin is a peculiar name."

"He doesn't usually come that fast, does he?" Primrose whispered, as Troy leaped over little Ranny's stick-horse in the drive and hurried toward the steps. "He's bringing something. My, it looks like Aunt Studney's sack, but of course it isn't."

"Let's still don't get up and look," muttered India, lying flat.

"I wouldn't have known him!" said Primrose. "But I always think of him as part horse—you know, the way he's grown to that black Isabelle in the fields."

"It's bigger than Aunt Studney's sack! Is old Aunt Studney dead yet?" asked Tempe, her fine brows meeting as she peered.

"No, indeed," Ellen said. "She still ain't studyin' us, either. She told Battle so yesterday, asking him for a setting of eggs. He's at the door."

"Here's Troy!" cried Dabney's voice. She was rushing down the stairs and letting him in.

Aunt Mac came through the parlor and by their sashes pulled the three ladies neatly away from the window, and went out again.

"You didn't kiss me!" cried Dabney.

But Troy was pushing his way into the parlor, intent. "Look," he said, "everybody look. Did you ever think your *mother* could make something like this? My mammy made these, I've seen her do it. A thousand stitches! Look—these are for us, Dabney."

"Quilts!" Dabney took his arm. "Shelley! Come in and look. Troy, come speak to Aunt Tempe—she's come for the wedding, Papa's sister from Inverness." But he flung her off and held up a quilt of jumpy green and blue. " 'Delectable Mountains,' " he said. "Pleased to meet you, ma'am. I swear that's the 'Delectable Mountains.' Do you see how any lady no higher'n a grasshopper ever sewed all those little pieces together? Look, 'Dove in the Window.' Where's everybody?"

They all came forward and watched Troy spread out the quilts, snatch them together, spread them out again. "Wedding presents." "They're lovely!" "Get up off the floor, India, or you'll get a quilt over you!"

"She sent so many," said Shelley, backing away a little each time she came forward.

"It gets cold in Tishomingo," said Troy gravely.

"Couldn't your mother come to the wedding, Troy?" asked Ellen gently. "We could send for her." Even if his mother wrote to him, she had not been sure he wrote to his mother.

"Not just to a wedding." He thoughtfully shook his head.

"What's the name of this quilt?" asked Dabney, arms on her hips.

"Let's see. I think it's 'Tirzah's Treasure,' but it might be 'Hearts and Gizzards.' I've spent time under both."

"Didn't you know either about George's predicament?" Aunt Tempe said to Aunt Primrose across the room. "I'm glad somebody else didn't know."

"He told me when I came in. Bless his heart! *She'll* come back," Aunt Primrose said, looking around Troy's arm.

"Ma pieced that top of a snowy winter," said Troy gravely staring, his eyes far away.

"I wish I could make something like that," said Aunt Primrose gallantly.

"Not everybody can," said Troy. "But 'Delectable Mountains,' that's the one I aim for Dabney and me to sleep under most generally, warm *and* pretty."

Aunt Tempe gave Ellen a long look.

"I think they are beautiful, useful wedding presents," said Ellen. "Dabney will treasure them, I know. Dabney, you must write and thank Troy's mother tonight."

"Let her wait till she tries them out, Mrs. Fairchild," said Troy. "That's what will count with Mammy. She might come if we have a baby, sure enough."

Aunt Primrose darted her little hand out, as if the quilt were hot and getting hotter, and Ellen and Dabney and Troy pulled it out taut in the air. The pattern shone and the ladies and Dabney all fluttered their eyelids as if the simple thing revolved while they held it.

"Look," said Ellen. "Troy, there's a paper pinned to this corner."

"Oh, that's Ma's wish," said Troy. "I noticed it."

"She says here, 'A pretty bride. To Miss Dabney Fairchild. The disappointment not to be sending a dozen or make a bride's quilt in the haste. But send you mine. A long life. Manly sons, loving daughters, God willing.' "

"That's Ma. She'll freeze all winter."

"Your pretty bride," said Dabney, going around. "How did she know I was pretty?"

"I don't know," said Troy. "I didn't give her much of a notion." He bent to her disbelieving kiss. "I guess you'd better get these off the floor and fold them nice, Dabney. And lay them on a long table with that other conglomeration for folks to come see."

The dinner bell rang. Battle and the boys came in rosy and slicked, playing with the barking dogs. Orrin had on his pompadour cap. George came down with Ranny riding him, knees on his shoulders. Ranny had the family telescope up to his eye, and turned it with both hands about the room, exclaiming.

"Who do you see in this room?" George was asking him

quietly. "Do you see Mama having secrets with Aunt Primrose and Aunt Tempe and Aunt Jim Allen?" They went toward them.

"Yes, sir!"

"I always thought Robbie was a very *strenuous* girl," said Aunt Primrose hesitantly, looking up at George.

"She's *direct*," said Ellen.

"She has her cheek," Tempe snapped, while Jim Allen was still asking pleadingly, "Who, who?"

"She has the nerve of a brass monkey," said George, and Ranny crowed from his head. George's forehead, nose, and cheeks still fiery from the sun, he seemed to be beaming now at the sight of his sisters all gathered, with a midday fragrance of stuffed green peppers and something else floating over them like a spicy cloud.

They're both as direct as two blows on the head of a nail, George and Robbie, Ellen was thinking with surprise. George was so tender-hearted, his directness was something you forgot; when he was far away, in Memphis, she thought of him—as she always thought of the man or the woman—as at Robbie's *mercy*. Robbie, anywhere, was being direct.

"I've racked my brains to think of something we can tell the Delta," Tempe declared, with Ranny's telescope turned on her. "Mary Denis named her *baby* for you, George, and you yell and run off like a maniac when I try to inform you."

"How's Mary Denis?" said George. "Tell the Delta about what?"

"About Robbie Reid, your wife," said Tempe. "You have to tell the Delta something when your wife flies off and you start losing your Fairchild temper. Right at the point of another wedding! You should have thought of it when you married her, woke up the night. Ranny, is that the manners your Uncle George teaches you? That's staring."

"I don't see Robbie," Ranny said, turning George with his digging knees. He looked through the front window, out at the glare. "I just see Maureen chasing a bird, and Laura turning round and round in the yard."

"Call them in," growled Battle.

"Tell the Delta to go to Guinea," said Ellen stoutly.

Aunt Mac came up the hall, her strong voice singing, belligerently sad, " 'O where hae ye been, Lord Randall my son? . . . O mother, mother, mak my bed soon. . . .' "

"Of course Mary Denis is thin as a rail. Mercy," Tempe said to Lady Clare, who appeared too and circled round her, ecstatically walking on her knees and drinking something green. "Don't you drink that in here—ink? Take it on out, I can't watch you."

"Well, is everything all pretty near ready now?" Troy's voice was asking.

"I see Dabney kissing Troy," Ranny announced.

"Oh, Troy, the altar rocks!" Dabney cried.

"Put a hammer in my hand, I'll knock it into shape before we sit down to dinner!"

"I see Lady Clare drinking Shelley's ink," said Ranny dreamily.

"Lady Clare, you know what happens when you show off," Aunt Primrose said, putting her finished bridesmaid's mit to her lips and biting the thread.

"She doesn't care," said Ranny, smiling, at the telescope. "She doesn't care."

"I seem to hear the dinner bell," said Aunt Jim Allen.

"Roy, close your book." Ellen kissed the top of his head, and he looked up with sucked-in breath.

"Laura and Maureen," said Battle, with the condensed roar in his fatherly voice carrying out the window, "will you obey me and come to the table before I skin you alive and shake your bones up together and throw the sack in the bayou? And Mary Lamar Mackey," he said, to the other direction, "will your ditty wait?"

"Oh, Papa, you're so *hot*," said Shelley. She pulled at his starched coat sleeve and tried to kiss him, and he spanked her ahead of him to the table.

"Miss Priss! Do you love your papa, not forget him?"

"Naturally," said Aunt Tempe, when Roy with his eyes bright told what George did, about the Yellow Dog on the trestle, "he did it for Denis."

She smiled and fanned with the Chinese fan she brought from Inverness, nodding at them. Dabney, who loved her father and adored George, knew beyond question when Aunt Tempe came and stated it like a fact of the weather, that it was Denis and always would be Denis that they gave the family honor to. She held Troy's hand under the table and accepted it with a feeling not far from luxuriousness: Denis was the one that looked like a Greek God, Denis who squandered away his life loving people too much, was too kind to his family, was torn to pieces by other people's misfortune, married beneath him, threw himself away in drink, got himself killed in the war. It was Denis who gambled the highest, who fell the hardest when thrown by the most dangerous horse, who was the most delirious in his fevers, who went the farthest on his travels, who was the most beset. It was Denis who had read everything in the world and had the prodigious memory—not a word ever left him. Denis knew law, and could have told you the way Mississippi could be made the fairest place on earth to live, all of it like the Delta. It was Denis that was ahead of his time and it was Denis that was out of the pages of a book too. Denis could have planted the world, and made it grow. Denis knew what to do about high water, could have told you everything about the Mississippi River from one end to the other. Denis could have been anything and done everything, but he was cut off before his time.

He could have one day married some beautiful girl worthy of him (Mary Lamar Mackey would have grown up to him), leaving Virgie Lee (Denis's choice was baffling, not to be too much brooded on) to somebody she would better have tried to live with; he would have had a beautiful child—a son—a second Denis, though not his father's equal. It was a shame on earth that Maureen, though George would naturally risk his life for her, was the only remnant of his body; she bore no more breath of resemblance to him than she did to, as Aunt Jim Allen always remarked, the King of Siam; if anything, she took after her mother, though her hair was light. It would be wrong to see in her dancing up and down any bit of Denis's tender mischief or marvelous cavorting.

"These fields and woods are still full of Denis, full of Denis," Tempe said firmly. "If I were to set foot out there by myself, though catch me!—I'd meet the spirit of Denis Fairchild first thing, I know it."

She looked pleased, Dabney thought, as if she were molli-
fied that Denis was dead if his spirit haunted just where she
knew. Not at large, not in transit any more, as in life, but
fixed—tied to a tree. She pressed Troy's hand, and he pressed
back. Poor Denis! she thought all at once, while Maureen,
eyeing her, stuck out her tongue through her smiling and
fruit-filled mouth.

V

IT WAS MORNING, the day of the rehearsal. Roy ran out of the house and scattered some crumbs to the birds. Ellen saw him from her window—his face tender-eyed under the blocky, serious forehead and the light slept-on hair pushed to the side, with a darker shadow the size of a guinea egg under the crest. Alone in the yard, he said something to a bird. This was her last day with her daughter Dabney before she married. How she loved her sons though!

"This is Dabney's wedding rehearsal day," Ellen said, turning to the old great-aunts, with Roxie by her offering them a second cup of black coffee while breakfast was getting ready.

"Gordon, dear, I'm hot," said Aunt Shannon fretfully. She lay back with her soft black Mary Jane slippers crossed, on Aunt Mac's chaise longue, frowning slightly at the mounted blue butterflies on the wall.

"She thinks none of the rest of us know it's September," growled Aunt Mac. She snapped her watch onto her bosom. "Nobody but Brother Gordon killed in the Battle of Shiloh. Foot!"

The two old sisters were not too congenial, had never been except for a little while when Battle's generation were growing up and absorbing their time, and in recent years the belief on Aunt Shannon's part that she was conversing with people whom Aunt Mac knew well to be dead seemed a freer development of the schism. Far back in Civil War days, Ellen had been told or had gathered, some ineradicable coolness had come between them—it seemed to have sprung from a jealousy between the sisters over which one agonized the more or the more abandonedly, over the fighting brothers and husbands. With the brothers and husbands every man killed in the end, the jealousy did not seem canceled by death, but extended by it; memory of fear and the keeping up of loyalty had its rivalries too—made them endless and now wholly desperate, for no good was ever to come of anguish any more and so it never had when anguish was fresh.

Aunt Shannon now, with her access to their soldier brothers

Battle, George, and Gordon, as well as to James killed only thirty-three years ago in the duel, to her husband Lucian Miles and even to Aunt Mac's husband Duncan Laws, was dwelling without shame in happiness and superiority over her sister. Poor Aunt Mac did indeed seem to think less of her husband now, in spite of herself (she made little flung-off remarks about his family, "Columbus new-comers") when Aunt Shannon spoke casually to "Duncan, dearie," and bent her head, as if he had come up behind her while she was knitting to give her a little kiss on the back of the neck, as indeed he had done often long ago.

"The wedding's right here. Are we ready, Aunt Mac?"

"Duncan, dearie, there's a scrap of nuisance around here ought to be shot," said Aunt Shannon, glancing sideways without stirring. "You'll see him. Pinck Summers, he calls himself. Coming courting here."

"Duncan Laws will shoot who I tell him, thank you," said Aunt Mac. "Shannon, be ashamed of yourself for getting your time so mixed up. Vainest of the Fairchilds!—Well, then, Ellen, go on to Dabney! Wake her up!"

But Dabney had ridden out on her red filly before any of them were awake, out through the early fields. Vi'let had not yet swept the night cobwebs from the doors, and she had dashed through shuddering, with fighting hands, and pushed open the back gate into the early eastern light which already felt warm and lapping against her face and arms. In her stall the little filly looked at her as if she were waiting for her early, there was a tremor to go in her neck and side. Howard's little boy was sitting in the hay and he saddled the filly and put Dabney on and held the gate. She rode out looking back with her finger to her lips—Howard's boy put finger to lips too, and jumped over the ditch watching her go. She thought she would ride out by herself one time. She had even come out without her breakfast, having eaten only what was in the kitchen, milk and biscuits and a bit of ham and a chicken wing, and a row of plums sitting in the window.

Flocks of birds flew up from the fields, the little filly went delightedly through the wet paths, breasting and breaking the dewy nets of spider webs. Opening morning-glories were turned like eyes on her pretty feet. The occasional fences smelled sweet, their darkened wood swollen with night dew like sap, and following her progress the bayou rustled within, ticked and cried. The sky was softly blue all over, the last rim of sunrise cloud melting into it like the foam on fresh milk.

With her whip lifted Dabney passed Troy's house, and passed through Mound Field and Far Field, through the Deadening, and on toward the trees, where the Yazoo was. Turning and going along up here, looking through the trees and across the river, you could see Marmion. Around the bend in the early light that was still night-quiet in the cypressy place, the little filly went confidently and fastidiously as ever.

Dabney bent her head to the low boughs, and then saw the house reflected in the Yazoo River—an undulant tower with white wings at each side, like a hypnotized swamp butterfly, spread and dreaming where it alights. Then the house itself reared delicate and vast, with a strict tower, up from its re-flection, and Dabney gazed at it counting its rooms.

Marmion had been empty since the same year it was com-pleted, 1890—when its owner and builder, her grandfather James Fairchild, was killed in the duel he fought with Old Ronald McBane, and his wife Laura Allen died broken-hearted very soon, leaving two poor Civil War–widowed sis-ters to bring up the eight children. They went back, though it crowded them, to the Grove, Marmion was too heart-break-ing. Honor, honor, honor, the aunts drummed into their ears, little Denis and Battle and George, Tempe and Annie Laurie, Rowena, Jim Allen and Primrose. To give up your life because you thought that much of your *cotton*—where was love, even, in that? *Other* people's cotton. Fine glory! Dabney would not have done it.

The eagerness with which she was now going to Marmion, entering her real life there with Troy, told her enough—all the cotton in the world was not worth one moment of life! It made her know that nothing could ever defy her enough to make her leave it. How sweet life was, and how well she could hold it, pluck it, eat it, lay her cheek to it—oh, no one else knew. The juice of life and the hot, delighting taste and the fragrance and warmth to the cheek, the mouth. She hated the duel for her grandfather, actively, while the little filly trembled

with impatience under her hand and hated being kept standing still. Everybody in the family had nearly forgotten the old
duel by now (it was "bad about Marmion," they "abandoned
the place") except Dabney, whom it had lately come to hor-
rify. She would not leave Marmion, having once come to it,
if there were duels for any cause. What was the reason death
could be part of a question about the crops, for instance?

Yes, honor—she had been told when she asked questions
as a little girl, Marmion was empty out in the woods because
Old Ronald McBane at Old Argyle had not protected his
landing where some of the people's cotton for miles around
was shipped from his gin; Grandfather, who had a gin too,
had accused him of it, had been challenged, called out to
pistols on the river bank, had been killed instantly. But both
gins went on the same. Dabney had always resisted and
pouted at the story when any of the boys told it—when they
said "Bang bang!" she covered up her ears and wept, until
they comforted her and gave her something for having made
her cry. She knew, though—even the surrender of life was the
privilege of fieriness in the blood. She felt it in herself, but
would anything ever make her tell, ever find it out? Not while
she could resist and lament the fact that dear life would surrender itself for anything.

The sun lifted over the trees and struck the face of Marmion; all the tints of cypress began to shine on it, the brightness of age like newness. Her house! And somehow the river
always seemed swift here, though it was the same river that
passed through Fairchilds under the bridge where the cotton
wagons went over as noisily as a child beating a tin pan, and
passed the Grove where the aunts sat on the porch and cried
for a breeze from it. As a child she would run off here and
throw sticks in, just at this spot, convinced that they would
tear around the curve where the river looked fast, only to see
them gently waltz and drift here and there. . . . She threw a
stick in again, and once more it went slowly. The river was
low now. In the spring it would be up over where she was
now. The little filly turned with Dabney, willfully, and took
the path back toward Shellmound.

"I will never give up anything!" Dabney thought, bending
forward and laying her head against the soft neck. "Never!

Never! For I am happy, and to give up nothing will prove it. I will never give up anything, never give up Troy—or *to* Troy!" She thought smilingly of Troy, coming slowly, this was the last day, slowly plodding and figuring, sprung all over with red-gold hairs.

Shelley couldn't stand him because he had hair in his ears. She called him Hairy Ears—Dabney smiled biting her lip at that small torment. The truth was, slowness made any Fairchild frantic, and Dabney delighted now again in Troy's slowness like a kind of alarm. "Papa never gave up anything," she was thinking. "I am the first thing Papa has ever given up. Oh, he hates it!" He would not tell her how he really felt about her going to Troy—nobody would. Nobody had ever told her anything—not anything very true or very bad in life.

Proud and outraged together for the pampering ways of the Fairchilds, she put the little switch to her filly where she had kissed her. The rehearsal was tonight. If they didn't say anything to her now, or try to stop her, it was their last chance.

And let them try! Just now, while they never guessed, she had seen Marmion—the magnificent temple-like, castle-like house, with the pillars springing naked from the ground, and the lookout tower, and twenty-five rooms, and inside, the wonderful freestanding stair—the chandelier, chaliced, golden in light, like the stamen in the lily down-hanging. The garden—the playhouse—the maze—they had all been before her eyes when she was all by herself, even her own boat landing!

Then after she got in and was living there married, she wanted it to rain, rain—sound on the roof like fall, like spring, bend the trees and the lightning to glare and show them trembling, lifted, bent, come-alive, the way trees looked from windows during storms at night. She wanted this to be outside, and inside herself, sitting in dignity with her cheek on her hand.

She rode by the thick woods where the whirlpool lay, and something made her get off her horse and creep to the bank and look in—she almost never did, it was so creepy and scary. This was a last chance to look before her wedding. She parted the thonged vines of the wild grapes, thick as legs, and looked in. There it was. She gazed feasting her fear on the dark, vaguely stirring water.

There were more eyes than hers here—frog eyes—snake eyes? She listened to the silence and then heard it stir, churn, churning in the early morning. She saw how the snakes were turning and moving in the water, passing across each other just below the surface, and now and then a head horridly sticking up. The vines and the cypress roots twisted and grew together on the shore and in the water more thickly than any roots should grow, gray and red, and some roots too moved and floated like hair. On the other side, a turtle on a root opened its mouth and put its tongue out. And the whirlpool itself—could you doubt it? doubt all the stories since childhood of people white and black who had been drowned there, people that were dared to swim in this place, and of boats that would venture to the center of the pool and begin to go around and everybody fall out and go to the bottom, the boat to disappear? A beginning of vertigo seized her, until she felt herself leaning, leaning toward the whirlpool.

But she was never as frightened of it as the boys were. She looked in while she counted to a hundred, and then ran. Behind her the little filly had been stamping her foot. She climbed on her and kissed her neck, and galloped back into the fields, the Deadening, Far Field, Mound Field, back to Shellmound. When she went under Troy's window she drew the reins a moment and cried out rapidly, tauntingly, all run together like one word,

> Wake up, Jacob, day is breaking!
> Pea's in the pod and the hoe-cake's baking!
> Mary, get your ash-cake done, my love—!

Was he awake? Did he hear? She rode flying home, and began calling "Mama! Roxie! Roxie! Papa!" How hungry she was!

2

"Shelley!" Ellen called at the foot of the stairs.

"Ma'am?" came Shelley's ladylike voice from around several corners in the upper regions. Where on earth was she?

"She's painting her name on her trunk to go to Europe," India said at her mother's feet. She kept her informed about what everybody was doing at all times, which she knew though she herself, as now, might be cutting paper dolls out of the *Delineator* on the hall floor with Laura and Roxie's little Sudie; she seemed truly the only one who knew.

"I want you to go to the store for me and get me a spool of strong string for Howard's altar!" called Ellen in a patiently high voice. "The pony cart's out front now, while it's still a little cool! And go to Brunswick-town and take Partheny a cup of that broth Roxie's pouring off and tell her if she's over being mindless to come up without fail to help in the kitchen! What else? Oh, my old garnet pin, Shelley! Tell Partheny Miss Ellen wonders if she could think what happened to it—you might try her memory a little! She came up and cooked for your papa's birthday and I had it on my dress. But tell her to be here tomorrow morning with the birds!—You can take Laura and India with you," she added in her normal voice. "Where's Lady Clare?"

"On the joggling board, joggling," said India.

"Yes'm, Mama! In a minute," called Shelley. "I'm all covered with black!"

"Oh, gracious," called Ellen perfunctorily. "Mind you invite Partheny to the wedding! She *loves Dabney*!"

Tempe was coming in the side door, they had heard her exclaiming in the yard. ("Poor Tempe, if there's a flower, she wants it!" Primrose always sighed.)

"Did the mosquitoes get you, Tempe?"

"I'm peppered!"

"We can go see Partheny without Shelley," said India, her face close to Laura's. She poked her scissors at Laura's heart. "We'll go with each other."

"Let me at the phone," said Aunt Tempe. "Pinck's going to have to get me some little fluted-paper salted-nut holders! It occurred to me in the garden—twelve silver ones won't go anywhere. I'll catch him at the Peabody!"

Nothing tired Ellen herself more than the spectacle of marital bullying, but it was the breath of life to Tempe, spectacle and all. She sailed among the children to the telephone, while little India smiled in the wake of her pleasure in demanding one more little old thing from Pinck.

"Oh, Mama," cried Shelley, running down the stairs into her mother's arms, as though something dreadful had that moment happened. "It's the only pin you ever really had. I don't count your sunburst! Oh, Mama, and it's lost!"

"Tragedy," remarked Tempe, turning from Pinck's voice at the receiver, "I'm surprised more things aren't lost around here than there are."

"Why, Shelley," Ellen said in surprise. "You mustn't start taking things that hard."

"Maybe *I* lost it!" said Shelley.

"Straighten your shoulders, dear. Just ask Partheny—she won't know anything, very likely. It's only a pin. Don't forget the string. Don't let the children go off without you. Oh, and bring Ranny back! Battle set his heart on getting Ranny's hair cut to show a little of his ears, so they won't think he's a girl at the wedding, and nobody with him but Tippy."

"Let's sneak off from Shelley," said India to Laura. They threw down their scissors and paper dolls and trailed toward the door.

George walked through, and the children all swept around him. Tempe took hold of him. Caught in their momentum, he looked out at Ellen perfectly still, as if from a train window.

"No, I'm going to the Grove and have dinner with Jim Allen and Primrose," he was saying.

"Today?" Tempe exclaimed.

"Has the wedding anything to do with today? That's tomorrow." He teased Tempe, but went out the front door. Through the side lights Ellen saw him stretch out in the porch hammock and lie prone as if asleep when Troy rode Isabelle up in the yard and called "Hi, George!" with his arm raised in that rather triumphant way. She waited a moment watching him, feeling that there was something radical in George, or that some devastating inner picture of their unnecessary ado would flash before his vision now and then. There was a kind of ascetic streak in him, even, she felt timidly. Left to himself, he might not ask for anything of any of them—not necessarily. . . . No, she could not think that for more than a moment. He was too *good*. He would not wish them any way but the way they were. But she, herself, wished they could all be a little different on occasion, more aware of one another when they were all so close. They should know of one an-

other's rebellions, *consider* them. Why, children and all re-
belled!

Laura and India were hunching down the steps like dwarfs
together under the big black umbrella that completely obliterated their shadows down to their trotting feet.

"Wait-wait-wait!" cried Shelley. She ran flying out the door
lacing her fresh middy, and tying it with the impatient knot
of a tomboy. Her hair from under her tight headband blew
straight back in the wind. Her cheeks were both smudged
with shiny black lacquer. She pretended not to see Uncle
George, for she did not beg him to come or tell him good-
bye.

"I had to finish my name," she said to India and Laura.
"Looks like you all could wait that long."

"She wants her name in *black*. When will it be ready?" cried
India.

"It won't be dry until eleven o'clock tonight," said Shelley.
"Do I smell?"

"Uh-huh."

She dipped between them and took the umbrella up to her
height and tilted it stylishly. Three pairs of leg shadows jiggled
on the grass. Above them, Roy was sitting on the roof and
singing, "'My name is Samuel Hall and I hate you one and
all, damn your eyes!'"

"Just don't look at him and he'll come down," said Shelley.
"Now you can come with me, but don't touch me." They
sat in the pony cart and Shelley drove Tiny down the road.
India and Laura carefully held the umbrella over her and made
faces behind her back. "I'm still full of breakfast," Laura ventured to say.

No one on the street of Fairchilds spoke any way but beau-
tifully-mannered to Shelley, all the men promptly swept off
their hats. No one told her her face was dirty, and India was
waiting until they got home to make her look in the glass.
They drove up and down the street three times and had Coca
Colas, speaking to people over and over, with all the men's hats
going up and down. India cried joyously, "Hi, Miss Thracia!
Hi, Miss Mayo!—Oh, I'm so lonesome at Shellmound!"

she sighed to Laura. "Miss Mayo has an oil painting that winks its eye."

Laura remembered Fairchilds—the notice nailed to the post-office wall warning people not to be defrauded by the Spanish swindle, the blind man standing up singing with his face to the Yazoo River, the sign, "Utmost Solitude," in Gothic letters over the door of a lady dying with T.B., who would not let Dr. Murdoch in. When they went in the post office, she saw the notice still there—and so the swindle was still going on—and recognized the cabinet photographs of the postmistress's family sitting around her ledge, and the framed one hanging over the window. At the barber shop they stopped and laughed. All wrapped up, Ranny was getting his hair cut, biting his lip. Sue Ellen's little girl Tippy was holding his hand, and swinging her foot. They threw him an encouraging kiss.

They passed the store by.

"Later," said Shelley.

She turned the pony into a short sunny road behind the compress that seemed to dip down, although it was level like everywhere, into the abrupt shade of chinaberry trees and fig trees.

Brunswick-town lay all around them, dead quiet except for the long, unsettled cries of hens walking around, and the whirr of pigeons now and then overhead. Only the old women were home. The little houses were many and alike, all white-washed with a green door, with stovepipes crooked like elbows of hips behind, okra, princess-feathers, and false dragonhead growing around them, and China trees over them like umbrellas, with chickens beneath sitting with shut eyes in dust holes. It was shady like a creek bed. The smell of scalding water, feathers, and iron pots mixed with the smells of darkness. Here, where no grass was let grow on the flat earth that was bare like their feet, the old women had it shady, secret, lazy, and cool. A devious, invisible vine of talk seemed to grow from shady porch to shady porch, though all the old women were hidden. The alleys went like tunnels under the chinaberry branches, and the pony cart rocked over their black roots. Wood smoke drifted and hung in the trees like a low and fragrant sky. In front of Partheny's house, close up to her porch, was an extra protection, a screen the same size as the house, of thick butter-bean vines, so nobody could see who might be home. The door looked around one side, like a single eye around a veil.

The girls climbed out of the pony cart and Shelley led the way up the two steps and knocked three times on the closed door.

In good time Partheny came out and stood on the porch above them. She was exactly as she had always looked, taller than a man, flat, and narrow, the color of midnight-blue ink, and wore a midnight-blue dress reaching to and just showing her shrimp-pink toes. She did not appear mindless this morning, for she had put a tight little white cap on her head, sharp-peaked with a frilly top and points around like a crown.

"Parthenia," said Shelley, speaking very politely, as she excelled in doing, "we wanted to invite you to Miss Dabney's wedding."

"Wouldn't miss it!" Partheny said, rolling her protruding eyes and looking somber.

"Mama says for you to come up with the birds in the morning."

"Thank you, ma'am."

"And Partheny," Shelley said, "Mama is so sad, she missed her garnet pin. It was Papa's present."

"Mr. Battle's present!" Partheny said dramatically.

"Yes, and, Partheny, Mama wondered if maybe while you were cooking for Papa's birthday barbecue, if maybe you might have just seen it floating around somewhere—if maybe you could send word to her where you think it might be. Where to look."

"Oh-oh," said Partheny regretfully. She shook her white crown. "I surely don't know what best to direct your mother, Miss Shell, where she could look. Hush while I think."

"Mama thinks now it's been lost all summer, and she just noticed it was gone," said Shelley.

"Now ain't that a shame before God?"

"Yes, indeed, it is," said Shelley. "Papa gave that pin to Mama before they were married." She was all at once carried away, and fell silent.

"What kind of hat is that?" asked India, passionately springing forward.

"Oh, Miss India Bright-Eyes! It's a drawer-leg," said Partheny, giggling up very high. "Miss Shell, don't you go back tellin' your Mama you caught me with no drawer-leg on my old head!" Then she took a serious step at them.

"Well."

"I like it," said India.

"Yes, it's real pretty, Partheny," said Shelley in a kind of coaxing voice.

"How is your mama—not speaking of garnet present?" asked Partheny.

"She's fine. She's not going out, right now."

Partheny gave them a bright look, like a bird. All of a sudden she gave a little cackle, bent down, and said, "Step inside—don't set your heels down, I've been mindless four and a half days. But let me just look around in parts of the house. Don't suppose that pin could have flown down *here* anywhere, do you?"

They went inside, Partheny shaking her head somberly, India dragging them forward. Partheny looked, patting the bed quilt and tapping the fireplace, and then disappearing into the other room where they could hear her making little sympathetic, sorrowful noises, and a noise like looking under the dishpan.

The three girls sat on one of the old Shellmound wicker settees, in a row. Laura's mouth was a little open; she was surprised to learn, this way, that Aunt Ellen had ever had such a fine present given to her. Uncle Battle himself had given it to her, she had lost it, and now Partheny was back there playing-like looking for it.

"What don't happen to presents!" Partheny cried out from the other room, in genial outrage.

Laura stole a glance at Shelley. She was sitting caught here in a boxy, vine-shadowed little room decorated with chicken feathers and valentines, with a ceiling that made her almost bump her head and a closeness that did make her droop a little. Now was a good time to ask Shelley something. Just as she opened her mouth, India threw herself abruptly to the floor. She caught a guinea pig.

"Put him down," whispered Shelley.

"You make me," said India, and sat holding the squirming guinea pig and kissing its wrinkled forehead.

Laura put her weight on Shelley's arm. "Can I give Uncle George a wedding present?" she whispered.

"Uncle George? You don't have to give him anything. India, put him down," whispered Shelley. She did not turn her head, but fussed at both of them looking straight in front of her. . . . This was a lowly kind of errand, a dark place to visit, old Partheny was tricky as the devil. Only—suddenly the thought of her mother's loss swept over Shelley with such regret, indignation, pity as she was not in the least prepared for, and she almost lost her breath.

"I want to give Uncle George a present, and to not give Dabney a present. I chose between them, which was the most precious."

"That was ugly," Shelley whispered, as if she had never heard of such a thing.

"Precious, precious guinea pig," India whispered on Shelley's other side.

Laura tugged her arm.

"Give him a kiss," whispered Shelley. "India, put him down before he bites you good."

India kissed the guinea pig passionately, and Laura said, "No, I want to give him not a kiss but a present—something he can keep. Forever."

"All right! When we go by the store, you can *find* something to give him, if you have to."

"Will that be my present, all mine?"

"Yes, all yours," whispered Shelley. "You do try people, Laura, I declare!"

"Precious, heavenly guinea pig! I bite thee," said India.

"Just don't you all touch me," said Shelley, and at that moment Partheny appeared in the room again, coming silently on her long bare feet. There was no sign of the guinea pig in India's arms, only a streak on the floor as it ran under Partheny's skirt. The little girl was leaning on her hand, dreamy-eyed.

This time Partheny brought something, which her long hands went around and hid like a rail fence. "Ain't no garnet present anywhere around," she said. She was smoking her pipe as she talked. "I ransacked even de chicken house—felt under de hens, tell your mama. Nary garnet present, Miss Shell. I don't know what could have become of Miss Ellen's pretty li'l garnet present, and her comin' down agin, cravin' it, who knows. Sorry as I can be for her."

"But what have you got?" cried India, jumping up and trying to see.

"But! Got a little somep'm for you to tote back," Partheny said, suddenly leaning forward and giving them all a look of malignity, pride, authority—the way the old nurse looked a hundred times intensified, it seemed. "Little patticake. Old Partheny know when somep'm happ'm at de big house— never fool yo'se'f. You take dis little patticake to Mr. George Fairchild, was at dis knee at de Grove, and tell him mind he eat it tonight at midnight, by himse'f, and go to bed. Got a little white dove blood in it, dove heart, blood of a snake— things. I just tell you enough in it so you trus' dis patticake."

"What will happen when he eats it?" cried India, joining her hands.

"Mr. George got to eat his patticake all alone, go to bed by himse'f, and his love won't have no res' till her come back to him. Wouldn't do it for ever'body, Partheny wouldn't. I goin' bring Miss Dab heart-shape patticake of her own—come de time."

"How did you know *she*'d ever gone, Partheny?" Shelley whispered, so India and Laura couldn't hear her any more than they could help.

"Ways, ways."

"Thank you, Partheny, but you keep the patticake."

"No! I bid to carry it! I'll make him eat it!" cried India. "Uncle George will have to swallow every crumb—goody! Oh, look how black it is! How heavy!"

India ran out before Shelley could catch her, the cake in both hands up over her flying hair.

"Then take it!" cried Shelley after her.

"I'm still taking Uncle George *my* present," Laura said doggedly.

Partheny followed them out to the porch. "Tell Miss Dab I'm comin'. Surely hopes she be happy wid dat high-ridin' low-born Mr. Troy. *You* all looks pretty." She watched them down the steps and out the gate. As they put up the umbrella she considered them gone, for she nodded over to a hidden neighbor and drawled out, "Got a compliment on my drawer-leg."

"Are we going to the store now?" asked Laura.

"Look. Do you want to go by the cemetery and see your mother's grave?" asked Shelley in a practical voice. "We're near it now."

"Not me," said India, and jumped out of the pony cart with Partheny's cake, when Shelley drew the reins.

"All right," said Laura. "But I want my present for Uncle George before dinner."

The cemetery, an irregular shape of ground, four-sided but narrowing almost to a triangle, with the Confederate graves all running to a point in the direction of the depot, was surrounded by a dense high wall of honeysuckle, which shut out the sight of the cotton wagons streaming by on two sides, where the roads converged to the railroad tracks, the river, the street, and the gin. The school, where the Fairchild children all went, was across one road, and the Methodist Church, with a dooryard bell in a sort of derrick, was across the other. The spire, the derrick, and the flag pole rose over the hedge walls, but nothing else of Fairchilds could be seen, and only its sound could be heard—the gin running, the compress sighing, the rackety iron bridge being crossed, and the creak of wagon and harness just on the other side of the leaves.

A smell of men's sweat seemed to permeate the summer air of Fairchilds until you got inside the cemetery. Here sweet dusty honeysuckle—for the vines were pinkish-white with dust, like icing decorations on a cake, each leaf and tendril burdened—perfumed a gentler air, along with the smell of cut-flower stems that had been in glass jars since some Sunday, and the old-summer smell of the big cedars. Mockingbirds sang brightly in the branches, and Fred, a big bird dog, trotted through on the path, taking the short cut to the icehouse where he belonged. Rosebushes thick and solid as little Indian mounds were set here and there with their perennial, worn little birdnests like a kind of bloom. The gravestones, except for the familiar peak in the Fairchild lot of Grandfather James Fairchild's great pointed shaft, seemed part of the streaky light and shadow in here, either pale or dark with time, and ordinary. Only one new narrow stone seemed to pierce the air like a high note; it was Laura's mother's grave.

All around here were the ones Laura knew—Laura Allen, Aunt Rowena, Duncan Laws, Great-great-Grandfather George, with Port Gibson under his name in tall letters, the slab with the little scroll on it saying Mary Shannon Fairchild. A little baby's grave, son of Ellen and Battle. Overhead, the enormous crape-myrtle tree, with its clusters of golden seed, was the same.

"Annie Laurie," said Shelley softly, still in that practical voice that made Laura wonder. It always seemed to Laura that when she wanted to think of her mother, they would prevent her, and when she was not thinking of her, then they would say her name. She stood looking at the mound, green now, and Aunt Ellen or Uncle Battle or somebody had put a vase of Maréchal Niel roses here no longer ago than yesterday, thinking of her for themselves. . . . It was late in January, the funeral. But all Laura remembered about that time was a big fire—great heaps of cottonstalks on fire in the fields and thousands of rabbits jumping out with the Negroes chasing after them. . . . "Have you seen my letter?" was all she could say, as Shelley took her hand.

"What letter?" asked Shelley, letting go and looking down at her frowning.

Laura had got a letter from her father which, as usual, somebody else opened first by mistake, and which she then passed around and lost. She nearly cried now, for she could not remember all it said. She suffered from the homesickness of having almost forgotten home. She scarcely ever thought, there wasn't time, of the house in Jackson, of her father, who had every single morning now gone to the office and come home, through the New Capitol which was the coolest way, walked down the hill so that only his legs could be seen under the branches of trees, reading the *Jackson Daily News* so that only his straw hat could be seen above it, seen from a spot on their front walk where nobody watched for him now.

Why couldn't she think of the death of her mother? When the Fairchilds spoke so easily of Annie Laurie, it shattered her thoughts like a stone in the bayou. How could this be? When people were at Shellmound it was as if they had never been anywhere else. It must be that she herself was the only one to struggle against this.

She tried to see her father coming home from the office, first his body hidden by leaves, then his face hidden behind his paper. If she could not think of that, she was doomed; and she was doomed, for the memory was only a flicker, gone now. Shelley and Dabney never spoke of school and the wintertime. Uncle George never spoke of Memphis or his wife (Aunt Robbie, where was she?), about being a lawyer or an aeronaut in the war. Aunt Ellen never talked about Virginia or when she was a little girl or a lady without children. The most she ever said was, "Of course, I married young." Uncle Battle did talk about high water of some year, but was that the worst thing he remembered?

And it was as if they had considered her mother all the time as belonging, in her life and in her death (for they took Laura and *let* her see the grave), as belonging here; they considered Shellmound the important part of life and death too. All they remembered and told her about was likely to be before Laura was born, and they could say so easily, "Before—or after— Annie Laurie died . . . ," to count the time of a dress being made or a fruit tree planted.

At that moment a tall man with a bouquet of Memphis roses and fern in green paper strode by. He tipped his hat to Shelley, and then puckering his handsome, pale lips, looked down at the Fairchild graves. "How many more of you are there?" he said suddenly.

"More of us? Seven—eight—no—I forgot—I forgot the old people—" Shelley gripped Laura's hand again. "Dr. Murdoch, this is my cousin—"

"You'll have to consider your own progeny too," said Dr. Murdoch, rubbing his chin with a delicate touch of his thumb. "Look. Dabney and that fellow she's marrying will have three or four at the least. That will give them room, over against the Hunters—have to take up your rose bush." He wheeled about. "Primrose and Jim Allen naturally go here, in line with

Rowena and What's-his-name that was killed, and his wife. An easy two here. George and the Reid girl probably won't have children—he doesn't strike me as a family man."

"He is so!" flashed Shelley.

"Nope, no more than Denis. I grew up with Denis and knew him like a book, and George's a second edition. Of course, grant you, he's got that spirited little filly the Reid girl trotting with him. You—what are you going to do, let your little sisters get ahead of you? You ought to get married and stop that God-forsaken mooning. Who is it, Dickie Boy Featherstone? I don't like the white of your eye," and all at once he was pulling down Shelley's lower eyelid with his delicate thumb. "You're mooning. All of you stay up too late, dancing and what not, you all eat enough rich food to kill a regiment, but I won't try to stop the unpreventable."

He turned abruptly and stepped off a number of steps. "You'll marry in a year and probably start a houseful like your mother. Got the bones, though. Tell your mother to call a halt. She'll go here, and Battle here, that's all right—pretty crowded, though. You and your outfit can go here below Dabney and hers. I know how it could be done. How many more of you are there? I've lost track. Who's this?" and he stopped his stepping off in front of Laura and glared down at her.

"Aunt Annie Laurie's daughter," said Shelley and with a trembling finger pointed at the new shaft.

"Ah!" He made a wry face as if he would prefer they hadn't mentioned Annie Laurie. "Jackson's a very unhealthy place, she talked herself into marrying a business man, moving to Jackson. Danced too much as a girl to start with, danced away every chance she had of dying an old lady, and I told her so, though she *looked* good. It's God's wonder she ever had *you*, and kept you *alive*!" He gave Laura a slight push on the shoulder. "Of course you were born *here*. *I* brought you into this world and slapped you to ticking, Buster." He flicked her collarbone with his knuckle. "Stay away from Jackson. Hills and valleys collect moisture, that's my dogma and creed."

"We have to go now, Dr. Murdoch, we're so busy at our house. We've got all the company in the world," said Shelley.

"What are you going to do about Virgie Lee, let her in?

She'd go in. Be a good thing if Maureen would up and
die—that aunt of yours, too, Aunt Shannon—both of 'em,
Mac's a thousand years old."

"Will you excuse us, Dr. Murdoch?"

"But—can't do a thing about Delta people," said Dr. Murdoch. "They're the worst of all. One myself, can't do a thing
about myself."

He glared at them and swung off.

Shelley stood where she was and rubbed her eye tenderly,
like a bruise.

"When are you going to get married, Shelley?" asked Laura
faintly.

"Never," said Shelley.

"Me neither," said Laura.   *great!*

After Dr. Murdoch, how beautiful the store looked!

Any member of the Fairchild family in its widest sense, who
wanted to, could go into the store, walk behind the counter,
reach in and take anything on earth, without having to pay
or even specify exactly what he took. It was like the pantry at
Shellmound. Anything was all right, since they were all kin.

And no matter what any of them could possibly want, it
would be sure to be in the store somewhere; the only require-
ment was that it must be looked for. There was almost absolute surety of finding it. One day on the ledge with the
hunting caps, India found a perfect china doll head to fit the
doll she had dropped the minute before.

At the moment nobody seemed to be keeping the store at
all, except little Ranny, whom Tippy must have set down
in here to wait; smelling of violets, he was bouncing a ball
in a cleared space, his soft voice going, "—Twenty-three,
twenty-four—last night, or the night before, twenty-four robbers at my back door—" There were some old fellows ninety
years old sitting there around the cold stove, still as sleeping
flies, resting over a few stalks of sugar cane.

Laura, who loved all kinds of boxes and bottles, all objects
that could keep and hold things, went gazing her fill through
the store, and touching where she would. At first she thought
she could find anything she wanted for a wedding present for
her uncle George.

Along the tops of the counters were square glass jars with
gold-topped stoppers—they held the kernels and flakes of
seed—and just as likely, crusted-over wine-balls, licorice sticks,
or pink-covered gingerbread stage-planks. All around, at many
levels, fishing boxes all packed, china pots with dusty little lids,
cake stands with the weightiest of glass covers, buckets marked
like a mackerel sky, dippers, churns, bins, hampers, baby baskets, popcorn poppers, cooky jars, butter molds, money safes,
hair receivers, mouse traps, all these things held the purest
enchantment for her; once, last year, she threw her arms
around the pickle barrel, and seemed to feel then a heavy,
briny response in its nature, unbudging though it was. The
pickle barrel was the heart of the store in summer, as in winter
it was the stove that stood on a square stage in the back, with
a gold spittoon on each corner. The name of the stove was
"Kankakee," written in raised iron writing across its breast
which was decorated with summer-cold iron flowers.

The air was a kind of radiant haze, which disappeared into
a dim blue among hanging boots above—a fragrant store dust
that looked like gold dust in the light from the screen door.
Cracker dust and flour dust and brown-sugar particles seemed
to spangle the air the minute you stepped inside. (And she
thought, in the Delta, all the air everywhere is filled with
things—it's the shining dust that makes it look so bright.) All
was warm and fragrant here. The cats smelled like ginger when
you rubbed their blond foreheads and clasped their fat yellow
sides. Every counter smelled different, from the ladylike smell
of the dry-goods counter with its fussy revolving ball of string,
to the manlike smell of coffee where it was ground in the
back. There were areas of banana smell, medicine smell, rope
and rubber and nail smell, bread smell, peppermint-oil smell,
smells of feed, shot, cheese, tobacco, and chicory, and the
smells of the old cane chairs creaking where the old fellows
slept.

Objects stood in the aisle as high as the waist, so that you
waded when you walked or twisted like a cat. Other things
hung from the rafters, to be touched and to swing at the
hand when you gave a jump. Once Laura's hand went out
decisively and she almost chose something—a gold net of blue
agates—for Uncle George. But she said, sighing, to Ranny

running by, "I don't see a present for Uncle George. Nothing you have is good enough!"

"Nine, ten, a big fat hen!" Ranny cried at her, with a radiant, spitting smile.

But Shelley had stiffened the moment she entered the store. Sure enough, she could hear somebody crying, deep in the back. She went to look, her heart pounding. Robbie was sitting on the cashier's stool, filling the store with angry and shameless tears, under a festoon of rubber boots.

Shelley stood beside her, not speaking, but waiting—it was almost as if she had made Robbie cry and was standing there to see that she kept on crying. Her heart pounded on. Robbie's tears shocked her for being unhesitant—for being plain, assertive weeping for a man—weeping out loud in the heart of Fairchilds, in the wide-open store that was more public than the middle of the road. Nothing covered up the sound, except the skipping of Laura up and down, the little kissing sound of Ranny's bouncing ball, and the snore of an old man. Shelley stood listening to that conceited fervor, and then Robbie raised her head and looked at her with the tears running down, and then made an even worse face, deliberately—an awful face. Shelley fell back and flew out with the children. An old mother bird dog lay right in the aisle, her worn teats flapping up and down as she panted—that was how public it was.

3

Robbie bared her little white teeth after Shelley Fairchild and whatever other Fairchilds she had with her. The flat in Memphis had heavy face-brick pillars and poured-cement ornamental fern boxes across a red tile porch. It was right in town! The furniture was all bought in Memphis, shiny mahogany and rich velvet upholstery, blue with gold stripes, up and down which she would run her fingers, as she would in the bright water in a boat with George. There were soft pillows with golden tassels, and she would bite the tassels! Two of the chairs were rockers to match the davenport and there were two tables—matching. The lamps matched, being of turned mahogany, and there were two tall ones and two short ones, all with shades of mauve gorgette over rose China silk. On the mantel, which was large and handsome made of red brick, was a mahogany clock, very expensive and ticking very slowly. The candles in heavy wrought-iron holders on each side had gilt trimming and were too pretty to be lighted. There were several Chinese ash trays about. (Oh, George's pipe!) The rugs were both very fine, and he and she went barefooted. The black wrought-iron fire-screen, andirons, and poker set were the finest in Memphis. Every door was a French door, the floors were hardwood, highly waxed, and yellow.

His books had never a speck of dust on them, such as the Shellmound books were covered with if you touched them. His law books weighed a lot and she carried them in her arms one by one when she moved them from table to chair to see all was perfect, all dusted. She was a perfect housekeeper with only one Negro, and one more to wash. How fresh her curtains were! Even in the dirtiest place in the world: Memphis.

Only the bedroom was still not the way she wanted it. She really wanted a Moorish couch such as Agnes Ayres had lain on in the picture show, but a mahogany bed would come in a set with matching things and she knew that would please George, new and shiny and expensive. Just yet they had an old iron bed with a lot of thin rods head and foot, and she had painted it. There were unnoticeable places where the paint had run down those hard rods, that had never quite got dry, and when George went away on a case or was late coming home she would lie there indenting these little rivers of paint with her thumbnail very gently, to kill time, the way she would once hold rose petals on her tongue and gently bite them, waiting here in the store, the days when he courted.

They lived on the second floor of a nice, two-story flat, and nobody bothered them. The living room faced the river with two windows. In front of those she had the couch so they could lie there listening to the busy river life and watching the lighted boats on summer nights. As long as they stayed without going to bed they could hear colored bands playing from here and there, never far away. The little hairs on her arm would rise, to think where she was. Then they would dance barefooted and drink champagne, and sometimes in the middle of the day they would meet by appointment in the New Peabody by the indoor fountain with live, pure Mallard ducks in it!

"Are you waiting on people?" asked a slow-talking man in front of her. It was Troy Flavin, the Fairchild overseer, his red hair on end.

"I'm not waiting on people, I'm just waiting. Looking for somebody," she said, opening her own eyes wide, expecting him to see who she was.

"Oh, I beg your pardon." Suddenly he swept his straw hat upwards from his side and fanned her face with it, vigorously. When she bent away he held her straight on the stool and fanned her as firmly as if he were giving her medicine. "Is it the heat? Who're you looking for?" He did not recognize her at all—maybe the heat had him.

"None of your business! Well, all right, stop fanning and I'll tell you. For George Fairchild."

He looked down and put his head on one side as if he talked to some knee-high child. "Why didn't you ask me somebody hard, from the way you're about to cry about it?"

"I'm not! Where is he?"

"Could put my finger on George Fairchild this minute, I'm marrying *into* that family, come eight o'clock tomorrow night."

"Not Shelley! Oh—Dabney!"

She began to laugh, and he said, "You look familiar."

"Don't you know me? I'm Robbie Fairchild. I'm George's wife."

Miss Thracia Leeds came into the store and fingered over the ribbon counter, like a pianist over trills. "Why, hello, Robbie, are you back at the store?"

"Well, George's right there at Shellmound in the porch hammock, if you want him," said Troy. "His wife? You look like you've been to Jericho and back, so dusty."

"I've been leaving him—that's what I've been doing. If anybody wondered!"

"In the porch hammock, he *was*," said Troy, with some

reserve in his voice. Then he added politely, "Dabney's who I'm carrying—you know, Mr. Battle's girl, not the oldest—the prettiest. High-strung sometimes, though!"

"High-strung!" said Miss Thracia with much sarcasm.

"But they're all high-strung. All ready to jump out of their skins if you don't mind out how you step. 'Course, it would be worse for a *girl*, marrying into them."

"I didn't *marry into* them! I married George!" And she beat his hat away, for he started that again—as though he had brought some insufferably old argument into her face.

"Well, it's a close family," Troy said laconically, catching his hat. "Too close, could be."

"A family *can't* be too close, young man," said a new voice. Miss Mayo Tucker had come in.

Robbie rocked gently on her stool, and like a courtesy Troy put his hand over her flushed forehead as if trying to feel there how dangerously close the Fairchilds were. Miss Maggie Kinkaid stood behind Miss Mayo and asked Robbie, if she had come back to work, if she would make good a nest egg, since the other one broke.

"I might have known! I might have known he wouldn't hunt for me—I could kill him! Right back at Shellmound in a hammock," Robbie cried. "I thought he might drag the river, even."

"Drag which river? Why, Dabney wanted George here, is why he's here," Troy said, looking down at her in concern. "*Dabney* sent for him. He's my what-you-call-it—best man. They didn't care for Buster Daggett, for that friend of mine over at the ice and coal."

"Buster Daggett, I don't wonder," remarked Miss Mayo. "Robbie, did I hear you'd run away, and George Fairchild used to beat you unmercifully in Memphis? Cut me off a yard of black sateen, child, you're right at it."

Robbie laughed and brushed at her eyes. "Dabney's marrying—marrying you? You're the overseer out there."

"Sure I am. How'd you know?"

"We've *met*," said Robbie with energy. "Don't you remember me on the trestle—that day? I remember you. All you did was keep looking up at the sky and saying, 'Why don't she storm?'"

"And she didn't?" Troy smiled in delight after a moment. "That day! I don't remember but one thing. I got engaged up yonder!"

"You got engaged, and George Fairchild missed by a hair letting the Yellow Dog run over him for the sake of a little old crazy! Never thinking of me!"

To her surprise, Troy Flavin became more dignified than before. "Yes, your husband'll make you worry-like," he said. "It'll come up."

Robbie with furious neatness cut off a yard of sateen, tied it up, and rang up thirty cents on the cash register.

"You're Robbie, George's wife. People've been norating about you, sure!" said Troy, watching her speed. "Well, you're just in time."

"I bet it's a big wedding and all. Did Miss Tempe make herself come? How's Mary Denis?" asked Miss Thracia.

"They've come from far and near, Fairchilds," said Troy. "You *could* have been too late." He momently reversed the fanning hat and fanned himself. "But now you'll see the wedding."

"Me! Who's going to invite me?"

"I invite you," said Troy. "Now I've invited me somebody." He stared at her appreciatively. Then he put his hat, carefully, over her head to make her laugh, and spread a big hand sprinkled with red hair over each of her shoulders.

"Which way is this? Set me straight, did you run off and leave George, or did he run off and leave you? I believe those Fairchild men are great consorters," said Miss Mayo. "Does he make any money in the law business? It's bad luck for a girl to put a man's hat on."

"It would be fun to walk in *during* it, and make George and everybody jump," Robbie said, looking up at Troy and smiling for the first time, under the yellow brim.

"What! Not during the wedding!"

"Oh, look at me forget about *you* being there."

"It would cause a stir," he said, and balanced a pencil on his finger. "Furthermore, I'd be scared of Aunt Mac. Why don't you go walk in now? What's keeping you, if you're going in the end? like I say to myself."

"Do you mean to say, Robbie Reid, you had gone off and

left George Fairchild and now you're just *coming back?*" said Miss Thracia. "I know what he ought to do to you."

"Must I go now, and push him out of the hammock?" said Robbie softly. Her eyelids fell, as if she were being lulled to sleep. She thought Troy was very kind, and clever. Tears ran down her face.

"That sounds better than the other," said Troy. She jumped off the stool. "And considering we're next thing to kin,—go wash your face."

She gave him back his hat and he stood holding it politely.

"And to tell you the truth," he said when she came in from the little back porch with a clean face, "I feel without doubt you ought to be getting somewhere near your husband, not sitting here baking by yourself in this hot store."

Robbie went out, past Miss Thracia, Miss Maggie, and Miss Mayo, fluffing her hair. "See if you think she's going to have a baby," said Miss Maggie. "I wonder if it will be a boy or girl and how they'll divide up the land in that case."

"She's not," said Miss Mayo definitely.

With a start Troy went to the door and looked up and down the street. "I forgot to wonder how she'd get there," he said.

India was walking up the sidewalk eating ice, with her eyes shut. She opened her eyes and saw Troy.

"Troy Flavin! I've got something for you," she said, her face alight. She put something in his hands. "A cake! Dabney baked it with her own hands, just for you."

"Well, it surprises me," Troy told her, accepting it. "I didn't know she could even make light bread."

India turned a handspring and looked back over her shoulder at him—it was a look so much like Dabney's that he started again, and he called after her, "Much obliged!" But she too had got out of sight.

4

Robbie saw it would be a long hot walk in the boiling sun. But Troy Flavin had been right, though high-handed, for somebody that came from "away"—anything was better than that oven of a store. She couldn't stand it any longer. And, oh, George must have known he could come and get her, Shelley must have tattletaled, and when she had come as far as Fairchilds, as far even as the store—! She passed the shade of the cemetery and took the road. Off there was the bayou, but if she was going back to George in the hot sun, then she was going in the hot sun. She glanced through the distant trees; the whirlpool was about there. She and George had once or twice gone swimming in that, once at night, playing at drowning, first he and then she sinking down with a hand up. There were people she would like to see go down in that, and a snake look good at them.

She was in the road through the Fairchild Deadening. What a wide field! All this was where the old Fairchilds had started, deadened off the trees to take the land a hundred years ago. She could hardly see across. The white field in the heat darted light like a prism edge. She put a hand over her eyes, but the light came red through her fingers. She knew she was a small figure here, and went along with a little switch of elderberry under the straight-up sun.

Caught in marriage you were then supposed to fling about, to cry out and ask for something—to expect something—what was the look in all unmarried girls' eyes but the challenging look of knowing what? But Robbie—who was greatly in love and so would freely admit everything—did not know what. It was not this!

In the depths of her soul she had at first looked for one of two blows, or magic touches, to fall—unnerving change or beautiful transformation; she had been practical enough to expect alternate eventualities. But even now—unless the old bugaboo of pregnancy counted—there was no eventuality. Here she was—Robbie, making her way, stamping her feet in the pink Fairchild dust, at a very foolish time of day to be out unprotected. There was not one soul to know she was desperate and angry.

The Fairchild women asked a great deal of their men—competitively. Miss Tempe in particular was a bully, or would have been, without the passive, sweet Miss Primrose and Miss Jim Allen to compete with another way. Naturally, the Fairchild women knew what to ask, because in their kind of people, the Fairchild kind, the women always ruled the roost; Robbie believed in her soul that men should rule the roost. (George, showing how simple and difficult he was in a Fairchild man's way, did not betray it that there *were* two kinds of people.) It was notoriously the women of the Fairchilds who since the Civil War, or—who knew?—since the Indian times, ran the household and had everything at their fingertips—not the men. The women it was who inherited the place—or their brothers, guiltily, handed it over,

In the Delta the land belonged to the women—they only let the men have it, and sometimes they tried to take it back and give it to someone else. The Grove had been left to Miss Tempe and she married Mr. Pinckney Summers (a terrible drinker) and moved to Inverness, presenting it to George— and George had told his unmarried sisters, Primrose and Jim Allen, that they could live there. Marmion belonged by rights to that little Maureen, for whom Miss Annie Laurie Fairchild had felt that wild concern some ladies feel for little idiot children, even the wicked ones—though if she knew, she would be sorry now, with her own child cheated. She had given Marmion to Denis when she married and went out of the Delta, and now of the two children would it in all strictness be Maureen's? A joke on the Fairchilds. And Shellmound— Miss Rowena, the quiet one, the quiet old maid, had let Mr. Battle have it before she ever lived in it herself; no one could ever be grateful enough to Rowena! Not then, not now, when she was dead and triumphantly beyond gratitude, but Robbie would tell anybody that Miss Rowena was *forgotten*, if a Fairchild could be. She let all her brothers take from her so, she *let* them! Robbie shivered for Miss Rowena. All the men lived here on a kind of sufferance!

She had never thought it strange in her life before, having no land or possessions herself—Reids and Swansons had never become planters—but now she did. It was as if the women had exacted the place, the land, for something—for something they had had to give. Then, so as to be all gracious and noble, they had let it out of their hands—with a play of the reins— to the men. . . .

She remembered all at once a picture of some old-time Fair-child lady down at the Grove. On a picnic, playing, Robbie had got wet in the river and Miss Jim Allen had not been able to rush her into the house fast enough, to get the river off her—she had put her in a little parlor to sit on a plaid while she readied a bedroom that couldn't have helped but look as perfect as possible already—and looking down at Robbie was the old-time Fairchild lady with the look on her face. It was obviously turned upon her husband, upon a Fairchild, and it was condemning. Robbie had been caught staring up at it (she still knew the outside of the Fairchild houses better than the inside) when Miss Jim Allen ran back in. "That's Mary Shannon," Miss Jim Allen had said, as though she told her the name of a star, like Venus, so generally known that only poor little visitors come up from holes in the river bank would need to be told. "That's Mary Shannon when she came to the wilderness."

And of course those women knew what to ask of their men. Adoration, first—but least. Then, small sacrifice by small sacrifice, the little pieces of the whole body! Robbie, with the sun on her head, could scream to see the thousand little polite expectations in their very smiles of welcome. "He would do anything for me!" they would say, airily and warningly, of a brother, an uncle, a cousin. "Dabney thinks George hung the moon," with a soft glance at George, and so, George, get Dabney the moon! Robbie was not that kind of woman. Maybe she was just as scandalous, but she was born another kind. She did want to ask George for something indeed, but not for the moon—not even for a child; she did not want to, but she had to ask him for something—life waited for it. (Here he lay in a hammock, just waiting for her to walk this whole distance!) What do you ask for when you love? If it was urgent to seek after something, so much did she love George, that that much the less did she know the right answer.

Then, at the head of a railroad trestle, in high heels, fuming and wondering then if she had a child inside her, complaining to him that she worshiped his life, she had tried and been reproved, denied and laughed at, teased. When she jumped up for him to look back at and heed, not knowing how love, anything, might have transformed her, it was in terror that she had held the Fairchilds' own mask in front of her. She cried out for him to come back from his danger as a favor to her. And in his forthright risk of his life for that crazy child, she had seen him thrust it, the *working* of the Fairchild mask, from him, on his face was an elation of throwing it back at her. He reached out for Maureen that demanded not knowing any better. . . .

In Robbie's eyes all the Fairchild women indeed wore a mask. The mask was a pleading mask, a kind more false than a mask of giving and generosity, for they had already got it all—everything that could be given—all solicitude and manly care. Unless—unless nothing was ever enough—and they knew. Unless pleading must go on forever in life, and was no mask, but real, for longer than all other things, for longer than winning and having.

an absolute net changing

She shaded her eyes and turned looking for one tree. She was so little she could take refuge in an inch of shade. Finally she saw a cotton shed that looked not too far to get to before she dropped in the heat. She had had the foresight to bring a sack of pickles and a box of cakes.

But when she stepped into the abrupt dark, she jumped. There was a Negro girl there, a young one panting just inside the door. She must have been out of the field, for sweat hung on her forehead and cheeks in pearly chains in the gloom, her eyes were glassy.

"Girl, I'm going to rest inside, you rest outside," said Robbie.

Like somebody startled in sleep, the girl moved out a step, from inside to outside, to the strip of shade under the doorway, and clung there. Her eyes were wild but held a motionless gaze on the white fields and white glaring sky and the dancing, distant black rim of the river trees.

Robbie ate the cool wet pickle and the little cakes. She had run off from her sister Rebel now, who would about this time begin to wonder where she was. She stretched her bare feet, for her high heels had made them tired. It was nice in here. She felt as if she were in a shell, floating in that sea of light, looking out its mouth with good creature comfort.

The moment she had thought over with the most ruin to her pride was the one after the train had actually stopped. George was safe, and the engineer had leaned out. George had suddenly leaped up from where he had fallen on the swampy earth, to greet him. "Oh, it's Mr. Doolittle!" he had said.

The engineer had raised his stripey elbow, saluted George, and said, "Excuse *me*." "You nearly got a whole mess of Fairchilds that time! Where do you think you're taking that thing?" George had shouted. "Taking it to Memphis, ever heard of it?" Mr. Doolittle had said—what absurd conversation men could indulge in with each other, at the most awful moments! Oh, Robbie could have killed them both. "It was somebody I knew!" George scoffed, right in bed, groaning for sleep. "Mr. Doolittle wasn't going to hit me!" When she knew all the time that George was sure Mr. Doolittle *was*. Until she couldn't stand it any longer. He would not say anything more; he wasn't used to saying anything more to women.

Robbie sat still, cross-legged, on the floor of the cotton house, with a forgotten motion fanning herself with her skirt. Across her vision the Negro clung and darted just outside, fitful as a black butterfly, perhaps crazy with the heat, and beyond her the light danced. Was this half-way? Her eyes fastened hypnotically on the black figure that seemed to dangle as if suspended in the light, as she would watch a little light that twinkled in the black, far out on the river at night, from her window, waiting.

The pure, animal way of love she longed for, when she watched, listened, came out, stretched, slept content. Where he lay naked and unconscious she knew the heat of his heavy arm, the drag of his night beard over her. She knew what he cried out in his sleep, she was outside herself as a cup those three drops fell in. She breathed the night in beside him, away off from dreams and time and her own thoughts awake—the companion of his weight and warmth. Then she was glad there was nothing at all, no existence in the world, beyond George asleep, this real and forgetful and exacting body. She slept by him as if in the shadow of a mountain of being. Any moon and stars there were could rise and set over his enfolding, unemanating length. The sun could lean over his backside and wake her.

She heard the Fairchilds' plantation bell ring in the dense

still noon. Dinner. She drew her breath in fiercely as always
when the fond, teasing, wistful play of the family love for
George hung and threatened near. Nothing was worthy of
him but the pure gold, a love that could be simply beside
him—her love. Only she could hold him against that grasp,
that separating thrust of Fairchild love that would go on and
on persuading him, comparing him, begging him, crowing
over him, slighting him, proving to him, sparing him, comforting him, deceiving him, confessing and yielding to him,
tormenting him . . . those smiling and not really mysterious
ways of the Fairchilds. In those ways they eluded whatever
they feared, sometimes the very thing they really desired. . . .

Robbie desired veracity—more than she could even quite
fathom, as if she had been denied it, like an education at
Sunflower Junior College; from a kind of poverty's ambition
she desired it—as hard and immediate a veracity as the impact
of George's body. It meant coming to touch the real, unde-
ceiving world within the fairy Shellmound world to love
George—from all she had spent her life hearing Fairchild,
Fairchild, Fairchild, and working for Fairchilds and taking
from Fairchilds, with gratitude for Shelley's dresses, then to
go straight through like parting a shiny curtain and to George.
He was abrupt and understandable to her as the here and
now—and now had become a figure strangely dark, alone as
the boogie-man, back of them all, and seemed waiting with
his set mouth open like a drunkard's or as if he were hungry.
She, plain hard-head who never dreamed, dreamed every
night now she saw him like that, until the image had become
matter-of-fact as some glimpse of him on a daylight street
corner in Memphis watching her coming. It was a nightmare,
Rebel would shake her till she woke up in terror. Where are
you? the cry would be in her throat. What if it was she who
had run away? It was he who was lost, without her, a Fairchild
man, lost at Shellmound.

Robbie drew up sharply; she heard a horse. The next minute she heard Troy Flavin's voice call out, "Go on, Pinchy!
Go on! I get tired of seeing you everywhere!"

Robbie looked out the door. Troy laughed at her. "I wondered how far you'd get," he said. "Jump up in front of me
and ride."

"No, sir," said Robbie. Then because she always told everything, she said, "I want it to be real hard, like this, to make him feel worse."

Troy put his thumb knuckle in his mouth and bit it gently. Then he got off his horse meditatively, telling her to wait. He came holding out a little round cake affair with one big bite gone, for Robbie to see.

"You're a married woman," he said. "Taste this," and watched her take a bite.

"It tastes like castor oil," said Robbie.

"Dabney made it for me. But myself, I don't think that positively requires me to eat it all." He clapped his hands at Pinchy, hovering.

"Oh-oh," said Robbie. "It tastes plenty awful. I do pride myself I could cook better than that when I was a bride."

"Well, I think myself something spilled in it. Such a big kitchen to try to cook anything in. I'll just tell her plainly, try again."

"She might pull your eyes out, on her wedding day," Robbie said darkly.

"Here, Pinchy—here's a cake, Pinchy," said Troy. "Eat it or give it to the other Negroes. Now scat!" He clapped his hands at her skirt.

Pinchy, with the cake, moved on stiffly, out into the light, like a matchstick in the glare, and was swallowed up in it.

"Hate to ride off and leave a lady," said Troy, "but surprise your husband if that's the way you want. A wet leaf on the head prevents the sunstroke."

He galloped toward Shellmound.

"My nose itches," said Troy in the parlor. "Company's coming."

"I'll tell you how to make the best mousse in the world," said Aunt Tempe.

"How?" cried India.

"Take a pair of Pinckney's old drawers." Aunt Tempe began to describe how she made gelatin. The boys were coming in one by one, with wet hair and glowing fiery cheeks, and grabbing up their books. Lady Clare swayed in, in a lady's dress and Dabney's pink satin shoes.

Shelley, pulling Laura, flew in out of breath.

"I'm a wreck! Partheny's got something of yours, Mama, but she wouldn't give it to me for fear she didn't know what a garnet was, and India bit a guinea pig and ran away."

"Not for good, I'm afraid," said Battle. "She beat you home."

"Wait! *Then*, we saw old Dr. Murdoch in the cemetery taking flowers to his wife's grave and he poked me in the eye and hit Laura after her mother died, and he said there wasn't enough room in our lot for all of us," Shelley said furiously.

"Where is he? I'm going to kill the man yet," Battle cried, jumping to his feet.

"I forgot the string for Howard's altar," Shelley said tremulously, and ran to the door in tears and cried pausing there against the wall. Bluet ran in and hid her face in her skirt.

"Shut up if you want me to kill him!" cried Battle.

"Remember, dear, he's the smartest man in the Delta," Ellen said, and he sat down again truculently.

"He is not!" Shelley sobbed.

"Don't cry! He's any old fool," Troy exclaimed suddenly. His face was glowing-red and concerned; could it be that he had never seen Shelley cry before? There was a feeling in the room, too, that this was the first time he had ever addressed Shelley directly.

"He's a fool, a fool, a fool!" Laura cried in triumph, hopping forward.

Ellen felt a stab of pain to see her. It seemed to her that being left motherless had made little Laura feel *privileged*. Laura was almost dancing around Troy.

Shelley, with a fresh burst of tears, ran out of the parlor.

"Troy," Aunt Tempe said, leaning her cheek on her forefinger, "you are speaking of one of our closest friends, a noble Delta doctor that has brought virtually every Fairchild in this room into the world."

"Laura McRaven," Battle was saying rapidly, "go directly and wash your mouth out with soap. You know better than to call anybody a fool. Your mother told you that."

"Old Dr. Murdoch, I despise him," said Laura, preening for one more moment.

"Who doesn't?" said Aunt Shannon, with lucid eyes.

"You could have cussed him out if you wanted to, and we'd all listened. But you call him a fool, or anybody in the Yazoo-Mississippi Delta a fool, and I'll blister your behind good for you. Switch for that right in this room. Now march in the kitchen and tell Roxie to wash your mouth out with soap. And tell her to hurry and get something on the table. You contradicted your aunt, too."

"Yes, sir. He stood on my mother's grave!" said Laura, and opened her mouth and cried. That was not quite true, but at the moment she thought she could go out crying if Shelley could.

She waited for Uncle Battle to clap his hands together and shoo her. But it was Troy's words that hung in the parlor air, not hers. Aunt Tempe, it was easy to see, had made up her mind about him. Troy, who stood with his feet apart on the hearth rug, with his eyes a little cast up, was capable of calling the Fairchilds some name or other too, without much trouble, the way he spoke up. Laura had to go get her mouth washed out with soap for *Troy*.

"Well," said Ellen. "We'd better eat, if we're so righteous. I'm *certain* Dabney's back with the groceries. Don't I hear Roxie's bell?"

Sure enough, as if in answer, the dinner bell rang.

"Here I am!" cried Dabney, rushing in radiant in a fresh blue dress, closing her little blue ruffled parasol as she came.

"You all can come to some old crumbs and scraps," said Roxie in the door. She looked hardest at Dabney and said, "Lucky for you we can wring a chicken and had a *ham* left."

"I forgot the groceries," Dabney whispered to Troy as she kissed him.

There was a new commotion in the hall. It was Pinck.

"Uncle Pinck!"

"Did you get the shepherdess crooks?" asked Aunt Tempe forthrightly from across the room.

"Tempe, I didn't," said Uncle Pinck. "I tried, God knows—couldn't even *find* the place. However, Dabney, look in front of the house."

Dabney ran to the window. "A Pierce-Arrow? Oh, Uncle Pinck, you shouldn't!"

"Well, I couldn't get the damn crooks," said Uncle Pinck.

"I thought Uncle Pinck was a man of influence," said India anxiously.

They laughed affectionately at Aunt Tempe. That was what she thought.

"But, oh, I'd so much rather have my shepherdess crooks!" Dabney cried at the window.

"Well! All I can say is, Pinck Summers didn't give his own baby grandson a Pierce-Arrow," Aunt Tempe said.

Uncle Pinck was going around kissing everybody, his prematurely white hair bobbing, bending down with his handsome lips and his sober breath.

"No matter what anybody omits or commits in September, good people," he said, and kissed Aunt Tempe loudly, "it's because: it's hot as fluzions."

Aunt Tempe hit him with the Chinese fan from Inverness.

5

At first Robbie thought wildly that they were making a to-do over her return. From the porch she smelled the floors just waxed, and at the windows saw the curtains standing out stiff-starched, and flowers even in the umbrella stand. Then she remembered once more—Dabney was getting married.

Of course George was not in the hammock! There was no sign of him or of any Fairchild. There was not even a sound, except the tinkle of chandelier prisms in the hall breeze. They were probably back there eating—they always were. She reached inside and tapped with the knocker on the open door—an absurdly tiny sound to get into that big house. Nobody answered the door at all. They were all back there in oblivion, eating.

Immediately, from within the house, a burst of unmistakable dinner-table laughter rose and went round its circle. The Fairchilds! She would make them hear. She beat on the screen door and on the thick side lights with her small fist, in which were wrinkled up together a wet handkerchief and a pinch of verbena she had taken from the front gate.

Little Uncle came toward the door, and then backed up and called Roxie through the back porch. Miss Robbie, the one Mr. George threw himself away on, stood knocking.

Roxie came and let her in, and for a moment Robbie nearly wavered. Everybody would be hard to confront at noon dinner. Suppose she just fainted? That would scare George. Roxie, her hands out like baby wings, turned and tiptoed, absurdly, down into the dining room. Robbie could hear what was said.

"Miss Ellen, surprise. Miss Robbie cryin' at de do'."

"Well! Good evening." That was Miss Tempe, all right, in the austere voice she admitted surprise with.

"Well, tell her quickly to come on back in the dining room and have dessert with us, Roxie," said Ellen. Of course as if nothing had happened! No shout from George, no sign.

Robbie came through the dining-room archway a little blindly—she had collided with Vi'let carrying an armload of fresh-pressed evening dresses up the hall. But George was not in here. "Where's George?" she asked.

"Say! Where's George?" asked Troy suddenly, looking up and down the table.

"At the Grove eating Aunt Primrose's guinea fowl," said India or somebody.

"He's left out for the Grove," Troy said, squinting up at Robbie, as if his eyes flinched.

"That booger! Did he know you were coming?" asked Battle, glancing up at her with bright eyes above the napkin he put to his lips.

She tried to shake her head, while Little Battle was dragging a chair up to the table for her, and Mr. Battle and Mr. Pinck and the boys were getting to their feet. "Won't you have some dinner? You must have some dinner," Ellen said anxiously, but "No, thanks," Robbie said. They all insisted on getting her kiss, passing and turning her from one to the other around the table. "Oh, Aunt Robbie, I love you, you're so pretty," said Ranny. Then Roxie was clearing off. They had been eating chicken and ham and dressing and gravy, and good, black snap beans, greens, butter beans, okra, corn on the cob, all kinds of relish, and watermelon-rind preserves, and that good bread—their plates were loaded with corncobs and little piles of bones, and their glasses drained down to blackened leaves of mint, and the silver bread baskets lined with crumbs.

"Won't you change your mind?" Ellen begged earnestly. But Robbie said, "No, thank you, ma'am."

Then Roxie was putting a large plate of whole peaches in syrup and a slice of coconut cake in front of her—she was seated between Shelley and Dabney—and bringing more tea in, and Mr. Battle was going on in a loud, sibilant voice which he used for reciting "Denis's poetry."

> "You shun me, Chloe, wild and shy,
>   As some stray fawn that seeks its mother
>   Through trackless woods. If spring winds sigh
>   It vainly strives its fears to smother.
>
> "The trembling knees assail each other
>   When lizards stir the brambles dry;—
>   You shun me, Chloe, wild and shy,—"

"Where have you been, Aunt Robbie?" asked Laura.

> "As some stray fawn that seeks its mother.
>
> And yet no Libyan lion I—"

"Battle," said Ellen.

> "—No ravening thing to rend another!
>   Lay by your tears, your tremors dry . . ."

"Try your nice peach—you look so hot," Ellen whispered, pointing.

Then a silence fell, like the one after a flock of fall birds has gone over. Uncle Pinck Summers, who had passed Robbie at forty miles an hour in the road and covered her with a cloud of his dust, stared at her as if in clever recognition. Robbie had worn a dust-colored pongee dress, bought in Memphis, with a red silk fringed sash, and on the side of her hair a white wool tam-o'shanter—but what could get as many wrinkles just from sitting down in some little hot place, as pongee? She felt wrinkled in her soul. And she trembled at the mention of lizards; they ran up your skirt.

"Well, my dear, I suppose wherever you were, your invitation to the wedding reached you," Miss Tempe said. "And you made up your mind to accept!"

"I'm afraid you just missed George," Ellen said, all afresh, and added in haste, "He happened to go to eat dinner with his sisters at the Grove—but he'll be back. He always takes a nap here—where it's quiet."

"He must have gone another way, then. I saw every inch of the road," Robbie said aloud, without meaning to.

"We didn't quite expect you," Battle said heavily, again over the folds of his napkin.

The family were having just a pieced dessert, without George to fix something special for—some of Primrose's put-up peaches and the crumbs of the coconut cake; Ellen was sorry Robbie had picked just this time. "Wouldn't you *try* a little dinner? Let me *still* send for a plate for you. You don't like the peaches!"

"No, thank you, Mrs. Fairchild." *why not "Ellen"*

"There's plenty more food! Enough for a regiment if they walked in!" Dabney was saying with a new, over-bright smile she had—was it her married smile, that she would practice like that?

"I'm not to say hungry," Robbie said. She bent over her plate and tried to take a spoonful of her whole peach while they all looked at her, or looked at Ellen.

This child was so unguarded—in an almost determined way. She would come, not timidly at all, into Shellmound at a time like this! Shelley sat actually cringing, while Dabney was giving her mother a conspirator's look, as if they should have expected this. Aunt Tempe's elevated brows signaled to Ellen. As if she would ever truly run away and leave him! Ellen could have asked Tempe: she never would. She would say she would, to have them thinking of explanations, racking their brains, at a time like this, and then run back and show herself to make fools of them all. *like a stand off or duel someone always loses*

Aunt Shannon gazed out the window, at a hummingbird in the abelias, but Aunt Mac sat up stiffly; it would show the upstart a thing or two if they ceased being polite and got anything like a scene over with at once.

Only Mary Lamar had excused herself, some moment or other, and beyond call again in her music was playing a nocturne—like the dropping of rain or the calling of a bird the notes came from another room, effortless and endless, isolated from them, yet near, and sweet like the guessed existence of mystery. It made the house like a nameless forest, wherein many little lives lived privately, each to its lyric pursuit and its shy protection. . . .

Ellen saw Shelley look at the girl failing at her peach and say nothing to her. And Robbie was scarcely listening to anything that was being said (Orrin was politely telling her about the longest snake he had ever seen). She would only look down and try to eat her peach. She was suffering. Her eyelids fell and opened tiredly over her just-dried eyes. The intensity of her face affected Ellen like a grimace.

When Ellen was nine years old, in Mitchem Corners, Virginia, her mother had run away to England with a man and stayed three years before she came back. She took up her old life and everything in the household went on as before. Like an act of God, passion went unexplained and undenied—just a phenomenon. "Mitchem allows one mistake." That was the saying old ladies had at Mitchem Corners—a literal business, too. Ellen had grown up not especially trusting appearances, not soon enough suspecting, either, that other people's presence and absence were still the least complicated elements of what went on underneath. Not her young life with her serene mother, with Battle, but her middle life—knowing all Fairchilds better and seeing George single himself from them— had shown her how deep were the complexities of the everyday, of the family, what caves were in the mountains, what blocked chambers, and what crystal rivers that had not yet seen light.

Ellen sighed, giving up trying to make Robbie eat; but she felt that perhaps that near-calamity on the trestle was nearer than she had realized to the heart of much that had happened in her family lately—as the sheet lightning of summer plays in the whole heaven but presently you observe that each time it concentrates in one place, throbbing like a nerve in the sky.

"Roxie, bring us just a *little* more iced tea," she called, as if she asked a boon.

Then a little jumpily they all drank tea while Robbie turned her peach over and over in the plate.

"Do you start to school next year, Little Battle?" Lady

Clare broke the silence in a peremptory conversational voice nearly like Aunt Tempe's.

"Yes, but I *hate* to start!" cried Little Battle.

"Well—why don't you cut your stomach out?"

"I'm going to take you out of here," said Aunt Tempe, motionless.

"Oh, Troy," India said, leaning forward so that she could watch Shelley, Dabney, and Laura, all three, "did you eat the cake Dabney sent you? How did it taste?"

"This isn't the time to speak of the cake," Troy said, and stared back at India. She giggled, and cutting her eye at Shelley said contritely, "Oh, me."

But suddenly Lady Clare, her fiery Buchanan hair spangling her Fairchild forehead, put out her tongue straight at Robbie and pulled down red eyelids. "This is the way *you* look!"

"You almost ruined my wedding!" cried Dabney, and then as if in haste she had said the wrong thing she put her hand comically to her lips. "I couldn't get married right if George wasn't as happy as I am!" she said, leaning intensely toward Robbie, as if to appeal to her underlying chivalry.

"*Why* have you treated George Fairchild the way you have?" said Tempe across from her. "Except for Denis Fairchild, the sweetest man ever born in the Delta?"

"How could you?" Shelley suddenly gushed forth tears, and Orrin had to get his dry handkerchief out for her and run around the table with it.

Robbie drew in her shoulders, to give Shelley room, and looked with burning eyes at the slick yellow peach she had not made a dent in. What vanity was here! How vain and how tenacious to vanity, as to a safety, Shelley and Dabney and all were! What they felt was *second*. They had something else in them first, themselves, that core she knew well enough, why not?—it was like a burning string in a candle, and *then* they felt. But it was a second thing—not all one thing! The Fairchilds! The way that Dabney rode her horse, when she thought herself unseen!

Robbie was not afraid of them. She felt first—or perhaps she was all one thing, not divided that way—and let them kill her, with her wrinkled dress, and with never an acre of land among the Reids, and with a bad grief because of them, but she felt. She had never stopped for words to feelings—she felt only—with no words. But their smile had said more plainly than words, Bow down, you love our George, enter on your knees and we will pull you up and pet and laugh at you fondly for it—we can! We will bestow your marriage on you, little Robbie, that we sent to high school!

"Do you like butter?" asked a soft voice.

"Yes," said Robbie, looking around the table, not quite sure from which direction that had come.

"Then go sit in the gutter," said Ranny.

"Excuse yourself and leave the table, Ranny," said Battle.

"Oh, let him stay, Papa, he was trying to be *nice*," said Orrin and Roy together.

"Now you think up one," said Ranny to Robbie.

"I can think up one," growled Battle. "Why isn't George here where he belongs? What are we all going to do, sit here crying and asking riddles? Excuse me! That boy's *never* here, come any conceivable hell or high water!"

How unfair! Why, it's the exact opposite of the truth! Robbie looked up at Battle furiously. That's always when George is here—holding it off for you, she thought. If *he* were here and I came in he would make everything fine—so fine I couldn't even say a word . . . and never tell them what I think of them . . .

All at once Vi'let came calling out in a lilting voice down the stairs and appeared in the doorway with both arms raised. "Bird in de house! Miss Rob' come in lettin' bird in de house!"

"Bird in de house mean death!" called Roxie instantly from the kitchen. She ran in from the other door, and the Negroes simultaneously threw their white aprons over their heads.

"It does mean that," said Troy thoughtfully. He pushed back his chair and slowly removed his coat and pushed a sleeve up. "A bird in the house is a sign of death—my mammy said so, proved it. We better catch her and get her out."

The Fairchilds jumped up buoyantly from their chairs. Orrin was the first out of the room, with the men next, and the children next, then Dabney and Shelley. Ellen looked after them. It was not anything but pure distaste that made them run; there was real trouble in Robbie's face, and the Fairchilds simply shied away from trouble as children would do. The beating of wings could be heard. Frantically the girls ran somewhere, their hands pressed to their hair. The chase moved down the hall—seemingly up the back stairs. . . . . "Get it out! Get it out!" Shelley called, and Little Battle called after her, "Get it! Get it!"

"*I* shall go to the kitchen and make a practice cornucopia for tomorrow," said Aunt Tempe rather grandly. "I am too short of breath to chase birds, neither am I as superstitious as my brother, or my nephews and nieces. Will you excuse me, Ellen?"

And only Aunt Mac and Ellen were left to attend to Robbie now. No, Aunt Shannon did rock on in her corner; George had brought her, when he came (stopping to remember her always!), something fresh to embroider on.

Robbie did not seem to know whether she had let the bird in or not; she did not know what she had done. Running out, the children wore smiles in their excitement and even took a moment to look expectantly at Robbie, who stood up. They left their mother in the dining room with the little figure of wretchedness, who stood up staunch as the Bad Fairy, and cried, "I won't fool a minute longer with that round peach!" *great*

Aunt Mac moved into a comfortable rocker and even eyed the peony-flowered bag that held her Armenian knitting. Stone-deaf as she was, she probably neither divined nor cared that there was a bird in the house, but she knew enough not to knit. She gave a positive nod, a little cock, of her top-knotted head and made her curls bounce.

Ellen looked sighing from Aunt Mac to Robbie. Mr. Judge Reid, a Justice of the Peace, was her father; he was dead now—Dr. Murdoch threw up his hands on the case, in public, years before he died, he had some hopeless thing. "I don't see why you don't shoot yourself," he said. Mr. Judge had married Irene Swanson, the daughter of Old Man Swanson; she was trying to be a schoolteacher. Old Man Swanson was an old fellow at the compress, who stuttered. Every little boy in this part of the Delta proverbially cut up by talking and walking like Old Man Swanson. They could all hobble, the way his back hurt, into the store and ask for some s-s-s-sweet s-s-s-s-s-spirits o' niter. And mock him, little boys and their little boys, eventually to his own granddaughter working there; Robbie tried to be a schoolteacher too (the lower grades), but her sister Rebel had run off with that drunkard, and of course the board had thrown her out. George, who had not seemed to mind courting over the counter, as Battle called it, must have had to listen to that deathless joke of poor Old Man Swanson's stutter a thousand times, right through his kisses.

"Don't clear off now—little while yet," Aunt Mac called toward the Negro-deserted kitchen. "Of course you only married George for his money," she continued without a break, in that comfortable sort of voice in which this statement is always made.

Robbie answered, lifting her voice politely to the deaf, "No, ma'am. I married him because he begged me!" Then she sat down, in the dining-room chair with its carved basket of blunt roses that always prodded the shoulder blades at emphatic moments.

To be begged to give love was something that she could not have conceived of by herself, and she assumed no one else could conceive of it. Now for a moment it struck Robbie and also Ellen humbly to earth, for it implied a magnitude, a bounty, that could leave people helpless. Robbie knew that now, still, George in getting her back would start all over with her love, as if she were shy. It was his way—as if he took long trips away from her which she did not know about, and then came back to her as to a little spring where he had somehow cherished only the hope for the refreshment that all the time flowed boundlessly enough. As if in his abounding, laughing life, he had not really expected much to his lips! Well, she was always the same, the way a little picnic spot would remain the same from one summer to the next, under its south-riding moon, and he was the different and new, the picnicker, the night was the different night.

Luckily Aunt Mac did not hear Robbie's answer, or suppose there could be one; she was an old lady. But the Fairchilds half-worshiped alarm, and Ellen knew just how they would act if they could hear Robbie say "He begged me"—as well as if they had never left the room. It was a burden of responsibility, the awareness that had come to supply her with the Fairchild accompaniment and answer to everything happening, just as if they all were present, that unpredictable crowd; the same as, thinking in the night, she referred to Battle's violent and intricate opinions when his sleeping body lay snoring beside her.

Now when Robbie said "He begged me," and sat down, Ellen could see in a mental tableau the family one and all fasten an unflinching look upon George. . . . It was a look near to reproach, though George, exactly like little Ranny, would sit innocent or ignorant in the matter of reproach, blind to the look, but listening with great care for what would come next. The most rambunctious of the Fairchild men could all be extremely affected by nervous changes around them, things they could not see, and put on a touching protective serenity at those times, a kind of scapegoat grace, which only reminded Ellen of pain—as when Dr. Murdoch, a rough man, set Orrin's broken arm and Orrin quite visibly filled himself with blissful trust to meet the pain he thought was coming. . . . The family of course had always acknowledged by an exaggerated and charming mood of capitulation toward George that George was mightily importunate—yet they had to reproach him, something made them or let them, and they would reproach him surely that they had never been granted the sight of him begging a thing on earth. Quite the contrary! Surely he took for granted! So he begged love— George? Love that he had more of than the rest of them put together? He begged love from Robbie! They would disbelieve.

"Then he risked his life for—for—and you all let him! *Dabney* knew the train was coming!"

"Now, listen here, Robbie, we all love Georgie, no matter how we act or he acts," said Ellen. "And isn't that all there is to it?" All of a sudden, she felt tired. She was never surer that all loving Georgie was not the end of it; but to hold back hurt and trouble, shouldn't it just now be enough? She had said so, anyway—as if she were sure.

But she sighed. There was a tramping upstairs and around corners, a sudden whistle of flight in the stair well, the tripping cries of her daughters in laughter or flight, and then vaguely to Ellen's ears it all mingled with the further and echoing sounds of a worse alarm. Dimly there seemed to be again in her life a bell clanging trouble, starting at the Grove, then at their place, the dogs beginning to clamor, the Negroes storming the back door crying, and the great rush out of this room, like the time there was a fire at the gin.

"Get it out! Get it out!" It was one cry, long lasting, half delight, half distress, all challenge.

"He won't be pulled to pieces over something he did, and so he ran away," said Robbie, her voice suddenly full. "Sure I came here to fight the Fairchilds—but he wasn't even here when I came. *Shelley* warned him. All the Fairchilds run away."

"Where have you been, Robbie Reid?" asked Aunt Mac. "You've got a piece of cotton or a feather, one, in your hair." Aunt Shannon with rising voice hummed a girlhood ballad.

"There is a fight and it's come between us, Robbie," said Ellen, her voice calm and a little automatic. "But it's not over George, we won't have it. And how that would hurt him, and shame him, to think it was, he's so gentle. It's not right to make him be pulled to pieces, and over something he did, and very honorably did. There's a fight *in* us, already, I believe—*in* people on this earth, not between us, and there is a fight in Georgie too. It's part of being alive, though you may think he cannot be pulled to pieces."

Another near flutter of wings, a beating on walls, was in the air; but the throbbing softly insinuated in a strange yet familiar manner the sound of the plantation bells being struck and the school bell and the Methodist Church bell ringing, and cries from the scene of the fire they all ran to, cries somehow more joyous than commiserating, though it threatened their ruin.

Robbie stood up again. Her poor wrinkled dress clung to her, and her face was pale as she said, "If there's a fight in George, I think when he loves me he really hates you—hates the Fairchilds that he's one of!"

"But the fight in you's over things, not over people," said Ellen gently. "Things like the truth, and what you owe people.—Yes, maybe he hates some thing in us, I think you're right—right."

But Aunt Mac was answering Robbie too, knocking her folded fan on the arm of her chair. "You'll just have to go on back if you're going to use ugly words in here," she was saying. "You're in Shellmound now, Miss Robbie, but I know where you were brought up and who your pa and your ma were, and anything you say don't amount to a row of pins."

"Aunt Mac Fairchild!" said Robbie, lifting her voice again, and turning to the old lady her intense face. "Mrs. Laws! You're all a spoiled, stuck-up family that thinks nobody else is really in the world! But they are! You're just one plantation. With a little crazy girl in the family, and listen at Miss Shannon. You're not even rich! You're just medium. Only four gates to get here, and your house needs a coat of paint! You don't even have one of those little painted wooden niggers to hitch horses to!"

"Get yourself a drink of water, child," said Aunt Mac, through her words. "You'll strangle yourself. And talk louder. Nobody's going to make me wear that hot ear-phone, not in September!"

"Of course not, dear heart!" Aunt Shannon remarked.

Robbie sank into her chair and leaned, with her little square nails white on her small brown fingers, against the side of the table. "My sister Rebel is right. You're either born spoiled in the world or you're born not spoiled. And people keep you that way until you die. *The people you love* keep you the way you are." _no escape_

"Why, Robbie," said Ellen. "If you weren't born spoiled, George has certainly spoiled you, I can *see* he has. And I've been thinking you were happy, surely happy."

"But he went to the Grove for dinner, when Miss Primrose had guinea for him, he couldn't stay for me! *Troy* knew I was coming!"

"If George knew you were coming, it was his deepest secret," said Ellen. "He just went to his dinner, he had a royal meal waiting for him at the Grove, and he went and ate it like any man, a sensible human being."

"He always goes to you. He always goes when you call him," said Robbie. "If *Bluet* would call him!" Her small fingers, with one of Mashula's rings, curled into fists in the cake crumbs over the cloth, and then opened out and waited as Ellen spoke.

"But George loves us! Of course he comes. George loves a great many people, just about everybody in the Delta, if you would count them. Don't you know that's the mark of a fine man, Robbie? Battle's like that. Denis was even more, even more well-loved. Why, George loves countless people."

"No, he doesn't!" Robbie looked at her frantically, as if Ellen had told her just what she feared. "I'm going to l-leave out of here," she said, with a sob like a little stutter in her words. "Mr. Doolittle. He loves him," she said seemingly to herself, to mystify herself.

"Well. You love George," Ellen told her, as if there were no mystery there. There was a faint little scream from a bedroom, ending in laughter—Dabney's.

Robbie looked around the room fatalistically—was she too imagining all the Fairchilds' rapt faces? "Maybe he didn't run away from me," she said. "But he let me run away from him. That's just as bad! Oh, I wish I was dead." Her brown eyes went wide.

A boy's gleeful cry rose from upstairs, from Ellen's and Battle's room. "Don't," Ellen whispered, not to Robbie. Then she could hear—from where, now, it did not matter—the most natural and yet the most terrible thing possible to hear just now—laughter, laughter filled with the undeniable music of relief.

Robbie flinched—at her own words, perhaps.

"Don't you die. You love George," Ellen told her. "He's such a splendid boy, and we have all of us always honored him so." She leaned back.

"It's funny," Robbie said then, her voice gentle, almost confiding. "Once I tried to be like the Fairchilds. I thought I knew how." When there was no answer from Ellen, she went on eagerly and yet sadly, "Don't any other people in the world feel like me? I wish I knew. Don't any people somewhere love other people so much that they want to be—not like—but the same? I wanted to turn into a Fairchild. It wasn't that I thought you were so wonderful. And I had a living room for him just like Miss Tempe's. But that isn't what I mean.

"But you all—you don't ever turn into anybody. I think you are already the same as what you love. So you couldn't understand. You're just loving yourselves in each other—

yourselves over and over again!" She flung the small brown hand at the paintings of melons and grapes that had been trembling on the wall from the commotion in the house, forgetting that they were not portraits of Fairchilds in this room, and with a circle of her arm including the two live old ladies too. "You still love *them*, and they still love you! No matter what you've all done to each other! You don't need to know how to love anybody else. Why, you couldn't love *me*!"

She gave a daring little laugh, and let out a sigh that was a kind of appeal after it. Ellen sat up straight with an effort. In the room's stillness, in Aunt Mac's stare and Aunt Shannon's sweet song, the absence of the Fairchilds and the quiet seemed almost demure, almost perverse. There was a festive little clatter from Tempe in the pantry, laughter coming downstairs.

Then there was George in the door, staring in.

Ellen got up and took hold of the back of her chair, for she felt weak. She held herself up straight, for she felt ready to deliver some important message to George, since he had come back. She was moved from her lethargy, from hearing things, a fluttering in the house like a bodily failing, by a quality of violation she felt quivering alive in Robbie, and looking at George she grew courageous in his implied strength. Yet in the same moment, for her eyes, he stood with his shirt torn back and his shoulders as bare (she thought in a cliché of her girlhood) as a Greek god's, his hair on his forehead as if he were intoxicated, unconscious of the leaf caught there, looking joyous. "Is it out? Is the fire out?" she asked. Her hand held tightly to little Laura McRaven's blue hair ribbon that lay caught over the chair back, flung behind her. Then, "Georgie," she said, "don't let them forgive you, for anything, good or bad. Georgie, you've made this child suffer."

The Yellow Dog had not run down George and Maureen; Robbie had not stayed away too long; Battle had not driven Troy out of the Delta; no one realized Aunt Shannon was out of her mind; even Laura had not cried yet for her mother. For a little while it was a charmed life. . . . And after giving George an imploring look in which she seemed to commit herself even further to him and even more deeply by wishing worse predicaments, darker passion, upon all their lives, Ellen fell to the floor.

6

Primrose and Jim Allen came in through the archway behind George, wearing their Sunday hats, and both gave little
screams—first the little screams of mild surprise or greeting
with which they always entered Shellmound, and then second
screams of dismay. "Oh, Primrose," said Jim Allen, and stopping still they shook their flowered heads at each other as if
there were no more to be done.

Tempe, coming that instant into the room with a pastry
cornucopia on a napkin, shrieked to hear her sisters and then
to see Ellen being lifted in George's arms. Then she said
calmly, "Fainted. I have these spells myself, semi-occasionally.
They are nothing to what I used to have as a girl.—I bet the
bird came in here!" She shuddered.

The new screams in the dining room brought in a roomful
of Fairchilds with amazing quickness. Robbie backed against
the china closet. Orrin was carrying a stunned or dead bird
in his cupped hands. The girls, fingers still darting reminis-
cently to their hair, all fell kneeling, in a stair-steps, around
the settee. George was taking off their mother's shoes. Ellen
lay with her eyes closed, and with her childlike feet propped
shallowly on the inclining end under the fern.

George pushed the children a little. He rushed from Ellen's
side to fill a glass from a decanter on the sideboard, and as he
went back to her with it, he leaned out and brushed Robbie's
wrist with his free hand. Next time he went by, for water, he
bent and kissed her rapidly, and asked in pure curiosity that
gave her a fierce feeling of joy, "Why did you throw the pans
and dishes out the window?" Then he was touching Ellen's
lips with various little glasses of stuff, frowning with con-
centration.

"I thought I saw Battle go by with a wild look, did you?"
said Tempe. "Battle! You can come in, she's not dying!"

Battle came in and roamed up and down the room and now
and then gave a touch or shake to Ellen's shoulder. Bluet
climbed up beside her mother and sang to her softly and leisurely, "Polly Wolly Doodle All the Day," crowding her a little
where she was stretched out. It was taking some time to revive
her, she was too clumsy now for other people to make easy.

There was a tight ring of Fairchilds around her. Maureen every now and then went around the table, arms pumping, long yellow hair flying.

Roxie pressed her forefinger under her nose. Poor Miss Ellen just wasn't strong enough *any longer* for such a trial. She wasn't strong enough for Miss Dabney and Miss Robbie and everything *right now*. One time before, Miss Ellen fainted away when everybody went off and left her—it was when the gin caught fire—and she had lost that little baby, that came between Mr. Little Battle and Ranny. Wasn't it pitiful to see her so white? Poor Miss Ellen at *this time*.

Robbie caught glimpses of the white face from her distance outside the ring.

"Rub her wrists, George," pleaded Battle.

It was Mrs. Fairchild's tenth pregnancy. But oh, why had she waited to faint just at this moment? Why couldn't Battle bring his own wife to? For the same reason the bird had got in the house when she came in, Robbie thought; for the reason Aunt Primrose killed her guinea fowl today for George: the way of the Fairchilds, the way of the world.

Ellen opened her eyes, then closed them again.

"I saw her peep," said Roxie. "Now then. Git to work, Vi'let, Little Uncle!"

"Half an hour," Tempe announced to Ellen, as if that would gratify a lady who had fainted.

"Oh, Mama!" cried Dabney. "Shelley, bring a pillow to prop her up."

"We caught the bird, Mama," said Ranny clearly. "It was a brown thrush. It was the female."

"It could have flown around our house all day and night with a thousand windows and never found the way out," said Little Battle. "I didn't think we was going to catch it, but Orrin caught it with Papa's hat and batted it to the wall."

Ellen opened her eyes. Orrin held out the still bird. *"Veni, vidi, vici!"* he said.

Dabney was leaning over her mother accusingly. "Mama! What happened? I know! You were upset about me."

"I'm all right," said Ellen, lifting one arm and pulling Dabney's hair low over her forehead the way she thought it looked nicer.

"Mama! Oh, Mama!"

Shelley, wordless beside Dabney, knelt on as if in a dream.

"I have the same thing, every now and then," said Aunt Tempe. "I nearly died when Mary Denis married—could scarcely be revived."

"Mama! Do you *want* me to get married?"

"Certainly she doesn't," said Tempe with surprise.

"Oh, she does too," said Primrose.

"I think about your happiness," said Ellen, in the thoughtful, slow voice of people coming out of faints.

"Oh, then!" Dabney jumped up, whirled, and with a scatter of tissue-paper and ribbons she flung wide her newest present, which somebody had put on the table ("A Point Valenciennes banquet cloth!" exclaimed Tempe. "Who from?") and pulled it to her with it spreading behind her like a peacock tail, and pranced around. Then she spread it out before her with her arms wide and smiled tenderly over it at her mother, as if from a balcony. "Don't you see you don't need to worry?" she asked, showing how wide, how fine, how much in her possession she had everything, all for her mother to see.

Shelley, getting up to look, turned on her heel, to go write in her diary. Then she turned back; belatedly, the dining room's one forlorn figure had printed itself on her mind.

"Don't you want to take a bath, Robbie?" she asked meditatively. "Where'd Little Uncle put your suitcase?"

"It got lost when I turned George's car over in a ditch and wrecked it," Robbie said, rocking gently on her high heels from one to the other.

"What?" cried George across the room, with his finger on Ellen's pulse.

"Right out of Memphis, and the day I left," Robbie said with some satisfaction.

"You haven't a stitch but what's on your back?" cried Tempe. "Fathers alive, what a state to come to a wedding in!"

George looked at Robbie intently, without smiling, across the still prancing Dabney, who marched between them.

Battle let out a generous laugh and ambled over to give Robbie a spank. "I'm going to get you a horse to ride for the next time you run away—no, a safe old mule with a bell around the neck. Hear, George?"

"Do you feel stronger?—How'd you get here?" George patted Ellen's hand. His voice for both women had an intolerant sound that made him seem trapped. Tempe made her way toward him and with a smile of mischief popped a pastry into his mouth.

"Do you know that she walked from Fairchilds?" said Ellen, turning her face toward the room. "And nobody's even offered her a bath till Shelley just now, or a place to lie down? Robbie, you lie down *here*."

George glared across the room. "What? You fought the mosquitoes clear from Fairchilds? I ought to whip you all the way home."

"By yourself? You could easily have met a mad dog," said Aunt Jim Allen, who had been able to hear all this.

"Don't chide her, Georgie," said Aunt Primrose. "She won't do it again, will you, Robbie?"

Robbie was basking a little, and fanned her face with the back of her hand.

"Well!" said Troy. "Now then. I've got to get back to East Field before dark." He picked up Aunt Tempe's cornucopia which went to bits under his thumb. "Oh-oh. Something you made me, Dabney?"

Dabney was still prancing—she seemed to see nobody in the room, and was smiling with her lower lip caught under her pretty teeth. "Dabney can't cook!" Tempe and several more cried together.

"She evermore can't," said Troy.

"I'm awfully sorry *I* can," said Aunt Tempe severely.

" 'Fare thee well,' " sang Bluet, patting her mother with soft raps like drum beats, her eyes gazing blissfully at Dabney in the glittering train. " 'Fare thee well, fare thee well, my fairy fay . . .' "

"The right place for a tablecloth is on a table, though," said somebody—Troy. He gazed at Dabney, side-stepped her path, and left the room.

7

"Want to get out?" asked Roy, just outside the dining-room arch. He and Laura both stood there, chins ducked. "Come on, Laura." He had seen a lady's hand reach out and pull his father in.

"All right." She loved Roy—his scars, bites, scabs and bandages, and intricate vaccination—his light eyes and his sunburn, little berry-colored nipples. The minute he was out of the dining room he was with a visible flash naked to the waist, flat and neat as a hinge in his short pants with the heavy leather belt that was too big around for him, so that he seemed to walk stepping in a tub. Roy was eight. He still shivered to hear the hounds in the night. He was giving her an intent, sizing-up look.

"You'll have to tote my turtle," he said. "The whole time, and keep him right side up and not set him down anywhere, if you come with me."

"Oh, I will," Laura promised, shuddering.

"You'll have to wait till I find him, so you can carry him."

India skipped out, her heavy straight hair swinging behind like a rope; she carried a stack of crackers in her mouth and skipped from side to side, going off to eat by herself.

"Do you want to come, India?" asked Roy, running up with his turtle.

"No," said India, who could talk plainly with anything in her mouth. "Do you want Maureen to come?"

"O-nay, I-day on't-day."

"Let's all the girls go sit in the chinaberry tree and see who is the one can make their crackers last the longest," said Lady Clare, coming out; she seemed tired—company always was.

"You have to chunk at Maureen, or she'll come." India picked up a stone and threw it.

"Don't hit her," said Laura.

"You *can't* hit her," said India scornfully.

"India, let us take Bluet!" said Roy crazily.

"Take me," said Bluet, clasping Roy around the knees and kissing them fervently.

"Not this time, Roy. I need her here." They all skipped off except Maureen, who did not go away but did not come either, this time. She only threatened, taking stamping steps forward with one foot.

They ran down to the bayou, the turtle in Laura's hands bouncing against her diaphragm. Roy went between two close Spanish daggers and she went after him. The bayou had a warm breath, like a person.   *an image*

"Is that your boat?" cried Laura.

"It's as much mine as anybody's. I'll take you for a row if you get in," said Roy, stepping in himself.

The boat was in a willow shadow, floating parallel to the bank—dark, unpainted, the color of the water. She would have to step deep. A fishing bucket was in it, and also one oar where a dark line of water went like a snake along the bottom. "Here's the other oar," she said; it was resting on a dogwood tree. She stepped down in, and he instructed her to sit at the other end of the boat and be quiet. "I know how," said Laura. On her lap the turtle looked out. Roy pushed off, his old tennis shoes splashed water which ran under her sandals, and he sat down and looked nowhere, frowning in the sun. The boat was cut loose but almost still, for as a current urges a boat on, the lack of current seems to pull it back, not let go. Laura could not see beyond a willow branch that hung in her face. Then with a gruff noise the oars went into the water, with the unwilling-looking, casual movement of Roy's arm. The water was quieter than the land anywhere.

"Let me row," said Laura.

"Be quiet," said Roy. He took his tennis shoes slowly off and put them on the little seat between them. He hooked his toes. At the stroke of his oars a shudder would interrupt the smoothness of their motion.

The bayou was narrow and low and soon the water's edge was full of cypress trees. They went in heavy shade. There were now and then muscadines hanging in the air like little juicy balls strung over the trees beside the water, and they rode staring up, Roy with his mouth open, hoping that grapes might fall. Then leaves cut out like stars and the early red color of pomegranates lay all over the water, and imperceptibly they came out into the river. The water looked like the floor of the woods that could be walked on.

"Are we going down the river?" asked Laura.

"Sure. And the Yazoo River runs into the Mississippi River."

"And it runs into the sea," said Laura, but he would say no more.

As they went down the Yazoo, a long flight of ducks went over, going the way they were going, the V very high in the sky, very long and thin like a ribbon drawn by a finger through the air, but neither child said anything, and after a long time the ducks were a little wrinkle deep down in the sky and then out of sight.

On the other side of the river from where they had come, facing them, Laura saw what they were getting to, a wonderful house in the woods. It was twice as big as Shellmound. It was all quiet, and unlived in, surely; the dark water was going in front of it, not a road.

"Look," she said.

Roy glanced over his shoulder and nodded.

"Let's go in!"

There was a dark waterlogged landing, and Roy got the boat to it neatly and ran the chain around a post. He jumped out of the boat and Laura climbed out after him. "Bring my turtle, remember," he said. She brought it, like a hot covered dish. They were in a wood level with the water, dark cedar trees planted in some pattern, some of them white with clematis. It looked like moonlight.

"Why, here's Aunt Studney, way over here!" cried Roy. "Hi, Aunt Studney!"

Laura remembered Aunt Studney, coal-black, old as the hills, with her foot always in the road; on her back she carried a big sack that nearly weighted her down. There at a little distance, near the house, she was walking along, laboring and saying something.

"Ain't studyin' you."

"That's what she says to everybody—even Papa," said Roy. "Nobody knows what she's got in the sack."

"Nobody in the world?"

"I said nobody."

"Where does she live?" asked Laura a little fearfully.

"Oh, back on our place somewhere. Back of the Deadening. You'll see her walking the railroad track anywhere between Greenwood and Clarksdale, Aunt Studney and her sack."

"Are you scared of Aunt Studney?" asked Laura.

"No. Yes, I am."

"I despise Aunt Studney, don't you?"

"Papa's scared of her too. Me, I think that's where Mama gets all her babies."

"Aunt Studney's sack?"

"Sure."

"Do you think *Ranny* came out of that sack?"

"Sure. . . . I don't know if *I* came out of it, though." Roy gave her a hard glance, and looked as if he might put his fist to her nose.

"I wonder if she'd let *me* look in—Aunt Studney," said Laura demurely.

"Of course not! If she won't let any of *us* look in, even Papa, you know she won't let *you* walk up and look in."

"Do you dare me to ask her?"

"All right, I dare you."

"Double-dog-dare me."

"I just dare you."

"Aunt Studney, let me look in your sack!" screamed Laura, taking one step in front of Roy and waiting with open mouth.

"Ain't studyin' you," said Aunt Studney instantly.

She stamped on, like an old wasp over the rough, waggling her burden.

"Look! She's going in Dabney's house!" cried Roy.

"Is this Dabney's house?" cried Laura.

"Cousin Laura, you don't know anything."

"All right: maybe she's gone in to open her sack."

"If she does, we'll run off with what's in it!"

"Oh, Roy. That would be perfect."

"Be quiet," said Roy. "How do you know?"

"All right: you go in front."

They went up an old drive, made of cinders, shaded by cedar and crape-myrtle trees which the clematis and the honeysuckle had taken. There were iron posts with open mouths in their heads, where a chain fence used to run. Taking the posts was a hedge that went up from the landing, higher than anybody's head, with tiny leaves nobody could count—boxwood; it was bitter-green to smell, the strong fearless fragrance of things nobody has been to see.

When they came to the house, there was a dead mockingbird on the steps. They jumped over it, Laura not looking back—dead birds lay on their sides, like people. Roy reached down and touched the bird to see how dead it was; he said it was hot. The porch was covered with leaves, like the river, and there were loose, joggling boards in it. The door was open.

Roy and Laura, Laura with the turtle against her, held in the crook of her arm now like a book, went in a vast room, the inside of a tower. Their heads fell back. Up there the roof, if there was one, seemed to fade into the light. Before them rose two stairs, wooden spirals that went up barely touching at wavery rims, little galleries on two levels, and winding into the depths of light—for Laura had a moment of dizziness and felt as if she looked into a well.

There was an accusing, panting breathing, and the thud of a big weight planted in the floor. "Look," said Laura. Aunt Studney, whom she had forgotten about, was in the middle of the room, which was quite empty of the furnishings of a house, standing over her sack and muttering.

"I know," said Roy impatiently. He was regarding the chandelier, his hands on his hips—probably wishing it would fall. Laura all at once saw what a thing it was too; it was as prominent as the stairs and came down between them. Out of the tower's round light at the top, down by a chain that looked the size of a spider's thread, hung the chandelier with its flower-shaped head covered with clusters of soft and burned-down candles, as though a great thing had sometime happened here. The whole seemed to sway, to almost start in the sight, like anything head downward, like a pendulum that would swing in a clock but no one starts it.

"Run up the stairs!" cried Roy, starting forward.

"Aunt Studney," whispered Laura.

"Well, I know!" cried Roy, as if Aunt Studney were always here on his many trips to this house.

"Did you say this was *Dabney's* house?" asked Laura. There

were closed doors in the walls all around, and leading off the galleries—but not even an acorn tea-set anywhere.

"Sure," said Roy. "Make yourself at home. Run up the stairs. (What's in your bag, Aunt Studney?)"

Aunt Studney stood holding her sack on the floor between her feet with her hands knotted together over its mouth, and peeping at them under an old hat of Mr. Battle's. Then she threw her hands up balefully. Laura flung out and ran around the room, around and around the round room. Roy did just what she did—surprising!—and so it was a chase. Aunt Studney did not move at all except to turn herself in place around and around, arms bent and hovering, like an old bird over her one egg.

"Is it still the Delta in here?" Laura cried, panting.

"Croesus, Laura!" said Roy, "sure it is!" And with a jump he mounted the stair and began to run up.

Laura probably would have followed him, but could not leave, after all, for a little piano had been placed at the foot of the stair, looking small as a fairy instrument. It was open. In gold it said "McClarty." How beautiful. She set the turtle down. She touched a white key, and it would hardly sink in at the pressure of her finger—as in dreams the easiest thing turns out to be the hard—but the note sounded after a pause, coming back like an answer—a little far-off sound. The key was warm. There was a shaft of sun here. The sun was on her now, warm, for—she looked up—the top of the tower was a skylight, and around it ran a third little balcony on which— she drew back her finger from the key she had touched—Roy was walking. And all at once Aunt Studney sounded too—a cry high and threatening like the first note of a song at a ceremony, a wedding or a funeral, and like the bark of a dog too, somehow.

"Roy, come down!" Laura called, with her hands cupped to her mouth.

But he called back, pleasure in his voice, "I see Troy riding Isabelle in Mound Field!"

"You do not!"

All at once a bee flew out at her—out of the piano? Out of Aunt Studney's sack? Everywhere! Why, there were bees inside everything, inside the piano, inside the walls. The place was alive. She wanted to cry out herself. She heard a hum everywhere, in everything. She stood electrified—and indignant.

"Troy! Troy! Look where I am!" Roy was crying from the top of the house. "I see Troy! I see the Grove—I see Aunt Primrose, back in her flowers! I see *Papa*! I see the whole creation. Look, look at me, Papa!"

"If he saw you he'd skin you alive!" Laura called to him. The bees, Aunt Studney's sack, the turtle—where was he?— and Roy running around going to fall—all at once she could not stand Dabney's house any longer.

But Roy looked down (she knew he was smiling) from the top, peering over a shaky little rail. "Aunt Studney! Why have you let bees in my house?" he called. The echoes went flying around the walls and down the stairs like something thrown down. It so delighted Roy that he cried again, "Why have you let bees in my house? Why have you let bees in my house?" and his laughter would come breaking down over them again.

But Aunt Studney only said, as if it were for the first time, "Ain't studyin' you," and held the mouth of her sack. It occurred to Laura that Aunt Studney was not on the lookout for things to put in, but was watching to keep things from getting out.

"Come back, Roy!" she called.

"Not ready!"

But at last he came down, his face rosy. "What'll you give me for coming back?" he smiled. "Aunt Studney! What's in your sack?"

Aunt Studney watched him swagger out, both hands squeezing on her sack; she saw them out of the house.

Outdoors it was silent, a green rank world instead of a playhouse.

"I'm stung," said Roy calmly. With an almost girlish bending of his neck he showed the bee sting at the nape, the still tender line of his hair. A submissive yet arrogant pleasure seemed to radiate from him, having for its source the angry little bump. Now Laura wished she had one. When they went through the deep cindery grass of the drive she saw the name Marmion cut into the stone of the carriage block.

Suddenly they cried out in one breath, "Look."

"A treasure," said Roy, calmly still. Catching the high sun in the deep grass, like a penny in the well, was a jewel. It might have been there a hundred years or a day. They looked at each other and with one accord dropped down together into the grass. Laura picked it up, for Roy, unaccountably, held back, and she washed it with spit.

Then suddenly, "Give it here," and Roy held out his hand for it. "You can't have that, it's Mama's. I'll take it back to her."

Laura gazed at it. It was a pin that looked like a rose. She knew it would be worn here—putting her forefinger to her small, bony chest. "We're where we're not supposed to be looking for anything," she said, as if something inspired her and made her clever, turning around and around with it as Roy tried to take it, holding it away and hiding it from Aunt Studney's fastening look, for Aunt Studney with her sack was suddenly hovering again. "You can't have it, you can't have it, you can't have it."

Roy chased her at first, and then seemed to consider. He looked at Laura, and the pin, at Marmion, Aunt Studney, even the position of the sun. He looked back at the river and the boat he had rowed here.

"All right," he said serenely.

They walked down and got back in the boat. They moved slowly over the water, Roy working silently against the current. Yet he seemed almost to be falling asleep rowing—he could sleep anywhere. His gaze rested a thousand miles away, and now and then, pausing, he delicately touched his bee sting. Presently he rocked the boat. He never asked even a word about his turtle.

"The only place I've ever been in the water is in the Pythian Castle in Jackson with water wings," said Laura. "Tar drops on you, from the roof."

"*What?*"

Roy dragged in the oars, got on his feet, and threw Laura in the river as if it were all one motion.

As though Aunt Studney's sack had opened after all, like a whale's mouth, Laura opening her eyes head down saw its insides all around her—dark water and fearful fishes. A face flanked by receding arms looked at her under water—Roy's, a face strangely indignant and withdrawing. Then Roy's legs drove about her—she saw Roy's tied-up toe, knew his foot, and seized hold. He kicked her, then his unfamiliar face again met hers, wide-eyed and small-mouthed and its hair streaming upwards, and his hands took her by her hair and pulled her up like a turnip. On top of the water he looked at her intently, his eyelashes thorny and dripping at her. Then he pulled her out, arm by arm and leg by leg, and set her up in the boat.

"Well, you've been in the Yazoo River now," he said. He helped her wring out her skirt, and then rowed on, while she sat biting her lip. "I *think* that's where Aunt Studney lives," he said politely once, pointing out for her through the screen of trees a dot of cabin; it was exactly like the rest, away out in a field, where there was a solitary sunflower against the sky, many-branched and taller than a chimney, all going to seed, like an old Christmas tree in the yard. Then, "I couldn't believe you wouldn't come right up," said Roy suddenly. "I thought girls floated."

"You sure don't know much. But I never have been in the water anywhere except in the Pythian Castle in Jackson with water wings," she said all over again.

They went from the river back into the bayou. Roy, asking her pardon, wrung out his pockets. At the right place, willow branches came to meet them overhead and touched their foreheads where they sat transfixed in their two ends of the boat. The boat knocked against the shore. They jumped out and ran separately forward. Laura paused and lifted up her hair, and turned on her heels in the leaves, sighing. But Roy ran up the bank, shaking the yucca bells, and disappeared in a cloud of dust.

India walked down to meet Laura and they walked up through the pecan grove toward the shady back road, with arms entwined. India was more startling than she because she was covered with transfer pictures; on her arms and legs were flags, sunsets, and baskets of red roses.

Dabney was at the gate.

"Where have you been?" asked Dabney, frowning into the sunset, in a beautiful floating dress.

"Where have *you* been?" said India. They passed in.

"It's nearly time for rehearsal. She's waiting for Troy," India said, as if her sister could not hear. On the gatepost itself sat Maureen, all dressed in another new dress (she had the most!) but already barefoot, and looking down at all of them, her fists gripped around her two big toes.

"I'm dripping wet," Laura murmured. They walked on twined together into the house. "Do you want to know why?" Mary Lamar was playing the wedding song. Laura's hand stole down to her pocket where the garnet pin had lain. For a moment she ached to her bones—it was indeed gone. It was in the Yazoo River now. How fleetingly she had held to her treasure. It seemed to her that the flight of the ducks going over had lasted longer than the time she kept the pin.

Roxie with a cry of sorrow had fallen on her knees behind Laura to take up the water that ran from her heels.

"Shelley did this," India remarked contentedly to the bent black head, and pulled up her skirt and stuck out her stomach, where the word Constantinople was stamped in curlicue letters.

"Lord God," said Roxie. "Whatever you reads it's a scandal to the jaybirds."

India, softly smiling, swayed to Laura and embraced and kissed her.

"Hold still both of you," said Battle over their heads. "No explanations either one of you." He switched them equally, his white sleeve giving out a starch smell as strong as daisies, and went up and down their four dancing legs. "A man's daughters!" He told them to go wash their separate disgraces off and be back dressed for decent company before he had to wring both their necks at one time.

"Laura!" India cried ecstatically in the middle of it. "Lady Clare's got chicken pox!"

Then she won't be the flower girl! and I can! Laura thought, and never felt the pain now, though it was renewed.

8

"Your flower girl," Aunt Tempe announced a little later at the door of the parlor, where the family were gathering for the rehearsal supper party—the clock was striking one, which meant seven—"has the chicken pox—unmistakably. She is confined to my room." She turned on her heel and marched off, but came right back again.

"Lady Clare's brought it from Memphis!" Ellen gasped. She reclined, partly, there on the horsehair love seat. Battle had told her to deck herself out and *lie* there, move at her peril.

"I have to take her to Memphis to get those Buchanan teeth straightened," Tempe said shortly. "All life is a risk, as far as that goes."

"Look out for the bridesmaids!" warned Roxie. "Miss Dab, look out for your bridesmaids and fellas!" She giggled and ran out, ducking her head with her arm comically raised before Mr. Battle. It was the children that stalked in at the door, fancily bearing down on all the canes and umbrellas in the house, Ranny at the front, Bluet at the back, with India and Laura in starchy "insertion" skirts and satin sashes falling in at the last minute.

"We're the wedding!" said Ranny. "I'm Troy! Oof, oof!" He bent over like an old man. "Shepherd crooks have come!" cried Little Battle, hooking Maureen with Aunt Mac's Sunday cane.

"Stop, Ranny, you're going to get the chicken pox," said his mother.

"Papa!" cried Dabney.

There were further cries in the yard and in the back of the house.

"Hallelujah! Hallelujah! Pinchy's come through!"

Roxie rushed in a second time, but seriously now, bringing Vi'let and embracing her, with some little black children following and appearing and disappearing in the folds of their skirts, and Little Uncle marched in with his snowiest coat standing out, and stood there remote and ordained-looking.

"Hallelujah," he said.

"Well, hallelujah," said Aunt Tempe, rather pointedly. George smiled.

Some open muffler roared in the yard.

"Dabney!" cried a chorus of voices, and the real bridesmaids ran in, in a company, all in evening dresses ready to go to the Winona dance afterwards. The boys ran in, some in blazers, and started playing with the children, lifting Ranny to the ceiling, kissing Aunt Tempe, spanking Bluet, and pulling Laura's hair.

"Oh, you all, the crooks haven't come! I'm a wreck," said Dabney in their midst.

"They'll be here tomorrow, precious," said Aunt Tempe. "They won't disappoint you, ever in this world."

"Shoo, shoo! All children git out!" shouted Battle. "We've got to rehearse this wedding in a minute, shoo!" But the children all laughed.

"Who's that?" Dickie Boy Featherstone was asking.

"Oh, Robbie," said Dabney, "this is Nan-Earl Delaney, Gypsy Randall, Deltah and Dagmar Wiggins, Charlsie Mc-Leod, Bitsy Carmichael," and she pulled all the bridesmaids forward with a fitful movement like flicking things out of a bureau drawer, "and then, there's Pokey Calloway, Dickie Boy Featherstone, and Hugh V. McLeod and Shine Young and Pee Wee Kuykendall and Red Boyne. They're in the wedding. She's my aunt-in-law—isn't that it, Mama?"

"Aunt?" said Red Boyne. "Aren't you going to the dance?"

"And you already know the best man, Robbie," said Dabney, nervously smiling. "It's George."

"Aunt Ellen," said Laura, kneeling at the love seat. "I've already had chicken pox."

"All right, dear," said her aunt. But it did not seem to occur to her that now Laura might be slipped into the wedding in the place of Lady Clare. And Laura, staring at her, suddenly wondered where, truly where, the rosy pin was. She got to her feet and backed away from her aunt slowly—she wanted to know in what wave. Now it would be in the Yazoo River, then it would be carried down to the Mississippi, then . . .

"When's that dish-faced preacher of yours coming, Ellen? Did you remind him?" said Battle, sprawling gently on a mere edge of the love seat, as if to show them all he would not take up too much room.

"This is his *business*, dear," said Ellen.

"Where's *Troy?*" cried some bridesmaid.

"We could have a little wine now," Ellen said to Shelley.

"With that excitement in the kitchen, there's no telling how or when or in what state our supper will get to us, when the rehearsing's done. Take my keys."

"Mama, they're the heaviest and most keys in the world."

"I know it! Some of them are to things I'll never be able to think of or never will see again," said Ellen.

One of those inexplicable pauses fell over the room, a moment during which Aunt Shannon's voice could be heard in another part of the house, singing "Oft in the Stilly Night." Then Ellen pulled out a key. "This one's to your father's wine, though—to the best of my knowledge. Do you know that little door?"

Robbie sat in the middle of the whirl. Where was George now—she thought she had heard his voice. . . . Something in her had taken note of every dress on Vi'let's arm even when she came storming through the door of Shellmound, and now she saw that Mary Lamar Mackey wore the Nile-green tulle that had the silver sash, and Aunt Tempe had on the Chinese coat of yellow velvet with roses and violets printed on it, the most dazzling bright spot in the room. Shelley wore the tea-rose silk dress with the gathered side panels, and Dabney the white net with the gold kid gardenia on the chest. Robbie herself had on a dress of Dabney's—a black chiffon one that felt no different from a nightgown. Mary Lamar Mackey was playing "Constantinople." The bridesmaids and groomsmen were dancing in the music room around the piano and across the hall and around the table in the dining room to cup up nuts in their hands.

"Dabney, don't you ever drag Troy over the country to the dances with you?" asked Uncle Pinck, with Aunt Tempe pinning a Maréchal Niel bud in his lapel.

"Troy wouldn't get up on the floor with me, Uncle Pinck, if it was the last thing he did on earth!" cried Dabney. She was dancing with Red Boyne. "I tell him I think he's just too big and clumsy to *learn*." It was a reason for loving him, but Uncle Pinck did not seem to understand this at once, from the bemused look that came on his face. Very daintily he took a little glass of wine—Shelley and Roy were passing it.

"You can't drink wine and not eat cake!" said Battle. "Look here. What kind of house is this?"

"It will spoil your supper afterwards, dear," said Ellen. "The rehearsal supper."

"I say let's have cake!" said Battle rambunctiously.

"Well . . . somebody will have to get it then, it looks like," said Ellen with an uncertain movement, which Battle stopped. "Roxie! Howard! Somebody!" he shouted. George moved through the room and Ellen called, "Just bring that one in the glass stand, and a sharp knife—bring more plates, those little Dabney plates."

"Are those the best?" asked Battle, falling back, and she said, "Well, they're from the Dabneys: yes."

"I'm holding back my cornucopias," said Tempe flatly. "You needn't think you'll gobble those up till the proper moment."

Mr. Rondo arrived, and not being able to make himself heard at the door, rapped on the windowpane, causing the bridesmaids to scream at that black sight through the wavery glass. Aunt Tempe insisted on his taking her chair and a little wine and even changed her mind about the cornucopias. She said she would go back and fill them with cherries.

"I'm especially pleased to see you, Mrs. Fairchild," Mr. Rondo told Robbie. "I was inquiring about you earlier in the week," and she fluffed her hair a little and faint color came in her cheeks.

"Now where's Troy?" asked Uncle Pinck. "Still, Primrose and Jim Allen haven't got here. Has anybody ever got here from the Grove less than an hour or two late?"

"Here's Troy," said Little Battle, prancing up. "I'm Troy!"

"Be Troy, Little Battle," said Battle. "Listen, Pinck. Ask him where he's from."

"Where are you from, Troy?" asked Uncle Pinck, drawling his words and bobbing his distinguished white head.

"Up near the Tennessee line," said Little Battle, in the voice of Troy. "Mighty good people up there. Have good sweet water up there, everlasting wells. Cool nights, can tolerate a sheet in summer. The land ain't what you'd call good."

"Little Battle, Little Battle," said Ellen anxiously.

"Isn't it lonesome, Troy?" prompted Battle.

"Lonesome? Not now. One of my sisters married a supervisor. Now we enjoy a mail and ice route going by two miles from the porch. Just reach down the mountain."

"Papa!" cried Shelley. "George!"

"And the road's got a bridge in, and a little sprinkle of gravel on it now. And my mammy's health is good, got a letter from her in my pocket. I'll read it to you—Dear Troy, be a good boy. I would write more but must plead company. Have called in passing to mail this for me. Your ma."

"The letter's too much!" cried Ellen, extremely upset, and addressing herself to Mr. Rondo.

But Dabney leaned on the mantelpiece, her cheek in her hand, and smiled at them all a moment; all their eyes were on her. Aunt Tempe, who had laughed till she cried, brought her the first cornucopia on the tray. "Here, dear heart." Dabney could see Troy's eyes open wide at the sight of Aunt Tempe tonight. Troy did venerate women—he thought Aunt Tempe should be home like his mammy, making a quilt or meditating words of wisdom, as he said his mother sat doing instead of getting lonesome. Dabney smiled at Aunt Tempe, who had been going to Delta dances for thirty years.

She had never put on her grown-up mind, Dabney thought fondly—as if her grown-up mind were a common old house dress Aunt Tempe would never want to be caught in. She did not want to be venerated . . . Dabney ran after her and kissed her soft, warm cheek. You never had to grow up if you were spoiled enough. It *was* comforting, if things turned out not to be what you thought. . . .

Dabney looked around the room, the big parlor where they all sat now, eating and waiting, with the western sun level with the windows now, and a hummingbird just outside drinking and suspending herself among the tall unpruned topknots of the abelias. Somewhere the dogs were barking fitfully at the guineas or the birds that had begun to fly over. . . . Her mother in a dress with a bertha was dutifully holding a tiny glass of cordial, sitting on the love seat beside her father who was leaning behind her, his brows contorted but unwavering, as though he had forgotten his expression. Maureen sat on the floor meekly bending her head to have her shining hair patted, and her mother's hand patted there. George came and stood in front of the mantelpiece, and looked out beside her.

And the bridesmaids were only there to fill up the room. . . .
"You're a genius, Tempe," said Battle, after he let her put a
cornucopia in his mouth.

Dabney gazed at them thinking, I always wondered what
they would do if I married somebody they didn't want me to.
Poor Papa is the only one really suffering. All her brothers
would try to hold her and not let her go, though, when the
time came actually to leave the house. Her mother had
fainted—but Dabney had not believed too well that the fainting counted as a genuine protest—her mother did not have
"ways." "Your mother *lacks ways*," Aunt Tempe always said
to the girls, darkly.

"Another new dress, Tempe?" asked her father, who ad-
mired Tempe very much while he ran from her voice. Aunt
Tempe hit him with her fan. "This old thing? I had it before
Annie Laurie died. . . ."

Battle, catching Dabney's eye, looked poutingly across the
room. "He didn't do it for you, eh, Robbie?" he said teasingly. Dabney looked at George, where he stood there at the
middle of the mantel, looking out, and she moved away, to
take a bite of a bridesmaid's cake.

It seemed to Ellen at moments that George regarded them,
and regarded things—just things, in the outside world—with
a passion which held him so still that it resembled indifference.
Perhaps it *was* indifference—as though they, having given him
this astonishing feeling, might for a time float away and he
not care. It was not love or passion itself that stirred him,
necessarily, she felt—for instance, Dabney's marriage seemed
not to have affected him greatly, or Robbie's anguish. But
little Ranny, a flower, a horse running, a color, a terrible story
listened to in the store in Fairchilds, or a common song, and
yes, shock, physical danger, as Robbie had discovered, roused
something in him that was immense contemplation, motionless pity, indifference. . . . Then, he would come forward all
smiles as if in greeting—come out of his intensity and give
some child a spank or a present. Ellen had always felt this in
George and now there was something of surprising kinship in
the feeling; perhaps she had fainted in the way he was driven
to detachment. In the midst of the room's commotion he
stood by the mantel as if at rest.

Robbie looking at him from across the room smiled faintly. "You were so sure of yourself, so conceited! You were so sure the engine would stop," she murmured, like a refrain, like one last refrain—they had had no time alone; here nobody had. So she spoke as though no one else but George were in the room. It was something not a one of them had ever thought of. . . . Battle groaned, then raised up on his elbow to hear more.

George stood drinking his home-made wine by the summer-closed fireplace. A tinge of joyousness pervaded him still, for Ellen, he had a rampant, presiding sort of attitude. The others had all thrown themselves down, in the soft flowered chairs, or else they danced at the room's edges, in and out the door.

"The Dog didn't hit us," George said, speaking with no mistake about it straight across them all, tenderly and undisturbedly, to Robbie. "I don't think it matters what *happens* to a person, or what comes."

"You didn't think it mattered what happened to Maureen?" Robbie lowered her eyelids. His words had hurt her. Under Ellen's hand Maureen began to chug. "Choo—choo—"

George was still a moment, then crossed the room and pressed Robbie's arms, pinned them to her side so that he seemed to hurt her more.

"To *me*! I speak for myself," he said matter-of-factly. Battle made a rude sound. "Something is always coming, you know that." For a moment George moved his gaze over the bobbing and shuttling bridesmaids to Ellen. "I don't think it matters so much in the world what. Only," he bent over Robbie with his look gone relentless—he was about to kiss her, "I'm damned if I wasn't going to stand on that track if I wanted to! Or will again."

Perhaps he is "conceited," thought Ellen tiredly.

"Ah! Doesn't that sound like his brother Denis's very words and voice?" cried Tempe, passing by with her little silver dish. "He would murder me if I contradicted him, and he loved me better than anybody in the world."

George did kiss Robbie.

"But you're everything on earth to me," Robbie said plainly. Mr. Rondo put his fingertips to his brow. With an extremely conscious, an almost brazen, power of explicitness that seemed to match George's, Robbie was leaving out every other thing in the world with the thing she said. The *vulgar* thing she said! Aunt Tempe cast her eyes simply up, not even at anybody.

For Tempe, her young brother George, who pulled Ranny out of the path of mad dogs, was simply less equal to pulling Dabney out of the way of Troy Flavin, Mary Denis out of the way of Mr. Buchanan, or himself out of the way of Robbie Reid, much less of trains turned loose on the railroad tracks. Deliver her from any of them, she didn't care what mercifully got her out of their path. Of course if anything ever did bear down on her, Pinckney would be in Memphis, she knew that much. Nobody could really do anything about her ever except Denis. How idle other men were! It was laziness on men's part, the difficulties that came up in this world. A paradise, in which men, sweating under their hats like field hands, chopped out difficulties like the green grass and made room for the ladies to flower out and flourish like cotton, floated vaguely in Tempe's mind, and she gave her head a toss.

Ellen leaned back against Battle's long bulk, sipping her cordial, and under her gaze her family, as they had a trick of doing, seemed to separate one from another like islands being created out of a land in the sea that had sprawled conglomerate too long. Under her caressing hand was Maureen. The Dog had stopped in time not to kill her. Here in the long run so like them all, the mindless child could not, as they would not, understand a miracle. How could Maureen, poor child, see the purity and dullness of *fact*, of the outside-world fact? Of something happening? Which was miracle. Robbie saw the miracle. Out of fear and possession, perhaps out of vulgarity itself, she saw. Not by George's side, but tagging behind, in the clarity of wifely ferocity, she had seen the true vision, and suspected it.

For Robbie, a miracle in the outer world reflected the worse on her husband—for her it made him that much more of a challenger, a proud defier that she had to protect. For her his danger was the epitome of the false position the Fairchilds put him in. Ellen saw clearly enough that George was not a challenging man at all; was he "conceited"—Robbie's funny little high-school word? He was magnificently disrespectful—that was what Ellen would have called him. For of course he saw death on its way, if they did not.

No, the family would forever see the stopping of the Yellow Dog entirely after the fact—as a preposterous diversion of their walk, resulting in lovers' complications, for with the fatal chance removed the serious went with it forever, and only the romantic and absurd abided. They would have nothing of the heroic, or the tragic now, thought Ellen, as though now she yielded up a heart's treasure.

Here they sat—all dreamily now, each with a piece of cake to spoil his supper—their truest selves, like their truest aberrations and truest virtues, not tampered with. Here in the closest intimacy the greatest anonymity lay, and a kind of basking, a kind of special pleasure, was in it. She heard Jim Allen and Primrose coming in that old electric car, that they had a colored preacher to drive . . .

Georgie had not borne it well that she called him heroic, as she did one day for something; but this, she saw now, was not for the reason that the heroism was not true, but that it too was after the fact—a quality of his heart's intensity and his mind's, too intimate for her to have looked into. That wild detachment was more intimate than desire. There was something unfair about that. Would Robbie's unseeing, fighting anger suit him better, then, than too close a divination? Well, that depended not on how Robbie loved him but on how he loved Robbie, and on other things that she, being mostly mother, and being now tired, did not know. Just now they kissed, with India coming up close on her toes to see if she could tell yet what there was about a kiss.

The whole family watched them "make up." And how did George himself think of this thing? They saw him let Robbie go, then kiss her one more time, and Battle laughed out from the pillows.

George wished it might yet be intensified. Inextinguishable, the little adventure, like anything else, burned on.

In the music room Mary Lamar resumed playing "Constantinople" and the bridesmaids, rising a little blankly as if from sleep or rest, took the groomsmen and began to dance here in the room, and around George and Robbie there in the center. Aunt Tempe too, with her finger drawing little circles, kept time. While George was kissing Robbie, Bluet had him around his knees and kissed him down there, with such fervor that she sat down, sighing. Then George and Robbie were dancing too—how amazingly together they went. In and out wove little Ranny, waving a pretended shepherd crook, shouting "I'm the wedding!" and stamping the floral wreath in the rug.

"Oh, Aunt Ellen," said Laura once more, coming forward. "Could I be in the wedding instead of Lady Clare? Because . . ."

"Why, yes, dear," said Ellen, "of course."

Then Bluet wandered by, dead on her feet, dragging Mashula's dulcimer, which she had asked for and someone had given her.

"Bluet, aren't you asleep? Bluet!" she cried, suddenly realizing the hour.

"Nobody put me to sleep," whispered Bluet. Ellen caught hold of her and kissed her—her seriousness sweeter than Ranny's delight now.

"Where do you think you're going now, Ellen?" said Battle.

He held her down a minute and she thought tenderly, there's no reason in the world why he should have been cowed in his life by Denis and George. . . .

"I'm going to put my baby to bed. You can't hold me down from that." She left them carrying Bluet in her arms, giving Robbie a soft, open look as she went out.

Tempe sighed. Ellen simply didn't know how to treat Robbie Reid—she should have just let *her* at her! But then Ellen was a very innocent woman, Tempe knew that. There were things you simply could not tell her. Not that Ellen hadn't changed in recent years. That shy, big-eyed little thing Battle had brought back with him from school dying laughing at her persistence in her own reticent ways . . . Ellen had come far, had yielded to much, for a Virginian, but still now a crowd, a roomful of people, was not her natural habitat, a plantation was not her true home.

"I'm the wedding!" Ranny was still calling, running by and twirling Tempe round. "I'm the wedding!" He carried a little green switch now for a stick, with peach leaves on it. In that moment Tempe, laughing, experienced not a thought exactly but a truer thing, a suspicion, that what she loved was not gone with Denis, but was, perhaps, perennial.

"Oh, there's always so much—so *much* happening here!" she cried contentedly to one of the bridesmaids, the McLeoud girl.

Robbie put her hand up to her head a minute as she danced, against the whirl. Dabney was dancing before her, by herself, eyes shining on them all. . . . Indeed the Fairchilds took you in circles, whirling delightedly about, she thought, stirring up confusions, hopefully working themselves up. But they did not really want anything they got—and nothing really, nothing really so very much, happened! But the next moment Miss Primrose and Miss Jim Allen arrived with so much authority and ado that she almost had to believe in them.

"This is our third trip between the Grove and Shellmound today," said Miss Jim Allen, almost falling against Battle in the door. "Nobody let us in!"

"Pinchy's come through."

"Of course."

"It's a wonder poor Primrose is not dead from carrying those Japanese lanterns in all by herself!"

"Why didn't you holler?" said George, still dancing.

Primrose and Jim Allen looked in at the room, playfully holding up their little unlighted paper lanterns.

"Oh, George, George, I'm *still* ashamed that guinea hen was tough!" Primrose cried.

"Why, it was deliciously tender," said George, over Robbie's shoulder.

"George! Was it?"

Robbie knew he smiled, with his chin in her hair. Well, the comfort they took in him—all the family—and that he held dear, was a far cry from *knowing* him. (They did a trick step.) The Fairchilds were always seeing him by a gusty lamp—exaggerating, then blinding—by the lamp of their own indulgence. While she saw him lighted up by his own fire—no one else but himself was there, a solid man, going through the world, a husband. It was by his being so full of himself that she felt the anger, the love, pride, and rest of marriage.

But oh, when all the golden persuasions of the Fairchilds focused upon him, he would vaunt himself again, if she did not watch him. He would drive her to vaunt herself too. After the Yellow Dog went by, he had turned on her a look that *she* would call the look of having been on a debauch. She could not follow. Sometimes she thought when he was so out of reach, so far away in his mind, that she could blame everything on some old story. . . . For he evidently felt that old stories, family stories, Mississippi stories, were the same as very holy or very passionate, if stories could be those things. He looked out at the world, at her, sometimes, with that essence of the remote, proud, over-innocent Fairchild look that she suspected, as if an old story had taken hold of him—entered his flesh. And she did not know the story.

She beat her hand softly, in time to "Constantinople," on George's hard back, for whatever threatened to waste his life, to lead him away, *even if he liked it,* she was going to go up against if it killed her. He laughed, and she bit him through his sleeve. Shelley saw her. *protect him*

"I wonder where Troy went, Mr. Rondo," said India.

It was a little before then that Laura started up and raced out of the parlor. She met Aunt Ellen carrying Bluet and pressed thin as a switch against the stair banister as she hurried, to let them by. It was out of love and the logic of love, and the thrill of loss she had, that she had seen a vision of Uncle George's own pipe as a present for him.

She slid still flatly and on tiptoe into the dining room. Nobody was there. Only the stack of plates for the supper and the flowers in the vases were there to see. On the chair under the lamp lay Uncle George's pipe, where by her memory he had left it. She took the pipe up and holding it gently, its stem to her nose, she started away.

All at once Aunt Shannon's voice spoke. She was sitting in the rocker she sat in all the time, only Laura had not noticed her. She was sewing on a little piece of embroidery.

"Denis," she was saying pleasantly, in an after-thought tone of voice, "I meant to tell you, little Annie Laurie's here. Set her heart on being in your wedding."

a beautiful little piece of it

Anxious as she was to get away with the pipe, Laura had to wait to hear what Aunt Shannon said about her mother.

"Has a little malaria, I'm sure," murmured Aunt Shannon. "But looks a hundred times better already, now that she's here with *us*.—Gals are growing too fast. That's all." Aunt Shannon rocked a little and then bit off her thread, and that was all she ever told Denis about Laura's mother.

Uncle George's pipe was perceptibly warm. It smelled stronger than Laura had guessed—it smelled violently. But she bore that, and crept out with it and edged up the stairs, meeting nobody. She knew where to hide the pipe—in her hat, which lay up in the wardrobe not to be touched till the day she put it on for the Yellow Dog to go home. The hat was a grand hiding place for her present for Uncle George, and the pipe was the thing he would want.

"Do you realize, dear hearts, that we have been waiting all this time on His Honor the Bridegroom?" said Aunt Tempe.

"Ah! What time is it?" inquired Mr. Rondo, but nobody answered. The piano was playing something soft and "classical," and George was passing cake among the fast-breathing, fallen bridesmaids all around the room.

"Not a *soul* to send for him."

Shelley did not want to stay, did not want to go and look for Troy. She saw Maureen grow overjoyed at the sight of the cake. "I take-la all your cake-la," she said, taking two big handfuls.

"Not for me, not for me," she murmured, stunned at the sight of George at that moment offering the loaded plate to her. It seemed to Shelley all at once as if the whole room should protest, as if alarm and protest should be the nature of the body. Life was too easy—too easily holy, too easily not. It could change in a moment. Life was not ever inviolate. Dabney, poor sister and bride, shed tears this morning (though belatedly) because she had broken the Fairchild night light the aunts had given her; it seemed so unavoidable to Dabney, that was why she cried, as if she had felt it was part of her being married that this cherished little bit of other people's lives should be shattered now. Dabney at the moment cutting a lemon for the aunts' tea brought the tears to

Shelley's eyes; could the lemon feel the knife? Perhaps it suffered; not that vague vegetable pain lost in the generality of the pain of the world, but the pain of the very moment. Yet in the room no one said "Stop." They all lay back in flowered chairs and ate busily, and with a greedy delight anticipated what was ahead for Dabney. . . . All except Shelley, who stared at George as he held the cake plate before her. She realized he was looking at her inquiringly. "Aren't you famished?" It occurred to her that he suffered no grievance against the hiding and protesting that went on, the secrecy of life. What was dark and what shone fair—neither would stop him. She had to love him as she loved the darling Ranny. For who was going to look after men and boys like that, who would offer up everything? She took his cake.

"Shelley, *you* go," said Dabney, smiling. "You go to the office and get Troy. Tell him we're all mad and we'll break his neck if he's not here in a minute."

9

Shelley ran out, down the steps, and across the grass in her satin slippers. The air was blue. She heard the falling waves of the locusts' song, as if the last resistance of the day were being overcome and the languor of night would be soon now. She could see the lightning bugs plainly even between flashes of their lights—flying nearly upright through the blueness, tails swinging, like mermaids playing beneath a sea. She went along the bayou, by the startling towers of the yuccas, and heard only faintly the sounds of the house behind her.

Theirs was a house where, in some room at least, the human voice was never still. Laughing and crying went rushing through the halls, and assuagement waylaid them both. In contrast, the bayou, in its silence, could seem like a lagoon in a foreign world, and a solitary person could walk beside it with inward, uncomforted thoughts. The house was charged with life, the fields were charged with life, endlessly exploited, but the bayou was filled with its summer trance or its winter trance of sleep, its uncaught fishes. And the river, that went by the Grove. "Yazoo means River of Death." India was fond of parading the thing they learned in the fourth grade, and of parading morbidity before Shelley anyway, but Shelley looked back at her unmoved at the word. "Snooty, that's what you are," said India.

"River of Death" to Shelley meant not the ultimate flow of doom, but the more personal vision of the moment's chatter ceasing, the feelings of the day disencumbered, floating now into recognition, like a little boat come into sight; and tenderness and love, sadness and pleasure, being let alone to stretch in the shade. She thought this because of the way the Yazoo looked, its daily appearance. River of the death of the day the Yazoo was to Shelley, and their bayou went in and out of it like the curved arm of the sleeper, whose elbow was in their garden.

Then Shelley ran along the bayou. Oh, to be beyond all this! To have tonight, tomorrow, over! The office, one of the houses none of the girls ever paid any attention to, was down near their bridge, on the other side. She felt the breath of air from the bayou as she ran over, and heard the clothes-like rustle of the fig trees that shaded the other bank. It was not yet dark—it would never get dark. The pervading heat and light of day lasted over even into night—in the pale sky, the warm fields, the wide-awakeness of every mockingbird, still this late in the year. They could mate another time before it was cold.

Yes, there was a light in the office. And Troy was keeping them all waiting! To show him what she thought of him, and rather shocking herself, she walked in with the briefest of knocks.

The green-shaded light fell over the desk. It shone on that bright-red head. Troy was sitting there—bathed and dressed in a stiff white suit, but having trouble with some of the hands. Shelley walked into the point of a knife.

Root M'Hook, a field Negro, held the knife drawn; it was not actually a knife, it was an ice pick. Juju and another Negro stood behind, with slashed cheeks, and open-mouthed; still another, talking to himself, stood his turn apart.

Shelley ran to Troy, first behind him and then to his side. Wordlessly, he pushed her behind him again. She saw he had the gun out of the drawer.

"You start to throw at me, I'll shoot you," Troy said.

Root vibrated his arm, aiming, Troy shot the finger of his hand, and Root fell back, crying out and waving at him.

"Get the nigger out of here. I don't want to lay eyes on him."

"Pinchy cause *trouble* comin' through," said Juju to the other boy as they lifted Root and pulled him through the doorway.

"All right, who're you now?" Troy said, before he spoke to Shelley.

"I's Big Baby, de one dey all calls."

"All right, stop making that commotion and tell me what's got hold of you. Alligator bite your tail?"

"Mr. Troy, *I* got my seat full of buckshot," said the Negro, in confessional tones.

Troy groaned with him, but laughed between his drawn lips. "Find me that ice pick. Pull down your clothes, Big Baby, and get over my knee. Shelley, did you come in to watch me?"

"I can't get past—there's blood on the door," said Shelley, her voice like ice.

"Then you'll have to jump over it, my darlin'," said Troy, sing-song.

Shelley halfway smiled, with the sensation that she had only seen a man drunk. The next moment she felt a sharp, panicky triumph. As though the sky had opened and shown her, she could see the reason why Dabney's wedding should be prevented. Nobody could marry a man with blood on his door. . . . But even as she saw the reason, Shelley knew it would not avail. She would jump as Troy told her, and never tell anybody, for what was going to happen was going to happen.

"Mr. Rondo's waiting," she said. "We're all ready, when you are. You have to practice coming into the parlor."

"I'll be there in due time, Shelley," said Troy evenly. He held the ice pick in a hand bright with red hairs, and red hairs sprang even from his ears.

Shelley jumped over the doorsill.

Running back along the bayou, faster than she had come, Shelley could only think in her anger of the convincing performance Troy had given as an overseer born and bred. Suppose a real Deltan, a planter, were no more real than that. Suppose a real Deltan only imitated another Deltan. Suppose the behavior of all *men* were actually no more than this—imitation of other men. But it had previously occurred to her that Troy was trying to imitate her father. (Suppose her *father* imitated . . . oh, not he!) Then all men could not know any too well what they were doing. Everybody always said George was a second Denis.

She felt again, but differently, that men were no better than little children. She ran across the grass toward the house. Women, she was glad to think, did know a *little* better—though everything they knew they would have to keep to themselves . . . oh, forever!

After, at last, the rehearsal, and the supper, and the Winona dance, Shelley, in a cool nightgown, opened her diary.

What could she put down? . . . "First, the wrong person has eaten Partheny's cake," she wrote, "like in Shakespeare . . ."

There was a whirr and a clawing at the window screen back of the light. A big beetle, a horned one, was trying to get in. All at once Shelley was sickeningly afraid of life, life itself, afraid *for* life. . . . She turned out the light, fell on her bed, and the beating and scratching ceased.

VI

NEXT MORNING Pinchy was setting the table and Aunt Mac was at the china closet loudly counting the glasses of each kind. Horace was hosing down the Summers's car and in a mystifyingly high falsetto he was singing "Why?" Howard, with Maureen running about the foot of his ladder, was with almost imperceptible motions hanging paper lanterns in the trees, gradually moving across the yard like the movement of shade under the climbing sun. In the soft early air—Ellen stood at her window, with Battle asleep—in which there was a touch, today perhaps the first touch, of fall, the sounds of the busy fields came traveling up to the yard, the beat and sashay of a horse's feet. Though by another hour the fields would seem to jump in the sight with heat, now there was over them—and would be later when evening would come—the distance and clarity of fall, out of which came a breath of cool. Ellen took it, the breath, and turned to wake Battle.

"When does Primrose Fairchild think she can make that ton of chicken salad, if she doesn't come on?" cried Tempe aloud in the kitchen as the clock was striking the dot of something. Some of the roast turkeys and the ham were lined up in the middle of the kitchen table, and the oven gave off waves of fire and fragrance. Roxie was cooking breakfast over a crowded little unused stove in another part of the kitchen, followed by Ranny begging sticks of bacon, and stamping her foot at some kittens that ran about over there. "I bet Jim Allen is trying to make mints. That can keep you running crazy all day, and with a wedding waiting on you. Roxie, where are the Memphis mints?"

"Great big pasteboard box yonder in de pantry, Miss Tempe," called Roxie. "Have to untie you de ribbon to git you a taste. But you ought to see dem Memphis ice slippers! Green!"

Tempe went from the pantry to the back-porch icebox. "And hard as rocks—*I* know," she said. "And slippery—! People'll lose them off their plates and they'll slide across the floor from here to yonder, oh me. It's an old story, Roxie, weddings to me." She slammed the icebox door, after taking out a little piece of celery.

"Yes, ma'am, sure is. Old story."

"Who's going to make the beaten biscuit, Roxie? I have to have the kitchen to myself when the cornucopias are made! I'll kill anybody making beaten biscuit around me."

"Miss Tempe, you sure will. Miss Ellen say she make one or two ovens of biscuit while you all be taking your napses."

"Good idea. *Everything* would be done more satisfactorily if you could do it with most people asleep. I don't think that's even remotely near the number of pickled peaches it will take for going around the hams and turkeys!" She started counting on her fingers. Ranny offered her a bite of bacon and she bent and took it.

The Memphis flowers had come down just right, on the Yellow Dog that morning, and Miss Thelma had sent them up on horseback, the boxes tied over Sammie McNair's saddle, with Sammie holding Miss Thelma's umbrella over them.

"Oh, mercy—the bride's bouquet! We ought to look at it," Tempe said darkly, as Sammie got off to have breakfast with them.

"Why?" asked India, appearing in her nightgown.

"Just to be sure."

India in a moment had the bouquet out, and held it up at arm's length over her head. "Are you sure, Aunt Tempe?"

"We'll have to doctor it a little, just as I thought," Aunt Tempe said, "take out those common snapdragons. Vi'let! You can take Miss Dabney's bouquet and all these flower boxes to the springhouse, Vi'let, but keep their paper around them so not even your breath touches them."

"Ain't they pretty?" Vi'let cried. "Oh. Oh!"

"There's a ladybug on Dabney's," said Bluet, gazing up. She had come out in her nightgown too.

"I bid it!" India went off with the ladybug on the back of her hand, Bluet following hopefully, asking the ladybug if the trip from Memphis wasn't simply *smothering*.

*

In a little while here came bumping a wagon. "It's the cake!" said Tempe clairvoyantly. It was the cake, in the tallest box yet from Memphis.

"Now the cake will have to be lifted out by everybody, on the cutting board—there's no two ways about that, if you don't want a ruined toppling thing," said Aunt Mac with spirit.

"One strong, sure-footed man might be the best," said Tempe, "*I* would think."

"Go to grass," said Aunt Mac. Vi'let ran for the old cutting board in the attic, big as the head of a bed, and she, Howard, and Little Uncle began to get the cake on it and so down from the wagon. Old Man Treat, a passer-by who had driven the cake up specially for Miss Thelma at the post office, was not allowed to put in a word or move.

"Mercy! Open it first!" cried Tempe. "So it won't rub off on the box! So we can see it!" They opened the box and stripped it back, like the petals of a flower. Mr. Treat looked over his shoulder. There it was, the tall white thing, shining before God in the light of day. It was a real fantasy! Only God knew if it was digestible.

Ellen already held the door, and some of the girls in their nightgowns and kimonos came out watching.

"It's leaning! It's leaning!" cried India, laughing and joining her hands.

"It looks like the Leaning Tower of Pisa," said Shelley critically.

"Well, it cost your father thirty-five dollars," Ellen told her. "It's no wonder it looks like something or other—do you think, Mr. Treat?" she threw in, for she remembered he was a distant cousin of the Reids.

"Talk about spun sugar!" said Tempe. She gave a little smack. In her arms, forgotten, were the early-cut flowers from the yard. "I think they did real well, considering it was all done by telephone. Now did they forget the ring and thimble and all inside?"

"That's something we won't know till the cake's cut and eaten," said Ellen. "That's too late to tell Memphis about."

"I'm going to cut the ring!" sang India.

"Who're you going to marry, child?" asked Aunt Tempe.

"Dickie Boy Featherstone! No, Red Boyne."

"Red hair!" cried Aunt Tempe exasperated. "What has happened to this clan? Don't you dare do it, India."

"All my children will be ugly like Lady Clare."

"And she upstairs with the chicken pox, shame," said Ellen. "Stand here by me, India."

"There will be no holding Lady Clare when they're all in their dresses, I'm afraid," said Aunt Tempe, flinching now as she watched the cake actually being lifted down. "I'm not saying she won't fight her way to the wedding after all—you watch that cake, Howard! Do you know what'll happen to you if you drop that?"

"Yes, ma'am. *Dis* cake not goin' drop—no'm."

"That's what you *say*. You have to *carry* it straight up, too."

"Little Uncle, you kind of go *under*—like that. Spread your arms out like a bird—now. That's grand, Little Uncle."

"I'm a wreck," said Shelley. "I'm glad Dabney's not here watching. Oh, Croesus, I wish old Troy Flavin would just *quit wanting* to marry Dabney!"

"Don't frown like that, you'll hurt your looks, Shelley. A fine time now, for Troy Flavin to do a thing like that," said Aunt Tempe. "You all set the cake where it's going to *go*, on the middle of the dining-room table. We'll just have to eat like scaries all day and not do any shaking or stamping."

"Can you all tell the middle of the table?" asked Ellen anxiously as the cake went in the door. "You run in, India, and show them with your finger, right in the center of that lace rose that's the middle of Mashula's cloth. This was certainly nice of you, Mr. Treat. Run lightly, India, don't shake the house, from now on."

George, coming downstairs, held still with his eye on the cake—it was crossing the hall. Howard, Vi'let, and Little Uncle with the cake coming in were meeting Bitsy and some of the field Negroes, Juju and Zell, carrying a long side-table out.

"No collisions, I tell you!" cried Tempe, at the heels of the cake party.

"You've got to find a level place in the yard to set that down now, Bitsy," said Ellen, in the voice of one who is not sure there are any level places in the Delta.

"Yes, ma'am! Dis table goin' to go down in a *level* place."

"Where's Robbie, Georgie?"

"She's still asleep," said George, running down and kissing them. "All of you look beside yourselves!"

"I think Robbie's going to sleep the day away! Like Dabney."

"That's *all right*, she was good and tired," said Ellen.

"Well! It looks like she could show some interest. After all, there's a wedding in the house!" Tempe said. George grinned and snapping off a Michaelmas daisy from her armful handed it to her.

"Where's my pipe, girls?" he said.

Bluet went in and woke up Dabney, carrying her coffee, with her sisters watching in the door. "Wake up, Dabney, it's your wedding day," she said carefully.

"Oh!" Dabney sat bolt upright. She seized the cup and drank off the coffee. Then she fell back, pulling Bluet up in the bed with her. She pressed the little girl to her.

"Precious! Precious!"

They all laughed and came in, and saw that she got up. They brought her down to the table and made her eat her breakfast. They all sat down around her wedding cake.

"It didn't break?" smiled Dabney, giving it a bright glance as she ate a plum. She and Shelley looked at each other, their kimono sleeves, pink and blue, fluttering together in the morning wind.

"Oh!" exclaimed Tempe, rising from her breakfast and running to the window. "Lady Clare's out there talking to a mad dog!" She turned to George—and time was when he would have dashed out of the house to hear that, but not now. He smiled absently and ate a bite of his mackerel. Pattering out the door, Tempe sighed. She ran through the sun as she would run through a pounding rain, and took hold of Lady Clare, who was in her nightgown and all spots.

"Don't you know strange dogs may be mad dogs?" she said, running in with her. "Probably *are* mad dogs. I fully expected something to happen to you, Lady Clare. A time like this and a house like this—!"

The strange dog—mad or not, Lady Clare would never know—looked after their retreat and trotted off to the bayou bank.

"How do I look, Aunt Ellen?" cried Laura, running into the parlor, where Ellen was getting the smilax hung. Mary Lamar, in a yellow kimono, was kneeling over the stool running her hands over the piano keys. Laura had on Lady Clare's flower-girl dress, without the petticoat. "Shelley's trying it on!"

"Mercy, I see your knees. But Primrose can let out the hem for you in two shakes of a lamb's tail when she ever gets here."

"Do I look like the flower girl?" asked Laura. "Shelley wants to know."

"Mama, will she do?" called Shelley's voice from the upper regions. This was the callingest house! thought Laura anxiously.

"You couldn't look *more* like one," Ellen said, and held her tight. "You'll have to put a little of Dabney's or Shelley's face powder over those old bites—where have you been?—and let somebody turn your hair over their finger, and you'll be splendid. Run back and tell Shelley to get the dress off you quick now. Would you like your hair up on old rags all day?"

"Oh, Aunt Ellen!"

"All right, I'll tie you up myself. I wish you'd prevail on India to wear curls just for tonight. She won't let anybody touch her."

"Mama used to curl my hair in curls," said Laura shyly. "Mary Lamar—what are you playing?" and she walked near the music, spreading her dress.

"It's not always anything," said Mary Lamar in a soft voice. "I'm improvising."

Up close, beautiful Mary Lamar's arm showed great covering freckles below the chiffon sleeve, her arms were leopard-like!

"Well, Pinchy," said Dabney, frowning.

There stood Pinchy in the dining room, swatting an old September fly. For a few days a creature of mystery, now that she had come through she was gawking and giggling like the rest.

"You swat every fly, Pinchy. That's what you're for, now, this whole day," she said sternly.

"I'll git 'em," said Pinchy.

On the back porch, surrounded by fireless-cooker pots and cake pans of cut flowers, Shelley and Dabney were making shiny bows. Battle wandered out.

"What are those made of, now?"

"Material," said Dabney.

Nobody else seemed to be around, except Ranny, who sat on the back steps motionless, looking at his father over a bright beard of what seemed also to be material.

"Well, Dabney, little girl, I wanted to confer my blessing, my paternal blessing," Battle said rather heartily.

"Two princess baskets of pink and white Maman Cochet roses, Miss Tessie at the icehouse sent up, Dabney," said Ellen, carrying them onto the porch. "She sent them over by *twins.*"

"Then it was every one she had," called Tempe's voice from within. Her brother looked in the direction of her voice as if in a moment he would comprehend Tempe.

"Who sent these real late Cape jessamines—Miss Parnell Dortch?" Shelley leaned over and buried her face in them while Vi'let held them out.

"Yes, Miss Parnell." Ellen whispered, "I don't know what we'll do with old Roxie's nasturtiums—little bitty short stems, look, they don't even peep over that shoe box. But it was every nasturtium Roxie had—she *loves Dabney.*"

"We can float them in an old card tray. She'll be looking for them at the wedding," Shelley said.

"She used to let me pick them, nasty-turtiums," said Dabney idly. "I'd pick them and eat them all the way from the stems up, when I was little."

"Then you can eat these," said Ellen with a little laugh. She leaned on the door.

"Come here and let me kiss you, puddin'," Battle said.

But, "Look at Miss Bonnie Hitchcock's *fern,*" groaned Shelley.

Four little colored boys holding a tub balanced on the handle of a broom staggered up the back path. Tub, boys, and all were in the shade and glow of an enormous fern that tilted its weight over them and fluttered its fronds in every direction like a tree in a gale.

"Mama! She sent that up for Aunt Annie Laurie's funeral!" Dabney said in an awe-struck voice.

"We almost never got it back to her after *that*," Shelley said doubtfully. "Or did we?"

"I don't want it where it was before," said Dabney.

"Dabney!" Battle said. "Come kiss me."

"It can go behind Jim Allen and India serving punch," said Ellen. "It will go fine there. It won't do anything but hide the china closet. If we could put it by the outdoor table! But that would hurt Miss Bonnie's feelings—it will have to come in the house."

"Mama, I think it's so tacky the way Troy comes in from the side door," said Shelley all at once. "It's like somebody just walks in the house from the fields and marries Dabney."

"You're sure you wouldn't rather have a trip to Europe than get married?" Battle remarked into the air off the porch. "Ranny, will you take off that beard, or stop looking at me?"

Dabney ran to her father, the shiny material in hand, and laughed as his whispering lips tickled the nape of her neck. "Or go back to college?" he said.

"Horrors, Papa," she said.

"You don't have but one silver champagne bucket, I know that," said Tempe, stepping out dramatically from the kitchen. "Why didn't I think to bring you mine? It would have been no trouble in the world. Mercy!" she spoke to the fern, which was at the door.

"It's grown, Mama!" said Dabney, leaning back as the fern went by, vibrating and seemingly under its own power, up the steps and across the back porch. Battle pinned her backwards against him and kissed the crown of her head.

"Well, one thing," said Tempe in a low voice to Shelley, looking after the fern with a sigh of finality, "when people marry beneath them, it's the woman that determines what comes. It's the woman that coarsens the man. The man doesn't really do much to the woman, I've observed."

"You mean Troy's not as bad for us as Robbie," whispered Shelley intently.

"Exactly!"

"Don't stop, don't stop! This way!" Ellen hurried ahead of the fern and led it into the house.

"The crooks have come, the crooks have come!" cried Orrin, racing in. "Dabney, I brought your crooks! Watch!" He reached in Little Uncle's arms as Little Uncle ran up with yellow sticks everywhere, and began throwing them in the air like a juggler. All the children ran picking them up—each got one.

"Orrin!"

"I was watching for the Dog! I saw them take everything off, and I wanted to bring you the crooks ahead of everything, Dabney! Only I went in swimming a minute—I was on Junie—"

"Oh, Orrin! Oh, I hate to go off and leave you and every-body!" Dabney kissed his smiling lips, and he untied her sash behind her.

"Give me one," she said, looking at the running children. "Ranny, I want that one."

"What's that old Bojo brought on the mule?" asked Ellen.

"Aunt Primrose's cheese straws," said Shelley, rushing to lift the lid of the corset box. "From the secret recipe!"

"I just have to have *one*," said Aunt Tempe, putting in her hand. "Excuse me, you all."

Dabney took the box, laughing, and ran to the kitchen.

Aunt Studney was in the kitchen taking a little coffee. Howard's little boy, Pleas, who was on the back porch twisting smilax on the altar, came stealing in behind Roxie and tried to look in Aunt Studney's sack. But Aunt Studney was up with a kettle off the stove and like lightning poured it over him, making him yell and run off as if the devil had him.

"Why, Aunt Studney," said Dabney. "I wanted to invite you to my wedding!"

"Ain't studyin' you," said Aunt Studney. She lifted her cof-fee cup in her quick, horny hand that was bright pink inside, and drank. Then she was gone with her sack.

*

Primrose and Jim Allen came up to Shellmound only in time to sit down to dinner, to Battle's teasing. And as it turned out, Primrose was making the chicken salad (which Roxie had luckily cut up for her), Ellen baking the beaten biscuit with Robbie (swallowed in a Fairchild apron) watching the pans, Tempe rolling out her cornucopias, and Roxie and Pinchy squeezing the fruit for the punch all in the kitchen together. Jim Allen had spent the morning making green and white mints, which they all declared were better than the Memphis mints, so she lay down and dozed a little on a bed.

"Mr. Horace," Vi'let said, coming through the shade in the yard with more napkins dry enough to iron, "you standin' up pretty good." All Horace had to do was wash cars and shine them, and get his flashlight ready for tonight, make sure it would burn. Preacher, the Grove chauffeur, who thought yesterday he had better not try to carry so much as a paper lantern in his old age, never do anything except drive an electric automobile, felt younger today and said he would be glad to fish seeds out of cook's juice, give him a spoon. Some wagons loaded with planks came up in the yard and Howard was told to fix a dancing place as he saw fit, but hurry! out of an old landing Mr. Battle was sending up from the river. "Mr. Battle sure love doin' things at las' minute, don't he, Miss Ellen?" laughed Howard from the top of his ladder, making it sound attractive, even irresistible of Mr. Battle.

"Don't you fall off that ladder, Howard, before you come down and nail those planks! Dancing on the platform's what the lanterns are *for*."

"No'm, I ain't goin' fall off *dis* ladder. Dance, yes, ma'am!"

Laura heard behind the bathroom door sounds of great splashing, and in between the splashes Dabney's voice, talking to Bluet.

"Now, Bluet, you mustn't ever brag."

"What's brag?"

Splash, splash.

"And, Bluet, you mustn't ever tell a lie."

"What's tell a lie?"

Splash, splash.

Laura banged on the door. "Let me in! I have to get ready too!"

They let her in. There were all the girls—tall Shelley too, naked and splashing. And they had Ranny, so little and sweet still. There was water everywhere, even dotting the fireplace like beads on a forehead. Bluet was in the center of the big pedestaled bathtub and they were squeezing washrags over her and putting soap on her hands, which she stuck forward for them. Bluet, her long hair pinned up in a topknot, was very serious today, at the same time slithering like a fish.

"And, Bluet," said Laura comfortably, "you mustn't ever steal."

"Don't *you* tell me," said Bluet gently, "just Dabney," and they all dashed her with water.

Finally, people began to come out in the halls or downstairs dressed. "Orrin! You look like a man!" cried Ellen. "Oh, the idea!"

"Mr. Ranny growin' up too, in case nobody know it," said Roxie. "Miss Ellen, did you know? That little booger every mornin' befo' six o'clock holler out de window fo' me. 'Roxie! I need my coffee!' and make me come right up."

"The idea!" said Ellen.

When the clock struck for seven, Laura in the flower-girl dress brought the pipe out of the hat and stood in the decorated hall with it until she saw George come through there. She followed him and confronted him at the water cooler on the back porch. Lizards were frolicking and scratching on the wire outside, being gazed at from inside by the old cat Beverley. Nobody else was around.

Bringing it slowly from behind her sash, she gave the pipe to him very slowly, inching it out to him to make the giving longer. At first he did not seem even to understand that he could take it, for she was so ceremonious.

"I wanted to give you a present you really wanted to get, so I kept it away from you a while," explained Laura. He bent his handsome head. He listened to her closely—that was the way Uncle George always listened, as if everyone might tell him something like this. "I wanted to surprise you," she said.

"Yes, honey." He kissed her right between the eyes. He took the pipe. "Thank you," he said. "You're growing up to be a real little Fairchild before you know it."

She was filled with happiness. "Is there any other thing I could give you after this, for a present?" she asked finally.

Instead of saying "No" he said gently, "Thanks, I'll let you know, Laura."

More happiness struck her like a shower of rain. She looked at him dazzled. "Tonight?"

"It might be later," he said. He pulled her hair a little then, her curls. When she waited shyly, he put the pipe in his mouth, lighted it, puffed out a strong cloud, and nodded his head at her to show her the pipe was nice to get back.

Then they both had a drink of water out of the spigot, he drinking from the tarnishy cup, she from the ridgy glass.

"Why is smoke coming out of the hall chimney?" asked India, walking in at the side door. She had been trying out her shepherdess crook.

"Smoke?"

In the hall Roy in his everyday clothes lay on the floor painting with Laura Allen's watercolors. Six or eight pictures—he finished them rapidly—were laid around the stove where his fire dried them as quickly as possible, though the heat did curl the older ones up tight.

"Roy!" cried Dabney in tears. "I'm going to get married in this house in fifteen minutes. Everybody will perish from the heat!"

"It was already as hot as it could be," said Roy. "This fire feels cool to me."

"Do you want your papa to stop Dabney's wedding to give you a switching?" asked Ellen. "I thought you were all in your white suit."

"I'll be there when you look for me," said Roy agreeably.

"Then run!"

"I thought you loved me," said Dabney. She and Shelley and Mary Lamar were all three in tears.

"Shelley, hush crying, who'll be next?" said Ellen, and Bluet came up and cried loudly.

"My God, girls!" shouted Battle, taking a step sideways.

"Stop your tears! Can't raise you, can't even marry you, without the shillelagh all over the place."

"What is the picture of, Roy?" asked India in practical tones.

"Lady Clare being hanged by the pirates. That's her tongue sticking out."

"Well, now, it's through, then," said Ellen. "Run! Make Orrin part your hair. It's the first time he's ever wanted to use the paints, as far as I know, Battle."

2

The bridesmaids came all of a company and flew upstairs to Shelley's room to get into their bridesmaid dresses, with Vi'let and Pinchy to put them over their heads, hot from the iron. "Ever'body git a crook," said Little Uncle, mincing it over and over, where they gathered in the upstairs hall. "Got you a crook, missy? Here a pretty one for you," as if shepherdess crooks were the logical overflow from Fairchild bounty. Old Partheny had come up just at the time she pleased, the time for Dabney to be putting on her wedding dress and be ready to stamp her foot at the way it did, and now appeared at the head of the back stairs clothed from top to bottom in purple. She went straight and speaking to nobody to Dabney's closed door and flung it open. "Git yourself here to me, child. Who dressin' you? Git out, Nothin'," and Roxie, Shelley, and Aunt Primrose all came backing out. The door slammed.

Downstairs, with all the boys in white suits gallantly running about, the family gathering in the parlor around Ellen and Battle greeted the arriving families of the wedding party and too-early arrivers for the reception from the more distant plantations. Aunt Mac and Aunt Shannon came in on Orrin's arm, one at a time. Aunt Mac wore her corsage of red roses and ferns on the shoulder opposite the side with her watch, so she could keep up with things. Aunt Shannon proceeded uncertainly and yet with pride, her little feet in their comfort slippers planted wide apart, as a year-old child walks, her hot little hand digging into Orrin's arm. White sweet peas were what Aunt Shannon wore, and she liked them.

"It's time we were sitting down, now, as many as can," said

Ellen, and all at once sank, herself, into one of the straight chairs before the altar.

All the windows were full of black faces, but the family servants stood in a ring inside the parlor walls. Pinchy stole in, all in white, and she looked wild and subdued together now in that snowiness with her blue-black. Maureen went up to her and gave her a red rose from her basket, not being, as a flower girl, able to wait. Partheny stood at the front of all the Negroes, where the circle had its joining, making the circle a heart. Her head was high and purple, she was thistlelike there, and perhaps considered herself of all the Negroes the head and fount. Man-Son, Sylvanus, Juju, more than that were all in the hall, spellbound and shushing one another. Aunt Studney, wherever she was, was keeping out of sight.

Uncle Pinck, who was laughing at something, hushed suddenly, Mr. Rondo had taken his place, and music began. The groomsmen entered, and then people leaned backwards from the doorway, so that everybody could see what came down the stairs. In twos the bridesmaids began coming, they entered and arranged themselves in front of the boys, fanning out from Howard's altar, deep to pale, dark to light in their pairs, fading out to Shelley, who entered trembling and with excruciating slowness, her sleeves aquiver. Their crooks they held seriously in front of them in their right hands, each crook crowned with Memphis flowers tied on with streamers. India came in, throwing petals, and Maureen, then Laura came in down the little path between people where she was supposed to walk; at last she was out before everybody, one of the wedding party, dressed up like the rest in an identical flower-girl dress, and she scattered rose petals just as quickly as India, just as far as Maureen. Did it show, that her mother had died only in January? Mary Lamar, in place at the piano, played in that soft, almost surreptitious fashion of players of wedding music.

It was Shelley that Ellen was watching anxiously. Ever since Dabney had announced that she would marry Troy, Shelley had been practicing, rather consciously, a kind of ragamuffin-ism. Or else she drew up, like an old maid. What could be so wrong in everything, to her sensitive and delicate mind? There was something not quite *warm* about Shelley, her first child.

Could it have been in some way her fault? Ellen watched her anxiously, almost tensely, as if she might not get through the wedding very well. Primrose was whispering in Ellen's ear. Shelley would not hold her shepherdess crook right—it should be straight in line with all the other girls' crooks—look how her bouquet leaned over. Like a sleepy head, Ellen thought rather dreamily in her anxiety.

"Crook like the others, dear," whispered Primrose from her front chair. She made a quick coaxing motion with her little lacy mits (she had indulged herself with a pair just like the bridesmaids').

Shelley, with a face of contrition, held her shepherdess crook like the others. Aunt Primrose had such an abundance of small, hopeful anxieties—the mere little ferns and flowers of the forest she had never guessed could be! Shelley was glad to hold her crook right.

Troy came in from the side door, indeed like somebody walking in from the fields to marry Dabney. His hair flamed. Had no one thought that American Beauty would clash with that carrot hair? Had no one thought of that? Jim Allen blinked her sensitive eyes.

Robbie looked up at George, who had entered with Troy and stood up beside him, listening and agaze at his family. In the confusion she had been seated a little toward the back. There was no one looking at him—except a bridesmaid to primp for a moment, push at a curl, or long-legged Laura that smiled—there was no one seeing him but herself. George was not the one they all looked at, she thought in that moment, as he was always declared to be, but the eye that saw them, from right in their midst. He was sensitive to all they asked of life itself. Long ago they had seized on that. He was to be all in one their lover and protector and dreaming, forgetful conscience. From Aunt Shannon on down, he was to be always looking through them as well as to the left and right of them, before them and behind them, watching out for and loving their weaknesses. If anything tried to happen to them, let it happen to him! He took that part, but it was the way he was made, too, to be like that.

But there was something a little further, that no one could know except her. There was enough sweetness in him to make him cherish the whole world, but in himself there had been no forfeiture. Not yet. He had not yielded up to that family what they really wanted! Or they would not keep after him. But where she herself had expected light, all was still dark too.

He wanted her so blindly—just to hold. Often Robbie was back at the time where she had first held out her arms, back when he came in the store, home from the war, a lonely man that noticed wildflowers. She could not see why he needed to be so desperate! She loved him.

But he turned his head a little now and glanced at her with that suddenness—curiosity, not quite hope—that tore her heart, like a stranger inside some house where he wanted to make sure that she too had come, had really come.

It was all right with her, she wanted him to look at her and see that. She was rising a little on her chair as if she would stand up, while the music swelled—looking over Aunt Tempe's hothouse corsage and meeting the dark look. Somehow it was all right, every minute that they were in the one place.

There was a groan from upstairs, as at a signal given perhaps by Mary Lamar's rising music, and Battle, his skin, too, fiery red against his white clothes, brought Dabney down and entered with her on his arm.

In the early morning, climbing out of bed, Dabney had looked out her windows, walked around her room; at her door she had looked out and down the sleeping hall, out through the little balcony under its ancient awning. There were soft beats in the air, which she dreamily identified as her father's sleeping snorts. The sun, a red ball down East Field, sat on the horizon. Faint bands of mist, in the fading colors of the bridesmaids' dresses, rose to the dome of clear sky. And that's me, she had thought, pleased—that little white cloud. She had got back in bed and gone back to sleep. And she felt she had not yet waked up. Though Partheny had just come up to her and seemed to shake at everybody and everything in her room, wild old nurse—the way a big spider can shake a web to get a little straw out, seeming to summon up all the anger in the world to keep the lure of the web intact.

"Never more beautiful!" whispered Primrose.

That is what will always be said about a bride, thought Tempe, suddenly agitating her fan. And they all look dead, to my very observant eye, or like rag dolls—poor things! Dabney is no more herself than any of them.

Ellen looked at Battle as he sat down beside her, and took his hand.

Ranny in his white satin walked in on some kind of artificial momentum, bearing the ring on the pillow, never looking behind him though everyone was murmuring "Sweet!"

Then the women put their handkerchiefs to their eyes. Mr. Rondo married Dabney and Troy.

3

"Nobody from Virginia came, eh, Ellen?" asked somebody—Dr. Murdoch.

"Not this time," said Ellen, blushing somewhat. A piece of the family sat about in the dining room, more guests had poured in and been greeted and now stood eating food or carrying it out, or danced all over the downstairs, or sat in every chair in the house and halfway up the stair steps. Little Uncle, with a retinue, carried the tray that was bigger than he was, taking champagne around. The fans blew the candles. The children ran outdoors, chasing each other around the house, those that should be in bed wild with the rest.

"Tell about when your mama came!" Was that Orrin or Battle?

"The idea!"

She saw Mr. Rondo seat himself in their little group—and it was so hot for a preacher, too, poor man; he looked so resigned, yet cheerful.

"Mama!" said Ellen softly. "I've been thinking of her tonight.—Well, I was fixing to have Shelley, and Mama was alive. Mama came down from Virginia to stay with me. We were living at the Grove. So Mama was up when I called her, it was before day, and sent and got Dr. Murdoch. The Fairchilds turned out to be late getting there, or couldn't come—Aunt Mac was sick and Aunt Shannon, who was the busiest woman in the world then, had to be waiting on her hand and foot, and Primrose and Jim Allen were still out at a dance."

"But already it wasn't doing them a smidgen of good, Tempe had cut them out," Battle said, tweaking Tempe's little diamond-set ear. He loved her absurdity and would fish it out of any story even if she wasn't in it.

"Dr. Murdoch," said Ellen, her voice a little livelier as she went, "was a young man starting out and he brought a brand-new gas machine with him in his buggy and had a little Negro specially to carry it in the house and then wait for it on the doorstep. As soon as he got here he just sneered at me, the way he would now, and said fiddle, I had all the time in the world and he was going to go and we could call him when I was good and ready. But Mama thought that was so ugly of him, and it was, Dr. Murdoch!—and she said, 'Don't you fret, Ellen, I'll cook him such a fine breakfast he wouldn't dare go.'

"Mama was from Virginia, so sure enough, she cooked him everything in the creation from batter bread on. She might even have had shad roe except I don't know where she would have found it. Dr. Murdoch sat down and ate like a king, all right, but he, or Mama one, forgot how early in the morning it was for all that. Poor Dr. Murdoch got the worst off he ever got in his life, I imagine, on that Virginia breakfast, and then of course he had to lie down and groan and feel sorry for himself, and the only bed he could get to with Mama helping him was mine, downstairs—Mama couldn't drag him all the way upstairs by his feet! She put him down by me. So I began to poke his side presently, to attract his attention.

"I poked his side and he just groaned. Finally he popped his eyes open and looked at me from the other pillow and said, 'Madam,' meaning Mama, 'will you please do such and such and kindly stoop over the gas machine and see if it is in order.' And Mama did what he said and took one breath and fell down in a heap.

"So Dr. Murdoch used some profane words, he thought Mama was snooty anyway toward the Delta, and he got up—he could have done it in the first place. He pulled Mama up and he put her on my bed. She opened her eyes and said, 'Is my baby born yet?'—like you were hers, Shelley.

"So Dr. Murdoch went over and he fiddled with the gas machine and he bent over and took a testing breath and he fell over. Mama just was not able to pick him up a second time, so we just let him alone, and I asked Mama to leave the room, I was shy before her, and I had the baby by myself—the cook came and she knew everything necessary—Partheny it was."

"Papa, where were you?" asked India, leaning on Mr. Rondo.

"Greenwood! And you hush, you weren't born yet."

"Aunt Shannon got there and was deviling Dr. Murdoch—oh, her positive manner then!—for being nothing but a green Delta doctor that couldn't even tend himself, and Mama was snooting Aunt Shannon—snooting things clear back to Port Gibson—!"

They laughed till the tears stood in their eyes at the foolishness, the long-vanquished pain, the absurd prostrations, the birth that wouldn't wait, and the flouting of all in the end. All so handsomely ridiculed by the delightful now! They especially loved the way it made a fool of Dr. Murdoch, who was right there, and Ellen, her eyes bright from the story, felt a pleasure in that shameless enough to make her catch her breath. Dr. Murdoch looked straight back at her as always, as if he counted her bones. She laughed again, pressing Battle's hand.

"Mama, don't tell how much I weighed," Shelley begged, darting in and darting out of their circle.

"You weighed ten pounds," said Ellen helplessly, for that was the end of the story.

The laughter focused on Shelley, and she fled from the room, almost upsetting the aunts.

"One little glass of champagne and I don't know bee from bumble!" cried Aunt Primrose. "And neither do you, Jim Allen!" India sprang up between them and joining hands swung the ladies off. Dr. Murdoch, smiling handsomely, merged with the champagne drinkers over in the fern corner, where Uncle Pinck welcomed him by raising his glass.

"Well—it's over, the wedding's over. . . . Did you hear

how old Rondo threw in his prayer, 'Lord, I know not many people in the Delta love thee'?" Battle said, stretching himself up and then slapping Mr. Rondo's back as if he were congratulating him.

"Cut the cake! Cut the cake! Cut the cake!" cried Ranny, running through.

"I'm tired of the cake! All day long in front of us!" glowered Roy. "Cut it and get it over."

Dabney was brought in and given the knife, and she cut the first slice. Then the bridesmaids and all rushed to cut after her. "I'm cutting the ring!" India cried, and sure enough, she did. "I'm the next!"

"Here comes the picture taker, Aunt Tempe!" For Tempe had said she had taken the liberty of giving permission to the Memphis paper to send down. Now she said "Mercy!" and clutched her hair. "Oh, we're all flying loose."

Battle wanted the photograph taken of the whole family, not of simply the bride and groom. Taking absolute charge he grouped his sons and daughters around him the way he wanted them. "Get in here, Ellen!" he roared through the room.

They posed, generally smiling. "Say cheese," Aunt Primrose reminded them, and said it herself.

"Now we're all still!" cried Battle. "I'm still!"

"Domesticated." People still pointed at Battle Fairchild after twenty years of married life, as if he were a new wonder. Ellen stood modestly beside him, holding some slightly wilted bridesmaids' flowers in front of her skirt. She herself, it occurred to Ellen as she stood frowning at the hooded man with his gadget, was an anomaly too, though no one would point at a lady for the things that made her one—for providing the tremendous meals she had no talent for, being herself indifferent to food, and had had to learn with burned hands to give the household orders about—or for living on a plantation when she was in her original heart, she believed, a town-loving, book-loving young lady of Mitchem Corners. She had belonged to a little choral society of unmarried girls there that she loved. Mendelssohn floated for a moment through the confused air like a veil upborne, and she could have sung it, "I Would that My Love . . ."

The flashlight went off. Just as it did, Ranny saluted.

"You all moved," announced the photographer, looking out from his black hood. "Try again! You know what's in my satchel?" He patted it until they all attended. "Train victim. I got a girl killed on the I.C. railroad. My train did it. Ladies, she was flung off in the blackberry bushes. Looked to me like she was walking up the track to Memphis and met Number 3."

"Change the subject," commanded Aunt Tempe, who was the right-end figure of the group.

"Yes, ma'am. Another picture of the same pose, except the little gentleman that saluted. Everybody looking at the bride and groom."

"I'm holding it!" Battle cried, and the light flashed for the picture.

Ellen looked at the bride and groom, but if the first picture showed her a Mitchem Corners choral singer, then the second showed her seeing a vision of fate; surely it was the young girl of the bayou woods that was the victim this man had seen. Then Battle was giving her a kiss. George and Robbie danced off, the group broke, and more and more people were arriving at the house. They had better be standing at the door.

Everybody for miles around came to the reception. Troy said he did not know there could be so many people in the whole Delta; it *looked* like it was cotton all the way. The mayor of Fairchilds and his wife were driven up with the lights on inside their car, and they could be seen lighted up inside reading the Memphis paper (which never quite unrolled when you read it); in the bud vases on the little walls beside them were real red roses, vibrating, and the chauffeur's silk cap filled with air like a balloon when they drove over the cattle guard. Shelley's heart pounded as she smiled; indeed this was a grand occasion for everybody, their wedding was really eventful. . . . Lady Clare came down once—pitiful indeed, her spots all painted over with something, and for some reason clad in a nightgown with a long tear. "I'm exposing you! I'm exposing you all!" cried Lady Clare fiercely, but was rushed back upstairs. More champagne was opened, buffet was carried out, and all started being served under the trees.

Then Dabney changed from her wedding gown to a going-away dress and the new Pierce-Arrow was brought up to the door. Dabney began kissing the family and the bridesmaids all around; she ran up and kissed Lady Clare. When she kissed Aunt Shannon, the old lady said, "Now who do you think you are?"

A brown thrush in a tree still singing could be heard through all the wild commotion, as Dabney and Troy drove away, scattering the little shells of the road. Ellen waved her handkerchief, and all the aunts lifted theirs and waved. Shelley began to cry, and Ranny ran down the road after the car and followed it as long as it was in hearing, like a little puppy. Unlike the mayor's car that had come up alight like a boat in the night, it went away dark. The full moon had risen.

4

Then the party nearly all moved outdoors, where the lanterns burned in the trees. "I hear the music coming," said Laura, coming up and taking Ellen around the knees for a moment. The band came playing—"Who?" coming out over the dark and brightening fields above the sound of their rackety car—a little river band, all very black Negroes in white coats, who were banjo, guitar, bass fiddle, trumpet, and drum—and of course saxophone, that was the owner. Horace flagged them down with his flashlight. Howard showed them their chairs which he had fixed by the dance platform like a place for a select audience to come and watch a performance of glory. The dancing began.

At midnight, Shelley came in by herself for a drink of cool water. On the back porch the moths spread upon the screens, the hard beetles knocked upon the radius of light like an adamant door. She drank still swaying a little to the distant music. "Whispering" turned into "Linger Awhile."

Only that morning, working at the wedding flowers with Dabney, she had thought to herself, hypnotically, as though she read it in her diary, Why do you look out thinking nothing will happen any more? Why are you thinking your line of trees the indelible thing in the world? There's the long journey you're going on, with Aunt Tempe, leading out . . . and you can't see it now. Even closing your eyes, you see only the line of trees at Shellmound. Is it the world? If Shellmound were a little bigger, it would be the same as the world entirely. . . . Perhaps that was the real truth. But she had been dancing with George, with his firm, though (she was certain) reeling body so gaily leading her, so solicitously whirling her round. "Bridesmaid," he called her. "Bridesmaid, will you dance?" She felt it in his cavorting body—though she danced seriously, always moved seriously—that he went even among the dancers with some vision of choice. Life lay ahead, he might do anything. . . . She followed, she herself had a vision of choice, or its premonition, for she was much like George. They played "Sleepy Time Gal," turning it into "Whispering." Only the things had not happened to her yet. They would happen. Indeed, she might not be happy either, wholly, and she would live in waiting, sometimes in terror. But Dabney's marriage, ceasing to shock, was like a door closing to her now. Entering into a life with Troy Flavin seemed to avow a remote, an unreal world—it came nearest to being real for Shelley only in the shock, the challenge to pride. It shut a door in their faces. Behind the closed door, what? Shelley's desire fled, or danced seriously, to an open place—not from one room to another room with its door, but to an opening wood, with weather—with change, beauty . . .

There was a scratch at the back door, and Shelley unlatched it. Her old cat, Beverley of Graustark, came in. He had been hunting; he brought in a mole and laid it at her feet.

In the music room, with some of the lingering guests there, Tempe and Primrose sang two-part songs of their girlhood, arch, full of questions and answers—and Tempe was in tears of merriment at the foolishness she had lived down. Primrose with each song remembered the gestures—of astonishment, cajolery—and Tempe could remember them the next instant. The sisters sang beckoning and withdrawing like two little fat mandarins, their soft voices in gentle, yielding harmony still. But soon Tempe, who had only come inside looking for her fan, was back where the dancing was.

Ellen strolled under the trees, with Battle somewhere near,

looking among the dancers for her daughters. The lanterns did not so much shine on the dancers as light up the mistletoe in the trees. She peered ahead with a kind of vertigo. It was the year—wasn't it every year?—when they all looked alike, all dancers alike smooth and shorn, all faces painted to look like one another. It was too the season of changeless weather, of the changeless world, in a land without hill or valley. How could she ever know anything of her own daughters, how find them, like this? Then in a turn of her little daughter India's skirt as she ran partnerless through the crowd—so late!—as if a bar of light had broken a glass into a rainbow she saw the dancers become the McLeoud bridesmaid, Mary Lamar Mackey (freed from her piano and whirling the widest of all), become Robbie, and her own daughter Shelley, each different face bright and burning as sparks of fire to her now, more different and further apart than the stars.

She saw George among the dancers, walking through, looking for somebody too. Suddenly she wished that she might talk to George. It was the wrong time—she never actually had time to sit down and fill her eyes with people and hear what they said, in any civilized way. Now he was dancing, even a little drunk, she believed—this was a time for celebration, or regret, not for talk, not ever for talk.

As he looked in her direction, all at once she saw into his mind as if he had come dancing out of it leaving it unlocked, laughingly inviting her to the unexpected intimacy. She saw his mind—as if it too were inversely lighted up by the failing paper lanterns—lucid and tortuous: so that any act on his part might be startling, isolated in its very subtlety from the action of all those around him, springing from long, dark, previous, abstract thought and direct apprehension, instead of explainable, Fairchild impulse. It was *inevitable* that George, with this mind, should stand on the trestle—on the track where people could indeed be killed, thrown with their beauty disfigured before strangers into the blackberry bushes. He was capable —taking no more prerogative than a kind of grace, no more than an ordinary responsibility—of meeting a fate whose dealing out to him he would not contest; even when to people he loved his act was "conceited," if not absurd, if not just a little story in the family. And she saw how it followed, the

darker instinct of a woman was satisfied that he was capable of the same kind of love. Indeed, there danced Robbie, the proof of this. To all their eyes shallow, unworthy, she was his love; it was her ordinary face that was looking at him through the lovely and magic veil, little Robbie Reid's from the store.

George made his way through the dancers now, sometimes caught up by one, sometimes not. She thought that everything he did meant something. Not that it was symbolic—with all her young-girl's love of symbols she could scorn them for their meagerness and her fallible grasp—everything he did meant something to him, it had weight. That seemed very rare! Everything he lost meant something. . . . Of course . . . She did not need to know each little thing about him any more—to be a mother to him any more. She recognized him as far from kin to her, scarcely tolerant of her understanding, never dependent on hers or anyone's, or on compassion (how merciless that could be!). He appeared, as he made his way alone now and smiling through the dancing couples, infinitely simple and infinitely complex, stretching the opposite ways the self stretches and the selves of the ones we love (except our children) may stretch; but at the same time he appeared very finite in that he was wholly singular and dear, and not promisingly married, tired of being a lawyer, a smiling, intoxicated, tender, weatherworn, late-tired, beard-showing being. He came forward through a crowd and anybody's hand might beckon or reach after him. He had, and he gave, the golden acquiescence which Dabney the bride had in the present moment—which Ranny had. "Are you happy, Dabney?" Battle had kept asking her over and over. How strange! Passionate, sensitive, to the point of strain and secrecy, their legend was *happiness*. "The Fairchilds are the happiest people!" They themselves repeated it to each other. She could hear the words best in Primrose's gentle, persuading voice, talking to Battle or George or one of her little boys.

"Will you dance this with me, Ellen?" George asked.

"Don't you dare, Ellen," said Battle. "Do you want to kill yourself?"

Clumsily, with care, she put up her arms and took hold of his. She pressed his arms tenderly a moment, as if she could express it, that he had not been harmed after all and had been

experience is different for everyone

ready for anything all the time. She loved what was pure at its heart, better than what was understood, or even misjudged, or afterwards forgiven; this was the dearest thing.

"I would always dance with you as quick as anything," she told him. She felt lucky—cherished, and somehow *pretty* (which she knew she never was). There were some people who lived a lifetime without finding the one who relieved the heart's overflow. She bore a little heavily on George's arm. She would not know in her life, or ask, whether he had found the one. She was his friend and loved him. But starting new, she thought as the waltz played and they moved by a tree where a golden lantern hung, and without one regret for her life with Battle, she might have been the one. There was the mistletoe in the tree. It was like a tree, too—a tree within a tree.

"You're tired," he said.

"No, not tired, I haven't danced in a long time, I guess, and when now again?"

They danced, the music progressed, changed, and slowed. It was "Should Auld Acquaintance Be Forgot"—it was good night.

VII

THEN they were waiting for Dabney and Troy to come back, and for George and Robbie to go, for Laura to go—three days.

The first morning, they were all beating their aching heads, Battle and George groaning out pitifully, waked up by Ranny and Bluet with the birds. Mary Denis telephoned from Inverness that Baby George had gained an ounce, and asked, did Dabney get off? Mary Lamar was driven home, the house was more or less silent, and Uncle Pinck sat meditating out all alone by the sundial.

Ellen in the morning cool walked in the yard in her old dress, her scissors on a ribbon around her neck, and one of the children's school gloves on in case she wanted to poke around or pull much.

"Howard! Start the water running out here. Let it run from the open hose, soak everything." She reached down and pulled up, light as down, a great scraggly petunia bush turned white every inch. In those few days, when she had forgotten to ask a soul to water things, how everything had given up, or hung its head. And that little old vine, that always wanted to take everything, had taken everything—she pulled at a long thread of it and unwound it from the pomegranate tree.

The camellia bushes had all set their buds, choosing the driest and busiest time, and if they did not get water they would surely drop them, temperamental as they were. The grass all silver now showed its white roots underfoot, and was laced with ant beds up and down and across. And in just those few days, she must warn Battle, some caterpillar nets had appeared on the pecan trees down in the grove—he would have to get those burnt out or they would take his trees. Toward the gate the little dogwoods she had had brought in out of the woods or saved, hung every heart-shaped leaf, she knew the little turrety buds were going brown, but they were beyond help that far from the house, they would have to get along the best they could waiting for rain; that was something she had learned. Dabney loved them, too.

A bumblebee with dragging polleny legs went smotheringly over the abelia bells, making a snoring sound. The old crape myrtle with its tiny late old bloom right at the top of the tree was already beginning to shed all its bark, its branches glowed silver-brown and amber, brighter than its green. Well, the cypresses in the bayou were touched with flame in their leaves, early to meet fall as they were early to meet spring and with the same wild color. The locust shells clung to the tree trunks, the birds were flying over every day now, and Roy said he heard them calling in the night.

And there was that same wonderful butterfly, yellow with black markings, that she had seen here yesterday. It was spending its whole life on this one abelia.

The elaeagnus had overnight, it seemed, put out shoots as long as a man. "Howard, bring your shears, too! Did this look this way for the wedding? It's a wonder Tempe didn't get after us for that."

The robins fed like chickens in the radius of the hose. A whole tree was suddenly full of warblers—strange small greedy birds from far away, that would be gone tomorrow. The Shellmound blue jays fussed at them furiously. Old Beverley opened his eyes, closed them again. A Dainty Bess that wanted to climb held a cluster of five blooms in the air. "I can't reach," Ellen remarked firmly. She needed to take up some things that would go in the pit for winter, she wanted to flower some bulbs too. When, when? And the spider lilies were taking everything.

Her chrysanthemums looked silver and ragged, their few flowers tarnished and all their lower leaves hanging down black, like scraggly pullets, and Howard would have to tie them up again too. "Howard, remind me to ask Mr. Battle for three or four loads of fertilizer *tomorrow*." The dead iris foliage curled and floated wraithlike over everything. "Howard, you get the dead leaves away from here and be careful, if I let you put your hands any further in than the violets, do you hear?"—"*I* ain't goin' pull up anything you don't want me pullin' up, *no'm*. Not *this* time." She looked at the tall grass in her beds, as if it knew she could no longer bend over and reach it. What would happen to everything if she were not here to watch it, she thought, not for the first time when a child was coming. Of all the things she would leave undone, she hated leaving the garden untended—sometimes as much as leaving Bluet, or Battle.

"Now those dahlias can just come up out of there," she said, pausing again. "They have no reason for being in there at all, that I can see . . ." She wanted to separate the bulbs again too, and spread the Roman hyacinths out a little under the trees—they grew so thick now they could hardly bloom last spring. "Howard, don't you think breath-of-spring leans over too much to look pretty?"

"Yes, *ma'am*."

"Howard, look at my roses! Oh, what all you'll have to do to them."

"I wish there wasn't no such thing as roses," said Howard. "If I had my way, wouldn't be a rose in de world. Catch your shirt and stick you and prick you and grab you. Got thorns."

"Why, Howard. You hush!" Ellen looked back over her shoulder at him for a minute, indignant. "You don't want any roses in the world?"

"Wish dey was out of de world, Miss Ellen," said Howard persistently.

"Well, just hush, then."

She cut the few flowers, Etoiles and Lady Hillingtons (to her astonishment she was trembling at Howard's absurd, meek statement, as at some impudence), and called the children to run take them in the house. Bluet and Ranny and Howard's little boy had three straws down a doodlebug hole and were all calling the doodlebug, each using a separate and ardent persuasion.

In the house she could hear India and Roxie laughing in a wild duet, Roxie turning the ice cream freezer, and at an upper window Aunt Shannon singing. Poor Lady Clare was calling that she was going to drop her comb and brush out the window if nobody came to make her look pretty and sweet. Shelley had taken Maureen and Laura with her to Greenwood for the groceries—they were out of everything. (Should she keep Laura? Billie McRaven was solid and devoted, but he had *no imagination*—should she take Laura and keep her at Shellmound?) Aunt Mac, driven by Little Uncle, had set off to Fairchilds for the payroll, as she had decided to iron it this morning—too much had happened, said Aunt Mac, and it seemed a little cool. Ellen had no idea where Roy and Little Battle had gone, racing out by themselves, she hoped and prayed they were all right and on the place. But Dabney. If only she could see Dabney, if Dabney would be home soon. Time, that she had wanted to stand still in the garden, waiting for her to catch up, if only it would fly and bring Dabney home. Memphis for three days even *sounded* like Forever.

She might go see what the men wanted for dinner. They were gone, except for poor Pinck, but she would go stand at the empty icebox and see if something would come to her. Battle, after having the bell beat on, had addressed a back yard full of Negroes that morning, all sleepy and holding their heads. "This many of you all are going over to Marmion to-day, right now—start in on it. Men clear off and clear out, women do sweeping—and so forth. Want you all to climb over the whole thing and see what has to be done—I imagine the roof's not worth a thing. Don't you go falling through, and skittering down the stairs, haven't got the time to fool with any broken necks, Miss Dabney wants Marmion *now*. Take your wagons, shovels, axes, everything—now shoo. Orrin, you go stand over this.—I believe we can do it in three days," he said to Ellen.

"Three days!"

"Sure. I could get it done in one day, if I could spare that many Negroes—all but the fine touches!"

"It *is* hard on you," she had said, watching him sink groaningly into his hammock.

"The weather's liable to change any day now," he agreed, shutting his eyes. "Then the rains."

George had wanted to plunge straight into fishing again, set off for Drowning Lake down the railroad track, and wanted Robbie to go with him—the minute he was out of bed. George—men—expected a resilience in women that exasperated Ellen while she wanted to laugh. Robbie had reached up and rapped him over the head—he stood in his pyjamas in the kitchen casually taking a bacon bone from Roxie's fingers. Robbie made him take her to Greenwood after breakfast, to buy her a little dress and some kind of little hat, saying that then they might fish somewhere, if he had to fish, and it wasn't too late. He would tolerate exactly that treatment, that was what he wanted, and they went off cheerfully together, in Tempe's car.

Pinchy, passing by, looked at Ellen stupidly. When Pinchy was coming through, she had not looked at her at all, but simply turned up her face, dark-purple like a pansy, that no more saw her nor knew her than a pansy. Now, speaking primly, back in her relationship on the place, she was without any mystery to move her. She was all dressed up in her glittering white.

"Pinchy! Where are you going, Pinchy?"

"To *church*, Miss Ellen," said Pinchy, with a soft, lush smile. *"This* is *Sunday!"*

Sunday! What has come over Aunt Mac? Ellen wondered, stricken. She'll never forgive herself, when she gets to the bank. Or us! We have every one lost track of the day of the week.

Laura liked to go along for the groceries, because in the Delta all grocery keepers seemed to be Chinese gentlemen. The car moved rapidly through the white fields toward Greenwood. A buzzard hung up in the deeps of sky, as if on a planted fish pole. Not another living creature was in sight.

"Is it still Shellmound?" she asked, but nobody answered her. Shelley must be thinking. Laura looked with speculation at the pure profile, the flying hair bound at the temples. She had thought Shelley perhaps knew more than anybody in the family, until Dabney's wedding night came, and Shelley was scorned a little, out in the hall—she had heard it.

She and India had gone to bed in an opened-out cot outside their room, because Dickie Boy Featherstone and Red Boyne had been put in their bed. One of the McLeouds had the place downstairs on the settee, and she thought Uncle Pinck might have stayed where last she saw him, in the hammock out under the stars.

Shelley had come down the hall barefooted, with her hair down, in her white nightgown. "Oh, Papa," she had said, standing in the door. "How could you keep getting Mama in this predicament?"

"How's that?" Uncle Battle asked drowsily.

"You'll catch cold, Shelley, come in out of that hall draft," Aunt Ellen said.

"I said how could you keep getting Mama in this predicament—again and again?"

"A predicament?"

"Like you do."

"I told you we were going to have another little girl, or boy. It won't be till Christmas," Aunt Ellen said sleepily in the voice she used to India, and Shelley hearing it said, "I'm not India!"

"Mama, we don't *need* any more." Shelley gave a reason: "We're perfect the way we are. I couldn't love any more of us."

"I've heard that before," said Aunt Ellen. "And what would you do without Bluet now?"

"What do you mean—a predicament?" said Uncle Battle once more.

"I thought that was what people call it," Shelley faltered. "I think in Virginia—"

"Maybe they do. And maybe they're right! But it's damn well none of your concern tonight, girlie," said Uncle Battle. "Waking up the house that's just getting to sleep."

But Shelley hung there as if she had nowhere to go. Robbie and George were sleeping in her room, its door pulled to, and one of Robbie's shoes had been dropped in the hall, as though George had picked her up and carried her in barefooted. This was Dabney's wedding night and the clock was striking. "The gas machine," Shelley tried to say, through the noise. "I'm so *sorry*, Mama—"

"Get in out of the draft, Shelley," said Aunt Ellen. "Even on a still night like tonight there's always a draft in that hall. Come in or go out."

"I'm going," said Shelley.

"Skedaddle," said her father. "Come kiss me."

"Yes, sir."

"You've got a bed."

"I can see you shivering right through your nightgown—standing with your back to the moon," said Aunt Ellen reproachfully, and Shelley folded her arms across herself and ran out on tiptoe.

"I hear people!" called Bluet from the sleeping porch. "I hear fairies and elves and gnomes! I hear pretty little babies fixing to dance!"

"Lie back down, Bluet!" yelled her father from his bed. "Go back to sleep or I'm coming to break your neck!"

"Are they going to dance by the light of the moon?" Bluet softly called a very subdued question.

"Yes, they *are*," Ranny could be heard answering her in an aerial voice.

"I'm going to move to a raft on the river where I can sleep!" shouted Orrin—though it sounded a bit like Little Battle too.

Then there was only the murmur of the night, the gin. There was once the cry of a hound far off, and Laura thought, Roy heard that too, and shivered in his bed. She would tell him that there was no mention of Aunt Studney's sack, and another baby was coming; that would stop him as he flitted by.

When Shelley got the groceries from a nice Chinese man who immediately unlocked the store for her (for it was Sunday) she saw Mr. Rondo forlorn on a corner and invited him to ride back to Fairchilds; something or other had delayed him, they could not follow other people's profuse talk, and he wanted by all means to get to church. He insisted that Maureen was the very one he wanted to sit by, though she did not want him to pat her, it was plain to see. He even drove her to try to steal Laura's doll.

"Give my darling back to me!"

Laura lay back in the whizzing car, her head gently rolling against the soft seat and Shelley's arm, and brought Marmion, her stocking doll, up to her cheek. She held him there, though he was hot—hotter than she was—and smelled his face which became, quite gently, fragrant of a certain day to her; his breath was the wind and rain of her street in Jackson.

It was a day they—her mother, father, and herself—were home from the summer's trip. With the opening of the front door which swung back with an uncustomary shiver, a sudden excitement made Laura run in first, pushing ahead of her father who had turned the key. She ran pounding up the stairs, striking the carpet flowers with the flat of her hands. The house was so close, so airless, that it gave out its own breath as she stirred it to life, the scents of carpet and matting and the oily smell of the clock and the smell of the starch in the curtains. It was morning, just before a rain. Through the window on the landing, the street was in the shadow of a cloud as close as a wing, fanning their tree and rolling sycamore balls over the roof of the porch.

Her mother, delighting in the threat of storm, went about opening the windows and on the landing leaning out on her hand as though she were all alone or nothing distracted her from the world outside. Her father was at the hall clock, standing with his driving cap and his goggles still on, reaching up to wind it. "I always like to know what time it is." She listened for her mother's familiar laugh at these words, and could imagine even without looking around at her how she flickered her eyelids as she smiled, so her father would not appear too bragging of his virtues or herself too unapprecia-tive. The loud ticks and the hours striking to catch up re-sponded to him and rose to the upper floor, accompanying Laura as she ran from room to room, in and out, flinging up shades, passing and looking in the mirrors.

Before the storm broke, before they were barely settled or had more than their faces washed, Laura cried, "Mother, make me a doll—I want a doll!"

What made this different from any other time? Her father for some reason did not ask "Why another?" or remind her of how many dolls she had or of when she last said she was tired of dolls and never wanted to play with one again. And this time was the most inconvenient that she could have cho-sen. Her mother, though, simply smiled—as if she shared the same excitement. As though Laura had made a perfectly log-ical request, her mother said, "Would you like a stocking doll?" And she began to turn things out of her basket, a shower of all kinds of colorful things, saved as if for the sheer pleasure of looking through.

Laura gazed at her mother, who laughed as she pulled the colored bits out and flung them on the floor. She was wearing a blue dress—"too light for traveling"—her hair was flying from the wind of riding and the breath of outside, fair long hair with the bone hairpins slipping loose. She was excited, smiling, young—as the cousins were always, but as she was not always—for the air at Shellmound was pleasure and excitement, pleasure that did not need to be explained, tears that could go a nice long time unsilenced, and the air of Jackson was different.

It was like a race between the creation of the doll and the bursting of the storm. In its summer location on the sleeping porch, the sewing machine whirred as if it spoke to the whirring outside. "Oh, Mother, hurry!"

"Just enough to stuff him!" She put every scrap in—every bright bit she had, all in one doll.

Now she was sewing on the head with her needle in her fingers. Then with the laundry ink she was drawing a face on the white stocking front. Laura leaned on her mother's long, soft knee, with her chin in her palm, entirely charmed by the drawing of the face. She could draw better than her mother could and the inferiority of the drawing, the slowly produced wildness of the unlevel eyes, the nose like a ditto mark, and the straight-line mouth with its slow, final additions of curves at the end, bringing at maddening delay a kind of smile, were like magic to watch.

Her mother was done. The first drop of rain had not fallen.

"What's his name?" Laura cried.

"Oh—he can be Marmion," said her mother casually. Had she been, after all, tired? Had she wanted to do something else, first thing on getting home—something of her own? She spoke almost grudgingly, as if everything, everything in that whole day's fund of life had gone into the making of the doll and it was too much to be asked for a name too.

Laura snatched Marmion from her mother and ran out. She did not say "Thank you." She flew down the stairs and out the front door.

The stormy air was dark and fresh, like a mint leaf. It smelled of coming rain and leaves sailed in companies through the middle air. Jackson to come back to was filled with a pulse of storm and she stood still and felt it, the forgotten heartbeat, for of course it had not rained on them visiting. The ground shook to some thunder not too far to hear, or of which only one note could be heard, like the stroke of a drum as far as

Smith Park on band-concert nights. She ran to the corner, which was down a hill, down a brick sidewalk, and at the corner house she called Lucy Bell O'Malley. Sometimes it is needful to show our dearest possessions to a comparative stranger. Lucy Bell was not a very good friend of Laura's, being too little. Last Christmas Laura had been taken calling on Lucy Bell by a neighbor in order that she might see something Santa Claus had brought her—a Teddy bear with electric eyes. The O'Malley parlor had had curtains and shades drawn—it was still and dark, almost as if a member of the family had died. And on the library table glittered, on and off, two emerald-green eyes. The Teddy bear lay there, on his back. But he could never be taken up from the library table and loved, for out of his stomach a cord attached him to the lamp, and Lucy Bell could only stand by and touch him. His eyes were as hot as fire.

"Lucy Bell! Look at my doll! We just came back from a car trip!" (Why, they had been to the Delta—been here! To Shellmound. And come home from it—it was under its momentum that her mother had been so quick and gay.) "His name is Marmion!"

She did not remember a thing Lucy Bell said to that. But as she cried it all out to her she knew that the reason she felt so superior was that she had gotten Marmion the minute she wished for him—it wasn't either too soon for her wish or too late. She had not even known, herself, that she wanted Marmion before that moment when she had implored her mother, "Make me a doll!"

She turned around and ran back in the winglike dark, holding Marmion high, so that Lucy Bell's eyes could follow. She got home and watched it storm, she and her mother standing quietly at the windows.

Now she held Marmion close, looking out across his crooked flat eye at the flying cotton, the same white after white, the fire-bright morning. She could kiss his fragrant face and know, Never more would she have this, the instant answer to a wish, for her mother was dead.

"Ah," said Mr. Rondo from the back seat. "The Yellow Dog!" as if he knew that subject interested the Fairchilds.

The track ran beside them on its levee through the fields and swamps, with now and then some little road, like the Shellmound road, climbing over the track to go off into the deep of the other side. Laura and Maureen waved at the Dog as it came down going back to Yazoo City. The engineer looked out of his window. "Mr. Doolittle," said Mr. Rondo.

"Mit-la Doo-littla can-na get-la by!" called Maureen.

Laura looked up at Shelley, her head with the band around it, as if she thought so much that she had to tie her brain in, like Faithful John and his heart and the iron band. It was good that Shelley had not that kind of heart too.

At that moment, with no warning, Shelley took one of the little crossing roads and drove the car up over the track, in front of the Yellow Dog, and down the other side.

"If you tell what I did, Laura," Shelley said calmly, after she let out her breath, "I'll cut you to pieces and hang you up for the buzzards. Are you going to tell?"

"No," said Laura, before she was through. Shelley's desperate qualities, out of the whole family, were those in which she unreservedly believed.

"I hope you won't speak of this, Mr. Rondo."

"Oh, no, no . . . !"

"Or Papa'd break my bones," Shelley said deprecatingly.

With her chin high, she drove along this side of the tracks where no road followed, taking the ruts, while the wildflowers knocked up at the under side of the car. It had struck her all at once as so fine to drive without pondering a moment onto disaster's edge—she would not always jump away! Now she was wrathful with herself, she despised what she had done, as if she had caught herself *contriving*. She flung up her head and looked for the Dog.

"Run home, Miss Shelley Fairchild!" called Old Man Doolittle.

Oh, horrors, he had stopped the Dog again! There it waited on the track, before the crossing, as if politely! How patronizing—coming to a stop for them a second time. Who on earth did Old Man Doolittle think he was, that he could even speak to a Fairchild out of that little window! The Yellow Dog started up again and came on by, inching by, its engine, with Mr. Doolittle *saluting*, and four cars, freight, white, colored, and caboose, its smoke like a poodle tail curled overhead, an inexcusable sight.

"Damn the Yellow Dog!" cried Shelley. "Excuse me, Mr. Rondo."

"Quite understand," said that foolish little man; even Laura knew he would have been the last person knowingly to let prudence, and respect for the spoiled young ladies of Shell-mound, be damned, and on a Sunday morning.

They rode, one way or another, into Fairchilds. "Is that Aunt Virgie Lee?" cried Laura.

Shelley slowed the car down and spoke to Virgie Lee. Usually she would have tried to pass without seeming to no-tice—the wild way Virgie Lee looked in the face, her cheeks painted red as if she were going to meet somebody, and in the back, with her hair tied up in a common rope.

Virgie Lee Fairchild, shaking her hair, going along in the ripply shade under the corrugated iron awning over the walk, rustled a green switch in their faces. As a matter of fact, she was going toward the church, fighting off the dogs—the Bap-tist Church.

"Go away! Go away! Don't tamper with me! Go home to your weddings and palaver," she said throatily. In her other hand she carried a purse by its strap (the way no lady would), a battered contraption like a shrunken-up suitcase. She might never end up in church, at all. When she swung the purse and danced the leafy branch, her long hair seemed to move all over in itself, like a waterfall.

Maureen leaned out over the side of the car and laughed aloud at her mother.

The sight and sound of that so terrified Laura that she flung herself over the back of the seat and threw her arms around Maureen as if to pull her back from fire, and held her, calling her as if she were deaf, "Maureen, Maureen!"

Virgie Lee, who had never stopped for them, emerged in the naked sun of the road and went on, her black hair seeming if possible to spread in the morning light, growing under eyes that hardly believed it, like a stain.

"You see! She'll have none of us!" said Shelley, in her light voice that had the catch in it.

Mr. Rondo, probably remembering he had already been

asked not to mention one thing, looked polite, taking the shortest glance at Virgie Lee. If he seemed to recognize her at all, it was as a Baptist. Shelley whirled off up the street and across the bridge, and they put Mr. Rondo down at the Methodist stile, where he thanked them and took out his watch, which, Laura told Shelley, seemed to have stopped.

"Poor Ellen," said Tempe, clasping her softly, her delicate, fragrant face large and serious as it pressed Ellen's close. "This has nearly killed you. I know! But, child, it's what mothers are for." They embraced in the kitchen, with Ranny pulling his mother's skirt—only a baby still.

"Tempe, I couldn't have done it without you." It was true, and she held Tempe the longer for being tired, from everything, from waiting—from mentally taking out shrubbery, from trying to make Howard love roses, from trying to make Bluet not want chicken pox or anything else because Lady Clare had it, from letting Aunt Mac get clear to the bank on a Sunday morning . . . Look at me, am I sorry for myself? she thought, shaken, seeing a mist in Tempe's eye.

Aunt Mac as a matter of fact had long since returned from her trip, without announcing whether it was successful or not. She came sitting as straight as she sat going out, in the pony cart under its wide flounced umbrella, and alighted at the carriage block without the slightest remark or notice of the world. She made her way into the house, Roy running up from somewhere like a flash, with a cut on his foot bleeding (he was the most *courteous* of her boys!), and escorting her, holding her elbow on the flat of his hand like a fine tray. No word would ever be said to *her* about money! Sunday money or any other kind.

Battle woke up and called for her, Jim Allen and Primrose were driven home, and the boys left over from the dance last night ate breakfast and departed, Red Boyne leaving Shelley a wild note which India read out loud. George and Robbie —who had gone off hours ago to buy a little dress and hat—came back in two cars, with the joke between them that it was Sunday. "We bought a car, though!" said Robbie. "The man opened up everything for George, and sold him a Hudson Super-Six." Shelley and the children came in starved from Greenwood, but bringing groceries from some charitable man, thank goodness.

Then Ellen was saying, catching the little girl in the hall, "Laura, there's something to tell you. We want you to stay, to live with us at Shellmound. Until you go to Marmion, perhaps. . . . Would you be happy? Your papa would listen to reason, he hopes you'd be happy too. India would be glad . . . Something's got all the curl out of your poor hair!"

The visit, the round-trip ticket on the Dog, had been just a premonition—now they told her what would really be. Shellmound! The real thing might always dawn upon her slowly, Laura felt, hanging her head while Aunt Ellen sadly stretched a straight strand of her hair out on her finger. That feeling that came over her—it was of having been cheated a little, not told at once. And so she answered overly soon, overly brightly, "Oh, I want to! I want to stay!" Then she cried, "But I don't want to go to Marmion!"

"Marmion'll be yours, you know, when you want it. I reckon! Someday you'll live there like your Aunt Ellen here, with all your chillen," said Uncle Battle, looking around Aunt Ellen and stepping out from behind her.

"I will?" said Laura. "It's big—isn't it?"

"Now, Battle, that's all too complicated to think of now, here in the hall," said Aunt Tempe, passing by. "You let Dabney have Marmion now, she wants it!"

"Besides—do you ever trust Virgie Lee not to flare up?" Aunt Ellen seemed to brood for a moment, her fingers went still in Laura's hair. "She'll have none of us now, but . . ."

"Did you have a dream about Virgie Lee?" Uncle Battle laughed.

Laura felt that in the end she would go—go from all this, go back to her father. She would hold that secret, and kiss Uncle Battle now.

Uncle Battle laughed and gave her a little dressing on her skirt. "Big? You'll grow, Skeeta," he said. "But no need to hurry."

And there was Aunt Shannon.

"Aunt Shannon," said Battle gruffly, sent in. His softened

voice was always hoarse; India listened, as she passed with her doll. "There's a plenty of everything. There's a plenty all around you. All in the world to eat, no need at all hiding bread crusts in your room. And nobody is dreaming they could get you or harm you. I'm here. See me?"

She nodded her head, gently and then sharply, and regarded him; India leaned in the door. "My little old boy," she said, and patted him. "Oh, you have a great deal to learn. Oh, Denis, I wish you wouldn't go out in the world unshielded and unprotected as you are. I have a feeling, I have a feeling, something will happen to you. . . ."

"If it isn't the Reconstruction, it's things just as full of trouble to you, isn't it?" Battle said softly, letting her pat her little hand on his great weight, holding still. He changed the level of his voice. "I'll stay, Aunt Shannon. I'll stay. I'm here. Here I am."

"Good-bye, my darling," she said.

2

It was the first night Dabney and Troy were back, and George's and Robbie's last night at the place. They would have a little family picnic.

"I don't see a bit of use trying to sit down to a big supper tonight, after all we've been eating, wedding food, company food . . . We'll just have a little picnic," said Ellen at the dinner table.

"Come to the Grove!" cried Primrose. The aunts were on hand at Shellmound for the welcomes and good-byes, of course.

"Marmion!" said Battle. "By God, it's not too hot for a barbecue. Not if we keep good and away from the fire."

"Troy loves barbecue," said Dabney gravely. It was Tuesday. They had just been away three days, on account of the picking.

But it was too hot for a barbecue, as could be seen by four o'clock, and they took a cold supper.

"Let's try out your new car, Dabney," said Orrin. "See how it takes the ruts. I'll drive."

"Oh, you will? Child, no. Robbie, you have a new car too."
She turned an earnest look on Robbie.

"We just got it in Greenwood, on Sunday," smiled Robbie.

But they went in buggies and wagons when the time came,
prevailed on for the sake of the tangles and brambles across
the river.

"You know, old Rondo's quite a fellow," said Battle. "Let's
invite him on the picnic!"

"No, then we'd have to go to church some Sunday," Ellen
pointed out. She said she had better stay home and keep Aunt
Mac and Aunt Shannon company, and poor Lady Clare, who
would know something was going on, but Battle and George
would not hear to that. Ranny and Bluet went nicely to sleep
at dark (Bluet still wearing her wedding shoes in bed part of
the night) never knowing about any of it, though Lady Clare
tore some of her red hair as she watched them go, pulled it
out by the roots to see a picnic start off without her, and
screamed that she would tell her papa.

It was a starry night—truly a little cool; that was hard to
believe! Laura and India, in the back of the buggy with the
food, rode at the head, Little Uncle, invisible, driving. A little
black horse mule was pulling them. They dangled their feet
over the track, looking at the rest of the procession. With
them rode a freezer of ice cream, the huddled napkins of
chicken, turkey, and sandwiches, the covered plates with surprises, the boxes with the caramel and the coconut cakes and
Aunt Tempe's lemon chiffon pie. The jug of iced tea was
somewhere—they could hear it shake and splash.

It was a beautiful night. "Still powder-dry!" called Battle,
out into it. "How much longer?" They were taking the plantation road into Fairchilds, to cross the river and follow the
old track to Marmion. Cotton was everywhere, as far as the
sky—the soft and level fields. Here and there little cabins nes-
tled, far away, and dark as hen roosts. In some of the wagons
they were singing "Some Sweet Day." Laura was sleepy, very
sleepy. By night the Delta looked just like a big bed, the
whiteness in the luminous dark. It was like the clouds that
spread around the east for the moon, that the horses walked
through and the buggies rolled over.

"The bayou ghost didn't cry once at Dabney's wedding,"

said Shelley's voice as they went by trees. "Did you notice her not crying, anybody?"

"If she held back, us Fairchilds consider that as lucky as you'd want." That was George.

"Listen—is that the crying now?"

But it was some night bird.

Dabney kept telling of how they went to New Orleans, not Memphis, and fooled everybody.

"We watched the river . . . the sea gulls . . ."

"It's the same river, Memphis and New Orleans," said Laura, opening her eyes and speaking from the back of their leading buggy. "My papa has taken me on trips—I know about geography . . ." But in the great confines of Shellmound, no one listened.

The night insects all over the Delta were noisy; a kind of audible twinkling, like a lowly starlight, pervaded the night with a gregarious radiance.

Ellen at Battle's side rode looking ahead, they were comfortable and silent, both, with their great weight, breathing a little heavily in a rhythm that brought them sometimes together. The repeating fields, the repeating cycles of season and her own life—there was something in the monotony itself that was beautiful, rewarding—perhaps to what was womanly within her. No, she had never had time—much time at all, to contemplate . . . but she knew. Well, one moment told you the great things, one moment was enough for you to know the greatest thing.

They rolled on and on. It was endless. The wheels rolled, but nothing changed. Only the heartbeat played its little drum, skipped a beat, played again.

"Is all of this Shellmound?" called little Laura McRaven.

"Remains to be seen!" called Battle gaily back.

From the last wagon came a chorus that started at Dabney's high pitch and changed in the middle—

> "Ye flowery banks o' bonnie Doon,
> How can ye bloom sae fair!"

They were crossing the river, rolling across the bridge, which groaned only lightly under their buggy wheels and the hoofs of the little horse mule.

> "Wi' lightsome heart I pu'd a rose
> Upon a morn in June,
> And sae I flourished on the morn,
> And sae was pu'd or' noon."

They went through the tangles and brambles, singing, and India took Laura around the waist, they held each other in.

"My secret is," India said in her ear, "I'm going to have another little brother before very long, and his name shall be Denis Fairchild."

Another wagon began its soft singing.

> "Oh, you'll take the high road and I'll take the low
>   road,
>   And I'll be in Scotland afore ye."

"My secret is," Laura murmured, "I've been in Marmion afore ye. I've seen it all afore. It's all happened afore." They leaned their heads together.

> "But me and my true love will never meet again . . ."

They're singing to Uncle George that his wife has left him, Laura thought sleepily but open-eyed. And to Dabney that she and Troy will never meet again. It was a picnic night. All secrets were being canceled out, sung out.

Uncle George's wagon came in view. Robbie and Maureen and George made a jolted but steady triangle, with little black boys hanging on and spilling off and catching up behind. And George was left still the adored one for the picnic, loved by the whole long procession with a love going further than the love for Dabney though she was the girl and the bride. The picnic was to tell Dabney hello but George good-bye. She gazed back at him, a figure in white clothes, face and throat dark by the starlight and in the brambly road—looking up at that moment, as if something wonderful might happen to him tonight, where he was going in the wagon. Maureen, now in all contrariness tame as a pigeon, squatted at his knee. She was *mostly* gentle, Laura dreamily realized. It was only now and then that she showed what she could do, just like most people. And Uncle George was singing—not "Loch Lomond," or "Some Sweet Day," but something . . . He was not really singing any song that she knew. It was something different and playful. He could not carry the tune—or he was improvising. It was that. She listened to it.

That picnic night she felt part of her cousins' life—part of it all. She was familiar at last with that wonderful, special anticipation that belonged to the Fairchilds, only to the Fairchilds in the whole world. A kind of wild, cousinly happiness surged through her and went out again, leaving her on India's shoulder.

She heard Uncle George's soft tune climb and fall, learned it—and then he changed to a whistle, just like a bird.

Marmion's grove rose up ahead, but Laura was asleep.

They had eaten everything they could, everything there was, and lay back groaning on the plaids and rugs. Battle had indeed cleared all the brambles away, it was a picnic place now by the riverside. There was a smell of cut green wood. And a smell of smoke—Howard was wafting it gently over them from a distant fire, aided by six or eight. George lighted his pipe to drive away the mosquitoes Tempe could tell were still after her. The dogs had the bones, those good for them and not, and worked contentedly by the water, now and then lifting up, listening . . . Overhead, showing it was the first cool night on the Delta, the Milky Way came out and wound like a bright river among the stars.

Troy handed a muscadine to his wife, like a present, and she gave him a weak tap and lay still with it in her teeth. Troy wore a new seersucker suit whose stripes in the house had seemed vibrant as if lightning were playing around him, but out here he looked like any other man in an old costume. Somebody sighed deeply. Once somebody said, "Too bad Pinck had to go to Memphis *today*." Little Battle was asleep, his cheek on his fist. Roy sat wordless, his gaze passing with the pure contact of starlight over all around. Orrin wandered off, first one way, then another, whistling like a whippoorwill.

"Did you all know Rowena wanted to be buried over here?" Jim Allen said once, out into the night. "Well, she did. But she wasn't."

"Wake up, Laura!"

"Oh, let her sleep."

"George," said Battle from where he lay on Ellen's blanket, "did I ever hear you say what you'd do if you came back and took possession of the Grove again?"

"Sure—I'd change things."

The silence drifted.

"Why, George," Tempe remarked, she alone sitting erect, and wielding her own little fan, "that's where Primmy and Jim Allen Fairchild are counting on living. If you came back, would you run your sisters away?"

There were little sounds never far away—the river and the woods. Their picnic had scared up the peafowls and peacocks, very fierce, long since gone to the wild, and now and then they ran in the viny ways to the river. The tower of Marmion was there over the trees.

"Let's go in," said Shelley, rising up. "Who wants to go in Marmion?"

"Nobody!" said Battle. "You can't go in, I've had that door locked for just such as you."

"Oh, if I took over, they could stay with us as long as they enjoy it," George said. "Or I could build them their own house near by. Or they could move in Shellmound—Dabney'll be here, and Orrin soon off to school—old Shelley'll not be long with us, I imagine," and he gave her ribbon a touch and it came off.

"I think you'd be *right* to, George," said Primrose, trying to make her voice carry. "And it's been such a responsibility!"

"Further than cotton, I might try fruit trees, might try some horses, even cattle," said George, smiling in the starlight.

"You're crazy, man," Battle roared delightedly.

"Who knows, I might try a garden. Vegetables!"

"Vegetables!" They all cried out together. "What would the Delta think?" Tempe demanded.

"And melons where all that sand was deposited on the bottom there."

"Is it what Robbie wants?" asked Shelley.

"Robbie wouldn't want it at all, I'm afraid," George said. "Robbie's our city girl born."

"I'd probably hate it," said Robbie dreamily. She laughed

softly where she lay on her back beside him, looking up at the sky. The lady moon, with a side of her hair gone, was rising.

"George," said Primrose, her voice shaking a little. "I forgot to tell you until now—there are rats at the Grove."

George laughed out. "Afraid to tell me!" He got up from Robbie's side and walked over to where Primrose sat on her little stool to keep "the damp" from her. "Primmy. Yes, I know, it has rats, and a lot of things—a ghost to keep you awake, and also it's the place Denis was going to come back to and enjoy a long, voracious old age and raise a houseful of healthy offspring. Now what if I want in, and others out, even you, Primmy?" He spoke softly.

"Georgie!"

"George said, What if he took the Grove?" Tempe called to Jim Allen.

The Grove? Robbie was thinking. Well, for her, it would be that once more they would laugh and chase by the river. Once more she and Mary Shannon, well-known as that star Venus, would be looking at each other in that house. Things almost never happened, almost never could be, for one time only! They went back again . . . started over . . .

"Robbie," said India. "Are you going to have a baby?"

"India!" said Ellen, shocked. "What do you know about babies?"

"I won't tell you," said Robbie in a clear voice, still lying on her back, one arm flung out, looking up at the sky.

Battle laughed uproariously.

"Excuse my back, please, ma'am," said Troy to Tempe. He pivoted around and kissed Dabney. "Do we have to kiss in front of your whole family from now on, Dabney, now that we're married?" He set her up straight again like something he had knocked over and was putting back so no one would tell the difference.

"Yes!" She looked on him beaming, maternally—to tease him.

How quickly she had known she loved Troy! Only she had not known how she could reach the love she felt already in her knowledge. In catching sight of love she had seen both banks of a river and the river rushing between—she saw everything but the way down. Even now, lying in Troy's bared arm like a drowned girl, she was timid of the element itself. Troy set her up again, and she smiled, looking at him all over and around him, up at the two rising horns of his parted hair. They had fooled everybody successfully about their honeymoon, because instead of going to the Peabody in Memphis they had gone to the St. Charles in New Orleans. Walking through the two afternoons down streets narrow as hallways, they had had to press back against the curb, against uncertain dark-green doors, to let the streetcars get through. The streetcars made an extraordinary clangor at such close quarters, as they did in the quiet of night, and some of them had "Desire" across the top. Could that have been the name of a street? She had not asked then; she did not much wonder now.

"Old Georgie. If you took possession of the Grove, you'd change it, eh?" said Battle. Ellen was leaning against him, she rubbed his arm tenderly. "Well—Shellmound's open, Prim, bear it in mind."

"Uncle Denis would never do this," said India dramatically.

"India," said Ellen, "you don't even remember your Uncle Denis, and why are you so wide awake? Laura's asleep."

"No, I'm not!"

"Well, Denis wouldn't," said Tempe. "Selfish, selfish! Spoiling the picnic. I don't understand George, he was always supposed to be so unselfish, unspoiled, never do anything but kind things. Now listen, he's as spoiled as any of us!"

"Oh, foot, Tempe," said Primrose. "Can't you listen to man talk without getting upset? Can't you listen to George and Battle talking?"

"What would Jim Allen think?" Battle said, yawning.

"She hates rats." Primrose laughed breathlessly. "We're two old maids, all right!"

"Well, *take* it then!" said Jim Allen all at once.

Ellen sighed. Poor deaf sister, she could not listen to herself, hear how grudging she sounded.

"I'd let George build Jim Allen and me a little house quick as anything," said Primrose. "And furniture, there's enough beds and all in the attic for a world of houses here."

"Your night light will be gone," said India. "Dabney broke it for good, carrying it away."

There was another silence, but gentler, more restful.

"Come back, George," said Robbie.

"Bless your hearts, Primrose," said George. He kissed her and Jim Allen.

"It's got *rats!*" said Jim Allen, and she sank back, restfully, as if there were comforts, after all, in a little spitefulness.

"But I don't understand George at all," Tempe began again, as if George himself were not there, and he kissed her too. "You just want to provoke your sisters, you're just teasing."

"It's his house," said Ellen. (Had she started interfering with the Fairchilds again—this far along? She sounded to herself for a moment like herself as a bride.)

"But I didn't dream he wanted it," Battle said. "'Here, take the Grove,' he said to the girls, when they wanted to fool with a house. Did that sound like he wanted it?"

"Why not?" said Primrose proudly. "Anyway—he only said tonight 'If—then maybe.'"

"Oh, my." Dabney yawned in luxury. "I'm glad he doesn't want to take Marmion away from me."

"Shame on you, pussy," said Troy sharply, and she was quiet.

"Watermelons and greens!" Tempe still fumed softly. "Sisters out in the cold. George, sometimes I don't think you show the most perfect judgment." Then they both laughed gently at each other.

> "Oft in the stilly night,
> Ere Slumber's chain has bound me . . ."

They began to sing, softly, wanderingly, each his way. But Jim Allen, whose voice rose strongest, stretched tilted on her small plump elbow on the grassy blanket, was looking at Robbie Reid as if she were for the first time quite aware that her brother was married—not hopelessly, like the dead Denis, but problematically, not promisingly!

> "Oft in the stilly night—"

"I like your idea, George," Troy said with deliberation through the song. "Growing greens and getting some cows around. I love a little Jersey, more than anything."

George, with his left-handed throw, put pebbles in the Yazoo. "We'll keep in touch. . . ."

One great golden star went through the night falling.

"Oh!" cried Laura aloud. "Oh, it was beautiful, that star!"

"I saw it, I saw it!" cried India.

Dabney reached over and put her arm around her, drew her to her. "Yes. Beautiful!" India smiled faintly, leaning on Dabney's beating heart, the softness of her breast.

Then, "Oh, India, you still look so tacky!" cried Dabney breathlessly. "I thought you'd be changed, some! Oh, *Mama*, look at her!"

"Stand still, India," said Ellen.

But India darted off and ran to look in the river. She stood showily, hands on hips, as if she saw some certain thing, neither marvelous nor terrible, but simply certain, come by in the Yazoo River.

Laura lifted on her knees and took her Aunt Ellen around the neck. She held her till they swayed together. Would Aunt Ellen remember it against her, that she had run away from her when she fainted? Of course Aunt Ellen would never find out about the rosy pin. Should she tell her, and suffer? Yes. No. She touched Aunt Ellen's cheek with three anxious, repaying kisses.

"Oh, beautiful!" Another star fell in the sky.

Laura let go and ran forward a step. "I saw that one too."

"Did you?" said somebody—Uncle George.

"I saw where it fell," said Laura, bragging and in reassurance.

She turned again to them, both arms held out to the radiant night.

THE PONDER HEART

TO
MARY LOUISE ASWELL,
WILLIAM AND EMILY MAXWELL

M Y UNCLE DANIEL'S just like your uncle, if you've got one—only he has one weakness. He loves society and he gets carried away. If he hears our voices, he'll come right down those stairs, supper ready or no. When he sees you sitting in the lobby of the Beulah, he'll take the other end of the sofa and then move closer up to see what you've got to say for yourself; and then he's liable to give you a little hug and start trying to give you something. Don't do you any good to be bashful. He won't let you refuse. All he might do is forget tomorrow what he gave you today, and give it to you all over again. Sweetest disposition in the world. That's his big gray Stetson hanging on the rack right over your head—see what a large head size he wears?

Things I could think of without being asked that he's given away would be—a string of hams, a fine suit of clothes, a white-face heifer calf, two trips to Memphis, pair of fantail pigeons, fine Shetland pony (loves children), brooder and incubator, good nanny goat, bad billy, cypress cistern, field of white Dutch clover, two iron wheels and some laying pullets (they were together), cow pasture during drouth (he has everlasting springs), innumerable fresh eggs, a pick-up truck—even his own cemetery lot, but they wouldn't accept it. And I'm not counting this week. He's been a general favorite all these years. *he buys love*

Grandpa Ponder (in his grave now) might have any fine day waked up to find himself in too pretty a fix to get out of, but he had too much character. And besides, Edna Earle, I used to say to myself, if the worst does come to the worst, Grandpa *is* rich.

When I used to spot Grandpa's Studebaker out front, lighting from the country, and Grandpa heading up the walk, with no Uncle Daniel by his side, and his beard beginning to shake under his chin, and he had a beautiful beard, I'd yell back to the kitchen, "Ada! Be making Mr. Sam some good strong iced tea!" Grandpa was of the old school, and wanted people to measure up—everybody in general, and Uncle Daniel and me

narrative an aside

339

in particular. He and Grandma raised me, too. "Clear out, you all," I'd say to who all was in here. "Here comes Grandpa Ponder, and no telling what he has to tell me." I was his favorite grandchild, besides being the only one left alive or in calling distance.

"Now what, sir?" I'd say to Grandpa. "Sit down first, on that good old sofa—give me your stick, and here comes you some strong tea. What's the latest?"

He'd come to tell me the latest Uncle Daniel had given away. The incubator to the letter carrier—that would be a likely thing, and just as easy for Uncle Daniel as parting with the rosebud out of his coat. Not that Uncle Daniel ever got a *letter* in his life, out of that old slow poke postman.

"I only wish for your sake, Grandpa," I'd say sometimes, "you'd never told Uncle Daniel all you had."

He'd say, "Miss, I didn't. And further than that, one thing I'm never going to tell him about is money. And don't let me hear you tell him, Edna Earle."

"Who's the smart one of the family?" I'd say, and give him a little peck.

My papa was Grandpa's oldest child and Uncle Daniel was Grandpa's baby. They had him late—mighty late. They used to let him skate on the dining room table. So that put Uncle Daniel and me pretty close together—we liked to caught up with each other. I did pass him in the seventh grade, and hated to do it, but I was liable to have passed anybody. People told me I ought to have been the *teacher*.

It's always taken a lot out of me, being smart. I say to people who only pass through here, "Now just a minute. Not so fast. Could *you* hope to account for twelve bedrooms, two bathrooms, two staircases, five porches, lobby, dining room, pantry and kitchen, every day of your life, and still be out here looking pretty when they come in? And two Negroes? And that plant?" Most people ask the name of that plant before they leave. All I can tell them is, Grandma called it Miss Ouida Sampson after the lady that wished it on her. When I was younger, I used to take a blue ribbon on it at the County Fair. Now I just leave it alone. It blooms now and then.

But oh, when the place used to be busy! And when Uncle Daniel would start on a spree of giving away—it comes in

our clue to audience

sprees—and I would be trying to hold Grandpa down and account for this whole hotel at the same time—and Court would fling open in session across the street and the town fill up, up, up—and Mr. Springer would sure as Fate throttle into town and want that first-floor room, there where the door's open, and count on me to go to the movie with him, tired traveling man—oh, it was Edna Earle this, and Edna Earle that, every minute of my day and time. This is like the grave compared. *You're* only here because your car broke down, and I'm afraid you're allowing a Bodkin to fix it.

And listen: if you read, you'll put your eyes out. Let's just talk.

You'd know it was Uncle Daniel the minute you saw him. He's unmistakable. He's big and well known. He has the Ponder head—large, of course, and well set, with short white hair over it thick and curly, growing down his forehead round like a little bib. He has Grandma's complexion. And big, forget-me-not blue eyes like mine, and puts on a sweet red bow tie every morning, and carries a large-size Stetson in his hand—always just swept it off to somebody. He dresses fit to kill, you know, in a snow-white suit. But do you know he's up in his fifties now? Don't believe it if you don't want to. And still the sweetest, most unspoiled thing in the world. He has the nicest, politest manners—he's good as gold. And it's not just because he's kin to me I say it. I don't run the Beulah Hotel for nothing: I size people up: I'm sizing you up right now. People come here, pass through this book, in and out, over *an* the years—and in the whole shooting-match, I don't care *aside* from where or how far they've come, not one can hold a candle to Uncle Daniel for looks or manners. If he ever did a thing to be sorry for, it's more than he ever intended.

Oh, even the children have always reckoned he was theirs to play with. When they'd see him coming they'd start jumping up and down till he'd catch them and tickle their ribs and give them the change he carried. Grandpa used to make short work of them.

Grandpa worshiped Uncle Daniel. Oh, Grandpa in his panama and his seersucker suit, and Uncle Daniel in his red tie and Stetson and little Sweetheart rose in his lapel! They did set up a pair. Grandpa despised to come to town, but Uncle

Daniel loved it, so Grandpa came in with him every Saturday. That was the way you knew where you were and the day of the week it was—those two hats announcing themselves, rounding the square and making it through the crowd. Uncle Daniel would always go a step or two behind, to exchange a few words, and Grandpa would go fording a way in front with his walking cane, through farmers and children and Negroes and dogs and the countryside in general. His nature was impatient, as time went by.

Nothing on earth, though, would have made Grandpa even consider getting strict with Uncle Daniel but Uncle Daniel giving away this hotel, of all things. He gave it to me, fifteen long years ago, and I don't know what it would have done without me. But "Edna Earle," says Grandpa, "this puts me in a quandary."

Not that Grandpa minded me having the hotel. It was Grandma's by inheritance, and used to be perfectly beautiful before it lost its paint, and the sign and the trees blew down in front, but he didn't care for where it stood, right in the heart of Clay. And with the town gone down so—with nearly all of *us* gone (Papa for one left home at an early age, nobody ever makes the mistake of asking about *him*, and Mama never did hold up—she just had me and quit; she was the last of the Bells)—and with the wrong element going spang through the middle of it at ninety miles an hour on that new highway, he'd a heap rather *not* have a hotel than have it. And it's true that often the people that come in off the road and demand a room right this minute, or ask you ahead what you have for dinner, are not the people you'd care to spend the rest of your life with at all. For Grandpa that settled it. He let Miss Cora Ewbanks run it as she pleased, and she was the one let the sign blow down, and all the rest. She died very shortly after she left it—an old maid.

The majority of what Uncle Daniel had given away up to then was stuff you could pick up and cart away—miscellaneous is a good word for it. But the Beulah was solid. It looked like it had dawned on Uncle Daniel about *property*. (Pastures don't count—you can take them back by just setting their cows back on the road.) Grandpa was getting plenty old, and

unusual narration like a whisper us "...just between"

he had a funny feeling that once *property* started going, next might go the Ponder place itself, and the land and the crop around it, and everything right out from under Uncle Daniel's feet, for all *you* could predict, once Grandpa wasn't there to stop him. Once Grandpa was in his grave, and Uncle Daniel shook free, he might succeed in giving those away to somebody not kin or responsible at all, or not even local, who might not understand what they had to do. Grandpa said that *the moral* people exist in the realm of reason that are ready to take advantage of an open disposition, and the bank might be compelled to honor that—because of signatures or witnesses or whatever monkey-foolishness people go through with if they're strangers or up to something.

Grandpa just wanted to teach Uncle Daniel a lesson. But what he did was threaten him with the asylum. That wasn't the way to do it.

I said, "Grandpa, you're burning your bridges before you get to them, I think."

But Grandpa said, "Miss, I don't want to hear any more about it. I've warned him, now." So he warned him for nine years.

And as for Uncle Daniel, he went right ahead, attracting love and friendship with the best will and the lightest heart in the world. He loved being happy! He loved happiness like I love tea.

And then in April, just at Easter time, Grandpa spent some money himself, got that new Studebaker, and without saying kiss-my-foot to me, Grandpa and old Judge Tip Clanahan up and took Uncle Daniel through the country to Jackson in that brand-new automobile, and consigned him.

"That'll correct him, I expect," said Grandpa.

Child-foolishness! Oh, Grandpa lived to be sorry. Imagine that house without Uncle Daniel in it. I grew up there, but all you really need to know about is it's a good three miles out in the country from where you are now, in woods full of hoot-owls.

To be fair, that wasn't till after Grandpa'd tried praying over Uncle Daniel for years and years, and worn out two preachers praying over them both. Only I was praying against Grandpa and preachers and Judge Tip Clanahan to boot, because whatever *you* say about it, I abhor the asylum.

Oh, of course, from the word Go, Uncle Daniel got more vacations than anybody else down there. In the first place, they couldn't find anything the matter with him, and in the second place, he was so precious that he only had to ask for something. It seemed to me he was back home visiting more than he ever was gone between times, and pop full of stories. He had a pass from the asylum, and my great-grandfather Bell had been a big railroad man, so he had a pass on the branch-line train, and it was the last year we had a passenger train at all, so it worked out grand. Little train just hauls cross-ties now. Everybody missed Uncle Daniel so bad while he was gone, they spent all their time at the post office sending him things to eat. Divinity travels perfectly, if you ever need to know.

Of course, let him come home and he'd give away something. You can't stop that all at once. He came home and gave the girl at the bank a trip to Lookout Mountain and Rock City Cave, and then was going along with her to watch her enjoy both, and who prevailed on him then? Edna Earle. I said, "Dear heart, *I* know the asylum's no place for you, but neither is the top of a real high mountain or a cave in the cold dark ground. Here's the place." And he said, "All right, Edna Earle, but make me some candy." He's good as gold, but you have to know the way to treat him; he's a man, the same as they all are.

But he had a heap to tell. You ought to have heard some of the tales! It didn't matter if you didn't know the people: something goes on there all the time! I hope I'm not speaking of kin of present company. We'd start laughing clear around town, the minute Uncle Daniel hopped off the train, and never let up till Grandpa came chugging in to get him, to set him on the down-train. Grandpa did keep at it. And I don't know how it worked, but Uncle Daniel *was* beginning to be less open-handed. He commenced slacking up on giving away with having so much to tell.

The sight of a stranger was always meat and drink to him. The stranger don't have to open his mouth. Uncle Daniel is

ready to do all the talking. That's understood. I used to dread
he might get hold of one of these occasional travelers that
wouldn't come in unless they had to—the kind that would
break in on a story with a set of questions, and wind it up
with a list of what Uncle Daniel's faults were: some Yankee.
But Uncle Daniel seemed to have a sixth sense and avoid
those, and light on somebody from nearer home always. He'd
be crazy about you.

Grandpa was a little inclined to slow him down, of course.
He'd say, "Who?—What, Daniel?—When?—Start over!" He
was the poorest listener in the world, though I ought not to
say that now when he's in his grave. But all the time, whatever
Uncle Daniel might take it into his head to tell you, rest assured it was the Lord's truth to start with, and exactly the
way he'd see it. He never told a lie in his life. Grandpa
couldn't get past that, poor Grandpa. That's why he never
could punish him.

I used to say Mr. Springer was the perfect listener. A drug
salesman with a wide, wide territory, in seldom enough to
forget between times, and knowing us well enough not to try
to interrupt. And too tired to object to hearing something
over. If anything, he laughed too soon. He used to sit and
beg for Uncle Daniel's favorite tale, the one about the time
he turned the tables on Grandpa.

Turned the tables not on purpose! Uncle Daniel is a perfect gentleman, and something like that has to *happen*; he
wouldn't contrive it.

Grandpa one time, for a treat, brought Uncle Daniel home
to vote, and took him back to the asylum through the country, in the new Studebaker. They started too early and got
there too early—I told them! And there was a new lady busy-
ing herself out at the front, instead of the good old one.
"Low-in-the-hole!" as Uncle Daniel says, the lady asked *him*
who the old *man* was. Uncle Daniel was far and away the best
dressed and most cheerful of the two, of course. Uncle Daniel
says, "Man alive! Don't you know that's *Mr. Ponder?*" And
the lady was loading the Coca-Cola machine and says, "Oh,
foot, I can't remember everybody," and called somebody and
they took Grandpa. Hat, stick, and everything, they backed
him right down the hall and shut the door on him boom. And

the moral or rule

life is a series of stories/moments   *great!*

Uncle Daniel waited and dallied and had a Coca-Cola with his nickel when they got cold, and then lifted his hat and politely backed out the front door and found Grandpa's car with the engine running still under the crape myrtle tree, and drove it on home and got here with it—though by the time he did, he was as surprised as Grandpa. And that's where he ends his story. Bless his heart. And that's where Mr. Springer would turn loose and laugh till Uncle Daniel had to beat him on the back to save him.

The rest of it is, that down in Jackson, the madder Grandpa got, the less stock they took in him, of course. That's what crazy *is*. They took Grandpa's walking stick away from him like he was anybody else. Judge Tip Clanahan had to learn about it from Uncle Daniel and then send down to get Grandpa out, and when Grandpa did get loose, they nearly gave him back the wrong stick. They would have heard from him about *that*.

When Uncle Daniel got here with that tale, everybody in town had a conniption fit trying to believe it, except Judge Tip. Uncle Daniel thought it was a joke on the *lady*. It took Grandpa all day long from the time he left here to make it on back, with the help of Judge Clanahan's long-legged grandson and no telling what papers. *He* might as well not have left home, he wouldn't stop to tell us a word.

There's more than one moral to be drawn there, as I told Mr. Springer at the time, about straying too far from where you're known and all—having too wide a territory. Especially if you light out wearing a seersucker suit you wouldn't let the rummage sale have, though it's old as the hills. By the time you have to *prove* who you are when you get there, it may be too late when you get back. *Think* about Grandpa Ponder having to call for witnesses the minute he gets fifty miles off in one direction. I think that helped put him in his grave. It went a long way toward making him touchy about what Uncle Daniel had gone and done in the meanwhile. You see, by the time Grandpa made it back, something had happened at home. Something will every time, if you're not there to see it.

Uncle Daniel had got clear up to his forties before we ever dreamed that such a thing as love flittered through his mind.

He's so *sweet*. Sometimes I think if we hadn't showed him that widow! But he was bound to see her: he has eyes: Miss Teacake Magee, lived here all her life. She sings in the choir of the Baptist Church every blessed Sunday: couldn't get *her* out. And sings louder than all the rest put together, so loud it would make you lose your place.

I'll go back a little for a minute. Of course we're all good Presbyterians. Grandpa was an elder. The Beulah Bible Class and the Beulah Hotel are both named after Grandma. And my other grandma was the second-to-longest-living Sunday School teacher they've ever had, very highly regarded. My poor little mama got a pageant written before she died, and I still conduct the rummage sales for the Negroes every Saturday afternoon in the corner of the yard and bring in a sum for the missionaries in Africa that I think would surprise you.

Miss Teacake Magee is of course a Sistrunk (the Sistrunks are *all* Baptists—big Baptists) and Professor Magee's widow. He wasn't professor *of* anything, just real smart—smarter than the Sistrunks, anyway. He'd never worked either—he was like Uncle Daniel in that respect. With Miss Teacake, everything dates from "Since I lost Professor Magee." A passenger train hit him. That shows you how long ago *his* time was.

Uncle Daniel *thought* what he was wild about at that time was the Fair. And I kept saying to myself, maybe that *was* it. He carried my plant over Monday, in the tub, and entered it for me as usual, under "Best Other Than Named"—it took the blue ribbon—and went on through the flowers and quilts and the art, passing out compliments on both sides of him, and out the other door of the Fine Arts Tent and was loose on the midway. From then on, the whole week long, he'd go back to the Fair every whipstitch—morning, noon, or night, hand in hand with any soul, man, woman, or child, that chose to let him—and spend his change on them and stay till the cows come home. He'd even go by himself. I went with him till I dropped. And we'd no more leave than he'd clamp my arm. "Edna Earle, look back yonder down the hill at all those lights still a-burning!" Like he'd never seen lights before. He'd say, "Sh! Listen at Intrepid Elsie Fleming!"

Intrepid Elsie Fleming rode a motorcycle around the Wall of Death—which let her do, if she wants to ride a motorcycle

that bad. It was the time she wasn't riding I objected to—
when she was out front on the platform warming up her motor. That was nearly the whole time. You could hear her day
and night in the remotest parts of this hotel and with the sheet
over your head, clear over the sound of the Merry-Go-Round
and all. She dressed up in pants.

Uncle Daniel said he had to admire that. He admired everything he saw at the Fair that year, to tell the truth, and everything he heard, and always expected to win the Indian
blanket; never did—*they* never let him. I'll never forget when
I first realized what flittered through his mind.

He'd belted me into the Ferris Wheel, then vanished, instead of climbing into the next car. And the first thing I made
out from the middle of the air was Uncle Daniel's big round
hat up on the platform of the Escapades side-show, right in
the middle of those ostrich plumes. There he was—passing
down the line of those girls doing their come-on dance out
front, and handing them out ice cream cones, right while they
were shaking their heels to the music, not in very good time.
He'd got the cream from the Baptist ladies' tent—banana, and
melting fast. And I couldn't get off the Ferris Wheel till I'd
been around my nine times, no matter how often I told them
who I was. When I finally got loose, I flew up to Uncle Daniel
and he stood there and hardly knew me, licking away and
beside himself with pride and joy. And his sixty cents was
gone, too. Well, he would have followed the Fair to Silver
City when it left, if I'd turned around good.

He kept telling me for a week after, that those dancing girls
wore beyond compare the prettiest dresses and feather-pieces
he ever saw on ladies' backs in his life, and could dance like
the fairies. "They every one smiled at me," he said. "And yet
I liked Miss Elsie Fleming very well, too." So the only thing
to be thankful for is he didn't try to treat Intrepid Elsie
Fleming—she might have bitten him.

As for Grandpa, I didn't tell him about the twelve banana
ice cream cones and where they went, but he heard—he
played dominoes with Judge Tip—and as soon as he got home
from the Clanahans' he took a spell with his heart. The Ponder heart! So of course we were all running and flying to do
his bidding, everything under the sun he said. I never saw

such lovely things as people sent—I gained ten pounds, and begged people to spare us more. Of course I was running out there day and night and tending to the Beulah between times. One morning when I carried Grandpa his early coffee, which he wasn't supposed to have, he said to me, "Edna Earle, I've been debating, and I've just come to a conclusion."

"What now, Grandpa?" I said. "Tell me real slow."

Well, he did, and to make a long story short, he had his way; and after that he never had another spell in his life till the one that killed him—when Uncle Daniel had *his* way. The heart's a remarkable thing, if you ask me. "I'm fixing to be strict for the first time with the boy," was Grandpa's conclusion. "I'm going to fork up a good wife for him. And you put your mind on who."

"I'll do my best, Grandpa," I said. "But remember we haven't got the whole wide world to choose from any more. Mamie Clanahan's already engaged to the man that came to put the dial telephones in Clay. Suppose we cross the street to the Baptist Church the first Sunday you're out of danger."

So up rose Miss Teacake Magee from the choir—her solo always came during collection, to cover up people rattling change and dropping money on the floor—and when I told Uncle Daniel to just listen to that, it didn't throw such a shadow over his countenance as you might have thought.

"Miss Teacake's got more breath in her than those at the Fair, that's what she's got," he whispers back to me. And before I could stop his hand, he'd dropped three silver dollars, his whole month's allowance, in the collection plate, with a clatter that echoed all over that church. Grandpa fished the dollars out when the plate came by him, and sent me a frown, but he didn't catch on. Uncle Daniel sat there with his mouth in an O clear through the rest of the solo. It seems to me it was "Work, for the Night Is Coming." But I was saying to myself, Well, Edna Earle, she's a Sistrunk. And a widow well taken care of. And she makes and sells those gorgeous cakes that melt in your mouth—she's an artist. Forget about her singing. So going out of church, I says, "Eureka, Grandpa. I've found her." And whispers in his ear.

"Go ahead, then, girl," says he.

If you'd ever known Grandpa, you'd have been as surprised

as I was when Grandpa didn't object right away, and conclude we'd better find somebody smarter than that or drop the whole idea. Grandpa would be a lot more willing to stalk up on a wedding and stop it, than to encourage one to go on. Anybody's—yours, mine, or the Queen of Sheba's. He regarded getting married as a show of weakness of character in nearly every case but his own, because he was smart enough to pick a wife very nearly as smart as he was. But he was ready to try anything once for Uncle Daniel, and Miss Teacake got by simply because Grandpa knew who she was—and a little bit because of her hair as black as tar—something she gets from Silver City and puts on herself in front of the mirror.

Poor Grandpa! Suppose I'd even *attempted*, over the years, to step off—I dread to think of the lengths Grandpa would have gone to to stop it. Of course, I'm intended to look after Uncle Daniel and everybody knows it, but in plenty of marriages there's three—three all your life. Because nearly everybody's got somebody. I used to think if I ever did step off with, say, Mr. Springer, Uncle Daniel wouldn't mind; he always could make Mr. Springer laugh. And I could name the oldest child after Grandpa and win him over quick before he knew it. Grandpa adored compliments, though he tried to hide it. Ponder Springer—that sounds perfectly plausible to me, or did at one time.

At any rate, Uncle Daniel and Miss Teacake got married. I just asked her for recipes enough times, and told her the real secret of cheese straws—beat it three hundred strokes—and took back a few unimportant things I've said about the Baptists. The wedding was at the Sistrunks', in the music room, and Miss Teacake insisted on singing at her own wedding— sang "The Sweetest Story Ever Told."

It was bad luck. The marriage didn't hold out. We were awfully disappointed in Miss Teacake, but glad to have Uncle Daniel back. What Uncle Daniel told me he didn't take to—I asked him because I was curious—was hearing spool-heels coming and going on Professor Magee's floor. But he never had a word to say against Miss Teacake: I think he liked her. Uncle Daniel has a remarkable affection for everybody and everything in creation. I asked him one question about her and got this hotel. Miss Teacake's settled down again now, and don't seem to be considering catching anybody else in particular. Still singing.

So Grandpa carried Uncle Daniel to the asylum, and before too long, Uncle Daniel turned the tables on Grandpa, and never had to go back *there*.

M EANTIME! Here traipsed into town a little thing from away off down in the country. Near Polk: you wouldn't have ever heard of Polk—I hadn't. Bonnie Dee Peacock. A little thing with yellow, fluffy hair.

The Peacocks are the kind of people keep the mirror outside on the front porch, and go out and pick railroad lilies to bring inside the house, and wave at trains till the day they die. The most they probably hoped for was that somebody'd come find oil in the front yard and fly in the house and tell them about it. Bonnie Dee was one of nine or ten, and no bigger than a minute. A good gust of wind might have carried her off any day.

She traipsed into Clay all by herself and lived and boarded with some Bodkins on Depot Street. And went to work in the ten cent store: all she knew how to do was make change.

So—that very day, after Uncle Daniel finished turning the tables and was just through telling us about it, and we were all having a conniption fit in here, Uncle Daniel moseyed down the street and in five minutes was inside the ten cent store. That was where he did all his shopping. He was intending to tell his story in there, I think, but instead of that, he was saying to the world in general and Bonnie Dee at the jewelry counter in particular, "I've got a great big house standing empty, and my father's Studebaker. Come on— marry me."

You see how things happen? Miss Lutie Powell, Uncle Daniel's old schoolteacher, was in there at the time buying a spool of thread, and she heard it—but just didn't believe it.

I was busy, busy, busy with two things that afternoon— worrying about what I'd say to Grandpa when he got back, and conducting my rummage sale in the yard. I might as well have been in Jericho. If Uncle Daniel had told me what he was going in the ten cent store to say—but I doubt strongly if he knew, himself, he's so sudden-quick—I could have pretty well predicted the answer. I could have predicted it partway. Because—Uncle Daniel can't help it!—he always makes every-

thing sound grand. Home on the hilltop! Great big car! Negroes galore! Home-grown bacon and eggs and ham and fried
grits and potato cakes and honey and molasses for breakfast
every morning to start off with—you know, you don't have
to have all the brilliance in the world to sound grand, or *be*
grand either. It's a gift.

The first thing I knew of what transpired was two hours
and a half later, when I was two dollars and ninety-five cents
to the good of the heathen, selling away to the Negroes as
hard as I could and dead on my feet in the yard. Then bang
up against the hitching post at the curb pulls in that Studebaker. It honks, and the motor huffs and puffs, and the whole
car's shaking all over like it does if you stop it too quick after
running it too long. *It's* been going all day, too. I shade my
eyes and who do I see but old Narciss at the steering wheel.
She's the cook out at the place. She's looking at me, very
mournful and meaning and important. She always does look
like that, but I never in my life knew she knew how to drive.

"Oh-oh," I says to the rummage sale. "Don't anybody
touch a thing till I get back," and march out to meet it. There
in the back seat sat Uncle Daniel big as life and right beside
him Bonnie Dee Peacock, batting her eyes.

"Uncle Daniel, dear heart, why don't you get out and come
in?" I says, speaking just to him, first.

And Eva Sistrunk, the one that's a little older than me, just
passing by with nothing to do, stopped in her tracks and politely listened in.

"Eva, how's your family?" says Uncle Daniel.

He was beaming away for all he was worth and shooting
up his arm every minute to wave—of course Saturday traffic
was traveling around the Square. Those people had just spent
the morning waving him good-by, seeing him off to the asylum with Grandpa. By next time around they'd know everything. I look straight at Narciss.

Narciss is biding her time till she's got a big crowd and an
outside ring of Negroes; then she sings out real high and sad,
"Mr. Daniel done took a new wife, Miss Edna Earle."

You can't trust a one of them: a Negro we'd had her whole
life long, older by far than I was, Grandma raised her from a
child and brought her in out of the field to the kitchen and

taught her everything she knew. Just because Uncle Daniel
asked the favor, because the Studebaker wouldn't run for him
the minute he got it back to where it belonged, Narciss
hitched herself right in that front seat and up to the wheel
and here they flew; got Bonnie Dee from in front of Woolworth's (and nobody saw it, which I think is worth mentioning—I believe they picked her up without stopping) and went
kiting off to Silver City, and a justice of the peace with a sign
in the yard married them. Uncle Daniel let Narciss pick out
where to go, and Narciss picked out Silver City because she'd
never been. None of them had ever been! It was the only spot
in Creation they could have gone to without finding somebody that knew enough to call Clay 123 and I'd answer. Silver
City's too progressive. Here they rolled back all three as
pleased and proud as Punch at what they'd accomplished. It
wasn't lost on me, for all the length Narciss had her mouth
drawn down to.

I hadn't even had my bath! I just stood there, in my rag-
gediest shade hat and that big black rummage sale purse
weighting me down, all traffic stopped, and Eva Sistrunk with
her face in mine just looking.

"So Miss Teacake's an old story," I said. "All right, Uncle
Daniel—this makes you two."

"Makes me three," he says. "Hop out a minute, sugar,
down in the road where Edna Earle and them can see you,"
he says to the child. But she sits there without a hat to her
name, batting her eyes. "I married Mrs. Magee and I married
this young lady, and way before that was the Tom Thumb
Wedding—that was in *church.*"

And it was. He has the memory of an elephant. When he
was little he was in the Tom Thumb Wedding—Mama's pageant—and everybody said it was the sweetest miniature wedding that had ever been held here. He was the bridegroom
and I believe to my soul Birdie Bodkin, the postmistress, was
the bride—the Bodkins have gone down since. They left the
platform together on an Irish Mail decorated with Southern
Smilax, pumping hard. I've been told I was the flower girl,
but I don't remember it—I don't remember it at all. And here
Uncle Daniel sat, with that first little bride right on tap and
counting her.

"Step out in the bright a minute, and see what I give you," he says to Bonnie Dee.

So she stood down in the road on one foot, dusty as could be, in a home-made pink voile dress that wouldn't have stood even a *short* trip. It was wrinkled as tissue paper.

And he says, "Look, Edna Earle. Look, you all. Couldn't you eat her up?"

I wish you could have seen Bonnie Dee! I wish you could. I guess I'd known she was living, but I'd never given her a real good look. She was just now getting her breath. Baby yellow hair, downy—like one of those dandelion puff-balls you can blow and tell the time by. And not a grain beneath. Now, Uncle Daniel may not have a whole *lot* of brains, but what's there is Ponder, and no mistake about it. But poor little old Bonnie Dee! There's a world of difference. He talked and she just stood there and took her fill of my rummage sale, held up there under the tree, without offering a word. She was little and she was dainty, under the dust of that trip. But I could tell by her little coon eyes, she was shallow as they come.

"Turn around," I says as nicely as I can, "and let's see some more *of* you."

Nobody had to tell Bonnie Dee how to do that; she went puff-puff right on around, and gave a dip at the end.

Uncle Daniel hollers out to her, "That's my hotel, sugar." (He'd forgotten.) "Hop back in, and I'll show you my house."

I could have spanked her. She hopped in and he gave her a big kiss.

So Narciss pulls out the throttle, and don't back up but just cuts the corner through the crowd, and as they thunder off around the Courthouse she lets out real high and sad, "Miss Edna Earle, Mr. *Sam* ain't back yit, is he?" She was so proud of that ride she could die. She and Uncle Daniel rode off with what they had 'em—proud together.

Before I can turn around, Judge Tip Clanahan bawls down out of the window, "Edna Earle!" His office has been in the same place forever, next door up over the movie; but that never keeps me from jumping. "Now what? What am I going to do with Daniel, skin him? Or are you all going to kill him first? I tell you right here and now, I'm going to turn him over to DeYancey, if you don't mind out for him better than that."

Judge Tip gets us out of fixes.

"And hurt Uncle Daniel's feelings?" I calls up. DeYancey is just his grandson—young, and goes off on tangents.

"Come one thing more, I'll turn him over," Judge Tip bawls down to the street. "Where are we going to call the halt? Look where I'm having to send after Sam, none too sure to get him. I can't make a habit of that."

I left the whole array down there and climbed straight up those hot stairs and said to his face, "You ought to be ashamed, Judge Clanahan. I do mind out, everybody living minds out for Uncle Daniel, the best they can; it's you and Grandpa go too far with *discipline.* Just try to remember Uncle Daniel's blessed with a fond and loving heart, and two old domino cronies like you and Grandpa can't get around that by marrying him off to"—I made him a face like a Sistrunk—"and then unmarrying him, leaving him free for the next one, or running off with him to another place. That's child-foolishness, and I don't like to be fussed at in public at this time of the afternoon."

"Go on home, girl," says Judge Tip, "and get ready for your grandfather; he's loose and on his way. Already talked to DeYancey on the long-distance; don't know why he couldn't wait. I got no intention of washing my hands of Daniel or any other Ponder, and I'm not surprised for a minute at anything that transpires, only I'm a quiet studious man and don't take to all this commotion under my window." It woke him up, that's what.

"I don't see why there has to be any commotion anywhere," I says—and down on the street I made up my mind I'd say that to everybody. "People get married beneath them every day, and I don't see any sign of the world coming to an end. Don't be so small-town."

That held them, till Grandpa got back.

He got back sooner than I dreamed. I shook my big purse at him, when the car went by, to head him off, but he and DeYancey just hightailed it straight through town and out to the place. Nearly everybody still in the house along the way got out front in time to see them pass. I understand Miss Teacake Magee even drove by Ponder Hill, pretending she was looking for wild plums. I said, Edna Earle, *you'd* better get on out there.

All right, I said, but let me get *one* bath. It generally takes three, running this hotel on a summer day. I said shoo to the rummage sale and let them go on to the store.

While I was in the tub, ring went the telephone. Mr. Springer got to town just in time to answer it. I had to come down in front of him in my kimona, and there was DeYancey, calling from the crossroads store; I could hear their two good-for-nothing canaries. I fussed at him for not stopping here with Grandpa, because he might know I'd have something to tell him.

DeYancey said *he* had a surprise for *me*, that he'd better not tell me in front of a lot of people. I could have sworn I heard Eva Sistrunk swallow.

"Tell me quick, DeYancey Clanahan," I says. "I've all but got my hat on now—I *think* I know what it is."

DeYancey only starts at the beginning. He said he and Grandpa pulled up under the tree at the Ponder place and went marching in by the front door. (I told him they hadn't been beat home by much. Mr. Springer called from his room that to Silver City and back and to the asylum and back is just about equal distance.) DeYancey said they heard running feet over their heads, and running feet on the stairs—and whisk through the old bead curtains of the parlor came somebody that poor Grandpa had never laid eyes on in his life or dreamed existed. "She'd been upstairs, downstairs, and in my lady's chamber," says DeYancey. "She was very much at home."

"No surprise so far," I says. "Bonnie Dee Peacock."

"All in pink," he said, like I wasn't telling him a bit. "And she'd picked one of Narciss's nasturtiums and had it in her mouth like a pipe, sucking the stem. She ran to the parlor windows and took a good look out of each one." He said Uncle Daniel came in behind her and after he kissed Grandpa, stepped to the mantel and rested his elbow on it in a kind of grand way. They smelled awful smoke—he had one of

Grandpa's cigars lighted. Narciss was singing hallelujah some-where off.

I said, "But DeYancey, you're leaving out what I want to hear—the words. What did Grandpa say?"

DeYancey said Grandpa *whispered*.

"I don't believe you."

DeYancey said, "It's all true. He whispered, and said 'They're right.'"

"Who?" I said.

"Well, the Clanahans," said DeYancey. "He whispered—" and DeYancey whispered, all hollow and full of birdsinging over the wires, with Lord knows who not with us—"'When the brains were being handed around, my son Daniel was standing behind the door.'"

"Help," I said. "And did Uncle Daniel hear it? Let me go, DeYancey, I haven't got time for conversation. I've got to get out there and stand up for both of them."

"Don't you want to hear the surprise?" he says.

Well, he *did* have a surprise; he just had to get to it. Do you know it turned out that she'd just married Uncle Daniel *on trial*? Miss Bonnie Dee Peacock of Polk took a red nasturtium out of her mouth to say that was the best she could do.

After that, Grandpa just pounded with his stick and sent DeYancey out of his sight, with a message he would speak to me in the morning. And when he was getting his car out of the yard, DeYancey said, Narciss had the fattest chicken of all down on the block, and hollered at him, "We's goin' to keep her!" and brought her ax down whack.

"Just hang up and go home and take a bath, DeYancey," I says. "I've heard all I'm going to. I'm going to put on my hat."

Well, it's our hearts. We run to sudden ends, all we Ponders. I say it's our hearts, though Dr. Ewbanks declares Grandpa just popped a blood vessel.

Grandpa, Uncle Daniel, and Bonnie Dee still in pink were all about to sit down. I was just walking in the door—smelled chicken. Uncle Daniel says to me, "Just in time, Edna Earle. Poor Papa! You know, Edna Earle, he's hard to please."

And lo and behold.

*

We had the funeral in the Presbyterian Church, of course, and it was packed. I haven't been able to think of anybody that didn't come. It *had* mortified the Sistrunks that following behind one of them so close would come a Peacock; but with Grandpa going the sudden way he did, they rallied, and turned up in their best, and Miss Teacake asked to be allowed to sing. "Beautiful Isle of Somewhere" was her choice.

Uncle Daniel held every eye at the services. That was the best thing in the world for Uncle Daniel, because it distracted him from what was going on. Oh, he hates sickness and death, will hardly come in the room with it! He can't abide funerals. The reason every eye was on him was not just because he was rich as Croesus now, but he looked different. Bonnie Dee had started in on him and cut his hair.

Now I'll tell you about Bonnie Dee. Bonnie Dee could make change, and Bonnie Dee could cut hair. If you ask me can I do either, the answer is no. Bonnie Dee may have been tongue-tied in public and hardly able to stand in high heels, till she learned how, but she could cut your hair to a fare-ye-well, to within a good inch of your life, if you put a pair of scissors in her hand. Uncle Daniel used to look like a senator. But that day his hair wasn't much longer than the fuzz of a peach. Uncle Daniel still keeps it like that—he loves him- *great* self that way.

Oh, but he was proud of her. "She's a natural-born barber," he said, "and pretty as a doll. What would I do without her?" He had the hardware salesman bring her a whole line of scissors and sharp blades. I was afraid she'd fringe every-thing in the house.

Well! Ignorance is bliss.

Except Bonnie Dee, poor little old thing, didn't know how to smile. *Yawned* all the time, like cats do. So delicate and dainty she didn't even have any heels to speak of—she didn't stick out anywhere, and I don't know why you couldn't see through her. Seventeen years old and seemed like she just stayed seventeen.

They had that grand Narciss—had her and never appreci-ated her. It didn't seem to me they ate out there near enough to keep her happy. It had turned out Narciss could sit at a wheel and drive, of course—her and Grandpa's Studebaker both getting older by the minute, but she could still reach the pedals and they'd still catch, a little. Where they headed for, of course, was right here—a good safe place to end up, with the hitching post there to catch them at the foot of the walk. They sashayed in at the front—Narciss sashayed in at the back—and all ate with me.

That's how everybody—me and whoever was in here at the time, drummers, boarders, lawyers, and strangers—had to listen to Uncle Daniel mirate and gyrate over Bonnie Dee. With her right there at the table. We had to take on over her too, every last one of us, and tell him how pretty and smart we thought she was. It didn't bother her one whit. I don't think she was listening to amount to a row of pins. You couldn't tell. She just sat and picked at the Beulah food like a canary bird, and by the time Uncle Daniel was through eating and talking and pulled her up, it would be too late for the show for everybody. So he'd holler Narciss out of the back and they'd all three hop back in the car and go chugging home.

Now the only bad thing about the Ponder place is where it is. Poor Grandpa had picked him a good high spot to build the house on, where he could see all around him and if anybody was coming. And that turned out to be miles from anywhere. He filled up the house with rooms, rooms, rooms, and the rooms with furniture, furniture, furniture, all before he let Grandma in it. And then of course she brought her own perfectly good rosewood in right on top of it. And he'd trimmed the house inside and outside, topside and bottom, with every trimming he could get his hands on or money could buy. And painted the whole thing bright as a railroad station. Anything to outdo the Beulah Hotel.

And I think maybe he did outdo it. For one thing he sprinkled that roof with lightning rods the way Grandma would sprinkle coconut on a cake, and was just as pleased with himself as she was with herself. Remarkable. I don't think it ever occurred to either one of *them* that they lived far out: they were so evenly matched. It took Grandpa years to catch on it was lonesome. They considered *town* was far.

I've sometimes thought of turning that place *into* something, if and when it ever comes down to me and I can get the grass out of it. Nobody lives in the house now. The Pepper family we've got on the place don't do a thing but run it. A chinchilla farm may be the answer. But that's the future. Don't think about it, Edna Earle, I say. So I just cut out a little ad about a booklet that you can send off for, and put it away in a drawer—I forget where.

So the marriage trial—only it had completely left our minds it was one—went on for five years and six months, and Bonnie Dee, if you please, decided No.

Not that she said as much to a soul: she was tongue-tied when it came to words. She left a note written in a pencil tablet on the kitchen table, and when Narciss went out to cut up the chicken, she found it. She carried it to Uncle Daniel in the barn, and Uncle Daniel read it to her out loud. Then they both sat down on the floor and cried. It said, "Have left out. Good-by and good luck, your friend, Mrs. Bonnie Dee Peacock Ponder." We don't even know which one of them it was *to*.

Then she just traipsed out to the crossroads and flagged down the north-bound bus with her little handkerchief—oh, she was seen. A dozen people must have been in the bushes and seen her, or known somebody that did, and they all came and told me about it. Though nobody at all appeared to tell me where she got off.

It's not beyond me. You see, poor, trusting Uncle Daniel carried that child out there and set her down in a big house with a lot of rooms and corners, with Negroes to wait on her, and she wasn't used to a bit of it. She wasn't used to keeping house at all except by fits and starts, much less telling Negroes what to do. And she didn't know what to do with herself all day. But how would she tell him a thing like that? He was older than she was, and he was good as gold, and he was prominent. And he wasn't even there all the time—*Uncle Daniel* couldn't stay home. He wanted her there, all right, waiting when he got back, but he made Narciss bring him in town first, every night, so he could have a little better audience. He wanted to tell about how happy he was.

The way I look back at Bonnie Dee, her story was this. She'd come up from the country—and before she knew it, she was right back in the country. Married or no. She was away out yonder on Ponder Hill and nothing to do and nothing to play with in sight but the Negroes' dogs and the Peppers' cats and one little frizzly hen. From the kind of long pink finger-nails she kept in the ten cent store, that hadn't been her idea at all. Not her dream.

I think they behaved. I don't think they fought all over the place, like the Clanahan girls and the Sistrunk boys when they marry. They wouldn't know how. Uncle Daniel never heard a cross word in his life. Even if Bonnie Dee, with her origins, could turn and spit like a cat, I hardly think she would around Uncle Daniel. That wouldn't be called for.

I don't blame Bonnie Dee, don't blame her for a minute. I could just beat her on the head, that's all.

And I did think one thing was the funniest joke on her in the world: Uncle Daniel didn't give her any money. Not a cent. I discovered that one day. I don't think it ever occurred to him, to give anything to Bonnie Dee. Because he *had* her. (When she said "trial," that didn't mean anything to Uncle Daniel that would alarm him. The only kind of trials he knew about were the ones across the street from the Beulah, in the Courthouse—he was fond of those.)

I passed her some money myself now and then—or I bought her something ladylike to put on her back. I couldn't just leave her the way she was! She never said more than "Thank you."

Of course, Uncle Daniel wasn't used to money, himself. With Grandpa in his grave, it was Mr. Sistrunk at the bank that gave him his allowance, three dollars a month, and he spent that mostly the first day, on children—they were the ones came out and asked him for things. Uncle Daniel was used to purely being rich, not having money. The riches were all off in the clouds somewhere—like true love is, I guess, like a castle in the sky, where he could just sit and dream about it being up there for him. But money wouldn't be safe with him a minute—it would be like giving matches to a child.

Well! How the whole town did feel it when Bonnie Dee lit out!

When we sat in here night after night and saw that pearly gray Stetson coming in view, and moving up the walk, all we could do was hope and pray Uncle Daniel was here to tell us she was back. But she wasn't. He'd peep in both windows from the porch, then go around by the back and come in through the kitchen so he could speak to Ada. He'd point out what he'd have on his plate—usually ham and steak and chicken and cornbread and sweet potatoes and fried okra and tomatoes and onion-and-egg—plus banana pie—and take his seat in the dining room and when it came go "Ughmmmmmmm!" One big groan.

And I'd call everybody to supper.

Uncle Daniel would greet us at the table. "Have you seen her, son? Has a soul here seen my wife? Man alive! My wife's done left me out there by myself in the empty house! Oh, you'd know her if you came across her—she's tiny as a fairy and pretty as a doll. And smart beyond compare, boys." (That's what she told him.) "And now she's gone, clean as a whistle." There'd be a little crowd sitting close on both sides before he knew it. And he'd go into his tale.

It would be like drawing his eye-teeth not to let him go on and tell it, though it was steadily breaking his heart. Like he used to be bound and determined to give you a present, but that was a habit he'd outgrown and forgotten now. It was safer for his welfare to let him talk than let him give away, but harder on his constitution. On everybody's.

But I don't think he could bring himself to believe the story till he'd heard himself tell it again. And every night, when he'd come to the end, he'd screw his eyes up tight with fresh tears, and stand up and kiss me good night and pull his hat down off the rack. So I'd holler Narciss out of the kitchen for him—she came out looking sadder and sadder every time too—and she'd carry him on home. I knew he'd be back the next night.

Eva Sistrunk said she couldn't make up her mind whether it was good or bad for this hotel—though I don't believe she was asked. Things would look like a birthday party inside, such a fine crowd—some out-of-town people hanging onto the story and commiserating with Uncle Daniel, and the Clay people cheering him on, clapping him on the shoulder. Everybody here, young or old, knew what to say as well as he did. When he sat there at the big middle table he always headed for, all dressed up in sparkling white and his red tie shining, with his plate heaped up to overflowing and his knife and fork in hand, ready and waiting to begin his tale of woe, he'd be in good view from the highway both north and south, and it was real prosperous-looking in here—till he came to the part about the note, of course, and how Narciss lightfooted it out to the barn and handed it to him so pleased, where he was feeding his calf—and he broke down at the table and ruined it all.

But that's what he came in here for—cry. And to eat in company. He ate me out of house and home, not so much to be eating as to be consoling himself and us (we begged him to eat, not cry), but some nights, when he had a full house, I had to flit along by the back of his chair and say under my breath, "Uncle Daniel! F. H. B.!"

He'd just catch me and say, "Edna Earle! Where do you suppose she could've got to by this time? Memphis?" Memphis was about the limit Uncle Daniel could stand to think of. That's where everybody else had it in mind she went, too. That's where *they'd* go.

Somebody'd always be fool enough to ask Uncle Daniel how come he didn't hop in his car and drive on up to Memphis and look for Bonnie Dee, if he wanted her back that bad. Some brand-new salesman would have to say, "It can be driven in three hours and forty-five minutes."

"Believe that's just what I'll do, sir!" Uncle Daniel would say, to be nice. "Yes sir, I'll go up there in the cool of the morning, and let you know what I find, too." "Miss Elsie Fleming—I wonder where *she* is," he said now and then, too. Well, he just never can forget anybody.

But he wouldn't dream of going to Memphis, to find Bonnie Dee or Intrepid Elsie Fleming or you or anybody else. Uncle Daniel belongs in Clay, and by now he's smart enough to know it; and if he wasn't, I'd tell him.

"Never mind, Uncle Daniel," I'd come up again and say when the tears fell. "Have a Fatima." He adores to smoke those. I order off after them for him, and always keep an extra supply on hand. And I'd light him one.

I don't really think Uncle Daniel missed Bonnie Dee as much as he thought he did. He had me. He appeared at the

Beulah every night of the world, sure as shooting, and every morning to boot, and of course when he came down sick out there, he hollered for Edna Earle.

I locked up the Beulah—well, it wouldn't lock, but I spoke to it and said "Burglars, stay away"—and went out to Ponder Hill in my trusty Ford to take care of him. When I got there, I missed Grandpa meeting me in the hall and telling me this had put him in a quandary.

The house is almost exactly the same size as the hotel, but it's a mile easier to run. If you know what you want done, you can just ask in the morning for how many Negroes you want that day, and Uncle Daniel hollers them in for you out of the fields, and they come just like for Grandpa. They don't know anything, but you can try telling them and see what happens. And there was always Narciss. By now she had a black smear across all her aprons, that the steering wheel made on her stomach; she sat up so close to the windshield to see how to drive. I made her get back to the stove.

I missed my city lights. I guess electricity was about the bane of Grandpa's life, next to weakness of character. Some power fellow was eternally coming out there and wanting to string it up to the house, and Grandpa'd say, "Young man, do you want to draw the lightning out here to me when I've done everything I know how to prevent it?" and throw him out. We all grew up learning to fend for ourselves. Though *you* may not be able to read in the dark, I can. But all the other children and grandchildren went away to the ends of the earth or died and left only me and Uncle Daniel—the two favorites. So we couldn't leave each other.

As a matter of fact, when I went back in that house to look after Uncle Daniel when he was sick, I'd have been lonesome myself if I hadn't liked to read and had good eyes. I'm a great reader that never has time to read.

Little old Bonnie Dee had six years of *True Love Story* and six years of *Movie Mirror* stacked up on the sewing machine in my room (she never hesitated to shift the furniture) and the hatrack in the hall, and down behind the pillows on the sofa. She must have read her heart out. Or at least she'd cut all the coupons out with her scissors. I saw by the holes she'd left where she'd sent off for all kinds of things—you know,

gaps in her stories

wherever they showed the postman smiling in the ad. I figured she must have got back, sometime or other, twenty-four samples of world-famous perfumes; and a free booklet on how to speak and write masterly English from a Mr. Cody who looks a great deal like Professor Magee from Clay, who's been dead for years; and a free piano lesson to prove you can amaze your friends; and a set of Balzac to examine ten days free of charge, but she must have decided against it—I looked everywhere. So there were holes in the stories all the way through, but they wouldn't have lasted me long anyway. I read *The House of a Thousand Candles* for the thousandth time; and the rest of the time I cleaned house. The hotter it is, the faster I go.

Uncle Daniel was happy no matter what I was doing. He wasn't really sick: I diagnosed him. Oh, he might have had a little malaria—he took his quinine when I gave it to him. Mainly, he just didn't want to be by himself. He wanted somebody closer than three miles away when he had something to say *right then*. There's something I think's better to have than love, and if you want me to, I'll tell you what it is—that's company. That's one reason Uncle Daniel enjoyed life even in Jackson—he was surrounded there.

moral teacher

"Why don't you come on into town, Uncle Daniel," I said, "and stay at the Beulah with me? I need to get the windows washed there too."

"No indeed," he says. "If she comes back, she'll come back here where she left off. Pretty thing, if she'd come in the door this minute, I'd eat her up."

But, "Oh, Edna Earle, where did she go?" That's what he began and ended his day with, that was the tail to all his stories. "Where has Bonnie Dee gone?" So after I'd heard that refrain enough times, I took myself into town and climbed the stairs to Judge Tip Clanahan's office. I caught him with his feet up on the wall, trying on fishing boots. I'm afraid DeYancey was already fishing.

great

Well, as I opened the subject by saying when I sat down, I can't *help* being smarter than Uncle Daniel. I don't even try, myself, to make people happy the way they should be: they're so stubborn. I just try to give them what they think they want. Ask me to do you the most outlandish favor tomorrow, and

I'll do it. Just don't come running to me afterwards and ask me how come.

So we compromised on a three-day ad in the Memphis *Commercial Appeal*. (Judge Tip wanted to let well enough alone.) Because it developed that Mr. Springer—my friend— had come through yesterday, and sailed right on to Silver City for the night; but had idled his engine long enough at the drugstore corner to call to DeYancey Clanahan, who was getting a haircut from Mr. Wesley Bodkin next door, to tell him *he* saw Bonnie Dee Peacock the day before in Memphis, when he was passing through. Saw her in Woolworth's. She was trying to buy something. And had her sister with her. Mr. Springer told DeYancey and Mr. Bodkin that he raised his hat and tendered a remark to her, and she put out her tongue at him. That was enough for Mr. Springer.

Looks like he would have come straight to me with that, but he said he didn't know where I was. Everybody else knew where I was. Everybody knows where everybody is, if they really want to find them. But I suppose if the door to the Beulah is ever pulled to, and Ada's not out cutting the grass, Mr. Springer will always assume that I'm dead.

Well, I mailed in the ad without saying a word to the post office, and sat back with folded hands. Judge Tip and I didn't breathe a word of what we'd done. Uncle Daniel hopes too much as it is. And he'd rather get a surprise than fly. Besides, it would have hurt his feelings more than anything else I know of to discover the entire world could pick up the morning paper and read at a glance what had happened to him, without him being the one to tell it.

Lo and behold, they printed it. I put it in the form of a poem while I was about it. It's called "Come Back to Clay."

Bonnie Dee Ponder, come back to Clay.
Many are tired of you being away.
O listen to me, Bonnie Dee Ponder,
Come back to Clay, or husband will wonder.
Please to no more wander.
As of even date, all is forgiven.
Also, retroactive allowance will be given.
House from top to bottom now spick and span,

Come back to Clay the minute you can.
Signed, Edna Earle Ponder.
P.S. Do not try to write a letter,
Just come, the sooner the better.

Judge Tip horned in on two lines, and I don't think he helped
it any. But it was better then than it may sound now. I cut it
out and put it in a drawer to show my grandchildren.

I don't believe for a minute that she saw it. Somebody with
bright eyes, who did, went and told her. And here she came.
Nine forty-five the next morning, in she walked at the front
door. She looked just exactly the same—seventeen.

The first I knew about it, Uncle Daniel hollered from the
dining room out to me in the kitchen, "Edna Earle! Edna
Earle! Make haste! She's fixing to cut my throat!"

I'd been up for hours. I was having Narciss put up his
peaches. But I came when he called, spoon and all. He'd
jumped up on top of the dining room table where he'd been
having a little buttermilk and crackers after breakfast.

I said, "Why, climb down, Uncle Daniel, it's only Bonnie
Dee. I thought that was what you wanted! You'll spill your
milk."

"Hallelujah!" hollers Narciss behind me. "Prayers is answered."

Here she came, Miss Bonnie Dee, sashaying around the
table with her little bone razor wide open in her hand. So
Uncle Daniel climbed down, good as gold, and sat back in
his chair and she got the doodads and commenced to lather
his face, like it was any other day. I suppose she always shaved
him first thing, and in the dining room!

"*Good* evening," I says.

"Miss Edna Earle," Bonnie Dee turns and remarks to me,
"*Court's* opened." There she stood with that razor cocked in
her little hand, sending me about my business. "Keep hands
down," she pipes to Uncle Daniel, bending down toward him
just as bossy, with her little old hip stuck out behind, if you
could say she had hips. And when he reached for her, she went
around to his other side. I believe she'd missed him.

So I just politely turned on my heel, leaving them both

there with fourteen perfect quarts of peach preserves cooling on the back porch behind me. But before I could get down the front steps—

"Miss Edna Earle! Miss Edna Earle!" Narciss came streaking out after me. "Call Dr. Lubanks!"

"I imagine I can handle it," I says. "What is it?"

"It's him," says Bonnie Dee in the door behind her, on one foot.

"Say please, then," I says, and when she did, I went back in. I thought there'd be a little tiny cut on one cheek. But there he stretched. What had happened was, poor Uncle Daniel had gotten out of the habit of knowing what to expect, and when Bonnie Dee came real close to his eye with that razor, biting her tongue as she came, he'd pitched right out of his chair—white as a ghost with lather all over his cheeks and buttermilk dotting his tie.

"Narciss!" I says. "Holler for the closest!"

Grandpa considered he had a perfectly good way of getting in touch with the doctor or anybody else: a Negro on the back of a mule. There's a white man sitting at the crossroads store with a telephone and nothing to do all day but feed those birds.

Dr. Ewbanks had this to say, after he'd come and we'd all finished a good dinner: "Daniel, you know what? You've got to use more judgment around here. You've got a racing heart."

"Sure enough?" says Uncle Daniel. He'd been almost guarded with Dr. Ewbanks ever since Grandpa's funeral. But he smiled clear around the table at that word "heart." "You hear that, Edna Earle? Hear that, sugar? It's my heart. Promise you won't ever go scootin' off again, then scare me that way coming back."

And Bonnie Dee crosses her heart, but looking around at us all while she does it, like she don't know which one to cross it to, me or Uncle Daniel or Dr. Ewbanks or Narciss or the kitchen cat. Dr. Ewbanks winks at her, and when Uncle Daniel runs around the table, so pale and proud, to get a kiss from her, she says, "Aren't you 'shamed! You always do the wrong thing."

I'll never forgive her.

I had her retroactive allowance right there in my pocket-book—I'd been about to forget it. I replaced my napkin, marched out to the parlor, straight to Grandma's vase on the table. It's two babies pulling a swan and holding something I always thought was a diploma. It had never held anything but calling cards before. I wish you could have seen it the way I left it, stuffed and overflowing with money. You would have wondered what had happened to the parlor table.

And here at the Beulah, coming in singing, Uncle Daniel commenced on, "Oh, my bride has come back to me. Pretty as a picture, and I'm happy beyond compare. Edna Earle got her back for me, you all, and Judge Tip Clanahan sewed it up. It's a court order, everybody. Oh, I remember how I fretted when she tried to run away."

"So do I," I says. "You cried on my shoulder."

"Did I?" he says. "Well, I don't have to cry any more. She's perched out there on the sofa till I get home tonight. I'll hug her and kiss her and I'll give her twenty-five dollars in her little hand. Oh, it would do you good to see her take it."

I put my finger on his lips.

I can't think just what they call that in Court—separate maintenance, I think it is. Only, Uncle Daniel and Bonnie Dee weren't separate as long as he maintained her, is what the difference amounted to. Old Judge Clanahan is pretty well up on things for a man of seventy-five. Uncle Daniel was so happy it was nearly more than he could stand. I sometimes feared for his heart, but he'd forgotten all about that; or she'd made him ashamed of it, one.

He even quit coming to town so much; he'd just send for me to come calling out there if he wanted company. And when I walked in, he'd beam on me and make me look through the bead curtains into the parlor. There she'd be, Bonnie Dee Peacock, curled up on Grandma's rosewood sofa, busy in the light of the lamp—spitting on her finger, turning through the magazines, cutting the coupons out by the stack and weighting them down under the starfish, and eating the kind of fudge *anybody* can make.

And after all I did, lo and behold! Poor Uncle Daniel—here he came around the Courthouse Square all by himself one day, in the middle of hot afternoon, carrying both the suitcases and wearing two hats. I was out in my flowers in front, getting a few weeds out of the ground with my little old hatchet.

"Edna Earle!" he starts calling as soon as he sees me. "Have you got a few cold biscuits I could have before supper, or a little chicken bone I could gnaw on? Look! I've come."

I jumped up and shook my hatchet at him. "Has she gone again?" I said. "Now she said she wouldn't—I heard her."

"Edna Earle, she didn't go a step," says Uncle Daniel, setting down his suitcases real gentle before me and taking off both hats. He'd walked all the way in, but made it all in one trip. "She didn't break her promise," he says. "She run me off."

And he walked in and made himself at home right away and didn't take it as hard as you'd imagine. He was so good.

And to tell you the truth, he was happy. This time, he knew where she was. Bonnie Dee was out yonder in the big old lonesome dark house, right in the spot where he most wanted her and where he left her, and where he could think of her being—and here was himself safe with Edna Earle in the Beulah Hotel, where life goes on on all sides. I moved out a lazy drummer and gave Uncle Daniel that big front room upstairs with the Courthouse out the window—the one where he is now. Christmas came, then spring, then Court, and everything in the world was going on, and so many more people were here around than out in the country—than just Bonnie Dee, the Peppers, and the Negroes, the Negroes, the Peppers, and Bonnie Dee. He had a world more to see and talk about here, and he ate like it.

You know, whatever's turned up, we've always *enjoyed* Uncle Daniel so—and he's relied on us to. In fact, he's never hesitated to enjoy himself. But Uncle Daniel never was a bit of good with nothing to talk about. For that, you need a *drama* Sistrunk. Something had better happen, for Uncle Daniel to appreciate life. And if he wasn't in the thick of things, and couldn't tell you about them when they did happen, I think he'd just pine and languish. He got that straight from Grandma. Poor Bonnie Dee: I never believed she had one whit of human curiosity. I never, in all the time she was married to Uncle Daniel, heard her say "What next?"

About the time she ran him off is when she began ordering off after everything. The Memphis paper did that. With her name in it that one time, she tried a whole year of it, and here it came, packed with those big, black ads. (Well, her name *was* in again. Mercy on us.)

We heard about the ordering from Narciss, when we saw Narciss in Bonnie Dee's pink voile dress she got married in, parading through Sistrunk's Grocery with a store-bought watermelon wrapped in her arms. Narciss said sure she was dressed up—she spent all her time now saying "Thank you!" As for Miss Bonnie Dee, her new clothes were gorgeous, and she hoped for some of those too some day, when they got holes. Narciss said there were evening dresses and street dresses and hostess dresses and brunch dresses—dresses in boxes and hanging up. Think of something to wear. Bonnie Dee had it.

And *things* began to pour into that house—you'd think there wouldn't be room. Narciss came chugging into town more times a week than ever, to claim something mighty well wrapped and tied, at the post office or the freight depot, and ride it home on the back seat.

Bonnie Dee even got a washing machine.

"She'll find she's going to need current out there," I says one day. "She may not be prepared for that."

"Yes'm she is," says Narciss. "She prepared. White man back agin yesterday."

"Does she remember it's Grandpa's house she's in?" I says, and Narciss drove off in a fit of the giggles, going zigzag.

But Bonnie Dee kept the washing machine on the front porch, just like any Peacock would be bound to do. Narciss didn't have any idea how to work any machinery but a Studebaker car. I wonder how many of those things they ever did bring under control. I told Narciss I was sure they came with directions hanging on, if there were eyes to read them.

I imagine Bonnie Dee was making hay while the sun shone. Because sure as you're born, if she hadn't run Uncle Daniel off, he'd be there giving things away as quick as she could get them in the door, or up to the porch. She was showing how *she* felt about things. Poor Bonnie Dee, I sometimes do think! Of course down payments were as far as her mind went.

And to crown it all, she got a telephone.

I passed by the place myself, going for a quick ride before dark with Mr. Springer when he was tired (so tired I drove) and Uncle Daniel sitting up behind. Bonnie Dee was out in the yard fully to be seen, in a hunter's green velveteen two-piece dress with a stand-up collar, and Narciss was right behind her in blue, all to watch the man put it in. They waved their hands like crazy at the car going by, and then again going back, blowing dust on all that regalia. Do you think it's ever rung once?

Of course I never asked Uncle Daniel why she ran him off, and don't know to this day. I don't want to know.

So Uncle Daniel was happy in the Beulah and Bonnie Dee was out yonder dressing up and playing lady with Narciss. And it got on toward summer again, but I just couldn't throw myself into it. My conscience pricked me. And pricked me and pricked me. Could I go on letting Uncle Daniel think *that* was the right way to be happy? Could you let your uncle?

I don't know if you can measure love at all. But Lord knows there's a lot of it, and seems to me from all the studying I've done over Uncle Daniel—and he loves more people than you and I put together ever will—that if the main one you've set your heart on isn't speaking for your love, or is out of your reach some way, married or dead, or plain nitwitted, you've still got that love banked up somewhere. What Uncle Daniel did was just bestow his all around quick—men, women, and children. Love! There's always somebody wants it. Uncle Daniel knew that. He's smart in a way you aren't, child.

And that time, he did it talking. In Clay he was right on hand. He took every soul I let in at the Beulah straight to his heart. "Hello, son—what's news?"—then he'd start in. Oh,

the stories! He made free with everybody's—he'd tell yours
and his and the Man in the Moon's. Not mine: he wouldn't
dream I had one, he loves me so—but everybody else's. And
things couldn't happen fast enough to suit him. I used to
thank my stars this was a Courthouse town.

Well, if holding forth is the best way you can keep alive,
then *do* it—if you're not outrageously smart to start with and
don't have things to do. But *I* was getting *deaf*!

So one Friday morning at nine-thirty when we were sitting
down to our cokes in the dining room, I made up my mind
to say something. Mr. Springer happened to be here. And Eva
Sistrunk had wandered in and sat down—invited herself.

I waited till Uncle Daniel took a swallow—he was giving
Mr. Springer's brother-in-law's sister a major operation in
Kansas City, Missouri; and thank goodness we never laid eyes
on *her*, before her operation or after. Then I said, "Uncle
Daniel, listen just a minute—it's a little idea I woke up with.
Why don't you try not giving Bonnie Dee the money this
Saturday?"

Did I say he'd gone on giving her the money? And that
Judge Tip Clanahan and Mr. Bank Sistrunk were both threatening to wash their hands of us for letting her treat us that
way.

But I'm a Ponder too. I always got twenty-five dollars in
fives from Eloise at the bank, and Uncle Daniel and I climbed
in my trusty Ford, every Saturday afternoon after dinner, and
ran the money out there. I took it up to the door, folded
inside an envelope, and Uncle Daniel sat and watched from
the car. Somehow he didn't seem to want to go in, just catch
his glimpse. He's a real modest man, you know, and would
never push his presence on you unless he thought you wanted
him; then he would.

I was perfectly willing about it. I just prissed across the yard
and up the steps to the porch and around the washing machine to the front door and called for Narciss. If there'd been
a doorbell, I'd have rung it, at my own birthplace. I wore
white gloves and a hat, as it was. And Narciss would be waiting to go to town, and holler "Miss Bonnie Dee!" And
Bonnie Dee would sashay to the door wearing some creation
and put out her little hand—not always too shining—and take

the envelope. Uncle Daniel didn't get to see much of her—just a sleeve.

"Ta ta!"

"You're welcome."

In the car Uncle Daniel raised his hat.

And Narciss caught a ride to town on our running board.

Once or twice Bonnie Dee had looked out as far as the road, and waved a little bit, but not too hard.

So now I said to Uncle Daniel—in front of the others, to hear how it sounded—"Why don't you try not giving the money to Bonnie Dee? Maybe stop her charge account at Sistrunk's Store too. Nobody can live on chicken and ham forever! And see what transpires. What do you say, Uncle Daniel?"

He says with round eyes, "What would we do on Saturday?"

"What did you used to do?" I says. "What do you think of that idea, Mr. Springer?"

Mr. Springer said he thought there was nothing to lose.

"What do you think, Eva?" I said, because there she was, fastened to her straw.

"I think just like Mr. Springer, there's nothing to lose," is all Eva says. Eva can draw you a coat-of-arms—that's the one thing she can do, or otherwise have to teach school. That's ours, up over the clock: Ponder—with three deer. She says it's not her fault if the gold runs—it's the doorbell ringing or something. She never does *anybody*'s over.

"I think we'll try it, Uncle Daniel," I said. "I made my mind up while the rest of you ate ice."

So I politely kept that Saturday's money for Uncle Daniel, and spoke to the butcher too. And guess what day she sent for us: Monday.

You never saw a happier mortal in your life. He came hopping up those stairs lickety-split to tell me.

I was up there in my room, reading some directions. That's something I find I like to do when I have a few minutes to myself—I don't know about you. How to put on furniture polish, transfer patterns with a hot iron, take off corns, I don't care what it is. I don't have to *do* it. Sometimes I'd rather sit still a minute and read a good quiet set of directions through than any story you'd try to wish off on me.

"Oh, Edna Earle," he says. "What do you think? It worked!"

And all of a sudden I just felt tired. I felt worn out, like when Mr. Springer stays over and makes me go to one of those sad, Monday night movies and never holds my hand at the right places. But I'll tell you what this was: a premonition. Only I couldn't quite place it at the time.

Uncle Daniel was out of breath and spinning his best hat on his finger like a top. "I got the word," he says. "She sent it by three different people—the ice man, the blackberry lady, and the poor blind man with the brooms that liked-to never found me, but *he* told it the best. I was in the barbershop, you know. I just brought the whole string back with me to the hotel and gave them cigars out of the drawer; they all said they smoked. She says to come on. Says to come on before it storms, and this was to you, Edna Earle: please to go by the ice house on the way and put fifty pounds on your bumper for her. Come on, Edna Earle," he says, putting his hat on and putting mine on me. "Come see Bonnie Dee welcome me home. I don't want you to miss it. Where's Mr. Springer? I'd like him to come too."

"Mr. Springer has just bolted out of town," I says. "I heard the car take the corner." Mr. Springer was the perfect listener until he had to go.

"Come without him," says Uncle Daniel, pulling me out of my poor chair. "But make haste. Listen to that! Bonnie Dee was right—she always is—it's fixing to storm." And sure enough, we heard it thunder in the west.

I never thought of the ice again until this day. Bonnie Dee wouldn't have hesitated asking for the moon! That there should be a smidgen of ice left in Clay at that hour is one of the most unlikely things I ever heard of. What was left of the public cake on the Courthouse steps had run down in a trickle by noon.

Well, to make a long story short, Bonnie Dee sent him word Monday after dinner and was dead as a doornail Monday before supper. Tuesday she was in her grave. Nobody more surprised than the Ponders. It was all I could do to make Uncle Daniel go to *that* funeral.

He did try to give the Peacocks his cemetery lot, but I doubt if he knew what he was doing. They said they bury at Polk, thank you.

He didn't want to go to Polk for anything, no indeed he did not. I had to make him. Then after he got dressed up and all the way down there, he behaved up until the last as well as I did; and it was scorching hot, too. I hope the day they bury me will be a little cooler. But at least people won't have so far to come.

I believe Polk did use to be a town. Mr. Springer told us how to get to it. (He was shooting through Clay headed *east* by Tuesday—there's a great deal of wonder-drug trade going on in all parts of Mississippi.) You start out like you were going to Monterrey, turn at the consolidated school, and bear right till you see a Baptist steeple across a field, and you just leave the gravel and head for that, if you have good tires. And that's Polk. The Peacocks live out from it, but trade there, and, as they said, bury there.

Well, their church is a shell—all burnt out inside. The funeral was further still, at the house.

Portulaca in pie pans was what they set along the front porch. And the mirror on the front of the house: I told you. In the yard not a snap of grass—an old auto tire with verbena growing inside it ninety to nothing, all red. And a tin roof you could just imagine the chinaberries falling on—ping! And now the hot rays of the sun.

The funeral was what you'd expect if you'd ever seen Polk—crowded. It was hot as fluzions in that little front room. A lot of Jacob's-Ladder tops and althea blooms sewed on cardboard crosses, and a salvia wreath with a bee in it. A lot of ferns hauled out of creek bottoms and drooping by the time they got ready for them. People, people, people, flowers, flowers, flowers, and the shades hauled down and the electricity burning itself up, and two preachers both red-headed; but mainly I felt there were Peacocks. Mrs. Peacock was big and fat as a row of pigs, and wore tennis shoes to her daughter's funeral—I guess she couldn't help it. I saw right there at the funeral that Bonnie Dee had been the pick.

We went by in the line, Uncle Daniel tipping on his toes. Such cracks in the floor, and chickens right under your feet! They had the coffin across the hearth on kitchen chairs.

Bonnie Dee was holding a magnolia a little too big for her size. She really did look seventeen. They had her in a Sunday-go-to-meeting dress, old-timey looking and too big for her—never washed or worn, just saved: white. She wouldn't have known herself in it. And a sash so new and blue and shiny it looked like it would break, right out of the Polk general merchandise, tied in a bow around a waist no bigger than your thumb.

When you saw her there, it looked like she could have loved *somebody*!

Uncle Daniel pulled loose from me and circled back. He had Mrs. Peacock by the hand in no time. He said, "Mrs. Peacock, let me tell you something. Your daughter's pretty as a doll."

And Mrs. Peacock says, "Well sir, that's just the way I used to look, but never cared to brag."

They had one big rawboned country preacher on one side of Bonnie Dee, to get up and say look what gold and riches brought you to, and at such an early age—and the other big rawboned country preacher on the other side, to get started praying and not be able to stop. That one asked heavenly mercy for everybody he could think of from the Peacocks on up to the President of the United States. When he got to Uncle Daniel's name I was ready for him and gave Uncle Daniel a good pinch at the right minute. (He generally beams to hear his name called.) My rocking chair was dusty, but at least I got to sit down.

During the service, half the Peacocks—the girls—were still as mice, but the boys, some of them grown men, were all collected out on the porch. Do you know what they did out there, on the other side of the wall from us? Bawled. Howled. Not that they ever did a thing for their sister in life, very likely, or even came to see her, but now they decided to let forth. And do you know all through everything the broom was still standing behind the door in that room?

Once outside, up on the hill, I noticed from the corner of my eye a good many Peacocks buried in the graveyard, well to the top of the hill, where you could look out and see the Clay Courthouse dome like a star in the distance. Right *old* graves, with "Peacock" on them out bold. It may be that the Peacocks at one time used to amount to something (there *are* worthwhile Peacocks, Miss Lutie Powell has vouched for it to Eva Sistrunk), but you'll have a hard time making me believe they're around us. I believe these have always been just about what they are now. Of course, Polk did use to be on the road. But the road left and it didn't get up and follow, and neither did the Peacocks. Up until Bonnie Dee.

It was there at the graveside that Uncle Daniel had his turn. There might have been high foolishness or even trouble— both big red-headed Baptist preachers took hold of him. It was putting her in the ground *he* didn't like.

But I said, very still, "Look, Uncle Daniel. It looks right cool, down yonder in the ground. Here *we* are standing up on top in the burning heat. Let her go."

So he stepped back, for me.

While they were laying on the ferns, away down below us a freight train went by through the empty distance, and the two littlest Peacocks, another generation coming up, stepped forward and waved it out of sight. And I counted the cars— not because I didn't know any better, like them, but because I couldn't help it right then. I counted seventy-nine.

Going back down the hill, Uncle Daniel offered Mrs. Peacock a new pick-up truck for her to haul their watermelons to market; he'd noticed through a slit in the shade, during all that praying, that they were about ripe over the fence, and he complimented the Peacocks on them and said he hoped they'd bring him one. The girls said all right, they would. If he hadn't been so shy with the Peacock boys, he might have given them something; but they didn't get a thing, for the way they acted.

And then, when we got home, they *charged* us.

I know of a case where a man really murdered his wife, with a sure-enough weapon, and her family put on her tombstone, "Vengeance is mine, saith the Lord, I will repay." And his family—the nicer people—had to go take it off with a cold chisel when her family wasn't looking. Ancient history. But thank goodness the Peacocks hadn't heard about that. They just charged us in Court.

Because of course the minute the funeral was over good, and the county paper came out with Eva Sistrunk's write-up and poem, that county attorney we wished on ourselves, Dorris R. Gladney—no friend of the Ponders—out he sailed in a black Ford older than mine, and searched out the Peacocks in Polk and found them, too, and told them what they could do.

They charged Uncle Daniel with murder.

So LAST WEEK it came up on the docket—it hadn't been anything much of a docket before that, and they shoved a few things out of the way for it.

Old Judge Waite was sitting on the case. Judge Tip Clanahan is not really a judge. What he is is a splendid lawyer and our best friend, even if he is a thousand years old and can't really see where he's going. But lo and behold, Judge Tip told me, just before we got off to the start, he had to let DeYancey, his grandson, argue Uncle Daniel's case, because he never realized how his strength was leaving him, and he had to go to Hot Springs.

"I was always partial to Daniel, but I'm getting too old for him now," he says. "I got to go to Hot Springs tomorrow."

I knew Grandpa was turning in his grave. "Go out of town?" I says. "You think I'm going to forgive you for it when you get back?"

He gives me a little pinch. The day I don't rate a pinch of some kind from a Clanahan, I'll know I'm past redemption—an old maid.

Uncle Daniel has always considered DeYancey one of his best friends, and was always partial to him until this happened. DeYancey came out and announced that Uncle Daniel wasn't going to open his mouth at his own trial. Not at all, not a word. The trial was going to proceed without him.

It would be like this. I was to testify about what happened. That's very important. Dr. Ewbanks was to testify from the medical point of view. And a few other odds and ends. But Uncle Daniel, the main one, was just supposed to sit there and be good, and not say anything at all. And he felt left out. He didn't understand a bit. It was so unlikely! Why, he loves the limelight.

Everybody in town was indignant with DeYancey when they heard. More than one member of our congregation baked and sent Uncle Daniel his favorite cake—banana—and a Never Fail Devil's Food came from the Clanahans the day Judge Tip went off. Miss Teacake sent a beautiful Prince of Wales cake in black and white stripes—her specialty, but I couldn't help thinking of *convicts* when I sliced it. The bank sent a freezer of peach ice cream from their own peaches, beautifully turned and packed. Uncle Daniel got the idea things must be more momentous than he thought. And we couldn't let a soul get near enough to him for him to do any talking beforehand— that was the hardest part.

Of course they hadn't done anything *about* Uncle Daniel: he didn't have to *go* anywhere. They knew where he was: with me.

"They're letting you roam," says DeYancey to Uncle Daniel.

"Roam?" says he.

"Now that isn't anything for you to worry about," says DeYancey. "Just means they can count on you for coming." As if they could keep him away.

But DeYancey Clanahan was here roaming around with him. I never saw the like—he was his shadow! He said, "Come on in the dining room, Daniel, I want to practice you not talking." That was easier in the dining room than anywhere else, but it wouldn't be clear sailing anywhere. Uncle Daniel couldn't bear to hear out what DeYancey was saying, that was always the trouble.

He managed to keep up his appetite, anyway. When the day came, he was up with the sun as usual, and looking pretty cheerful at breakfast. He had on his new white Sunday suit and white shirt with the baby-blue pinstripe in it, and snow-white shoes and his Sunday tie. He set out when breakfast was over and got a fresh haircut at the barbershop and came back looking fat and fine to me, with a little Else Poulsen rose in his lapel.

Well, the town was jam-packed. Everybody and his brother was on hand, on account of Uncle Daniel's general popularity—and then people not knowing the Ponders but knowing *of* them are just about everywhere you'd look. It was a grand day, hot but with that little breeze blowing that we get from the south.

Uncle Daniel and I didn't get there either early or late, but just on time, and Uncle Daniel had to speak to a world of people—but just "Hello." He was delighted at where our seats were saved—inside the railing. That was the furthest down front he'd ever sat anywhere. I kept my gloves on, and shook open my Japanese fan, and just fanned.

Of course, inside the Courthouse was hot, and one ceiling fan sticks, and the Peacocks coming to town and crowding their way in behind us made the courtroom a good deal hotter.

They came in a body. I didn't count, either time, but I think there were more Peacocks if possible at the trial than at the funeral. I imagine all Polk was there with them; there were people we'd never laid eyes on before in our lives.

The immediate Peacock family had paraded into town in Uncle Daniel's pick-up truck that he'd sent them, as pretty as you please. To see them in Polk was bad enough, but you ought to see them in Clay! Country! And surprised to death at where they found themselves, I bet you a nickel, even if they were the ones started this.

We saw them come in; I turned right around and looked. Old lady Peacock wagged in first, big as a house, in new bedroom slippers this time, with pompons on the toes. She had all of them behind her—girls going down in stairsteps looking funnier and funnier in Bonnie Dee's parceled-out clothes, and boys all ages and sizes and the grown ones with wives and children, and Old Man Peacock bringing up the rear. I didn't remember him at all, but there he was—carrying the lunch. He had a face as red as a Tom turkey and not one tooth to his name, but he had on some new pants. I noticed the tag still poking out the seam when he creaked in at the door.

They're not dying out. Took up the first two rows, with some sitting on laps. And I think it was their dog barked so incessantly at all the dogs in town from the Courthouse porch. Now that the boys weren't bawling, they sat there with their mouths wide open. The biggest ones' babies just wore their little didies to court, one of them with a brand-new double holster around on top, about to fall off. Couldn't a one of them talk. And of course there was eternal jumping up from the Peacocks to get water. Our drinking fountain in the Courthouse quit working years ago, so it's heaped up with concrete to cover the spout and rounded off and painted blue—our sheriff's wife's idea—and you have to know where to go if you're honestly thirsty.

Uncle Daniel spoke to the Peacocks, but then I saw his face light up, like it only does for a newcomer in his life. And in sailed that lawyer, Dorris R. Gladney. Long, black, buzzardy coat, black suspenders, beaky nose, and on his little finger a diamond bigger than mine, but not half as expensive. Walked too low, and got up and sat down too fast, like all the Gladneys. We all know people who're in a terrible hurry about something! And I understand Mr. Gladney has been peppered with buckshot on several occasions in the course of his career—shows you what kind of people he's thrown with. He rushed up and down the room several times, to show he'd come, and patted the little Peacocks on the head, but they didn't smile an inch.

Then in came DeYancey, real pale, and he patted Uncle Daniel and *he* smiled. And all around us, everybody in the courtroom was talking ninety to nothing when old Judge Waite brought down the gavel and the whole conglomeration sat up.

The other side was first.

Mr. Truex Bodkin came on to start—was led on, rather—he's blind. He's the coroner.

"Heart failure," he said. "Natural causes—I mean *other than* natural causes, could be. That's what I meant—could've been other than natural causes."

"This is the case of the State versus Daniel Ponder we're on today," says the Judge. "Put your mind to your work. Suppose I acted that way." Poor old blind Truex is led back. And do you know who was called next? Nobody you'd ever hear of in a thousand years.

Would you guess, that after all that had been done for him, Uncle Daniel had taken it on himself to send Bonnie Dee *his own message*? That same Saturday I stopped the money, he did it. By word of mouth, of course. And he picked out the slowest, oldest, dirtiest, most brainless old Negro man he could find to send it by. I thought it showed a little ingratitude.

It was Big John—worked for us out there since time was: I don't know what he *did*. Always wore the same hat and shoes and overalls, and couldn't sign his name if life depended. Old man lives off by himself, a way, way back on the place—wonder how far anybody would have to go to find him. *I* never saw where he lived. First, Uncle Daniel had had to send a little Negro from the barbershop to get the old one to come in and *learn* the message. Whole thing took all day.

All the money Big John's ever made is right on him now, in his overall pocket, if somebody hasn't taken it again—that's all he wants it for, to carry it around. I expect he's been robbed a hundred times, among the Negroes, but he'll always ask you for money any time he sees you. Of course he and Uncle Daniel get along *fine*. He used to work in the flowers, if you could keep him out of the beds. Dug holes for Grandma; *that's* what she did with Big John.

So here he was. Around his hat is a bunch of full-blown roses, five or six Etoiles in a row, with little short stems stuck down in the hatband—they're still growing in Grandma's garden, in spite of everything.

"Did Mr. Daniel Ponder send word by you to his wife, Miss Bonnie Dee Ponder, on the fourteenth day of June of this year?" is what old Gladney asks him.

Big John agrees with you every time. He nods his head, and the roses bow up and down.

"Now I can tell you're a reliable Negro," says old Gladney. "And I just want you to tell me what the message was. What did Mr. Daniel tell you to say to the lady?"

Big John has a little voice like a whistle the air won't come through just right.

"Go tell Miss Bonnie Dee—go tell Miss Bonnie Dee—" He's getting started.

"Keep on. Tell Miss Bonnie Dee what?"

Big John fixed his mouth, and recited it off. " 'I'm going to kill you dead, Miss Bonnie Dee, if y' don't take m' back.' "

I would have thought Big John would get the message wrong, to begin with—that's one reason I'd never have picked him. But there was no mistaking that—he got *Uncle Daniel's* right!

Old man Gladney says after him, real soft, " 'I'm going to

kill you dead, Miss Bonnie Dee—' Did he laugh, I wonder, when he said that?"

DeYancey took objection to that, but Big John didn't even know what laugh was. He just scratched his head up under his hat.

"What made you remember it so good, Uncle?"

Big John still only scratched his head. Finally he says, " 'Cause Mr. Daniel give me a dime."

That was all he could think of. But I knew it was because of that high esteem Big John held Uncle Daniel in, that made him remember so fine. I must say Uncle Daniel held esteem for Big John, too. He always did like him—because of the money he could deposit on him, and then he didn't mind old dirty people the way you and I do. He let Big John come around him and listened to what he said, both. They listened to each other. When you saw them walking white and black together over the back lot, you'd have thought there went two Moguls, looking over the world.

Speak direct to us

"And what word did Miss Bonnie Dee send back?" says old Gladney. But Big John could remember that about as well as the frizzly hen that comes up to the back door.

"Her didn't have nothing to give me," was the best he could do.

"But Mr. Daniel Ponder did send this message to Miss Bonnie Dee Peacock Ponder, paying you for its safe delivery, Uncle, only two short days before her death: 'I'm going to kill you dead if you don't take me back.' Didn't he?"

"Ain't said to *me*, to *her*," Big John whistled out. "Ain't said to me *that* time. I ain't doin' nothin'. Only but what he tell me."

"That's right. 'I'm going to kill you dead, Miss Bonnie Dee'—and now he's done it," says old Gladney sharp, and no matter how DeYancey's objecting, Big John's agreeing like everything, bobbing his head with those flowers on it under everybody's nose.

DeYancey doesn't want to ask him anything—makes a sign like he's brushing flies away.

"Well, go on, Uncle, I'm through with you," says Gladney.

"He won't go away if you don't give him a nickel," I remarks from my seat.

"What for?" says old Gladney, but forks over, and the old man goes off real pleased. I must say the whole courtroom smelled of Big John and his flower garden for a good time afterward.

"I think as a witness, Mr. Gladney, Big John Beech was worth every bit of that," says DeYancey.

But Uncle Daniel looked to me like his feelings were already hurt. Big John up there instead of him.

Well, of course I hid it—but *I* was surprised myself at a few who were chosen as witnesses. Here rose up somebody I'd never expect to see testifying in a thousand years—Miss Teacake Magee. Old Gladney begins to tackle her.

"Mrs. Magee, you were married to the defendant, Mr. Daniel Ponder, for two months in the year 1944, were you not?"

Miss Teacake had cut bangs, and was putting on that she could barely whisper; the Judge had to tell her to speak up so people could hear.

"And divorced?"

You couldn't hear a thing.

"Why were you divorced, may I ask?" says old Gladney, cheerful-like.

"I just had to let him go," whispers Miss Teacake. That's just what she always says.

"Would you care to describe any features of your wedded life?" asks old Gladney, and squints like he's taking Miss Teacake's picture there with her mouth open.

"Just a minute," says the Judge. "Miss Edna Earle's girl is standing in the door to find out how many for dinner. I'll ask for a show of hands," and puts up his the first.

It was a table full, I can tell you. Everybody but the Peacocks, it appeared to me. I made a little sign to Ada's sister she'd better kill a few more hens.

Then Gladney gives a long look at the jury and says, "Never mind, Mrs. Magee, we understand perfectly. You'd rather keep it to yourself that you were harboring a booger-man. I won't ask you for another word about it."

Miss Teacake's still looking at him pop-eyed.

Old Gladney backs away on her easy, and DeYancey hops over and says, "Miss Teacake, just one question will clear this up, for us and you both, I think. In the period of this, your second marriage, did you ever at any time have cause to fear the defendant? Were you scared of Daniel, in other words?"

"Listen here. I don't scare that easy, DeYancey Clanahan," says Miss Teacake in her everyday voice. They tell her just to answer the question. All she says is, "Ever since I lost Professor Magee, I've had to look after myself." She keeps a pistol by her bed, and for all I know, it's loaded.

"But you did ask Mr. Ponder to go. Would anything ever induce you to ask him to come back?" says old Gladney, pointing a finger.

And she hoots out "No!" and scares herself. But by that time they're through with her.

She was mighty dressed up for that five minutes. Had a black silk fan she never did get worked open. Very different from appearing in church, appearing in a court trial. She said afterwards she had no *idea*, when she was asked to testify, that it might be for the other side.

And here next came Narciss—her whole life spent with the Ponders, and now grinning from ear to ear. And she had that little black dog of hers with her. She didn't know any better than let him come, so there he trotted. And her black umbrella she came to town under was folded up and swinging by her skirt.

"Woman, were you working in the Ponder house on the day of which we speak, Monday afternoon the sixteenth of June?" says old Gladney.

"Just let me take off my shades," says Narciss. In town, she wears black glasses with white rims. She folds them in a case that's a celluloid butterfly, from Woolworth's, and says she was there Monday.

He asked her what she was doing the last thing she did for Mrs. Ponder, and when she got around to that answer, she said, "Draggin' old parlor sofa towards the middle of the room like she tole me."

"What for?"

"Sir, lightnin' was fixin to come in de windows. Gittin' out de way."

"Was Mrs. Ponder there in the parlor with you, woman?"

"She ridin' de sofa."

All the Peacocks laughed in court. They didn't mind hearing how lazy they were.

"Was Mrs. Ponder expecting company?"

"That's how come I ironed her apricots dress, all dem little pleats."

"And company came?"

Narciss looked around at me and slapped her leg.

"Who was it? Tell who you saw."

Narciss took him down by telling him she didn't see; but it was us. She ran out of the room first, but she had ears. They let her tell just what she heard, then.

Narciss said, "Hears de car Miss Edna Earle ride around in go umph, comin' to a stop by de tree. Hears Mr. Daniel's voice sound off in a happy-time way, sayin' Miss Bonnie Dee was sure right about de rain. Hears it rainin', lightnin' and thunderin', feets pacin' over de yard. And little dog barkin' at Miss Edna Earle 'cause she didn't bring him a sack of bones."

"So you could say who the company was," says old Gladney, and Narciss says, "Wasn't no spooks." But Judge Waite wouldn't let that count, either question or answer.

"Did Mrs. Ponder herself have a remark to make?" says old Gladney.

"Says, 'Here dey come. Glad to see *anybody*. If it gits anybody, hope it gits dem, not me.'"

Uncle Daniel turned around to me with his face all worked in an O. He always thought whatever Bonnie Dee opened her mouth and said was priceless. He recognized her from *that*.

"Sh!" I said to him.

"Keep on," says old Gladney to Narciss.

"Can't keep on. I's gone by den."

"But you do know this much: at the time you left the parlor, and heard the company coming across the yard and talking, Mrs. Ponder was alive?"

Narciss gave him the most taking-down look she knows. "Alive as you is now."

"And when you saw Mrs. Ponder next?"

"Storm pass over," says Narciss, "I goes in de parlor and asks, 'Did I hear my name?' And dere Mr. Daniel and Miss Edna Earle holding together. And dere her, stretched out, all dem little pleats to do over, feets pointin' de other way round, and Dr. Lubanks snappin' down her eyes."

"Dead!" hollers Gladney, waving his hand like he had a flag in it. Uncle Daniel raised his eyes and kept watching that flag. "And don't that prove, Narciss, the company had something to do with it? Had everything to do with it! Mr. Daniel Ponder, like Othello of old, Narciss, he entered yonder and went to his lady's couch and he suffocated to death that beautiful, young, innocent, ninety-eight-pound bride of his, out of a fit of pure-D jealousy from the wellsprings of his aging heart."

Narciss's little dog was barking at him and DeYancey was objecting just as hard, but Narciss plain talks back to him.

"What's that you say, woman?" yells old Gladney, because he was through with her.

"Says naw sir. Don't know *he*; but Mr. *Daniel* didn't do nothin' like dat. His heart ain't grow old neither, by a long shot."

"What do you mean, old woman," yells old Gladney, and comes up and leans over her.

"Means you ain't brought up Mr. Daniel and I has. Find you somebody else," says Narciss.

Gladney says something about that's what the other side had better try to do. He says that's just what he means, there *wasn't* anybody else—since nobody would suspect Miss Edna Earle Ponder of anything—but he stamps away from Narciss like she'd just cheated him fine.

Up jumps DeYancey in his place, and says, "Narciss! At the time you heard company running across the yard, there was a storm breaking loose, was there not?"

"Yes *sir*."

"All right, tell me—what was the reason you only stayed to *hear* the company, not see them? Your best friends on earth! When they came in all wet and wanting to be brushed off, where were you?"

"Ho. I's in de back bedroom under de bed," says Narciss. "Miss Edna Earle's old room."

"Doing what?"

"*Hidin'*. I don't want to get no lightnin' bolts down me. Come lightnin' and thunder, Mr. DeYancey, you always going to find me clear back under de furthermost part of de bed in de furthermost back room. And ain't comin' out twell it's over."

"The same as ever," says DeYancey, and he smiles. "Now tell me this. What was Miss Bonnie Dee herself generally doing when there was such a thunderstorm?"

"Me and Miss Bonnie Dee, we generally gits down together. Us hides together under Miss Edna Earle's bed when it storms. Another thing we does together, Mr. DeYancey, I occasionally plays jacks with her," says Narciss, "soon as I gits my kitchen swep out."

And at first Bonnie Dee just couldn't stand Negroes! And I like her nerve, where she hid.

"But that Monday," says DeYancey, "that Monday, she didn't get down under anything?"

"She pleadin' company. So us just gits de sofa moved away from de lightnin' best we can. Ugh! I be's all by myself under de bed—listenin' to *dat*." Narciss all at once dies laughing.

"So you can't know what happened right afterward?"

"Sir? I just be's tellin' you what happened," says Narciss. "Boom! Boom! Rackety rack!" Narciss laughs again and the little dog barks with her.

"Narciss! Open your eyes. Both of 'em." And DeYancey gave a whistle. Here came two little Bodkin boys, red as beets, wearing their Scout uniforms and dragging something together down the aisle.

"DeYancey, what is that thing?" asks Judge Waite from the bench.

"Just part of a tree," says DeYancey. He's a modest boy. I don't think it had been cut more than fifteen minutes. "You know what tree that is?" he says to Narciss.

"Know that fig tree other side of Jericho," says Narciss. "It's ours."

"Something specially big and loud *did* happen, Narciss, the minute after you ran under the bed, didn't it?"

DeYancey shakes the tree real soft and says, "Your Honor, I would like to enter as evidence the top four-foot section of the little-blue fig tree the Ponders have always had in their yard, known to all, standing about ten feet away from the chimney of the house, that was struck by a bolt of lightning on Monday afternoon, June the sixteenth, before the defendant and his niece had ever got in the house good. Had they gone in the side door, they would very likely not be with us now. In a moment I'll lay this before Your Honor and the jury. Please to pass it. Look at the lightning marks and the withered leaves, and pass it quietly to your neighbor. I submit that it was the racket this little-blue fig tree made being struck, and the blinding flash of it, just ten short feet from the walls of the Ponder house, that caused the heart of Mrs. Bonnie Dee Peacock Ponder to fail in her bosom. *This* is the racket you heard, Narciss. I told you to open your eyes."

Narciss opened her eyes and shut them again. It was the worst looking old piece of tree you ever saw. It looked like something had skinned down it with claws out. DeYancey switched it back and forth, sh! sh! under Narciss's nose and all at once she opened her mouth but not her eyes and said:

"Storm come closer and closer. Closer and closer, twell a big ball of fire come sidlin' down de air and hit right *yonder*—" she pointed without looking right under DeYancey's feet. "Ugh. You couldn't call it pretty. I feels it clackin' my teeths and twangin' my bones. Nippin' my heels. Den I couldn't no mo' hear and couldn't no mo' see, just smell dem smokes. Ugh. Den far away comes first little sound. It comes louder and louder twell it turn into little black dog whinin'—and pull me out from under de bed." She pointed at the dog without looking and he wagged his tail at her. Then Narciss opens her eyes and laughs, and shouts, "*Yassa! Dat* what git her! *You* hit it!" And all of a sudden she sets her glasses back on and quits her laughing and you can't see a thing more of her but stove black.

All I can say is, that was news to me.

"And *then* you heard the company at the door," says DeYancey, and they just nod at each other.

Old Gladney's right there and says, "Woman, are you prepared to swear on the Holy Scripture here that you know which one came in that house first—those white folks or that ball of fire?"

"*I* ain't got nothin' to do wid it," says Narciss, "which come in first. If white folks and ball of fire both tryin' git in you all's house, you best let *dem* mind who comin' in first. *I* ain't had nothin' to do wid it. *I* under de bed in Miss *Edna Earle's* old room."

She just washed her hands of us. You can't count on them for a single minute. Old Gladney threw his hands in the air, but so did DeYancey.

"Come on, Sport," says Narciss, and she and Sport come on back up the aisle and stand at the back for the rest of it.

So about all old Gladney could do was holler a little—I'll skip over that—and say, "The prosecution rests." That looked like the best they could do, for the time being.

THERE WAS a kind of wait while DeYancey rattled his papers. I never knew what was on those. While he rattled, he had those little boys haul the fig tree around the room again, and up the aisle and back and forth in front of the jury, till Judge Waite made them quit and brush him off, and then they propped it up against the wall, in the corner across from the Confederate battle flag, where I reckon it still may be, with poor little figs no bigger than buttons still hanging on it. As Uncle Daniel said, we'll miss those.

The Peacocks were all looking around again. I don't know what they came expecting. Every once in a while, old man Peacock had been raising up from his seat and intoning, "Anybody here got a timepiece?" And Mrs. Peacock had settled into asking questions from the people behind her and across the aisle, about Clay—mostly about how many churches we had here and the like. To tell you the truth, Mrs. Peacock talked her way through that trial. If there was one second's wait between things, *she'd* say something. Once she says, "Anybody able to tell me what you can do about all this swelling?" and shows her fingers. "Wake up in the morning all right, and then, along towards now, I look like you'd chopped my fingers all off and stuck 'em back on again." She was right. But she wasn't spending the day in a doctor's waiting room. The Peacock girls sat with their arms tight around each other's necks like a picture-show party—it was hard to tell where one left off and the other began. The littlest brother, about eight, walked up and down with a harmonica in his mouth, breathing through that. The babies kept sliding off laps and streaking for the door, and somebody had to run after them. And of course there was eternal jumping up for water from everybody, and a few water fights—one right in the middle of Miss Teacake's spiel. It was hot, hot, hot. Judge Waite was heard to remark from the bench that this was the hottest weather ever to come within his jurisprudence.

Finally, DeYancey got started and said that what he was

undertaking to prove was that the Peacocks didn't have a case on earth. He said it would be very shortly seen that Bonnie Dee was beyond human aid already by the time Uncle Daniel and I put our foot over the sill of the door to that house. I laid my hand on Uncle Daniel's knee. He smiled at me just fine, because here came the blackberry lady, the ice man, and the blind man with the brooms—people he was glad to see again. They fell over each other testifying that Bonnie Dee had sent for Uncle Daniel. They just opened their mouths once and sat down.

Then Dr. Ewbanks. Busy, busy, busy and a widower to boot—everybody has to take him when they can get him. He had an Else Poulsen rose on too.

He told the Court a little white boy called up his house on the telephone from the crossroads store near Ponder Hill that day and told the cook he was wanted out at Mr. Sam's in a hurry, and hung up; and she sent her little boy Elder, who hollered at him, and Dr. Ewbanks was fishing away on Clanahan's Lake, and it was commencing to pour down there too, but he made it on back to shore and back home and out to the Ponders as quick as he could get there in the pouring-down, and found his patient stretched on the sofa there in the parlor with life extinct. He found Uncle Daniel and me needing more attention than she did. He put it down death by misadventure.

When Gladney asks him, he says no, he didn't notice signs of a struggle of any kind; the lady's heart had just up and failed her. It happened sometimes. And if that was how the Ponders had walked in on her and found her, it would never occur to him to doubt a Ponder's word.

Old Gladney scratched his head and pretended to think. "Doc," he says, "what makes the heart fail? What would make a poor young lady's heart fail, without giving warning?"

Dr. Ewbanks waved his hand. "Say fright. Fright due to the electrical storm we had roaming over the countryside at that time," he says. "That's reasonable. Why, a bolt of lightning just narrowly missed *me*, out in my boat on the lake, before I could get it turned around."

Old Gladney edges up and takes a smell of Dr. Ewbanks'

rose. He says, "Doctor, how many other cases of the same kind you come across since that storm?"

Dr. Ewbanks says Bonnie Dee was the only case he had, he was glad to say.

"Lightning never strikes twice in the same place, I believe the old saying goes," says Gladney. "Maybe the Ponder family feels like they're all out of danger now, and maybe the Ewbankses do too."

The jury—one or two Ewbankses and Peppers and a Sistrunk connection or two and a Clanahan by marriage, plus a handful of good old Bodkins—and I wish you'd been here for the selection of the jury!—just looked back at Gladney. He wheels on Dr. Ewbanks with coattails flying. "Would you swear, Dr. Ewbanks, that the death you ascribe to heart failure might not also be ascribed to suffocation?"

"That distinction would be perfectly pointless, Mr. Gladney. Misadventure, Mr. Gladney, in case you'd like to remember this for future occasions," says Dr. Ewbanks, who didn't like anybody to go smelling his rose, "is for all practical purposes an act of God. Like when the baby gets the pillow against its face, and just don't breathe any more." He stands up and smiles. "That answer your question?"

He gave us a nod, and went up the aisle and sat down by Miss Teacake Magee. He'd told me, before the start, he might not be able to stay long enough to see how the case came out; but he did.

And I was next.

I wore this dress—I wear it for everyday, now—and a big Milan hat that's seen me through flood and fire already—but my other glasses, and my dinner ring.

By the time I got settled in the witness chair, DeYancey had his coat off and his tie undone and his collar open. He's not his grandfather in court, by any means. And he called me "Ma'am" for the occasion—I could have killed him.

"Now, ma'am," he says. "The State has been having themselves quite a time over a message Mr. Daniel Ponder is supposed to have sent his wife just two days before her death. If we're to rely on the word of Big John Beech, this message ran, 'I'm going to kill you dead, Miss Bonnie Dee, if you

don't take me back.' Now, ma'am, did you ever hear remarks
like that spoken in the Ponder household?"

"Why, certainly," I says. "It was a perfectly normal household. Threats flew all the time. Yes, sir. 'I'm going to kill
you dead—' The rest of it goes, 'if you try that one more
time.'"

"Have there been instances in your presence when Mr.
Daniel Ponder said those very words to Miss Bonnie Dee?"

"Plenty," I says. "And with no results whatever. Or when
she said it to him either."

"Can you tell us right now of one occasion when Mr.
Daniel said it to her?"

"Very probably he said it the first time Bonnie Dee tried to
cut up a leg of his Sunday pants to make herself a skirt out
of," I says.

They objected to that—I don't know why. It was exactly
what she made.

"But whatever and whenever the occasion for that remark,
it was a perfectly innocent remark?" says DeYancey.

"I should hope so."

"So that when Mr. Daniel Ponder sent word to Miss Bonnie
Dee that he was going to kill her if she didn't take him back,
in your estimation it meant nothing like a real threat?"

"Meant he got it straight from Grandma," I says. "That's
what it means. She said 'I'm going to kill you' every other
breath to him—she raised him. Gentlest woman on the face
of the earth. 'I'll break your neck,' 'I'll skin you alive,' 'I'll
beat your brains out'—Mercy! How that does bring Grandma
back. Uncle Daniel was brought up like anybody else. And
had a married life like anybody else. I'd hate to hear the things
the *Clanahans* say brought back to my ears! Mr. Gladney
didn't need to traipse over the fields and find him an old
Negro that can't talk good through his windpipe to tell the
Court what word Uncle Daniel sent his wife—I could have
repeated it without ever hearing it at all, if I'd been asked."

"Thank you, ma'am, I believe you," says DeYancey. "And
I believe as well as anything in this world that those words
never meant a thing."

After that, I testified in no uncertain terms that our visit
out there that day was Bonnie Dee's idea, pure and simple.

"Uncle Daniel had been asked to leave in the first place," I says. "Being a gentleman, he would surely wait to be asked to come back before he *went*."

"And you went with Mr. Daniel Ponder for this reunion, ma'am?"

"Would I have missed it for the world?" I said, and looked out at the courtroom. I was certainly on the side of love—that's well known and not worth denying. I said, "How would he have gotten out there otherwise? I drove. Drove us out there at forty, my limit, and pulled up under the pecan tree in the front yard. It was beginning to lightning and thunder at the crossroads; fixing to pour down as we turned in the gate. As I look back—" DeYancey held up his hand, but I went right on and said I had a premonition. You remember it.

"Now tell what you found," says DeYancey, "when you all went in the parlor."

"At first," I says, "I didn't know where I was. Because the furniture was all crazy. And it was so dark. Not any of the lights would turn on, after she had them put in! We tried 'em. Hard to see what she *was* doing. But it lightninged."

"Go on and tell us," he says.

I said, "Well, she *had been* piled up on the parlor sofa in the middle of the room with the windows all down, eating ice out of a tea glass in her best dress. And pushing up candy on the blade of a knife out of a turkey platter she'd poured it out in. I noticed the texture was grainy." I wanted them to see I couldn't hide anything.

"What was she doing now, ma'am?"

"Piled up on the sofa in her best and that's all."

"You mean dead?"

"As a doornail," I says. "I mean what I say, as I always do."

"And how did you know she was dead, ma'am?" asks DeYancey.

I told him it was because I had sense enough to. And I said, "Not a thing would revive her."

"What did you do, ma'am?"

"I hollered. 'Narciss!' I hollered. Because that Negro'd been here in the house since before I was born. 'Narciss!' But she'd gone to cover like a chicken in the daytime when something comes over the sun. 'Narciss!' And not a peep. Not even boo."

Narciss laughed from the back of the courtroom to hear how she did.

"So I ran and reached the spirits of ammonia myself from the top shelf in the bathroom, and ran and held it to her—while you could have counted to a hundred, but it didn't do her a speck of good, as I could have told you beforehand."

"Didn't you try calling any white people?" says DeYancey, trying to hurry me.

"Front and back. I hollered for Otis and Lee Roy Pepper—they're white; they're responsible for running the place. But they didn't come when I called them—they never do. Turned out they were getting drenched to the skin under a persimmon tree a mile and a half away. So I had to stop a child of ten in his hay wagon, sheltering under a tree, and send him out in it to the crossroads to use the phone at the store and try to find the doctor. *Then* Dr. Ewbanks was out of human cry, till a little nine-year-old colored boy got to him with a bucket on his head. It's a wonder we ever got a doctor to her at all, all of us put together," I says. "No one has ever seen that little white boy or that hay wagon since."

"What was your uncle doing at this time?" asks DeYancey, offhand.

"I quieted him down," I says real calm, so he wouldn't look up. He was looking at the floor. "I told him just to sit there quiet while I listened for her heart. And every time my uncle says, 'Edna Earle, Edna Earle, what do you hear?' I have to say, 'Nothing yet.' 'Then what's that *I* hear?' he says, and I says, 'You must hear your own heart.' "

I heard a real deep sigh come up from everybody, like a breeze. It settled me some. I saw Eva Sistrunk taking out her handkerchief.

"Finally, though, here trotted Dr. Ewbanks in from Clanahan's Lake, in his boots and soaking wet and a dirty duck hat on his head full of water, tracking swamp mud and leaves through the house. He was surprised to see *me*. He was extremely fishy. I think he had some baits in a tin can he forgot to take out. I saw an awful-looking knife sticking out, and my uncle turns his eyes on it too.

" 'Where's my patient?' says Dr. Ewbanks, and poor Uncle Daniel falls right over at his feet."

Then I told all about Uncle Daniel stretched out on the floor and giving him the spirits of ammonia and how he groaned and how pitiful it was and we couldn't lift him, and I heard everybody in court beginning to cry, I believe—but Uncle Daniel was the loudest. He was looking at me now.

"Well," says DeYancey, "to go back a moment to the deceased. When you discovered Mrs. Bonnie Dee Ponder the way she was, ma'am, you were sorry and upset—but were you greatly surprised?"

"Why, no," I says. "Not greatly surprised. I've been more surprised in my life by other sudden deaths in this town."

"Just tell us how long ago you might have been prepared for something like this."

"She was always out of breath, like somebody that's been either working or talking as hard as they could go all day," I says. "For no reason. She weighed less than a hundred pounds on my scales in the Beulah lobby—I weighed her. Before she married Uncle Daniel, she fainted in Miss Eva Sistrunk's and my presence in Woolworth's one day, just because the fan went off. Of course, everybody knows Woolworth's would be the most breathless spot in creation to *stay* in."

"So as her niece-in-law, you would testify that Mrs. Bonnie Dee Ponder, to the best of your memory and knowledge, was always frail?"

"A gust of wind might have carried her away, any time." I thought of blowing a kiss out the window to show them, but I felt Uncle Daniel's eyes still on me.

"Your witness," says DeYancey, with a bow to old Gladney.

I looked at Gladney and he looked at me, and drew his hand up to his chin. Grandma Ponder said, "Show me a man wears a diamond ring, and I'll show you a wife-beater." There he was.

He says to me, "Mizriz Ponder?" That's what he calls me—Mizriz. He likes to act country, but he don't have all that far to go—he *is* country. "So threats to kill husband or wife never amounts to a hill of beans around here?"

"Depends on who says it," I says, very cool. "It would be different if you take somebody like Williebelle Kilmichael, out in the country. She really empties a load of birdshot into her husband's britches, every so often. Whenever he stands up all through Sunday School, you can be pretty well sure what's happened. Williebelle Kilmichael does it all the time—because she means it. Grandma didn't mean it, Grandpa didn't mean it, I don't mean it—Uncle Daniel don't mean it. You don't mean it."

Just then, too late, I remembered where Mr. Gladney had been peppered, so we heard. He was somebody that knew somebody'd meant it. But I went on fanning, and he went on looking like an old deacon, and opened his mouth and said:

"Well—it may not mean a thing in general, to send a lady a message you're going to kill her if she don't please you, but *what if the day after, she's found dead?*"

"It was two days after. Then everybody's sorry," I says. The Judge makes me change my answer to say it still don't mean anything. "Except love, of course. It's all in a way of speaking," I says. "Putting it into words. With some people, it's little threats. With others, it's liable to be poems."

He says, "All right, Mizriz Ponder, set me straight about something else. I've been worrying about that storm that come up right the same time as your visit—wasn't that too bad for everybody! What worries me most about it is how that ball of fire ever got into you all's house out there. To the best of my memory, every time I ever passed that house, it was covered with lightning rods."

"You're behind the times," I says. "Look up over your head next time you go out of the Courthouse. The first time I had men on the roof after Grandpa Ponder was gone, fixing the holes, I had those things pulled down; Grandma never could stand them. And the Courthouse took them off my hands. Judge Tip Clanahan thought they added enough to the Courthouse to justify the purchase."

"I'm way behind the times," says old Gladney. "Can't keep up with you at all. Now a ball of fire, like that nigger of yours saw, I've got yet to see one—and might not know one if I met it in the road."

"If you don't know what a ball of fire looks like by this time, I'm afraid it's too late to tell you," I says.

He says, "Don't tell me you've seen one, too."

I says, "As a matter of fact, I was the one saw the ball of fire in the Ponder house, the day of the trouble. I saw it the closest-to of anybody."

"Now that'n," he says. "Then you're the very one I ought to ask. Which-a-way did that'n get in, and which-a-way did it get out?"

"You've never been inside our house, Mr. Gladney," I says. "But I'll try to tell you. In down the front chimney. Careened around the parlor a minute, and out through the hall. And if you've never seen a ball of fire go out through bead curtains, it goes as light as a butterfly with wings."

"Do tell!—And what was Mrs. Bonnie Dee Ponder doing," he hollers, "while you was in the parlor *with* her, miratin' at a ball of fire that was supposed to be scarin' her to death? And who else was in there besides? Now the cat's out of the bag!"

Would *you* have known what he was up to? I could have bitten my tongue off! But I didn't show it—I just gave a laugh.

"I beg your pardon, Mr. Gladney," I says. "You aren't a bit straight. The ball of fire you keep going back to was coming out of the parlor when I saw it. That's how I knew where it had been. When Uncle Daniel and I were heading in through the front door of the house, it was heading out the parlor through the curtains—those bead curtains. We practically collided with it in front of the hatrack. I remember I said at the time, 'Whew, Uncle Daniel, did you see that? I bet that scared Bonnie Dee Peacock!' It skirted on down the hall and streaked out the back somewhere to scare the Negroes."

And I sails from the witness stand. I wasn't going to hear another word about balls of fire *that* day.

"Now they've found a witness!" says old Gladney to my back. "A fine witness! A ball of fire! I double-dog dare Mr. Clanahan to produce it after dinner!"

Well, everybody had a good time over that. But when I sat down again by Uncle Daniel, he looked at me like he never saw me before in his life.

"Speaking of dinner," says Judge Waite. "Recess!"—and I

could have kissed him, and Ada's sister too, that stood in the door with her finger up.

We had all that company to crowd in at the Beulah dinner table, had to serve it twice, but there was plenty and it was good; and everybody was kind enough to tell me how I did (except Judge Waite, who sat up there by me without opening his mouth except to eat) and made me feel better. I hardly had a chance to swallow my fresh peach pie. When somebody spoke to Uncle Daniel, I tried to answer for him too, if I could. I'm the go-between, that's what I am, between my family and the world. I hardly ever get a word in for myself.

Right across the street were the Peacocks perched on the Courthouse stile, in stairsteps, eating—in the only shade there was. I could tell you what they ate without even seeing it— jelly sandwiches and sweet milk and biscuit and molasses in a tin bucket—poked wells in the biscuit to hold the molasses—and sweet potatoes wrapped in newspaper. That basket was drawing ants all through my testimony, I saw them. The Peacocks finished up with three or four of their own watermelons that couldn't have been any too ripe, to judge by what they left lying on the Courthouse grass for the world to see and pick up.

I certainly was unprepared for what DeYancey Clanahan did after lunch. He asked permission to call up a surprise witness; and he called up one of those blessed Peacocks.

It was one of Bonnie Dee's little old sisters—Johnnie Ree Peacock. The same size and the same hair, and batting her eyes! And there was most of Bonnie Dee's telephone-putting-in costume—very warm for June. And in the most mosquitery little voice you ever heard in your life, with lots of pauses for breath, she testifies that no, she and Bonnie Dee were not twins, they just came real close together, and their mama used to play-like they were twins. You could tell from listening at Johnnie Ree that she didn't have the sense her sister did, though Bonnie Dee never had enough to get alarmed about. Just enough to get married on trial.

Johnnie Ree said Bonnie Dee never did a thing to be ashamed of in her life. And neither did she.

"Even in Memphis?" says DeYancey, prancing around her.

That's what I mean by a tangent. DeYancey didn't have any business starting to prove that Uncle Daniel *ought* to have got after Bonnie Dee. He just ought to stick to proving that he didn't. He hadn't told me at all, eating that pie, that he was thinking of doing that. If he had, he'd have had another think coming. I didn't want any harm done to Bonnie Dee now! I don't have an ounce of revenge in my body, and neither does Uncle Daniel. The opposite.

"I believe it to be a fact, Miss Peacock, that you once enjoyed a trip to Memphis, Tennessee, with your sister," says DeYancey, and Johnnie Ree's face lights up a smidgen.

She says "Yessir."

I saw it then. Oh, I did well not to make up my mind too hastily about Ovid Springer. I congratulate myself still on that, every night of the world. Mr. Springer would not have hesitated to blacken Uncle Daniel's name before the world by driving sixty-five miles through the hot sun and handing him over a motive on a silver platter. Tired traveling man if you like—but when it came to a murder trial, he'd come running to be in on it. DeYancey had taken time from dinner to catch him on the telephone—he was eating cold cuts in Silver City—and he was headed here, as I found out later, but he had a flat tire in Delhi. I'm afraid that's a good deal like Mr. Springer, from beginning to end. Of course, he never had anybody to look after him.

So Johnnie Ree was just a substitute. But she didn't know it.

DeYancey says, "What kind of time did you have in Memphis?" and she says "Nice," and he says, "Tell us about it."

"Here?" she says.

"Why not?" says DeYancey, smiling that Clanahan smile.

According to Johnnie Ree, in her little mosquito voice, they walked around blocks and blocks and blocks of sidewalks in Memphis without coming to anything but houses, and when they came to stores they rode up and down in stores, and went to movies. Never saw the same show twice. By the second day they started going in the morning and didn't stop all day. Four in one day was their goal. Johnnie Ree wanted to stop and tell us all *Quo Vadis*, as if it had never been to Clay, but DeYancey broke in to ask her where did they stay in Memphis and Johnnie Ree said *she* didn't know: it said "A Home Away from Home." There was a fern a yard broad sitting on the buttress out front that looked like it could eat them up, and that was how she could tell the house from some others that said "A Home Away from Home" too.

And they didn't care to board with the lady, but ate in cafeterias, because you could pick out what you wanted. They had store-bought watermelon in round slices, and store-bought cake that tasted of something queer, like paregoric. Johnnie Ree's voice got a little stronger on the subject of watermelon.

I suppose her tales of Memphis would have gone on the rest of the afternoon (what a blessing that Bonnie Dee didn't *talk* but took after her father!) and everybody was sleepy after dinner anyway, except all of a sudden Uncle Daniel *noticed* her. Noticed Johnnie Ree. (She was on the premises at the funeral, but nothing looked the same then.) I heard his chair scrape. His eyes got real round, and I put my hand on his knee, like I do in church when he begins to sing too fast.

"Why, Bonnie Dee kept something back from me," he says. "Look yonder, Edna Earle. I'm seeing a vision. Why didn't you poke me?"

I says, "Oh, she's got on rags and tags of somebody else's clothes, but she looks like the last of pea-time to me." I still hold that Bonnie Dee was the only pretty one they had.

But it was her clothes that Uncle Daniel was seeing.

"Wait till the trial's over, Uncle Daniel," I whispers, and he subsides. He's forgotten the way he looked at me—he's good as gold again.

So Johnnie Ree, who'd talked on and on, and on and on, says, "So we got back home. The end." Like a movie.

"And you behaved like a lady the whole time?" asks De-Yancey.

"Yes sir. As far as I know."

"And Bonnie Dee behaved?" cried DeYancey.

"Oh, Bonnie Dee *sure* behaved. She stayed to home."

"What's that?" says DeYancey, stock still. "Who's this sister you've been telling us about? Who did go on this fool's errand, anyway? We were given to understand by a witness now racing toward us to testify, that it was you and your sister Bonnie Dee that were up in Memphis on the loose."

"Bonnie Dee's not the only sister in the world," says Johnnie Ree. "Stand up, Treva."

And up pops a little bitty one. She held her gum still, and turned all the way around, and stood there, till Johnnie Ree says, "Sit down." She was well drilled. Treva had a pin pulling her front together, and guess what the pin was—a little peacock with a colored tail, all kinds of glass stones. I wouldn't be surprised if that wasn't the substance of what she brought back from Memphis.

DeYancey groans. "Mrs. Bonnie Dee Ponder never went herself at all?"

"She was ready to hear what it's like the way we told it. But me and Treva was the ones went, and Bonnie Dee stayed home with Mama," says Johnnie Ree. "She give us two twenties and a five and a ten, and part of her old-lady clothes. So she could get a whole bed to herself and eat Mama's greens."

"But never went?" DeYancey groaned—*everybody* groaned, but the Peacocks.

"She said she was an old, married lady. And it was too late for her to go."

"Why, Mr. Clanahan," says Judge Waite. "I believe you've been wasting our time."

Johnnie Ree brings up her fingers and gives three little scrapes at DeYancey. When she came down, her whole family was just as proud of her as if she'd been valedictorian of the graduating class. The other side didn't want to ask her a thing. She'll remember that trial for the rest of her days.

B UT MERCY. Uncle Daniel was stirring in his chair.

"DeYancey," he says. "You've got a hold of me. Let-a-go."

"Never mind," says DeYancey. "Never you mind."

"I'm fixing to get up there myself." That's what Uncle Daniel said.

"Take the stand? Uh-uh, Daniel. You know what I told you," says DeYancey. "What I told you and told you!"

"Let-a-go your side, Edna Earle," says Uncle Daniel.

"Dear heart," I says.

"It's way past my turn now," says Uncle Daniel.

"Let-a-go."

"Edna Earle, he said he wouldn't—didn't you hear him?" says DeYancey across Uncle Daniel's little bow tie.

"You all didn't tell me I was going to have to do so much listening. It ain't good for my constitution," says Uncle Daniel.

I just drew a deep, big sigh. Sometimes I do that, but not like then, in public.

"What's this new commotion? Is this a demand to testify I'm about to hear? I expected it," says the Judge.

I just looked at him.

"That's what it's mounting up to be, Judge," says De-Yancey, and he all but wrings his hands then. "Judge, do you have to let him?"

"If he so demands," says Judge Waite. "I've been sitting on the bench a mighty long time, son, since before you were born. I'm here to listen to any and all. Haven't been surprised so far."

"Daniel," DeYancey turns back and says. "If you stand up there, you got to fire me first."

"I'd hate that," says Uncle Daniel, really sorry. "But I'd rather be up there talking myself than hear you and every one of these other folks put together. Turn-a-loose."

"Daniel, it looks to me like now you got to choose between you and me who knows best," DeYancey says.

"I choose me," says Uncle Daniel.

"Don't you think, Daniel, you need to think that over a minute?" says Judge Waite, leaning down like he's finally ashamed of himself.

"Not a bit in the world," says Uncle Daniel.

"Miss Edna Earle's trying her best to say something to you," says Judge Waite.

"I'm going to beat her if she don't stop. And I'm going to *fire him*," says Uncle Daniel. "DeYancey, you're fired."

"Here and now?" says DeYancey, like his heart would break, and Uncle Daniel says, "Sure as you're born. Look— my foot was about to go to sleep." And up he rises.

"Who's going to ask you the questions up there?" says DeYancey, with one last try.

"*Questions!*" says Uncle Daniel. "Who you think I am?"

"Wait, Daniel Ponder," says the Judge. "You've been here enough times and sat through enough sessions of Court to know how it's done as well as I do. You got to let somebody ask you the questions before you can do the talking. I say so."

"Then I choose this gentleman here," says Uncle Daniel— pointing straight at old Gladney, nearly in his open mouth. "I've had my eye on him—he's up and coming. Been at it harder than anybody and I give him a little pat on the back for it. DeYancey's spent most of his time today trying to hold us all down. Run home, DeYancey. Give your grandfather my love."

The judge just made a few signs with his hands, and threw himself back in his chair.

There it came: "Mr. Daniel Ponder!"

Uncle Daniel listened to his name, and just beamed. I wish you could have seen him then, when he walked up there and faced us. He could always show his pleasure so! Round and pink and grand, and beaming out everywhere in his sparkling-white suit. Nobody'd still have a coat on in weather like this—you'd have to be Uncle Daniel, or a candidate.

They let Uncle Daniel hold up his hand and swear, and old Gladney loped over to him, and eyed him, looking up. Uncle Daniel didn't care to sit down. He'd always rather talk standing up.

"Mr. Ponder?"

And Uncle Daniel looked over his shoulder for Grandpa. Nobody had ever called him Mr. Ponder in his life. He was thrilled from the start.

"Mr. Ponder, what is your calling or occupation?" says old Gladney. "Your line of work?"

"Work?" says Uncle Daniel, looking all around, thrilled. "What would I want to work for? I'm rich as Croesus. My father Mr. Sam Ponder left me more than I'd ever know what to do with."

Old Gladney keeps on. "Did you love your wife, Mr. Ponder? I refer to your second wife, Mrs. Bonnie Dee."

"Yes indeed. Oh, I should say I did. You would have loved her too, Mr. Gladney, if you could have had the chance to know her," says poor Uncle Daniel.

"You loved Bonnie Dee," says old Gladney, still keeping on. "You expect the Court to believe that?"

"They've heard it before," Uncle Daniel said, "every one of 'em. She wasn't any bigger than a minute—and pretty as a doll. And a natural-born barber. I'll never find another one like her." But for a second his poor eye wandered.

"And did your wife Bonnie Dee return your love?" asks Gladney.

"Well now, that depended, sir," says poor Uncle Daniel, with the best will in the world. "Edna Earle could have told you all about that. She kept tabs on it." The whole thing might have come out then and there, the whole financial story of the Ponder family. Of course everybody in the room was familiar with it, but nobody wanted to *hear* it.

"On Monday, the sixteenth of June, Mr. Ponder, would you say she loved you?" says old Gladney. "Or loved you not?" He laughed.

They had to recall to Uncle Daniel the day that was—he's the worst person in town on dates and figures—but he said, "Oh, yes indeed, sir. She loved me then."

"Well, Mr. Ponder! If you loved your wife as you declare, and thought there was nobody like her, and your wife—as it depended or not—loved you, and on June the sixteenth she showed she did love you by sending you three proved invitations to return to her side—what did you want to go out there and kill her for?"

Old Gladney shot his old bony finger right in Uncle Daniel's face, surprising him to death. I don't reckon he'd ever really taken it in what the charge was.

Nothing happened in the courtroom except some babies cried.

"Was it because you told her you would? . . . Tell us about it," says old Gladney, real smiley.

They ought never to have let Uncle Daniel up there if they didn't want to hear the story. He smiled back. I tried to hold him with my eye, but it didn't work—not with him up on a stage.

He says, "Do you know, all in all, I've seen mighty little of that girl? First she came, then she went. Then she came, then she run me off. Edna Earle knows, she keeps tabs. Then three kind friends brought word in one day I was welcome. It already looked dark and commenced rumbling towards the west, and we lit out there lickety-split. Now when we got there, I went to hug my wife and kiss her, it had been such a time, Mr. Gladney; but you might hug your wife too hard. Did you ever do that?" asks Uncle Daniel.

Old Gladney says, "No-o-o." People started to laugh at him, then changed their minds and didn't.

"It's a way too easy to do," says Uncle Daniel.

"Sure enough?" says old Gladney, and steps close. "Show me."

Uncle Daniel stood there and hung his head, ashamed of that old fool.

"I'm impervious, I guarantee you," says that old lawyer. "Go ahead, show me what a hug too hard is."

"But that time I didn't," Uncle Daniel tells him. "I went to hug her, but I didn't get to."

"Is that so? How come you didn't get to?" says old Gladney, still close.

That little frown, that I just can't stand to see, came in Uncle Daniel's forehead, and everybody caught their breath but me. I was on my feet.

"Never mind, Uncle Daniel," I calls up. "I've told that."

Judge Waite and old man Gladney and DeYancey Clanahan all three poked their fingers at me, but didn't really notice what I said; nobody noticed. Even Uncle Daniel.

Old Gladney keeps right on. "Listen close to my next question, Mr. Ponder. I know you can answer it—it ain't hard.
When you ran into the parlor to hug her—only you didn't
get to—did Bonnie Dee speak to you?"

DeYancey was leaping up and snapping his fingers, objecting his heart out, but what good does objecting to Uncle
Daniel do? You just get fired. Uncle Daniel would have fired
the angel Gabriel, right that minute, for the same thing. You
never could stop Uncle Daniel from going on, once you let
him know he had your ears. And now everybody was galvanized.

"Hollered! She hollered at me. 'I don't appreciate lightning
and thunder a bit!' " said Uncle Daniel—proudly. And in her
voice. He did have it down to a T, like he could always do
bird calls. He looked over our heads for Narciss, and smiled
at her.

Everybody let out one of those big courtroom sighs.

"She spoke. She hollered. She was alive and strong," says
Gladney. "And what did *you* say, sir?"

Uncle Daniel changed. He got carnation-color. He looked
down at the Stetson between his fingers and all that time went
by while he turned it round and then sighted through the
ventilation holes he'd cut in the crown. Then he said quick,
"I said 'Catch her, Edna Earle!' "

Gladney says, "Bonnie Dee was running?"

"No, falling," says Uncle Daniel. "Falling to the floor."

"And did Miss Edna Earle catch her?"

"No, sir," says Uncle Daniel. "She can't catch."

I could have died right there.

"And what had you done to her first?" whispers old
Gladney.

Uncle Daniel whispers back, "Nothing."

"You laid hands on her first!" yells Gladney.

"On Bonnie Dee? No, you can hug your wife too hard,"
says Uncle Daniel, "when you haven't seen her in a long time.
But I didn't get to. Dr. Ewbanks had to raise me up and tend
to me. I'm more poorly than I look."

"I congratulate you just the same," says Gladney, straight-
ening up. "You got a reliable memory. You set us going on
the right track. You got the most reliable memory in Court.

We'll see who can remember the rest of it now. Much obliged—Mr. Ponder."

"Daniel!" says DeYancey, pushing in front of Gladney and pulling Uncle Daniel by the sleeve. "I know you fired me, but we've got to disregard it—everything! Listen to me: were you ever in the asylum?"

"Look, Tadpole," Uncle Daniel says—he still calls De-Yancey that from the time they played so nicely together, "if there's anybody knows the answer to that already, it's you and your granddaddy. Your granddaddy got me in, him and some-body else." Till that good day, Uncle Daniel had never men-tioned Grandpa's name from the time he died.

"Thanks, boy," says DeYancey, and to Gladney he says, "That's the witness. I ask that his evidence be stricken—"

Old Gladney was already wheeling back in his coattails. "Mr. Ponder! Were you *discharged* from the asylum?"

"Why, sure," says Uncle Daniel. "Look where I am. Man alive, if Judge Clanahan could get me in he could get me out. Couldn't he, Tadpole? Where is he, by the way—I've missed his face. Give him my love."

"Thank you, Mr. Ponder—I thank you. That'll be all. I'd now be very happy to cross-examine Miss Edna Earle Ponder once more, if she don't mind," old Gladney says.

But Uncle Daniel says, "Wait. You want the story, don't you? There's a world more to it than that. I can beat Edna Earle the world and all telling it. I'll start over for you."

And I knew he did want to tell it—I was the one knew that better than anybody. But I leaped up one more time where I was.

"Never mind, Uncle Daniel! Listen to Edna Earle," I says. "If you tell that, nobody'll ever be able to believe you again—not another word you say. You hear me?"

He needn't think I was going to let him tell it now. After guarding him heart and soul a whole week—a whole lifetime! How he came into the parlor all beaming pleasure and went shining up to her to kiss her and she just jumped away when the storm went boom. Like he brought it. And after she'd gone to the trouble to send for him, and we'd gone to the trouble to come, she just looked at him with her little coon eyes, and would have sent him back if I hadn't been there.

She never said good evening to me. When I spoke she held her ears. So I sat myself down on the piano stool, crossed my knees, and waited for the visit to start.

Uncle Daniel sat down beside her and she wouldn't even look. She pulled herself in a little knot at the other end of the sofa. Here came a flash of lightning bigger than the rest, and thunder on top of it, and she buried her face in the pillow and started to cry. So the tassel of Grandma's antimacassar came off in Uncle Daniel's hand and he reached out and tickled her with it, on the ankle.

The storm got closer and he tickled a little more. He made the little tassel travel up to her knee. He wouldn't call it touching her—it was tickling her; though she didn't want one any more right now than the other.

Of course, Uncle Daniel and I had both been brought up to be mortally afraid of electricity ourselves. I'd overcome it, by sheer force of character—but I didn't know Uncle Daniel had. I believe he overcame it then. I believe for Bonnie Dee's sake he shut his own ears and eyes to it and just gave himself up to trying to make her stop crying.

And all the while it was more like a furnace in there, and noisy and bright as Kingdom Come. Grandpa Ponder's house shook! And Bonnie Dee rammed harder into the pillow and shrieked and put out her hands behind her, but that didn't do any good. When the storm got right over the house, he went right to the top with "creep-mousie," up between those bony little shoulder blades to the nape of her neck and her ear—with the sweetest, most forbearing smile on his face, a forgetful smile. Like he forgot everything then that she ever did to him, how changeable she'd been.

But you can't make a real tickler stop unless you play dead. The youngest of all knows that.

And that's what I thought she did. Her hands fluttered and stopped, then her whole little length slipped out from under his fingers, and rolled down to the floor, just as easy as nod, and stayed there—with her dress up to her knees and her hair down over her face. I thought she'd done it on purpose.

"Well!" I says to Uncle Daniel. "I don't think it's such a treat to get sent after. The first thing Bonnie Dee does when we get here is far from ladylike." I thought that would make her sit up.

"Catch her, Edna Earle," he says. "Catch her." That's when he said it.

I marched over and pulled up her hand, and it hung a weight in mine like her ball and jacks were in it. So did her other hand when I pulled it. I said "Bonnie Dee Peacock."

That's when the ball of fire came down the chimney and charged around the room. (The ball of fire Narciss took for her story.) That didn't scare me. I didn't like it, but it didn't scare me: it was about as big as your head. It went up the curtains and out through them into the hall like a butterfly. I was waiting for Bonnie Dee to answer to her name.

When she wouldn't do it, I spread back that baby hair to see what was the matter. She was dead as a doornail. And she'd died laughing.

I could have shaken her for it. She'd never laughed for Uncle Daniel before in her life. And even if she had, that's not the same thing as smiling; you may think it is, but I don't.

I was in a quandary what to do. I had hold of her, and nobody ought to stay on the floor. It was still carrying on everywhere you looked. I hauled her back up on the sofa the best I could. She was trouble—little as she was, she was a whole heap heavier than she looked. And her dress was all over the place—those peach-colored pleats blinking on and off in the lightning, and like everything else you touched, as warm as dinner plates.

Poor Uncle Daniel had never stirred an inch since she went out of his reach, except to draw up his feet. Now, after where I put her back, and let her be, he hitched both arms around his knees and stayed that way.

Of course I couldn't go off and leave him there, to get help. I only ran after the ammonia, and that only takes a second, because I know where to find it. In the bathroom I glanced in the mirror, to see how I was taking it, and got the fright of my life. Edna Earle, I said, you look old as the hills! It was a different mirror, was the secret—it magnified my face by a thousand times—something Bonnie Dee had sent off for and it had come. I ran back, but the laugh didn't go away—for all I went out of the room a minute, and for all Uncle Daniel sat still as a mouse, and for all the spirits of ammonia I offered her or the drenching I gave her face. That ice in her glass was all water now.

I never thought of the telephone! I got the boy on the hay wagon by the simple expedient of opening the window and hollering as loud as I could, till it brought him. In came Dr. Ewbanks, finally, in his boots, and pushed that yellow fluff back just the way I did.

"You don't mean she's flew the coop?" he says.

And Uncle Daniel didn't wait. He tumbled headlong to the doctor's feet, and didn't know any more about *that*. Thank the Lord for small favors.

Well, I could have told the courtroom that as well as Uncle Daniel, and carried it on a little further. But I had too much sense to even try. I never lied in my life before, that I know of, by either saying or holding back, but I flatter myself that when the time came, I was equal to either one. I was only thankful I didn't have to explain it to Grandpa.

Maybe what's hard to believe about the truth is who it happens to. Everybody knows Uncle Daniel Ponder—he wouldn't have done anything to anybody in the world for all you could give him, and nobody, you'd think, would do anything to him. Why, he's been brought up in a world of love.

So I stopped the words on his lips, from where I stood. "You can't tell it, Uncle Daniel," I says firm. "Nobody'll believe it."

"You can tell *me*, Mr. Ponder," says old Gladney. "Remember, you picked me out. I'll believe it, easy as pie. What had you gone and done to that precious girl?"

"That's enough, Uncle Daniel," I says, real firm and real loud. "You can't answer that. You can't tell it to a soul."

And Uncle Daniel's mouth opens—and sure enough, he can't.

Uncle Daniel stood still a minute on the witness stand. Then he flung both arms wide, and his coat flew open. And there were all his pockets lined and bursting with money. I told you he looked fat. He stepped down to the floor, and out through the railing, and starts up the aisle, and commences handing out big green handfuls as he comes, on both sides. Eloise Clanahan climbed over her new beau and scooted out of the courtroom like the Devil was after her.

"What is this-here?" says Gladney. Poor man, he was taken by surprise. He ran and caught onto Uncle Daniel's coattails. "Come back, man, the trial's not over!"

That's all *he* knew.

"What is this?" says DeYancey. "Edna Earle, what have you brought on?"

And "Order!" says the Judge.

Uncle Daniel doesn't say anything, but reaches in with both hands. He brings out more money than you could shake a stick at. He made every row, like he was taking up collection in church, but doing the very opposite. He reached in and reached in, handed out and handed out. He was getting rid of it all right there in Court, as fast and businesslike as he could.

Everybody in town, Ewbankses, Magees, Sistrunks, old Miss Ouida Sampson that hadn't been out of her house in years but wanted to be carried to this, and couldn't hear a word that was said, but put out her little skin-and-bones hand now for what came her way; and all the children in town (they were loose) and total strangers who'll always go to anything, and the coroner, that blind Bodkin, everybody that could walk and two that couldn't, got some.

Some put their hands out like they were almost scared not to. The Peacocks hung back the longest, with their mouths open, but the little ones in diapers soon began to strike out and run after floating bills that got loose and were flying around. And old Gladney sends up a cry to the Peacocks then, "Grab what you can get!"

There was Bedlam. And passing the window Uncle Daniel let fly some bills that they never found, and I reckon the dogs chewed them up. Uncle Daniel was only trying to give away all he had, that's all. Everything to his name.

Old Mr. Jeff Ewbanks—he's Dr. Ewbanks' father and the mayor, frail, frail—he says, "Stop him, Miss Edna Earle! Stop him, young lady!"

Now I'll tell you something: anything Uncle Daniel has left after some future day is supposed to be mine. I'm the inheritor. I'm the last one, isn't that a scream? The last Ponder. But with one fling of the hand I showed the mayor *my* stand: I'd never stop Uncle Daniel for the world. This was his day, and anyway, you couldn't any more stop Uncle Daniel from giving away than you could stop a bird from flying.

Of course the *lawyers* couldn't do anything; DeYancey was fired, to boot. And Judge Waite wasn't even born in this county. Finally, it was too much for guess who?

It was Miss Lutie Powell who spoke up *directly* to Uncle Daniel. She was his old teacher, that's who *she* was. Afraid of no man. She points her palmetto at him and says, "Go back to your seat this minute, Daniel Ponder. Do you know how much money you've thrown away in the last five minutes? Have you any idea of how much you've got left? What do you say to me, Daniel?"

It froze Uncle Daniel for about one half minute. Then he just skipped Miss Lutie and went on.

Next, Mr. Bank Sistrunk stands up and roars out, "Daniel Ponder! Where did you *get* that money?"

It was too late then.

"Well," says Miss Missionary Sistrunk—the oldest one, returned from wildest Africa just twenty-four hours before—"the Ponders as I've always been told did not burn their cotton when Sherman came, and maybe this is their judgment."

"Take that back, Miss Florette," I says over people's heads. "The Ponders did not make their money that way. You got yours suing," I says. "What if that train hadn't hit Professor Magee, where'd any Sistrunks be today? Ours was pine trees and 'way after Sherman, and you know it."

"'Twas the same Yankees you sold it to!" That was Mr. Sistrunk. Why, he was beside himself. But Uncle Daniel just then got to him and gave him a single hundred-dollar bill, and shuts him up. You know, I think people have lost the power to be ashamed of themselves.

After all, it was our bank—Mr. Sistrunk just ran it. It turned out later that Uncle Daniel had gone to the bank early that morning—he was roaming—right after his haircut, and nobody was there yet but Eloise. So Uncle Daniel just took the opportunity of asking for it all: he asked Eloise for it and Eloise just gave it to him. She said she did it to cheer him up.

It took every bit the bank had that day, and then they owed him some. They still do. The bank had never, never, never let Uncle Daniel get his hands on cash. It's just a rule of Clay. Mr. Bank Sistrunk says he's going to have to let Eloise Clanahan go.

And you know—she was right. It *was* cheering him up. There on Uncle Daniel's face had come back the ghost of a smile. By that time, I think that all he wanted was our approval.

(And I don't give a whoop for your approval! You don't think I betrayed him by not letting him betray himself, do you?)

speaks directly to us

Most people were on their feet in Court by then, and some crying—old ladies that remembered Grandma—and Judge Waite just sits there, leaning his head on his hand. Then leans it on the other hand. Then stands up and raises both arms, without words. That's the way DeYancey behaved too, but more like a jack-in-the-box, being younger. I just sat there and took note.

I don't think any of those people that day would have ever accepted it from Uncle Daniel—money!—if they'd known what else to do. Not to know how to take what's offered shows your manners—but there's a dividing line somewhere. Of course they could have taken it and then given it back to *me*, later. Nobody ever seemed to think of that solution, except Edna Earle Ponder. Surely they're not beginning to be scared of *me*.

And Uncle Daniel had got right back to where he started from. He went from giving away to falling in love, and from falling in love to talking, and from talking to losing what he had, and from losing what he had to being run off, and from being run off straight back to giving away again.

Only it was worse than before, and more public. The worst thing you can give away is money—I learned that, if Uncle Daniel didn't. You and them are both done for then, somehow; you can't go on after it, and still be you and them. Don't ever give me a million dollars! It'll come between us.

directly to us

I wish you could have seen Miss Teacake Magee when she saw Uncle Daniel coming. She let out two little hoots, like a train going round the bend, and fell over with her cheek on

Dr. Ewbanks' shoulder. Uncle Daniel put a little money in her lap anyway, and gave her knee a stir.

The Judge charged the jury somewhere along there, but I don't remember a bit of what he said, and doubt if he does either, and they just went around the door and came right back, hating to miss anything in the courtroom. Uncle Daniel heard the commotion of them coming in and worked back that way and let fly a great big handful over their heads.

And all the children were jumping up and down and running around Uncle Daniel for dear life and calling him, and he threw them the change out of his pants pockets, like he always did. He didn't realize they grew up right there and wanted some big money now.

The Baptist preacher—Brother Barfield, always on hand— rose up and made his voice heard over the storm. (Our preacher was home praying for us, where he belonged.) He said he thought all the money here unclaimed by Mr. Daniel Ponder (*that* was a funny way to put it) should be turned over to the Baptist Church, which needed it. But old lady Peacock—and such a Baptist, you remember *two* preachers at the funeral—hollers back gay as a lark, "Finders keepers!" and showed him her hands full.

"Si-lence!" says Judge Waite. He's famous for that cry. That may be why they got him for this trial. But he was shaking both fists, too. I don't know that I ever saw him that wild before. "Let the public please to remember where they are at. I have never, in all my jurisprudence, seen more disrespectful behavior and greater commotion and goings-on at a trial. Put that right in the record, Birdie Nell. This jury, *mirabile dictu*, has reached a verdict. Now you *hear* it."

So the jury said Not Guilty. It almost got lost in the rush. Anyway, that old Gladney cringed. I hoped he was done for, but I expect he's not—he's probably going straight ahead from here and will end up Governor of Mississippi. Nobody showed a sign of going home.

Uncle Daniel saw that, and patted all over his pockets and threw the children what you could see was the last few pennies he could find. When it was all gone, he just went through the motions—like scattering chickenfeed.

"Edna Earle," he calls to me at last, "you got any money?"

"No, Uncle Daniel," I calls back, "I haven't got any money."

"Well, mine's all vamoosed," he says, and just stops. He spreads his hands. Eva Sistrunk had the nerve to tell me later that everybody felt so bad about Uncle Daniel at that moment that if he hadn't been so prominent and who he was, they would have taken up a collection for him. Like he was anybody else just acquitted of murder!

So that was about all.

There's no telling how much the Peacocks got—but remember how many there are, and how many hands that made. I'm sure I saw one of the babies eating money. Furthermore, before they left, the Peacocks had claimed kin with poor old Miss Ouida Sampson, but I don't believe she knew a thing about it. She just nods her head that way—whatever happens.

Well! I'd hate to have to go through it all again.

Outside, everybody was running ahead down the Courthouse steps—ahead of Uncle Daniel and me. We came down together. I heard the Judge's wife blowing the horn for him, but he was going down real heavy and slow and leaning on DeYancey Clanahan, and then I saw DeYancey hurrying off to get drunk. That's the Clanahan failing. Old Gladney came last of all, and all alone, and jumped in his Ford and hit the highway.

There was a little crowd held up at the stile, and a minute when we caught up with the Peacocks. Uncle Daniel pulled at the corner of Johnnie Ree's dress as she was going over the top and asked if he could come take her riding one of these days.

But she says, "No thank you!" It's all gone to her head as quick as that.

For a minute he just stood still in the bright sun, like the cake of ice that was melting there that day.

"Come with me, Uncle Daniel," I says, and put my arm through his.

Uncle Daniel comes on with me, real quiet, over the stile to the street full of cars getting started and going home. We go fronting through the children still clinging around, that don't understand there's not any more left.

And here came Mr. Springer, for the Lord's sake, chugging around the corner. Uncle Daniel didn't even see him. We crossed the street while Mr. Springer had to hold the brakes for us. I didn't give a good continental.

Oh, for a minute in the street there, I wished that Uncle Daniel had just whipped out and taken a stick to Bonnie Dee—out of good hard temper! Of course never meaning to kill her. And there *is* temper, on Grandpa's side. Uncle Daniel was just born without it. He might have picked up Grandpa's trusty old stick hanging right there on the hatrack where Grandpa left it, and whacked her one when she wasn't glad to see him. That would have gone down a whole lot easier in Clay. Even with the Peacocks, who didn't know anything was out of the way till a man like Gladney spotted it right through a poem and had to haul off and tell them about it. Sometimes I think old Gladney dreamed the whole thing up himself, for lack of something to do, out of his evil mind.

Well, if he did, the verdict served him right.

"Edna Earle," says Uncle Daniel, when I got him safe through the street and the front door of this hotel, "I've got good news for you. I'm coming to live with you for keeps. In the best room you can give me in the Beulah Hotel."

I says, "Grand." I says, "That's the room you're in already, Number One at the head of the stairs."

He hung his hat there and went right on through the lobby and started up that staircase without looking around for a soul—and there really wasn't a soul. I stood there at the foot and watched him go. I started to call to him I'd give him the hotel back. But I thought the next minute: no use starting him off again.

He got as far as the landing and turned around and called down, "You fooled me up yonder at Court this afternoon, Edna Earle, I declare you did. But never mind—I'm staying just the same. You didn't fool me as bad as Bonnie Dee did."

"Well, I hope not," I said. "You better go on up and wash your face and hands, and lie down till you're ready for your supper. Just let me call you."

But he don't enjoy it any more. Empty house, empty hotel, might as well be an empty town. He don't know what's become of everybody. Even the preacher says he has a catch in his back, just temporary. And if people are going to try being ashamed of Uncle Daniel, he's going to feel it. *I'm* here, and just the same as I always was and will be, but then he never was afraid of losing me.

So Grandpa's house is standing out there in grass. The Peppers are keeping on with the crop, though they don't have a notion who for, or where they stand. Who does?

You see, that money has come between the Ponders and everybody else in town. There it still is, on their hands. (I'm sure the Peacocks have spent theirs in Polk, without a qualm—for something they don't have the ghost of a use for.) Here Clay sits and don't know what to do with it. All dressed up and no place to go, so to speak. There's been talk, I hear, of something civic—an arch to straddle the highway with the words in lights, "Clay. If You Lived Here You'd Be Home Now." I spot that as a Sistrunk idea.

And I haven't seen a soul in here in three days. You'd think Eva Sistrunk, at least, would be beginning to get lonesome. So I wasn't sorry to see you come in. Uncle Daniel will express a welcome too. You're the first!

He comes down a little later every night. One of these times I'm going to start him on a good course of calomel-and-quinine. I'm a pretty good doser myself. But it's time now supper was ready.

Narciss! Put three on the table!

At least I've got somebody now that can cook—if she just would. But Narciss don't cook good any more. I hate to tell you—her rice won't stand apart. She don't cook any better than Ada or Ada's sister ever did. She claims she's lonesome in town.

And you know, Bonnie Dee Peacock, ordinary as she was and trial as she was to put up with—she's the kind of person you do miss. I don't know why—deliver me from giving you the *reason*. You could look and find her like anywhere. Though I'm sure Bonnie Dee and Uncle Daniel were as happy together as most married people.

And it may be anybody's heart would quail, trying to keep up with Uncle Daniel's. But I don't give Bonnie Dee Peacock too much credit for trying.

I'm going to holler—*Uncle Daniel!*

I'd like to warn you again, he may try to give you something—may think he's got something to give. If he does, do me a favor. Make out like you accept it. Tell him thank you.

Uncle Daniel? Uncle Daniel! We've got company!

Now he'll be down.

LOSING BATTLES

To the memory of my brothers,
Edward Jefferson Welty
Walter Andrews Welty

Characters in the Novel

TIME:
A summer in the 1930's
PLACE:
The hill country of northeast Mississippi

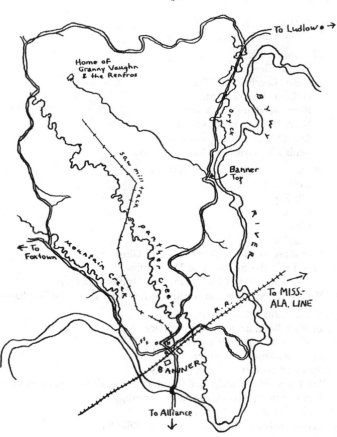

Part 1

WHEN the rooster crowed, the moon had still not left the world but was going down on flushed cheek, one day short of the full. A long thin cloud crossed it slowly, drawing itself out like a name being called. The air changed, as if a mile or so away a wooden door had swung open, and a smell, more of warmth than wet, from a river at low stage, moved upward into the clay hills that stood in darkness.

Then a house appeared on its ridge, like an old man's silver watch pulled once more out of its pocket. A dog leaped up from where he'd lain like a stone and began barking for today as if he meant never to stop.

Then a baby bolted naked out of the house. She monkey-climbed down the steps and ran open-armed into the yard, knocking at the walls of flowers still colorless as faces, tagging in turn the four big trees that marked off the corners of the yard, tagging the gatepost, the well-piece, the birdhouse, the bell post, a log seat, a rope swing, and then, rounding the house, she used all her strength to push over a crate that let a stream of white Plymouth Rocks loose on the world. The chickens rushed ahead of the baby, running frantic, and behind the baby came a girl in a petticoat. A wide circle of curl-papers, paler than the streak of dawn, bounced around her head, but she ran on confident tiptoe as though she believed no eye could see her. She caught the baby and carried her back inside, the baby with her little legs still running like a windmill.

The distant point of the ridge, like the tongue of a calf, put its red lick on the sky. Mists, voids, patches of woods and naked clay, flickered like live ashes, pink and blue. A mirror that hung within the porch on the house wall began to flicker as at the striking of kitchen matches. Suddenly two chinaberry trees at the foot of the yard lit up, like roosters astrut with golden tails. Caterpillar nets shone in the pecan tree. A swollen shadow bulked underneath it, familiar in shape as Noah's Ark—a school bus.

Then as if something came sliding out of the sky, the whole

tin roof of the house ran with new blue. The posts along the porch softly bloomed downward, as if chalk marks were being drawn, one more time, down a still misty slate. The house was revealed as if standing there from pure memory against a now moonless sky. For the length of a breath, everything stayed shadowless, as under a lifting hand, and then a passage showed, running through the house, right through the middle of it, and at the head of the passage, in the center of the front gallery, a figure was revealed, a very old lady seated in a rocking chair with head cocked, as though wild to be seen.

Then Sunday light raced over the farm as fast as the chickens were flying. Immediately the first straight shaft of heat, solid as a hickory stick, was laid on the ridge.

Miss Beulah Renfro came out of the passage at a trot and cried in the voice of alarm which was her voice of praise, "Granny! Up, dressed, and waiting for 'em! All by yourself! Why didn't you holler?"

This old lady's one granddaughter was in her late forties, tall, bony, impatient in movement, with brilliantly scrubbed skin that stretched to the thinnest and pinkest it could over the long, talking countenance. Above the sharp cheekbones her eyes were blue as jewels. She folded the old lady very gently in her arms, kissed her on the mouth, and cried, "And the birthday cake's out of the oven!"

"Yes, I can still smell," said Granny.

Miss Beulah gave her call that clanged like a dinner bell: "Come, *children*!"

Her three daughters answered. The Renfro girls ran out of the still shadowy passageway: Ella Fay, sixteen, the only plump one; Etoyle, nine, fragrant of the cows and the morning milk; and Elvie, seven, this summer's water hauler, with her bucket and ready to go. They lined up and put a kiss apiece, quick as a bite, on Granny's hot cheek.

"Happy birthday, Granny!" all three of them said at the same time.

"I'm expecting to see all my living grandchildren, all my great-grandchildren, and all the great-great-grandchildren they care to show me, and see 'em early," said Granny. "I'm a hundred today."

"Don't contradict her," Miss Beulah commanded as Etoyle

opened her mouth. "And Granny, you'll get the best present of all—the joy of your life's coming home!"

Granny nodded.

"Won't that be worth the waiting for?" cried Miss Beulah. Then she patted the old lady's trembling hand.

From the waterless earth some flowers bloomed in despite of it. Cannas came around the house on either side in a double row, like the Walls of Jericho, with their blooms unfurled— Miss Beulah's favorite colors, the kind that would brook no shadow. Rockets of morning-glory vines had been trained across the upper corners of the porch, and along the front, hanging in baskets from wires overhead, were the green stars of ferns. The sections of concrete pipe at the foot of the steps were overflowing with lacy-leaf verbena. Down the pasture-side of the yard ran a long row of montbretias blazing orange, with hummingbirds sipping without seeming to touch a flower. Red salvia, lemon lilies, and prince's-feathers were crammed together in a tub-sized bed, and an althea bush had opened its flowers from top to bottom, pink as children's faces. The big china trees at the gateposts looked bigger still for the silver antlers of last year's dead branches that radiated outside the green. The farm track entered between them, where spreading and coming to an end it became the front yard. It lay before them in morning light the color of a human palm and still more groined and horny and bare.

"He can come right now," said Granny.

"Then suppose you eat fast enough to be ready for him," said Miss Beulah.

Granny rocked herself to her feet and, fighting help, found the passage. Miss Beulah kept behind her, not touching her, as though the little pair of shoulders going low and trembling ahead of her might be fragile as butterfly wings, but framing her with both arms. The little girls followed, making up for going slowly by jumping all the way.

Then Vaughn Renfro, the younger brother, who had finished doing what there was still nobody but him to do, catching and killing the escaped rooster and his whole escaped flock, put down his hatchet. He stepped up onto the porch and washed at the basin on the table. Taking the rag again, he swabbed the new dust off the mirror, so that it ran with a color delicate as watermelon juice on a clean plate, and looked at his face in there. This year he had turned twelve.

Then he clomped in after the girls and women.

Distance had already vanished in the haze of heat, but the passageway down which they had just gone was bright as the eye of a needle. The other end was sky. The house was just what it seemed, two in one. The second house had been built side by side with the original—all a long time ago—and the space between the two had been floored over and roofed but not to this day closed in. The passage, in which Granny's old loom could stand respected and not be in the way, was wider than the rooms on either side. The logs had been chinked tight with clay and limestone, in places faced with cedar board, now weathered almost pink. Chimneys rose from the side at either end. The galleries ran the full width of the house back and front, and under the roof's low swing, the six slender posts along the front stood hewn four-square and even-spaced by rule of a true eye. Pegs in the wood showed square as thumbnails along the seams; in the posts, the heart-grain rose to the touch. The makings of the house had never been hidden to the Mississippi air, which was now, this first Sunday in August, and at this hour, still soft as milk.

When Granny, Miss Beulah, and the children took their places at the kitchen table, Mr. Renfro came in and joined them. He was smaller than Miss Beulah his wife, and walked with a kind of hobble that made him seem to give a little bow with every step. He came to the table bowing to Granny, to his wife, to his children, bowing to the day. He took his place at the foot of the table.

"Now where's *she?*" asked Miss Beulah.

The three young sisters raising their voices together called through their noses, "Glo-ri-a! Sister Gloria!"

From the company room up front a sweet cool voice called back, "We're busy right now. Go on without us."

"Well, ask the blessing like a streak o' lightning, Mr. Renfro," Miss Beulah told her husband. "The rest of us has got a world to do!"

All heads were bowed. Mr. Renfro's was bald, darkened by the sun and marked with little humped veins in the same pattern on both sides, like the shell of a terrapin. Vaughn's was silver-pink, shaved against the heat, with ears sticking out like tabs he might be picked up and shaken by. Miss Beulah and her three daughters all raked their hair straight back, cleaved it down the middle, pulled it skin-tight into plaits. Miss Beulah ran hers straight as a railroad track around her head; they were tar-black and bradded down with the pins she'd been married in, now bright as nickel. The girls skewered their braids into wreaths tight enough to last till bedtime. Elvie's hair was still pale as wax-beans, Etoyle's was darkening in stripes, Ella Fay's was already raven. Granny's braids were no longer able to reach full circle themselves; they were wound up behind in two knots tight as a baby's pair of fists.

After the Amen, Mr. Renfro bent over and gave Granny her birthday kiss.

She said, "Young man, your nose is cold."

Miss Beulah flew to wait on them. "Now eat like a flash! Don't let 'em catch you at the table!"

"Who'll be the first to get here?" Ella Fay began.

"I say Uncle Homer will be the *last*, because we're counting on him and Auntie Fay to bring the ice," said Etoyle.

"I say Brother Bethune will be the last, because he's got to fill Grandpa's shoes today," said Elvie, an owlish look on her thin little face.

They all looked quickly at Granny, but she was busy licking up syrup in her spoon.

"I say Uncle Nathan will be the last," said Ella Fay. "He's coming afoot."

"And doing the Lord's work along his way," Miss Beulah said from the stove. "He'll never fail us, though. He's Granny's oldest."

"Jack will be the last."

"Who said that? Who said my oldest boy will be the last?" Miss Beulah whirled from the stove and began stepping fast around the table, raising high the graniteware coffee pot, with its profile like her own and George Washington's at the same time, and darting looks at each member of the family under it before she quickly poured.

"It was Vaughn," said Etoyle, smiling.

"Vaughn Renfro, have you taken it in your head to behave

contrary today of all days?" cried Miss Beulah, giving him a big splash in his cup.

"Jack's got him the farthest to come. Providing he can get him started," said Vaughn, his stubborn voice still soft as a girl's.

Etoyle laughed. "How do *you* know how far it is? *You* never been out of Banner!"

Vaughn's blue eyes swam suddenly. "I've been to school! I seen a map of the whole world!"

"Fiddle. My boy'd get here today from anywhere he had to," said Miss Beulah loudly. "He knows exactly who's waiting on him."

Granny, with her spoon to her lips, paused long enough to nod.

"And as for you, Mr. Renfro!" Miss Beulah cried. "If you don't stop bringing a face like that to the table and looking like the world might come to an end today, people will turn around and start going home before they even get here!"

At that moment the barking of the little dog Sid was increased twenty-fold by the thunder of shepherd dogs and the ringing clamor of hounds. Ella Fay, Etoyle, and Elvie ran pounding up the passageway, ahead of everybody.

The three girls lined up on the gallery's edge and even before they could see a soul coming they began their waving. Their dresses, made alike from the same print of flour sack, covered with Robin Hood and his Merry Men shooting with bow and arrow, were in three orders of brightness—the oldest girl wore the newest dress. They were rattling clean, marble-ized with starch, the edging on the sleeves pricking at their busy arms as sharp as little feist teeth.

A wall of copper-colored dust came moving up the hill. It was being brought by a ten-year-old Chevrolet sedan that had been made into a hauler by tearing out the back seat and the window glass. It rocked into the yard with a rider on the running board waving in a pitcher's glove, and packed inside with excited faces, some dogs' faces among them, it carried a cargo of tomato baskets spaced out on its roof, hood, and front fenders, every basket holding a red and yellow pyramid of peaches. With the dogs in the yard and the dogs in the car all barking together, the car bumped across the yard to the pecan tree, and halted behind the school bus, and then the dust caught up with it.

Uncle Curtis Beecham, next-to-oldest of Miss Beulah's brothers, climbed down from the wheel. He walked low to the ground and stepped tall, and bore shoulder-high on each slewed-out palm a basket of his peaches. Behind him a crowd of his sons and their jumping children and their wives hurrying after them poured out of the car, the dogs streaking to the four corners of the farm.

The Renfro sisters ran to take Uncle Curtis's baskets and put the little points of their tongues out sweetly to thank him.

"A new roof! You got a new roof!" Uncle Curtis shouted to his sister Miss Beulah, as though her ears wouldn't believe it.

"Jack's coming home!" she shrieked. "My oldest boy will be here!"

"That roof's sound as a drum," said Mr. Renfro, lining up on the porch with Miss Beulah and Granny. "Or better be."

"Oh, I don't blame you a bit for it," Aunt Beck protested. She climbed the steps in the wake of Uncle Curtis. Her pink, plain face was like a badge of safety. Over her pink scalp, tiny curls of a creamy color were scattered in crowds, like the stars of a clematis vine.

"You brought your chicken pie," Miss Beulah said, relieving her of the apron-covered dishpan.

"And Jack's exactly who I made it for," said Aunt Beck. "If I made my good chicken pie, he'll come eat it, I thought, every dusty mile of the way."

She and Uncle Curtis were from the Morning Star community. She kissed Granny, and kissed Mr. Renfro along with Miss Beulah and the girls, calling him Cousin Ralph. Then she went back to Granny and kissed her again, saying, "Granny stays so good and brave! What's her secret!"

The old lady took her seat in the rocking chair. She precisely adjusted her hat, a black plush of unknowable age. Her purplish-black cambric dress was by now many sizes too large and she was furled in by it. She had little black pompons on the toes of her sliding-slippers.

"Here's more!" screamed Etoyle.

Coming out of the dust that still obliterated the track appeared an old pickup riding on a flat tire, packed in behind with people too crowded in to wave, and with babies hanging over the sides on their folded arms, like the cherubs out of Heaven in pictures in the family Bible. This belonged to Uncle Dolphus and Aunt Birdie Beecham, of Harmony. In another minute the truck emptied. Little Aunt Birdie and the daughters came speeding ahead of the others, under every sort of hat and bonnet, as if dust and heat and light were one raging storm directed at women and girls. All were laden.

"If there's anything I do abhor, it's coming through the broad outdoors!" cried Aunt Birdie with elation. "New tin! Why, Beulah Renfro! What'd you give for it?"

"Ask Mr. Renfro!"

"And what's the excuse?" Aunt Birdie cried, hugging her.

"My boy's coming! My boy's coming!" cried Miss Beulah. "He's coming to surprise Granny—we just somehow know it."

Aunt Birdie with a squeal of joy opened her arms and ran to Granny. She was faded but still all animation, as if long ago she'd been teased into perpetual suspense.

"Happy birthday, Granny! Jack's coming! Won't that make up for everything?" she cried into the old lady's ear.

"My ears are perfectly good," Granny said.

Then the little Beechams came up and tried to present Granny with a double armload of dahlias, each stalk as big as a rag-doll, a bushel of plushy cockscomb, and cooking pears tied in an apron. Miss Beulah rushed to her rescue.

Uncle Dolphus, the middle Beecham brother, walked heavily across the porch and put his black-browed face down close to Granny's and kissed her. "All right, we'll help you wait on him," he told her.

As his own grandchildren swarmed around, Granny put kisses on top of their heads like a quick way to count them. From the little girls' crowns, the hair fell in sun-whitened strands as separate and straight as fork tines over the dark yellow underneath. The little boys' heads, being shaved, were albino white or even a silver gray, like the heads of little old men. Every little mouth said, "Happy birthday, Granny Vaughn!"

"Jack's coming! Jack's coming!" Miss Beulah was shrieking anew. With a sharp smell of leaking gasoline, another car had drawn up in the yard behind Uncle Dolphus's old Ford. It was another old Ford, sagging with weight, but carrying only two people.

"It's Uncle Percy and Aunt Nanny, Granny!" yelled Etoyle.

"I can still see," said Granny.

Aunt Nanny Beecham hauled herself up the steps as though she had been harnessed into her print dress along with six or seven watermelons, and only then did she try to speak. "Jack's coming? For keeps?" She looked around, already winking. "Well, where's Gloria?"

"She's over the ironing board, I reckon," Miss Beulah said.

"Wouldn't you know it?" Aunt Nanny gave over to Miss Beulah a dishpan full of honey-in-the-comb robbed that morning, tossed in peaks and giving off a clover smell as strong as hot pepper. "Got a baby here for me?" she hollered.

"Granny's being so brave behind you," Aunt Beck gently reminded her, and Aunt Nanny nearly fell over herself to hug the old lady, the cheeks in her big face splashed over red with blushes.

Uncle Curtis's sons and Uncle Dolphus's grandsons helped carry in the new load. They brought in tomatoes and bell peppers, some fall pears, and a syrup bucket full of muscadines—all that set of children were now at large with purple hands. They brought dahlias with scalded leaves hanging down their stems like petticoats, darker and heavier prince's-feathers that looked like a stormy sunset, and a cigar box full of late figs, laid closely, almost bruising each other, in the leaves and purple and heavy as turned-over sacks, with pink bubbles rising to the top and a drunk wasp that had come with them from Peerless. They brought watermelons. They brought one watermelon that was estimated to weigh seventy-five pounds.

Uncle Percy followed it all silently. Because his voice was weak and ragged, he was considered a delicate man. He lifted up for Granny's eyes a string of little fish, twitching like a kite-tail. "Happy birthday," he said, his Adam's apple trembling like one of the fishes.

"You could fry all those in one skillet," said Granny. "I'm planning a little bigger dinner than most of you seem to think."

"And won't you be glad to see that big brother of yours come home?" Aunt Birdie cried to Vaughn.

"I don't care if he don't get here till tomorrow," said Vaughn.

"That boy's grown two feet higher since Jack's been away," said Uncle Curtis, as though that explained him.

"But if he don't get a little wider somewhere, we won't be able to see him much longer or find him when we want him," said Aunt Nanny, giving Vaughn a pinch at the waist.

"I don't care if he don't get here till the *next* reunion," Vaughn said.

"All right, Contrary!" called Miss Beulah, coming in with a pitcher and a Mason jar packed tight with flowers. "Right now you can go to the cemetery in the wagon for me. There's a foot-tub already loaded in it, and go get that churn of salvia for Mama and Papa Beecham. These dahlias go to Grandpa Vaughn. Sam Dale Beecham gets the milk-and-wine lilies in this fruit jar—I advise you to hold it steady as you can between your feet."

"Yes ma'am."

"And you know what to bring back with you! Don't leave a solitary one."

"Yes ma'am."

"Go flying. And if you meet that blessed mortal in the road, turn right around and come back with him!" yelled Miss Beulah after Vaughn. "Give him the reins! Let him drive!"

As Vaughn rattled off in the hickory wagon, Miss Beulah threw up her hands. "He'll never be Jack," she said. "Says the wrong thing, does the wrong thing, doesn't do what I tell him. And perfectly satisfied to have you say so!"

"Beulah, this may be Jack coming this minute," warned Aunt Birdie.

Vaughn had waited to let it by. An old Ford coupe, that looked for the moment like a black teakettle boiling over and being carried quick off the stove, crossed the yard. It bounced to a stop in the last bit of shade under the pecan tree, and

Etoyle screamed prophetically, "It's Uncle Noah Webster back in Banner! Bringing his new wife to show us!"

The next minute, a big, mustached man with plugged watermelons under both arms and both his hands full took the force of Etoyle's running against his knees. He laughed and kept coming, carrying her with him at a run. Etoyle grabbed the banjo from one fist, Mr. Renfro took the watermelons and laid them on the porch.

"Now be careful, Sissy! That's a pretty—it'll break!" Uncle Noah Webster cried as he let Miss Beulah take the wrapped-up present out of his other hand. Then he kissed her with such a bang that she nearly dropped it. He flung his free arms around Granny, chair and all. "If you ain't the blessedest!"

"What are you doing here?" said Granny in a defensive voice. "Thought they told me you was dead."

He hugged her till she tried a smile on him, and then went all but galloping over the porch, the yard, hugging his brothers, kissing their wives, throwing their children up in the air and catching them. Clapping Mr. Renfro on the back, he roared, "Who you trying to fool with that new lid on the old house?"

"Play 'I Had a Little Donkey,' Uncle Noah Webster!" cried Etoyle.

"I'm looking for Jack!" Uncle Noah Webster hollered, with a swing of his banjo. "Ain't he here yet?"

"No, but he's coming!" cried Miss Beulah. "He's coming, to make Granny's heart glad!"

"Why, Sissy, I'm as sure of that as you are," cried Uncle Noah Webster. "And I thought if Jack can make it, I can! Where's that sweetheart of his?"

"She's putting the baby to sleep now," said Elvie, looking solemn. "So that when she opens her eyes, Jack will be here."

"Uncle Noah Webster, look behind you!" said Ella Fay.

Walking toward them came the new member of the family, Aunt Cleo, from South Mississippi, Uncle Noah Webster's new wife. She wore a dress of shirting in purple and white stripes, with sleeves so short and tight that her vaccination scar shone at them like a tricky little mirror high in her powerful upper arm.

"We try to be ready here for all comers," Miss Beulah said,

facing her. "Make yourself at home. I reckon you know who I am."

"Is that your husband? He take a nail in his foot already this morning?" Aunt Cleo asked as Mr. Renfro hobbled forward.

"No'm, a little piece of dynamite accounts for that," said Miss Beulah.

"A wonder it didn't carry off more of him than it did," said Aunt Cleo.

"Well, don't think he did it just for you," said Miss Beulah. "He got on crutches just in time for our wedding day, twenty-four years ago. Here's my grandmother and she's ninety today!"

"Oh, I've nursed 'em like *you*!" said Aunt Cleo, bending down to see Granny closer. "Pat pat pat pat pat."

"Well, you needn't come patting after me," said Granny. "I'd just have to stop what I was doing and run you off, like I do some others."

"Here's my daughters," said Miss Beulah. "They've reached seven, nine, and sixteen."

"Three generations and all fixing their hair in the same pig-tails. You-all must be a mighty long ways from civilization away up here," Aunt Cleo said.

The girls ran.

"It's a bigger reunion than I ever dreamed, congratulations," said Aunt Cleo.

"Listen!" Aunt Nanny cried. "But it ain't started yet, Cleo." And as Aunt Cleo began again looking around her, Aunt Nanny cried, "You'll know when it starts, all right, you'll hear the bang! That's when our boy makes it on back home. Jack Renfro!"

"Where's he?" asked Aunt Cleo.

"In the pen," came a voice that was all but a whisper—Uncle Percy's.

"The pen! The state pen? Parchman?"

"What's Noah Webster been doing all this time if he hasn't told you all the sad story?" asked Aunt Birdie.

"What did Jack do?" Aunt Cleo cried.

"Not a thing," came a chorus right on top of her.

"That's enough," said Miss Beulah.

"Then show me—who'd he marry before he went? Bet you he made sure of somebody, didn't he, to come home to?"

"Yonder she comes!" cried Ella Fay. "She likes you to wait as long as you can, then she comes out looking cooler and cleaner than you do."

"Who's this streaking up behind me?" asked the old lady. "Declare yourself."

The young girl just stepping out of the company room came forward. Dressed up in white organdy, smelling like hot bread from the near-scorch of her perfect ironing, she said, "It's Gloria."

All but Granny took a deep breath.

"A redhead. Oh-oh," said Aunt Cleo.

"You're standing on your tiptoes looking just about good enough to eat! Right this minute!" Uncle Noah Webster shouted. He ran up onto the gallery and gave her a big hug and kiss.

"Don't she look like somebody stepped out of a storybook?" exclaimed Aunt Beck in her compassionate voice.

"You look good and cool as a fresh cake of ice, sure enough," Aunt Birdie told her.

"Don't even all that hair tend to make you hot?" asked Aunt Nanny. "It'd roast me, just being the color it is."

"Well, in spite of even that hot dress, and curly hair, you contrive to look cooler right now than we do," said Aunt Birdie. "We're good and jealous, Gloria."

"When she wants to use it, Gloria's still got the prettiest thank-you in the family," said Aunt Beck in her gentle voice.

"Well, and I'd just like to know why she *wouldn't* have!" Miss Beulah said.

Gloria sat down in front of them all on the top step, a long board limber as leather and warmer than the skin, her starch-whitened high-heeled shoes on the mountain stone that was the bottom step. In four yards of organdy that with scratching sounds, like frolicking mice, covered all three steps, she sat with her chin in her hand, her head ablaze. The red-gold hair, a cloud almost as big around as the top of an organ stool, nearly hid what they could peep at and see of her big hazel eyes. For a space about the size of a biscuit around the small, bony points of her elbows, there were no freckles; the inner sides of her arms, too, were snowy. But everywhere else, every other visible inch of her skin, even to her ears, was freckled, as if she'd been sprinkled with nutmeg while she was still dewy and it would never brush off.

Ella Fay chanted, "Sit still, Sister Gloria, keep your hands folded, don't let your dress get dirty. You just keep yourself looking pretty and be ready for your husband." The two younger sisters chanted it after her, smiling, "Keep your hands folded!"

"Yes sir, you're still here!" Uncle Noah Webster jumped heavily to the ground, ran around in front of Gloria and looked up the steps at her, slapping his hands down on his knees. "Cleo, two years ago this little bride was just as green as you are." The fading mustaches hung like crossed pistols above his radiant smile, and he cried to Gloria, "Did any of 'em ever succeed in making you tell how you ever decided to marry into this ugly family in the first place?"

"Here comes somebody new, just in time to stop her," announced Aunt Cleo.

Vaughn was driving up into the yard with the tables from the church dinner grounds thumping in the back of the wagon and a passenger sitting up on the seat beside him; for a minute all they could see of her was a stylish hat with a quill slanting up from the crown. Then she put her leg over with the high white man's sock and the winter shoe.

"That's Mr. Renfro's old maid sister Lexie. Oh, ever at the wrong time!" cried Miss Beulah, running out.

The lady got down from the wagon in her Sunday dress, and reached up for a big oilcloth portmanteau and pulled it down herself.

"I stood for an hour! I'd already walked as far as across the bridge, and I stood there at the store waiting on an offer of a ride. Some of you went right by me," said Miss Lexie Renfro.

"It's that gripsack you've got along with you. They might wonder if they'd have you to carry from now on," said Miss Beulah. "I'm not sure you can find any room left to set it down here."

"Everything I've got will fit right in there together." said Miss Lexie. "Then I can tell myself I don't have to go back if I don't want to."

"Don't take a bite out of Lexie, that's a nice dog," Miss Beulah told one of the shepherds and faced Miss Lexie as she came walking up the steps.

"I borrowed a little bit of this and a little bit of that from her pantry, and made my donation to the reunion," Miss Lexie said, poking around in her portmanteau and then handing out a flattish parcel.

"What is it?" asked Miss Beulah before she'd take it.

"A pound cake. It won't kill anybody," said Miss Lexie.

Miss Beulah unwrapped it from the sheet of *The Boone County Vindicator*, and it was tied again in an old jelly-bag darkened with berry stains. She held it up by the drawstring.

"Don't everybody look at me like I'm the last thing of all," Miss Lexie said. "My sister Fay hasn't come, or her husband Homer Champion, I beat Nathan Beecham, and Brother Bethune's not yet in sight. None of which surprises me."

"No, and *Jack's* still got to come!" cried Miss Beulah.

"Now that *would* surprise me," said Miss Lexie.

"He's coming! And you needn't ask me how I know it," cried Miss Beulah.

"What kind of a postcard did he manage to send you?" asked Miss Lexie.

"My oldest boy never did unduly care for pencil and paper," Miss Beulah retorted. "But you couldn't make him forget Granny's birthday Sunday to save your life. He knows who's here and waiting on him—that's enough!"

Miss Lexie Renfro dipped her knees and tipped herself back, one tip. She didn't make a sound, but this was her laugh.

"Take your hat off, then, Lexie," said Miss Beulah.

"When I saw that hat coming, I thought—I thought you were going to be somebody else," Gloria told Miss Lexie.

"I'm wearing her Sunday hat. I make no secret of it. She'll never need a hat again," Miss Lexie said. "Miss Julia Mortimer's out of the public eye for good now."

Mr. Renfro came forward to carry in her portmanteau. "You just come off and leave your lady, Lexie?" he asked his sister.

"I may be more needed here than there, before the day gets over with," she answered.

Granny poked her shoe.

"You a nurse?" Aunt Cleo called, as Miss Lexie exchanged short greetings with the Beechams all around her and refused a seat on a nail keg.

"Well, let's say I know what to do just about as well as the next fella," said Miss Lexie.

"You've run up on the real thing now, sister," Aunt Cleo said. "And I could tell you tales—!"

Vaughn, having led the mule out of the yard, lifted out of the wagon bed the cedar buckets and milk buckets full of water drawn from Grandpa Vaughn's old well, the only one that hadn't run dry. He lugged them to the house, replenished the drinking bucket on the porch, lugged the rest to the kitchen. Then he let Mr. Renfro take an end of each of the tables he had brought up from the dinner grounds at Damascus Church in Banner, along with one or two of their better benches, and help him get them down out of the wagon.

"Vaughn! Hurry up, and get your other clothes on! Don't entertain the reunion looking like that!" called Miss Beulah.

Now there was family everywhere, front gallery and back, tracking in and out of the company room, filling the bedrooms and kitchen, breasting the passage. The passageway itself was creaking; sometimes it swayed under the step and sometimes it seemed to tremble of itself, as the suspension bridge over the river at Banner had the reputation of doing. With chairs, beds, windowsills, steps, boxes, kegs, and buckets all taken up and little room left on the floor, they overflowed into the yard, and the men squatted down in the shade. Over in the pasture a baseball game had started up. The girls had the swing.

"Been coming too thick and fast for you?" Aunt Birdie asked Aunt Cleo.

"Everywheres I look is Beecham Beecham Beecham," she said.

"Beulah's brothers. Except for one, that circle is still unbroken," said Miss Lexie Renfro. "Renfros come a bit more scarce."

"Where they all get here from?" cried Aunt Cleo, looking full circle around her.

"Everywhere. Everywhere you ever heard of in Boone County—I can see faces from Banner, Peerless, Wisdom, Upright, Morning Star, Harmony, and Deepstep with no trouble at all."

"And this is Banner. The very heart," said Miss Beulah, calling from the kitchen.

"Never heard of any of it," said Aunt Cleo. "Except Banner. Banner is all Noah Webster knows how to talk about. I hail from Piney."

"I at present call Alliance my home," said Miss Lexie. "That puts me across the river from everybody I see." She went to put her hat away and came struggling backwards up the passage to them dragging something.

Miss Beulah shrieked, "Vaughn! Come get that away from your Aunt Lexie!" She was running behind it—a cactus growing in a wooden tub. "Little bantie you, pulling a forty-pound load of century plant, just to show us!"

"I've pulled a heavier load than this. And the company can just have that to march around," Miss Lexie said. "Give 'em one thing more to do today besides eat and hear 'emselves talk."

The cactus was tied up onto a broomstick but grew down in long reaches as if trying to clamber out of the tub. It was wan in color as sage or mistletoe.

"It's threatening to bloom, Mother," Mr. Renfro warned Miss Beulah.

"I see those buds as well as you do. And it's high time, say I. Bloom! Bloom!" she cried at it gaily. "Yes, it's making up its mind to bloom tonight—about time for 'em all to go home, if it knows what's good for it."

"Can't tell a century plant what to do," said Granny.

"Now, let that be enough out of you, Lexie. Set," said Miss Beulah. "And help us look for Jack."

"Jack Renfro? He won't come. He hasn't been in there long enough yet, by my reckoning," said Miss Lexie. She had a gray, tired-looking face, gray-speckled hair cut Buster Brown with her own sewing scissors that were swinging wide on the ribbon tied around her neck as she walked around looking for something to do. "Better start thinking what *you'll* look like if he *don't* get here," she said to Gloria. Her foot in its black leather, ragged-heeled shoe, feathered with dust, and wearing a skinny white sock, stepped on the end of Gloria's sash.

"What's she want to walk off and leave good company for?" asked Aunt Cleo the next minute. "She too good for us?"

For Gloria walked down the yard away from the house, through the circles of squatters, until she was all by herself. Her high heels tilted her nearly to tiptoe, like a bird ready to fly.

"Hair that flaming, it looks like it would hurt her," murmured Aunt Beck. "More especially when she carries it right out in the broil."

All the aunts, here on the gallery, were sheltering from sun as if from torrents of rain. Ferns in hanging wire baskets spread out just above their heads, dark as nests, one for each aunt but Aunt Lexie, who wouldn't sit down.

Aunt Nanny shaded her eyes and asked, "How far is Gloria going, anyway?"

Down near the gate, a trimmed section of cedar trunk lay on the ground, silver in chinaberry shade. Clean-polished by the seasons, with its knobs bright and its convolutions smooth-polished, it looked like some pistony musical instrument.

"That's her perch," said Miss Beulah as Gloria sat down on it with her back to them, her sash-ends hanging down behind her like an organist's in church.

"She's got to be ready for her husband whether he gets here or not," Aunt Beck said softly. "But she's young, she can stand the disappointment."

"She's too young to know any better. That's the poorest way in the wide world to bring him," Aunt Birdie said. "Getting ready so far ahead of time, then keeping your eyes on his road."

"Set still, Sister Gloria, keep your hands folded!" Jack's little sisters chanted together. "Don't let your dress get dirty! You got plenty-enough to do, just waiting, waiting, waiting on your husband!"

"When I can't see her determined little face any longer, but just her back, she looks mighty tender to my eyes," Aunt Beck said in a warning voice to the other women. "Around her shoulder blades, she looks a mighty tender little bride."

A big spotted cat, moulting and foolish-looking, came out onto the porch, ramming its head against their feet, standing on its hind legs and making a raucous noise.

"He's kept that up faithful. He's looking for Jack," said Etoyle. "That cat's almost got to be a dog since Jack's away."

"Think he'd better whip up his horse now and come on," said Granny.

"He's coming, Granny, just as fast as he can," Aunt Birdie promised her.

Aunt Nanny teased, "Listen, suppose they was all ready to let those boys out, then caught 'em in a fresh piece of mischief."

"They'd just hold right tight onto their ears, then," said Miss Lexie. She had a broom now and was sweeping underneath the school chair, the only one where nobody was sitting.

"You wouldn't punish a boy on his last day, would you?" Uncle Noah Webster asked. "Would you now, Lexie?"

"Yes, I would. By George, I took my turn as a teacher!" Miss Lexie cried.

Vaughn ran the little girls out of the swing, and while the uncles climbed to their feet to watch he started setting out the long plank tables. There were five, gray and weatherbeaten as old rowboats, giving off smells of wet mustard, forgotten rain, and mulberry leaves. None of them were easily persuaded to stand true on their sawhorse legs. Vaughn looked down an imaginary line from the big bois d'arc to the chinaberry. Unless Gloria were to move from where she sat, there would have to be a jog in the middle of it.

Close to the house, the company dogs had fallen into long slack ranks, a congregation of leathery backs jolted like one long engine by the force of their breathing. Over the brown rocks of their foreheads flickered the yellow butterflies of August like dreams, some at their very noses. Sid, tied in the barn behind, did the barking all by himself now. His appeals, appeals, appeals rang out without stopping.

"I guess," said the new Aunt Cleo, "I guess I'm waiting for somebody to tell me what the welcome for Jack Renfro is all about! What's he done that's so much more than all these big grown uncles and boy cousins or even his cripple daddy ever done? When did he leave home, and if he ain't let you have a card from him, what makes you so sure he's coming back today? And what's his wife got her wedding dress on for?"

Aunt Cleo had been left the school chair to sit on. She leaned her elbow on the writing-arm and crossed her feet.

Then the uncles stretched and came strolling back to the house. Uncle Noah Webster skidded across the porch floor, riding his splint chair turned backwards, so as to sit at her elbow.

"If you don't know nothing to start with, I don't reckon we could tell you all that in a hundred years, Sister Cleo," said Aunt Birdie. "I'm scared Jack'd get here before we was through."

"Take a chance," she said.

There was not a breath of air. But all the heart-shaped leaves on the big bois d'arc tree by the house were as continually on the spin as if they were hung on threads. And whirly-winds of dust marched, like scatterbrained people, up and down the farm track, or pegged across the fields, popped off into nowhere.

"Can't she wait till Brother Bethune gets here for dinner and tells it to us all at the table? Surely he'll weave it into the family history," pleaded Aunt Beck.

"This'll be his first go at us," Uncle Percy reminded her.

"If he shows up as poor in comparison to Grandpa Vaughn at the reunion as he shows up in the pulpit on Second Sundays, I'll feel like he won't even earn his dinner," said Uncle Curtis.

"Brother Bethune is going to do the best he can, and we all enjoy the sound of his voice," said Aunt Birdie. "Still, his own part in this story's been fairly stingy. I wouldn't put it past a preacher like him to just leave out what he wasn't in on."

"What I mainly want to hear is what they sent Jack to the pen for," said Aunt Cleo.

Miss Beulah marched right away from them and in a moment her set of bangs and clatters came out of the kitchen.

Then a mockingbird pinwheeled, singing, to the peak of the barn roof. After moping and moulting all summer, he'd mounted to his old perch. He began letting loose for all he was worth, singing the two sides of a fight.

Their voices went on with his—some like pans clanking on the stove, some like chains dropping into buckets, some like the pigeons in the barn, some like roosters in the morning, some like the evening song of katydids, making a chorus. The mourning dove's voice was Aunt Beck, the five-year-old child's was Aunt Birdie. But finally Aunt Nanny's fat-lady's voice prevailed: "Let Percy tell! His voice is so frail, getting frailer. Let him show how long can he last."

Only at the last minute did Aunt Cleo cry out, "Is it long?"

"Well, crops was laid by one more year. Time for the children to all be swallowed up in school," Uncle Percy's thready voice had already begun. "We can be sure that Grandpa Vaughn had started 'em off good, praying over 'em good and long here at the table, and they all left good and merry, fresh, clean and bright. Jack's on his best behavior. Drove 'em off in the school bus, got 'em all there a-shrieking, ran and shot two or three dozen basketball goals without a miss, hung on the oak bough while Vaughn counted to a hundred out loud, and when it's time to pledge allegiance he run up the flag and led the salute, and then come in and killed all the summer flies while the teacher was still getting started. That's from Etoyle."

"But it don't take Ella Fay long!" prompted Aunt Nanny.

"Crammed in at her desk, she took a strong notion for candy," Uncle Percy quavered. "So when the new teacher looked the other way, she's across the road and into the store after it."

"And shame once more on a big girl like that," said Miss Lexie.

"Well, wouldn't you have liked the same?" Uncle Noah Webster teased. "A little something sweet to hold in your cheek, Lexie?"

"Not I."

Aunt Nanny winked at the porchful. "The first day *I* had to go back to Banner School, I'd get a gnawing and a craving for the same thing!"

"And been switched for it!" they cheered. "By a good strong right arm!"

"It didn't take Ella Fay but one good jump across a dry mudhole to the store. And old Curly Stovall's just waiting."

"Stovall? Wait a minute, slow down, halt," interrupted Aunt Cleo.

"You're a Stovall," several guessed.

"Wrong. I was married to one, the first time round," she said. "My first husband's folks comes from Sandy. It's a big roaring horde of 'em still there."

"The first Stovalls around here walked into Banner barefooted—three of 'em, and one of 'em's wife. I don't know what description of hog-wallow they come from," said Mr. Renfro, passing by in the yard, "but the storekeeper then alive put the one in long pants to work for him. Stovalls is with us and bury with us."

"Visit their graves," Aunt Beck invited Aunt Cleo. "They need attention."

"Don't you-all care for the Stovalls?" she asked, and Uncle Noah Webster slapped a hand on her leg and gave a shout, as though watching her find this out was one of the things he'd married her for.

"If I was any kind of a Stovall at all, I'd keep a little bit quiet for the rest of this story," came the bell-like voice of Miss Beulah up the passage out of the kitchen.

"Well, Ella Fay didn't much more than get herself inside the store than she had to start running for it," said Uncle Percy.

"What had she done?" Aunt Cleo challenged them.

"Not a thing in the world that we know of but grow a little during the summer," Uncle Percy went on mildly. " 'Well,' says Curly, 'look who they're sending to pay the store.' 'I didn't bring you anything, I come after a wineball,' she says, as polite as you are. 'Oh, you did?' " To speak the words of rascals, Uncle Percy pitched his poor voice as high as it would go into the confidential-falsetto. " 'And it'll be another wineball tomorrow,' he says, 'and another one the tomorrow after that, every school morning till planting time next spring—I can't afford it. Not another year o' you!' Jumps up.

'When am I ever going to get something back on all that candy-eating?' says he to her. And she starts to running."

"Tell what he's like, quick," said Aunt Birdie.

"He's great big and has little bitty eyes!" came the voice of Ella Fay from where she was pulling honeysuckle off the cow shed. "Baseball cap and sideburns!"

"She's got it! Feel like I can see him coming right this minute," said Aunt Nanny, hitching forward in her rocker.

" 'Don't you come a-near me,' Ella Fay says. She trots in front of Curly around the store fast as she can, threading her way—you know how Banner Store ain't *quite* as bright as day."

"Pretty as she can be!" exclaimed the aunts.

"If only she didn't have the tread of an elephant," said Miss Beulah in the kitchen.

"Girls of his own church will run from him on occasion, so I'm told. Better Friendship Methodist is where he worships, and at protracted meetings, or so I'm told, every girl younger'n forty-five runs from him," said Uncle Percy primly.

"Every bit of that is pure Baptist thinking," said Aunt Beck. "I'd like you to remember there's plenty of other reasons, just as good, to keep out of that storekeeper's way, and my sympathies go out to his sister. She can't even *bring* him to church."

"Well, he's coming behind Ella Fay and says, 'Your folks been owing me for seed and feed since time was—and when's your dad going to give me the next penny on it! You-all never did have anything and never will!' And he's just about to catch her. She turns around, reaches in, slides out in his face the most precious treasure there is, a gold ring! And that's just the way her mind works," said Aunt Nanny proudly.

"She's borrowed it out of Granny's Bible for the first day of school," said Aunt Birdie. "Yes sir, and had it tucked in where Granny tucks her silver snuffbox."

"Little devil," said Aunt Nanny.

"And he put out his great paw and taken it! Of course she right away asks him to please kindly give that back."

"And he wouldn't give it back?" a chorus of cries came, as hilarious as if none of them here had ever heard. "And what excuse did he offer for such behavior?" said Aunt Birdie in sassy tones.

"Oho, she didn't give him time to resurrect one. Out of that store she flies! Not even his wineball would she take—spit it right out in the road. And put out her tongue at him, to remind him just who she was," cried Aunt Nanny, hitching herself forward a little farther.

"Pure gold?" Aunt Cleo asked.

Uncle Noah Webster rumbled at her: "Our dead mother's. Granny's keeping it in her Bible. That's your answer."

"What was a half-grown girl like that doing with it?" she asked.

"Carrying it to school. She'd already shown it to the other girls," Aunt Beck said with a sigh. "I don't know yet how she escaped having the teacher take it up, first thing."

"Teacher's too young and green," voices teased.

Gloria sat on, before their eyes, with her back to them. Out beyond the gate, the heat flickered and danced, and devil's whirlwinds skittered across the road.

"Ella Fay Renfro'd go parading off in your *hat* if you didn't stop her," Miss Lexie Renfro said.

"She's over-hungry to be gauding herself up, living in the land o' dreams," said Aunt Nanny, winking. "Something like me, back when I was a schoolgirl."

"All right, then what does she do?" cried Aunt Cleo.

"Planted herself right there in the road and bawls: 'Big booger's got Granny's gold ring!' Etoyle says that's the swiftest she ever saw her brother Jack brought out of his desk."

"Oh, Jack is *so* dependable!" sighed Aunt Beck.

"Is it always Jack?" asked Aunt Cleo.

"Try hollering help yourself one time and see," cried Miss Beulah from the kitchen.

"Sprung over his desk like a blessed deer and tore out of the schoolhouse and in that store he prances. And in two shakes Jack Renfro and Curly Stovall's yoked up in another fight."

"A schoolboy fighting an old man?" cried Aunt Cleo.

"Listen, Curly Stovall ain't old. He's just mean!" Uncle Noah Webster told her.

"And Jack wasn't due to be a schoolboy much longer!" grinned Aunt Nanny. "He didn't know it but his days were already numbered."

"Listen, Sister Cleo, here's what Curly Stovall is: big and broad as the kitchen stove, red in the face as Tom Turkey, and ugly as sin all over. Old Curly Stovall ain't old and I don't think he'll *get* old," said Uncle Dolphus.

"The Mr. Stovall I buried was old," she said. "Creepin'!"

"You can forget him." Uncle Dolphus brought the front legs of his chair down hard. "Had they but saved it for Saturday!" he cried to his brothers. "It wasn't only that we had to miss a good one. But fifteen or twenty more fellows at least would've been on hand, and ready and able to tell it afterwards, in Court or out, and help us give the world a little better picture of the way we do it in Banner."

"But like it was, everybody's busy getting in the last of their peas," said Uncle Percy. "Well, Curly skinned Jack's ear, and Jack had to skin Curly's ear, and so on, and old Curly's getting pretty fractious, and calling now for his pup to come and take a piece out of Jack's britches. He comes, and Jack's little dog Sid that's there waiting for the end of school, he frolics in too, with a kiss for that ugly hound! 'Sic 'em, Frosty!' Curly hollers, and if you'd been there, you'd had to stand well out of the way, or hid behind the pickle barrel. Curly even calls for his sister! Calls for Miss Ora to come out of the dwelling house back of the store and swat Jack with her broom."

"She's a pretty good artist with that broom, but she don't always make an appearance when she's called," giggled Aunt Birdie. "That's her reputation."

"A good thing for 'em both they didn't call for Lexie," said Miss Lexie. "I'd killed both of 'em right on the spot, before they went an inch further."

"If you'd got close enough to the store, you might've caught a flying rattrap, sure enough." Uncle Curtis told her. "But you couldn't expect to put a stop to Jack and Curly. Your broom ain't any longer than Miss Ora's."

"'Hand over the ring! Where you got it hid?' Jack keeps hollering. 'What'd you do, swallow it?' he says.

"'Let go my windpipe,' says Curly. 'And quit turning my store upside down—I put it in my safe.'

" 'Bust it open!' says Jack.

" 'I ain't a-gonna!'

" 'Don't make so much racket,' says Jack. 'The new teacher's over there trying to get a good start. Speak more quiet.'

" 'Make me!' says Curly.

"So Jack he brought down on Curly's crown with a sack of cottonseed meal—"

"Without warning?" Aunt Cleo cried.

"—of cottonseed meal that Curly had standing right there. Busted the sack wide open and covered that booger from head to foot with enough fertilize to last him the rest of his life. Then didn't old Curly whirl!

"Jack says, 'Hold it, Curly! Vaughn, go back to your desk!' Yes, that little feller's slipped out and followed his big brother into battle."

"Couldn't the new teacher hold onto her pupils any better'n that?" teased Uncle Noah Webster. "In my day, the teacher wielded a switch as long as my arm!"

"You can't keep children of *mine* shut up in school, if they can figure there's something going on somewhere!" Miss Beulah called above the sudden spitting of the skillets in her kitchen. "They're not exactly idiots!"

" 'Vaughn, get out of men's range,' says Jack. And Vaughn's still little enough to back off like his brother tells him, but big enough not to back no further than the best place to see. He squats him on the roof of the pump box and could see and hear."

"Here it comes!" sang the aunts.

"Jack dives right over the counter into Curly and butts him out of reach of that old piece-of-mischief that Curly was whirling for, and it was loaded, you bet, and steers him out from behind that counter to the one clear spot in the middle of the floor—and the whole store busts wide open. All in a golden cloud of pure cottonseed meal."

"That's when I wish I could've waded in on top of 'em!" hollered Aunt Nanny. "Wielding the battle-stick I stir my clothes-pot with!"

"The whole schoolhouse must've been equally ready to

pop!" cried Aunt Birdie. "And the teacher, of course, she couldn't do any good."

"Maybe not a *teacher*. But what was Gloria doing all this time? Where was *she*?" asked Aunt Cleo. "She must come into this somewheres."

"If you teach, you're expected to go on teaching whatever happens," said the voice of Gloria. She spoke from her seat on the log.

"Until you die or get married, one," Aunt Birdie agreed.

"You mean *Gloria* was the teacher?" shrieked Aunt Cleo.

"That was only my first day." Gloria turned her head only the least bit to tell them. "I wasn't blind to what went on. I was taking full stock of that commotion from my windowsill, abreast the pencil sharpener. All the while careful to keep the brunt of the children behind me instead of where they were struggling for, so they couldn't learn the example that was being set. And teaching them a poem to hold them down, the one about Columbus and behind him lay the gray Azores."

"And when Curly stretched his arm for the gun?" cried Aunt Birdie.

"I rang that dinner bell," said Gloria.

"If Ella Fay could've just lasted till then! She had jelly in all her biscuits in her dinner pail, besides the rest of her dinner!" Miss Beulah cried from the kitchen.

" 'Curly, hear that bell? It's dinner time already,' says Jack. 'Give me the ring and be quick about it—you wouldn't want me to keep the new teacher waiting on me.'

" 'I ain't going to bust open that safe,' says Curly.

" 'Stay put, then,' says Jack. 'And I'll come back after dinner and bust it open for you.'

" 'What's gonna hold me?' says Curly.

" 'Well, what's that coffin been doing here in our way so long?' says Jack, and packs him in so quick!"

"Where'd it come from in such a hurry?" Aunt Cleo asked.

"Made for him. Made just to hold Curly, thanks to Miss Ora his sister," said Uncle Curtis. "It wasn't nothing new. All his trade was pretty well used to falling over it. She had Willy Trimble to get busy on that coffin when Banner in general and her in particular had it settled Curly's about to go in it—back when the Spanish Influenza was making its rounds. Then of course old Curly jumped up and fooled her. Well, that mistake is still taking up room in Curly's store to this day."

"Cleo, that's some coffin," said Uncle Noah Webster. "Made out of two kinds of wood, cedar and pine. It would hold two of you. If it wasn't Sunday, you could step in the store and take a look at the size of it."

"If it wasn't Sunday she could step in and take a look at the size of Curly," said Uncle Percy primly.

"Vaughn says, 'You can't do that to our storekeeper!'"

" 'Just because nobody ever has?' says Jack."

"Didn't Curly Stovall object to being treated like that in his own store?" asked Aunt Cleo.

"He let it shortly be known he wasn't too happy about it," whispered Uncle Percy. "Stuffed in backwards the way he was, yellow as sin from cottonseed meal, and boxed in as pretty as you please—all that was lacking was the lid on."

"Squeezed in tight on his old tee-hiney!" cried Aunt Birdie.

"Right smack on his old humpty-dumpty!" shouted Aunt Nanny.

"To a tighter fit than any galvanized tub ever give him. And chalked up the side of it's running the words 'Cash Sale Only, Make Me an Offer!' I reckon up till that very day, old Curly'd been basking in the notion somebody'd come along from somewheres and cart that thing off his hands." Uncle Noah Webster groaned with laughter. "Curly says, 'Jack, wait! You go off to eat and leave me like this for my trade to find?' 'I better make sure,' says Jack, and runs a little clothesline around. Laces him tight and ties the ends behind, so fat arms can't reach. Like Nanny here—can't untie her own apron strings."

" 'Twas a mighty poor trick to play, then!" Aunt Nanny cried, delighted.

Uncle Percy went on. "Vaughn says, 'Now can I pop him?' And Jack says, 'You trot yourself back to the teacher and hand in your slingshot before she can ask you for it,' he says. 'That's a teacher I want us to hang onto. Help me keep her rejoicing in Banner, so she'll stay.' Vaughn told it on him.

"And without a word Jack skips to the safe, rakes off a forest of coal oil lamps and chimneys that's crowding the top of it, squats him under it, and ups with the whole thing on his back. Packs it right on top of him! You can bet Curly loved seeing that safe get up and walk away from him—about as well as he'd love a dose of Paris green!" sang out Uncle Noah Webster, and Uncle Percy went wavering on:

"Out Jack goes, staggers down the steps of the store, and starts across the road. The children's got their lunch pails open, they's already gobbling, but the teacher's still on the doorstep pumping that bell. I reckon now's when she drops it."

"And I reckon he was fixing to drop that safe, there at her feet," said Aunt Beck gently. "But when he gets there, she's ready for him."

They paused to look at Gloria. Small girl cousins had been drawn to her now, and marched in a circle around her, every little skirt a different length from the others.

> "Down on this carpet you must kneel
> Sure as the grass grows in this field,"

the little girls were singing, loud through their noses.

" 'You can't bring that to school,' says Miss Gloria. 'School is not the place for it. Just keep your antics to the store.' And she says, 'If all this was to make me sit under the oak tree with you and open our lunch side by side, you've gone the wrong way about it, Jack Renfro,' she says."

"My lands," said Aunt Cleo, leaning back in her chair.

"Little Elvie told it on her—she can copy Gloria just like Poll Parrot," Aunt Nanny grinned.

" 'If you took up a ton on your back to let me know how good and strong you are, I'm not going to give you the satisfaction of laying it down,' she says. 'You can just keep on going. Carry it on home and see what your grandpa will say. I've already sent your sister crying home ahead of you. And here!' She prisses to meet him, and hangs his own lunch pail on his other hand. Then she's strapping up his history and arithmetic and geography and speller, and saddling 'em around his neck. 'Go on,' she says. 'See how far this performance will carry you. If I'm going to hold down Banner

School, I need to see right now what my future's going to be like.' "

"No wonder she had her pupils running out the door! I'm surprised they didn't go climbing out the windows as well," said Aunt Nanny, slapping her lap.

" 'And come right straight back! And bring me a written excuse from your mother for coming home before school is out. Or take your punishment!'

"Off he staggers."

"Say, wasn't Jack showing off a good bit for the first day of school, when you start to adding it all up?" asked Aunt Cleo.

"Oh, no more than the teacher," said Miss Beulah coolly, standing there to look at her.

A couple of butterflies flew over Gloria where she sat on her log, particles whirling around each other as though lifted through the air by an invisible eggbeater. But she sat perfectly still and stared straight ahead.

"Well, I'm ready to hear the rest!" said Aunt Cleo. "How big a safe is it?"

"It's as big as a month-old calf!" cried Aunt Nanny.

"Well, how big is Jack?"

"He's Renfro-size!" said Miss Beulah. "But he's all Beecham, every inch of him!"

"How come he didn't just crack open that safe and try carrying home nothing but the ring?" asked Aunt Cleo.

"Do you think he had all day?" cried Aunt Birdie.

"Pore Jack! How he made it up that first hill is over and beyond my comprehension," said Aunt Nanny.

"Pore Jack! It's just a wonder he didn't fall flat on his face, once and for all," said Aunt Beck.

"Carrying the safe on his back, and books and lunch pail and the rest of the burdens he's had piled on him, one on top the other! He ate the lunch, got rid of that much load—we don't need to be told that," cried Aunt Nanny.

"Didn't the safe alone pretty soon start weighing a ton?" asked Aunt Cleo.

"It's only a wonder he didn't go through a single bridge with it," Uncle Percy conceded. "It had to weigh as much as a cake of ice the same size, but a safe don't melt as you go, more is the pity."

"I could see him coming when he started up through the field," said Miss Beulah. "Oh, I wish I'd turned him around right there!"

Ella Fay in the front yard giggled. "And Mama yells, 'What're you bringing now, to get in my way?' I was crying so hard I couldn't tell her!"

"The day before, he'd brought up them old pieces of concrete pipe he'd unearthed from some bridge that's gone, and upended them there by the foot of the steps for his mother to plant—so the new teacher'd see 'em when she went up the steps or down!" cried Miss Beulah. "And now this!"

"Jack struggles through the gate and the yard and drops his load to the ground at the front steps. 'Here's Papa something to open,' says Jack."

"What ways and means has Mr. Renfro got?" asked Aunt Cleo, as Mr. Renfro came around the house carrying a watermelon. "He don't look like he's got too many left."

"Never mind, he didn't get the chance," said Miss Beulah.

"You knew something would go awry, you was just waiting for the first hint!" Aunt Birdie said, tugging on Aunt Cleo's hefty arm. "Well, by the time that safe hits home soil, it's already open! The door's hanging wide—"

"And the cupboard was bare," whispered Uncle Percy. He turned to Granny. "There's no more ring than I can show you right now in the palm of my hand."

Granny looked back at him through the long slits of her eyes.

"*Now* what does Jack say?" Aunt Cleo asked.

" 'Bring me a swallow,' he says. So Ella Fay holds the dipper and when he can talk he says, 'If Curly wants that safe now, after the behavior it's give me, he's going to have to come with his oxen and haul it down himself.' Then he gives his mother the gist, and says, 'Don't worry about the ring, Mama. Tell Granny not to worry—somebody with bright eyes can help me find it.' And he says, 'The new teacher told me not to come back without a written excuse.' 'I wouldn't write you an excuse this minute to please Anne the Queen,' says

Beulah. 'I'm too provoked to guide a pencil, and what do you suppose Grandpa's going to be?' 'Then I got to make haste,' says Jack. 'If I ain't back by the last bell to take my punishment, she's liable to kill me!' Whistles for Dan. Onto his back and shoots off like a bolt."

"And why ain't he back?" asked Granny. "I've heard this tale before."

"Never mind, Granny, he's on his way right now," boomed Uncle Noah Webster. "That's what we're doing—bringing him."

"Who'd opened the safe?" asked Aunt Cleo.

"Nobody." Uncle Noah Webster beamed at her. "It'd opened itself. Jack'd already hit the ground with it a time or two, coming."

"Wouldn't *you* have?" Miss Beulah cried. "It was as big as a house and twice as heavy!"

"Well, now, I wouldn't say it's all that sizeable," said Mr. Renfro, coming around the house with another melon to put on exhibition. "Or all that heavy. I reckon the sides of the thing may have a certain amount of tin in 'em, Mother. Or you'd expect it to go through the store floor."

"How do you know, Mr. Renfro?" asked Aunt Cleo.

"Used to be my safe," he said. "Used to be my store."

"My!" she said. "How did you come so far down in the world, then?"

"And my daddy's before me," he said. "And away back yonder, his granddaddy made the first start—trading post for the Indians. Come down to me and I lost it."

"The year we married," said Miss Beulah. "Never mind going any further."

"I *see* all the rest," Aunt Cleo told her.

"Just you be assured that that safe weighs a ton," said Miss Beulah. "I heard the noise the *ground* made when the safe came down and shook it. Just exactly like thunder."

"Let's be fair, and say it wasn't any more the fault of the safe than the fault of this here soil," said Uncle Curtis. "Banner clay is enough to break even a man's back, when rain is withholden. Ain't that the case, Mr. Renfro?" he asked. "Growing watermelons is about the best it can do now, ain't it?"

Mr. Renfro thumped his melon and left again for more.

"And just to think of an ignorant boy walking along this hilly old part of the world, dropping out pennies and nickels and dimes and quarters behind him! Wheresoever that boy walked there was good money laying in his tracks, and he didn't know it!" Aunt Cleo cried.

They all laughed but Miss Beulah.

"It was the *ring* he lost!" she shrieked. "What he went to all the trouble for!"

"How's Curly Stovall getting along?" Aunt Cleo cried.

"In his coffin? He ain't any better," said Uncle Noah Webster, giving her a clap on the shoulder.

"Curly in his own coffin is a picture I'd give anything in this world to see to this day, and just listening to his choice remarks," said Uncle Curtis. "It happened on the wrong day of the week and that's the only thing that's the matter with it."

"I reckon those precious children's the only ones got a decent look at him," said Aunt Cleo.

"That teacher, the minute they's through gobbling, she lines 'em up and marches 'em right back inside the schoolhouse," said Aunt Nanny. "They never knew what they missed. And she didn't know no more about any coffin than they did!"

"Thought she could see so good with those bright eyes," said Aunt Birdie.

"What good's her eyes? In the first place, the store scales is standing right in front of the door, trying to block you. And in the second place, it's dark inside," Aunt Beck gently reminded them.

"You don't know what's there till you get in the store, and even when you can see it, sometimes it'll bump you," said Uncle Curtis. "That coffin."

"And now there's Curly stuck in it, as tight as Dick's hatband, going sight unseen," said Uncle Percy.

"Stuck and still wearing his baseball cap," said Aunt Nanny, grinning. "Sideburns thick with meal. Like bunches of goldenrod hanging to his ears, Etoyle says."

"How'd Etoyle get a look?" asked Aunt Cleo.

"She ate the fastest and run the quickest, then told her

story and didn't find any believers," said Ella Fay in the yard. "She's not but in the fourth grade and everybody knows she embroiders."

"Well, what does Curly Stovall do?" asked Aunt Cleo.

"Hollers," whispered Uncle Percy. "And not a soul can he summons. Calls again for Sister Ora. But she don't come till she's ready."

"She can't hear Curly half the time for the reason she's talking to *him*," said Aunt Birdie. "When he's in the store she's talking to him from the house. When he's in the yard she's talking to him from the store. I bet you she was there in the house talking to Curly the whole time. And he had to hear all she had to say, stuck in his own coffin."

"I'm glad he did," said Uncle Dolphus. "And for the good it done him."

"So nothing he could do but go on raising as much racket as he was able. But who was he going to bring? It wasn't Saturday. You could holler your own head off, but that don't guarantee you'll draw a soul if it ain't no further along than Monday," Uncle Percy went on.

"If I couldn't get anybody by hollering, I believe I'd use the telephone," Aunt Cleo said. "If I found myself in as friendless a spot as he's in."

"Sister Cleo, you must have walked in that store in some dream and seen where that coffin was put. It's put facing the post where the only phone in seven earthly miles is hooked up," said Aunt Birdie.

"That's right, and after while, old Curly got his head poked out, in between them hanging boots and trailing shirt-tails, and butted the receiver off," said Uncle Percy, and went into falsetto: "Hello? Find me the law! I'm tied up! Been robbed!"

"Miss Pet Hanks is Central in Medley. That means she's got a Banner phone in her dining room," said Aunt Birdie. "Sometimes when you're trying to tell somebody your woes, you hear her cuckoo clock."

"Well, you know her laugh. Miss Pet Hanks comes right back out of the receiver at him and says, '*You're* the law, you old booger!'"

"Ha, ha," said Ella Fay, coming out into the yard. She carried the preacher's stand out in front of her and placed it in the shade, ready to twine it in honeysuckle vines.

"Sure, by that time hadn't we started Curly on his way up? He was the marshal. So Miss Pet just lets him stew in his own juice awhile. She's got that job for life," Uncle Curtis said.

"Didn't one earthly soul come in?" cried Aunt Cleo.

"Do you count Brother Bethune? When he comes in it's with the one idea of helping himself to some shells out of the box. He calls to Curly how many he's taking, and goes his way. Curly don't let even a Baptist preacher have anything free. And it takes more than a Methodist storekeeper getting stuck in his own coffin to take Brother Bethune's mind off his own business," whispered Uncle Percy.

"Oh, I'm beginning to feel sorry for Curly, I can't help it," Aunt Beck warned them. "It's a human deserted from far and near."

"Are you telling me Gloria wouldn't cross a dirt road herself to help a human fight free of his coffin?" asked Aunt Cleo. "What was she doing?"

"Teaching," spoke up Gloria. "Teaching 'Sail on! Sail on!'"

"She was in her schoolroom where she belonged, trying her little best to hold down a flock of children she was just beginning to learn the first and last names of," said Aunt Beck gently.

"I was getting through my first day about as well as I expected," said Gloria from the yard. "Then when the storekeeper started making more noise than all seven grades put together, it was time to step out on the doorstep and speak to him."

"Oh-oh!" cried Aunt Nanny.

"I called for his attention. I said this was the teacher! I told him he was interrupting the recitation of a hard-learned piece of memory work and not doing the cause of education any good. And I told him all that work to attract attention had better stop right quick, because my opinion of Banner was fast going down."

"Oh-oh!" several exclaimed.

"He gave very little more contest till he heard my last bell," said Gloria. "People will learn to measure up if you just let them know what you expect of them."

"Where'd she get all that?" giggled Aunt Birdie, and Miss Lexie dipped her knees and rocked back to laugh.

"Green or not, if she'd been doomed to teach on, little Gloria might have needed to be reckoned with," said Aunt Birdie. "Some day."

"Don't forget. She knew who to copy," said Miss Lexie.

"Then I reckon Curly Stovall just had to wait for Jack to come on back to have enough mercy to pull him loose and finish the fight," said Aunt Cleo. "Who won?"

"Know what? Jack never did get back to the store to so much as even untie him," Uncle Percy put his head on one side and told her. "You can try naming your own reason."

"Curly Stovall belongs to be tied. That's one," Aunt Birdie offered.

"It's a plenty. But there was some reason why somebody did untie him," Uncle Percy went on.

"It was Aycock Comfort and he don't need no reason," said Uncle Curtis.

"Who's Aycock Comfort and what's wrong with *him*?" asked Aunt Cleo.

"He's a Banner boy and a friend of Jack's. What's wrong with him is he ain't Jack," said Uncle Noah Webster, with an expansive smile for his brothers.

"Had Aycock followed Jack over from school, like he follows him everywhere else? And straggling?" asked Aunt Birdie.

"Aycock ain't even reported to school. Ain't even heard there's a new teacher. He's just ready for a sour pickle. It's just as Miss Ora Stovall finds it's time to slice off some meats for her greens," said Uncle Percy. "She walks in on the vision of Curly in the coffin and she lets forth one cackle. 'I'm going to put that in the paper!' she says. She writes Banner news for *The Boone County Vindicator.* 'What happened to you?' 'School threw open this morning!' he says. 'Get me out of this harness!' 'Jack Renfro must have made up his mind mighty sudden to go on with his education,' she says, seeing what kind of knots it was. "If you-all just wouldn't bring it in the store!' 'If you could just get me loose!' says Curly. So

Aycock borries the knife out of the store cheese and saws through the clothesline with it. And Curly hollers, 'Now who's going to buy that, Aycock, after you been slicing on it?' Pore Aycock, it looks like anywhere he goes he has a hard time finding him any gratitude."

"One more way he's a different breed from Jack," said Aunt Beck.

"So Miss Ora says, 'Take your pickle and go, Aycock, and stand out of busy folks' way. Me and Brother don't want to see this high varnish get scratched.' Plants her feet. Takes a good hold of that brother of hers and she pulls. And she pulls. Till out he comes like a old jaw tooth, hollering. She had to give the pull of her life to do it, and declares to the passing public she ain't over it yet," Uncle Percy said.

"And as soon as she's out of the way, Curly whirls and cuts off Aycock's shirt-tail. And if Aycock don't pick up a little two-ounce popcorn-popper and come running at him while he's nailing it up!"

Uncle Noah Webster said, "Percy, you don't give Aycock no credit at all. I feel like it was at least a churn dasher!"

"Well, he's running full-tilt with it. And right in time for the crack, in comes Homer Champion!"

"That's my sister Fay's husband," Miss Lexie told Aunt Cleo. "I'm going to get you one person told before you ask."

"And look out for him today," said Uncle Noah Webster. "He's a certified part of this reunion."

"Well, Homer comes rattling up and bringing in his bucket of eggs—he's on his egg route. 'Homer Champion,' says Curly, 'you're justice of the peace—why won't you come to the phone? I been smothered, tied and robbed, pulled on by a hundred and seventy-five pound woman, and hit a good lick with a churn dasher! Made a monkey out of by who ought to be in school, talked back to by a eight-ounce schoolteacher! Everything but have my phone used free! Well, here's Aycock by the ear—I caught you one of 'em. And you can catch you the other one. You grab hold of Jack, put 'em under arrest, and haul 'em off to jail, both of 'em.'"

"'Did I understand you to say *Jack*?' says Homer Champion.

" 'Now he's a safe robber!' says Curly. 'You can catch him easy when he gets back to drive the school bus.'

"But Homer Champion says, 'Curly Stovall, did you suppose you could trick me that easy into riding my own wife's brother's oldest boy through the country clear across Boone County all the way to Ludlow to put him in jail—the whole Banner School basketball team in one?' 'That's what I want,' says Curly. 'I got a good mind to throw something at you,' Homer says. Or so he tells it.

" 'Now will all three of you get out from under my feet so I can clean up the store?' says Miss Ora, coming in to take the eggs away from 'em. 'Before that tide of children floods in here when the last bell rings? I wish you didn't have to act so countrified.' She sends Curly to the pump to wash some of it out of him."

"If I'd been Curly, I'd been mad at all of 'em, her included," said Aunt Cleo.

"He wasn't overly pleased," said Uncle Curtis. "Now, it's the last bell, and without a minute wasted in pours the whole horde of children for their penny stick of fresh gum to chew in the bus going home. Then they all pour out into the bus, and Jack ain't quite back yet."

"Didn't the new teacher know enough to wait on him?" teased Aunt Birdie.

"She says, 'Long skinny red-headed boy without any books, come here to me.' That's Aycock, standing there gawking at her. 'What is your name and grade?'

" 'Aycock Comfort, and I thought I'd quit.'

" 'I'm putting you to further use,' says she.

" 'Well, I'm not the one they generally calls on,' says Aycock.

" 'You're more than tall enough to see over the steering wheel,' she says. 'I'll let you carry this load of children as far as they live.'

" 'If I can get it to crank, all right,' says Aycock. 'I rather drive a pleasure car, but slide in.' The Comforts never says 'Thank you' for a favor. They say that's because they're fully as good as you are. But the teacher don't slide in with *him*. 'Just carry the children,' she says. 'I need to wait for the elected driver to get back here so I can give him his punishment. You are just the substitute.'

"Put Aycock right back in the seventh grade. He'd been out of school four years, but Jack had had to give it up for five, so as to give the little ones a chance to start. And now, for the new teacher's sake, he's determined to do everybody's work and let her teach him too. The whole five months of it out of the year." Uncle Percy's voice failed him for a minute.

"Little did Jack know, when he started back to school that morning to try out the new teacher!" Aunt Nanny said with a wide smile.

"Little did Gloria know!" Aunt Beck said. "With the tumult over, I reckon she just sat down in the school swing to wait for him."

"He had to ride her home on his horse, holding on behind him!" said Aunt Nanny.

"Why, Nanny, he sat her up in the saddle, and come home leading him," said Miss Beulah. "And the cows had been calling to him since sundown."

Gloria raised and let fall her shoulders in what looked like a sigh. Out there with her flew the yellow butterflies of August—as wild and bright as people's notions and dreams, but filled with a dream of their own; in one bright body, as though against a headwind, they were flying toward the east.

"All right, did the ring ever turn up?" asked Aunt Cleo.

"Cleo, what in the name of goodness did you think we ever started this in order to tell? No'm!"

"Sure enough? How hard you look for it?" she asked.

"Listen! We *all* looked till the sun went down and we was putting our eyes out trying to see," said Miss Beulah, coming to the head of the passage. "Combing the woods and pasture and that creek bank and the weeds and the briars! Here on this farm it was every hill of corn, every stick of beans—and Jack had those rows as clean as I keep this house, didn't he? And this family knows *how* to look! If something's trying to hide from us, we'll find it! But the blessed ring fooled us."

"Ha ha," Ella Fay spoke from the yard.

"And I've got a good eye on you!" Miss Beulah called to

her. "I want to see you twine Grandpa's stand so thick with honeysuckle that Brother Bethune'll have a hard time finding *it*."

"Well, if you didn't see the ring anywhere, I hope you got all the money picked up," said Aunt Cleo.

"*What* money? Curly's money?" Uncle Noah Webster was asking through their shouts of laughter. "Have you heard of anybody yet that pays that billy goat cash?"

"Will you tell me where on earth they elect to keep what they run the store on?" Aunt Cleo demanded to know. "They have to keep change."

"In Ora's purse I think you'll find the majority of it today the same as then. Though I'm not trying to tell you she ain't got a sugar bin too, if you want to go knocking down the door and tromping in the house to make sure," said Miss Beulah. "I don't. I don't go *in* their house."

"Sister Cleo," Uncle Curtis said, "before Curly slapped in that gold ring, he'd put very little else in that safe worth taking out."

Aunt Birdie said, "Miss Ora kept a thing or two of hers in there that she don't consider it nobody's business to go through."

"Her pincushion, her needles and thread, and her scissors are all things I've seen her reach out of there," Aunt Beck said. "Her specs. Bah."

"And there's that big pot o' rouge she piles on her cheeks on Saturday," said Aunt Nanny.

"The only thing anybody ever found was the mortgages," whispered Uncle Percy. "They was all together in one pile in the bed of Panther Creek. Hadn't been a single drop of rain to fall."

"Who found those? The mortgages?" Aunt Beck asked with a sigh.

"Vaughn Renfro, the little brother, and run to carry 'em straight back to the store—all Curly had to do was snap on a new rubber band. Ants had eat up the old one, but left the signatures alone. Sure is a pity the weather had been so dry."

"Just pull me out of this chair. Lead me in your woods. If all you want's that ring, I bet I could turn it up," Aunt Cleo said with spirit.

Miss Beulah was back out here, holding an egg in her hand as if ready to crack it. "Sister Cleo, if you're the one knows and can tell where that ring rolled to, you'll get a more whole-hearted welcome out of this family than you'll ever know what to do with," she said. "But the truth is you don't know, nor I don't, nor anybody else within the reach of my voice, because that ring—it's our own dead mother's, Granny's one child's wedding ring, that was keeping safe in her Bible—it's gone, the same as if we never had it." She returned to the kitchen, and hard, measured strokes began in a bowl of batter.

Granny spoke. "Time's a-wasting."

"There, Granny, never mind," said Aunt Birdie. "We're all remembering it's your birthday."

"Bring him here to me, will you?" said Granny. "Don't keep Granny waiting a good deal longer."

"That's what we're doing, Granny—we're bringing him," said Uncle Noah Webster, going over to pat her shoulder, fragile as a little bit of glass. "Just as fast as we can."

"And next morning at the earliest," Uncle Percy continued, "weaving up the road to the house comes Homer Champion's chicken van from Foxtown. And when it bucks to a stop, it's two of 'em hops out—Homer and Curly Stovall! Just like they's buddies.

" 'Here's your proof, Homer Champion! Here's my safe, and Jack's turned it over to babies to play with!' says Curly. 'If they won't give it back, you can arrest him!' And it's Etoyle and Elvie and Vaughn, Beulah's three youngest, playing store to their hearts' content under a chinaberry tree. And they don't do a thing but quick sit down on that safe in a pile. Precious children, they don't get many play-pretties up this way.

" 'Climb off my safe!' says Curly. 'If you don't, old Homer'll carry you to jail, all in one load!'

"And Elvie don't do a thing but open the safe and tuck her little self inside and slam the door on him.

" 'Quit, you little mischiefs. Give it back to him like he says,' says Homer. 'The safe ain't hurt none, Curly, just the door needs a little lining up and oiling so it don't hurt your ears. Let's don't have hard feelings. Let's all just be friends.'

"Old Curly scrapes the other two children off the safe and

yanks that door open and shakes Elvie by the foot. 'Hand me the money out!' he hollers.

" 'We never had any money but chinaberries, we're too little,' pipes Elvie out of the safe.

"And Curly, the big bully! Has to haul out Elvie kicking and fighting, and he pulls that safe right out through their little arms that's twined around it! Elvie cried for her safe till dark.

"Etoyle knows enough to holler Jack from the barn. Here he comes, straight from the cow, carrying two full buckets, calling to say it's never too early for company, and asking if they won't come sit on the steps and enjoy a glass of foaming milk and the sunrise.

" 'Jack, you're under arrest!' says Homer.

"Jack threw the first bucket so fast! All that new milk right in Curly's face."

"Why not Homer Champion's?" objected Aunt Cleo.

"Sister Cleo, it's Homer that's arresting him, but he's married into our family—Mr. Renfro's and Miss Lexie's sister is his wife. And you know how Jack holds the family. And all ladies especially he holds in terrible respect."

"Drummed it into him as a child!" cried Miss Beulah.

"Jack, though, had to set one bucket down before he could throw the other one—he's like anybody else—and before you know it, old Homer's give it back to him, the whole thing plumb in the face. Blinds him! Curly and Homer acting in harness lifts him blind-struggling right into Homer's van with the chickens. Somewheres they find room in there for the safe too, and Curly climbs in after it and sits on it—Etoyle was quick enough to see he was holding his nose. Homer slams 'em all in together and drives off, without ever giving this house the benefit of a good morning. Little Elvie has to go to the kitchen and cry, to break the news."

"Hasn't Homer Champion changed his tune?" asked Aunt Cleo.

"He's a little bit primed this morning. And a good thing he didn't catch any of that milk, because it ain't the drink he's most overly fond of," said Uncle Curtis.

"I still don't see why Curly Stovall couldn't do his own arresting," said Aunt Cleo. "A marshal's got every right in the world and a justice of the peace is very little better than he is."

"Curly knew better, that's why! So off Jack's carted to Fox-town and shooed in jail. And Etoyle said Homer warned him before they started that if he give any more trouble resisting arrest he'd get a bullet ploughed through his leg."

"Etoyle embroiders. What are you doing sitting down with company now, Etoyle Renfro?" asked Miss Lexie.

"I love to hear-tell."

"You slip in here for what's coming next? In time to hear how your poor mother cried?" Aunt Beck reproached her.

"Now, I'm not going to try to tell the way Beulah per-formed that night," Uncle Percy whispered. "I ain't got the strength to do it justice."

"And you wasn't here to see it!" called Miss Beulah.

"Well, how did Gloria here perform?" asked Aunt Cleo.

"Cleo! Gloria hadn't got to be a member of the family *that* quick!" The other aunts laughed, and Aunt Nanny called, "Had you, Gloria!"

Gloria sat without turning around or speaking a word.

"Has she got good sense?" Aunt Cleo wanted to know.

"No indeed, she's addled," Miss Beulah came out to tell her. "And there's not a thing I or you or another soul here can do about it. It'll take Jack."

"I'm wondering by now why even Homer Champion don't get here," said Aunt Cleo. "Unless he's waiting for Jack to get here first."

"Oh, I can tell you exactly what Homer's doing. He's sit-ting jammed in a hot pew somewhere, waiting on the final Amen so he can shake hands with the whole congregation when they're let out the door," said Miss Beulah.

"The biggest, fullest, tightest-packed Baptist church he can find holding preaching today," said Aunt Beck.

"Then he'll hurry to shake hands again in front of the Fox-town ice house," said Uncle Percy. "He'll catch the Meth-odists going home to dinner."

"He'll figure a way to jar loose a few Presbyterians before the day of worship is over, if he can find some," said Miss Lexie.

"How's Curly Stovall putting in *his* last Sunday?" asked Aunt Cleo.

"He'll think of some such thing as a fish-fry to sew up all the infidels," said Miss Beulah, going.

"He figures he's got the Christians hooked like it is, blooming storekeeper!" recited Elvie, in her mother's voice.

"What're you doing here, child?" cried Aunt Beck.

"Keeping the flies killed."

"Well, sweetheart, your Uncle Homer Champion and Curly Stovall is in eternal tug-of-war for the same office now," Uncle Noah Webster told her. "You ain't likely to understand all you hear till you get up old enough to vote yourself."

"Both in the run-off?" asked Aunt Cleo.

"Why, of course. And I don't know how in the nation old Homer's going to cheat him out of it," said Uncle Noah Webster. "Homer's my age. He can't keep a jump ahead of Curly much longer."

"Now to me," Uncle Percy was quavering, "what they ought to had sense enough to do was throw this case out that selfsame day in Foxtown."

"Think of the trouble it would have saved!" Aunt Beck sighed.

"To me and the majority," Uncle Curtis said, "Jack had acted the only way a brother and son could act, and done what any other good Mississippi boy would have done in his place. I fully expected 'em to throw the case right out the window."

"With nothing but a good word for Jack," said Aunt Birdie.

"Well, if Jack's that lucky, then Curly's just wasting his time trying to arrest him," said Aunt Cleo.

"Well, Jack *wasn't*, and Curly *wasn't*. So don't go home," Aunt Nanny teased her.

"Well, they was mighty hard up for a spring docket in Ludlow if Jack's the worst fellow they could get Foxtown to furnish," said Uncle Curtis.

"All right, Sister Cleo, would *you* call that a case?" asked Aunt Birdie in sassy tones.

They cried, "We're testing you."

"Now wait, now wait," said Aunt Cleo. "I might could."

"Why, you could no more call that a case for court than I

could call my wife flying!" said Uncle Percy. He put his hand on Aunt Nanny's shoulder.

"I *might* could," said Aunt Cleo. "Even if all Jack got home with was the empty safe, I reckon you could call that safe-cracking. I don't know what else you could call it."

The beating in the kitchen stopped again. Miss Beulah came out onto the porch. "If Jack had wanted to steal something, Sister Cleo, he could have run off with Curly's fat pig and butchered it and done us all a little good at the same time! My son is not a thief."

"If a boy's brought up in Grandpa Vaughn's house, and knows drinking, dancing, and spot-card playing is a sin, you don't need to rub it into his hide to make him know there's something a little bit the matter with stealing," Uncle Noah Webster cried.

"Throwing his case out of court," said Uncle Curtis, "was the only thing for Homer Champion to do, so he didn't. He bound Jack over to the grand jury. Homer swore he couldn't afford to do anything else. They'd call him playing favorites. And said Jack hadn't done himself a world more good the way he treated the Foxtown jail," said Uncle Dolphus.

"Started nicking his way in a corner, prizing his way out as soon as he'd cleaned up his first dinner plate," said Uncle Percy. "He worked faithful. But Jack is a Banner boy, and how was he to know that if you dug your way through the brick wall of the Foxtown jail with your pie knife, you'd come out in the fire station? Chief looks up from the checkerboard and says to him: 'Son, I don't believe I ever seen you before. You better turn around and scoot back in till they make up their minds what to do with you.' And helped him scoot."

"Well, when they got Jack told they'd have to lock him up a little better now and keep him till spring, Jack just told *them* he's a farmer," said Uncle Curtis. "Jack told *them* just exactly who he was and just exactly where he lived. 'I got my daddy's hay to get in the barn, his syrup to grind, his hog to kill, his cotton to pick and the rest of it,' he says. 'His seed in the ground for next year. And I got my schooling to finish. I can't be here to sit and swing my foot while you scare up somebody to try me,' he says.

"So they told Jack, 'Go on, then.' And one of the other

prisoners says, 'We don't keep room in the Foxtown jail for the likes of you country boys.' "

"And they let him go?" cried Aunt Cleo.

"Look out, don't start to saying something good about the courts, Foxtown or anywhere else!" yelled Miss Beulah. "Not when Homer had the further crust to tell Jack if he didn't show his face in Ludlow Courthouse on the very stroke of the clock when they called his name, he could look forward to being arrested the same way all over again. Don't thank Homer! And don't let me hear anybody start thanking Curly Stovall for putting up that bail!" She went.

"Now that was right outstanding of a Stovall," said Aunt Cleo. "Say as much."

"How else did he think Renfros was going to live? How else did he figure he stood a chance of getting a penny out of 'em?" laughed Uncle Noah Webster. "Oh, Jack he did sweat, early and late. And just when we didn't need it, rain. And court creeping closer and closer. So the time come when we couldn't stand sight of his face any longer and we had to tell him, 'Jack! Before you get drug off to be tried in Ludlow, what would you most rather have out of all the world? Quick!' And quick he says, 'To get married!' Didn't surprise nobody but his mother."

"You couldn't say Jack hadn't been showing signs. Now the year before, our guess would have been the little Broadwee girl," said Aunt Birdie.

"Imogene? The one that's timid?" grinned Aunt Nanny.

"Yes and she's sitting there still."

"He's chased 'em all some. But when he singles out who he wants to carry *home*, he singles out the schoolteacher!"

"Was that a pretty good shock?" asked Aunt Cleo.

"Being as she's already living here in the house and eating at the table, no'm," said Aunt Nanny.

"Gloria had a choice too, even if you leave Aycock out. Curly Stovall was right across the road from that schoolhouse, with nobody but Miss Ora to look out for, enjoying a job on the public. And in his store carried all she wanted. But she turned up her little nose at him."

"He didn't make a good impression on me, from the first time I saw him," Gloria called in.

"But that year it's our turn to board the teacher, no hope of rescue," said Miss Beulah, coming to the head of the passage. "We'd spent the summer highly curious to see what they'd send, after the last old maid give up the battle. Well, here she came. The old fella that got it for superintendent of schools carried her up here in a car that's never been seen in my yard before or since—purse in both hands, book satchel over her shoulder, valise between her feet, and her lap cradling a basket of baby chicks for her present to whoever was to board her. I had a feeling the minute she pulled off her hat—'Here's another teacher Banner won't so easily get rid of.'"

All at once Lady May Renfro, aged fourteen months, came bolting out into their midst naked, her voice one steady holler, her little new-calloused feet pounding up through it like a drumbeat. She had sat up right out of her sleep and rolled off the bed and come. Her locomotion, the newest-learned and by no means the gentlest, shook the mirror on the wall and made its frame knock against the house front like more company coming.

"Who you hunting?" Aunt Nanny screeched at the baby.

Lady May ran through their catching hands, climbed down the steps in a good imitation of Mr. Renfro, and ran wild in the yard, with Gloria up and running after her.

"Where's your daddy, little pomegranate?" they hollered after her flying heels. "Call him! Call him!"

Elvie came third, following solemnly with the diaper.

Lady May ran around the quilt on the line and Gloria got her hands on her. There behind the quilt she knelt to her, curtained off from the house; the quilt hung motionless, just clear of the ground. It was a bed-sized square that looked rubbed over every inch with soft-colored chalks that repeated themselves, more softly than the voices sounding off on the porch. From the shadow of an iron pot nearby, rising continuously like sparks from a hearth, a pair of thrushes were courting again.

The sugar sack Gloria pinned about her baby's haunches blushed in the light and sparkled over with its tiny crystals that were never going to wash out of it. Around their shoulders the air shook with birdsong, never so loud since spring.

On all the farm, the only thing bright as the new tin of the roof was the color of Gloria's hair as she bent her head over her baby. It was wedding-ring gold.

"Act like you know what you're here for, Lady May," she told the smooth, uplifted face.

The child looked back at her mother with her father's eyes—open nearly to squares, almost shadowless, the blue so clear that bright points like cloverheads could be seen in them deep down. Her hair was red as a cat's ear against the sun. It stood straight up on her head, straight as a patch of oats, high as a little tiara.

"Just you remember who to copy," Gloria told her child.

She came leading Lady May to the house and through their ranks and inside the company room and out again, and this time the little girl was tiptoeing in a petticoat.

"Have a seat with us," said Aunt Nanny. "That's better."

Gloria sat down on a keg and Lady May climbed onto her lap. She turned her little palms up in a V. Her eyebrows lifted in pink crescents upturned like the dogwood's first leaves in spring. Her unswerving eyes looked straight into her mother's.

"Learn to wait," said Gloria, pulling both baby hands down.

So the baby sat still, her lashes stiff as bird-tails; she might have been listening for her name.

"Honey, where did Banner School ever get you from?" asked Aunt Beck, leaning forward. "Has this reunion ever asked you and ever got a full reply?"

"Miss Julia Mortimer was training me to step into her shoes," said Gloria.

"Whose shoes?" asked Aunt Cleo, and everybody groaned.

"The oldest teacher that's living. She was giving me my start," said Gloria.

"You meant to teach more than the single year?" exclaimed Aunt Birdie. "Never dreamed!"

"When I came, I could see my life unwinding ahead of me smooth as a ribbon," said Gloria.

"Uh-oh!" said Aunt Cleo.

"All I had left to do was teach myself through enough more summer normals to add up to three years, and I could step right into Miss Julia's shoes. And hold down Banner School forevermore."

"But then she just happened to run into Jack," said Aunt Nanny, with a strong pinch for Gloria's arm.

"So I wonder what was everybody's first words to Jack when he says he wants to marry his teacher?" asked Aunt Cleo.

Miss Beulah called, "I told him, 'Jack, there's just one thing you need for that that you're lacking. And that's the ring. Remember the gold ring Granny was keeping in the Bible? She might have spared it to a favorite like you, at a time like this, and where did it go?'"

"I reckon his mother had him there," said Aunt Birdie.

"No she didn't. Jack said, 'Mama, I'm going to afford my bride her own ring, like she wants, and all I need is a little time.' Time! He thought he had all the time he was going to need. You had to feel sorry for the child. Sorry for both of 'em."

"Well, I see you got you one anyway," Aunt Cleo said to Gloria. "What'd you have to do? Steal it?" She laughed, showing her tongue.

"Mind out, Sister Cleo, Gloria don't like to tell her business," Miss Beulah called, while Gloria laid her cheek to the baby's. Lady May's fast hands pulled the mother's hairpins out, and the curls rolled forward over them both.

"Gloria taught Banner School a whole year long for that little ring, that's what I think," said Aunt Birdie, giggling.

"A teacher always gets a warrant she can trade with," said Miss Lexie. "It means the same as a salary. And it just depends on the teacher—what she decides to use it for, if and when and how soon. If she don't starve in the meantime."

"If you used up your warrant for your ring, what'd you have left over for that wedding dress?" asked Aunt Cleo. "I only ask because I'm curious."

"It's homemade."

"You just can't see how much sewing there is to it, because of all that baby in her lap," Aunt Nanny said.

"Just a minute! If it tore!" Gloria cautioned two little girls who had come up from either side to stare and were now holding her sleeves and the hem of her skirt between their fingers. "I rather you stood back a distance." Her short puff sleeves were ironed flat into peaks stuck flat together and canvas-stiff, almost as if they were intended to be little wings.

"Full, full skirt and deep, deep hem," said Ella Fay, bumping through them on her way into the house now. "Organdy and insertion, flower-petal sleeves, and a ribbon-rose over the stomach above the sash. That's the kind of wedding dress *I* want."

"You could almost wear hers. I can see now there's a lots of material going to waste in that," said Aunt Cleo. "Despite that baby taking up the most of her lap." She laughed. "So you was here, ready, and waiting all this time?" she asked Gloria. "Well, where'd you hold the wedding? Your church right on the road? Or do you all worship off in the woods somewhere?"

"I'm surprised you didn't see Banner flying by on your way here, Sister Cleo," said Uncle Curtis. "Didn't Noah Webster show you which church was ours?"

"I keep my eyes on the driver," she said.

"Listen, Grandpa Vaughn downed enough trees himself to raise Damascus Church. Hewed them pews out of solid cedar, and the pulpit is all one tree. And in case you're about to tell us you still don't remember it, you might remember the cemetery on beyond—it's bigger than Foxtown's got to this day."

"How many came to the wedding? Church fill up to the back?"

"Stand up now and count!" Miss Beulah cried, clattering some pans together. "And you can add on the ones still to come today—Nathan, bless his heart, Fay and Homer Champion, Brother Bethune—"

"And Jack!" they cried.

"I'd call it a fair crowd," said Uncle Curtis. "I seen Aycock Comfort propped in a window—that's what room we had left for a Methodist."

"Blessed Grandpa joined those two blushing children for life in Damascus Church on a Sunday evening in spring," said Aunt Birdie. "If I forget everything else alive, I'll remember that wedding, for the way I cried."

"Oh, Grandpa Vaughn out-delivered himself! Already the strictest marrier that ever lived—and the prayer he made *alone* was the fullest you ever heard. The advice he handed down *by itself* was a mile long!" cried Uncle Noah Webster. "It would have wilted down any bride and groom but the most sturdy."

"And Curly Stovall come down the aisle and clapped his hand on Jack's shoulder in the middle of it, I've already guessed," said Aunt Cleo.

"Sister Cleo! Curly Stovall would not dare, would not dare to walk in Damascus Church with Grandpa Vaughn standing up in his long beard and looking at him over the Bible!" Aunt Birdie cried. "And Curly ain't even a Baptist."

"Not even for the scene it'd make?" she asked them.

Miss Beulah marched in on her. "I just came to be told the name of the church *you* go to," she said.

"Defeated Creek Church of the Assembly of God. One mile south of Piney."

"Never heard of a single piece of it." She about-faced and marched out again.

"It's after we're back at the house here, Sister Cleo, cooling off with Beulah's lemonade, and seeing the sun go down, that old Curly sneaks up the road on Jack for the second time. Says Curly, 'Eight o'clock in the morning by the strike of the courthouse clock, they'll be calling your name in Ludlow!' And just to be sure Jack will answer, he gets him thrown in the Ludlow jail on his wedding night!" said Uncle Noah Webster. "And don't you know Curly enjoyed doing it?"

"Suppose *you'd* put up the bail!" Aunt Cleo said. "But what about Grandpa Vaughn—wasn't he still awake, to scare off all comers?"

"Grandpa wasn't going to stand in the way of justice, Sister Cleo. Only unless Curly had tried that in church, before Grandpa had married 'em. *Then* Curly'd seen what he got out of Grandpa."

"Or even what he got out of Jack," said gentle Aunt Beck.

"I still hold Jack Renfro wasn't *born* that easy to take by surprise," said Aunt Birdie in loyal tones.

"His wedding night may have been the prime occasion they could risk it," Uncle Curtis said.

"Who'd Curly bring along to partner him this time?" Aunt Cleo asked. "He still playing with Homer Champion?"

"Oh no, he's already declared for office against Homer!" cried Uncle Noah Webster. "Old Curly's brought Charlie Roy Hugg, the one that's got the Ludlow jail."

"What's *his* style?"

"Drunk and two pistols. Makes his wife answer the phone."

"We got his twin in Piney."

"Sister Cleo, this entire family had to sit where we're all sitting now and see Jack Jordan Renfro carried limp as a sack of meal right off this porch and down those steps on his wedding night. He's open-mouthed."

"Just the caps of his toes dragging," said Etoyle, smiling.

"Curly had to hold up his other arm. And partly hold up Charlie Roy Hugg before they all got on and fired off. And at Banner Store there sits Aycock on the bench like he's waiting for a ride. Charlie Roy stops and Curly hops out of the sidecar and they fold Aycock in. Charlie Roy carried those boys away to Ludlow in a weaving motorcycle—too drunk to drive anything better."

"If Charlie Roy Hugg hadn't been kin to Aycock's mother, and hadn't had an old daddy living in Banner, I believe Jack might have come to and tended to him before they got to Ludlow, right from where he's holding on behind him," said Uncle Curtis.

"He may have had the most he could do just keeping Charlie Roy awake. I believe Aycock went to sleep on both of 'em in the sidecar. Twenty-one miles is a heap of distance after the sun goes down," said Uncle Percy, whispering. "And with all the creeks up. And Mrs. Hugg give 'em a room in the jail and no pie at all with their supper."

"That wasn't any kind of a way to treat one of mine," Granny said. "No, it wasn't. Tell 'em I said so. I'm in a hurry for him back."

"We told 'em. Maybe they've already sent him. Maybe he's here in this crowd now, and you just can't see him," teased Aunt Cleo.

"Hush up, Sister Cleo! None of that! Take your nursing tricks away from here!" cried Miss Beulah.

Uncle Noah Webster leaned away out from his chair and caught a baseball flying in from the pasture. Prancing down the steps, he wound up and threw it back into the game. "So the next thing we knew," he cried, coming back, straddling the chair as he sat down again, "there we all was at the trial. Cleo, I wish it had been your privilege to be with us our day in court."

"Even if I'd known it was going on and got a free ride to Ludlow, my first husband wouldn't have let me sit with you all: he was still living," said Aunt Cleo.

"Excuse me," said Uncle Noah Webster.

"Though I love a good trial as well as the next fellow," she said.

"We'd had to squeeze to make room for one more, down front where we was all sitting. Grandpa was holding down one end of our pew, just a little bit more bent over on his cane than before, and Beulah held down the other end, with the rest of us in between. It's a wonder everybody could get there! It wasn't like it was any other time of year. It was spring! The whole world was popping, needing man. Oh, it needed Jack bad! And the wedding and the trial, that made two days in a row. But everybody was there, all but Nathan— he was out of reach. The majority of Banner community was there, right behind us. Harmony had another record attendance, to make Dolphus and Birdie feel real good, and Morning Star to a man was packed in behind Curtis and Beck, and I think Percy and Nanny drew at least their side of Panther Creek. Even a few Ludlow folks was there, with nothing better to do, I reckon, than come to get a peep at a bunch of country monkeys." Uncle Noah Webster smiled at them tenderly.

Uncle Percy downed a gourdful of water and shook his head. "From the opening tune he give on the gavel," he said, "I commenced praying that Judge Moody might drop dead before the trial was over and the whole thing be called off out of respect. Can happen! I never witnessed it myself, but there's such a thing in the memory of Brother Bethune—he's there telling it while Judge Moody's bringing us to order.

" 'You're pleading innocent, I suppose,' says he to Jack.

" 'Yes sir, I'm needed,' says Jack.

"Judge Moody calls, 'Hush that crying! Or I'll send the whole crowd out and order the doors shut. This is a court-room.' That'll give you some idea. 'Call Marshal E. P. Stovall,' he says."

"Who in the world was that?" asked Aunt Cleo.

"That's Curly. His mama named him Excell Prentiss. In he comes, parading that coffin behind him. Mr. Willy Trimble's holding up the foot," said Uncle Curtis.

"Wearing his Sunday harness, sporting a tie," said Aunt Nanny. "Red tie. You could have packed Curly back in that coffin and sent him straight to meet his Maker without a thing more needed."

"And Mr. Willy was saying down the aisle, 'If anybody in Ludlow wants one just like it, you're looking at the artist right now.'

" 'Stand that thing in the corner until it's called for and show some respect for this court!' Judge Moody says to Curly. I don't know why I took heart," said Uncle Percy in a wa-vering voice. "Then they carried in the safe and the Judge wants a good look at that."

"Just as empty as before?" asked Aunt Cleo.

"Not only that, a bird had built a nest in it."

"Oh, we know how to make things dangerous around here!" cried Uncle Noah Webster. "And she was setting!"

" 'Am I going to have to forgo examining that safe in the face of a nesting robin?' That's the Judge," said Uncle Percy.

"Well, it was spring!" Aunt Nanny interrupted. "That's what Curly got for leaving the safe out front with the door wide open to show the passing public what had happened. I'd been surprised if there *wasn't* a nest in that safe, by the time it comes to the trial.

"Jack says, 'Judge Moody, I hate to come in the courthouse and act like I know more than you do, but that's a purple martin.'

" 'What kind of a *safe* is that?' says Judge Moody. 'And I want the best answer I can get from the owner.'

"Curly tells him it's a Montgomery Ward safe with a Sears Roebuck door.

" 'You kept it locked?' says Judge Moody, and Curly says

he didn't have to just exactly lock it if he leaned on it good. 'Can you tell me why you don't keep it locked?' says Moody, and Curly says it's because every time he locks it it costs him another sack of coal to get Mr. Willy Trimble to stop his horses and open it again. And he says when that door is leaned on good, it's stuck so tight nothing will open it but a good rain of blows from his own fist in just the right tender spot on top, and that's where he keeps his lamps setting."

"To me, that safe looked as poor an excuse for something to make a big fuss over as anything you could hope to see at a trial," Uncle Curtis said.

"Oh, the safe was on show, the coffin was on show, everything was on show but the ring! The only thing in the world that would have told the true story and spoken for itself!" screamed Miss Beulah. "That's missing!"

"That safe was the evidence, Beulah," said Uncle Noah Webster. "And was that little rooster martin loud!"

"Hen never budged, either," Uncle Percy whispered. "Not for something as unparticular as a wagon-ride to Ludlow and a courthouse trial and the same ride home again. She set right through it all."

"Don't you know she got hungry?" cried Aunt Nanny.

"She hatched 'em, too, later on," said Aunt Birdie. "It was Ora's cat that finally made a meal of 'em."

"Well, they couldn't blame Jack for that!" Aunt Beck said. "He was too far from us all to save baby birds by that time!"

"It's money they worry about in town," said Uncle Curtis.

"Curly had 'em sized up! He give a song and dance about how poor he stayed, never getting paid like he ought by the poor farmers, then to lose his safe, only to get it back full of chinaberries. I'm surprised he didn't show 'em the chinaberries," Uncle Percy said. "But finally he's through and it's Jack's turn." Uncle Percy lifted his hand for quiet and went into falsetto. " 'I'm going to question this boy myself,' Judge Moody says, and bangs till the family's all in their seats and the dogs from Banner gives up on their barking. Then says to Jack, 'All right, you heard the charge. Now did you do all that to Marshal Stovall?'

" 'Yes sir, and a little bit more.'

" 'Well, what did you do it for?'

"Jack says, 'Well, it's because he's aggravating.'

"Judge Moody cracks down with the gavel. 'No clapping and stamping in the courtroom while I'm on the bench!' he calls to the congregation. 'Try and remember you all are in Ludlow, and in this room on sufferance,' he says, and asks Jack, 'What's "aggravating" mean in your book? Give me one example,' he says.

" 'He'd just have to show you himself,' says Jack."

"Well, Jack's a bashful boy," said Aunt Birdie loyally.

"Sure-enough?"

"You'd been bashful too, Sister Cleo," said Aunt Beck, "if you'd been a boy no more than eighteen years old and just got married the night before by Grandpa Vaughn to your schoolteacher, and woke up in jail in Ludlow to be tried by a hard-to-please stranger sitting over you and in front of all your aching family and a pretty good helping of the public. And if you was the only one of 'em standing up."

"What's the trouble, couldn't Jack put up a good story?" Aunt Cleo asked. "That's what he's up there for."

"He's twenty-one country-miles from home!" Uncle Noah Webster cried.

Miss Beulah came out drying her hands on her apron. "And we knew full well he wasn't going to stand up in front of the public and tell 'em any of our business. Wasn't going to call his sister's name, even! Though she did keep standing up and setting down and standing up again, waving at him, like she's trying to tell him go ahead."

"Felt cheated, didn't she?" grinned Aunt Nanny.

"Just hungering to get up there herself and cry for a crowd of strangers!" Miss Beulah marched off again.

"Vaughn felt mighty put-upon too. Jack had told us the best place for Vaughn Renfro was setting on the steps outside and holding the dogs. Vaughn was there, boo-hooing," Aunt Nanny said with a grin.

"Judge Moody says, 'Hush that crying! Why aren't these children in school?' Then he asks Jack how many times along the way did he drop that safe, and Jack says he hadn't kept count. 'I just dropped it to mop my neck, like you're mopping yours now, sir,' he says. 'I reckon it's even hotter in Ludlow than it is in Banner.' "

"Of course it was! I could see it rolling off of both of 'em," said Aunt Birdie.

"And I was sweating right along with 'em! Pouring! Oh, I wouldn't live in a paved town for all you'd give me!" cried Aunt Nanny.

"And the flies!" Aunt Birdie said.

"Judge Moody says to Jack, 'The storekeeper aggravated you, so you carried off his safe. Was it your idea to rob him?' 'No sir,' Jack says, 'just to aggravate him.' 'Yet all that was in the safe managed to get out, vanish, disappear, melt away, never to be found,' says the Judge."

"Ain't Percy grand? He gets 'em all down pat," said Aunt Birdie. "I wish I was married to him," she told Uncle Dolphus. "He'd keep me entertained."

"Oh, I wish you could have been there, Cleo!" Uncle Noah Webster cried again into her face.

"I'd been sitting with Mr. Stovall and pulling for the other side," she reminded him.

" 'The picture I get's a familiar one,' the Judge says. Sounds not far from mournful about it, though. 'You folks around Banner trade at Stovall's store, vote him into office, and raise the roof when you feel like it.' " Uncle Noah Webster smiled.

"And keep coming back some few miles to do it," added Uncle Percy. "Though the Saturdays now is few and far between."

"And if you *don't* give Curly your vote, what happens to your store credit? I don't know what could be easier to understand," said Uncle Dolphus.

" 'Baiting the storekeeper and thumbing your nose at the peace officer,' Moody says. 'Blessed with Excell Stovall, Banner is able to accomplish both at the same time.' "

"Moody didn't know any of that for sure—how could he?" said Uncle Dolphus. "He just makes a living off of guessing. Gets paid for it. Bound to be lucky some time."

"And then it all comes out—what Moody's up to," quavered Uncle Percy.

Miss Beulah in her kitchen yelled, "I'll tell you! He made a monkey out of Jack."

"That's right, Beulah. I can hear his voice right now." Uncle Percy prettily piped: " 'How long will it take people to start showing some respect for those they have raised to office?' "

"Whoa, I don't know as I go along with that," cried little Aunt Birdie.

"Look first!" cried Aunt Nanny. "And see if it's Curly Stovall!"

"*Or* Judge Moody!" they joined in.

"Judge was bound to miss the gist, and he's missed it now," said Uncle Curtis.

"That Judge Moody's whole battle cry was *respect.* I don't believe any of that courtroom was too well pleased. They wasn't prepared for anything they hadn't come to hear," whispered Uncle Percy.

"Why, I saw *Curly* baffled!" Uncle Noah Webster cried, and let out a laugh that sounded like reckless admiration.

" 'You-all go right ahead taking things in your own hands. Well,' says Moody, 'I'm here today to tell you it's got to stop.' He says, 'You can't *go* knocking the law down if it gets in your way, you can't keep *on* packing up the law in the nearest crate big enough to hold it'—nods at the coffin—'and go skipping out the store with a safe, so-called'—nods at the mother-bird—'and all without offering this court any better reason than "He's aggravating." Aggravating!'

" 'Judge, I reckon to do justice to Curly, you got to see him in Banner,' says Jack. 'The best place is his own store, and the best time is Saturday.'

" 'I'm doing the justice around here,' says Moody. 'When I need outside help, I'll ask for it. What if he is aggravating!'

" 'I'd like you to see him try cutting off your shirt-tail and nailing it to the beam before you make up your mind, sir,' says Jack, still polite about it. He just gets the gavel."

"But didn't you-all have a lawyer furnished to pull a better story out of Jack?" asked Aunt Cleo. "You can get those free."

"If that's what you want to call the fellow," said Uncle Curtis. "He was not there on my invitation, and I think I speak for the family. He got as much in the way as he knew how, I imagine. A good deal of what he said was drowned out. Never caught even his first name, doubt if I'd know him again if I was to see him coming."

"Well, when Moody finally pounds 'em quiet, he leans out over Jack," said Uncle Percy, "and says, 'Tell me one last thing: would you do it again?' "

"Why, Jack's as dependable as the day is long!" Aunt Birdie cried out.

"And Jack gives a great big smile to Gloria and says, 'Well, sir, I'm a married man from now on. And I reckon my wife would have to pass a law about that.'

"Bang bang and thump thump thump, says the gavel. Judge Moody tells Jack, 'Come on back here. Don't you realize the jury hasn't been charged and brought in a verdict and I haven't passed sentence yet?' Jack had been about to sit down with his family. 'I'm about to make a living example out of you, young man!' And there's a groan you could hear from one end of the State of Mississippi to the other, I bet—it's this family. 'You're going to be a lesson to the rest,' says Judge Moody, and gives the jury a strict piece of his mind too, like they's no better than the rest of us poor humans, and sent 'em out. They turned right around and came back, while Jack's still puzzling over it."

"How'd you-all like the verdict?" asked Aunt Cleo.

"Of guilty?" everybody cried, while Uncle Noah Webster sank back in the seat of his chair and opened both arms to them all, as if to bring in the word once more.

"And what of?" he begged them.

"Aggravated battery!"

"—whatever that is!" called Miss Beulah in the suddenly gay, sharp voice of the cook whose pan is ready to come out of the oven no matter what happens, and she ran feverishly onto the porch with a pan of hot gingerbread clutched in the folds of her apron.

"And robbery," said Elvie solemnly, coming behind her mother to serve the buttermilk.

At Granny's chair first, they found her with head bowed in sleep, and tiptoed past her.

"Aggravated battery and robbery, I bet you fainted," said Aunt Cleo in congratulatory tones, biting into a hot square.

"Jack all but did!" cried Aunt Birdie.

"Pole-axed is a little more like it," Aunt Nanny said, cradling a thick brown square in both hands before the big bite.

"What surprised us was the courthouse didn't fall down."
Uncle Curtis reached for his portion. "When the judge says,
'Two years in the state pen, time off for good behavior.'"

"Then Grandpa Vaughn put his head right down on his
cane in front of him," said Uncle Percy, his wary eye on
Granny.

"We did our share of helping out his groans!" cried Aunt
Nanny. "Homer Champion didn't do so bad himself. He was
ever'where at once, begging 'em all for their sympathy."

"Vaughn come in with the dogs in time to hear Moody say
the pen. And I saw Vaughn—he bit himself. Just turned away
from Jack and took a big plug out of his arm," said Aunt
Birdie.

"Bet Curly kicked up his heels," Aunt Cleo said. "Wasn't
he well pleased?"

"In hog heaven. Invited everybody there but us to a fish-
fry the next Sunday, told Judge Moody to come too and bring
his wife if he had one. He didn't come and didn't send any
wife either," said Uncle Noah Webster.

"Good. I'd hate the rankest stranger to get their notion of
Banner hospitality from Curly's fish-fry. Stovalls fry their fish
with the hides on," grinned Aunt Nanny.

Miss Beulah cried, "The rest was all in Damascus that Sunday listening to Grandpa heal our hearts by telling us of
Heaven to come. We could smell Curly's smoke the whole
sermon long. He'd dance on your grave." She whirled fiercely
with the hot pan. "If I'd known what that Judge was fixing
to do to Jack, I'd stood up in the courtroom right quick and
told him a thing or two to his face he'd still remember! After
all, I'm the boy's mother!"

"Beulah, I bet you could have!" They helped themselves in
quick turn as she passed them the pan.

"For two cents I'd a-done it, too!"

"The way you know how to let fly, Beulah, if I'd been
Judge Moody you'd have silenced *me*," said Aunt Birdie.

"Oh, I'd silenced him," said Miss Beulah, and she ran out
and ran back with her second panful. "I'd silenced him, all
right. Let 'im try it again, he'll never ruin my boy but once."

"My eyes see a sunbonnet coming this way," said Etoyle,
chewing.

"Little Mis' Comfort, coming all this way up?" asked Aunt Nanny.

"It'll just be to peep at us," said Miss Beulah. "She'll just come far enough up our road to count us. She'll turn around in a minute and trail home." She laughed. "She said she's having a hen and cooking a mess of collards for Aycock, and I bet not a bit of that's so."

"You think Aycock's coming home too?" Miss Lexie asked.

"Jack's coat-tails is where he lives. He couldn't stay anywhere by himself," she said.

"Why isn't she home, then, and preparing?" cried Aunt Birdie.

"I doubt you she's even set bread," said Miss Beulah.

"Hasn't she called on kin to come be with her when he walks in?" asked Aunt Beck. "Help hold her up?"

"Besides Mr. Earl Comfort, and nobody wants Earl, there's just Mr. Comfort *to* call, and he's been gone."

"Mr. Comfort and little Mis' Comfort, they didn't gee," said Miss Lexie comfortably.

"Does this mean Aycock went to the pen with Jack?" Aunt Cleo asked.

"How'd you get so behind! Yes'm, at least Jack had Aycock with him, to keep him from being so altogether homesick. We slept better at night for that," said Aunt Beck.

"How come Aycock had to pay the penalty like Jack?" Aunt Cleo asked. "What had *he* lost?"

"Because when Aycock had his turn in court, he stood up and said he's going too! 'And how are you going to qualify yourself for the pen?' says Moody. Aycock says he'd been in the store from the beginning, propped up behind the pickle barrel. He'd set still and let goods go flying over his head if they wanted to, let Jack have the gun pulled on him and Curly be boxed and tied, must have seen the safe get carted off, heard out all Curly's racket. And hadn't done a thing but enjoy himself and put away pickles." Uncle Noah Webster slapped Aunt Cleo's leg. "But the Judge comes down on his gavel and says, 'Well, I see no reason why I can't make a lesson of you too.' Verdict was guilty as charged."

"Goodness, that was over in a hurry," Aunt Cleo said.

"Aycock goes to the pen as big as Jack. Whether he'll come

home as big is another question. The Comforts don't know what the word reunion means," said Uncle Curtis.

"Never did I have any use for those Comforts at all, they're the nearest to nothing that ever did come around here. I'm sorry we have 'em. Even the mother is a failure," said Miss Beulah.

"She's gone now," said Etoyle.

"She hadn't the least idea how to put a face on it!" said Miss Beulah.

"And there *you* was, high and dry! Wouldn't we all have hated to be in your shoes!" Aunt Birdie cried to Gloria.

"Had you finished your good-byes?" asked Aunt Beck sadly.

"No ma'am," Gloria said. "But we got our promises made. We're going to live for the future."

"Bet that made you cry!" said Aunt Nanny.

"She hasn't cried yet!" said Miss Beulah. "Not a single time when I was looking at her!"

Gloria closed her eyes. Everybody watched her cheeks. They were as speckled as sweet warm pears, but just as tearless.

"You was crying inside," Aunt Beck told her.

"Didn't you have anybody with good shoulders to cry on? Where's *your* family?" asked Aunt Cleo.

"Sister Cleo, you're asking that to the only orphan for a mile around," said Aunt Birdie. "We'll have to forgive you for your question this time."

"Who was your mama and papa?" asked Aunt Cleo.

"Nobody knows," said Gloria.

"Did they burn up, fall in, or what?"

"Nobody knows," said Gloria.

"Gloria's a little nobody from out of nowhere," said Aunt Beck fondly.

"She's from the Ludlow Presbyterian Orphan Asylum, if you want to hear it exactly," said Miss Beulah. "And how she turns all that around into something to be conceited about is a little bit more than I can tell you."

"Found on a doorstep?" cried Aunt Cleo.

"A little better than that. You may hear about it one day," said Aunt Beck soothingly. "For right now, her new husband's just been dragged away from her. And she still hasn't cried."

"What about the one that was trying to make a teacher out of you before it happened?" Aunt Cleo asked Gloria. "You could have cried on her. She'd have been the very one to offer."

"I never went back to see Miss Julia Mortimer and give her the chance."

"Well, excuse me! No wonder you're sitting up on that powder keg in your wedding dress today!" cried Aunt Cleo.

"I don't know today who I relish blaming the most—Judge Moody or old Curly Stovall," said Aunt Birdie.

"Moody!" Miss Beulah cried. "Moody! For the name he laid on my son. I just hope Jack's feelings get over it before mine do."

"I'll be glad to say Moody," said Aunt Beck.

"And there Jack went, trusting him!" yelled Miss Beulah. "The poor fool, I reckon he thought he was safe because he's needed. I learned my lesson then!"

Aunt Nanny said, "But it was Curly that took that ring like it was even change. I more than blame him, I look down on him. And more than that, I'm not going to vote for him Tuesday."

"Curly'd do the same thing over again, it's the only way he knows to behave at all," said Aunt Birdie. "Blame him and he don't care! Your votes is all he cares about. I swear he's too mean to live."

"And it's not like Curly would have left a wife, had somebody hauled in the store and *killed* him. He's too mean to marry! That's what I told his own preacher, Brother Dollarhide, that was taking up half my seat at the trial," said Aunt Nanny.

"Old Curly was baptized a Methodist to boot, if you can picture him being just a month old," said Uncle Percy. "A big bawler."

"While I put Judge Moody down as a Presbyterian. For one good reason. The whole way through that trial, his mouth was one straight line. He didn't look out on that crowded courtroom and smile once. Not one time." Uncle Noah Webster laid a crumb-stuck hand on his wife's leg.

"And if he never lets me see his Moody face again for the

rest of his life," Miss Beulah shouted, as if she were still the length of the passage away from them, "that'd be the first kind thing I could find to thank him for."

"He's through with us now, Mother," said Mr. Renfro.

"Of course that judge never got it through his head what it was all about!" yelled Miss Beulah. "Born and bred in Ludlow, most likely in the very shadow of the courthouse! A man never spent a day of his life in Banner, never heard of a one of us!"

"I don't think there's a heap you can say on behalf of that *jury*," said Uncle Curtis. "I wonder where they ever resurrected a bunch like that."

"All right, if I had that jury back together before me, I wouldn't mind taking a minute to skin 'em alive right now for my own satisfaction," said Miss Beulah, passing her pan again fast. "All twelve of 'em quick just for doing what Moody told 'em."

"Now and then I have to feel provoked with even Ella Fay for letting people suppose she'd trade treasure for a little bit of store candy—a precious gold band, the only one like it in Christendom!" Aunt Beck said, tears rising to her eyes.

"How long had she had it?" Aunt Cleo asked.

"A day."

"Granny kept it in the Bible knotted to a good stout string," said Miss Beulah, addressing her words to the chair where the sleeping old lady was cradled. "I thought all we had to guard it against was children swallowing it."

"All of 'em striving as one, they succeeded. That's how I look at it," said Aunt Birdie. "They locked up the sweetest and hardest-working boy in Banner and Boone County and maybe in all Creation."

"But he never got a whipping at home, I reckon, for all the trouble he caused you?" asked Aunt Cleo.

"We whipped Ella Fay," said Miss Beulah.

"Hey, Ella Fay, did you cry, darlin'?" Aunt Birdie called.

"You could've heard me clear down to the store," Ella Fay called from inside the house.

"Good."

"But I'd stick that ring in his face again if I had it back right now," she called sweetly.

"How many more chances do you suppose you've got coming to you?" called her mother sharply.

"Well, a lot grew out of one little ring, didn't it?" remarked Aunt Cleo.

"Even Sister Cleo sees that! And I'll tell you once more that's exactly what old Judge Moody lost sight of!" cried Miss Beulah. "The ring itself!"

"Not having it there in front of his eyes to remind him," said Aunt Beck sympathetically.

"Yes'm, it would've been a little mite different for Jack and us all today if he'd contented himself with spilling open that safe there in the store, and fishing out the ring, and carrying the ring home in his shirt pocket, and delivering it back to Granny. But he's a man! Done it the man's way," said Aunt Nanny.

"He did his best," Miss Beulah cried. "And it was a heap more trouble! For everybody!"

Mr. Renfro ran his eye over the parade of melons he had lined up there on the porch, then passing along them spanked each one. They resounded like horses ready to go.

"Oh, I've brought mine up on praise!" cried Miss Beulah, glaring after him.

"You get the credit, Beulah!" Aunt Birdie cried. "You get the credit for the wonderful children they are!"

"And I'll keep it up to my dying day!" she shrieked in their faces. "Praise! With now and then a little switching to even it up."

"It's the girls that gets the switchings," Elvie said, and bolted.

Aunt Nanny grinned and said, "And all this time, that ring may be laying down yonder in the Banner road in front of Stovall's store, looking no more'n a little bit of tin, a piece of grit! Bet it is right now! But you've all walked on it a hundred times! And if it had teeth it'd bite you."

"I tell you lost's lost," said Miss Beulah, and passed the pan with the last piece of gingerbread in it, which Miss Lexie didn't mind taking. "And my son in the pen for the trouble he took to save it."

"So here's all these little sisters and a little brother, with a cripple daddy and with uncles that's had to scatter, and

Grandpa and Granny Vaughn and their broken hearts, and Beulah that's beside herself for a spell, all doing without Jack. And after Jack had stayed out of school himself to give the little ones their chance, they had to pass up their own schooling half the time, smart as they was—" Uncle Percy was trying to get the story back from them.

"Well, Vaughn did Jack's work and some of mine, and I did his, and the girls they scrubbed and hauled and fetched and carried, and did every bit of their own part, and that was the system we used," said Miss Beulah.

"And Vaughn trying to trot even for little Mis' Comfort when his mother told him," said Aunt Birdie.

"I couldn't let her accept charity!" cried Miss Beulah.

"She did it anyway, behind your back," said Aunt Beck. "Our preacher carried her with him to the courthouse and they came back with a big box of commodities."

"Pity *her*!" came cries.

"Our preacher says further there wasn't anything worse served him in the United States Army than what he got at Boone County Courthouse last December."

"And here was the baby put in *her* appearance. Lady May Renfro, bless her little heart, she come as soon as she could," Aunt Beck said.

Lady May's neck, like the stem of a new tulip, held poised its perfect little globe. She had heard her name. Throwing her arms wide, she jumped from her mother's knee to the floor.

"Look how that baby can already fly!" said Miss Lexie in a voice of present warning, as Lady May ran about the porch sounding off louder than before.

"I'm going to catch you and run off with you, Britches!" Aunt Nanny called after her flying heels. "Who you hunting?"

"Pore little Lady May's running in her petticoat and it reaches to the calf of her leg," said Aunt Cleo. "Who made that!"

It had been made like a doll dress from a folded sugar sack, round holes cut for neck and arms, then stitched down the sides. A little flounce edged the bottom, a mother's touch.

"It allowed for her to grow like she's been growing—fast as a beanstalk," said Miss Beulah. "Do you raise any objection to that?"

"No'm," she said. "That's nature, you got to accept it."

"Well, *we've* been feeling mighty sorry for her!" Miss Beulah retorted.

The baby scrambled down the steps and out into the yard. In her shoes coated white with cornstarch, their high heels tipping her a little forward, Gloria went after her. She walked fast but didn't quite run, the way a thrush skims over the ground without needing to use wings.

"Don't fall down! Don't rake your dress on the rosebush! You've got to both be ready for Jack, got to look pretty for him!" came Etoyle's cry.

The baby ran behind the quilt again and Gloria caught her on the other side. But she was already sliding, slick as a fish, from her arms and running ahead of her mother again.

Aunt Nanny headed off Lady May, and breathing hard she crouched and scooped up the baby in her arms. "I've come to steal you!" But Lady May squirmed free and charged up and down a little path that kept opening between their knees, over their patting feet.

"Well, in case anybody forgets how long Jack Renfro's been gone, feel the weight of *that*," said Miss Lexie, and stopping the baby with a broom, she caught her and loaded her onto Granny Vaughn's lap.

Even before her eyes opened, Granny had put both arms out. Lady May, the soles of her feet wrinkling like the old lady's forehead, went to the weakest and most tenacious embrace she knew. They hugged long enough to remind each other that perhaps they were rivals.

"And what's Jack know about his baby?" asked Aunt Cleo.

"Not a thing in this world. She's his surprise!" cried Aunt Birdie. "What else would she be?"

"Yes sir! I've already started to wondering when she's going to talk and what she's fixing to say," Miss Lexie said.

Lady May made a dart from Granny to Gloria, and Gloria took her up on her lap and began to make her a hat from the nearest plant stand within reach. She pinched off geranium leaves, lapping them over the child's head, fastening them with the thornless stems from the pepper plant and the potted fairy rose that she bit to the right length. Some little girls drew near in a ring to watch, their hair falling beside their cheeks in pale stems, paler across the scissors' slice, like fresh-cut lily stalks. Now Lady May had a hat.

"But where's she going, where's she going so soon?" Uncle Noah Webster teased Gloria.

"That's for the future to say," she replied.

Aunt Birdie said staunchly, "Well, a son can do something that's a whole heap harder to bear than what Jack did."

"That's right, he could've kilt somebody," said Aunt Cleo. "And been sentenced to die in the portable electric chair— they'd bring it right to your courthouse. And you-all *could* be having his funeral today, with a sealed coffin."

They cried out at her.

Aunt Beck said in shocked tones, "Now I'm not *blaming* the boy!"

"Find fault with Jack? I'd hate to see the first one try it," said Aunt Nanny.

"I'd hate to see anybody in the wide world try it!" Aunt Birdie cried.

"It'd be the easiest way to kill him," said Miss Beulah.

"If ever a man was sure of anything at all, I was sure I had to give this house a new tin top to shine in Jack's face the day he gets home," said Mr. Renfro. "That roof speaks just a world, speaks volumes."

"Mr. Renfro give up just about all we had left for that tin top over our heads," said Miss Beulah. "He had to show the reunion single-handed the world don't have to go flying to pieces when the oldest son gives trouble."

"You hammer that tin on by yourself?" protested Aunt Beck. "Since he wasn't even here to help you? Cousin Ralph, I'm more than half surprised you didn't crack at least your collarbone for today."

"He had so-called help. And I'll tell you what I got tired of was Mr. Willy Trimble scurrying and frisking around like a self-appointed squirrel up over my head," said Miss Beulah. "He was neighborly to offer, but he's taken liberties ever since. It's still our roof!"

"Paid for with what?" the new Aunt Cleo asked in complimentary tones.

"Take comfort. Our farm ain't holding together a great deal better than yours, Mr. Renfro," said Uncle Curtis.

"Maybe me and Beck did raise a house full of sons, and maybe not a one of 'em had to go to Parchman, but they left home just the same. Married, and moved over to look after their wives' folks. Scattered."

"Why, of course they did," said Aunt Beck softly.

"But all nine!" said Uncle Curtis. "All nine! And they're never coming home."

"I'm thankful they can still get back all together at the old reunion," said Uncle Percy, looking over at the ball game in the pasture. "Who are they playing—their wives?" But as he stood looking, he exclaimed in his faint voice, "Look where the turkey's walking."

The Thanksgiving turkey, resembling something made on the farm out of stovepipe and wound up to go, walking anywhere he pleased with three months yet to stay alive, paraded into a grease-darkened, grassless patch of yard with a trench worn down in the clay, an oblong space staked out by the stumps of four pine trees.

"I *thought* there's something about the place that's unnatural!" said Uncle Noah Webster. "Beulah!" he hollered. "Where's Jack's truck, Jack's precious truck? It ain't picked up and gone to meet him, has it?"

"One guess."

"Oh, the skunk!" the uncles shouted, all rising.

"Now you Beechams might as well sit down. It was nothing but a dirty piece of machinery," Miss Beulah said.

"Curly didn't even let Jack get home first to make it go," said Uncle Noah Webster.

"Jack was so purely besotted *with* it, I'd been more greatly surprised to learn something hadn't happened *to* it," Uncle Dolphus said.

"But a truck? How did Jack ever get hold of such a scarcity to start with?" asked Aunt Cleo. "You-all don't look like you was ever that well-fixed."

"It fell in his lap, pretty near. Jack's just that kind of a boy, Sister Cleo," said Aunt Beck.

"The last time I seen it enthroned in your yard, Beulah, it was still asking for some little attention," said Uncle Curtis. "I don't guess it improved a great deal with the boy away."

"I hadn't let the children touch it!" she declared. She put

up her hand. "And listen, everybody, don't let on to Jack
about his filthy truck—not today. Don't prattle! Owing to the
crowd, he might not see it's gone any quicker'n you did.
Don't tell him, children!" she called widely. "Spare him that
till tomorrow."

"Just lay the four stumps with some planks, like it's one
more table. And Ella Fay can have it covered up with a cloth.
That wouldn't be a hard trick at all," said Aunt Nanny. "I'll
eat at it!"

"And there's another thing that's gone he'll come to find
out," said Uncle Curtis. "That's the Boone County Courthouse. It burned to the ground, they don't like to think how."

"How many here got to see it?" asked Aunt Cleo.

Aunt Nanny said, "Me and Percy got invited to ride over
with our neighbors and wait for the roof to fall in. And guess
who come in sight with the fellows bringing things out, the
water cooler and such as that. My own daddy! I hadn't seen
him in five years, and then he was too busy to wave back. He
was rescuing the postcard rack with all those postcards of the
courthouse."

"It burned right at commodity time," said Uncle Percy.

"And whenever I think of it going up in smoke, I think of
all that sugar!" said Aunt Nanny.

"Never mind. With the welcome he's got waiting, he won't
ever start to count what's gone," said Aunt Beck.

"If he tries, then that roof ought to be enough to blind
him," said Aunt Birdie, "the sweet trusting boy. It blinded
me."

"And then when he sits, Brother Bethune will forgive him
here at the table for his sins," said Aunt Beck. "I just hope
he won't disappoint everybody. I know he's got your church
now, all you Baptists—"

"Beck, if you can't forget you're the only Methodist for a
mile around, how do you expect the rest of us to forget it?"
said Miss Beulah. "It don't take a Methodist to see Brother
Bethune as a comedown after Grandpa. Who wouldn't be?"

"There must be a dozen other Baptist preachers running
loose around the Bywy Hills with their tongues hanging out
for pulpits," argued Aunt Beck.

"There's a right good many who'd be tickled to steal Damascus away from him this very day," Miss Beulah granted her. "Brother Yielding of Foxtown would dearly love to add it to his string. But Brother Bethune is the one who grew up in Banner, and you've got to put up with him or explain to him that there's something the matter with him, one. So he can't be touched."

"I just feel at a time like this he won't be a match for us," Aunt Beck said with a sigh.

"Yes, it's Grandpa we need, and Grandpa's in the cemetery. It was a year ago tonight we lost him," said Uncle Curtis.

"Well, but if you had one to die, Jack could have got a pass home," said Aunt Cleo. "Ain't that good old Mississippi law? They'd let him come to the funeral between two guards, then be led back. Handcuffed."

They cried out again. Only Granny was peaceful, head low.

"Sister Cleo, we didn't tell him about Grandpa. Jack's got that to learn today, it's part of his coming home," said Miss Beulah. "It's what's going to hurt him the most, but I can only hope it'll help him grow up a little."

"He's already a father," said Uncle Dolphus.

"He don't know that either," said Aunt Nanny.

"That's right. We'll bring out that little surprise just when he needs it most, won't we?" Aunt Birdie cried.

"She's my surprise to bring," Gloria said.

"Well, ain't *you* about ready to cry a little bit about everything, while you still got time?" Aunt Cleo asked, pointing to Gloria.

Gloria shook her head and set her teeth.

"What we say here at home is," said Miss Beulah, "Gloria's got a sweet voice when she deigns to use it, she's so spotless the sight of her hurts your eyes, she's so neat that once you've hidden her Bible, stolen her baby, put away her curl papers, and wished her writing tablet out of sight, you wouldn't find a trace of her in the company room, and she *can* be pretty. But you can't read her."

"She can roll up her hair in the dark," said Elvie devotedly.

"*There's* a sweet juicy mouthful singing!" Aunt Nanny told Lady May, when just then the mourning dove called. "It won't be long before the boy gets home who'll treat you to a morsel of that."

"I wouldn't let her have it," said Gloria. "She's a long way off from eating tough old bird."

"Listen! But I've seen 'em when their mothers' backs was turned, and they'd be sitting up eating corn on the cob!" cried Aunt Cleo.

"Stop, Sister Cleo. Gloria don't want to tell her business," Aunt Beck gently warned.

"Well, ain't you a little monkey!" Aunt Cleo laughed at Gloria, but nobody laughed with her.

Mr. Renfro counted them and then one by one he took the torpedo-shaped watermelons and loaded them carefully back into the cool cave underneath the porch.

Aunt Birdie suddenly asked, "Where *is* Parchman?"

"A fine time to be asking," said Uncle Dolphus.

Uncle Curtis said, "Well, only our brother Nathan's ever seen for himself where it is, I believe I've heard him say."

Vaughn, at the water bucket, pointed straight through them. "Go clean across Mississippi from here, go till you get ready to fall in the Mississippi River."

"Is he in *Arkansas?*" cried a boy cousin, raising a baseball bat. "If he is I'm going over there and git him out."

"Arkansas would be the crowning blow!" Miss Beulah cried. "No, my boy may be in Parchman, but he still hasn't been dragged across the state line."

"Jack's in the Delta," said Uncle Curtis. "Clear out of the hills and into the good land."

They smiled. "That Jack!"

"Where it's running with riches and swarming with niggers everywhere you look," said Uncle Curtis. "Yes, Nathan in his travels has spied out the top of its water tower. It's there, all right."

"The spring after Jack went, General Green about took over your corn, remember?" Uncle Dolphus said to Mr. Renfro, who at last came hobbling up the steps and bowing into their company. "And today, your whole farm wouldn't hardly give a weed comfort and sustenance."

Uncle Noah Webster clapped Mr. Renfro on the back and cried in the tones of a compliment, "Looks like ever' time we had a rain, you didn't!"

"And the next thing, everything's going to dry up or burn

up or blow up, one, without that boy. Is that your verdict, Mr. Renfro?"

"While Jack's been sitting over there right spang in the heart of the Delta. And whatever he sticks in the ground, the Delta just grows it for him," whispered Uncle Percy.

"I'm sorry I even asked where it was," said Aunt Birdie. "I wonder now how early a start he made, if he's got all that distance to cover."

"He better start hurrying," Uncle Dolphus said. "Busted out of jail in Foxtown in less than twenty-four hours—I see little reason why he can't make it back from Parchman in a year and a half."

"Hush!" cried Miss Beulah.

"You can't get out of Parchman with a pie knife," cried Uncle Noah Webster.

"Men, hush!" ordered Miss Beulah. "He's coming just as fast as he can. He ain't going to let it be the end of the world today—he'll be right here to the table."

"And a good thing Jack knows it. Because the truth of the matter is," Aunt Beck murmured, gazing at the old lady in her rocker, "if we had to wait another year, who knows if Granny would've made it?"

There came a sound like a pistol shot from out in the yard. All heads turned front. Ella Fay had cracked the first starched tablecloth out of its folds—it waved like a flag. Then she dropped it on the ground and came running toward them, screaming. Dogs little and big set up a tenor barking. Dogs ran from all corners of the yard and from around the house and through the passage, streaking for the front gate.

Aunt Nanny grabbed the baby from Gloria's knees and ran to hide her in the company room, screaming as if she herself had nearly been caught in her nightgown. Miss Beulah raced to Granny's side. The barking reached frantic pitch as a whirlwind of dust filled the space between the chinaberry trees. As even those chatterers on the back porch and those filling the house started up through the passage, the floor drummed and swayed, a pan dropped from its nail in the kitchen wall, and overhead even the tin of the roof seemed to quiver with a sound like all the family spoons set to jingling in their glass.

Riding a wave of dogs, a nineteen-year-old boy leaped the

steps to a halt on the front gallery. He crashed his hands together, then swung his arms wide.

"Jack Jordan Renfro," announced Miss Lexie to the company. "Well: you brought him."

He might never have been under a roof from the day he
left home until this minute. His open, blunt-featured face in
its morning beard had burned to a red even deeper than the
home clay. He was breathing hard, his chest going up and
down fast, his mouth was open, and he was pouring sweat.
With his eyes flared wide, his face smileless as a child's, he
stood and waited, with his arms open like gates.

Then it seemed that the whole reunion at once was trying
to run in.

"Why ain't you nearly perished?" Miss Beulah shrieked as
she shouldered her way through the rest and smacked his face
with kisses.

"What did you bring me?" yelled Etoyle.

"What did you bring me?" yelled Elvie. They both beat
their fists against him. Elvie beat on his legs, crying with joy,
then found a cockleburr to pull off his pants, and Etoyle with
a scream of triumph pinched a live June bug that was riding
his sleeve—the torn sleeve that flowed free from his shoulder
like some old flag carried home from far-off battle.

"Where's mine?" teased the boy cousins. "Where's mine,
Jack?"

Ella Fay ended her shrieks at last and ran to get her hug.
Then Vaughn came across the floor in long strides, his heavily
starched pants weighted down by the deep folds at the bottom. He had put on his print-sack school shirt, new and read-
able front and back, from which the points of his collar were
damply rising. Jack lunged forward looking ready to kiss him,
but Vaughn said, "I've got on your pants." He had with him
a pair of dried cornstalks, and offered them. Jack took one
and for a moment the brothers jousted with them, shaking
them like giant rattles, banging them about like papery clubs.

"Was you a trusty?" Vaughn asked, then fled.

"And oh but he's home tired, limping and sore after all his
long hot way!" screamed Aunt Birdie, pulling down Jack's

head to kiss his cheeks and chin, while Aunt Nanny bear-hugged him from behind.

"Honey, you don't know yet how hard we've been waiting on you," said Aunt Beck, with great care ripping a briar away from his pants leg. "I wish you did."

"Never wrote your family once—I got that out of your daddy," Miss Lexie was sweeping up the cakes of clay and strings of briars his shoes had tracked in. "Might as well be coming back from the dead."

"Don't he get here fat and fine, though?" Aunt Nanny still squeezed him around the ribs. "Believe you put a little meat on your bones while you was away!"

"But I venture to say they never did succeed in feeding you like we're fixing to feed you today," said Aunt Birdie, pulling him loose.

"Well, did you bring us a rain?" Uncle Noah Webster was shouting at him as though from a rooftop.

The uncles plunged forward to pull on him and pound him, while Etoyle and Elvie sat on the floor and each anchored one of his feet.

"Where's Gloria? Gloria, Glo-ri-a! Here's him! You forgotten how to act glad? Girl, can't you find him, can't you fight your way through us?" It was the aunts screaming at her, while the uncles said to the aunts, "Hold back, then."

They divided and there stood Gloria. Her hair came down in a big puff as far as her shoulders, where it broke into curls all of which would move when she did, smelling of Fairy soap. Across her forehead it hung in fine hooks, cinnamon-colored, like the stamens in a Dainty Bess rose. As though small bells had been hung, without her permission, on her shoulders, hips, breasts, even elbows, tinkling only just out of ears' range, she stepped the length of the porch to meet him.

"Look at that walk. *Now* I'd know her for a teacher anywhere," said Aunt Cleo.

Jack cocked his hands in front of his narrow-set hips as she came. Their young necks stretched, their lips tilted up, like a pair of rabbits yearning toward the same head of grass, and Jack snapped his vise around her waist with thumbs met.

"First kiss of their lives in public, I bet a hundred dollars," Aunt Cleo observed.

"Speak, Jack, speak!" shrieked his mother.

"Speak, Jack!" they were crying at him. "You ain't gone deaf and dumb, have you?"

"A new roof! I could see it a mile coming!" His lilting voice came at last. "What's happened?"

"Bless his heart!" Miss Beulah thankfully cried.

"Well, I believe it's one thing that may be on tight, son," said Mr. Renfro. He still stood back, with his arms hugged together in front and the prong of his chin in his hand. But as Jack started parting his way toward him, Granny made a little noise of her own.

"Look who's been waiting, just a speck!" Uncle Noah Webster shouted, as Jack, spinning and sweeping her from her feet, brought Granny up to meet him, chin to chin.

"Ain't you got me a little sugar?" she inquired.

"I didn't quite hear Grandpa's thunder as I came through the lot," Jack told her after she'd got her kiss, still holding her up where he could see her. "Where have you got him hid, Granny?"

"Jack, we've lost Grandpa," Miss Beulah called up, hands frantic at her lips.

"We lost Grandpa Vaughn, one year ago today," Uncle Curtis said, and as all went quiet, like the rattle of tiny drums came the sound of one more kettle coming to a boil in the kitchen.

"You never stopped coming for long enough to see if there's a new grave in the cemetery with fresh flowers on it?" Miss Beulah asked, reading his face. "It would have been staring right at you."

"It was the last place I thought to look," gasped Jack.

"Yes, son. And oh but you know how an old lady grieves! We was all worried for fear we couldn't keep her for you, either," Miss Beulah cried.

Granny, up in the air, only looked him back cockily in the eye. Carefully he lowered her down to the floor, and when she got her footing he brushed some of his dust off her sleeves.

"Oh, Jack's cheek is ready to wipe," said Aunt Birdie.

"We've got a mighty good little surprise ready for now," Aunt Nanny said.

"When people need it most! That's the time to bring it out," said Aunt Birdie.

"Gloria! What have you got for Jack? Ain't it just about time to show him?" The crowd caught up with her in the kitchen, clamoring to her.

"I'll be the judge," said Gloria from the stove.

Jack came plunging into the smoke and steam, turned her around, circled the table at a hop, counting his mother's cakes out loud, stealing a wing from the mountain of fried chicken heaped on the bread board, and kissed the icing off the blade of a knife. Then, sinking into the kitchen rocker, he took off his shoes and held them out to the nearest sister.

Under the red dust that coated them the uppers were worn nearly through. Their soles were split. The strings hung heavy with dust and weeds and their own extra knots. They were the shoes he had left home in. Elvie bore them off to the company room, while Jack lifted a crock from the table and drank off the top of the milk.

"And here's who's been doing the most of that barking," cried Aunt Nanny.

Sid ran in panting, a festive-looking little dog with a long coat, black and white with a marking down his breast like a flowing polka-dot tie. He was like a tiny shepherd. Jack gathered him onto his knee, raised the moulting cat to his shoulder, and rocked the two together.

"What would we have done if you *hadn't* got here and *wasn't* sitting right now in that chair?" Miss Beulah screamed at him.

"Well, Mama, I believe I'm right on time," he said with milky mouth.

"Jack Renfro, you're home early, by my reckoning," Miss Lexie Renfro now marched up and said with the bang of her own kiss. "Now how'd you get rewarded like that?"

"Aunt Lexie, what they told me it was for was my behavior."

"Surprised *they'd* know good behavior when they saw it!" snorted his mother, and forced a saved-up square of gingerbread whole into his mouth.

Chewing softly, he kept his eyes on Gloria, and now in a wreath of steam she came toward him. She bent to his ear and whispered her first private word.

"Jack, there's precious little water in this house, but I saved you back some and I've got it to boiling."

"Whose is it?" he whispered back.

"Lady May's."

The whole round circle of blue showed in his eyes.

"There's a foot tub waiting in you and Vaughn's old room. Scrub. Then you can shave those whiskers so they won't scare somebody else." She put into his groping hand the lump of sweet-soap, gave him a towel she had ready, stiff as pasteboard from the clothesline and hot too, and walked ahead of him carrying from the stove the boiler of slightly milky, steam-breathing water.

"I've been in the river already," he said humbly there at her heels.

"Like I couldn't help but know!"

The front porch that he had emptied of all company by going back to the kitchen was for the moment still deserted. It was only draped with their coats, set about with their packed buckets and bundles, and its floor was bulging as if pressed up from below by Mr. Renfro's melons underneath.

Jack came leaping over a banjo laid on a folded coat, and straddling a bucket of zinnias he planted himself before the mirror. She pointed out to him where all this time they'd kept his shaving brush in the dish. Then she put into his hand the razor she'd stropped.

"Don't just look at me," she said.

The mirror was mottled like a bird egg. He filled it with his urgent face.

"She's being a real little wife, she's making him earn his surprise," said Aunt Birdie. A circle had re-formed on the porch.

"Now that cheek looks more like you. It would take more'n the whole wide world to change you, Jack," said Aunt Beck.

"Don't let those fingers slip! I bet he's already lost a gallon of sweat just proving how glad he is to see us," said Aunt Birdie.

Aunt Cleo pushed in front of the others, leaned over Jack's shoulders, and got into the mirror with him.

"Who you think this is?" she asked.

He almost cut his cheek. Everybody laughed but Gloria, Granny Vaughn, Miss Beulah, and Aunt Cleo.

"Her story is," said Aunt Nanny, "your Uncle Noah Webster gave the Market Bulletin a free ad for a settled white Christian lady with no home ties and drawing a pension to come keep house for him."

"Wasn't that just the same as handing Aunt Lexie an invitation?" he asked, shaving his perplexed jaw.

"You know I'd be turned down," Miss Lexie said.

"The bus halted at Foxtown store," said Aunt Nanny. "And when she climbed off it was Cleo. 'Well, now that I've seen your house,' she says to Noah Webster when she's ready to go, 'suppose you ride back with me and I'll show you mine.' Well, he climbed on."

"I ended up my ad, 'Don't care if you drink, dip, cuss, flirt or philander, just so you can wield a broom and enjoy the banjo,' " said Uncle Noah Webster.

"I started not to even come," Aunt Cleo said.

"I got a pretty fair little set of answers altogether," said Uncle Noah Webster.

"You're still gettin' 'em. Bulletin never did know how to *quit* running an ad," said Uncle Dolphus. "Mailman says if you don't want 'em, he does."

"But Jack," said Uncle Noah Webster, "it was when I spotted the name Stovall peeping out of Cleo's answer that I saw the first familiar thing. I'd found my pick!"

"And guess what she is," they cried. "A Stovall's widow."

Gloria had to take the razor or it would have fallen out of his hand.

"Not Curly!" the circle, all except smiling Aunt Cleo, cried into his boiled, well-alarmed face.

"For a minute you had me thinking somebody had fell for Curly, married him, and the shock had killed him," Jack told Aunt Cleo. He beat his hands and face with Gloria's towel, and put his welcome on Cleo's cheek.

"And she keeps house for him fine except they're married

and living in hers, and it's clear down away from us all in South Mississippi," Aunt Birdie said.

"He thinks we've forgiven him for it," called Miss Beulah.

Gloria took hold of Jack's still undried wrist, and led him straight from the porch to the door of the company room, then stopped him.

"You can't come any farther till the reunion's over—the company room is chock-full," she told him. She pushed open the door upon thick hot air as palpable as a wedge of watermelon. "Take your nose back," she warned him, and pressed the door against his naked toes, leaving only a crack.

Inside a ring of ladies' hats and tied-up presents, the width of the bed was filled with babies, as many as a dozen, all of them asleep, tumbled on top of or burrowed into one another. Gloria hovered for a minute over the baby whose eyelids were not quite sealed, and whose girl-hair streamed soft as a breath against a mother's palm. As if to show she remembered the way she'd looked when she first came, Lady May buried her face away from the light, and down the nape of her neck lay the same little trigger of hair, nasturtium pink.

Then Gloria pulled her valise from under the bed and took something out. When she slipped into the passage again, she was holding it up—a store shirt, never worn.

"Somebody that's never seen you before wants to see you a little better adorned," she whispered. "Curly Stovall traded me this for black walnuts, Jack. I picked 'em all up between here and the store, just keeping to my way. A barrel full."

"The hog," he said hoarsely.

Without ever taking his eyes from her, and without moving to get the old shirt off till she peeled it from his back, he punched one arm down the stiffened sleeve. She helped him. He drove in the other fist. It seemed to require their double strength to crack the starch she'd ironed into it, to get his wet body inside. She began to button him down, as his arms cranked down to a resting place and cocked themselves there. The smell of the cloth flooded over them, like a bottle of school ink spilled—the color was blue, a shade that after a few boilings in the pot would match her sky-blue sash.

By the time she stood with her back against the door to get the last button through the buttonhole, he was leaning like the side of a house against her. His cheek came down against hers like a hoarse voice speaking too loud.

Then the voices of others, that tread which was only just a little lighter than feet, ran over them. Somebody else was arriving.

"Uncle Homer and Auntie Fay and the ice has made it in. And Uncle Homer says for Jack to come hopping, Sister Gloria." There was Elvie's little announcing face. She was holding a present tied up in the shape of an owl and another hat for the bed.

Jack still had his weight against Gloria. She straightened him up and led him back into the midst of them.

With only two newcomers, the porch now looked crammed so full that the standing room seemed to reach even beyond the floor's edge. The only thing that held the reunion from falling off appeared to be the double row of cannas that ran around it.

Aunt Nanny gave a boy's whistle as Jack walked in again, Gloria at his shoulder. "Whoo-ee! Who you dressed up for?" "Now he looks ready!" came welcoming cries. "Where'd you get that shirt? Who had that waiting for you, how'd she get that paid for?" "Ask her whereabouts is your *big* surprise!"

Auntie Fay, a little woman twice as frail as Miss Lexie and Mr. Renfro, but wearing pink in her cheeks, grabbed Jack with a shriek and with a second shriek let him go as though she'd grabbed the hot stove by mistake.

Uncle Homer Champion clicked across the floor in western boots. He carried his black alpaca coat hanging from his thumb down over the back of his shoulder. He hung it up on the antlers and then took his hat off too and hung it on top. When he turned around, a necktie with green bluejays on it was blazing down his front.

"Jack Renfro! What do you mean by showing up the Sunday before election day?"

"You've still got till Tuesday, Uncle Homer," Jack said, shaking hands. "I just had till today." His voice still croaked. "Please bring me a swallow," he told Gloria, and with his starched arm reached for the gourd she carried to him, drank, and handed it back.

"Sit down!" Uncle Homer said.

The whole company, as far as could, sat. Only the school chair was left vacant; Jack sat down in that. Gloria perched just above him on the writing-arm, where she could look down on his face.

"In all this great and sovereign State of Mississippi, how far out of your way did you have to travel today to find you trouble?" Uncle Homer began.

"I thought I was coming in a pretty straight line, sir," said Jack. When he listened to Uncle Homer it was the same as when he listened to all his family—he leaned forward with his clear eyes fixed on the speaker as though what was now being said would never be said again or repeated by anybody else.

"But you found you a car in the ditch, didn't you—while you was still a good mile from Banner?"

"Put shoulder to wheel and upped him out," said Jack. "Is that Buick back in again?"

Auntie Fay drew breath and shrieked, "Willy Trimble, trust him, saw you do it! And declared it to Homer!"

"Just tell, Jack. Who was it at the throttle of that Buick?" asked Uncle Homer. "They might all like to hear it."

"A stranger for sure. He'd never tumbled in a Boone County ditch before, to judge by the slang it drove him into using," said Jack. "An old fellow, that couldn't climb out very fast."

"Homer, won't you set and butter you a biscuit?" cried Miss Beulah. She faced him with a plate full.

"Beulah, you'd stop the very preacher about to deliver your own funeral oration to see if you couldn't make him feel more at home," said Uncle Homer. He took a biscuit but remained on his feet. "Jack, I'd be more careful before I called that man old. You could call that man more in the prime of life, about like you'd call me. Jack! Did you just get out of the pen today so's to shoulder the very man that *sent* you there up out of the ditch?" he cried, and slapped butter on his biscuit.

Jack leaped up. He nearly fell backwards, recoiling, over a basket of dishes and a pillowcase stuffed with knives and spoons. Children ran up and grabbed him.

"It was the Judge?" yelled Etoyle. "O glory."

"Jack Jordan Renfro," came a chorus of aunts, as he slowly sat down again under Gloria's eyes.

"Judge Oscar Moody in the flesh," said Uncle Homer, and bit in. "That's exactly who you stopped and acted the Good Samaritan to before you'd so much as got home."

"Now you better think up a good one," said Aunt Cleo.

"All my children is too quick," Miss Beulah said. "Just too quick."

"Gloria, I think he needs another surprise fast," said Aunt Beck. But Gloria stayed where she was, peering into Jack's face.

"Speak, Jack!" cried Uncle Homer.

"All I need to tell is a Buick pleasure car only about five years old was spinning nice and pretty towards Banner cross-roads, and Mr. Willy Trimble entered the story," said Jack.

"So Mr. Willy turned right across its path," said Uncle Curtis.

"Who *is* Willy Trimble?" asked Aunt Cleo.

"He's such an old bachelor that the way he cleans out his fireplace is to carry the ashes through the house, shovel-load at a time, and dump 'em out through the front door," said Miss Lexie Renfro. "That answer your question?"

"His ditch is pretty well all cinders," said Jack. "And that's the one that Buick went in."

"And when the fella saw where he was put—" Uncle Percy prompted.

"The same as any mortal that fell in the ditch, he hollers get-me-out, and the same as any Good Samaritan alive, Jack done it," cried Miss Beulah. "He can't help it. We make no secret of it."

"How did a man of Judge Moody's reputation find help so quick? To be right particular, how did he find Jack?" asked Uncle Curtis.

"You was riding on his tire," Vaughn said.

"I don't know how a little schoolboy like you would know that," cried Jack. "We was, though. Me and Aycock had caught on behind that Buick between Peerless and Harmony. It was heading right for Banner."

"But son, was that becoming?" cried Miss Beulah.

Jack told her, "Mama, we'd already covered ground with

three preachers, and we'd sat up front and heard 'em out for miles, and been invited to three sermons and three Sunday dinners and one river baptizing, and then I reasoned we'd get home faster if we caught on with somebody with more of their mind on the road. And when we did, that's the very fellow that before you could turn around twice was in the ditch."

"But then what?" cried Aunt Birdie.

"He was glad to have help offered!" Jack cried.

"If Willy Trimble's ditch is the ditch I'm thinking about, that Judge might've been glad to have help offered from Lucifer himself," said Aunt Nanny.

"It didn't take me but a minute to up him," said Jack.

"And wasn't you sorry then?" Aunt Birdie reproached him.

"I didn't know who it was!" cried Jack.

"Willy Trimble must have spread it like only he knows how. Everybody knew it at the ice house. Laughed!" Uncle Homer said.

"And Homer didn't dream, till he heard about that, that Jack would even get turned loose today!" Auntie Fay told them.

"Jack, you ought to be examined," said Uncle Homer. Elvie, making a sorrowful face, brought him a glass of buttermilk with a piece of his own ice in it.

"Why didn't that miserable Aycock warn you what you was doing? What was you carrying *him* along for?" Aunt Nanny cried.

"I believe when we hit the bottom of the ditch is right exactly when Aycock said 'Good evening,' Aunt Nanny, and struck off home to his mama," said Jack. "He was just about as close home as he could get."

"If we'd just been there, coming in the road behind you!" cried Uncle Dolphus.

"We'd hollered quick. *'Watch out who you're saving, Jack!'*" cried Aunt Birdie.

"Beulah, that boy's led a sheltered life," said Uncle Homer in a heavy voice. "And it don't seem to me now that he's remedied that a *great* deal where he's been."

"Some day it'll happen," Aunt Nanny cried. "He'll have a jolt and an awakening."

"Why can't Jack ever look and see where he's headed?" Uncle Homer pointed a buttery finger at Jack. "Couldn't you even spare a glance through the window into that car to see who might be driving?"

"We was riding back there with most of the dust for company, Uncle Homer," said Jack. "I did see as far as a cake I'm pretty sure was a chocolate, riding under a napkin in the back seat. I don't know where it went when we hit. Mr. Willy's team broke aloose and split up and they went on to Banner. The white one climbed to Better Friendship Church and the black one got all the way down under the bridge. I shouldered the Buick up onto the road. And on it went without me. Caught and brought both mules back and got Mr. Willy hitched up again. Then I come running on home and never thought about a one of 'em again."

"Judge Moody might even have made you his passenger and rode you home for your trouble, put you out right here at your door, and let you thank him in front of the whole reunion, and you *still* wouldn't have caught on!" Uncle Homer said. "That's what I believe of you."

"Yes, you'd have just thanked him for the ride," said Aunt Beck sadly. "You're the densest thing sometimes. Oh, I take that back!"

"Just let Moody dare to come up in my yard!" shrieked Miss Beulah. "Just let him show his Moody face at this reunion. He'll hear *me* tell him who he is!"

"Mama, I saw his face when he climbed out of his car, to get a look at the damage. I don't believe there was a *whiff* of the courthouse clinging to him," said Jack.

"Well, who did he look like?"

"He looked more like a bank robber than any judge. He had a white handkerchief tied across his nose and hanging down over his chin," said Jack.

"I guess he don't care for your dust," said Aunt Cleo.

"It was Judge Oscar Moody in the flesh, and you saved him," Uncle Homer said. "Wait till the rest of the voters hears about it."

"And they will," said Auntie Fay. "I've learned that much just putting up with Homer."

"Jack, you did Judge Moody a favor in return for him sending you to the pen. That's what it adds up to," Uncle Homer said.

"And it wasn't even hard!" Jack said. "Ditch was powder dry! Looks to me like Banner ain't had rain in a hundred years!"

"Now all it lacks is for *Curly* to tell me about it. How much notice do you think that gives me, Jack, to think up an answer and get it back to the population?" asked Uncle Homer.

"Sir Pizen Ivy is what me and Aycock called that Judge every day alive at Parchman!" said Jack in a hoarse voice.

"Then didn't know him when you met him in the road," said Aunt Cleo. "Sounds to me like a joke on *you*."

"Leave him alone!" every one of them hollered at her, all except Uncle Homer and Gloria.

"I think it's a joke on the whole reunion," said Aunt Cleo.

"Who's that?" asked Uncle Homer. He told Aunt Cleo, "Lady, you don't vote around here."

"She's a Stovall's widow. That's a shock, ain't it?" Aunt Nanny said to Uncle Homer.

"No, Nanny Broadwee. Even a Stovall in with this reunion today don't surprise me a whit." Uncle Homer told Aunt Cleo, "And you're about what I'd expect at this stage of the game."

Jack crouched forward in the chair, hands on his knees. Miss Lexie studied him. "Brother," she said to Mr. Renfro, who stood with his chin in his hand, contemplating Jack too, "these children of yours are the least prepared to be *corrected* of any I ever ran up against. How they'll conduct themselves on the Day of Judgment I find it hard to imagine."

"All I can say is, Jack, I'm glad you ain't old enough to vote," said Uncle Homer. "Or I believe you'd vote against me."

"Homer! That's a terrible thing to say!" cried Auntie Fay. "Vote against his own family?"

"And *for Curly?*" Uncle Dolphus cried.

"Homer Champion, my boy would do anything for his family, anything in the world!" cried Miss Beulah. "*Look* at him! He'd vote for you if that's what's asked of him, and not even stop there!"

"If it hadn't been for this family," Uncle Homer said, glaring around at the reunion, "I'd been no telling how high up now. Maybe even sheriff."

"Perish the day!" cried Miss Beulah. "Mr. Renfro, if you don't find something to say to this boy, you're going to have him feeling ashamed of himself in a mighty few minutes! Look at him biting his lip!"

"Judge Moody didn't make a single mistake to give himself away?" asked Aunt Beck, as if it might even then not be too late.

"He just showed himself for a stranger," said Jack. "Offered to pay me for my help. I told him I *lived* around here and it would vex me pretty hard to have to take his money."

"Oh, my boy sounds pitiful," said Miss Beulah. "Pitiful!" She stamped her foot.

"Mama!" cried Jack. "Listen: if that was the Judge and he's so smart, how come *he* didn't know *me*?"

"That's my boy!" shouted Uncle Noah Webster, and his brothers said, "He's right!"

"What good did it do him to make a living example out of me if he wasn't going to know me the next time he saw me?" Jack cried.

"And what business did he have in our part of the world anyway?" cried Miss Beulah. "Homer Champion, tell me that! What you need is a little more buttermilk to wash those crumbs down with!"

"He's politicking. That's what everybody's doing today and that's what Moody's doing. Politicking!" cried Auntie Fay. "He's got to run for office the same as other people! The sands is running out for him as fast as they is for Homer!"

"Judges ain't elected, Sister Fay, it wouldn't be safe," said Uncle Curtis.

"Where do we get so many, then?"

"For aught I know or ever give thought to it, they's self-appointed," he said.

"And that's exactly what they act like!" cried Miss Beulah. "One in particular!"

"If his memory's gotten that poor since I been gone, then I ain't much past letting him know *yet*," said Jack.

"You mean you'd go hunt him?" Uncle Percy whispered. "Now?"

"I'd know that Buick if I saw it a mile away," said Jack.

"Then what?" Uncle Noah Webster hollered.

"I'd tell him who that Samaritan was, and no two ways about it!"

"You got to do more than announce yourself in this world, Jack," said Uncle Curtis. "We proved that in court. You're going to just about need to run headlong into the man and butt him with it like a billy goat, to make him pay you heed. But we'll be right behind you to a man. Won't we, sons?" he asked.

"Yes sir!" they cried, a chorus of uncles and boy cousins.

"If you've already rescued somebody, he's rescued," said Miss Lexie Renfro. "So give up right now."

"Now Lexie, what we all want is a second chance!" Uncle Noah Webster cried. "That's all we're asking for, ain't it, boys?"

"You saved the wrong man, but you can always go back and make him feel bad about it. That's still your privilege, I should hope," said Aunt Birdie to Jack.

"Jack, I just wish you could steal back and ruin his day," said Aunt Nanny. "That would sure help my feelings more than a little."

"Jack, honey, you don't know and never will dream what we've been through, just knowing where they had you," said Aunt Beck, the gentlest of the aunts always. "Grieving for you! Then at last to see you come—and you've saved your Judge's life before you even reached your door."

"Where you reckon he's got to by now?" Aunt Cleo asked. "Timbuktu?"

Jack shot to his feet.

"Hold yourself in one piece, son," said Uncle Noah Webster fondly. "And remember one blessed thing: he's a man that ain't at home around here. He won't know one road from another when he gets to a forks, and it's ten to one he's already lost. Lost upon the face of the wilderness! That make you feel any rosier?"

"Noah Webster, you act like you know where the man's headed," said Mr. Renfro, rocking on his feet.

"And what's him heading anywheres got to do with it?" cried Aunt Birdie loyally. "He's on our roads!"

"At least we've got bad roads!" Aunt Beck cried.

"He'll double on his tracks. These roads alone will see to that," Uncle Curtis predicted.

"And then I know what," Etoyle said, turning herself in circles to make herself dizzy. Aunt Birdie beat her to saying it: "You-all could wait for him at a real good place and when he comes past, hop on him!"

Jack made a sudden plunge for the water bucket.

"Judge Moody could end up pop in the Bywy River!" said Auntie Fay. "That's what I've been trying to get at ever since I walked in this house!"

"Well, it ain't going to be allowed!" cried Miss Beulah.

"Or just start him out across our bridge, that may be all it needs!" Aunt Nanny cried.

"The good old Banner bridge!" said Aunt Birdie. "That'd make an everlasting good drop. If it's ever going to fall in now's the day."

"No decent floor to it hardly at all," Miss Beulah said to Mr. Renfro fiercely. "Speak, Mr. Renfro, tell him what he's waiting to hear you say!"

"The old Bywy ain't deep enough in August to go over his head, Beulah. It's just deep enough to give 'im a splash," said Uncle Noah Webster with his face already beaming. "I feel like I'm getting younger by the minute!"

"When do you suppose the supervisor we all voted for is going to fix our bridge?" Aunt Beck asked, pulling him back by the arm.

"Not today!" Uncle Noah Webster cried gaily, jumping to his feet.

"I've got that supervisor in my pocket, if you all get me elected. But take care of that bridge while you got it, boys," Uncle Homer cried, pounding his fist on a barrel top. "Why does everybody think because it's falling to pieces it's a good place to have a big time on? You're misinterpreting my remarks."

"Jack ain't going to see a flea hurt, you know that!" Miss Beulah said frantically to her brothers.

Jack looked over the rim of the dipper and said, "I'm feeling harder and harder at Judge Moody. I don't think nothing much could stop me from announcing myself to him and telling him who it is that's back."

"That's right, Jack. He made a monkey out of you. Now you can make a monkey out of him," said Aunt Birdie. "That's all the reunion is asking of you."

"I tell you not so fast!" Uncle Homer shouted, with biscuit crumbs flying from his tie.

"Homer is so fickle," Miss Beulah cried. "Sometimes I wonder if he knows whose side he's on himself. He started this!"

"Jack, you *nearly* messed me up last time—getting yourself sent to the pen," said Uncle Homer. "Now you're trying to mess me up again by coming home and reminding the voters we got one like you in the family."

"Oh, go to grass!" said Miss Beulah, and ran to the kitchen.

"Homer," said Mr. Renfro, coming forward, and leveling his forefinger at Uncle Homer, "if you're speaking now of votes, my boy leaving home for the pen is just about what give you your margin in the first place. I can recall the day when you come in ninth for coroner. You wouldn't have an office to be holding *onto* if it wasn't for Jack."

"Liked on all sides as that sweet starving boy is!" cried Miss Beulah, running back in with a platter set around with hot biscuits opened and filled with melted butter in one half and pools of blackberry jelly in the other. "Yes, Homer arrested Jack, his own nephew-in-law, then electioneered for a fresh term as justice of the peace on how bad he hated to do it. Asked the voters to show they found it in their hearts to feel sorry for him. And voters is such fools! And I was one right along with 'em."

"Come on, boys!" cried Uncle Noah Webster.

"Has he even had a decent breakfast?" Miss Beulah reproached them all, while Jack was shaking his head and opening his mouth at the same time.

But before she could pop a biscuit in, the boy cousins cried:

"Hey! Jack! Are we supposed to spend the whole day waiting on you to catch up at the table?"

The men were all on their feet. At the same time the porch

seemed full of liver- and lemon-spotted dogs. The barking had started over.

"Nathan ain't going to go exactly into raptures over this!" Miss Beulah cried despairingly at them. "Remember I've still got one more brother to come!"

"Beulah, by the time Nathan makes it in, things is going to be all over," Uncle Noah Webster said, "and skies clear."

"Now, then," said Uncle Curtis, "how are we all going? I ain't inclined to walk it."

At this moment Gloria rose, turned on her little white heel, and went inside the house.

"Well, you can't all load on one mule, can you?" Mr. Renfro said.

"Well, want to trust that rattletrap of ours?" asked Uncle Curtis.

"I got a slow leak in my gas tank," said Uncle Percy. "It may not last me and Nanny back to Peerless like it is, but we can always *start* in our jitney."

"There's a good old-timey Ford in my little family now that'll go anywhere and do anything. It's true the radiator's boiled over twice since it started climbing hills on the way up," said Uncle Noah Webster. "I ain't yet tried it going down."

"Well, everybody can see the nigh front tire on my son's contraption is down again flat," said Uncle Dolphus. "What do you think of all going in it?"

"You'll have to go back to driving the school bus!" cried Elvie. Under the tree it stood headed downhill and first in line, with a chunk under the wheel. It was wrapped in dust as in a pink baby blanket.

Vaughn said, "You can't. You ain't the driver, Jack, not any longer."

"I'm telling you all one thing! If I had my good truck finished now, there wouldn't be any question! I wouldn't *hear* no other offer!" Jack cried. "That is, if you-all wouldn't mind riding like we do at Parchman, standing up! It'd block any man's road—"

Jack had turned himself around to look. Ready on the

moment, Ella Fay raised her lovely goose-white arms and flung wide the last tablecloth and spread it over the vacancy there.

"Jack," Miss Beulah said, "ready for some more bad news?"

"I think I'm about to guess it already, Mama," he told her.

"What's this?" Uncle Homer demanded to know. "I don't *see* that truck."

"Won't you sit back down, Homer?" Miss Beulah cried. "You need a little more biscuit to come out even on your buttermilk." She laid her hands on Jack's arms. "There's a little story about Stovall and that truck, Jack," she said. "We had to mortgage it."

Jack looked without words from one face to another.

"Curly hauled it right back to where you got it," Etoyle told Jack. "Drug it with oxen."

"He's looking almost pale," Aunt Birdie said, and Aunt Beck tremulously called for him, "Gloria!"

"I'm right in here, tending to some of my business," she called out the window of the company room. "While I can hear every word being said."

"Hauled the whole thing away?" cried Jack. "The *whole thing*?"

"Nothing left but that miserable spot of grease," said Miss Beulah.

"The skunk!" Jack cried.

"*Now* choose between us!" said Uncle Homer Champion to the world.

"Well, he'll never get that engine to hitting without me, that's one thing left to live for!" Jack shouted.

"Saturday's still coming!" Uncle Dolphus cried, to some cheers.

"All right, Vaughn, pull Dan out of the pasture and shoot the bridle on him. I'll ride ahead and the rest can follow. I'll give Dan a treat he's been going without for a long time," said Jack.

"Tell me something more easy," said Vaughn.

"Has he missed me too bad to thrive?"

"We had to part with Dan too, Jack," said Miss Beulah.

"Whoa, Elvie!" he cried, as she burst into tears for him.

He broke from them, hurled himself over the steps and started racing toward the pasture, the barn, turning everywhere at once.

"Would you completely spoil his welcome?" Miss Beulah shrieked at Elvie and all the little girls. "You crybabies'll do it yet!"

"My! Who's Dan?" asked Aunt Cleo.

"It's Jack's stud, Jack's stud," they told her.

"That Dan was a horse in a million," said Uncle Noah Webster.

"That horse was as good and spoiled as anybody in this family," said Miss Lexie Renfro.

"Fib to him a little bit!" pleaded Aunt Birdie.

The cousins were chasing Jack and one of them called, "Come on back, Jack, Curly didn't get your stud." Jack stopped in his tracks.

"We had to shoot him," Aunt Beck compassionately called. "He's still taking it hard," she turned and said. "Look where he's biting down on that lip."

"And you know, it seemed like he wasn't hardly worth the powder it took," Curtis Junior kept talking persuasively as the cousins crept up on him.

"Lead me to his grave."

They grabbed him.

"Jack! Watch out! *Please* don't get your family to feeling so sorry for you before you go!" Aunt Beck begged him from the porch.

"You can't find his grave! He was drug off to the renderers," said Etoyle, hands joined at her breastbone. "Clear to Foxtown! I watched him go."

"Gloria!" he hollered.

"Be patient," her sweet voice called back. "I'll be with you when everything's all ready."

"I always said my horse was going to be buried under trees," Jack gasped out.

"We had to have coal and matches and starch," Miss Beulah listed for him. "And flour and sugar and vinegar and salt and sweet-soap. And seed and feed. And we had to keep us alive. Son, we parted first with a nanny goat, then a fat little trotter. Then the cow calved—"

"Mama, I ain't going to make you tell me any more of the tale," said Jack. "Not in front of all of 'em."

"And how is old muley?" asked Aunt Nanny.

"Bet's been doing it all, if you'd like to see her stagger," Miss Beulah replied.

"I was reading the signal from that roof pretty well," said Jack at last. "Judge Moody's got a lot on his head. I got a lot more to tell him now besides my name. Bring me my shoes."

Then Gloria came out onto the porch with his shoes in her hand. At the same minute she released Lady May from her skirts into their midst.

Jack came hurling himself up the steps. When he saw the baby aiming straight as a cannonball for him, he opened his mouth and gave a great shout. Then she veered and ran back to her mother. Jack threw himself over and stood on his head. As Lady May gazed at him, her eyes open all the way like vinca flowers at midday, he slowly pedalled his feet in the air.

"Jack!" They all began talking at once, moving their circle closer around the three of them.

"Jack! You're home after nearly two long years away—and here's your baby."

"Here's your surprise!"

"Here's your reward."

"Hold it, Jack!" Uncle Noah Webster cried when he wobbled.

"Don't he appear a little small, though, for all he's done and still got to do?" asked Aunt Cleo, her head on the horizontal.

"He's sparing—I never knew there to be a sin in that," said Miss Beulah. "All Renfros is sparing, and they just about never wear out. Now us Beechams, when we go, we go more in a flash, call it a blaze of glory."

The new shirt turned over on its tails all in one piece, like a board on its hinges, uncovering the full stretch of Jack's roasted back and the pair of pants he'd come home in—so worn and faded that they had no more color than skimmed milk. The frayed holes gaped like fish-mouths up both legs.

Lady May drew closer to him, dressed in her first colored dress, her leaf hat, and sliding-new baby shoes buttoned tight with a frill of blue sock falling over the tops. She looked at the holes in Jack's pants, all the way up, like a little buttoner, till her gaze was elevated to his feet. She moved closer, under those feet that were walking upside down on the air, dusty and with leaves sticking to the raw and bleeding toes.

"Look. He already worships her," said Aunt Beck.

Then he tumbled over, as if toppled by the baby.

"Now look at the smile he's brought to that little face! Jack's a real artist!"

Now he squatted before her, face to face. "Come here, baby, come here, baby," his lilting voice said. "Bring me what you've got."

The baby passed and re-passed him.

"He's winning her."

She kept returning him looks of her own, steady and solemn, like a woman trying on a hat. When she stood still, he laid his arms out on the air, and she walked in. He gave her a hug that looked strong enough to break her bones.

"Look at her go right to him. Look at her give him her own play-pretty!" It was her mother's comb.

"Where's mine?" one of the cousins teased the baby, but Aunt Beck said, "Hush, there's been enough of that."

Jack flicked the comb through his own sopping hair and sawed it down through the starch of his shirt pocket and put it out of sight. Lady May's mouth opened round as a plum.

"That fourteen-month-old thinks Jack is *her* surprise," said Aunt Birdie.

"Hi, Lady May," said Jack. "Lady May Renfro, how do you do?" He gave her a kiss, which she returned.

"Listen. Listen at that—he called that baby by her name," Aunt Nanny said.

"Gloria told!" cried Aunt Birdie.

"Gloria told him what she had."

"That baby's no more surprise than I am!" cried Aunt Nanny.

"*I'm* not afraid of pencil and paper," said Gloria.

"I caught her going to the road and giving letters to Uncle Sam!" cried Etoyle. "Plus the fresh egg for the stamp!"

"Lady May all along was supposed to be his surprise. *Now* what is she?" cried Aunt Birdie.

"She was my surprise to tell," Gloria said.

"You've been just the least little bit sneaky, it seems to me," Aunt Nanny said, starting to grin.

"And where do you suppose Gloria ever got her such a dress?" cried Aunt Birdie.

Lady May's first real dress was not made of Robin Hood flour sacks, it was not handed down from Elvie. It was solid blue and had pockets—starched till the pocket flaps stood out like little handles to lift her by.

"I cut it out from mine," Gloria said. "That's the dress I wore the day I came here."

"At least I'm glad you didn't let Curly Stovall cheat you with it at his store," said Aunt Beck sympathetically.

"Look, now it's made that baby cry. She's caught on! She's no surprise at all! She heard you, poor little old thing!" said Aunt Birdie.

Jack picked her up. "Whitest little biddy!" he said softly.

"She's without blemish," said Gloria, reaching for her. "Her skin's like mine, tender tender. Till now, I've kept her pretty well shielded in the house."

He lifted the leaf hat to see what was under it, and the baby's red cockscomb sprang up like a Jack-in-the-box. Then here came his smile. It was as big as a house.

"Welcome home from the pen!" roared Uncle Noah Webster.

Lady May in her mother's arms put out a little crow.

"Laugh, baby! Ladybird, laugh, that's right!" cried Uncle Noah Webster.

"And now let's us get going!" cried some boy cousins.

While his big arched smile, gratitude and gratification in equal parts, still held on his face, Jack dropped to the floor and laced on his shoes that Gloria had scrubbed ready for him.

"Oh, ever'thing happens at once!" Uncle Noah Webster cried and almost kissed Aunt Cleo. "I wouldn't take a pretty for still being alive and able to come today!"

"All right, Homer Champion, see what you accomplished, bringing in that story!" raged Miss Beulah.

"Ain't you coming with us, Homer?" teased Uncle Noah Webster.

"Now listen here, bunch of idiots!" cried Miss Beulah.

"Good-bye, Granny," Jack whispered to her nodding head. "Good-bye, Mama, all my sisters and aunts and girl cousins! Good bye, Gloria—you can play with our baby girl till I get back. Keep dinner waiting!"

"Your mother is going right ahead and spread dinner when the shade gets to those tables in the front yard!" cried Miss Beulah. "And if you're all still alive, you'd better be right back here and ready to eat it! Jack, watch these idiots and don't let 'em do anything more foolish than they can help in honor of you coming home, and you lead 'em right back here, do you heed me?"

There was a general surge of men and boys departing from the house. Bird dogs, coon dogs, and squirrel dogs were jumping and pawing the air and racing for the gate, every one giving his bark.

"Let every one of you come back to your seats," came the uplifted voice of Gloria. "I don't want man or boy to leave this house, or budge an inch till Jack gets back. This is Jack Renfro's own business. And nobody's coming with him but me and the baby."

They all stopped where they were. A long shout travelled all the way down the scale. Gloria lifted her old teacher's satchel from among the plunder on the floor and hung the strap over her shoulder.

Jack's blue eyes had opened nearly to squares. He was the one to move first—he ran and brought her a dipper of water.

"No thank you," she said. "I never have got used to Banner water, and try to do without it."

"Are you really braving it?" asked Aunt Birdie in a faint voice. "Tagging along through the broil behind Jack?"

"Now I know she's addled," said Aunt Cleo.

"Waiting is the hardship," Aunt Beck said gently. "That was her part."

"But it's over! Now it's all over! Don't she know her hardship is ended?" asked Aunt Birdie.

The uncles had fallen back onto chairs as though Gloria had blown them all down with a puff of her breath.

"Just sit tight and hold my dogs, boys," Jack ordered his cousins.

"She ain't even going to let the dogs go?" they cried.

"Just one," said Gloria.

"Sid, I reckon your day has about come," said Jack.

"That dog ain't good for a thing but friendship. And you ought to learned that by now, Jack," said Uncle Dolphus as Sid rose on his hind legs.

"Oh, please wait, son!" shrieked Miss Beulah. "You haven't even had a word from your father yet!"

"Well, the roof wasn't exactly lost on him," said Mr. Renfro.

Granny opened her eyes and said, "Who now? Who's trying to sneak away from Granny?"

Jack ran to her. "I still got a little bit to do to finish getting myself home, Granny," he told her. "But it can't take long, not with the help I got." He hugged her and whispered, "You'll see us all back together again at the table." Then he swung the baby up against his hip.

"Jack's going to make a wonderful little mother himself," predicted Aunt Beck.

"Tell 'em good-bye, Lady May!" said Jack. "Wave at 'em!" Lady May, from under his arm, waved like Elvie, quick-time. He laid the palm of his other hand between Gloria's shoulder blades, pivoted her around, and they skimmed together down the steps.

Ella Fay, in the yard with all her tables spread, watched them go. "Bring me something!" she called after them.

"Even if the reunion was to stop this minute, it would have been worth coming through the dust for," Aunt Birdie said.

"You just can't read her!" Miss Beulah exploded. "It's Gloria I'm talking about. Why, I reckon this minute is all in the world she's been waiting on."

Part 2

T HE DUST Uncle Homer had made still rolled the length
of the home road, like a full red cotton shirtsleeve. Jack
led off through the fields. Lady May was riding his shoulder,
Gloria with her satchel marched right beside him on the narrow path.

"I hated to go off and leave the rest of 'em if it hurt their
feelings," Jack said. "But they've all growed old, that's the
shock! If they'd come, we'd had to find a place for 'em all to
sit down."

The farm was as parched now as an old clay bell of wasp
nest packed up against barn rafters. As the roar of the reunion
grew faint behind them and even the barking toned itself
down, heat, like the oldest hand, seized Jack and Gloria by
the scruff of the neck and kept hold. They marched through
the cornfield, all husks, robbed of color by drought as if by
moonlight, through the cotton that had struggled no higher
than halfway to Jack's knees. Jack dropped on one knee and
thumped a melon his father had overlooked.

"Don't crack Lady May one," said Gloria. "I'm not anxious
for her to start on common ordinary food."

"What're you trying to tell me, Possum?" he asked, turning
his head to look at her.

The mule stood waiting by the pasture gate, as if thunder-
struck at some idea that was floating around in the air.

"Want to see if Bet can carry us all three without any nonsense?" Jack cried as if inspired.

"I never had the wildest dream of going on a mule," said
Gloria.

"She's still better than nothing and she knows it herself,
bless her old black heart!" He went and hung his free arm
around her neck. "She's getting a little scrawny, I'll have to
feed her."

Under the shade tree shaped like a rising bird, two cows
stood nose to nose in the cow-brown pond, motionless; the
water in the middle was deep enough to cool their bags, but
just barely. The rest of the pond baked its bottom like a mud-

pie made by Elvie last summer. They walked through waist-
high spires of cypress weed, green as strong poison, where the
smell of weed and the heat of sun made equal forces, like foes
well matched or sweethearts come together. Jack unbuttoned
his new shirt. He wore it like a preacher's frock-tailed coat,
flying loose. They passed the cane mill and came to the top
of the rise where a crop of spears, old iron spikes man-made
and man-high, made a hollow squarish circle like a crown, and
an old oak tree standing within it poured black shade over it.
Inside lay buried old Captain Jordan under a flat tablet black
as a slate, like a table that he had all to himself. A bushel of
Granny's red salvia gushed from a churn on top of it. Bees
were crawling like babies into the florets. Beyond this was the
last fence, and there the bantam flock pecked, like one patch
quilt moving with somebody under it.

Jack helped Gloria through the fence after him. Then side
by side, with the baby rolled next to Jack's naked chest, they
ran and slid down the claybank, which had washed away until
it felt like all elbows, knees, and shoulders, cinder-hot. Bare
Banner clay was the color of red-hot iron. The bank pitched
them into the bed of a rusty sawmill track, overgrown like the
bed of an untended grave. A stinging veil of long-dead grass
flowed to meet their steps and hid cow-pats dry as gunpowder.
Keeping time with each other they stepped fast without missing a tie—domino-black, flat-sunk, spongy as bread, sun-
cooked, all of them. Sumac hung over the way ahead, studded
with long heads like red-hot pokers. On the curve they
mounted their rails and walked balancing, each with an arm
arched overhead. Gloria slipped first. Jack reached for her and
led her over the trestle, bleached like a ghost-trestle, then he
soared into the creek bed, caught the baby from her arms,
hopped Gloria down, and beat their way along a strip of path
slick as leather. It was like walking through a basket.

"Lady May," Jack said, "you have to remember that when
the old Bywy backs up in Panther Creek, it's an ocean where
we're stepping."

"And right now it's extra-mosquitery," said Gloria.

Jack tucked the baby inside his shirt.

The high shoulders of the Bywy Hills rose ahead, near but
of faint substance against the August sky. They looked no

more than the smudges Lady May might have made on the
pages of the Renfro Bible, turning through them with her fast
little hands.

They climbed up past the old chimney that stood alone.

"But I know this is snakey," said Gloria, pulling back a little
as Jack led her over the old hummocks, deep in vines too thick
to see the ground through, where Grandpa Vaughn's own
early home used to be, like breastworks for some battle once
upon a time. Then, on the well path, piney shadows, falling
soft about them, slid down their arms and sides into the early-
fallen pine needles. The path was a carpet that threw off light
like running water. They began to run, Gloria in front—Jack
had the baby. A pack of courting squirrels electrified a pine
tree in front of them, poured down it, ripped on through
bushes, trees, anything, tossing the branches, sobbing and
gulping like breasted doves, and veered the other way. Gloria
slid on the straw, tripped on a root, and was thrown to her
knees. Jack sank to his right there on the spot, and released
the crowing baby. The final glare dropped from them like a
set of clothes. The big old pine over them had shed years of
needles into one deep bed.

Around the circle of needles, slick and hot and sweet as skin
under them, and dead quiet, they chased each other on the
hobble, fast as children on their knees, around and around the
tree. A family of locust shells with wide-open backs went praying up the trunk. Each time she turned to go the other way,
Gloria re-gathered an armload of skirt to her breast. With
flushed eyes and faces straight ahead, they kept from running
into each other or into the baby, who now made efforts to
join in. His face rushed like an engine toward hers.

They hugged as they collided, gasping and wet. Their hearts
shook them, like two people pounding at the same time on
both sides of a very thin door. Then Gloria threw back her
head, with all the weight of her curls, and said, "Jack! This
isn't what we came out for!" She pulled herself to her feet.
Lady May came, still running hard, into her legs, and she
gathered up both baby and satchel before Jack climbed upright again.

Even after they started again on the path, the well at the
end of it seemed to go on turning. In its canopy of trumpet-

vines it only slowed down gradually, like a merry-go-round after a ride.

Jack stepped to the well for them, and after the wait it took to get the splash and haul the bucket up, its long, long shriek came up with it. By the time he came bringing the jelly glass full, Gloria and Lady May were waiting all fresh, seated straight up on a fallen tree, and Gloria was daintily strapping up her satchel.

They passed the jelly glass back and forth, Lady May sitting between them, and then Gloria emptied what was left onto the ground. It was swallowed up at once there, leaving only a little deposit of what looked like red filings.

They stood up together. In another step they were back on the farm track. Jack threw out both arms and went first, to bar Gloria and the baby from coming too fast down the perpendicular, and they were here, in a cloud of dust. Banner Road ran in front of them, standing table-high out of the ditch.

Here the road had all but reached its highest point. It came winding and climbing toward them between claybanks that reared up grooved and red as peach pits standing on end. Little pink and yellow gravelstones, set like the seeds in long cuts of watermelon, banded all the banks alike, running above the road—more gravel than the road had ever received in its life. Growing along the foot of the banks the branchy cosmos stood man-tall, lining the way. Their leaves and stalks looked dust-laden as the old carpentered chairs that take their places by more travelled roadsides in summer, but the morning's own flowers were as yellow as embroidery floss.

"Not a soul's been raising new dust. We beat Judge Moody altogether! And we're travelling with a baby and he ain't," said Jack. With Lady May astride his neck he jumped the ditch, and held out his hand. Gloria jumped to him.

Directly in front of them across the road, Banner Top rose up. In shape it was like a wedge of cake being offered to them, icing side toward them, point facing away. With Jack going in front, carrying both baby and satchel, they proceeded up to the peak of the road and came back onto Banner Top by the gentler slope where the path crawled. There was a barbed-wire fence that ran with the banks on this side of the road, climbing and dipping at sharp angles and pendant with small "Keep Off" signs ruby-red with rust, like the lavalier chains draped across the pages of a mail-order catalogue.

Jack walked a high step over the wire, holding the baby, then helped Gloria under it.

"Getting up on a rise! That's what I was homesick for," said Jack.

Up here, limestone cropped out of the clay and streaked it white. The real top of Banner Top was like part of a giant buried cup lying on its side. Taking Gloria's hand in his free one Jack made straight across it. The way underfoot was ridged with little waves the size of children's palms. There were places clean and white as if a cat's tongue had licked them. The clay that there was set with shallow trenches, and all around the edge it was scallopy with seats and saddles. The jumping-off place itself was grooved like the lip of a pitcher, sandy, peach-colored, grainy, and warm until long after dark in summer—it faced the summer moonrise. A tall old cedar tree was stubbornly growing out of the end and standing over it. A scattering of plum bushes, delicate and quivering, already hung with orange-colored fall plums of the kind whose sucked skins tasted like pennies, furnished the only screen to keep passers in the road from seeing exactly who was up here and what their business might be.

"Now, Lady May. The first thing you do is look out and see what you got around you," Jack told the baby. "This right here is Banner Top, little girl, and around us is all its brothers and sisters." He had set the baby up to ride his shoulders. As far as eye could see, the world was billowing in its reds and pinks that the heat had pearled over and the dust had coated until it seemed that everything swam as one bubble. The sky itself looked patched here and there with the thin pink plaster of earth.

"Mind you don't step too close," said Gloria, getting behind them. "Lady May doesn't care for steep places."

"You might even call this a mountain," Jack invited Lady May. "If you do, I ain't going to argue with you."

Now the baby obscured Jack's head. Her little draped behind, white as a tureen, rested on his neck, and she looked with all the hair of her own head standing up.

"And winding along the edge of everywhere is the old Bywy. Right now it's low as sin and you can't see it. If this was bare winter, you could look right through yonder and see Grandpa's church pointing up its finger at you."

Both the baby's hands pulled gently at the tufts of Jack's hair as he turned with her, a little at a time, showing her the world.

"You can't see dear old Banner from here. By the road it's five miles away, at the bottom of the ridge. But it's right—where—I'm pointing," Jack told her. "Like a biddie under a wing. You just follow the road."

He reached for Gloria's arm and steered her, taking them back across the Top to where it hung over Banner Road. It ran deep between its banks that were bright as a melon at that instant split open. It came over its hill, rushed to the bottom, and disappeared around a claybank.

"Right here in the world is where I call it plain beautiful," said Jack. "That way is Banner." He pointed. "And that's the other way. Your guess is as good as your daddy's which end of the road that old booger's on now."

Lady May pointed her finger straight forward.

"Why, that's Grandpa's chimney again," Jack told her.

Back on the other side, it stood drinking up the light, red like the claybanks, the same clay.

"Oh, Grandpa Vaughn! I come listening for his voice all the way up to the house this morning. And believed when he kissed me good-bye he'd live to be a hundred," said Jack.

"Showing how much more you count on everybody than I do," said Gloria. "Get back from this edge."

Jack squeezed Lady May's thin leg a little. "And listen to me: that was the strictest mortal that ever breathed. He's asleep in the ground now, and don't have us to pray over any longer. And I miss him! I miss his frowning presence just as I get myself ready to perform something."

"If you're wishing for somebody who's hard to please and wouldn't too well like what you're planning on now, there's one standing over your shoulder and alive this minute," said Gloria. "Now, haven't we had enough of Lover's Leap?" she cried.

"That's what they call Banner Top if they weren't born here," Jack told Lady May, smiling. "Gloria, there's just one word I want to tell you about where they had me for a year and a half: it was flat."

The baby complained, and Jack whispered to her, "Getting homesick? Then I can show you right back where we started. That new tin giving us the signal from away across yonder"—he pointed far—"is the roof of our house." He pointed to the farm track, red as a strand of mitten-yarn, where it showed along the curving ridge, draping it, to fall in easy stages till the last minute, when it cut through the claybank and dropped twelve feet into Banner Road, with the ditch across its foot. "And that's our road. It comes out right under our feet. Who's that holding up the mailbox?" And he told her, "Uncle Sam."

The wooden figure stood at the foot of the farm track like a paper doll made out of a plank, weatherbeaten but recognizable by its pink-tinted stripes and the shape of its overlarge hat. It held out the mailbox on a single plank arm.

"I brought you here by the short-cut," said Jack.

"Now explain to your baby what we're all here for," Gloria challenged him.

"Family duty," Jack told Lady May. "And it won't take longer than a snap of your own little finger to get Judge Moody tucked away in a ditch like he was in, long enough to learn his lesson. To save precious time, I'm going to see to it that the ditch he goes in now is one he can get *himself* out of, for a change."

"And what easy ditch do you know of?" asked Gloria.

"Ours. You just jumped it."

He trotted with the baby along the edge to where the bank stood steepest over the road. In the thin fold of the clay wall at the top, a round peephole had in some past time been leisurely carved. It gave a view of the road around the turn, toward Banner.

"Now look through that and tell me if you see anybody coming." Jack let Lady May peep, she smiled, and then he peeped and cried, "You do! You see Brother Bethune! He's coming up the road on foot and the least bit weaving!"

"That's who has to take Grandpa Vaughn's place," said Gloria. "He's in Damascus pulpit on Second Sundays. And today he's taking Grandpa's place at the reunion."

"Giving us the family history?" cried Jack. "He's licked to start with!"

"He's heard our voices. Now look who you're bringing right up here," said Gloria.

The old man came right on up Banner Top, climbing the path like a rickety ladder of his dreams. It was when he got to the top that he stumbled and fell. He kept hold of his gun, but everything else on him pitched to the ground. Jack and Gloria raised him to his feet and straightened him up between them.

"Don't tell me where I am," the old man warned them, as Gloria beat his hat for him and put it on his head and Jack beat the dust out of his black serge pants, dropped the tuning fork back into his shirt pocket, and scooped up his Bible, and the baby stood and watched and put her finger into her mouth. "Or where you think I'm headed. I want to tell *you*. It'll all come back to me in good time."

Brother Bethune's Bible, bound in thin black leather skinned to the red of a school eraser, looked as if it had come to his door every Sunday by being thrown at it, rolled up like the Ludlow Sunday newspaper. Its pages, with rain-stained pink edges, looked as loose and fragilely layered as the feathers of a shot bird as Jack picked it out of a plum bush and blew on it to fly the dust.

"That looks like mine," said Brother Bethune, reaching for his Bible and rolling it up to go back in his pocket. "Just stand still. I want you folks to keep me company right here till I can tell you who you are."

"Jack, I wonder if this means everybody in Banner has forgotten you?" whispered Gloria.

"I hope not. And I'd be pretty quick to remind 'em!" he exclaimed. Then he cautioned her in a low voice, "But don't tell him. You got to let him do it his own way, he's old and a preacher."

"He may be with us all day."

"Suppose Judge Moody come spinning in sight before

Brother Bethune knows it's me?" Jack whispered. "And I'd just have to hold my mouth shut?"

"You should have thought of that before you started."

"Vaughn!" Jack shouted, and made the sound of the name like a tree falling.

"Now you can't catch me. Vaughns is all gone, I know that much—played out and gone to mouldering," said Brother Bethune, his face beginning to light up.

Jack shouted, "If you want to start learning to be a Good Samaritan, we need a buggy ride from the mailbox!" Then he bent to Brother Bethune. "I'm just going to whisper you one thing, sir: your gun is loaded."

Brother Bethune looked back at him in a fixed way. The skin on his bony, motionless face looked like the skin on chicken gravy when it has been allowed to cool, even to the little flecks and spots of brown trapped in it. "I know good and well I'm supposed to be carrying comfort and solace to somebody," he said.

"Not today!" Jack warned him. "You can take my word for it, you're headed where you can just lend your presence in the absence of somebody mightier, eat your share, and offer a few kind words in return for hospitality."

"No death in the family, sudden or otherwise?" Brother Bethune argued. He looked from Jack to Gloria to the baby. "Now who in the world is that!" He tried to poke his finger into the baby's mouth, his own mouth stretching in delight.

The trotting of hooves and the creaking of an axle sounded, as if approaching from down under, and stopped in the road just below them. They ran to peer down over. The dust climbed to their level in clouds like boxcars. As the red faded, then turned transparent, the first thing they could see was mule ears scissoring. Then they saw a bonnety hat, stationary, at the low point of the settling dust.

"Met your mule! She's headed for the cemetery. Want to ride home with me?" called the driver.

"You don't want to go with him, sir," said Jack to Brother Bethune. "I'll just tell you one thing more—it's Mr. Willy Trimble."

"The biggest old joker in Christendom!" said Brother

Bethune, looking pleased as at a favorite game. "No sir, can't catch me! No, I ain't ready yet to ride in your old wagon, not till I'm ready for Kingdom Come! Ha! Ha! Ha!" Brother Bethune shouted laughter into the dust rising again as the team started on its way. Then he asked a bit quaveringly, "Am I all that far from some cold water?"

Jack went, and the well-pulley gave its squeal. He came back bringing the jelly glass full, all its faces stained tea-color from the beady Banner water.

"It's warm as pee," pondered Brother Bethune, then gave a cry. "The water give it away! It's Banner! Today is First Sunday! And I'm good old Brother Bethune!"

"So far, he's remembering everything in one grand rush," said Jack.

Brother Bethune pivoted on his gun and fixed him with his loving, gimlet eye. "It's the Prodigal Son."

"Yes sir, looks like I'm just about to make it," said Jack. He blushed. On his skin shone the crystal tracks, like snail tracks at sunup, of Lady May's confidences and kisses up to now.

"Hi, Ladybug," the old man said gaily, coming to try Lady May again. "There now. Churning my finger to pieces with your little tongue? Can't talk yet? When they going to carry you to church?" He gazed at Gloria; he didn't look as sure about her. "Mother still living?" he asked in the tones of a compliment.

"I'm an orphan, sir," she said.

He made a shaming sound back at her.

"And Banner is not my home."

Brother Bethune struck a sudden attitude and fixed his eye on the jumping-off place. A small head protruded over it with the motion of a hen's. Like a long black stocking being rolled out through the wringer, all of it came up over the edge and moved on into the open over the flag-red ground and the milk-white limestone in the direction of Banner Road. Brother Bethune showed an incredulous face, on which the old nose, dark as a fig in its withering days, dangled over a mouth as wide-open as a man's who was hearing this told in a story. An instant later he'd brought his heels together and fired his gun. Glistening, the snake appeared for a moment at the heart of the dust that played like a whirly-wind at their feet, and kept playing.

Rocketing hooves seemed to cover all the countryside at the same time, and the figure of Vaughn appeared as if flying upright above the top of the bank opposite. He was standing up in the wagon and driving Bet as if all their lives depended on it. He whipped the mule down the farm track and jumped her and the rocking wagon over the ditch and only brought them to a halt halfway down the hill on Banner Road.

Brother Bethune, his finger and thumb both rainbow-colored with tobacco stain, pared away at the well-toothed brim of his hat. He reloaded. "Now bring on the next one," he told Lady May. "You know they ranges in pairs."

Lady May had not shut her wide-open mouth. She sat on Gloria's arm staring at him.

Here came Vaughn running straight to the snake. "I'll carry that man back with me to show to Granny!" he shouted, plunging his arm in and holding up the running, perhaps headless, coils.

"It's an old story to Granny," said Jack. "No call for you to go carrying 'em home anything but Brother Bethune by himself."

"Didn't first catch on he's a rattler, sir!" Vaughn shouted.

Brother Bethune laid on his shoulder a hand that appeared weighty enough to sink him. "All poisonous snakes you can tell 'em because they crawls waverly, son. If a snake ain't coming with the idea to kill you, he crawls straight."

"In my judgment, you all ought to see the rattlesnakes at Parchman before you jump to a verdict," said Jack. "Throw that thing clear away from here, Vaughn. Anywhere but our ditch."

Vaughn squatted down, picked up the snake afresh with both hands under it, as if it were a fainting woman, and bore it slowly to the jumping-off place and threw it over the drop.

"Banner Top looks very natural," observed Brother Bethune. He pivoted. "And round, Baptist faces even more so. Many another one waiting on my words at your reunion."

"What lost you your bearings, sir?" asked Jack kindly.

"I'd like to tell you," said Brother Bethune. "A great big pleasure car in a cloud of dust and pine cones like to hit me right in the middle of the road, and that's what spooked my mule. Stranger asked me what road could he take to get him to Alliance and not have to cross the river on Banner bridge. He talked a little uncomplimentary about it."

"Brother Bethune, I'd love to know what answer you had for him," Jack said.

"Told him to turn around the first chance he got and go back to Halfway Forks and try it all over. 'Don't waver,' I told him, 'just keep to the straight and narrow, every opportunity comes along,' I told him, 'and you'll get to Grinders Mill in a little while, and see a bridge. Or there used to be one when I was taken there as a boy.' He didn't look too well pleased. But listen, Tiny—he spooked my mule," said Brother Bethune into Lady May's still horrified gaze. "Oh, what a day for upsets, Baby Child! I'll tell you where I hope my mule's gone—home."

"Thank you, Brother Bethune," said Jack.

"You're welcome, Prodigal Son."

"Now Vaughn," said Jack, "if you're cleaned off good, carry Brother Bethune on up to the reunion. Why didn't you bring Grandpa's buggy?"

"That mule can't learn Grandpa's buggy," said Vaughn. "She hitches to the wagon."

"See that Brother Bethune don't spill another time," said Jack. "And tell Mama to keep holding dinner—Brother Bethune's sent Judge Moody to Grinders Mill for me."

"*Is* that who that was!" said Brother Bethune over his gun shoulder as Vaughn took him by the trigger finger and led him down the bank to the wagon. "I declare it to be a small world." He set his foot in its high-topped shoe into Vaughn's hands and took the boost onto the wagon seat. He drew into his lungs a sweet, suspiring smell.

"I reckon you know you been breaking the Sabbath, son," said the old man, with one long-legged maneuver transferring himself to the nest of new hay in the bed behind. As the wagon rattled up the home road, he raised his gun high, and Lady May broke her silence and let out a shriek at it.

"Brother Bethune's going to drive all the snakes out of this end of Boone County if he don't slow down," said Jack. "Poor old chicken snake—I reckon he lived around here pretty close and was just paying his ordinary call for a sip of water."

"Why can Judge Moody be trying to seek out Alliance?" wondered Gloria.

"Well, he'll never start across at Grinders," said Jack. "Not if he knows anything about a bridge at all. And if he's gone all the way to Grinders on that road, he'll reason it out: any road that looks like it's working that hard against nature, it must have *somewhere* better to go than Grinders. He'll take the fork that brings him on around and back into Banner Road by keeping up with Panther Creek every switch of the way, if he's smart. I'm as sure as I am of anything in this world, Gloria, he'll roll right past here about forty miles further on from now."

Holding her hand, he had been leading her back toward the jumping-off place. Now he drew his finger down through the bow of her sash, and the whole dress stood away from her like a put-up tent. The sash itself slid down to her shoes. His arm went around her waist, and with her holding the baby they all sat down together.

Here in the best patch of shade, an apron of old cedar roots, long exposed to the elements and rubbed smooth as horn, was spread out under them.

Lady May had lost her hat, but she still had her little shoes on. "Carry Jack a secret," said Gloria. She whispered into the baby's ear and sent her tiptoeing. Lady May wrapped Jack's head in her arms and made humming sounds into his ear.

"I got it! Take Mama this'n from me!" he cried.

But when Lady May came to blow in her ear, Gloria reached for her, took her on her lap, and opened her own bodice.

Jack jumped to his feet, then suddenly crashed to the ground again as though the baby had tripped him.

"Possum, that's the last thing in the world I was picturing you doing," he broke out.

"Maybe it'll do you good."

"She's got teeth!"

"That's to show you how long you stayed gone. And let me tell you she's proud of those little teeth, too, every single one."

"Holy Moses!" He propped up on one elbow and looked at Gloria's sweetly lowered face. She raised her eyes and appraised him back.

"Get used to being a father, please kindly."

"She could eat a plateful, the same as you and me. Why, she's going to wear you out. She's a little pig, ain't she?"

"When you got your first look at her this morning, you weren't scared of a baby."

"Then, she made me feel right at home. She cannonballed in like a little version of Mama."

"And you stood on your head for her."

He couldn't take his eyes away. "She's such a sweet, helpful little thing, now ain't she!" he exclaimed. Lady May set a sidelong gaze on him while she held Gloria's breast in both hands, like a little horn blower whose hoots and peeps were given mainly with the eyes. "I reckon she can do everything in the world, next to talking."

"Don't criticize her!" cried Gloria. "If she could talk now, she would tell you you can't just prance back like this and take it for granted that all you have to do is come home—and life will go on like before, or even better."

"Trust your dad," he told the baby.

"The system you're trying won't work," Gloria said. "I wouldn't need to bring you down to earth if I wasn't your wife."

He smiled at her.

"I feel like you missed my last letter by coming home today," Gloria said.

"That's all right—you already had all the other letter writers in the world licked."

"I'm glad for you and sorry for the rest of the prisoners going deprived."

"Never mind about them. What they had was family coming to beg for 'em," he said, fanning her and the baby with his shirt-tails.

"Beg for 'em?"

"The smartest they had, the pick of their family. That's who'd be elected to come to Parchman and beg. Or else how would the poor lonesome fools ever get out of there? Renfros and Beechams and Comforts relied a hundred percent on me and Aycock's own behavior to turn the trick. Now that's the slow way."

"How could I have got myself to Parchman?" she cried.

"They call it Visiting Day."

"Coming afoot? All the way to Parchman?" Gloria cried.

"You could've brought me a bottle of Banner water. And a pinch of home dirt—I could have carried that around in my shoe. I'd be looking for you on Visiting Day. Uncle Homer's got the surest transportation, but he wouldn't have begged for me as hard as you. You got to beg pretty wholehearted before old Parchman will listen."

"I didn't know Parchman would behave like that," said Gloria.

"You got to aggravate 'em until they do." He fanned them.

"I had a baby. That's exactly what I was doing!"

He looked at her over the baby's little crop of hair. "And I wouldn't have had you set your little foot in a place like Parchman for all you'd give me! You know that, Beautiful. I was trying to make you smile. Where I'm proud and glad to have you is right here at home in Banner, exactly the way you are."

"Then why do you tease me?" she whispered.

"Honey, Judge Moody's gone to Grinders Mill."

"You went farther than Grinders Mill."

"I'm back."

"And look what you're doing first thing."

"Is she satisfied now?" he loudly answered her, for the baby just then dodged from her mother to complete a yawn. He jumped up. "I believe she's sleepy. How sound does our baby sleep?"

Lady May's little hand dropped like a falling star. More slowly, her eyelids fell.

"She goes to the Gates of Beyond, just like you," whispered Gloria.

He took the shirt off his back and folded it and took up the limp baby in it and walked to where the shadow of the tree reached into the feathery plum bushes. He laid her down and wrapped her lightly in his sleeves, and saw that she had a little canopy of light boughs, with a plum hanging as if it might fall in her mouth.

He turned, and Gloria darted. Once more they were running as hard as they could go, Gloria in front, rounding the
bank its whole way around, swiftly past the piecrust edge,
streaking by the peephole, clicking across the limestone,
bounding over the hummocks, taking the hollow places skip
by skip without a miss, threading serpentine through the plum
bushes, softly around the baby, and back to the tree, where
he reached with both hands and had her. Catching her weight
as though he'd trapped it, he lowered her into the seat that
looked out over the drop and got in with her.

The tree trunk, as high up as the hitching limb, was well
carved; it was wound up in strings and knots of names and
initials as if in a clover chain. In the upper gloom of branches,
two doves like two stars flew in, then flew out again, out over
the unseen river.

"When will we move to ourselves?" Gloria whispered.

"I believe that's what you was saying to me the last thing
before I left home for the courthouse."

"Our wedding day. It was those very words."

"They sound a familiar tune."

"And I wrote you the same words too, didn't let you forget
'em all the time you were gone."

"I so much rather hear your sweet voice saying 'em," he
gasped, and taking her by the hand he laid his mouth over
hers.

When she could speak, she said, "Stop. What is the most
important thing in all the world?"

"I reckon what we need right now is a scout," he said without pulling his face off hers. "Now Vaughn would come if I'd
give him another holler. Little fellow just sits there listening."

"No, I want Vaughn to remember you later as a good example."

"Or Aycock. Aycock'd do anything for me and I'd do anything for him. He'd keep a lookout—"

"Jack, I want you to give him up."

"Give up *Aycock*?"

"He's good-for-nothing and spineless. And now he's back
home with a prison record besides."

"He's an old Banner boy! He just ain't had all the good
things I have—has no daddy at home, no mama able to keep

on the subject, no sisters and brothers to call on—no wife! Not to mention a sweet, helpful little girl-baby."

"I wouldn't let Aycock touch the hem of her garment," she said. "If it wasn't for all the other people around us, our life would be different this minute."

"Who wants it different?" he whispered.

"Your wife."

He rolled closer.

"And here you are, going right back down in the road to more trouble, the minute you let go of me," she said, as he clasped her close.

"Just because something may give me a little bit of trouble, you don't see me go backing away from it, do you?" He rubbed his cheek against hers. "I'm beholden to the reunion to keep it running on a smooth track today, for Granny's birthday to be worth her living to see. For Mama's chickens not to go wasted, and for all of 'em that's travelled through dust not to go home disappointed. It's up to me to meet that Judge, Possum, sing him my name out loud and clear, and leave him in as good a ditch as the one he had before I saved him. That's all."

"Then it's up to your wife to pit her common sense against you, Jack," she said, catching her breath.

"Honey, Judge Moody's gone to Grinders. And our baby's lying safe where we can see her, in the Land of Nod." His arms reached all the way around her.

"Oh, Jack, I ought to've hit you over the head with your mother's cornbread irons, back when you first began! Beat you back over to your side of my desk with the blackboard eraser! Never kept you in after school to learn 'Abou Ben Adhem' by heart!"

"I like to never did learn it."

"I couldn't forget a word if I tried."

"Don't say it now," he begged, short-breathed. "I doubt if they come any longer."

Her face with a thousand freckles on it was moving from side to side like a tiger lily trying not to give out perfume.

"Possum!" he croaked.

She skinned loose from the knot of his arms and for a minute sat up over him. She brought down the sides of her fists on his naked chest as if it were solid oak, and his heart seemed to jump out of it, almost into visibility.

"Do you still think you're going to pick up living right where you left off?" she asked fast.

"Did something put the idea in your precious little head I can't?"

"This is the time I've been guarding myself against for a year, six months and a day," she gasped, but if he heard more than the first words he didn't show it, for the whole weight of his head rammed upward, blundered against her neck, and then moved in a blind way up her face, his cheek hot as a stove on hers, something hotter splashing between them that could have been tears.

"Oh Jack, Jack, Jack, Jack—now you've bumped my head on something hard—"

He had rolled over with her and stopped breathing. Without stopping to be sorry for her head he crammed kisses in her mouth, and she wound her arms up around his own drenched head and returned him kiss for kiss.

But almost at once three or four nervous hounds began licking the back of Jack's neck and the sole of Gloria's foot that lay outside its shoe.

"Boo!" said a sober young man who came stalking up onto Banner Top with a guitar under his arm. Jack and Gloria sprang apart.

"Aycock! Seems like it was a hundred years ago when I last saw you!" said Jack. "How did you find your little mama?"

"Mad at me. What did they say when you come walking in?"

"They seemed to think it was right well timed," said Jack. "They had a big welcome on their faces. Then the news started trickling from 'em."

"Bet you had a sizable amount to listen to."

"Grandpa Vaughn is gone, Aycock, been laid in the ground while they had me off yonder where I didn't know it."

"Well, at least you know where he is," said Aycock. "Not like my dad. We don't know what's become of him at all."

"He didn't even take anybody with him? Your Uncle Earl?"

"Uncle Earl would rather do anything than leave Banner,"

said Aycock. He had such a short face that all his life he must have looked as he did now, ready to cry. His hair was the rust of a cedar bush winter-killed, even had the bush's shape and crinkly texture.

"Somebody watched me coming through the peephole. It was a red-headed baby," said Aycock.

"If she hasn't waked up and worked her way clear out of her harness!" Jack jumped up and ran to meet the baby, welcomed her, and swung her down in front of Aycock.

"Goodness-a-life. Which is it?" Aycock said.

"A girl! Wearing a dress to prove it!" Gloria said.

"Goodness-a-life." Aycock folded down into a squat. "Whose big shoe are you carrying?"

"I wonder if Aycock brought one good excuse along for coming up here," said Gloria.

"Mama said she heard gunfire overhead. So I come to see if you was still living, Jack," said Aycock. "While you was hearing the bad news, did you hear anything about Poison Ivy Moody?"

"I was just fixing to break it to you!" Jack cried.

"How long did it take you to find it out?"

"Uncle Homer told me. He made it in right behind me," Jack said. "Who told you?"

"I looked," Aycock admitted.

"You sound like you was expecting to see him! If you was on the watch for a judge on your way home from the pen, Aycock, I wasn't!" said Jack. "And when Mr. Willy Trimble merrily turned in front of his Buick and down he went, if that didn't give him first marks of being a stranger! And I took him for one."

"He looked the same to me as he done in Ludlow courthouse," said Aycock. "Like a sinner, more or less."

"Well, all I got to do now is shoo him back in a ditch just as good as he was in, and call it evens," Jack said, buttoning on his shirt.

"Don't one ditch satisfy 'em at home?"

"No, Aycock, he managed that much by himself. And I didn't have the sense or stamina to leave him floundering!" said Jack. "My family is just about on the verge of having a fit over it."

"How many you got up there today?"

"It's the whole reunion!"

"Has that already come around again?"

"My little granny's birthday come around again, and now it's my welcome home. It's going on right now."

"They waiting dinner on you?"

"How could they eat till I get back?"

"Always glad I ain't you," said Aycock.

"They'll wait," said Jack. "For one thing, Uncle Nathan's still got to come, from who only knows how far!"

"Jack, didn't you see what's right in your face? You bumped my head on it," said Gloria. She pointed back to a little wooden sign staked low to the ground not far from the jumping-off place. Its black letters were still running with bright fishtails of paint.

" 'Destruction Is At Hand,' " Jack read off affectionately. "Bless Uncle Nathan's heart, he *has* made it in!"

"They'll soon be gobbling, Jack," said Aycock. "I wouldn't mind being one at the table."

Lady May was creeping close on him, where he still squatted there. Tipping his sassafras-colored head to one side, Aycock laid the guitar over his knee. At the first chord he squinted an eye upward and his voice became a tenor.

> "Bought me a chicken and my chicken pleased me
> And I tied my chicken be-hind a tree
> And my chicken said 'Coo-coo, coo-coo, coooo!'
> Anybody that feeds his chickens,
> Feed my chicken too."

Lady May opened her own mouth wide, held her breath. Her eyes followed Aycock's sideburns moving with his singing—they were long as cat-scratches.

> "Bought me a hen and my hen pleased me—"

"Aycock, you made her cry," said Jack.

"Then Great Scots-a-life! Are you planning to try running that Judge in a ditch with a crying baby *girl* to be your partner?"

"She was having the time of her little life till Aycock Comfort came along," said Gloria. She put up her arms, lifted her hair high to the crown and tied it furiously tight but didn't bind it, so it flared from the ribbon like the petals of a flower. Her head was glary as a trumpet flower against the hot green cedar shade. Aycock didn't look straight at her. His eyes went sleepy and even his ears turned gold.

With both hands, Jack worked the slipper back onto Gloria's slick, hot little foot. "I don't believe that shoe was ever *made* for serious hopping," he said. "I'm proud my wife and baby got nothing more to do than sit in the shade and watch me." Then he jumped up by Aycock. "Son, if what you're trying to do is come in on it, I better save time and invite you now."

"Jack!" Gloria cried out.

"Would make it seem like olden times, Jack," said Aycock. "But you got a majority on it?"

"She's my wife!" protested Jack. "How could Gloria be sitting here at my feet and not be for whatever I do?" And up she jumped.

"Then all we got to worry about is him. We can't get old Poison Ivy by wishing. He's got to come along, Jack," said Aycock.

"He's trying to get across the river to Alliance, that's his aim," Jack told him. "What his story is, I don't know."

"If he's using Banner Road, ain't nothing going to stop him. It throws him right on the bridge."

"He don't overly care for the looks of our bridge," said Jack.

"That could be why he run up in our yard, skinned around the martin houses, and gone again like a lost soul," said Aycock. "He was just using us to turn around."

"In your very yard?" cried Jack. "What did your mother say?"

"She complained of the dust. Next thing, she complained of gunfire up over her head."

"She heard Brother Bethune delivering judgment on a chicken snake. Before that, he talked Judge Moody into going all the way to Grinders Mill in the hope of a better-looking bridge. But he's going to find that old covered bridge at Grinders is going without a floor. I don't believe even the mill still calls itself in commission."

"Jack, where did you learn so much about Grinders Mill?" Gloria objected.

"Parchman. Ask me about anywhere! I reckon for every spot there is, there's somebody in the pen going homesick for it. Old trusty told me every inch of Grinders, the same as I told him Banner," said Jack. "I only hope now there isn't one of his kin standing there with little enough to do to tell Judge Moody he could bump three miles further on and be poled across the river at Wisdom's Point. Aycock'll guarantee that."

"Be ready for a shock," Aycock told him. "The ferry at Wisdom ties up on Sunday now. Uncle Joe Wisdom has been converted and spends the whole day in church shouting repentence. I'll bring you that much from Mama."

"Thank her for the best news she could have sent me. Now, unless they teach a Buick to swim, it's Banner bridge or nothing for Judge Moody. And he's going to make up his mind to it. He'll come puffing along again, any time now, gritting his teeth for it. He's more or less like me, not the kind to give up in the face of a little hardship," said Jack.

"Jack, I hope you're wrong," said Gloria, while he capered to the front of the bank and hung over the road.

"We'll land him in my own ditch kissing the mailbox!"

"That's bringing it close to home," said Aycock at his shoulder.

"It's not a bad ditch, Aycock. It's the ditch the school bus has deepened out for itself by eternally trying to get up out of our road and go to school."

"But you know what?" said Aycock. "If it's the second time he's run in a ditch in one day, he might think it was being done on purpose with him in mind."

"But that's the whole blooming idea, Aycock! That's the beauty of it," said Jack. "That's when I announce myself to him, the minute the dust starts clearing and he puts his head up!" He sprang onto Aycock's back, the guitar wobbled in the air, and the boys began leapfrogging.

"Well, old Poison Ivy ain't going to love me and you a bit the better for it," said Aycock, tumbling and rolling over.

"Love us!" Jack cried, sitting on him. "Aycock, I'm going to a heap of trouble just to blooming well keep him from it!"

"A man as out-of-patience as the Judge might for all I know

send me and you both back to Parchman for it! First thing
Monday morning!"

"I ain't ever going anywhere that flat again, and that's all
there is to it. Shinny up the tree, Aycock, and watch till you
see him coming."

"She's beating me to it," Aycock pointed. "Which one was
that?"

A Robin-Hood patterned dress was already halfway up to
the first limb of the tree, with rosy arms reaching, sunburned
feet tucking up behind.

"They've grown, every one of 'em," said Jack. "Etoyle
looks as broad as Ella Fay now, sitting on that hitching limb."

"I'm here to see the look on Judge Moody's face!" Etoyle
sang.

"Well, you've got more society here than a little bit. And
all girls," said Aycock in polite tones. "Will I have time to
enjoy my first sip of Banner water?"

"My eyes see dust!" sang Etoyle from the tree. "Somebody's a-coming!"

Gloria snatched up the baby and followed Jack and Aycock
to where the front of the bank overlooked the road. It
dropped away on both sides below them, like a sash picked
up in the middle on a stick. The ditch ran with it, sometimes
on one side and sometimes on the other. Then both ends of
the road went out of sight in identical blind curves.

"Banner Road is just plain beautiful," said Jack. Then a puff
of dust showed along the next ridge over, as though a match
had been laid to a string in Freewill whose other end was here
at Banner Top. "That's him. He's coming the long way
round."

For a few minutes, a buzzard flying slow as a fence-walker
along the rim of trees seemed to be in a bigger hurry. Then
the dust was a growing cloud. Presently there came a sound
from the road itself, thin as that of a veil being parted.

"He's passing the supervisor's house. I hear the gravel,"
said Aycock. Thoughts seemed to chase one another up and
down his forehead, rippling it like a squirrel's tail.

"Is it fair for me to warn him?" Etoyle called.

"Want me to send you back to help Mama?" shouted Jack.
"Keep count of the Dry Creek bridges, and when it's six,

holler! Gloria! Hold our baby high out of the dust! Aycock! At the last minute you're hanging onto my britches!"

"Not everybody goes rushing into trouble as headlong as you, Jack!"

"Man alive, let go of my britches! Want me to come away and leave 'em?" Jack yelled. "We got to charge down fast and shoo him in! He ain't going to wait on us!"

"I changed my mind," said Aycock.

Jack's pants gave a rip, Aycock let him go, and Gloria handed him his baby.

"If you can't be a better example to Lady May—*hold* her!" Gloria's arm circled up in a teacher's best gesture, and it threw her off balance. She staggered backwards, and as her skirt blew up at the edge of the bank, spread, shone like a pearl, she wheeled and her shoes started sliding with her down toward the road.

Jack spun on Aycock. "Hold the baby!"

"You hold it."

"You hold it! I got to catch Gloria!"

"I don't know how to hold no baby! I just got back from the pen a while ago—I'm like to drop it!"

"Take hold of her and she takes hold of you!"

"Six!" sang Etoyle from the tree.

Jack held out the baby to Aycock, he parried with his guitar. Lady May gave a shriek. She turned herself around and plastered herself to Jack's chest, legs like a frog's. Binding him around the neck with her arms, ramming her head into his croaking throat, she pumped out soft, anticipatory cries on her own little bellows.

Jack's eyes bulged. His toes suddenly turned unnaturally outwards.

"Stop, Jack, stop, Jack, S-T-O-P stop!" Gloria's voice called from below, fading while it spelled. "Lady May hates downhill!"

A mockingbird threw down two or three hard notes on him like a blacksmith driving in nails, and he went rigid. Hugging Lady May to him, taking short, frantic steps as though he'd been caught naked, he hopped over the edge into Gloria's dust and went down, rigid and upright, first at a zigzag and then, shuddering on his heels, straight down a washboard of clay. He yelled, but the baby now made no sound at all except for clapping together the soles of her bare feet just above his belt-buckle. At the skin of his chest her little mouth nibbled—it might have been everything feminine laughing at him. He landed in a bed of yellow cosmos. On his face a wide, frantic smile of paternity flashed on and off again, as he raised the baby in his arms like a bunch of flowers for Gloria.

She had not been able to stop until she went down on both knees into the ditch at the foot of the mailbox, with her arms around it.

Lady May's hot little foot slammed Jack across the windpipe. She slid down him, left him with his breath cut off and both feet ploughed out in front of him, while she set forth across the road. Each bare foot hopped from the heat of the dust. She had the crow of a tattletale. She hooked onto her mother, made sounds at her ear, then started back, hopping for Jack. This was the moment the car came thundering for the top of the hill, a sunset of red dust fanning into high air, bank to bank.

Jack staggered to his feet. Gloria sprang to hers, ran after the baby, collided with Jack, who was spun around so hard that he fell backwards into his own ditch this time, and she captured the baby by throwing herself down on top of her, and lay flat there in the middle of Banner Road as if she waited in the path of a cyclone.

The car took the only way left open and charged up Banner Top in a bombardment of pink clods like thrown roses. Aycock appeared in its train of dust. He was running after it, waving his guitar. He caught hold and was borne on up as if by some large, not local, bird. The car never stopped. The dogs streaked with it, barking it further off the road. Dust solid as a waterfall poured over the bank along whose roof the car rolled on, tossing a fence post, mowing down plum bushes. There was a shriek out of Etoyle, a blow, a scraping sound, a crack, then silence, even from the dogs.

Jack picked up his family. He stood holding Gloria's face between his hands, while Lady May stood spread-eagled against his legs, then he gathered the baby up fast and hugged her and Gloria together.

What looked like big Buicks of dust hung stalled in the air

until they slowly turned pink and then gauzy. The cedar tree with Etoyle standing at the top emerged first. Then the car emerged; it was still there, standing still, in a position right beyond the tree. It couldn't be anywhere but on the jumping-off place. Then the dogs came to life and tried to bark it on over as fast as possible.

Jack lunged to go.

"Jack! Don't desert me!" Gloria cried.

"He saved my wife and baby!" he yelled, as she grabbed him.

"Stay with 'em!"

"But I got to be quick if I'm in time to catch him!"

"I see his face!" called Etoyle.

The driver's door had opened, and Judge Oscar Moody climbed out of the car. He stood coated, hulking in seersucker, a middle-aged man in a little sea of plum bushes. In a voice hoarse from dust he called, "Young lady!"

"We're still living! You still living?" hollered Jack.

Then the door on the passenger side of the car opened, and somebody else got out. Judge Moody came around the tree to get to the other side of the car, and then came leading forward a middle-aged lady. Through the scarves of dust she appeared dressed for church. She was all in white, wearing a wide-brimmed hat, carrying a purse the size of a plum bucket. Judge Moody took her arm and they came, wobbling a little, across Banner Top.

"Here Judge Moody comes," said Etoyle, hunkering down and sliding down the face of the bank into the road. "And his mother with him."

"His wife," Gloria cried.

Jack said, "His what? I never had a notion there *was* a Mrs. Judge Moody! What's she doing along?"

Judge Moody set his foot on the bottom wire of the fence where it was still standing, and the lady came through head-first, like a novice.

"Jack, try to make up your mind there's a wife for everybody," said Gloria in a voice that trembled.

"Sister Gloria, you scraped one knee," said Etoyle. "It's losing blood. But what if they'd aimed a little sharper at my tree?"

Gloria let out a short scream. Jack squatted, kissed the blood off her knee, and brushed her skirt in modest places until the pink dust re-formed and put up a gauze screen around them for a minute. He rose, put his lips to her ear, and whispered, "Face 'em, from now on. Your dress is tore behind."

Gloria took the handkerchief from her pocket, cleared away a coating of dust and tears from the baby's face, set her on her feet, and then cleared her own face. "And my baby's lost her little new shoes!"

"He saved you! And I reckon his wife was sitting there to help him," said Jack and more resolutely still she worked on his face.

"And now here they both come to eat us up," said Gloria.

The Moodys reached the road and started for them. Judge Moody had tied a handkerchief over his mouth and nose, and Mrs. Moody carried his Panama hat along with her purse.

Judge Moody in a strong, slow voice called through his handkerchief the same words. "Young lady!"

"That's you, Gloria," said Etoyle. "Maybe he'll march you to jail."

"You were right in front of my wheels. I might have run over you and killed you. Are you harmed?" called Judge Moody.

"No sir, only bleeding a little," answered Gloria.

"We could have run right smack dab into you! And that one was blocking off that other little road, the only way we could turn," said Mrs. Moody, pointing her finger at Jack. "And there was another one, scooting through the bushes— brandishing something! Everywhere you looked there was another one."

"And there was one in the tree," said Etoyle. "I wasn't scared."

"I saw you first, girl." Mrs. Moody pointed at Gloria. "Clinging to that mailbox like Rock of Ages. And the next minute you were streaking across the road! Yes, you *think* nobody lives on a lonesome road like this," she complained, "and then out of the middle of nowhere some little somebody jumps out at you, runs you off the road before you know it—"

"Little somebody? That's my wife you saved!" cried Jack, his face glowing at the Moodys.

Lady May lifted one foot and wailed.

"Good Lord! And where did that infant come from?" asked Judge Moody, as Jack scooped her triumphantly into his arms.

"Yes sir, here is our first," Jack said, holding up Lady May with a grip around her knees. She swayed, wandlike.

"Didn't you see her, Oscar? That baby just streaked across!" said Mrs. Moody. "And then this girl came from right yonder and threw herself down on her like one possessed. Spang in the middle of the road."

"I'm going to tell a lot of people on you," Etoyle told Gloria.

"Is that infant harmed?" asked Judge Moody.

"No sir, I was right on top of her," said Gloria.

Judge Moody groaned.

"But you saved 'em both!" cried Jack.

Gloria put her hand on his sleeve. "I don't want my husband too quickly blamed for the way he let his baby slide out of his grasp," she told Judge Moody. "This is the first time he's ever been anywhere in her company in his life, or hers, your honor."

"Girl, how in the world do you know who we are?" Mrs. Moody exclaimed.

"We are still within my circuit, Maud Eva. I suppose I'm pretty well known wherever I go," said Judge Moody.

"Well, thank goodness for small favors," she said. "I'm glad somebody knows *you*, because I certainly don't even know where I am."

"Where you are now," came the slow voice of Aycock, and everybody hushed—only his dogs barked with him, "is called Banner Top around here. Others call it Lover's Leap. It's the highest known spot in the Banner community."

"Aycock beat all of you. He got *in* the car," said Etoyle.

"The car! Look at the *car*!" yelled Jack, and he hurled himself straight up the clay wall.

Out on the shelf of clay that was the jumping-off place, the five-passenger sedan sat shining in its original paint, all but one fender still undented, its windshield and back window still unstarred, its back bumper flashing dusty light at them from below the spare tire. The tree was behind it. The Buick had skinned past the trunk, the tree had creaked back into place as if after a gust of wind, and now the old cedar stood guard just behind the left rear fender.

Jack pounded toward it.

"Buick ended up better than the way you first had it figured, Jack." Aycock was sitting up in the middle of the back seat.

"I got to figure again pretty fast," said Jack.

"It's like I told you. A ditch for the second time in a row wouldn't have made us popular at all."

"Shut up, Pete! Shut up, Queenie and Slider!"

This time when the dogs stopped barking, everybody cried out, Aycock along with the rest. The sound that made itself heard was unmistakable, though soft as a teakettle singing beyond the boil: the Moodys had climbed out and gone off and left the Buick with its engine running.

Aycock's foot, shorn of its shoe now and arched as if in fastidiousness, appeared over the rear door.

"Keep your foot!" shouted Jack. "Stay where you are till you hear from me! Aycock! This Buick couldn't be in a much sweeter fix had you been the driver!" He put out his hand and laid it with care against the side of the hood. "Like she's wondering if she can go ahead and fly," he said, looking respectful. "Well, she's going to find out in another two shakes, if she ain't real careful."

"Young man!" Judge Moody called through his dust protector. "I don't think that car needs much more encouragement before it'll go over—stand back!" He put out a foot.

All Aycock's dogs rushed down the bank and started barking at him. Mrs. Moody was already saying, "Oscar Moody, come back here. You're fifty-five years old, had a warning about your blood pressure, suffer from dust and hay fever, and insisted on wearing your best seersucker today. You stay put—you hear me? You can give those boys directions—"

"Stand back!" called Judge Moody. "Away from that car!"

"Grab it!" shrieked Mrs. Moody.

Jack bent his head studiously toward the hood, put his ear

next to it. "Nothing to worry about here!" he called. "It's her own original sweet-singing engine this Buick's travelling on, and not much hotter than I am."

Wrapping his new shirt-tail over his hand, he reached for the radiator cap. The Buick responded by rocking back to front, as if the back and the front end were on the two pans of a balance scale.

"Show that car a trifle more respect!" Mrs. Moody protested.

When Jack took a step back from it, it kept rocking.

"I'm humanly certain I pulled that emergency brake," Judge Moody said. "If I'm not a complete ass, I pulled it."

"Judge Moody, you didn't pull it. And she's still in gear," Jack now called back. "But no harm done—your wheels is a hundred percent off the ground."

"Come back, you heard me. I don't want to lose you *and* the car! I don't know where I am or how I'd get home," Mrs. Moody cried to her husband, while the dogs barked in front of him.

"She didn't stop for the tree—what's holding her?" Jack shouted. He dropped to the ground and rolled fast underneath the Buick. He rolled out again and scrambled to his feet. "Let's all hope he's planted that one there to stay. Judge Moody, you're resting on top of the hickory sign my Uncle Nathan's drove in the ground and donated to the passing public just in time—the paint's still wet! Well, that was *one* way to stop!" He came trotting to face the road. "I'm ready with my verdict. Here it is. If one living soul adds on to the driving end of that car, or if another living soul is taken away from the hind end—" He raced back to the car, stuck his head in, and said, "Aycock, I got word for you: you can't get out."

"Can I sit up to the wheel?" asked Aycock.

"Ride where you are! Lean *back*!" Jack hollered.

"But that leaves us hanging over *nothing*!" Mrs. Moody cried in her husband's face.

"Well," said Judge Moody. "One thing sure. A good garageman had better be sent for *now*, to bring that car down before something more happens to it."

"But you got a Good Samaritan right here!" Jack called.

"I'm not asking for a Good Samaritan, I'm asking for a man with some know-how," called Judge Moody. "And a good piece of road equipment."

"But you saved my wife and baby!" cried Jack, running to lean over the bank above him. "I can't let some stranger shove his way in and help your car off Banner Top, not while I'm living, no sir!"

"I want that car off of there," said Judge Moody.

"And in the road! In the road!" cried Mrs. Moody. "And listen! It's my car, I'll have you all know!"

"It's her car," said Jack hoarsely to Aycock. He pleaded down to her, "Mrs. Judge, don't have a fit. If you won't, I'll hop to the wheel and back this Buick off Banner Top like such a streak of lightning she won't even know what's grabbed her."

"Jack!" cried Gloria, but Mrs. Moody wildly cried over her, "All right! I don't care who does it, just so you do it in time and don't get a scratch on the finish! I only want to see that car down in the road!"

"Headed which way?" asked Jack.

"Young man!" said Judge Moody. "I'd like to point out something. There is a tree behind that car. It isn't going to get up out of the ground and walk off for you."

"All I need is an inch—I can *make* a inch! Just to give myself one inch to cut the wheel! It'll be over before you know it, Aycock," said Jack, running to the Buick and setting his hand on the door.

"I reckon I better go on up there and put the quietus on that boy," Judge Moody said. "Young lady, you are not the only member of your family who's too precipitous." As he spoke through the handkerchief, the baby leaned from Gloria's arms to watch it talk.

"Oscar! If you won't consider your blood pressure, consider mine. You stay down here where I've got you," said Mrs. Moody. "Don't set your foot an inch up that bank, or I'll tell Dr. Carruthers on you the minute we get home."

"All it needs is one good push," said Judge Moody, and the baby showed her mirth.

"Girl, *you* go. Can't you talk your husband out of trying to rescue my car, till my husband thinks of something better?"

Mrs. Moody asked Gloria. "If you can't, I'll have to tie Judge Moody up."

"If you will kindly hold my baby, I'll see how well I can discourage him," Gloria said, and she went lightly up the diagonal toe-holds, the way she would have shown off the staircase in her own imaginary house.

When she tripped to the car, Jack was wiping the dust off the windshield, using the sleeve of his shirt.

"Jack, I don't know which is worse," said Gloria. "What you thought you were going to do, or what you're ending up doing. For the sake of the reunion you were willing to run Judge Moody in the ditch. Now for his sake you are just as willing to break your neck."

"I'll be all through in a minute—now that I can see out through the glass where I'm going."

"Here I come!" Aycock suddenly piped in falsetto.

Jack jumped backwards and one foot slipped off the edge. He saved himself. One hollow root, broken off short, was trained onto space like the barrel of a cannon, and he grabbed it. One leg thrashed for a place on another root that plunged downward like a mermaid's tail. He fought his way back over the top.

"Hey, Aycock," he said, "I bet if you and me could be down on the Bywy fishing, this Buick'd look like a peanut balanced on the end of a nose!"

Gloria clasped Jack and pressed her dizzy head against his throbbing shoulder. "Jack, I've come just in time to put a limit on you."

"What's that you say, Possum?"

"I'll let you be a Good Samaritan one last time. But providing you use some of my common sense. I'm not letting you to the steering wheel!" she cried.

"But honey," he said, "who knows better than you what a good driver I am?"

"That's driving the school bus down Banner Road with me sitting right at your back," she said. "That's not backing Judge and Mrs. Moody's polished Buick sedan down Lover's Leap with me watching—and breaking your neck!"

He stared. "I reckon you know that means find a slow way, Possum," he brought out.

"The slower the better," she said. She took one step toward the car. Aycock, at the side window, sat in profile, leaning back. Because of the way it grew, his hair looked like a sofa pillow with small tassels at the corners, worn pitched low on the forehead.

"Aycock Comfort, don't you holler 'Here I come' once more till you've got solid ground in front of you. I'll be listening," she said.

"Yes ma'am."

Jack handed Gloria down to the road, looking fondly as ever in all directions over the tall red lumps of clay and the yellow-fringed clambering road and the ditch that kept up with it, and the flower-hugged syrup stand and the Uncle Sam mailbox and the home track, falling between its own rosy banks and buckled like a little hearth in firelight.

"Never mind, Lady May! Nothing about it's got your daddy licked, not as long as he can tackle it on home grounds," he said.

"Young man, have you been made to understand to keep hands off of that car?" Judge Moody asked.

"Yes sir," Jack said. "My wife's done passed a law."

"Not any too soon. You almost went over all by yourself," said Mrs. Moody. "You've started looking to me like the kind who might scratch the finish. That car's been mighty lovingly cared for. I don't want to see it getting in any more trouble today than it's in already."

"Trouble!" Jack cried. "That's one thing I never look for. Ask my wife!" He turned to the Judge. "But if it suits your wife and my wife any better, I'll go up real easy behind the Buick, hitch to the spare with the best puller I can find, and pull her down, hind-end foremost. Mrs. Judge didn't let you start out without rope and tackle, did she, sir?"

"The rope and tackle, and all the tools," intoned the Judge, "are inside the car, safely stowed under the back seat."

"Aycock, hear what you're setting on?" Jack called, and then said, "Never mind, Mrs. Judge. I never seen the fix yet there wasn't some way out of."

"But I want to hear it first," said Judge Moody.

"My system is be ready for what comes to me in a good strong flash!" said Jack.

Judge Moody said, "But the way I prefer to do it is calling up my own garageman, even if we have to wait a little longer on him."

"Seek an outsider?" cried Jack. He gave Gloria and the baby a stricken look.

"Now there ought to be a store, reasonably there's some little store at a crossroads nearby with a telephone in it," Judge Moody said.

Up on Banner Top, Aycock laughed.

"You mean Banner! Curly Stovall closes up on Sunday, sir," Jack told Judge Moody.

"Get your storekeeper to open up, if that's the only phone there is," said Judge Moody.

"Yes, you could pull him out of church," agreed Mrs. Moody. "I'm sure he's no more than a Baptist."

"Old Curly uses Sunday to go fishing," said Jack. "He's floating down the Bywy, no question about it. But his store's shut just as tight as if he's a Christian in good standing. The old bench is pulled just as solid across the door."

"Who's got a phone in the house?" asked Judge Moody. "The nearest."

"Miss Pet Hanks."

"Where does the lady live?"

"Medley. That's five miles going the other way—you passed her house coming. She's who rings two longs and a short in Curly's store when somebody wants to talk to Banner."

"You might just as well go back to Ludlow," Mrs. Moody told her husband. "And use the one in your den."

"Then the store at the *next* benighted crossroads!" Judge Moody cried.

"Everywhere it's the same story, Judge: shut tight," Jack said. "Everything but the Foxtown icehouse is keeping Sunday."

"Where's that singing?" Mrs. Moody sharply inquired.

"When the wind veers just a little bit to the west, and it's First Sunday, you'll hear the Methodists letting off from Banner," said Jack.

" 'Throw out the life line! Throw out the life line!' " sang the Methodists. " 'Someone is sinking today.' "

"Then what are we supposed to do?" Mrs. Moody asked.

"Stand here together and wait for the first person to come along?"

"Mrs. Judge, generally the first ones to come along the road ain't exactly the ones you'd have picked," said Jack. "Now, all I need to do is holler. There's a hundred up there just waiting." Taking in a barrelful of air, he squared his mouth to holler. But Gloria shook her head at him, and he swallowed it.

"I thought till today I knew any cranny of the county you might try to show me," said the Judge to his wife. "But where's any hundred people along this road?"

"It's the gathering of his family," Gloria told the Moodys. "I don't think it's more than fifty, but that's the way they count." She told Jack, "The way your family loves to tell stories, they wouldn't hear the Crack of Doom by this time. You'll have to send up there and pull one of 'em loose by the hand."

"All right, Etoyle," said Jack.

"Hooray!" she yelled.

"Without doing the St. Vitus Dance, just tell 'em I miscalculated a shaving on what I'd be running into," said Jack. "You might give 'em the idea I could use a rope. And some of their strength."

"But don't embroider!" Gloria called after the whooping child.

" 'Miscalculated' will tell my family all they need to know," Jack said. "So don't be downhearted, Mrs. Judge! Help'll come fast. All I need 'em to bring is the equal of your car to pull with. Uncle Homer's up there with a pretty good answer."

"Uncle Homer!" Gloria exclaimed.

"Well, some day he can be expected to improve—he's been married into the family for a good long while," said Jack. "Why wouldn't this be the day? Judge and Mrs. Judge, there's seats right behind you where you can fit right into the shade."

Straddling the ditch in the shade of a mulberry tree, some planks were nailed between two-by-fours to make Jack's roadside stand. The dust was on each plank like a runner of figured pink velvet.

"I'll stay right here on my own two feet. I'm not going to

make myself comfortable till I see what happens to my car, thank you," Mrs. Moody said. "And that goes for my husband too."

Footing the bank along the ditch now there was a carpet-runner of shadow. Judge Moody walked it, to stare up the farm track that came cutting down through the bank, its clay walls, like its floor, scarred as if by battle. Dust lay in the old winter-made ruts, deep as ashes on an unraked hearth; it was dust sifted times over, quiescent now. At the foot of the track, where the wooden Uncle Sam stood as high as the Judge's waist, Judge Moody reached inside his coat to his breast pocket, as if to make sure that what he carried himself was comparatively safe.

"This is not where *I* come from," Gloria assured Mrs. Moody as the two of them stood together under the mulberry tree. "When I started out as a teacher, they handed me Banner School."

"A teacher? Well, you're just talking to another one," said Mrs. Moody, her eyes not leaving her car. "I taught nine years before Judge Moody came galloping along. I don't suppose there's a Mississippi girl alive that hasn't taken her turn teaching some lonesome school—but that serves as no excuse to me for jumping out of the bushes unannounced, dressed like a country bride, and scaring people that have cars off the road."

On Banner Top, Jack stood guard by the Buick, his arms folded and his legs crossed. The tree's shadow draped him there like a piece of sacking with holes through it. Everywhere else, the light drenched all that side of the road from top to bottom.

"Well, here we are," said Aycock. "I reckon Sir Poison Ivy is wishing him and his car was a mile away from here."

"And I'm going to do my best to get him started," said Jack.

"Let him stew a little while, Jack. I got me a seat in a pleasure car, riding here free, and I kind of hate to give it up."

"Aycock, you may not be in a hurry, but Judge Moody is. And it's still his car. Or his wife's, that's the same thing. I'm going to get it back on the road for him if it's the last thing I do," said Jack. "That's for saving my wife and baby like he did."

"He ain't done nothing for me yet," said Aycock. "Glad I don't owe him nothing."

"I'm trying to count up how many Uncle Homer will come bringing," said Jack. "For all I know, leaving the ladies out, it'll be the whole reunion. And I couldn't begrudge 'em if they want to help pull." He shoved out an arm and tried it against the tree.

"This here tree's been hitched to and carved on and chased around and climbed up and shot at so many times already," said Aycock, "if much more was to happen around this tree, it might not even stand for it."

"It's been a good old tree," said Jack. "And I aim to take care of it."

The cedar had suffered from the weather, and was set with the pegs of many lost branches; some of the stumps were onion-shaped, as though the branches had been twisted off by teasing boys whose names a good teacher could call right now. The upper trunk was punctured like a flute to give entry to woodpeckers or owls.

"Old-timers hung a rascal from this tree, my grandmaw used to tell. Jack, it wouldn't hold the rascal now," said Aycock.

"What I'm going to ask it to do is a little less than that," said Jack. "All you got to do is lean back and wait."

"Shall We Gather at the River" rose and faded on the air, and the stitching sound of the Buick's motor played on the midday silence. Then the distant sound of a pick-axe travelled to them, slow blows falling on dry ground somewhere below, spaced out with hollers of protest in between.

"That digs like my Uncle Earl," remarked Aycock. "On Sunday, too. Wonder who's played a joke on him?"

"I just want the world to know," Mrs. Moody raised her voice and called to the surrounding hills, "I wouldn't have budged from my cool house in Ludlow this morning except to go to Sunday School if I hadn't had my husband's conscience to contend with. And look where that's brought me."

"Could we possibly get rid of these dogs?" asked Judge Moody. As he paced, Queenie, Pete, and Slider were weaving hot circles around him.

"They won't bite, sir," said Jack. "They're just asking you what you want with Aycock."

Mrs. Moody suddenly exclaimed, "Where did those people spring from?"

A line of grown men and boys was coming over the crest of the road headed in the Banner direction. They kept the same distance apart from one another, and might have all been mounted on a single platform, some creeping flatcar, that moved them upgrade as a body by a pulley under them. They were all eating watermelon, their eyes raised to Banner Top.

"*They're* not bringing any help," said Mrs. Moody.

"The Broadwees are still living!" said Jack, and at his wave they made a rush for the roadside stand, where the first-comers took seats as if their names were on them.

"Hey, Jack. Hey, Aycock. Where you been!" the various ones began in hooting voices.

"Well, look whose car that is!" said the biggest Broadwee. "How about a good push, Jack? What you studying about?"

"There's a sample. There's what's wrong with this end of Boone County, *right there*," said Mrs. Moody, pointing her finger along the double row of Broadwees.

"Watch what you're saying, boys," Jack called. "There's ladies present."

"Hey, Teacher," cried one to Gloria. Then "Boo!" they all said at once to the baby, who had anticipated their greeting by starting to cry.

"You all be careful around my baby, it's a girl. She don't take to seeing roughnecks or hearing slang language," said Jack.

"Boo! Boo! Boo!" the Broadwees called systematically and in unison at the baby, like some form of encouragement practiced in their family.

"If you-all got nothing to do but sit and wait, start showing some manners!" Jack shouted. "And look out for your feet in front! Somebody may come out of my road in a bigger hurry than you are."

"A bite on the hook already, Jack," called Aycock. "Somebody's putting dust in your road."

"It's Uncle Homer for sure! He's yielding to the day!" Jack came scudding down the bank. "Judge Moody, here comes Uncle Homer and a load of helpers!"

Gloria caught him by the hand. "Uncle Homer's never come to your help yet," she said. "If he comes now, I'll have to take back my opinion of him."

Dust like a flapping blanket appeared back among the trees. A wall of dust rose on the farm track and toppled downward, there was a bang at the ditch, and a light delivery van came into view struggling to get up into the road.

"Am I to be towed by that?" asked Judge Moody.

"And just as church would be letting out at home!" cried his wife.

The van, as it pulled up its last wheel and turned toward Halfway Forks, showed its panel side painted with a big chicken dressed up in a straw hat, bow tie, and cane, while down over its head swung an axe of Pilgrim Father's size. It skidded, something was thrown out, and it ripped past them all. So empty of a load was it that its rear half danced all the way down the road, dust rising like a series of camp tents going up on the zigzag behind it. Tied onto its back doors, like an apron on backwards, there'd been a strip of oilcloth lettered "Let Homer Do It. There Is No Substitute for Experience."

"Didn't even wait to bring his own dog," said Jack. "Something about the way he handles himself makes you believe he'd be part-willing to take the joy out of life. Well, there's only one of Uncle Homer."

"I was right about him, anyway," said Gloria.

"Not a hundred percent," said Jack. He picked up what Uncle Homer had thrown at them—a length of chain, a little shorter than the length of Jack's arm. He held it up, to the Broadwees' cackle.

"Well, this means they know. That's how I read this chain," said Jack. "So help is still forthcoming, somewhere behind."

"They're all up there just sitting and listening to 'emselves talk, Jack," said Gloria.

"Recounting for Granny some tale or another about me?" he wondered.

"This is going to be another one if you aren't careful."

"There's another cloud of dust coming from the other way," said Mrs. Moody.

"And a whopper!" said Jack. "What that means is Better Friendship has turned 'em loose and a lot of hungry Methodists are headed home for dinner."

"Church people! Now they'll be my answer," said Mrs. Moody. "They'll stop and help." She composed a long face and moved forward.

"Watch out for your feet, Mrs. Judge," cautioned Jack.

Mrs. Moody raised Judge Moody's hat and started to wave it at the line coming, buggies and some wagons and a clacking Ford coupe all in one cloud of dust.

"What are your Methodists *like*?" Mrs. Moody cried, as one after the other they went driving past her.

"Well, Aycock is one," said Jack.

"Why won't they stop for a fellow worshipper, at least?" she cried, still waving Judge Moody's Panama.

"His attendance has been middling-poor," Jack answered. "For the last year and a half it's been down to nothing. His church may have forgotten what he looks like."

"I'd just like to see a bunch of Presbyterians try to get by me that fast!" said Mrs. Moody.

"There went Preacher Dollarhide, I believe. He must have worked up a fairly decent appetite," observed Jack, as the Ford coupe rushed the length of Jack's ditch and got past a buggy.

"Why, you didn't even help me make 'em stop!" Mrs. Moody exclaimed. "I believe you waved 'em on by!"

"It's my wife and baby Judge Moody saved, Mrs. Judge," Jack told her gravely. "And I feel right particular about my help."

"Now watch out—there's something else coming down that funny little road," warned Mrs. Moody.

Something that resembled a fat moon drawn in pink chalk had popped up on the rise of the farm track. It just sat there for the moment, as if waiting to be believed. It was the Banner school bus with the dust of all summer on it. It looked empty.

Then Elvie's little face could be made out, framed in the lower half of the steering wheel.

Judge Moody jabbed a finger. "That child going for help?"

"It's her opinion she *is* the help!" said Jack.

"I object to being at the mercy of a school bus fully as much as my husband objects to a chicken wagon," Mrs. Moody said, as it waited there above them, with its jawless face, every metal part below the headlight sockets gone. "Now that's just not going to tow me."

"Not towed! Not with the Buick still trying so hard to go the other way!" cried Jack. "You're about to be one end of the best tug-o'-war ever seen around Banner!"

"Under no circumstances!" exclaimed Judge Moody.

"Judge Moody, I ain't going to hear No!" cried Jack. "Ears Broadwee, you and Emmett get up and give Judge and Mrs. Moody your seats on my syrup stand. Show some manners! You forgotten all you know while I been gone?"

They scrambled to their feet, strung themselves out along the foot of the bank, elbowing their way in with the cosmos.

"Judge Moody, they wouldn't make school buses if they couldn't stand their share of punishment," said Jack. "Take heart, because this is the one I used to drive myself." He hollered, "Let 'er come!"

"Clear the way or be run over," came Elvie's serious voice, and the school bus came dropping toward them, not running on its engine. It came like an owl on the glide, not quite touching the banks on either side. Scraped-up and bulging like the Ark, it slammed into the ditch, then on one bounce was elevated onto Banner Road, in perfect starting position to go to school. "I coasted!" she shrieked at Judge Moody, who sank to a seat on the stand to let her coast on past him, headed down the hill. Queenie, Pete, and Slider tore after it barking, Queenie on her way frisking wildly around a Broadwee, nipping him and then running off with his cut of watermelon.

"Keep a hold, Elvie!" Jack was running alongside. "Begin thinking where you'll stop."

"It's a relic, that's all it is!" called Mrs. Moody after all of them.

"Elvie Renfro, *can* you stop?" called Gloria, and the bus

swerved at last and gave a big crack as it put itself back in the ditch again nearly at the bottom of the hill. The signal arm flipped out and, bright as a bunch of nasturtiums, rusty water spurted from the capless radiator.

Elvie sprang out into Jack's arms, carrying her water bucket.

"Oh, I always said I was going to drive one of them things before I died," said Elvie, raised in the air. "I wisht it'd been full of all the little girls I know, that's all."

"That was real sisterly, Elvie. Thank you," said Jack. "Who give you the first push?"

"Nobody. I pulled out the chunk and run for it," she said. "Say, will it crank?"

Jack had scrambled into the driver's seat. His foot beat the floor.

"What you fixing to do with it?" called Elvie adoringly. "Give Moody a last push?"

"Whoa, Elvie! I'm fixing to save him!"

She shrieked and ran for home.

The engine turned over once and died. Stomp as he would, Jack got no more sign out of it. "One more vacation has ruined one more battery," he said. "Every year, this old bus needs a little more encouragement to go. I feel sorry for this year's driver."

"Then feel sorry for your own brother," said Gloria.

"Vaughn Renfro?" he yelled.

"Instead of the most popular, the best speller gets it now," Gloria said.

"Well, he's already let a seven-year-old girl get the thing away from him!" Jack cried.

"I hate to see the next piece of help that comes out of *that* little road," said Mrs. Moody.

"You're about to see it now," called Aycock.

There was a clopping and a jingling, and Etoyle came riding down the track astride the mule, bareback, loaded with trace chains. She was barefooted, sawing Bet's ribs with her heels. When she fetched out onto the road, she bent over in a fit of laughter, and everybody could see her little flat chest ridgy as a church palm-fan, naked and quivering inside her dress.

"What's the word from home?" Jack greeted her over the barking.

" 'Don't let that baby fall.' "

"Ain't they been brought more up to date than that?" He took the chains, helped giggling Etoyle to the ground, then he sat up sideways on Bet and scratched her forehead. The mule wagged him up the road and onto the path up Banner Top, between fallen fence posts, through the plum bushes onto the clicking limestone. His shoulders were jolted as if by hard sobs, but when Bet turned him around at the tree they could see his face shining with pleasure.

He dropped to the ground and went fast to work with the chains. Bet posed sideways to the road; her markings were like the brown velour swag that goes over the top of a Sunday School piano. Then he slid astride her.

"Come on, Jack boy! Now!" shouted one of the Broadwees.

> "What's the matter with Ren-fro?
> He's all right!"

the Broadwees sang.

"Jack's not playing basketball any longer," Gloria broke out. "He's got his diploma."

"He's hitched that chain around that tree and the car, yes. But when the unknown quantity starts to pulling?" Judge Moody stood up.

"That tree's gonna give," chanted the Broadwees, and Mrs. Moody turned and commanded them: "Suppose you just pray."

Jack spoke into Bet's ear. But, drooping a long, kid-white, white-lashed eyelid, she balked.

"You want me to swap you for a chain-saw?" cried Jack.

There was an explosion, and he all at once sat on empty air. The trace chains flew in two as Bet shot, in a rippling cloud of pink, madly down to the road. Jack pounded down the face of the bank to head her off. The Moodys rose to the plank of the syrup stand, where they stood with uncertain footing, and the Broadwees had already scattered. Gloria hugged Lady May tightly and hid the baby's face, while Jack ran to throw out his arms to guard them, and Bet went picking her way up the home track, as if to tell her story.

"Did you hear that bang?" Mrs. Moody asked her husband. "It sounded almost like a blowout."

"The one thing it couldn't be," he said.

"Yes sir," Jack called when he returned to the car. "Mrs. Moody's right. A blowout—that's what Bet was objecting to. It was your spare."

The baby, hearing the Broadwees laugh, wailed very loud, and the Broadwees helped her by bellowing, "Boo, boo, boo!"

"Just keep on," Gloria addressed them. "Boo some more. I want you to show our visitors just how ill-behaved Banner can be. Do your most, Emmett, Joe, VanCleave, Wayne, T.T., and Ears Broadwee. I expect it of you."

"Sorry, Teacher. Sorry, we're sorry," they said, drooping.

"All right, boy, when're you going to start getting the kind of help that'll do us some good?" Mrs. Moody asked Jack, pointing her finger at him.

"Don't be downhearted, Mrs. Judge! I've got a full reunion still to draw on!"

"And not one is going to do you a bit more good than your little seven-year-old crybaby sister," cried Gloria.

He scudded down to the road. "Sweetheart!"

"The most they ever do for you is brag on you."

He bent to search her face, while the baby placed a tear-covered hand against his cheek and patted it.

"Gloria," he said gently. "You know all the books, but about what's at home, there's still a little bit left for you to find out. Not all of 'em brag so foolish—here comes Papa right now."

"Well, I rather your papa than your mama," called Aycock.

Mr. Renfro had come into sight on the farm track. Elvie came with him, singing:

> "Yield
> not to temp-
> ta-
> tion
> for
> yielding is
> sin,"

as she came down the steep track. Giving one skip to either side, she kept time to the homesick, falling tune in a sweet voice like plucking strings. Little by little, like a pigeon stepping down a barn roof, Mr. Renfro stepped his way behind her, then together they made the high step out of the ditch onto the road.

Mr. Renfro lifted his old felt hat to Mrs. Moody and Gloria, acknowledged Lady May's stare of recognition with one of his own, then came in a Sunday manner up to the Judge.

"Old man, are you connected to the telephone?" asked Judge Moody before he could begin. "Excuse me, but I believe I'm in a bigger hurry than you are."

With his drill shirt and pants Mr. Renfro had put on a mended dark blue suit coat, tight on his body as a boy's or even a girl's jacket. His shirt was still buttoned tight to his Adam's apple, and a pinch of traveller's joy had been freshly poked into his lapel.

"There's a telephone down to what's known as Stovall's store in Banner if anybody's getting ready to have a fit," he said.

"Then you can just go back, old man," Mrs. Moody exclaimed. "We know enough about that already."

"Why, this is Mr. Renfro," he said. "I reside right up that road." He turned to Judge Moody, who still wore the handkerchief across his lower face. "Been carrying Mrs. Moody for her Sunday ride? I hope she's fairly well. You seen anything lately of my son?" He gave a formal scan of the road.

"Take a peep over your head, sir," said Elvie, giggling.

Mr. Renfro glanced up Banner Top, then whistled.

"Papa!" said Jack, as he came running from the well, bringing him a glass of water. "You didn't need to be the one to come. What brought you forth?"

"Sensed undue commotion," said Mr. Renfro after he had drunk. "Nobody that left the house come back, and the mule come back by herself." He pointed at Banner Top. "I don't right exactly know how you managed it."

"I can't take the full credit, sir," Jack said, as Gloria blushed. "We all kind of managed it together."

"I'm glad to hear you admit it, son. You couldn't bring something like that to pass just by trying," Mr. Renfro said.

"But I don't see how you could hardly improve on it for showing how to go about a thing the wrong way." He handed Jack the glass and struck out across the road and set his good foot on the bank that ran straight up.

"Papa, it don't need you!" Jack said, catching up with him and stopping him, giving an earnest look into his face.

"Mr. Renfro," Gloria said, "what the rest of us are busy doing is finding a way to bring the car down in the road again without letting Jack drive it."

"Well, I kind of wonder, now, which one of you's been giving the other more trouble," said Mr. Renfro, eyes bright, looking from Jack to Judge Moody. "It's a good thing for everybody I come along."

"Papa," said Jack, "there's no call for you to be in a rush about it."

"Why, there most certainly is a call," said Mrs. Moody.

"The old cedar tree is your drawback," said Mr. Renfro. "That's plain to see from right here. Yes, and that's a pretty stubborn old cedar. I'd like to up it out of your way for you."

"Oh yes, and scar the finish of my automobile!" exclaimed Mrs. Moody. "You're not going to come chopping around my car with any old axe."

"Papa, that Buick got where it is by cheating its way around that tree. We got to pull it back the same way—that's the answer."

"May be your answer, son. I got a more seasoned one," said Mr. Renfro. He tilted back his head and ran his gaze up the tree. "Good people, I can tell you pretty quick what's called for, and that is to spring it."

"What do you mean, spring it?" Mrs. Moody asked.

"Well, talking won't bring it down," he said kindly.

"Just a minute, mister," Judge Moody said. "I'd better talk to you next, and quick, I think."

"Let's you and me go up there," said Mr. Renfro, giving him a sudden grin of conspiracy. "We ain't too old for a little sortie to the top, are we? I reckon you're about my age."

"Papa, Mrs. Judge would have a fit," Jack stammered out.

"My son thinks his dad may be a speck out of practice. But I think if you asked enough of the right people, you'd find

I'm pretty well known around Banner for the results I get," said Mr. Renfro to the Moodys.

"I'd like to point something out!" Judge Moody was saying.

"Mr. Renfro, we've got Aycock sitting *in* the car," Gloria said.

"Now I wouldn't a-done that either," he said instantly.

"It's his fault," Mrs. Moody cried.

"Well, now," said Mr. Renfro. "That changes the picture. It means going a little less heavy on the charge than I was first inclined."

"Charge?" asked Mrs. Moody, while the Judge could be heard breathing.

"Plain, common old dynamite, it's the reliable," said Mr. Renfro quietly.

"Preposterous!" said Judge Moody. The baby, who had been growing restless, smiled as his new word came popping through the handkerchief.

"I can just see visions of that! To be saved from falling to the bottom of nowhere by getting blown sky-high with a stick of dynamite!" said Mrs. Moody. "Honestly!"

"I'd have to send home for the materials, that's all. I've got bringers," said Mr. Renfro. "Sunday don't put a stop to me a minute, not when it's a need of setting my son a little straighter."

Jack laid both his hands on his father's shoulders, and Gloria spoke. "Mr. Renfro, Jack doesn't need you to rally up your dynamite for him. All he needs is a wife's common sense, and he's got that right here."

Mr. Renfro gave her the same kind of little bow that he often gave Miss Beulah.

"That's right," said Jack. "I could've already jumped that Buick around that tree and backed her down in a cloud of fiery dust in her own tracks, but Gloria run in too quick with her common sense."

"And here's a piece of mine: I'm not going to let any old man go lighting a stick of dynamite under my car, Oscar," said Mrs. Moody. "I warn you."

"Under the tree," Mr. Renfro corrected her gently. "Well,

sir, we all have to stop doing what our good ladies tells us not to, and try to make out with doing what's left," he said to Judge Moody, the light going out of his eyes. "If you rather get Stovall, and for what Stovall charges, I won't be mad at you. Now what he'll come up with is a pair of oxen. Just as set on mischief as they can be, both of 'em, as you'll know if you can read the glints in their eyes right well. And you ain't going to like Stovall's work or be crazy about his behavior or his oxens' behavior. And I'm not promising that after he's had his go at you, you won't all run crying back to me." Mr. Renfro put his hat back on. "And now I must plead company. The good ladies is about to make use of some tables spread under the trees. Jack," he turned to his son and said, "it's dinner time."

"Thank you, Papa. Tell Mama to please keep holding it."

"Papa's feelings is hurt," said Elvie, patting her father's hand.

"Papa, Elvie let the school bus run right smack dab in the ditch," said Etoyle, popping down off the syrup stand.

"Why, come back to me, Elvie. Can't you show respect for your family any better than that? That's Vaughn's bus." Mr. Renfro pointed at Banner Top as though nothing unusual attached to it any longer. "Growing up there you'll find a crop of switches. Bring me one."

"Papa, me and Etoyle ain't allowed to go up there, we're too little! That's for sweethearts!"

"Prance."

Frantically, Elvie climbed up and hopped back down. Mr. Renfro took a switch, the lightest of the three she offered, and gave her legs the least brief stinging. Then he dropped the switch, lifted his hat, sent a reserved glance all the way around him, then whistled to the baby once like a far-away train, and mounted his road. Elvie passed him, speeding home to start her crying ahead of him.

The baby, looking over her mother's arm, peep-eyed at Judge Moody with the puff of her sleeve.

"That infant ought to be home," he fumed. "The help of babies and old men is getting us nowhere."

"Of course none of these people have any idea of how to get that car down. They're all one family!" said Mrs. Moody.

"Judge and Mrs. Judge, don't be downhearted. Banner is still my realm," Jack said.

"It doesn't sound like your realm to me," said Mrs. Moody. "If you don't have the phone or the team of oxen or any way to get visitors out of here."

"We got people," said Jack. "The best thing in the world."

"I don't need anything but a single piece of machinery in good working order and a tow line," said Judge Moody.

"And a driver," said Jack. "If you'd just waited and tried us about next Saturday, you'd had it all—me and my truck and a tow rope all ready for your holler."

"All I hope is by that time we're not still up there teetering!" Mrs. Moody cried.

Around the legs of both Moodys, Aycock's bony hounds endlessly darted and shied, loudly sniffing, like ladies being unjustly accused.

"Could we possibly get rid of these dogs?" asked Judge Moody.

"Can I whistle 'em inside with me?" Aycock called.

"No!" everybody cried, and Jack said, "They'd be in the driver's seat in no time."

There was another explosion. Jack charged up the bank.

"That was your right front!" he called in a moment. "A good old Firestone tire with the tread still on it. I believe they're overheating. One way to stop 'em is let the air out of the others before they start copying!"

"Keep your hands off—they're safer just blowing out," said Judge Moody. "Dear," he said to his wife, "how much air did you have put in our tires?"

"The maximum," she said. "I always order the maximum when I get anything for you."

"The maximum air? Then just give the others time," said Judge Moody. He looked at the car and gave a short bark of laughter.

"Now cut it out, Oscar. You're about to start feeling sorry for yourself. I'll tell you one thing," Mrs. Moody said. "If that car hasn't fallen to its destruction before much else happens, it wasn't intended to fall."

"How much longer do you think Providence is prepared to go on operating on our behalf?" the Judge asked her.

"Keep talking like that and it'll fall right now!" she exclaimed. "Oscar, instead of tempting Providence, you'd do better to head on down this road to that store that's all locked up. And if you don't see the man around, climb in through the window."

"And you know what somebody'd pop up and call it? Trespassing," said Jack.

"Yes, I'd call it that," said Judge Moody. "But if we knew where this man was to be found—if we had his ear in this—"

"He's safe out in a rowboat," cried Jack. "Though if he only knew what you wanted with him, he'd be right there to say No! And I'd tackle him for you on the spot, and while you cranked up Miss Pet Hanks, I'd be setting on his chest where I could pound some willingness in him."

"There's not too much wrong with any of that, that I can see," said Mrs. Moody in a piteous voice. "Not if it allows you to use the telephone, Oscar."

"Direct me instead to the man with those oxen," Judge Moody told Jack.

"Still out floating in a boat, still the same scoundrel," said Jack. "And anything else you want to think of, that you'd like to have, old Curly's the one that's got it."

"If we had nothing but a good solid truck!" stormed Judge Moody.

"He's got it. He's got mine!" Jack told him. "With no right in the world to a single bolt of it. Before I got the last lick on it, he got ahold of it and they tell me it's down there inside his old iron shed with the iron shutter rung down on it and the padlock staring at you! Laying in a few more pieces now than it was when it's ornamenting my front yard, from the benefit of the trip! I bet you a penny he wishes he hadn't done it."

"Somebody might have to walk all the way to Foxtown," Judge Moody said to his wife. "And call from that icehouse."

"They haven't got a phone. They don't need a phone," said Jack. "But outside help—even if you could try 'em, ain't they shut? It's Sunday in the courthouse too, ain't it?"

"Then what is the answer, in all the sovereign State of Mississippi?" demanded the Judge of his wife.

"You've still got to prove it to me you want to *get* where

you're going," said Mrs. Moody. "I see plenty of misgivings in your face."

"Right through the handkerchief?" asked Etoyle curiously.

"Right through the handkerchief," said Mrs. Moody.

When he gave a hapless swing of the arms, she walked up to him. "All right, dear." She put his hat on him. She took him by the shoulders and said, "March. To the ends of the earth if need be. Only bring me back somebody with the wherewithal and the gumption to get it back for me."

"Just so he keeps in hollering distance of Banner Top," said Jack. "We don't want Judge Moody to get lost."

"Lost? What do you think he is now?" said Mrs. Moody.

Judge Moody stood still a moment longer, then faced in the direction away from Banner.

"If you come to anybody with some boiled peanuts, I could go through a pack of 'em right now!" Aycock called down.

"Buster, you pay attention to *your* job!" cried Mrs. Moody.

"In what manner and at exactly what moment did he ever get *in* that car?" Judge Moody paused to ask her. "Did you see him do it?"

"No, dear. I was too busy trying to steer you," she said.

But it was getting hotter everywhere before they were faced with another red cloud of dust, travelling from the direction of Halfway Forks. Coming out of it was a grinding noise.

Gloria clutched Jack by his belt. He was holding Lady May, and her little face rose just above his like a head-lamp, where she had wrestled her way up his neck and now clamped his ears with her elbows. "Jack, there's something I haven't told you."

"Save it till after dinner," Jack urged Gloria.

"Here it is. There's somebody in the world, and not very far away, that could pull that car down in a second, if he wanted to."

"Then he's got to have something with more power than a dozen mules he can pull *with*!" he cried.

"He has," she said. Closer now a chirping as from a load of baby chicks was added to the grinding.

"My truck! Or I'll eat it! I can just look in your face and

read how right I am!" he gasped. "Curly's got it on the road without me!"

"Life don't just stop!" she cried.

"Holy Moses!" he yelled, and the baby clapped her hands over his mouth, opening her own wide.

At first only two yellowed globes, that caught light from the sun, could be seen through the dust, set like the eyes of a locust in the roof. Then a pair of oxhorns could be made out pushing up the road toward them, with a spread wider than the fenders behind them, all but scraping the banks.

"Why, here comes the very thing!" Mrs. Moody exclaimed. "Like it sprung right out of the ground! Providence sent that. My husband only had to turn his back."

Jack pulled Lady May over his head as he would pull off a tight undershirt and set her on the ground, and staggered for a minute.

"I hated to break it to you—I waited till it was the last minute, before you'd find it out for yourself," Gloria said.

"You was just being the best little wife you knew how," he agreed in a painful voice. Then all of a sudden he shouted, "Mrs. Judge! Now I'm going to save your car by hook or by crook! Honey, you and Lady May get back from the road, about as far as the well," he cried to Gloria.

"But Jack, you know what we are here for!"

"Then put your heads down!"

"To think you would ask me to hide," she said sadly, going behind the syrup stand into the goldenrod and cosmos and down on mulberry leaves with her baby.

"Go home, Queenie! Go home, Pete and Slider! Go ask Aycock's mama for your bone. There ain't going to be nothing here for you!" Jack told the dogs. They skidded in their tracks, then turned and loped off down the road. Gloria from her hiding place let out a cry—in Queenie's mouth were both of Lady May's shoes. "And you lean back, Aycock, just look straight ahead where you're going! Old Curly's rolling right here in my truck, never dreaming." He whirled and disappeared up the farm track.

Mrs. Moody was already advancing into the center of Banner Road. She stood waving her purse, as steadily as a train brakeman with a lantern, guiding the truck to a stop. Strips

of adhesive tape rayed sunset style from a hole in the middle
of the windshield, but a large red face showed itself around it
and advanced out the window and held itself there cheek up,
as if waiting for a kiss. It was slick and jowled as a big vine-
ripe bell pepper.

"Lady," said the thin voice of a fat man, "is that your car
gone through the fence up there?"

"Of course it's mine!" she said. "Can't you see me flagging
you down?"

"Then what's it doing on Banner Top? Can't you read?
Every one of those signs along that fence says 'Keep Off.'
You're trespassing."

"Trespassing! On as wild and forsaken a spot on earth for
a hot and breathless Sunday as I ever saw in my wildest
dreams?" she cried. "Don't make me indignant!"

"Who told you you could run a pleasure car up yonder and
leave it, lady? That's a spot just waiting to give trouble. Full
of temptations of all kinds. You know what that car's asking
for?"

"Listen here, I want to talk business with you, mister," said
Mrs. Moody. "Do you know who I am?"

A head of cosmos wagged, and Jack came down the home
track with his spring-heeled walk.

"Can you tell a stranger which is the quickest way to Banner?" he asked.

"Huh?" Then the deacony voice changed into a roar. A
two-hundred-pound man in the prime of life rocked out of
the cab, his boot heels striking the road and reviving the dust.
He threw out both red arms. Jack at the same moment
charged on him, and they began pumping on each other's
backs.

"Thought you wasn't due till hog-killing time!"

"Trying to run off with my truck, you skunk!" Jack cried.
"Giving her the last lick behind my back!" He scooped up a
chunk from the ditch and ran to lay it under a front wheel.

Curly Stovall's curls were stacked like three-pound scale
weights across the breadth of his forehead; they bounced with
his laughter. Behind him, the truck's hood, fenders, and the
railings around its bed all jumped too under their thatches of
dust with the commotion of the motor. Some fishing canes

lashed to the cab roof sawed on one another, and the open door danced on its single hinge.

"Yeah, I did that truck a favor, Jack!"

"She sure stuttered hard enough getting up this hill," said Jack, and ran up the hood. The engine stormed in all their ears.

"I want to talk business," Mrs. Moody called, raising her voice against it.

"Curly, I'm holding my judgment till I see her tested!" cried Jack.

"Wait till you see her going down," said Curly Stovall. "I'm on my way home now."

"How's Miss Ora, and how did you get away from her?" asked Jack. "How's the old store? Falling to pieces?"

"Jack, times is no better since you left. Nearly all my trade's trying to get me to starve to death, I can't get a bit of satisfaction. Ain't hardly a Banner soul going to make a crop again."

"Whose troubles am I here to listen to? Yours or mine?" called Mrs. Moody, standing close.

"There wasn't but one answer, Jack. Run for office," said Curly.

"I hate for poor, hard-working Miss Ora to see how bad you'll get beat," said Jack.

"By Homer and that rattle-trap, shimmy-tail chicken wagon of his? Wait for Tuesday's explosion! This truck is my answer to Homer. A solid-built, all-round, A-one, do-all truck!" Curly Stovall's voice rose to a tenor yell over the clamorous motor. "It's ready for anything and everything, you name it—from hauling in their hay for 'em to pulling 'em out when they get stuck, before they go out of sight in Banner mud. Any act of neighborly kindness a justice of the peace can offer will be furnished cheap at the price."

Mrs. Moody pinched each one of them by his shirtsleeve. "Look at my car!" she cried.

"That's where I been this morning, doing a few little neighborly acts of kindness. I been to see the bedridden," said Curly Stovall. "And the shut-ins. Promised 'em I'm coming back on Tuesday and carry 'em every one to the polls. Old Mr. Hugg clapped his hands!"

"What you fixing to do right now, Curly?" asked Jack.

"It's a big all-out fish-fry on the sandbar! It's my last Sunday and I'm showing my hospitality."

"Look at my car!" Mrs. Moody cried, shaking her purse at him.

"Go a step further and you're going to be in badder trouble," he said.

"I have no intention of going a step further!" she cried.

"Why, do look at that car up there. Like a ladybug on a red rose!" said Jack. "How did a lady driver ever find her way up by herself?"

Curly Stovall squinted, then suddenly pointed his finger. "Not by herself! She's got another one in that car right now. Yonder's a man's head." He raised his prim voice another octave. "Hey, blooming idiot! This is the law! We discourage fools from riding up there on dangerous ground, you hear me? Bring that Buick back down here and set it in the road!"

Aycock was now holding an imaginary steering wheel in front of him, giving it some fast spins.

"Curly, squint harder. That fellow's in the *back* seat. He's nothing but just a harmless passenger," said Jack. "Don't let him fool you."

Curly turned to Mrs. Moody. In a voice beginning to sound almost respectful he asked, "How long a while you had that Buick and him up there, lady?"

"Forever is what it seems like!" she cried.

"Well, tell your blooming passenger to step up front and grab the wheel and pitch on down here," Curly Stovall cried. "We don't tolerate showing off like this from the passing public."

"Now listen," Mrs. Moody said with spirit. "It's my car. That idiot or any other idiot is not to touch that wheel, not for love or money."

"Then I got something to tell you. If you don't make him drive it off there in a pretty big hurry and of your own sweet accord, lady, I'm going to go up there and *haul* it down *for* you. Tied to the tail of my truck," Curly Stovall said primly, as Jack slapped both knees.

"The very thing I wanted!" cried Mrs. Moody. "If men would ever stop long enough to heed what's being told 'em!

Now hurry! Before my husband gets back, hear? Wait till he finds I stayed right in one place and without budging accomplished twice as much as he could."

"It'll be a dollar," said Curly Stovall. "In cash."

"Now wait, are you somebody reliable?" she asked at the same time.

"Reliable?" cried Jack. "Lady, this is old Curly Stovall. Everybody knows him! He's the storekeeper in Banner and he's a rascal and a greedy hog and a few more things—you can rely on him for all of 'em. Go ahead and show her, Curly—start riding!" He slammed down the hood of the truck. When he muffled the motor as he did, the soft lisp of the Buick engine went floating over their heads.

A thin little cry came from Curly Stovall's deacony mouth. "You trying to tell me that car's sitting out on the edge of nowhere with nobody to the wheel and nothing in front to stop it, and running on its engine?"

"Just breaking its heart to go over," said Jack.

"Then what's it waiting on! What's been holding it back?" Curly shouted at him.

"The Lord is looking after me and my husband," said Mrs. Moody in a sharp voice. "That's what's been holding it back! Now, then!"

"Cut that engine!" cried Curly Stovall.

"The fellow's arms ain't long enough, unless he grows 'em longer, waiting on your help," said Jack. "You heard this lady pass the law he can't move from where he's riding."

"Let him try budging one inch," said Mrs. Moody.

"Oh, I know better than to budge," said Aycock at once.

"Wait," Curly said. "That voice had a Banner ring."

"Open them coon eyes a little wider," said Jack. "Ain't there the least little bit about that pumpkinhead to remind you of somebody you know?"

Aycock screwed his head clear around and grinned out the back window like a Jack-o'-lantern.

"Aycock Comfort!" Curly Stovall yelled. "What're you doing home and in a Buick car on Banner Top?"

"Just sitting," said Aycock.

"You didn't get there by yourself!" Curly whirled on Jack. The curls rolled down on his forehead as he lowered his head and said, "*Now* things is taking on the complexion of the rest of your tricks, Jack Renfro. Now it's starting to look natural and sound natural and feel natural around Banner! I feel like I just had a good dose of tonic! All right, what's been your hand in this?"

"I'm the Good Samaritan! And I've been it just about all day!" Jack hollered.

"You run this lady's car up on Banner Top yourself and for my benefit, didn't you, and just waited till I come along?"

"Honestly!" cried Mrs. Moody.

"Curly, I be dog if I did!" said Jack. "And this poor lady, I'd had her down long ago and she knows it, only I got the news broke to me this morning that even before you stole my truck you already went off with my horse!"

"How did your mule handle it?"

"About the way you reckon!"

"I wouldn't have your mule for all you'd pay me!"

"Is anybody listening to me?" cried Mrs. Moody.

"Lady, I just went up a dollar on you," said Curly Stovall, not moving from where he stood, gazing upward.

"As long as that Buick's holding to the same spot, Curly, she'll behave," Jack told him. "She's reposing in the sweetest balance you ever saw in your life, with her frame sitting right on a hickory sign donated to Banner Top by my Uncle Nathan, and not a minute too soon."

"I wouldn't trust any of his work, he lives without a penny," said Curly Stovall.

"You just wouldn't hardly believe what's the case up there. You wouldn't hardly believe the balance she's in, without giving her a little rock to test her yourself," said Jack. "There she sits, singing along, good as gold, fighting along against the laws of gravity, and just daring you to come near her. But the lady wants her down and you want her down—"

Curly Stovall leaned back against the truck, his purpled arm resting on the cab window. "Jack, I swear I don't know what I been doing without you."

"I'd been here the whole time, had the sayso been mine."

"No sir, there ain't nobody upped to start a blessed thing under my nose, not since you been gone. Banner just as well been dead!"

"It won't take long to wake it up now!" Jack said. "Me, you, and Aycock all doing our part!"

"Start, then!" cried Mrs. Moody. "Get busy! And remember! Don't get on the inside of my car, don't scratch the outside finish, and don't be in too big a rush coming down and tip over my chocolate cake—"

There came a loud report from the Buick.

"What was that?" asked Curly Stovall in a thin voice.

"Blowout number three," Jack told him. "I'm betting it's the other front wheel."

"Hurry, mister!" Mrs. Moody cried, as Curly made a lunge toward Jack and put up a fist. They both began weaving with their feet.

"Lady, how Jack prevailed on you to run your own car up there to start with, I still ain't made up my mind. How Aycock's keeping it from taking off the ground, it's a little early to ask him. All I got to tell you is Jack Renfro's home again and it's starting to get away too natural around Banner!"

"But aren't you going to keep your word?" Mrs. Moody cried.

"You ain't caught me as easy as you think, lady," said Curly, dancing on his toes. "Because listen to me—I don't do Sunday business! 'Tain't the law and 'tain't Christian!"

"And that's all I'm waiting for!" Jack shouted, and made a leap for the open cab door.

Curly was ready for him, spun him around, and climbed up and rammed himself in behind the steering wheel.

"Have I spoken of Providence too soon?" Mrs. Moody cried.

"Hitch over! Either move your carcass or get out!" Jack yelled.

"What're you trying to do now, steal my truck?" Curly yelled back. The engine was still pounding, the sheaf of fishing canes arching above the cab roof and hanging over the sides quivered their length like the whiskers of some oversized store cat.

"I'm taking the wheel! I'm going up and get this lady's suffering Buick down, what do you reckon?" yelled Jack. "I'm going to fire up this truck and save that Buick right in front of your eyes!"

"Oh, is that the case!" said Curly. "First you coaxed that car up Banner Top, by ways best known to you, planted Aycock inside, and you rigged up a trap for me so pretty I nearly fell in. All I had to do was rebuild the truck and pump in three gallons of gas and drive it past the right place at the right time, and turn it over to you to save one more lady. All right, I'm going to tell you what *is* the case! *I'm* going to go ahead and save her while you watch, and not charge you a dime for the privilege or your daddy a dime. I'll just charge the lady."

"Hurrah!" Mrs. Moody cried to Heaven. "He's giving in!"

"And you want to know why I'm treating you like a son, Jack? It's because old Curly Stovall is sorry for you!" Curly hollered.

"Jack! Jack, you're going right pale!" cried Gloria, running out from behind the syrup stand with the crumbles of mulberry leaves pressed into her flashing legs. She set Lady May down on her own little feet and tried to help Jack rise.

"Well, hello, Peaches!" said Curly Stovall.

"*Sorry* for me? Did you hear Curly say it? Nobody ever dared in his whole life to be sorry for Jack Renfro! Nobody in Banner or nowhere else ever so much as threatened to be sorry for me!" said Jack, holding onto Gloria.

"That's the way it used to be, but it ain't that way no longer!" Curly hollered. "It's time you had your eyes opened, Jack—you come home to be pitied!"

Jack staggered where he stood. Gloria fanned his face with little bats of both hands. Lady May held to her mother's knees and wailed.

"Curly don't know what he's talking about, Lady May," said Jack, and she wailed louder. He took a running jump and landed with both feet on the running board.

"Jack, you ain't got a prayer of getting this truck away from me, don't you know it?" said Curly, inside.

"When it's mine already? Something I made out of nothing, using about a ton of my own sweat?" Jack wrenched at the vibrating door against Curly's pull. "Man alive, I'm taking what belongs to me!"

Curly Stovall leaned out the window into Jack's face, his small mouth stretching into a grin. "Then ask your daddy!

What do you think he give me to pay for that new tin roof? To keep folks from feeling sorry for your whole family?"

Jack tumbled backwards and sat down in the road. Lady May shrieked and Gloria ran and threw herself at him. "Lady May means she never loved you worse than now—seeing you so crestfallen," she whispered, clutching him.

Curly blew the horn on the truck, adding to the racket a sound like the buzzing of a hundred flies.

"Come back here!" cried Mrs. Moody, as he raised the throttle.

"Didn't you hear me say I was on my way to a fish-fry I'm giving myself?" he called out the window.

"But you're who Providence sent, you big bully!" Mrs. Moody cried.

"I can't be late to my own fish-fry, can I? The sandbar's loading up with voters now. I got a lot of brethren waiting on me," said Curly. "And my *ice* is melting!"

"With a lady in trouble like mine, you're going off and *eat*?" she cried.

"Ladies tells Jack Renfro what to do, but they ain't got me by the nose," said Curly, as Jack got himself to his feet. "You all can try looking for me after milking time in the morning. I'll come back and see what story the night has told."

"Serve you right if by milking time in the morning there's nothing here left for you to save!" Mrs. Moody cried as the wheels passed over the chunk and the truck started rolling down Banner Road. "Oh, why wasn't my husband here to take charge of that man? I doubt if he even realized who I was."

The truck plunged.

"Curly, that was a close call you had, a close call!" Jack yelled as he ran to keep up with it. "You nearly got yourself in a fix you couldn't even get out of by tomorrow, didn't you?"

"Drop back, you're licked!" called Curly. "Go on home and tell 'em! While I wind up my campaign in a blaze of glory!" Then there was a volley of backfire.

"We'll see who gets the glory!" Jack yelled into it. He stood still in the road, his back to the others, looking after the truck. Bales of dust tumbled behind it, then it made the blind curve

and went out of sight. "I still, I *still* don't see how he ever
got the thing on the road without me—his *or* mine," he said.
"So far as I could tell, those horns is the extent of everything
he thought of that I hadn't thought of first."

Gloria ran to him, brought him the baby.

"Gloria! What would you rather most of all I'd do to that
skunk now?" he begged her to tell him.

"Give him up!" she cried.

"I'm on your side now, Gloria," said Etoyle. "Know why?
Because you're the one that's bleeding."

"I should hope I am!" cried Gloria.

At the same time, there came a second clattering up the
road from the direction of Halfway Forks. As wheels rattled
to a stop, and an axle creaked, dust went up like a big revival
tent with the flaps popping.

"Oscar!" Mrs. Moody cried when the white triangle of
handkerchief emerged. Then, as the rest smoked into view,
she said, "You've brought me nothing but another old man,
with a team that looks about ready to fall down."

Halted at the start of the downgrade, Mr. Willy Trimble's
mules with forefeet splayed might have just alighted from the
upper air and struck Banner clay too hard.

"I expect it's the other way round, Mrs. Judge, and Mr.
Willy found *him*," Jack told her. "He lives in the road. Good
evening, Mr. Willy, the world treating you all right?"

"Ready for me to hitch my rope to your circus and give it
a pull?" asked Mr. Willy, squinting up from under his hat brim
at Banner Top.

"No sir, we still ain't reached that point yet," said Jack.

"Not saying I would if you's to ask me. Looks like it might
be liable to hurt my reputation to touch it," said Mr. Willy.

Judge Moody was climbing down from the wagon still
wrapped like a burglar against the dust. "I reckon I got fooled
at the forks," he began.

"You ought to have stayed here! I managed to get hold of
a great big truck!" said Mrs. Moody. "But there's strings tied
to it."

"No Sunday business?" Judge Moody sighed.

"First the man *threatened* me with bringing down my
car. Then he discovered that's what I wanted. So he said no

Sunday business. I offered him everything in your pants pocket, but he went off to a fish-fry! At the last minute he said he'd come back here in the morning, and I consider I'm lucky just to be here—you might have had to bail me out of jail for trespassing!"

"Did you get his name?" asked Judge Moody.

"Oh, it's the same one, the storekeeper," she said. "He did have a truck after all—I'll spare you what I had to stand here and listen to!"

"You did a better job than I did, Maud Eva. I got to a forks. I could see just one house. In the teeth of a dozen dogs I pounded, but nobody came."

"That was the Broadwees' house, sir. Even the women don't stay home on Sunday," said Jack.

"I found him drooping, and carried him back to you, lady. Told him better to stay put with who he's with," said Mr. Willy. "Stand still: your answer always comes along."

"Yes indeed, I've seen just about every sample of it, counting you! And now I doubt if there's anybody left at this end of the world *to* come," Mrs. Moody said with indignation in her voice. "Just take a look at the emptiness of this road."

There were only the claybanks and themselves. Where the Broadwees had been standing there was a newly gouged-out "B" like a cat sitting on its tail, and the two halves of a watermelon, eaten out, had been left beside the syrup stand like a pair of shoes beside a bed.

"It's dinner time," said Jack. "And even the Broadwees has bowed out. I reckon they're down at the fish-fry."

"Oscar," Mrs. Moody said, "you are to shanghai the next thing on wheels that dares to come along here and make 'em carry you back to civilization where you can beat somebody over the head till they come and haul us."

"Cock your ears right now!" Etoyle cried.

Something came quaking over a Dry Creek bridge. Then a confused noise moved toward them up the road, again toward Banner, a rumble and creaking accompanied by a full register of women's voices.

"Shanghai that!" said Mrs. Moody. A short broad bus, painted blue, came over the rise.

"Why, that's a church bus, Mrs. Judge, and it's headed the other way—he can't turn *them* around," said Jack. "And it's packed tight. I wonder where it's coming from and where it's going so late."

The bus sagged sideways, behind Mr. Willy Trimble's wagon, then stopped. Out of every paneless window an excited face appeared.

"Gloria Short!" one of them cried, and then a smiling middle-aged lady in white hat and white dress leaned out of a forward window as far as her waist. "Dressed up and waiting by the side of the road! You looking for a ride?"

"No, Miss Pet, I'm not dressed up like this to go travelling," said Gloria.

"You look like you're fixing to get married all over again. What did you do to get so skinny?" another one cried. "Well, I believe it's becoming to you."

Jack came and stood in the road beside Gloria, and rested his hand on her shoulder.

"I see now what you're dressed up for! You got your husband back," said the smiling lady, who had the voice of a tease.

"I got him back this morning, Miss Pet."

"And I hope you were ready for him!"

"Tried to be."

"How many ladies is it?" Jack wondered aloud.

"This is a busload of schoolteachers, all of them teachers but Miss Pet Hanks," Gloria told Jack. "It looks like all the teachers of the Consolidated School System of Boone County. This is the first time any of them's come to see me since I was married."

His lips moved to her ear. "Honey, ask those teachers what they want with you now."

"You got some mighty dressed-up friends, too," said Miss Pet. "You-all doing your visiting here in the road?"

"They're waiting to leave in their car. Try looking straight up over my head," said Gloria.

"Why, that's Lover's Leap," said Miss Pet Hanks with a wink. "As we used to call it. And yonder's somebody hugging somebody in the back of that car in broad, open daylight."

"It's not somebody, it's just a guitar he's hugging," said Etoyle, who had been running and skipping up and down, up and down the bank without attracting much notice.

"He'd do better to back up instead. I wouldn't give you two cents for where I think he's headed," said a teacher.

"Looks like he aimed for the moon and didn't quite get there. I rather they all stayed on the ground," said the flower-hatted driver.

"He's about to go off over the edge of doom and there's not much you and I can do about it, Mrs. Grierson. We're only teachers," said a cranky voice from nearer the back.

"Some of *your* work?" Miss Pet Hanks playfully pointed her finger out the window at Jack.

Gloria said, "Jack's here to help, he feels called on."

"Then I only hope you've been standing by to keep him from making any more mistakes," said Miss Pet.

"That's exactly what I'm doing," Gloria said.

Jack gripped her closer. "Honey, ask 'em what's the calamity," he whispered.

"I declare, Gloria, we picked a busy day to find you, didn't we?" teased Miss Pet Hanks.

"We're not sparing any effort," said Gloria. "It may be a long story yet, getting that car down without a scratch."

"Well, I daresay it was quite a story how it got up there," said the cranky voice.

"It'll fall, and solve your problems," two other voices said in unison and then everybody in the bus laughed and the two speakers made a wish on it.

"Aycock Comfort!" Miss Pet Hanks exclaimed, as his face turned full toward them. "Imagine you being where you are!"

"Is he kin to any *Mrs.* Comfort?" asked a new and timid voice from the crowded, benchlike seat at the back end of the bus. "Mrs. Comfort that lives in walking distance of Banner School and wants to board the teacher?"

"Sure! If that's all you ladies came for, just keep going," Jack said. "Take the last chance you get to turn off before you start down to the bridge—you have to squeeze around a big old blackjack oak, but if the school bus can make it, you can."

"If there's one thing I was hoping I wouldn't get, up here, it was bad news," said Aycock in the car.

"Good-bye, then," said Jack to the teachers.

"Good-bye," said Gloria.

Leaning out of the windows, some of them standing and peeping over the others' shoulders, they looked down from the bus at Gloria. They themselves were rainbow-dressed in Teachers' Meeting dresses of spring crêpe, teachers' hats shading their rouge spots, and their voices competed together like sisters'.

"Gloria Short, we're going all the way to Alliance," Miss Pet Hanks called through the others. "Miss Julia Mortimer dropped dead this morning and I rounded up every teacher I could find and said, 'Let's all go!'"

Gloria stood as if she had been struck in the forehead by a stone out of a slingshot.

"She took a fall in her own home," said an old lady's voice. "Nobody with her. Somebody had to *find* her. Home's the most dangerous place after all, they say."

Jack was supporting Gloria—she looked ready to fall backwards.

"I spread the news, the minute somebody started trying to find her doctor. It went through me," said Miss Pet Hanks. "Gloria, I rung two longs and a short all morning long in Stovall's store and nobody ever came to the phone to take the message. Well! Some exchanges would give up, but that isn't my style." She laughed excitedly.

"Is Gloria crying? I don't think she's crying yet," said a voice farther back in the bus.

"The baby's crying," said another.

"And so," said Miss Pet Hanks, "as long as we could come by Banner as easy as any other way, and we still had one seat, I says, 'Let's pile in the new teacher that goes to Banner School and dump her where she boards, and let's hunt up Gloria Short on Banner Road—and she can have Myrtle Ruth's seat and ride with us the rest of the way to Alliance.' I says, 'Kill two birds with one stone! Be inexcusable to go all that way with an empty seat.'"

As if on signal, the door of the bus swung open and the

breath of the engine and the smell of candy mints spread out into the road.

"Come ride with a whole load of teachers and me! All going to pay tribute!" cried Miss Pet.

"She's quaking a little. Maybe she's going to have a fit," said a teacher.

"No she ain't," said Jack. He clamped Gloria to him.

"The reason I'm one of the bunch is somebody had to be smart enough to think up the trip," said Miss Pet. "We've got 'em from Gowdy, Roundtree, Stonewall, Medley, Foxtown, Flowery Branch, Freewill. And you're the last on the line."

"We started the minute church let out," said one of the other voices. "We borrowed the Presbyterian bus because it stays the hardest-scrubbed—it's from Stonewall. Isn't it the luckiest thing it's a Sunday she picked? Suppose it had been a school day, like tomorrow. We'd been cooped up."

"I'm never cooped up. I never consider myself cooped up," said Miss Pet Hanks, turning her head from side to side. "I'm a free soul, I am."

"Come on. You're still one of us, Gloria Short. Even though you didn't wear too well or last as long as we did," said the driver. "You can come without a hat—join the ride."

"Because remember all you owe her," said the old voice from back within.

"Owes her even more than we do. Owes her the most of all," said another voice.

"The most of all!" they chorused.

"Besides owing her part of your education, you were just an orphan!" said Miss Pet Hanks. "I reckon I know how you begun!"

"She loved you the best and prized you the most—*you* started out with three strikes against you," said the strict voice.

"What was the third strike?" asked Etoyle, with a pull on Gloria's sash.

Gloria handed her Lady May, then slowly tears ran down both cheeks.

"It was my inspiration to pick you up and carry you just the way we found you!" cried Miss Pet.

"You certainly made yourself easy enough to find, Gloria," said the driver. "We couldn't have missed you."

"And you aren't glad after all to see some fellow teachers again?" asked one. "Don't you appreciate still being counted?"

"Does your baby cry like that all the time?" the new teacher's tiny voice asked.

"She's crying for me." Gloria turned her face into Jack's shoulder and he patted her a little faster.

"All this happening to you on one pretty Sunday, I *wanted* to come hunting you and find out how you'd take it. I *wanted* to say 'Come ride with us' to see how quick you'd jump in," said Miss Pet Hanks, turning her rose face in its wide-brimmed hat from side to side again, as if to accept praise from all corners of the world. Judge and Mrs. Moody stood as still as the Uncle Sam by the road. Judge Moody with his head sunk.

"You wanted to kill two birds with one stone," Etoyle reminded Miss Pet Hanks. "Now I see the other bird. I see the new teacher's face staring, the one we're going to get tomorrow, oh-oh!"

"Raise your head, Possum. I'm here," Jack told Gloria.

"No, let her cry," voices said. "It's good for her. Good if she could cry a little harder."

"Listen at her now," said a teacher to the others. "Makes you wonder how often she's cried when there's nobody to hear her."

"Sure is lonesome up Banner way. I'd forgotten how lonesome," said another.

"This is getting close to Miss Julia's old stamping grounds, right here," said Miss Pet Hanks.

"Yes'm, another five miles or so further on, and at the bottom of the hill just before you get to that bridge. There's Banner School, if it hasn't blown away," the driver said.

"And how many tracked here once, going to school to Miss Julia? I did!" cried Miss Pet.

"Trudged! We didn't have a bus like that one yonder, did we? School buses! What they do best is get away from the driver," said the flower-hatted driver of the church bus.

"Look at that one. Glad it's over in the ditch if *I've* got to pass it."

"When I was growing up close to Medley and trudging to school at Banner, the way there wasn't as forlorn-looking as it is today," said Miss Pet Hanks. "Not to me."

"Not to me either, young lady," said Mr. Trimble from his wagon. "Remember me, anybody? I'll try you, Thelma Grierson: *'Willy Trimble?—Hope Not!'* I sat behind you."

"Willy Trimble, you put my pigtail in your inkwell," replied the driver. "I remember you and I want you to hitch yourself a little closer to that ditch and hold onto those mules. Thirty ladies want to get by you."

"That's right—that dishpan full of chicken salad don't want to wait much longer. Try Gloria Short one more time, and if she won't jump in we'll go on without her, carrying a perfectly good empty seat across that bridge," said Miss Pet Hanks.

Jack said, "I'll speak for her. She ain't coming with you. I'm not letting her, that's why."

A black-bonneted, wrinkled face leaned out of a back window and the strict voice said, "Gloria Short, I'm as old as Julia myself. I think you just better find something to do with that husband of yours and climb on board and ride to Alliance while you get the chance. Or what's to keep you from being sorry in afteryears?"

Gloria put up her head and asked the busful, "What makes you think a mother would run off and leave her baby?"

"It's the other way round," said Etoyle, jumping up and down beside her, pointing her finger up. "Look in the peephole!"

Jack pounded down the road. In the upper wall of the bank where Banner Top rose straightest from the downslant of the road, the peephole faced them at this hour with a shadowless rim, showing the circle of sky no brighter than the clay around it, just a different color of the same substance, like a seal on a document. Lady May's face showed itself in it, peeped, went away. It reappeared, peeped, went away.

Jack was already clawing himself up the steep smooth wall below her, thrashing and swinging his body. In an instant he was halfway to the top, hanging spread-eagled to catch his first breath.

The baby's face went away and out poked her foot with its little shoe gone. From below, it looked white and airy as a waving handkerchief.

"Jack! Climb! Climb for your baby!" Gloria screamed.

Then Lady May's little leg and behind entered the hole and nearly came too far, like a too-small cork. At once she busied herself with trying to turn around in the hole, as if she meant all the time to take a seat there facing front, and all of a sudden she did it.

"Aycock! Jump! Run to my baby and catch her britches!" Jack hollered, while he scrambled, inches at a time.

"Come on in here with me, baby," Aycock called.

"She's just got herself too big a crowd," moaned Gloria.

"I'm praying," chattered Mrs. Moody, holding onto her husband.

"Don't let that baby fall!" cried Etoyle.

Judge Moody lurched forward, but Mrs. Moody pulled him back by his coattail. "You'll just scare her, make her fall quicker, that's what you're good for," she said, with her teeth chattering.

Lady May watched them all from where she sat in the hole as if she were at home in the automobile tire that hung in the tree, waiting to be swung from behind. Jack took a recovering step and balanced on an outcrop of goldenrod. The sun had moved; only above him was the wall still rose red. That below was in deep brown shade, as if a big wave had come up out of the Bywy and filled everything but where the baby was. Out of it reached his shirtsleeves.

Lady May put up her arms and dropped to Jack's, straight into his chest, where he folded her in.

Mrs. Moody grabbed Judge Moody at the same time and cried, "Couldn't you kill both of 'em!"

"What a trip already! And we're not even to the bridge!" cried Miss Pet Hanks.

Jack was studiously backing down the bank with Lady May. Once they were at the bottom, she hollered, turned herself upside down in the fold of his arm, and drove her little heel straight into his eye.

"Well, I've got me a tomboy," announced Jack.

He walked up the road carrying her, smoothing back her

hair, clearing her forehead, baring her ears, giving her a wan, older face. She looked back at him soberly now, flat-headed, as if water were streaming from her, as if she knew she'd been bodily snatched from something and was now beginning to wonder what it was.

"That little hidey-hole she found keeps the heat like Mama's oven," Jack told Gloria, giving the baby over. "No wonder she was ready to jump out like a little grain of pop-corn."

Lady May with one hand knocked her mother's dress ajar and set a fist around the nipple inside. Her tuning-up sounds stopped abruptly. Gloria curved her arm around her and bent her head over her.

"This is going beyond the pale," Mrs. Moody said to her husband.

"Can't you understand?" Gloria asked the busload. "I've got my hands so full!"

"Oh. Of the living," said one of the voices, gone flat.

"Stay right where you are, Gloria," said the driver. "Seeing is believing."

"Bye-bye, Gloria! You're needed here. Your baby said it for you!" called Miss Pet Hanks. "And she looks exactly like you, congratulations. Mr. Willy Trimble, this is the first time I ever saw you but I know who you are: pull over further in that ditch and let thirty schoolteachers and a lady by, please kindly."

Mr. Willy pulled over, saying, "I do like it when I come across a please, no matter how late."

Jack spurted forward to give the bus a push, and the engine at length turned over, a tenor engine that sounded fighting mad. With all the teachers looking back, the bus went past them, went past the wagon and then the school bus. Shutting off the throttle, the driver took it to the bottom of the hill on the glide.

Mr. Willy Trimble took off his bonnety hat and leaned down from his wagon toward Gloria. "That's right, daughter. This morning it was," he said. "Down fell she. End of *her*. You're looking at the very one found her."

Judge Moody, out in the road, put his hands to his cheeks

and rolled the tied-on handkerchief up into a ring around his forehead, and there was his naked face.

Lady May gave an outcry. Perhaps she had simply expected that under that handkerchief there was a face like Jack's, or Mr. Renfro's or Bet's, or even no face at all—but not one she had never seen before, not one more new hot red face. And with it all in view, and the long lines creasing it, his eyes seemed to everybody there to show for the first time, brown and sad.

"All right, Oscar. And now let me tell you something more," said Mrs. Moody. "That church bus would have let you jump in with them. They had a seat for you. Men are the rankest cowards!" She stood up too. "Now what?"

"Judge and Mrs. Judge," Jack said, "there ain't all the time there was. I ain't going to let anybody at all stand out on Banner Road, roofless and perishing, with the sun already started down the sky. Now your Buick's got seven or eight good inches of gas to go—she can purr right ahead without the benefit of you watching, just as long as Aycock donates his weight to your balance. I invite you to come to our reunion."

"Jack!" Gloria cried out faintly.

"Nothing is too good for Judge Moody, he saved my wife and baby. If I hadn't been here for Lady May this time, he'd have had to save her again." He turned around and planted himself in front of the Judge. "But Judge Moody, before you start to thanking me, wait. Think back. Have you ever seen me before, sir?" Jack drove his face close and stared at him.

Judge Moody took a step back. From behind him Mrs. Moody suddenly exclaimed, "I have! I have! Oscar, I swear it."

"I believe you are getting to look a little bit familiar to me too," said Judge Moody. "Now from how long ago—?"

Jack stood closer, his eyes open to squares.

"This very morning!" Mrs. Moody cried at him. "Our car went in the ditch and the first one to come along was you."

Judge Moody groaned. "A good safe ditch. A perfectly good safe ditch. I have no doubt it was you, and you ought to have left us there."

"But who was that Good Samaritan?" asked Jack urgently. "Go back farther than the ditch, Judge Moody. My name is *Jack Jordan Renfro*. That's what I came here to tell you and it looks like I finally caught up with the chance. Jack Jordan Renfro, from Banner." He looked Judge Moody intently in the face and got his stare returned.

"Son, I bet you a nickel we've had you behind bars!" said Mrs. Moody in a sudden flash.

"For doing what?" challenged Etoyle.

Judge Moody had fixed him with his eye. "Are you the fellow that subjected me to the screeching mother bird in court? And corrected the court on the name of the bird?"

"That's right! It was a purple martin. Start with her and you may remember it all in a grand rush," said Jack.

"What was your case?" Judge Moody asked. "You tell me."

Gloria, still giving the baby her breast, said in a voice from which exhaustion was not now far away, "Your honor, I'm here to tell you Jack Renfro's case in two words—home ties. Jack Renfro has got family piled all over him."

"Proud of it," said Jack. "And they had 'em a sorry time of it, Judge, while I was away ploughing Parchman."

"I expect so." Judge Moody sighed. "Though I'm also sure that the first time they showed up like this and put in a plea for you"—without really looking at Gloria and the baby he nodded their way—"Parchman turned you loose, didn't they? Don't tell this court about home ties, I'm entirely familiar with 'em. How long have you been out?"

"Got in this morning, sir, in time to get the reunion warmed up to a good start," said Jack. "I wish you could've seen my baby streak in to surprise me."

"I saw her try it on me. What did I sentence you for?" asked Judge Moody, as if he barely could hold back a coming groan.

"Aggravated battery," said Jack. "And I might just as well have held my blow, sir—he's the same old Curly today."

"The same storekeeper that's going to bring the truck—when he feels like it?"

"There ain't but one!" said Jack.

"They're all in this together," said Mrs. Moody.

"And your partner?" Judge Moody looked up at the car. "Back from Parchman?"

"Fresh back from Parchman, sir, ain't had his dinner yet either, any more than you or I. But there's a plenty of everything where you and Mrs. Judge are invited if you hurry right now. They're only waiting on sight of me to sit down," Jack said.

The air rang as if all the pots and pans had dropped at once onto the iron top of a kitchen range somewhere. Gradually the reverberations died down.

"What was that?" Mrs. Moody asked, her hand on Judge Moody.

"That was good old Banner bridge," Jack said. "The church bus has just made it to the other side." He jumped to Mr. Willy's team and took hold of the white mule's bridle. "You could carry these folks to my house, couldn't you, Mr. Willy?"

"Don't approve of Sunday pleasure riders. And I ain't going to carry no crying baby anywhere—anything I do hate, it's baby-crying."

"You don't hear Lady May. She's sound asleep now," Gloria said in a whisper.

"All right, let 'em climb on and see if I will," said Mr. Willy. He spoke to the mules, and after they each took a juicy bite of cosmos they brought the wagon up out of the ditch and waited there.

"Look at your old wagon coming apart, Mr. Willy," said Etoyle as she skinned up the side and peeped in.

The high sides, like a skimpily mended fence, had missing places as wide as windows between some of the uprights. Scraps of lumber were visible lying on the floor by a pile of quilts, and a quota of chairs stood in a double row. The wagon gave off a smell like a busy sawmill's.

"Other people won't give me a chance to fix my own, girlie," said Mr. Willy. "They just won't leave me alone." He turned sideways on the seat and said to the Judge, "I'll sharpen your plough-point, mend your harness, fix your wife's sewing machine, and the rest of it. Banner's my home. Try me." His hat, that he wore year-round, had its wintry, dust-packed brim pulled down like a black sunbonnet around his withered cheeks.

"Just a minute," said Mrs. Moody. "Just one minute!" She elbowed past her husband to go around and get a look at the wagon from behind. "Oscar, this is the very same old fellow that started our trouble this morning, and I said I hoped I was never going to see him again on my road."

Judge Moody stood beside her. "Well, you've hit on a fact," he said. "Old man, you wouldn't let my car pass you, I'd have had to go in the ditch—"

"Well, to let you pass me, *I'd* had to go in the ditch," said Mr. Willy. "Figure it out."

"—and finally you turned right across the road in front of me, and forced me—"

"Thought everybody knew that's where I lived," said Mr. Willy. Only Etoyle, scampering over the wagon, laughed.

"Well, Maud Eva, and here we are in the heat of sun," said Judge Moody. "Now that you know the worst, do you think you can bring yourself to mounting this wagon and getting under the shelter of this boy's roof, and leaving the car where it is?"

"Oh, the car's not going to fall now. It's certainly been given every opportunity there is to fall," said Mrs. Moody in a surprised and almost offended tone of voice. "If the Lord had intended my car to fall, don't you think He'd have gone ahead and seen about it before all this came along? I do."

Judge Moody turned around, plodded to the foot of the bank and called in a hoarse voice up to Aycock. "Now I expect to find this car right in the same place when I get back. And you still in it. Is that understood?"

"Are you-all saying good-bye?" Aycock called.

"Can I trust you?"

"Yes sir, you can trust me," called down Aycock. "Anybody that wants to is welcome to trust me."

"Sure you can, sir. Aycock's the best friend I got and my closest neighbor," Jack said. "I only hope your Buick was listening as well as he was to what you said."

"Speaking of excuses nobody in their right minds would believe," said Mrs. Moody, pointing up at the Buick, "if you'd tried to *make up* an excuse for not getting where you were going, Oscar, you couldn't have beat that."

"I'm not much on making excuses, Maud Eva—"

"It's the last thing they'd believe," she said, still pointing. "The real excuse doesn't ever carry weight at all. It's just as well you're not going to get the chance to offer it."

Judge Moody was leading her to the wagon. The nailed-on ladder came down the wagon side nearly to the road. Mrs. Moody put her foot up. "All right, Oscar, but just remember this was *your* decision."

"Is this your ice, Mr. Willy?" Down in the bed of the wagon, Etoyle lifted the quilt from what it was covering. "Who's that for?" she asked as she jumped from the high board side into Jack's arms.

"Nobody from Banner," Jack told her with a pat on the head, and she danced away.

"Oscar, do you see what I see?" Mrs. Moody bumped back against the Judge. "Honestly!"

It was a new pine coffin, still a little rough-looking—the source of the medicinal smell that had kept coming out of the wagon while it waited in the road.

"I'm the artist," said Mr. Willy Trimble. "Got the lining to fit it with, and plane it some more. I'm just going down to the old sawmill." He nodded toward Banner. "There's still a whole raft of cedar boards back in yonder from Dearman's time, laying in that wilderness of honeysuckle. Pretty well seasoned by now. Any fellow can go stepping in there and help himself to some sound timber if he ain't afeared of snakes. Nobody to tell him halt. I'm finishing up this one special for a present. Aim to carry it across the river to Alliance." He took his hat off and folded it to point with into the distance ahead.

"Well, sir, you can just carry it *right on*," said Mrs. Moody. "Go right on to Alliance, and without benefit of the Moodys' company. Go on, shoo!" She stamped her foot in the road. "Get up, horse!" she cried to the mules.

Mr. Willy put his hat back on. A wasp staggered from its brim, then, carrying its legs like a basket, took off swinging into the air. He brought out into Banner Road and rattled off down it and disappeared around the blind curve, leaving them his dust.

"You didn't really hurt his feelings," Etoyle told Mrs. Moody. "Mama says it can't be done, no matter how hard you might try."

At the same time, another clatter filled their ears. A whirlwind of dust was rising on the home track. The same as the other time, Vaughn came at them driving the mule from a stand on the seat of the wagon as though all their lives depended on him. Bet jumped the ditch and the wagon seemed for a moment to fly to pieces, but before it could turn over, Jack got the mule halted.

"What does Mama say?" he asked Vaughn, picking him up from the road and setting him back on the seat.

"Said even if the world was coming to an end here, the reunion was ready to sit down."

"All right, Vaughn. I believe we're as ready as they are. But who you're carrying to the table is Judge and Mrs. Judge Moody."

Vaughn opened his mouth. Jack helped Mrs. Moody and the Judge up onto the spring seat beside him.

"What word do I take Mama along with 'em?" Vaughn broke out.

"Mama knows what to do," Jack said. "Just keep down to a trot and don't spill 'em. The rest of us will walk it and get there the same time as you," he told the Moodys.

"The school bus!" yelled Vaughn, in the minute between when his old dust faded and his new dust was still to be raised. "Look where you put the Banner School bus!"

"You got it to keep up with for a whole year, Vaughn. You ought to've started sooner," said Jack. He gave Bet a spank.

At the last minute, Etoyle sprang and made a jump into the wagon. She dropped down into the hay behind the Moodys and smiled at them.

"No, Mischief, you can't hold my baby again," Gloria said, as Etoyle held out her arms from the moving wagon. "She didn't get up Lover's Leap all by herself."

"And here *we* go up this funny little road," said Mrs. Moody.

As though he needed to wring out something, Judge Moody wrung out his handkerchief, then scraped it over his cheeks and brow and tied it on again.

When the dust began to rise behind the wagon, Etoyle stood and waved at the only one she could still see above it, Aycock. "Sweet dreams!" she called. The smile of pure happiness on her face was the same one she'd welcomed Jack home with this morning.

"How late is it drawing on to be?" Aycock called.

"Don't fret. One of my sisters'll find her way back to pitch you a chicken leg," said Jack.

"Stop her. I want a can of sardines and a can of Vyenna sausages and a pick to punch it open. And the kind of pickles Miss Ora Stovall knows so well how to cure," he called. "Those're what I been homesick for."

"Save 'em for Saturday," Jack advised.

"Can I keep Queenie? She'll be good, she's the mother dog."

"She took off, leading those two other scampers. They'll get home without you. But I'll run tell your mama you're safe and sound before she sets in to calling you," said Jack.

Now he and Gloria and the sleeping baby were the only ones in the road, and the sound of all wheels had faded. He set his hands in place around her waist and asked, "Ready for home?"

They started up the track, and Jack steered them toward the well. Its smell came to meet them, like that of a teakettle that has been steaming away, out of mind, on the back of the stove all day. Under the big pine was Gloria's satchel lying forgotten, already velvety pink. The wooden cover over the well had the heat of a platter under the Sunday hen. Through Jack's hands the rope ran down in a long coarse stocking of red, and then he drew the bucket up on its shrieking pulley. They shared the glassful. Then Jack, looking at Gloria's face, poured her another glassful and handed it to her.

"You can count on one thing, Gloria," he told her. "Before the day's out I'm going to see that you get your good-byes said to your Miss Julia Mortimer."

She spilled the water and dropped the glass. "Jack!"

"You needn't have worried—I wasn't going to let you get carried off by a gaggle of geese," he said, brushing the drops off her skirt, chasing the glass. "We ain't that bad off yet, that my wife has to be *come after* in time of trouble. We still got a wagon and mule to our names."

"Are you sending me back where I came from?" she cried.

"I'm carrying you. I'm going with you, not letting you go anywhere by yourself, sweetheart."

"I don't want to go! I've *said* my good-byes to Miss Julia!"

"But she's the one who was good to you. Your main encourager."

"Then listen! Miss Julia Mortimer didn't encourage me to marry you, Jack!" cried Gloria.

"What?"

"She was against it and gave that out for her opinion."

The pupils of his shocked eyes nearly overflowed the blue. *"Why?"*

"She said it promised too well for future trouble."

"She came out with the bare naked words?"

"Trouble and hardship."

"Gloria, next to losing Grandpa, this is the worst news to welcome me yet," he said.

"And the only letter I ever did find in that mailbox for me was from her," said Gloria.

"What did it say? Get it out, honey," said Jack.

Gloria hugged the baby closer. "It said for me to come to Alliance and she'd tell me what would become of me. To my face," she whispered. "I never went!"

"Because how could you get there?" he said. "You couldn't even get to Parchman to beg for me."

" 'Don't marry in too big a hurry,' she said."

"Possum, then what would she have had you do?"

"Teach, teach, teach!" Gloria cried. "Till I dropped in harness! Like the rest of 'em!"

He gripped her.

"Do you blame me for keeping out of her sight?" she asked.

"But it was so remarkable of her," he said, staring. "She knew what would happen without even laying eyes on me. Didn't even know me."

"She knew *of* you."

He held her close to him, her face spangled with its freckles and beginning tears as if dragonfly wings were laid across it.

"Don't cry. Don't cry about it now," he said, his cheek on hers.

"I waited so long on today! I thought I was ready for anything, if you'd just come—reunion or no reunion. Then first Judge Moody and now Miss Julia Mortimer! I blame them both for where we find ourselves right now."

"You can't blame who you love," he said.

"I can. I blame Miss Julia Mortimer."

"You can't blame somebody after they're dead," he said.

"I can."

As they stared at each other, he suddenly jumped her aside, for a wasp came swinging toward her temple, like a weight on a thread. He beat it off, beat the air all around her, stamped on the wasp, and brushed her carefully again, although nothing had touched her. Nothing had bothered the baby, who lay against Gloria's bosom, open-mouthed in sleep.

"*You* can't blame anybody *living*," she accused him.

"Now I can't blame Judge Moody. He saved—" He drew her near, stroking her forehead, pushing her dampening hair behind her ears.

"Sending for me to tell me what she thought of our future! An old maid, and a hundred and one years old!"

"Old people want to tell you what's on their mind, regardless of what it is or who wants very bad to know it," whispered Jack. He went on stroking her, as if she might have fallen and hurt herself, or the wasp had stung her after all. "And they pick the time when they want to tell it. It's always right now—they don't like to wait. You just got to expect it."

"I've hoped against hope she was wrong through and through!" Gloria's tears ran down the face he was kissing.

"Poor little old fat Possum," he whispered. "I see now what you've been doing all this time without me. Thinking. Broodering."

"The very last time I was over the bridge, she tried to talk me out of listening to you. That's when you were still my pupil."

"And when you took my side," he asked her, stroking her forehead where it was so hot, "wouldn't she pay regard to your common sense?"

"Jack, she pooh-poohed it. She laughed at me." Then every bit of her was ready to dissolve in tears. He sank to the ground along with her and the baby, and took them on his lap—onto his old torn pants, whitened and crumbling along the seams as though they'd been trimmed in crusts of bread.

"I'd wondered why she didn't come to our wedding," he said. "But I see now why she couldn't show her face."

"I wouldn't have told you she laughed. Only if I hadn't, you would have carried me straight to her wake," she whispered.

"Now you've had one to laugh at you, and I've had one to be sorry for me," said Jack.

She sobbed.

"Never mind, honey. I ain't ever going to laugh at you, and you ain't ever going to feel sorry for me. We're safe."

"That's being married," she agreed between sobs.

"And never mind, sweetheart, we're a family. We've still got the whole reunion solid behind us."

"Oh, if we just had a little house to ourselves, no bigger than our reach right now," she whispered. "And nobody could ever find us! But everybody finds us. Living or dead."

He cradled her flaming head against his shoulder. He held her in his arms and rocked her, baby and all, while she spent her tears. When the baby began to roll out of her failing arm, he caught her and tucked her into the pillow of the school satchel. Then he picked up Gloria and carried her the remaining few steps to that waiting bed of pinestraw.

When the sun had moved, Jack said, "And they're waiting dinner on us." They stood up together and Jack lifted Lady May—the limp child whose cheek had been pressed pink by a little buckle, whose feet were bare as a beggar's.

A flock of birds, feathers of that blue seen only in the loneliest places, flitted across the path that started home. From behind them, a string was plucked, then another—a tune.

"I reckon what Aycock spent his year, six months and a day missing was his guitar," said Jack. "He's serenading himself now. I wonder what told him he was going to need that before he got back home this time."

"And now, Jack," said Gloria, when they were back on the

short-cut, "the reunion sent you to get rid of Judge Moody and what you've done is invite him home with you. And his wife along with him. This time, they'll kill you."

He smiled at her.

"Or they'll just have to give up and cry," she promised him.

"Little chicken, before you stopped, you'd cried enough for all of 'em."

"Those tears were saved up, Jack. I had to get that crying done before I could go any further."

He gave a nod, as when she mentioned her common sense to him.

Dense mounds of blackberry bushes held their own through the sheets of dust, looking like giant iron cooking pots set the width of the home pasture. Above the trees on the last rise, the roof began to flash. They could already hear the great hum. Lady May began rubbing her eyes.

"All I ask is you let me wash my face first," said Gloria. "To be ready for 'em."

"That's my little wife," Jack said, tying her sash for her.

Part 3

THE SHADE had circled around to the front yard. The tables appeared to have opened and bloomed. They reached in a jointed line from the bois d'arc tree all the way down the yard, almost as far as the post with the bell on it. Elvie solemnly drew apart the sacks and unveiled the ice.

Miss Beulah ran to the old lady's chair. "Granny, are you of a mind to let Brother Bethune use the Vaughn Bible to-day?" she asked.

"Not until he shows me his right to be here at all," said Granny. "Who went so far as to let him through the bars?"

"Brother Bethune's carrying a Bible of his own, Mother," said Mr. Renfro.

"He can pocket it," said Miss Beulah. "I wouldn't trust it to have everything it needs in it. Bring the Renfro Bible, Elvie, off the table in the company room. All right, Curtis, Dolphus —one two three!"

Rocker and all, Granny Vaughn was lifted high and carried through the crowd. Little clouds of fragrance seemed to go with her. The day had brought out the smell of her black dress, a smell of black, of her trunk and its brass lock, and there was a little vinegary smell that lasted longer, from the washing of the hand-worked lacy collar that went raying around her neck.

Elvie came back out of the house, the Renfro Bible the only thing showing above her prancing legs. As she dumped it into Brother Bethune's lap, its lid banged, heavy as a table top, and let out a smell loaded as a kitchen cabinet's. Brother Bethune rose with it sprawled in his own arms and first led the company, then trailed them, as in long spreading scatters through the solid shade of the house and the floating shade of the trees they moved toward the tables, with Miss Beulah calling and pointing them out where to go, or taking them by the shoulders and steering them there.

Granny, transported to the head of the top table and given some dahlias to hold, sat with head cocked. Brother Bethune and his stand were wedged into the tree roots by her side, in

608

between her and Grandpa's chair. A tub of lemonade was fitted in too, next to the stand, so strong-scented that it drew tears.

"Table looks almost too pretty to be molested!" Uncle Noah Webster hollered from the foot, sitting high on the sugar barrel. Granny's table was seated round with her grandchildren—the Beechams and their wives, and Mr. Renfro and his sisters. Beyond the tables, the overflow sat on the ground at the cloths and quilts spread in surrounding diamonds, and the edges of the crowd reached back up into the wagons.

Uncle Nathan remained standing at Granny's back, his hand on her chair, a fixture there from now on. He had hair streaked with white, tangled and falling to his shoulders. His old coat and pants had been patched again on top of last year's patches and, though neat, had been put on rough-dry. He gave off a steam that spoke of the river and now and then of tar. His face was brown and wrinkled as the meat of a Stuart pecan.

"You a bachelor?" asked Aunt Cleo.

"And the oldest Beecham boy," said Miss Beulah, stepping up beside him. "Nathan never fails us. If only we could keep him!"

Aunt Nanny still held a baby boy on her lap, and only stopped tickling him and gave him up when Brother Bethune made a sign. He threw open the Bible and flung back his hand, as if to show he could start on any page it wanted him to. Without a glance downward, he smiled.

"Well, look at me!" said Brother Bethune. "I'm proud I made it. The way it is lately, every year that's rolled around, there'd be a Bethune to go. For a while it looked like this year it was going to be me. But as precious friends will remember with me, the Lord took two others instead. Lowered Sister Viola in her grave in Banner Cemetery and they was fixing to cover her. My oldest brother Mitchell says, 'Hand me the shovel, Earl Comfort, I want to just shovel a little dirt on her coffin, it's the last thing I'll ever get to do for her.' And he did and the next minute the shovel flew and dirt flew and Mitchell was down kicking on the ground! It was Sister all over again! I throwed my weight on him, that's what I did for Sister, but I couldn't help but see his face was already going black. Oh, I held a fast grip on him. But he threshed right ahead. Until he's gone like Sister, and gone before she's even covered." He crowed. "And listen, then they couldn't get *me* up! And I couldn't get myself up! Well, Mitchell he made two and I all but made three—three Bethunes to go in one year and pretty near all in one day. There you are now, match that."

"I wish Brother Bethune would reserve some of that story for use in the pulpit," came the voice of Aunt Birdie. "It's not all that much, and those not in the family can get tired of it."

"And so," Brother Bethune continued in a key a notch higher, "this beautiful old home, this happy family, the bounty of God's blessings and all His wonderful gifts to Man is making our hearts glad this evening. Now if you was to ask me what exactly in the Book it looks like to me this minute"— he snapped over a page in the Bible which cracked like a whip and flourished the smell of honeysuckle—"I'd answer you quick: Belshazzar's Feast. Miss Beulah may have even out-provided it! And I bet it's as good as it looks."

Miss Beulah edged near enough to warn him: "Grandpa Vaughn made himself wait. He got the blessing said and the history every bit delivered and the lesson of it through our heads before he even looked at the table."

"It's Belshazzar's Feast without no Handwriting on the Wall to mar it," Brother Bethune went smoothly on, "and no angel, so far, to come and take the glory and credit away."

"Is he coming to Jack fairly soon?" whispered Aunt Birdie among the *Menes* and *Tekels* of Brother Bethune. "And forgive him quick and get it over?"

"Birdie, Jack hasn't reached the table yet. Everything in its time," said Uncle Curtis.

"Though I hope Ralph Renfro's not planning on acting like Belshazzar's daddy—that's Nebuchadnezzar going out to eat grass," Brother Bethune said slyly. "I'd like you to show me enough grass around here would satisfy a rabbit, Ralph, un-less you count what's took over your cotton. Lord, you sure need a rain." He got his laugh from the men. "All right, then! Bow your heads and hush your babies, I'm fixing to ask the blessing."

When Brother Bethune addressed the Lord, he threw his voice as far as the top of the bois d'arc tree over Granny's head. It was this big tree that at this hour had taken command of the yard. Its look was this: if disaster ever wants to strike around here, let it try it on this tree. The top had spread almost as wide as the roof, which it had shaded blue as a distant mountain. Its hard, pronged branches could never be well concealed by leaves so constantly stirring, shimmering without a breath of air. Brother Bethune had leaned his gun against the trunk.

"Know another who draws his prayers out to too great length," said Granny when Brother Bethune had finished. "I'm putting a stop to it."

Then quickly Miss Beulah, with Ella Fay and Elvie to help her, began garlanding movements around behind them, offering them more to eat before they started, and telling them right and left the only good way to eat it.

"And keep your eyes peeled for Jack!" Miss Beulah cried over their heads while they were reaching. "Sometimes taking the first juicy bite is all that's needed to bring him."

"Those children's just like little pigs—what one won't eat, the other will. Look at 'em go!" said Aunt Nanny behind her drumstick.

"We are fortunate to have Granny Vaughn still with us today and in her right mind. Her living grandchildren and great-grandchildren are making her happy and going to fill her lap with presents as soon as I let 'em at her. First I'll look out over your heads and tell you who I *don't* see," began Brother Bethune.

"Now that's not what I came to hear," said Aunt Birdie to the top table.

"Let Brother Bethune warm up a little bit for the rest of us. You ain't eaten the crust off one little wing yet," Uncle Dolphus told her.

"One who is living but not present is Homer Champion," Brother Bethune told them. "Homer Champion is ready to give his soul to keep on being what he is now come Tuesday: justice of the peace. Well, I haven't heard his excuse yet, but you know something? I believe we got as many as we need without Homer."

"Jack is a different matter," Aunt Beck was saying, when Brother Bethune rattled a page of the Bible for attention.

"All right! Granny Vaughn is the Miss Thurzah Elvira Jordan that was, born right here in this house, known far and wide in the realms of the Baptists for the reach of her voice as a young lady. She is one of our oldest citizens today, beaten only by Captain Billy Bangs, who has reached to the age of ninety-four and still going to the polls. Granny is mighty pretty, she's kind and courageous, sweet, loving, faithful, frisky, and outspoken. It is said that Death loves a shining mark. So we had all best be careful of Granny, precious friends, and treat her nice for the year to come, because she's shining mighty hard. Ain't that so, Granny Vaughn?"

Granny's eye met his perfectly. She was sucking on a little chicken bone.

"I believe it is true that her eye can still see to thread her own needle, though we won't make her prove it at the table," Brother Bethune went on. "She still gets up at four in the morning, sees to her chickens—"

"As if I'd let her," said Miss Beulah, marching to her grandmother with platter piled high with the white pieces.

"She started in at an early age, reared a lovely young lady that's in the graveyard, and then she started all over again on that daughter's family. And here they are, all living but one! She has had her trials in this vale of tears and still, as all can see, she's never yet bowed her head. As I look out over that sweet old head and count 'em—raise your hands!—I see six living grandchildren, thirty-seven or thirty-eight living great-grandchildren—and others galore. I see faces from Banner, Deepstep, Harmony, Upright, Peerless, Morning Star, Mountain Creek, and one who makes the whole wide world his home." He flung out a hand at Uncle Nathan. "According to her years, she is about to live up her life here on earth, and may expect any day to be taken, but we hope she will be spared to bring her precious presence to one more reunion."

"When he gets as far as Jack, I'm going to tell him to slow down a little," said Aunt Birdie. "I want to listen to every word when he forgives that sweet mortal."

Aunt Beck said, "We want Jack to get to the table first, to

be forgiven. And Gloria and the baby in their place beside him, so we can cry for all of 'em."

"Jack won't disappoint us," Aunt Nanny said. "By this time he wouldn't even know how."

"It's Brother Bethune that ain't measuring up like he ought to," said Aunt Birdie. "What he's reeling off is tailored to fit any reunion he's lucky enough to get invited to."

"He uses the same old thing on all the Baptists—I expected that," said Aunt Beck.

"You'd both take it worse if he was to come up and beat Grandpa, wouldn't you?" asked Mr. Renfro. "Give him a little rope, ladies."

"Granny's granddaddy built this house. Built it the year the stars fell," said Uncle Curtis, talking along with Brother Bethune and raising his voice a little over the preacher's. "Jacob Jordan was his name, Captain Jordan was the way he liked to be known. He perched him here in the thick of the Indians, overlooking the stage road that come threading through the canebrakes up to Tennessee. It's still the road that comes to the house." He turned to gaze up at it. "It's got a chimney stack inside that's five foot deep and five foot wide. And after Captain Jordan's son settled for a Carolina bride, Granny herself was born squalling in that very room, by the licking fire."

"In August?" Elvie cried. "On the first Sunday in August?"

Granny studied her through the long narrow slits of her eyes.

"Winter used to come early around these parts," said Uncle Percy. "Lots of old tales about those winters. I believe 'em."

Granny put down a crumb and raised her fist ready for the next sentence.

"And by the time old Grant come over the horizon and put a cannon ball in that chimney, she was big enough to scamper out in the yard in her little flounce and boots and shame 'im for it to his face!" said Uncle Curtis.

"Just wish she'd been a year older, she'd done better'n that," Granny said, looking amused.

"What happened to Captain Jordan?" some child prompted.

"Died brave. His son died brave. And there's one of those

Jordans, Jack Jordan, they had to starve to death to kill him," Uncle Curtis told.

"Couldn't dent a crack in my chimney, send all the volleys you want to," said Granny, and she ate her crumb.

"Preacher Vaughn he grew up in Banner too," said Brother Bethune. "Spent his whole life here."

"Grandpa's daddy was the builder of the first house in the town of Banner," Uncle Curtis prompted him.

"And that's a good smart piece away from where he ended up here," said Brother Bethune.

"Banner's just a good holler. It's the road that's winding," said Mr. Renfro.

"I believe there's nothing left of the first Vaughn house today," said Brother Bethune. "Banner's getting along without it."

"Grandpa's daddy raised that house out of his own oaks, pines, and cedars, and then he raised the church. He'd preach in the church on Sunday and the rest of the week he could stand on his own front porch and have it to look at," said Uncle Curtis. "Old house burned. Though not within living memory of any except Granny."

"When I was a boy, there's still a chimney standing, looked big enough to roast an ox," said Mr. Renfro. "It was backed up to the river. Then the chimney went. Then the whole back end of the bank where it stood, that went. Tumbled and sunk itself in the river. Delivered itself to the Bywy. I always got the general idea that Grandpa Vaughn just didn't care for that at all."

"He still had his old horse switch. Right here," said Uncle Percy.

Granny raised her wavering finger as if it could find what to point at. It was the big bois d'arc tree, right behind her.

"Yes sir, old-timers used to call that tree Billy Vaughn's Switch," said Uncle Curtis. "He'd stick it in the ground when he got down from his horse, trotting up here to court Granny, and one night he forgot it. Come up a hard rain, and the next thing they knew, it'd sprouted."

The tree looked a veteran of all the old blows, a survivor. Old wounds on the main trunk had healed leaving scars as big as tubs or wagon wheels, and where the big lower branches had thrust out, layer under layer of living bark had split on the main trunk in a bloom of splinters, of a red nearly animal-like.

"Too late to pull it up now," said Granny, looking from one face to another, all around her table.

"Well, but there's bodocks and bodocks growing between here and the road," said Elvie. "They're lining our way. They couldn't *all* be Grandpa Vaughn's horse switches from when he came riding to see Granny and get her to marry 'im."

"Who says they couldn't?" Granny said swiftly.

"Granny's good husband, Preacher Vaughn, came here to this beautiful old house to live on their wedding day, and I believe he'd just surrendered to the ministry too, both at the age of eighteen. Mr. Vaughn is the living example of a real, real Baptist," Brother Bethune was declaring, and he smiled as his hand went reaching over his face. "I wonder does he recall with me a little story. I was taken along with him as a little feller, for company, to a Methodist revival being held one August over to Better Friendship. All went well as long as he could enjoy good singing and sermons and the shade of their trees, but after that, they started up one thing he hadn't counted on, poor man. Infant baptism! Such heartfelt groans you never heard in your life as good Preacher Vaughn give out that day, with his head dropped down on the back of the bench in front of us—suffering for them poor little Methodist babies."

A humming began to come from all the aunts at the table. When they looked at Granny, Granny looked back at them without blinking, as if she'd long ago decided how much it was worth her while to set them right about anything.

"One of the babies was Clyde Comfort," mused Brother Bethune.

"Aycock's daddy? I believe if Grandpa could see Mr. Comfort today, he'd groan again," Mr. Renfro said.

"And if Mr. Comfort could see Grandpa in our midst right now, he'd turn tail another time," said Aunt Nanny, helplessly winking.

"Oh yes, you could hear Preacher Vaughn well above them Methodist babies and the way they was crying." Brother

Bethune let out a bark of laughter. "Ain't that so, Preacher Vaughn?"

Aunt Beck cried out in panic.

"Brother Bethune, you jumped your track a little ways back down the line there," called up Uncle Curtis primly, while some of the young girls at the table below cackled out like old women. "You know we lost Grandpa Vaughn."

"I declare, Brother Bethune, your memory's come to be no longer than your little finger!" Aunt Nanny called admiringly.

"Get up to date!" shrieked Aunt Birdie.

"You're hanging right over the Vacant Chair, Brother Bethune! You've left your hat in it! If it had teeth, it'd bite you!" cried Uncle Dolphus.

"Don't you know what happened to Grandpa?" screamed Miss Beulah, her arms around Granny. "Can you think of a single other reason on earth why you should find yourself standing here at the table and making the effort to take his place at the reunion?"

"You're right," said Brother Bethune in a congratulatory voice, "we lost him, he left us just about exactly a year ago, at the age of eighty-nine. Stopped speaking, didn't care any longer for earthly food, then couldn't lift up his head, then perished. With all these blesseds around him and pleading him to stay."

"Wasn't that way at all," said Miss Beulah.

"I'm sure those are just the same words he uses for everybody," said Aunt Beck. "I advise you to get rid of him, before the next reunion."

She whispered, but Granny looked back at her in a fixed manner. Something about her glittered—the silver watch pinned to her front, worn like the medal she'd won by Grandpa's dying first.

"And I'm sure Granny Vaughn will forgive me for the first slip I've made all evening, and agree it was a mean trick to play on the new preacher, to see how far he'd go. Wasn't it?"

"Last year's reunion I wish we all could have skipped," said Aunt Beck, letting out a sigh.

"Jack was gone from sight. Grandpa Vaughn was groaning

so, I asked him if he couldn't allow himself to give the history
and the sermon to us sitting down. If he had, it might have
saved his life!" said Miss Beulah. "We might have kept him
till today."

"He died at you-all's reunion?" cried Aunt Cleo, and biting
her lip, turned for a fresh look at Granny.

"No, Sister Cleo, he waited till after good-nights was over
and good-byes was said and we'd all gone home to bed," said
Uncle Curtis.

"In the barn," said Uncle Percy in a whisper.

"When he didn't come to bed, and didn't come, Granny
went out there all by herself and found him, with a lantern.
He'd fell over from his knees. But he had a nice sweet bed of
hay under him," said Miss Beulah fiercely.

"I'll never forget Grandpa at that last reunion," said Uncle
Curtis. "Oh, he thundered! He preached at us from Romans
and sent us all home still quaking for our sins."

"We didn't know, till Mr. Renfro rode the horse into the
daylight to tell us, how shortly he lasted after 'Blest Be the
Tie,'" said Uncle Percy in a whisper.

They all stole glances at Granny. Her fingers reached for
Grandpa's watch on her dress front. She opened it for a look,
quick as she'd open a biscuit to make sure it was buttered,
and shut it again.

"I think we're brave to keep coming, times like these," said
Aunt Beck. "All of us, plain brave."

"I let my thoughts dwell for a minute on harvest time in
Heaven," Brother Bethune called, passing behind her. He'd
interrupted himself to line up with the children before the
cake of ice. Dense with ammonia, like fifty cents' worth of the
moon, it stood melting in its blackening bed of sawdust. He
chipped some off into his cup to cool his lemonade, and came
striding back talking.

"Granny Vaughn and Grandpa Vaughn—oh, they was David
and Jonathan," Brother Bethune went gleefully on. "After
Grandpa left this sorry old world, Granny appeared for a while
to be trailing a wing. Yes sir, we in Banner told one another,
he will soon have the old lady wooed upward. We know he's
been hungry for her! I expect while we set around her here
today, Grandpa in Heaven is busy wondering why in the world

she don't pick up her foot and track on up there with him. But I expect she's got her answer ready."

"Suppose you try taking a seat," Granny was heard to say. "Go over there in the corner." She pointed to the old cedar log.

"And behind him in the world Preacher Vaughn left five living grandsons, and only one keeping on with the Lord's work today—and then it's pretty much where and when he feels it coming over him." Brother Bethune right-faced toward Uncle Nathan.

Uncle Nathan, back of Granny's chair, inclined his gypsy head in acknowledgment.

Aunt Cleo pointed at him with a pie-shaped wedge of cornbread. "You all got one in the family? Then why did you invite another one to do the preaching?" she asked them.

Miss Beulah said promptly, "Nathan's too modest, Sister Cleo, to think he could take Grandpa's place. Most everybody knows better than to try it."

"Why don't he eat, then?" asked Aunt Cleo. "If he won't preach, why don't he eat?"

"Sister Cleo, he didn't come to eat either. Just make up your mind you don't always know what a man's come for," Miss Beulah advised her. "And some I'd think twice before I'd ask."

"There was only one Beecham daughter, there was Miss Beulah alone!" cried Brother Bethune. "And Miss Beulah Beecham she will ever be. And I want her to save me back some of those chicken gizzards she's provided such a plenty of, I want to carry 'em home for my supper—does she hear me? Miss Beulah, who ain't going to let no one in the world go hungry as long as she can trot, took for loving husband Mr. Ralph Renfro, who is yet with us today. He's here somewhere, trying to keep up with his children and stay alive!" Brother Bethune laughed. "Beulah and Ralph all their lives has worked right in harness together, raised a nice set of girls with a boy at each end. The girls is unclaimed as yet, but the oldest one is liable to surprise us any minute." He paused to let Ella Fay, wherever she was, stamp her foot.

"And *that's* making a mistake," Miss Beulah said, running

around with the platter. "One day, Brother Bethune is going off the track and he'll stay off."

"I'm getting downright impatient listening for him to forgive Jack and get the hard part over," Aunt Birdie said as Brother Bethune lifted his voice and veered away into the Renfros.

"He can't do his forgiving till Jack gets here, unless he's willing to waste it," said Uncle Curtis.

"Grandpa Vaughn would have done it either first, or last, if he was going to do it at all," Aunt Nanny said. "Not just slip it in somewhere."

Uncle Curtis said, "He wouldn't have done it at all."

"Papa," said Elvie, standing at her father's ear, "peep behind you. Here's them."

At the same moment, Etoyle seized her skirt and cracked it like a whip to get the dust out, and came rushing into the yard. She butted her head into Miss Beulah's side and embraced her.

"Lady May jumped through the peephole! Jack caught her! But he couldn't miss, she came like a basketball!" she cried.

"Oh, it's not so. But what's this?" And Miss Beulah was marching toward the wagon. Judge Moody, wincing as if his bones creaked, got down and held his hand for his wife.

"Is somebody dead up here? I never did see so many," exclaimed Mrs. Moody.

"You see exactly how many we've got, with three more to be counted," Miss Beulah cried. "And if you came here expecting to find a bunch of mourners, you're in the wrong camp." Now she and Judge Moody stood eye to eye over the heaped-up platter she was carrying. "I bet you a pretty I can tell you who you had to thank for your invitation. What have you done with my oldest boy this time? I can tell that's your wife," she went on. "And I can see you're famished, parched and famished, in another minute you'll drop. Trot after me. Might as well shuck off your coat, Judge Moody, and don't dawdle."

"He's kept his coat on before me through it all this far— he can keep it on for the rest of the time, thank you," said Mrs. Moody.

"Vaughn! It's time for that spare on the porch!" yelled Miss Beulah, and Vaughn came bringing the school chair. It was a heavy oak piece with a hole bored clean through its back, the seat notched, the desk-arm cut like a piecrust all around and initialed all over. As Vaughn strong-armed it over his head, the deathless amber deposits of old chewing gum were exposed underneath.

"All right, sir. That gives you a little table all to yourself," said Miss Beulah.

"Mama, who is that? Is that the Booger?" asked a little child from the crowd as Judge Moody wedged himself in under the desk arm, and Brother Bethune caught his eye and waved at him.

"Mrs. Judge, Mr. Renfro is busy offering you his chair— slide in. And where are *your* children? How many've you got and what have you done with 'em?" Miss Beulah asked, coming at Mrs. Moody's heels.

"I was never intended to have any," said Mrs. Moody, looking out from under the brim of her hat as she squeezed in between Aunt Miss Lexie Renfro and Aunt Birdie and sat on a hide-bottomed chair.

Miss Beulah forked two crusty wings from her platter down before her. "You-all can start at the beginning and I reckon by trying you may be able to catch up," she said. "Yonder's my grandmother at the head of this table, she's ninety years old today. Try not to have her object to you. She's getting all the excitement she needs the way it is, and still got a while to wait to blow out her candles."

Granny's eyes hadn't left her plate, but Uncle Nathan, behind her, slowly raised his arm to hail the newcomers.

"Who's that familiar-looking old man doing the talking?" asked Mrs. Moody, and just then Brother Bethune waved his hand at her.

"And so here we all are, with very few skips and some surprises." Brother Bethune was keeping right on, in the argumentative voice of one who habitually brings comfort to others. His words ran on over Granny's bobbing head and down her table, over the rest of the tables and the sitters on the ground, went scaling up into the leaves, lighting on the chimney with a mockingbird, skimming down to the lemonade. Every now and then his eyes went to the cake of ice, as they might have gone to a clock-face. "They have journeyed over long distances and perilous ways to get here. Won't it be sorrowful if they don't all get home tonight! Let us hope they do—without losing their way or swallowing too many clouds of dust or having their horses scared out from under 'em or their buggies upsetting and falling in the river." He spread his arms. "Or meeting with the Devil in Banner Road."

"How long will this go on?" Mrs. Moody turned and whispered over her shoulder to Judge Moody behind her.

The school chair he sat in was crowded up against the althea bush. Mr. Renfro had hitched a keg up close to his other side, and sat just behind Judge Moody's elbow, eating off his lap. A little black and white dog came trotting up, lay at the Judge's feet, and began licking his shoe.

"Just eat like everybody else, Maud Eva. It can't be helped," he said, and set his teeth into a big chicken back.

"You let the children beat you to the finish, Brother Bethune —here's the birthday cake coming!" Miss Beulah cried. She caught Brother Bethune by his suspenders, turned him around, and pointed for him.

Coming out of the passage and around the cactus to cross the porch, and down the steps and over the yard, winding in and out among the sitters on the ground, Miss Beulah's and Mr. Renfro's three girls were joined in parade. Their dresses had been starched so stiff that they kept time now with their marching legs, like a set of little snare-drums. Elvie at the rear looked almost too small to keep up. Etoyle had splashed her face clean, and along with her shoes she had added her school-band coat, emerald green. Epaulettes the size of sunflowers crowded onto her shoulders and poked her dress out in front. The cake was carried by Ella Fay at the head of them, with twelve candles alight, their flames laid back like ears. In a hush that was almost secrecy, it was set on the table in front of Granny's eyes. For a moment nothing broke the silence except a bird shuffling about in the althea bush like somebody looking through a bureau drawer where something had been put away.

Then Granny rose to her feet, her own crackling petticoats giving way to quiet the way kindling does when the fire catches. She stood only by her own head taller than her cake with its candles and its now erect, fierce flames. With one full blow from her blue lips, breath riding out on a seashell of pink and blue flame, Granny blew the candles out.

"She'll get her wish!" cried a chorus of voices.

"Yes sir, Mis' Vaughn is right remarkable," said Brother Bethune, looking at her from the drawn-back face of caution.

Granny accepted the knife Miss Beulah offered, she placed the blade and sank it in. The cake cut like cream.

"I made it in the biggest pan I had," said Granny. "If it don't go round, I'll have to stir up another one."

While the birthday cake and its companion cakes went on their rounds, all sank back in a murmuring soft as a nest. Then suddenly Jack's dogs tore loose from their holdings and streaked through the reunion, turning over one or two sitters on the ground, their voices pealing. Shouts and cheers rose up on the edge of the crowd, then spread, and the dogs poured up the front steps and clamored on the porch.

Jack, Gloria, and the baby burst shining out of the passage.

"They set down without us," gasped Jack.

"I see the Moodys, first thing," Gloria said. "Their faces stick out of the crowd at me like four-leafs in a clover patch. Now see what kind of welcome you get."

Jack, washed and curried and with his shirt buttoned together, though it was tucked into the same ragged pants, went leaping into the reunion. Miss Beulah, with her arms open, clapped him against her.

"Son, what will you bring home to your mother next?" she cried, hugging him tight.

"Bring yourself forward, Jack! Fight your way in, and take your place at the table! Here comes the bashful boy!" roared Uncle Noah Webster, as they made a path for him to Granny. Behind him walked Gloria, gleaming and carrying Lady May, who was wide-awake with both clean little feet stuck out.

Jack bent to kiss the old lady, her mouth busy with coconut. She gave him a nod. She put out her hand and found Lady May's little washed foot and clasped it, as if to learn who else had come. Then she let them by.

"Uncle Nathan!" Jack cried. "When I see your face, I know

Jack Frost is coming not far behind! I want you to know that's
a good strong sign you planted on Banner Top."

"What did that one say?" asked Uncle Nathan in a modest
voice, but just then Lady May's little feet, like two pistols,
were stuck right in his chest, and he drew back.

Other arms reached for Jack, more hands pulled him along,
and he made his way down Granny's table kissing and being
kissed by the aunts, being pounded on by the uncles, with
Gloria coming along behind him with a crowing Lady May.

"Jack, you got here in time for it," Aunt Beck told him.

"Though I don't exactly approve of Moody being here for
everything," said Aunt Birdie.

"Never mind, Jack, we know you just can't help it," said
Aunt Beck. "I'm not blaming you. I'm just glad to see you
still alive. And ready for what's coming."

"We are all pleased and proud to welcome the oldest son
of the house back into our midst—Jack Renfro!" Brother
Bethune was calling out in competition. "He has been away
and dwelling among strangers for the best part of two years!
Though Jack has been away from our beck and call, we are
sure without needing to be told that he's back here today the
same as he ever was, and will be just as good a boy after
getting home as he was before he went. Jack is just a good
Renfro boy of the Banner community that we have all knowed
since birth. Ain't that right, precious friends?"

Some shouts of approval could be heard through the noise,
and Brother Bethune continued in rising shouts of his own.
"Jack was getting to be one of the best-known farmers of this
end of the ridge! He raised all his folks' cotton and corn,
sorghum, hay and peas, peanuts, potatoes, and watermelons!
And all needing him as bad as I ever saw crop needing man!
He'd grind him his cane at the right time and sell his syrup
to the public!" As Jack made his way down the table, Brother
Bethune's tongue got faster and faster. "Cuts him and sells
him his wood in winter, and all of it goes to Curly Stovall—
the Renfros don't even get the sawdust! Ha! Ha! Ha! Slops
him a pig or two! Concerned in raising him a herd of milkers!
And his daddy's still got two left for him to start over with!
Best of all, he helps his father and mother by living with 'em!
And now! Now that he's come through all his trials and

troubles unscathed and is about to take up where he left off
and get everybody back to as good as before—all right, then!
Today, the one that gets the baby-kiss for coming the farthest
is—Jack Renfro! How do you like that for a change, Brother
Nathan? All right, Jack!" shouted Brother Bethune, though
he could scarcely have been heard by now over the other
shouts, the teasing, and the dog-barking. "You wasn't a lick
too soon!"

A baby, like something coming on wings, was shoved into
Jack's face. It was still Lady May, in Aunt Nanny's hands.

"Haul yourself off the sugar barrel, Noah Webster—that's
Jack's," said Miss Beulah, and he had to bring up a stepladder
for himself and wedge it in on the other side of Aunt Cleo,
almost in Miss Lexie Renfro's lap. Miss Beulah pushed Jack
onto the barrel there at the foot of the table, where he and
Granny could face each other, and cried, "Now, start catching
up!" as she turned a dozen pieces of chicken onto a platter
in front of him. "All right, Gloria," she said. "Now you. I
saved you the baby-rocker."

Gloria lowered herself and slid in. The rocker, there below
Jack's barrel, was slick as a butter paddle and so low to the
ground that her chin was barely on a level with the edge of
her plate. The baby sat on her lap; only her little cockscomb
could have been visible to those up and down the table.

"Did Brother Bethune forgive Jack? Or not?" Aunt Birdie
was asking the other aunts.

"If forgiving Jack was what he was doing, I'd hate to think
that's his best effort," said Aunt Beck.

"Judge Moody and Mrs. Moody! I hope your appetite is
proving equal to the occasion," Jack was saying, while the
pickled peaches and the pear relish, the five kinds of bread,
the sausages and ham—fried and boiled—and the four or five
kinds of salad, and the fresh crocks of milk and butter that
had been pulled up out of the well, were all being set within
his reach. And then Aunt Beck's chicken pie was set down
spouting and boiling hot right under his nose. "Mama'll take
it pretty hard if you go away leaving a scrap on your plate,"
he told the Moodys.

Brother Bethune had come down to the World War. "All
the Beecham boys but the youngest and the oldest went over

with me to the trenches and ever' last one of 'em but the youngest got back like me with their hides on. I don't know how they did it, exactly, but I do know it's a good deal more like the Beechams than it is like the Bethunes. A few scratches here and a few medals there to be put away and buried with 'em, but they come back the same old Beecham boys they always was, and just the good old Beecham boys we still know 'em to be. Like they'd never been gone."

"If we go German-hunting again, I say don't let's us leave even a nit over there this time!" shouted Uncle Noah Webster. Laughter spilled out of his mouth like the cake crumbs.

"They say the next time, them Germans is coming over here after us," whispered Uncle Percy.

"Let 'em come try!" shouted Uncle Dolphus.

"Will we arm ourselves as did the knights of old? Or will we turn and run, like that jack rabbit I see yonder?" asked Brother Bethune, arm shooting out to point, as every head turned to follow. Then came the laugh.

"Brother Bethune, I declare, you might get somewhere yet," Uncle Dolphus declared, and Uncle Curtis said, "You're not Grandpa Vaughn, but at least you know better now than try to be."

Brother Bethune cleared his throat and looked all about him. "The old homestead here looks very natural," he said, wearing the face of good news. He wheeled back to them so fast that he might have been expecting to find somebody already gone.

"Crops not what they used to be," said Uncle Curtis, as though Brother Bethune needed prompting.

He went on in soothing tones. "I don't reckon good old Mississippi's ever been any poorer than she is right now, 'cept when we lost. And in all our glorious state I can't think of any county likelier to take the cake for being the poorest and generally the hardest-suffering than dear old Boone." Sighs of leisure and praise rose to encourage him, and Brother Bethune paused to suck up some lemonade. Then his smile broke. "Looks like some not too far from the sound of my voice is going to have to go on *relief* for the first time. Ha! Ha!"

"Not Ralph Renfro," Mr. Renfro promised him shortly. He

was at the lemonade tub too. He filled his cup and sat down again beside Judge Moody, so as to take pleasure in him.

"I believe we might even do a little material complaining around Banner, if we try right hard," said Brother Bethune, managing to dip up a little more for himself by tilting the tub against his knee. "Floods all spring and drought all summer. We stand *some* chance of getting *about* as close to starvation this winter as we come yet. The least crop around here it would be possible for any man to make, I believe Mr. Ralph Renfro is going to make it this year."

"Good old Brother Bethune," somebody was murmuring out in the crowd, "he's warming up now."

"No corn in our cribs, no meal in our barrel, no feed and no shoes and no clothing—tra la la la!" he sang to the littlest one he could see, a baby tied in the wheelbarrow. "No credit except for the kind of rates nobody is inclined to pay. Pigs is eating on the watermelons. All you people without any watermelons come on over to my house. Too cheap to haul from the field this year! And yet! It'd be a mighty hard stunt to starve a bunch like us." He spread his teasing smile over them all. "I reckon we'll all, or nearly all, hold out for one more round." As they cheered him on he called over them, "We got hay made and in the barn, we'll soon have some fresh meat, the good ladies has stocked the closet shelf with what garden we saved by hauling water. We got milk and butter and eggs, and maybe even after today's slaughter there'll be a few chickens left. And if we must needs accept them old commodities again from Uncle Sam, come about Christmas time, here's hoping he will have the preferences of Boone County better in mind than he did last year and leave out his wormy apples, ha ha! I expect he's found out by now we can be a little more particular here than the next fella!"

"Tell us some more!" the men cried, their voices aching with laughter the same as his, while Miss Beulah behind Jack's shoulder cried, "Ready for your next plateful? Here's the sausage I saved you from last year's hog! Here's some more home-cured ham, make room for more chicken. Elvie! Buttermilk! This time bring him the whole pitcher!"

"I would like to draw you a picture of Banner today," said Brother Bethune, gazing upwards, with his lips smacking over the name just as they smacked over "Bethune." But when he finished—"In Stovall's cornfield, only this morning, I saw a snake so long it was laying over seven and a half hills of corn. I didn't get him, either, precious friends! There was the other one coming, and I stood there torn between 'em, let the pair of 'em get away. There's a lesson in that!"—Aunt Cleo said, "He almost makes me glad I don't live here."

"That's because you've listened to the wrong preacher," said Aunt Beck.

"Now *I* didn't *recognize* Banner," claimed Aunt Birdie, pointing her finger at Brother Bethune. "And I was a Lovat and grew up right there, with the river right under my door. If that was Banner, I certainly wasn't hearing any compliments for it."

"I don't think that's high enough praise you've given the neighborhood, Brother Bethune," said Aunt Beck. "I miss something in your words. Can't you make that church rivalry sound a little stronger?"

Brother Bethune only looked down at them all from Grandpa's old place. "Banner is better known today for what ain't there than what is," he said. "I can truthfully say it hasn't growed one inch since I been preaching."

"It's been growing, but like the cow's tail, down instead of up!" cried Uncle Noah Webster. "Cleo, the old place here was plum stocked with squirrel when we was boys. It was overrun with quail. And if you never saw the deer running in here, I saw 'em. It was filled—it was filled!—with every kind of good thing, this old dwelling, when me and the rest of us Beecham boys grew up here under Granny and Grandpa Vaughn's strict raising. It's got everlasting springs, a well with water as sweet as you could find in this world, and a pond and a creek both. But you're seeing it today in dry summer."

"It's parched," said Uncle Dolphus. "Just like mine. So dry the snakes is coming up in my yard to drink with the chickens."

"And it's a shame and a crime about them web worms, too," said Aunt Nanny, looking to the other end of the yard where the majestic pecan tree rose, full of years. The caterpillar nets that infested it gave it the surface of some big old clouded mirror.

"It's loaded, though," said Mr. Renfro. "If you doubt that, Nanny, all you got to do is make a climb up there and count what's coming."

"I've about decided that nothing's going to kill some bearers," said Aunt Birdie. "Regardless of treatment."

"And won't you be glad when those little hard nuts start raining down," said Aunt Beck. "They're the sweetest, juiciest kind. The hardest to crack always is."

"None of you have much, do you?" said Aunt Cleo.

"Farming is what we do. What we was raised for," said Uncle Curtis in a formal manner, from there at Granny's right.

"Farmers still and evermore will be," said Uncle Dolphus, farther around on her left.

"We're relying on Jack now. He'll haul us out of our misery, and we thought he was going to haul us with that do-all truck." Uncle Curtis's long face cracked open into its first smile. "Since all my boys done up and left my farm."

"Mine too. That's only the way of it," whispered Uncle Percy.

"But all nine of mine," said Uncle Curtis, turning in his chair to gaze around at the crowd. "The only chance I get to see 'em, over and beyond the Sundays when their wives can drive 'em to church, is the reunion."

"What did they leave home for? Wasn't there enough to go round?" teased Aunt Cleo.

"It's the same old story," said Uncle Dolphus. "It's the fault of the land going back on us, treating us the wrong way. There's been too much of the substance washed away to grow enough to eat any more."

"Now well's run dry and river's about to run dry. Around here there ain't nothing running no more but snakes on the ground and candidates for office. And snakes and them both could do that in their sleep," said Uncle Dolphus.

"Too bad we boys had to ever leave Grandpa and Granny and the old farm," Uncle Curtis said. "All we boys had to come away and leave the old place so as to get by. We all tried not to take ourselves too far."

"I was the last of Granny's boys to go. I stayed to be the

last one, didn't I, Granny?" Uncle Noah Webster asked from his ladder.

"Benedict Arnold," she said.

"How come everybody moved away?" Aunt Cleo teased. "Hungry?"

"There's only so much of everything," Aunt Nanny said.

"Takes a lot of doing without," Aunt Beck said serenely.

"Well," said Mr. Renfro, "we was never going to move, me and Beulah. Granny's got us. And now, Jack and his family —we got them."

Everybody looked at Jack and Gloria, as they pulled a wishbone between them.

There came a louder report. Kneeling on the ground, Mr. Renfro had split open the first watermelon. He rose with the long halves facing outward from his arms, like the tablets of the Ten Commandments. He served Granny first, then around he started, cracking his melons, making his bows, putting down a half at each place.

Brother Bethune was going on, too, telling of the wanderings of his father and the one time he got help from an angel on Banner Road.

Aunt Birdie, unable to contain herself any longer, put her head around and said, "Jack boy, when Judge Moody finishes his dinner, you reckon he'll arrest you? Is that his idea, you reckon?"

"Well, it couldn't have been his idea when he started out, Aunt Birdie," said Jack. Over his watermelon he gave a smile at Judge Moody. "He'd sentenced me himself and he can count. He'd know I wasn't even due back here till tomorrow."

"Explain a little something right quick to Judge Moody, son," directed Miss Beulah, who was following Mr. Renfro, taking around the salt. "He looks like he's getting ready to lay down his knife and go home."

"I don't want to hear any further," Judge Moody said to Jack.

"Our reunion is one that don't wait, sir," Jack said at the same time. "Nobody, not even my wife, would have forgiven me for the rest of my life if I hadn't showed up today."

"You escaped?" Gloria cried out.

"Horrors!" cried Mrs. Moody.

"It was up to me," Jack said. "What good would it have done anybody for me to get back here tomorrow?"

Aunt Nanny was already laughing. "How'd you get rid of your stripes, darlin'?" she called out. "Ain't you supposed to wear striped britches? I don't see any!"

"Sh!" came from Uncle Curtis.

"Scaled the wall, I suppose, then fell off like Humpty Dumpty," Aunt Birdie said. "Or did you scoot right quick through the fence?"

"Out of Parchman? You couldn't find a fence," said Jack. "Aunt Birdie, Parchman is too big to fence. There's just no end to it, that's all."

"You didn't just walk out of Parchman," muttered Judge Moody.

Jack said, "I come out on Dexter."

"I don't follow," said Judge Moody.

"Get up on a horse and just *ride* him out of there on a Sunday morning, while it's still cool—that seemed reasonable, and it was reasonable," said Jack. "I rode Dexter. He knows me. There's a overseer that rides him every day but Sunday. The kind of horse Dexter is, he's almost an overseer himself. He took me overseeing all over those acres, and finally he conducted me out onto a little road that meant business."

"Was Aycock riding on behind you?"

"Aunt Birdie, riding double could have caused somebody to look twice. Aycock come along behind the horse's tail, crouching lower than the cotton."

"Jack, you ought to have kept that a dim secret," Gloria whispered to him. "But you don't know how—somebody's got to keep your secrets for you."

"Roped my shirt and tied him to a shady cottonwood and talked to him and left him, and now if you're ready to laugh, Aunt Nanny," said Jack, "I don't even know whose pants these are I jumped into." She shrieked. "I traded with a clothesline. At first we couldn't find but one pair of pants. Aycock nearabout had to wear a bedspread. But we persevered, and the first preacher that came pitching down the road, we jumped in the car with him. And the story he told us, to get us to Winona! How somebody'd burnt down our courthouse!"

"Well, you can just go and change those pants instead of telling it here," said Miss Beulah.

"Keep on the pants you've got, Jack," Aunt Birdie begged him. "We're used to 'em now. Tell us the rest, do, please!"

"He just rode a plough horse out of Parchman," said Judge Moody to his wife, who was looking at him.

"Being church time, the roads was fairly well packed with Good Samaritans. Judge Moody was one and didn't know it." Jack turned to the Judge. "For about as long as it takes to tell it, I was riding behind on your spare, sir, and so was Aycock. Then we all went in together into Mr. Willy's ditch."

Judge Moody sat with a fixed expression on his face, while Mr. Renfro looked at him with enjoyment.

"Reckon they might come after him yet—using bloodhounds? It's a good thing we've got their equals!" Aunt Birdie squealed.

"I believe they'll let well enough alone," Mr. Renfro said to Judge Moody.

"If I was Parchman, I would," Mrs. Moody vowed, while the Judge just looked at her.

"I missed getting my good-bye present of new shoes," Jack told Gloria a little apologetically. "But I'll donate those wholehearted to whoever would rather say good-bye to the pen tomorrow than today. I had to get me back for Granny's birthday Sunday!"

Aunt Birdie again shook her spoon at Judge Moody. "What was *he* doing on Banner Road, then?"

"Now we won't ask him for his story," said Miss Beulah. "The man's been tackling our roads, and at the first little bump and skirmish he lands himself in a ditch, and here he is. I think that'll do."

"Why, it won't do at all," Mrs. Moody began, but Etoyle set down her melon, joined her hands at her breast, and cried, "In the ditch? Judge Moody's car's gone straight up Banner Top!"

" 'Tisn't so!" said Miss Beulah fiercely to Mr. Renfro, who sat there at Judge Moody's elbow with pleasure in his face.

"On Banner Top? Out on the flirting edge of nowhere? Is

that right?" Aunt Nanny cried to the Moodys. "And don't know how to get down?" She shook with laughter.

Mrs. Moody pointed her finger across the table at Gloria's bright crown. "Give credit where credit is due," she said. "She's the one ran out of the bushes and right under our wheels, calling us by name. She's the one drove us right up that wall!"

Mrs. Moody said more but it was drowned out in the cheering that rose from the table.

"Look who's set here quiet as a mouse for two years! Bless your heart!" Uncle Noah Webster jumped off the stepladder and kissed Gloria, leaving cake-crumbs on her face.

"Gloria Short! I declare but you're turning out to be a little question mark! I'm wondering what you'll do next!" cried Aunt Birdie.

Aunt Nanny cried, "Now that's what I call trying to make yourself a member of the family. Stopped 'em right in their tracks? Sent 'em skywards?"

"Don't! Please don't brag on me," Gloria begged them. "Or at least, if you're going to start, don't brag on me for the wrong thing."

"I've been telling Gloria she should've stayed home with the ladies, but I eat my words this minute," said Aunt Beck, rising and coming to kiss her as if to make amends in public.

"Just let 'em have a little pleasure out of it, honey," Jack bent and said into her ear.

"She only gets the credit for not knowing no other way to stop. She had up too much steam!" cried Etoyle.

"I fell on my knees! I'm ashamed of what happened," Gloria cried, with her face almost as flaming as her hair.

"First time that young lady ever said she done anything to be ashamed of in her life, ain't it?" exclaimed Aunt Nanny with a broad smile.

"And I've listened," agreed Miss Beulah.

"I might have been killed! And my baby in my arms!" cried Gloria.

"And who saved you from it? Jack Renfro," said Miss Beulah, leading a chorus of answerers, some of whom were still trying to reach Gloria to hug and spank her.

"I was doing my best to *save Jack*," Gloria corrected them as she worked free.

They laughed, loud with affection, at Jack. He'd risen up still holding his watermelon to his cheek, harmonicalike. He had eaten it down so close to the rind that the light of the sky shone through it now. "You *what*, honey?"

"That was what I started out to do!" Gloria cried. "I was going to save him! From everybody I see this minute!"

"Miss Gloria! I believe you're getting to be a little bit more of a handful than this family had bargained on!" Uncle Noah Webster sang out in pure hilarity.

"I'm keeping on trying! I'll save him yet!" she cried. "I don't give up easy!"

Aunt Beck said, "You know, I reckon there's nothing too much for a schoolteacher to try."

Jack shouted, "It's thanks to Judge Moody we still got her! He saved my wife and baby!"

"How in the wide world did you come to let Judge Moody save your wife and baby for you?" Miss Beulah cried. "With all this saving, where were *you*?"

"I was making such haste after Lady May that I sent Jack spinning in the ditch," said Gloria. "But if Judge Moody hadn't come along just at that minute, we would all have been all right and jumped right back on our feet."

Jack bent his brow on her.

"It was Judge Moody's own fault he had to save us," Gloria told them all clearly.

Judge Moody was heard saying to his wife, "The real culprit is that baby, of course. She ran between them—she was a moving target."

"That's right, blame a little suckling babe," said Mrs. Moody.

Miss Beulah blazed, "There's nothing you can say about that baby that's any fault of her own."

"But this is the first I realized that *all* plans has miscarried," said Auntie Fay Champion.

"And the car sitting this minute on Banner Top. You just come off and left it, Judge Moody, at the first crook of the finger?"

"I don't believe it's still there, Beulah," said Uncle Dolphus consolingly. "And I ain't going to take a hot walk yonder to prove it, either."

"I took the walk, saw it for myself," said Mr. Renfro. "And as far as the car goes, the car's up there and running in pretty good tune."

"And it's got somebody in it to hold it down! One guess! Aycock!" Etoyle screamed.

"Oh, for a minute I thought you was going to say 'Jack' once more," gasped Aunt Birdie.

"Aycock Comfort's deposited in your car and still behaving himself?" Miss Lexie Renfro asked Judge Moody coolly, speaking to him for the first time. "Well, I'm gratified to hear it. I expect Parchman did Aycock that much good. I wish you could find and send his daddy."

"Mama, as long as Aycock stays put, he's safe as we are," Etoyle said. "Jack says so."

"And if he budges, he's a gone gander. What about the rest of it?" screamed Miss Beulah. "These boys, these men, they don't realize anything!"

"Realize what, Mother?" Mr. Renfro asked her.

"What makes you think that's the end of the story? Somebody's still going to have to coax that car *down*. Suppose you never thought of that, any of you?" Miss Beulah cried. "What goes up has got to come down! Regardless! I declare there's no end sometimes! So you're elected, Jack."

"The home team might want me, all right," Jack said. "But the last I heard, Judge and Mrs. Judge are holding out together for old Curly."

"Curly Stovall and that brace of wore-out oxen? I declare, Judge Moody, that booger'll find a way to horn in on all you've got," said Miss Beulah.

"That baby may still be baby enough for what she's up to, but if she's old enough to wear pockets!" exclaimed Aunt Cleo.

Gloria, down low as she was, almost too low for it to be seen across the table, had opened her dress behind the screen of one hand.

"All the same, that baby's had some little threads of white

meat, some crumbles of hard-boiled egg, a spoonful of corn-bread soaked in buttermilk, and a pickle," said Aunt Nanny. "From her father. And I saw her waving his drumstick in her little fist."

"Give us some more, Brother Bethune," called Uncle Noah Webster. "You can't give up yet."

Brother Bethune called that the prize for being the oldest here today went to Granny Vaughn. "Now the prize for the youngest!" he called, and up was rolled this year's new baby, lying bound around the middle to a pillow in a wheelbarrow, hands and feet batting like two sets of wings. "Now the prize for having the most descendants after Miss Granny Vaughn herself—stand up, Curtis Beecham!" Aunt Cleo was named the prize winner for being the newest bride, Uncle Percy for being the thinnest, Aunt Nanny for being the fattest.

"Grandpa never gave a prize in his life for being fat," said Miss Beulah. "You had to *do* right. And if you *did* right, you were considered having prize enough already. Weren't you, Granny?"

The old lady's head drove back from her plate for a minute, as though buggy wheels had started rolling under her chair.

"And now poor Jack! Judge Moody comes along Banner Road and right on time for him to put that truck to proof. And no truck," said Aunt Nanny.

"Yes, Judge Moody, we all know better'n you do what you stand in need of," said Uncle Percy in his whisper. "Too bad you picked the wrong day to get it."

"If Jack ever gets through today alive, then gets back that truck and makes it go, I hope I for one am still on earth that day and with the eyesight left to see it perform," Uncle Dolphus said. "Jack's all but convinced his family it could even plough."

"What ever happened to bust it in the first place?" asked Aunt Cleo. "Running over some fool in the road? I don't think Jack's too careful with what's his." She looked at him with his second half of melon.

"Until it was busted, it never got to be Jack's," said Aunt Nanny, winking.

"Has there been something wrong with it?" asked Mrs. Moody.

"It started away from Curly's store in Banner on a Saturday morning, and the Nashville Rocket comes up the track. We was sitting there on the store porch, telling each other our woes, when there comes quite a crack," said Uncle Dolphus.

"It got hit by a train?" cried Mrs. Moody.

"It stopped the Nashville Rocket on the crossing, yes'm."

"This truck is something that had to be picked up out of the cinders of the railroad track?" asked Mrs. Moody.

"Jack picked it up. Had to wade to get it. There's a river of hot Coca-Cola and a mountain of broken glass trying to stop him—it was a Coca-Cola truck," said Aunt Birdie.

"Jack could have sliced an artery and no woman the wiser at home," said Aunt Beck.

"The only Cokes left standing for a mile around was the ones old Ears Broadwee had just finished delivering to Curly," Uncle Percy whispered.

"That was one sticky cow-catcher," said Uncle Dolphus.

"I'm surprised at the Coca-Cola people. It sounds to me like one more case of a careless driver," said Mrs. Moody to her husband.

"Watch out! That's my kin," said Aunt Nanny.

"I reckon there wasn't enough left of him for you-all to pick up and bury," said Aunt Cleo. "Have his funeral with a sealed coffin?"

"Didn't get a scratch. That was Ears Broadwee. He'd just been in the store, swapping yarns with Jack and Curly and the boys. Claims he ain't heard that train yet," said Aunt Nanny. "Ears was glad to be furnished an excuse to find him a job that would keep him nearer home. He's still looking, you-all. He may have to go to the CC Camp if something more to his liking don't come along."

"His touch is pure destruction, all right," said Uncle Noah Webster. "That truck wasn't much better than a chicken crate that's been waltzed around by a cyclone. The Nashville Rocket was right on time."

"The Coca-Cola people were a good deal put out. They sent one fellow here from Alabama to look at it. He just turned around and went back," said Uncle Dolphus. "Well, they can afford it."

"So it's pretty well scattered there on Curly's store yard,

laying on his property. 'Who you reckon's going to make me the right offer for that International truck, Jack?' Curly says. 'Look there, not a part in it is over a year old.' Well, that got 'em all to drooling.''

"It still looks to me like Curly ought to have thanked Jack for just hauling it this far off his premises," said Aunt Birdie. "Instead of charging him out of his corncrib. Hear, Jack?"

"Jack's trying to eat! He's got to catch up with you, not listen to you," said Miss Beulah. "To make a long story short, that truck, or what was left of it, ended up right here in our yard. Jack didn't ask his mother first, just started bringing it. Scrap!"

"Well, Mother, there's the old forge down yonder in the back," said Mr. Renfro. "And there's a raft of lumber standing on end in the barn, well seasoned, waiting on somebody to find good use for it. I told Jack what I'd do, faced with his problem, was finish taking it to pieces first. And start from scratch."

"How did Jack get the thing up to the house from the store yard? Did it have a steering wheel?" asked Aunt Cleo.

"Sister Cleo, he pounded him a sled together and loaded on and drug up this part and that part, Dan and Bet both pulling. And it all went right over yonder," said Miss Beulah, turning around to point with her long horn-handled fork. "There was four young pines growing just right to suit him. He chopped 'em off equal and mounted the frame of that truck with its corners sitting where you could see the stumps, if anybody'd get up and move away for a minute. It was a sight!"

"It was beautiful to Jack," said Aunt Nanny, grinning. "Oh, Jack was in a big hurry for that truck."

"I still wonder what he needed it for. You-all are clear off the highway or even a good gravel road," said Aunt Cleo. "What did he have that was so much to haul? I haven't seen it yet."

"It was his dream to provide," said Aunt Beck, though her eye was still on Brother Bethune, who had announced he was preaching on the subject "Be Humble." "And then to get hauled away like that himself!"

"And wouldn't it have done a perfect job of carrying a load

of us to church and not let our shoes get nasty? And all winter long, from where we lived in mud, he could've been picking us up and carrying us to see him play basketball for Banner! Tore away like he was, he couldn't even be on the team!"

"Don't, Birdie, you're making us feel so sorry for him," pleaded Aunt Beck, looking back and forth between Jack and Brother Bethune.

"And more than that, it would've carried us to the courthouse faster and in a lot more style than we had, when it came time for his trial," Aunt Birdie said to the Moodys. "We could've passed the whole string of 'em going, and let 'em eat our dust coming home too, after we got our hearts broken in Ludlow."

"But what was *his* hurry for?" asked Aunt Cleo. "It wasn't to go and be tried!"

"He's courting! Of course, he got married before he got the truck finished," said Aunt Nanny. "It was a race with Nature, and Nature run ahead of all the hammering he could do."

"Shining at the end of the rainbow was Gloria Short," said Aunt Beck ardently.

"Where? Where was that?" asked Aunt Cleo.

"Where? Right here in this house," said Miss Beulah repressively. "Not twenty feet from where she sits now. She was in our company room, when she wasn't out in the kitchen with me, ironing her blouses."

"The new schoolteacher, soft, green, and untried," Uncle Noah Webster reminded her, smiling.

"Jack didn't think he ought to ask her to marry him if he couldn't even invite her to go riding on Sunday in something besides the school bus," said Aunt Nanny.

"Gloria's so much of a one to like nice things and nice ways and sitting up out of the dust to ride where you're going," said Aunt Birdie. "Two on horseback's not much her style. You'd never suppose that where she got to be Lady Clara Vere de Vere was in the Ludlow Orphan Asylum."

"Well, as school drew to a close, things got to growing mighty serious," said Uncle Noah Webster. "Jack was prepared to hand over a decent billy goat to Curly for what

Curly's still got of the truck. It was trade-as-you-go right straight along, need I say!"

"And what was still Curly's?" asked Aunt Cleo.

"A whole heap of the engine," said Aunt Birdie, quick, like a good guesser.

"Be humble!" shouted Brother Bethune.

"That's right, Birdie," said Uncle Noah Webster. "Where the running parts was supposed to be, it still looked like a mule had taken a healthy bite right out of the middle. What Curly held onto till the last thing was the engine."

"Then it sounds to me like somebody went out of their way to trade Jack something that was looks only," said Aunt Cleo, and she gave a laugh. "Well, I'd say the fault was Jack's for not getting the engine part first."

"Jack thinks the other fellow is as honest and true as he is!" cried Miss Beulah furiously, still patrolling. "Even the hogs in this world! Keep going, Brother Bethune!" she cried. "Some people have still got the grace to listen."

"Curly mounted that engine on the post out in front of the store like a curiosity," Uncle Curtis said.

"And it was a freak to look at!" cried Aunt Nanny to Mrs. Moody. "You ever see one? It looks like some crawler you tie on the other end of your fishing line. Every time you tried to go in Curly's store to so much as wish for something, you had to duck for that engine."

"I hate to think that's what makes 'em go," said Aunt Beck.

"Why didn't Jack just swipe it?" Auntie Fay asked.

"Too honest. Too honest and too busy! When Jack wasn't driving the school bus and getting his cotton up and fighting General Green in the corn and tending to the last of his education, he was courting strong," said Aunt Birdie.

"Never anybody but the same schoolteacher?" Aunt Cleo asked.

"R-r-ruff!" Aunt Nanny growled. She grabbed Lady May over onto her lap, and growled at her like a wildcat and shook her. "That's right, Cleo."

"Well, Curly Stovall had Jack in a cleft stick with that engine."

"You're evermore right. Till finally he broke down and

promised Curly the livest of his calves!" cried Uncle Noah Webster.

"Just for that dirty engine, a pretty little nuzzling calf with a white face," Miss Beulah said to Mrs. Moody, as she passed. "Ain't men fools?"

"Jack by that time was *dying* to get married," said Aunt Nanny, looking at him eat, and taking another bite with him.

"Do you wonder what Curly Stovall could still find to ask for, after he'd taken Jack's calf and staked it out along with his billy goat?" asked Aunt Birdie. "All right, he said the one thing Jack needed to do now so as to carry that engine home was talk the new teacher, Miss Gloria Short, into taking Miss Ora's seat in the boat and go floating with Curly on Sunday evening as far as Deepening Bend and watch him catch his supper!"

"Not a bad fight resulted," said Brother Bethune, aside.

"And there was no call for them to go to battle," said Gloria. "I'd already made my mind up what I thought of both of them, and was ready to put it in plain words if they'd only asked me."

All the uncles broke out in delighted laughter.

"That battle come close to taking the cake," said Uncle Curtis.

"Seldom seen one like it," said Uncle Dolphus.

"The last real good and worthwhile battle that's been fought for a worthwhile cause *in* the store," said Uncle Percy, "the last one before Jack was drug from us."

"Jack tied Curly up in the same old knots and trussed him in the same style?" Aunt Cleo asked.

"Well, this was the time that Jack got beat," said Uncle Curtis. "But it did us all so much good, because what it left us with, after Jack got hauled to the pen, was a peaceful feeling of having something to wait for. 'There'll be another Saturday,' says Jack, while we wrench on his good right arm and sink it back in the socket for him." He patted Jack's busy shoulder and turned and told Judge Moody, "Well, that's the Saturday we're waiting for now."

"And now Curly Stovall's got the whole shootingmatch back again?" Aunt Cleo said, laughing.

"That's right! Ain't it, Jack? Oh, I'm glad to see him go

after that third melon with such appetite, but you'd think he hadn't had a bite of dinner at all," said Aunt Birdie.

"Yes'm, I suppose if Curly could finish the work it takes, he'd even start coming to church in that truck on Sunday. The hypocrite!" said Aunt Beck to Brother Bethune.

From Brother Bethune's side, Miss Beulah said, "Finish it? He wouldn't know which end to start. He can't even untie a knot in a little bit of clothesline, he can't get a store safe to stay locked."

"The truck is finished." Gloria stood up, appearing to them suddenly out of the low rocker. "We have seen it—Jack, Mrs. Moody, Lady May and me, Aycock, and all the churchgoing Methodists. Judge Moody came close to seeing it, but he missed it. It's going to pull the Moodys' car to the road, if it can."

"Jack's truck? It's riding?" shouted Uncle Noah Webster. "What kind of bad news is this you're bringing on a spotless fine day?"

"Foot! I can't believe Stovall had sense enough to know what it needed without Jack standing there to tell him," cried Miss Beulah.

"Must be something wrong with it. Surely now!" The uncles were all exclaiming to one another.

"Of course, nobody can promise you how far he'll get with it," said Mr. Renfro to Judge Moody. He had brought himself another glass of lemonade and sat down again close beside the Judge to watch him eat—Judge Moody was still no further along than chicken. "I'm just sorry to hear he's cranked it."

Uncle Noah Webster was shouting with delight into Judge Moody's face. "But *now* we've got something! *Now* we've got a war on that's like old times! Jack and Curly buttin' head-on again! And you in the middle! And old Aycock sitting holding his breath for everybody. Good old days has come back to Banner, Judge Moody! For a while I thought there wasn't much left for me to get homesick for."

"Poor old car," said Judge Moody to his wife.

"If nobody has any better idea tomorrow than they have today of what the word rescue even means!" said Mrs. Moody. "The very first fellow that came along today was sporting a chicken van, but would he stop? He sailed right by our signals of distress and went out of sight."

"He ain't too popular here at the reunion, either," said Miss Beulah grimly.

"Homer's got his own ideas," said Mr. Renfro, looking with interest at Judge Moody, who was still struggling with Miss Beulah's pickled peach. "I'll tell you how Homer's inclined, give you a little story. Now he used to make his syrup in my cane mill. The last time, he had Noah Webster to pull in the cane, while he's in the middle feeding it, and I was there to do the boiling, and our mule was grinding it. So Jack come along to get some skimmings, and somehow, someway, Jack put a scare in that mule. It was Bet with her blinders on. Bet commenced running away as fast as she could go," he said, smiling when the Judge looked up at him with a frown. "She had to go in a circle, it was the best she could do at the time, tied to the long arm of a cane mill. And old Homer's caught in the middle, ducking. Every time Bet come around, Homer tried to beat that pole and scramble out of the pit, and she wouldn't let him. His head would peek up, he'd start his foot, and here she come again, with the dogs giving very best encouragement. But as to Homer Champion, the family knows it, the world knows it, and Bet knows it—he just wasn't born to get out of a cane mill surrounded by a runaway mule. He's born to duck."

"I knew I ought to stopped Bet for him, Auntie Fay, but I just couldn't bring myself to get in a hurry about it," said Jack, a bite on the way to his lips.

"That was Homer's last batch," said Mr. Renfro. "And about the last batch our mule had anything to do with. It *was* the last. You couldn't persuade her to make any molasses for you today, Judge Moody. Although that was the smoothest-tasting that Bet ever made. Her last batch was her best, made for Homer."

"Oh, we've been at the mercy of that mule today too," said Mrs. Moody. "Only Providence got that truck ready for us."

"Stovall tied a string to the truck, didn't he? Said he'd make you wait till tomorrow to do business, didn't he?" challenged Miss Beulah. "And between 'em all, Judge and Mrs. Judge, they've left you high and dry with no place else to go, haven't they? I can tell by the downtrodden looks on both your faces."

"Give us some more, Brother Bethune! Don't let us think you're falling by the wayside!" The call floated up from the company.

"Don't you stop too soon, sir," said Aunt Beck.

"Well, let me welcome a surprise visitor to our midst!" Brother Bethune called. "Judge Oscar Moody, of our county seat of Ludlow! Let's all see him stand and take a bow! I know he's as happy as I am to see where he's found himself today. And the lady setting in front of him is none other than his good wife and helpmeet. Stand up, Mrs. Judge! I wasn't fixing to get me a wife till I finished hunting, and still without a wife to this day," he turned around and said to his gun.

"Why did we stand up?" Judge Moody asked his wife.

"I normally stand up when it's asked of me," she said. "Now, we can sit down." She sat.

But Brother Bethune became suddenly stern, as though he had had to pull the chair out from under Judge Moody. "Now sir! Now that you're here in our midst, Judge Moody, what you reckon we better do with you? I'm going to tell you." While they all, at last, hushed and waited, he waited with them. Then he addressed the Judge in the flat tones of inspiration. "We're going to forgive you."

"Forgive him?" cried Jack, with a leap to his feet, and Etoyle, turning loose from her swinging rope, performed, in the emerald coat, the jump she'd practiced for and alighted on his back. He staggered forward. All the faces, filled to bursting with the occasion, turned from the Judge to Jack, and back and forth.

"Brother Bethune! Brother Bethune! I wonder did you listen good to what you just finished saying?" Jack cried, though the reunion was already humming with fresh pleasure. "What's my family going to think of you?" Etoyle with a shout bounced to the ground and steadied his leg.

"Watch out, Oscar. You're blushing," said Mrs. Moody.

The color rose to his very forehead, as though he had prepared himself for the guilty part. "Forgive me? For what?" he asked.

"Don't try and forgive us for walking in on you. We were invited," Mrs. Moody warned everybody.

"That's plain hospitality," said Uncle Noah Webster, slapping Aunt Cleo on the back. "That ain't no guarantee you ain't going to be forgiven when you get there."

"No sign you are, either," Jack protested. "Brother Bethune! It seems to me like your memory comes and goes at a mighty fast trot today."

Judge Moody looked at his wife.

"Well, after all, you put my car where it is and then made me come off and leave it," she said.

"I'll forgive you for that," Aunt Birdie offered.

"A little forgiveness never hurt anybody," Mrs. Moody said.

"You think it's fitting and proper for them to make a clown of me?" Judge Moody asked her.

"I'll forgive you for bringing your wife," cried Aunt Nanny.

"That'll do, that's a plenty," cried Uncle Noah Webster, and the others began letting out cries and calls more and more hilarious at the sight of the Judge's face and of Jack's face, right together.

"Why is it necessary to forgive me?" Judge Moody demanded.

"That's what I want to know! Judge Moody, I got the same low opinion of it you got!" said Jack.

"Judge Moody, you do like the majority begs and *be* forgiven," Brother Bethune said with a spread of his great long arms. "Be forgiven for sweet forgiveness' sake, Judge Moody dear. Forgiveness would suit us all better than anything in this lonesome old world."

"And make this a perfect birthday for Granny!" said Uncle Percy, putting all his might into his voice.

"Oh, what's been let loose?" cried Miss Beulah. "It's the second time today I've had to ask this bunch of people that!"

"Well, I'm not going along with 'em, Mama," said Jack. "Not this time."

"What's a reunion for!" bellowed Uncle Noah Webster, while Aunt Birdie, charmed clear out of herself, threw open her arms and cried to the Judge, "I forgive you for livin'!"

Judge Moody again looked at his wife.

"That's about the limit," she told him, and he swung around from them all. "Cut it out, Oscar. You're just feeling sorry for yourself," she called, for he'd started away from his school chair, stumbling over some bright green bois d'arc fruits that rolled on the ground the size of heads. "Come on back here. You're not going to leave me sitting by myself! And you have nowhere to go."

"Come on back, Judge Moody," cried Brother Bethune in a voice of sweet invitation. "Don't you want to come back and hear yourself be forgiven?"

"No sir. I do not," said Judge Moody.

"Look! Jack's dog is *bringing* him back!" came laughing cries.

"I don't know why, but I never could teach that dog good sense!" cried Jack, as Sid ran with authority at Judge Moody's heels, driving him back, and as the Judge sank down again into the school chair, some hand rewarded the dog's jaws with birthday cake.

"What does this mean?" Judge Moody asked Jack.

"My family can't bring 'emselves to say it, Judge," Jack told him. "And not much wonder. They're trying to forgive you for sending me to the pen." He stared around him. "Judge Moody, I just don't hardly know what my poor family's thinking about."

"I'll forgive you for pronouncing judgment on Jack Renfro!" cried Aunt Birdie, and she gave a clap of the hands, while Jack groaned.

"No!" said Judge Moody. "I wasn't feeling my way along that road to come to this—"

"He's where he is now because he's lost," said Mrs. Moody. "But can you show me a man anywhere that's got the fortitude to admit that for himself? No."

"I forgive you for being lost," said Aunt Beck.

"—and I don't want your forgiveness for being a fair judge at a trial. I don't deserve *that*."

"Judge Moody, me and you feel the same way about it!" cried Jack.

"Look at the boy, Judge Moody. Jack Renfro might just as well have been a boy was never heard of around here for the treatment he got from you in Ludlow. I don't believe his mother will ever get over it," said Uncle Curtis. "You need some pretty tall forgiving for that."

Miss Beulah marched up to Judge Moody with the cake plate and its crumbling remains held up in front of her chest to offer. "Don't tell me, sir, you have nothing to be forgiven for, I'm his mother."

"But the fact remains that whatever judgment I passed on this boy I'd be very apt to pass again, if the same case came to court," said Judge Moody.

"I knew it!" said Uncle Dolphus.

Brother Bethune was coming around the table and now he walked close to Judge Moody and linked arms with him. "I even forgive you myself for calling me 'old man,' but don't try it again very soon," he said. "Come with me—march one step further and you can take a bow," he coaxed the Judge. "I'm going to let you meet her. Mis' Vaughn, here's who's come forty-five miles to wish you happy birthday."

"In whose place? Who are you trying to fool?" Granny asked Judge Moody.

Miss Beulah ran to protect her, but she had already found the little wilted bunch of dahlias and swatted feebly at Judge Moody. He backed away, and Jack caught him, then guided him out of Granny's hearing.

"I'm sorry, Judge Moody—Granny's jealous of who tries to get in our family," Jack said. "But her shooing you off don't make me forgive you any the faster! Judge Moody, here you are because you and Mrs. Judge would be roofless in Banner and in danger of starving without us. And you're welcome to the table. And I owe you a raft of gratitude for veering and not killing my wife and baby. And I'm going to get your car back the way it was going in Banner Road. But I ain't going to forgive you for sending me to the pen! Because listen, Judge Moody, you caused all these you see here smiling to do without me for a year, six months and a day while I was ploughing Parchman. And I take it right hard, and it gives me right much of a shock on the day of my welcome home, to hear 'em all forgiving you for it—all but Granny." He gave Granny a look, and then cried, staring all around, "Is the whole rest of the reunion going to forgive him? Mama, Papa, sisters, brothers, aunts, uncles, cousins? Every last one except my wife?"

"I told you so," said Gloria.

"It's all part of the reunion. We got to live it out, son," said Mr. Renfro.

"No sir, I don't forgive you, Judge Moody," Jack told him. "Oh, I'm boiling for 'em still, for the way you deprived 'em. And *now* hear 'em!"

"Jack, make up your mind your family is always going to stay one jump ahead of you," said Gloria.

"I don't forgive you at all, sir," said Jack in a clear, loud voice.

"All right! Fine! I prefer it that way," Judge Moody said with some vigor. "Thank you."

"You're more than welcome," said Jack. He thrust out an arm, and he and Judge Moody shook hands.

"None of this would have happened if Grandpa Vaughn had had this reunion in charge," said Miss Beulah. "And least of all this headlong forgiving of the first craven soul that comes and offers. Oh, Grandpa Vaughn, I miss your presence!"

"We're just at the wrong end of Boone County!" Mrs. Moody burst out.

"Can I just tell *you* something?" interrupted Miss Beulah. "That coconut cake's so tender I advise you to eat it with a spoon."

"And now who wins for giving the biggest surprise?" Brother Bethune called, sweeping Lady May up out of her mother's lap and running with her back to his place, then setting her onto his gun shoulder. "It's a pretty little girl— the one you see raised at last above your heads. She answers to the name of Lady May."

"And if that ain't the longest upper lip in Boone County!" said Aunt Nanny.

Lady May, who had drawn a deep breath, took a look down at everybody, and then it came.

"And I want to take this opportunity to say," said Brother Bethune right over the baby's crying, almost crying himself, "that never have I seen any more of a family gathered together since the Bethunes started to go. There's been a Bethune and a Renfro to go every year, till this year somebody fooled us out of the Renfros. Wonder whose turn it'll be next time, Mr. Ralph?" Brother Bethune cranked his head around the baby's kicking legs and put it to him. He ripped out a bandanna, paused to mop his face, then the baby's, and drove on. "At no reunion the summer long have I enjoyed any better attention or seen any better behavior. The interruptions has been few and far between. And the boat—the boat this little baby, the youngest Renfro walking today, is travelling up on the river of life, I hope the oar of faith and the oar of works will row that little boat clear to the gates of Heaven."

He shut his mouth in a black line, put Lady May down on the ground, and from all around the yard the other babies all cried with her.

"And now, precious friends—if you think *this* is a big reunion! If you think *this* is a pretty full count and a brave showing! Wait! On the Day of Judgment and at the Sounding of the Trumpet—!"

"*I* can wait!" sang out Uncle Noah Webster.

"Why, Banner Cemetery is going to be throwed open like a hill of potatoes!" Brother Bethune cried. "All those loving kin who have gone before, there they'll all be—waiting for you and me! How will you start behaving *then*, precious friends? I'll tell you! You'll all be left without words. Without words! Can you believe it? Think about that!"

He threw out his arms and stood there, open-mouthed.

"Ain't we given him a splendid time?" Aunt Birdie exclaimed.

"Sometimes I think it was an old bachelor like Brother Bethune that thought up reunions in the first place," said Aunt Nanny.

"Three cheers for Brother Bethune!" shouted Uncle Noah Webster.

"Brother Bethune has not accepted many earthly titles," croaked Brother Bethune. "He is content to be one of God's chosen vessels."

"Three more cheers for Brother Bethune!"

"Never asked the church for a cent of money and never needed such. Without script or purse," he whispered, as the cheers died down.

"That's right, Brother Bethune. Sit down, Brother Bethune," several voices invited him.

"I may not have very many earthly descendants," Brother Bethune in an unmollified voice went on. "If you want to come right down to it, I ain't got a one. Now I *have* killed me a fairly large number of snakes. I have kept a count of my snakes I have killed in the last five years, and up to and including this Sunday morning, the grand sum total is four hundred and twenty-six."

They cheered.

"Brother Bethune holds the title of champion snake killer of this entire end of the county," contributed Uncle Curtis. "And I suppose he limits himself to the Bywy on this bank and five or six little branches of it. Is that so, Brother Bethune?"

"It is so so far," said Brother Bethune, still not sitting down.

"You use the old-time twelve-gauge shotgun, I believe," said Mr. Renfro. "That is your main weapon."

"It is my only weapon," said Brother Bethune. He threw out an arm for it, where it stood against the tree—as long as he was, its barrels silver-bright—and shook it at Uncle Nathan, who slowly saluted him back with his paint-stained hand.

Brother Bethune sat down with a groan. His eyes went first to the cake plate, where the last slice of birthday cake stood caving into its crumbs. With the flat of her knife, Granny rapped his reaching fingers.

But here ran Miss Beulah, who set a plate in front of Brother Bethune and rained down on it a collection of chicken gizzards, clattering like china doorknobs. She forked onto the plate the last pickled peach, so heavy it would hardly roll. Brother Bethune gave a hoarse sound of appreciation.

"Did Brother Bethune forgive Jack?" Aunt Birdie asked.

"No, he didn't. He was on the track, but he swerved," said Uncle Curtis.

Mr. Renfro split open seven or eight more watermelons and passed them around. Each time, he gave a different girl the bursting red heart to drown her face in. Each time, giggling, the girl accepted it.

"Listen, I want to know something," said Aunt Birdie. "If it wasn't to make trouble for our boy today, why did you come along Banner Road at all? Judge Moody, will you tell me?"

"My presence in this end of the county has nothing to do with him or the rest of this crowd," said Judge Moody. "I'm here on an errand of my own. I was doing my best to find a way across that river, that's all."

"But we didn't want to get up on that bridge," said Mrs. Moody.

"Shied at the bridge? Well, I don't entirely blame you," said Mr. Renfro.

"Why, of course they don't want to cross that," said Aunt Beck. "Neither do I. And I don't."

Miss Beulah said, "I reckon they must know the story."

"No," said Judge Moody warningly. "I just took a good look at it."

"That bridge is a bone of contention between two sets of supervisors, now that's one safe thing to say about it," said Mr. Renfro. "It's crossing the river between rival counties, you know. Boone on this side, Poindexter on the other."

"There's a sign hanging from the top saying 'Cross at Own Risk,'" said Judge Moody.

"With a skull and crossbones on it," said Mrs. Moody. "Do you argue with that?"

"And the same sign hangs for them on the other side," said the unexpected deep voice of Uncle Nathan.

"Boone and Poindexter, each one of 'em owns that bridge as far out as the middle," said Mr. Renfro. "Let something get the matter with it and the blame goes flying backwards and forwards, thick and fast. And that's about the end of it."

"I'd hate to hear the story," said Mrs. Moody accusingly.

"Clyde Comfort had been out gigging frogs that night, and was just pulling in," said Mr. Renfro, setting down his glass of lemonade. "And passing under the bridge in his boat, he chanced to look up. And he seen the three-quarter moon shining at him just like the bridge wasn't there. There's been a great big bite taken out of the floor of that bridge on the

Boone County side, right where it leaves the bank at Banner, and the moon's peeping through at Clyde just like through a gap in the clouds. The first few rows of planks had give way and fell in, or somebody had carried 'em off out of meanness, nobody ever knew. If they'd been pitch pine, I wouldn't have put it past Clyde Comfort himself to run off with 'em, to feed the fire in his boat," he assured Judge Moody. "Well, while he sat there marvelling, he says, he heard a horse and buggy come tearing down the hill into Banner, lickety-split for the bridge. And it's still dark. The pine-knots burning down in Clyde's boat and the three-quarter moon in the sky, that's all the light there was anywhere. And about that same time, Clyde out of the other eye saw him a big fat frog, the kind he was looking for all night, just setting there waiting on him. What was Clyde going to do, hop out and skin up that bank to holler to 'em when he didn't know who—or not lose that frog? Well, he took the path of least resistance. Clyde liked to tell it longer than that, but that's the substance."

"Mr. Renfro, are you trying so hard to entertain Judge Moody that you'd give 'im that story from the other side?" cried Miss Beulah. "What that story is about is Mama and Papa Beecham being carried off young and at the same time, how that bridge flung 'em off and drowned 'em in that river one black morning when the Bywy was high, and afterwards being found wide apart."

"Oh, at least I've heard that one," protested Aunt Cleo.

"Our papa was a Methodist circuit rider, from over in Poindexter County," Miss Beulah began. "And he circuited around here for the declared purpose of finding himself a wife. Clapped his eyes *one time* on Ellen Vaughn stepping out of her father's church one pretty Sunday, and it was all over for Euclid Beecham."

"I wish I'd had a penny for every time I've listened to this one," Mr. Renfro told Judge Moody, but Miss Beulah drove on, and everybody listened except Gloria.

"She did more than marry Euclid Beecham, she made him give up being a Methodist too. And Granny and Grandpa took him in hand and made a pretty good farmer out of him, to boot. Oh, Ellen and Euclid's wedding! That's the one I wish I had a picture of!" she cried. "Rival preachers to marry 'em—Grandpa Vaughn and the Methodist. And the time of year when everything was all bowery. Wasn't it, Granny?''

"Time of locust bloom," Granny admitted.

"And it was two rings to that wedding," Miss Beulah went on. "She gave hers to him, he gave his to her."

"I reckon they did have a plenty more of everything in those days," said Uncle Percy in a whisper. "Long Hungry Ridge must have been a fair prospect then."

"And all this countryside hitched in the grove at Damascus Church and there was singing you could hear for a mile, and Mama and Papa was young and known to all around, and everybody said it was the prettiest couple ever to marry in Banner. Said they could hardly wait to see their children."

"Thick and fast we got here! Nathan the oldest, then Curtis, then Dolphus, then Percy, then me, then Beulah, and then Sam Dale the baby," said Uncle Noah Webster.

"Euclid got what he bargained for," said Mr. Renfro.

"And every last one of those children good as gold, bright and sweet-natured and well-mannered," continued Miss Beulah, still speaking as if from hearsay, or from beyond the grave.

"Well, we know what happened," said Aunt Cleo.

"Papa couldn't help it if he's good-looking beyond the ordinary," said Miss Beulah. "He couldn't help it if he's baptized in the cradle. Couldn't even help it if they named him Euclid, poor little old soul." Suddenly she folded her arms and cried, "I just wish he'd learned how to stop a runaway horse a little better! That's what I wish!"

"Maybe he'd done better if his wife hadn't been holding the reins," said Mr. Renfro.

"I'm going right ahead and tell it!" cried Miss Beulah. "You can't stop me. Now of all the children, Noah Webster was the one awake and was here on the spot to witness 'em go."

"*This* Noah Webster?" Aunt Cleo asked.

Miss Beulah raced on. "He run out when he heard the barn door open, run out in his little gown with a 'Stop, Papa and Mama! Wait a minute!' Almost catches onto the horse but just not high enough. So he just hollers 'Granny!' instead. Well, they was going right on, straight out to the gate, and Granny comes running to stop 'em and nearly got caught and

mashed to pieces between the buggy shaft and the tree—"
She jabbed her finger at the section of cedar down in the yard.
"She run-run-run down the hill after 'em, calling 'em back
here."

"Granny *running*?" Vaughn yelled out in horror.

"She jumped on her horse and whipped him up and followed behind 'em trot-a-trot, trot-a-trot, galloping, galloping, but her smart horse stopped dead at the bridge when he
got her there. Because he smelled the danger and seen the
hole, and there's the buggy-horse kicking down under, and
the top of the buggy out in the water, standing up like a sail."

Uncle Curtis, Aunt Nanny, Uncle Percy, all but Uncle
Nathan, with single accord flung up their arms in the air, and
Uncle Noah Webster held his transfixed wide over his head.

"The beginning of the bridge was just a big hole, and nobody saw fit to tell 'em, and it throwed both of 'em out and
drowned 'em in the Bywy River and left us orphans all in the
twinkling of an eye," said Miss Beulah. "The Bywy was running high, was full that spring, and I don't know how far
downstream they put up the struggle, or what may have tore
'em out of each other's arms. They wasn't found too almighty
close together."

"Did they ever find the horse?" yelled Vaughn.

"He didn't manage to hit the water. Had to shoot him."

"Poor Noah Webster always tries to put in that he blames
himself for that trouble. And it does look like there ought to
been a wide-awake boy could have got his father and mother
to hear him when he opened his mouth," said Miss Beulah,
striking her own breast.

"Somebody was running away from us children, that's what
I believed at the time and still believe," said Uncle Noah Webster. "If I hadn't believed it, I wouldn't have stationed myself
in the road and waited for 'em. I'd have been in the bed,
tumbled in with the rest of you. Because unless I dreamed it,
I didn't know yet about the Bywy bridge getting a hole in it,
didn't know any more than they did. I just knew I was in
pretty bad danger of losing 'em."

"If they hadn't been who they was, his own mother and
father, they might have done different. They only thought he
was trying to go with 'em, I reckon. Didn't even turn their

heads. If it'd been anybody but a Comfort out gigging on the river! And of course *Granny* couldn't do anything to stop 'em!" said Miss Beulah in anguish. "Papa was fished out by evening, right where he went in. But where was Mama?" she cried at the company.

"I stood on Banner Top and watched 'em dynamite for her. Two days," said Mr. Renfro. "Old river was running by me faster than I could run, trailing its bubbles."

"But at Deepening Bend, she came up by herself, Mama did. Beulah's too little to remember it, she says," Uncle Dolphus said, sadly teasing.

"It's a wonder to me that river didn't swallow a whole lot of other people that morning who was behaving just as mule-headed," said Aunt Birdie, giving a deep sigh. "That's what still scares me."

"Old bridge has seen some progress. We keep the floor patched at *our* end, and keep driving spikes in the runners to hold 'em from flapping. But give it high water, or a little mischief, and it's still sure death," Uncle Curtis said to Judge Moody. "From my own bed, I've heard it sing all night and with nobody on it, when a north wind blows."

"Take me back to the bridge a minute. What errand was they both so bent on when they hitched and cut loose from the house so early and drove out of sight of Grandpa and Granny, children and all, that morning?" It was Aunt Beck with the gentle voice who prodded.

"Now that's a deep question," said Aunt Nanny.

"Beck, that part of the story's been lost to time," said Uncle Curtis, looking over at his wife. "I think most people just give up wondering, in the light of what happened to 'em on the way."

"Something between man and wife is the only answer, and it's what no other soul would have no way of knowing, Cousin Beck," said Mr. Renfro, and he climbed to his feet and made his way back to the lemonade tub.

"At any rate, by patience and waiting they was able to hold a double funeral," said Aunt Beck to Mrs. Moody. "That's always a comfort."

"At the double funeral," said Miss Beulah, her eyes burning at her grandmother, "it was the same church, with the same

two rival preachers, but Grandpa Vaughn overpowering, and
with all the little children lined up—that was us—bawling like
calves in a row, I'll be bound, though I don't have a speck of
recollection."

"So before it's too late," said Aunt Nanny, "those that's
bringing comfort make up their minds to take one of them
two rings off. Not let 'em go in the ground taking just all
there was of them. They taken Ellen's for the reason she was
the most pitiful."

"And who got it?" asked Aunt Cleo.

Miss Beulah's warning hand came up and fixed itself in the
air. The skin on her fingers was swollen and silvered until it
was like loose, iridescent scales. Her own wedding band would
never come off unless and until she lay helpless in her turn,
for it was too deeply buried in the flesh.

"It went in Granny's Bible," whispered Aunt Beck, shaking
her head.

"I thought it right to bury the ring with my daughter."
Granny spoke, and their voices hushed for hers. "I thought it
seeming. It was callers to the house saw fit to meddle. With
Ellen in her coffin, they came circling round and stripped the
ring from her finger. I never saw a one of 'em's face before."

Aunt Nanny winked once at the other aunts.

"That's it. That's the way of it, Granny," Aunt Beck said,
and the women rose, came around Granny and said, "So often
the way. The world outside don't respect your feelings, even
to the last."

"And it's the ring Ella Fay carried to school that morning?
Are we back around to that?" Aunt Cleo asked.

"It's the same gold ring, and all the one sad story," Miss
Beulah said, patting Granny's shoulder, smoothing out the
lace collar. "You didn't hear but the Renfro part this morning."

"Sit patient," Mr. Renfro said. "That's all you had to
do."

"Oh, yes, it takes Ella Fay *one day of school* to come home
crying without it. It'd take her a mighty long year to learn
the way to scrub and hoe and milk and slop the pigs and the
rest of it wearing a wedding band of her own and not lose
it!" Miss Beulah laid her own ringed hand on the table. Aunt
Beck and Aunt Birdie raced to lay their hands down with it

and Aunt Nanny slapped hers down on top, and suddenly they all laughed through their tears.

"So to finish the story, Granny just tied on her apron, dusted off her cradle, and started in all over again with another set of children," Uncle Percy said.

"Yes, then it was our blessed little Granny that licked us all into shape," said Uncle Curtis. "With Grandpa towering nearby to pray over our failings. We would have been a poor sort today if we'd had to raise ourselves, wouldn't we, Granny?"

"We didn't believe in letting anybody go orphans in our family," said Miss Beulah.

"They might have even tried to separate us!" cried Uncle Noah Webster.

"That was surely acting a Christian twice in a lifetime!" Aunt Beck called to Granny. "Bringing all these up!"

"We was all fairly good children," said Miss Beulah. "Sam Dale was the best of all, being the baby."

"All except curly-headed Nathan," said Uncle Percy. "I can hear Grandpa saying it to Granny now, behind closed doors. 'Conquer that child! Stand over him, whip him till he's conquered!' Didn't he, Granny?"

"Come around from behind me," Granny said, "you who I'm guarding back there."

"This forty-pound melon is so good and sweet I believe even you could be tempted, this go-round, Brother Nathan," said Mr. Renfro. He stood offering him the heart on a fork.

"Don't be too hard on yourself, Nathan dear," said Miss Beulah. "You're here only one day and night in the year—all of us wish you wouldn't spend every minute of it standing up and not taking a bite at all."

Uncle Nathan put up his hand and said, "No, Brother Ralph, I'd be much obliged if you'd give it to one of the children."

"Hey!" Aunt Cleo cried. "Ain't that a play hand?"

Uncle Nathan's still uplifted right hand was lineless and smooth, pink as talcum. It had no articulation but looked caught forever in a pose of picking up a sugar lump out of the bowl. On its fourth, most elevated finger was a seal ring.

"How far up does it go?" asked Aunt Cleo.

"It's just exactly as far as what you see that ain't real," said Miss Beulah. "That hand come as a present from all his brothers, and his sister supplied him the ring for it. Both of 'em takes off together. Satisfied?"

"For now," Aunt Cleo said, as they all went back to their seats.

"I've just been to wake Sam Dale," said Granny. "He'll be along in a little bit."

Their faces were stilled for a moment, as though the big old bell standing over them in the yard had laid a stroke on the air.

"Who's Sam Dale?" asked Aunt Cleo.

"Jack's the nearest thing to Sam Dale we've got today," Miss Beulah said in a voice of urgent warning.

"Though Sam Dale left us before he ever got himself sent to the pen for something, I'll tell you that!" Aunt Birdie said in a voice helplessly gay. "If I hadn't married Dolphus, I'd *married* Sam Dale! I believe he was sweet on me."

"Yes, he was sweet on a plenty, but not as many as was sweet on him," said Miss Beulah. "Every girl in Banner was setting her cap for Sam Dale Beecham, and Jack went through the same hard experience."

"Sam Dale got out of marrying any of 'em—the hard way, though," said Mr. Renfro.

Then suddenly Miss Beulah folded her arms and said in a flat voice, "In all our number we didn't have but one with the looks to put your eyes right out, and that was our baby brother Sam Dale."

"Uh-oh," said Aunt Cleo. "Something happened to *him*, I bet."

"Will you try not to pull it out of us?" Miss Beulah cried, still standing with folded arms.

Aunt Beck said, "His is one story I wish we never had to tell."

"Handsome! Handsomer than Dolphus ever was, sunnier than Noah Webster, smarter than Percy, more home-loving than Curtis, more quiet-spoken than Nathan, and could let you have a tune quicker and truer than all the rest put together," said Miss Beulah.

"He sounds like he's dead," said Aunt Cleo.

The shade was deep and widespread now. The old bell hanging from its yoke on the locust post was the only thing in the yard still beyond shade's reach. The wisteria that grew there with it looked nearly as old as the bell; its trunk was like an old, folded, gray quilt packed up against the post, and the eaves made a feathery bonnet around the black, still, iron shape.

"He'd better come to the table in a hurry now, or miss his treat," Granny said, her finger trembling above the cake plate. "A fool for sweets ever since I put the drop of honey on his tongue to hush his first cry."

Uncle Noah Webster offered Aunt Cleo the dripping heart of his melon, and she took it in bites from the point of his knife, but still she said, "Are you all going to humor her? Just because she's old?"

Miss Beulah threw open her arms and brought her hands fast together in a clap. "Come, *children*!" she yelled.

Then an avalanche of the waiting children came down on Granny. "I'm not a baby," she said, putting out her little hands. One hand closed around a bag of red-hot-poker seed, and in the other was set a teacup quaking in its saucer. At the same time she was asked to unwrap a can of talcum powder.

"There's something you can make live through the winter!" "And that's something will bloom for you before you know it!" They all encouraged her.

Elvie came with the speckled puppy carried high to her cheek, his rump filling the cup of one careful hand, and with a sigh she gave him up, sank him into Granny's lap. "He'll run anything with fur on it. He'll retrieve anything with feathers on it," she said in the gruff voice of Uncle Dolphus. The puppy yawned into Granny's face. In the open pan of his muzzle a good-sized acorn would have fitted closely. "He'll do it all."

"Now what's that? It's that Christmas cactus coming around again," said Granny. "If there's one thing I'm ever tired of!"

"Then ain't these beautiful? And when Old Man Winter's at your door, how you'll love to eat on 'em," said Uncle Percy, coming himself to bring her a bottle of his own hot peppers steeping in vinegar and turned blue, red, and high purple. "Pretty as chicken gizzards to me."

The Champions' present, wrapped up like an owl, was an owl—in brown china, big as a churn, with potbelly, sunflower-yellow feet, and eyes wired to flash on and off.

"Like I didn't have enough of those outside without bringing one inside. Believe I'll like the next present better. I know what *this* is," Granny told them, as she took a box covered in yellowing holly paper from four children and clawed it open on her knee. She shook out the new piece-quilt. A hum of pleasure rose from every man's and woman's throat.

When the mire of the roads had permitted, the aunts and girl cousins had visited two and three together and pieced it on winter afternoons. It was in the pattern of "The Delectable Mountains" and measured eight feet square, the slanty red and white pieces running in to the eight-pointed star in the middle, with the called-for number of sheep spaced upon it. Then Aunt Beck had quilted it on her lap with her bent needle.

Granny's eyes tried to see into theirs while she shimmered it at them. She turned and held it the other way to show the sky-blue lining. Peering at them, she put it next to her cheek.

"Finished it last night. Took me just about all night," she said. "Pricked my finger a time or two."

"She'll be buried under that," said Aunt Beck softly.

"I'm going to be buried under 'Seek No Further,'" said Granny. "I've got more than one quilt to my name that'll bear close inspection."

The network of wrinkles in her face shifted a little, and deep within it for a moment her eyes shone blue as theirs. She bored her eyes into the nearest one there—it was Lady May.

"Look who's standing there for her!" said Aunt Nanny. "Don't she look like a little firecracker about to go off?"

The baby had come as close as she dared to all the presents, without having risked yet putting her hand on the puppy.

"What have you got for Granny, Lady May?" cried Aunt Birdie.

"I want a kiss," said Granny, leaning toward the baby. "I want lovingkindness."

Lady May bolted.

Miss Beulah threw back her head and in an unwavering note gave them the pitch. All their voices rose as one, with Uncle Noah Webster trailing his echoes in the bass.

"Gathering home! Gathering home!
Never to sorrow more, never to roam!
Gathering home! Gathering home!
God's children are gathering home."

As they sang, the tree over them, Billy Vaughn's Switch, with its ever-spinning leaves all light-points at this hour, looked bright as a river, and the tables might have been a little train of barges it was carrying with it, moving slowly downstream. Brother Bethune's gun, still resting against the trunk, was travelling too, and nothing at all was unmovable, or empowered to hold the scene still fixed or stake the reunion there.

Part 4

T HEY SANG for a while longer, still in their chairs but settled back, some of them singing with their eyes closed.
On the tables before them there were only the scraps and the
bones, the boats of the eaten-out watermelons; yet still, now
and again, a white chicken feather floated down from the sky
and did a brief spin on the grass, or a curl of down landed on
one of the tables.

"Why does she sing so old-timey?" Aunt Cleo asked.
Granny was a jump ahead of everybody else with her fa-so-la,
on up to the Amen of "Blessed Assurance."

"She sings it that way because that's the way she likes to
hear it," Miss Beulah told her. "If that ain't the way you want
it, my little granny's going to go you one better than you
want."

By now the girls' and boys' baseball game had started again
in the pasture. There was a board laid across the cedar trunk
and little girls were seesawing.

"There's Gloria's perch those children are making free
with," observed Miss Lexie.

"I don't need it any more, thank you," Gloria said.

She was coming out of the house now at Jack's shoulder;
he was carrying a syrup bucket stuffed to the top.

"After Aycock gets his satisfaction out of this, I'll carry
word to little Mis' Comfort where he is, so she can give up
and go to bed," Jack told Granny's table.

"Is he going to eat it like a horse?" cried Miss Beulah.

"Promise me. Promise me when you get up there you
won't try anything single-handed, young fellow," said Mrs.
Moody.

"Yes, I'd like to have your word on that too," said Judge
Moody.

"Single-handed—that ain't the way we do it around Banner," Jack told them. "And I already promised Curly the same
thing. We're saving the Buick till in the morning."

He bounced kisses on Gloria's and his mother's cheeks and
on Granny's chin, and walked away. There was nothing of the

661

world to see any longer below their gate, only the low roof of dust lying over the road, fine-stretched and unbroken as skin, and Jack went down through that and out of sight.

"Don't like the way they keep sneaking in and out on me," said Granny.

"Never you fear," Miss Beulah said to her quickly. "He'll be back when we want him, he's not one to fail us."

"Seems to me you've let an awful lot hinge on Aycock. I wonder if you know a great deal about his appetite," Mr. Renfro said to Judge Moody. "I think of the time Jack got home from a little hunting and Aycock tagged along with him, and it was supper time." He hitched his keg a little closer to Judge Moody, there at his elbow, "Well, to let Aycock have a sample of what hospitality means around here, Beulah fried up Jack's squirrels along with the rest of supper, and she set those on a platter in front of Aycock's plate while he's eating. And remember, Mother, how one after the other he forked those over and et 'em all? Et fourteen squirrel? I counted, because that's how many times he apologized, once for each squirrel, saying he hadn't had a real solid meal since morning." Mr. Renfro sat looking into Judge Moody's face. "All them mouth-watering squirrels went into Aycock's mouth one by one, while we mostly just set and felt sorry for him," he said. "There don't seem to be nothing there to tell him when he's reached the point of enough."

"Jack can handle Aycock," said Miss Beulah.

"Then tomorrow there's Curly Stovall, and that tree to get around," said Mr. Renfro. "And it's a pretty stubborn old tree."

"Jack Renfro will find his own way," said Miss Beulah. "He's come along too splendid now to get himself licked in the morning."

"What a fellow's got to do is suit his strategy to the tree," Mr. Renfro said to Judge Moody. "I think now of a tree that must've been forty foot up to the first good branch when I come up against it. A honey tree that was, a poplar. You could hear those bees just boiling inside—oh, they was working heavy. So the way I licked it, I went and got me a good augur—inch-and-a-half, I reckon. Bored me a hole in the trunk and drove me in a peg and climbed up and stood on that.

Drove me in the next one. Well, sir, I pegged me a ladder all the forty foot up that tree trunk, winding my way around it two or three times, and when I pulled up to that hollow limb, was it ever a-roaring around my ears! I hadn't climbed all that way without a saw at my belt. Sawed it through and let it down gentle on my rope, honey, bees, and all, the whole limb, until there, where she's standing down on the ground waiting, was Beulah's honey."

"Oh, *she* was the one making you," said Aunt Cleo.

"Beulah let it out some way—I managed to get it out of her—that however I could manage to reach it, she'd pretty dearly like to have it," said Mr. Renfro. "Truth is she'd been heartbroken going without it. Like Mrs. Moody'd be without her car, if my guess is any good."

"Can you see today where you went up, Papa?" asked Elvie from a branch of the bois d'arc.

"All healed over. Oh no, the tree's grown all over that now," he said. "If it's standing at all, that is."

"I wouldn't mind having another sample of that very honey," said Miss Beulah right behind him.

"I was a climbing fool," said Mr. Renfro to Judge Moody.

"We've got more company," called Etoyle up above Elvie. "Watch out, Gloria!"

The squeak of an axle cut through a song somewhere and the head of a white horse came swinging up through the dust, and its wagon with an old man driving it came past the seesawing children and tunnelled into the shade under the boughs. The dry yard, packed though it was with people, wagons, and cars, sounded hollow under the wheels like the floor of an empty barn.

"Willy Trimble, I'm always just on the point of forgetting about you!" Miss Beulah cried out like the best praise she had for him.

Mr. Willy saluted back by holding up his whip as if to crack it. Gloria jumped as if to get ready to run.

"What do you think you're doing here, Willy Trimble?" asked Miss Beulah. "We're holding our family reunion, or trying to, the best way we can."

"Happy birthday," Mr. Willy called down to Granny as he reined in.

"Go back where you came from," she suggested.

Mr. Willy got down from the wagon, gave them all a nod. "How're you, Lexie?"

"I'm livin'." That was the most that question ever got out of her.

Mr. Willy cocked his head at her. "And who's looking after your lady while you're gallivanting?"

"A nurse. One that's seven years old. I let him wear my Mother Hubbard tied up high around his neck. It's a little boy that can't know much," she said. "Lives down the road. And he don't know what Miss Julia Mortimer will do and Miss Julia Mortimer don't know what he'll do. So they're evens."

"And what are you going to have to give that little-old boy when you get back?" asked Aunt Cleo.

"A whipping if he breaks something!" cried Miss Lexie.

"Suppose she's played us all a trick," said Mr. Willy Trimble.

As Gloria's breath came fast, Miss Lexie said, "Now that I'm not there to soldier her, you couldn't surprise me with anything she'd try."

Miss Beulah hummed her high note with which she corrected the pitch of the congregation in church. "Let's not be served with any of your story today, Lexie," she said.

"Miss Julia took a tumble. And I'm the one found her," Mr. Willy Trimble said, his expression all self-amazement. "She'd made it down to the road, and pitched in the dust. I raised her up. Her face told its story."

"Now who's Miss Julia Mortimer?" asked Aunt Cleo into the sudden quiet.

"Hush up!" came a big chorus.

"Down fell she. End of *her*. And her cow was calling its head off," Mr. Willy Trimble said.

"It's not fair!" cried out Gloria.

Etoyle and Elvie jumped down from the tree. Locking knuckles they went spinning together around and around in a chicken fight, while the aunts gathered themselves to their feet.

"Gloria, sounds like it's your turn to go," said Aunt Nanny.

"That's right! You just better switch on over there the

soonest way you can," said Aunt Birdie. "There'll be work cut out for you to do, girlie."

"You owe her a debt of gratitude, Gloria," said Aunt Beck, coming to give her an embrace. "I'm sorry *for* you."

"Find somebody to take you, and go on. That's better than standing here crying," Aunt Nanny said, coming toward her. "There'll be ones there to cry with you."

"She's not crying yet," said Etoyle.

"Don't start tormenting her," said Aunt Beck. Now the aunts were passing her from one to the next to hug her and kiss her cheek. "I know you're being pulled two ways," she said to Gloria.

"Life's given to tricks like that," scoffed Miss Beulah at Granny's chair. "You just have to be equal to the pulling."

"It's not fair," Gloria was saying to each one who kissed her.

"I carried her in out of the sun, and then raised a good holler," Mr. Willy went on. " 'Anybody here?' And you know who it was? Little fellow from down the road, crying like he'd just took a whipping from somebody. I give him a drink of water and sent him home."

"And I'd like to know if any of this explains what you're doing *here*, Willy Trimble!" cried Miss Beulah.

"Well, do you know I just been run off from *there*?" Mr. Willy asked them all around. "I got it made to a T, a nice coffin, got all the way over there with it, and the crowd in the yard run me off. Like they'd never heard of such a thing or heard of me either. She's already fitted, they says. Don't need any present. I thought they'd be having a fit over it and welcome me with open arms. Seems like they opened up and got her one in Gilfoy. It's a Jew. They don't believe in Jesus—I reckon Sunday's just like any other day to him. When I went breaking the Sabbath for her! Then for it to get thrown back at me."

"I hope you didn't come bringing it here," warned Miss Beulah.

"I felt like I'd tailored my work to suit her," Mr. Willy said in a voice grown more and more proudly aggrieved. "I considered it dovetails correct, it's good good wood, there's not a thing cheap about it from one end to the other, or a thing shoddy about the way I fashioned it—squared off the ends and rabbitted them joints and the rest of it. I had full faith in it. For one thing, you know who taught me how to use a handsaw? She did."

"Exactly when?" asked Miss Lexie Renfro.

"Miss Julia Mortimer elected me every year I showed up at school to split up the wood for the potbelly stove, and I proved to her what I was good at. Oh, when I finally got my toolbox, time I was forty, I made her chicken coops a-plenty, flower-boxes, yard seats, porch swings, and till I got 'em right, too. She was ever the least bit hard to please. I don't believe, if she was still listening, she'd stop me from saying that. She was pretty smart, herself! She could have made her own coffin if she thought she had to. Of course, her *eye* was true, she couldn't help how true her eye was," apologized Mr. Willy. "As a child I recall her tacking up a crokersack over a busted school window on a snowy day. With a good ten or twenty tacks in her mouth all at one time, she'd *pp pp pp pp pp* not a miss. They all went in straight. And still hearing the history lesson. I told 'em my story in Alliance. It didn't budge 'em."

"Maybe it wasn't them to blame. Maybe it was you," said Miss Beulah.

" 'Why, I'm the one milks for her!' I says. 'I wanted to do something for her. She taught me to use hammer and saw when I was a shirt-tail lad, I've made many a coffin in Banner, and now I made hers. I made her a beauty.' They just went back in the house and left me with it."

"Willy Trimble, I'm going to tell you something, if you're all that anxious to find out," said Miss Beulah. "The main thing you know how to do is overstep. Just because you milk for a lady don't mean you're welcome, the next thing, to make her coffin. And until you get an invitation, you ought to stay home."

"Well," he said, "she told me herself, when I was that shirt-tail lad, she thought I'd wind up making hers in the end, her coffin."

"Let me tell you right here and now, I don't want you making mine," said Miss Beulah. "And nobody else's you might have an eye on."

"I owed it to her, that's how I figured it," he went right

on. "After she taught me just about everything I know. Once I got started, I just never looked back."

"Mr. Willy, between here and the schoolhouse I can count nine Uncle Sams, and they every one looks like you," said Etoyle.

"Well, I'm the artist," he said benevolently. "And it's all because she put a hammer in my hand. And it was for her I commenced writing my name with the question mark after it. 'Willy Trimble?' "

"She told you to?" asked Uncle Percy respectfully.

"Well, she told me not to. That's the way I'm down on the poll books today: 'Willy Trimble?' But she rammed a good deal down me, spelling, arithmetic—well, history's where she fell down," he said. "There's a heap of history I don't know, standing right here before you." He scraped his foot, gave them a bow. "But she knew it all. She had it by heart. There's just one thing Miss Julia come to find she couldn't do as well as I could, and that's to milk a cow. She got too old, and there wasn't anybody else, and she got me to do that for her." He turned and gave Gloria a bow to herself. "You want to climb on now?" he asked her. "I'll head back over. I ain't too proud to try anybody a second time. Maybe you could get *me* in."

"Pshaw!" said Miss Beulah.

"Gloria's staying right here! She don't want to leave the reunion!" cried Aunt Birdie. She put up a loyal fist. "We wouldn't *let* you go, you belong where you are, with us," she told Gloria.

"We had to tease you, just the first minute, because you was looking so found out, Gloria," said Aunt Nanny, poking her, and then pushing her back down into the baby rocker.

"Nobody's going over there with you, Willy Trimble," Miss Lexie Renfro said sharply.

"Then I reckon I'll just visit here a while, with some other folks that's left out," he said.

"Left out?" screamed Miss Beulah. "Mr. Willy, let's not have one of your jokes." She threw up her hands.

"I'll tell you one thing sure. I wouldn't go back over there unless I was sent for," said Miss Lexie Renfro.

"Lexie, you're supposed to be there now," said Aunt

Nanny, with a wink at the table. "And I bet you was paid for it."

"I don't suppose you heard anybody over there call my name?" Miss Lexie asked, defying Mr. Willy, and he shook his head at her.

"But we can spare you," said Miss Beulah. "If that's what you want."

"There's others!" said Miss Lexie. "And people can always find you if they want you."

Aunt Beck said, "Well, I don't know about that. And I'm afraid, Lexie, you'd have a hard time persuading any of us to go with you."

"To the wake of somebody you don't know? I can't think of more than once or twice I've ever been persuaded," said Aunt Cleo.

"Somebody we don't know?" came a chorus from all around.

"You *all* know her?" asked Aunt Cleo.

"Know her?" a whole chorus cried. "Suffered under her!" cried Aunt Birdie.

"We all *had* her! She was our teacher, all the long way through Banner School," said Aunt Beck. "That's how well we know her, and so do a hundred other people born just as unlucky."

"Well, they know how to give you a hard time," Aunt Cleo said with an easy nod. "Whatever this one was like, though, I bet you I had one in Piney that would outshine her."

"Bet you a hundred silver dollars you didn't!" Uncle Noah Webster said.

"Mine was a regular hornet's nest to run up against," said Aunt Cleo. "I'm surprised the majority lived through mine. The only thing about mine is, I can't remember her name."

"You'd never forget the name of Miss Julia Mortimer," Aunt Beck said. "Or ever hope Miss Julia Mortimer would forget yours."

"She taught every single soul I see, leaving out three or four. Why, it's like coming back to school right here, as good as over there, gathered in her own house right now," said Mr. Willy, looking around him.

Brother Bethune excused himself and went off with his gun.

"How many's she got over yonder already?" asked Auntie Fay.

"She's got your husband, if that's what you're asking. Got all Alliance, half of Ludlow, and most of Foxtown. A little sprinkling from Freewill," said Mr. Willy. "It's as many as you got."

"That's as many as she taught, all right," said Miss Beulah. "Oh, and teach us she did. Here's one I bet she remembered right up to the end."

"She taught you, Mama?" Etoyle cried. "How could a teacher be as old as that?"

"She taught me," said Miss Beulah coolly. "She's responsible for a good deal I know right here today."

"Beulah, I want you to save and give her that compliment when you get to Heaven with her," said Uncle Curtis. "I bet she never expected to draw one out of you."

"Who do you suppose started the woman off? How do you suppose she'd get started teaching without having some Beechams to teach?" Miss Beulah asked Etoyle and Elvie, who stood with their arms wound around each other's waists.

"Miss Julia taught me, and that was back-breaking effort," said Uncle Noah Webster to the children. "But I reckon she about cut her teeth on Nathan. He was her shining light."

"She taught us every one. I can see her this minute while I tell it, thumping horseback to school, wrapped up in that red sweater," cried Aunt Birdie. "Red as a railroad lantern, of her own knitting. Ready to throw open school and light straight into us."

"I remember her waiting for us on the old doorstep, a-ringing that bell. She had more arm than any other woman alive," said Uncle Curtis. "That was her switching arm, too."

"She didn't scare the girls with her whistling switch. She scared 'em off by expecting a whole world *out* of 'em," said Aunt Beck.

"She used the same weapon on the boys," Uncle Dolphus argued. " 'Where's your ambition bump?' And she'd rub her chalky hand over our pore hot skulls."

"Though sometimes she'd only come and stand close while you sat trying. Like if she could just blow on you, you would know the right answer," said Aunt Beck.

"She had designs on everybody. She wanted a doctor and a lawyer and all else we might have to holler for some day, to come right out of Banner. So she'd get behind some barefooted boy and push," said Uncle Percy. "She put an end to good fishing."

"She'd follow you, right to your door!" Uncle Dolphus said.

"Taking over more'n her territory, that was her downfall," said Miss Beulah, nodding. "Made herself fair nuisance with the boys in particular. When these Beecham boys was shirt-tail lads, they was fairly high-spirited."

"Miss Julia Mortimer and her whistling switch put an end to their dreams," Aunt Nanny teased.

"That's right! Not many escaped her yardstick. Boys, she wanted us to learn something if it was to kill us," Uncle Percy said with ragged voice. He had started to whittle his stick of wood.

"She held that five months took out of our lives every year wasn't punishment enough. She had us commencing our schooling in August instead of November. And after planting time was over in spring she called us back and made us finish what we'd started, beginning at the very spot we'd left off," said Uncle Dolphus. "She was our bane."

"She drove what she could into us," said Miss Beulah. "But nobody could hold a Beecham boy down. Not if you was to kill yourself trying. Nobody could but Grandpa."

"Outside the home, we boys was more used to sitting on the bridge fishing than lining the recitation bench. Now she wanted that changed," said Uncle Curtis.

"She thought if she mortified you long enough, you might have hope of turning out something you wasn't!" cried Uncle Noah Webster.

"And then she'd take the credit!" cried Miss Beulah. "Where ninety percent of the time, the credit was owing to the splendid mothers at home!"

" 'Children never change,' she'd say. 'They come to school three kinds—good, bad, and hungry,' " said Miss Lexie, making a face like a hungry one.

"It appeared to be her notion nobody around here could give their children enough to eat at home," said Uncle Curtis, looking innocent. "Every Monday morning on her horse, she carted milk to school in a ten-gallon can—and give that milk to children at dinner time to wash their biscuit down with."

"Of course we had to pour ours right out on the ground," said Aunt Nanny. "Broadwees is as good as she is."

"She told us a time or two what her aim was! She wanted us to quit worshipping ourselves quite so wholehearted!" cried Miss Beulah, and set her hands on her hips.

"Maybe just about then is when we quit worshipping her," Uncle Curtis said.

"If I ever worshipped Miss Julia Mortimer, it was a pretty short romance!" shouted Uncle Dolphus.

"Deliver me from the schoolroom," said Aunt Birdie with finality. "I hate the very thought now of trying to teach anybody anything. If they came begging to me, I'd have to send 'em to you, Beck."

Auntie Fay primmed her lips. "Remember the day I got to be one of you?"

"Here goes Sissie. All right! Tell yours," said Miss Lexie sardonically.

"I wasn't but five years old that morning—and it all went dark, dark in the house, and I ran and got the door open. I says, 'Something's *coming*!' I heard it! 'Get out, Lexie! Run!' It was the *wind* I heard. The air was too thick to see through. Too thick to breathe any of. Too strong to stand up in. And I went down on my hands and knees and I shut my eyes and crawled," said Auntie Fay. She was telling it with her eyes shut. "Blind crawled."

"Where was you going?" asked Aunt Cleo. "Did you think it would do you any good?"

"I was crossing the road to go to school but I didn't know it," said Auntie Fay.

"You went off and left me," said Miss Lexie.

"You was kept home from school with the chicken pox. I *called* you."

"The rest of us children was already right where we belonged, inside Banner School with Miss Julia Mortimer telling us it was the best place to be," said Miss Beulah with her straight-lipped smile. "She taught right ahead. We could perfectly well hear all outdoors fixing to come apart. I reckon most of Banner was trying to get loose and go flying. All of a sudden, the schoolhouse roof took off and went right up to the sky. The cyclone was on top of Banner School like a drove of cattle. There was our stove, waltzing around with our lunch pails, and the map flapping its wings and flying away, and our coats was galloping over our heads with Miss Julia's cape trying to catch 'em. And the wind shrieking like a bunch of rivals at us children! But Miss Julia makes herself heard all the same. 'Hold on! Hold onto each other! All hold onto me! We're in the best place right here!' Didn't she?" she cried to the others.

"I thought I saw her throw herself down on the dictionary once, when it tried to get away," said Aunt Birdie. "But I didn't believe my eyes."

"Where was *you*?" Aunt Cleo pointed at Auntie Fay. "You started this."

"I was out on the schoolhouse step, hollering 'Let me in!' " she said. "And it seemed to me like they was trying a good deal harder to keep me out. Till Miss Julia herself got the door open and grabbed for me. And the wind was trying its best to scoop me and her and all of 'em behind her out of the schoolhouse, but she didn't let it. She had me by the foot and pulled me in flat. She pulled against the wind and dragged me good, till I was a hundred percent inside that schoolhouse."

"Finally we got the door shut again, and Miss Julia got on her knees and leaned against it, and we all copied her, and we held the schoolhouse up," said Aunt Birdie. "Every single one of us plastered with leaves!"

"And that chair—that's when this house was delivered that school chair, the one you're holding down this minute, Judge Moody. It blew here," said Miss Beulah, pointing at him. "And the tree caught it—Billy Vaughn's Switch did. If it hadn't, it might have come right in the house through that window into the company room. That chair's the only sample of the cyclone this house got. I reckon Grandpa was pretty strongly praying."

"What did it do to the store?" asked Aunt Cleo. "Stovall's store?"

"It was Papa's store then. Well, sir, the roof took off and it was just like you'd shaken a feather bolster and seen it come open at the seam," said Mr. Renfro. "I was watching the whole thing get away from Papa. Everything that'd been inside that store got outside. Blew away. And the majority of our house went right along to keep it company."

"What happened to the bridge?" asked Mrs. Moody.

Auntie Fay rattled her little tongue.

"No it didn't. It didn't even wiggle. I was paying it some mind, I was under it," said Mr. Renfro to his sister. "I was going a little tardy to school that morning, and when I heard the thing coming, the bridge is what I dove under. And it wasn't in the path, that bridge. No, the storm come up the river and it veered. The bridge stood still right where it was put, and a minute away, the rest of the world went right up in the air."

"It picked the Methodist Church up all in one piece and carried it through the air and set it down right next to the Baptist Church! Thank the Lord nobody was worshipping in either one," said Aunt Beck.

"I never heard of such a thing," said Mrs. Moody.

"Now you have. And those Methodists had to tear their own church down stick by stick so they could carry it back and put it together again on the side of the road where it belonged," said Miss Beulah. "A good many Baptists helped 'em."

"I'll tell you something as contrary as people are. Cyclones," said Mr. Renfro.

"It's a wonder we all wasn't carried off, killed with the horses and cows, and skinned alive like the chickens," said Uncle Curtis. "Just got up and found each other, glad we was all still in the land of the living."

"You were spared for a purpose, of course," said Mrs. Moody.

"Everybody made it the best way they could till Banner got pieced back together. Grandpa Vaughn did a month's worth of preaching on destruction—it was all Banner but the Baptist Church. And if you want to count the bridge," said Uncle Curtis.

"It made another case of having to start over. You just don't quite know today how your old folks did it," said Mr. Renfro.

"Miss Julia was as wrong as you could ever hope about the

best place to be," said Miss Beulah. "If it hadn't been for the children holding it up, that schoolhouse would have fallen right on top of 'em, and her too!"

"And in return, did we get a holiday out of that cyclone? Why, no," said Uncle Curtis. "That same day, and the first thing anybody knew, Miss Julia made all the fathers around here get together and give the schoolhouse the first new roof in Banner, made out of exactly what they could find. And she never quit holding school while they was overhead pounding. Rain or shine, she didn't let father or son miss a day. 'Every single day of your life counts,' she told 'em all alike. 'As long as I'm here, you aren't getting the chance to be cheated out of a one of 'em.' "

"Everybody went off that morning and left me," said Miss Lexie.

"Yes, Lexie elected to stay home by herself and the whole house blew away and left her in the frame of the front door, standing in her petticoat and all come out in spots. Wasn't that forlorn?" teased Aunt Birdie.

"Well, you've been going from one's house to another's ever since, Lexie," Miss Beulah pointed out. "You've made up for it now."

"I remember another time, when the river was high and Miss Julia Mortimer asked us how many in the room couldn't swim," said Uncle Curtis. "And at the show of hands she says, 'Every child needs to know how to swim. Stand at your desks.' And with us lined up behind her she taught us how to swim." Uncle Curtis flailed his arms. "The river was lapping pretty well at the doorstep at the time. The last thing she'd have thought of was send us home. When she thought we could swim, she went back to the history lesson."

"Foot. Nothing fazed her," said Aunt Nanny.

"She was ready to teach herself to death for you, you couldn't get away from that. Whether you wanted her to or not didn't make any difference. But my suspicion was she did want you to *deserve* it," Uncle Curtis stated.

"How did she last as long as she did?" marvelled Aunt Beck.

"She thought if she told people what they ought to know, and told 'em enough times, and finally beat it into their hides, they wouldn't forget it. Well, some of us still had her licked," said Uncle Dolphus.

" 'A state calling for improvement as loudly as ours? Mississippi standing at the foot of the ladder gives me that much more to work for,' she'd say. I don't dream it was so much palaver, either," said Miss Beulah. "She meant it entirely."

"That's what comes of reading, bet your boots," said Uncle Curtis.

"Full of books is what she was," said Aunt Beck.

"Oh, books! The woman read more books than you could shake a stick at," said Miss Beulah. "I don't know what she thought was going to get her if she didn't."

"She'd give out prizes for reading, at the end of school, but what would be the prizes? More books," said Aunt Birdie. "I dreaded to win."

"And memory work! Every single 'and' and 'but' in the right place. I'd like to know if her own memory lasted as long as she did," said Aunt Nanny.

Uncle Dolphus, tilting his chair back, crossed his legs at the knee. " 'Hark, hark the lark at Heaven's gate sings!' "

"Dolphus, you dog," they cried back at him.

"I love coffee, I love tea, I love the girls and the girls love me!" shouted Uncle Noah Webster as the handclapping stormed.

"If it was Miss Julia Mortimer taught you to recite that, I'm a billy goat," grinned Aunt Nanny.

"Yes'm, she taught the generations. She was our cross to bear," said Uncle Dolphus as the laughter died away. " 'Hark hark.' "

For the moment after, the only sound was that of Brother Bethune hitting the tobacco can he was shooting at somewhere behind the house.

"I'd got over there sooner, and found Miss Julia Mortimer sooner," Mr. Willy Trimble then said, "if she'd ever been persuaded to give a morning yell. I listen for Captain Billy Bangs, listen for Brother Bethune, and they listen for me—"

"What's a morning yell for?" interrupted Aunt Cleo.

"Mainly to show you're still alive after the night," he told her.

"You've got Noah Webster now," Miss Beulah told her. "You can afford to keep still."

"It's the time-honored around here, for us old folks left dwelling to ourselves. A chain of 'em—one hollering across to the next one. So then if somebody breaks it, we know what it is," said Mr. Willy, putting his tongue into the corner of his smile. " 'Sound travels over water,' I told Miss Julia. 'You can holler 'cross the Bywy. I'll hear.' "

"She wasn't dwelling to herself, I was right there to watch her till this morning," said Miss Lexie. "But I didn't want to fail the reunion. I'd get myself talked about."

Mr. Willy did not cease regarding them. His eyes, where the whites showed above the rounds, were wary as a feeding rabbit's.

Aunt Nanny cocked her head. "Come on, tell it. There's some more. You found her: she hadn't drawn on her hose?"

"Did she speak to you?" Aunt Beck in a voice of dread asked.

"Yes'm. Before I got her picked up. She said, 'What was the trip for?' "

"The trip?" several of them chorused.

"But she hadn't been anywhere, had she?" asked Aunt Beck.

"We was equals. I didn't come with any answer," said Mr. Willy. "Well, she picked the wrong one to ask. It's the chance you are always taking as you journey through life. I just raised her up and carried her to her bed. But she didn't even know that. She was past it."

Granny was glaring up at him from the head of her table.

"And now they're all moving in on her and they'll set up with her all night," he told her.

"Granny's not scared of old Willy Trimble," said Miss Beulah, there at her side.

"She's sized him up," said Granny.

"Granny's not scared of Satan himself, is she?" cried Uncle Noah Webster.

"She's pretty venturesome," said Granny.

"And they'll bury her in the morning," Mr. Willy told them at large. "Want to go?" He smiled for them like a little girl. Then he pulled a chair quick under him and sat on it as if modesty had captured it for him. It was Brother Bethune's, only one chair away from Granny's own. "Now I didn't come to the table to catch your bites," he declared.

"Will you take a slice of cake in spite of yourself?" Miss Beulah cried at him, glaring. "Then take some of Lexie's pound cake that's going begging."

"I ain't choicy," he said, using both hands.

"Well, Gloria, if you hadn't changed your ways, an end like that was what might've been in store for you," said Aunt Birdie. "Glad you're married now?"

Aunt Cleo pointed at Gloria. "What makes me wonder is the school system. How'd it ever get ahold of *her*?"

"Gloria Short won the spelling match from over the whole state when they held it in Jackson and she was twelve years old. In the Hall of Representatives in the New Capitol. Schoolchildren against the Legislature—Miss Julia Mortimer's idea. And an orphan spelled down grown men. It gratified Miss Julia's soul, she said," recited Miss Lexie Renfro. "She coached that child so she could go to Alliance High School and keep up with ordinary children, till she got a diploma like they did, and she boarded her in her own home while she did it. She put her on the bus after that and sent her to Normal, headed to be a teacher. Miss Julia Mortimer was given to flights like that."

"How did she get to be so rich?" asked Aunt Cleo.

"A teacher? Not by teaching," said Mrs. Moody. "Ask one."

"She sure didn't have anything of her own! In that case she'd have quit," said Aunt Cleo.

They laughed at her. "Miss Julia Mortimer quit?"

"Taught to put herself through school in the first place," said Miss Lexie. "Just like anybody else."

"The year she boarded me and sent me to high school, she had Banner School to keep open herself. And she said she'd do that if she had to walk over the backs of forty supervisors. That's when she put some cows in the back and fenced her pasture," Gloria related. "And we milked them, before school and after."

"I never milked for her," said Miss Lexie, and Mr. Willy Trimble laughed. "Contending with a pasture full of cows takes about the same amount of strength out of you as teaching a schoolroom full of children, I'd judge. But she contended—because she was of the opinion nothing could lick her."

"Then she had fruit bushes and flower plants for sale, and good seed—vegetables. She had a big yard and plenty of fertilizer," said Gloria. "She'd sell through the mail. She wouldn't exchange. But she'd work just as hard trying to give some of her abundance away."

"Well, you have to trust people of the giving-stripe to give you the thing you want and not something they'd be just as happy to get rid of," said Miss Beulah.

"She put her lists in the Market Bulletin. She had letters and parcel post travelling all over Mississippi," Gloria said.

"I don't imagine she ever made her postman very happy," said Aunt Birdie. "Carrying on at that rate with that many poor souls makes work for others."

"One year, she sent out more little peach trees than you can count, sent them free," said Gloria, and they laughed.

"Her switches?" Uncle Noah Webster teased.

"These were rooted," said Gloria. "Came out of her orchard. She wanted to make everybody grow as satisfying an orchard as hers."

"I believe you. Listen! I got a peach tree from her, travelling through the mails. And so did everybody on my route get one. Didn't ask for it," said Uncle Percy. "Why'd she waste it on me? I'm not peach-crazy."

"I remember too. I only supposed it was from somebody running for office," said Aunt Birdie. "And voted accordingly."

"I give her peach tree room, and saw it get killed back the second spring. Didn't remember it was hers. Don't know how it would have eaten," said Uncle Curtis.

"It would have eaten good and sweet," said Gloria. "She wasn't fooling."

"I plain didn't plant mine," said Uncle Percy.

"Good ole blood-red Indian peach will ever remain my favorite," said Aunt Nanny. "I could eat one of mine right now."

"Did she keep you trotting?" asked Aunt Cleo of Gloria.

"She expected me to do my part," Gloria replied. "I hoed. And dug and divided her flowers and saved the seed, measured it in the old spotted spoon. Took the cuttings, wrapped the fresh-dug plants in fresh violet leaves and bread paper—"

"You sound homesick," said Aunt Beck. "Or something almost like it."

"And packed them moist in soda boxes and match boxes to mail away. I wrapped her directions around the peach trees and tied them with threads and bundled them for the postman."

"You was trying to keep on like Miss Julia herself? With those dreamy eyes? Honest?" asked Aunt Birdie.

"You copy who you love," Aunt Beck said.

"Unless you can get them to copy you," said Gloria. "But when I was young, Miss Julia filled me so full of inspiration, I even dreamed I'd pass her. I looked into the future and saw myself holding a State Normal diploma, taking the rostrum and teaching civics in high school," she told Judge Moody. "I'd keep on making the most of my summers, and finish as the principal. I always thought I'd wind up in Ludlow."

"Well, Jack wound up in Ludlow, and I can't say much for it," said Miss Beulah.

"Miss Julia undertook it, and she wanted me to undertake it after her—a teacher's life," said Gloria. She sat up as tall as she could in the middle of them, her face solemn as a tear drop, her head well aflame in the western light. "Her dearest wish was to pass on the torch to me."

"The torch?" asked Etoyle, dancing closer.

"What she taught me, I'd teach you, and on it would go. It's what teachers at the Spring Teachers' Meeting call passing the torch. She didn't ever doubt but that all worth preserving is going to be preserved, and all we had to do was keep it going, right from where we are, one teacher on down to the next."

"And the poor little children, they had to pay," said Aunt Nanny.

"Anybody at all that would come to her wanting to learn, she'd welcome a chance at them," said Gloria. "They didn't have to be a child."

"Who're you starting to take up for, girl?" Aunt Nanny cried, to tease her.

Uncle Noah Webster laughed. "Didn't there use to be a story that she even tried to teach Captain Billy Bangs? He come up like Granny in the bad years after the war, and in his case never got any schooling from his mother."

Gloria said, "She liked to say, 'If it's going to be a case of Saint George and the Dragon, I might as well battle it left, right, front, back, center and sideways.'"

"I'm glad Banner School didn't hear about that," said Miss Beulah. "Or me either, while I was one of her scholars. I'd had to run from a dragon, though that's about the only thing."

"She was Saint George," Gloria corrected her. "And Ignorance was the dragon."

"Well, if she sent you to high school and coached you in the meanwhiles, and was fighting your way to a diploma from Normal for you, she must have come mighty near to thinking you was worth it, Gloria," Aunt Beck said in comforting tones as she searched the young girl's face. "A heap of times, people sacrifice to the limit they can for nothing. But now and then there'll be a good excuse behind it."

"But the time came and I didn't want her sacrifice," Gloria said. "I'd rather have gone without it. And when the torch was about to be handed on to me for good, I didn't want to take it after all."

"For how long did you keep fooling yourself?" asked Aunt Cleo. "I don't see many lines across your brow."

"I finished Alliance High and crammed at Normal and studied in summer and took an exam and got my two-year certificate. Then I took Banner School to gain the experience to help earn the money to get back to Normal and win my diploma to keep on teaching—"

"And run bang into Jack Renfro," said Aunt Nanny, with a strong pinch at her from behind.

"Wait, wait, wait!" little Elvie cried. "What's Normal? Don't skip it! Tell it!"

"It's true, Gloria, you're the only one in sight that's been or is ever likely to go there," said Aunt Birdie. "Put it in a nutshell for us."

"Not enough of anything to go round, not enough room, not enough teachers, not enough money, not enough beds, not enough electric light bulbs, not enough books," said Gloria. "It wasn't too different from the orphanage."

"Was it pretty?" begged Elvie.

"Two towers round as rolling pins made out of brick. On top of the right-hand one was an iron bell. And right under that bell in the tip-top room was where they put me. Six iron beds all pointing to the middle, dividing it like a pie. When the bell rang, it shook us all like a poker in the grate," said Gloria. "I can hardly remember anything about Normal now, except the fire drills."

"Tell the fire drill!" cried Elvie.

"A black iron round thing four stories tall, like a tunnel standing on end, and a tin chute going round and round down through it," said Gloria. "You have to jump in, stick your legs around the one in front and sit on her skirt and the next one jumps in on yours, and you all go whirling like marbles on a string, spinning on your drawers—they grease it with soap—round and round and round—it's everybody holding on for dear life."

"Do you come out in a somersault?" asked Elvie.

"You pray all the way down somebody will catch you. Then you stand up and answer to roll call."

"I'm a-going," said Elvie.

"It's already too crowded," said Gloria. "Just us giving the history teacher the kings of England was liable to bring the roof down, and we practiced gym outdoors. When it rained, the piano had to be rolled like a big skate right into the post office, that was the basement. While you were trying to dance the Three Graces for the gym teacher, everybody else stood in your path reading out loud from their mother's letters and opening their food from home. We just had to dance around them."

"Do it now!" said Elvie.

"I said I hoped never to be asked to do that dance again."

"Didn't you appreciate a good education being handed to you on a silver platter?" asked Miss Lexie Renfro with a sharp laugh.

"There was too much racket," said Gloria. "Too big a crowd."

"Oh, but didn't you love it?" Mrs. Moody broke in. "A bunch of us in Ludlow still get in the car and go back there every spring to see 'em graduate."

"Come and see me!" Elvie invited her. "That's where I'm going. I'm going to come out a teacher like Sister Gloria."

"You've got a mile to go," Miss Lexie told her.

"Everybody was homesick, homesick, homesick," Gloria said.

"Who was *your* letters from?" asked Ella Fay.

"Miss Julia Mortimer, telling me to make the most of it, because it comes your way only once," said Gloria.

"That's a fact," said Mrs. Moody. "I majored in gym," she went on. "Led the school-wide wand drill. I still have my Zouave cap." Judge Moody bent a surprised look on her. *"Ta-ta ta da!"* She gave him back a bar of the *Hungarian Rhapsody.* "Then I had to go forth and teach Beginning Physics. That's what they were all starved for."

"I can't hardly wait," said Elvie.

"For right now, you start getting busy with the fly swatter," Miss Beulah told her.

"So here came Gloria to take her turn at Banner School, and she run bang into Jack, only to have Miss Julia herself to face. I declare, Gloria!" Aunt Birdie exclaimed. "I wish you had the power of the Beechams to draw us a picture. I'd dearly loved to have been hiding behind the door the day you broke it to Miss Julia Mortimer you was leaving the schoolhouse and becoming a married woman."

Gloria rose to her feet from the baby-rocker. Aunt Nanny reached out and caught the baby.

"It's a sweet little story, I know," said Aunt Beck.

"Nobody's listening but we women," Aunt Nanny said. "The men are all about ready to fall asleep anyway, Curtis is nodding, and Percy is already whittling to his heart's content."

"Tell it. Maybe we can help you," said Aunt Birdie.

Uncle Noah Webster reached his hand up the neck of the banjo, as the other hand stole to the strings and began to pluck out softly "I Had a Little Donkey and Jacob Was His Name," without giving the tune its words.

"It was the last time I went across to see Miss Julia," said Gloria. "It was Sunday before my reports were due, the first reports after spring planting. Her bank going up the road to her house was a sheet of white, all irises and pheasant-eye. We had tender greens and spring onions with our chicken. The Silver Moon rose was already out, there at the windows—"

"It's about to pull the house down now," said Miss Lexie.

"The red rose too, that's trained up at the end of the porch—"

"That big west rose? It's taken over," nodded Miss Lexie.

"She'd filled the cut-glass bowl on the table," said Gloria. "With red and white."

"She didn't cut 'em any longer," Miss Lexie said, as if she were bragging on her. "The reds hung on the vine all over everything, and turned blue as bird-dog tongues."

"Leave the child alone, Lexie. Nobody asked you to help tell," said Aunt Birdie.

"I was sitting with her at the dining room table after dinner, under those frowning bookcases, and I had my report cards spread out all over the table, making them out."

"Skip those!" cried Aunt Nanny.

"And I spilled her ink," said Gloria. "And after we rescued the reports and mopped the table, I said, 'Miss Julia, listen. Before I go back to Banner, I've got something to tell you that'll bring you pain, and here it is. I may not ever be the wonderful teacher and lasting influence you are. There's a boy pretty well keeping after me.' And she said, 'A Banner boy? Well, give me his name and age and the year I taught him, and I'll see if I can point out an answer for you.'"

"Gloria, you've got her down perfect!" cried Aunt Birdie. "Go on!"

"So I handed her his report. 'Still a schoolboy?' she says. I told her he'd had to stay out of school and that's why he was coming so late, and she'd never got to teach him. I said *I* taught him and that was half my trouble, because I couldn't run from him. She said, 'I'm looking right now at who he is, and I see exactly your trouble. I'll go over a few questions with you.'"

"Poor Gloria!" breathed Aunt Beck.

"She said, 'In the first place, how did you get him to start back to school, once he was loose?' I told her, 'I let him be the one to drive the school bus.' She said, 'What way did you find to get him to study his lessons? Though it seems to have done little good.' I told her by asking him to run up my flag, cut and saw my wood, and keep up my stove so the whole school wouldn't either freeze us or burn us down, and watch my leaks and my windows and doors so we wouldn't have a chance to float out of sight or all get blown away. And he's studying between times before he knows it.' She said how did I keep him with open book on pretty days? I said, 'On pretty days, I might be driven to keeping him in after school.' I said, 'After he carries the children home to their mothers, he turns the bus around and sails back. He washes my boards and beats my erasers and sweeps my floor and cuts my switches and burns my trash and grinds my pencils and pours my ink, and takes down my flag—and all the time I'm right behind him, teaching him.' She says, 'After that, how do you make sure he doesn't forget it the minute you finish?' I said, 'He carries me home. And I live at their house. We have all the evening,' I said."

"Go on," said Aunt Nanny. "Don't stop and dream on us."

"Miss Julia said, 'And what about now, after the seed's in the ground and before the crops are laid by? How far away from school is he now?' And I told her how even now he was still coming to run up my flag and salute it with me and coming back to help me home in the evenings. And on the days he missed all the recitations, I had that much more to catch him up on. When I saw the very most of Jack, I told her, it seemed like those were the same days when I had to take off from his attendance and mark him an absence from school. I told her the family was still trying to scrape a living from this old farm, the circle still unbroken, nine mouths to feed, and he's the oldest boy."

"Well, and just who is that, now, that you're making sound so pitiful?" cried Miss Beulah, still being everywhere at once, as if she'd be too busy to sit down to listen to foolish chatter.

"Did she say she'd love to meet him?" asked Aunt Beck.

"She didn't think that was necessary," Gloria said. "I tried telling her she'd never laid eyes on Jack. 'Scholastic average 72, attendance 60, and deportment 95 is a pretty clear picture to me of the two of you,' she said. 'You've awarded him a general average of 75 and two-thirds.' I said, 'And 75 is passing.' 'Passing so far,' she says. 'Is he going to be present on examination day and sit down and take those seventh-grade examinations? Remember, I'm the one who made those examinations out.' 'He'll take 'em if I have anything to do with it!' I told her. 'And win his diploma?' And I tell her I've already got his diploma filled out—all but for the Superintendent's signature and the gold seal. 'Miss Julia, I'm going to hang onto Jack and pull him through. And as soon as he gets his feet on solid ground, I'm going to marry him.' 'Marry him?' she said."

"Did she appear satisfied?" Aunt Birdie asked, nodding Gloria ahead. "And tell you to go on, keep a-courting?"

"Exactly the opposite," said Gloria. " 'Marry him! And leave Banner School without its teacher?' she says. And she jumped right up and it shook the china closet behind her, and said, 'Oh, you can't do that!' "

Aunt Nanny slapped her lap, on either side of the baby, and Aunt Birdie's high giggle led the laughing.

"She said, 'It's a thoroughly unteacherlike thing to do,' " Gloria went on. "She said, 'Instead of marrying your pupil, why can't you stick to your guns and turn yourself into a better teacher and do him and the world some good?' "

There was a fresh burst of womanly laughter, and along with that and the tickling notes of the banjo, one low groan from a man joined in—it could only have come from Judge Moody.

"I wonder what Miss Gloria *won't* decide to tell us," remarked Miss Beulah. "Something's happened somewhere to loosen her tongue."

"Keep on, Gloria! Gloria, I declare! After all the good excuse you'd put up!" cried Aunt Birdie. "Could you still go her one better?"

"I told her I wanted to give all my teaching to one," Gloria said. And as they sat silenced, she added, "That's when she laughed at me."

"You can't stand that," said Miss Beulah. "No, not from anybody, not you."

"Did you wilt?" asked Aunt Nanny.

Gloria's eyelids dropped shut and trembled. Then she went on. "Miss Julia said my story was one that had been heard of before now. She said I wasn't the first teacher in Creation to be struck down by tender feelings the first day I threw school open and saw one face above all the rest out in front of me. She said teachers falling in love with their first pupils was old at the Flood. But it didn't give them any certificate to stop teaching."

"Those words must still be in letters of fire on your poor brain," said Aunt Beck.

"What did you do? Laugh or cry?" said Aunt Nanny. "Tell you what I'd done—I'd run." As she hollered it, Lady May scampered down and ran from her.

"I argued as good as she did," Gloria said. "I asked her if she could give me just three good reasons right quick why I couldn't give up my teaching and marry that minute if I wanted to."

"Was she stumped?" asked Aunt Birdie eagerly.

"She thought she had them," said Gloria. "She told me, 'All right, Gloria. One: you're young and ignorant—each one of you as much as the other.' That wasn't so. 'Two: sitting and hanging your heels over Banner Top in the moonlight, you don't dream yet where strong feelings can lead you.' That wasn't so. 'And three: you need to give a little mind to the *family* you're getting tangled up with.'"

"For mercy's sakes! Only one of the biggest families there is!" cried Miss Beulah. "And one of the closest!"

"And it's exactly where they put me down with my valise," said Gloria.

"Well! Stacey Broadwee, Ora Stovall, and Mis' Comfort and me, we all drew straws for the teacher," said Miss Beulah to the company. "And who do you reckon got the little one?"

"Miss Julia didn't let up," said Gloria. " 'Here's reason four, for good measure: do you know who you are? Just who are you? You don't know,' she says. 'Before you jump head-long, ask yourself a few questions.'"

"And as if that wasn't our business more than hers!" said

Miss Beulah. She added to Gloria with a show of sarcasm, "And I suppose she was ready with an answer for that too?"

While Uncle Noah Webster leaned toward her and picked at another chorus, Gloria was shaking her radiant head. "She said if only Mississippians had birth certificates and would be like other people! 'It wouldn't kill them,' she said. 'It's no insult to be asked to prove who you are. It wouldn't hurt a soul to be ready to furnish some proof of his existence at the right time. And nothing would be lost but a little fraction of the confusion.' "

In the disapproving quiet that came after her words, Judge Moody could be heard clearing his throat.

"There's a good long page, ain't there now, in everybody's family Bible for writing 'em down?" asked Uncle Curtis.

"For writing down ours. But Gloria's lacking in the ones to do the writing," Aunt Beck sadly reminded him.

"You're *here*, aren't you?" Aunt Birdie said with a scandalized laugh at Gloria.

"Miss Julia told me there was a dark thread, a dark thread running through my story somewhere," Gloria went on. "Or my mother wouldn't have made a mystery out of me. And I owed it to myself to find out the worst, and the quicker the better."

"The worst! And how did you like that?" grinned Aunt Nanny.

"I said it suited me all right kept dark the way it was. I didn't mind being a mystery—I was used to it. And if I was born a mystery, I'd be married a mystery."

"And die one?" prompted Aunt Beck.

"Miss Julia still wasn't satisfied?" asked Aunt Birdie, looking into Gloria's face. "I'd have been."

"She said it was a piece of unwisdom."

"Was that all?" asked several.

"No. 'Use your head,' she said. 'Find out who you are. And don't get married first,' she said. 'That's putting the cart before the horse.' "

"But you did that very thing, didn't you?" said Aunt Birdie sympathetically. "Don't blame you a solitary bit."

"She said, 'Go back to Banner School. Give out your reports tomorrow—and make those children work harder. Then teach out your year as you promised. And meantime, get your own eyes open. You're in the very best place to get a little light on yourself. Banner's the side of the river you surely were born on. You were found in Medley—that's in walking distance of Banner School. Get to work on yourself. And I'll work on you, too.'"

"Ouch!" cried Aunt Nanny.

"She said where there was a dark thread running, she hated to think of it being unravelled by unknowing hands, and after it's too late—when she couldn't be standing there to see it done right. She said every mystery had its right answer—we just had to find it. That's what mysteries were given to us for. And she didn't think mine would be too hard for a good brain."

"Poor Gloria!" murmured Aunt Beck. "I bet you wished mighty hard you hadn't got her started on you."

"You're lucky it didn't do her any good," said Aunt Birdie. "You're the same little question-mark as ever, ain't you?"

"How did you discourage her, Gloria?" asked Aunt Nanny.

"I snapped the elastic band around my reports, and took the roses she gave me with 'em, and went out of her house and into the spring, and took my road," said Gloria. "And Jack was there at the other end of the bridge, waiting for me. Whistling."

"Oh, I bet you skipped!" said Aunt Nanny.

"And never went back," said Miss Lexie, looking at her.

"And never give another thought to who you were," said Aunt Birdie stoutly. "And how would you have had the time, anyway, after that?"

"I didn't see how she could be right about the best place to look—about my beginnings being anywhere around here. I'd already seen all there was to Banner, the first day."

"Not grand enough for Miss Gloria?" Miss Lexie rocked back on her heels, giving her silent laugh.

"In my heart of hearts, I thought higher of myself than that." Gloria lifted her chin and opened her eyes wide upon them. "I still do."

Granny's tiny voice spoke.

Uncle Noah Webster stopped his tune at once, everybody

hushed talking and laughing, and Miss Beulah said, "What is it, what's that, Granny?"

She said, "Sojourner."

Miss Beulah went hurrying toward her chair. "Are you telling us something, Granny?"

"Prick up your ears. Once is all I'm going to tell it," Granny said. "Sojourner. That's your mother." She flicked her fan at Gloria. "Fox-headed Rachel."

All eyes travelled back to Gloria. She stood staring.

"Granny, Granny, wait a minute—I can't put my finger right quick on who Rachel Sojourner is!" cried Miss Beulah. "There's no Sojourners I know of!"

"Sure you know! Sure you remember!" said Aunt Nanny. "I do."

"Where'd they live?" asked Aunt Cleo. "In Banner, sure-enough?"

"Yes'm, clear to the bottom of the hill," Aunt Nanny said. "Lower than Aycock. They did! Nobody with the name left now." She slapped herself on her lap. "And Rachel is the one Miss Julia Mortimer taught sewing to—the little girl on the end of the recitation bench. Yes'm. Rachel couldn't learn to do mental arithmetic, so while the rest of us was firing off to beat the band, she sat like Puss—just pointing the tip of her little tongue out, and putting in a seam."

"Taught her to sew right here." Granny's voice came again. "Saw she's starving. Called her into my own house. 'You can help me with this brood, mending their stockings. At least you'll get fed.'"

"You're bringing her back to me," said Miss Beulah, in wary tones. "I don't see her face yet, but I'm beginning to hear just a little—hear the laughing. Yes, in this house, I'd hear the boys tease her, circling around her at the quilting frame, or the loom, maybe, tease her while she treadled. I can hear her laugh floating through the breezeway—and I can see her weak eyes now. She worked—or she laughed—till the coming tears would put her eyes right out. I'll remember two or three other failings about her too, in a minute," she added, her eyes moving to Gloria. "Yes, I'm about to see her pretty well."

"Tossing her mane," said Granny. "Fiery mane."

As Gloria let out a gasp of protest, Miss Beulah kept on. "And it was Nathan knew best how to make her cry."

"But was as still about her as that hunk of firewood going to waste down there in the yard," Granny said, looking around her and then up into Nathan's face.

"Couldn't help teasing Miss Rachel, Granny!" said Uncle Noah Webster. "I remember her for the very reason."

"But we had one she could count on. Sam Dale would never tease her," said Uncle Curtis, and instantly the tears stood in Miss Beulah's eyes.

Granny's head drove back against her chair as if it had started on its rockers to run off with her, like a buggy. "Mr. Vaughn put a stop to her foolishness, sent her on," she said. "Well, that's who you are. You're Rachel's."

"It's just because Granny is so old that you believe her," Gloria said in a rush to the company. "If she wasn't your granny, celebrating her birthday, you'd think she could be as wrong as anybody else."

"All I hope is Granny didn't hear that," Miss Beulah whispered.

"And you all believe her because *you're* old!"

"Gloria, you're showing yourself to be a handful today, whoever you got it from!" said Aunt Nanny, laughing.

"I'm not hers. I'm not Rachel's. I'm not one bit of hers," said Gloria.

"Well, where did she come from?" asked Aunt Cleo. "Gloria right here, I mean."

"Oh, that little story's fairly well known, as far as it goes," said Miss Beulah.

Aunt Nanny, shooing at a game of "Fox in the Morning, Geese in the Evening" which just then swept over the yard like a gust of wind, was already telling it. "The home demonstration agent of Boone County come out and found her new-born on her front porch one evening. In her swing. Tucked in a clean shoe box."

"You was tiny," Aunt Cleo told Gloria.

"She was red as a pomegranate, and mad. Waving her little fists, the story goes," said Aunt Nanny fondly. "So the home demonstration agent—that was Miss Pet Hanks's mother, and while she lived she's in the same house in Medley where Miss Pet's still answering the phone—Mis' Hanks, the minute she saw what she had, and even though it was her busy day, she planked that baby in her old tin Lizzie and bounced all the way to Ludlow. And it was dewberry time, ditches full of 'em, bushes just loaded, begging to be picked on both sides of the road all the way. Made her wish she had time to stop and enjoy 'em, while she could."

"Must have been shortly before our Easter Snap," said Aunt Beck.

"It was."

"What day do you call your birthday?" Aunt Cleo pointed at Gloria.

"April the first!" she said with defiance.

"I wish I'd known you was going begging!" Aunt Nanny cried to her through the others' laughter. "I'd opened both arms so fast! I always prayed for me a girl—though I'd have taken a boy either, if answer had ever been sent." She puffed on. "Mis' Hanks carried you straight to the orphan asylum and handed you in. 'Here's a treat for you,' she says to 'em. 'It's a girl. I even brought her named.' She named you after her trip to Ludlow. It was a glorious day and she was sorry she had to cut her visit so short. Gloria Short."

"It wasn't bad for a name for you either, Gloria—you was born with a glorious head of hair and you was short a father and a mother," said Aunt Birdie.

"It might be a sweeter name than you'd gotten from either one of them, for all you know, Gloria," said Aunt Beck.

"I would have named myself something different," said Gloria. "And not as common. There were three other Glorias all eating at my table."

"Considering who found you, be thankful you wasn't named Pet Hanks and been all by yourself," said Uncle Noah Webster.

"That's right. Now *they* know how to inflict you!" said Aunt Birdie. "The papas and mamas. Mama and Papa named me Virgil Homer, after the two doctors that succeeded in bringing me into the world. It wasn't till I tried saying it myself and it came out 'Birdie' that I ever got it any different."

"I named all mine a pretty name, every one of 'em," said Miss Beulah. "Give 'em a pretty name, say I, for it may be the only thing you *can* give 'em. I named all mine myself, including little Beulah, that didn't live but a day."

"I'm Renfro now," said Gloria.

"And in just no time!" said Miss Beulah. She studied Gloria with her head on one side. "Sojourner. That makes you kin to Aycock. And Captain Billy Bangs is stumping back there somewhere behind you. Reckon you'll be as long-lived as him?"

"I don't believe I'm Rachel's!" Gloria cried.

"It fits perfect," Miss Beulah said. "Only too perfect if you knew Rachel."

"But I was a secret," Gloria protested. "Whosoever I was, I was her secret." She jumped up, her head like a house afire.

"You might have been Rachel's *secret*, all right—but Rachel's story is a mighty old story around Banner, and now it comes crowding back in on me, the whole thing, coming like we'd called it," said Miss Beulah. "I reckon everybody and his brother heard that story once upon a time, and lived just about the right length of time to forget it."

"What about Rachel? Have you got *her* somewhere where you could corner her and ask her?" asked Aunt Cleo.

"You'll have to wait till you meet her in Heaven if you want to get it from Rachel," said Miss Beulah.

"Then how can you-all be so sure beforehand?" cried Gloria. "How do you know I'm Rachel's secret?"

"If Mis' Hanks was the only soul in Medley that Rachel Sojourner knew well enough to speak to, that's the one she'd give her baby to. Wouldn't she?" Aunt Birdie asked her.

"But Mis' Hanks might have known others going unmarried besides Rachel who had babies to give. She was the home demonstration agent, after all. Went countywide, pushed in everywhere," argued Aunt Beck for Gloria.

"But Rachel's baby has to be *somewhere*," said Miss Beulah. "And I think with Granny that somewhere is right here."

"I'm not Rachel's," said Gloria. "The more you tell it, the less I believe it."

Aunt Nanny said, grinning, "Well, listen—mothers come different. Mama had two, and gave away both of 'em, me and my sister, when we was squallers, and she didn't need to at all—it just suited her better. She's up the road with Papa now, busy living to a ripe old age."

"But she was a Broadwee," Miss Beulah reminded her. "Tough as an old walnut."

"Old Man Sojourner, after Rachel had been laid in the ground, he reached in the chink of the chimney-piece and pulled all the money out that was being saved to bury he and his wife, and sold the cow to boot, all to put up a stone to Rachel's memory. It's still there—a lamb, and not very snowy," said Aunt Nanny. She reached out and gave Gloria a spank.

Gloria cried out, "It's the grave that looks ready to go slipsliding down the hill and into the Bywy!"

"That's right," said Miss Beulah. "And by this time the whole tribe has pretty well followed suit and gone to the grave behind her. I reckon what keeps Captain Billy Bangs alive is purely and solely trying to outlive Granny." Then she took a step toward Gloria. "I ought to have known you on sight, girl. The minute you walked in my house with your valise and satchel and the little setting of eggs for the teacher's present, and unsnapped the elastic on your hat. You might have been poor, frail, headstrong little-old Rachel Sojourner all over again. Why didn't I just stop in my tracks long enough to think a minute?" She looked at Granny. "Why, that day, when Granny came in from the garden with a bushel of greens in her apron, she stopped in front of you and said, 'Aren't you under the wrong roof, little girl?' "

" 'No ma'am,' I told her. '*I* haven't made a mistake—I'm the teacher.' And her greens fell right down on the floor, for us to pick up," said Gloria.

Miss Beulah put a hand on the old lady's shoulder and told Gloria, "You might've been the very same, the one that used to come to this house and help sew and stay a week at a time in our company room, sleeping with the teacher. Maybe it was hoped Miss Julia Mortimer's head on the next pillow could talk some sense into her head!"

"Miss Julia Mortimer," Miss Lexie retorted to Gloria before she could speak, "is exactly who *found* Rachel Sojourner, when that girl was fixing to die. Quivering and shaking she

was, on the Banner bridge. Miss Julia was driving across in
her flivver, late leaving the schoolhouse, and it's changing—
turning cold, and getting dark. There's Rachel! Her sewing
pupil, that couldn't learn mental arithmetic. Miss Julia
stopped and commanded her to halt right there and stop giving the appearance of being about to jump in the river and
climb in the car instead, and backed all the way back across
the bridge, turned around in the school yard, and headed for
Ludlow, lickety-split. 'You're on your way to a doctor, girl,'
she said. 'No time to waste sitting down and waiting for *him*.
You're blue!' she said. 'Have you got any stockings on? What
do you mean, walking out without stockings—it's icy!' The
thermometer's dropped about forty degrees at a gallop—it's
April. Miss Julia stopped the flivver in the middle of the road,
tore off her own stockings, put them on Rachel struggling,
and wrapped her up in her own cape too, I wouldn't put it
past her, and rode her to Ludlow. By the time Miss Julia's
blowing her horn at the doctor's front door, Rachel's an icicle.
But Rachel tells the doctor, when she can chatter, 'I don't
care if it kills me, I wouldn't be caught dead in Miss Julia's
old yarn stockings.' She'd taken 'em right off again—using, I
reckon, the last ounce of strength she had left. Then she went
into a hard rigor. She wasn't going to wear Miss Julia Mortimer's old yarn stockings to Ludlow, and the cold got to her
bones. That's how she got pneumonia. She died when her
crisis came."

"I bet Miss Julia didn't even catch a cold out of it," said
Aunt Birdie, shivering.

"Oh, she's iron," said Aunt Nanny.

All went quiet, except for those somewhere at the outer
edges who were singing a round, *". . .gently down the stream.
Merrily merrily . . ."*

"Lexie, how is it you can furnish such a story?" asked Miss
Beulah. "You must have picked that up from Miss Julia herself."

"On one of her sunny days, back when, when she had confidence in my nursing, she let me have it," said Miss Lexie.
"But if there was a baby anywhere in it, she left it out for my
benefit."

"Well, Rachel had already had the baby," Aunt Beck divined.

"Do you reckon Rachel told Miss Julia some of her story on that long freezing ride?"

"No, not if she wouldn't wear her stockings," Aunt Birdie said.

"She'd just left her baby, and felt like it was a good time to come on home," said Aunt Beck. "She could stand, and no more, I feel sure. Just put one foot in front of the other. And when she got to Banner—"

"The Easter Snap got her," said Aunt Nanny, chopping at Beck with her hand.

"It dovetails perfect," Aunt Beck said to Gloria. "Just too perfect."

"I firmly believe the Sojourners wouldn't let Rachel back in the house when she tried 'em. That was one tale," said Aunt Birdie. "Remember, now? What else drove her out on the bridge for Miss Julia's eagle eyes to find?"

"Old Man Sojourner, when they sent for him to come after her at the end of it, had to take his wagon all the way to Ludlow. And he had another long ride back to Banner, bringing her home to bury," said Miss Beulah. "That would have given him time to think."

"That's what brought forth the lamb," said Aunt Beck to Gloria.

"Well, she'd long since left our house, and good riddance!—Oh, she came back once. She came back once, I knew as soon as I'd got the words out of my mouth. To help Granny out when I was busy fixing to marry Mr. Renfro," said Miss Beulah. "Still sewing she was, then. Do you remember her being here, Mr. Renfro? I expect you don't—just the groom."

"Oh, without a question. I remember the dewberry-picking race," he said.

She gave a short laugh. "Oh, yes, that came to try our nerves," she said. "That was Rachel and one of these boys."

"That was Sam Dale Beecham," said Mr. Renfro. "Sam Dale and Rachel, each of 'em claimed in front of the whole table to be the best and fastest and most furious dewberry picker in the world. So nothing to do but for each to take a bucket and set on out to prove it. When each one's bucket got full, they'd scamper back to the house here, empty the buckets in the big washtub, then scamper out again. Every trip, they'd just meet each other again back at the tub. They picked from first thing in the morning till last thing in the evening, when it was still a tie—am I right?"

"Don't remind me of any more," said Miss Beulah.

"They filled the tub and every bucket on the farm, and Sam Dale finally had to hollow him out a poplar log and fill that and come carrying it in over his shoulder. And Rachel still showed her bucket full to match him."

"It must have been a plentiful year," said Aunt Nanny.

"It was more than that, it was a matter of each of 'em vowing they could beat the other and neither being willing to give in," said Aunt Birdie.

"They *called* it a tie," said Miss Lexie.

"Blessed Sam Dale let her tie him," said Aunt Beck sweetly.

"And where did all that carrying-on leave the rest of us?" Miss Beulah cried. "Poor Granny was back in the kitchen up to her elbows in dewberries. What was she going to do with so much blooming plenty, and with a wedding right at her heels? She put up forty-nine quarts of dewberries that night before she give up and went to bed. Or was it sixty-nine, or ninety-six?"

Granny replied with a nod to all these numbers.

"Well, it may have been a tie the way you tell it, but I think Granny come out ahead," said Aunt Nanny.

"By the time you was ready to be born, Gloria, looks like the dewberries had come around again," said Aunt Birdie.

Gloria cried, "I wish you-all wouldn't keep on. I know I'm better than Rachel Sojourner and her lamb. Nobody here or anywhere else can make me believe I'm in the world on account of any fault of hers." She threw back her mane.

"Oscar, can't you do 'em some good?" asked Mrs. Moody. "That would make some of this worthwhile."

"Things that should be a matter of record in Boone County just aren't," said Judge Moody. "I can't remedy that, Maud Eva."

"There ain't no more records. Not now, Judge Moody. They went," said Mr. Renfro.

"I know about the courthouse fire," said Judge Moody

drily. "We're still holding court in the Primary Department of the First Baptist Church."

"Squatting on Sunday School chairs," said Mrs. Moody, with a short laugh for him in the chair that held him now.

"Yes. I didn't have to come to Banner to find out what happened in Ludlow," said Judge Moody. "But what about the doctor who attended this girl? There'd be his record—or if that's thrown away, he might come up with it out of his own memory, if he was tantalized long enough."

"I think Rachel had that baby *by herself*," said Aunt Birdie, with a storyteller's snubbing look. "Did the best she could, gave it away to the one who'd know best what to do with it, and let the good Lord take her."

"Oscar, you know full well they could never get a doctor to plough his way up here," said Mrs. Moody. "You'd have to go down on your knees to one and beg him!"

"Well," said Mr. Renfro, with a warm eye cocked on Judge Moody, "I didn't know that, and so when we had one ready to be born—" Miss Beulah gave a short laugh, and he went on. "I hopped to the store and took the phone and asked 'em to put me in touch with a doctor in Ludlow, and the doctor said all right, he'd come. 'Come to the old Jordan house,' I says. 'Everybody can tell you where that is.' Well, it was already darkening up considerable by the time I got back here, and I see there's a storm rising I never had quite seen the like of. I got a little anxious for fear a big tree might blow down right on the road and catch the doctor before he could get here. Lightning and thunder just flying! I was walking the gallery here, looking out for him. Never had seen the doctor and the doctor hadn't ever seen me, but I told Beulah when a man said he's coming he meant it, and for her just to hold on.

"Saw him coming, just burning the wind! He had a good horse under him, and the fire was just flying when the shoes hit down on those stones. First thing he did when he pulled up here was hand me down a great big gun he'd been carrying across his lap. I was the least bit surprised, I was half-expecting it to be his doctor bag, but that was the next thing he handed me. Then his saddlebags.

" 'You do a lot of hunting around here?' he says, hopping down, and he wasn't much older than I was, and I says, 'I sure do, Doctor.' 'Well,' he says. 'I thought this sounded like a real good part of the world to go out and get squirrel. So tomorrow,' he says, 'if it clears and all, tell you what—let's me and you go out and get us a bagful.'

"So the baby come that night, true to Beulah's prediction, and the next day was clear—beautiful!—and me and the doctor went hunting. And that doctor, he didn't go home for a week. Not till Grandpa invited him to come hear his sermon. He and I was out on the ridge every day of the world and we got all the squirrels your very own heart could wish for. Granny cooked all he could eat every night, and beyond that, when he finally told us good-bye, he had his saddlebags just loaded with pretty dressed squirrel. When he left me and Beulah and the baby and the old folks, he said he'd never had such a pleasant visit in his life. Carruthers was his name."

"Gerard Carruthers?" protested Mrs. Moody.

"How much did he charge?" asked Aunt Cleo. "Plenty?"

"I'm sure it wasn't too steep a bill for all he gave us," said Mr. Renfro. "I reckon he knew when he started how little well we'd be able to pay it."

"Grandpa Vaughn gave him something to put in his purse, I know," said Miss Beulah. "No, we weren't going to be thought beggars here!"

"So he's been up here too," said Judge Moody. "You got Gerard Carruthers too."

"That's Judge's doctor," cried Mrs. Moody. "Imagine getting him way up here!"

"It was some several years ago," said Mr. Renfro. "Jack was the baby."

"He even wanted to name the baby, on top of the rest of it," said Miss Beulah. "I wouldn't allow him. 'That's Jack Jordan Renfro,' I told him."

"Try and get him to pay a house call today," said Mrs. Moody.

"Lady May got here fine without a doctor," said Gloria. "And I didn't die either, like I might have, if I was a Sojourner."

"You had Granny," a chorus of voices rose to tell her.

"Beulah had Granny too," said Granny. "Good thing."

"But even Granny can't prove I'm Rachel's," said Gloria. "Nobody can."

"Then watch out—I can show you the proof right now," said Aunt Birdie with fresh glee. "It's coming right out to meet you this minute, and in front of our eyes."

From under the skirts of the tablecloth Lady May came crawling out on hands and knees. Somewhere down there she had found a bone. She gave her mother a shout, as though she'd beat her to it. The bone had a live jacket of tiny ants.

"Like mother, like daughter! Isn't that the old-timey rule? See there?" Aunt Birdie sang in a charmed voice.

Gloria opened her mouth but stood speechless.

"Go back, Red Roses," Aunt Beck warned Lady May.

"Come here, Britches!" cried Aunt Nanny, and with a red arm she swept the child up. "Yes, you was a pretty good little secret yourself, wasn't you?" she asked her.

"And don't you wish she was yours?" The other aunts stood up around Lady May, opening their arms. "Come be mine!" "Come be mine!" They took her bone.

"Gloria, we didn't come here to cry," Aunt Beck said. "If we'd wanted to do that, we could've just stayed home, couldn't we, everybody?"

"There's two now," said Aunt Nanny, as Lady May, from there in her lap, joined her mother in tears.

"There, let her go. I'll tell you who it is she likes, it's the men," said Aunt Birdie. "She'll grow up to be a heartbreaker too, just watch."

Lady May, down on her feet, ran past the uncles too, all sweeping their arms out to catch her, and saddled herself on Judge Moody's foot in its city shoe. At once it stopped swinging, though she belabored his silk-clad ankle with her little hand.

Miss Beulah had been raising her voice at the aunts. "Birdie Beecham, and every one of you, now I want you to know something: I taught my boys to do the right thing, do you hear me? Jack Renfro never gave Banner community the first cause for complaint! He'd treat a girl strictly the way he's been everlastingly told! And if something's wrong, *she's* to blame."

"I always told myself the same thing you do, Beulah," said Aunt Beck soothingly. "About my nine boys."

"Hey! You mean to tell me Gloria here jumped the gun?" exclaimed Aunt Cleo.

Gloria stood straight and defied them, the same as when she had had to tell them her birthday was April Fool's Day.

Aunt Nanny made a reach at Gloria and gave her a spank. "Stand up there, Gloria! In your skirt there, where the sash is trying to hide it—you got a rip. Been in the briar patch with it?"

"Gloria, peep behind you. Did you know you look like you just met up with a biting dog?" asked Aunt Birdie.

"Is that the only Sunday dress you got?" Aunt Cleo asked.

"My wedding dress!" said Gloria.

"Homemade?" asked Aunt Cleo.

"Yes ma'am."

"Bet you made it on yourself, with nobody to tell you how," Aunt Cleo said.

"Thank you. I did."

"But I'll tell you one thing about it: it don't fit you very perfect," said Aunt Cleo. "You work with a pattern?"

"I remember seeing you wear it on your wedding day," said Aunt Beck. "And you simply looked like all the brides that ever were."

"I believe it's that sash that makes it so old-timey-looking," Mrs. Moody now joined in.

"Yes'm, brought-in like that with a sash a mile high, she looks suffocated," said Auntie Fay.

"But so many brides have the tendency," said Aunt Beck.

"She's wearing it as tight as Dick's hatband now," said Aunt Nanny, as she tested the sash.

"Pull it," said those around her.

Aunt Nanny drove her finger through the knot and the sash slipped, fell with the heaviness of an arm down the skirt to Gloria's feet.

"Lands! Will you look at the wealth of material she allowed herself in that skirt!" exclaimed Aunt Birdie. "Had to rope yourself in to be sure you was there, Gloria."

"Now wait a minute. I never noticed anything wrong with the *dress*," said Miss Beulah. "It just looks like a good many widths of material went into it. Takes an hour to iron it, but suppose you just call it a little roomy—that's better than one that'll pinch you after a while."

"I believe that sash by itself must've weighed a ton," said Aunt Nanny.

"It did," said Gloria, looking down where it made a gleam like water around her. "It's slipper satin." She gathered it up carefully and Aunt Nanny took it away from her.

"Holy Moses! Where'd a schoolteacher get hold of slipper satin!"

"She sacrificed," Aunt Beck said, as if that should be enough.

Aunt Birdie went on. "Yes, and look at that little vein of pink running along the edge of it there. That sash has been light-struck."

"It might be an old piece of goods," said Aunt Nanny.

"It is not!" Gloria cried. "No ma'am, I bought it new and paid for it. Nothing I have on is second-hand!" All the while, more of the aunts were coming to pat the dress at Gloria's shoulders and waist and here and there, as if trying to find her in it.

"It's swallowed her whole," said Aunt Nanny. "It's waiting on her to grow some."

"I don't see how she could have tracked around all day in a dress that's ten miles too big for her, and expected only compliments," said Aunt Cleo. She picked up the edge of the hem. "It don't even look very snowy to me."

"It was brand-new material! I'd spent my whole life wearing second-hand!" said Gloria. "And wishing for new! And I made me this."

"Gloria just considers she's made to look the bride regardless," teased Aunt Nanny. "Getting a head-start with those curls."

"Let her have it her way. But it's still a mighty good country saying—like mother, like daughter. She's Rachel's child, and yonder rides somebody to prove it," Aunt Birdie said, starting to giggle at Judge Moody with the baby on his foot.

"Who said it needs proving! I know she's Rachel's child!" insisted Miss Beulah. "All I needed to do was stop and look straight at her. But if Rachel's your mother, it's picking out your father that's going to be the uphill work," she told Gloria.

Gloria opened her mouth as if on the verge of shrieking.

"Rachel took to going Sunday-riding with call-him-a-Methodist," said Aunt Nanny, eyes glinting.

"Are you putting the blame for the father on the Methodist?" asked Aunt Cleo.

"Well, you know how Baptists stick together," said Aunt Beck. "They like to look far afield to find any sort of transgressor."

"Let's not go any further with it," said Miss Beulah urgently. "Let's stop before we get started. Let's perish the whole idea."

Gloria put one hand and then the other hand too on her mouth.

Granny's voice spoke. "Sam Dale Beecham. Sam Dale Beecham was going to marry fox-headed Rachel."

There was uproar at the table. Gloria's shriek came out and ran through the middle of it.

"Granny, you've got Sam Dale on the brain! Do you know what you're saying?" Miss Beulah cried out, running back to the old lady's chair.

Granny glared at the company. The rheumy blue eyes looked lit up as with fever.

"No, Granny dear. Sam Dale wouldn't have got a girl in trouble, and then gone off and left her," said Uncle Noah Webster. He put the banjo down, out of sight.

"Oh, if only he might have!" cried Miss Beulah in great agitation.

"No, Sam Dale was too good. Too plain good," Uncle Curtis stated. "Granny, all we boys know that."

"I don't think he had a single mean trick in him," said Uncle Noah Webster, shaking his head soberly. "Or even a mean thought about a one of us. Or about a soul in Banner, or the wide world if you want to carry it that far."

"Oh, I won't be a Beecham!" cried Gloria.

Granny was looking at the still silent Uncle Nathan. "Go get the Vaughn Bible, from under my lamp," she told him, her lifted forefinger pointing straight up.

But Elvie, too quick for Uncle Nathan, ran and came staggering back with it, carrying it between her legs, barely able to keep it off the ground. She just made it to Granny's lap. She knelt in front of Granny's knees, facing out, and bent her little back forward to help hold up the weight.

Granny fished in her pocket and brought up a pair of spectacles, fished again and brought up a blackened and silky dollar bill which she polished them with. With the spectacles on her nose, she raised the Bible's cover and turned to the first page.

She dwelt for a moment over the angel-decorated roster of births and deaths set down in various hands, then lifted and wet her finger and began turning systematically through her Bible—not as though she needed to hunt for what she wanted but as though she were coming to it in her own way. Those nearest her saw the lock of Ellen's hair when it went by in Chronicles, pale as silk. Deep in the crease of First Thessalonians lay Grandpa's spectacles. Granny poked them free and put them on top of hers. Here came the ribbon that had held Ellen's ring, like a pressed flower stem without its flower. Then she turned one more page and drew out what looked like a brownish postcard. It had lain in its place so long that it had printed the page brown too, with a pattern like moiré.

"Let 'em hear that and see how they like it," she told Uncle Nathan.

But Miss Beulah flew between them and seized it herself and brought it to her eyes, picture side up. "It's Sam Dale! It's Sam Dale Beecham in his soldier suit!" she cried. "I never saw him dressed in it except when we buried him."

"The message is spelled out on the other side," Uncle Curtis told her, but she could not take her eyes from the picture. They waited until at last she turned the card over and cried out again. " 'Dear Rachel'!" Her voice suddenly lost all its authority as she began to read aloud from the written words. In monotone, halting herself every few words, she read, " 'Dear Rachel. Here I am in—front of the—mess tent. Excuse me for—just wearing my'—something—'*blouse* but it is so hot in'—something—'in *Georgia*. Here is a—present for our—baby save it for when he gets here. Bought it with today's—

pay and'—something—'*trust* it keeps good time. I miss one and all and wish I was in Banner.' Something—'Sincerely your husband Sam Dale Beecham.'"

Gloria cried out but didn't move. Miss Beulah bent and peered into her grandmother's face. "Sam Dale put the words on that but he never sent it. Did he?"

"It was bundled with his things. This and the watch. I got 'em when I got back Sam Dale," said Granny. "It's a likeness. I can peep at it, before I get my prayers said."

"Well, now, ain't that pitiful," Miss Beulah was murmuring. Then she cried in a loud voice of release and joy, "Ain't that pitiful! Oh, all these years!" She turned the card first to the faded handwriting, then to the picture, turned it back and forth faster and faster, as if trying through her tears to make the two sides one, bind them. "You held it in, kept it hid. Granny, what have you been saving this for?"

"Till I was a hundred years old and had my grandchildren and great-grandchildren all around me, all with ears pretty well cocked to hear it," Granny replied. She frisked the postcard out of Miss Beulah's fingers, returned it to her Bible, and shut up the Bible. Elvie sprang up and went hauling off with it.

"Fan me, Granny," Miss Beulah said, kneeling at the old lady's chair. "Oh, cool my forehead a little." She hugged Granny's knees and laid her cheek down on the ancient, un-stirring lap. "Sam Dale got to be a father after all."

"He was not my father!" Gloria cried out.

"But he wasn't too good to be, he tells you right on the card he wasn't," said Aunt Birdie. "He must have had a reason mighty like you to want to marry little-old Rachel Sojourner."

"Oh, I believe he had, I believe he knew what he was say-ing!" Miss Beulah cried, as Granny laid on the crown of her head a dispassionate look.

"I hope Beulah ain't happy too soon," said Aunt Birdie.

"Beulah's got more fortitude than some," said Aunt Beck gently. "Yet, if the right story comes along at the right time, she'll be like the rest of us and believe what she wants to believe."

"I wish I'd known, I wish I'd been allowed to know," Miss

Beulah said. "Then, when I could see the handwriting on the wall, I could have smiled to myself over this child and my boy Jack. Well, I'd have thought, even this may turn out all right in the end, with Beecham blood on both sides." She suddenly climbed to her feet and threw open her arms to Gloria, who burst into tears.

"Rachel's the one you take after," Miss Beulah said, lifting the girl's convulsed, streaming face in her hand. "There's very little Beecham in your gaze. I don't see the first glimmer of Sam Dale. Yes, your face is Rachel's entirely, and with all the wild notions in it. Makes me remember how she used to vow she was going clear to Ludlow some day, and live in style."

"And the mane," said Granny.

"But never mind, Granny—she's here. Gloria's here, and she's proof, living proof! I didn't do hurt to my own, after all. I can die happy! Can't I?" Miss Beulah's voice rose exultant. Gloria wept. And Judge Moody, whose head with its long forehead, long nose, long upper lip and chin, and long, close-set ears had been tilted back as if out of reluctance to listen, made a melancholy sound in his throat. The cheers were coming from everybody else, drowning out all three.

"Well, Gloria! We told you, didn't we? We told you who you are. Ain't you going to say thank you?" asked Aunt Birdie with excitement, staggering up from her chair.

"I never heard Gloria say thank you for anything yet," said Miss Beulah. "But that won't stop me from hugging her now."

"You didn't need to find out for yourself, Gloria. You didn't need Miss Julia's helping hand. You had us," said Aunt Birdie. "I don't consider we had to go to too much trouble, to figure you out. Here's a kiss for you."

"Pull me up!" said Aunt Nanny, then came toward Gloria, walling up like a catalpa tree in full bloom. "Welcome into the family!"

The uncles were all rising too, laughing and pressing in, all but Uncle Nathan.

"I don't want to be a Beecham!" Gloria cried. "Now it's ten times worse! I won't be a Beecham—go back! Please don't squeeze me!"

Over their heads, the chimney swifts circled as if a crooking finger below held them on tight strings. As though in some evening accord with the birds, the aunts came circling in to Gloria, crowding Miss Beulah to one side—all the aunts and some of the girl cousins. They had Gloria out in the clear space in the middle of the yard, moving her along with them.

"London Bridge is falling down," some voice sang, and a trap of arms came down over Gloria's head and brought her to the ground. Behind her came a crack like a firecracker—they had split open a melon.

She struggled wildly at first as she tried to push away the red hulk shoved down into her face, as big as a man's clayed shoe, swarming with seeds, warm with rain-thin juice.

They were all laughing. "Say Beecham!" they ordered her, close to her ear. They rolled her by the shoulders, pinned her flat, then buried her face under the flesh of the melon with its blood heat, its smell of evening flowers. Ribbons of juice crawled on her neck and circled it, as hands robbed of sex spread her jaws open.

"Can't you say Beecham? What's wrong with being Beecham?"

Lady May, as if catapulted into their midst, arrived and stood rooted, her mouth wide open and soundless, the way she'd watched Brother Bethune go bang with the gun. The next minute Miss Beulah snatched her up and carried her off.

"Jack!" called out Gloria. But they were ramming the sweet, breaking chunks inside her mouth. "Jack! Jack!"

"He went to take Aycock some bread and water." That was Aunt Beck's voice—one voice the same as ever, trying to bring comfort.

"Say Beecham!" screamed Aunt Nanny.

"Don't you like watermelon?" screamed Aunt Cleo. "Swallow, then! Swallow!"

"I declare," murmured the voice of Mrs. Moody to the side, "I haven't seen something like this in years and years."

"Say Beecham and we'll stop. Let's hear you say who's a Beecham!"

"Fox in the morning!" called some little girls playing in the distance. *"Geese in the evening!"* Up in the tree, Elvie passed to and fro in her swing and gave the scene below the deadly eye of a trapeze artist whose turn would come next. The chim-

ney swifts ticked in the deepening sky overhead, going round and round, tilting, like taut little bows drawn with arrows ready. In her chair, Granny sat with the face of a cornshuck doll, a face so old and accomplished that it might allow her to sleep with her eyes open.

"Come on, sisters, help feed her! Let's cram it down her little red lane! Let's make her say Beecham! *We* did!" came the women's voices.

"What you so proud about?" Aunt Nanny held high a hunk of melon as generous as a helping at the table. They were crying with laughter now. "Say who's a Beecham! Then swallow it!"

Gloria tried to call Jack once more.

Somebody shouted, "Wash it down her crook!"

Elvie in her swing said, "If she swallows them seeds, she'll only grow another Tom Watson melon inside her stomach."

A melony hand forced warm, seed-filled hunks into Gloria's sagging mouth. "Why, you're just in the bosom of your own family," somebody's voice cried softly as if in condolence. Melon and fingers together went into her mouth. "Just swallow," said the voice. "*Everybody's* got *something* they could cry about."

"I think she's lost her breath now. She's just letting us sit on her," said a voice that sighed.

"Sometimes women is too deep for me. But I reckon it's only for the good reason that I never had any sisters," pronounced Miss Beulah from the porch, in the voice of lofty argument she used with Lady May.

The aunts were helping each other to their feet. Gloria lay flat, an arm across her face now, its unfreckled side exposed and as pale as the underpelt of a rabbit. The swifts were gone out of the sky, perhaps all down their chimney.

"Remember when she first come to Banner? She wasn't as determined then as she got to be later. She was scared as a little naked bird. Wonder why!" said Aunt Nanny.

"Far from what she knew," said Aunt Beck. "That's in her face again now."

"Got here and didn't even know how to pull mustard," said Aunt Birdie.

"Yes, she knew that. She was brought up an orphan, after all," Auntie Fay said.

"What do men see in 'em?" whispered Miss Lexie.

Miss Beulah came marching to Gloria and planted her feet beside her. "Gloria Beecham Renfro, what are you doing down on the dusty ground like that? Get up! Get up and join your family, for a change." Miss Beulah reached down, took Gloria by the arm, and pulled her to her feet.

"I still don't believe I'm a Beecham," she came up saying. The watermelon juice by now had chalked her face pink and stiffened her lips as it dried.

"Gloria," said Miss Beulah, "go back in the house and wash that face and get rid of some of that tangly hair, then shake that dress and come out again. Now that's the best thing I can tell you."

"No thank you, ma'am." She stood right there. "I'm standing my ground," she told everybody.

"And look at her," said Miss Lexie. "I guess you-all will make me be the one to fix her so we can stand the sight of her." She walked up to Gloria and clapped a hand on her shoulder as if she'd been empowered to arrest her. "You need a little trimming done on you. Gonna run?" Miss Lexie invited her. Her fingers made sure of the needle she carried in her collar. She threw out her hand at random, a thimble was tossed from among the aunts, and she cupped it to her breastbone to catch it. Then she threw forward her Buster Brown bob and pulled off over her head the ribbon that carried her scissors with her everywhere.

"Lexie, you always bite off more than you can chew," said Miss Beulah. "And this house never allowed sewing on Sunday."

"I'm not going to come out of my dress for anybody," said Gloria, arms clamped to her sides.

"We know you're modest," teased Aunt Nanny.

"You just stand still, and tell it to stay light," said Miss Lexie to Gloria. "The men ain't going to pay a sewing session a bit of attention, and Jack ain't here to worry about."

On her saying that, the uncles turned their chairs a little bit, and Mr. Renfro got up and hobbled away, as if to see how many more of his watermelons still waited in reserve under the porch. With a long sound like a stream of dry seed being poured into an empty bucket, the song of the locusts began.

"I'll tell you one thing about that dress—you can't hurt it now! Not after the travelling it's done today," Aunt Nanny said gaily, "and the waltzing around it's had." She swung the sash she held.

"I found my patch ready-made," said Miss Lexie, ripping.

"Will you please spare my pocket?" cried Gloria.

"I've already got it," said Miss Lexie and slipped it wrong side out.

"No wedding dress I ever saw *had* a pocket," said Mrs. Moody.

"It was carrying my wedding handkerchief," said Gloria.

"Looks prettier if you hold it," said Miss Lexie, handing it up. "And you might want to drop some tears, who knows? Just for a change."

Miss Lexie began snipping at the hem of Gloria's dress. "I worshipped her! Worshipped Miss Julia Mortimer!" she suddenly declared from behind Gloria, close to her there near the ground. She brought out her words as loudly or as softly as she ripped, as if to keep up with her thread. "She lived and boarded with us, right across the road from the schoolhouse, and taught me as far as the seventh grade. She encouraged me too, when I was coming up. For all anybody here knows, I might have had my sights set too on stepping into her shoes." She paused to rock on her heels where she squatted, giving her silent laugh. "But they die," she said. "The ones who think highly of you. Or they change, or leave you behind, get married, flit, go crazy—"

"Lexie, has anybody asked you for your story?" Miss Beulah asked, still patrolling the yard, down as far as where some boy cousins were tinkering under two of the cars, keeping her eye on the whole scene.

"My memory reaches back to where she first came to Banner," said Miss Lexie, going after the thread. "But it was before that that Grandfather Renfro said, 'I've lived a long time and come a long way to find out there's a rushing river still left between my folks and something they ought to have on the other side. And I'm going to pray till I find a way for mine to get ahold of it.' He meant a good schooling. He'd had Papa and his two little sisters going to Alliance. It meant two of 'em riding the horse to a place up the river, and the little one hanging on behind to ride the horse back home. Then they rowed 'em across and walked the rest of the way."

"Where was the bridge?" Aunt Cleo was asking.

"Nobody'd dreamed yet we needed one," Miss Beulah said forbiddingly.

"Man would pole you across for the promise of a fat hen or a sack of potatoes," said Granny. "A fellow thought twice about it, then, whether he wanted quite as much as he thought he did to be on the other side."

"Grandfather took all this to the Lord," said Miss Lexie, "and the Lord told him it would be a lot better if they built a school on this side of the Bywy and let the *teacher* do the crossing. So as to save time and trouble and to cheat the bad weather, she could board on the Banner side during the week. Well, then!"

"You mean to say we owe Banner School to a Renfro? Never dreamed that!" Aunt Nanny cried, and called, "Why, Mr. Renfro!"

"And Miss Julia Mortimer was the living answer to Old Preacher Renfro's prayer? I never knew that either!" cried Uncle Noah Webster.

"Well, not right directly," said Mr. Renfro. "There had to be a generation go by before something more come of it. They had to build the schoolhouse. And after it's built and standing there, there was a little breathing space while they could hope the teacher they prayed for'd never come."

"But here she came. Miss Julia Mortimer," said Miss Lexie, snipping and ripping, squatting her way around Gloria's skirt. "Solid as a rock and not one bit of nonsense, looking like the Presbyterian she started out to be. First thing, she clamped down on the men and made 'em fence the yard to keep us in and saw out more windows to see our lessons by, and she scrubbed it inside out and scoured it without any help, raised up a ladder and painted it herself inside and out. 'That's a good start, now,' she says when it's white and got a flagpole. 'And I'll keep lessons going till you find somebody better.' That's how she got herself in harness."

"Where did they even *find* her!" exclaimed Aunt Birdie.

"They didn't have to find her. She'd found them. Banner School was ready for a teacher, and that was all she needed," said Miss Lexie.

"How old was you then, Lexie?" asked Aunt Nanny. "How old are you *now*?"

"I'm old enough to remember the first morning," said Miss Lexie, "with a mind still clear. She steps to the front and says, 'Children of Banner School! It's the first day for both of us. I'm your teacher, Miss Julia Mortimer. Nothing in this world can measure up to the joy you'll bring me if you allow me to teach you something.' "

"And Banner was glad to get her!" Miss Beulah said. "Oh, yes, Grandpa offered up a prayer of thanks for her and asked the Lord to spare her."

"At first everybody must have been as happy as she was," said Miss Lexie. "Fell in love with each other! I've come to believe that's a bad sign. The next thing they knew, Miss Julia Mortimer was saying that poor attention and bad behavior on a Monday would always be punished on a Tuesday. On Tuesday, here came all the children to school and some leading their fathers. So Miss Julia said 'Good morning!' to all alike, and then she called up the pupils that hadn't behaved on Monday, like Earl Comfort, and one by one she gave 'em a little token of her meaning with her fresh-cut peach-tree switch. Then she says, 'Now. If any of these fathers who were so brave as to come to school this morning feel prompted to step up too, I'm ready for them now. Otherwise, they can all stay right there on the back bench and learn something.' And invited up old Levi Champion first—Homer's daddy."

"He run," said Mr. Renfro. He sat down by Judge Moody and smiled at him. "I know that without being there. She meant her words entirely, the lady did. Then and every other time she delivered herself."

"From that day on, she was a fixture at Banner School," said Miss Lexie. "She wouldn't have given it up for anybody. Now, *your* turn," she told Gloria. She went on. "Promptly, she nailed a shelf there under the front window and called it the library. She took her own money to fill up that shelf with books."

"She made salary, didn't she?" asked Aunt Cleo.

"The first month, the way the old folks remembered it, they paid her with seventeen silver dollars. But afterwards, they wasn't ever able to come up to that brave start," said Miss Beulah.

"They knew about warrants, even in the early days. Teachers just got a warrant," said Mr. Renfro. "And there come up Mr. Dearman—"

"Perish the name!" cried Miss Beulah.

"Well, he was going around the country buying up teachers' warrants at a discount," said Mr. Renfro. "That's telling the least of him, Mother."

"No matter how, Miss Julia got books and came bringing 'em. I bet you Banner School had a library as long as your arm," cried Aunt Birdie, as though she saw a snake.

"Then what happened to it? It was gone by the time I came along," said Auntie Fay.

"It got rained on, darlin'," said Aunt Nanny, letting her grin show. "I believe the teacher was young enough to cry."

"She only started it again. And kept her map of the world hanging up year in, year out," said Aunt Birdie. "And did it rattle on a March morning!"

"And we're not on it," said Miss Beulah. "Miss Julia said—"

" '*Put* Banner on the map!' " came a chorus, the men joining in.

"We know the rest!" said Miss Beulah. "That'll do for her now, Lexie."

"I worshipped her as a child, though please don't ask me to find you the reason for it now, now that I've seen her go down," Miss Lexie said. "I cried when she had to leave our house for this one."

"Stayed with me first," said Granny, looking at them sideways out of the slits of her eyes.

"Don't start getting jealous, Granny!" Uncle Noah Webster said. "You didn't *want* the teacher, did you? Grandpa and us children filled up the house for you, didn't we?"

"Everybody had to have her. The Comforts, they had their crack at her too. Come the long winter evenings, they all had to crowd mighty close together in the room with the fire to both see and keep warm by. And she'd stand up and read to 'em! Made 'em mad as wet hens. They had to hush talking, else be called impolite," said Aunt Nanny. "I used to be there and in the same boat with 'em, because, you know, that's who Mama gave me to."

"*Read* to 'em? At *home*?" Aunt Birdie cried.

"It was her idea, not theirs," said Aunt Nanny. "*Old* Mis' Comfort says nobody'd ever know what her and the children suffered, with that teacher cooped in with us all winter. Old lady's dust now, but she one time heard Miss Julia out to the tag end of her piece in the reader, and then that old lady spit in the fire and told the teacher *and* her own daughter—who'd just had a baby without sign of wedding band—'Now be ashamed *both* of ye.'"

"That's enough," said Miss Beulah.

Miss Lexie said to Gloria, "If anybody's trying to cut under you, hold still." She looked up at the rest of them, from under her Buster Brown bangs, and said, "But I didn't come in that class. She *encouraged* me. She *made* me work."

"That's her case, all right," said Auntie Fay. "Lexie went charging through Banner School and got her diploma right on time. And she went and lived in Ludlow in a Baptist preacher's widow's boarding house, and in the afternoons and all day Saturday wrapped packages in the corner department store. We didn't think she was strong enough to go to high school too."

"I had my sights set," said Miss Lexie, squinting her eye now at the scissors in her hand. "But it took more strength than I had—I fell down on Virgil, and wasn't shown any mercy."

"They was just trying to keep you out of State Normal," said Auntie Fay provocatively.

"I thought I could teach just as well without Virgil," said Miss Lexie. "And I could have, if they hadn't given me Banner right on top of Miss Julia. They'd put her out to pasture—against her will entirely and much to her surprise—it's nothing but a state law. And who would dare come after her? I tried holding 'em down. But my nerves weren't strong enough. I switched to caring for the sick."

"Uh-oh!" said Aunt Cleo.

"And then it came. The Presbyterian sisterhood in Alliance sent out a call on both sides of the river for a settled white Christian lady with no home ties."

"Oh, *those* are the scum of the earth!" Mrs. Moody burst out. "We had one of those for our preacher's widow! Got her the same way!"

"And I presented myself," Miss Lexie said. She was under Gloria's arm now, snipping higher, at the gathers of her waist. Gloria had to keep both arms raised while Miss Lexie went around her, smelling of sour starch. "I left Mr. Hugg for her. I thought the change would have to be for the better."

"I don't know about the rest of it, but it looks to me like you've got a few ties," remarked Mrs. Moody, as if a nerve still throbbed.

"The one thing I was sure of was I was the best she could do," said Miss Lexie. "And that's what I told her. You're supposed to turn when I punch you," she said to Gloria. "Have to get you from all sides. You would suppose she'd count it a blessing, getting for her nurse somebody she'd once put to work and encouraged. Somebody that knew her disposition and couldn't be surprised at her ways. Another teacher."

"Look where it's brought both of you," said Miss Beulah. "That's a good place to stop your story now, Lexie."

"For how long was she gracious?" asked Aunt Cleo with a short laugh.

"I wish I'd kept count of the few days," said Miss Lexie. "She was the same to everybody, though. The same to people in Alliance as she was to me, no favorites. All her callers fell off, little at a time, then thick and fast. She made short work of the sisterhood in Alliance."

"The very ones that went out of their way to bribe you to be her nurse?" asked Aunt Cleo, giving a nod.

"Miss Julia sent them packing when they came calling and told her the angels had sent me," said Miss Lexie. "When they told her she'd finished her appointed work on earth and the Lord was preparing to send for her and she ought to be grateful in the meantime. She clapped at 'em—they left backing away."

"She was a Presbyterian, and no hiding that. But was she

deep-dyed?" asked Aunt Beck. "There's a whole lot of different grades of 'em, some of 'em aren't too far off from Baptists."

"I don't care to say," said Miss Lexie after a moment.

"I suppose they were right there again the next day, and the next," said Aunt Cleo, nodding. "The sisterhood."

"After Miss Julia Mortimer dismissed them?" Miss Lexie exclaimed. "No, nobody tried it again, and then she wondered what had happened to everybody. What had happened to *her*?"

"That's the ticket," said Aunt Cleo. "Well, whatever it was, it wasn't your fault."

"So they made me have her by myself. Sunday after Sunday we'd sit there and wait and nobody'd peep their heads in at all. 'Are they keeping absent on purpose to miss today's lesson?' she'd ask. And she'd struggle to her feet and walk to the front porch and ask, 'Where's Gloria Short?' You were right in style when you didn't come," Miss Lexie said, close to Gloria's back. "There Miss Julia Mortimer and me would sit, getting older by the minute, both of us. Both foxed up for Sunday, I saw to that. Her on one side of the porch and me on the other, her in the wickerwork rocking chair and me in the oak swing. Pretty soon she'd stop rocking. 'And what're you doing here, then?' says Miss Julia to me. 'Suppose you take your presence out of here. How can I read with you in the house with me?' She'd put her foot right down. I'd put my foot down. She'd stamp: one. I'd stamp: one. After all, we'd both learned our tactics in the schoolroom. In my opinion it didn't matter all that much any longer who'd taught who or who'd started this contest. We'd stamp, stamp—and one-two-three she'd kilter."

"And where was you, Lexie?" cried Aunt Birdie.

"Right behind her!" Miss Lexie called, right behind Gloria. "Don't!" Gloria cried.

"Don't, yourself. Stop quivering, because I'm fixing now to take a great big whack out of your skirt. I had to puff a little bit to catch Miss Julia. She was too used to charging off in a hurry. She was looking all at one time in the vegetable patch and in the shed where her car gathered dust and behind the peach trees and under the grape vine and even in the cow pasture, to see where the bad ones were hiding. There was I, chasing her over her flower yard, those tangly old beds, stumbling over 'em like graves where the bulbs were so many of 'em crowding up from down below—and on to the front, packed tight as a trunk with rosebushes, scratch you like the briar patch—and down into those old white flags spearing up through the vines all the way down her bank as far as the road, thick as teeth—and there in the empty road she'd even crack open her mailbox, and look inside!"

"How long did she keep it up, looking for company?" asked Aunt Cleo. "A week? A month?"

"Longer! If you could see today the trough her feet have worn under that old wickerwork chair in the yard—she had me lug it right off the porch to where she could sit and watch the road. Like children wear under a swing," said Miss Lexie. "I used to say, 'Miss Julia, you come on back inside the house. Hear? People aren't used to seeing you outside like this. They aren't coming visiting. Nobody's coming. And what if they did, and found you outside with your hair all streaming?' I'd say, 'Why are you turning so contrary? Why won't you just give up, Miss Julia, and come on in the cool house with me?' And when she was inside again, then she turned around and ran me out and dared me to come back in! 'Get out of here, old woman!' And she's full eleven years older than me!"

"She's a scrapper, all right." Granny was nodding her head. "Knew it the minute I got my first look at the girl, teaching her elders."

"She put up her fists next?" asked Aunt Cleo.

"If I got to the door and locked it first, she'd try to get out of her own house," Miss Lexie said. "Shake—she'd shake that big oak door! You ever see a spider shake his web when you lay a pine-straw in it just for meanness? She could shake her door like a web was all it was. I felt sometimes like just everything, not only her house but me in it, was about to go flying, and me no more'n a pine-straw myself, something in her way."

"I'm ready for you to stop," whispered Gloria.

"I tied her, that was the upshoot," said Miss Lexie. "Tied her in bed. I didn't want to, but anybody you'd ask would tell you the same: you may have to." Gloria tried to move, but Miss Lexie gripped her that moment by the ankle and said, "Don't shift your weight."

"If Lexie can find something to do the hard way, she'll do it," said Miss Beulah. "Setting a patch in that skirt, now, with the girl inside it!" She paced around them.

"It's a matter of being equal to circumstances," Miss Lexie asserted. "Every day, Miss Julia there in her bed called me to bring her her book. 'Which book?' I ask her. She said just bring her her book. I couldn't do that, I told her, 'because I don't know which book you mean. Which book do you mean?' Because she had more books than anything. I couldn't make her tell me which book she meant. So she didn't get any."

"Book! It looks like of all things she'd have been glad she was through with and thankful *not* to have brought her!" exclaimed Aunt Birdie.

"Bet Gloria could have picked one out," teased Aunt Nanny.

"Gloria, I think it was really you that must have disappointed her the most," said Aunt Beck, as though she offered a compliment. "She hoped so hard for something out of you."

Gloria cried out.

"Elvie, bring me a row of pins!—But no, you never came to see your old teacher, all the time she lay getting worse," said Miss Lexie. "She was peeping out for you, right straight along. First she'd say, 'Gloria Short will be here soon now. She knows it's for her own good to get here on time.' Even in bed, she'd lean close to her window, press her face to the glass even on rainy mornings, not to miss the first sight of Gloria coming."

"Where was you hiding, girl?" Aunt Cleo cried with a laugh.

"Hiding? I was having a baby," Gloria broke out. "That's what I was doing, and you can die from that."

"You can die from anything if you try good and hard," said Miss Beulah.

"I said, 'Oh, she's just forgotten you, Julia, like everybody else has,'" said Miss Lexie.

Granny had begun to look from one face to the next, her

breath coming a little fast. Miss Beulah saw, and went to stand beside her.

"So the next thing, didn't she ask me for her bell. She wanted the school bell!" said Miss Lexie.

"Why, that's a heavy old thing," said Uncle Curtis. "Solid brass and a long handle—"

"She couldn't have raised it. Never at all. Never again in her life. And I told her so. 'And no matter if you could,' I reminded her, 'you haven't got the school bell. Banner School's got it! It doesn't belong to you,' I said. 'Banner School's got the bell and you've been put out to pasture— they're through with you.' I thought that would finish the subject. But 'Give me back my bell,' she'd say. And look at me, with living dread in her face."

"Dread?" scoffed Miss Beulah, staunch beside Granny.

"You're hurting me," whispered Gloria.

"It's not me, it's my scissors. I'd say, 'Julia'—I'd got to the point where I didn't call her anything but Julia—'what is it you *want* that bell for? Give me a good reason, then maybe I'll get it for you. You want to bring 'em, make 'em come? Or is this the way you're going to drive 'em off if they try? Make up your poor mind if the world is welcome or unwelcome. The world isn't going to let you have a thing both ways.' "

"You can't always easily fool 'em," said Aunt Cleo. "I'm a real nurse, *used* to all that, *used* to going in other people's houses, and just like today becoming one of the family. I've had a worlds of experience, now, just a worlds. And I could tell *you* tales, now."

Miss Lexie said, "And she looks me back in the face trying to think of an answer, and all she can think of to say, and she said it loud and clear, was 'Ding dong! Ding dong bell!' "

"But where was her mind?" cried Miss Beulah.

"I asked her, plenty of times," said Miss Lexie.

"But why wasn't Miss Julia content with her lot?" asked Aunt Beck in a low voice. "Like an ordinary Christian?"

"An ordinary Christian wouldn't want to wear her red sweater and keep her shoes on in bed," said Miss Lexie. "And if she didn't know what she was doing, any better than that, bed was right where she belonged. And I wasn't to touch her fingernails, either. They grew a mile long. She said she wanted to be ready for me."

"She must have put up some battle, for somebody that's part-paralyzed," said Aunt Birdie.

"She wasn't paralyzed anywhere. That would have made it easier."

"But I happen to know about a lady who wouldn't cut her own toenails," Aunt Cleo said. "And she wasn't paralyzed, either. Until they crossed each other over all her toes and weaved back and forth over her feet sharp as knives, and she finally had to go with 'em to the hospital. The doctors said they'd met with a lot before, but not that. Her funeral was held with a sealed coffin."

"They could never have paralyzed Miss Julia Mortimer," said Miss Lexie. "I'd say, 'Why don't you quit fighting kind hands?' She'd say, 'Only way to keep myself alive!' Knocks my arm back with her weak little fist. 'I *love* you,' I says. 'You used to be my inspiration.' 'You get out of my house, old woman. Go home! If you've got a home,' she says."

"She hit the nail on the head when she said you didn't have elsewhere to go," said Miss Beulah. "Not unless you went back to Mr. Hugg, took care of him again." She patted Granny's bent shoulder.

"Then she quoted some poetry at me. I don't mean Scripture," said Miss Lexie.

"Sure-enough, Lexie, we didn't mean to ask you all that," said Aunt Birdie.

"Old Lexie's truly been stirring up the bottom," said Aunt Nanny.

"Lexie, you'd take all night long to sew up a little hole in your stockin'!" cried Miss Beulah.

"I take pains with all I do and I want my results to show it."

"You've got coming night to contend with now. I warned you," Miss Beulah said.

"Oh, I'm used to putting out my eyes! Here's where you climb up and stand on a chair for me," said Miss Lexie to Gloria. "I'm tacking your fresh hem in. Oh, she never forgot she had something to tell *you*."

Mr. Willy Trimble hopped to bring Miss Lexie up her own

chair, and she took it and shooed him back. She drew a needle from her collar with a thread that was never seen, lost like the outlines of Gloria's dress now in the glow of evening that was all around them. She went to work on Gloria where she stood with arms slowly lifting, legs ladylike, feet one in front of the other on the rush seat.

"If it'd been me doing it, I wouldn't have used my scissors and cut my thread behind me. I'd have it now to put in over again," said Auntie Fay.

"Sissie, do you forget I'm the one taught you to sew?"

"How late in the game was it, Lexie, when Miss Julia took it in she'd met her match?" asked Aunt Nanny.

"If the news ever sunk in, she kept it a pretty good secret," said Miss Lexie. "I reckon what it amounted to was the two of us settling down finally to see which would be first to wear the other one out."

"There you give a perfect little picture of the battle of nursing," said Aunt Cleo.

"But it was only if I'd hold out her pencil to her that she'd come quiet."

"A pencil?" cried Aunt Birdie. "A common *pencil?*"

Gloria drew breath. She was turned to face the deep blush of distance, out of which the cows were coming in now, the three in a line. Their slow steps were not quite in time to the tinkling, as though their thin-worn bells rang for what was behind them, down the reach of their long, back-flung shadows, back over Vaughn's shoulder and his shadow as he drove them home.

"Yes'm, pencil! And you want to see the way she wrote?" asked Miss Lexie, and she showed them, while her hands went on sewing.

"Wrote with her tongue spreading out?"

Miss Lexie smacked her lips at them. "Like words, just words, was getting to be something good enough to eat. And nothing else was!"

"Lexie, you're about to ruin this reunion in spite of everything, giving out talk of death and disgrace around here," exclaimed Miss Beulah. She cried to the others, "Take away her needle, if that's what sewing brings on."

Granny's eyes raced from one face to another, as though

here at her table she had somehow got ringed around by strangers. She breathed in shallow gasps, striving hard to hear the voices.

"I wouldn't have wanted to be shut up with Miss Julia Mortimer too long, myself. She might have brought up with something I wasn't inclined to hear," said Aunt Birdie.

"She was just doing harm to herself, wearing herself out like that," said Aunt Beck.

Miss Lexie cried out, "I didn't think just writing letters could hurt her! But reckless? She'd tell 'em! Let 'em know she's afraid of nothing! Speak out whatever's the worst thing she can think of! Holler to the nurse for tablet and pencil! Lick and push! Lick and push! Fold it and cram it in the envelope till it won't hold one word more! Bring up the stamp out of hiding! And say, 'Mail it, fool!' "

"Oh, were those real letters?" asked Aunt Beck.

"Is there some other kind?" asked Judge Moody from his same school chair. The ladies paused at his voice, and Gloria's hands let fall her handkerchief and reached up to her cheeks.

"I've heard that licking an indelible pencil was one sure way to die," Aunt Birdie said.

"I've seen her wetting that pencil a hundred times a day—it wasn't very sharp. Opened up that old Redbird school tablet and up would come her pencil and out would go her tongue and away she'd fly," said Miss Lexie. "And send that old purple pencil racing, racing, racing."

"Didn't you tell her it'd kill her?" asked Aunt Nanny.

"For the thanks I'd get?" Miss Lexie dipped back to laugh.

Gloria said over her head, "She wouldn't have quit writing just for your satisfaction. I've known her to correct arithmetic papers with a broken arm. But I never knew her to lick a pencil before."

"What'd you do with those letters, Lexie? Throw 'em in the pig pen?" cried Miss Beulah.

"I don't want to say."

"You threw 'em in the pig pen. So I guess it didn't make any difference who they was to."

"I said, 'Listen, Julia. If you've got something this bad to say about human nature,' I said, because I skimmed one or two of 'em over, 'why don't you go ahead and send it to the

President of the United States? What do you want to waste it on us for?' "

"And I'd believe it of her! My, she was vain! Was vain!" Miss Beulah cried, in a voice of reluctant admiration. "To the end, I should say?" she asked Lexie.

Miss Lexie replied without a sound—only opened her mouth as for a big bite.

"Yet, the littler you wish to see of some people, the plainer you may come to remember 'em," said Miss Beulah, with some darkness. "Even against your will. I can't tell you why, so don't ask me. But I can see that old schoolteacher this minute plainer than I can see you, Lexie Renfro, after your back's turned."

"In the long run, I got her pencil away from her," said Miss Lexie, speaking faster. "I could pull harder than she could."

"What'd she do then?" asked a voice.

"She just wrote with her finger."

"What'd she use for ink, a little licking?"

"Yes'm, and wrote away on the bedsheet."

There was a stifled sound from Judge Moody. Aunt Beck said with a sigh, "I'm glad for you you couldn't tell so well by then what she was saying."

"And I pulled off the hot sheet and she wrote on, in the palm of her hand."

"Wrote what?"

"Fuss fuss fuss fuss fuss, I suppose," Miss Lexie cried.

The chorus of locusts came through the air in waves, in a beat like the brass school bell wielded with full long arm, all the way up to the yard, to the forgotten tables, to the house, to where the setting sun had spread its lap at that moment on the low barn roof.

"Lexie, will you please quit going around on your knees and with your tongue hanging out?" asked Miss Beulah. "There's some may not be able to appreciate that."

Even when it was Miss Beulah, Granny gave each speaker a bewildered look, her little head shaking as it turned from one to the other.

"I was tacking in my hem," said Miss Lexie, staggering to her feet.

"Well, we're all getting there, I suppose. And it won't be long before the baby of us all—!" Aunt Beck murmured.

"Oh, I could tell it wouldn't be long," said Miss Lexie. "I hid her pencil, and she said, 'Now I want to die.' I said, 'Well, why don't you go ahead and die, then?' She'd made me say it! And she said, 'Because I want to die by myself, you ever-present, everlasting old fool!'"

"She didn't know what she was saying," said Aunt Beck.

"That's just what she did know!" said Miss Lexie.

"Take away her needle," Miss Beulah commanded.

"Some things you don't let them make you say," said Miss Lexie. "And I don't care who they are."

"But does that mean it's better to just come off and leave 'em?" asked Aunt Beck, and slowly one of her hands went in front of her face to shield it.

"I had the reunion to come to, didn't I?" Miss Lexie retorted.

The barn was a gauzy pink, like a curtain just pulled across a window, and Vaughn was coming in now with the cows and the dogs. With the sun as low as where the cows swung their heads, the brass nubs on their horns sent a few last long rays flashing. Then all marched slowly into the folds of the curtain.

"One thing I didn't hear, if you told it," Aunt Cleo said. "I'd like to know what disease was eating of her. Did anybody ever find out, or did they tell?"

"Old age," said Miss Lexie. "That do?"

"Now are you satisfied, Lexie? Now will you set?" cried Miss Beulah.

"You don't get over it all that quick—what some of 'em make you do," returned Miss Lexie. "But I'm *through*!" she said to Gloria, as though the girl had cried out. She dipped her head close to Gloria's leg and bit off the thread. "It was nothing to hurt you, now was it?" She lifted the girl, roughly enough, and set her down on warm ground.

"At least we know who it is, can see who you are now, Gloria," said Aunt Birdie.

"Look at those skinny little legs, everybody, like a sparrow's," said Aunt Nanny, coming to tie on her sash.

"Petticoat shows now," said Auntie Fay.

"And remember from now on," Aunt Beck said, "every

little move you make, Gloria, is still bound to show on that sash. Every little drop you spill. Every time you get up or down, it'll tell on you."

"Hey, Gloria," said Aunt Cleo. "With all those scraps and without half trying"—she pointed to them, organdie scraps as pale as the scraps of tin that still lay around from the roofing, ready to cut open a foot—"you could make Lady May a little play wedding dress, just like yours."

"Where is my baby?" Gloria cried.

Aunt Nanny barred Lady May's path with a big quick arm. She caught the child up and hugged her. "And you was a pretty good little secret yourself, wasn't you?" she asked her.

Lady May struggled, got free of her, ran from her and from her mother too, and vanished behind the althea bush with its hundreds of flowers already spindling, like messages already read and folded up.

Miss Lexie gathered up the scraps and balled them, to drop into her own gingham pocket.

"Last reunion, it was Mr. Hugg. And we had it all to hear about him," said Auntie Fay.

"I knew you'd say that, Sissie."

"Hugg? Thought he had the Ludlow jail," said Aunt Cleo.

"Jailer had a daddy, didn't he? This is his daddy," said Miss Lexie.

"Isn't *he* worse than *her*?"

"I sit there and he lays there, Fay. When I see his eyes fly open, I get ready for him."

"Sister Cleo, Lexie first took care of an old man in the bed named Jonas Hugg, kept house for him, fed him and his frizzly hen. And the old man'd just as soon pitch the plate of grits back in her face if she tried to get him to eat it," giggled Auntie Fay.

"Looking back, I don't mind Mr. Hugg one bit," warned Aunt Lexie. "I don't mind him any longer."

"And if she went for more grits, peed in the bed to pay her back for it."

"I'm above it," sang Miss Lexie. "I'm above it. Him and his money belt too. He's just exactly one hundred percent what he seems. Bad Boy."

"Why did you ever bother to leave him for her? They're all the same," Aunt Cleo told Miss Lexie.

"No. Mr. Hugg cries. And the *first* day, he clapped his hands together just to see me coming!" said Miss Lexie. "He was glad to see me at first and didn't hide it."

"The thing to remember is they change," said Aunt Cleo, with a nod toward Granny. "And you and me will do the same, I hate to tell you."

From the moving swing above them, Elvie pointed to far away, to the edge of what they could see. There stood the moon, like somebody at the door. One lop-side showing first, the way a rose opens, the moon was pushing up through the rose-dye of dust. The dust they'd breathed all day and tasted with every breath and bite and kiss was being partly taken from them by the rising of the full, freighted moon.

"When I first went to Miss Julia, I loved her more than Mr. Hugg, now I love Mr. Hugg more than her—wish I was back with him now! These are his socks," Miss Lexie said, cocking her ankle for them. "I'm still busy wearing out some of his socks for him."

A thrush was singing. As they all fell quiet, except for Miss Lexie dragging her own chair back to the table, its evening song was heard.

Granny heard that out too. Then she whispered, and Miss Beulah put her head down.

"I'm ready to go home now."

Miss Beulah put her arms around her. Granny, as well as she was able, kept from being held. "Granny, you *are* home," said Miss Beulah, gazing into her grandmother's face.

"What's she getting scared of?" asked Aunt Birdie.

"Granny's not scared of anything."

"Afraid we'll all go off and leave her?" asked Aunt Beck.

"Please saddle my horse," Granny said. "I'd like you to fetch my whip."

"Granny, you're home now." Miss Beulah knelt down, not letting the old lady with her feeble little movements escape out of her arms. "Granny, it's the reunion! You're having your birthday Sunday, and we're all around you, celebrating it with you just like always."

"Then," said Granny, "I think I'd be right ready to accept a birthday present from somebody."

Miss Beulah moved a step back from Granny's chair, and there she sat where everybody could see her. Her lap was holding a new white cup and saucer, and on the ground around her rested everything else she had untied from its strings and unshucked from its wrappings, all their presents—a pillow of new goose feathers, a pint of fresh garden sass, a soda-box full of sage, a foot-tub full of fresh-dug, blooming-size hyacinth bulbs, three worked pincushions, an envelope full of blood-red Indian peach seeds, a prayer-plant that had by now folded its leaves, a Joseph's-coat, a double touch-me-not, a speckled geranium, and an Improved Boston fern wrapped in bread paper, a piece of cut-glass from the mail order house given by Uncle Noah Webster, a new apron, the owl lamp, and, chewing a hambone, the nine-month-old, already treeing, long-eared Bluetick coonhound pup that any of her great-grandchildren would come and take out hunting for her any time she was ready. And there behind her, spread over her chair and ready to cloak her, was "The Delectable Mountains."

"You've had your presents, Granny. You've already had every single one," said Miss Beulah softly.

Granny covered her eyes. Her fingers trembled, the backs of her hands showed their blotches like pansy faces pressed into the papery skin.

"Just look around you," said Miss Beulah. "And you've thanked everybody, too."

Then Granny dropped her hands, and she and Miss Beulah looked at each other, each face as grief-stricken as the other.

By now, the girls' and boys' softball game had gone on, it seemed, for hours. But now the teams trailed in, Ella Fay Renfro in front tossing a sweat-fraught pitcher's glove. Children too tired to sing or speak could still blow soap-bubbles through empty sewing spools, or hold out their arms and cry. Little boys raised a ring of dust around them too, galloping on cornstalk horses and firing a last round of shots from imaginary pistols over their heads. A hummingbird moved down the last colored thing, the wall of montbretias, as though it were writing on it in words.

At that moment the distant reports stopped. There was a sound like a woodpecker at work: Uncle Curtis snoring in his chair. In the school chair, Judge Moody sat very still too, with his hand over his eyes.

"I believe your husband's reached the Land of Nod, with my husband," Aunt Beck told Mrs. Moody. "Is that chair where he's going to sleep tonight?"

"And still I'd know him for a judge," said Miss Beulah, slowly turning around to her company again. "Look at that dewlap. I suppose a man like him goes right on judging in his sleep."

"He's not asleep," said Mrs. Moody. "Far from it."

"Oh, come—come—come—come," the bass voice of Uncle Noah Webster started off, and they came in with him, *"Come to the church in the wild wood, oh come to the church in the dell."* After that, Miss Beulah, with a churning fist, led them through *"Will there be any stars, any stars in my crown when at evening the sun goeth down?"*

Mr. Willy Trimble, who didn't sing, got to his feet and waited on them to finish.

"Well, I'll tell you a little something *I* know *they* don't know about," said Mr. Willy. "Goes clear back to early morning, when I carried Miss Julia up to her house and safe inside. Laying spang in the middle of the kitchen table, instead of a spoon-holder or a piece of flypaper or a nice pie, was this." He reached for his back pants pocket and brought out a narrow, stiff, blue-backed book, handling it like a little paddle.

"I'd know that a mile away," said Miss Beulah, coming and taking it out of his hands, then immediately thrusting it back. "It's the speller. Oh, how I could beat the world spelling! I could spell everybody in this reunion down right now," she offered. "Give me a word."

"Can't think of any," several immediately said.

"Extraordinary," said Miss Beulah. "E-x, ex, t-r-a, tra, extra, o-r, or, extraor, d-i, di, extraordi, n-a-r-y, nary, extraordinary. Does any of my sisters-in-law here present remember *that* spelling match?"

"You got it spelled but wet your britches," Aunt Nanny said, pointing a finger at her.

"Laugh, then! I spelled you all down with that word like a row of tin soldiers."

"One thing I can tell you: she kept that book by her and it's all she did keep by her, after she got like she was. Now what was it doing out on the kitchen table?" demanded Miss Lexie. "It lived under her pillow, with her hand over it. Once she had it, try and prize it loose. Finger by finger! You couldn't."

"Well, under her pillow's where it was," said Mr. Willy, sounding apologetic. "I didn't like to say where, but it was. I laid her down and trying to ease her fiery head, I jerked out what was so ungiving beneath it. She didn't say 'Put it back,' didn't say not to. She was past it."

Miss Lexie peeked, on tiptoe, over Mr. Willy's shoulder. "Look at the cover-boards," she said with an odd look of pride. "After I got her pencil hid, she did that work with a straight pin."

The white gouges in the dark blue, with faint-hyphenated scratches fraily joining them together, Miss Beulah followed from point to point with a slow-moving finger. "M-Y-W-I-L-L," she spelled out.

Judge Moody, sitting crammed in the school chair, lifted a face strained around the eyes, filling now with a martyred look, as though he might be sitting in Ludlow, back home in the courthouse again. "I'll take charge of that speller, if you please," he said. "I think there may be a document preserved inside it that was meant to be delivered to me."

Hands passed him the speller through the dumbfounded silence. Judge Moody lifted the speller and shook it. Nothing dropped out of the pages, though birds came down low into the althea bush behind him, as silent as petals shedding from a dark rose.

He laid the book down on the desk-arm and opened it, letting the pages riffle by, back to front. When he came to the flyleaf at the beginning, he sat back, drew with care from his breast pocket his spectacle case, and hooked the horn-rim spectacles on. They watched him study that narrow page. There was handwriting on both sides of it. Then, without raising his head, he began pounding with the flat of his hand on the desk-arm of his chair.

"Judge Moody." Miss Beulah ventured close. "I've heard you more than a time or two try to put a word in edgewise. Are you about to tell us you come into this story too?"

Judge Moody pulled himself out of the chair and climbed, heavy and rumpled-looking, to his feet.

"Mama," patiently asked the same child's voice that had asked it before, "is that the Booger?"

"I'm an old friend," he said. "Now this is written in her own hand, and my name is on it." He offered the open book to their unwilling gaze, exposed it there for a moment. Then he took it back under study. He began to frown, turning slowly ahead in the book, shifting its angle this way and that. "It's written right on the spelling pages," he muttered. "And the pencil's a little hard to read. Now, will you listen, please? This concerns you all."

Exclamations of dismay rose from the whole crowd.

"What's the substance of it?" Uncle Curtis asked. "Could you just give us that?"

Judge Moody took his eyes from the page and told them. "The substance? Yes. You're all mourners."

Miss Beulah even laid a hand behind her ear, as the groans gave way to a straining hush over all the reunion.

"You are every one going to attend her burial," Judge Moody said.

They cried out.

"We're invited, sir?" asked Mr. Renfro.

"Not invited. Told. You'd all just better good and well be there," said the Judge, reading on ahead to himself.

"The whole reunion? Is she counting me?" asked Aunt Cleo. "Well! I'm famous!"

"The reunion is still not quite everybody. She says everybody. I gather from her words if you ever went to school to Miss Julia Mortimer, you are now constituted her mourner," said Judge Moody.

"What's constituted?" the aunts asked one another, while some of the uncles rose to their feet.

"Whoa! Slow down a minute for us," said Uncle Noah Webster, trying to laugh.

" 'A plain coffin, no fuss . . . Father Stephen McRaven, if he remembers how hard I tried to teach him algebra, can try praying me into Eternity. St. Louis, Missouri, will find him . . .' Here," said Judge Moody. " 'The Banner School roll call is instructed to assemble in a body inside the school yard. The old, the blind, the crippled and ailing, and the congenital complainers may assemble inside the schoolhouse itself, so far as room may be found on the benches at the back. For the children, there is positively to be no holiday declared.' "

"Why do we have to go back to school? We've done with all that," said Uncle Curtis.

"And at the signal, we all go marching over the bridge in a long, long line to Alliance?" cried Uncle Dolphus. "She's not asking much!"

"May I have quiet restored?" said Judge Moody. "You won't need to go to her. She's coming to you."

"Whoa!" called Uncle Noah Webster again, and Uncle Curtis asked, "Judge Moody, are you certain-sure you know what that book's saying?"

The Judge's mouth had drawn down. He continued, " 'The mourners will keep good order among themselves and wait till I reach the schoolhouse. Good behavior is requested and advised on the part of one and all as I am lowered into my grave—' " He looked at what was coming and for a full minute stopped reading aloud. Then he went on—" 'already to have been dug beneath the mountain stone which constitutes the doorstep of Banner School. The stone is to be replaced at once after the grave is filled, so the children will be presented with no excuse for staying home from school. In case of rain, the order of events will proceed unchanged.' " Judge Moody closed the book with the sound of a crack of thunder, then gave them the last words. " 'And then, you fools—mourn me.' " He lifted to them a face that was long and lined.

" 'Whosoever shall say, Thou fool, shall be in danger of hell fire!' " said Brother Bethune, as he came and joined the table again. He sat down, giving off a smell of steaming Bible and gunpowder smoke.

"If this ain't keeping after us!" Uncle Dolphus cried. "Following us to our graves."

"You're following her," said Judge Moody.

"Well," said Miss Beulah, "she may be dead and waiting in her coffin, but she hasn't given up yet. I see that. Trying to regiment the reunion into being part of her funeral!"

"Well, you can't make people come to see you buried just by trying the same tricks you used on 'em when you was alive," said Aunt Nanny.

"Who's going to not mind her, and stay home? I'm just not too sure I can be in her parade. I'm going to have to ask Miss Julia's ghost to excuse me," said Aunt Birdie in a child-like voice, beginning to giggle.

"I've been in a heap of your dust today already," said Auntie Fay.

"How's she going to get us back home?" Uncle Noah Webster inquired. "She's burying herself and just leaving us standing in the school yard. I live in South Mississippi now!"

"As for me, I'm not a child," said Uncle Percy, whittling. "To be told."

"I'm not a child either," said Aunt Nanny.

"I'm a child," said Etoyle, hopping up among them. "And I like funerals."

"Well, listen to me. I ain't a-going," said Uncle Dolphus. "Now what's she going to do about it?"

"I might have gone back and pitched in today, if anybody'd asked or sent for me. But they didn't," said Miss Lexie. "And now, I'm not real sure I'll even go and swell their number to see her buried. I might ask myself first, who'll mourn *me*?"

"Well, you may wake up feeling more like charity in the morning, Sister Lexie," Brother Bethune said heavily. "Me and you both. Take it from me, Sunday can get too crowded."

"Miss Julia didn't stint herself when she called on everybody to be present!" said Aunt Nanny. "Greedy thing."

"But you go expecting too much out of other souls all your life and the day comes when you may have tried 'em too far," Miss Beulah said. She cocked her head at Judge Moody. "Well, I can say this much to you, sir: all it'd take to keep the whole nation away would be for you to stand up like she wanted you to and let 'em know they's whistled for."

"I wish she'd minded her own business and not ours," said Aunt Birdie.

"She never did that in her life. And so brag on her, brag

on her all you want! But I'll tell you this when you've finished," Miss Beulah warned them all. "She never did learn how to please."

"No," said Uncle Curtis, "she never. You're right, Beulah, and you nearly always are." Miss Beulah nodded. "Knowing the way to please and pacify the public and pour oil on the waters was entirely left out when they was making her pattern."

"Maybe that wasn't what she was trying for," Aunt Beck said. "Since she was going about the other thing just as hard as a steam engine."

"Beck is always in danger of getting sorry for the other side," said Miss Beulah.

"Didn't even know how to please when she picked a day to die, to my notion!" cried Aunt Birdie loyally. "But she didn't damage our spirits much—howsoever she might have liked to. Not ours!"

" 'I am in school to learn.' That was her cry. To this day I can see Earl Comfort being sent to the board to write it a hundred times. And every single line of it going right downhill," said Uncle Dolphus.

"And if she's going in a grave down at the schoolhouse, it's old Earl himself will be the one has to dig it for her," said Uncle Noah Webster. "Don't imagine he's too pleased at her yet."

"And she couldn't beat time when she marched us," said Aunt Birdie. "She run ahead of us."

"No, she couldn't beat good time. And I say give me a teacher who can do it all. Or else don't let her even start trying," said Uncle Percy. "It's her fault, right now, we don't know as much as we might. Stay poor as Job's turkey all our lives. She ought to made us *stay* in school, and learn some profit."

"Yes siree. If she was all that smart, why couldn't she have done a little better work on you and I?" Uncle Curtis asked.

"She read in the daytime." Mr. Renfro's lips were judicious as he looked at Judge Moody. "When she boarded with us, she did. And that was a thing surpassing strange for a well woman to do."

"Well, I expect what happened to her was she put a little

more of her own heart in it than she knew. And tried to make her teaching all there was," said Aunt Beck. "She was in love with Banner School." Awe and compassion together were in her voice.

"All she wanted was a teacher's life," Gloria said. "But it looked like past a certain point nobody was willing to let her have it."

"Well, it's too late to change it now," said Miss Beulah.

"When she could be sitting at the foot of Judgment this minute? I reckon it is too late!" said Aunt Birdie.

"She knows more than we do now," Aunt Beck reproached them gently.

"There was only one Miss Julia Mortimer, and I'm glad. But she didn't spare herself for that reason. She *once* was needed, and could tell herself that," Aunt Beck said. "She had that."

"Not in the end," Miss Lexie claimed. "That failed her in the end."

"What did she finally get like? Drawing to the end?" asked Aunt Cleo.

"She was getting a good deal like Mr. Hugg, or he's getting like her, take your pick. Old men and old women, they lose that too," said Miss Lexie, with what appeared to be contentment.

"Sister and ladies, she's dead and not even covered," said Mr. Renfro then, so softly that his voice barely made its tunnel through theirs. "Let's leave her lay. We've lived through it now."

"And Banner School makes just one more thing that's *happened* to me," Aunt Birdie confided to them. "It must've been pure poison while it lasted, but it didn't leave me any scars. I was so young, and it was so far-fetched. And I've gone a long ways ahead of it now!" She blew a kiss at Gloria. "And you will too!"

Uncle Nathan now broke his long silence to say, "Many a little schoolhouse I pass on the mountainside today is a sister to Banner, and I pass it wondering if I was to knock on the door wouldn't she come running out, all unchanged."

"I can still hear her, myself," said Uncle Noah Webster, gazing at his brother Nathan as he might at some passing spectacle. "Saying the multiplication table or some such rig-marole. Her voice! She had a might of sweetness and power locked up in her voice. To waste it on teaching was a sin."

"She spent her life in a draught!" said Aunt Birdie. "If I'd had to take her place for even a day, I'd have died of pneumonia."

"What other mortal would know the way to die like she did? Just met her end all by herself—what other mortal would succeed?" cried Aunt Beck. "Even if they wanted to, for some contrary reason."

"Going to meet it by herself in the road! Taking a chance of being found not even exactly decent. I can't hold with that or give it my understanding," Aunt Birdie said soberly.

"It seems to me like a right unkind thing to do unto others," Aunt Beck said as if unwillingly. "Getting 'em all to feel like traitors, or even worse."

But Miss Lexie said, "She was equal to it."

"I could have told you she was threatening the schoolhouse," said Auntie Fay. "Only it don't amount to a row of pins."

"Sissie, what do *you* know about her and the schoolhouse?" asked Miss Lexie.

"Homer says the board of supervisors got a letter from Miss Julia Mortimer—and that must have been through *your* fault, Lexie. Homer was tittering over it—said she told 'em like it was her royal due she wished to be buried right there by the schoolhouse when her time came. Those supervisors today, they were mostly boys of Banner School, and she just *told* 'em."

"The *bad* boys of Banner School," Miss Lexie amended. "That's why Homer Champion's so thick with 'em, he's another one."

"The supervisors didn't answer her letter and they voted her down," said Auntie Fay. "The supervisors said Nay."

"It don't sound highly Christian to me either," said Aunt Beck.

"Homer said the supervisors said that if you was to take the stone out of place for even long enough to sink her grave, the whole schoolhouse would give in and fall down in a heap," said Auntie Fay.

"I can easily picture it," said Miss Lexie. "I don't need any supervisors to tell me. Grandfather Renfro started with that stone when he built that schoolhouse, and he meant it to stay. He didn't mean it to come out for anybody. And didn't think to foresee any such mischief out of the teacher, I don't care how long she'd labored or how crazy it had run her. I'm only surprised that bunch of supervisors had the gumption to stand up for the schoolhouse against her."

"It was unanimous," said Auntie Fay. "Homer heard the same thing from all of 'em."

"Neither am I very happy about her wish," muttered Judge Moody. "About what I read between the lines." He took out his handkerchief and blotted his forehead.

"Can you be buried anywhere you want to?" Mrs. Moody asked him. "Just anywhere you want to?" She gave an abandoned wave of the hand.

"I don't know, as I stand here. The question has never come up in a form like this, not in my experience," he muttered. "At any rate, law or no law, she ought to have been talked out of it. She'd no business to humble herself—"

"Humble herself?" Miss Beulah laughed out loud. "She's about as humble as I am serving a grand dinner to a hundred!"

"It wasn't like her. It shows how poorly off she had gotten to be," he said.

"Well, I'll tell you what: I'm ashamed of her now," Miss Beulah said as she folded her arms. "That's the windup of her story for me, I'm ashamed *of* her and *for* her."

"She was so wrought," Aunt Beck said with a sigh.

"She ought to have married somebody," said Aunt Birdie. "Then what she wanted wouldn't mean a thing. She would be buried with him, and no questions asked."

"Where was Miss Julia Mortimer born, for pity's sakes?" asked Aunt Cleo. "Is there some reason why they can't go against her wishes and carry her back there?"

"Born in Ludlow! She sold her house behind her, to go on teaching. So, where she had left to go, when they put her to pasture, was across the river—the house her mother came from," said Miss Lexie. "But you can't miss it. She lives on Star Route, in sight of the Alliance water tank. The hot afternoons while she's asleep and I've walked to the Jew's store and back for a needle and thread for me and a fresh cake of soap for her! It's all of a mile and a half."

"She came out of Boone County, the same soil we did. What made her to be Miss Julia Mortimer, only the good Lord can tell you," said Uncle Curtis.

"You'll have to put her *somewhere*," said Aunt Cleo.

"Watch out, Oscar," said Mrs. Moody.

He stood there looking as if he'd found his hands too full, holding the speller, and he answered his wife by taking a step to lay it in her lap. His hand reached into the breast pocket of the coat he'd kept on all day, and he brought out an envelope, dusty, flattened, and bent. From this he pulled forth some folded sheets covered on both sides with handwriting.

"How'd you get *that*?" Miss Lexie sharply cried.

"It reached me through the U.S. Mail. It came to my post-office box in Ludlow," he said.

"Lexie, I thought you threw those letters in the pig pen," said Miss Beulah.

"I *mailed* 'em. I couldn't think to my soul what else to do with 'em!" cried out Miss Lexie. "I may not have mailed 'em right on the day she told me. I had more to do than go trotting to the mailbox every whipstitch."

"Don't read it to us!" cried more than one voice at Judge Moody.

It was almost too late to see to read. The world had turned the hyacinth-blue that eyes see behind their lids when closed against the sun. The moon was all above the horizon now. It looked as though it had been added to with a generous packing of Banner clay all around.

"I couldn't have imagined it this morning," Judge Moody said. "When I set out with this letter in my pocket, I couldn't have imagined ending up in circumstances under which I would share it with anybody. I hadn't even meant to show it to my wife." Abruptly he spread out the page. The paper was thin, unlined, not the kind that comes in a school tablet; even in the poor light it looked all but transparent. The high, precise steeples of handwriting, a degree uphill on one side of the page and a degree downhill on the other, appeared one puzzle that crossed and locked in the middle.

"Looks like it's our fate to sit through one more lesson," protested Aunt Birdie. "Ain't we remembered enough about Miss Julia Mortimer?"

"Your memory's got a dozen holes in it. And some sad mistakes," said Judge Moody.

They sat stiffly, as though some homemade thing they'd all had a hand in, like the quilt, were being criticized.

" 'I have always pretty well known what I was doing.' "

At the opening words he read, they all shouted. He might have just flashed Miss Julia's face on the screen of the bois d'arc tree with a magic lantern. Even Aunt Beck laughed, putting a corner of her handkerchief to her eyes.

Judge Moody ignored them and read on. " 'All my life I've fought a hard war with ignorance. Except in those cases that you can count off on your fingers, I lost every battle. Year in, year out, my children at Banner School took up the cause of the other side and held the fort against me. We both fought faithfully and single-mindedly, bravely, maybe even fairly. Mostly I lost, they won. But as long as I was still young, I always thought if I could marshal strength enough of body and spirit and push with it, every ounce, I could change the future.' "

"I can't understand it when he reads it to us. Can't he just tell it?" complained Aunt Birdie.

"Come on, tell us what it says, Judge Moody," said Aunt Nanny. "Don't be so bashful."

Judge Moody with a rattle turned the page over and read on. " 'Oscar, it's only now, when I've come to lie flat on my back, that I've had it driven in on me—the reason I never could win for good is that both sides were using the same tactics. Very likely true of all wars. A teacher teaches and a pupil learns or fights against learning with the same force behind him. It's the survival instinct. It's a mighty power, it's an iron weapon while it lasts. It's the desperation of staying alive against all odds that keeps both sides encouraged. But the side that gets licked gets to the truth first. When the battle's over, something may dawn there—with no help from the teacher, no help from the pupil, no help from the book. After the lessons give out and the eyes give out, when memory's trying its best to cheat you—to lie and hide from you, and you know some day it could even run off and leave you, there's just one thing, one reliable thing, left.' "

"Wait," said Aunt Birdie. "I don't know what those long words are talking about."

"What long words?" said Judge Moody. He read on. " 'Oscar Moody, I'm going to admit something to you. What I live by is inspiration. I always did—I started out on nothing else but naked inspiration. Of course I had sense enough to know that doesn't get you anywhere all by itself.' " Judge Moody's mouth shut for a moment in a hard line. " 'Now that the effort it took has been put a stop to, and I can survey the years, I can see it all needs doing over, starting from the beginning. But even if Providence allowed us the second chance, doubling back on my tracks has never been my principle. Even if I can't see very far ahead of me now, that's where I'm going.' "

"I wish we didn't have to hear it," Aunt Beck said, sighing.

"I don't know how much time goes by in between the parts of her letter, when the writing gets worse," said Judge Moody under his breath, frowning at the page. " 'I'm alive as ever, on the brink of oblivion, and I caught myself once on the verge of disgrace. Things like this are put in your path to teach you. You can make use of them, they'll bring you one stage, one milestone, further along your road. You can go crawling next along the edge of madness, if that's where you've come to. There's a lesson in it. You can profit from knowing that you needn't be ashamed to crawl—to keep on crawling, to be proud to crawl to where you can't crawl any further. Then you can find yourself lying flat on your back—look what's carried you another mile. From flat on your back you may not be able to lick the world, but at least you can keep the world from licking you. I haven't spent a lifetime fighting my battle to give up now. I'm ready for all they send me. There's a measure of enjoyment in it.' "

"Now I know she's a crazy," Miss Beulah was interrupting. "We're getting it right out of her own mouth, by listening long enough."

" 'But I've come to a puzzler. Something walls me in, crowds me around, outwits me, dims my eyesight, loses the pencil I had in my hand. I don't trust this, I have my suspicions of it, I don't know what it is I've come to. I don't know any longer. They prattle around me of the nearness of Heaven. Is this Heaven, where you lie wide-open to the mercies of others who think they know better than you do what's best—what's true and what isn't? Contradictors, interferers, and prevaricators—are those angels?' " Aunt Birdie gave out a little scream but Judge Moody didn't stop for it. " 'I think I'm in ignorance, not Heaven.' "

"How can you see any longer to give us those words?" Miss Beulah asked from where she stood stock-still at her grandmother's chair.

"I have read the letter to myself, before now," Judge Moody said. It was the rose-light from the sun already down that he read by. The moon did not yet give off light—it was only turned to the light, like a human head. He read on. " 'I'm right here on my old battleground, that's where I am. And there's something I want to impart to you, Oscar Moody. It's a warning.' "

"Oscar, listen to me," said Mrs. Moody. "I suggest you sit down."

" 'There's been one thing I never did take into account,' " he continued. " 'Most likely, neither did you. Watch out for innocence. Could *you* be tempted by it, Oscar—to your own mortification—and conspire with the ignorant and the lawless and the foolish and even the wicked, to *hold your tongue?* " Judge Moody steered the sheet of paper around where a few more lines of writing ran under his eyes along the margin. " 'Oscar Moody, I want to see you here in Alliance at your earliest convenience. Bring your Mississippi law with you, but you'll have to hear the story. It leads to a child. If I'm finally to reach my undoing, I won't be surprised to meet it in a child. That's what I started with. You'd better get here fast.' " He stood still, lowering the letter in his hands.

"Is that all?" asked Granny dismissively.

"Listen at Gloria," Aunt Nanny said. "She's shedding tears."

"That's right, Gloria. Now's a good time," Aunt Beck said lovingly. "A few tears for somebody else, you can spare those."

"They're not for somebody else," wept Gloria.

Miss Lexie Renfro had stalked her way forward. She cried to the Judge, "When did that come?"

"The letter? I've been carrying the letter around in my coat pocket for the better part of a month," Judge Moody said in his hard voice.

"Let's see that envelope." Miss Lexie filched it out of his hand. "An old one she used over again—it's the one the light bill came in. *I* didn't mail that. Don't blame me. I wouldn't have wanted the mail rider to see it." She put it back into his hand.

"It's a wonder you ever opened such a thing after it got there, Oscar," said Mrs. Moody. "That paper it's written on has got a mighty suspicious gold edge. And those rounded corners. Don't tell me it's the flyleaf out of her Testament."

Judge Moody stood silent.

"You can make sure by smelling it," prompted Mrs. Moody, to no avail.

"I'll tell you how she must have put one over on me," said Miss Lexie. "It must have been still only July, for her to write it. I was getting overtired of always tying her sheet. She found her chance, I reckon. Pulled up on the back of the chair till she could stand. Walked with the chair going in front of her, carrying the letter, out to the chicken house and robbed a nest. Walked back with her chair, carrying the letter plus the egg—she always had a pocket—down the hill to her mailbox, and put the letter there for the mail rider, along with the egg to pay him for the stamp. She learned one thing from the way it's done in Banner! Then she made it back with her chair to her bed. And I never knew I slept more than thirty minutes at a time."

"Can't trust yourself any longer," Aunt Nanny told her.

"Or I might even have been gone to town to pay the light bill," said Miss Lexie. "If I'd found *my* chance."

"The time, the effort, the trickery even, it cost that beleaguered woman to get this to me!" Judge Moody stared at Miss Lexie briefly and then widened his gaze to take in them all. "The complete and utter mortification of life! Of course," he said, "this required an answer in person."

"But here you are," said Mrs. Moody.

"Exactly," he said.

"You said 'Anything for Miss Julia!' " Mrs. Moody said.

"Look here, Judge Moody," interrupted Miss Beulah. She stopped her pacing. "I just this minute got a pretty good inspiration of what's the matter with you—you're kin to that woman!"

All cried out but the sleepers.

"Beulah, it's true! That's got to be it. That's his secret!" Aunt Birdie cried. "That's why he's so mad at everybody."

"Explains a whale of a lot!" Uncle Noah Webster cried.

"And so we've been allowed to talk about somebody who's kin to present company?" Miss Beulah moved in on Judge Moody. "While you set here in our midst and let us rake her up one side and down the other, and never once put claim on her? Never give out one peep you was armed with a letter from her till you got good and ready and thought it was a good time to spring it?" She drew up her hand and pointed a finger at him. "Treatment I wouldn't mete out to my worst enemy! Cheating on my hospitality like that!" She whirled on Mrs. Moody. "And you let him!"

Judge Moody had been holding up his hand toward her, palm flat. When he could be heard again, his voice was quiet. "Just a moment. I am not kin to Miss Julia—there are other ties."

"You wasn't *married* to her!" Uncle Noah Webster hollered out. "You can't stand here and tell us that, not after you brought your wife along to hear you!"

"I wouldn't mind, when you're ready, hearing a little more about you and Miss Julia myself," said Mrs. Moody to her husband.

"There are other ties," Judge Moody repeated.

"We don't appreciate a comer like you getting up in our midst and making us listen to ourselves being criticized," said Uncle Percy in a whisper. "If she couldn't be kin I just wish anyway she'd taught you."

"So she did," said Judge Moody.

Aunt Nanny stamped her foot and hollered "Don't believe it!" over the clamor of his listeners.

"She coached me," said Judge Moody. "The house I grew up in in Ludlow was right across Main Street from hers."

"That old house with the stone dragons?" asked Mrs. Moody.

"Missionary stock," he said with a nod.

"Judge Moody's just one of her Ludlow pets," said Miss Lexie, and she tried her laugh.

"One summer," said Judge Moody. "Myself along with some other high school boys who aimed for college. She coached me in rhetoric, and I won first place in the Mississippi Field Meet."

"Oscar, your blood pressure," said Mrs. Moody as if in despair, but he deepened his voice and mocked himself. " 'Archimedes said: "Give me a standing place and I will move the world." ' "

"Never mind. If you lived across the street from her, you were in a dangerous enough place," said Miss Beulah.

"Then what?" asked Mr. Renfro to lead him on.

"When I came home to practice, and pretty soon was made district attorney, she climbed the stairs to my office one day to say she was proud of me."

"She was claiming you," said Miss Lexie. "Taking the credit for you."

Judge Moody was still.

"He don't know her the way we did," said Aunt Birdie. "See if you can tell us her horse's name," she challenged him.

"When she left Ludlow for good, to track across the county and give her life to Banner School, she was driving an automobile. A Ford coupe, a thank-you present from Senator Jarvis the year he went to Washington. I remember her style of backing out: she set the throttle, fixed her eyes straight ahead on the back wall of the garage, and erected a perpendicular on it," said Judge Moody. "She was teaching herself to drive. I used to wonder how many innocent bystanders she scattered without knowing it." He took out his handkerchief and wiped it over his face.

"So there was a time when *you* laughed at her too," Mrs. Moody told him.

"I don't suppose even a Ford could get over these roads, not in winter," he said.

"Was that good-bye?" asked Mr. Renfro.

"A little later on, at her request, I sold the house for her, the old Mortimer house," he said.

"That means she wrote to you before. She had the habit of writing to you," said Mrs. Moody.

"I handled things, acted for her once or twice," he sighed. "That little inheritance. Taxes."

"So you wrote to her."

"Yes," he said. "On occasion."

"So not only was she writing letters. She was getting 'em," said Aunt Beck mournfully.

"What did you do with the letters that came for her, Lexie?" asked Miss Beulah. "Throw 'em in the pig pen?"

"I don't care to say," said Miss Lexie.

"That's what you threw in the pig pen."

"Who was the best judge! She was too sick and bad off to be bothered with something she would have to give her mind to."

"Oscar, you're rocking on your feet," said Mrs. Moody. "Sit down, you're just feeling sorry for yourself, standing up."

"And then this morning," said Judge Moody, reaching again inside his coat and bringing out another rumpled envelope, "in my box I found this. The envelope is one of my own, used over again. No letter inside, only a map she'd drawn me, showing how to get from Ludlow to Alliance and where she lived. That's when I gave up and started."

"I mailed it when I could, and not before!" cried Miss Lexie.

"And it's a maze," he said, squinting down at the old bill on which a web of lines radiated from some cross-mark ploughed into the center. "Just a maze. There wasn't much right about her thinking any longer. I didn't try to go by it—but I lost my own way on Boone County roads for the first time I can remember. I could almost believe I'd been *maneuvered* here," he said in grieved, almost hopeless tones. "To the root of it all, like the roots of a bad tooth. The very pocket of ignorance." He raised his head suddenly. "What have I been thinking of? I came here and stood up and read her letter to you. And you," he turned and said to his wife. "I've broken her confidence."

"I think that was unlawyerlike," she told him.

Judge Moody was struggling to get the map and the letter back inside their envelopes. "All the same, in my judgment, this bunch had it coming," he said.

"I'd just like to hear now, Oscar," said Mrs. Moody, "what you were doing getting letters like that at the office, and I didn't even know about it."

"Maud Eva," he said. "Why, she felt free—"

"It irks the fire out of me!" Mrs. Moody exclaimed.

"Both of us wrote, occasionally," he said.

"You and a poor, lonesome, old maid schoolteacher?" asked Mrs. Moody.

"Not always—" He stared down at her. "Why, every young blade in Ludlow was wild about Miss Julia Mortimer at one time."

"When she was young?"

"When all of us were young."

"A country schoolteacher? Why, that's no more than I was," said Mrs. Moody, eyebrows very high. She asked, "And you did your full share of courting her?"

"Oh, no. There were plenty without me, from Ludlow and all around. Herman Dearman, even, from this neck of the woods and crude as they come—even he aspired to her, knowing no better. She didn't discourage him enough—perhaps didn't know how," said Judge Moody. "Perhaps was able to even see something in him."

"Aspired!" said Mrs. Moody.

"He came to a sorry end, I believe."

"Sorry is right," said Uncle Curtis.

"There, that's enough," said Miss Beulah.

"So did Gerard Carruthers," said Judge Moody.

"So did he what?" asked his wife.

"Aspire. He trotted off and worked himself to the bone in Pennsylvania Medical School to come home and set up a country practice, you know," said Judge Moody. "He had a fond allegiance to her. And he kept coming, didn't he, attending her?"

"He was a liquorite, now that was his trouble," Miss Lexie replied. "He came. But in the end she dismissed him, and he went."

Judge Moody persisted. "She's made her a Superior Court judge, the best eye, ear, nose, and throat specialist in Kansas City, and a history professor somewhere—they're all scattered wide, of course. She could get them started, lick 'em into shape, but she couldn't get 'em to stay!"

"You stayed," said Mrs. Moody.

He sat down hard in the protesting chair.

"That irks the fire out of me," Mrs. Moody said again. "There's still something from way back somewhere that you haven't told me. I can tell by looking at the way your hair's all standing on end. What did you do, propose to her? To have her turn you down?" she pressed.

He put his hand over his eyes. "That's not it."

"Well, did she propose to you?" cried Aunt Nanny with a daring grin.

"Like you did to Percy?" a chorus called.

"It was owing to her I made the decision I did. That's right. She expressed her satisfaction that I hadn't chased off somewhere but was staying here, working with my own. In consequence, I never moved out of the state, or to a better part of the state."

"Oh, my! To think if only you had left!" Miss Beulah sighed.

"I had chances, you know, Maud Eva. I'm where I am today because she talked me into staying, doing what I could here at home, through the Boone County Courts." After a pause he said, "Well, and I never fully forgave her."

"Who did you take it out on?" Miss Beulah asked with a sage face.

Judge Moody turned again to his wife and seemed to repeat the question to her silently. As the company looked at him they could see his lined face glisten. He said, "Well, it's owing to her we're both here."

"Here? Right here?" asked Miss Beulah.

"Where I am on earth. Yes ma'am, here in the middle of you all right now. She's still the reason," Judge Moody said. "Mrs. Moody was shrewd—I wasn't anxious enough at all to see Miss Julia today, find out what had happened to her—I admit that, Maud Eva. I suffered an attack of cowardice, there on the road."

"I don't know why you keep addressing these complaints to me," said Mrs. Moody. "I made a six-egg cake, and piled on that icing, and skipped Sunday School too on account of your conscience, and I rode up front with you. I've been trying to get you there all day."

"I was already too late when I started," he said. "She said come and she meant *now*."

"She wouldn't have known you by the time you got there anyway," Mrs. Moody all at once told him. "Might not have known who she was herself, after you made the trip." She threw up her hands.

He struck at the breast pocket of his coat where the letters were. "She knew exactly who she was. And what she was. What she didn't know till she got to it was what would *happen* to what she was. Any more than any of us here know," he said. As she stared at him he added, "It could make you cry."

"All I know is we're all put into this world to serve a purpose," said Mrs. Moody.

"It could make a stone cry," said Judge Moody.

Around them the white tablecloths, clotted with shadows, still held the light, and so did old men's white shirts, and Sunday dresses with their skirts spread round or in points on the evening hill. The tables in their line appeared strung and hinged like the Big Dipper in the night sky, and the diamonds of the other cloths seemed to repeat themselves for a space far out on the deep blue of dust that now reached to Heaven. Now and then a flying child, calling a name, still streaked through everybody, and some of the die-hards turned themselves round and round or rolled themselves over and over down the long front hill, time after time, toward an exhaustion of joy.

Mrs. Moody still leaned toward her husband. "Yet you vow it was all platonic?"

Silence that was all one big question opened like a tunnel, long enough for all the birds in Boone County to have flown through in one long line going to roost.

"Don't try to read any secrets into this, Maud Eva," said Judge Moody then.

"Your real secrets are the ones you don't know you've got,"

said his wife, as if she'd been irked into knowing that, and she still waited on his answer.

"I'm not kin to her, was only once living nearby, only counted as a summer pupil, didn't try to propose to her, didn't do all my duty by her, she gave me advice I took and cherished against her, and when at the last she sent for me, I failed to get there: I was her friend, and she was mine."

"Well, she was older than you, you fool," said Mrs. Moody.

"Ten years," he said, staring as if aghast into the purple of first-dark.

"Then what's got wrong with you, after all this time?"

In a voice so still and so stubborn that he might have been speaking to himself alone, Judge Moody said, "Nothing wrong. Only I don't care quite the same about living as I did this morning."

"I feel like we've *been* to her wake," Mrs. Moody accused him.

"Watch out, everybody!" Elvie sang.

"Look! Granny's rising up out of her chair," said Uncle Percy hoarsely.

With the cup, the saucer, the pincushions tumbling, the quilt sliding down behind her, the little puppy sleepily following a few steps, Granny walked by herself into the middle and stood before them, at the height of a boy cousin. She lifted both little weightless hands. Miss Beulah started on the run toward her, then arrested herself.

Shoulders high, hands stiff but indicating the least little movement from side to side, Granny stood gathering herself, and then, in a quick, drumbeat voice just holding its own against the steady, directionless sound of crickets, she began to sing. Uncle Noah Webster rose, put his foot on the seat of a chair, and raised his banjo to his knee. Picking lightly, he fell in with her.

"Is it 'Frog Went A-Courting' or 'Wondrous Love'?" Aunt Birdie whispered. "Sounds like a little of both."

She knew every verse and was not sparing them one. When the verses were all sung, Granny, giving them calculating looks, kept on patting her foot. Uncle Noah Webster kept up with her, the banjo beat on, and as her left hand folded itself small as Elvie's against her hip, she gave a pat with her right foot and was lifted bodily straight up—Uncle Curtis was ready for her—to the top of her own table and set down carefully among the platters and what was left of everything. Uncle Noah Webster's hand came down sharp on the strings, and under its long skirt her foot, her whole leg, was lifted inches high to paddle the table in time to another chorus. The little black sliding-slipper with the silk-fuzz pompon on the toe must have been a dozen years old, though it was as good as new.

"With that little patting foot, she comes in right on time," said Uncle Dolphus. "Something she never showed us before."

"Just so we ain't seeing the last of Granny!" mourned Aunt Beck.

She danced in their faces.

"Mama, tell her it's Sunday," Elvie whispered.

"You got the brain of a bird? She's got track of what day this is better than you have, better than anybody here," said Miss Beulah fiercely, leaning forward and ready to spring. "Her own birthday."

Then Granny's old black hem began to trail and catch itself across the dishes behind her as she started to walk off the table.

"Catch-her-*Vaughn*!" screamed Miss Beulah in panic.

Electrified, the little boy opened his arms but like everybody else stood rooted where he was. It was Jack, racing in at that moment and flinging aside his empty bucket that rolled clang-clanging down the hill behind him, who got there and did the catching.

"Well. I've been *calling* ye times enough." In Granny's eyes gathered the helpless tears of the rescued. As he held her, she put up her arms to him. Her sleeves fell back. Moving like wands, her two little arms showed bare, strung and knotted with dark veins like long velvet Bible markers. Her hands reached for Jack's face. Then a faint cry came, and her face, right in his, broke all to pieces. "But you're not Sam Dale!"

Miss Beulah spread the birthday quilt over the chair and Jack carefully set her down within it.

"Granny, you just slipped back a generation there for a little," said Uncle Noah Webster fondly, bending over her.

"Put the blame right on Brother Bethune," urged Aunt Beck, fanning her.

"She's all right, Granny's all right," said Miss Beulah in a desperate voice.

The old lady still looked at Jack in a fixed manner. Dust as if from a long journey twinkled back at the moon from the high plush crown of her hat. "Who are you?" she asked finally.

He dropped to his knees there beside her and whispered to her the only answer there was. "It's Jack Jordan Renfro, Granny. Getting himself back home."

Part 5

T HE SUBSTANCE fine as dust that began to sift down upon the world, to pick out the new roof, the running ghost of a dog, the metal bell, was moonlight.

"Nightfall!" said Aunt Birdie. "When did that happen!"

"And they've started back to biting," said Aunt Nanny, spanking at her own arms and legs and at the invisible cloud of mosquitoes around her head.

"Let's get Granny's little soles off this ground!" cried Miss Beulah. "We don't want the dew to catch her!"

By Jack alone the old lady was lifted up in her chair and carried through the crowd back to the porch and to her old place at the head of the steps. The others began to follow more slowly. Groaning, carrying their chairs, they moved away from the tables and through the yard back again to the house. Those who could found the same places for their chairs that they had marked out this morning. As many others, who sat on the ground or lay with their heads in somebody's lap, elected to stay right where they were, not to move until they had to.

At Granny's back, with his wild gypsy hair pale in the moonlight, Uncle Nathan again took up his post with his hand on her chair. Judge Moody brought up his wife's chair and seated her, and when he brought the school chair up he placed it within the radius of Granny's rocker, where her small black figure in its little black hat waited perfectly still. He sat down there beside her.

"And we're sitting here in the dark, ain't we?" said somebody.

"If a stranger was to come along and find us like this, how could he tell who's the prettiest?" teased Aunt Birdie.

"Turn on them lights, then, Vaughn!" Uncle Dolphus called. "Why did you let 'em snake in here and hook you up to current for? For mercy's sakes let's shine!"

Suddenly the moonlit world was doused; lights hard as pick-axe blows drove down from every ceiling and the roof of the passage, cutting the house and all in it away, leaving them an island now on black earth, afloat in night, and nowhere, with only each other. In that first moment every face, white-lit but with its caves of mouth and eyes opened wide, black with the lonesomeness and hilarity of survival, showed its kinship to Uncle Nathan's, the face that floated over theirs. For the first time, all talk was cut off, and no baby offered to cry. Silence came travelling in on solid, man-made light.

"Now that's better," Mrs. Moody said. "Seems like we're back in civilization for the time being."

"Gloria!" Jack cried. "Where is our baby girl?"

He leaped back into the dark. They watched until they saw him come walking up out of it, carrying the baby. One of Lady May's arms hung over his shoulder, swinging lightly as a strand of hair.

"She had her a nest all made in the grass," Jack said as he came up the steps. He stopped before Granny in her chair and then rocked the baby downwards into the old lap. The baby was gone in sleep, where any nest is the same.

"Jack, I called and called you and you didn't come. Mr. Willy Trimble invited himself here and told the whole reunion on Miss Julia, how she died by herself and let him find her," cried Gloria. "Miss Julia and Judge Moody were two old cronies!"

He stopped her, his face struggling. "I was listening. I was standing to the back. I heard that teacher's life." Then he broke out, "That sounds about like the equal of getting put in the Hole! Kept in the dark, on bread and water, and nobody coming to get you out!"

"Jack—oh, don't let it spoil your welcome!" Miss Beulah said wildly.

"And she ain't calling you. They quit calling you after they're dead, son," said Uncle Dolphus.

"I'd rather have ploughed Parchman," said Jack to Judge Moody. Then he placed his hands on Gloria's shoulders. "I'm thankful I come along in time to save my wife from a life like hers."

"But were you here to see what your family did to *me?*" Gloria cried. "That's when I wanted you! That's when I called you. Listen to me—they pulled me down on dusty ground and got me in a watermelon fight!"

"I know you proved equal to that," Jack said, his voice soft again for her. They stood right under the naked light where it blazed the strongest, facing close; he was patting her on the shoulder.

"They didn't hesitate to wash my face in their sticky watermelon juice!"

"And you let 'em? What's happened to your old fight since morning?" he teased under his breath.

"They washed out my mouth with it! And I called 'Jack! Jack!' and you didn't come. They found the tear in my dress and Aunt Lexie sewed it right up on me in front of all, sticking her needle and scissors into my tender side. They all banded together against me!"

"Anyway, they've quit making company out of you, Possum," he said softly. "You're one of the family now."

"Oh, Jack," she said, all the more despairingly, "they say I'm your own cousin."

"Well, the sky hasn't fallen," he said, and smiled at her.

"May yet," said both Miss Lexie and Uncle Percy.

"They say Sam Dale Beecham's my daddy though he had no business being," Gloria rushed on.

"Uncle Sam Dale? Why, bless his mighty heart!" Jack cried, turning toward Granny. But she sat silent, looking straight ahead.

"And my mother was Rachel Sojourner, who never taught a day. They never had time to get married, they both of them died, all apart from each other, and here I am now. One way or the other, I'm kin to everybody in Banner," she said in a voice of despair.

"They'll be proud to hear it," Jack told her, and he stood back to hold her at arm's length as though never had she been more radiant.

"And my *baby* is kin to everybody," she mourned.

"This makes my welcome even better this time than it was this morning!" he cried.

"I might as well never have burned Miss Julia Mortimer's letter!"

"You got one too?" cried Aunt Nanny. "Glad it's gone!"

"It's still in words of fire on my brain. It said if I was going to marry who I threatened to marry, to stop right there. And come to see her—there were still things I needed to know," said Gloria. "She said she'd been delving into her own mind, and was still delving."

"Just to see what she could find?" cried Aunt Birdie.

"I was praying against her!" cried Gloria.

"What's delving?" Aunt Beck asked miserably, and Aunt Nanny asked, "Gloria, what did you *do*?"

"Tore up that letter. Put the pieces in the stove. Never answered. Never went. I got married!"

"Decided to fly in her face and go ahead with it anyway. Without telling no more than Jack himself, I bet a pretty penny, without telling the Beechams, without telling the Renfros, or Granny, or Grandpa, or the Man in the Moon. Pretty brave," said Aunt Birdie. "Or else pretty sneaky."

"I just try to mind my own business," said Gloria. "It hasn't been easy!" she cried to Mrs. Moody.

"Didn't you realize, young lady?" Judge Moody asked her. "Do you *ever* realize your danger?"

"But I didn't have to believe her just because she's Miss Julia!" Gloria said. "I had eyes of my own. And if I was an unmarried Banner girl's child, like she'd have me believe, all I had to do was take one look around the church at my own wedding, and see the whole population gathered, to know what family I was safe with. There was just one unmarried lady." Gloria turned and faced Miss Lexie. Shouts of appreciation rose up for a moment.

Gloria hushed them all with her pleading hand. "Miss Julia didn't tell me it was my *father* to be scared of. Or that my mother even had to be dead."

"She'd been saving the worst till she got you there," said Aunt Beck, shaking her head over at where she thought Alliance lay.

"I'd still like to know what Miss Julia Mortimer was so busy warning *you* for, Gloria!" cried Miss Beulah. "*You* did the only safe thing in the world—married your own cousin and found a home."

"Not safe," said Judge Moody. He spoke from his same school chair but it was closer to them now, and his voice louder. "Not safe if that's what *has* happened, and supposing the State has any way to prove it."

"We proved it, right yonder at the table," said Miss Beulah.

"I don't think much of your proof—I listened, without being able to help myself," the Judge said, while the chair creaked under his weight. "In fact, there's not a particle of it I'd accept as evidence. Fishing back in old memories. Postcard from the dead. Wise sayings."

"But we settled it," cried Aunt Nanny from among the exclaiming aunts.

"By a watermelon fight. In court we settle problems a little differently."

"*I* didn't say I'd ever believe it! No matter how many tried to make me," Gloria said. "I go by what I feel in my heart of hearts."

"Feelings!" added Judge Moody.

"And what's your feelings now, Miss Gloria?" cried Miss Beulah.

"They don't change! That I'm one to myself, and nobody's kin, and my own boss, and nobody knows the one I am or where I came from," she said. "And all that counts in life is up ahead."

"You're an idiot," Judge Moody told her, not unkindly. "The fact is, you could be almost anybody and have sprung up almost anywhere."

"Why, Oscar," said Mrs. Moody. "That's strong words."

"I'm ready for 'em."

Jack grabbed hold of Gloria and drew her back and put himself in front of her.

But Gloria came around Jack and on toward the Judge. She told him with a musing face, "Why, at the first warning she gave—I thought I might even be *hers*."

"Miss Julia's?" There were gaping mouths all the way around the bright porch.

"My lands," said Aunt Birdie. "That's what I call using the unbridled imagination."

"Why else would I have ever thought I could be a teacher?" Gloria put it to them, and this time a louder groan rose out of Judge Moody. "That would have explained everything. If once *she'd* made a mistake—and had me."

"No hope. No, she's never made a mistake, on purpose or otherwise," said Miss Beulah. "And I think if she had, she'd stuck right to her guns, Gloria, and brought you up for the world to see and brag on. She wouldn't make a mystery out of you. Had no use for a mystery."

"And it takes two!" cried Aunt Nanny.

"But she saved me from the orphanage—even if it was just to enter me up at Normal," argued Gloria. "She encouraged me, she wanted me to rise."

"I don't suppose for a minute Miss Julia saw the danger ahead. I think she had all the blindness of a born school-teacher," said Aunt Beck, a little pleadingly.

"What Miss Julia didn't figure out like she ought was a nameless orphan can turn out to be a raving beauty," said Aunt Birdie. "More than likely will."

"Judge Moody, you ain't got fault to find with anybody here but me, have you?" Jack asked.

Squinting and scowling in the light that beat down, the Judge looked at him. "Jack," he said, calling him by name for the first time, "the thing that strikes me strongest is that you didn't know you were marrying your cousin—if you *were* marrying your cousin."

"No sir," Jack stammered, "I wasn't worrying about who she used to be before I married her!"

"Jack, you didn't know?" Aunt Birdie asked.

"Jack? Jack know?" they chorused at her all around, as Miss Beulah gave a short laugh.

"No, but *she* did. *She* had knowledge," Miss Beulah said. "You didn't warn Jack away from you, even a word, did you, Miss Gloria?"

"But Judge Moody!" said Gloria. "Then Miss Julia let fly at me a second letter! She wrote and told me the wedding would be scratched off the books and Jack would have to go to the pen—"

"Well, Jack did!" Uncle Noah Webster said. "In his own way he managed it!"

"What came over her? What did she have against these two sweethearts?" Aunt Birdie cried. "What was the woman think-ing of?"

Judge Moody said, "The innocent. She thought of the child."

Gloria slowly bowed her head.

"Miss Julia was able to conjure up Lady May without even seeing her? Just laying over there in Alliance?" cried Aunt Nanny.

With one accord, everybody turned to Miss Lexie, who stared them down.

"That baby was never on my lips. Not with all I had to contend with! All I ever told Miss Julia Mortimer was I supposed Gloria had forgotten her, the same as everybody else had," Miss Lexie vowed.

"Did she ask you straight to your face, Lexie?" asked Auntie Fay.

"By the time that baby'd arrived in the world, I was making her right sure she didn't know anything but what went on inside her own head," said Miss Lexie.

Granny's little black shoulder started to tremble again. The baby in her lap never stirred but slept with her face turned up bared to the light, her lips parted.

" 'Baby'? Is that what her letter said, Gloria?" asked Aunt Beck. "The naked word?"

"The letter said a baby, if one was to get here, might be deaf and dumb."

They laughed all around but hushed on the instant.

"No. More than that. There's a worse danger than that," Judge Moody said, scowling down at Gloria.

"And my baby would go without a name," she said, not raising her head.

"With a name like Lady May?" Jack cried, looking aghast.

Even at the sound of her name, the baby didn't wake or stir.

"And what's wrong with a family any way you can get one?" cried Aunt Nanny.

"And all the while, when I was waiting on my husband, sitting apart from the others on my cedar log, quieting my baby, singing to her, all I could think of were the two words I'm scaredest of, null and void," Gloria cried out. "In Miss Julia's handwriting!"

"And the pen? Watch out, Jack, they could come after you again," said Uncle Curtis. "And run you back in for getting married."

"For marrying Gloria?" he cried.

"Catch him, Gloria, don't let him topple over on you!" cried Aunt Nanny.

But Jack had turned around to Judge Moody. "If I've done something wrong, I'd kind of like to be told about it, sir. I'd like to hear the reasoning, Judge Moody—hear it from you," he said. "Now it looks to me like the law'd do better to run me in if I hadn't."

"No. It was wrong to get married," Judge Moody said. "If you two young people are related within the prohibited degree, then you ran head-on into a piece of Mississippi legislation—I think they passed it about ten years ago. And I reckon they'd be in their rights if they arrested you for it. You could be tried—"

"Tried?" screamed Miss Beulah.

"And if convicted—"

"I'd be convicted all right! When I married Gloria I married her on purpose!" Jack cried. "All right. If they want two more years of my life for that, it's worth it. Here I am, sir."

"And if convicted," Judge Moody went on in spite of women's cries, "you'd get a fine or a ten-year sentence in the penitentiary—"

Gloria sank to the floor and wrapped her arms around one of Jack's legs, screaming "No!"

"—or both, and the marriage would be declared void. That's now State law."

"And Miss Julia Mortimer was the one who dug that up," Aunt Birdie marveled.

"And before this ever happened may have helped get the law passed," said Judge Moody briefly.

"Young people have 'em a hard time starting out always," pleaded Aunt Beck. "They're going to overcome this, aren't they?"

"This is different from me and you, Beck," said Miss Beulah. "All the time Jack took, all the load he shouldered, and all the trouble he went to, even blackening his name going to Parchman, was in order to marry his own cousin and have Judge Moody come back and open the door so Curly Stovall could walk in the house and arrest him all over again."

"I'd welcome Curly to try it!" Jack said, with some of his color returning. He lifted Gloria to her feet and they stood with their arms wrapped around each other's waists.

"I still think it's the sweetest thing in the world," said Aunt Beck.

"But Mississippi law is bound and determined it ain't going to let you drink or marry your own cousin!" shouted Uncle Noah Webster. "It's too pleasurable!"

Mrs. Moody said to Gloria, "You broke the law worse than that boy did."

"Ma'am?"

"Look what you made of that baby—"

"My baby!" Gloria ran a step, took the limp child into her arms. "She's speckless!" Then under the bright lights she saw the first freckle lying in the hollow of the baby's throat, like a spilled drop of honey.

"—and *knowing!* And *knowing!* Then, when this baby grows up and starts finding out a thing or two for herself—" Mrs. Moody shook her head at her.

"Couldn't she find it in her heart to forgive her own mother?" cried Gloria. "*I* did!"

Judge Moody in his melancholy voice remarked, "Forgiving seems the besetting sin of this house."

"With good reason!" said Mrs. Moody. "Though I wouldn't know any more about cousins marrying being wrong than they did," she confessed. "Somehow, I always thought it was the thing to do."

"Well, then we're lucky it wasn't what you did," Judge Moody told her.

"And now, lo, it's a sin!" said Mrs. Moody.

"Oh, I suppose it just aggravates whatever's already there, in human nature—the best and the worst, the strength and the weakness," Judge Moody said to his wife. "And of course human nature is dynamite to start with."

"Oh, when I'd thought, for a minute, that with Beecham blood on both sides the world would turn out all right!" Miss Beulah cried out, her imploring voice still going toward Granny, who sat fixed and silent.

"You ain't too well-schooled along the highways and by-ways of Mississippi law, Mother, that's all," said Mr. Renfro kindly. "But Judge Moody is, and he's setting right here to aim it at us."

"And *I* thought when I came to Banner to teach my first school, I was going forth into the world," said Gloria.

"Instead, you was coming right back to where you started from," said Aunt Birdie. "Just as dangerous as a little walking stick of dynamite."

"That's right! You come here danger personified," said Aunt Beck.

"Living danger. You come here and started waving your little red flag at Jack," teased Aunt Nanny.

"Waving a red flag? I was trying to save him!" Gloria cried. "I've been trying to save him since the day I saw him first. Protecting his poor head!"

"From what?" Miss Beulah demanded, both hands on hips.

"This mighty family! And you can't make me give up!" Gloria threw back her hair, and a few dried watermelon seeds flew out from it. "We'll live to ourselves one day yet, and do wonders. And raise all our children to be both good and smart—"

"And what is it you think *I've* done, right here?" Miss Beulah interrupted in a voice of astonishment.

"What are you trying to say, girl?" Aunt Birdie cried.

"I'm going to take Jack and Lady May and we're going to get clear away from *everybody*, move to ourselves."

"Where to? To the far ends of the earth?" cried Aunt Beck, as Jack stifled a sound in his throat.

"Carry me with you," begged Etoyle, jumping up.

"Carry me," begged Elvie.

"Carry me, carry me!" cried a chorus of sadly teasing uncles and one or two distant voices joining in.

"And just how do you think you're going?" Miss Beulah demanded to know.

"That's still for the future to say." And she looked out to see the distance, but beyond the bright porch she couldn't see anything at all.

"Poor Gloria," said Aunt Beck. "Given fair warning, she was. She knew she was risking Jack too. Honey, why did you marry our boy? I think you can tell it to us now."

There in blinding light Gloria cried out, "It's because I love him worse than any boy I'd ever seen in my life, much less taught!"

Jack turned the color of a cockscomb flower as he stood rigid by her side.

"There. That was tore out of her," said Miss Beulah.

"I didn't have to believe Miss Julia Mortimer if I didn't want to," Gloria repeated. Then she came headlong at Judge Moody, holding her baby bucketed, and Lady May's little legs stuck out pointed at his head like two guns even though she was asleep. "Is that what's at the end of your Sunday errand, sir? Did you come all the way to Banner to make Jack's baby and mine null and void, and take Jack away from me again?"

"My errand could be in no way so interpreted," he said drily.

"If you could just turn around, go back to Ludlow again and not do anything more to me and Jack. If you could just see your way. If you could just be that yielding, sir," said Gloria softly. "Then I'd forgive even her. Miss Julia."

"Forgive!" He did look ready to shake her. "You, whose fault it all is! You and your everlasting baby's!"

"Well, I would forgive her."

"It's just as wrong now as it was then, when she found out about what she was doing, isn't it, Oscar?" Mrs. Moody prodded her husband. "If they were first cousins on their wedding day, they'll be first cousins again in the morning."

"Yes. If," he said.

"Are they going to be hounded till they die?" Mr. Renfro asked Judge Moody, and Miss Beulah whirled on Mr. Renfro to say, "And I thought you knew what you was doing when you hammered a new roof on the house!"

"No, before that happens, they could pack up and take this infant with them and go live in Alabama," said Judge Moody.

"Alabama!" cried Jack, a chorus of horrified cries behind him. "Cross the state line? That's what Uncle Nathan's done!"

"It's not over a few dozen miles. Cousins may freely marry across the Alabama line and their offsprings are recognized," Judge Moody said.

"You want me and Gloria and Lady May to leave all we hold dear and all that holds us dear? Leave Granny and everybody else that's not getting any younger?" Jack's eyes raked across all their faces.

"There ain't no end, it looks like, to what you can lose and still go on living," Uncle Curtis pointed out.

"Why, it would put an end to the reunion," Jack said. Gloria, at the sight of his face, pressed herself and the baby close to him.

"There's the answer to your wish. Didn't it come in a hurry!" cried Aunt Nanny. "Ain't that what you been wishing for, Gloria, a good way to leave us?"

"Not by being driven!"

"So Miss Julia Mortimer couldn't stop you from marrying Jack by fair means or foul," Aunt Birdie said to Gloria. "Just couldn't prevent you."

"And I wish I could let her know now," said Gloria softly.

Women's voices echoed peacefully around her. "Let her know what?"

"How wrong she was. How right I was. She only needed to see my baby. And I was going to carry her over there!" said Gloria. "I was only waiting till she could talk."

Again Judge Moody groaned.

"Judge, I believe you'll make up your mind to forget this blood-kin business," Mrs. Moody said.

"What? Now, just a minute, don't go so fast, Maud Eva!" he said. His face grew darker as the blood ran into it. "I would just like a little evidence. My kind of evidence." He scowled around at the family. "Though as far as that goes, there's very little of that left now for any of us—that we were ever born, were married, had children—that any of our family have died, where they're buried."

"You've got your family Bible, haven't you, with it all down on the page?" cried Miss Beulah.

"No deeds to say whose the land is. No tax receipts, no poll books. There's no written proof left that any of us at all are alive here tonight. We're all in the same boat."

"What kind of people would burn down a courthouse?" cried Mrs. Moody.

"Varmints," said Granny. "They're all around us."

"Well, go on from there," said his wife impatiently to the Judge.

"And here," he said, with his eye on her, "they've told a patched-together family story and succeeded in bringing out no more evidence than if their declared intention had been to conceal it. Now this cousin story may be fact, but where is the present proof of it?" he asked the company. As Miss Beulah started to speak, he shook his head at her. "I saw there was a postcard," he told her. "It was signed 'Your loving husband.' That could have been their manner of speaking, you know, calling themselves husband and wife, real enough to them—meaning to make it a lawful union when he got his soldier's leave. But a postcard isn't the same evidence as a license to marry, or a marriage certificate, and even that—"

"It's better! There's a whole lot more of Sam Dale in that postcard, if you know how to read it!" Miss Beulah cried. "And Granny saved it from destruction, kept it in her Bible, showed it to you! Granny's word is as good as gold, don't you believe it? She's better than any courthouse, anywhere on earth."

"Oh, yes. Yes ma'am, I believe her word," Judge Moody said, moving his weight a little, leaning forward to let Granny hear him. "But I'm not wholly persuaded that this lady is always saying exactly what you think she's saying. Be reminded it's her birthday. She's a privileged character."

Granny's eyes moved along their slits and fixed on him. She still didn't speak. The others looked at him too, except for Jack, Gloria, and the baby, who clung together all one.

"Look at 'em, all hugging. They's victims of justice, all three," Aunt Birdie said, pointing. "I love 'em more than ever. What's ever going to become of 'em?"

Miss Beulah glared at Judge Moody. "Well, you don't have long to enjoy your little bit of foolish hope, do you?" she said. "But we've got to look after that little scandalous, haven't we?" She came to meet Judge Moody eye to eye, just as when he came breaking in at the dinner's start. "And with you to listen, and Granny not moving to stop me, I guess I'm going to have to tell it. And save 'em myself."

"Now, Mother," said Mr. Renfro.

"I believe to my soul we're misjudging one, and him not here tonight to stand up for his own innocence, and that's

Sam Dale Beecham. And so I'm just going to silence you, everybody!" said Miss Beulah.

"Mother, I believe I'm going and put up the evening bars," said Mr. Renfro, leaving them.

"I know good and well I punished the poor little fellow when he was in dresses and I was too little to know better how to watch over him!" cried Miss Beulah. "Judge Moody, Sam Dale wasn't no more likely than you are now to be responsible for Gloria being in the world."

"Don't, Beulah," Aunt Beck pleaded. "We didn't come here to cry, I keep on telling us."

"Something happened earlier than anything else to Sam Dale Beecham, and the main reason I'm in torment when I think about him is they all blame me. Yes sir, you do!" she cried to Granny, whose expression did not change.

"Mama," said Jack, "you wouldn't do harm to your own little brother. Now that's something you ain't going to make us believe."

"Then try listening," she said harshly. "Sam Dale's a little fellow sitting up close to the big hearth—still in dresses. I was supposed to be minding him but I don't know and can't ever remember what I was doing instead. Coal flew out of the fire and hit in his lap. Oh, it was a terrible thing! Granny called for some slippery elm for it and I said I'd go, I'd go! And instead of settling for the first elm I could find—instead of settling for the closest-to, I had to send myself farther and farther and farther, hunting for the *best*! For what's good enough to help what I'd done? They thought when I came running back late with that slippery elm that I'd dawdled along the way."

"Wasn't all your fault, Beulah," said Aunt Beck, as the silence lengthened itself. "No big sister nor anybody else could tell a spark to keep from flying out of the fire."

"Grandpa whipped me himself. The only time in his life. Granny still lives to blame me," Miss Beulah told Judge Moody, bending forward to see into his averted face. "They had me to grow up in torment for little Sam Dale."

"Jack's stricken, Beulah. Jack can't stand to hear 'em cry," said Aunt Beck.

"Neither can Oscar," said Mrs. Moody.

"Beulah always feels like she has to tell some of that story to the old folks before she lets us go," Aunt Beck said, sighing. "But I never heard it come out sounding any sadder than today, now that she's given us all of it."

"Is it evidence?" Mrs. Moody asked her husband.

"Hearsay. Hearsay," Judge Moody's voice rumbled, and when it stopped there was a silence of fresh amazement.

"Well, I don't know what the whole *world's* hanging on by!" cried Aunt Birdie in a voice of indignation. "While it's waiting to get proved it's there according to Judge Moody!"

"This one's a sadder story. But not for that reason does it stand up any better as proof," said Judge Moody quietly to Miss Beulah. "They didn't have a doctor, I suppose," he said, and waited for what seemed a long time.

When Granny spoke, she said to Miss Beulah with shaking lips, "They've just carried me the message. He didn't last through the crisis."

"God takes our jewels," came the soft response from the porchful.

Judge Moody said over them in a heavy voice, "Never mind any more. I've succeeded only in worrying another old lady."

Granny said, "Far from home. Under Georgia skies . . ."

"It's that baby. I think we'll have to close one eye over that everlasting baby," Judge Moody said in the same heavy voice. "You end up doing yourself the thing you hate most, the thing you've deplored the loudest and longest," he said to Uncle Nathan, the one who was looking at him now, with fixed eyes, over Granny's bowed head. "Here I am, taking the law into my own hands."

"Well," said Uncle Percy in a remote whisper, "that ain't such a poor idea. It's a whale of a lot better idea than going to Alabama."

"Take the law in your own hands? These people have never let it *out* of their own hands," Mrs. Moody said to her husband. "And I think that goes for your precious Miss Julia too. A tyrant, if there ever was one. Oh, for others' own good, of course!"

"Hush, everybody," Miss Beulah commanded. "Judge Moody's standing up again. I think this time he's going to do his part for the reunion."

For a moment he stood silenced. "It's that baby," he said. "I think we'll have to leave it that what's done is done. That there was no prior knowledge between the partners. And no crime."

"We can just bury it. With all else she knew," said Mr. Renfro, walking back from just within the passage and standing beside him. "The schoolteacher."

"Well, it's wonderful the way the Lord knows how to work things out," said Aunt Birdie brightly to Judge Moody.

"I hope that means the world's all right again! And that Jack can stay home a little longer this time!" cried Aunt Beck.

"I knew that's what you were going to have to do," Mrs. Moody said to her husband. "You'd have saved time and caused fewer tears to do it when I told you."

"I suppose, if I was the first of Miss Julia's protégés, this girl was her last," said Judge Moody with a sigh.

"She expected too much out of you too, Oscar," Mrs. Moody said, and he all at once sat down. "*Now* what have I said wrong?"

"Are you going to say 'Thank you,' Gloria?" asked Aunt Beck anxiously.

Mrs. Moody was holding Gloria's eye. "You had a talent for spelling. And some early determination." She granted her two short nods. "And what did you have besides?"

"She was an orphan child with nothing in this world and nobody knew who she was—" began Aunt Birdie.

"Youth," Judge Moody said shortly. "Her life before her."

Lady May opened her mouth and let out a long, welling cry.

Gloria said, "Miss Julia saw *promise* in me," and opened her bodice.

"Poor little scrap of mischief!" Mrs. Moody broke out. "She can't satisfy nature like that. And honestly, if a child is old enough to wear *pockets*—"

"She eats at the table too!" Gloria cried back at her. "She gets common, ordinary food just as well as this. What I'm seeing to is she doesn't *starve*!"

Dead silence greeted her. Aunt Nanny grabbed Jack and seemed to hold him from falling. Miss Beulah came up to Gloria in measured steps. Then she said, "All I'm thankful for this late, Gloria, is that Grandpa Vaughn didn't last long enough to hear that. Has a soul in this household ever been allowed to starve yet?"

"And when Jack jumps out in those fields tomorrow, he'll resurrect something out of nothing. Don't you know he will?" cried Aunt Birdie.

Aunt Nanny said, "And Jack will butcher the hog. You'll tide yourselves over, one year more. And the cow will freshen—"

"I beg your pardon," Mrs. Moody said to Gloria.

"Granted," said Gloria, nursing.

"You see, Judge Moody, and Mrs. Moody, now that Jack has come home to stay, everything's going to look up. It'll all be on his shoulders," said Uncle Curtis. "Trust him."

"Young man!" cried Mrs. Moody. "Jack! Merciful fathers! Is my car still there where Judge left it?"

"Running in good tune," said Jack, standing with his hand on the baby's head. "Uncle Nathan's piece of work is still holding. I went down and apologized for Aycock to his mother, and when I told her where he's spending the night she gave the credit entirely to me. And Aycock says he enjoyed his dinner and the same thing again for supper would be all right."

"Then what took you so long?" cried Miss Beulah. "Too much tried to happen while you tarried!"

"I had to tell Aycock about the new teacher that's come to board at their house, Mama," said Jack. "Young, green, and untried, and just the right medicine for him. I'm going to get behind him and help him marry her."

"I forgot all about what was pitched on the edge of a forty-foot drop!" said Mrs. Moody. "And oh, Oscar, where are we going to lay our heads tonight?"

"I very much fear that by this time that question's been settled for us," Judge Moody said.

"I think it's about time for us to take a little prettier view of ourselves," said Miss Beulah. "Go bring out my wedding," she told Elvie. "Stand on a chair and reach careful."

Elvie trotted inside, then there came from the company room a shattering noise. It sounded like handclapping. She came hurrying back with something made out of thin cardboard that had rolled up tight from both ends. Miss Beulah took it carefully and opened it out as if she uncoiled a spring, then carried it over to Granny's chair to hold it where the old lady's eyes might fall on it and where the rest might stand to see. It was nearly two feet long, seven or eight inches high.

"The only picture that ever was made of our whole family," Miss Beulah said, while a crowd gathered behind her shoulders.

The earlier company had lined up three deep that day on the front porch and steps of this house where they themselves were now. They stood then in April light; the house stood dark, roof and all, as a woodsy mountain behind the water-splash of the bride.

"That's me," said Miss Beulah. "That's you, Granny. And there's Grandpa, Granny."

At the apex of the group stood a medium-tall, upright lady with black hair showing under her hat, with her hand over the arm of the man standing in a preacher's stance; a crack in the surface had split his beard like lowered antlers.

The old lady didn't say a word.

"Remember, Mr. Renfro? The man on the mule that happened along to take the picture? Cranked it off, packed up and rode away, never saw him or his mule again. You fished out and paid that fellow I never knew what, and it was a month coming! Rolled like a calendar! I remember how hard it was for fingers to get it unrolled. It's been propped twenty-five years on its shelf with two flatirons to hold it, but it still likes to roll up on you—step on the wrong floorboard and see."

"I give him a silver dollar for it," said Mr. Renfro. "And never saw that man evermore."

"Just one of life's wayfarers, a picture-taker," said Miss Beulah. "You was up on crutches before that picture got back to us."

Mr. Renfro, the groom, was seated by the standing bride; he was in a chair with one of his legs offered to the forefront of the picture, set out on a cot like a loaf on a table; and the very bedspread on the cot was the one just inside the window on the company bed, visible now in the hot electric light.

"But you kept right on, Brother," said Miss Lexie.

"I had to come behind Dearman and get the stumps out for a mighty lot of people," Mr. Renfro said. "In those days I was called on here, thither, and yon."

"Be grateful you was on earth to be in the picture at all," said Miss Beulah. "Look, it's got all the Beecham boys together, standing shoulder to shoulder. There's precious Sam Dale, Granny!"

The old lady didn't give out a word.

"Did he have inkling?" asked Aunt Cleo.

"Does he look like it?" countered Miss Beulah. "Look at that face—there's nothing in it but plain goodness, goodness personified."

"But it's in twice," said Etoyle.

Evidently by racing the crank of the camera and running behind backs, Sam Dale had got in on both ends of the panorama, putting his face smack and smack again into the face of oblivion. Though too young and smooth to print itself dark enough not to fade, his face could not be mistaken; the hair stood straight up on his forehead, luxuriant as a spring crop of oats.

"Wasn't that a little mischief-making of him?" murmured Aunt Beck.

"That was being eighteen years old and fixing to march off to war," said Miss Beulah shortly.

"Only one of the boys was married yet," said Aunt Birdie. "So that only gave the right to Nanny to be in the picture."

"Look, oh look, in those days Percy was bigger than Nanny. Now it's the other way round," said Aunt Birdie. "I always forget what tricks time likes to play."

Aunt Nanny's finger flattened on the blur where someone had moved, and she asked, "Rachel Sojourner?"

"Oh, those slipping fingers!" cried Miss Beulah. "Don't bring back to me, please, how she tried to button me up in that dress—I thought those fingers'd never get to the foot of the row! Slipping, hurrying, and ice cold!" She pulled away Nanny's finger. "But what's she doing hiding in my wedding picture, and I never saw her before?"

"She's been in the company room with you all this time, Gloria," said Aunt Beck. "Your mother."

"I can't see what this girl looked like," said Gloria, coming at last to look at the picture with them.

"She didn't hold still. Beulah, this picture's filling up with the dead," said Aunt Beck. "After this year, let's not try taking it off its shelf any more."

"I'll hand you this much: looking at it today you get the notion there was nobody on earth but Renfros," said Miss Beulah. "And it was a big tribe to start with. They didn't ever outshine the Beechams, but they did threaten once to out-crop 'em. All them's Renfros! That's Mr. Renfro's father and mother, cocking their heads at each other. Dust these many years. All them's Renfros! That's Fay, with her finger in her mouth. And not a living man of 'em walking around today but the bridegroom I took for my husband."

Mr. Renfro made her a bow.

"What kind of a dandy is this?" asked Aunt Cleo, whose finger was moving behind theirs, more slowly. "Walking cane! And a straw hat with a stripey band on it. A flowing tie! Is that Noah Webster?"

"That's Nathan!" a chorus cried full of glee.

"Well, he's got both hands," Aunt Cleo challenged them. "Was he born like you and I?"

"That picture was taken before he surrendered to the Lord," said Miss Beulah. "That's enough of the picture. Carry it back in the house and stand it back on the shelf with my switches."

"They didn't have many pretty ones," Aunt Cleo said, her finger still moving slowly across the picture, across Miss Lexie's face, then stopping. "I'd have to give the prize to that one."

"Pull back your finger!" said Miss Beulah, pulling it back for her. "That's not Vaughn, not Beecham, not even Renfro, that's no kin to anybody here, and to my mind hadn't much business here at my wedding. Grandpa and Granny Vaughn was boarding her here at the time of the big occasion. Now who's the answer?"

She was standing the last one on the back row, her head turned away from the crowd and ignoring the camera, looking off from this porch here as from her own promontory to sur-vey the world. The full throat, firm long cheek, long-focused eye, the tall sweep of black hair laid with a rosebud that looked like a small diploma tied up in its ribbon, the very way the head was held, all said that the prospect was serious.

"Miss Julia Percival Mortimer," Judge Moody said, standing with them, looking down.

"She'll never git it all on one tombstone," said Aunt Cleo. "Just what I've been telling Noah Webster Beecham."

Mrs. Moody remarked, "It doesn't sound to me like she's even very sure of a grave."

"Where was I?" Elvie asked, her eyes still fixed on the photograph.

"Lucky for you, you was nowhere on earth yet!" said Miss Beulah. "Now that you're here, put this picture back where it belongs. Granny dear, don't you want to see it? Just one more time before it goes?"

Granny waved it away. Elvie skipped.

"Look-a-there! Look at our light!" cried Etoyle, and some of the aunts involuntarily shielded their eyes.

Within the opening of the passage, the bright bulb on its cord rose up toward the ceiling, slowly, then dropped in fits and starts, then zoomed up with the speed of a moth. Close to the ceiling, into which its cord disappeared, the bulb clung for a minute, then dropped and danced to a standstill.

"Well, now you're haunted," said Miss Lexie.

"It's starting afresh!" said Elvie.

"Jack!" yelled Miss Beulah, as the cord moved like a fishing line with a bite on it.

"I think now that whoever said ghosts is right, not that I ever held with ghosts. I'm a pretty good Presbyterian, back home," Mrs. Moody said.

"Jack! Jack! Ever out of sight when most needed. Vaughn, you climb a piece of the way up under the roof, take a poker, and just poke for a second at what's doing that," said Miss Beulah. "Come back and tell us what we've got there. I bet you a pretty it's alive, now."

"Who's going to wait on me like that when I get old?" crowed Miss Lexie, as Vaughn slowly went. "Not a soul, not a blessed soul!"

"You'll have to go to the poor farm," Aunt Cleo told her without taking her eyes from the ceiling. "If they still got room for you."

"I'll come wait on you, Aunt Lexie," cried Elvie, jumping up and down to watch the ceiling. "As long as I ain't too busy school-teaching. And if I don't get married or have children before I know it. Look!"

"Ha ha ha!" Etoyle cawed out. Now the light was being let down on its cord, jerky as a school flag down its mast.

Then all the lights went out. It seemed a midnight moment before the moonlight gathered its wave and rolled back in.

"Well, that's one more system that today's put out of commission," said Uncle Curtis, as if with favor.

In a moment they heard Vaughn come running up the passage, and now they made him out—he came cradling something alive. All around, the dogs put up a clamor.

"Here's who it was, Mama. Playing with us all from over our heads."

"Uh-*huh*," said Miss Beulah. "What did I tell you!"

"Horrors," said Mrs. Moody. "Is that a monkey?"

"Don't try to put him in my lap," said Aunt Cleo. "I mean it."

"Hey, Coony!" cried the little girls.

"He was just tantalizing you, Mama," said Vaughn pleadingly.

"Eternal, everlasting mischief!" stormed Miss Beulah. "There's always *that* you can count on! I said I wasn't going to have coon or possum under my roof and I'm not," she went on, with repeated pokes testing the coon's needly teeth on her finger. "Yes sir, and you're one little scrap of mischief I mean to send right back where it started from."

While the boy cousins tried to keep back a battery of hounds, two enormous yellow globes moved out of the passage. Etoyle had gone for the oil lamps, even while Miss Beulah was calling over the frenzied barking of the held-back, straining dogs, "Bring the lamps! Don't leave your great-grandmother sitting in the dark!" Etoyle brought the lamps to the coon.

The coon, circular-eyed, lamp-eyed itself, fluffed up and drew one long breath, hoarse and male.

Then it got itself thrust into the lap of Ella Fay, who hollered, "Jack!"

"Hold him, Ella Fay, hold him!" shouted the uncles. "That's not the way! He's scrambling!"

"Don't let him run off with anything belonging to me," said Aunt Cleo. "Oh, they're great for thieving."

"Oscar, I want to go home," said Mrs. Moody piteously.

Held up by Elvie, Lady May was shaken awake again to see the coon. When she saw it, her eyes went three-cornered and her cheeks went plump as two Duchess roses on a stem.

"Look at that smile. There it comes! And it's her mother's. And looks like you're going to have to work just as hard to get it," Aunt Birdie said.

"Mama, I believe he knows you're the cook," pleaded Vaughn. "See how he wants to follow you. Let's keep him, let's keep him! When I get him chained up and you bring him some food in a saucer, he'll quit his monkeying. I want to name him Parchman."

"He'll go!" said Miss Beulah. "And I don't want to have any coon-and-dog battle on the premises. Boys! Tighten up on those visiting dogs! Come here to me, Sid."

Little Sid, to their laughter, ran at even draw with the head of the pack as the coon streaked straight to meet them. In the moonlight Sid showed his teeth like a row of lace.

"I give the coon fifty-fifty and the dogs fifty-fifty," said Uncle Curtis in leisurely tones.

"There's a little more racket out there than I like to hear," moaned Miss Beulah.

The dogs' tails, white and moonlit and all beating at once, disappeared last, speeding down the hill towards joy. But a boy cousin came plodding back into view to tell them, "He got away. Coony got away. It looked like he was heading for Banner Top."

"That coon didn't put up the fight those dogs expected of him," said Uncle Dolphus. "He'd been suffocating under that roof too long, that might have been his trouble. Better luck next time!"

The moon shone now at full power. The front gallery seemed to spread away and take the surrounding hills and gullies all into its apron. Banner Top seemed right in their laps. Banner itself all but showed itself over the rim, as though the only reason why anything on earth was still invisible tonight was that it had taken the right steps to make itself so.

"You know, I can hear that thing running from here," said Aunt Beck. "Mrs. Judge, your motor sounds to me like the old courthouse clock trying to strike again, and not making it."

"You sure are stranded here," said Mrs. Moody. "Mercy, what a long way off from everything!"

"Long way off? They're right in the thick," cried Aunt Birdie. "This is where I wish I was when I get hungry to see something happen."

"In my young days," said Brother Bethune, "I incurred the wrath of the law-abiding, one sweet summer's night."

"Brother Bethune!" the aunts turned slightly in their chairs to exclaim. "Never dreamed that," said one.

"Are you trying to tell us you got yourself marched off to jail?" Miss Beulah asked.

"I'm trying to tell you I incurred the wrath of the law-abiding. There was at one time a little whiskey-making going on in and around these peaceful moonlight hills. And I supplied 'em the sugar."

"Brother Bethune!"

"Every last one of us got caught. Yes, in my day revenuers roamed these moonlight roads as thick as thieves. But I was the only one arrested that they let run back in his house a minute. They said I could gather up my Bible."

"They owed you at least that much!" hollered Uncle Noah Webster. "What happened to the makings? They drink it up then and there?"

"I went on out through the back window," said Brother Bethune. "Into the moonlight."

"Well, it done you good to come out and tell us, didn't it?" said Aunt Birdie. "Now we know at least one thing *you're* sorry for."

"Brother Bethune, I think you might go back to it," Miss Beulah broke out. "Go back to making your moonshine. There's less chance of mistakes than there is in trying to preach the Lord's Word. Grandpa's turned in his grave more than once or twice today."

"Beulah! Do you know what you're saying?" Uncle Curtis asked her.

"I was young and untried," said Brother Bethune. "Needing to be shown the way, that's all."

"Well, the Lord only knows how I'm going to get home, even if I live till morning," Mrs. Moody said.

"Mrs. Judge, you and Judge Moody's welcome to our company room," Mr. Renfro said immediately. "Where's my wife? Hear it polite from her."

"My car sitting up on the edge of nowhere, with nobody but a booby in it," Mrs. Moody went on. "I guess before morning he'll find my chocolate cake, and just sink his teeth in it."

"Well, sir, I'll be looking in next week's *Boone County Vindicator* to read what's the outcome. Ora Stovall is the Banner correspondent, she'll get it all in. If the worst should happen to your car, most readers will say it served Curly just about right," said Uncle Dolphus.

"What about the way it'll serve me?" asked Judge Moody.

"It won't be that bad," Uncle Noah Webster promised him.

"Mother, hurry to invite 'em," said Mr. Renfro, looking about for her. "Or they'll go!"

"If you still got no place to be till morning, Judge and Mrs. Moody," said Miss Beulah finally, "we got our company room. I'll just move Gloria and the baby out of it before Jack gets in it, and now that Jack's home, I'll move Elvie out of it too and put Elvie on Vaughn's cot on the back porch, since Lexie's in with the other two girls, and Vaughn can sleep where he's inclined."

"Well, if that's not any trouble," said Mrs. Moody, while Elvie cried.

"But you'll have to wait on it," Miss Beulah said. "You can't even see your way in till some of this company starts saying goodnight and takes babies and hats and all away from the bed."

All the women and nearly all the men sat with some child's arm hanging a loop around them. Other children, still wide enough awake, ran stealthily behind the chairs, tickling their elders with hen feathers. Sleeping babies had been laid on the company bed long ago, there were sleepers on pallets in the passage, and others slept more companionably among the chair-legs and the human feet on the gallery floor, like rabbits in burrows, or they lay unbudging across laps.

"Well, you're visiting an old part of the country here," said Mr. Renfro. "If you was to go up Banner Top and hunt around, Judge Moody, you'd find little hollows here and there where the Bywy Indians used to pound their corn, and keep a signal fire going, and the rest of it. But there ain't too much of their story left lying around. I'm afraid you could call them peace-loving."

"Indian Leap," said Granny.

"That's the name my grandmother called it too. Blue Knob is another old-timey name for it," said Aunt Beck.

"There's nothing blue about Banner Top," laughed Aunt Nanny. "It's pure barefaced red."

"You ever seen it in the evening from Mountain Creek?" asked Aunt Beck. "I was born in Mountain Creek. And from there Banner Top is as blue as that little throbbing vein in Granny's forehead."

"The Indians jumped off from there into the river and drowned 'emselves rather than leave their homes and go where they'd be more wanted. That's Granny's tale," said Uncle Curtis.

"There's a better name than any, and that's the one it got christened by those that walked it here all the way from Carolina in early times and ought to knowed what they was talking about," Mr. Renfro said to Judge Moody. "Renfros, that is. They called the whole parcel of it Long Hungry Ridge."

"If tonight was as much as a hundred or more years ago," Uncle Curtis said, addressing the Moodys, "you might not have had such an easy time finding us. There was just the thin little road, what you might call a trail, mighty faint, going along here through the standing forest. So dim and hard to find in the trees that they thought it would be the best judgment in the long run to ring a bell to let the travelers know where they was. Once an hour they had to remember to ring it, and regular, or the woods would have been full of lost travellers, stumbling on one another's heels. That was back in the days when there was more travelling through here than lately—folks was in a greater hurry to get somewhere, you know, while the country's new."

"There it is," said Miss Beulah. "Straight ahead of your noses."

The black iron bell hung from its yoke mounted on a black locust post that stood to itself. The leaves of a wisteria climbing there made a feathery moonlit bonnet around the bell.

"I've read somewhere about a bell like that on the Old Grenada Trail," Judge Moody said to his wife. "Doubt if that one still exists."

"That's the Wayfarer's Bell," said Miss Beulah. "And it was here before any of the rest, I reckon. Before Granny was born."

"I rang it this morning, a little before sunup," said Granny.

"Yes, Granny dear," said Uncle Percy, his voice nearly as much of a whisper as hers.

She nodded to either side of her. "Brought you running, didn't it?"

"You missed things," called Auntie Fay serenely, as the Champions' chicken van bounced into the yard and stopped under a moonstruck fall of dust. "Gloria's born a Beecham, she's Sam Dale's child—that's the best surprise that was brought us. She's here tonight as one of the family twice over.—Oh no she isn't!—Well, believe what you want to."

"Well, chickens come home to roost," said Uncle Homer, stumbling once on the steps, the bright hearth of moonlight.

"We got a little extra company as usual," Auntie Fay kept on. "Two that turned up with no place to sleep."

Uncle Homer came on into the lamplight. "Judge Moody! What's that man doing in this house?"

"He's spending the night," said Auntie Fay. "Beulah's just asked him in spite of herself."

"Judge Moody, you was asked for over at Miss Julia Mortimer's all evening long!" cried Uncle Homer. "Doc Carruthers was about to go hunting the roads to see if you'd fell in somewhere. I had to rake up a dozen excuses for you."

"*You* did? You're the very fellow rode right by us this

morning and left us to languish!" Mrs. Moody said. "And my car clinging to the edge of nowhere. If clinging it still is."

"It is," said Uncle Homer. "It evermore is, ma'am. Still clinging. I'm glad to be able to bring you the comforting word. I saw it again on my way back, just passed it."

"Possum," said Jack, low, "don't tell Mama, but Uncle Homer's back here the worse for wear. We ought to have been over yonder for the family in place of him. Paying respects is not Uncle Homer's long suit."

"I don't suppose you heard anybody over there call my name, Homer Champion?" Miss Lexie said, coughing from her dry throat.

"I don't believe the splendid name of Renfro ever came up," he said.

"I would have gone back and pitched in today, if anybody'd asked for me and sent after me. But they didn't," said Miss Lexie. "I listened hard to be asked for and I wasn't."

"Lexie, are you working up for a crying spell at this late hour?" Miss Beulah asked.

Miss Lexie raised her voice. "I can get my feelings hurt, the same as anybody else!"

"When I cry, I go off somewhere and cry by myself," Miss Beulah said, taking a step away from her high on tiptoe to show her, "and I don't come back till I'm good and over it. But if her crowd adds up to more than we've got here, Homer Champion, I'll eat that table out there—I promise you!"

"If she's got a crowd now, they didn't come paying her any attention while she's sick, any more than this crowd here," said Miss Lexie.

"Well, darlin', maybe all of 'em was waiting for now," Aunt Beck said in consoling tones.

"That whole house is busy filling up with big shots! They're everywhere, with hardly room left for the homefolks to sit down," Uncle Homer was saying. "It ain't just Boone County that's over there. I saw tags tonight on cars from three or four different counties, and that ain't all—they're here from Alabama, Georgia, Carolina, and even places up North!"

"Found their way all right," said Mrs. Moody, with a glance toward her husband.

"A Willys-Knight from Missouri liked-to crowded me off

my own road! And Father Somebody-Something, that's who's going to preach her funeral, and he wears a skirt. He's a big shot from somewhere too, just don't ask me where," said Uncle Homer.

"That's no Presbyterian!" flashed Mrs. Moody. "No *Southern* Presbyterian!"

"The nearest one he reminds me of is Judge Moody," said Uncle Homer.

"What bridge were all these crossing on?" Judge Moody asked.

"Dear old Banner bridge is the one I use. And you know who sent a telegram he wishes he was coming to the funeral tomorrow? Governor Somebody from I forgot to listen where! Getting telegrams is pretty high style," said Uncle Homer.

"All right for high style. But the way we've been told, Miss Julia herself is still going without a place to be buried," said Auntie Fay.

"That's a false charge," said Uncle Homer, holding up his hand. "When Miss Julia Mortimer's letter came down on the supervisors to give her right-of-way to a grave under the schoolhouse doorstep and they said Nay, I went to work on it myself—until I got her a site in dear Banner Cemetery. That's hitting it pretty close to her mark, ain't it?"

"In Banner Cemetery? Homer Champion! You're bringing her right smack in our midst?" cried Miss Beulah wildly. "She's going to be buried with us?"

"Beulah, I got the site from Earl Comfort in return for a Comfort site and a Jersey cow. He said he couldn't afford to turn it down, and little Mis' Comfort could milk her for him. Mr. Comfort's got to be buried in Ludlow among strangers for his brother's pains, and little care I. Getting Miss Julia buried to Banner's credit is worth a heap to me," said Uncle Homer. "I can always point to it."

"Well, old Earl come just about as close to digging his own grave as a man could get, and still tell it," said Mr. Renfro. "Eh, Willy Trimble?"

But Mr. Willy Trimble sat there very papery, still as a finished fly in a web, his eyes shut.

"Homer Champion is not ungrateful," said Uncle Homer.

"Let that never be told against him. Miss Julia Mortimer made me what I am today, and you could have heard me declaring so tonight if you'd been there. I grew up only a poor Banner boy, penniless, ignorant, and barefoot, and today I live in Foxtown in a brick veneer home on a gravel road, got water in the kitchen, four hundred chickens, and filling an office of public trust, asking only—"

"I'm never a particle surprised at you, Homer," said Miss Beulah. "You'd find a platform anywhere at all."

"So she'll be going in in the morning," Uncle Homer went on, clapping Brother Bethune on the shoulder. "And you can have your whack at her. I think you can look for a good crowd."

But Brother Bethune now slept too, with his head thrown back and his mouth open. They had a glimpse of his old wrong tongue, shining like a little pocket-mirror back there. It was reflecting the moon.

"Damascus Church don't even have an organ," said Aunt Beck.

"The best sounding-board in the world! That's all!" exclaimed Miss Beulah. "And voices do the rest. When Damascus lights into a hymn, the countryside will know what it's in praise of!"

"The funeral won't be ours. Just the burial, Sister Beulah," said Uncle Homer. "Wait till Brother Bethune sees him coming—his rival in the skirt. Boys, they're having 'em a high old time over yonder, let me tell you."

"How much of a one have *you* had?" Aunt Cleo asked. "Let me get a good look at your eyes."

"Besides the rest, Mr. Ike Goldman of Goldman's Store brought in a trayload of eats you never seen the like of," said Uncle Homer. "And decorating a silver tray was a bottle of something—the bought kind—and some little glasses the size of a lady's thimble! Some of those Presbyterians made out like they'd rather go home, but there was plenty of the other kind that helped themselves."

"If you'd rather be celebrating at her house than mine, just turn around and go back over there, Homer," said Miss Beulah to his face. "A hundred to one they haven't started missing you yet."

"Is it going on all over her house?" Aunt Beck asked.

"It's Bedlam," said Uncle Homer, as though satisfied. "It's pure unadulterated Bedlam over there. Cigars!"

"Well, Homer," said Miss Beulah, "you may have gained yourself a margin of votes today by racing off from your own family and rubbing shoulders with a crowd of mourners—but no further stars in your crown, not if I had any say-so about it. And I doubt if the eats could come up to mine—they had pretty short notice."

"Chicken predominated," said Uncle Homer. "Chicken predominated." Suddenly he sat down.

Again quiet threatened. Only a few children still had their eyes open. Wild with asking a riddle one minute, they would be stopped by sleep the next, as though a cup were being passed around the company, and having tasted what was in it they fell back open-lipped one after the other, even the most stubborn. Now their elders had their own silence left to them.

"And on moonlight nights like tonight," said Granny, "they'd mount 'em the same steed and ride 'em up the road and down the road, then hitch the bridle to the tree. That's after I was safe under the covers and Mr. Vaughn had left off his praying and settled in to snore."

"Who, Granny?" the aunts were all asking her.

"Just told you. The schoolteacher. Ain't that who you're trying to bury?" she asked.

"Miss Julia Mortimer? Granny!" Uncle Percy, Uncle Curtis, and Uncle Dolphus all exclaimed at her in shocked voices. Uncle Noah Webster asked, "Granny dear, are you telling us about Miss Julia Mortimer and a sweetheart?"

"Call him Dearman. That's his moniker," said Granny.

The laugh that rose and fell around her was one of dismay.

"Who can believe that?" challenged Miss Beulah. "Well, I'm not saying I can't. A rascal like him's just the kind that some over-smart old maid would take a shine to."

"Some did consider her beautiful of face as a girl. Haven't you ever marvelled to hear that?" said Aunt Birdie.

"Miss Julia Mortimer had ears set close to her head, little

ears that run up in points—like Judge Moody's and mine," said Mr. Renfro in candid vanity.

"If she'd married Dearman! It would have been a different kettle of fish," said Aunt Nanny.

"We would have escaped from a lot," agreed Aunt Beck. "But would *she* have been as satisfied, with only a husband to fuss over instead of a whole nation of ignorant, squirming schoolchildren?"

"Watch out, Beck. Watch out for your sympathies," said Aunt Birdie.

"Don't talk about Dearman around here," said Miss Beulah.

"What's his story? Ain't he the one you come home from German-hunting and found in charge of your store?" Aunt Cleo asked Mr. Renfro. "Oho-oho."

"I didn't go German-hunting," Mr. Renfro replied.

"He managed to blow himself up right here at home," said Miss Beulah.

"I didn't have a bit of excuse in the world, I was right here in Banner, and watching him, and lost it to him. Mr. Dearman," Mr. Renfro said. "The store I had from my daddy."

"Shucks," said Aunt Cleo.

"I was *out* of the store some, blowing stumps, cleaning up after him—he needed somebody knowing how to do that," said Mr. Renfro. "And hunting some. And he all at once had my business. There ain't hardly what you could call a story to it."

"It's your story. Not Dearman's. You don't know your own story when you hear it," Miss Beulah said. She whirled on Aunt Cleo. "All right. Dearman is who showed up full-grown around here, took over some of the country, brought niggers in here, cut down every tree within forty miles, and run it shrieking through a sawmill."

"Did he cut your trees?" Aunt Cleo asked.

"Did you see any giants left, coming?"

"Went through our hills and stripped 'em naked, that's all!" Aunt Nanny cried. "I kept asking how he got in here and found us!"

"Followed the tracks. The railroad had already come cutting through the woods and just barely missed some of us.

Yes'm, he put up a sawmill where he found the prettiest trees on earth. Lived with men in a boxcar and drank liquor. Pretty soon the tallest trees was all gone."

"Reckon you-all got something for 'em," said Aunt Cleo.

"By then we was owing to Dearman," said Mr. Renfro.

"We didn't even get the sawdust!" cried Uncle Noah Webster to his wife.

"It was a tearing ambition he had to make all he could out of us. And even some of our girls listened to his spiel and was sweet on him," said Uncle Percy. "I hated that."

"What he left us was a nation of stumps," said Mr. Renfro.

Granny put out both hands in an amazingly swift predatory gesture.

"That's him!" said Miss Beulah. "Just a great big grabber, that's what Dearman was."

"Well, that's the way to get something," said Aunt Cleo, grinning at them.

"I believe down your way was exactly where he come from, Sister Cleo," Uncle Curtis said.

"He did. Manifest, Mississippi, is where he sprung from," said Miss Beulah.

"That's a familiar-sounding name, Dearman," said Aunt Cleo.

"He's what levelled Piney!" Uncle Noah Webster told her. "Why, I've learned that since I've been living in your house and going to the barber shop. Those forest pines he took right in his maw. And when he first showed up there he didn't have but two goats."

"And when he left it he had all the money he needed and a gang to go with him and they just started up the railroad track," said Uncle Dolphus.

"Then after the store he took my house away from me," Mr. Renfro went on. "I had a little bad luck just at the perfect time to suit his needs, and he put me out and moved himself in. Thinking he was going to dwell in it forever, I reckon, and lord it over Banner forever and aye. He didn't get to do that."

"That's enough!" warned Miss Beulah. "He was just a glorified Stovall. Now will everybody please forget about him?"

"I don't know what Beulah could have married me for,

after that. Unless she did it just to show she felt sorry for me," Mr. Renfro said.

"Go to grass," said Miss Beulah. "And now you've told more than enough, haven't you?"

"What happened to Dearman?" asked Aunt Cleo.

"I sent him home," said Granny.

A long sigh travelled over the company, like the first intimations of departure.

"Poor Brother Bethune. His memory has tried to serve him one time too many, look at him," said Aunt Nanny.

"He may last. May last another go-round. May not last," said Aunt Birdie. "Poor Brother Bethune. I'm a little inclined to pinch him."

"Wake him up and see if he knows who's got him!" said Aunt Nanny.

"No, Mr. Willy Trimble's just as sound asleep as he is. Tilted right together, look at the picture. Foreheads kissing like something could run right out of one head and into the other one."

"And wouldn't it surprise them both if it did!"

"Nathan, what're you fixing to do to start us home? Blow or pray?" Uncle Noah Webster called.

Uncle Nathan slowly walked out from behind Granny's chair, where she sat all motionless. He raised his right hand. Then his arm jerked aside. His nose darkened the center of his face.

"Uh-oh," said Aunt Cleo. "He's fixing to go."

"He's fixing to go, right now!" cried Brother Bethune, jumping out of his sleep and coming as if to pounce.

Miss Beulah was ahead of him. Running, she caught hold of her eldest brother under his arms and let his head tumble into her breast. She planted her feet and stood propping him up.

"Don't try to speak a word," she said between her teeth. "Now don't be foolish. I've got you."

He jerked back his head and jerked open his mouth longways at her, but no sound came out. Neither did he seem to draw breath. Presently he leaned forward again and coughed.

"Do I see blood on his shirt?" asked Aunt Lexie.

"A little bite of watermelon," said Miss Beulah fiercely. "Get back if you don't know the difference." Moving her hand like one feeling her way, Miss Beulah patted Uncle Nathan on his great head of springing, doglike hair. Presently he raised his head and looked at her, gray-faced.

"Now what came over you?" she asked calmly. "You be quiet like I said. Don't jabber."

"Well, what's *he* got to hide?" asked a voice.

"Sister Cleo, I don't know what in the world ever guides your tongue into asking the questions it does!" Miss Beulah cried. "By now you ought to know this is a strict, law-abiding, God-fearing, close-knit family, and everybody in it has always struggled the best he knew how and we've all just tried to last as long as we can by sticking together."

Now Jack came up and put an arm around his uncle. "Every word Mama's saying is true, Uncle Nathan. You're back with us. You can feel comforted like I do." He looked into the old, dark-burned, age-stained face. "Some day, Uncle Nathan, I wish you'd tell it," he broke out. "What ever caused you to go off like that among strangers, and never stay still, and only let us see you at reunion time. You make me wonder tonight if what you had to do was as bad as aggravated battery."

"Whatever that is," said Miss Beulah in strong, prohibitive tones.

Uncle Nathan moved; he turned his shaggy head toward Jack and spoke. "Son, there's not but one bad thing either you or I or anybody else can do. And I already done it. That's kill a man. I killed Mr. Dearman with a stone to his head, and let 'em hang a sawmill nigger for it. After that, Jesus had to hold my hand."

"Now what did you want to tell that for?" said Miss Beulah shortly, her voice the only sound that was heard. "We could've got through one more reunion without that, couldn't we? Without you punishing yourself?"

But Uncle Nathan's face shone. It looked back at them like a dusty lantern lighted.

"Don't show us the stump! Don't show us that," came voices.

But he did. He took off his hand and showed them the

stump. There was good moonlight to see it by, white and clean with its puckered stitching like a flour sack's.

"Is that the hand that did it?" asked Miss Lexie behind his back. "Didn't he ever tell it before, Beulah? Didn't anybody know besides just you, you and Granny?"

"Lexie Renfro, he told Miss Julia Mortimer. And she told him, and I heard her: 'Nathan, even when there's nothing left to hope for, you can start again from there, and go your way and *be good*.' He took her exactly at her word. He's seen the world. And I'm not so sure it was good for him," said Miss Beulah.

Brother Bethune with a shocked face asked Uncle Nathan, "Why didn't you break down and tell the preacher, if you sinned that bad?"

"The preacher was Grandpa," said Uncle Nathan. Then he stalked back and stood in his place again, behind Granny's chair.

"Did it for Sam Dale," said Granny. She turned her head around and looked Uncle Nathan in the face.

Judge Moody, his face fixed, had watched him in dead silence. Uncle Nathan now returned his look but it was a moment before he seemed to place the Judge.

"You're journeying to Alliance," he said then. "I left Alliance this morning and walked *here*. I believe in the old method of travelling."

Miss Beulah took a step back and asked in horror, "Did you try to pay her one of your breakfast-time visits this morning, dear? Miss Julia Mortimer?"

"Jesus Lord told me not to," he said.

"You see a good reason why I told you not to harp on Dearman, Mr. Renfro?" Miss Beulah broke out.

But Mr. Renfro in his chair gave no answer. The only sound coming out of his open mouth was like dry seed being poured between two buckets, back and forth.

"Never said Sam Dale was the father," said Granny. She gave a minute nod at Judge Moody. "Going to marry the girl, I said. Think Sam Dale was pulling her out of a pickle."

"Granny!" Miss Beulah ran to the old lady. She picked up a church fan and fanned her.

"Granny, you're playing with us now, ain't you? With your grandchildren and all? With the reunion that's gathered round to celebrate the day with you?" Uncle Curtis stood and asked her.

"Hush. She wouldn't play with us about Sam Dale," said Miss Beulah. "She's saying things the way they come back to her at their own sweet will. Maybe she's not right in step with the rest of us any longer—that's all."

"Think he's pulling her out of a pickle," said Granny.

"Granny, which would you rather? Keep Sam Dale perfect, or let him be a father after all?" Miss Beulah asked, her voice pleading.

"It's not a matter we can settle by which we'd rather," said Judge Moody down a long sigh. "You can't change what's happened by taking a voice vote on it."

Miss Beulah begged. "Granny, you can't have Sam Dale both ways."

"And carry him a generous slice of my cake," Granny ordered her.

"Hey, don't she know the difference yet? Who's alive and who's dead?" asked Aunt Cleo in a nurse's whisper.

"She knows we're all part of it together, or ought to be!" Miss Beulah cried, turning on her. "That's more than some other people appear to have found out."

"You could be anybody's," said Mrs. Moody to Gloria. "My husband was speaking truer than he knew."

Gloria turned toward Granny.

"Don't make an ell's worth of difference, does it? If you're not Sam Dale's," said Granny, waving her away.

Jack held his arms out. He clasped Gloria as she threw herself against him. "She's Mrs. J. J. Renfro, that's who she is," he told the reunion. "Grandpa married us in Damascus Church and she's my wife, for good and all. And that's the long and the short of it."

He turned with her and they walked the short way down the steps into the yard and sat on the old cedar log in the moonlight and began looking at each other.

"There was a time, some years back, when I didn't deplore her presence here." Granny was speaking. "Mr. Vaughn is so much given to going out of sight to do his praying before we blow out the lamp. And she and I could set and catch our breath when the day's over, and confab a little about the state the world was in. She picked up a good deal from me."

"Who's that? Miss Julia Mortimer for the last time, Granny?" asked Aunt Birdie.

"Too bad she wasn't able to put two and two together," Granny said. "Like I did."

"But all that happened a mighty long time ago," Aunt Birdie objected during the hush that followed.

"You forget feelings, Birdie! Feelings don't get old!" Aunt Beck said, with all the night's agitation. "We do, but they don't. They go on."

In her soft yellow lamplight, Granny smiled, showing her teeth like a spoonful of honeycomb. "She was young herself once. And if she was, I was. Put that in your pipe and smoke it."

Uncle Nathan stepped down from them and went to his pack, which was still under the tree where he had dropped it. Groping in it, he brought up his cornet and readied it.

"Play 'Poor Wayfaring Stranger'!" came a call.

"Play 'Sweet and Low' for me!"

When they all stopped asking, he played them "Let the Lower Lights Be Burning." He needed nothing but his good left hand.

"Makes the hair of my skin stand on end. Like I was pulling okra," said Aunt Nanny. "To hear him reach with his horn like that."

"That's right, that's the way. Blow 'er over Jordan, Nathan," called Uncle Noah Webster. "Blow Miss Julia Mortimer over Jordan."

Uncle Nathan held the last note. He held it till none of them listening had any breath of their own left—then he ceased. Miss Beulah looked at Granny. So did they all. Though the hills were ringing still, Granny nodded in her chair.

Miss Beulah drew the lamp away from her face. One bit of brightness still gleamed about her—the silver wire of Grandpa's spectacles she had put away in her lap. There behind her, spread over her chair and ready to cloak her, was "The Delectable Mountains," known to be green and red and covered with its ninety-and-nine white sheep, but now a piece and puzzle of the dark.

Jack and Gloria sat side by side on the old cedar log, close together, their backs to the crowd. Around them, though they appeared not to know it, the girl cousins as if with one accord began stirring about, cleaning up after the day. They cleared off the tables, carried platters and watermelon plates and cloths back to the kitchen or the back porch. The cake of ice had disappeared, the lemonade tub had nothing left but hanging crusts of sugar and a pavement of seeds. From the complaint they made, there had been little left to feed the company dogs. The cows were calling, taking turns.

Presently Uncle Nathan passed close by the porch, going down into the yard carrying upright a hoe with rags draped about the blade in a sort of helmet. There was a cutting smell of coal oil where he walked. After a moment, a red torch shot up fire, moved; then an oval, cottony glow, like utterly soft sound, appeared in the dark—how close, how far, how high up or low down, was not easy for the eye to make sure. Then it went out, and appeared almost at once in a new place.

"We've lost him, I know, to the Book of Revelation," said Miss Beulah. "But once a year I feel like he still belongs to us. Right now, he's burning the caterpillar nests to finish up the day for the children."

Their eyes as they watched all reflected the fiery nests in dancing points.

"And at the same time, it's a hundred thousand bad little worms that's curled up and turned black for every touch he gives," said Aunt Birdie. "You can be thankful for that much deliverance."

Uncle Nathan carried his torch past Jack and Gloria as though he didn't see them. Neither did Jack and Gloria seem to know he went by. They sat without moving, kissing each other.

"Mr. Renfro, do you dream at all of what's coming next?" cried Miss Beulah.

He didn't move. Only, while they looked, the wilted snippet of traveller's joy slid out of his shirt pocket and dropped to the floor.

Granny, the moment she was touched, put up her head warily.

"The joining-of-hands!" Miss Beulah at her side put out the cry. "Everybody stand! It's time for the joining-of-hands!" She threw out her arms. "Where's Jack? Sometimes just making your circle will bring him in. Stand up, catch Granny, don't let her fall now! Pull up Brother Bethune before he's slipped clear down out of reach! Stand up! Judge Moody, stoop a little, catch hold of Elvie's hand. Mrs. Judge, I've got you." She shook Mr. Renfro and got a cry out of him. "Drag Nathan in where he belongs!" came her urgent voice. "Now, are we a circle?"

By now the chairs were pushed back out of the way and as many of the reunion as could worked themselves into a circle in the expanded space of the porch. The rest of them carried the circle down the steps and along the flower rows and around from tree to tree, taking in the well-piece and the log seat and the althea bush and the post with the Wayfarer's Bell on it, encompassing the tables and the bois d'arc tree.

"Are we a circle?" cried Miss Beulah again, and she struck off the note.

Then they had the singing of "Blest Be the Tie." There was only one really mournful voice—Judge Moody's.

"And will you give us the benediction, Brother Bethune?" cried Miss Beulah. "Are you fully awake?"

For a moment Brother Bethune tottered, but Vaughn caught him and held him by the waist to steady him. His arm shot into the air and his voice exploded: "God go with us all!"

"Amen," said the voices around the circle.

"Now," said Miss Beulah warningly, "would anybody care for a further bite before starting on their road?"

"I couldn't get another bite in me if you was to stand before me with gun loaded, Beulah," Uncle Dolphus said, leading a chorus of No's.

Uncle Noah Webster and Uncle Dolphus gave a brotherly shout together. Unregarded, a flower had opened on the shadowy maze of the cactus there on the porch with them.

"Well, I reckon that's what you've all been waiting for," said Miss Beulah.

"We scared it into blooming after all," said Aunt Birdie, sashaying towards its tub. Little groups in turn looked down in a ring at the spectacle, the deep white flower, a star inside a star, that almost seemed to return their gaze, like a member of the reunion who didn't invariably come when called. The fragrance, Aunt Beck said, was ahead of the tuberose.

Only Granny sat and stared rigidly before her.

"Leave her alone," said Uncle Curtis.

"Granny's almost a hundred," whispered Uncle Percy, trying to tiptoe going by her.

"Granny heard the Battle of Iuka. Heard the volleys," said Uncle Dolphus, circling around.

"Talked back to General Grant. Remembers the conversation," said Aunt Beck, pausing at the still chair.

"Mrs. Moody thinks she wants to say something," Miss Beulah said.

"You've produced a night-blooming cereus!" repeated Mrs. Moody. "I haven't seen one of those in years."

"Yes'm, whatever in the nation you called it, it bloomed," said Miss Beulah. "Even if it never does us the favor again."

"Wait on it a little longer and there'll be another one," said Uncle Noah Webster. "I love 'em when they smell sweet."

"And not a drop of precious water did I ever spare it," said Miss Beulah. "I reckon it must have thrived on going famished."

Not a groan but a long expenditure of breath was heard.

"I think Judge Moody had best be excused to bed," said Miss Beulah to Mrs. Moody, and she took one of the lamps and started inside. "That man's ready to drop."

Uncle Homer threw out an arm to keep Judge Moody from passing. "Oh, we're going to tend to that road better—wait till I get to be supervisor," he said. "Roads—mosquitoes— our many cemeteries—mad dogs—floods—I'll get my hands on all of 'em. Some day we'll even do something about that bridge. Though no use us fixing our end any better till they fix theirs!"

"Oscar, just beat your way around him," said Mrs. Moody, as she herself went stepping over the sleeping twins who lay entwined on the threshold of the passage, their twin peashooters pressing crosses into their naked chests.

"Here's the company room—be careful how you step," Miss Beulah's voice came from inside. "And don't bump your head. The only thing I still haven't offered you is my night-gown—could I help you to it through the door? It's fresh and it's cool—I starched it this morning—and the only one to my name. It's going on eleven years old."

"You didn't suppose I would *undress*, did you?" exclaimed Mrs. Moody's voice.

"Do you want to let Judge Moody tell you goodnight, Granny? He's bowing to you," said Mr. Renfro at the old lady's chair. "You remember Judge Moody."

"Thought I sent him to Coventry," Granny said.

Judge Moody slipped around her and followed his wife inside. His voice came out saying, "But if that's to be our bed, I'd like this one last baby carried away from it." When Miss Beulah returned to the porch she was holding her—it was Lady May, still dressed, and sound asleep. Gloria took her and carried her to a shadowy corner, out of the glare of the moonlight, and sat down with her, to watch the reunion go.

Mr. Willy Trimble came up to Granny. "Then keep a close watch on this young lady, folks," he said, putting his long, joker's face down beside Granny's unblinking one. "If she starts to cutting up and you-all don't want her, send for me and I'll come back after her and have her for mine."

All at once, and at the very end of her day, Granny decided to take off her hat. Elvie received it from her—it sank heavy as a setting hen in her small arms. She ran into the house with it, blowing on it, as though in its dust lived a spark.

Granny was staying.

"Now I got far to go. And no mule. And Willy Trimble has whispered in my ear I still got to turn around and get me back to the cemetery in the morning," said Brother Bethune. "I'm just good enough to get her into the ground," he said, after he'd found his gun. "She's still being a schoolteacher about it, up in Heaven. I'm the one she couldn't bring to school."

"Now you're paying for it," said Aunt Birdie.

"She tried. But she just couldn't lure me inside the school-house," Brother Bethune went on. "I went right along with my daddy where he's going and helped him preach. Sung the duets with him, standing on a chair. It was an outdoor life, and I don't see nothing wrong with it *yet*."

"All right. You gave us as good today as you knew how," Miss Beulah cried at him. "You can go if you want to."

"And I'll tell you what you can give me for coming. The surprise of a nice nanny goat tied to my front porch one moonlight night," Brother Bethune replied.

"Granny, when it comes around to your next birthday, do you want to invite Brother Bethune and give him another chance?" asked Miss Beulah.

"See him in Tophet first," said Granny.

"Granny's going to be my next girl," said Mr. Willy. "I lost me one girl this morning, but I believe I already found me another'n."

"Willy Trimble, if you come a step closer—!" cried Miss Beulah. "Didn't you feel your foot stepped on in 'Blest Be the Tie'?"

"And take that jade of yours off somewhere and leave her," Granny told him in dismissal. "She's been cropping my flowers."

Brother Bethune elected to keep Mr. Willy Trimble company. They rode off together with the gun pointing up like a mast on the wagon seat between them.

"And where do you think *you're* going?" Granny asked inside a circle of her grandsons. They bent above her, squatted before her, patted her knee, took her by the hand, tried to kiss her face.

"Are you trying to tell me you're leaving me too?" she asked.

"Granny, there's stock at home waiting to be fed, and bawling, no doubt," Uncle Curtis said gently.

"Then what are you running off for?" asked the old lady.

The great-grandchildren were already loading up the wagons and finally mended cars. "Love you a bushel and a peck, Granny. Many happy returns!" One by one her great-grandchildren began putting kisses on Granny's face. They walked off from her carrying their own children stretched out in their arms, or hauled up over their shoulders, arms and legs dangling, little girls' hair streaming silver. Children that had barely waked up carried children still asleep. The whistled-up dogs flowed at their heels.

"Who're you trying to get away from?" asked Granny. "Come back here."

"Go if you must, but you can't get away without these!" Miss Beulah shrieked.

At some moment during the day she had found time to run out and cut the remainder of her own flowers against their departure. She was ready to load everybody home. Here was the duplication of what they'd come bringing here—milk-and-wine lilies, zinnias, phlox, tuberoses.

"Who's running off with my posies?" asked Granny.

Now the uncles were shaking hands with each other and with Mr. Renfro, then Jack.

"Well, we brought you, Jack. We brought you back home," said Uncle Curtis.

"And my wife and I are much obliged to one and all," said Jack.

"I should say on the whole, Jack, we let you back in the ranks of the family pretty easy today. Didn't make it too hard on you," said Uncle Dolphus.

"If only he didn't have in-the-morning to go through with!" cried Aunt Birdie.

"He's young!" said Aunt Beck.

"Stay," Granny said.

"And little-old Gloria! We made you really and truly one of us today," said Aunt Birdie, kissing her good-bye. "You can always be grateful, and show it as well as you can."

"You're one of the family now, Gloria, tried and true. Do you know what that means? Never mind! You're just an old married woman, same as the rest of us now. So you don't have to answer to the outside any longer," Aunt Beck said, putting an arm around her.

"Just put that dress away more careful when you take it off tonight. They can bury you in it, child," said Aunt Birdie. "Put yours away like I did."

"If it'd been my dress, it'd stayed deep down in its trunk today! If I'd get my wedding dress out and try wearing it again in front of this crowd, I'd expect you all to fall into a hard fit of laughing," said Miss Beulah, trying to persuade Aunt Nanny down the steps.

"I'll tell you something," said Aunt Nanny with what looked like pride. "If my wedding dress could talk, I'd burn it."

"Reckon Lady May's got just one little word? One little word to say about it all before we go?" Aunt Birdie cried into the oblivious face.

"Nothing ever wakes her but the sun coming up and feeling the fresh pangs of hunger," said Gloria.

"I never said I wanted you to go," Granny said.

"Here's one that's staying till tomorrow," said Miss Lexie. "Because I want to see the behavior. I'd like to see 'em finish what they started today."

"And because starting with tonight you got nowhere to go," said Miss Beulah. "Unless you happen to worship sleeping between Ella Fay and Etoyle."

Miss Beulah stood accepting their thanks. "Fay, I was crazy about you at one time," she told her. "Because you weren't Lexie. And look what's happened to you. You're Homer's wife." They put their tired arms around each other.

"Miss, you must wear stockings on your arms when you work in the field," said Aunt Cleo, pinching Ella Fay's shoulder. "Or they'd never be white in the moonlight like that."

"That's one secret you guessed, Aunt Cleo," said Etoyle.

"How old is Ella Fay getting to be?"

"She'll be seventeen on Groundhog Day next year," said Miss Beulah.

"Why's she hanging back?"

"Now from what? I thought you were on your way!" cried Miss Beulah.

"Sister Beulah, let me inquire, have you ever been into the deep subject with Ella Fay?" Aunt Cleo kept on.

"Listen, will you tell us good-bye and crank up?"

"Truly I mean it. You've got a growing girl on your hands."

"I'd as soon start worrying over Vaughn!" said Miss Beulah violently.

"Her *feet* are growing," said Mr. Renfro.

"My mama never went into the deep subject with me. And

you know what? I've always felt a little sorry for myself," remarked Auntie Fay, waiting now up inside the chicken van.

"But I haven't been told what the commotion is all about," said Granny. "What the headlong rush is for."

"Bless your heart, Granny Vaughn! Good-bye, good-bye, Jack! Brought you home by all of us working together, didn't we? Good-bye, Beulah, sweet dreams, Mr. Renfro. Ain't you growing faster than ever, Ella Fay?" Uncle Homer was hugging the Renfro girls. "I swear, Ella Fay, I wouldn't be surprised if we couldn't find a way when Tuesday dawns to let you vote."

"Hush up! She don't even want to," said Miss Beulah. "My children have learned to wait for everything till it's the right time for them to have it. Wish somebody'd taken the time and trouble to teach a few of their elders that lesson."

"Jack'll go on working the rest of his life to pay for that roof," said Uncle Noah Webster with a mighty slap of congratulation on Mr. Renfro's back. "You've got an acre of tin up there. It'll take it all the rest of the night to cool off." He gave Jack a fierce smile and wrung his hand as if he couldn't stop. Then he smacked Gloria's cheek with a last big kiss that smelled of watermelon. "Gloria, this has been a story on us all that never will be allowed to be forgotten," he said. "Long after you're an old lady without much further stretch to go, sitting back in the same rocking chair Granny's got her little self in now, you'll be hearing it told to Lady May and all her hovering brood. How we brought Jack Renfro back safe from the pen! How you contrived to send a court judge up Banner Top and caused him to sit at our table and pass a night with the family, wife along with him. The story of Jack making it home through thick and thin and into Granny's arms for her biggest and last celebration—for so I have a notion it is. Eh, Nathan?" He raised his arm high to salute the oldest brother. "I call this a reunion to remember, all!" he called through the clamoring goodnights. "Do you hear me, blessed sweethearts?" He swung over to Granny's chair and folded his arms around her, not letting her go, begging for a kiss, not getting it.

"Benedict Arnold," she whispered. Then as Aunt Cleo came to pull him away, Granny spoke to her too, and said, "But I'll give you a pretty not to take him."

"Remember, there's a South Mississippi too!" Uncle Noah Webster called when they were both up inside the cranked car. "It ain't all that far on a pretty day!" He leaned out and looked back at them while he drove away. They could see the gleam of his homesick smile beneath the crossed-pistols mustache.

"Now we know that nothing in the world can change Noah Webster," said Miss Beulah. "Even the one he's picked."

"Oh, Grandpa Vaughn, if only you'd lived to see!" Aunt Birdie said, hugging Jack. "Jack, listen, when you went to the pen, it's just about what carried Grandpa off, precious!"

"Mr. Vaughn never knows when it's bedtime. Have to go out there with a lantern and prod him again," Granny said.

"Listen. Thunder," said Aunt Beck. "Did I hear distant thunder?"

"I don't believe it," said Uncle Dolphus bluntly. "By now I'm not ready to be fooled by any more of folks' imagination. It ain't ever going to rain." He shook hands with Mr. Renfro. "But your hay's just aching to be cut. You're about to realize you one crop in spite of yourself, Mr. Renfro." The horn of the pickup was bleating out there; all the children were packed back inside. He hugged Miss Beulah and bent to say good-night to his grandmother.

"Now I once thought I had a *big* family," said Granny. "What's happening to 'em?"

"Come see us!" came calls as the pickup started off on its freshly patched tire to Harmony. "Come before Old Man Winter's broke loose and we all have to try to keep from going out of sight in mud!"

"Shame on ye. *Shame* on ye," said Granny, as their dust began to rise.

"I've still got a craving under my breastbone for a little more of that chicken pie, Beck," Aunt Nanny said as they parted.

"You'll have to wait for next year."

"Then good-bye, good-bye! Good-bye, Jack boy—kiss that baby for me. Good-bye, Beulah, and sweet dreams, Judge Moody in there! I'm too tired out from laughing to climb up in my car and go home. Help me, Jack," Aunt Nanny gasped.

"All I need to do is start," said Uncle Percy, holding up

his new twelve-link chain he'd whittled. Then in their cloud of ghostly dust they were gone.

"Remember to look on Banner Top when you get to the road!" called Etoyle, running after them, waving. "If you want to see what'll keep you laughing all the way to Peerless!"

"Granny will be all right in the morning," said Aunt Beck, putting her arms around Miss Beulah. "When she thinks back on today she'll wish she could have it to live all over again." She smiled on Gloria. "And you don't want to be another one any longer, not another schoolteacher, do you, Gloria? And change the world?"

"No ma'am, just my husband. I still believe I can do it, if I live long enough," Gloria said.

Uncle Curtis hugged Granny without words. She kissed him—then saw him leave her anyway.

"I don't know who I've thought about more times today than I have Grandpa. Blessed Grandpa!" said Aunt Beck, softly patting Granny's cheek, then tiptoeing away.

"Don't listen to him," said Granny. "Listen to me."

She watched the old Chevrolet hauler, loaded with so many people that it was almost dragging the ground, go down into the dust, the last one.

"Parcel of thieves! They'd take your last row of pins. They'd steal your life, if they knew how," Granny said.

"Granny, don't you know who dearly loves you?" Miss Beulah asked, clasping her. "Don't you remember the hundred that's been with you all day? Giving you pretties, striving to please you—"

"Thieves all," said Granny.

Uncle Nathan kissed Granny on the forehead, the little vein throbbing there. He was to sleep outdoors under his tent. He declared he preferred it.

"But I don't want to lose ye," said Granny after him into the night.

After Uncle Nathan had gone, only Miss Lexie was left of all the day's company.

"Would you stay with me, please?" Granny asked Miss Lexie. "My children have deserted me."

But Miss Lexie seemed not to hear, staring at the old cactus where another and still another bloom drifted white upon the dark. "Yes, and those'll look like wrung chickens' necks in the morning," she said. "No thank you." She went inside.

"Now, many happy returns of the day, Granny Vaughn," said Mr. Renfro, bending to her cheek, but she only let his kiss touch her little withering ear.

"Suppose something had happened to me while you gapped," she said, and he bowed his way inside.

When nothing of them was left out there but their dust behind them, Granny still summoned them. "Thieves, murderers, come back," she begged. "Don't leave me!" Her voice cracked.

Jack knelt at the foot of the rocker and looked up at her face. Presently her head was brought down. Then she saw he was there. For a little while she gazed at him.

"They told me," she said, her voice barely strong enough to reach him, "you'd gone a long time ago. Clean away. But I didn't believe their words. I sat here like you see me—I waited. A whole day is a long wait. You've found Granny just where you left her. You sneaked back when nobody's looking, forged your way around 'em. That's a good boy."

Jack held still under her eyes. Nobody made a sound except Lady May in her mother's arms, who sent up a short murmur out of her dream.

Granny lifted both her little trembling hands out of her lap and took something out of her bosom. She held it before her, cupped in her hands, then carried it toward him. Her face was filled with intent that puckered it like grief, but her moving hands denied grief. Then, in the act of bending toward him, she forgot it all. Her hands broke apart to struggle toward his face, to take and hold his face there in front of her. It was the little silver snuffbox that Captain Jordan in his lifetime had come by, that had been Granny's to keep for as long as anybody could remember, that rolled across the floor and down into the folds of the cannas.

Jack let her trembling fingers make sure they'd found him, move over his forehead, down his nose, across his lips, up his cheek, along the ridge of his brow, let them trace every hill and valley, let them wander. He still had not blinked once when her fingers seemed to forget the round boundaries belonging to flesh and stretched over empty air.

Jack rose and put his arms around her. Miss Beulah said, "It's her bed she wants!" and swung up the lamp and led the way. Jack lifted the old lady to her feet, she gasped, and then he picked her up in his arms. He carried her, her bare head drooped quiet against his chest, down the passage to where Miss Beulah waited holding the lamp at the open door.

Later, an arm stretched out of the dark of the passage with some starched gowns and folded mosquito netting laid over a load of quilt.

"Thank you, Mama," said Jack, receiving it.

Gloria sat in Granny's rocker and undressed the sleeping baby. She raised the little arms one at a time and pulled her out of her sleeves. She shucked her out of her petticoat and little drawers and lifted her by her two feet and changed her.

"She's a sweet, trustful little thing. I believe altogether she enjoyed this day more than anybody," Jack said, gazing.

"Do you know what? You fell in love with this baby," Gloria told him. "I watched you do it."

"What a little hugger! And I believe she's going to be smart too."

"She's our future, Jack. I wish you'd look at your baby's bites! Her whole little body's given over," Gloria said. "She looks like she's been embroidered in French knots. Those are what she got going through it all with her daddy." She popped the baby's nightgown over her head. When the little cockscomb came out at the top, Jack laughed.

"I see her new tooth in her little objecting mouth," he said, and then kissed the baby good-night.

Gloria rose and stilled the rocker till it stood like a throne and laid the baby down in it. She opened out the length of mosquito netting and with one fling spread it over Lady May, chair, and all.

Then she took first turn undressing in the dark passage and putting on her gown, and while Jack did the same she ran on quick bare feet to the quilt, flung it wide, and spread it on the floor. Dropping to her knees she patted it perfectly free of wrinkles. It was ready by the time Jack in his gown came running out, catching all the moonlight down his front, and before she could get her hand over his mouth he had given his holler.

The pallet seemed thinner than paper, and was already the warmth of the floor underneath. Long since faded, blanched again tonight by moonlight, it showed a pattern as faint as one laid by wind over a field of broomsedge. It was the quilt that had baked on the line all day, and its old winter cleanness mixed with today's dust penetrated their very skins with a smell strong as medicine. There was no pillow to spare for this bed, no up and down to it.

A female voice, superfine, carrying but thin as a moonbeam, strung itself out into the night: "Ay-ay-ay-cock!"

"I can't help thinking about my luck," said Jack in a hoarse whisper. "I'm a married man and Aycock ain't. And suppose I was in his place!"

"Don't let it go to your head," Gloria said and laid her palm there. His forehead was as burning as Lady May's, and under the bridge of her hand his eyes shone unevenly moonlit.

"Gloria, we won our day," said Jack.

There was a secret sound, something that rasped on the ear over and over like the chirp of a late cricket. In the company room, Judge Moody was winding his watch.

"We've still got in-the-morning, Jack. The Moodys are in our bed," Gloria reminded him in a whisper.

"They've beat us to that," he said. "They got there first."

"Your school diploma is nailed up over their heads. It's all we've got, because our wedding license is burned up along with the rest of the courthouse."

"Our courthouse caught afire?" he exclaimed. "Why wasn't I home! I'd helped 'em put it out."

"My son in the pen," Miss Beulah's voice said, travelling up the passage from the dark bedroom. "My son had to go to the pen."

Jack's head rolled away from Gloria's. "Mama must've been up and at it today for 'most as long as I have," he said presently. "She's bone tired."

"She'll forget what she's saying to your daddy," Gloria promised him. "She's old. She'll soon be asleep, just like he will."

"I wish I could do something for the boy," Mr. Renfro's voice said.

"Not something foolish," said Miss Beulah's.

"I'd do anything in the world to help that boy and his pride," came Mr. Renfro's voice.

"That didn't keep you from putting-out for Judge Moody," said Miss Beulah's.

"I took a shine to the fellow, you're right. I couldn't tell you why," Mr. Renfro's voice agreed. "I just did, that's all. If he'd stay a week, I'd take him turkey-hunting."

"And call it helping Jack?"

"I'd like to help 'em both out, Mother. If I was a little younger, I believe I could help both of 'em at the same time."

"I tried getting home before today," Jack whispered, head still turned to the outdoors. "Don't let on to Mama, to make her feel worse. The day I got there, I started trying finding a way. When I heard about our baby, I went out stooping, went through a watermelon field. Stooping—like I was thumping melons from row to row to find us boys a good one. At the last minute I stooped low out of there, but they knew that trick. Don't tell Mama how easy they caught me—it would break her heart. I put in all my time and every bit of my thinking on the subject. I tried for the reunion last year. They caught me."

"I don't see how they charged all that up to good behavior," Gloria whispered.

"Today was my last chance of making my escape. I took it. One more day, and I'd had to let 'em discharge me."

"Of course the boy didn't do what Nathan did," said Mr. Renfro's voice.

"I've got it to stand and I've got to stand it. And you've got to stand it," said Miss Beulah's voice. "After they've all gone home, Ralph, and the children's in bed, that's what's left. Standing it."

Jack turned to Gloria.

"Say now you'll love 'em a little bit. Say you'll love them too. You can. Try and you can." He stroked her. "Wouldn't you like to keep Mama company in the kitchen while I'm ploughing or fence-mending, give her somebody she can talk to? And encourage Ella Fay to blossom out of being timid, and talk Elvie out of her crying and wanting to grow up and be a teacher? You can give Etoyle ladylike examples of behavior. And on bad winter evenings, there's Vaughn. All you need to do with him is answer his questions. Honey, won't you change your mind about my family?"

"Not for all the tea in China," she declared.

"Once it's winter, Papa just wants to put up his foot and see pictures in the fire. You could crack his pecans for him, perched there on the hearth. And there's precious little Granny—I asked her when I told her good-night if *she* wouldn't love *you* and she said she would, she nodded."

"You're so believing and blind," Gloria said. "About *all* of 'em—they don't even have to be girls."

"The whole reunion couldn't help but love you—the prettiest one of 'em and still looking just like a bride."

"They didn't hesitate to wash my face in their sticky watermelon juice!"

"Poor face," he said tenderly, drawing his hand down her cheek, turning her face to his.

"What they said was we'd been too loving before we got married!"

"And if we hadn't, I'd like 'em to tell me when we'd had another chance at it!" he burst out.

"They tried making me your cousin, and almost did."

"Be my cousin," he begged. "I want you for my cousin. My wife, and my children's mother, and my cousin and everything."

"Jack, I'll be your wife with all my heart, and that's enough for anybody, even you. I'm here to be nobody but myself, Mrs. Gloria Renfro, and have nothing to do with the old dead past. And don't ever try to change me," she cautioned him.

"I know this much: I don't aim to get lonesome no more. Once you do, it's too easy to stay that way," said Jack.

"I'll keep you from it," she vowed.

"And you'd better."

"Jack, the way I love you, I have to hate everybody else."

"Possum!" he said. "I ain't asking you to deprive others."

"I want to."

"Spare 'em a little bit of something else," he pleaded.

"Maybe I'll learn after a long time to pity 'em instead."

"They'll take it a good deal harder!" he cried.

She drew still closer to him.

"Don't pity anybody you could love," whispered Jack.

"I can think of one I can safely pity."

"Uncle Nathan? Love him."

"Miss Julia."

"I know she hated to breathe her last," he said slowly. "As much as you and me would." He took her hand.

"Are you trying to say you could do better than pity her?" Gloria asked him. "You never laid eyes on her."

"I reckon I even love her," said Jack. "I heard her story."

"She stands for all I gave up to marry you. I'd give her up again tonight. And give up all your family too," she whispered, and felt him quiver.

"Don't give anybody up." He stroked her. "Or leave anybody out. Me and you both left her out today, and I'm ashamed for us."

"There just wasn't room in today for it," she said. "Or for feeling ashamed either."

He said, "There's room for everything, and time for everybody, if you take your day the way it comes along and try not to be much later than you can help. We could go yet, and be back by milking time. There's still the same good reason."

She put her mouth quickly on his, and then she slid in her hand and seized hold of him right at the root. And so she convinced him that there is only one way of depriving the ones you love—taking your living presence away from theirs; that no one alive has ever deserved such punishment, although maybe the dead do; and that no one alive can ever in honor forgive that wrong, which outshines shame, and is not to be forgiven until it has been righted.

Moonlight the thickness of china was lying over the world now. The Renfro wagon stood all alone where the school bus used to stand, muleless, empty, its spoked iron wheels clear-cut as the empty pods of fallen flowers. The shadows of the trees stretched downhill, lengthened as if for flight.

"You'll never get away from me again," Gloria whispered. "Not in your wildest dreams."

She reached for Jack's hand. It was hot as the day, with calluses like embedded rocks. It was fragrant of sweat, car grease, peach pickle, chicken, yellow soap, and her own hair. But it was dead weight, with fingers hanging limp as the strands of wilted weed that dangled through the crack in Mr. Willy Trimble's wagon. She stroked his lips and they moved at her touch and opened. He let out a snore. Everything love had sworn and done seemed to be already gone from him. Even its memory was a measure away from him and from her too, as apart as the cereus back there in its tub, that was itself almost a stranger now, having lifted those white trumpets.

Vaughn thought the house was asleep, but for a little distance as he rode away he listened behind him—he might still hear his name called after him. For a year and a half it had been "Vaughn! Vaughn!" every minute, though it would turn before he knew it back into "Jack!" again.

Or would it? Had today been all brave show, and had Jack all in secret fallen down—taking the whole day to fall, but falling, like that star he saw now, going out of sight like the scut of a rabbit? Could Jack take a fall from highest place and nobody be man enough to say so? Was falling a secret, another part of people's getting tangled up with each other, another danger to walk up on without warning—like finding them lying deep in the woods together, like one creature, some kind of cricket hatching out of the ground, big enough to eat him or to rasp at him and drive him away? The world had been dosed with moonlight, it might have been poured from a bottle. Riding through the world, the little boy, moonlit, wondered.

Grandpa Vaughn's hat came down low and made his ears stick out like funnels. Over and under the tired stepping of Bet, he could hear the night throb. He heard every sound going on, repeating itself, increasing, as if it were being recollected by loud night talking to itself. At times it might have been the rush of water—the Bywy on the rise in spring; or it might have been the rains catching up after them, to mire them in. Or it might have been that the whole wheel of the sky made the sound as it kept letting fall the soft fire of its turning. As long as he listened, sound prevailed. No matter

how good at hollering back a boy might grow up to be, hollering back would never make the wheel stop. And he could
never out-ride it. As he plodded on through the racket, it rang
behind him and was ahead of him too. It was all-present
enough to spill over into voices, as everything, he was ready
to believe now, threatened to do, the closer he might come
to where something might happen. The night might turn into
more and more voices, all telling it—bragging, lying, singing,
pretending, protesting, swearing everything into being, swearing everything away—but telling it. Even after people gave up
each other's company, said good-bye and went home, if there
was only one left, Vaughn Renfro, the world around him was
still one huge, soul-defying reunion.

Bet twitched her ears when he rode her out into Banner
Road. In the moonlight the car on Banner Top looked like a
big, shadowy box mysteriously deposited there at the foot of
the tree, not to be opened till morning. For a moment, he
thought he heard somebody up there, moving. He thought
he saw men flitting in the moonlight, like bats—he thought
he could see the ears of Ears Broadwee.

He could have shouted when he saw the school bus again,
peacefully stranded in the ditch.

He trotted downhill to it, reined in. He slid from Bet's
back. Then with the chain he'd brought he hitched her to the
bus, took her around the neck, and led her; and without the
slightest fuss about it, there in the moonlight the bus creaked
once, rose out of its berth, and surfaced to the road.

"Without Jack, nothing would be no trouble at all."
Vaughn spoke it out. He laid his hand on the radiator, with
its armor of moonlit scorch and rust, warm as a stove in which
the fire has been banked all day. He carried well water to it
in Grandpa's hat. Climbing in through the still-open door, he
took the steering wheel. It was warm and sticky as his own
hands. He coasted the bus the rest of the way down the first
hill, and before it reached the bottom up came a froglike
chirping, then a sound like a slide of gravel, then bang, bang,
bang—the engine was running for Vaughn just as any engine
in the world ought to do.

If it would be morning now! He thought of tomorrow with
such sharp pain that he might have just been asked to give it

up. He so loved Banner School that he would have beaten sunup and driven there now, if the doors had had any way of opening for him.

Gritting his teeth, he backed the bus up again, far enough to turn in at his own road, accomplishing the drop and hurdle of the ditch.

The row of bois d'arc trees that lined the home road stirred like birds in their feathers in the moonlight. Some of the trunks were four or five trunks sprouted from one old stump, fused now into one, like a rope swollen barrel-thick. Where the big split stump was like two bears dancing, he turned off to the best hiding place he knew. A little way off from the truck, pale oaks hid the moon; heads of stars like elderberry bloom filled the space between the trees. He cut off the engine. Very loud and close he heard:

> "Who cooks for you?
> Who cooks for me?
> AHA HA HA HA HA HA HA!"

He saw the owl sitting in a dead sycamore that had become a wreath of moonlight.

Biting mosquitoes were everywhere; he plucked them from his breast like thorns. But he kept one hand on the steering wheel. The bus, as long as he held the wheel, held him all around, and at the same time he could feel that bus on its own wheels rolling on his tongue, like a word of his own ready to be spoken, then swallowed back into his throat, going down, inside and inside. And at the same time, the sky that he could see went on performing—more stars fell, like a breaking chain.

Before he left the bus here, ready and secret till morning, he made sure of the book he had been sitting on, the new geography that he'd traded out of Curly Stovall. He dragged it to his cheek, where he could smell its print, sharper, blacker, dearer than the smell of new shoes.

Then he got on Bet when she caught up with him and rode her on home. He rode Bet to the barn and attended to her, and rounded the house for the water bucket.

Down past the empty tables, he saw the Wayfarer's Bell against the stars, elevated and gathered into itself. It was just

as ever, but nobody was lost any more. Might it give sound
of its own accord on some night like this? It was the one voice
that hadn't spoken. Vaughn's heart quailed. The Wayfarer's
Bell would not speak in silver like the rest of the night. It was
iron, with an iron tongue, and it would say "Iron"—and go
on saying it, go reaching with it all over the world. Though
no one was lost any more, there could be no bell that does
not say "I will ring again."

Uncle Nathan's tent was under the pecan tree like a pair of
big black-spread wings that had dipped near to the ground to
hover there all night. Among all who slept here slept one who
had killed a man. But he might not be asleep. Perhaps Uncle
Nathan never slept.

Vaughn went to the water bucket, and the dipper rattled in
it—it was empty. He climbed the steps, and there lay Jack and
Gloria asleep on the porch, in his way. They were lying one
behind the other in running positions. Though they lay perfectly still, they looked like race runners all the same. Jack's
head was thrown back, but Gloria was in front. He had never
before seen her barefooted, much less asleep—now he saw her
blistered heels. The moonlight lay on her back-flung hair like
ashes over coals. He stepped over Jack and waded through
the moonlight around her forward, unshielded arm. Had she
still counted as a teacher, had she not married Jack, it would
have said in her voice: "I am not asleep." He could smell
their sweat—it went against his face as would the moist palm
of a hand. Then he saw—the smell must be coming from the
flowers. They looked like big clods of the moonlight freshly
turned up from this night—almost phosphorescent. All of him
shied, as if a harness had bloomed.

Veering, he almost collided with the baby. He had forgotten
there was a baby. She was lying up over the sleepers in the
hide seat of Granny's rocker, with something gauzy wrapped
around her, as though she'd been in that spokey cart clear to
the moon and back.

He got by her, and his shirt-tail brushed the spokes of
Granny's spinning wheel, which by daylight's gloom stood
like a part of the wall but was now lit up. It softly struck like
a clock. He tiptoed into the now moonlit passage. A nail
nailing its shadow to a high board was where Uncle Noah

Webster's banjo always hung before he went to live with Aunt
Cleo. There the loom stood, open to the night like the never-
closed-in passage itself. The moon picked out its spider web.
It looked as tall as Banner bridge, and better made, stretching
from the old loom to the ceiling of the passage. His mother's
broom tore it down every morning, it was back new every
night.

But here, with people on every side and behind every door,
no more voices came—only knocks, night-sounds. Even from
the heart of the house no sound came now except the beat,
beat that was given off by the swifts in the chimney, where
they stirred and shifted, a hundred deep or more.

Then all of a sudden there came through the passage a current of air. A door swung open in Vaughn's face and there
was Granny, tiny in her bed in full lamplight. For a moment
the black bearskin on the floor by the bed shone red-haired,
live enough to spring at him. After the moonlight and the
outdoors, the room was as yellow and close as if he and
Granny were embedded together in a bar of yellow soap.

"Take off your hat," Granny's mouth said. "And climb in
wi' me."

He fled out of her dazzled sight. "She didn't know who I
was," he told himself, running. And then, "She didn't care!"

He ran on, onto the back porch and past moonlit Elvie
reigning on her cot, and forgetting the kitchen where there
might be water in the bucket, he stumbled out of the house
and ran for the barn. He got himself inside, met the old smells
thick as croker sacks hanging from the rafters, so thick he
seemed to have to part them with his arms. He heard Bet still
feeding, saw the dark shape of the broken buggy, which the
muffled clucking of nesting hens seemed to be moving on oars
down the night. The stall was full of the electrical memory of
Dan the horse, the upper regions full of Grandpa Vaughn's
prayers. Granny's side saddle hung on the wall in the dark,
invisible but in its place, and he saw it in his mind, the leather
crumbling and flaking like sycamore bark. Brother Bethune's
mule had found his way to the Renfro barn; Vaughn saw the
whites of his eyes, but they were to him only the extra eyes
of confusion, and he pulled himself up the ladder into the

loft. While saying his prayers, he tumbled over from his knees and was asleep before his forehead rolled on the floor.

Silent as the pulse itself that went beating on through sleep, there was lightning deep in the south, like the first pink down in the kindling—only a muscle that moved, like a bird in the net. A sky-wide stretch of cottony cloud came up and spread itself, so it appeared, under the moon, pallet-like. A different air streamed slowly toward the house and stirred the moon-struck nightgowns on the porch.

The cloud showed motion within, like an old transport truck piled high with crate on crate of sleepy white chickens. The moon, like an eye turned up in a trance, filmed over and seemed to turn loose from its track and to float sightless. First floating veils, then coarse dark tents were being packed across the sky, then the heavy, chained-together shapes humped after them.

Lightning branched and ran over the world with an insect lightness. Eventually, thunder followed. A ragged cloud ran in front, the moon was round for a minute longer, like a berry in the open beak of a bird, then it was swallowed.

Then thunder moved in and out of the house freely, like the voice of Uncle Noah Webster come back to say once more, "Good-night, blessed sweethearts."

Then the new roof resounded with all the noise of battle. With the noise and the smell as sudden as from water being poured into a smoking skillet, in the black dark it began to rain. Miss Beulah, who sprang up as at the alarm of fire, ran through the house slamming everything tight shut, company room included. Elvie, perhaps in her sleep, rose long enough to set two cedar buckets outside on the back steps.

Jack and Gloria never stirred.

Hearing what sounded like great treads going over her head, the baby opened her eyes. She put her voice into the fray, and spoke to it the first sentence of her life: "What you huntin', man?"

Miss Beulah ran out onto the porch, snatched up the baby, and ran with her back to her own bed, as if a life had been saved.

Part 6

"GRANNY'S SLEEPING her little head off this morning," said Miss Beulah, running around the kitchen table, where Mr. Renfro, the Renfro girls, Miss Lexie, and Uncle Nathan were eating breakfast by lamplight.

"Paying for yesterday," said Miss Lexie.

"Rewarding herself! Getting a good start on ninety-one!" Miss Beulah corrected her.

"I got my own pants back," said Jack, coming in. Yesterday's shirt was tucked inside, with the starch gone but with most of the dust cracked out of it. He was steering Gloria to the table. A sober-looking Lady May trotted at their heels.

"Jack Renfro, look at you! What's the matter with your blessed eye!" Miss Beulah shrieked.

"Mama, it's just something that happened to it down in the road—away back yesterday, as long ago as before dinner. I can still see out of the other one."

"That's the one to mind out for this morning, when you rush back in," she said, helping his plate from the hot skillet.

Lady May stood up to the table, not tall enough to see, but she could reach plates.

"Where's Judge and Mrs. Judge? Still enjoying the company bed?" asked Jack.

"Why, Vaughn's gone in the wagon to carry 'em to Banner Top," said Miss Beulah. "You never saw two people in so great a hurry. You'd think, after being forgiven in front of a hundred, after eating the most chicken, sleeping all night in the weightiest featherbed in my house—you'd think they'd feel beholden enough, those blessed Moodys, to eat as hearty a breakfast as they could swallow? Not on your life. I fried up every morsel I had left over to spread company breakfast, and they didn't deign. They left it for you."

Ella Fay laughed. She was all excitement and clattering feet this morning. "You ought to have seen Judge Moody hop right over your nose, Jack!"

"I didn't hear him go hop," said Jack, softly into Gloria's ear. It was brightly exposed. This morning her load of hair,

810

straight as a poker, was carried all on top of her head, close-packed as a fine loaf.

"You was dreaming! Till I took pity on you and shook water on both your faces," said Miss Beulah, nodding to their faces, held cheek-together. "But Vaughn had to hitch the wagon and trot 'em there, they wouldn't wait."

"Why, there's still plenty of time. Both me and Curly got to milk," said Jack. "What drove 'em?"

"It's raining, son," said Mr. Renfro. "Getting pretty slick up there."

"And is that the whole story?" Miss Beulah cried at him.

"Your own daddy's another one that didn't wait on you, Jack," said Miss Lexie.

Miss Beulah put the biscuit pan in Mr. Renfro's face. "All those poor souls down in Banner Cemetery must've thought it was Judgment Day last night. Bang! Right over their heads. I bet you succeeded in waking your own father—for long enough to disappoint him, anyway."

"It would have taken a better job than that to wake Grandpa Vaughn," Miss Lexie retorted. "If he was as wedded as Papa to the Sounding of the Trumpet, he was a lot more of the disposition to sleep through it. Bang, bang, bang, indeed I heard it."

Jack said, with his cheek against Gloria's, "I don't remember the least bang."

"Well, it wasn't the bang I wanted," said Mr. Renfro. "I forgot to cap my fuse. And right to this minute, I can't think of a good reason for it."

"Papa," cried Jack, "what's this story you're telling me, sir?"

"Though for one thing, my fuse was a little dried, a little caked—at the time I played it out, I was critical of it," Mr. Renfro went on. "Results was a little beneath what I'd term my standard."

"Who told you to try it at all?" Miss Beulah cried.

"I did nick the old cedar to a certain extent, son," said Mr. Renfro. "You ought to find when you get there I made it a little bit easier for you to start out this morning."

"*Sir?*" cried Jack.

"You'd *better* start worrying. Didn't you *hear* your daddy setting off that blast in the night?" cried Miss Beulah. "What's getting wrong with your ears, now?"

"I reckon that's about when I dreamed I was behind the wheel of my truck," Jack said. "Aycock didn't show too strong an objection?"

"He was enough trouble just being there," said Mr. Renfro. "I don't harm a neighbor, you know. I've learned by my time of life you've got to go a little slower than you would be inclined, because wherever you put your foot down there's a fool like Aycock that don't know enough not to keep out of your way."

Vaughn whirled in on them, raindrops flying. "The car's still there and Banner Top's still there, but their looks are ruined. You can't see the worst till it gets good day," he cried. He was back in his knee pants.

"I didn't even rise up when it started to raining," said Jack to Gloria.

"You missed the racket on the new roof?" cried Vaughn. "I give up."

"Well, don't sit down—you haven't got time to eat breakfast, Vaughn Renfro. Scoot! Up, the rest of you children! You've got your chores to finish and then school to track for, and Vaughn's got the teacher to tell he's misput the bus. There's only one new pair of shoes to be ruined, there's a mercy."

"Think how many's waiting on that bus to come along and pick 'em up this first morning. Well, they'll give up, sooner or later, and walk to school like I did," said Miss Lexie. "Do 'em that much more good."

"Vaughn'll catch a whipping at the door. I'll give him one myself when he gets back this evening, with a little extra for the hay he's lost his daddy," said Miss Beulah.

"If everybody hadn't wanted the gathering and all to wait on Jack!" Vaughn cried. "I could have had the hay saved!"

"It was what you felt called on to cut and leave laying in the field, Contrary, that's out yonder to spoil now," said Miss Beulah. "Yes sir, school is right where you're going. Put down that chicken bone."

Ella Fay jumped up clattering, Etoyle and Elvie moved morosely to follow, and they all went around the table telling Uncle Nathan and Miss Lexie good-bye.

"Me and Etoyle wanted to go help Jack," said Elvie.

"A fine way to get to be a teacher!" said Miss Beulah.

"Oh, yes, they'd like all life to be one grand reunion and never stop," said Miss Lexie. "I'm glad it's over. Taking it all in all, Beulah, I consider yesterday came just about up to scratch. It compares with the others. I was only afraid your little old granny might wonder where we got those Moodys. But she didn't."

"She took them in her stride, along with you and the rest of it," said Miss Beulah. "And if you're going to take any of my dewberry jelly, take it! If not, put back the spoon."

"The reunion didn't come up to *my* idea," said Ella Fay. She tarried in the kitchen door in Gloria's old teaching dress—the blue sailor with the flossy white stars on the collar and the skirt with the kick-pleats in it. "Curly Stovall was left out of the invitations, that's why!"

Miss Beulah ran and caught up with her in the passage. "All right, New Shoes! I'm fixing to smack you hard right across those pones of yours, where you need it most," she cried. "And for the rest of your punishment, you're to come straight home from school today and tell me something you've learned."

"Feed the stock. Lead the cows to pasture, Vaughn," said Mr. Renfro. "You heard your mother. The reunion is over with."

"I ain't done anything," said Vaughn.

"Then keep still," said Uncle Nathan. He pointed a loaded fork at Vaughn. He ate something out of his pack for breakfast, with a little home syrup poured over it.

"Everybody is liable to get a surprise yet," said Vaughn, as he struck off for the barn.

"Uncle Nathan, you ain't leaving?" cried Jack, when a moment later Uncle Nathan began handing around tracts out of his pack—the one about the crazy drunkard that he carried the most of. "Are you trying to tell us you won't stay for hog-killing time like you always do?"

"I must needs be on my way," said Uncle Nathan. His

patched sleeve still smelled of coal-oil and a little scorching from last night.

"Nathan, have you even set long enough under my roof to dry out a little?" cried Miss Beulah. "Let me feel your thatch."

"Sister, I must needs not stop to take comfort."

"You won't even stop in Banner to help bury Miss Julia Mortimer?"

He shook his wet locks. "If the Lord has left me to outlast her, He must want me to go my road further than I ever gone it before," he told her, and hoisted his pack.

"Then put a kiss on Granny's cheek without waking her up," she told him.

"Good-bye, good-bye, Uncle Nathan!" yelled the three girls' voices from the barn lot, when Uncle Nathan's footsteps were heard measuring their way through the mud. "See you next reunion!"

"There's a chink of light out yonder now," said Mr. Renfro.

"They can't start till I get there!" Jack cried, jumping up. He laid a restraining hand on Gloria's shoulder. "Honey, I wouldn't have you get your little feet wet. Don't you come traipsing after me. It won't take long at Banner Top—it can't!" He kissed the baby, who was holding a little ham bone in her lips like a penny whistle, kissed everybody, ran up the passage, shouted, "Milk for me, Vaughn!," gave a warbling whistle, and ran splashing off with the dogs. They heard Bet thudding away with him.

Miss Beulah took off her apron.

"Now, Mother, are you ready to set down for the first time?" asked Mr. Renfro.

She cried loudly, "Set down? I'm going to Banner Top! Why, you couldn't hold me! Stovall and Moody are about to come to grips with their two machines! If my boy's ready to turn in the performance I think he is, it's a mother's place to be there and see it done right!"

"It's raining like it almost means it," said Mr. Renfro.

"I'm neither sugar nor salt, I won't melt. And morning rain's like an old man's dance, not long to last," Miss Beulah recited. "What I'm asking is, is anybody at this table coming with me?"

"Don't believe I'll venture from the house," said Mr. Renfro in mild tones. "If you ladies will excuse me."

"He's got that old dynamite headache," said Miss Beulah. "I'll only say it one more time, Mr. Renfro, and I'm through: from now on, you let other folks go out in the night and blow things to pieces, and you stay home. There's too much of the Old Boy in you yet."

"He'll shortly blow up something else. He won't learn, he's a man," said Miss Lexie.

"Yes sir, your touch is pure destruction!" Miss Beulah told him and ran to her kitchen. "I'll consider you were drunk on lemonade," she said when she marched back, Mr. Renfro's hat on her head.

"I really ought not to keep Mr. Hugg waiting," Miss Lexie said. "Especially when I'm coming to be his surprise. Jack may have to do without me watching him."

"I'm not going to beg you, Lexie Renfro," said Miss Beulah. "You can take your stand at our mailbox and get carried off either of two directions. Elmo Broadwee can carry you on his route and when he gets to Mr. Hugg's he can set you down with his nickel's worth of ice. Or you can change your mind and go the other way with the mail rider. Then you could get put down at that funeral. Couldn't she, Gloria?"

"If she's ready for it. And not scared of Miss Julia any longer," Gloria said, standing up in her church dress of deep blue dotted swiss with white piqué collar and cuffs.

"Still, I missed everything yesterday," argued Miss Lexie, rising too, and shaking crumbs on the floor for someone else to sweep up.

"Nobody's compelled to watch my boy's performance that don't want to," said Miss Beulah.

"Ask 'em who's going to stay home with me," said Mr. Renfro to Lady May, and Gloria handed her over. Lady May went to him as good as gold and gave him her tract, too.

On the ridge of the new roof the mockingbird sat silent, all chest, like a zinc bucket filled to the top, all song contained. What looked at first glance like a herd of strange cows come up into the yard overnight were only the tables of yesterday, stripped and naked, gleaming like hides in their sheen of rain. It was a tobacco tin in the weeds that shone like a ruby; what crouched like a possum under the althea was somebody's lost apron. A peashooter dangled from its sling down the back of the school chair. The night-blooming cereus flowers looked like wrung chickens' necks. Miss Lexie, coming out onto the porch wearing a pillowcase over her hat, pointed them out.

Miss Beulah came pulling the old wool brim down squarely over her forehead and said, "Gloria Renfro, is all that hair you've got going to be enough to keep you dry?"

Gloria popped a blue straw sailor onto her head and snapped the elastic under her chin. "No ma'am, I've still got the same hat I came here in."

There was a sudden fusillade of sounds at their backs. Vaughn was feeding the pig. They had only to turn their heads to see all the refuse of yesterday, corncobs, eggshells, chicken bones, chicken trimmings, chicken heads, and the fish heads, all jumping together in the blue wash of clabber, all going down. Rusty looked back at them, with tiny eyes. He had the old, mufflered face of winter this morning and fed sobbing with greed, champing against blasts he was never going to feel.

"That reminds me, I've thought of a very good way to fix Mr. Hugg, when I get back to him in a little while," Miss Lexie said, hooking arms with the other two ladies on the slippery yard. "It's to give him every single thing he wants. Everything Mr. Hugg asks for—give it to him." She glared.

"All right, Lexie, go ahead," said Miss Beulah. "Just so it don't mean you cart him here to me."

"He'll get the surprise of his life, won't he?"

"Now Vaughn!" Miss Beulah was calling over her shoulder. "After he's gobbled that, turn the old sinner loose again. There's still plenty he can root out, not very far away. But he did look sassy tied up there for the reunion!"

"Gloria Renfro, how did you *ever* switch that car away up there? If you told it yesterday, I reckon I was too busy to listen." Miss Beulah stopped still in the middle of Banner Road and stared upward from beneath the row of rain beads on Mr. Renfro's hat.

"I scared it up," said Gloria, giving a skip over the ditch

and arriving beside her. "I only wish it was in my power this morning to scare it down again."

No Moodys were in evidence. Jack stood on Banner Top by himself, hands on hips, studying the scene.

The Buick seemed not to have changed its position at all, though there was a lick of scorch up the back of it and its back window had stars. But the tree was out of the ground and hanging top-down over the jumping-off place. All its roots had risen together, bringing along their bed of clay, as if a piece of Boone County had decided to get up on its side. The solid wheel of pocked and bearded clay looked like an old white summer moon, burnt out on the edge of the world.

Miss Beulah was climbing the path up, making haste toward the Buick. "With a living Comfort inside it. I marvel," she said. "Or *is* he inside, I wonder? Comforts generally acts by contraries, but you'd be nothing but a fool to count on it."

"Sure, he's in there, Mama," said Jack, still studying the car. "Asleep on all fours, like a bird dog."

"Right where you left him? Oho!" Miss Beulah scoffed. "If that'd been a Beecham or a Renfro so treated, do you suppose the world had been safe from us last night?"

"Never knew the world *was* safe," hummed Miss Lexie, who had halted right at the mailbox, where she stood a head taller than Uncle Sam. "Well, the sight's not a great deal different from the way I had it pictured."

"Mr. Renfro was being modest for a change when he said he took a little nick out of that tree," said Miss Beulah. "I don't think it's going to be with us very much longer."

"It's clinging," said Jack. "Waiting to see what's the next thing to come along."

Nothing but memory seemed ever to have propped the tree. Nothing any stronger than memory might be holding it where it was now—some last tag end of root, that was all. There was just a round mass of clay, hanging with roots, like a giant lid raised and standing open, letting out an aromatic smell. There in the rain, its underside went on raining, itself, into the hole, the starved clay raining down dryness from the old, marrowless, pink-and-white colored roots.

"What do you think of it now, Jack?" called Judge Moody's

voice. He and Mrs. Moody came in sight from the top of the farm track, where they had been sheltering under a tree. They made their slow way down into Banner Road.

"I'll tell you what I think," said Miss Beulah. "It's lacking very little. It's a very nearly perfect example."

"What of?" asked Miss Lexie.

"Man-foolishness," said Miss Beulah. "Ever heard of it?"

"One of these days I'm going to have to agree with your mother about something, Jack," said Gloria into his ear. "I hope she never finds out."

"Papa was trying to help," Jack said. "He's got him a reputation that's going to kill him one day yet."

"I want a good answer," said Judge Moody from the road. "What's the size of the situation now?"

"Well, sir, my way down was already closed off north, south, and east," Jack called. He made a step forward and went down up to his belt buckle. "And now Papa's cut off my west. Well, it's just a hole. Nothing but a hole," he said, climbing out. "And I believe that big pleasure Buick'll clear it! If she's persuaded the right way—and I'm counting on my truck just as strong as I can count!"

"Where is it, then? Is that truck going to fail us too?" asked Mrs. Moody.

They all stared down Banner Road. In the row with them, the cosmos flowers barely stirring on their stems under the fine soft rain were washed bright as the embroidery on the pillowcase Miss Lexie wore over her hat. There came a sound like a swelling, heavier rain.

"Yonder's your answer! Coming right now! Bigger and brighter than ever!" Jack hollered. He seized Gloria and Miss Beulah each by a hand and ran with them down to the road.

"Is that the same truck? It doesn't look the same as yesterday," Mrs. Moody greeted them.

"It's backing," Jack told her. "It's been coming uphill from Banner."

"It even looks to me like it's got a dog driving it," Mrs. Moody argued.

"Suppose you say no more, dear, and just give it a chance to get here," said Judge Moody in heavy tones.

Jack stood in the middle of the road while the truck backed

up toward him, holding a muddy chunk raised in his hand ready to brake the wheels on top. This morning, the fishing poles had gone, and draping the rear was a strip torn off a bolt of kitchen oilcloth, on which words written in red paint with a stick were now coming close enough to be read: "Excell (Curly) Stovall for Justice of the Peace. Leave It To Curly."

"Rain curtains!" Jack hollered, as the truck drew closer. "Who parted with those?"

"Brother Dollarhide for a gallon of gas. Where's he hiding—the fellow that belongs to that Buick?" came the muffled voice from within the cab.

"He's standing right here with his wife, waiting on you. Whoa!" The truck drew even with his feet and Jack blocked the wheel. Ten or fifteen of Curly's hounds at once poured out from the bed behind onto the road and surrounded Jack, Judge Moody, and the ladies, their tails like a dozen fairy wands all trembling towards trouble.

"Then tell him it's going to be a dollar to go up and a dollar to come down. The whole business is going to set him back two dollars," called Curly Stovall. "Cash."

"If the fellow doesn't know any better than that, let's just keep him in the dark about what they'd charge in Ludlow," Mrs. Moody murmured to her husband.

"I am not reassured," said Judge Moody.

"It's a bargain, Curly!" Jack sang out. "So stick your head out of them pretty curtains now, it's time to see where you're going."

The curtains on the driver's side parted. A yell came out. "Jack! Hey! Look yonder at Banner Top! Who got here first?"

"Papa," answered Jack. "Don't worry. It's just minus one tree."

"And what am I going to hitch to? Drat your hide!"

"Careful how you talk, Curly. We got a pretty fair crop of ladies scared up for a rainy morning," said Jack. "And lined up here to watch us."

"First and foremost his mother!" cried Miss Beulah, and as she spoke the cab door on the passenger side swung out and down stepped one more lady, with the only umbrella for a mile around already raised.

"Why, Curly, you brought Miss Ora! Who's holding the store down—Captain Billy Bangs?"

Everything waited while the fat lady picked her way through the mud. "Granny Vaughn live through her birthday? Jack get his welcome without it leaving any scars? Get any surprise visitors?" Miss Ora Stovall asked Miss Beulah. "I believe I'm looking at two of those right now." She edged in on the Moodys, so she could stand between them. "How're you feeling?" she began. "I'm Ora Stovall, weigh more than I should, never married, but know how to meet the public, keep up with what's going on. Enjoying your visit? What do you think of Banner? Like to hear about the biggest fish-fry that ever was?"

"All right, Jack Renfro and Curly Stovall!" Miss Beulah called over dogs, engine clatter, Miss Ora and all. "The visitors may have all day to talk, but the Renfros haven't! Now get on up there and perform! And keep in mind a mother's here to watch you."

"I'm the owner of the car, if you please!" Mrs. Moody exclaimed.

Through the rain curtains, canvas that had come to be the texture of old velvet, slit with isinglass lights and a few peep-holes, Curly's voice called out, "Lady! This ain't the same job I took on yesterday!"

Jack flung himself onto the running board. "Curly, things change overnight, you got to be ready for that. We got a job this morning as whopping big as both our reputations put together!"

"And how you think we're going to do it!"

"By you sticking to the wheel and me doing the engineering!" He hopped to the road. "All right, Curly! Crawl! Back like you're going, right on up the bank, just back on up to me." He ran up the slippery clay, both arms beckoning.

"Shucks. Hindways?" Miss Beulah objected.

"Mama, in my truck, as long as you want your gas to feed steady, you got to pamper it on the upgrade. Give her the throttle, Curly! Don't be bashful!" Jack called.

From the road they watched it. With a long chain of noises like a string of firecrackers set fire to, the truck began to plough its way upward. The rain had washed it, so now, in part, it was the old International blue. With the spots and circles of oil that had worked their way through the finish, it was iridescent as butterfly wings as it quivered its way up. On the brow of the cab the original wording had emerged, "Delicious and Refreshing."

"What do those blasted horns mean?" Judge Moody asked.

"They mean I made a good trade out of Captain Billy Bangs! Who wants to know?" came Curly's voice back.

Sid, having barked the truck off the road in spite of a dozen hounds, was still after it, and flung himself like a bullet at the windshield, already stuck up with adhesive like a cut face.

"Mind out for your bob-wire fence!" Jack sang, as something flew up from under the back wheels like a whip. "You strung it there—just to trip your own self up with the first time you tried for the top! And the next thing is you got to straddle a hole about the same size you are. Keep your eye cocked on me."

"What caused a tree to just up and get out of the ground?" Curly hollered, over the hole.

"It was old and ready to fall—Lady May Renfro could've pushed it over with her little finger," Jack cried. "All right, whoa!" He skidded to put a chunk in front of the truck's front wheel. "Now! Pitch me your rope!"

The cab door swung open long enough for an arm-throw, and a black coil crossed through the air and slammed Jack wetly in the chest. He spun and crouched with it behind the truck, shoulders pumping as he worked with his knots. In a moment he'd jumped around to the back of the Buick. As he attacked that, a shaking of bells thrilled the air.

"Somebody, somebody for sure, climbed up here in the night and tied cowbells on this Buick!" Jack called. "Only the Broadwees would have had that little to do." Then he rose and yelled into the car, "Wake-up-Jacob! Wake up! Ain't you about ready to quit riding?"

"Is it daylight?" came Aycock's sleepy voice from inside.

"And raining. All right, Aycock, you can get out now—I'll count three. When I count three, Curly, you start pulling!" Jack yelled. "And when you do, remember yours ain't the only engine that's running! Once Aycock jumps and the Buick's out of balance, she'll start pulling against you! All right—ready?"

"Jack Renfro, you can finish this by yourself!" yelled Curly. "I'm going back to Banner right now."

"You're tied!" Jack shouted. "You and the Buick's hitched to one rope and hitched good! *One!*"

"Do you reckon we've got a chance?" Mrs. Moody asked her husband.

"I should say what chance we have depends on Jack," he said, eyes never leaving him.

"I can vouch for that!" Miss Beulah agreed. "Don't count on either one of those two machines. As for the truck Jack's so in love with, it's got parts from everything that's ever passed through Banner and lost a particle. It's an example of a grab-bag to me. And more'n likely it'll fly to pieces the first chance it gets, if you want my unvarnished opinion."

"Two!" yelled Jack.

"I ain't playing!" roared Curly.

"Curly, Aycock, there ain't no time left for anybody to act bashful," Jack said. "If you want any glory, you can't quit now!"

"You want to change places?" cried Curly.

"Two and a half!" yelled Jack.

"I dread this," said Miss Beulah, taking off Mr. Renfro's hat and emptying some rain out of the saucer of the brim, never taking her eyes from on top.

Jack opened his mouth again.

The Buick's rear door shot open then and Aycock came tumbling out into Jack's spreading arms. Both boys fell, Jack rose, picked up Aycock and stood him up stiff with his hair dry and on end. Then Aycock danced sideways into the plum bushes and while they waited on him they could all hear through the sound of the rain what he was doing.

"Three!" Jack was calling urgently. "Three! And watch out down in the road!"

The rope had already stretched out straight—the Buick had already moved forward. A loud report cracked out from underneath it and something went spinning.

"Yonder went Uncle Nathan's sign!" hollered Jack, as the

truck backfired, crawled forward, then was jerked to a halt. The Buick, on solid ground, was running the other way. Jack raced to catch it. But even before he got there its wheels rolled to a stop. Then they began to roll the other way. The Buick was moving with the roaring, recovering truck. It was coming on the rope, slowly away from the edge, swaying, like a lady coming out of church—one of its tires was not flat.

"Well," said Jack, watching the car, "she just plain run out of gas. Ain't that your opinion, Aycock?"

"I seen we needed some," Aycock said.

"In a minute she'll be coming down behind you, Curly!" Jack hollered. A whip of barbed wire flew up from under the truck and Curly yelped like a woman scared by a mouse, and braked the truck with a sharp turn of the wheels. The engine choked and died. The Buick, just at the crown of Banner Top, presented with a slack in the rope, rolled back to where it had come from, and on past it. It proceeded on its original forward way over Banner Top, disappearing with the moderate speed of an elevator going down. The truck rose up like a tin monkey on a string, until both its back wheels entered the tree hole and stayed there.

"Well, this isn't what *I* came to see!" said Miss Ora Stovall. "What about you?"

An upward avalanche pounded its way to Banner Top from the road. With Jack holding both arms wide to keep them safe behind him, Gloria, Miss Beulah, the Judge, and Mrs. Moody all crowded together in the clouds of exhaust and cedar fumes, to look down.

The automobile was hanging by the rope and the tree beside it was hanging by its own last roots, like two things waiting for the third.

"Oscar, I feel like I can draw my first breath," said Mrs. Moody. "It's happened."

"Not what you *wanted*?" he broke out.

"No, but now it's not still ahead of us."

"Some of it is," he said.

The Buick had descended as far as the drop of the rope allowed: its nose hung within five or six feet of the ledge below. Its wheels turned innocently in free air. The rope held, held, until holding was hardly believable any longer, until it seemed tenuous as a sound—a long, last, feathered note from Miss Beulah singing "Blessed Assurance," holding even after the rest of the choir and the congregation had given up.

"From here, I would call things a tie," said Miss Lexie. She still stood in position at the mailbox.

"That's right. As long as they're hanging on tight to each other, both of 'em's as safe as you are, Aunt Lexie," Jack said.

The rain curtains were torn aside and a face red as the hidden sun looked out of the truck.

"I see you, you old infidel!" Miss Beulah screamed. "That's all I needed! How do you like what you've done to us now?"

"Tuck back in there, Curly!" cried Jack.

"But the truck's coming out of the hole!" hollered Curly.

"Not this way!" Jack warned him. "Start driving. Drive the other way, Curly, drive as hard as you can!"

The truck engine gave out a piercing, froglike chirping.

"The throttle!" yelled Jack. "The Buick's gaining on you, Curly! The Buick's pulling too much weight!"

"I'm coming out of the hole!" Curly warned. "In spite of all, I'm coming out! Like a old jaw tooth!"

"I just wish you'd gobbled a bigger breakfast before you come!" Jack yelled.

"She's coming!" shouted Curly. "Think I won't jump? You can catch me too!"

Jack whirled, grabbed the rope and pulled leaning back toward the truck, pulled till he sat down pulling, and was hauled to his knees and forward down onto his stomach and dragged, by the inch, till he hung head-first over the drop, yelling, "Gloria! Take ahold of me! Just anywhere you can find!"

Gloria slid behind him into the bucket-like seat that sweethearts had worn over the years into the jumping-off place, and clamped her arms around his bulging legs. His feet locked together behind her. Judge Moody, breathing heavily over her head, wrapped his hands around the rope and pulled with Jack and the truck. Mrs. Moody, planting her feet apart, got his suspenders in her fists and sawed on him, while Miss Beulah dug her hands into Mrs. Moody's girth, rammed herself back against one leg, and hauled on her, setting up a steady rhythm.

"The way to do it is make a human chain," Miss Lexie instructed them from her place at the mailbox.

"I'm driving hard, Jack! But I ain't getting anywhere!" called Curly.

"Just hold things like they are so they don't get any worse!" yelled Jack.

"How far is that thing now from touching the ledge?" asked Judge Moody.

Jack screwed around his head. "In my judgment, about as far as me to you, sir." He slid for an instant. Gloria's arms locked his feet to her breast. "Closer!"

Down there the ledge was spread with rose briars in ten-foot rays and dotted with chewed plum bushes. In the scoop of the gully below it, the little sprung-up cedars pointed up darkly out of the clay, like the hairs in Brother Bethune's ears.

"Are we reaching clear back to my truck, Mama?" Jack called.

"How long do you think I am?" she yelled. "But we got two more in the road and one more idler on top! March here behind me, Aycock Comfort. Squat. Sit on my foot. Brace that leg of mine, Foolish!"

"Then if the rope comes in two, all the line'll fall back on top of me," he said, not coming.

"Pore you. And what about Jack, when he flies the other way?" Miss Beulah flung at him scornfully.

"If Miss Ora would volunteer to set her two hundred pounds' worth down on the bumper of my truck, and kind of tread backwards with her feet, that wouldn't hurt any-thing," gasped Jack. "But even if she could hear me, I can't ask her—it's so little of a compliment."

"Get up here, Ora Stovall!" yelled Miss Beulah.

"I'm going to put you in the paper and that's all! When it rains, I'm a regular little kitty," Miss Ora called at once from the top of the bank opposite, where she had climbed to see better, out from under her big umbrella black as a buzzard's wing.

"Oh, I can't think Providence has delivered us this far in order to desert us now! Surely help will come," Mrs. Moody said faintly over the creaking of her corset as Miss Beulah hauled on her. "But please don't in the meantime cut my wind."

"The ones I'd call for first are already with us, this time," Jack gasped. "There ain't any better than who's right here pulling, Mrs. Judge!"

"I don't trust that infidel Stovall to stick to the wheel a minute, Jack," said Miss Beulah. "You know what he's thinking of? His own hide!"

"I wish everybody would be less loudly critical for a minute and let me think," Judge Moody said.

"Let him think!" hollered Jack.

"Better hurry," said Miss Lexie. "World isn't going to stand still and wait on you."

"Lexie, for the second time, come catch on to my waist!" Miss Beulah said in a loud voice.

"I've got to save my strength for battles later on," said Miss Lexie. "Mr. Hugg is a ton."

"I'm driving but I ain't getting anywhere!" called Curly. "Sinking, that's all."

"That's a fellow!" called Jack.

"When it falls, will it fall on that little shelf down there?" asked Mrs. Moody fearfully.

"If it don't skip," Jack called. "Uncle Nathan's sign skipped right over it, though. Yonder *it* lays, too far down to even read. I'm glad Uncle Nathan got back on his road before he learned what become of that one."

"But what's at the bottom?" Mrs. Moody cried.

"The Bywy River," said Jack. "Low as it is now, you could walk the sandbar from right under here clear to Banner bridge without getting wet."

She gave a little cry.

"Jack," said Judge Moody, "I think if we could very gently lower the car the rest of the way to that ledge, it would have a better chance. While we still have time. And strength."

"That's giving in, Oscar," protested Mrs. Moody.

"The other thing against it is the rope won't stretch like I will," gasped Jack.

"Jack, what are you going to do?" Gloria pleaded.

"I'm going to hang here pulling as long as you can hold my feet, Possum," he gasped.

A racket was heard in the road.

"Ha, ha, Homer Champion," came Miss Ora Stovall's voice

in greeting as the wheels skidded to a stop. "Take a look at Brother!"

"Where?" came Uncle Homer's voice. "Hey, what's going on here?"

"Want to be part of the human chain?" yelled Jack.

"That sounded like Jack Renfro!" exclaimed Uncle Homer. "Where's he? Was he speaking to me?"

"He's hanging over the living edge!" yelled Miss Beulah.

"Sister Beulah!" shouted Uncle Homer. "Here, what's the big idea?"

"Just seeing how long we can keep us all in one piece, I reckon!" Jack said in short breaths. "Glad to have you if you want to add on!"

"Every dog has his day, huh?" laughed Miss Ora Stovall. "Look at Brother right on top."

"On top? Is Stovall in charge of that *truck*?" Uncle Homer hollered.

"Curly!" Jack yelled, but already the truck shuddered as its door opened and Curly hopped out in boots into the naked air, and heavy-shouldered as if doubled over in knots of laughter, he cut a short caper, his face beaming from side to side, and then he was back inside again.

"I saw what you did, you old rangatang!" yelled Miss Beulah. "Not content with all you caused already, you try to make an end of us too!"

"Never mind, Mama. When Curly hit that door open, this one answered," called Jack. "So we're still matched."

The Buick's back seat had been jolted forward and had turned loose all the tools, with a wheel of never-used towline that rolled and wobbled on the ledge, printing its track, then lay down under their eyes.

"Everything in its own good time, Possum," said Jack in short breaths. "There's everything I stood in need of yesterday."

"Look where you've succeeded in raising my rival to!" Uncle Homer cried. "Don't you know what'll happen? Hold him there long enough in the public eye, and they'll vote for him!"

"My boy's keeping one end of this man-foolishness from running off with the other, with his bare hands, and you just think about Tuesday!" said Miss Beulah. "We got no time to waste listening to pretty speeches, get on up here before I throw something at you!"

"Don't fret, Uncle Homer. If Curly had his way this minute, he'd be away from here and down on solid ground where you are," called Jack.

"The heck I would," said Curly. He sounded the truck's horn; it hummed like a distant swarm of bees.

"The heck he would," said Uncle Homer. "Sitting pretty where you got him planted! And if you want the public to decree Stovall is the man better fitted for worthy office than your own in-law, you keep him where he is, from now right on up till when the polls open. The only thing he lacks now is cowbells."

With effort, Jack managed to work the rope a fraction, and faintly the Buick's cowbells rang from below.

"If you want the rest of the story, Uncle Homer, at the other end of this rope we got a Buick out of gas," he called.

"It'll be a landslide!" howled Uncle Homer. "I don't see why you don't charge to see it!"

"Champion, do you really reckon this exhibition is going to gain Stovall votes?" Miss Lexie demanded to know. "I wonder could you once be right about anything?"

"I know people. I know people," bawled Uncle Homer, as if his heart would break.

"So I suppose you'll stand there wishing the rope would snap!" Miss Beulah yelled. "Till it does! Politics! I wouldn't have son of mine enter politics if it was the last door open to him on earth!"

"Uncle Homer, the ladies are growing a little frail," Jack panted out. "Don't you want to lend your strength to keep Curly where we got him?"

"I'm all that's lacking, am I?" Uncle Homer shouted. "You ought to go back to Parchman, Jack! Next time, stay through the primary and the run-off too!" The van skidded away and down out of hearing, and Curly Stovall let out a rocking laugh from the truck.

"There it came! My guitar," Aycock said, peering over the brink. He took a hop into the air and landed on the ledge with both feet.

"You come off and left it behind when you jumped? I hope you find it still in tune!" Jack called.

The car's headlights just cleared the rusty top of Aycock's head as he loped underneath and picked up the guitar from the mud. "Well, I reckon I better get on home and speak to Mama," he said, as he hauled himself up by protruding tree roots onto the top. Nursing his guitar, he gave a small wave of his free hand as if he were closing a little purse, and started away. "I'll see is she still mad at me."

"Don't you care to see the end?" Jack called.

"I just as soon hear you tell it," said Aycock. "All I'm truly wondering about this minute is how cold will my grits get before I make it home. Cold till the butter won't melt?"

"Trifling! And always will be. Parchman was too good for you, Aycock Comfort! Go home and tell your mother I said so!" cried Miss Beulah.

"All you needed was to get married, Aycock," Jack said. "Ought to brought you a wife home ahead of time, like I did, and had her gripping your feet now."

"Not yet awhile," Aycock said politely. He stopped at Miss Beulah's position and stood with his head on one side and his wetting hair lying on his neck like the feathers of a Rhode Island Red. "Mis' Renfro, I feel like Mr. Renfro kind of aimed to blow me up."

"I've got just enough patience left to ask you one question," she yelled. "How did Mr. Renfro get himself up here last night?"

"He creeped," said Aycock. "Then he creeped down again. If he'd told me ahead what he's going to do, he'd had me out in his lap. Come the bang, I thought I'd wait to see what else was coming, before I set foot outside. His dynamite ain't the freshest in all the world."

"Dynamite?" Curly Stovall's head came out through the rain curtains.

Judge Moody suddenly broke out: "We're all holding on here now by the skin of our teeth! Can't conversation ever cease? Can't anybody offer just a single idea? What're we going to do about this?"

"You could cut that rope," suggested Aycock. "Save time." He tiptoed away across the mud puddles.

"We have now been holding on for eleven and a half minutes," said the Judge.

"Judge Moody, I kind of believe your watch has stopped," Jack gasped. "Can you still hear it running?"

"Please, *you* let me try to think," said Judge Moody.

"What's the matter, Gloria?" called Jack. "When you gave that sigh, it travelled right on through my toes and down me to the top of my head."

"I don't see our future, Jack," she gasped.

"Keep looking, sweetheart."

"If we can't do any better than we're doing now, what will Lady May think of us when we're old and gray?"

"Just hang onto my heels, honey," he cried out.

"We're still where we were yesterday. In the balance," Gloria said.

"Don't give up, baby," said Jack as her chin came to rest between the heels of his muddy shoes, with their wet soles splitting apart, their tops worn down to sandbar pink, their strings sodden and metal-heavy with mud and weed, his wedding shoes. "Just put your mind on what me and you will be doing this same day next year. That's what I told myself last year in the old pen."

"Jack, only you would still think it was all going to be all right!"

"I still believe I can handle trouble just taking it as it comes," he gasped.

"It takes thinking! We've got to think!" Judge Moody broke out.

"Jack, now the blood is all running to your head!" Gloria cried.

"Just so he don't fall and land on it," Miss Beulah cried from the end of the line. "Precious head!"

Hot tears coursed through the rain on Gloria's face. "Oh, Jack," she whispered to his heels. "I don't see how you've stayed alive for as long as you have."

"He don't know when he's licked. That's how!" said Miss Beulah.

"I ain't never licked!" cried Jack.

The rope went singing in two. As it cracked Jack free he rose, spread his arms, and came down in the fallen tree. The

Judge, his wife, and Miss Beulah were flung backwards to the ground, but Gloria dived the other way. Her hat popped off and went sailing down through space.

"And there she goes after him again!" came Miss Beulah's wild cry.

Both Jack and Gloria were in the tree, tumbling toward each other. The cedar trunk rolled once, as if a wave came all the way up from the river and went under it, but it stayed attached, hanging onto its very last roots. Branches sharp-cracked at Jack's and Gloria's knees and shoulders and around their heads, and pitched them against each other, buoyed them up and dropped them. Like runaways caught in a storm and living through it, they drove out with their arms and legs and went down shouting. Still the tree held to its shape—like a summer's-old nest that had itself fallen out of some greater tree or vine, with all its yesterdays tangled up in it now. The two of them fell together through what was once the roof of the tree onto the ledge, landing right side up, looking at each other, weak with accomplishment.

Cowbells were still shaking a little, close to their ears.

"Well, the auto evermore landed where it hurts, didn't it?" Miss Beulah cried.

The Buick stood on its nose on the rose-pink ledge.

Jack was climbing back to his feet. "Curly! If you couldn't bring a better rope than that, I'd just as soon you hadn't brought none!"

"It was a World Wonder Number Two Grade," shouted Curly, still inside the noisy truck.

"I think it was just a plowline with a little pitch on it!" Jack was tenderly lifting Gloria up out of the broken branches. He drew little twigs from her hair.

"What's wrong with the knots you tie!" Curly hollered back.

"They're still tied! They're the same Jack Renfro knots they ever was! Curly, that rope of yours busted in the *middle*!"

"Wasn't ever used but once before. And that was to pull one little calf away from his mother."

"You brought the wrong rope."

"On its very nose. And it wasn't for lack of me trying to see the thing done right," said Miss Beulah. "Well, things could be a lot worse, though. Machines could both be piled up down at the bottom and two or three people with a leg or an arm or two broken."

"I suppose you're happy," Mrs. Moody said to her husband. "There it is. On that ledge."

"It brings some relief," he said. "Of course it's temporary."

"It looks to me just a whole lot like it's permanent," she told him.

"Well, it's temporary, Maud Eva," he said.

At that moment there came something like a thunderclap behind them, and a cloud of larkspur-blue swallowed up all of Mrs. Moody and a part of Miss Beulah. The truck sprang up like some whole flock of chickens alarmed to the pitch of lunacy, fell, bounced, bounced again.

"Curly," Jack was hollering, "I believe you must be driving over one of Brother Bethune's snakes!"

The truck came to rest ten feet away in some plum bushes, the dogs streaking circles around it, barking. Curly Stovall, as soaking-wet as if he'd been outside with other people, leaped the second time from the cab and stamped through mud back to the jumping-off place and yelled at Jack, "All right, what was that?"

"Curly, you know Papa planted a little of his dynamite up here, trying to do me a favor," Jack said. "And he did."

"We already heard from that once!" shouted Curly.

"And now you've heard from it again," said Miss Beulah, looking him in the eye. "Some folks' dynamite blows up once and gets through with it, but you don't reckon on that little from Mr. Renfro."

"He's using dynamite that's mighty old, then!" Curly stormed. "And there ain't no guarantee on what *old* dynamite is *ever* going to do!"

"If it hadn't been good for one extra bang, I can think pretty fast where *you'd* be, Stovall," said Miss Beulah. "Still in that hole! Well on your way to China! Oh, that smell, Mr. Renfro!" She cast up her eyes. "That smell! Worse than a whole roomful of Cape Jessamines at funeral time."

Mrs. Moody let out a cry.

The tree had begun to move. It was leaving them. First it

went slowly, and then it was bounding, rolling unevenly down on its wheel of roots and clay, diminishing under their eyes, firing off fainter sounds, until it was quiet and still—only a bundle in the grayness below, of no more size or accountability than a folded umbrella.

"Mrs. Moody scared it down," said Gloria.

"Thank Mr. Renfro instead—it was that last bang shook it," Miss Beulah contradicted her.

"And now the Buick's got a sweet path open in front of her," said Jack. "Back to the road where she started."

"You call that a path?" asked Judge Moody, frowning down.

"It finds its way out here from the road, threading down to the river," said Jack. "Gloria, keep as far back from me as you can." He picked her up and swung her around behind him.

"Hold onto him, girl!" cried Mrs. Moody.

"I'm only fixing to level you, Mrs. Judge," Jack said.

"With what?" Judge Moody demanded.

"Nothing but my own main strength, sir, that's the safest," Jack said.

"Don't move. Wait for me," ordered the Judge.

The car stood with its underside exposed in full to face Judge Moody as he tramped around the fishing path onto the ledge. Away from the road, or even the sight of the road, rising up on a ledge by itself, with a clay wall going up on one side and the rain falling to the houseless distance down the other, it might have been some engine of mysterious invention, its past unknown, its function obscure, possibly even illegal—like some whisky still come upon without warning in a clearing in the woods.

Judge Moody stood there in front of it, Gloria stood behind, Mrs. Moody and Miss Beulah overhead, and Curly Stovall was somewhere back there laughing.

"As Jack's wife, I would rather nobody breathed," said Gloria.

Jack stepped before the car and stood under it with his back turned, flexed his arms, squatted once, then squared his knees. He cleaned off his bloody hands on his pants, then, as slowly as if he were already lifting its weight, he pushed his arms upward and took hold of the car.

"Now watch! Reminds me of Samson exactly!" Miss Beulah cried frantically—she was standing on the jumping-off place. "Only watch my boy show the judgment Samson's lacking, and move out of the way when it starts coming!"

Jack staggered and then jumped as if out from between a set of jaws, and the Buick came down like the clap of thunder after a very near strike of lightning.

"And she's ready to haul!" he yelled, as Judge Moody caught him.

"My cake!" exclaimed Mrs. Moody.

The Buick's other doors one after the other fell open, like pockets being turned out, and up the path from under the ledge ran little spotty wild pigs, like the church carpet come to life, and they gobbled up the cake that had spilled out of the front seat into the rain. Bringing up the wild pigs from behind came Rusty, the pig from home.

"All right, Stovall, now it's your turn," Judge Moody called.

"I quit! I ain't going to drag you no further and you can't make me—I'm the law, mister," said Curly.

"Curly, Judge Moody's the law too," said Jack. "I hope you ain't so ungrateful that you'd forget Judge Moody."

"What Judge Moody? *That* Judge Moody?" Curly cried. "I didn't know I was ever going to see *that* Judge Moody again! Not around here."

"How many do you think there are?" Mrs. Moody exclaimed. "Are you trying to suggest to me there's some other Judge Moody? Don't waste my time."

"Maud Eva," began Judge Moody.

But there was suddenly added to the throbbing of the truck a rattling sound. Curly whirled. Jack rushed the clay wall, grabbing at cedar roots, cedar sprouts, rose briars, his legs wheeling him finally over the top, where Miss Beulah spanked him on.

The empty truck was jolting headlong toward the road, skating in and out of the tracks it had made backing up. It was held back only a little by its laboring engine and by the brief fingering of plum bushes. It banged into Banner Road, a puddle walling up in front of it, then through its shower limped on across the road as if pretending something was broken, and threw itself into the ditch, ushering a part of the syrup stand with it and still dragging a long clay tail behind, which was its end of the rope.

"All right now, that splashed my dress," Miss Lexie greeted it at the mailbox.

"I'm staying right here with mine," Mrs. Moody was calling.

"All right, Jack, *you* done that. You jolted it. You shook Banner Top, letting that Buick down. This truck, the way it's put together, it feels ever' little shake and shiver," Curly accused him.

"Well, one thing leads to another, that's all," said Miss Lexie. "That's why I stay out of it."

Each section of the truck stood just a jot away from its neighbors, like the plated hide of the rhinoceros on its page in the geography book. Everything about it seemed a little out of its place except the license tag, an ancient one turned gold, from Alabama, which still hung upside down. The back wheels were as solid with mud as the balled roots of a tree out of the ground, but the front wheels and both horns were dripping with thinner, fresher mud like gingerbread batter.

"She's a little whopper-jawed now," Jack agreed, while he shouldered the truck back into the road and headed it toward the crowd of cosmos that concealed the fishing path. "But looks ain't everything. I'll do a little more tightening on her, the first chance I get." He climbed into the cab. "Here's hoping I didn't crack the ledge with that Buick like I cracked my truck," he said to Gloria as she reached the road still running.

"Get back to the other one," she said. "The Moodys are having a fit."

On the ledge, Judge Moody stood with his hand on the open car door, one foot on the running board. "I'm on my way out of here now, Maud Eva," he said.

She screamed again. "Jack, don't let my husband set foot in my car! Where's that truck? Drag it away from him!"

"My truck is waiting on a little further encouragement to

get her clacking again, Mrs. Moody," Jack said. "I know what it needs, right now."

"Never mind," Judge Moody interrupted. "I'm driving my own car out of this place, young man."

"Don't let him, Jack. Look down under him!" cried Mrs. Moody. "If he tries, take the wheel out of his hands. Dr. Carruthers would faint!"

"Wait in the road, Maud Eva. Will you young people help my wife to the road? If you don't object, everybody please wait in the road till I come driving out." He added more calmly, "I believe I can do better if you're not standing over me. I may be peculiar that way."

"What you are is out of gas, sir," Jack reminded him. "I'll bring you back some of mine."

"Then I've had my say," said Mrs. Moody. "I'm not going to offer another word, Oscar, until we get home."

Jack hunted up a chewed section of rubber tube in the bed of the truck, unstuck a rusty bucket from the ground under the syrup stand, emptied out the rainy leaves, and then sucked and siphoned into the bucket some gasoline out of the tank. "With the mileage he's been getting, this ought to carry him to Banner," he said, running back with the handleless bucket in his arms.

"He owes me four bits more now," said Curly Stovall.

They heard cowbells before they saw it. Then, streaked with clay, hung with briars, the emblem gone from its radiator top, its bumper swallowed up, both headlights blinded, the Buick bumped its way into view, listing sideways and fanning up mud. Judge Moody was visible at the wheel in spite of the mesmerizing rainbows flashing through the drizzle from cracks in the windshield. It churned hard before climbing its way up into the road, and then coming out between bowed-over heads of cosmos, it bumped around to where Mrs. Moody was waiting.

"You bring it to me covered with mud!" she cried.

"And it's got a few other serious things the matter with it," said Judge Moody.

"Her nose is a little bit out of kilter," Jack said. "And that's reasonable. She's been standing on it."

"The first thing to do is remove those cowbells," directed Mrs. Moody, and already Jack was pulling them off like so many cockleburs.

"Listen to the engine, Maud Eva. The way it's running leaves something to be desired," Judge Moody said.

"She'll make it to Banner," said Jack. "You could call it all downhill. Pull her up where I show you, Judge Moody, sir, in front of my truck—" He was shoving the truck, pointing it down the road.

"Instead of you pulling me, now I'm pulling you?" broke out Judge Moody.

"We'll all go in one," said Jack.

"Rescuing some woebegotten homemade truck that couldn't even get up the steam to rescue me?" exclaimed Mrs. Moody. "I can just see visions of that!"

"We're all going the same place, Mrs. Judge! Curly, I'm going to let you ride in my truck, all the way, sitting high to the wheel if you want to. And Judge Moody's Buick'll bring you in behind him."

"Right under the nose of my trade?" he yelled. "My voters?"

"Curly, make up your mind to be towed," said Jack.

"There's always *something* to come along to shorten the tail of the rabbit. Remember that, Stovall," said Miss Lexie Renfro.

Judge Moody had just backed the Buick into place.

"But I don't hear it choking any longer, Oscar," said Mrs. Moody.

"Neither do I. No, I can't get another spark out of it, I'm afraid," said Judge Moody.

"So you brought it here to me and that's as far as you can go," Mrs. Moody said to the Judge. "That was a short distance.—Stay out! Stay out! I don't want to see you getting in my engine, even with my car on the ground!" she called at Jack's back—he'd rattled up the hood. "Oscar, blow the horn at him!"

Jack put up his head. "Listen!"

It was another horn that blew. The flying school bus came down on them, around the mailbox and past the truck and the Buick, and Jack with a shout ran chasing it.

"Stop! Stop!" he hollered, until the stop-flag dropped down, the bus swerved, and he caught hold of it.

Vaughn put his head out the window.

"Scoot out and give me your bus," said Jack.

"I fixed it easy. I'm on my way to school!" Vaughn cried.

"Just what we need, and just in time, and I hadn't even missed it!" Jack said.

"It's my first day to drive it," Vaughn cried. "I ain't even let my sisters in on it, to cramp my style—they walked the sawmill track." The engine kept on with its excited, sibilant sound like uncontrolled whispering.

"Vaughn, it can be your first day tomorrow." Jack with a still bleeding hand reached in and patted Vaughn's scrubbed one. "Just get it in line at the front of that Buick and hop out. I only wonder if you sparked that battery the way I would."

"It's no blooming fair," said Vaughn, accepting it.

"The rain has washed that thing off some," said Mrs. Moody, looking disapprovingly at where the headlight sockets were still empty and the grille and the front bumper were both still missing. This morning, dimples as big as children's faces were visible, pressed into the yellow fenders. The metal of the body showed itself punctured and in places burned. The words "Banner Bob Cats" had come out across the front under the roof. "It's bound to be the same bus. And we're going behind it, Oscar?"

Judge Moody's cheeks puffed out, holding in his reply.

"All right, Vaughn, you go hunt Judge Moody's towline. Look under the jumping-off place, down on the ledge, if we still got a ledge," said Jack. "I'm going to give his rope a fair try."

"My tools and my towline are back in the car where they belong," said Judge Moody. "Under the back seat." He began to get them out again, while Jack went leaping up the other bank.

In a moment there came a kettle-drumming that went sounding on forever, it seemed, before it was swallowed up. "We got one sturdy fellow!" Jack said, running back to them. Stained red and black, and heavy as a live snake, it hung looped and dripping over his scratched, muddy arms.

"You let that bucket fall back in, Jack, and there went one thing you won't get back just by asking for it," said Miss Beulah. "That well goes to China, and your Great-great-granddaddy Jordan himself was the stubborn old digger. Might even be his bucket."

"And that's what you'll use to pull a truck and a car both from here to Banner?" asked Miss Lexie. "Tied to the Banner School bus? It's a well rope, is all it is."

"If a thing didn't have but one use to it, Lexie, I'd just let you have it," said Miss Beulah. "Mind!" she cautioned Jack. "That soppin' rope's heavier than you are!"

"Mama, I believe this morning it's wetter outside that well than in," he told her, as the two brothers went hurriedly to work knotting, Vaughn doing just as Jack did.

"Still not enough to get us all in one!" said Jack. "Now what?"

"I brought along a rope of my own," said Vaughn, with a glance up Banner Top. "In case what happened to him was to happen to me." From under the driver's chair in the school bus he got out a neatly coiled rope with a big knot in it. Mr. Renfro's axe and a length of chain were stowed there too. Jack had it all out of his hands at once.

Only a few moments later he hopped to his feet and asked Mrs. Moody, "Will you have a seat in the school bus now, Mrs. Judge? It'll give you a front view of the road."

"Not in my seat!" Gloria pleaded.

"Thank you, I'll ride where I can keep the best eye on my car limping along in front of me," she said.

"You choose the truck?" exclaimed Judge Moody.

"Then it's a little bit careful with where you put your feet, Mrs. Judge," Jack said, boosting her into the cab of the truck, "while I work you in from behind."

Mrs. Moody screamed, "Why, there's no floor!"

"Hook one foot onto that good two-by-four across the front end there, Mrs. Judge, and swing the rest of you over," Jack said. "Mind out for biting springs."

"She's got a horse blanket to her," Curly Stovall said, pointing.

"Curly, the only reason I'm letting you back in this truck one more time is my wife wouldn't trust nobody but me to drive the school bus," said Jack. "Judge Moody, I'd be obliged if you'd set between 'em, and while Mrs. Judge keeps her eye on the Buick, you keep your eye on Curly."

"That is what I intend doing. I'll keep my eye on everybody," he said. He climbed in, Curly Stovall pushed in after him and threw his weight on the steering wheel, and Jack's dogs and Curly's dogs leaped into the bed of the truck together. "But I will not travel with those dogs—Bedlam on top of Bedlam," the Judge said. "Dismiss those dogs."

"And they're wet in addition to the rest," said Mrs. Moody.

Jack ushered the dogs out, and they split as if for a race, some of them pounding down the road and the rest trundling one another onto the path that started around Banner Top.

"Now, have you boys got all that hitched perfectly? I'm not sure yet I place what's holding all that array in one piece, exactly," Miss Beulah cried.

"Trace chains, well rope, Moody towline, fence wire, and Elvie's swing, ma'am," called Vaughn.

"Well, I'm not as sure as you are that Elvie was through with that swing. Jack, whatever happens, promise you come back with that swing to give back to Elvie. She'll cry if you don't," said Miss Beulah, all agitation now, her hand already starting up as if to wave good-bye.

Now Jack whistled and was answered by a whinny.

"What do we need with that terrible mule?" Mrs. Moody exclaimed as Bet showed herself at the top of the farm track.

"All going in one," said Jack. "And I believe Bet's recruited me one extra on her own."

The black mule and then a white mule came slipping down the home track, passing and re-passing each other.

"Brother Bethune's mule has just been waiting to be shown the way home," said Vaughn. "He won't need to eat no more for a week."

"By the time we're loaded with children too, we're going to need that extra mule power," said Jack. "Add him on."

"What children?" cried Mrs. Moody.

"The schoolchildren. Vaughn ain't the only one. Mrs. Judge, we got to deliver all the poor little souls that's starting to school this morning," said Jack. "If they're late, the teacher'll give 'em a hiding."

"Now there's Vaughn on Bet, partnered with Brother Bethune's mule, both heading up the school bus with Jack at the wheel, and the truck with Stovall and the Moodys inside, and the Moodys' pleasure car tied on in the middle. Like a June bug about to be hauled home to dinner by a doodlebug and a yellow butterfly and a couple of ants," said Miss Lexie. "There! I've got something to tell Mr. Hugg."

"No, Vaughn! You hitched to the wrong end. You and the mules are going last!" Jack hollered. "You're the brakes!"

"Don't you know how to pull the emergency?" Vaughn said with scorn.

"I know how. But if there's one thing in the world I wouldn't put my faith in, Vaughn, it's the emergency on the Banner School bus," said Jack. "You've got two good mules. Each with their own good record of behavior. I trust one as much as I do the other."

"But they've never worked together," Judge Moody interpreted.

"And they won't gee," said Miss Lexie.

"I'm counting on 'em," said Jack. "I want 'em right behind."

"Here comes somebody else. But I don't reckon he's any help," said Miss Beulah. "He's just the letter carrier."

"You can pass us right here if you whip your pony up fast and follow the tracks through my ditch, Mr. Wingfield!" Jack called.

"No letter for you," said the mailman to Gloria. "You mailing one on the route?"

"I don't ever have to write any more letters," she told him.

"I'm glad *for* you."

"If it isn't the iceman too!" said Miss Beulah. "Look, coming the other way. Watch out, everybody, you'd hate to collide with that ice."

"It's my ride," said Miss Lexie, handing her a wad of damp cloth. "I enjoyed wearing your pillowcase." For the moment, she exposed to the rain Miss Julia Mortimer's birdwing. After the ice wagon had maneuvered its way around, Jack ran back to boost Miss Lexie up.

"Miss Lexie? You still teaching the public?" asked the driver of the ice wagon as Miss Lexie rose foursquare into the air.

"If I said I'd given it up long ago, that make you any happier?"

"I heard they're fixing to bury one now in Banner," he said when she was up on the box beside him.

"Get a wiggle on," said Miss Lexie. "Carry me till you can set me down at old man Hugg's front gate."

"There goes Lexie, back to something she knows," said Miss Beulah, as the ice wagon banged on away.

Then Miss Ora Stovall stepped on the running board of the truck. "Hope you don't mind if I slide in on your lap," she said, and sat down on Mrs. Moody. She was the only clean, dry person left. White powder on her face gave her a complexion that seemed to have a pile, like cat's fur. Her cheeks were burdened down with a pink like that of excitement, which extended all the way to her ears.

Mrs. Moody, with Miss Ora on top of her, put up one hand overhead, exploring. It stayed helplessly raised.

"It's raining," she told Judge Moody piteously. He reached and brought the curtained door shut on roofless, floorless space.

Jack leaned out of the bus. "Now, who're we about to go off and leave if she don't run for it?"

Gloria ran and hopped lightly up the steep iron step, swung herself inside, and perched on the seat behind the driver's, where she folded her hands over the back of his wobbly chair.

"Don't let that parade get away from you, Vaughn! Vaughn can't rob a hen's nest without Jack to tell him. Vaughn is not Jack, and never will be," Miss Beulah confided at the top of her voice into the truck.

"Oh, Jack," Gloria sighed at the same time into Jack's ear from behind him, "this is the way we started out. Our first day."

They shot forward. Creaks, booms, gunlike reports, the rattling of bolts, splashings underneath, and the objections of mules from behind added themselves to the high-pitched motor of the school bus leading.

"We thought things was bad *last* year," Miss Ora began to Judge Moody. "Thought we was poor *then*. Compared to now we was all millionaires and didn't know it!"

There was not a close fit to the hood covering the truck's engine. A piece of the motor was almost under their noses, glistening like a chocolate cake. Mrs. Moody peeped around Miss Ora and saw it.

"Suppose it starts working!" she exclaimed. "Oh, what'll I do with my feet?"

"Hold 'em!" Jack called back.

The three big hulks ploughed their joined-up way down Banner Road, moving as they'd never been before and never would be again, in one another's custody and in mule custody, above the ragged gullies and under the shaved clay hills that were shining as though great red rivers were pumping through their hearts.

The rain, that was falling on everything more gently than the rays of yesterday's sun, had been just enough to spoil the hay and to part Sid's hair down the middle. He was joining them now, going first, leading them all. As they came along faster he ran faster too, jumping over puddle after puddle, rocking himself like a little chair to jump over the big ones.

"I'm taking the liberty of unsnapping these rain curtains," said Mrs. Moody. "If they were doing any good for the roof of my head, I wouldn't object, but they are decidedly mildewed."

"Don't ask me to hold 'em! I've got all I can hold. All," said Miss Ora. In her lap, besides the umbrella, was a big purse of black leather that was turning gray along the seams and around the corners, the same gray that hair turns in old age.

Mrs. Moody gave the curtains to Judge Moody to hold. She peeped again, ran her eyes up and down the claybanks and frowned at the sky on top. The procession dipped across a creek bridge, limber as a leather strap.

"It's just some more of what was served to us yesterday," she said.

"No, the world doesn't do much changing overnight," said Judge Moody.

"And this is the edge of nowhere, no two ways about it. Don't try telling me there's people living along here," Mrs. Moody said, when big shepherd-type dogs ran out from where they guarded the entry to some little track, barking to greet Sid, trying to bite at the tires of the school bus, barking everything on past.

"Follow them buggy tracks back far enough and you'll see

houses for 'em. Oh, there's plenty customers still hanging on." Miss Ora laughed there on Mrs. Moody's knees.

"Brakes, Vaughn!" Jack sang out, and the line of them jerked, tugged almost to a stop. A handful of children with schoolbooks held over their heads waited by the side of an Uncle Sam mailbox.

"To the back!" Gloria commanded as the children scrambled shrieking inside with her, while their dogs, the shepherd-type, like members of the neighborhood family, then tried to get on the bus.

"Get back in that road, Murph!" said Jack. "Get that tail out of here. Sid's the only dog that knows how to ride with me." He whistled and Sid entered and sat up by the gear box, panting. He sat as close to Jack's foot as Gloria sat close to his head.

Judge Moody pointed suddenly across the two ladies. "I believe there's my ditch. There it is, Maud Eva! Take a look."

"Horrors, you made me see a snake in it about nine feet long," said Mrs. Moody. "Dead, I devoutly trust."

"Yes sir, along here gets to be a fairly good-size dreen," said Miss Ora. "Don't it, Brother? Panther Creek gets in a hurry sometimes to get to the old Bywy."

"Brakes!" called Jack.

"My opinion is we're going to bang together so hard next time we stop that I'm going to spill somebody," Mrs. Moody warned.

"But Mrs. Judge, we got to gather up all these children regardless!" Jack called. "They've got one in every cranny, waiting in the rain, with nothing to their poor shaved little heads but a schoolbook or two. You wouldn't want 'em left behind and missing a day of school."

A sled, with a front guard like the foot of a little bed, stood hitched to a gray mule, waiting where there was no mailbox but only a clearing in the cut-over woods to let a track through. A little boy jumped off the sled from behind his father who stood to drive.

"Patient as Job," said Jack, throwing open the door to let the little boy in.

"Now let that be enough," Mrs. Moody prayed to the dripping sky.

Judge Moody pointed again. "No, *that's* my ditch! There it is, Maud Eva. This is the right one."

"You've already forgotten," she said. "Well, that one's got some kind of a warning planted down in there, plain to see. Take a look yourself."

It was a new sign, its paint shining wet in long black fish-tails.

" 'Where Will YOU Spend Eternity?' " Miss Ora read off for them. "I can tell you without a bit of trouble who to thank for that."

"I'm not going in again," said Judge Moody.

"Old Nathan Beecham. He's a crank. He comes this way once a year and you never see the last of it," Miss Ora told him. "I'll tell you who else lives on that road, Mr. Willy Trimble. He's a bachelor. Down yonder's his chimney." It was of mud, lumpy as an old stocking on an old leg. "He's a pretty old fixture of this community."

"Well, just keep on twisting and winding," said Mrs. Moody to her own car going in front of them. "I suppose we've got to get past everything there is before we're there."

On top of the bank could be seen a roof and, higher than that, gourds hanging in rows, strung on lines between thin poles, like notes on a staff of music, each painted skull-white with a black opening.

"All right, that's Brother Bethune's house," said Miss Ora. "He's a Baptist preacher and a moonshiner, and that's his bluebird houses."

Now, election posters for races past and still to come embraced the bigger tree trunks. There were the faces of losers and winners, the forgotten and the remembered, still there together and looking like members of the same family. Every time there was Curly Stovall on a tree there was Uncle Homer on the next one, but only Uncle Homer's qualifications were listed in indentation like a poem on a tombstone:

EXPERIENCED
     COURTEOUS
LIFELONG BAPTIST
     MARRIED
RELIABLE
     JUST LEAVE IT TO HOMER.

"It ain't far now! We're coming to Aycock's house," said Jack.

Against the sides of the road bank, like the two halves of a puzzle, lay a parted bedstead, every iron curlycue of it a flower of rust.

"Look what little Mis' Comfort is trying to wish off on the public now," said Jack. "I believe that's Aycock's own bed."

"No," said Gloria. "That's been rusting even longer than you and Aycock have been gone. It's Mr. Comfort's."

"If he ever is planning on coming home, he's got one of the poorest welcomes I ever saw waiting on man. I almost hope he's dead," said Jack. "Brakes!"

"What are we stopping for now?" protested Mrs. Moody, as they slowed down under a big blackjack oak that a little path climbed up under.

"Aycock!" Jack hollered. "Where's the teacher?"

Over their heads was a house perched even with the edge of the bank, on struts. Aycock was visible sitting on the porch floor with his knees crossed and legs hanging over; he was crouched over his guitar. Without interrupting the rise and fall of his hand, he called, "She hoofed it. I told her the school bus wasn't anything to count on."

"He's happy right where he is. He'll sit there serenading himself till he's seen the train go by," said Jack as the procession leaped forward.

"The train?" repeated Mrs. Moody.

"You know, Maud Eva, it's due in Ludlow at ten fifteen," said Judge Moody, looking at his watch.

"Banner's on the crossing," said Miss Ora. "They call it a blind crossing."

"The train better stop for it," said Mrs. Moody.

"*We'd* better stop. The Nashville Rocket doesn't know Banner's on the map," said Judge Moody. "Any more than you did yesterday."

"They know now!" Jack sang out. "Ever since he got stopped by my truck, Mr. Dampeer always blows for Banner about forty times! Don't worry, Mrs. Judge, he won't hit my truck a second time!"

"On the last dip, I bet you a nickel we're going to give 'em a free show, Brother," said Miss Ora.

"I swear you Bob we've risked life and limb every inch of the way since we left home, Oscar," Mrs. Moody said. "And going on a mercy errand!"

"Listen, now somebody's coming up behind us," Curly Stovall said.

"Who?" objected Miss Ora.

"I can hear 'em. It's another horse or mule back yonder, crowding the two we got," said Curly.

Miss Ora stuck her head out. "I'll tell you who it is, it's old Mr. Willy Trimble," she said, and yelled, "*Willy Trimble?— Hope not!* What're you coming after us for?—He's pulling a load of flowers in his old wagon," she told Judge Moody. "He's funeral-crazy. I can tell you where he's going."

"I know already," he told her.

"Well, excuse *me*," Miss Ora exclaimed. "Excuse me for living."

For a straight strip downhill the road ran between equally high carved banks shining wet on either side and too close for comfort, like the Red Sea in the act of parting as pictured in the Bible. Two wooden churches hung over them from opposite sides of the road, as if each stood there to outwait the other and see which would fall first.

"Methodist—Baptist," said Miss Ora Stovall with a wag of her head. She asked Mrs. Moody, "I'm Methodist, which are you?"

"I'm neither one, and gladder of it every minute."

Jack was waving his hand out of the school bus. Brother Bethune stood on the Baptist porch watching them go by, in a coat from which the pocket flaps stood out like stove lids, a sheltering dog under each drumming palm.

"Looks like I've been stood up!" he called back. "Where's my crowd?"

Mrs. Moody gave a little shriek and, even under the weight of Miss Ora on her lap, she drew up her legs and held her feet. They were looking down a gap between banks red as live coals onto a streak of river with a bridge across it.

"Brakes!" Judge Moody said loudly.

"School bus goes down this hill every morning and crawls back up every evening!" Jack called as down they plunged. "If anything ever happens to put a stop to that, it's going to be about twice as hard to get an education!"

"It's running away with us," whispered Mrs. Moody. "With all of us!"

"Now I can see it! Almost under my nose!" Jack called. "The blessed water tank that spells out Banner." He let out a shout. "Brakes, Vaughn! Whip 'em just as hard as you can labor—in the direction of home!"

"Oh, Jack!" said Gloria.

"Blow my horn, Curly, if you're coming that close behind!" yelled Jack.

"Pray!" cried Mrs. Moody.

And the children all with one accord began to sing,

> "O hail to thee, Banner School so fair,
> The fairest school in the land!"

"I'm going to put it all in the *Vindicator*. Watch out, Freewill! Banner's going to beat you this week! You won't have as much as we have to toot your horn about," bragged Miss Ora Stovall.

"Be ready for the shock if that engine catches, Curly!" hollered Jack. "We're gonna level out in a minute!"

The claybanks flew up behind them, the smell of the river came forward in their place. Honeysuckle and trumpet vines whipped out at the school bus, at the Buick, the truck. A little crossroad peeped up for a minute. "The blind crossing!" Judge Moody cried, warning, while the children all sang the louder, *"Beyond compare! Beyond compare!"* and they rushed upon the railroad track and were bounced in quick turn over it, while old circus posters on the side of a store went by like a flurry of snow in their faces, and they rushed on to where the road widened at a water tank and just as quickly narrowed again to meet the bridge, and just before the bridge they swung off to the right into the open level of a school yard and around it in a pounding circle, taking the shocks of humping tree roots, and seemed to be running straight into the schoolhouse—it pressed close like a face against a win-dowpane—while the children yelled to finish the song,

> "We rally to thee!
> To the purple and gold!"

and the truck engine suddenly caught and fired off and braked them from behind as the bus came up against the basketball goal post and stopped to its tired crack.

"Oh, Jack. It was like it used to be," Gloria sighed. She had been sprung over his chair from behind him, into his lap.

"I ain't lost my touch?" he asked tenderly.

"Hardly any."

"You can sit up and look, Mrs. Moody!" Jack called. "You're in Banner!"

"Praise Allah," she said.

Only Mr. Willy Trimble, with hat lifted, had kept going straight ahead, taking mules and wagon on the jump onto the old cable bridge that ran unsupported as an old black tongue put out by Banner at the other side. The noise was like forty anvils making a chorus.

"Run for it!" Jack cried, throwing open the bus door. The laughing children poured out, jumped the puddles to the schoolhouse step, and shoved their way inside.

"All right, Vaughn! Cut a-loose!" said Jack. "We don't need you any longer!"

Immediately the mules, unshackled, ran past the school and then, one with neck laid over the other's neck, turned back the way they'd come.

Vaughn stood on the bus step. "Sister Gloria, would you please to find me my books? They're where I was going to sit on 'em to reach up to my steering wheel."

"Rise up, Jack. They're still as good as new," Gloria lied, placing the warm books in Vaughn's arms.

"You can drive it home," said Jack. "Don't forget all you learned on the way down, and remember it's the oppo-site."

"He's drenched," Gloria said to Jack. "That green teacher ought to excuse him from sitting three in a seat until he dries out in the cloakroom."

"No'm, it just feels good to my skin," said Vaughn. "You can't be the teacher any longer."

Painted in another year, the schoolhouse had the ghostly whiteness of a bottle from which all the milk had just been poured. A line of crayoned and scissored bonnety daffodils, pasted on the windowpane before the break-up of school for spring planting, was still there. Now the window filled from behind with laughing faces. The teacher Vaughn was so ready to worship appeared in the doorway. The jonquil smell of new pencils ground to a point for the first day, smells of rainy hair and flattened crumbs, flowed out of the schoolhouse around her as she held out her hand.

Holding his books circled close to his ribs, Vaughn cleared the mud puddle and the mountain stone both in one leap and landed almost in the teacher's arms.

"Vaughn's big brother he's been to the pen," some children's voices began to chant as he got inside.

Jack plunged out of the bus and jumped Gloria to the ground. He raced to the truck, pulled Curly bodily out of it, then leaped into the driver's seat himself.

He ran both arms under the steering wheel and embraced it. Butting the Buick ahead, he drove the truck at thirty miles an hour, while it roared back at him, swinging it under the sycamore boughs to bring off a wide left turn out of the school yard, straddling the mud puddle as he crossed the road, roaring past the giant sunflowers lined up all the way to the store like a row of targets, with Miss Ora sliding from Mrs. Moody's lap onto Judge Moody's and back again, and stopped with the Buick's nose an inch short of the telephone pole. He unhitched the two machines and drove the truck to the other side of the yard and evened it with the Buick so that they stood matched.

An old man sat on the bench on the store porch above them, feet planted and wide apart, hands gripping the seat.

"Well, if it's not Captain Billy Bangs, gathering up strength to vote tomorrow!" cried Jack.

"Today is election day," said the old man. "Ain't it?"

"No sir, you're going to have to wait for tomorrow to get here," said Jack, and he leaped onto the porch to shake the old man's hand. "Captain Billy, I want you to know Judge Moody and Mrs. Judge Moody from Ludlow—they spent last night in my bed and they just had a ride from Banner Top in my truck."

"Train's late," Captain Billy told them. "Life ain't what it used to be." There was still some red in his beard.

"Well, all I hope is when they read about it in the *Vindicator* they'll appreciate what I went through," said Miss Ora Stovall. "Give me a strong pull out of here, Brother."

When she was out of the truck, Judge Moody helped his wife slide off the horse blanket to get her feet on the ground, where rivulets the orange of inner tubes played over the clay-packed gravel in front of the store.

Banner School and Stovall's store sat facing each other out of worn old squares of land from which the fences had long ago been pulled down, as if in the course of continuing battle. The water tank was shimmering there above the railroad track like a bathing pigeon in the fine rain. Around its side, under the word BANNER, letters that stretched so wide as to appear holding hands spelled "Jack + Imogene." Beyond that, there were two ancient, discolored sawdust piles standing in a field of broomsedge like the *Monitor* and the *Merrimac* in the history book, ready to fight again. A beckoning fringe of old willows grew all around their bases.

Once through Banner, the road climbed steep as a stepladder onto the bridge that was suspended narrow and dark as an interior hallway between the banks of the Bywy, somewhere down there out of sight.

"Why, we're right back in mortal sight of *that*!" Mrs. Moody's face, looking at the way they'd come, became mapped in pink. "For all we've travelled!"

"It's never been any secret that on Banner Top they've almost got Banner in their laps," said Gloria. "I'm glad it's further than it looks, or nobody'd ever be out of everybody else's call."

"And is that the road we just came down?" Mrs. Moody demanded.

"The thing that looks like a sliding board is. That's the straight part," said Jack.

"Those same two churches!" protested Mrs. Moody.

"And here is Curly's store, where you can ask for anything you want," said Jack.

As he spoke, a busy-walking little person switched out of the store and down the steps. She popped her eyes and put out her tongue at Gloria.

"Hi, Imogene," said Jack.

"Jack Renfro, listen-a-here, the first thing you do, I want you to climb up and scrub your name off that water tank where you wrote it up there with mine," she said. "You can leave my name up there *all by itself*. I evermore mean it."

"Just as cute and bowlegged as ever," Jack said to Gloria as Imogene Broadwee wagged herself away. "And the very one for Curly here to marry. I'm going to tell him a good way to go about it."

"I'm going to use the telephone," Judge Moody interrupted. "Better late than never." He climbed the steps of the store. Nailed one to a post across the front were posters, each with its picture of Curly wearing a hat, and coming out from the crown on rays were the different words "Courteous," "Banner-Born," "Methodist," "Deserving," and "Easy to Find." A hide was stretched and nailed on the wall over the doorway, where it appeared to hover, like a partly opened black umbrella not too unlike Miss Ora's. Judge Moody stumbled over the scales as he found his way in.

The smells of coal oil, harness, cracker dust, cloth dye, and pickles clung about the doorway. Judge Moody could be only dimly seen where he stood at the telephone; among the boots and halters hanging from the beam above his head, shirt-tails of every description, old and new, were visible like so many fading banners of welcome.

"Hey, Curly, today is here at last!" Ella Fay Renfro cried.

There where the sawmill spur came out of the bushes into the railroad track, she and Etoyle and Elvie stepped off into Banner. Ella Fay piled her books on the little sisters and sent them dragging themselves inside the school. With a skip she came running across the road.

A fatuous look spread over Curly's face and he said, "Well, look who they're sending to pay the store!"

Jack punched him in the nose.

"And there go Brother and Jack again, not looking a bit

different or a day older since the last time they was at it. But
you do, and I do," Miss Ora Stovall remarked to Gloria. "Just
don't bring it in the store!" she yelled at them, as Captain
Billy Bangs drummed his heels on the porch floor and gave a
clap once or twice with his hands.

Jack drove his fist again and Curly, losing his baseball cap,
staggered backward until he fell against the open door of the
truck and slid to the ground. Some whimpers began coming
out of his mouth like small, squeezed tears.

"Jack, that hurt!" Gloria cried. "I hope landing that blow
was an accident, not something you learned at Parchman."

Ella Fay squatted down, put both her little white hands
around the ham of Curly's arm, and said, "I was only coming
to ask him for a dime's worth of candy corn."

"Haul up, little sister!" Jack told her. "Didn't you learn
you a lesson when he took Granny's gold ring?"

"I should worry, I should care!" said Ella Fay. "I made *him*
give *me* something!" With all the haste her wet fingers could
manage, she unlaced the throat of Gloria's sailor dress, turned
back the collar, and displayed what she wore on a calendar
cord tied around her neck: a pearl-handled pocketknife an
inch long. Both little fingers extended, she rapidly undid the
knot behind, and with a brief scream of pleasure showed it to
them in turn, laid on her sweet, horny, greedy little palm. "So
we're evens. We exchanged," she said, blushing at last.

"Why, you little sneak!" cried Gloria.

"But that's all we did," said Ella Fay back. "So what if the
old ring did go down the mouse-hole? I know who'd get me
a new one. Hear, Curly?"

Curly Stovall laughed and sat up. Re-tying her calendar
cord, dropping the knife expertly down her front while she
gave a brimming glance around her, Ella Fay told Gloria,
"Watch and see! I can be a bride too. You can't always be the
one and only!" She turned and pounded splashing into the
schoolhouse.

"Curly! You threatening to marry Ella Fay? Curly! That's
coming into my family!" Jack said.

"Jack, you're turning red all over," said Gloria. "You're
going to pop."

"Curly! Our battles'll be called off before they start! We'll all be one happy family!" Jack cried. "I'll have to bow you a welcome into my own house where I can't lather you!" He pulled Curly to his feet and yelled in his face, "With Uncle Homer out of the running, we'll even have to vote for you from now on!"

"And you all vote as a family. That's a hundred votes right there," said Curly. He put his baseball cap on again, visor to the back.

"Curly, I'd give you something. I'd almost give you the truck, like it stands, not to marry into us. Want it for a present?"

Curly stopped laughing and put out his jaw. "I ain't going to take no present off of you."

"I'd just as soon give it to you as look at it," said Jack hotly.

"Jack!" screamed Gloria, running to stand beside it.

"It's yours! It's yours, Curly, take it! I dare you!" said Jack.

"I ain't gonna!" shouted Curly.

"It's yours on a silver platter. Take it right now! And get out of my family before you get in it."

Curly's fist landed under his jaw. Jack rose on his toes as if about to fly, then toppled, and the foot of the telephone post cracked him on the forehead. He rolled over and spread out on his back. His good, wide, blue eye was still fixed where he had just turned it—the blue was nearly out of sight in the corner, as if something might still be coming around the edge of his cheek.

"Jack! Jack!" said Gloria. "Can you see day?"

"Now gimme that shirt-tail, boy!" Curly shouted. He whipped out his big hunting knife, and rolled Jack over and cut his shirt-tail off.

"Oscar, aren't you going to referee?" cried Mrs. Moody, as the Judge reappeared on the porch.

"Maud Eva, I am not a referee," said Judge Moody.

"Well, I am! Listen here, Buster, Jack was down there on the ground lying helpless as a babe!" Mrs. Moody cried to Curly. He ran with the shirt-tail past her into his store. "And you big bully you, you cut his shirt-tail off!" she called after him. "That's no fair!"

"I knew it would happen some day," said Gloria. She had Jack's head in her lap, and sank back against the telephone post that rose like the gnawed pith of a giant stalk of sugar-cane behind her.

"It'll learn him! Trying to give me his truck! What's he trying to call himself? Rich?" cried Curly, hammering the shirt-tail to the cross-beam with all the other shirt-tails.

"I can't even get hold of the operator," said Judge Moody through the blows.

"If anybody's dead, she's at the funeral," said Miss Ora Stovall. "Gets her a crowd and *goes*. Try her about dinner time."

"Just lie there," said Gloria, stroking Jack's brow. "You don't know a thing that's going on."

"We're stranded. Worse than yesterday. Stranded," said Judge Moody to his wife. He pointed. "And what's the boy doing down on the ground?"

"Didn't you hear the crack to his head?" Mrs. Moody asked. "I don't see why his wife doesn't simply shake him."

"Completely stranded," Judge Moody said, and over the river a church bell rang. In the rainy air it was no more resonant than a bird call. Now, on this side of the river, from up the road, a car descended into Banner and ran through it onto the bridge.

The air rang as though anvils were being struck for a mile around. Before the bridge had stopped swaying, another car followed the first one down Banner Road, and two more, travelling close together as if keeping each other company, ploughed splashing up out of the crossroad coming from Foxtown, streaked and redwheeled with mud, all of them. They all went the same way, onto the bridge, under the old tin sign saying CROSS AT OWN RISK. Miss Ora Stovall had already put her finger out and started counting them.

"These people don't know it, but they're lucky not to be meeting that funeral," shouted Mrs. Moody over the racket. "It's nothing but a one-way bridge."

"They're going to the funeral, I should say," said Judge Moody, looking at his watch again.

"Oh, Jack," Gloria said under the clanging, "you don't even hear our bridge. When we were young we used to chase each other on it, back and forth, like running through a cat's-cradle."

Another car bounded past. "Not one soul looks this way. You'd think they'd inquire if there'd been an accident," shouted Mrs. Moody.

"They're from Ludlow," said the Judge.

"Then I should be thankful they're *not* looking."

"They're driving like they're mad," said Miss Ora Stovall, looking satisfied.

"I expect they've already tried every other road they can find," said Mrs. Moody.

Finally there was only the barking of the dogs and the chirping of the truck in their ears. The truck motor, all by itself, still ran, having never been cut off. Mud still poured from it as it shook, thick drops like persimmons being steadily rolled out of buckets.

"Well, you only had to wait," said Mrs. Moody, still speaking loudly. "It comes without being called, Judge. Here's your wrecker."

"Now *that's* something *new*," said Miss Ora.

A wrecker clattered up out of the crossroad and over the railroad track into Banner. It had had a coat of red paint, but the black hieroglyphics of a more recent soldering job overlaid the paint on most of the body parts. Rocking and splashing through the puddles, it made its way past the Buick and went straight for the truck. It backed up in front of it. On the driver's door was lettered in black, as if by a burning poker, "Red's Got It."

The driver got out, hopped a puddle, landed in front of Curly Stovall, and said, "How much did you bet you'd never see me again?"

"Mr. Comfort!" said Curly.

"And look there. Who give him that souvenir?"

"He bumped his own head to make that rising. And his eye just got a kick from a dear little baby," Gloria retorted. She held Jack's head in her lap. His good eye was still rolled as if to see around the corner of her knee.

"You give us a shock, Mr. Comfort!" cried Curly. "Who's letting you run around loose in that wrecker?"

"Started working for old Red this morning. First job he give me was come over to Banner and haul him in this truck."

"Come back and see me day after tomorrow, Mr. Comfort. Better make it Saturday," said Curly urgently.

"I may not have to work on Saturday," said Mr. Comfort. "Hope not."

"Oscar, aren't you going to speak to him?" cried Mrs. Moody. "He'll go off without my car if you don't speak to him. He's shifty-eyed."

"Just a minute, there. Mister, do you see this Buick?" asked Judge Moody.

"Yes sir, looks like a booger's had a fit in it," said Mr. Comfort. "But I didn't have no orders about a Buick. My orders was Stovall's truck."

"Well, it just don't do any good to say good-bye to anybody," said Miss Ora Stovall.

"But you can't carry it off now!" Curly cried, blocking the older man's way.

"Old Red got wind a while ago he better git it while the gitting is good," said Mr. Comfort. "Make way, Curly."

"What's he want with your truck, Brother?" asked Miss Ora Stovall. "Is it a prime secret?"

"Wants the parts," said Mr. Comfort. He ducked around Curly, hopped puddles to the truck. He started thumping its sides as if it were a watermelon and he were a judge of ripeness. "Is it at all in good shape?" he asked with pursed lips. "Seems like I already smell a little smoke somewhere."

"It's most likely coming out from a thin place in your own hide," Captain Billy Bangs said from the bench.

Curly was splashing around Mr. Comfort, who was trying to hitch a chain, while his dogs came and tried unsuccessfully to bite through Mr. Comfort's boots.

"Hey, Jack!" Curly hollered. "Jack, are you dead, possuming, or what?"

"Wake him up, girl! Give him a slap!" Mrs. Moody called. "We need him quick."

"He's sleeping so trustfully," said Gloria. She laid her ear to his chest. "His heart is beating right along with mine."

"Do you want him to be *sorry*?" cried Mrs. Moody. "Listen,

that rascal's running off with his truck when he doesn't know it—and won't take the Buick to the shop like Judge told him. Swat him!" she cried to Curly, as Mr. Comfort put out a hand and cut off the truck's motor.

"He's an old man!" bawled Curly. "He's Aycock's long-lost daddy!"

Mr. Comfort wiped off his hands and vaulted the step into the wrecker's cab.

"Mr. Comfort, ain't you staying here even long enough to vote?" cried Curly.

"I'm voting in Foxtown now."

"Mr. Comfort, I could tell you some news you might be interested in hearing," called Miss Ora Stovall. "This very morning they're burying another lady in your grave. Don't you want to stay for that?"

"No, I'll just be running on. I just come to git this truck while the gitting's good. Tell my little family hello and to keep praying for me," called Mr. Comfort.

The wrecker engine started with a sound as mild as a sneeze, then delivered a volley of backfiring. The two vehicles began moving together. The wrecker shook harder than the truck; it looked as if the pieces of the bed they had passed on Banner Road might have gone into making it.

The melodious hoot of the diesel streamliner made itself heard in the distance. It warned Banner softly over the river hills, coming closer, sounding louder and sweeter, its pitch rising.

"Pour a bucket of water over his head right quick, girl!" said Mrs. Moody.

"This is *my* husband," said Gloria.

A roar began to dip and wave on the air, and Gloria with her hand warded them off as the wrecker drew the truck around them and out of the store yard, on toward the railroad track.

A deep organlike note vibrated throughout Banner. Jack reached out a hand, feeling about in space, and as the train sprang as if out of the store onto the blind crossing, he got to his feet, staggering. Eyes focused ahead, he moved his lips. "Where went my truck?"

Gloria pointed for him, and by the time he turned right-

about there was only the train to see. It was going at eighty
miles an hour, all heat, with the sunflowers and the elderberry
bushes bowing, sucked in as if by a storm running on its belly.
For a moment or two the heads of strangers rode by at lighted
windows, and when the road could be seen again on the other
side, it was already empty, only a few live sparks dancing on
it. The dogs that had raced the train to the other end of the
school yard stood convulsed with barking until their voices
became audible once more. Then the last, soft, lapping sounds
of the train were gone too. Like the truck and the wrecker, it
had vanished.

"The junk man got it!" Gloria cried.

"You're dreaming!" cried Jack.

"Took it away while you didn't know the difference."

"But I hadn't been at my wheel but a minute! Didn't drive
it a whole lot over thirty yards!" Jack cried.

"Now it's going to Old Red in Foxtown. And Old Red is
going to take it back to pieces," said Gloria. "That's what he
wants with it."

"He's the renderer!" said Jack. "He's who got my horse!
My horse first and now my truck!"

"That's how the world treats you, Jack, when you don't
know any better. Now do you see?"

"Curly!" Jack spun around. "What new bargain have you
been striking behind my back?"

"Jack, what that truck was was my vote getter!" hollered
Curly. "Old Red owns Foxtown! Like I own Banner. And he
swore—"

"You traded this truck for the Foxtown votes. *I* see," remarked Mrs. Moody. "There's no abiding mystery to me
about politics."

"I thought I could trust him till tomorrow. But he's pulled
a triple double-cross," cried Curly. "I sure wasn't looking for
nobody to come for the truck till after the votes was in and
counted!"

"But it's gone!" Jack cried again. "And in the twinkling of
an eye!"

"Homer Champion is an everlasting unmitigated blooming
skunk," said Curly, grabbing him. "He's the lowest thing that
crawls."

"And he must have a mind like chain-lightning to go with it," said Jack. "To come back with an answer that quick after you were crowing over him on Banner Top."

"He's thick with Old Red, as thick as he can be!" cried Curly.

"Uncle Homer may be doddering before long, but this time he wasn't asleep at the switch. He won't lose by much," said Jack. "Thanks to you for selling away my truck!"

"Old Red knew it wasn't in the bargain for him to come for that truck till after Tuesday's celebration. And you didn't reckon I was going to let him *have* it, did you?"

"You just did!" cried Jack.

"I couldn't hit Mr. Comfort! He sent Mr. Comfort!"

"Yes, Jack, to add insult to injury, Mr. Comfort came back to be the one to haul it," said Gloria. "And nobody stopped him."

"To think that's the way Mr. Comfort elected to put in his appearance. After all this time, being given up maybe for dead!" said Jack.

"It's these daddies that need the whippings," said Miss Ora.

"At least he gets a better mark than Ears Broadwee for beating the train to the crossing," said Jack.

"He didn't have a minute to spare," said Gloria. "Suppose the train had been on time?"

"You're a fine one to criticize!" Mrs. Moody exclaimed. "Who wouldn't throw a bucket of water on her husband? Just let him lie there while that old monkey got away with it."

"I wanted you to wake up right on time to see what they all would do without you, Jack," said Gloria. "Judge Moody showed his colors too—all he did to help was stand there and say 'Stranded. Stranded!'"

"Stranded?" Jack cried. "Who's stranded?"

Over the water, the bell rang again, faint as an echo. "I missed the funeral service in Alliance," said Judge Moody.

"You ain't going to miss the burying in Banner!" cried Jack. "No sir. I made you a promise to get you back on your road, and I'm going to keep it yet. They ain't in sight yet. I'm going to patch you up in time to join in with the parade to the cemetery. And that's your road home, Judge Moody—after we bury her, you just keep on going. With good luck getting through Foxtown, you'll be back at the courthouse by dinner time." He spun around. "All right, Curly, where's your newest tires?"

On a pipe coming out of the wall three used tires hung like ringers in a game of quoits. "You're going to need ever' one I got," said Curly, rolling them out. "I'll put 'em on for three dollars and your old tires, mister."

"Three won't take me anywhere," said Judge Moody, coming down the steps into the yard.

"The best-looking one in sight is Judge Moody's spare," said Jack. "All it ever had was one blowout. Patch it and it can go on a front." He dived down in the bob-tailed shirt and crawled under the Buick with the jack.

When the Buick stood up on four slick, gray, pumped-out tires, Judge Moody climbed into the driver's seat.

"I'm still unable to get a spark," he said. "I didn't expect to."

"Keep your head out of my engine, Jack Renfro!" Mrs. Moody cried.

Jack's hands and face were hidden from them. "One wire is pulled just a little bit loose from your coil," he said. "There, it's hanging in two."

"Leave it. Leave it in two. Leave it that way, Jack," Judge Moody said.

Jack shuttered down the hood, clambered inside the Buick as Judge Moody squeezed out of the driver's seat, and seized the wheel as if it were a pair of vibrating handlebars on a motorcycle. With the noise of a motorcycle, the engine leaped to life.

"How do you account for that? How do you suppose you fixed that wire?" Judge Moody asked over the motor's singing.

"I used some of my spit. I believe it might even hold you as far as the courthouse," Jack said as he jumped out.

Judge Moody heaved a long sigh.

"Was it all that hard, Oscar?" asked his wife, getting in beside him.

"Everything's hard," he said. "Or it's getting that way."

"Do you want me to tell you what your next birthday will be?" she asked.

"No," he said, and she told him.

"Pump me in a dollar's worth of gas, then," he called to Curly Stovall.

"That makes two. And it's a dollar for the trip to Banner Top and a dollar for the trip down," Curly reminded Judge Moody as he paid him. "And three tires."

"Seven whole dollars! And I want to add to that that you've been thoroughly objectionable and I won't soon forget you," said Mrs. Moody.

"And sixty cents more for the rope," said Curly. "I ain't going to be able to use it again or sell it either."

"Sixty *cents!*" Mrs. Moody screamed. "Is that the rope we were all hanging onto? Is that what he supposed our life was worth?"

"Keep it. I'll charge the rope to Jack," Curly said, as Miss Ora Stovall came and took the bills out of his hand, folded them, and snapped them inside her purse.

Curly Stovall went into the store and came back with his candidate's hat on, placed down low over his brow.

"Now, hurry up, funeral!" Miss Ora called. "It's just quit raining for you."

"Funeral coming?" asked the wavery voice of Captain Billy Bangs. He put his old hands tight on his knees. "Is it Elvira Vaughn?"

"No sir, she started on ninety-one this morning," said Jack.

"Just wanted to see if I could catch you," said the old man. "She still putting up with Billy Vaughn?"

"We buried Grandpa, Captain Billy," said Jack in a low voice.

"Well, I like to see who I can catch," said Captain Billy. "Who are they fixing to bury now?"

"Miss Julia Mortimer, sir."

"Oh, is that the case with her," he said and fell silent.

"I want to get home," said Mrs. Moody from the Buick. "Bury the woman and get home."

"There's been some starch taken out of you too, dear," Judge Moody said then, and he put his hand down on her knee.

"White piqué wasn't intended to be worn a second day. Much less to graveside services in falling rain," she said. "But can we *not* go, Oscar? And then be able to forgive ourselves?"

"Oh, we're going," he said. "We always were."

"If you so decree. But I wish you could see yourself!" she cried. She aimed a finger at his seersucker trousers where he had gone down in the mud. "People from Ludlow, and Presbyterians from everywhere, will wonder what you've been doing down on your knees."

"Let them wonder," he said.

She gave him a short laugh. "And when they see this car, and look for the winged Mercury I had especially put on the radiator! They'll say it's lucky you had me along to vouch for who you are." Judge Moody glanced at her and she said, "And I'll tell you something. One thing along with us is still snowy—Maud Eva Moody's gloves! They've never come out of my purse until this minute." She drew them forth.

"Put them on," he said. He turned and leaned out of the Buick. "We'll say good-bye. You kept hold of us all for a pretty good little while there this morning, Jack."

"I was proud to do it." He blushed. "The one thing I wasn't ready for was a poor excuse for a rope!"

"Well, I hope—I hope you save the hay," said Judge Moody.

"Thank you, sir."

Judge Moody put out his rope-burned hand, Jack put up his bloody one, and they shook.

"The one you'd been happy to see in the ditch, you saved and shook hands with," said Gloria in a low voice.

"I know it," said Jack.

"I didn't want you risking your neck either time."

"I'm proud you helped me in spite of yourself," said Jack, bending to kiss her cheek. "Like a little wife."

"It's hard to help somebody and keep them out of trouble at the same time," she said. "But through it all I tried to keep my mind on the future."

"Leaving what was going on to me. That was a good wifely way," he said.

"But you'll do it again," she cried. "Put me in the same fix! You risked your life for them! And now look at you."

"Look at his eye," Mrs. Moody called over to her. "That's from his own family. His own child gave him that."

"It was a love-tap," said Jack and grinned as he went to shake Mrs. Moody's gloved hand.

"And look at your hands, Jack! They're rags!" said Gloria.

"You can put a little goose grease on 'em for me when it's all over and we get home," he said tenderly. He washed them under the pump, then said, "Come stand close." He kissed a finger and rubbed her cheek with it. "I think I must have given you a little smear on your cheek."

"Blood?" she asked.

"Only about fifty percent. The rest is pure Banner clay. Now I reckon we're as ready as we'll ever be for that funeral."

"Come on, funeral!" called Miss Ora Stovall.

"You and the girl haven't got a way to ride," said Judge Moody. "You can ride in the back seat of our car to the cemetery."

"I'd hate us to sit on that velvet," said Jack. "The Buick on the inside is as good as it ever was—when you get it home, you can find something and pound the dust out of it."

"They're young, Oscar," said Mrs. Moody. "They can walk."

"We're not tired," agreed Jack. "There's a pretty good short-cut. Aren't you ready for a march, Gloria?"

"You still don't know the worst," Gloria said. "Prentiss Stovall finally got your shirt-tail, Jack. And nailed it to his beam."

Jack went scarlet. He brought up a clenched fist, but Gloria laid her hand on his arm, over the muscle. "Too late now," she said. "You can't get another minute of it in. I see what's coming."

Slowly their arms went around each other's waists. Moving together, they walked the last few steps down the road to the old plank platform of the bridge.

The opposite bank of the river was high, and not red clay but limestone. It rose shell-white out of the water, washed and worn into the shapes of tall, waisted spools, of forts with slits, old towers cut off at the top. The high-water mark was a golden band of rust nearly as high as the bridge floor. Where the bridge reached it, the stone was wrinkled in rings like a pair of elephant legs braced to hold it up.

As the slow-moving procession followed the line of the

bank and then turned to pour down its road toward the
bridge, down-floating wands of light and rain tapped it here
and there. As it reached the bridge, loose planks began to play
like a school piano. The stringy old cables squealed, the floor
swayed. Behind the hearse the line seemed to narrow itself,
grow thinner and longer, as if now it had to pass through the
eye of a needle. And the eye of the needle was the loudest
place on earth.

Yet a moment came when the procession stretched and covered the full length of the bridge. The clatter of the cables
stopped, the floor drummed in a different key. As it ran full
from one end to the other, the bridge become nearly as quiet
as the river.

"Hope they don't fall through with her at our end," said
Miss Ora Stovall. "That wouldn't do our reputation very
much good."

"Miss Julia came over that bridge every Monday morning
for a good many years," said Judge Moody. "It would do well
to bear her weight one more time."

Arms entwined, Jack and Gloria stepped down out of the
way, their feet on a path that led down under the bridge.
Below, the river bed reached out from the bank a bare,
pocked, uneven white floor, over which ran strands and knotted ropes of red water. Beyond the farthest shelf of rock,
nearly all the river there was was flowing by in one narrow
channel. A child might have jumped it. And between here and
there, the whole limestone floor was ignited with butterflies,
lit there and remaining as if fastened on. Without rising, some
of them opened and closed their yellow wings, like mutes
speaking with their hands.

As Jack and Gloria waited, the hearse trundled down off
the bridge almost over their heads. Its most recent coat of
paint, wrinkled like oilcloth, shone in the lightless air because
it was wet.

Curly Stovall, standing at attention beside his gas pump,
removed his hat and held it over his heart. Miss Ora stood
beside him, counting those going by with a gesture from her
folded umbrella. Cars with headlights burning on dim followed close one behind the other, and now and then would
come a wagon, all alike filled with hatted passengers. At every

departure off the bridge, the noise of those still coming was increased a little more.

The church bus came off the bridge washed to a blue as acid and strong as a stand of hydrangeas nobody could ever make bloom pink. It crawled past Jack and Gloria, windows packed with returning faces. "You haven't got very far since yesterday!" the driver called as she went by.

Behind that came school buses, one after the other. Two looked worse than the Banner School bus, two looked better, and one was like the Banner bus all over again. Their special racket brought the children inside Banner School to the window. Through the paper flowers they watched the buses ride past full of schoolteachers.

"It's a holiday!" cried Miss Pet Hanks, leaning out of one of them. "News went out far and wide! Spread like wildfire! Everybody knows it but Banner! I couldn't get anybody to answer the phone. Children running wild all over Boone County so the teachers could come to her funeral."

Judge Moody at the wheel of his car softly groaned.

"That's your fault, Oscar, for not being on the job," said Mrs. Moody. "You were supposed to prevent anything of the kind."

Rocking over the railroad track, the procession was turning down into the Foxtown road that ran almost hidden between high banks of elderberry, following the track and the river.

"Count the license tags from away!" Miss Ora Stovall's head turned from one side to the other for every vehicle that passed. "She taught all those folks. They're all sprung from around here, no doubt about that. Those're the ones got up and left home. I never supposed they'd show up here again till it's time for us to bury *them*."

On the bench by himself up on the porch, Captain Billy Bangs didn't rise—he was too old to rise. "She taught me. She taught her elders. Because after the Surrender, they didn't leave us no school to go to. She taught me the world's round," he said. " 'We ain't standing still, Captain Billy,' she says. 'No sir, the world's round and goes spinning.' 'And if that's what it's doing, daughter,' I says back to her, 'I'd hate to think there's a can of kerosene setting anywheres on it.' "

Captain Billy, who had slowly been raising one hand, finally touched one trembling finger to the brim of his hat.

The hearse had reappeared heading the long line climbing now up the cemetery hill. And at the same time, with a masterpiece of racket, Mr. Willy Trimble came last off the bridge and brought silence. His wagon was loaded with what looked like a bale of honeysuckle. The little boy who lived down the road from Miss Julia's house in Alliance rode among the vines to keep them from flying loose. As they passed Banner School, he faced the window-packed schoolhouse, laid his thumb to his nose, and played on all his fingers at the imprisoned children.

"Now or never!" cried Mrs. Moody, grabbing the wheel along with her husband and helping him make the turn. The Buick moved slowly out of the store yard and edged into place behind Mr. Willy at the end of the line.

"His steering's going to veer him a little from now on," murmured Jack. "But I believe Judge Moody would rather I left him to find that out for himself."

"Well, they every one of 'em made the bridge. It'd been something extra if they hadn't," said Miss Ora Stovall. "But there's hardly an inch I've got left to fill up my Banner Notes anyway. With the crowd for the fish-fry and the crowd for that reunion and the crowd for this funeral, that's a big set of names. Willy Trimble is getting his in three times. Wait for me!" She was stopping to put Orange Crushes and Grapettes and Cokes into the barrel with the fresh ice. "They won't be very cold, but they'll sell. After you been to a funeral, you're glad to drink 'em warm or any other way you can get 'em," she said.

Then she and Curly, Jack and Gloria set off to follow on foot. Jack's little dog Sid was at Jack's heels, jumping the puddles.

"I'm staying right here," said Captain Billy.

"Honey, I'm sorry I can't put you in my truck," Jack said as they trudged up the short-cut. "So I could carry you like Judge Moody's carrying Mrs. Judge."

"Jack, do you know what that truck turned out to be? It

was just a play-pretty," said Gloria. "A man's something-to-play-with."

"It was my sweat."

"It finished up being nothing but a bone of contention."

"But I wasn't through with it!" he cried. "And neither was old Curly!"

"I'd already learned enough about it to satisfy me. It was never going to carry *us* anywhere. We'd always have to be carrying *it*," said Gloria. "I didn't feel all that sorry to see it go."

"Honey, you're a soldier," he said.

The path was one that led to the dinner grounds lying back of Damascus Church. Here it was empty like an empty room, exhausted of sound like a schoolroom in summer. There was a smell that had steeped for years, of horses and leather and waiting and dust, and the ghost-smell of mulberry leaves and wet mustard belonging to the tables that had gone to yesterday's reunion and were waiting now on Jack to bring back. Where each table had stood was a trough in the ground like that under a children's swing or an old person's chair by a roadside.

When they came to the old iron fence in its honeysuckle, Jack helped Gloria over it where two waist-high homemade ladders clasped in each other's arms made a stile. Across an acre of billowing ground, the funeral procession was now inching to its destination.

Grandpa Vaughn's grave was the brightest thing in sight. It was still an elevation, red as new brick, with only a few strands of grass hanging out of the clay, each a foot long, bleached but alive. The fruit jar of Granny's seed dahlias stood on it; having lived through yesterday's sun they had bowed to the rain this morning.

Jack dropped down and with his planting hand he straightened and firmed the small wooden cross, frail as kite-sticks.

"And I'm going to afford him a tombstone some day if it's the last thing I ever do," he said, jumping up.

The billowy Vaughn graves seemed to be shoving against one another for first place, tilting with their markers—some of iron, crested like giant doorkeys that might unlock at any moment.

"Where we're walking now is where Granny'll go," Jack said. "The last Vaughn in the world! And not weighing much more for all her years than our baby weighs now. When I lifted her up for her birthday hug, she near-about shot out of my hands!"

The whole expanse they were crossing had the look of having been scythed yesterday. It smelled of hay that had been rained on. Even though it was wet, their own footsteps sounded on the bristles as though they were walking over some old giant's stubbled chin. They walked faster.

"There's Mama and all of 'em's mother and dad going by," Jack said, his hand going out to the double-tablet over the single grave, with only one grave close to keep it company. "Yet when you think back on the reunion and count how many him and her managed to leave behind! Like something had whispered to 'em 'Quick!' and they were smart enough to take heed." An old crape myrtle stood with branches weighted down by rain and casting the preponderance of its bloom over Sam Dale Beecham. It grew with half a dozen trunks, not round but like girls' arms, flat-sided; with the drops of rain to honeycomb them the panicles of bloom looked heavy as flesh and twice as pink. Sam Dale Beecham's marker had darkened, its surface like the smooth, loving slatings of a pencil on tablet paper laid over a buffalo nickel, but the rubbed name and the rubbed chain hanging in two, its broken link, shone out in the wet. A grasshopper of shadowless green and of a mouse's size sat hunched there. It flew up before their hurrying steps and vanished in the stubble.

"Let him hop!" said Jack. "Sam Dale Beecham wasn't hardly older than I am now when they put him in that grave of his."

"He'd be old like the rest of 'em now. Even if he was just the baby brother," Gloria reminded him, "if he hadn't died, he'd be old, and expecting to be asked to tell everything he knew."

Her feet almost stumbled—there were also three small stones, three in a row, like loaves baked by different hands but all bearing the same one word, "Infant." Two were Aunt Nanny's and Uncle Percy's, all they'd had, and the other was Miss Beulah's last.

"Honey, no time to stand still! They can bury people before you know it," said Jack, swinging Gloria over a mud puddle.

"You didn't hear Brother Bethune bury Grandpa. It was like the reunion, never-ending."

"I hope nobody got forgiven before he was through!"

An army of tablets, some black as slates, marked half a hill-load of husbands and wives buried close together—all the Renfros. This time, Aunt Lexie and Auntie Fay, Uncle Homer Champion, Mr. Renfro and Miss Beulah, their children—Jack and Gloria themselves, and Lady May Renfro—were the skips. The original grasshopper was repeated here too, repeated everywhere and a hundred times over, grave-sitting or grave-hopping in the stubble, rising up in front of their hurrying feet and dropping behind them after they passed, grasshoppers by the hundreds.

They had made the short-cut to the little road, and along its side, in among the honeysuckle-shrouded trees and the Spanish daggers in their lowlit bloom, the cars and wagons, horses and buses had been already left behind. There was the Buick, its engine softly running at low throttle. Next to it was the postman's pony and cart, mail left in a cigar box, gathered in by a rubber band. There was Uncle Homer's van with a fresh sign decorating it, "It's Homer's Turn." The school buses had put new scrapes on one another's sides trying to line up where they wouldn't get stuck. The church bus had been left with its door open; every seat was laid with a hat, for a little rain still dripped from the branches of cemetery trees. Mr. Willy Trimble's mules stood docile, cement-gray, like monuments themselves, quietly eating honeysuckle off the fence.

"We made it," Jack whispered, lips warm at Gloria's ear. "We're just in time."

The hearse was already backed in among the graves. It was standing still, and Gloria and Jack flew past it and joined the crowd.

They rounded a great clump of ribbon-grass as high as a haystack, out of which Rachel Sojourner's grave seemed to slide, ready to go over the edge of the bank, like a disobedient child. The small lamb on its headstone had turned dark as a blackened lamp chimney.

The crowd was forming around three sides of the new grave hole. Where Mr. Comfort had been supposed to go was the last grave at the river end of the cemetery. At its back stood only an old cedar trunk, white against gray space. Its bark was sharp-folded as linen, it was white as a tablecloth. Wreaths and sprays of spikey florist flowers from Ludlow—gladioli and carnations and ferns—were being stood on their wire frames around the grave, and the homemade offerings—the flower-heads sewn onto box-lids and shirt cardboards, and the fruit jars and one milk can packed with yard lilies and purple phlox and snow-on-the-mountain—were given room to the side.

Jack held Gloria's hand and led her out in front of the known and the unknown faces around them, making for right in front. As though magnetized to the tallest monument in the cemetery, both Curly Stovall and Uncle Homer Champion stood at Dearman's grave, both glaring straight in front of them, both with their candidate's hats laid over their hearts. A little taller than they were, Dearman's shaft rose behind them, on its top the moss-ringed finger that pointed straight up from its hand in a chiseled cuff above the words "At Rest."

"That boy walking in front of you has brought himself to a funeral without a shirt-tail behind," said a voice at their backs.

"It's Jack Renfro. I feel like telling his mother," said somebody else.

"*She's* not much better. Look at *her* collar and cuffs. Look at her skirt."

"They're married. And I heard that before you could shake a stick at him, he'd gone to the pen for a hold-up."

"She'll have to stick to him now. They've got a baby not even weaned. I've laid eyes on it."

"He's probably the best she could do. Little old orphan! If she didn't want to teach school the rest of her days."

"Look at his eye when he turns around to look back at us. You know what? I saw his baby kick him in that eye. Right out in the public yesterday. I saw his baby jump and saw him catch her and she delivered him something special."

"He could still wear a shirt-tail to a funeral."

"Just keep your mind on what's coming, honey," Jack whis-

pered to Gloria. "You've done grand so far, been a soldier as
good as Mama."

"I don't think they've got any business at a funeral," said
the voice of a very old man or a very old woman.

The grave hole, up close, smelled like the iron shovel that
had dug it and the wet ropes that would harness the coffin
down into it. As though thirsty and greedy enough to take
anything, it had swallowed all the rain it had received and
waited slick and bright. The raw clods grubbed out of the
ground outshone those on Grandpa Vaughn's now older
grave; they had been piled un-gravelike as a heap of dug sweet
potatoes on the far side of Mr. Earl Comfort standing there
on a trampled clump of cemetery iris.

"I never saw so many grayheads in one place at one time,"
said Miss Ora Stovall's voice. "There wouldn't even be time
now to count 'em. And look at that one! What does *he* call
*him*self?"

It was the priest in his vestments. His skirts dragged rhyth-
mically over the objecting stubble. Behind him marched the
pallbearers; Judge Moody with his own bared head was first
on the right.

"That pallbearer came in such a hurry he hasn't even
shaved," came a voice.

The coffin had been draped with the Mississippi flag.

"If I know that flag, it's one that's been wrapped up all
summer, lying on top of a school piano with the march music.
Let's just hope it didn't sour," came a carrying voice from
where the schoolteachers stood, all sticking together.

As the pallbearers reached where they were going, owls in
a stream, one after the other, came up out of the old cedar
tree. Owls lifted like a puff of smoke over the priest and the
pallbearers and the coffin as it rocked once, suspended over
the grave, lifted over the morning's crowd, over monuments
and trees, and away. Even the last old cedar was inhabited.

The priest stood imperturbable, waiting on the pallbearers'
final success, on the silence of those present. A little blackface
robin sat reared back near the opened ground, watching all
their moves, as if to see what was in it for him. Then the priest
opened his mouth and words came out—unfamiliar in Banner
Cemetery, not a one of them understood. His syllables fol-

lowing one another fell like multiple leaves in the rain. Then he made a movement with his hands, and his head turned an inch or two. He seemed to be yielding gracefully to some offer of assistance.

"Where's Brother Bethune? It's his turn," whispered Jack.

The priest gave him only a moment, wherever he was, and went on without him. He lifted both hands and spoke in a low voice and rapidly, keeping to the same tongue. When he came to a stop, Mr. Willy Trimble came scrambling toward him with the agility of a roof-climber over the graves between, both his arms loaded with honeysuckle, and said for Brother Bethune, "Amen." Mr. Earl Comfort took a step forward in a patched red rubber boot, and then the first clods fell.

At once the crowd broke, moved, and started streaming away. The priest had got away first, before they knew it.

"And I reckon all that was just to say 'Ashes to ashes and dust to dust,'" said a voice. "Worshipped himself, didn't he? Just loved hearing the sound of his own voice."

"Where was good old Brother Bethune? He's going to be disappointed when he gets here."

"Neglect!" said a heavy, red-flushed pallbearer in a limp Palm Beach suit, striding there between the Moodys towards the cars. "Neglect, neglect! *Of course* you can die of it! Cheeks were a skeleton's! I call it starvation, pure and simple."

"She's past minding now, Dr. Carruthers," said Mrs. Moody.

"And now I mind!" he said.

"And she'd already completed her task here on earth. But I do think she could have given in enough to allow down-to-earth Presbyterians to take charge of her funeral. All that jabber we got here in order to be served with! Just because she once taught that fellow algebra!"

The three of them picked their way out among the graves and disappeared through the trees. "You pick a funny time to laugh, Oscar," Mrs. Moody's voice said, fading.

Then there was only the racket of departure, and Mr. Earl Comfort, with a groan as though he needed help, was filling the grave.

"Look! We're to ourselves, Jack," said Gloria.

He drew her close and led her a little distance away, toward the edge of the bank. Rachel Sojourner's ribbon grass had a rainy sheen—it was like last night's moonlight hanging in threads. Down below their feet was the river.

The Bywy, running close to the Banner side here, where it was called Deepening Bend, was the color of steeping tea, clearer at the top. Stranded motionless just under the surface, a long and colorless tree lay crosswise to the current they couldn't see, and heaped in its arms, submerged, were white and green leaves and the debris it had caught. Lying under the water with the drifts of fine rain on it, it was like a fern being pressed in a book.

"Oh, this is the way it could always be. It's what I've dreamed of," Gloria said, reaching both arms around Jack's neck. "I've got you all by myself, Jack Renfro. Nobody talking, nobody listening, nobody coming—nobody about to call you or walk in on us—there's nobody left but you and me, and nothing to be in our way."

He stood in her arms without answering, and she dropped her own voice to a whisper. "If we could stay this way always—build us a little two-room house, where nobody in the world could find us—"

He drew her close, as if out of sudden danger.

The first sun had started to come out. Light touched the other side of the river, the other bank went salt-white. A shadow plunged down a fold of rock where the cave was, a black opening like a mouth with song interrupted. The banks of the other side shelved forward with the sun, close enough to show the porous face of the stone. It was like a loaf sliced through with a dull knife. The high-water mark was yellow and coarse as corn meal, and travelling along its band some wavery letters spelled out "Live For Him."

"I'm glad Uncle Nathan didn't ever have to go to the pen. They would never have let him put up his tent and bring his own syrup. Or be an artist," said Jack presently. "As long as I went and took my turn, maybe it's evened up, and now the poor old man can rest."

"He'd have to be talked into it," said Gloria.

"At the next reunion I might get a chance to speak to him."

"He only washes in the Bywy River. I hope he won't come."

"He loves his grandma," said Jack. "And I rather hear his cornet blow for a poor soul than a hundred funeral orations, long or short." He took her hand to lead her out the way they had come. "I'm sorry you had to lose your teacher," he said. "But I'm glad I could get you here on time and you got your respects paid."

Gloria didn't speak until they got to the fence. Then she said, "Miss Julia Mortimer didn't want anybody left in the dark, not about anything. She wanted everything brought out in the wide open, to see and be known. She wanted people to spread out their minds and their hearts to other people, so they could be read like books."

"She sounds like Solomon," said Jack. "Like she ought to have been Solomon."

"No, people don't want to be read like books."

"I expect she might be the only one could have understood a word out of that man burying her. If he was a man," said Jack. "She was away up over our heads, you and me."

"Once. But she changed. I'll never change!" she cried out to him, and he clasped her.

While he helped her back over the stile, the sun came following fast behind them. The cemetery everywhere began to steam. The gravestones looked small and white and alike, all like one gathering of eggs let carelessly roll from an apron.

They came out through the dinner grounds and on around the church. Damascus was a firm-cornered, narrow church resting on four snowy limestone rocks. It stood even with the bank to face Better Friendship Methodist Church across Banner Road. This morning the rained-on wooden face of Damascus had a darkness soft as a pansy's. The narrow stoop was sheltered by two new-looking boards at a right-angle; under this, like an eye beneath an eyebrow, a single electric light bulb was screwed into the wall. Its filaments showed a little color, like weak veins—somebody had turned on the current and it was working. Two wires bored into the wall, and a meter box hung by the closed door, bright as a watch. Up above, the steeple was wrapped around and around up to its point in tin, like an iris bud in its gray spring sheath.

"Jack, the last time we stood together on the steps of Damascus, we were just starting out! Getting up the courage to walk inside and down the aisle where Grandpa Vaughn was waiting at the foot, ready to marry us," said Gloria.

"Too late!" said Brother Bethune, coming out. "I waited and nobody came. 'Where's my bride and groom?' I kept asking. 'Where's my crowd?' It's a shame the way you all treat me. I wasn't even sure your floor was going to hold me. And I drawed my finger 'cross the lid of your Bible, and if I could've thought of my name right quick, I had enough dust right there to write it in. And look at me teeter! Porch like this could pitch a hungry preacher right out on his head. Pitch him clean to the road! You're letting 'em undermine your church, clawing up here with that road, and what's fixing to cave in the hind end—your river? Front and back, you're being eat out of here." Brother Bethune inched down the steps, leaving the door wide open behind him. He pointed back up with his gun. "Why don't you paint it?" he asked. "It's going to rot! There's only one thing I feel like is going to save this church at all—I just know it's Baptist. The same as I know I am. And why don't you try getting married on a Sunday? That's what Sunday's for."

"If Grandpa was back on earth to hear him, he'd bore a hole right through him now with his eyes," whispered Jack, as Brother Bethune tramped over the irises down to the road. "Grandpa Vaughn *built* Damascus."

"One ordinary look should have told even Brother Bethune we were married," said Gloria.

His mule walked out of the hitching grounds and trotted down to the road after him, while Bet stood waiting her turn in the shade.

"He's climbing on," said Jack. "As long as his mule knows him, he's safe. He'll get carried to the right place."

The sun came out as if for good. All at once they were standing again in a red world. Their skin took the sharp sting of heat. At the foot of the road, on which Brother Bethune was trotting down to Banner, the shadow of the bridge on the river floor looked more solid than the bridge, every plank of its uneven floor laid down black, like an old men's game of dominoes left lying on a sunny table in a courthouse yard at dinner time. Along the bank of the river, the sycamore trees in the school yard were tinged on top with yellow, as though acid had been spilled on them from some travelling spoon. The gas pump in front of Curly's store stood fading there like a little old lady in a blue sunbonnet who had nowhere to go.

"Between 'em all, they've taken away everything you've got, Jack," said Gloria.

"There's been just about a clean sweep," he agreed.

"Everybody's done their worst now—everybody and then some," she said. "They can't do any more now."

He set his lips on hers. "They can't take away what no human can take away. My family," he said. "My wife and girl baby and all of 'em at home. And I've got my strength. I may not have all the time I used to have—but I can provide. Don't you ever fear."

"I'll just keep right on thinking about the future, Jack."

He interrupted her with a shout. Down on the dim, steamy pasture between Curly Stovall's back shed and the river, something white was moving, erratic as a kite in a windy sky.

"Dan!" he shouted. "I'm looking straight at Dan!"

The horse ran lightly as a blown thistledown out of the open pasture gate, around Curly's house and store, over the road, across the school yard and once around the school, down the railroad track to the water tank and around it and back, running on his shadow. He ran all over Banner in those few bright minutes. He ended up in the school yard, and paced deliberately up to the basketball goal post, his old hitching post, which leaned over him with its battered ring of sunlit rust. He stood as if listening for his name.

"Dan!"

The horse lifted on his hind legs and turned around on his shadow. He came down in a red splash that shot up man-high and fell behind him. He came a graceful step or two up Banner Road, and there was nobody out to see him, tossing his mane and tail, while Jack laughed until tears popped out on both cheeks.

"Dan, you're alive. You lived through it!" He stood in the road and threw open his arms.

The horse came a little way farther, close enough to show he was still white, though his coat was rough. His mane and tail had been combed only by the rain. Jack gave his sweet, warbling whistle. But the horse with a wayward toss of his head turned around in the road and trotted back down again, his tail streaming bright as frost behind.

"He's fickle," Gloria told Jack. "Dan is fickle. And now he's Curly's horse and he's let you know it. Oh, Jack, I know you'd rather he was rendered!"

"No, I rather he's alive and fickle than all mine and sold for his hide and tallow," said Jack. He still stood in the road with his arms out. "Why hasn't Curly already pranced out on his back in front of me then? What's he saving the last for?—There's just one answer. He's waiting till he can catch him." Gloria slowly nodded. He went on, "And I expect this morning Captain Billy Bangs let him out of the pasture. We all went off and left Captain Billy with nothing else to do— he can't vote till tomorrow." He cupped his hands to his mouth and yelled, "All right, Curly! I saw him! I'll be down to get him when the time's good and ripe!"

"That's what Prentiss Stovall wants you to do," said Gloria. "He'll be justice of the peace by day after tomorrow. Oh, Jack, does this mean it'll all happen over again?"

"It's a start," said Jack. Then he swung around. "But for right now, Gloria, there's a lot of doing I got to catch up with at home. We got to eat! That's the surest thing I know. But I still got my strength."

Bet came down into the road.

"The surest thing I know is I'll never let you out of my sight again. Never," Gloria swore. "I never will let you escape from me, Jack Renfro. Remember it."

"It's the first I knew I was trying," he said, with his big smile.

He lifted her and set her up on Bet's waiting back, and took Bet by the bridle and led her. They started for home.

"And some day," Gloria said, "some day yet, we'll move to ourselves. And there'll be just you and me and Lady May."

"And a string of other little chaps to come along behind her," said Jack. "You just can't have too many, is the way I look at it."

Sid twinkled out of the church. He had gone straight through Damascus Church, in at the back and out at the front, as though it were a tree across a ditch. He came in springs down the bank and ran up the red road, tail jumping like a ringing bell as he sped for home, and growing smaller and smaller up ahead.

Jack and Gloria went along behind him, and the sun gave Banner Road no more shade now—it was noon. One of his eyes still imperfectly opened, and the new lump blossoming on his forehead for his mother's kiss, Jack raised his voice and sang. All Banner could hear him and know who he was.

> "Bringing in the sheaves,
> Bringing in the sheaves!
> We shall come rejoicing,
> Bringing in the sheaves!"

THE OPTIMIST'S DAUGHTER

For C.A.W.

One

I

A NURSE held the door open for them. Judge McKelva going first, then his daughter Laurel, then his wife Fay, they walked into the windowless room where the doctor would make his examination. Judge McKelva was a tall, heavy man of seventy-one who customarily wore his glasses on a ribbon. Holding them in his hand now, he sat on the raised, thronelike chair above the doctor's stool, flanked by Laurel on one side and Fay on the other.

Laurel McKelva Hand was a slender, quiet-faced woman in her middle forties, her hair still dark. She wore clothes of an interesting cut and texture, although her suit was wintry for New Orleans and had a wrinkle down the skirt. Her dark blue eyes looked sleepless.

Fay, small and pale in her dress with the gold buttons, was tapping her sandaled foot.

It was a Monday morning of early March. New Orleans was out-of-town for all of them.

Dr. Courtland, on the dot, crossed the room in long steps and shook hands with Judge McKelva and Laurel. He had to be introduced to Fay, who had been married to Judge McKelva for only a year and a half. Then the doctor was on the stool, with his heels hung over the rung. He lifted his face in appreciative attention: as though it were he who had waited in New Orleans for Judge McKelva—in order to give the Judge a present, or for the Judge to bring him one.

"Nate," Laurel's father was saying, "the trouble may be I'm not as young as I used to be. But I'm ready to believe it's something wrong with my *eyes*."

As though he had all the time in the world, Dr. Courtland, the well-known eye specialist, folded his big country hands with the fingers that had always looked, to Laurel, as if their mere touch on the crystal of a watch would convey to their skin exactly what time it was.

"I date this little disturbance from George Washington's Birthday," Judge McKelva said.

Dr. Courtland nodded, as though that were a good day for it. "Tell me about the little disturbance," he said.

"I'd come in. I'd done a little rose pruning—I've retired, you know. And I stood at the end of my front porch there, with an eye on the street—Fay had slipped out somewhere," said Judge McKelva, and bent on her his benign smile that looked so much like a scowl.

"I was only uptown in the beauty parlor, letting Myrtis roll up my hair," said Fay.

"And I saw the fig tree," said Judge McKelva. "The fig tree! Giving off flashes from those old bird-frighteners Becky saw fit to tie on it years back!"

Both men smiled. They were of two generations but the same place. Becky was Laurel's mother. Those little home-made reflectors, rounds of tin, did not halfway keep the birds from the figs in July.

"Nate, you remember as well as I do, that tree stands between my backyard and where your mother used to keep her cowshed. But it flashed at me when I was peering off in the direction of the Courthouse," Judge McKelva went on. "So I was forced into the conclusion I'd started seeing behind me."

Fay laughed—a single, high note, as derisive as a jay's.

"Yes, that's disturbing." Dr. Courtland rolled forward on his stool. "Let's just have a good look."

"*I* looked. I couldn't see anything had got in it," said Fay. "One of those briars might have given you a scratch, hon, but it didn't leave a thorn."

"Of course, my *memory* had slipped. Becky would say it served me right. Before blooming is the wrong time to prune a climber," Judge McKelva went on in the same confidential way; the doctor's face was very near to his. "But Becky's Climber I've found will hardly take a setback."

"Hardly," the doctor murmured. "I believe my sister still grows one now from a cutting of Miss Becky's Climber." His face, however, went very still as he leaned over to put out the lights.

"It's dark!" Fay gave a little cry. "Why did he have to go

back there anyway and get mixed up in those brambles? Because I was out of the house a minute?"

"Because George Washington's Birthday is the time-honored day to prune roses back home," said the Doctor's amicable voice. "You should've asked Adele to step over and prune 'em for you."

"Oh, she offered," said Judge McKelva, and dismissed her case with the slightest move of the hand. "I think by this point I ought to be about able to get the hang of it."

Laurel had watched him prune. Holding the shears in both hands, he performed a sort of weighty saraband, with a lop for this side, then a lop for the other side, as though he were bowing to his partner, and left the bush looking like a puzzle.

"You've had further disturbances since, Judge Mac?"

"Oh, a dimness. Nothing to call my attention to it like that first disturbance."

"So why not leave it to Nature?" Fay said. "That's what I keep on telling him."

Laurel had only just now got here from the airport; she had come on a night flight from Chicago. The meeting had been unexpected, arranged over long-distance yesterday evening. Her father, in the old home in Mount Salus, Mississippi, took pleasure in telephoning instead of writing, but this had been a curiously reticent conversation on his side. At the very last, he'd said, "By the way, Laurel, I've been getting a little interference with my *seeing*, lately. I just might give Nate Courtland a chance to see what he can find." He'd added, "Fay says she'll come along and do some shopping."

His admission of self-concern was as new as anything wrong with his health, and Laurel had come flying.

The excruciatingly small, brilliant eye of the instrument hung still between Judge McKelva's set face and the Doctor's hidden one.

Eventually the ceiling lights blazed on again, and Dr. Courtland stood, studying Judge McKelva, who studied him back.

"I *thought* I was bringing you a little something to keep you busy," Judge McKelva said in the cooperating voice in which, before he retired from the bench, he used to hand down a sentence.

"Your right retina's slipped, Judge Mac," Dr. Courtland said.

"All right, you can fix that," said Laurel's father.

"It needs to be repaired without any more waste of precious time."

"All right, when can you operate?"

"Just for a scratch? Why didn't those old roses go on and die?" Fay cried.

"But this eye didn't get a scratch. What happened didn't happen to the outside of his eye, it happened to the inside. The flashes, too. To the part he sees with, Mrs. McKelva." Dr. Courtland, turning from the Judge and Laurel, beckoned Fay to his chart hanging on the wall. Giving out perfume, she walked across to it. "Here's the outside and here's the inside of our eye," he said. He pointed out on the diagram what would have to be done.

Judge McKelva inclined his weight so as to speak to Laurel in her chair below him. "That eye wasn't fooling, was it!" he said.

"I don't see why this had to happen to *me*," said Fay.

Dr. Courtland led the Judge to the door and into the hallway. "Will you make yourself comfortable in my office, sir, and let my nurse bother you with a few more questions?"

When he returned to the examining room he sat in the patient's chair.

"Laurel," he said, "I don't want to do this operation myself." He went on quickly, "I've kept being so sorry about your mother." He turned and gave what might have been his first direct look at Fay. "My family's known his family for such a long time," he told her—a sentence never said except to warn of the unsayable.

"What is the location of the tear?" Laurel asked.

"Close to central," he told her. She kept her eyes on his and he added, "No tumor."

"Before I even let you try, I think I ought to know how good he'll see," said Fay.

"Now, that depends first on where the tear comes," said Dr. Courtland. "And after that on how good a mender the surgeon is, and then on how well Judge Mac will agree to take our orders, and then on the Lord's will. This girl remembers." He nodded toward Laurel.

"An operation's not a thing you just jump into, I know that much," Fay said.

"You don't want him to wait and lose all the vision in that eye. He's got a cataract forming on his other eye," said Dr. Courtland.

Laurel said, "Father has?"

"I found it before I left Mount Salus. It's been coming along for years, taking its time. He's apprised; he thinks it'll hold off." He smiled.

"It's like Mother's. This was the way she started."

"Now, Laurel, I don't have very much imagination," protested Dr. Courtland. "So I go with caution. I was pretty close to 'em, there at home, Judge Mac and Miss Becky both. I stood over what happened to your mother."

"I was there too. You know nobody could blame you, or imagine how you could have prevented anything—"

"If we'd known then what we know now. The eye was just a part of it," he said. "With your mother."

Laurel looked for a moment into the experienced face, so entirely guileless. The Mississippi country that lay behind him was all in it.

He stood up. "Of course, if you ask me to do it, I will," he said. "But I wish you wouldn't ask me."

"Father's not going to let you off," Laurel said quietly.

"Isn't my vote going to get counted at all?" Fay asked, following them out. "I vote we just forget about the whole business. Nature's the great healer."

"All right, Nate," Judge McKelva said, when they had all sat down together in Dr. Courtland's consulting office. "How soon?"

Dr. Courtland said, "Judge Mac, I've just managed to catch Dr. Kunomoto by the coat-tails over in Houston. You know, he taught me. He's got a more radical method now, and he can fly here day after tomorrow—"

"What for?" Judge McKelva said. "Nate, I hied myself away from home and comfort and tracked down here and put myself in your hands for one simple reason: I've got confidence in you. Now show me I'm still not too old to exercise good judgment."

"All right, sir, then that's the way it'll be," Dr. Courtland said, rising. He added, "You know, sir, this operation is not, in any hands, a hundred per cent predictable?"

"Well, I'm an optimist."

"I didn't know there were any more such animals," said Dr. Courtland.

"Never think you've seen the last of anything," scoffed Judge McKelva. He answered the Doctor's smile with a laugh that was like the snarl of triumph from an old grouch, and Dr. Courtland, taking the glasses the Judge held on his knees, gently set them back onto his nose.

In his same walk, like a rather stately ploughboy's, the Doctor led them through the jammed waiting room. "I've got you in the hospital, they've reserved me the operating room, and I'm fixed up, too," he said.

"He can move heaven and earth, just ask him to," said his nurse in a cross voice as they passed her in the doorway.

"Go right on over to the hospital and settle in." As the elevator doors opened, Dr. Courtland touched Laurel lightly on the shoulder. "I ordered you the ambulance downstairs, sir—it's a safer ride."

"What's he acting so polite about?" Fay asked, as they went down. "I bet when the bill comes in he won't charge so polite."

"I'm in good hands, Fay," Judge McKelva told her. "I know his whole family."

There was a sharp, cold wind blowing through Canal Street. Back home, Judge McKelva had always set the example for Mount Salus in putting aside his winter hat on Straw Hat Day, and he stood here now in his creamy panama. But though his paunch was bigger, he looked less ruddy, looked thinner in the face than on his wedding day, Laurel thought: this was the last time she had seen him. The mushroom-colored patches under his eyes belonged there, hereditary like the black and overhanging McKelva eyebrows that nearly met in one across his forehead—but what was he seeing? She wondered if through that dilated but benevolent gaze of his he was really quite seeing Fay, or herself, or anybody at all. In the lime-white glare of New Orleans, waiting for the ambulance without questioning the need for it, he seemed for the first time in her memory a man admitting to a little uncertainty in his bearings.

"If Courtland's all that much, he better put in a better claim on how good this is going to turn out," said Fay. "And he's not so perfect—I saw him spank that nurse."

2

Fay sat at the window, Laurel stood in the doorway; they were in the hospital room waiting for Judge McKelva to be brought back after surgery.

"What a way to keep his promise," said Fay. "When he told me he'd bring me to New Orleans some day, it was to see the Carnival." She stared out the window. "And the Carnival's going on right now. It looks like this is as close as we'll get to a parade."

Laurel looked again at her watch.

"He came out fine! He stood it fine!" Dr. Courtland called out. He strode into the room, still in his surgical gown. He grinned at Laurel from a face that poured sweat. "And I think with luck we're going to keep some vision in that eye."

The tablelike bed with Judge McKelva affixed to it was wheeled into the room, and he was carried past the two women. Both his eyes were bandaged. Sandbags were packed about his head, the linen pinned across the big motionless mound of his body close enough to bind him.

"You didn't tell me he'd look like that," said Fay.

"He's fine, he's absolutely splendid," said Dr. Courtland. "He's got him a beautiful eye." He opened his mouth and laughed aloud. He was speaking with excitement, some carry-over of elation, as though he'd just come in from a party.

"Why, you can't hardly tell even who it is under all that old pack. It's big as a house," said Fay, staring down at Judge McKelva.

"He's going to surprise us all. If we can make it stick, he's going to have a little vision he didn't think was coming to him! That's a *beautiful* eye."

"But *look* at him," said Fay. "When's he going to come to?"

"Oh, he's got plenty of time," said Dr. Courtland, on his way.

Judge McKelva's head was unpillowed, lengthening the elderly, exposed throat. Not only the great dark eyes but their heavy brows and their heavy undershadows were hidden, too, by the opaque gauze. With so much of its dark and bright both taken from it, and with his sleeping mouth as colorless as his cheeks, his face looked quenched.

This was a double room, but Judge McKelva had it, for the time being, to himself. Fay had stretched out a while ago on the second bed. The first nurse had come on duty; she sat crocheting a baby's bootee, so automatically that she appeared to be doing it in her sleep. Laurel moved about, as if to make sure that the room was all in order, but there was nothing to do; not yet. This was like a nowhere. Even what could be seen from the high window might have been the rooftops of any city, colorless and tarpatched, with here and there small mirrors of rainwater. At first, she did not realize she could see the bridge—it stood out there dull in the distance, its function hardly evident, as if it were only another building. The river was not visible. She lowered the blind against the wide white sky that reflected it. It seemed to her that the grayed-down, anonymous room might be some reflection itself of Judge McKelva's "disturbance," his dislocated vision that had brought him here.

Then Judge McKelva began grinding and gnashing his teeth.

"Father?" Laurel moved near.

"That's only the way he wakes up," said Fay from her bed, without opening her eyes. "I get it every morning."

Laurel stood near him, waiting.

"What's the verdict?" her father presently asked, in a parched voice. "Eh, Polly?" He called Laurel by her childhood name. "What's your mother have to say about me?"

"Look-a-here!" exclaimed Fay. She jumped up and pattered toward his bed in her stockinged feet. "Who's *this?*" She pointed to the gold button over her breastbone.

The nurse, without stopping her crochet hook, spoke from the chair. "Don't go near that eye, hon! Don't nobody touch him or monkey with that eye of his, and don't even touch the bed he's on, till Dr. Courtland says touch, or somebody'll be mighty sorry. And Dr. Courtland will skin me alive."

"That's right," said Dr. Courtland, coming in; then he bent close and spoke exuberantly into the aghast face. "All through with my part, sir! Your part's just starting! And yours will be harder than mine. You got to lie still! No moving. No turning. No tears." He smiled. "No nothing! Just the passage of time. We've got to wait on your eye."

When the doctor straightened, the nurse said, "I wish he'd waited for me to give him a sip of water before he took off again."

"Go ahead. Wet his whistle, he's awake," said Dr. Courtland and moved to the door. "He's just possuming." His finger beckoned Laurel and Fay outside.

"Now listen, you've got to watch him. Starting now. Take turns. It's not as easy as anybody thinks to lie still and nothing else. I'll talk Mrs. Martello into doing private duty at night. Laurel, a good thing you've got the time. He's going to get extra-special care, and we're not running any risks on Judge Mac."

Laurel, when he'd gone, went to the pay telephone in the corridor. She called her studio; she was a professional designer of fabrics in Chicago.

"No point in you staying just beca   ᵃid so,"
said Fay when Laurel hung up. She

"Why, I'm staying for my own s
cided to put off the other necessa
the time both of us can give hin
to being tied down."

"O.K., that's not a matter of
in a cross voice. As they went '
leaned over the bed and said, '
hon."

Judge McKelva gave out a shocking and ragged sound, a snore, and firmed his mouth. He asked, "What's the time, Fay?"

"That sounds more like you," she said, but didn't tell him the time. "It was that old *ether* talking when he came to before," she said to Laurel. "Why, he hadn't even mentioned Becky, till you and Courtland started him."

The Hibiscus was a half hour's ride away on the city's one remaining streetcar line, but through the help of one of the floor nurses, Laurel and Fay were able to find rooms there by the week. It was a decayed mansion on a changing street; what had been built as its twin next door was a lesson to it now: it was far along in the course of being demolished.

Laurel hardly ever saw any of the other roomers, although the front door was never locked and the bathroom was always busy; at the hours when she herself came and went, the Hibiscus seemed to be in the sole charge of a cat on a chain, pacing the cracked-open floral tiles that paved the front gallery. Long in the habit of rising early, she said she would be with her father by seven. She would stay until three, when Fay would come to sit until eleven; Fay could ride the streetcar back in the safe company of the nurse, who lived nearby. And Mrs. Martello said she would take on the private duty late shift for the sake of one living man, that Dr. Courtland. So the pattern was set.

It meant that Laurel and Fay were hardly ever in the same place at the same time, except during the hours when they were both asleep in their rooms at the Hibiscus. These were adjoining—really half rooms; the partition between their beds was only a landlord's strip of wallboard. Where there was no intimacy, Laurel shrank from contact; she shrank from that thin board and from the vague apprehension that some night she might hear Fay cry or laugh like a stranger at something she herself would rather not know.

In the mornings, Judge McKelva ground his teeth, Laurel ⟨to⟩ him, he waked up, and found out from Laurel how ⟨and⟩ what time her watch showed. She gave him his ⟨. . .⟩ she fed him she could read him the *Picayune*. ⟨. . . his⟩ being washed and shaved she went to her

time suspended

own breakfast in the basement cafeteria. The trick was not to miss the lightning visits of Dr. Courtland. On lucky days, she rode up in the elevator with him.

"It's clearing some," Dr. Courtland said. "It's not to be hurried."

effort to stop movement

By this time, only the operated eye had to be covered. A hivelike dressing stood on top of it. Judge McKelva seemed inclined to still lower the lid over his good eye. Perhaps, open, it could see the other eye's bandage. He lay as was asked of him, without moving. He never asked about his eye. He never mentioned his eye. Laurel followed his lead.

a △

Neither did he ask about her. His old curiosity would have prompted a dozen specific questions about how she was managing to stay here, what was happening up in Chicago, who had given her her latest commission, when she would have to go. She had left in the middle of her present job—designing a theatre curtain for a repertory theatre. Her father left his questions unasked. But both knew, and for the same reason, that bad days go better without any questions at all.

unusual

they shared.

He'd loved being read to, once. With good hopes, she brought in a stack of paperbacks and began on the newest of his favorite detective novelist. He listened but without much comment. She went back to one of the old ones they'd both admired, and he listened with greater quiet. Pity stabbed her. Did they *move too fast* for him now?

grief

Part of her father's silence Laurel laid, at first, to the delicacy he had always shown in family feelings. (There had only been the three of them.) Here was his daughter, come to help him and yet wrenched into idleness; she could not help him. Fay was accurate about it: any stranger could tell him the time. Eventually, Laurel saw that her father had accepted her uselessness with her presence all along. What occupied his full mind was time itself; time passing: he was concentrating.

She was always conscious, once she knew, of the effort being made in this room, hour after hour, from his motionless bed; and she was conscious of time along with him, setting her inner chronology with his, more or less as if they needed to keep in step for a long walk ahead of them. The Venetian blind was kept lowered to let in only a two-inch strip of March daylight at the window. Laurel sat so that this light fell into her lap onto her book, and Judge McKelva, holding himself motionless, listened to her read, then turn the page, as if he were silently counting, and knew each page by its number.

The day came when Judge McKelva was asked to share the room with another patient. When Laurel walked in one morning, she saw an old man, older than her father, wearing new, striped cotton pajamas and an old broadbrimmed black felt hat, rocking in the chair by the second bed. Laurel could see the peppering of red road dust on the old man's hat above his round blue eyes.

"This is too strong a light for my father, I'm afraid, sir," she said to him.

"Mr. Dalzell pulled the blind down during the night," said Mrs. Martello, speaking in a nurse's ventriloquist voice. "Didn't you pull it down?" she shrieked. Judge McKelva did not betray that he was awake, but the old man rocking appeared as oblivious as the Judge to the sound of their voices. "He's blind, and nearly deaf in the bargain," Mrs. Martello said proudly. "And he's going in surgery just as soon as they get him all fixed up for it. He's got a malignancy."

"I had to pull the vine down to get the possum," Mr. Dalzell piped up, while Laurel and the nurse struggled together to string the blind back into place. Dr. Courtland came in and did it.

Mr. Dalzell proved to be a fellow Mississippian. He was from Fox Hill. Almost immediately, he convinced himself that Judge McKelva was his long-lost son Archie Lee.

"Archie Lee," he said, "I might've known if you ever did come home, you'd come home drunk."

Judge McKelva once would have smiled. Now he lay as ever, his good eye closed, or open on the ceiling, and had no words to spare.

"Don't you worry about *Mr. Dalzell*," Mrs. Martello said to Laurel as they prepared one morning to change places. "Your daddy just lets Mr. Dalzell rave. He keeps just as still, laying there just like he's supposed to. He's good as gold. *Mr. Dalzell's* nothing you got to worry about."

3

"Nothing to do but give it more time," said Dr. Courtland regularly. "It's clearing. I believe we're getting us an eye that's going to *see* a little bit."

But although Dr. Courtland paid his daily visits as to a man recovering, to Laurel her father seemed to be paying some unbargained-for price for his recovery. He lay there unchangeably big and heavy, full of effort yet motionless, while his face looked tireder every morning, the circle under his visible eye thick as paint. He opened his mouth and swallowed what she offered him with the obedience of an old man—obedience! She felt ashamed to let him act out the part in front of her. She managed a time or two (by moving heaven and earth) to have some special dish prepared for him outside; but he might as well have been spooned out hospital grits, canned peaches, and Jello, for all that food distracted him out of his patience—out of his unnatural reticence: he had yet to say he would be all right.

One day, she had the luck to detect an old copy of *Nicholas Nickleby* on the dusty top shelf in the paperback store. That would reach his memory, she believed, and she began next morning reading it to her father.

He did not ask her to stop; neither could he help her when she lost their place. Of course, she was not able to read aloud with her mother's speed and vivacity—that was probably what he missed. In the course of an hour, he rolled his visible eye her way, though he rationed himself on the one small movement he was permitted, and lay for a long time looking at her. She was not sure he was listening to the words.

"Is that all?" his patient voice asked, when she paused.

"You got that gun loaded yet?" called Mr. Dalzell. "Archie Lee, I declare I want to see you load that gun before they start to coming."

"That's the boy. You go right on hunting all night in your mind," Mrs. Martello stoutly told Mr. Dalzell. She would never in a year dare to get so possessive of Judge McKelva, Laurel reflected, or find something in his predicament that she could joke about. She had gained no clue but one to what he used to be like in Mount Salus. "He's still keeping as good as gold," she greeted Laurel every morning. "It's nothing but goodness—I don't think he *sleeps* all that steady."

Mrs. Martello had crocheted twenty-seven pairs of bootees. Bootees were what she counted. "You'd be surprised how fast I give out of 'em," she said. "It's the most popular present there is."

Judge McKelva had years ago developed a capacity for patience, ready if it were called on. But in this affliction, he seemed to Laurel to lie in a *dream* of patience. He seldom spoke now unless he was spoken to, and then, which was wholly unlike him, after a wait—as if he had to catch up. He didn't try any more to hold her in his good eye.

He lay more and more with both eyes closed. She dropped her voice sometimes, and then sat still.

"I'm not asleep," said her father. "Please don't stop reading."

"What do you think of his prospects now?" Laurel asked Dr. Courtland, following him out into the corridor. "It's three weeks."

"Three weeks! Lord, how they fly," he said. He believed he hid the quick impatience of his mind, and moving and speaking with deliberation he did hide it—then showed it all in his smile. "He's doing all right. Lungs clear, heart strong, blood pressure not a bit worse than it was before. And that eye's clearing. I think he's got some vision coming, just a little bit around the edge, you know, Laurel, but if the cataract catches up with him, I want him seeing enough to find his way around the garden. A little longer. Let's play safe."

Going down on the elevator with him, another time, she asked, "Is it the drugs he has to take that make him seem such a distance away?"

He pinched a frown into his freckled forehead. "Well, no two people react in just the same way to anything." They held the elevator for him to say, "People are different, Laurel."

"Mother was different," she said.

Laurel felt reluctant to leave her father now in the afternoons. She stayed and read. *Nicholas Nickleby* had seemed as endless to her as time must seem to him, and it had now been arranged between them, without words, that she was to sit there beside him and read—but silently, to herself. He too was completely silent while she read. Without being able to see her as she sat by his side, he seemed to know when she turned each page, as though he kept up, through the succession of pages, with time, checking off moment after moment; and she felt it would be heartless to close her book until she'd read him to sleep.

One day, Fay came in and caught Laurel sitting up asleep herself, in her spectacles.

"Putting your eyes out, too? I told him if he hadn't spent so many years of his life poring over dusty old books, his eyes would have more strength saved up for now," Fay told her. She sidled closer to the bed. "About ready to get up, hon?" she cried. "Listen, they're holding parades out yonder right now. Look what they threw me off the float!"

Shadows from the long green eardrops she'd come in wearing made soft little sideburns down her small, intent face as she pointed to them, scolding him. "What's the good of a Carnival if we don't get to go, hon?"

It was still incredible to Laurel that her father, at nearly seventy, should have let anyone new, a beginner, walk in on his life, that he had even agreed to pardon such a thing.

"Father, where did you meet her?" Laurel had asked when, a year and a half ago, she had flown down to Mount Salus to see them married.

"Southern Bar Association." With both arms he had made an expansive gesture that she correctly read as the old Gulf Coast Hotel. Fay had had a part-time job there; she was in the typist pool. A month after the convention, he brought her home to Mount Salus, and they were married in the Courthouse.

Perhaps she was forty, and so younger than Laurel. There was little even of forty in her looks except the line of her neck and the backs of her little square, idle hands. She was bony and blue-veined; as a child she had very possibly gone undernourished. Her hair was still a childish tow. It had the tow texture, as if, well rubbed between the fingers, those curls might have gone to powder. She had round, country-blue eyes and a little feist jaw.

When Laurel flew down from Chicago to be present at the ceremony, Fay's response to her kiss had been to say, "It wasn't any use in you bothering to come so far." She'd smiled as though she meant her scolding to flatter. What Fay told Laurel now, nearly every afternoon at the changeover, was almost the same thing. Her flattery and her disparagement sounded just alike.

It was strange, though, how Fay never called anyone by name. Only she had said "Becky": Laurel's mother, who had been dead ten years by the time Fay could have first heard of her, when she had married Laurel's father.

"What on earth made Becky give you a name like that?" she'd asked Laurel, on that first occasion.

"It's the state flower of West Virginia," Laurel told her, smiling. "Where my mother came from."

Fay hadn't smiled back. She'd given her a wary look.

One later night, at the Hibiscus, Laurel tapped at Fay's door.

"What do you want?" Fay asked as she opened it.

She thought the time had come to know Fay a little better. She sat down on one of the hard chairs in the narrow room and asked her about her family.

"My family?" said Fay. "None of 'em living. That's why I ever left Texas and came to Mississippi. We may not have had much, out in Texas, but we were always so close. Never had any secrets from each other, like some families. Sis was just like my twin. My brothers were all so unselfish! After Papa died, we all gave up everything for Mama, of course. Now that she's gone, I'm glad we did. Oh, I wouldn't have run off and left anybody that needed me. Just to call myself an artist and make a lot of money."

Laurel did not try again, and Fay never at any time knocked at her door.

Now Fay walked around Judge McKelva's bed and cried, "Look! Look what I got to match my eardrops! How do you like 'em, hon? Don't you want to let's go dancing?" She stood on one foot and held a shoe in the air above his face. It was green, with a stiletto heel. Had the shoe been a written page, some brief she'd concocted on her own, he looked at it in her hands there for long enough to read it through. But he didn't speak.

"But just let me try slipping *out* a minute in 'em, would he ever let me hear about it!" Fay said. She gave him a smile, to show her remark was meant for him to hear. He offered no reply.

Laurel stayed on, until now the supper trays began to rattle.

"Archie Lee, you gonna load that gun or you rather be caught napping?" Mr. Dalzell called out.

"Mr. Dalzell reminds me of my old grandpa," said Fay. "I'm not sorry to have him in here. He's company."

The floor nurse came in to feed Mr. Dalzell, then to stick him with a needle, while Fay helped Judge McKelva with his supper—mostly by taking bite for bite. Laurel stayed on until out in the corridor the lights came on and the room went that much darker.

"Maybe you can sleep now, Father—you haven't been asleep all day," said Laurel.

Fay switched on the night light by the bed. Placed low, and not much more powerful than a candle flame, it touched Judge McKelva's face without calling forth a flicker of change in its patient expression. Laurel saw now that his hair had grown long on the back of his neck, not black but white and featherlike.

"Tell me something you would like to have," Laurel begged him.

Fay, bending down over him, placed her lighted cigarette between his lips. His chest lifted visibly as he drew on it, and after a moment she took it away and his chest slowly fell as the smoke slowly traveled out of his mouth. She bent and gave it to him again.

"*There's* something," she said.

"Don't let the fire go out, son!" called Mr. Dalzell.

"No sir! Everything around this camp's being took good care of, Mr. Dalzell!" yelled the floor nurse, coming to the door. "You just crawl right in your tent and say your prayers good and go to sleep."

Laurel stood, and said goodnight. "Dr. Courtland believes the time's almost here to try your pinhole specs," she dared to add. "Do you hear, Father?"

He, who had been the declared optimist, had not once expressed hope. Now it was she who was offering it to him. And it might be false hope.

There was no response in the room. Judge McKelva, like Mr. Dalzell, lay in the dark, and Fay crouched in the rocker, one cheek on the windowsill, with a peep on the crack.

Laurel went reluctantly away.

4

It was not that night but the next that Laurel, in her room at the Hibiscus, having already undressed, suddenly dressed again. As she ran down the steps into the warm, uneasy night, the roof light went on in a passing cab. She hailed and ran for it.

"You don't know how lucky you are, sister," said the driver. "Getting you something-to-ride on a night like tonight."

The interior of the cab reeked of bourbon, and as they passed under a streetlight she saw a string of cheap green beads on the floor—a favor tossed from a parade float. The driver took back streets, squeezing around at every corner, it seemed to Laurel, who was straining forward; but when she let down the window glass for air, she heard the same mocking trumpet playing with a band from the same distance away. Then she heard more than one band, heard rival bands playing up distant streets.

Perhaps what she had felt was no more than the atmospheric oppression of a Carnival night, of crowds running wild in the streets of a strange city. And at the very beginning of the day, when she entered her father's room, she thought something had already happened to Mr. Dalzell. He was up on a wheeled table, baldheaded as an infant, hook-nosed and silent—they had taken away his teeth. It was only that something was *going* to happen. A pair of orderlies came during Judge McKelva's breakfast to take Mr. Dalzell to the operating room. As he was wheeled out, no longer vigilant, into the corridor, his voice trailed back, "*Told* you rascals not to let the fire go out." They had still not brought him back when Laurel left.

A strange milky radiance shone in a hospital corridor at night, like moonlight on some deserted street. The whitened floor, the whitened walls and ceiling, were set with narrow bands of black receding into the distance, along which the spaced-out doors, graduated from large to small, were all closed. Laurel had never noticed the design in the tiling before, like some clue she would need to follow to get to the right place. But of course the last door on the right of the corridor, the one standing partway open as usual, was still her father's.   *not in the right place*

An intense, tight little voice from inside there said at that moment in high pitch, "I tell you enough is enough!"

Laurel was halted. A thousand packthreads seemed to cross and crisscross her skin, binding her there.

The voice said, even higher, "This is my birthday!"

Laurel saw Mrs. Martello go running from the nurse's station into the room. Then Mrs. Martello reappeared, struggling her way backwards. She was pulling Fay, holding her bodily. A scream shot out and ricocheted from walls and ceiling. Fay broke free from the nurse, whirled, and with high-raised knees and white face came running down the corridor. Fists drumming against her temples, she knocked against Laurel as if Laurel wasn't there. Her high heels let off a fusillade of sounds as she passed and hurled herself into the waiting room with voice rising, like a child looking for its mother.   *Robbie Lael*

Mrs. Martello came panting up to Laurel, heavy on her rubber heels.

"She laid hands on him! She sai̦   ⸺⸺ out of it, she'd—" The veneer of nurse sli̦ she pushed up at Laurel the red, s countrywoman as her voice rose taken ahold of him. She was ab̦ echoing. "I think she was fixing I think she thought she could! ̦ *that* mountain!" Mrs. Martell̦ nurse!" She swung her starch voice back toward Judge McK̦ with that woman? Does she ̦

At last her legs drove her. Laurel ran.

The door stood wide open, and inside the room's darkness a watery constellation hung, throbbing and near. She was looking straight out at the whole Mississippi River Bridge in lights. She found her way, the night light was burning. Her father's right arm was free of the cover and lay out on the bed. It was bare to the shoulder, its skin soft and gathered, like a woman's sleeve. It showed her that he was no longer concentrating. At the sting in her eyes, she remembered for him that there must be no tears in his, and she reached to put her hand into his open hand and press it gently.

He made what seemed to her a response at last, yet a mysterious response. His whole, pillowless head went dusky, as if he laid it under the surface of dark, pouring water and held it there.

Every light in the room blazed on. Dr. Courtland, a dark shape, shoved past her to the bed. He set his fingertips to her father's wrist. Then his hand passed over the operated eye; with its same delicacy it opened the good eye. He bent over and stared in, without speaking. He knocked back the sheet and laid the side of his head against her father's gowned chest; for a moment his own eyes closed.

It was her father who appeared to Laurel as the one listening. His upper lip had lifted, short and soft as a child's, showing ghostly-pale teeth which no one ever saw when he spoke or laughed. It gave him the smile of a child who is hiding in the dark while the others hunt him, waiting to be found.

Now the doctor's hand swung and drove for the signal button. "Get out in a hurry. And collar his wife and hold her. Both of you go in the waiting room, stay there till I come."

The nurse pushed into the room, with another nurse at her shoulder.

"Now what did *he* pull?" Mrs. Martello cried.

The other nurse whipped the curtains along the rod between the two beds, shutting out Mr. Dalzell's neat, vacated and the rocking chair with the felt hat hanging on it. With she kicked out of her way the fallen window blind on the floor.

d, using both hands, drew Laurel outside the time to lose." He closed the door on her.

But in the hall, she heard him give an answer to the nurse. "The renegade! I believe he's just plain sneaked out on us."

In the waiting room, Fay stood being patted by an old woman who was wearing bedroom slippers and holding a half-eaten banana in her free hand.

"Night after night, sitting up there with him, putting the food in his mouth, giving him his straw, letting him use up my cigarettes, keeping him from thinking!" Fay was crying on the woman's bosom. "Then to get hauled out by an uppity nurse who doesn't know my business from hers!"

Laurel went up to her. "Fay, it can't be much more serious. The doctor's closed in with Father now."

"Never speak to me again!" shrieked Fay without turning around. "That nurse dragged me and pushed me, and you're the one let her do it!"

"Dr. Courtland wants us to stay here till he calls us."

"You bet I'm staying! Just wait till he hears what I've got to say to him!" cried Fay.

"You pore little woman," said the old woman easily. "Don't they give us all a hard time."

"I believe he's dying," said Laurel.

Fay spun around, darted out her head, and spat at her.

The old woman said, "Now whoa. Why don't you-all take a seat and save your strength? Just wait and let them come tell you about it. They will." There was an empty chair in the circle pulled up around a table, and Fay sat down among five or six grown men and women who all had the old woman's likeness. Their coats were on the table in a heap together, and open shoeboxes and paper sacks stood about on the floor; they were a family in the middle of their supper.

Laurel began walking, past this group and the others who were sprawled or sleeping in chairs and on couches, past the television screen where a pale-blue group of Westerners silently shot it out with one another, and as far as the door into the hall, where she stood for a minute looking at the clock in the wall above the elevators, then walked her circle again.

The family Fay had sat down with never let the conversation die.

incessant chatter

MR. Dalzell's son

"Go on in there, Archie Lee, it's still your turn," the old woman said. *(pg 899)*

"I ain't ready to go." A great hulking man in a short coat like a red blanket, who was too gray-headed to be her child, spoke like her child and took a drink from a pint bottle of whiskey.

"They still ain't letting us in but one at a time. It's your turn," the old woman said. She went on to Fay. "You from Mississippi? We're from Mississippi. Most of us claims Fox Hill."

"I'm *not* from Mississippi. I'm from Texas." She let out a long cry.

"Yours been operated on? Ours been operated on," said one of the daughters to Fay. "He's been in intensive care ever since they got through with him. His chances are a hundred to one against."

"Go on in yonder, scare-cat," ordered the mother.

"They went in my husband's eye without consulting my feelings and next they try to run me out of this hospital!" cried Fay.

"Mama, it's Archie Lee's turn, and I come after you. Go yourself," said the daughter.

"I reckon you'll have to excuse me a minute," the old woman said to Fay. She began brushing at her bosom where Fay had cried, shaking herself to get the crumbs off her skirt. "I declare, I'm getting to where I ain't got much left to say to Dad myself."

"You know what his face looks like to me? A piece of paper," said a wizened-looking daughter.

"I ain't going to tell him that," said the old woman.

"Tell him you ain't got too much longer to stay," suggested one of the sons.

"Ask him if he knows who you are," said the wizened-looking daughter.

"Or you can just try keeping your mouth shut," said Archie Lee.

"He's your dad, the same as mine," warned the old woman. "I'm going in because you skipped your turn. Now wait for me! Don't run off and leave me."

"He don't know I'm living," said Archie Lee, as the woman

trudged through the doorway in Indian moccasins. He tilted up the bottle: Mr. Dalzell's son, long lost.

Fay sobbed the louder after the old woman went.

"How you like Mississippi?" Mr. Dalzell's family asked, almost in a chorus. "Don't you think it's friendly?" asked the wizened daughter.

"I guess I'm used to Texas."

"Mississippi is the best state in the Union," said Archie Lee and he put his feet up and stretched out full length on the couch.

"I didn't say I didn't have kin here. I had a grandpa living close to Bigbee, Mississippi," Fay said.

"Now you're talking!" the youngest girl said. "We know right where Bigbee is, could find it for you right now. Fox Hill is harder to find than Bigbee. But *we* don't think it's lonesome, because by the time you get all of us together, there's nine of us, not counting the tadpoles. Ten, if Granddad gets over this. He's got cancer." *The Pancreatit at y*

"Cancer's what my dad had. And Grandpa! Grandpa loved me better than all the rest. That sweet old man, he died in my arms," Fay said, glaring at Laurel across the room. "They died, but not before they did every bit they could to help themselves, and tried all their might to get better, for our sakes. They said they knew, if they just tried hard enough—" *blaming her father*

"I always tell mine to have faith," said the wizened daughter.

And as if their vying and trouble-swapping were the order of the day, or the order of the night, in the waiting room, they were all as unaware of the passing of the minutes as the man on the couch, whose dangling hand now let the bottle drop and slide like an empty slipper across the floor into Laurel's path. She walked on, giving them the wide berth of her desolation.

"Wish they'd give Dad something to drink. Wash his mouth out," said the old mother coming back—Laurel nearly met her in the door.

"Remember Mamie's boy?" Another family had come in, grouping themselves around the Coke machine. The man who was working it called out, "He shot hisself or somebody shot him, one. He begged for water. The hospital wouldn't give him none. Honey, he died wanting water."

"I remember Joe Boy Bush from Bruintown," a man retorted, turning around from the television screen. "He was laying there going without water and *he* reached himself over and bit that tube in two and drunk that glucose. And drunk ever' drop that was in it. And that fool, in two weeks he was up out of that bed and they send him home."

"Two weeks! Guess how long they've held us here!" cried Fay.

"If they don't give your dad no water by next time round, tell you what, we'll go in there all together and pour it down him," promised the old mother. "If he's going to die, I don't want him to die wanting water."

"That's talking, Mama."

"Ain't that true, Archie Lee?"

But Archie Lee lay on the couch with his mouth open.

"There's a fair sight. I'm glad his dad can't walk in on us and see him," said the old woman. "No, if Dad's going to die I ain't going to let him die wanting water!" she insisted, and the others began raggedly laughing.

"We'll pour it down him!" cried the mother. "He ain't going to stand a chance against us!" The family laughed louder, as if there could be no helping it. Some of the other families joined in. It seemed to Laurel that in another moment the whole waiting room would dissolve itself in waiting-room laughter.

Dr. Courtland stood in the doorway, the weight of his watch in his hand.

When Laurel and Fay reached him, he drew them into the elevator hall. The door to Judge McKelva's room stood closed.

"I couldn't save him." He laid a hand on the sleeve of each woman, standing between them. He bent his head, but that did not hide the aggrievement, indignation, that was in his voice. "He's gone, and his eye was healing."

"Are you trying to tell me you let my husband die?" Fay cried.

"He collapsed." Fatigue had pouched the doctor's face, his cheeks hung gray. He kept his touch on their arms.

"You picked my birthday to do it on!" Fay screamed out, just as Mrs. Martello came out of the room. She closed the door behind her. She was carrying a hamper. She pretended not to see them as she drummed past on her heels.

Laurel felt the Doctor's hand shift to grip her arm; she had been about to go straight to the unattended. He began walking the two women toward the elevators. Laurel became aware that he was in evening clothes. *in a hurry*

At the elevator he got in with them, still standing between them. "Maybe we asked too much of him," he said grudgingly. "And yet he didn't have to hold out much longer." He looked protestingly at the lighted floors flashing by. "I'd been waiting to know how well that eye would *see*!"

Fay said, "I knew better than let you go in that eye to start with. That eye was just as bright and cocky as yours is right now. He just took a scratch from an old rose briar! He would have got over that, it would all be forgotten now! Nature would have tended to it. But you thought you knew better!" Without taking her eyes from him, she began crying.

Dr. Courtland looked at her briefly, as if he had seen many like Fay. As they were leaving the elevator among all the other passengers, he looked with the ghost of a smile into Laurel's face. In a moment he said, "He helped me through medical school, kept me going when Daddy died. A sacrifice in those days. The Depression hit and he helped me get my start."

"Some things don't bear going into," Laurel said.

"No," he said. "No." He took off his glasses and put them away, as if he and she had just signed their names to these words. He said then, "Laurel, there's nobody from *home* with you. Would you care to put up with us for the rest of the night? Betty would be so glad. Trouble is, there's goings-on, and of course more to follow. Dell—our oldest girl's eighteen—"

Laurel shook her head.

"I've got my driver waiting outside, though," Dr. Courtland went on. "As soon as you-all finish at the office,

I'll send you where you're going, with something for you both to make you sleep."

"All I hope is *you* lay awake tonight and remember how little you were good for!" cried Fay.

He took them on, through the necessary office gates, and when they came outside the hospital into the air and the sounds of city streets and of tonight, he helped them into his car.

"I'll phone Adele," he said to Laurel. That was his sister in Mount Salus. "You can take him home tomorrow." Still he did not turn to go back into the building, but stood there by the car, his hand on the door he had closed. He gave the drawn-out moment up to uselessness. She felt it might have been the hardest thing he had done all day, or all his life.

"I wish I could have saved him," he said.

Laurel touched her hand to the window glass. He waved then, and quickly turned.

"Thank you for nothing!" Fay screamed above the whirr of their riding away.

Laurel was still gearing herself to the time things took. It was slow going through the streets. There were many waits. Now and then the driver had to shout from the wheel before they could proceed.

Fay grabbed Laurel's arm as she would have grabbed any stranger's. "I saw a man—I saw a man and he was dressed up like a skeleton and his date was in a long white dress, with snakes for hair, holding up a bunch of lilies! Coming down the steps of that house like they're just starting out!" Then she cried out again, the longing, or the anger, of her whole life all in her voice at one time, "Is it the Carnival?"

Laurel heard a band playing and another band moving in on top of it. She heard the crowd noise, the unmistakable sound of hundreds, of thousands, of people *blundering*.

"I saw a man in Spanish moss, a whole suit of Spanish moss, all by himself on the sidewalk. He was vomiting right in public," said Fay. "Why did I have to be shown that?"

"Where you come from?" the driver said scornfully. "This here is Mardi Gras *night*."

When they reached there, they found that the Carnival was

overflowing the Hibiscus too. Masqueraders were coming and going. The cat was off its chain and let inside; it turned its seamed face to look at them and pranced up the staircase and waited for them on the landing, dressed in a monkey coat sewn with sequins.

"All on my birthday. Nobody told me *this* was what was going to happen to me!" Fay cried before she slammed her door.

Her sobbing, the same two close-together, accusing notes running over and over, went on for a time against the thin sounding-board between the two beds. Laurel lay in the dark waiting for it to reach its end. The house took longer than Fay did to go to sleep; the city longer than the house. Eventually she heard the ludicrous sound of chirping frogs emerge from the now completed excavation next door. Toward morning there was the final, parting shot of a pistol fired far off. Nothing came after that; no echo.

They got away in the afternoon. Judge McKelva's body was on board the smooth New Orleans–Chicago train he had always so enjoyed travelling on; he had taken full pleasure in the starched white damask tablecloths, the real rosebud in the silver vase, the celery crisp on ice, the strawberries fresh from Hammond in their season; and the service. The days of the train itself were numbered now.

In the last car, the two women lay back in chairs in their compartment partitioned off from the observation section behind. Fay had kicked off her shoes. She lay with her head turned away, not speaking.

Set deep in the swamp, where the black trees were welling with buds like red drops, was one low beech that had kept its last year's leaves, and it appeared to Laurel to travel along with their train, gliding at a magic speed through the cypresses they left behind. It was her own reflection in the windowpane— the beech tree was her head. Now it was gone. As the train left the black swamp and pulled out into the space of Pontchartrain, the window filled with a featureless sky over pale smooth water, where a seagull was hanging with wings fixed, like a stopped clock on a wall. She must have slept, for nothing seemed to have changed before her eyes until the seagull became the hands on the clock in the Courthouse dome lit up in the night above Mount Salus trees.

Fay slept still. When Laurel had to touch her shoulder to wake her, Fay struggled and said, "Oh no, no, not any more!"

Two

I

THE ANCIENT PORTER was already rolling his iron-wheeled wagon to meet the baggage car, before the train halted. All six of Laurel's bridesmaids, as they still called themselves, were waiting on the station platform. Miss Adele Courtland stood out in front of them. She was Dr. Courtland's sister, looking greatly aged. As Laurel went first down the steps, Miss Adele softly placed her hands together, then spread her arms.

"Polly," she said.

"What are you here for?" asked Fay, as Laurel moved from one embrace into another.

"We came to meet you," Tish Bullock said. "And to take you home."

Laurel was aware of the row of lighted windows already sliding away behind her. The train gathered speed as swiftly as it had brought itself to a halt. It went out of sight while the wagon, loaded with the long box now, and attended by a stranger in a business suit, was wheeled slowly back along the platform and steered to where a hearse, backed in among the cars, stood with its door wide.

"Daddy wanted to come, Laurel, but we've been trying to spare him," said Tish, with protective eyes following what was happening to the coffin. Her arm was linked in Laurel's.

"I'm Mr. Pitts, hope you remember me," said the businessman, appearing at Laurel's other side. "Now what would you like done with your father?" When she didn't speak, he went on, "May we have him in our parlor? Or would you prefer him to repose at the residence?"

"My father? Why—at his home," said Laurel, stammering.

"At the residence. Until the hour of services. As was the case with the first Mrs. McKelva," said the man.

"I'm Mrs. McKelva now. If you're the undertaker, you do your business with me," said Fay.

Tish Bullock winked at Laurel. It was a moment before she

remembered: this was the bridesmaids' automatic signal in moments of acute joy or distress, to show solidarity.

There was a deep boom, like the rolling in of an ocean wave. The hearse door had been slammed shut.

"—and you may have him back in the morning by ten A.M.," the undertaker was saying to Fay. "But first, me and you need to have a little meeting of the minds in a quiet, dignified place where you can be given the opportunity—"

"You bet your boots," said Fay.

The hearse pulled away, then. It turned to the left on Main Street, blotted out the Courthouse fence, and disappeared behind the Presbyterian Church.

Mr. Pitts turned to make his bow to Laurel. "I'll return this lady to you by-and-by," he said.

Miss Adele took Laurel's coat over her arm and the bridesmaids gathered up all the suitcases. The old Bullock Chrysler had been waiting.

It was first-dark in the town of Mount Salus. They turned right on Main Street and drove the three and a half blocks.

The McKelva house was streaming light from every window, upstairs and down. As Tish passed the row of parked cars and turned up into the driveway, Laurel saw that the daffodils were in bloom, long streamers of them reaching down the yard, hundreds of small white trumpets. Tish lightly touched the horn, and the front door opened and still more light streamed out, in which the solid form of Miss Tennyson Bullock walked out and stood on the porch.

Laurel ran from the car and across the grass and up the front steps. Miss Tennyson—Tish's mother—was calling to her in ringing tones, "And he was such a precious, after all!" She folded Laurel close.

Half a dozen—a dozen—old family friends had been waiting here in the house. They came out into the hall from the rooms on both sides as Laurel walked in. Most of them had practiced-for smiles on their faces, and they all called her "Laurel McKelva," just as they always called her. Here at his own home, inside his own front door, there was nobody who seemed to be taken by surprise at what had happened to Judge McKelva. Laurel seemed to remember that Presbyterians were good at this.

But there was a man's deep groan from the dining room, and Major Bullock came swinging out into the hall, cutting through the welcomers, protesting. "I'm not even going to *have* it, I say. He was never sick a day in his life!" Laurel went to meet him and kissed his flushed cheek.

He was the only man here. It might have been out of some sense of delicacy that the bridesmaids and the older ladies, those who were not already widows, had all made their husbands stay home tonight. Miss Tennyson, who had relieved Laurel of her handbag and crushed gloves, smoothed back the part into her hair. She had been Laurel's mother's oldest friend, the first person she'd met when she came to Mount Salus as a bride.

Now she gave a sidelong glance at Tish and asked her, "Did Mr. Pitts manage to catch Fay?"

"He's going to return her to us by-and-by." Tish mocked him perfectly.

"Poor little woman! How is she taking it, Laurel?" asked Major Bullock.

At last she said, "I don't think I can safely predict about Fay."

"Let's not make Laurel try," suggested Miss Adele Courtland.

Miss Tennyson led Laurel into the dining room. The bridesmaids had been setting out a buffet. On the little side table, where Major Bullock, standing with his back to them, was quickly finishing up something, was the drinks tray with some bottles and glasses. Laurel found herself sitting at her old place at the dinner table, the only one seated, while everybody else was trying to wait on her. Miss Tennyson stood right at her shoulder, to make her eat.

"What are all these people doing in my house?"

That was Fay's voice in the hall.

"You've got pies three deep in the pantry, and an icebox ready to pop," said Miss Tennyson, going out to meet her. "And a dining room table that might keep you from going to bed hungry."

"Well, I didn't know I was giving a reception," said Fay. She came as far as the dining room doors and stared in.

"We're Laurel's friends, Fay," Tish reminded her. "The six of us right here, we were her bridesmaids."

"A lot of good her bridesmaids will ever do me. And who's making themselves at home in my parlor?" She crossed the hall.

"Fay, those are the last, devoted remnants of the old Garden Club, of which I'm now president," said Miss Tennyson. "Here now for—for Laurel's mother's sake."

"What's Becky's Garden Club got to do with me?" exclaimed Fay. She stuck her head inside the parlor door and said, "The funeral's not till tomorrow."

"They're a hard bunch to put off till tomorrow," said Miss Tennyson. "They picked their flowers and they brought 'em."

Laurel left her chair and went out to Miss Tennyson and the gathering ladies. "They're all Father's friends, Fay. They're exactly the ones he'd have counted on to be here in the house to meet us," she said. "And I count on them."

"Well, it's evermore unfair. I haven't got anybody to count on but me, myself, and I." Fay's eyes travelled to the one man in the gathering and she accused him. "*I* haven't got one soul." She let out a cry, and streaked up the stairs.

"Poor little woman, she's the helpless kind," said Major Bullock. "We're going to have to see about her." He looked around him, and there were the suitcases, still standing near the front door. Three of them: one was Judge McKelva's. Major Bullock loaded himself and walked upstairs with them. When he came back, almost immediately, his step was even heavier. Straight-armed, he carried at full length on its hanger a suit of black winter clothes. It swayed more widely than he swayed in negotiating the turn on the landing. There was a shoebox in his other hand and a leather case under his arm.

"She's sending me down to Pitts', Tennyson," he said. "Carrying him these."

"Naked through the streets?" Miss Tennyson objected. "But I suppose you couldn't let her go to the trouble of packing them."

"A man wanted to get out of the room," he said stiffly. But his arm gave at the elbow, and the suit for a moment sagged; the trousers folded to the floor. He stood there in the middle of the women and cried. He said, "I just can't believe it yet! Can't believe Clint's gone for good and Pitts has got him down there—"

"All right, I'll believe it for you," said Miss Tennyson, on her way to him. She rescued the suit and hung it over his arm for him, so that it was less clumsy for him and looked less like a man. "Now go on and do like she told you. You *insisted* on being here tonight!"

Upstairs, the bedroom door was rather weakly slammed. Laurel had never heard it slammed before. She went and laid her cheek for a moment against Major Bullock's, aware of the tears on it and the bourbon on his breath. He propelled himself forward and out of the lighted house.

"Daddy, wait! I'll drive you!" Tish called, running.

It was the break-up, and when they'd all said goodnight, promising to return in the morning in plenty of time, Laurel saw them to the door and stood waiting until their cars had driven away. Then she walked back through the parlor as far as the doorway into the library behind it. There was her father's old chair sitting up to his desk. *empty*

The sound of plates being laid carefully one on top of the other reached her then from the kitchen. She walked in through the pantry.

"It's I."

Laurel knew that would be Miss Adele Courtland. She had finished putting the food away and washing the dishes; she was polishing dry the turkey platter. It was a piece of the old Haviland in the small arbutus pattern—the "laurel"—that Laurel's mother had loved.

"Here in the kitchen it will all start over so soon," Miss Adele said, as if asking forgiveness.

"You can't help being good. That's what Father said about you in New Orleans," Laurel said. Then, "*He* was the best thing in the world too—Dr. Courtland."

Miss Adele nodded her head.

"What happened was not to Father's eye at all. Father was going to see," Laurel told her. "Dr. Courtland was right about the eye. He did everything right." Miss Adele nodded, and Laurel finished, "What happened wasn't like what happened to Mother."

Miss Adele lifted the stacked clean dishes off the kitchen

table and carried them into the dining room and put them away in their right places on the shelves of the china closet. She arranged the turkey platter to stand in its groove at the back of the gravy bowl. She put the glasses in, and restored the little wine glasses to their ring around the decanter, with its mended glass stopper still intact. She shut the shivering glass door gently, so as not to rock the old top-heavy cabinet.

"People live their own way, and to a certain extent I almost believe they may die their own way, Laurel." She turned around, and the chandelier threw its light down on her. Her fine-drawn, elegant face might almost have withered a little more while she was out here with the kitchen to herself. She wore her faded hair as she had always worn it from the day when she was Laurel's first-grade teacher, in a Psyche knot. Her voice was as capable of authority as ever. "Sleep, now, Laurel. We'll all be back here in the morning, and you know we won't be the only ones. Goodnight!"

She left by the kitchen door, as always, and stepped home through the joining backyards. It was dark and fragrant out there. When the Courtland kitchen light went on, Laurel closed her back door too, and walked through the house putting out lights. The only illumination on the stairs came from the lamp that they had turned on for her by her bed.

In her own room, she undressed, raised the window, got into bed with the first book her fingers found, and lay without opening it.

The quiet of the Mount Salus night was a little different now. She could hear traffic on some new highway, a sound like the buzzing of one angry fly against a windowpane, over and over.

When Laurel was a child, in this room and in this bed where she lay now, she closed her eyes like this and the rhythmic, nighttime sound of the two beloved reading voices came rising in turn up the stairs every night to reach her. She could hardly fall asleep, she tried to keep awake, for pleasure. She cared for her own books, but she cared more for theirs, which meant their voices. In the lateness of the night, their two voices reading to each other where she could hear them, never letting a silence divide or interrupt them, combined into one unceasing voice and wrapped her around as she listened, as still as if she were asleep. She was sent to sleep under a velvety cloak of words, richly patterned and stitched with gold, straight out of a fairy tale, while they went reading on into her dreams.

Fay slept farther away tonight than in the Hibiscus—they could not hear each other in this house—but nearer in a different way. She was sleeping in the bed where Laurel was born; and where her mother had died. What Laurel listened for tonight was the striking of the mantel clock downstairs in the parlor. It never came.

[handwritten annotation: and]
[handwritten annotation: a change]

2

At the inevitable hour, Laurel started from her bed and went downstairs in her dressing gown. It was a clear, bright seven o'clock, with morning shadows dappling the shine of the floors and the dining room table. And there was Missouri, standing in her hat and coat in the middle of the kitchen.

"Am I supposed to believe what I hear?" asked Missouri.

Laurel went to her and took her in her arms.

Missouri took off her hat and coat and hung them on the nail with her shoulder bag. She washed her hands, and then she shook out a fresh apron, just as she'd started every morning off during Laurel's mother's life in Mount Salus.

"Well, *I'm* here and *you're* here," said Missouri. It was the bargain to give and take comfort. After a moment's hesitation, Missouri went on, "*He* always want Miss Fay to have her breakfast in bed."

"Then you'll know how to wake her," said Laurel. "When you take it up. Do you mind?"

"Do it for him," said Missouri. Her face softened. "He mightily enjoyed having him somebody to spoil."

In a little while, just as Missouri walked out with the tray, Miss Adele Courtland came in at the back door. She was wearing her best—of course, she'd arranged not to teach her children today. She offered Laurel a double-handful of daffodils, the nodding, gray-white kind with the square cup.

"You know who gave me mine—hers are blooming outside.

Silver Bells," Miss Adele prompted her. "Is there a place left
to put them?"

They walked through the dining room and across to the
parlor. The whole house was filled with flowers; Laurel was
seeing them for the first time this morning—the cut branches
of Mount Salus prunus and crab, the thready yellow jasmine,
bundles of narcissus, in vases and pitchers that came, along
with the flowers, from houses up and down the street.

"Father's desk—?"

"Miss Laurel, I keep a-calling Miss Fay but she don't sit up
to her breakfast!" called Missouri on the stairs.

"Your day has started, Laurel," said Miss Adele. "I'm here
to answer the door."

Laurel went up, knocked, and opened the door into the big
bedroom. Instead of her mother's writing cabinet that used
to stand between those windows, the bed faced her. It seemed
to swim in a bath of pink light. The mahogany headboard,
rising high as the mantelpiece, had been quilted from top to
bottom in peach satin; peach satin ruffles were thrown back
over the foot of the bed; peach satin smothered the windows
all around. Fay slept in the middle of the bed, deep under the
cover, both hands curled into slack fists above her head. Laurel
could not see her face but only the back of her neck, the most
vulnerable part of anybody, and she thought: Is there any
sleeping person you can be entirely sure you have not misjudged? Then she saw the new green shoes placed like orna-
ments on top of the mantel shelf.

"Fay!" she cried.

Fay gave no sign.

"Fay, it's morning."

"You go back to sleep."

"This is Laurel. It's a few minutes before ten o'clock.
There'll be callers downstairs, asking for you."

Fay pushed herself up on her arms and cried over her shoulder, "I'm the widow! They can all wait till I get there."

"A good breakfast do you a lot of good," said Missouri,
bringing it in, letting Laurel out.

Laurel bathed, dressed. A low thunder travelled through
the hall downstairs and shook in her hand as she tried to put

the pins in her hair. One voice dominated the rest: Miss Tennyson Bullock was taking charge.

"So this time it's Clint's turn to bring you home," said an old lady's voice to her as she came down the stairs. All Laurel could remember of her, the first moment, was that a child's ball thrown over her fence was never to be recovered.

"Yes, daughters need to stay put, where they can keep a better eye on us old folks," said Miss Tennyson Bullock, meeting Laurel at the foot of the stairs with a robust hug. "Honey, he's come."

Miss Tennyson led the way into the parlor. Everything was dim. All over the downstairs, the high old windows had had their draperies drawn. In the parlor, lamps were burning by day and Laurel felt as she entered the room that the furniture was out of place. A number of people rose to their feet and stood still, making a path for her.

The folding doors between the parlor and the library behind it had been rolled all the way back, and the casket was installed across this space. It had been raised on a sort of platform that stood draped with a curtain, a worn old velvet curtain, only halfway hiding the wheels. A screen of florist's ferns was being built up before her eyes behind the coffin. Then a man stepped out from behind the green and presented a full, square face with its small features pulled to the center—what Laurel's mother had called "a Baptist face."

"Miss Laurel, I'm Mr. Pitts again. I recall your dear mother so clearly," he said. "And I believe you're going to be just as pleased now, with your father." He put out his hand and raised the lid.

Judge McKelva lay inside in his winter suit. All around him was draped the bright satin of a jeweler's box, and its color was the same warm, foolish pink that had smothered the windows and spilled over the bed upstairs. His large face reflected the pink, so that his long, heavy cheek had the cast of a seashell, or a pearl. The dark patches underneath his eyes had been erased like traces of human error. Only the black flare of the nostrils and the creases around the mouth had been left him of his old saturnine look. The lid had been raised only by half-section, to show him propped on the pillow; below the waist he lay cut off from any eyes. He was still not to be mistaken for any other man.

"You must close it," said Laurel quietly to Mr. Pitts.

"You're not pleased?" But he had never displeased anyone, his face said.

"Oh, look," said Miss Tennyson, arriving at Laurel's side. "Oh, *look*."

"I don't want it open, please," said Laurel to Mr. Pitts. She touched Miss Tennyson's hand. "But Father would never allow—when Mother died, he protected her from—"

"Your mother was different," said Miss Tennyson firmly.

"He was respecting her wishes," Laurel said. "Not to make her lie here in front of people's eyes—"

"And I've never forgiven him for that. Nobody ever really got to tell Becky goodbye," Miss Tennyson was saying at the same time. "But honey, your father's a Mount Salus man. He's a McKelva. A public figure. You can't deprive the public, can you? Oh, he's lovely."

"I would like him away from their eyes," said Laurel.

"It is Mrs. McKelva's desire that the coffin be open," said Mr. Pitts.

"See there? You can't deprive Fay," said Miss Tennyson. "That settles that." She held out her arms, inviting the room.

Laurel took up her place in front of the coffin, near the head, and stood to meet them as they came.

First they embraced her, and then they stood and looked down at her father. The bridesmaids and their husbands, the whole crowd of them, had gone from the first grade through high school graduation together, and they still stood solid. So did her father's crowd—the County Bar, the elders of the church, the Hunting and Fishing Club cronies; though they seemed to adhere to their own kind, they slowly moved in place, as if they made up the rim of a wheel that slowly turned itself around the hub of the coffin and would bring them around again.

"May I see him?" the Presbyterian minister's wife asked right and left as she elbowed her way in, as if Judge McKelva's body were the new baby. She gazed on him lying there, for a minute. "And here I'd been waiting to see who it was I was saving my Virginia ham for," she said, turning to Laurel and squeezing her around the waist. "It was *your mother* first told me how I could harness one of those and get it cooked so it was fit for anybody to eat. Well, it's headed right for your kitchen." She nodded back to the coffin. "I'm afraid my husband's running a little late. You know people like *this* don't die every day in the week. He's sitting home in his bathrobe now, tearing his hair, trying to do him justice."

"Why, here's Dot," said Miss Adele, posted at the front door.

To everyone in town, she was known simply as Dot. She came in with her nonchalant, twenties stalk on her high heels.

"I couldn't resist," she said in her throaty baritone as she approached the coffin.

She must have been seventy. She had been Judge McKelva's private secretary for years and years. When he retired, her feelings had been hurt. Of course, he'd seen to it that she was eased into another job, but she had never forgiven him.

"When I first came to work for him," said Dot, looking at him now, "I paid thirty-five dollars of my salary to a store in Jackson for a set of Mah Johng. It was on sale from a hundred dollars. I really can't to this very day understand myself. But, 'Why, Dot,' this sweet man says, 'I don't see anything so specially the matter with giving yourself a present. I hope you go ahead and enjoy it. Don't reproach yourself like that. You're distressing my ears,' he says. I'll never forget his kind words of advice."

"Mah Johng!" gasped Miss Tennyson Bullock. "Great Day in the Morning, I'd forgotten about it."

Dot gave her a bitter look, almost as if she'd said she'd forgotten about Judge McKelva. "Tennyson," she said across his body, "I'm never going to speak to you again."

Somebody had lit the fire, although the day was mild and the room close now, filling with more and more speaking, breathing people.

"Yes, a fire seemed called for," said Major Bullock. He came up to Laurel and scraped his face against hers as though his were numb. His breath had its smell of Christmas morning—it was whiskey. "Fairest, most impartial, sweetest man in the whole Mississippi Bar," he said, his gaze wavering, seeming to avoid Judge McKelva's face, going only to the hand that had been placed like a closed satchel at his tailored side. "How soon is that poor little woman going to bring herself downstairs?"

"Eventually," Miss Tennyson told him. Whatever she said, in times of trouble, took on all the finality in the world. Finality was what made the throb in her voice.

3

"Now what could *they* want," said old Mrs. Pease, who stood at the front window parting the draperies.

"Polly," warned Miss Adele.

Everyone turned, and those seated stood up, as two equally fat women and a man walked past Miss Adele into the parlor.

"I said this had to be the right spot, because it looks like the very house to hold a big funeral," said the old fat woman. "Where's Wanda Fay? I don't see her."

While she was speaking, the two women, old and young, were walking up to the coffin, and while they passed it, they looked in. Laurel heard herself being introduced by one of the strangers to the other.

"Mama, this is Judge and Becky's daughter," said the young woman.

"Becky's the one she takes after, then," said the mother, seating herself in Judge McKelva's smoking chair, which now stood nearest the casket. "You don't favor him," she told Laurel. "A grand coffin my little girl's afforded. Makes me jealous." She turned toward the man. "Bubba, this is Judge and Becky's daughter."

The man with them raised his arm from the elbow and waved at Laurel from close range. He wore a windbreaker. "Hi."

"I'm Mrs. Chisom from Madrid, Texas. I'm Wanda Fay's mother," the fat lady said to Laurel. "And this is some of my other children—Sis, from Madrid, Texas, and Bubba, from Madrid, Texas. We got a few others that rather not come in."

"Well, you're news to me," said Miss Tennyson, as if that were simply all there was to it.

Major Bullock came forward to greet them. "I'm Major Bullock!"

"Well, if you're wondering how long it took us, I made it from Madrid in close on to eight hours," the man in the windbreaker said. Madrid was pronounced with the accent as in Mildred. "Crossed the river at Vicksburg. And we're going to have to turn around and go right back. The kids wanted to all pile in, but their mama said you don't ever know what germs they might pick up in a strange place. And she's right. So I left 'em with her in the trailer, and didn't bring but one of 'em. Where's Wendell?"

"I reckon he's looking over the house," said the young woman. She was pregnant, rather than fat.

"Sis brought the whole brood of hers. Sis," said the man. "This is his first wife's daughter."

"I knew that's who she was, you didn't have to introduce us. Feel like I know you already," said the sister to Laurel.

And oddly, Laurel felt that too. Fay had said they didn't even exist, and yet it seemed to Laurel that she had seen them all before.

"I told my bunch they could just play outside in the front yard and watch for us all to come out," said Sis. "That seemed to pretty well satisfy 'em."

Old Mrs. Pease was already at the window curtains, and patting her foot as she peeped out between them.

Major Bullock looked gratified. "I summoned 'em up without any trouble at all," he said. "They were delighted to come." He threw a hopeful glance into the hall.

"You just forgot to warn *us*," said Miss Tennyson.

Laurel felt a finger twine its way around her own finger, scratch under the ring. "You have bad luck with *your* husband, too?" Mrs. Chisom asked her.

"Year after she married him," said old Mrs. Pease. "Gone. The war. U.S. Navy. Body never recovered."

"*You* was *cheated*," Mrs. Chisom pronounced.

Laurel tried to draw back her finger. Mrs. Chisom let it go in order to poke her in the side as if to shame her. "So you ain't got father, mother, brother, sister, husband, chick nor child. Not a soul to call on, that's you."

"What do you mean! This girl here's surrounded by her

shock

oldest friends!" The Mayor of Mount Salus stood there, clapping Laurel on the shoulder. "And listen further: bank's closed, most of the Square's agreed to close for the hour of services, county offices closed. Courthouse has lowered its flag out front, school's letting out early. That ought to satisfy anybody that comes asking who she's got!"

"Friends are here today and gone tomorrow," Mrs. Chisom told Laurel and the Mayor. "Not like your kin. Hope the Lord don't ask me to outlive mine. I'd be much obliged if He'd take *me* the next round. Ain't that a good idea, children?"

A little boy came into the room at a trot while she waited for an answer. He did not look at her or anybody else. He was wearing a cowboy suit and hat and double pistol holsters. He stopped when he saw where he was going.

"Wendell, you pull off your hat if you go any closer," said Sis.

The child bared his head, continued to the coffin, and stood there on tiptoe, at Laurel's side. His mouth opened. He was about seven, fair and frail. The ferocious face he looked at and his own, so near together, were equally unguarded.

"How come he wanted to dress up?" asked the child.

"Who promised if they could come in the house they wouldn't ask questions?" asked Sis.

"Yes, me and my brood believes in clustering just as close as we can get," said Mrs. Chisom. "Bubba pulled his trailer right up in my yard when he married and Irma can string her clothesline as far out as she pleases. Sis here got married and didn't even try to move away. Duffy just snuggled in."

"What's his name?" asked Wendell.

"Wendell, run up those stairs and see if you can find your Aunt Wanda Fay. Tell her to come on down and see who she's got waiting on her," said Bubba.

"I don't want to," said Wendell.

"What you scared of? Nothing's going to bite you upstairs. Go hunt her," said his father.

"I don't want to."

"She better hurry if she wants to see us," Bubba said. "Because we're gonna have to turn right around in a minute and start back to Madrid."

"Now, wait!" said Major Bullock. "You're one of the pall-bearers."

"What did he call you, Dad?" cried Wendell.

"It seemed only right," Major Bullock said to the room.

"Tell her to come double-quick," said Bubba to Wendell. "Run!"

"I want to stay here," said Wendell.

"I'm sorry. This is his first funeral," said Sis to Laurel.

"Let me show you Judge," Mrs. Chisom said placatingly to Bubba.

"I just finished seeing him," Bubba said. "I couldn't help but think he's young-looking for a man pushing seventy-one."

"That's right. Not a bit wasted. I'm proud for you, Wanda Fay," Mrs. Chisom said, addressing the ceiling over her head. "Your pa was wasted and they didn't have the power to hide it." She turned to Laurel. "But I reckon he'd lasted longer on nothing but tap water than anybody ever lasted before. Tap water, that's all Mr. Chisom could get down. I kept listening for some complaint out of him, never got one. He had cancer but he didn't whimper about it, not to me. That's because we both of us come from good old Mississippi stock!"

A big, apple-cheeked woman in a hairy tam smiled into Laurel's face from the other side. "I remember, oh, I remember how many Christmases I was among those present in this dear old home in all its hospitality."

This caller was out of her mind, yet even she was not being kept back from Judge McKelva's open coffin. By the rundown heels on her shoes as she lumbered toward her, Laurel knew her for the sewing woman. She would come to people's houses and spend the whole day upstairs at the sewing machine, listening and talking and repeating and getting everything crooked. Miss Verna Longmeier.

"And they'd throw open those doors between these double parlors and the music would strike up! And then—" Miss Verna drew out her arm as though to measure a yard— "then Clinton and I, we'd lead out the dance," she said.

In Mount Salus nobody ever tried to contradict Miss Verna Longmeier. If even a crooked piece of stitching were pointed out to her, she was apt to return: "Let him who is without sin cast the first stone."

"Oh, I've modeled myself on this noble Roman," declared the Mayor, sending out his palm above the casket. "And when I reach higher office—" He strode off to join the other members of the Bar. Laurel saw that they were all sitting more or less together on a row of dining room chairs, like some form of jury.

Miss Thelma Frierson creaked over the floor and stood above the casket. She had filled out the fishing and hunting licenses at her Courthouse window for years and years. Her shoulders drooped as she said, "He had a wonderful sense of humor. Underneath it all."

"Underneath it all, Father knew it *wasn't* funny," said Laurel politely.

"Too bad he ever elected to go to the hospital," old Mrs. Chisom said. "If he knew what ain't funny."

"I tell you, what they let go on in hospitals don't hardly bear repeating," said Sis. "Irma says the maternity ward in Amarillo would curl your hair."

"Doctors don't know what they're doing. They just know how to charge," said Bubba.

"And you know who I wouldn't trust for a blessed second behind my back? Nurses!" cried Mrs. Chisom.

Laurel looked over their heads, to where the Chinese prints brought home by an earlier generation of missionary McKelvas hung in their changeless grouping around the mantel clock. And she saw that the clock had stopped; it had not been wound, she supposed, since the last time her father had done duty by it, and its hands pointed to some remote three o'clock, as motionless as the time in the Chinese prints. She wanted to go to the clock and take the key from where her father kept it—on a small nail he'd hammered, a little crookedly, into the papered wall—and wind the clock and set it going at the right time. But she could not spare the moment from his side. She felt as though in death her father had been asked to bear the weight of that raised lid himself, and hold it up by lying there, the same way he'd lain on the hospital bed and counted the minutes and the hours to make his life go by. She stood by the coffin as she had sat by his bed, waiting it out with him. Unable to hear the ticking of the clock, she listened to the gritting and the hissing of the fire.

Dr. Woodson was saying, "Clint and me used to take off as shirt-tail lads with both our dogs and be gone all day up in the woods—you know where they used to call it Top o' the World? With the gravel pit dug out of the claybanks there. I've been his doctor for years, hell, we're the same age, but after all this time it hasn't been until now that something made me think about his foot. Clint went swinging on a vine, swinging too wide and too high, and soared off and came down on a piece of tin barefooted. He liked-to bled to death a mile from home! I reckon I must have carried Clint into town on my back and used strength I didn't know I had. You know Clint always gave you the impression you couldn't kill him, that nothing could, but I believe he really must have been kind of delicate."

Light laughter broke out in the room and hushed itself in the same instant.

"Is this it, Aunt Sis?" Wendell Chisom asked. "Is it the funeral yet?"

"It'll be the funeral when I say so," said Sis.

"After I'd *got* him here, he fell out cold. But there's houses in sight by then. It's where the Self-Serve Car Wash is now. I reckon I'm to blame for saving Clint's life for him that time!"

"Father *was* delicate," said Laurel.

"With everything that's the matter with me, you'd have thought he'd outlive me," the doctor went on.

"Not for me or you to ask the reason why," Mrs. Chisom told him. "It's like the choice between Grandpa and my oldest boy Roscoe. Nobody in Texas could understand what the Lord meant, taking Roscoe when He did."

"What happened to Roscoe, Grandma?" Wendell asked, abandoning the coffin to hang over her lap and look up into her face.

"Son, you've heard me tell it. Stuffed up the windows, stuffed up the door, turned on all four eyes of the stove and the oven," said Mrs. Chisom indulgently. "Fire Department drug him out, rushed him to the Baptist Hospital in the fire-wagon, tried all their tricks, but they couldn't get ahead of Roscoe. He was in Heaven already."

"He beat the fire engines? Was you there, Grandma?" Wendell cried. "You see him beat 'em?"

"I'm his mother. Well, his mother could sit and be thankful he didn't do nothing any more serious to harm his looks. He hated more than anything having remarks made against him. In his coffin he was pretty as a girl. Honey, he just stretched him out easy and put his head on a pillow and waited till he'd quit breathing. Don't you ever let me hear you tried that, Wendell," said Mrs. Chisom.

Wendell turned and looked back at Judge McKelva.

"Roscoe told his friends in Orange, Texas, what he was figuring on doing. When it's all done, they wrote and told me he'd called 'em up crying and they went and cried with him. 'Cried *with* him?' I wrote those people back. 'Why couldn't you-all have told his mother?' I can't get *over* people. I says on my card, 'I had the bus fare. I'm not that poor. I had the round-trip from Madrid to Orange and back again.' " She was patting both feet.

"He's better off, Mama," said Sis. "Better off, just like Judge McKelva laying yonder. Tell yourself the same thing I do."

"I wrote another card and said at least tell his mother what had been fretting my son, if they knew so much, and they finally got around to answering that Roscoe didn't *want* me to know," Mrs. Chisom said, her face arranging itself all at once into an expression of innocence. It lasted for only a minute. She went on, "Roscoe was my mainstay when Mr. Chisom went. They said, 'Prepare your mind, Mrs. Chisom. Mr. Chisom is not going to go anywhere but downhill.' They was guessing right, that time, the doctors was. He went down fast and we buried him back in Mississippi, back in Bigbee, and there on the spot I called Roscoe to me." She pulled Wendell to her now. " 'Roscoe,' I says, 'you're the mainstay now,' I says. 'You're the head of the Chisom family.' He was so happy."

Wendell began to cry. Laurel wanted at that moment to reach out for him, put her arms around him—to guard him. He was like a young, undriven, unfalsifying, unvindictive Fay. So Fay might have appeared, just at the beginning, to her aging father, with his slipping eyesight.

At that moment, Wendell broke from Mrs. Chisom and ran tearing toward the hallway. He threw his arms around the knees of an old man whom Miss Adele was just showing in from the hall.

"Grandpa Chisom! I can't believe my eyes! It's Grandpa!" Sis cried out.

Wendell at his side, the old man came slowly into the parlor and through the crowd, carrying a yellowed candy box in one hand and a paper sack in the other. Wendell had possession of his old black hat. He came up to Laurel and said, "Young lady, I carried you some Bigbee pecans. I thought you might not harvest their like around here. They're last year's." He held onto his parcels while he explained that he had sat up most of last night, after walking to the crossroads to flag down the bus at three this morning, and had shelled the nuts on the way, to keep awake. "Where I got lost was after I got inside of Mount Salus," he said, giving the box to Laurel. "That's the meats. You can just throw the shells away for me," he added, handing her the sack. "I didn't like to leave 'em in that nice warm seat for the next passenger." He carefully dusted his hands before he turned toward the casket.

"Who you think it is, Grandpa?" asked Wendell.

"It's Mr. McKelva. I reckon he stood whatever it was long enough," said Mr. Chisom. "I'm sorry he had to go while he's so many miles short of home."

"Out of curiosity, who does he remind you of?" Mrs. Chisom asked him as he gazed down.

The old man reflected for a minute. "Nobody," he said.

"Clint thought it was too good a joke not to play it on somebody!" Laurel heard behind her, at the end of a long spate of words.

She saw that most of the Bar had gathered themselves up and gone behind the screen of ferns, without being missed. They had retired into her father's library and were talking among themselves back there. Now and then she heard a laugh. She smelled the cigar smoke. They were all back there but Major Bullock.

"How's my fire?" cried Major Bullock. "Somebody tend to the fire!" he called toward the kitchen. "Important time like this, you can't do without a fire, can you?" But he kept his own watch on the doorway leading from the hall, and looked eagerly to see each one who came in.

Old Mrs. Pease kept a watch on the front walk through the parlor curtains, making herself at home. "Why, here comes Tommy," she said now. She might have been entertaining a notion of running him away, as she might have to run those Texas children if they played too near the house.

The caller entered the room without the benefit of Miss Adele, walking with a spring on the balls of his feet, striking his cane from side to side in a lordly way. He was Tom Farris, Mount Salus's blind man. Instead of going to the coffin, he went to the piano and tapped his cane on the empty piano stool.

"He's so happy," said Miss Tennyson approvingly.

He sat down, a large, very clean man with rotund, open eyes like a statue's. His fly had not been buttoned up quite straight. Laurel thought he had never been in the house before except to tune the piano, ages ago. He sat down on the same stool now.

"And under that cloak of modesty he wore, a fearless man! Fearless man!" Major Bullock suddenly burst into speech, standing at the foot of the coffin. "Remember the day, everybody, when Clint McKelva stood up and faced the White Caps?" The floor creaked agonizingly as he rocked back and forth on his feet and all but shouted, filling the room, perhaps the house, with his voice. "The time Clint sentenced that fellow for willful murder and the White Caps let it be known they were coming to town out of all their holes and nooks and crannies to take that man from the jail! And Clint just as quick sent out word of his own: he was going to ring that jail and Courthouse of ours with Mount Salus volunteers, and we'd be armed and ready. And the White Caps came, too— came a little bit earlier than they promised, little bit earlier than the rest of us got on hand. But Clint, Clint all by himself, he walked out on the front steps of that Courthouse and stood there and he said, 'Come right on in! The jail is upstairs, on the second floor!'"

"I don't think that was Father," Laurel said low to Tish, who had come up beside her.

Major Bullock was going irrepressibly on. " 'Come in!' says

the private lives

he. 'But before you enter, you take those damn white hoods off, and every last one of you give me a look at who you are!' "

"He hadn't any use for what he called theatrics," Laurel was saying. "In the courtroom or anywhere else. He had no patience for show."

"He says, 'Back to your holes, rats!' And they were armed!" cried Major Bullock, lifting an imaginary gun in his hands.

"He's trying to make Father into something he wanted to be himself," said Laurel.

"Bless his heart," mourned Tish beside her. "Don't spoil it for Daddy."

how true like a story

"But I don't think it's fair *now*," said Laurel.

"Well, that backed 'em right out of there, the whole pack, right on out of town and back into the woods they came from. Cooked their goose for a while!" declared Major Bullock. "Oh, under that cloak of modesty he wore—"

"Father really was modest," Laurel said to him.

"Honey, what do you mean? Honey, you were away. You were sitting up yonder in Chicago, drawing pictures," Major Bullock told her. "I saw him! He stood up and dared those rascals to shoot him! Baring his breast!"

"He would have thought of my mother," said Laurel. And with it came the thought: It was my mother who *might* have done that! She's the only one I know who had it in her.

"Remains a mystery to me how he ever stayed alive," said Major Bullock stiffly. He lowered the imaginary gun. His feelings had been hurt.

The mystery in how little we know of other people is no greater than the mystery of how much, Laurel thought.

"But who do you call the man, Dad?" asked Wendell, plucking at his father's sleeve.

"Shut up. Or I'll carry you on home without letting you see the rest of it."

"It's my father," Laurel said.

The little boy looked at her, and his mouth opened. She thought he disbelieved her.

The crowd of men were still at it behind the screen. "Clint's hunting a witness, some of the usual trouble, and this Negro girl says, 'It's him and me that saw it. He's a witness, and I's a got-shot witness.' "

consistent — he's funny

They laughed.

"'There's two kinds, all right,' says Clint. 'And I know which to take. She's the got-shot witness: I'll take her.' He could see the funny side to everything."

"He brought her here afterwards and kept her safe under his own roof," Laurel said under her breath to Miss Adele, who had come in from the door now; it would be too late for any more callers before the funeral. "I don't know what the funny side was."

"It was Missouri, wasn't it?" said Miss Adele.

"And listening," said Laurel, for Missouri herself was just then lit up by a shower of sparks; down on her knees before the fire, she was poking the big log.

enlightened

"I always pray people won't recognize themselves in the speech of others," Miss Adele murmured. "And I don't think very often they do."

The log shifted like a sleeper in bed, and light flared all over in the room. Mr. Pitts was revealed in their midst as though by a spotlight, in the act of consulting his wristwatch.

"What's happening isn't real," Laurel said, low.

"The ending of a man's life on earth is very real indeed," Miss Adele said.

"But what people are saying."

"They're trying to say for a man that his life is over. Do you know a good way?"

of being
lost

Here, helpless in his own house among the people he'd known, and who'd known him, since the beginning, her father seemed to Laurel to have reached at this moment the danger point of his life.

misunderstood
like
dissolving

"Did you listen to their words?" she asked.

"They're being clumsy. Often because they were thinking of you."

"They said he was a humorist. And a crusader. And an angel on the face of the earth," Laurel said.

like
Denis
in

Miss Adele, looking into the fire, smiled. "It isn't easy for them, either. And they're being egged on a little bit, you know, Laurel, by the rivalry that's going on here in the room," she said. "After all, when the Chisoms walked in on us, they thought they had their side, too—" *Great*

Delta
Wedding
in death
a hero

"Rivalry? With Father where he lies?"

"Yes, but people being what they are, Laurel."

"This is still his house. After all, they're still his guests. They're misrepresenting him—falsifying, that's what Mother would call it." Laurel might have been trying to testify now for her father's sake, as though he were in process of being put on trial in here instead of being viewed in his casket. "He never would have stood for lies being told about him. Not at any time. Not ever."

"Yes he would," said Miss Adele. "If the truth might hurt the wrong person."

"I'm his daughter. I want what people say now to be the truth."

Laurel slowly turned her back to the parlor, and stood a little apart from Miss Adele too. She let her eyes travel out over the coffin into the other room, her father's "library." The bank of greenery hid the sight of his desk. She could see only the two loaded bookcases behind it, like a pair of old, patched, velvety cloaks hung up there on the wall. The shelf-load of Gibbon stretched like a sagging sash across one of them. She had not read her father the book he'd wanted after all. The wrong book! The wrong book! She was looking at her own mistake, and its long shadow reaching back to join the others.

"The least anybody can do for him is *remember* right," she said.

"I believe to my soul it's the most, too," said Miss Adele. And then warningly, "*Polly—*"

Fay at that moment burst from the hall into the parlor. She glistened in black satin. Eyes straight ahead, she came running a path through all of them toward the coffin.

Miss Adele, with a light quick move from behind her, pulled Laurel out of the way.

"No. Stop—stop her," Laurel said.

Fay brought herself short and hung over the pillow. "Oh, he looks so good with those mean old sandbags taken away and that mean old bandage pulled off of his eye!" she said fiercely.

"She's wasting no time, she's fixing to break aloose right now," said Mrs. Chisom. "Didn't even stop to speak to me."

Fay cried out, and looked around.

Sis stood up, enormous, and said, "Here I am, Wanda Fay. Cry on me."

Laurel closed her eyes, in the recognition of what had made the Chisoms seem familiar to her. They might have come out of that night in the hospital waiting room—out of all times of trouble, past or future—the great, interrelated family of those who never know the meaning of what has happened to them.

"Get back!—Who told *them* to come?" cried Fay.

"I did!" said Major Bullock, his face nothing but delight. "Found 'em without a bit of trouble! Clint scribbled 'em all down for me in the office, day before he left for New Orleans."

But Fay showed him her back. She leaned forward over the coffin. "Oh, hon, get up, get out of there," she said.

"Stop her," Laurel said to the room.

"There now," said Miss Tennyson to all of them around the coffin.

"Can't you hear me, hon?" called Fay.

"She's cracking," said Mrs. Chisom. "Just like me. Poor little Wanda Fay."

"Oh, Judge, how could you be so unfair to me?" Fay cried, while Mr. Pitts emerged from behind the greens and poised his hand on the lid. "Oh, Judge, how could you go off and leave me this way? Why did you want to treat me so unfair?"

"I can tell you're going to be a little soldier," Major Bullock said, marching to Fay's side.

"Wanda Fay *needed* that husband of hers. That's why he ought to lived. He was a care, took all her time, but you'd go through it again, wouldn't you, honey?" asked Mrs. Chisom, pulling herself to her feet. She put out her arms, walking heavily toward her daughter. "If you could have your husband back this minute."

"No," Laurel whispered.

Fay cried into the coffin, "Judge! You cheated on me!"

"Just tell him goodbye, sugar," said Major Bullock as he tried to put his arm around her shoulders, staggering a little. "That's best, just plant him a kiss—"

Fay struck out with her hands, hitting at Major Bullock and Mr. Pitts and Sis, fighting her mother, too, for a moment. She showed her claws at Laurel, and broke from the preacher's last-minute arms and threw herself forward across the coffin onto the pillow, driving her lips without aim against the face under hers. She was dragged back into the library, screaming, by Miss Tennyson Bullock, out of sight behind the bank of greenery. Judge McKelva's smoking chair lay behind them, overturned.

Laurel stood gazing down at the unchanged face of the dead, while Mrs. Chisom's voice came through the sounds of confusion in the library.

"Like mother, like daughter. Though when I had to give up her dad, they couldn't hold me half so easy. I tore up the whole house, I did."

"Where's the doctor? In hiding?" old Mrs. Pease was saying.

"She'll get over it," said Dr. Woodson. All the men except for old Tom Farris, who sat just waiting, and Major Bullock following after Fay, had withdrawn to a huddle in the hall.

"Give me those little hands," Major Bullock's voice came from the library.

"She bites." Fay's sister. _great_

"And no wonder. It's hard to be told to give up goodness itself." Major Bullock.

Hearing his voice disembodied, Laurel realized he was drunk.

"Then why was he so _bad_?" screamed Fay. "Why did he do me so _bad_?"

"Don't cry! I'll shoot the bad man for you. Where is the bad man?" came the thin pipe of Wendell. "If you don't cry!"

"You _can't_ shoot him," said Sis. "Because I say so, that's why."

"Shake her," said Mrs. Chisom's appreciative voice.

"There's no telling when she last had a decent home-cooked meal with honest vegetables," said Miss Tennyson Bullock. "That goes a long way toward explaining everything. Now, this will be just a little slap."

In the moment of silence that came after that, Laurel looked at her father for the last time, when there was only herself to see him like this. Mr. Pitts had achieved one illusion, that danger to his lived life was still alive; now there was no longer that.

"He loved my mother," Laurel spoke into the quiet.

She lifted up her head: Tish was coming to stand beside her, and old Tom Farris had remained in attendance at the back of the room. Mr. Pitts had been waiting them out in the greenery. As he stepped forward and put his strength to his task, Tish very gently winked at Laurel, and helped her to give up bearing the weight of that lid, to let it come down.

Then Mr. Pitts, as if he propelled it by using the simple power of immunity, moved through their ranks with the coffin and went first; it had been piled over with flowers in the blink of an eye. Last of all came Miss Adele: she must have been there all the time, in the righted smoking chair, with her drawn forehead against its old brown wing.

Laurel, Miss Adele, and Missouri walked out together and watched it go. Children at play and a barking dog watched it come out, then watched the people come out behind it. Two children sat on the roof of a truck to wave at Wendell, with their hands full. They had picked the Silver Bells.

Mount Salus Presbyterian Church had been built by McKelvas, who had given it the steepest steps in town to make it as high as the Courthouse it was facing. From her place in the family pew, Laurel heard the seven members of the Bar, or their younger sons, and Bubba Chisom in his windbreaker bringing up the thundering weight of Judge McKelva in his coffin. She heard them blundering.

"Heavenly Father, may this serve to remind us that we have each and every one of us been fearfully and wonderfully made," Dr. Bolt said over the coffin, head bowed. But was that not Judge McKelva's table blessing? They were the last words Laurel heard. She watched him perform the service, but what he was saying might have been as silent as the movements of the handkerchief he passed over and over again across his forehead, and down his cheeks, and around.

Everybody remained seated while the family—the family was Laurel, Fay, and the Bullocks—walked back up the aisle first, behind the casket. Laurel saw that there had not been room enough in the church for everybody who had come. All around the walls, people were standing; they darkened the colored glass of the windows. Black Mount Salus had come too, and the black had dressed themselves in black.

All of them poured down the steps together. The casket preceded them.

"He'll touch down where He took off from," said Miss Verna Longmeier, at the bottom. "Split it right down the middle." Her hands ripped a seam for them: "The Mount of Olives." Triumphantly, she set off the other way.

There was a ringing for each car as it struck its wheels on the cattleguard and rode up into the cemetery. The procession passed between ironwork gates whose kneeling angels and looping vines shone black as licorice. The top of the hill ahead was crowded with winged angels and life-sized effigies of bygone citizens in old-fashioned dress, standing as if by count among the columns and shafts and conifers like a familiar set of passengers collected on deck of a ship, on which they all knew each other—bona-fide members of a small local excursion, embarked on a voyage that is always returning in dreams.

"I'm glad the big camellia will be in bloom," said Laurel. She felt her gloved hand pressed in that of Miss Tennyson, as Fay said from her other side:

"How could the biggest fool think I was going to bury my husband with his old wife? He's going in the new part."

Laurel's eye travelled among the urns that marked the graves of the McKelvas and saw the favorite camellia of her father's, the old-fashioned *Chandlerii Elegans*, that he had planted on her mother's grave—now big as a pony, saddled with unplucked bloom living and dead, standing on a fading carpet of its own flowers.

Laurel would hardly have thought of Mount Salus Cemetery as having a "new part." It was like being driven to the other side of the moon. The procession stopped. The rest of the way was too rough, as Laurel now saw, for anything except a hearse. They got out onto the grass and clay of the petered-out road. The pick-up truck had pulled up right behind the family's car, nearly touching it with the tin sign on its bumper. "Do Unto Others Before They Do Unto You."

"What're we here for?" asked Wendell, his voice in the open air carrying though light as thistledown.

"Wendell Chisom, they've got to finish what they started, haven't they? I told you you was going to be sorry you ever begged," said Sis.

They struck out across the field. There were already a few dozen graves here, dotted uniformly with indestructible plastic Christmas poinsettias.

"Now, is everybody finding the right place?" called Miss Tennyson, her eyes skimming the crowd that went walking over the young grass. "Somebody help old Tom Farris get where he's going!"

An awning marked the site; it appeared to be the farthest one in the cemetery. As they proceeded there, black wings thudded in sudden unison, and a flock of birds flew up as they might from a ploughed field, still shaped like it, like an old map that still served new territory, and wrinkled away in the air.

Mr. Pitts waited, one more time; he stood under the awning. The family took their assigned seats. Laurel had Fay on her right, sitting with a black-gloved hand held tenderly to her cheek. The coffin, fixed in suspension over the opened grave, was on a level with their eyes now.

Miss Tennyson, still on Laurel's left, murmured close to her ear, "Look behind you. The high school band. They better be here! Clint gave 'em those horns they're sporting, gave 'em the uniforms to march in. Somebody pass 'em the word to perk up. *Of course* they're not going to get to play!"

Under Mr. Pitts' awning Laurel could smell the fieriness of flowers restored to the open air and the rawness of the clay in the opened grave. Their chairs were set on the odorless, pistachio-green of Mr. Pitts' portable grass. It could still respond, everything must respond, to some vibration underfoot: this new part of the cemetery was the very shore of the new interstate highway.

Dr. Bolt assumed position and pronounced the words. Again Laurel failed to hear what came from his lips. She might not even have heard the high school band. Sounds from the highway rolled in upon her with the rise and fall of eternal ocean waves. They were as deafening as grief. Windshields flashed into her eyes like lights through tears. Beside her, then, Fay's black hand slid from her cheek to pat her hair into place—it was over.

"I want to tell you, Laurel, what a beautiful funeral it was," said Dot Daggett, immediately after Dr. Bolt had gone down the line shaking hands with the family, and they'd all risen. "I saw everybody I know and everybody I used to know. It was old Mount Salus personified." Dot looked up at Laurel out of her old movie-actress eyes. Kissing her hand to the others, she told them goodbye, cutting Miss Tennyson Bullock.

The members of the high school band were the first to break loose. They tore across the grass, all red and gold, back to their waiting jalopy. Wendell ran at their heels. In the road he found his truck. He climbed into the back of it and threw himself down on the floor and lay flat. *another story*

The rest of the company moved at a slower pace. "Somebody mind out for old Tom Farris!" called Miss Tennyson. Laurel, letting them go ahead, walked into the waiting arms of Missouri.

In the wake of their footsteps, the birds settled again. Down on the ground, they were starlings, all on the waddle, pushing with the yellow bills of spring. *hope*

setting—all chaos
4
restoring order

In the parlor, the fire had mercifully died out. Missouri and Miss Tennyson got all the chairs back into place in the two rooms here and the dining room, and the crowd of bridesmaids had succeeded among them in winding the clock on the mantel and setting the hands to the time—only ten minutes past noon—and starting the pendulum.

Miss Tennyson Bullock, from the dining room, gave out the great groan she always gave when a dish had been made exactly right; it was her own chicken mousse. She invited them in.

Fay stared at the spread table, where Miss Tennyson, Miss Adele, Tish, and some of the other bridesmaids were setting plates and platters around. Missouri, back in her apron but with cemetery clay sticking to her heels, was bringing in the coffee urn. Missouri looked at her own reflection in the shield of its side and lifted her smiling face to Laurel.

"Now!" she said softly. "The house looking like it used to look! Like it used to look!"

"So you see? Here's the Virginia ham!" said the minister's wife to Laurel, as if everything had turned out all right: she offered her a little red rag of it on a Ritz cracker. Then she scampered away to her husband.

As soon as she was out of the house, Major Bullock carried in the silver tray heavy with some bottles and a pitcher and a circle of silver cups and tall glasses.

"Wanda Fay, you got enough stuff in sight to last one lone woman forever," said Bubba Chisom, both his hands around a ham sandwich.

"I think things have gone off real well," said Fay.

"Poor little girl!" Major Bullock said. As he offered her one of the silver cups with whiskey and water in it—she let him go on holding it—he said again, "Poor little girl. I reckon you know you *get* the house and everything in it you want. And Laurel having her own good place in Chicago, she'll be compensated as equally as we know how—"

"Oh, foot," said old Mrs. Pease.

"I sure do know whose house this is," said Fay. "But maybe it's something a few other people are going to have to learn."

Major Bullock lifted the cup he'd offered to her and drank it himself.

"Well, you've done fine so far, Wanda Fay," said old Mrs. Chisom. "I was proud of you today. And proud for you. That coffin made me wish I could have taken it right away from him and given it to Roscoe."

"Thank you," said Fay. "It was no bargain, and I think that showed."

"Still, I did the best I could. And I feel like Roscoe sits up there knowing it now," said Mrs. Chisom. "And what more could you ask."

"You drew a large crowd, too," said Sis. "Without even having to count those Negroes."

"I was satisfied with it," said Fay.

"For the first minute, you didn't act all that glad to see *us*," said Sis. "Or was I dreaming?"

"Now, be sisters," warned old Mrs. Chisom. "And I'm glad you broke down *when you did*, Wanda Fay," she went on, wagging her finger. "There's a time and a place for everything. You try begging for sympathy later on, when folks has gone back about their business, and they don't appreciate your tears then. It just tries their nerves."

"Wanda Fay, I'm sorry I can't fool around here no longer," said Bubba Chisom, handing her his empty plate. "A wrecking concern hasn't got all that time to spare, not with all we got to do in Madrid."

"Come on, then," said Sis, who had pushed herself to her feet again. "Let's get going before the children commence to fighting and Wendell starts giving trouble again. Wendell Chisom," she said to the little boy, "you can take this home to your mother: this is the first and last time you're ever going to be carried to a funeral in any charge of me." She took Laurel's hand and shook it. "We thought a heap of your old dad, even if he couldn't stay on earth long enough for us to get to know him. Whatever he was, we always knew he was just plain *folks*."

Through the open front door could be seen the old grandfather already outside with his hat on, walking around looking at the trees. The pecan tree there was filled with budding leaves like green bees spaced out in a hive of light. There was something bright as well in the old man's hatband—the other half of his round-trip ticket from Bigbee.

"Wanda Fay," said Mrs. Chisom, "let me ask you this: who're you ever going to get to put in this house besides you?"

"What are you hinting at?" said Fay with a dark look.

"Tell you one thing, there's room for the whole nation of *us* here," Mrs. Chisom said, and stepping back into the hall she looked up the white-railed stairway. "In case we ever took a notion to move back to Mississippi." She went outside and they heard her stepping along the front porch. "It'd make a good boarding house, if you could get your mother to come cook for 'em."

"Great Day in the Morning!" exclaimed Miss Tennyson Bullock.

"Mama," said Fay, "you know what? I've got a good mind this minute to jump in with you. And ride home with my folks to Texas." Her chin was trembling as she named it. "Hear?"

"For how long do you mean to stay?" asked Mrs. Chisom, coming to face her.

"Just long enough."

"You going to rush into a trip right now?" Major Bullock asked, going to her other side.

"Major Bullock," she said, "I think when a person can see a free ride one way, the decision is made for them. And it just so happens I haven't unpacked my suitcase."

"I haven't heard your excuse for going yet," said Sis. "Have you got one?"

"I'd just like to see somebody that can talk my language, that's my excuse. Where's DeWitt?" Fay demanded. "You didn't bring him."

"DeWitt? He's still in Madrid. He's been in a sull ever since you married Judge McKelva and didn't send him a special engraved invitation to the wedding," said Bubba.

Fay gave them a tight smile.

Mrs. Chisom said, "I said, 'DeWitt, now! You're a brother just the same as Bubba is—and Roscoe was—and it's your place to get up out of that sull and come on with us to the funeral. You can take the wheel in Lake Charles.' But DeWitt is DeWitt, he expects his feelings to be considered."

"He speaks my language," said Fay. "I've got a heap to tell DeWitt."

"You may have to stand out in front of his house and holler it, if you do," said Bubba. "He's got folks' appliances stacked over ever' blooming inch of space. You can't hardly get in across those vacuum cleaners and power motors and bathroom heaters and old window fans, and not a one of 'em running. Hasn't fixed a one. He can't hardly get out of the house and you can't get in."

"I'll scare him out of that sull," said Fay.

"I think that's just what he's waiting for, myself," said Sis. "I wouldn't give him the satisfaction, if it was me."

Fay cried, "I don't even mind standing up in the back and riding with the children!" She whirled and ran upstairs.

"You'll wind up riding on my lap," said her mother. "I know you." She put her hand out and stopped a tray going by. "I wouldn't mind taking some of that ham along, though," she told Tish. "If it's just going begging."

Laurel followed Fay upstairs and stood in the bedroom door while Fay stuffed her toilet things into the already crammed suitcase.

"Fay, I wanted you to know what day I'll be leaving," she said. "So there'll be no danger of us running into each other."

"That suits me dandy."

"I'm giving myself three days. And I'll leave Monday on the three o'clock flight from Jackson. I'll be out of the house around noon."

"All right, then." Fay slammed her suitcase shut. "You just try and be as good as your word.—I'm coming, Mama! Don't you-all go off and leave me!" she yelled over Laurel's head.

"Fay, I wanted to ask you something, too," Laurel said. "What made you tell me what you did about your family? The time we talked, in the Hibiscus."

"What did I say?" Fay challenged her.

"You said you had nobody—no family. You lied about your family."

"If I did, that's what everybody else does," said Fay. "Why shouldn't I?"

"Not lie that they're dead."

"It's better than some lies I've heard around here!" cried Fay. She struggled to lift her suitcase, and Laurel, as if she'd just seen her in the deepest trouble, moved instinctively to help her. But Fay pushed on past her, dragging it, and hobbled in front of her, bumping her load a step ahead of her down the stairs. She had changed into her green shoes.

"I believe a few days with your own family would do you good," Miss Tennyson Bullock said. In the dining room, all of them were waiting on their feet. "Eating a lot of fresh vegetables, and so forth."

"Well, at least my family's not hypocrites," said Fay. "If they didn't want me, they'd tell me to my face."

"When you coming back?" asked Major Bullock, swaying a little.

"When I get ready."

The clock struck for half-past twelve.

"Oh, how I hate that old striking clock!" cried Fay. "It's the first thing I'm going to get rid of."

They were taking old Mr. Chisom as far as the bus station, to be sure he found it.

"You got a lot of fat squirrels going to waste here," the old man said, bending down to Laurel, and she was unprepared for it when he kissed her goodbye.

At last they were in the truck, rolling down the driveway to the street.

"Poor little woman. Got a bigger load than she knows yet how to carry by herself," said Major Bullock, waving.

Wendell was the only Chisom visible now, standing at the very back of the truck. He pulled one of his guns out of the holster and rode off shooting it at them. No noise came but his own thin, wistful voice.

"Pow! Pow! Pow!"

The few who were left walked back into the house. The silver tray on the hall table held a heap of calling cards, as though someone had tried to build a little house with them. Beside it lay a candy box with the picture of a pretty girl on the dusty lid.

"Old Mr. Chisom gave me all those pecans he brought," said Laurel, sighing. "I don't know why. Then he kissed me when he left."

"I believe he thought you must be Fay," said Miss Adele gently.

"I'm making myself a little toddy," said Miss Tennyson, adding sugar to something in a glass. "Do you know, Laurel, who was coming to my mind the whole blessed way through? *Becky!*"

"Of course," said Miss Adele.

"And all I did was thank my stars she wasn't here. Child, I'm glad your mother didn't have to live through that. I'm glad it was you."

"Foot! I'm mad at you for not getting the house," old Mrs.

Pease told Laurel. "After all, I'm the one that's got to go on living next door." She went home.

The others were leaving too. "Rupert, I could brain you for roping in those Chisoms," said Miss Tennyson, as the Major took her by the arm.

"I thought they'd be the answer to her prayers, poor little woman. And Clint jotted the list of 'em down for me just the day he took off for New Orleans. In case she needed 'em."

"And she did," said Miss Adele.

"I still can't believe it!" the Major loudly said, as the Bullocks helped each other toward the old Chrysler. "Can't believe we've all come off and left him in the ground!"

"Rupert," said Miss Tennyson, "now listen to me. Believe it. Now you get busy and believe it. Do you hear what I say? Poor Clinton's in Heaven right now."

Miss Adele took a step toward the kitchen, and then Missouri clinked some glasses back there. Miss Adele lifted her empty hands for a moment, and dropped them.

Laurel touched her own to one of hers, and watched her go.

perhaps to get rid of her!

Three

I

LAUREL, kneeling, worked among the iris that still held a ragged line along the back of the house up to the kitchen door. She'd found the dark-blue slacks and the blue cardigan in her suitcase—she'd packed them as automatically as she'd packed her sketchbook. She felt the spring sun gently stinging the back of her neck and she listened to other people talk. Her callers sat behind her and over to the side, in the open sunshine.

"Well, we got her out of the house," Miss Tennyson Bullock said. "Fay's gone!"

"Don't brag too soon," said old Mrs. Pease.

These four elderly ladies were all at home in the McKelva backyard. Cardinals, flying down from low branches of the dogwood tree, were feeding here and there at the ladies' crossed feet. At the top of the tree, a mockingbird stood silent over them like a sentinel.

"I used to waste good time feeling sorry for Clint. But he's in Heaven now. And if she's in Texas, I can just sit here in sunshine and be glad for *our* sakes," Miss Tennyson said. She had the ancient deck chair, which engulfed her like a hammock. "Of course, Major daily expects her back."

"Oh, but not to stay, do you think? In Mount Salus without a husband?" asked Mrs. Bolt, the minister's wife. She promptly reassured herself. "No, she won't last long. She'll go away."

"I wouldn't count on it if I were you," said old Mrs. Pease. "You got a peep at her origins."

"Ask yourself what other roof than this she'd rather have over her head, and you've got your answer," said Miss Tennyson.

"What did she do with herself while he was *here?*" exclaimed Mrs. Bolt.

"Nothing but sit-and-eat," said Miss Tennyson. "And keep straight on looking like a sparrow."

946

"She had to eat. Had nothing else to do to occupy her hands," said Mrs. Pease, holding up a perfectly enormous afghan she was knitting as if by the porcelain light of the dogwood tree.

"Oh, surely you know she was occupied enough with this great big house to care for." Miss Adele tilted up her face at it. The faint note of mockery that belonged in her voice had come back today. *the Bird*

"The house was not exactly a *sight*. Yes it was," said Miss Tennyson. "The way they set off and left it to come back to—I won't describe the way Adele and I found it."

"Their bed wasn't made," suggested the minister's wife.

"Well, if she made him happy. You've never caught me guilty yet of saying any more than that," said Miss Tennyson.

The wild phlox was blue as a lake behind Miss Adele Courtland as she said, "Oh, indeed he doted on her."

"Doted. You've hit on it. That's the word," said Miss Tennyson.

Laurel went on pulling weeds. Her mother's voice came back with each weed she reached for, and its name with it. "Ironweed." "Just chickweed." "Here comes that miserable old vine!" *setting*

"It couldn't be for her bridge game, if dote he did. Beggar-my-neighbor was more in her line of accomplishment," said old Mrs. Pease grimly.

"Oh, he doted on her, exactly like a man will. I'd only wish to ask your precious father one question, if I could have him back just long enough for that, Laurel," said Miss Tennyson, and with effort she leaned forward and asked it hoarsely: "What happened to his judgment?"

"He wasn't as old as all that," agreed Mrs. Pease. "I'm older. By a trifle."

"A man can feel compunction for a child like Fay and still not have to carry it that far," said Miss Tennyson. She called, "Laurel, do you know that when he brought her here to your house, she had very little idea of how to separate an egg?"

"And neither did he," said Miss Adele.

" 'Frying pan' was the one name she could give you of all the things your mother had in that kitchen, Laurel. Things like that get over town in a hurry, you know. I hate to tell you the upshot," said Miss Tennyson, "but on Sundays, when no power on earth could bring Missouri, they walked from church and took their Sunday dinner in the Iona Hotel, in that dining room."

On top of the tree, the mockingbird threw out his chest and let fall a cascade of song.

"Oh, it's been the most saddening exhibition within my memory," said old Mrs. Pease, crablike over her wool.

"Major and I just happen to walk that way too, when we go home from church. Sunday after Sunday we saw 'em through the dirty plate-glass window," said Miss Tennyson. "Billing and cooing. No tablecloth."

"A good thing you reminded me!" said Mrs. Bolt. "My husband hasn't yet rehearsed his Sunday sermon to me, and he's got just today and tomorrow." She took her leave.

"Shocked her, but that service of her husband's wasn't up to Clinton, either," said Miss Tennyson, settling back in the big old chair. "At the time, I didn't object—the catch came in thinking it over later."

"The whole day left something to be desired, if you want to hear me come right out with it," said old Mrs. Pease.

"Go ahead. I know you're blaming Major," said Miss Tennyson. "Why he had to get so carried away as to round up those Chisoms, I'll never know, myself. He said they were nothing but just good old Anglo-Saxons. But I said—"

"You can't curb a Baptist," Mrs. Pease said. "Let them in and you can't keep 'em down, when somebody dies. When the whole bunch of Chisoms got to going in concert, I thought the only safe way to get through the business alive was not say a word, just sit as still as a mouse."

"I, though, consider that the Chisoms did every bit as well as we did," said Miss Adele. "If we're going to dare mention behavior."

"Adele has the schoolteacher's low opinion of everybody," said Miss Tennyson.

"It's true they were a trifle more inelegant," said Miss Adele. "But only a trifle."

"The pitiful thing was, Fay didn't know any better than the rest of 'em. She just supposed she did," said Miss Tennyson.

setting [handwritten annotation]

"Did you hear her snub her sister? Refused to cry on her," said old Mrs. Pease.

"Well, we all knew exactly what the sort of thing *was* that Fay'd be good for," said Miss Tennyson. "Didn't make it go any quicker when it came. That slap I gave her took the starch out of *me*."

"Strangely enough," said Miss Adele, "I think that carrying-on was Fay's idea of giving a sad occasion its due. She was rising to it, splendidly.—By her lights!" she interrupted herself before the others could do it for her. "She wanted nothing but the best for her husband's funeral, only the most expensive casket, the most choice cemetery plot—"

"Choice! It looked right out on the Interstate! Those horrible trucks made so much whine, not a thing Dr. Bolt was saying could be heard. Even from our good seats," said Miss Tennyson.

"—and," continued Miss Adele, "the most broken-hearted, most distraught behavior she could manage on the part of the widow."

Singing over her words, the mockingbird poured out his voice without stopping.

"I could have broken her neck," said Miss Tennyson.

"Well, you couldn't expect her to stop being a Baptist," said old Mrs. Pease.

"Well, of course I'm a Baptist," said Miss Adele, the dimple coming into her cheek.

"Adele, you didn't care for Fay's behavior any more than the rest of us did," said Miss Tennyson.

"I saw you have to sit down," said old Mrs. Pease shrewdly.

"I give myself as bad a mark as anybody. Never fear," said Miss Adele.

"Well, I'm not ashamed of anything *I* did," said Miss Tennyson. "And I felt still more ashamed for Fay when she upped and told us goodbye and went off with the rest of the Chisoms. I reckon she thought we might not let her go. But we didn't beg her any too hard to stay, did we?" Miss Tennyson sank back deeper into the old chair.

"As a matter of fact," said Miss Adele, "Fay stuck to her guns longer than the rest of us, the ones who knew

Judge McKelva better, and knew everything better. Major Bullock got outright tipsy, and everybody that opened their mouths said as near the wrong thing as they could possibly manage."

"Adele! You just dearly love to punish yourself. You *hate* what you're saying, just as much as we do," declared Miss Tennyson.

"But I believe it."

"Well, I'm going right on blaming the Chisoms," said old Mrs. Pease. "They ought to have stayed home in the first place. All of 'em."

"I further believe Fay thought she was rising in the estimation of Mount Salus, there in front of all his lifelong friends," said Miss Adele. "And on what she thought was the prime occasion for doing it."

"Well, she needed somebody to tell her how to act," said Miss Tennyson flatly.

"I gathered from the evidence we were given that Fay was emulating her own mother," said Miss Adele, while the mockingbird sang.

"Why, Fay declared right in front of old Mrs. Chisom and all that she wished her mother hadn't come!" said Miss Tennyson.

"Nevertheless, that's who she emulated," said Miss Adele. "We can't find fault with doing that, can we, Laurel?"

Laurel, who had worked her way as far as the kitchen door, sat on the back step and gazed at the ladies, all four.

"I got the notion if Fay hadn't turned around quick, they might've just settled in here with her," said old Mrs. Pease. "When old Mrs. What's-her-name stepped off the reach of the front porch, I had an anxious moment, I can tell you."

"Are we all going to have to feel sorry for her?" asked Miss Tennyson.

"If there's nothing else to do, there's no help for it," said Miss Adele. "Is there, Laurel?"

"Well, answer!" exclaimed Miss Tennyson. "Are you prepared now to pity her, Laurel?"

"Cat's got her tongue," said old Mrs. Pease.

"I hope I never see her again," said Laurel.

"There, girlie, you got it out," said Miss Tennyson. "She's a trial to us all and nothing else. Why don't you stay on here, and help us with her?"

"Why not indeed?" said Miss Adele. "Laurel has no other life."

"Of course I must get back to work," said Laurel.

"Back to work." Miss Tennyson pointed her finger at Laurel and told the others, "That girl's had more now than she can say grace over. And she's going back to that life of labor when she could just as easily give it up. Clint's left her a grand hunk of money."

"Once you leave after this, you'll always come back as a visitor," Mrs. Pease warned Laurel. "Feel free, of course—but it was always my opinion that people don't really want visitors."

"I mean it. Why track back up to the North Pole?" asked Miss Tennyson. "Who's going to kill you if you don't draw those pictures? As I was saying to Tish, 'Tish, if Laurel would stay home and Adele would retire, we could have as tough a bridge foursome as we had when Becky was playing.'"

"Are you figuring on running me out, then? Or what?" asked old Mrs. Pease, who had tottered to her feet.

"No, play on as you're playing now," said Miss Adele, smiling. "Nate's adorable French wife in New Orleans would agree with Laurel perfectly: there's not enough Mount Salus has to *offer* a brilliant mind."

"There!" exclaimed Miss Tennyson. "I'd begun to despair that we could ever make Laurel McKelva laugh on this trip at all."

"I've got my passage," Laurel said. "The afternoon flight from Jackson on Monday."

"And she'll make it, too. Oh, Laurel can do anything. If it's been made hard enough for her," said Miss Adele. "Of *course* she can give up Mount Salus and say goodbye to this house and to us, and the past, and go on back to Chicago day after tomorrow, flying a jet. And take up one more time where she left off."

Laurel stood up and kissed the mischievous, wrinkled cheek.

"Laurel, look yonder. You still might change your mind if

you could see the roses bloom, see Becky's Climber come out," said Miss Tennyson softly.

"I can imagine it, in Chicago."

"But you can't smell it," Miss Tennyson argued.

All of them wandered toward the rose bed, where every hybrid tea stood low with branches cut staggered. They were hiding themselves in an opalescent growth of leaf. Behind them—Laurel took a few steps farther—the climbers rose: Mermaid, solid as a thicket, on the Pease side, and Banksia in its first feathery bloom on the Courtland side, and between them the width of bare fence where Becky's Climber belonged. Judge McKelva had recalled himself at Becky's Climber.

("I'd give a pretty to know what exactly that rose is!" Laurel's mother would say every spring when it opened its first translucent flowers of the true rose color. "It's an old one, with an old fragrance, and has every right to its own name, but nobody in Mount Salus is interested in giving it to me. All I had to do was uncover it and give it the room it asked for. Look at it! It's on its own roots, of course, utterly strong. That old root there may be a hundred years old!"

"Or older," Judge McKelva had said, giving her, from the deck chair, his saturnine smile. "Strong as an old apple tree.")

Sienna-bright leaves and thorns like spurts of match-flame had pierced through the severely cut-back trunk. If it didn't bloom this year, it would next: "That's how gardeners must learn to look at it," her mother would say.

Memory returned like spring, Laurel thought. Memory had the character of spring. In some cases, it was the old wood that did the blooming.

"So we've settled Laurel. But has anybody but Tennyson settled Fay? I don't see how we can think so," said Miss Adele, with the excruciated dimple making a shadow in her cheek. "When we really lack the first idea of knowing what to do with Clinton's little minx, whom he's left on our hands in such utter disregard for our feelings." She was doing her best, getting back into her form today.

"Short of crowning her over the head with a good solid piece of something," agreed Miss Tennyson. "She'll live for-

CLASS

ever and a day. She'll be right here when we're gone. Why do all the men think they need to *protect* her?"

"Major just slobbers over her," old Mrs. Pease agreed.

"But he wasn't the *prime* idiot. Wouldn't Clint be amazed if he suddenly had ears again and could hear us right now?" said Miss Tennyson with relish. "You know, I marvel at men."

"Laurel is who should have saved him from that nonsense. = Fay Laurel shouldn't have married a naval officer in wartime. Laurel should have stayed home after Becky died. He needed him somebody *in* that house, girl," said old Mrs. Pease. guilt

"But that didn't have to mean Fay," said Miss Tennyson. "Drat her!"

"She's never done anybody any harm," Miss Adele remarked. "Rather, she gave a lonely old man something to live for."

"I'd rather not consider how," interrupted Miss Tennyson primly.

"We just resent her, poor little waif," said Miss Adele. "And she can't help but know it. She's got more resentment than we have. Resentment *born*." Robbie Reid

"If I'd just known Clint was casting around for somebody to take Becky's place, I could've found him one a whole lot better than Fay. And right here in Mount Salus," Miss Tennyson was stung to say. "I could name one now that would have *leaped*—"

"He didn't find Becky in Mount Salus," Miss Adele reminded them, silencing all but the mockingbird.

"And of course that's one of the peculiarities Laurel inherited from *him*. She didn't look at home to find Philip Hand," said Miss Tennyson.

Laurel stood up.

"Laurel's ready for us to go," said Miss Adele, rising herself. "We've kept her out of the house long enough." setting

"No, don't ask us in, we'll leave you to struggle through the rest without us," said Miss Tennyson indulgently. She waved her way out toward the street. Old Mrs. Pease walked slowly away, folding her afghan, and turned through the gate that opened into her untrespassed garden.

the destructive forces
fresh air to breathe again
too stifling

As Laurel walked with Miss Adele toward her own opening in the hedge, there could be heard a softer sound than the singing from the dogwood tree. It was rhythmic but faint, as from the shaking of a tambourine.

"Little mischiefs! Will you look at them showing off," said Miss Adele.

A cardinal took his dipping flight into the fig tree and brushed wings with a bird-frightener, and it crashed faintly. Another cardinal followed, then a small band of them. Those thin shimmering discs were polished, rain-bright, and the redbirds, all rival cocks, were flying at their tantalizing reflections. At the tiny crash the birds would cut a figure in the air and tilt in again, then again.

"Oh, it's a game, isn't it, nothing but a game!" Miss Adele said, stepping gracefully into her own backyard.

2

Laurel faced the library. This was where, after his retirement and marriage, her father had moved everything he wanted around him from his office in the Mount Salus Bank Building on the Square.

Perhaps a crowded room, whatever is added, always looks the same. One wall was exactly the same. Above one bookcase hung her father's stick-framed map of the county—he had known every mile; above the other hung the portraits of his father and grandfather, the Confederate general and missionary to China, as alike as two peaches, painted by the same industrious hand on boards too heavy to hang straight, but hanging side by side: the four eyebrows had been identically outlined in the shape of little hand-saws placed over the eyes, teeth down, then filled in with lamp-black.

She saw at once that nothing had happened to the books. *Flush Times in Alabama and Mississippi*, the title running catercornered in gold across its narrow green spine, was in exactly the same place as ever, next to Tennyson's Poetical Works, Illustrated, and that next to Hogg's *Confessions of a Justified Sinner*. She ran her finger in a loving track across *Eric*

Brighteyes and *Jane Eyre*, *The Last Days of Pompeii* and *Carry On, Jeeves*. Shoulder to shoulder, they had long since made their own family. For every book here she had heard their voices, father's and mother's. And perhaps it didn't matter to them, not always, what they read aloud; it was the breath of life flowing between them, and the words of the moment riding on it that held them in delight. Between some two people every word is beautiful, or might as well be beautiful. In the other bookcase, which stood a little lower—maybe because of Webster's *Unabridged* and the McKelva family Bible, twin weights, lying on top—there was the Dickens all in a set, a shelf and a half full, old crimson bindings scorched and frayed and hanging in strips. *Nicholas Nickleby* was the volume without any back at all. It was the Gibbon below it, that had *not* been through fire, whose backs had come to be the color of ashes. And Gibbon was not sacrosanct: *The Adventures of Sherlock Holmes* looked out from between two volumes. Laurel dusted all of them, and set them back straight in the same order.

The library was a little darker now that one of the two windows that looked out on the Courtland side of the house was covered by Judge McKelva's office cabinet. This was jammed with lawbooks and journals, more dictionaries, his Claiborne's *Mississippi* and his Mississippi Code. Books, folders, file boxes were shelved with markers and tapes hanging out. Along the cabinet top his telescope was propped extended, like a small brass cannon.

Laurel slid back the glass doors and began to dust and put back neatly what she came to. His papers were in an order of their own—she thought it was that of importance to unimportance. He had kept civic papers dating from the days when he was Mayor of Mount Salus, and an old dedication speech made at the opening of the new school ("These are my promises to you, all the young people I see before me: . . ."). The promises had made them important to him. There was a bursting folder of papers having to do with the Big Flood, the one that had ruined the McKelva place on the river; it was jammed with the work he had done on floods and flood control. And everybody had already forgotten all about that part of his life, his work, his *drudgery*. This town deserved him no *misunderstood*

more than Fay deserved him, she thought, her finger in the dust on what he'd written.

Laurel took her eyes away from words and stood for a moment at the window. In the backyard next door, Miss Adele was hanging something white on the clothesline. She turned as if intuitively toward the window, and raised her arm to wave. It was a beckoning sort of wave. She beckons with her pain, thought Laurel, realizing how often her father must have stood just here, resting his eyes, and looked out at her without ever seeing her.

Yet he loved them as a family. After moving into town from out in the country, the Courtlands ploughed the field behind the house, and back of that, in the pasture, kept cows. In Laurel's early memory, Mrs. Courtland had sold milk and to Judge McKelva's disturbance had had her children drink it skimmed blue so she could sell all the cream.

It was not until that night when Dr. Courtland told her, that Laurel ever heard he owed part of his medical schooling to her father. Never had Judge McKelva been well off until the last few years. He had come unexpectedly into a little oil money from a well dug in those acres of sand he still owned in the country—not a great deal, but enough, with his salary continuing for life, to retire on free of financial worry. *"See there?"* he had written to Laurel—or rather dictated to Dot, who loved underlining his words on her typewriter. "There was never anything wrong with keeping up a little optimism over the Flood. How well would you like to knock off, invite a friend for company, and all go see England and Scotland in the spring?" The next thing she heard, he was about to marry Fay.

he broke his promise

She'd been all around the room, and now there was the desk. It stood in the center of the room, and it had been her father's great-grandfather's, made in Edinburgh—a massive, concentrated presence, like that of a concert grand. (The neglected piano in the parlor seemed to have no presence at all.) Behind the desk yawned his leather chair, now in its proper place.

great verb

Laurel walked around to it. There used to be standing on the desk, to face him in his chair, a photograph of her mother, who had been asked to stop what she was doing and sit on the garden bench—this was the strongly severe result; and the picture was gone. That was understandable. The only photograph here now was of herself and Philip running down the steps of the Mount Salus Presbyterian Church after their wedding. Her father had given it a silver frame. (So had she. Her marriage had been of magical ease, of *ease*—of brevity and conclusion and all belonging to Chicago and not here.)

But something had been spilled on the desk. There were vermilion drops of hardened stuff on the dark wood—not sealing wax; nail polish. They made a little track toward the chair, as if Fay had walked her fingers over the desk from where she'd sat perched on its corner, doing her nails.

Laurel seated herself in her father's chair and reached for the top drawer of his desk, which she had never thought of opening in her life. It was not locked—had it ever been? The drawer rolled out almost weightless, as light as his empty cigar box, the only thing inside. She opened the drawers one after the other on both sides of the huge desk: they had been cleaned out. Someone had, after all, been here ahead of her.

Of course, his documents he had placed in the office safe; they were in Major Bullock's charge now, and his will was in Chancery court. But what of all the letters written to him— her mother's letters?

Her mother had written to him every day they were separated in their married lives; she had said so. He often went about to court, made business trips; and she, every summer since she had married him, had spent a full month in West Virginia, "up home," usually with Laurel along. Where were the letters? Put away somewhere, with her garden picture?

They weren't anywhere, because he hadn't kept them. He'd never kept them: Laurel knew it and should have known it to start with. He had dispatched all his correspondence promptly, and dropped letters as he answered them straight into the wastebasket; Laurel had seen him do it. And when it concerned her mother, if that was what she asked for, he *went*.

But there was nothing of her mother here for Fay to find, or for herself to retrieve. The only traces there were of anybody were the drops of nail varnish. Laurel studiously went to work on them; she lifted them from the surface of the desk and rubbed it afterwards with wax until nothing was left to show of them, either.

That was on Saturday.

3

"Laurel! Remember when we really *were* the bridesmaids?" Tish cried as they sat over drinks after dinner. It was Sunday evening.

While the bridesmaids' parents still lived within a few blocks of the McKelva house, the bridesmaids and their husbands had mostly all built new houses in the "new part" of Mount Salus. Their own children were farther away still, off in college now.

Tish's youngest son was still at home. "He won't come out, though," Tish had said. "He has company. A girl came in through his bedroom window—to play chess with him. That's what she said. I think she's the same one who came in through his window last night, close to eleven o'clock. I saw car lights in the driveway and went to see. They call him every minute. Girls. He's fifteen."

"And remember Mama at the wedding," Tish said now, "crying when it was over, saying to your father, 'Oh, Clint, isn't it the saddest thing?' And Judge Mac saying, 'Why, no, Tennyson, if I had thought there was anything sad to be said for it, I should have prevented it.'"

"*Prevented* it? I never saw a man enjoy a wedding more," said Gert.

"Wartime or no wartime, we had pink champagne that Judge Mac sent all the way to New Orleans for!" one of the others cried. "And a five-piece Negro band. Remember?"

"Miss Becky thought it was utter extravagance. Child-foolishness. But Judge Mac insisted on it all, a big wedding right on down the line."

"Well, Laurel was an only child."

"Mother had a superstitious streak underneath," Laurel said protectively. "She might have had a notion it was unlucky to make too much of your happiness." From her place on the chaise longue by the window, she saw lightning flickering now in the western sky, like the feathers of a bird taking a bath.

"Judge Mac laughed her out of it, then. Remember the parties we had for you!" Gert gave Laurel a lovingly derisive slap. "That was before the Old Country Club burned down, there never was another dance floor like that."

"What kind of dancer was Phil, Polly? I forget!" Tish lifted her arms as though the memory would come up and dance her away to remind her.

"Firm," said Laurel. She turned her cheek a little further away on the pillow.

"Your daddy knew how to enjoy a grand occasion as well as we did—as long as it stayed elegant, and as long as Papa didn't get too high before it was over," Tish said. "Of course, Mama should have saved all her tears for her own child's wedding." Tish was the only divorcée, as Laurel was the only widow. Tish had eloped with the captain of their high school football team.

"But Miss Becky would rather go through anything than a grand occasion," said Gert.

"I remember once—it must've been the Bar Association Meeting, or maybe when he was Mayor and they had to function at some to-do in Jackson—anyway, once Judge Mac himself bought Miss Becky a dress to wear, came home with it in a box and surprised her. Beaded crepe! Shot beads! Neck to hem, shot beads," said Tish. "Where could you have been, Laurel?"

Gert said, "He'd picked it out in New Orleans. Some *clerk* sold it to him."

Music started up from off in another room of the house. Duke Ellington.

"The young don't dance to him. They play chess to him, I suppose," Tish said aside to Laurel. "And Miss Becky said, 'Clinton, if I'd just been told in advance you were going to make me an extravagant present, I'd have asked you for a load of floor sweepings from the cottonseed-oil mill.' Can't you hear her?" Tish cried.

"She wore it, though, didn't she?" one of them asked, and Tish said, "Oh, they'd do anything for each other! Sure she wore it. And the weight she had to carry! Miss Becky told

Mama in confidence that when she wasn't wearing that dress, which was nearly a hundred per cent of the time, she had to keep it in a bucket!"

The bridesmaids laughed till they cried.

"But when she wanted to justify him, she wore it! With an air. What floored me, Laurel, was him getting married again. When I saw Fay!" said Gert. "When I saw what he *had* there!"

"Mama, for his sake, asked at the beginning if she wouldn't be allowed to give some sort of little welcome for her—a sit-down tea, I believe she had in mind. And Fay said, 'Oh, please don't bother with a big wholesale reception. That kind of thing was for Becky.' Poor Judge Mac! Because except when it came to picking a wife," Tish said, smiling at Laurel, "he was a pretty worldly old sweet."

"Since when have you started laughing at them?" Laurel asked in a trembling voice. "Are they just figures from now on to make a good story?" She turned on Tish. "And you can wink over Father?"

"Polly!" Tish grabbed her. "We weren't laughing at them. They weren't funny—no more than my father and mother are! No more than all our fathers and mothers are!" She laughed again, into Laurel's face. "Aren't we grieving? We're grieving *with* you."

"I know. Of course I know it," said Laurel.

She smiled her thanks and kissed them all. She would see the bridesmaids once more. At noon tomorrow they were coming for her, all six, to drive her to her plane.

"I'm glad there's nobody else for you to lose, dear," Miss Tennyson Bullock said staunchly. She and the Major had driven over, late as it was, to tell Laurel goodbye.

"What do you mean! She's got Fay," Major Bullock protested. "Though that poor little girl's got a mighty big load on her shoulders. More'n she can bear."

"We are only given what we are able to bear," Miss Tennyson corrected him. They'd had such a long married life that she could make a pronouncement sound more military than he could, and even more legal.

Laurel hugged them both, and then said she intended to walk home.

"Walk!" "It's raining!" "Nobody ever walks in Mount Salus!" They made a fuss over letting her go. Major Bullock insisted on escorting her.

On this last night, a warm wind began to blow and the rain fell fitfully, as though working up to some disturbance. Major Bullock shot his umbrella open and held it over Laurel in gallant fashion. He set the pace at something of a military clip.

Major Bullock lived through his friends. He lived their lives with them—up to a point, Laurel thought. While Miss Tennyson lived his. In a kind, faraway tenor, he began to hum as they went along. He seemed to have put something behind him, tonight. He was recovering his good spirits already.

> "He rambled,
> He rambled,
> Rambled all around,
> In and out of town,
> Oh, didn't he ramble—"

The leafing maples were bowing around the Square, and the small No U-Turn sign that hung over the cross street was swinging and turning over the wire in trapeze fashion. The Courthouse clock could not be read. In the poorly lit park, the bandstand and the Confederate statue stood in dim aureoles of rain, looking the ghosts they were, and somehow married to each other, by this time.

"He rambled till we had to cut him down," sang Major Bullock.

The house was dark among its trees.

"Fay hasn't come," said the Major. "Oh, what a shame."

"I expect we'll just miss each other," said Laurel.

"What a shame. Not to tell each other goodbye and good luck and the rest, it's too bad."

Pushing his umbrella before them, Major Bullock took her to the door and went with her inside to turn on the hall lights. His mouth knocked against hers, as though it knocked perfunctorily on a door, or on a dream—an old man's goodnight; and she saw him out, lighted his way, then shut the door on him fast.

She had seen something wrong: there was a bird in the

bad tuck bird in house - Delta Wedding

house. It was one of the chimney swifts. It shot out of the dining room and now went arrowing up the stairwell in front of her eyes.

Laurel, still in her coat, ran through the house, turning on the lights in every room, shutting the windows against the rain, closing the doors into the hall everywhere behind her against the bird. She ran upstairs, slammed her own door, ran across the hall and finally into the big bedroom, where she put on the lights, and as the bird came directly toward the new brightness she slammed the door against it.

It could not get in here. But had it been in already? For how long had it made free of the house, shuttling through the dark rooms? And now Laurel could not get out. She was in her father's and mother's room—now Fay's room—walking up and down. It was the first time she had entered it since the morning of the funeral.

4

Windows and doors alike were singing, buffeted by the storm. The bird touched, tapped, brushed itself against the walls and closed doors, never resting. Laurel thought with longing of the telephone just outside the door in the upstairs hall.

What am I in danger of here? she wondered, her heart pounding.

Even if you have kept silent for the sake of the dead, you cannot rest in your silence, as the dead rest. She listened to the wind, the rain, the blundering, frantic bird, and wanted to cry out as the nurse cried out to her, "Abuse! Abuse!"

Try to put it in the form of facts, she ordered herself. For the person who wishes to do so, it is possible to assail a helpless man; it is only necessary to be married to him. It is possible to say to the dying "Enough is enough," if the listener who overhears is his daughter with his memory to protect. The facts were a verdict, and Laurel lived with this verdict in her head, walking up and down.

It was not punishment she wanted for Fay, she wanted acknowledgment out of her—admission that she knew what she had done. And Fay, she knew now, knew beyond question, would answer, "I don't even know what you're talking about." This would be a fact. Fay had never dreamed that in that shattering moment in the hospital she had not been just as she always saw herself—in the right. Justified. Fay had only been making a little scene—that was all.

Very likely, making a scene was, for Fay, like home. Fay had brought scenes to the hospital—and here, to the house—as Mr. Dalzell's family had brought their boxes of chicken legs. Death in its reality passed her right over. Fay didn't know what she was doing—it was like Tish winking—and she never will know, Laurel thought, unless I tell her. Laurel asked herself: Have I come to be as lost a soul as the soul Fay exposed to Father, and to me? Because unlike Father, I cannot feel pity for Fay. I can't pretend it, like Mount Salus that has to live with her. I have to hold it back until she realizes what she has done.

And I can't stop realizing it, she thought. I saw Fay come out into the open. Why, it would stand up in court! Laurel thought, as she heard the bird beating against the door, and felt the house itself shake in the rainy wind. Fay betrayed herself: I'm released! she thought, shivering; one deep feeling called by its right name names others. But to be released is to tell, unburden it.

But who could there be that she wanted to tell? Her mother. Her dead mother only. Laurel must have deeply known it from the start. She stopped at the armchair and leaned on it. She had the proof, the damnable evidence ready for her mother, and was in anguish because she could not give it to her, and so be herself consoled. The longing to tell her mother was brought about-face, and she saw the horror.

Father, beginning to lose his sight, followed Mother, but who am I at the point of following but Fay? Laurel thought. The scene she had just imagined, herself confiding the abuse to her mother, and confiding it in all tenderness, was a more devastating one than all Fay had acted out in the hospital. What would I not do, perpetrate, she wondered, for consolation?

She heard the bird drum itself against the door all its length from top to bottom. Her hands went to her hair and she backed away, backed out of the room entirely and into the little room that opened out of it.

It was the sewing room, all dark; she had to feel about for a lamp. She turned it on: her old student gooseneck lamp on a low table. By its light she saw that here was where her mother's secretary had been exiled, and her own study table, the old slipper chair; there was the brass-bound three-layer trunk; there was the sewing machine.

Even before it had been the sewing room, it had been where she slept in infancy until she was old enough to move into her own room across the hall. It was cold in here, as if there had been no fire all winter; there was only a grate, and it was empty, of course. How cold Miss Verna Longmeier's hands must have got! Laurel thought—coming here, sewing and making up tales or remembering all wrong what she saw and heard. A cold life she had lived by the day in other people's houses.

But it had been warm here, warm then. Laurel remembered her father's lean back as he sat on his haunches and spread a newspaper over the mouth of the chimney after he'd built the fire, so that the blaze caught with a sudden roar. Then he was young and could do everything.

Firelight and warmth—that was what her memory gave her. Where the secretary was now there had been her small bed, with its railed sides that could be raised as tall as she was when she stood up in bed, arms up to be lifted out. The sewing machine was still in place under the single window. When her mother—or, at her rare, appointed times, the sewing woman—sat here in her chair pedalling and whirring, Laurel sat on this floor and put together the fallen scraps of cloth into stars, flowers, birds, people, or whatever she liked to call them, lining them up, spacing them out, making them into patterns, families, on the sweet-smelling matting, with the shine of firelight, or the summer light, moving over mother and child and what they both were making.

It was quieter here. It was around the corner from the wind, and a room away from the bird and the disturbed dark. It seemed as far from the rest of the house itself as Mount Salus was from Chicago.

Laurel sat down on the slipper chair. The gooseneck lamp threw its dimmed beam on the secretary's warm brown doors. It had been made of the cherry trees on the McKelva place a long time ago; on the lid, the numerals 1817 had been set into a not quite perfect oval of different wood, something smooth and yellow as a scrap of satin. It had been built as a plantation desk but was graceful and small enough for a lady's use; Laurel's mother had had entire claim on it. On its pediment stood a lead-mold eagle spreading its wings and clasping the globe: it was about the same breadth as her mother's spread-out hand. There was no key in either keyhole of the double doors of the cabinet. But had there ever been a key? Her mother had never locked up anything that Laurel could remember. Her privacy was keyless. She had simply assumed her privacy. Now, suppose that again she would find everything was gone?

Laurel had hesitated coming to open her father's desk; she was not hesitating here—not now. She touched the doors where they met, and they swung open together. Within, the cabinet looked like a little wall out of a country post office which nobody had in years disturbed by calling for their mail. How had her mother's papers lain under merciful dust in the years past and escaped destruction? Laurel was sure of why: her father could not have borne to touch them; to Fay, they would have been only what somebody wrote—and anybody reduced to the need to write, Fay would think already beaten as a rival.

Laurel opened out the writing lid, and reaching up she drew down the letters and papers from one pigeonhole at a time. There were twenty-six pigeonholes, but her mother had stored things according to their time and place, she discovered, not by ABC. Only the letters from her father had been all brought together, all she had received in her life, surely—there they were; the oldest envelopes had turned saffron. Laurel drew a single one out, opened the page inside long enough to see it beginning "My darling Sweetheart," and returned it to its place. They were postmarked from the courthouse towns her father had made sojourn in, and from Mount Salus when he addressed them to West Virginia on her visits "up home"; and under these were the letters to Miss Becky Thurston, tied in ribbons that were almost transparent, and freckled now, as the skin of her mother's hands came to be before she died. In the back of the pigeonhole where these letters came from was some solid little object, and Laurel drew it out, her fingers remembering it before she held it under her eyes. It was a two-inch bit of slatey stone, given shape by many little strokes from a penknife. It had come out of its cranny the temperature and smoothness of her skin; it fitted into her palm. "A little dish!" Laurel the child had exclaimed, thinking it something made by a child younger than she. "A boat," corrected her mother importantly. The initials C.C.M.McK. were cut running together into the base. Her father had made it himself. It had gone from his hand to her mother's; that was a river stone; they had been courting, "up home."

There was a careful record of those days preserved in a snapshot book. Laurel felt along the shelf above the pigeonholes and touched it, the square boards, the silk tassel. She pulled it down to her.

Still clinging to the first facing pages were the pair of grayed and stippled home-printed snapshots: Clinton and Becky "up home," each taken by the other standing in the same spot on a railroad track (a leafy glade), he slender as a wand, his foot on a milepost, swinging his straw hat; she with her hands full of the wild-flowers they'd picked along the way.

"The most beautiful blouse I ever owned in my life—I made it. Cloth from Mother's own spinning, and dyed a deep, rich, American Beauty color with pokeberries," her mother had said with the gravity in which she spoke of "up home." "I'll never have anything to wear that to me is as satisfactory as that blouse."

How darling and vain she was when she was young! Laurel thought now. She'd made the blouse—and developed the pictures too, for why couldn't she? And very likely she had made the paste that held them.

Judge McKelva, who like his father had attended the University of Virginia, had met her when he worked one carefree year at a logging camp with quarters in Beechy Creek, where her mother had taught school.

"Our horse was Selim. Let me hear you pronounce his name," her mother had said to Laurel while they sat here sewing. "I rode Selim to school. Seven miles over Nine Mile

Mountain, seven miles home. To make the time pass quicker, I recited the whole way, from horseback—I memorized with no great effort, dear," she'd replied to the child's protest. "Papa hadn't had an entirely easy time of it, getting books at all up home." *treasured education*

Laurel had been taken "up home" since a summer before she remembered. The house was built on top of what might as well have been already the highest roof in the world. There were rocking chairs outside it on the sweet, roofless green grass. From a rocking chair could be seen the river where it rounded the foot of the mountain. It was only when you wound your way down the mountain nearly to the bottom that you began to hear the river. It sounded like a roomful of mesmerized schoolchildren reciting to their teacher. This point of the river was called Queen's Shoals.

Both Becky's father and her mother had been Virginians. *like the Beechers* The mother's family (fathered by a line of preachers and teachers) had packed up and gone across the border around the time of the Secession. Becky's own father had been a lawyer, too. But the mountain had stood five times as high as the courthouse roof, straight up behind it, and the river went rushing in front of it like a road. It was its only road.

They must have had names. Laurel never remembered hearing them said. They were just "the mountain," "the river," "the courthouse," parts of "up home."

In the early morning, from the next mountain, from one stillness to another, travelled the sound of a blow, then behind it its echo, then another blow, then the echo, then a shouting and the shouting falling back on itself. On it went.

"Mother, what are they doing?" Laurel asked.

"It's just an old man chopping wood," said "the boys."

"He's praying," said her mother.

"An old hermit that is," said Grandma. "Without a soul in the world."

"The boys"—there were six—saddled the pony for their sister; then they rode off with her. They lay on blankets and saddles under the apple tree and played the banjo for her. They told her so many stories she cried, all about people only she knew and they knew; had she not cried she would have never been able to stop laughing. Of her youngest brother, who sang "Billy Boy" and banged comically on the strings, she said, "Very well for Sam. He went out and cried on the ground when I married."

In sight of the door there was an iron bell mounted on a post. If anything were ever to happen, Grandma only needed to ring this bell.

The first time Laurel could remember arriving in West Virginia instead of just finding herself there, her mother and she had got down from the train in early morning and stood, after it had gone, by themselves on a steep rock, all of the world that they could see in the mist being their rock and its own iron bell on a post with its rope hanging down. Her mother gave the rope a pull and at its sound, almost at the moment of it, large and close to them appeared a gray boat with two of the boys at the oars. At their very feet had been the river. The boat came breasting out of the mist, and in they stepped. All new things in life were meant to come like that.

Bird dogs went streaking the upslanted pasture through the sweet long grass that swept them as high as their noses. While it was still day on top of the mountain, the light still warm on the cheek, the valley was dyed blue under them. While one of "the boys" was coming up, his white shirt would shine for a long time almost without moving in her sight, like Venus in the sky of Mount Salus, while grandmother, mother, and little girl sat, outlasting the light, waiting for him to climb home.

Wings beat again. Flying in from over the mountain, over the roof and a child's head, high up in blue air, pigeons had formed a cluster and twinkled as one body. Like a great sheet of cloth whipping in a wind of its own making, they were about her ears. They came down to her feet and walked on the mountain. Laurel was afraid of them, but she had been provided with biscuits from the table to feed them with. They walked about, opalescent and solid, on worm-pink feet, each bird marked a little differently from the rest and each with a voice soft as a person's.

Laurel had stood panic-stricken, holding a biscuit in a frozen gesture of appeal.

"They're just Grandma's pigeons."

Her grandmother smoothed Laurel's already too straight hair and pushed it behind her ears. "They're just hungry."

But Laurel had kept the pigeons under eye in their pigeon house and had already seen a pair of them sticking their beaks down each other's throats, gagging each other, eating out of each other's craws, swallowing down all over again what had been swallowed before: they were taking turns. The first time, she hoped they might never do it again, but they did it again next day while the other pigeons copied them. They convinced her that they could not escape each other and could not themselves be escaped from. So when the pigeons flew down, she tried to position herself behind her grandmother's skirt, which was long and black, but her grandmother said again, "They're just hungry, like we are."

No more than Laurel had known that rivers ran clear and sang over rocks might her mother have known that *her* mother's pigeons were waiting to pluck each other's tongues out. "Up home," just as Laurel was in Mount Salus, her mother was too happy to know what went on in the outside world. Besides, when her mother looked closely, it was not in order to see pigeons but to verify something—the truth or a mistake; hers or another's. Laurel was ashamed to tell anybody else before she told her mother; as a result the pigeons were considered Laurel's pets.

"Come on!" cried "the boys" to Grandma. "*Let* the little beggar feed her pigeons!"

Parents and children take turns back and forth, changing places, protecting and protesting each other: so it seemed to the child.

Sometimes the top of the mountain was higher than the flying birds. Sometimes even clouds lay down the hill, hiding the treetops farther down. The highest house, the deepest well, the tuning of the strings; sleep in the clouds; Queen's Shoals; the fastest conversations on earth—no wonder her mother needed nothing else!

Eventually her father would come for them—he would be called "Mr. McKelva"; and they would go home on the train. They had taken a trunk with them—*this* trunk, with all the dresses made in this room: they might have stayed always. Her father had not appeared to realize it. They came back to Mount Salus. "Where do they get the *mount*?" her mother said scornfully. "There's no 'mount' here."

Grandma had died unexpectedly; she was alone. From the top of the stairs Laurel had heard her mother crying uncontrollably: the first time she had ever heard anyone cry uncontrollably except herself.

"I wasn't there! I wasn't *there*!"

"You are not to blame yourself, Becky, do you hear me?"

"You can't make me lie to myself, Clinton!"

They raised their voices, cried out back and forth, as if grief could be fabricated into an argument to comfort itself with. When, some time later, Laurel asked about the bell, her mother replied calmly that how good a bell was depended on the distance away your children had gone.

Laurel's own mother, after her sight was gone, lay in bed in the big room reciting to herself sometimes as she had done on horseback at sixteen to make the long ride over the mountain go faster. She did not like being read to, *she* preferred to do the reading, she said now. " 'If the salt have lost his savor, wherewith shall it be salted?' " she had asked, the most reckless expression on her wasted face. She knew Dr. Courtland's step, and greeted him with " 'Man, proud man! Dress't in a little brief authority!' "

"Don't let them tie me down," her mother had whispered on the evening before the last of the operations. "If they try to hold me, I'll die."

Judge McKelva had let this pass, but Laurel had said, "I know—you're quoting the words of your own father."

She had nodded at them fervently.

When she was fifteen years old, Becky had gone with her father, who was suffering pain, on a raft propelled by a neighbor, down the river at night when it was filled with ice, to reach a railroad, to wave a lantern at a snowy train that would stop and take them on, to reach a hospital.

("How could you make a fire on a raft?" asked Laurel, here on this matting. "How could a fire burn on water?" "We had to have a fire," said her mother, sewing on her fingers. "We *made* it burn.")

In the city of Baltimore, when at last they reached the hospital, the little girl entrusted the doctors with what he had told her: "Papa said, 'If you let them tie me down, I'll die.' " He could not by then have told the doctors for himself; he was in delirium. It turned out that he had suffered a ruptured appendix.

Two doctors came out of the operating room, to where Becky stood waiting in the hall. One said, "You'd better get in touch with whoever you know in Baltimore, little girl." "But I don't know anybody in Baltimore, sir." "Not know anybody in *Baltimore*?"

This incredulity on the part of the hospital was the memory that had stayed sharpest in Becky's mind, although afterwards she had ridden home in the baggage car of the train, guided herself back to her mother and the houseful of little boys, bearing the news and bringing the coffin, both together.

Neither of us saved our fathers, Laurel thought. But Becky was the brave one. I stood in the hall, too, but I did not any longer believe that anyone could be saved, anyone at all. Not from others.

The house shook suddenly and seemed to go on shaking after a long roll of thunder.

"Up home, we loved a good storm coming, we'd fly outdoors and run up and down to meet it," her mother used to say. "We children would run as fast as we could go along the top of that mountain when the wind was blowing, holding our arms wide open. The wilder it blew the better we liked it." During the very bursting of a tornado which carried away half of Mount Salus, she said, "*We* never were afraid of a little wind. Up home, we'd welcome a good storm."

"You don't know anybody in Baltimore?" they had asked Becky.

But Becky had known herself. *self sufficient*

There had been so much confidence when first her vision had troubled her. Laurel remembered how her mother, early in the morning of her first eye operation (and after an injection supposed to make her sleepy), was affected with the gayest high spirits and anticipation, and had asked for her dressing case, and before the inadequate mirror had powdered and dabbed rouge on her face and put on a touch of lipstick and even sprayed about with her scent, as though she had been going to an evening party with her husband. She had stretched out her hand in exhilaration to the orderly who

came to wheel her out, as if after Nate Courtland had removed that little cataract in the Mount Salus Hospital, she
would wake up and be in West Virginia.

When someone lies sick and troubled for five years and is
beloved, unforeseen partisanship can spring up among the
well. During her mother's long trial in bed, Laurel, young
and recently widowed, had somehow turned for a while
against her father: he seemed so particularly helpless to do
anything for his wife. He was not passionately enough grieved
at the changes in her! He seemed to give the changes his same,
kind recognition—to accept them because they had to be only
of the time being, even to love them, even to laugh sometimes
at their absurdity. "Why do you persist in letting them hurt
me?" her mother would ask him. Laurel battled against them
both, each for the other's sake. She loyally reproached her
mother for yielding to the storms that began coming to her
out of her darkness of vision. Her mother had only to recollect
herself! As for her father, he apparently needed guidance in
order to see the tragic.

What burdens we lay on the dying, Laurel thought, as she
listened now to the accelerated rain on the roof: seeking to
prove some little thing that we can keep to comfort us when
they can no longer feel—something as incapable of being kept
as of being proved: the lastingness of memory, vigilance
against harm, self-reliance, good hope, trust in one another.

Her father in his domestic gentleness had a horror of any
sort of private clash, of divergence from the affectionate and
the real and the explainable and the recognizable. He was a
man of great delicacy; what he had not been born with he
had learned in reaching toward his wife. He grimaced with
delicacy. What he could not control was his belief that all his
wife's troubles would turn out all right because there was
nothing he would not have given her. When he reached a loss
he simply put on his hat and went speechless out of the house
to his office and worked for an hour or so getting up a brief
for somebody.

"Laurel, open my desk drawer and hand me my old
McGuffey's Fifth Reader," her mother would sometimes say
while she sat there alone with her. It had become a book of
reference. Laurel's hand, now, drew open the drawer of the

desk, and there lay McGuffey. She took it out and let it fall open. "The Cataract of Lodore." She could imagine every word on the page being recited in her mother's voice—not the young mother who had learned it on her mountain, but the mother blind, in this house, in the next room, in her bed.

> . . . "Rising and leaping—
> Sinking and creeping,
> Swelling and sweeping—
> Showering and springing,
> Flying and flinging,
> Writhing and ringing . . .
>
> Turning and twisting,
> Around and around
> With endless rebound;
> Smiting and fighting,
> A sight to delight in;
> Confounding, astounding—"

Whatever she recited she put the same deep feeling into. With her voice she was saying that the more she could call back of "The Cataract of Lodore," the better she could defend her case in some trial that seemed to be going on against her life.

> "And glittering and frittering,
> And gathering and feathering,
> And whitening and brightening,
> And quivering and shivering,
> And hurrying and skurrying,
> And thundering and floundering . . ."

Then when he'd come home, her father would stand helpless in bewilderment by his wife's bed. Spent, she had whispered, "Why did I marry a coward?"—then had taken his hand to help him bear it.

Later still, she began to say—and her voice never weakened, never harshened, it was her spirit speaking in the wrong words—"All you do is hurt me. I wish I might know what it is I've done. Why is it necessary to punish me like this and not tell me why?" And still she held fast to their hands, to Laurel's too. Her cry was not complaint; it was anger at wanting to know and being denied knowledge; it was love's deep anger.

"Becky, it's going to be all right," Judge McKelva whispered to her.

"I've heard that before."

One day her mother had from her torments gasped out the words, "I need spiritual guidance!" She, who had dared any McKelva missionary to speak his piece to her, sent out through Laurel an invitation to the Presbyterian preacher to call upon her soon. Dr. Bolt was young then, and appealing to women—Miss Tennyson Bullock used to say so; but his visit upstairs here had not been well taken. He had begun by reading her a psalm, which she recited along with him. Her tongue was faster than his. When he was left behind on everything he tried, she told him, "I'd like better than anything you can tell me just to see the mountain one more time." When he wondered if God intended her to, she put in a barb: "And on that mountain, young man, there's a white strawberry that grows completely in the wild, if you know where to look for it. I think it very likely grows in only one spot in the world. I could tell you this minute where to go, but I doubt if you'd see them growing after you got there. Deep in the woods, you'd miss them. You could find them by mistake, and you could line your hat with leaves and try to walk off with a hatful: that would be how little you knew about those berries. Once you've let them so much as touch each other, you've already done enough to finish 'em." She fixed him with her nearly sightless eyes. "Nothing you ever ate in your life was anything like as delicate, as fragrant, as those wild white strawberries. You had to know enough to go where they are and stand and eat them on the spot, that's all."

"I'll take you back to your mountains, Becky," her father had said into the despairing face after Dr. Bolt had tiptoed away. Laurel was certain it was the first worthless promise that had ever lain between them. And the house on the mountain had by that time, anyway, burned. Laurel had been in camp the summer it happened; but her mother had been "up home." She had run back into the flames and rescued her dead father's set of Dickens at the risk of her life, and brought the books down to Mount Salus and made room for them in the library bookcase, and there they stood now. But before she died it had slipped her mind that the house had ever burned down at all.

"I'll carry you there, Becky."

"Lucifer!" she cried. *"Liar!"*

That was when he started, of course, being what he scowlingly called an optimist; he might have dredged the word up out of his childhood. He loved his wife. Whatever she did that she couldn't help doing was all right. Whatever she was driven to say was all right. But it was *not* all right! Her trouble was that very desperation. And no one had the power to cause that except the one she desperately loved, who refused to consider that she was desperate. It was betrayal on betrayal.

In her need tonight Laurel would have been willing to wish her mother and father dragged back to any torment of living because that torment was something they had known together, through each other. She wanted them with her to share her grief as she had been the sharer of theirs. She sat and thought of only one thing, of her mother holding and holding onto their hands, her own and her father's holding onto her mother's, long after there was nothing more to be said.

Laurel could remember, too, her mother holding her own hands before her eyes, very close, so that she seemed to be seeing them, the empty, working fingers.

"Poor hands in winter, when she came back from the well—bleeding from the ice, from the *ice*!" her mother cried.

"Who, Mother?" Laurel asked.

"*My* mother!" she cried accusingly.

After a stroke had crippled her further, she had come to believe—without being able to see her room, see a face, to verify anything by seeing—that she had been taken somewhere that was neither home nor "up home," that she was left among strangers, for whom even anger meant nothing, on whom it would only be wasted. She had died without speaking a word, keeping everything to herself, in exile and humiliation.

To Laurel while she still knew her, she had made a last remark: "You could have saved your mother's life. But you stood by and wouldn't intervene. I despair for you."

Baltimore was as far a place as you could go with those you
wow loved, and it was where they left you.

Then Laurel's father, when he was approaching seventy, had
married Fay. Both times he chose, he had suffered; she had
seen him contain it. He died worn out with both wives—
almost as if up to the last he had still had both of them.

As he lay without moving in the hospital he had concentrated utterly on time passing, indeed he had. But which way
had it been going for him? When he could no longer get up
and encourage it, push it forward, had it turned on him,
started moving back the other way?

Fay had once at least called Becky "my rival." Laurel
thought: But the rivalry doesn't lie where Fay thinks. It's not
between the living and the dead, between the old wife and
the new; it's between too much love and too little. There is
no rivalry as bitter; Laurel had seen its work.

Later and later into the night, with the buffeting kept at its
distance, though it never let up, Laurel sat under the lamp
among the papers. She held in her hands her mother's yellowed notebooks—correspondence records, address books—
Virginia aunts and cousins long dead, West Virginia nieces and
nephews now married and moved where Laurel no longer
quite kept up with them. The brothers had moved down the
mountain into town, into the city, and the banjo player who
had known so many verses to "Where Have You Been, Billy
Boy?" had turned into a bank official. Only the youngest had
been able to come to Mount Salus to his sister's funeral. He
who had been the Evening Star climbed on two canes to her
grave and said to Judge McKelva, as they stood together,
"She's a long way from West Virginia."

A familiar black-covered "composition book" came off the
shelf and lay open on Laurel's lap to "My Best Bread," written out twenty or thirty years ago in her mother's strict,
pointed hand, giving everything but the steps of procedure.
("A cook is not exactly a fool.") Underneath it had lain something older, a class notebook. Becky had sent herself to
teacher's college, wearing the deep-dyed blouse. It was her
keeping her diagrams of *Paradise Lost* and Milton's Universe
that was so like her, pigeonholing them here as though she'd

be likely to find them useful again. Laurel gazed down at the careful figuring of the modest household accounts, drifted along the lined pages (this was an old Mount Salus Bank book) to where they eased into garden diaries and the plots of her rose beds, her perennial borders. "I have just come in. Clinton is still toiling. I see him now from my kitchen window, struggling with the Mermaid rose." "That fool fig tree is already putting out leaves. Will it never learn?"

The last pigeonhole held letters her mother had saved from her own mother, from "up home."

She slipped them from their thin envelopes and read them now for herself. Widowed, her health failing, lonely and sometimes bedridden, Grandma wrote these letters to her young, venturesome, defiant, happily married daughter as to an exile, without ever allowing herself to put it into so many words. Laurel could hardly believe the bravery and serenity she had put into these short letters, in the quickened pencil to catch the pocket of one of "the boys" before he rode off again, dependent—Grandma then, as much as Laurel now—upon his remembering to mail them from "the courthouse." She read on and met her own name on a page. "I will try to send Laurel a cup of sugar for her birthday. Though if I can find a way to do it, I would like to send her one of my pigeons. It would eat from her hand, if she would let it."

A flood of feeling descended on Laurel. She let the papers slide from her hand and the books from her knees, and put her head down on the open lid of the desk and wept in grief for love and for the dead. She lay there with all that was adamant in her yielding to this night, yielding at last. Now all she had found had found her. The deepest spring in her heart had uncovered itself, and it began to flow again.

If Phil could have lived—

But Phil was lost. Nothing of their life together remained except in her own memory; love was sealed away into its perfection and had remained there.

If Phil had lived—

She had gone on living with the old perfection undisturbed and undisturbing. Now, by her own hands, the past had been raised up, and *he* looked at her, Phil himself—here waiting, all the time, Lazarus. He looked at her out of eyes wild with the craving for his unlived life, with mouth open like a funnel's.

What would have been their end, then? Suppose their marriage had ended like her father and mother's? Or like her mother's father and mother's? Like—

"Laurel! Laurel! Laurel!" Phil's voice cried.

She wept for what happened to life.

"I wanted it!" Phil cried. His voice rose with the wind in the night and went around the house and around the house. It became a roar. "I wanted it!"

Four

S HE HAD SLEPT in the chair, like a passenger who had come on an emergency journey in a train. But she had rested deeply.

She had dreamed that she *was* a passenger, and riding with Phil. They had ridden together over a long bridge.

Awake, she recognized it: it was a dream of something that had really happened. When she and Phil were coming down from Chicago to Mount Salus to be married in the Presbyterian Church, they came on the train. Laurel, when she travelled back and forth between Mount Salus and Chicago, had always taken the sleeper—the same crack train she had just ridden from New Orleans. She and Phil followed the route on the day train, and she saw it for the first time.

When they were climbing the long approach to a bridge after leaving Cairo, rising slowly higher until they rode above the tops of bare trees, she looked down and saw the pale light widening and the river bottoms opening out, and then the water appearing, reflecting the low, early sun. There were two rivers. Here was where they came together. This was the confluence of the waters, the Ohio and the Mississippi. *In Huck Finn* They were looking down from a great elevation and all they saw was at the point of coming together, the bare trees marching in from the horizon, the rivers moving into one, and as he touched her arm she looked up with him and saw the long, ragged, pencil-faint line of birds within the crystal of the zenith, flying in a V of their own, following the same course down. All they could see was sky, water, birds, light, and confluence. It was the whole morning world.

And they themselves were a part of the confluence. Their own joint act of faith had brought them here at the very moment and matched its occurrence, and proceeded as it proceeded. Direction itself was made beautiful, momentous. They were riding as one with it, right up front. It's our turn! she'd thought exultantly. And we're going to live forever.

Left bodiless and graveless of a death made of water and fire in a year long gone, Phil could still tell her of her life. For *theme*

her life, any life, she had to believe, was nothing but the con-
tinuity of its love.

She believed it just as she believed that the confluence of
the waters was still happening at Cairo. It would be there the
same as it ever was when she went flying over it today on her
way back—out of sight, for her, this time, thousands of feet
below, but with nothing in between except thin air.

Philip Hand was an Ohio country boy. He had a country
boy's soft-spokenness and selfless energy and long-range
plans. He had put himself through architectural school—
Georgia Tech, because it was cheaper and warmer there—in
her country; then had met her when she came north to study
in his, at the Art Institute in Chicago. From far back, generations, they must have had common memories. (Ohio was
across the river from West Virginia; the Ohio was his river.)

But there was nothing like a kinship between them, as they
learned. In life and work and in affection they were each
shy, each bold, just where the other was not. She grew up in
the kind of shyness that takes its refuge in giving refuge. Until
she knew Phil, she thought of love as shelter; her arms went
out as a naïve offer of safety. He had showed her that this
need not be so. Protection, like self-protection, fell away from
her like all one garment, some anachronism foolishly saved
from childhood.

Philip had large, good hands, and extraordinary thumbs—
double-jointed where they left the palms, nearly at right angles; their long, blunt tips curved strongly back. When she
watched his right hand go about its work, it looked to her
like the Hand of his name.

She had a certain gift of her own. He taught her, through
his example, how to use it. She learned how to work by working beside him. He taught her to draw, to work toward and
into her pattern, not to sketch peripheries.

Designing houses was not enough for his energy. He fitted
up a workshop in their South Side apartment, taking up half
the kitchen. "I get a moral satisfaction out of putting things
together," he said. "I like to see a thing finished." He made
simple objects of immediate use, taking unlimited pains. What
he was, was a perfectionist.

But he was not an optimist—she knew that. Phil had

learned everything he could manage to learn, and done as much as he had time for, to design houses to stand, to last, to be lived in; but he had known they could equally well, with the same devotion and tireless effort, be built of cards.

When the country went to war, Philip said, "Not the Army, not the Engineers. I've heard what happens to architects. They get put in Camouflage. This war's got to move too fast to stop for junk like camouflage." He went into the Navy and ended up as a communications officer on board a mine sweeper in the Pacific.

Taking the train, Laurel's father made his first trip to Chicago in years to see Phil on his last leave. (Her mother was unable to travel anywhere except "up home.")

"How close have those *kamikaze* come to you so far, son?" the Judge wanted to know.

"About close enough to shake hands with," Phil said.

A month later, they came closer still.

As far as Laurel had ever known, there had not happened a single blunder in their short life together. But the guilt of outliving those you love is justly to be borne, she thought. Outliving is something we do to them. The fantasies of dying could be no stranger than the fantasies of living. Surviving is perhaps the strangest fantasy of them all.

The house was bright and still, like a ship that has tossed all night and come to harbor. She had not forgotten what waited for her today. Turning off the panicky lights of last night as she went, she walked through the big bedroom and opened the door into the hall.

She saw the bird at once, high up in a fold of the curtain at the stair window; it was still, too, and narrowed, wings to its body.

As the top step of the stairs creaked under her foot, the bird quivered its wings rapidly without altering its position. She sped down the stairs and closed herself into the kitchen while she planned and breakfasted. She'd got upstairs again and dressed and come out again, still to find the bird had not moved from its position.

Loudly, like a clumsy, slow echo of the wingbeating, a pounding began on the front porch. It was no effort any longer to remember anybody: Laurel knew there was only one man in Mount Salus who knocked like that, the perennial jack-leg carpenter who appeared in spring to put in new window cords, sharpen the lawn mower, plane off the back screen door from its wintertime sag. He still acted, no doubt, for widows and maiden ladies and for wives whose husbands were helpless around the house.

"Well, this time it's your dad. Old Miss been gone a dozen year. I miss her ever' time I pass the old place," said Mr. Cheek. "Her and her ideas."

Was this some last, misguided call of condolence? "What is it, Mr. Cheek?" she asked.

"Locks holding?" he asked. "Ready for me to string your window cords? Change your furniture around?" He was the same. He mounted the steps and came right across the porch at a march, with his knees bent and turned out, and the tools knocking together inside his sack.

Her mother had deplored his familiar ways and blundering hammer, had called him on his cheating, and would have sent him packing for good the first time she heard him refer to her as "Old Miss." Now he was moving into what he must suppose was a clear field. "Roof do any leaking last night?"

"No. A bird came down the chimney, that's all," said Laurel. "If you'd like to be useful, I'll let you get it out for me."

"Bird in the house?" he asked. "Sign o' bad luck, ain't it?" He still walked up the stairs with a strut and followed too close. "I reckon I'm elected."

The bird had not moved from its position. Heavy-looking, laden with soot, it was still pressed into the same curtain fold.

"I spot him!" Mr. Cheek shouted. He stamped his foot, then clogged with both feet like a clown, and the bird dropped from the curtain into flight and, barely missing the wall, angled into Laurel's room—her bedroom door had come open. Mr. Cheek with a shout slammed the door on it.

"Mr. Cheek!"

"Well, I got him out of your hall."

Laurel's door opened again, of itself, with a slowness that testified there was nothing behind it but the morning breeze.

"I'm not prepared for a joke this morning," Laurel said. "I want that bird out of my room!"

Mr. Cheek marched on into her bedroom. His eye slid to the muslin curtains, wet, with the starch rained out of them —she realized that her window had been open all night— where the shineless bird was frantically striking itself; but she could see he was only sizing up the frayed window cords.

"It'll get in every room in the house if you let it," Laurel said, controlling herself from putting her hands over her hair.

"It ain't trying to get in. Trying to get out," said Mr. Cheek, and crowed at her. He marched around the room, glancing into Laurel's suitcase, opened out on the bed—there was nothing for him to see, only her sketchbook that she'd never taken out—and inspected the dressing table and himself in its mirror, while the bird tried itself from curtain to curtain and spurted out of the room ahead of him. It had left the dust of itself all over everything, the way a moth does.

"Where's Young Miss?" asked Mr. Cheek, and opened the big bedroom door. The bird flew in like an arrow.

"Mr. Cheek!"

"That's about my favorite room in the house," he said. He gave Laurel a black grin; his front teeth had gone.

"Mr. Cheek, I thought I told you—I wasn't ready for a joke. You've simply come and made things worse than you found them. Exactly like you used to do!" Laurel said.

"Well, I won't charge you nothing," he said, clattering down the stairs behind her. "I don't see nothing wrong with you," he added. "Why didn't you ever go 'head and marry you another somebody?"

She walked to the door and waited for him to leave. He laughed good-naturedly. "Yep, I'm all that's left of my folks too," he said. "Maybe me and you ought to get together."

"Mr. Cheek, I'd be very glad if you'd depart."

"If you don't sound like Old Miss!" he said admiringly. "No hard feelings," he called, skipping into his escape down the steps. "You even got her voice."

Missouri had arrived; she came out with her broom to the front porch. "What happen?"

"A chimney swift! A chimney swift got out of the fireplace into the house and flew everywhere," Laurel said. "It's still loose upstairs."

"It's because we get it all too clean, brag too soon," said

Missouri. "You didn't ask that Mr. Cheeks? He just waltz through the house enjoying the scenery, what I bet."

"He was a failure. We'll shoo it out between us."

"That's what it look like. It's just me and you."

Missouri, when she appeared again, was stuffed back into her raincoat and hat and buckled in tight. She walked slowly up the stairs holding the kitchen broom, bristles up.

"Do you see it?" Laurel asked. She saw the mark on the stairway curtain where the bird had tried to stay asleep. She heard it somewhere, ticking.

"He on the telephone."

"Oh, don't hit—"

"How'm I gonna git him, then? Look," said Missouri. "He ain't got no business in your room."

"Just move behind it. Birds fly toward light—I'm sure I've been told. Here—I'm holding the front door wide open for it." Missouri could be heard dropping the broom. "It's got a perfectly clear way out now," Laurel called. "Why won't it just fly free of its own accord?"

"They just ain't got no sense like we have."

Laurel propped the screen door open and ran upstairs with two straw wastebaskets. "I'll *make* it go free."

Then her heart sank. The bird was down on the floor, under the telephone table. It looked small and unbearably flat to the ground, like a child's shoe without a foot inside it.

"Missouri, I've always been scared one would touch me," Laurel told her. "I'll tell *you* that." It looked eyeless, unborn, so still was it holding.

"They vermin," said Missouri.

Laurel dropped the first basket over the bird, then cupped the two baskets together to enclose it; the whole operation was soundless and over in an instant.

"What if I've hurt it?"

"Cat'll git him, that's all."

Laurel ran down the stairs and out of the house and down the front steps, not a step of the way without the knowledge of what she carried, vibrating through the ribs of the baskets, the beat of its wings or of its heart, its blind struggle against rescue.

On the front sidewalk, she got ready.

"What you doing?" called old Mrs. Pease through her window curtains. "Thought you were due to be gone!"

"I am, just about!" called Laurel, and opened the baskets.

Something struck her face—not feathers; it was a blow of wind. The bird was away. In the air it was nothing but a pair of wings—she saw no body any more, no tail, just a tilting crescent being drawn back into the sky.

"All birds got to fly, even them no-count dirty ones," said Missouri from the porch. "Now I got all that wrenching out to do over."

For the next hour, Laurel stood in the driveway burning her father's letters to her mother, and Grandma's letters, and the saved little books and papers in the rusty wire basket where pecan leaves used to get burned—"too acid for my roses." She burned Milton's Universe. She saw the words "this morning?" with the uncompromising hook of her mother's question mark, on a little round scrap of paper that was slowly growing smaller in the smoke. She had a child's desire to reach for it, like a coin left lying in the street for any passer-by to find and legitimately keep—by then it was consumed. All Laurel would have wanted with her mother's "this morning?" would have been to make it over, give her a new one in its place. She stood humbly holding the blackened rake. She thought of her father.

The smoke dimmed the dogwood tree like a veil over a face that might have shone with too naked a candor. Miss Adele Courtland was hurrying under it now, at a fast teacher's walk, to tell Laurel goodbye before time for school. She looked at what Laurel was doing and her face withheld judgment.

"There's one thing—I'd like you to keep it," said Laurel. She reached in her apron pocket for it.

"Polly. You mustn't give this up. You must know I can't allow you—no, indeed, you must cling to this." She pressed the little soapstone boat back into Laurel's hand quickly, told her goodbye, and fled away to her school.

Laurel had presumed. And no one would ever succeed in comforting Miss Adele Courtland, anyway: she would only comfort the comforter.

*

Upstairs, Laurel folded her slacks and the wrinkled silk dress of last night into her case, dropped in the other few things she'd brought, and closed it. Then she bathed and dressed again in the Sibyl Connolly suit she'd flown down in. She was careful with her lipstick, and pinned her hair up for Chicago. She stepped back into her city heels, and started on a last circuit through the house. All the windows, which Missouri had patiently stripped so as to wash the curtains over again, let in the full volume of spring light. There was nothing she was leaving in the whole shining and quiet house now to show for her mother's life and her mother's happiness and suffering, and nothing to show for Fay's harm; her father's turning between them, holding onto them both, then letting them go, was without any sign.

From the stair window she could see that the crab-apple tree had rushed into green, all but one sleeve that was still flowery.

The last of the funeral flowers had been carried out of the parlor—the tulips, that had stayed beautiful until the last petal fell. Over the white-painted mantel, where cranes in their circle of moon, the beggar with his lantern, the poet at his waterfall hung in their positions around the clock, the hour showed thirty minutes before noon.

She was prepared for the bridesmaids.

And then, from the back of the house, she heard a sound—like an empty wooden spool dropped down through a cupboard and rolling away. She walked into the kitchen, where through the open door she could see Missouri just beginning to hang out her curtains. The room was still odorous of hot soapsuds.

The same wooden kitchen table of her childhood, strong as the base of an old square piano, stood bare in the middle of the wooden floor. There were two cupboards, and only the new one, made of metal, was in daily use. The original wooden one Laurel had somehow passed over in her work, as forgetfully as she'd left her own window open to the rain. She advanced on it, tugged at the wooden doors until they gave. She opened them and got the earnest smell of mouse.

In the dark interior she made out the fruitcake pans, the sack of ice-cream salt, the waffle irons, the punch bowl hung with its cups and glinting with the oily rainbows of neglect. Underneath all those useless things, shoved back as far as it would go but still on the point of pushing itself out of the cupboard, something was waiting for her to find; and she was still here, to find it.

Kneeling, moving the objects rapidly out of her way, Laurel reached with both hands and drew it out into the light of the curtainless day and looked at it. It was exactly what she thought it was. In that same moment, she felt, more sharply than she could hear them where she was, footsteps that tracked through the parlor, the library, the hall, the dining room, up the stairs and through the bedrooms, down the stairs, in the same path Laurel had taken, and at last came to the kitchen door and stopped.

"You mean to tell me you're still here?" Fay said.

Laurel said, "What have you done to my mother's breadboard?"

"Breadboard?"

Laurel rose and carried it to the middle of the room and set it on the table. She pointed. "Look. Look where the surface is splintered—look at those gouges. You might have gone at it with an icepick."

"Is that a crime?"

"All scored and grimy! Or you tried driving nails in it."

"I didn't do anything but crack last year's walnuts on it. With the hammer."

"And cigarette burns—"

"Who wants an everlasting breadboard? It's the last thing on earth anybody needs!"

"And there—along the edge!" With a finger that was trembling now, Laurel drew along it.

"Most likely a house as old as this has got a few enterprising rats in it," Fay said.

"Gnawed and blackened and the dust ground into it— Mother kept it satin-smooth, and clean as a dish!"

"It's just an old board, isn't it?" cried Fay.

"She made the best bread in Mount Salus!"

"All right! Who cares? She's not making it now."

"You desecrated this house."

"I don't know what that word means, and glad I don't.

a reason for crass behavior of lower classes

But I'll have you remember it's my house now, and I can do what I want to with it," Fay said. "With everything in it. And that goes for that breadboard too."

And all Laurel had felt and known in the night, all she'd remembered, and as much as she could understand this morning—in the week at home, the month, in her life—could not tell her now how to stand and face the person whose own life had not taught her how to feel. Laurel didn't know even how to tell her goodbye.

"Fay, my mother knew you'd get in her house. She never needed to be told," said Laurel. "She predicted you."

"Predict? You *predict* the *weather*," said Fay.

You *are* the weather, thought Laurel. And the weather to come: there'll be many a one more like you, in this life.

"She predicted you."

Experience did, finally, get set into its right order, which is not always the order of other people's time. Her mother had suffered in life every symptom of having been betrayed, and it was not until she had died, and the protests of memory came due, that Fay had ever tripped in from Madrid, Texas. It was not until that later moment, perhaps, that her father himself had ever dreamed of a Fay. For Fay was Becky's own dread. What Becky had felt, and had been afraid of, might have existed right here in the house all the time, for her. Past and future might have changed places, in some convulsion of the mind, but that could do nothing to impugn the truth of the heart. Fay could have walked in early as well as late, she could have come at any time at all. She was coming.

"But your mother, she died a crazy!" Fay cried.

"Fay, that is not true. And nobody ever dared to say such a thing."

"In Mount Salus? I heard it in Mount Salus, right in this house. Mr. Cheek put me wise. He told me how he went in my room one day while she was alive and she threw something at him."

"Stop," said Laurel.

"It was the little bell off her table. She told him she deliberately aimed at his knee, because she didn't have a wish to hurt any living creature. She was a crazy and you'll be a crazy too, if you don't watch out."

"My mother never did hurt any living creature."

"Crazies never did scare me. You can't scare me into running away, either. You're the one that's got to do the running," Fay said.

"Scaring people into things. Scaring people out of things. You haven't learned any better yet, Fay?" Trembling, Laurel kept on. "What were you trying to scare Father into—when you struck him?"

"I was trying to scare him into living!" Fay cried.

"You what? You *what*?"

"I wanted him to get up out of there, and start him paying a little attention to *me*, for a change."

"He was dying," said Laurel. "He was paying full attention to that."

"I tried to make him quit his old-man foolishness. I was going to make him live if I had to drag him! And I take good credit for what I did!" cried Fay. "It's more than anybody else was doing."

"You hurt him."

"I was being a wife to him!" cried Fay. "Have you clean forgotten by this time what being a wife is?"

"I haven't forgotten," Laurel said. "Do you want to know why this breadboard right here is such a beautiful piece of work? I can tell you. It's because my husband made it."

"*Made* it? What for?"

"Do you know what a labor of love is? My husband made it for my mother, so she'd have a good one. Phil had the gift —the gift of his hands. And he planed—fitted—glued— clamped—it's made on the true, look and see, it's still as straight as his T-square. Tongued and grooved—tight-fitted, every edge—"

"I couldn't care less," said Fay.

"I watched him make it. He's the one in the family who could make things. We were a family of comparatively helpless people—that's what so bound us, bound us together. My mother blessed him when she saw this. She said it was sound and beautiful and exactly suited her long-felt needs, and she welcomed it into her kitchen."

"It's mine now," said Fay.

"But I'm the one that's going to take care of it," said Laurel.

"You mean you're asking me to give it to you?"

"I'm going to take it back to Chicago with me."

"What makes you think I'll let you? What's made you so brazen all at once?"

"Finding the breadboard!" Laurel cried. She placed both hands down on it and gave it the weight of her body.

"Fine Miss Laurel!" said Fay. "If they all could see you now! You mean you'd carry it out of the house the way it is? It's dirty as sin."

"A coat of grime is something I can get rid of."

"If all you want to do is rub the skin off your bones."

"The scars it's got are a different matter. But I'd work."

"And do what with it when you got through?" Fay said mockingly.

"Have my try at making bread. Only last night, by the grace of God, I had my mother's recipe, written in her own hand, right before my eyes."

"It all tastes alike, don't it?"

"You never tasted my mother's. I could turn out a good loaf too—I'd work at it."

"And then who'd eat it with you?" said Fay.

"Phil loved bread. He loved good bread. To break a loaf and eat it warm, just out of the oven," Laurel said. Ghosts. And in irony she saw herself, pursuing her own way through the house as single-mindedly as Fay had pursued hers through the ceremony of the day of the funeral. But of course they had had to come together—it was useless to suppose they wouldn't meet, here at the end of it. Laurel was not late, not yet, in leaving, but Fay had come early, and in time. For there is hate as well as love, she supposed, in the coming together and continuing of our lives. She thought of Phil and the *kamikaze* shaking hands.

"Your husband? What has *he* got to do with it?" asked Fay. "He's dead, isn't he?"

Laurel took the breadboard in both hands and raised it up out of Fay's reach.

"Is that what you hit with? Is a moldy old breadboard the best you can find?"

Laurel held the board tightly. She supported it, above her head, but for a moment it seemed to be what supported her, a raft in the waters, to keep her from slipping down deep, where the others had gone before her.

From the parlor came a soft whirr, and noon struck.

Laurel slowly lowered the board and held it out level between the two of them.

"I'll tell you what: you just about made a fool of yourself," said Fay. "You were just before trying to hit me with that plank. But you couldn't have done it. You don't know the way to fight." She squinted up one eye. "I had a whole family to teach *me*."

But of course, Laurel saw, it was Fay who did not know how to fight. For Fay was without any powers of passion or imagination in herself and had no way to see it or reach it in the other person. Other people, inside their lives, might as well be invisible to her. To find them, she could only strike out those little fists at random, or spit from her little mouth. She could no more fight a feeling person than she could love him.

"I believe you underestimate everybody on earth," Laurel said.

She had been ready to hurt Fay. She had wanted to hurt her, and had known herself capable of doing it. But such is the strangeness of the mind, it had been the memory of the child Wendell that had prevented her.

"I don't know what you're making such a big fuss over. What do you see in that thing?" asked Fay.

"The whole story, Fay. The whole solid past," said Laurel.

"Whose story? Whose past? Not mine," said Fay. "The past isn't a thing to me. I belong to the future, didn't you know that?"

And it occurred to Laurel that Fay might already have been faithless to her father's memory. "I know you aren't anything to the past," she said. "You can't do anything to it now." And neither am I; and neither can I, she thought, although it has been everything and done everything to me, everything for me. The past is no more open to help or hurt than was Father in his coffin. The past is like him, impervious, and can never be awakened. It is memory that is the somnambulist. It will come back in its wounds from across the world, like Phil, calling us by our names and demanding its rightful tears. It will never be impervious. The memory can be hurt, time and again—but in that may lie its final mercy. As long as it's vulnerable to the living moment, it lives for us, and while it lives, and while we are able, we can give it up its due.

From outside in the driveway came the sound of a car arriving and the bridesmaids' tattoo on the horn.

"Take it!" said Fay. "It'll give me one thing less to get rid of."

"Never mind," said Laurel, laying the breadboard down on the table where it belonged. "I think I can get along without that too." Memory lived not in initial possession but in the freed hands, pardoned and freed, and in the heart that can empty but fill again, in the patterns restored by dreams. Laurel passed Fay and went into the hall, took up her coat and handbag. Missouri came running along the porch in time to reach for her suitcase. Laurel pressed her quickly to her, sped down the steps and to the car where the bridesmaids were waiting, holding the door open for her and impatiently calling her name.

"There now," Tish said. "You'll make it by the skin of your teeth."

They flashed by the Courthouse, turned at the school. Miss Adele was out with her first-graders, grouped for a game in the yard. She waved. So did the children. The last thing Laurel saw, before they whirled into speed, was the twinkling of their hands, the many small and unknown hands, wishing her goodbye.

CHRONOLOGY

NOTE ON THE TEXTS

NOTES

Chronology

Scott, Robert Louis Stevenson, Mark Twain, Ring Lard-
ner, encyclopedias, and popular sentimental and didactic
fiction. Enjoys drawing and playing upright Steinway piano bought by mother with earnings from selling the milk
of her Jersey cow. Learns about photography from father,
who develops his own pictures, and from mother to study
Bible with use of a concordance. Goes to movies weekly.
A drawing by Welty is published in children's magazine
St. Nicholas in August 1920.

1921–24   Wins $25 prize in summer in Jackie Mackie Jingles contest
sponsored by Mackie Pine Oil Specialty Co., which sends
letter encouraging Welty to "improve in poetry to such
an extent as to win fame." Begins attending Jackson's
Central High School in fall 1921; publishes sketches and
poems in school newspaper and *St. Nicholas* and one of
her drawings is accepted by the Memphis *Commercial
Appeal.*

1925–26   Parents build new home on Pinehurst Street in Jackson.
Welty enrolls in fall 1925 at Mississippi State College for
Women in Columbus with plans to become a writer; shares
room in Old Main dormitory with three other students.
For first time, gets to know people from throughout the
state and is fascinated by their different accents. Tries
writing a novel; publishes sketches, poems, and stories in
campus newspaper, *The Spectator*, and two of her drawings
appear in campus magazine *O, Lady!* (later describes herself during these years as "a wit and humorist of the
parochial kind").

1927–29   Transfers to University of Wisconsin, Madison, for junior
and senior years; concentrates on literature and fine arts
and considers career as an artist. Studies literary modern-
ists including Virginia Woolf, Faulkner, and Yeats, who
becomes her favorite poet. Also reads Irish writer Æ
(George Russell) and Russian novelists. Feels lonely in
what she later describes as the "icy world" of Madison,
whose people "seemed to me like sticks of flint." Poem
"Shadows" published in *Wisconsin Literary Magazine*
(April 1928). Makes frequent visits to Chicago and spends
time at the Art Institute while waiting for train connec-
tions between Mississippi and Madison. Graduates with

B.A. degree in 1929. Becomes seriously interested in photography; uses Kodak camera with a bellows and develops her own prints.

1930   Begins one-year advertising course at Columbia University Graduate School of Business in New York City; rooms with friends from Jackson. Regularly visits galleries, museums, and theater, where she enjoys musical comedy and revues, as well as jazz clubs and vaudeville shows in Harlem.

1931–34   With jobs scarce in the Depression, returns home at completion of Columbia course in 1931. Shortly after, father becomes critically ill with leukemia and dies while receiving a blood transfusion from mother, with Welty at bedside. Welty gets work writing scripts, doing odd jobs, and editing *Lamar Life Radio News* at WJIX, first Jackson radio station, which is housed in Lamar Life building. Also works as Jackson social news correspondent for the Memphis *Commercial Appeal.*

1935–36   Works as publicity agent for the Works Progress Administration in Mississippi, traveling throughout the state to photograph and report on WPA projects and people they serve; uses Recomar camera and in 1936 buys a Rolleiflex. Prepares group of her photographs, titled "Black Saturday," in spring 1935 and sends them to New York publisher Harrison Smith, who rejects them. Visits New York City with the photographs; fails to find a publisher, but Lugene Opticians sponsors exhibition of 45 of the prints at Photographic Galleries, March 31–April 15, 1936, and that summer Samuel Robbins proposes mounting a second exhibit at the Camera House (it is held March 6–31, 1937). Welty applies for, but fails to receive, job as a photographer with the Resettlement Administration in New York City. Submits stories to prestigious little magazine *Manuscript,* published in Athens, Ohio, which accepts "Death of a Traveling Salesman" and "Magic." Begins receiving letters from publishers inquiring about her writing a novel; she suggests a collection of stories, but the proposal is not accepted. Meets at her home with friends including young writers Frank Lyell, Hubert Creekmore, Nash Burger, and composer and conductor Lehman Engel; dubs the group Night-Blooming Cereus Club.

1937   Works on short stories; sends several to Robert Penn Warren and Cleanth Brooks, editors of the newly established
Southern Review at Louisiana State University. Discour-
aged when they return "Petrified Man," which was previously rejected by other journals, Welty destroys the only
copy of it (when Warren expresses second thoughts about
the story, she rewrites it from memory). Six of Welty's
photographs appear in *Life* (Nov. 8, 1937) in conjunction
with story, for which she did research, about series of
deaths in Mount Olive, Mississippi, caused by new form
of the prescription drug sulfanilamide. Three other photographs are chosen for *Mississippi: A Guide to the Magnolia State* (published by Federal Writers Project in 1938).
Continues to circulate photographs, along with a collection of stories, to New York publishers, but they are rejected partly on grounds that the genre of photo-fiction is
saturated.

1938   "Lily Daw and the Three Ladies" (*Prairie Schooner*, Winter 1937) appears in *The Best Short Stories 1938*. Warren,
Brooks, and Katherine Anne Porter sponsor Welty in
Houghton Mifflin Fellowship contest for first novels; her
entry receives high rating but does not win. Ford Madox
Ford writes Welty in November praising her work; she
sends him a collection of her stories and he submits it to
publishers in England and America, but without success.

1939   "A Curtain of Green" (*Southern Review*, Autumn 1938) is
chosen for *The Best Short Stories 1939* and "Petrified Man"
(*Southern Review*, Spring 1939) for *O. Henry Prize Stories
of 1939*. Continues publishing in *Southern Review*. Visited
in autumn by John Woodburn, an editor and scout for
Doubleday, Doran to whom she has been recommended
by Brooks and Warren; he takes back a collection of her
stories but it is rejected.

1940   Learns that "The Hitch-Hikers" (*Southern Review*, Autumn 1939) has been chosen for *The Best Short Stories 1940*.
Takes on Diarmuid Russell, son of George Russell (Æ)
and a founder of new Russell & Volkening literary agency
in New York, as her agent in June; he begins working to
place her fiction in well-paying magazines such as *Atlantic
Monthly*, *The New Yorker*, and *Harper's Bazaar*, and seeks

publisher for a story collection. Welty spends part of summer on fellowship at Bread Loaf Writers' Conference in Middlebury, Vermont; sees Russell in New York in August and they begin close working relationship and enduring friendship. Concentrates on writing stories set in the Natchez Trace area; reads Robert Coates' *The Outlaw Years*. In early December, *Atlantic Monthly* accepts "Powerhouse" and "A Worn Path."

1941   Doubleday, Doran offers contract for story collection (published in November, with introduction by Katherine Anne Porter, as *A Curtain of Green*). "A Worn Path" wins second prize in the O. Henry Awards competition. Spends June–July on fellowship at Yaddo writers colony, Saratoga Springs, New York; shares housing with Katherine Anne Porter. Night-Blooming Cereus Club entertains Henry Miller during his three-day visit to Jackson; he offers to put Welty in contact with publishers in the pornographic market.

1942   Wins a Guggenheim fellowship for writing fiction in spring. *The Robber Bridegroom* is published by Doubleday, Doran in October. "The Wide Net" wins first prize in the O. Henry Awards competition for 1942. Hearing in November that Woodburn has left Doubleday for Harcourt, Brace, Welty decides to move with him.

1943   *The Wide Net and Other Stories* is published by Harcourt in September. "Livvie is Back" (later titled "Livvie") wins first prize in O. Henry Awards competition for 1943, "Asphodel" is included in *The Best American Short Stories 1943*, and "Old Mr. Marblehall" and "A Piece of News" are included in Brooks and Warren's textbook *Understanding Fiction*.

1944–45   Moves to New York City for summer to work for Robert Van Gelder at *The New York Times Book Review* (for reviews of books on the war, Welty writes under pseudonym "Michael Ravenna"); continues writing reviews after return to Jackson. Works on story "The Delta Cousins" based on stories and documents of friend John Fraiser Robinson's family; by January 1945 it "boils over" into a novel that she calls "Shellmound" (later *Delta Wedding*).

1946   Story "A Sketching Trip" wins mention in O. Henry
        Awards competition for 1946. *Delta Wedding* is serialized
        in *Atlantic Monthly* (Jan.–April 1946) and brought out as
        a book by Harcourt in April. Begins writing stories that
        are later collected in *The Golden Apples*. Travels in Novem-
        ber to San Francisco for a stay that stretches to four
        months; while there, writes story "Music from Spain,"
        sees a lot of John Fraiser Robinson, and makes new friends
        including Art and Antonette Fereva Foff, clients of
        Russell.

1947   Receives letter from E. M. Forster praising her work, par-
        ticularly *The Wide Net*. Delivers lecture at Northwest
        Pacific Writers' Conference at University of Washing-
        ton in August, then uses fee to stay in San Francisco
        until late November; buys new Royal typewriter. Contin-
        ues working on short stories and revises lecture to form
        first extended essay in literary criticism, "The Reading and
        Writing of Short Stories" (published in *Atlantic Monthly*,
        Feb. 1949).

1948   Despite urging of Russell that she finish revisions of *The
        Golden Apples*, goes to New York to collaborate with Hil-
        degarde Dolson on revue "The Waiting Room" (only
        Welty's skit "Bye-Bye Brevoort" is later produced). Also
        collaborates by mail with Robinson on screenplay of *The
        Robber Bridegroom* (completed in 1949, it is never
        produced).

1949   Hears that her Guggenheim fellowship has been renewed.
        After *The Golden Apples* is published by Harcourt, sails to
        Italy, where she sees Robinson, and to France where she
        travels with *Harper's Bazaar* editor Mary Louise Aswell.
        Goes on to England and then by ferry to Ireland; sends
        note to Elizabeth Bowen, who has reviewed Welty's work
        favorably, and is invited to visit her at home in County
        Cork.

1951   "The Burning," published in *Harper's Bazaar* (March
        1951), wins second prize in O. Henry competition for 1951.
        Travels to England in spring to deliver lecture at Cam-
        bridge University based on "The Reading and Writing of
        Short Stories"; visits Bowen in Ireland, where she works
        on "The Bride of the Innisfallen," and spends June to

mid-July in London; also sees Elizabeth Spencer and Stephen Spender. In late November accompanies Bowen to New Orleans and Shreveport on part of her American lecture tour.

1952–54　Elected to the National Institute of Arts and Letters in 1952. *The Ponder Heart* appears in *The New Yorker* (Dec. 5, 1953) and is published by Harcourt in January 1954; it is also a Book-of-the-Month Club selection. Writes "Place in Fiction" for Fulbright program held at Cambridge University in July 1954. *Selected Stories of Eudora Welty*, including *A Curtain of Green* and *The Wide Net*, published by Modern Library.

1955　*The Bride of the Innisfallen and Other Stories*, dedicated to Bowen, published by Harcourt in January. Delivers "Place in Fiction" at Duke University in February; meets Reynolds Price, then editor of student paper *The Archive*. Mother suffers a slow and difficult recuperation from eye surgery. While caring for her, Welty works on a "long story about the country" (eventually *Losing Battles*), writing brief vignettes and scenes which she keeps in shoe boxes for assembling later.

1956　With mother and Jackson friends who charter a plane for the event, attends New York opening on February 16 of Joseph Fields and Jerome Chodorov's adaptation of *The Ponder Heart*, starring David Wayne as Uncle Daniel and Una Merkel as Edna Earle, it runs for 149 performances. Returns to the city for May 22 opening at Phoenix Theatre of *The Littlest Revue* which includes Welty's 1948 skit "Bye-Bye Brevoort."

1959　Brother Walter dies in January.

1960　On Ford Foundation grant spends two seasons of study and observation at Phoenix Theatre in New York.

1962　Serves as guest lecturer at Smith College in Massachusetts in winter term; in May is chosen to present the National Institute of Arts and Letters' Gold Medal for Fiction to William Faulkner.

1963   In response to the assassination in Jackson on June 12 of Mississippi NAACP leader Medgar Evers, writes "Where Is the Voice Coming From?" (published in *The New Yorker*, July 6, 1963).

1964   Children's book *Pepe, The Shoe Bird*, with illustrations by Beth Krush, published by Harcourt, Brace & World Inc. in October.

1965   Russell circulates parts of *Losing Battles*, and in April Bennett Cerf at Random House offers a lucrative contract; Welty remains with Harcourt. Writes essay "Must the Novelist Crusade?" during civil rights disturbances in Mississippi.

1966   Mother dies on January 20 after a long and painful series of illnesses. Brother Edward dies on January 24.

1967   Welty completes a draft of "Poor Eyes" in May 1967, which Russell sends to *The New Yorker* (titled "The Optimist's Daughter," it appears March 15, 1969).

1968   "The Demonstrators" (*The New Yorker*, Nov. 26, 1966) wins first prize in O. Henry competition.

1969   Sends completed draft of *Losing Battles* to Russell in May 1969 and he sends it out for bids to several publishers. When Harcourt demands cuts, Welty terminates contract with them and in August signs with Random House for four books, including *Losing Battles*.

1970   *Losing Battles*, dedicated to her brothers, is published on Welty's birthday; it becomes her biggest seller and precipitates re-issues of her earlier works.

1971   *One Time, One Place*, photographs of Mississippi during the Depression (many part of the 1935 "Black Saturday" group), published by Random House in October. Welty receives nomination for 1971 National Book Award for *Losing Battles*.

1972   *The Optimist's Daughter*, a revision of *The New Yorker* text, published by Random House in spring. Welty wins

Pulitzer Prize for *The Optimist's Daughter* in April and in May receives Gold Medal of the National Institute of Arts and Letters; it is presented by Katherine Anne Porter.

1973   Honored by celebration of May 2, 1973, as Eudora Welty Day in Mississippi. Diarmuid Russell, who had retired in the spring because of illness, dies on December 16.

1978   *The Eye of the Story: Selected Essays and Reviews* published by Random House in April.

1979   Wins National Medal for Literature.

1980   *The Collected Stories of Eudora Welty*, published by Harcourt in October, wins the American Library Association Notable Book and the American Book awards. Awarded the Medal of Freedom by President Jimmy Carter at White House ceremony in June.

1983   Delivers William E. Massey Sr. Lectures in the History of American Civilization at Harvard University in April.

1984   *One Writer's Beginnings*, a version of the Massey lectures, is published by Harvard University Press and wins the American Book and National Book Critics Circle awards.

1987   Made Chevalier de l'Ordre des Arts et Lettres (France). Continues over the next decade to write occasional book reviews, introductory essays, and prefaces.

1989   *Eudora Welty Photographs*, including 226 photographs from the Welty collection at the Mississippi Department of Archives and History, published with foreword by Reynolds Price by University Press of Mississippi.

1996   Inducted into France's Légion d'honneur at ceremony held in Old Capitol building in Jackson.

Note on the Texts

This volume contains the complete novels of Eudora Welty: *The Robber Bridegroom* (1942), *Delta Wedding* (1946), *The Ponder Heart* (1954), *Losing Battles* (1970), and *The Optimist's Daughter* (1972).

Welty began writing her first novel, *The Robber Bridegroom*, which is set on the Natchez Trace, several years after visiting the area as an employee of the Works Progress Administration in Mississippi in 1935–36. She completed a draft titled "The Robber Bridegroom: A Tale" by the fall of 1940, and her agent Diarmuid Russell began submitting it to publishers and magazines that October. Welty apparently made some revisions in the story over the next few years, and she dropped the subtitle after Doubleday, Doran accepted the manuscript on May 29, 1942. *The Robber Bridegroom* was published by Doubleday on October 23, 1942. Welty made no further revisions in it (nor did she revise any of her other novels after their first book publication), and the text of the first Doubleday printing is used here.

Delta Wedding originated in an unpublished short story titled "The Delta Cousins." Welty revised the story after it was rejected by three magazines from late 1943 to early 1944, and by January 1945 she began expanding it into a novel titled "Shellmound." The novel was accepted by both Harcourt, Brace and *The Atlantic Monthly* in September 1945. Welty made revisions to the Harcourt galleys and also authorized changes to correct an error in the novel's chronology that was discovered by an editor. Now titled *Delta Wedding*, the novel appeared serially in *The Atlantic Monthly*, January–April 1946, and was published by Harcourt, Brace on April 15, 1946. This volume prints the text of the first 1946 Harcourt printing.

In early 1953 Welty read an unfinished version of *The Ponder Heart* to *New Yorker* editor William Maxwell, who responded enthusiastically and was later granted "first look" at the completed work. The novel was published in *The New Yorker* on December 5, 1953, and on January 6, 1954, by Harcourt, Brace, which used corrected *New Yorker* galleys as setting copy and then incorporated further revisions that Welty made in the resulting Harcourt galleys. The text printed here is of the first 1954 Harcourt printing.

Welty began writing *Losing Battles* in 1955 and worked on it intermittently over the next 15 years. She completed the final version of the novel in the spring of 1969, and the novel was published by Random House on April 13, 1970. This volume prints the text of the first 1970 printing.

The Optimist's Daughter was begun in the mid-1960s, while Welty was working on *Losing Battles*, and had as tentative titles "Baltimore," "An Only Child," and "Poor Eyes." Welty revised the work for book publication after a version titled "The Optimist's Daughter" appeared in *The New Yorker* on March 15, 1969. She completed the final draft in the autumn of 1971, and it was published as *The Optimist's Daughter* by Random House on March 23, 1972, the text reproduced here.

This volume presents the texts of the original printings chosen for inclusion here, but it does not attempt to reproduce features of their typographic design, such as display capitalization of chapter openings. The texts are printed without change, except for the correction of typographical errors. Spelling, punctuation, and capitalization are often expressive features, and they are not altered, even when inconsistent or irregular. Except for clear typographical errors, the spelling and usage of foreign words and phrases are left as they appear in the original texts. The following is a list of typographical errors corrected, cited by page and line number: 31.27, our; 99.34, fiixng; 112.8, glasess; 114.27, carried; 136.12, it that; 137.17, hurts; 138.36, them; 138.36, hold; 139.32, yawning; 141.8, night; 145.17, hand,; 147.15, ¶Everybody; 172.16, tougue; 178.33, everything The; 183.30, as it; 204.18, bridemaid's; 229.27, "She; 231.18, late. He; 236.33, then; 241.24, 'Here; 252.10, full. Sure; 254.40, You've; 268.20, 'You; 277.15, man were!; 307.36, "Im; 325.6–7 [no space]; 386.5, barbership; 485.23, aded; 498.11, out."; 530.35, them.; 536.3, King dom; 541.23, Grinder's; 548.6, Banner."; 570.26, But; 574.33, Elive; 582.2, and and; 670.37, hungry.; 676.7, "You; 676.8, hear."; 677.28, own?; 715.17, "Where's; 737.28, of my; 746.32, hubsand; 788.23, nets; 803.21, said.; 803.38, whispered,; 831.23, nose-pink.

Notes

In the notes below, the reference numbers denote page and line of this volume (the line count includes headings). No note is made for material included in standard desk-reference books such as Webster's *Collegiate, Biographical,* and *Geographical* dictionaries. Biblical references are keyed to the King James Version. Quotations from Shakespeare are keyed to *The Riverside Shakespeare*, ed. G. Blakemore Evans (Boston: Houghton Mifflin, 1974). For further background and references to other studies, see Michael Kreyling, *Author and Agent: Eudora Welty and Diarmuid Russell* (New York: Farrar Straus Giroux, 1991); Suzanne Marrs, *The Welty Collection: A Guide to the Eudora Welty Manuscripts and Documents at the Mississippi Department of Archives and History* (Jackson: University Press of Mississippi, 1988); Noel Polk, *Eudora Welty: A Bibliography of Her Work* (Jackson: University Press of Mississippi, 1994); *Conversations with Eudora Welty* (Jackson: University Press of Mississippi, 1984), ed. Peggy Whitman Prenshaw.

THE ROBBER BRIDEGROOM

1.1   THE ROBBER BRIDEGROOM] Cf. the Grimm Brothers tale of this title.

6.17   Mike Fink] Based on Indian scout, keelboatman, and trapper Mike Fink (1770?–1823), who became a frontier legend.

17.5   Old Natchez Trace] A 600-mile trail originally used by indigenous peoples and then by European explorers and settlers; it runs from the area of Nashville, Tennessee, to Natchez, Mississippi.

20.30   Dr. Peachtree] A few spankings with the branch of a peach tree.

45.14   Little Harp] Based on the bandit Wiley "Little" Harpe (1770–1804); Wiley and his brother Micajah "Big" Harpe (1768–99) were notorious for perpetrating acts of such pathological violence that they were shunned by other outlaws. Big Harpe was killed in Tennessee by vigilantes and Little Harpe was hanged near Natchez, Mississippi; the heads of both men were severed and displayed.

51.36   Old . . . Sea] In the *Arabian Nights* tale "Sinbad and the Sailor."

53.21–22   Fort Rosalie] French post and settlement established in 1716 at present Natchez, Mississippi.

58.35   almo] Alms; a small monetary donation.

DELTA WEDDING

90.2   *JOHN ROBINSON*]   A writer and good friend of Welty, Robinson (1909–89) worked with her on several projects, including the adaptation of *The Robber Bridegroom* from novel to (un-optioned) screenplay.

91.32   Madge Evans]   A stage and film actor, Evans (1909–81) began starring in films at the age of five.

93.34–35   "Abdul . . . Amir"]   "Abdulla Bulbul Ameer" (or "Abdul Abulbul Amir") by Percy French (1877); an arrangement of the song by Frank Crumit became popular in 1928.

97.4   "Break! Break! Break!,"]   First line and title of a sea poem (1842) by Tennyson; in Tennyson, the words are divided by commas.

97.14   Sir Harry . . . Jock."]   Lauder (1870–1950), Scottish music hall entertainer, singer, and author, wrote the song in 1904 and recorded it in 1910; Frank Folley collaborated with him on the lyrics.

97.22–23   Rabbit's Foot Minstrel]   Fats Chappelle's Rabbit Foot Minstrels; Ma Rainey and Bessie Smith were among the performers who toured with the troupe.

97.23–24   "Babes in the Wood,"]   Version of the old ballad "The Children in the Wood," a tragic tale; it appears, e.g., in *R. Caldecott's Picture Book (No. 1)* by English illustrator Randolph Caldecott (1846–86).

127.1   *Berengaria*]   Oceanliner of the Cunard and White Star lines; Gloria and Anthony Patch take passage on it in F. Scott Fitzgerald's *The Beautiful and Damned* (1922; see page 172.3 in this volume).

142.5   *Saint Ronan's Well*]   Medieval romance (1823) by Walter Scott.

144.32–33   "As . . . Ives."]   Anonymous riddle that continues: "I met a man with seven wives, / Each wife had seven sacks, / Each sack had seven cats, / Each cat had seven kits; / Kits, cats, sacks, and wives, / How many were going to St. Ives?"

155.3   Battle of Corinth]   Fought October 3–4, 1862, at Corinth, Mississippi.

172.3   *The Beautiful and Damned*]   See note 127.1.

178.11–12   'I'm . . . Araby!']   Opening of "The Sheik of Araby" (1921), music by Ted Snyder, lyrics by Harry B. Smith and Francis Wheeler.

199.13   *Quo Vadis?*]   Novel (1896) by Henryk Sienkiewicz (1846–1916).

204.2–3   'O where . . . soon.]   In "Lord Randal," a ballad.

212.26–27   Wake . . . love—!]   In the song "Cowboy's Gettin'-up Holler."

228.20–21   Agnes Ayers . . . show]   As Rudolf Valentino's co-star in *The Sheik* (1921).

323.10   Faithful . . . band.]   Cf. the Grimm brothers' "Faithful Hans" and "Iron Hans" (Hans is John in English).

THE PONDER HEART

338.2–3   ASWELL . . . MAXWELL]   Aswell (1902–84) was on the editorial staff of *Atlantic Monthly* (1932–35) and *Reader's Digest* (1935–41) before becoming fiction editor of *Harper's Bazaar* (1941–52), where she published several of Welty's stories. A novelist and short-story writer, William Maxwell published some Welty stories as an editor at *The New Yorker* (1936–76), and served as president of the National Institute of Arts and Letters, 1969–72; he married Emily Gilman Noyes in 1945.

344.16   Divinity]   A fudge-like confection made of sugar, eggs, water, corn syrup, and salt.

354.36   Irish Mail]   A type of three- or four-wheel child's vehicle propelled by a central lever, like a railway hand car.

365.13   "F. H. B.!"]   "Family Hold Back!"

365.34   Fatima]   A brand of cigarette.

367.11   *The . . . Candles*]   Meredith Nicholson's novel (1905) about a wealthy man who fakes his death in order to test his potential heirs.

405.40   *Quo Vadis*]   See note 199.13; the film (MGM, 1941) was directed by Mervyn LeRoy and starred Robert Taylor, Deborah Kerr, and Peter Ustinov.

LOSING BATTLES

457.6   Paris green]   An insecticide and pigment prepared as a very poisonous bright green powder consisting of cupric acetoarsenite.

543.30–31   'Abou Ben Adhem']   Poem (1838) by Leigh Hunt (1784–1859).

610.25–29   Belshazzar's . . . *Tekels*]   In Daniel 5, the words "mene, mene, tekel, upharsin" (numbered, weighed, and divided), written on the wall by a disembodied hand, foretell the defeat and death of Belshazzar, last regent of Babylon.

610.34–36   Nebuchadnezzar . . . grass]   In Daniel 5:18–21.

638.35–36   Lady Clara Vere de Vere]   A self-indulgent snob, the "daughter of a hundred earls," in Tennyson's 1832 poem of that title.

666.16   crokersack]   A bag made of burlap or coarse brown hemp.

675.21   'Hark, . . . sings!']   Shakespeare, *Cymbeline*, II.iii.20.

730.34–35   'Whosoever . . . fire!']   Matthew 5:22.

791.12   sent . . . Coventry]   Banished or ostracized him as undesirable.

841.19   gee]   Act in harmony; turn as a team (at driver's command).

THE OPTIMIST'S DAUGHTER

892.39   *Picayune*]   *New Orleans Times-Picayune*, a daily newspaper.

954.32   *Flush . . . Mississippi*]   Biographies, comic anecdotes, and satirical sketches concerning the justice system in the old Southwest, by Joseph Glover Baldwin (1815–64).

954.36–955.2   *Eric . . . Jeeves*]   Novels by, respectively, H. Rider Haggard (1891), Charlotte Brontë (1847), Edward Bulwer-Lytton (1834), and P. G. Wodehouse (1925).

955.24   Claiborne's *Mississippi*]   J. F. H. Claiborne, *Mississippi as a Province, Territory and State* (1880).

970.17–18   'If . . . salted?']   Matthew 5:13.

970.20–21   'Man . . . authority!']   Shakespeare, *Measure for Measure*, II.ii.117–18.

973.2   "The Cataract of Lodore."]   By Robert Southey (1774–1843).

986.4   Sybil Connolly]   Irish fashion designer of Welsh birth, known for her use of one-of-a-kind designs in Irish textiles.

Library of Congress Cataloging-in-Publication Data

Welty, Eudora, 1909–
  [Novels]
  Complete novels / Eudora Welty.
      p.   cm. — (The library of America ; 101)
    Contents: The robber bridegroom — Delta wedding — The Ponder
  heart — Losing battles — The optimist's daughter.
    ISBN 1–883011–54–X (acid-free paper)
    1. Southern States—Social life and customs—Fiction.   I. Title.
  II. Title: Robber bridegroom.   III. Title: Delta wedding.
  IV. Title: Ponder heart.   V. Title: Losing battles.   VI. Title:
  Optimist's daughter.   VII. Series.
  PS3545.E6A6   1998b
  813'.52—dc21   97–46702
                                                                 CIP

THE LIBRARY OF AMERICA SERIES

The Library of America fosters appreciation and pride in America's literary heritage by publishing, and keeping permanently in print, authoritative editions of America's best and most significant writing. An independent nonprofit organization, it was founded in 1979 with seed money from the National Endowment for the Humanities and the Ford Foundation.

This book is set in 10 point Linotron Galliard,
a face designed for photocomposition by Matthew Carter
and based on the sixteenth-century face Granjon. The paper
is acid-free Domtar Literary Opaque and meets the requirements
for permanence of the American National Standards Institute. The
binding material is Brillianta, a woven rayon cloth made by
Van Heek-Scholco Textielfabrieken, Holland. The compo-
sition is by The Clarinda Company. Printing and
binding by R.R. Donnelley & Sons Company.
Designed by Bruce Campbell.